THE POWER OF ONE

TANDIA

Bryce Courtenay was born in South Africa and now lives in Sydney, Australia. He is a creative director of George Patterson Advertising, lectures widely and also writes a weekly column for the *Australian*.

THE POWER OF ONE

TANDIA

Bryce Courtenay

William Heinemann Australia

Published 1992 by
William Heinemann Australia
a part of Reed Books Australia
22 Salmon Street, Port Melbourne, Victoria 3207
a division of Reed International Books Australia Pty Limited

Reprinted 1992 (three times)
Reprinted 1993

Typeset in 10pt Bembo by MacKenzies Typesetting
Printed and bound in Australia by Griffin Paperbacks

National Library of Australia
cataloguing-in-publication data:

Courtenay, Bryce, 1933-
The power of one; Tandia.
ISBN 0 85561 504 4.
I. Title. II. Title: Tandia.
A823.3

As a great admirer of the work of Dame Elizabeth Frink I have put many of her observations concerning her art into the dialogue which comes from the character Harriet in my novel *Tandia*. I have also used the concept of the walking Madonna, Frink's work of acknowledged genius done for Salisbury cathedral. Other than these obvious and I hope complimentary references, the character Harriet is not intended in any way whatsoever to depict Dame Elizabeth, who is not known personally to me. All the other characters, unless they are mentioned specifically by name as public figures of the time, are entirely fictional.

CONTENTS

THE POWER OF ONE

For Maude Jasmine Greer and Enda Murphy.
Here is the book I promised you so long ago.

ONE

This is what happened.

Before my life started properly, I was doing the usual mewling and sucking, which in my case occurred on a pair of huge, soft black breasts. In the African tradition I continued to suckle for my first two and a half years after which my Zulu wet nurse became my nanny. She was a person made for laughter, warmth and softness and she would clasp me to her breasts and stroke my golden curls with a hand so large it seemed to contain my whole head. My hurts were soothed with a song about a brave young warrior hunting a lion and a women's song about doing the washing down on the big rock beside the river where, at sunset, the baboons would come out of the hills to drink.

My life proper started at the age of five when my mother had her nervous breakdown. I was torn from my lovely black nanny with her big white smile and sent to boarding school.

Then began a time of yellow wedges of pumpkin, burnt black and bitter at the edges; mashed potato with glassy lumps; meat aproned with gristle in grey gravy; diced carrots; warm, wet, flatulent cabbage; beds that wet themselves in the morning; and an entirely new sensation called loneliness.

I was the youngest child in the school by two years, and I spoke only English, the infected tongue that had spread like a plague into the sacred land and contaminated the pure, sweet waters of Afrikanerdom.

The Boer War had created a great malevolence for the English, for the *Rooineks*. It was a hate that had entered their bloodstream and pocked the hearts and minds of the next generation. To their barefoot sons, I was the first live example of the congenital hate they carried for my kind.

I spoke the language which had pronounced the sentences that had killed their grandfathers and sent their grandmothers to the world's first concentration camps, where they died like flies from dysentery, malaria and black water fever. To the bitter Calvinist farmers, the sins of the fathers had been visited upon the sons, unto the third generation. I was infected.

I had had no previous warning that I was wicked and it came as a fearful surprise. I was blubbing to myself in the little kids' dormitory when suddenly I was dragged from under my horrid camphor-smelling blanket by two eleven-year-olds and taken to the seniors' dormitory, to stand trial before the council of war.

My trial, of course, was a travesty of justice. But then what could I expect? I had been caught deep behind enemy lines and everyone, even a five-year-old, knows this means the death sentence. I stood gibbering, unable to understand the language of the stentorian twelve-year-old judge, or the reason for the hilarity when sentence was passed. But I guessed the worst.

I wasn't quite sure what death was. I knew it was something that happened on the farm in the slaughter house to pigs and goats and an occasional heifer. The squeal from the pigs was so awful that I knew it wasn't much of an experience, even for pigs.

And I knew something else for sure; death wasn't as good as life. Now death was about to happen to me before I could really get the hang of life. Trying hard to hold back my tears, I was dragged off.

It must have been a full moon that night because the shower room was bathed in blue light. The stark granite walls of the shower recesses stood sharply angled against the wet cement floor. I had never been in a shower room before and this place resembled the slaughter house on the farm. It even smelt the same, of urine and blue carbolic soap, so I guessed this was where my death would take place.

My eyes were a bit swollen from crying but I could see where the meat hooks were supposed to hang. Each granite slab had a pipe protruding from the wall behind it with a knob on the end. They would suspend me from one of these and I would be dead, just like the pigs.

I was told to remove my pyjamas and to kneel inside the shower recess facing the wall. I looked directly down into the hole in the floor where all the blood would drain away.

I closed my eyes and said a silent, sobbing prayer. My prayer wasn't to God, but to my nanny. It seemed the more urgent thing to do. When she couldn't solve a problem for me she'd say, 'We must ask Inkosi-Inkosikazi, the great medicine man, he will know what to do.' Although we never actually called on the services of the great man it didn't seem to matter, it was comforting to know he was available when needed.

But it was too late to get a message through to Nanny, much less have her pass it on. I felt a sudden splash on my neck and then warm blood trickled over my trembling, naked body across the cold cement floor and into the drain. Funny, I didn't feel dead. But there you go. Who knows what dead feels like?

When the Judge and his council of war had all pissed on me, they left. After a while it got very quiet, just a drip, drip, drip from someplace overhead and a sniff from me that sounded as though it came from somewhere else.

As I had never seen a shower I didn't know how to turn one on and so had no way of washing myself. I had always been bathed by my nanny in a tin tub in front of the kitchen stove. I'd stand up and she'd soap me all over and Dee and Dum, the two kitchen maids who were twins, would giggle behind their hands when she soaped my little acorn. Sometimes it would just stand right up on its own and everyone would have an extra good giggle. That's how I knew it was special. Just how special I was soon to find out.

I tried to dry myself with my pyjamas, which were wet in patches from lying on the floor, and then I put them back on. I didn't bother to do up the buttons because my hands were shaking a lot. I wandered around that big dark place until I found the small kids' dormitory. There I crept under my blanket and came to the end of my first day in life.

I am unable to report that the second day of my life was much better than the first. Things started to go wrong from the moment I awoke. Kids surrounded my bed holding their noses and making loud groaning sounds. Let me tell you something, there was plenty to groan about. I smelt worse than a kaffir toilet, worse than the pigs at home. Worse even than both put together.

The kids scattered as a very large person with a smudge of dark hair above her lip entered. It was the same lady who had left me in the dormitory the previous evening. 'Good morning, Mevrou!' the kids chorused, each standing stiffly to attention at the foot of his bed.

The large person called Mevrou glared at me. '*Kom*,' she said in a fierce voice. Grabbing me by the ear she twisted me out of the stinking bed and led me back to the slaughter house. With her free hand she removed my unbuttoned pyjama jacket and pulled my pants down to my ankles. 'Step,' she barked.

I thought desperately, she's even bigger than Nanny. If she pisses on me I will surely drown. I stepped out of my pyjama pants, and releasing my ear she pushed me into the shower recess. There was a sudden hissing sound and needles of icy water drilled into me.

If you've never had a shower or even an unexpected icy-cold drenching, it's not too hard to believe that maybe this is death. I had my eyes tightly shut but the hail of water was remorseless, a thousand pricks at a time drilling into my skin. How could so much piss possibly come out of one person?

Death was cold as ice. Hell was supposed to be fire and brimstone and here I was freezing to death. It was very frightening, but like so much lately, quite the opposite to what I had been led to expect.

'When you go to boarding school you'll sleep in a big room with lots of little friends so you won't be afraid of the dark anymore.' How exciting it had all sounded.

The fierce hissing noise and the deluge of icy piss stopped suddenly. I opened my eyes to find no Mevrou. Instead, the Judge stood before me, his pyjama sleeve rolled up, his arm wet where he'd reached in to turn off the shower. Behind him stood the jury and all the smaller kids from my dormitory.

As the water cleared from my eyes I tried to smile gratefully. The

Judge's wet arm shot out; grabbing me by the wrist he jerked me out of the granite recess. The jury formed a ring around me as I stood frightened, my hands cupped over my scrotum. My teeth chattering out of control, a weird, glassy syncopation inside my head. The Judge reached out again, and taking both my wrists in one large hand he pulled my hands away and pointed to my tiny acorn. 'Why you piss your bed, Rooinek?' he asked.

'Hey, look there is no hat on his snake!' someone yelled. They all crowded closer, delighted at this monstrous find.

'Pisskop! Pisskop!' one of the smaller kids shouted and in a moment all the small kids were chanting it.

'You hear, you a pisshead,' the Judge translated. 'Who cut the hat off your snake, Pisskop?'

I looked down to where he was pointing, my teeth changing into a quieter timpani. All looked perfectly normal to me, although the tip was a bright blue colour and had almost disappeared into its neat round collar of skin. I looked up at the Judge, confused.

The Judge dropped my arms and using both his hands parted his pyjama fly. His 'snake', monstrously large, hung level with my eyes and seemed to be made of a continuous sheath brought down to a point of ragged skin. A few stray hairs grew at its base and, I must say, it wasn't much of a sight.

More serious trouble lay ahead of me for sure. I was a Rooinek and a pisskop. I spoke the wrong language. And now I was obviously made differently. But I was still alive, and in my book: where there's life, there's hope.

By the end of the first term I had reduced my persecution time to no more than an hour a day. I had the art of survival almost down pat. Except for one thing: I had become a chronic bed wetter.

It is impossible to be a perfect adapter if you leave a wet patch behind you every morning. My day would begin with a bed-wetting caning from Mevrou, after which I would make the tedious journey alone to the showers to wash my rubber sheet. When the blue carbolic soap was rubbed against the stiff cane bristles of the large wooden scrubbing brush I was made to use, fiercely stinging specks of soap would shoot up into my eyes. But I soon worked out that you didn't need the soap like Mevrou said, you could give the sheet a good go under the shower and it would be okay.

My morning routine did serve a useful purpose. I learned that crying is a luxury good adapters have to forgo. I soon had the school record for being thrashed. The Judge said so. It was the first time in my life that I owned something that wasn't a positive disadvantage to adaptation. I wasn't just a hated Rooinek and a pisskop, I was also a record holder. I can tell you it felt good.

The Judge ordered that I only be beaten up a little at a time. A punch here, a flat-hander there, and if I could stop being a pisskop he'd stop even that, although he added that, for a Rooinek, this was probably impossible. I must confess, I was inclined to agree. No amount of resolve on my part or saying prayers to Nanny or even to God seemed to have the least effect.

Maybe it had something to do with my defective acorn? I forced a hole in the side pockets of my shorts through which my forefinger and thumb would fit. I took secretly to pulling my foreskin and holding it over the tip of my acorn as long as I could in the hope that it would lose elasticity and render me normal. Alas, except for a sore acorn, nothing happened. I was doomed to be a pisshead for the rest of my life.

The end of the first term finally came. I was to return home for the May holidays: home to Nanny who would listen to my sadness and sleep on her mat at the foot of my bed so the bogey man couldn't get me. I also intended to enquire whether my mother had stopped breaking down so I would be allowed to stay home.

I rode home joyfully in the dicky-seat of Dr 'Henny' Boshoff's shiny new Chevrolet coupé. Dr Henny was a local hero who played fly-half for the Northern Transvaal rugby team. When the Judge saw who had come to pick me up, he shook me by the hand and promised things would be better next term.

It was Dr Henny who had first told me about the nervous breakdown, and he now confirmed that my mother was 'coming along nicely' but her nervous breakdown was still with her and she wouldn't be home just yet.

Sadly this put the kibosh on my chances of staying home and never leaving again until I was as old as my granpa, maybe not even then.

As we choofed along in the car, with me in the dicky-seat open to the wind and the sunshine, I was no longer a Rooinek and a pisskop but became a great chief. We passed through African villages where squawking chickens, pumping wings desperately, fled out of the way and yapping kaffir dogs, all ribs and snout and brindle markings, gave chase. Although only after my speeding throne had safely passed. As a great chief I was naturally above such common goings-on. Life was good. I can tell you for certain, life was very good.

Nanny wept tears that ran down her cheeks and splashed onto her huge, warm breasts. She kept rubbing her large, dark hand over my shaven head, moaning and groaning as she held me close. I had expected to do all the crying when I got home but there was no competing with her.

It was late summer. The days were filled with song as the field women picked cotton, working their way down the long rows, chatting and singing in perfect harmony while they plucked the fluffy white fibre heads from the sun-blackened cotton bolls.

Nanny sent a message to Inkosi-Inkosikazi to the effect that we urgently needed to see him on the matter of the child's night water. The message was put on the drums and in two days we heard that the great medicine man would call in a fortnight or so on his way to visit Modjadji, the great rain queen.

The whites of Nanny's eyes would grow big and her cheeks puff out as she talked about the greatness of Inkosi-Inkosikazi. 'He will dry your bed with one throw of the shin-bones of the great white ox,' she promised.

'Will he also grow skin over my acorn?' I demanded to know. She clutched me to her breast and her answer was lost in the heaving of her belly as she chortled all over me.

The problem of the night water was much discussed by the field women who pondered deeply that a matter so slight could bring the great one to visit. 'Surely a grass sleeping mat will dry in the morning sun? This is not a matter of proper concern for the greatest medicine man in Africa.'

It was all right for them, of course. They didn't have to go back to the Judge and Mevrou.

Almost two weeks to the day Inkosi-Inkosikazi arrived in his big, black Buick. The car was a symbol of his enormous power and wealth, even to the Boers, who despised him as the devil incarnate yet feared him with the superstition of all ignorant God-fearing men. None was prepared to pit the catechism of the Dutch Reformed Church against this aged black goblin.

All that day the field women brought gifts of food. By late afternoon a small mountain of kaffir corn and mealies, gem squash, native spinach and water melons had grown under the big avocado tree next to the slaughter house. Bundles of dried tobacco leaf were stacked up beside it and, separated by two large grass *indaba* or meeting mats, lay six scrawny kaffir chickens. These were mostly tough old roosters, four-hour boilers, their legs tied and their wings clipped. They lay on their sides with their thin, featherless necks and bald heads caked with dust. Only an occasional 'sck-wark!' and the sudden opening of a bright, beady eye showed that they were still alive, if not exactly kicking.

One especially scrawny old cock with mottled grey feathers looked very much like my granpa, except for his eyes. My granpa's eyes were pale blue and somewhat watery, eyes intended for gazing over soft English landscapes, whereas the old cock's were sharp as a bead of red light.

My granpa came down the steps and walked towards the big, black Buick. He stopped to kick one of the roosters, for he hated kaffir chickens almost as much as he hated Shangaans. His pride and joy were his one hundred black Orpington hens and six giant roosters. The presence of kaffir chickens in the farmyard, even though trussed and clipped, was like having half a dozen dirty old men present at a ballet class.

He greatly admired Inkosi-Inkosikazi who had once cured him of his gallstones. 'I took his foul, green muti and, by golly, the stones blasted out of me like a hail of buckshot! Never a trace of a gallstone since. If you ask me, the old monkey is the best damned doctor in the lowveld.'

We waited for Inkosi-Inkosikazi to alight from the Buick. The old medicine man, like Nanny, was a Zulu. It was said that he was the last son of the great Dingaan, the Zulu king who fought both the Boers and the British to a standstill. Two generations after the Boers had finally defeated his *impis* at the Battle of Blood River, they remained in awe of him.

Two years after that battle, Dingaan, fleeing from the combined forces of his half-brother Mpande and the Boers, had sought refuge among the Nyawo people on the summit of the great Lebombo mountains. On the night he was treacherously assassinated by Nyawo tribesmen he had been presented with a young virgin, and the seed of the second greatest of all the warrior kings was planted in her fourteen-year-old womb.

'Where I chose blood, this last of my sons will choose wisdom. You will call him Inkosi-Inkosikazi, he will be a man for all Africa,' Dingaan had told the frightened Nyawo maiden.

This made the small, wizened black man who was being helped from the rear of the Buick one hundred years old.

Inkosi-Inkosikazi was dressed in a mismatched suit, the jacket brown and shiny with age, the trousers blue pinstripe. He wore a white shirt meant to go with a detachable starched collar, the collarless shirt was secured at the neck with a large gold and ivory collar stud. A mangy-looking leopard-skin cloak fell from his shoulders. As was the custom, he wore no shoes and the soles of his feet were splayed and cracked at the edges. In his right hand he carried a beautifully beaded fly switch, the symbol of an important chief.

I had never seen such an old man; his peppercorn hair was whiter than raw cotton, small tufts of snowy beard sprang from his chin and only three yellowed teeth remained in his mouth. He looked at us and his eyes burned sharp and clear, like the eyes of the old rooster.

Several of the women started keening and were quickly rebuked by the old man. 'Stupid *abafazi!* Death does not ride with me in my big motor, did you not hear the roar of its great belly?'

Silence fell as my granpa approached. He briefly welcomed Inkosi-Inkosikazi and granted him permission to stay overnight on the farm. The old man nodded, showing none of the customary obsequiousness expected from a Kaffir and my granpa seemed to demand none. He simply shook the old man's bony claw and returned to his chair on the stoep.

Nanny, who had rubbed earth on her forehead like all the other women, finally spoke. 'Lord, the women have brought food and we have beer freshly fermented.'

Inkosi-Inkosikazi ignored her, which I thought was pretty brave of him, and ordered one of the women to untie the cockerels. Two women ran over and soon the chickens were loose. They continued to lie there, unsure of their freedom, until the old man raised his fly switch and waved it over them. With a sudden squawking and flapping of stunted wings all but one rose and dashed helter-skelter, their long legs rising high off the ground as they ran towards open territory. The old cock who looked like Granpa rose slowly, stretched his neck, flapped the bits of wing he had left, his head darting left and right, slightly cocked as though he were listening; then, calm as you like, he walked over to the heap of corn and started pecking away.

'Catch the feathered devils,' Inkosi-Inkosikazi suddenly commanded. He giggled, 'Catch an old man's dinner tonight.'

With squeals of delight the chickens were rounded up again. The ice had been broken as five of the women, each holding a chicken upside down by the legs, waited for the old man's instructions. Inkosi-Inkosikazi squatted down and with his finger traced a circle about two feet in diameter in the dust. He hopped around like an ancient chimpanzee completing five similar-sized circles, muttering to himself as he did so.

The incantations over, he signalled for one of the women to bring over a cockerel. Grabbing the old bird by its long scrawny neck and by both legs, he retraced the first circle on the ground, this time using the bird's beak as a marker. Then he laid the cockerel inside the circle where it lay unmoving, its eyes closed, a leg protruding from each wing. He proceeded to do the same thing to the other five chickens until each lay in its own circle in front of the crowd. As each chicken was laid to rest there would be a gasp of amazement from the women. It was pretty low-grade magic but it served well enough to get things underway.

Inkosi-Inkosikazi moved over and squatted cross-legged in the centre of the indaba mats and beckoned that I should join him. It was the first time he'd acknowledged my presence and I clung fearfully to Nanny's skirts. She pushed me gently towards him and in a loud whisper said: 'You must go, it is a great honour, only a chief can sit with a chief on the meeting mat.'

He had the strong, distinctly sweet smell of African sweat, mixed with tobacco and very old man. After all I had been through in the smell department, it wasn't too bad, and I too sat cross-legged beside him with my eyes glued to the ground in front of me.

Inkosi-Inkosikazi leaned slightly towards me and spoke in Zulu. 'Tomorrow I will show you the trick of the chickens. It's not really magic, you know. These stupid Shangaans think it's magic but they don't deserve to know any better.'

'Thank you, sir,' I said softly. I was pleased at the notion of sharing a secret. Even if it was only a trick, it was a damned clever one which might confound the Judge and the jury if I could get my hands on a stray chicken at school. My confidence in his ability to change my status as a pisskop was growing by the minute.

Inkosi-Inkosikazi indicated to Nanny that she should begin the matter of the night water. Two women were quickly delegated to start the cooking fire and the rest of the field women settled down around the indaba mats, taking care not to touch even the tiniest part of the edge.

African stories are long, with every detail cherished, scooped up for telling a thousand times over. It was a great moment for Nanny as she stood alone in the rapidly fading twilight and told her story. She spoke in Shangaan so that all could share wide-eyed and groan and nod and sigh in the appropriate places.

The hugeness of Mevrou with her moustache they found amazing, the injustice of the Judge and jury they took in their stride, for they all knew how the white man passes sentences that have no relationship to what has been done. The pissing upon me by the Judge and jury had them rocking and moaning and holding their hands to their ears. Such an indignity was surely beyond even the white man?

In the sudden way of Africa it was dark now. A piece of green wood crackled sharply in the fire sending up a shower of sparks. The leaping flames lit Nanny's face; there was no doubt that they would remember this teller of a great story of misery and woe. Tears flowed copiously as she told of how death finally arrived in a shower of icy piss that jetted from the loins of the great, moustached angel of perdition.

I must admit I was hugely impressed, but when Nanny got to the part where my snake had no hat which, in my opinion, was the most important bit of the lot, they cupped their hands over their mouths and, between the tears, they started to giggle.

Nanny concluded by saying that the business of my night water was an evil spell brought upon me by the angel of death with the moustache like a man and waterfall loins, so that she could return each morning to feed her great beating sjambok on my frail child's flesh. Only a great medicine man such as Inkosi-Inkosikazi could defeat this evil spell.

The light from the fire showed the deeply shocked faces of the women as Nanny finally sat down, heaving with great sobs, knowing that such a tale had never been told before and that it might live forever, warped into a Shangaan legend.

I can tell you one thing, I was mighty impressed that any person, most of all me, could go through such a harrowing experience.

Inkosi-Inkosikazi rose, scratched his bum and yawned. With the handle of his fly switch he prodded my weeping nanny. 'Get me some kaffir beer, woman,' he demanded.

Dee and Dum, the twin kitchen maids, served me my dinner, as Nanny was required to attend to the drinking and other needs of the scrawny old wizard. Both little girls were wide-eyed with the excitement of it all and told me I was the bravest person they had ever known.

By bedtime Nanny was at my side as usual, arriving with a large sweet potato, its tummy open with a spoon sticking out of the middle, tiny wisps of steam curling upwards, condensing on the handle. There is something about a sweet potato that cheers you up when you are low and celebrates with you when you are happy. Sweet potatoes baked in their jackets have a very large comfort factor built into them.

Nanny's excitement was still with her, she grabbed me and crushed me to her enormous bosom and laughed and told me how I had thrust greatness upon her with the coming of the old monkey who was, nevertheless, the greatest medicine man in all Africa; how the telling of the tale of the night water showed that a Zulu woman could be a teller of tales superior in every way to even the best told by the most eloquent Shangaan.

I pointed out that she had entirely missed the matter of my school record for canings. A large tear rolled down her cheek. 'In the matter of white man's punishment, the black people already understand that the body can be broken by a sjambok but never the spirit. We are the earth, that is why we are the colour of earth. In the end it is the earth which will win, every African knows this.'

Whatever all that was supposed to mean, it didn't answer my question. Nanny finally left me, but first she lit the paraffin lamp and turned it down low, but not so low that I wouldn't recognise the bogey man should he try to sneak into my room.

'Tonight Inkosi-Inkosikazi will visit in your dreams to find the way of your night water,' she said, tucking me in. The morning after the night Inkosi-Inkosikazi went walkabout in my dreams, he summoned me to sit alone with him again on the meeting mat. From an old leather bag he produced the twelve magic shin-bones from the great white ox. Then, squatting on his haunches as he prepared to throw the bones, he commenced a deep, rumbling incantation that sounded like distant thunder.

The strange bone-yellowed dice which would solve my bed-wetting habit briefly clicked together in his hands and then fell onto the ground in front of him. Inkosi-Inkosikazi flicked at them with his forefinger and, as he did so, tiny rolls of thunder came from his throat. With a final grunt he gathered them up and tossed them back into his ancient leather satchel.

Inkosi-Inkosikazi's eyes, sharp pins of light in his incredibly wrinkled face, seemed to look right into me. 'I visited you in your dreams and we came to a place of three waterfalls and ten stones across the river. The shin-bones of the great white ox say I must take you back so that you can jump the three waterfalls and cross the river, stepping from stone to stone without falling into the rushing torrent. If you can do this then the unfortunate business of the night water will be over.'

I nodded, not knowing what to say. After all, five-year-old kids are pretty rotten at riddles. His face became even more simian as he chuckled, 'When you have learned this lesson I will show you the trick of the chicken sleep.'

I had seen the faint marks of last night's circles, but no chickens. I guessed that they had been consigned to the communal tummy. I only hope he doesn't use one of Granpa's black Orpingtons, what a kerfuffle that would be, I thought.

'Now, listen to me carefully, boy. Watch and listen. Watch and listen,' he repeated. 'When I tell you to close your eyes you will do so. Do you understand?'

Anxious to please him I shut my eyes tightly. 'Not now! Only when I tell you. Not tight, but as you do when your eyes are heavy from the long day and it is time to sleep.'

I opened my eyes to see him crouched directly in front of me, his beautiful fly switch suspended slightly above my normal sightline. The fall of horsehair swayed gently before my eyes.

'Watch the tail of the horse.' My eyes followed the switch as it moved to and fro. 'It is time to close your eyes but not your ears. You must listen well for the roaring of water is great.'

A sudden roar of water filled my head and then I saw the three waterfalls. I was standing on an outcrop of rock directly above the highest one. Far below me the river rushed away, tumbling and boiling into a narrow gorge. Just before the water entered the gorge and churned white I noted the ten stepping stones, like ten anthracite teeth strung across its mouth.

Inkosi-Inkosikazi spoke to me, his voice soft, almost gentle. 'It is late, the bush doves, anticipating nightfall, are already silent. It is the time of day when the white waters roar most mightily as water does when it is cast in shadow.

'You are standing on a rock above the highest waterfall, a young warrior who has killed his first lion and is worthy now to fight in the legion of Dingaan, the great impi that destroys all before it. Worthy even to fight in the impi of Shaka, the greatest warrior king of all.

'You are wearing the skirt of lion tail as you face into the setting sun. Now the sun has passed beyond Zululand, even past the land of the Swazi and now it leaves the Shangaan and the royal kraal of Modjadji, the rain queen, to be cooled in the great, dark water beyond.

'You can see the moon rising over Africa and you are at peace with the night, unafraid of the great demon Skokijaan who comes to feed on the dark night, tearing its black flesh until, at last, it is finished and the new light comes to stir the sleeping herd boys and send them out to mind the lowing cattle.'

As I stood on the great rock waiting to jump, I could see the new moon rising, bright as a new florin above the thundering falls.

'You must take a deep breath and say the number three to yourself as you leap. Then, when you surface, you must take another breath and say the number two as you are washed across the rim of the second waterfall, then again a deep breath as you rise and are carried over the third. Now you must swim to the first stone, counting backwards from ten to one, counting each stone as you leap from it to the next to cross the rushing river.' The old medicine man paused long enough for me to work out the sequence he had given me. 'You must jump now, little warrior of the king.'

I took a deep breath and launched myself into the night. The cool air, mixed with spray, rushed past my face and then I hit the water below, sank briefly, rose to the surface and expelled the deep breath I had taken. With scarcely enough time to take a second breath I was swept over the second waterfall and then again I fell down the third roaring cascade to be plunged into a deep pool at the base of the third waterfall. I swam strongly and with great confidence to the first of the great stones glistening black and wet in the moonlight. Jumping from stone to stone I crossed the river, counting down from ten to one, then leaping to the pebbly beach on the far side.

Clear as an echo, his voice cut through the roar of the falls. 'We have crossed the night water to the other side and it is done, you must open your eyes now, little warrior.' Inkosi-Inkosikazi brought me back from the dreamtime and I looked around, a little surprised to see the familiar farmyard about me. 'When you need me you may come to the night country and I will be waiting. I will always be there in the place of the three waterfalls and the ten stones across the river.' Pointing to what appeared to be an empty mealie meal sack, he said: 'Bring me that chicken and I will show you the trick of the chicken sleep.'

I got up and walked over to the sack and opened it. Inside the sharp, beady red eye of the chicken that looked like Granpa blinked up at me. I dragged the sack over to where the previous circles he'd made in the dust had been and the old man rose and called over to me to draw a new circle in the dirt. Then he showed me how to hold the old rooster. This was done by securing the main body of the chicken under your right armpit like a set of bagpipes and grabbing it high up its neck with your left hand so that its featherless head is held between forefinger and thumb. Getting a good hold of its feet with your free hand, you dip the chicken towards the ground at an angle of forty-five degrees while squatting on the ground with the chicken's beak not quite touching the rim of the circle. The beak is then traced around the perimeter three times whereupon the bird is laid inside the circle.

The old man made me practise it three times. To my amazement and his amusement, the old rooster lay within the circle docile as a sow in warm mud. To bring the chicken back from wherever chickens go in such trying circumstances, all I needed to do was touch it and say in a gruff voice, 'Chicken sleep, chicken wake, if chicken not wake then chicken be ate!' Which is, I suppose, a pretty grim warning to a chicken.

I did not ask Inkosi-Inkosikazi how a Shangaan chicken could understand Zulu because you simply do not ask such questions of the greatest medicine man in all of Africa.

I was as yet unaware that this chicken was pretty exceptional, that the ability to understand a couple of African languages was probably not beyond him.

'The chicken trick is our bond. We are now brothers bound in this common knowledge and also the knowledge of the place in the dreamtime. Only you and I can do this trick or come to that place.'

I'm telling you something, it was pretty solemn stuff. With a yell across the farmyard the old man called for his driver who was asleep in the back of the Buick. Together we walked towards the big, black car.

'You may keep this chicken to practise on,' Inkosi-Inkosikazi said as he climbed into the back seat of the car.

As if from nowhere, the car was surrounded by field women who loaded up the trunk with the tributes they'd brought the previous day. Nanny handed the old man a small square of brightly coloured cloth into the corner of which were knotted several coins. Inkosi-Inkosikazi declined the offer of what was, for Nanny, two months' salary.

'It is a matter between me and the boy. This place is on my way to the Molototsi River where I go to see Modjadji, the rain queen.' He stuck his head out of the rear door window and gazed up into the sky. 'The rains have not come to Zululand, and in this matter her magic is greater than mine.'

The rains had been good north of the Drakensberg Mountains and now Nanny grew fearful as she asked for news of her people.

'The fields are ploughed three months and the seed maize is ready in the great seed pots, but the wind carries away the soil as we wait for the rains to come,' the old man sighed.

Nanny translated the news of the drought to the women. Drought is always news to be shared among the tribes. The women broke into a lament, doing a shuffling dance around the Buick and singing about the great one who brought the rains, gave barren women the sons they craved and cured the bite of snakes, even of the great black mamba.

Inkosi-Inkosikazi stuck his ancient head out of the window again and shook his fly switch impatiently. 'Be gone with you, you stupid old crows, sing for Modjadji the rain queen, this old rain maker has failed to squeeze a drop from the sky.'

With a roar from its mighty V8 engine, the big, black automobile shot down the road, raising a cloud of dust behind it.

By the time the holidays were over Granpa Chook, for that was what I had called my chicken gift, and I were practically inseparable. Calling a chicken a 'chook' was a private joke my mother and I had shared. We had received a bunch of photos from a distant cousin in Australia, one of which had shown a small boy not much older than me feeding the chickens. On the back of the photo was written: 'Young Lennie, feeding the chooks on the farm in Wagga Wagga.' We had called the two old drakes who always quacked around the farmyard together Wagga Wagga, and had started referring to Granpa's black Orpingtons as 'the chooks'.

Granpa Chook was, I decided, a splendid name for the scraggy old rooster who came running the moment I appeared at the kitchen door. There was no doubt about it, that chicken had fallen for me. I don't mind admitting, I felt pretty powerfully attracted to him as well.

We practised the chicken trick for a couple of days but he got so smart that the moment I drew a circle in the dust he stepped into it and settled down politely. I think he was only trying to be co-operative, but it meant that I had lost all my power. Granpa Chook was the first living creature over which I held power and now this not-so-dumb cluck had found a way of getting back on even terms which was damned annoying if you ask me.

TWO

The holidays came to an end. My bed-wetting habit had, of course, been cured, but not my apprehension at the prospect of returning to boarding school. As for my hatless snake, I'd asked Inkosi-Inkosikazi about that and he'd hinted that we were similarly unique which was why we were so special. It was comforting at the time, but now I wasn't so sure.

Nanny and I had a good old weep on the last evening at home. She packed my khaki shorts and shirts and two pairs of pyjamas and a bright red jumper my mother had sent from the nervous breakdown place. We laughed and laughed, in between crying of course, because one sleeve was about ten inches shorter than the other. Nervous breakdowns probably do that sort of thing to people's knitting. By unpicking it at the shoulders Nanny made it into a nice red jumper.

We set out after breakfast in Granpa's old Model A Ford truck. On the way we picked up fat Mrs Vorster, the widow who owned the farm next door. Granpa spoke no Afrikaans and she no English so she thumped up and down in silence with her chins squashing onto her chest with every bump of the old truck.

I was delighted to be in the back with Nanny and Granpa Chook, who was concealed in the mealie sack where he lay so still you'd have sworn he was an empty sack. Nanny was going to town to send money to her family in Zululand to help with the terrible drought.

Granpa Chook's wing feathers had practically grown again and by taking a run-up, his long legs pumping up and down, he could take off and land high up on a branch anytime he liked. I have to admit, while he was heavier, he wasn't any prettier. His long neck was still bare and his head still bald, his cock's comb was battered and hung like an empty scrotum to one side of his head. Compared to the black Orpingtons he was a mess.

We stopped at the school gates and Nanny handed me the suitcase and the bag with Granpa Chook playing possum. 'What have you got in the bag, son?' Granpa asked.

Before I could reply Nanny called from the back, 'It is only sweet potatoes, baas.'

The tears were as usual running down her cheeks and I wanted to rush back and hide myself in her big safe arms. With a bit of a backfire and a puff of blue exhaust smoke the truck lurched away and I was left standing at the gates. Ahead of me lay the dreaded Mevrou, the Judge and the jury and the beginning of the power of one, where I would learn that in each us there is a flame that must never be allowed to go out. That as long as it burns within us, we cannot be destroyed.

I released Granpa Chook from the sack and gave him a pat. Pisskop the Rooinek, possessor of a hatless snake, was back in town. But this time, for damn sure, he was not alone.

The playground was empty as we crossed it; Granpa Chook darted here and there after the tiny green grasshoppers that landed on its hot, dusty surface. They too seemed to be in enemy territory for not a blade of grass grew on the sun-baked square of earth. To make it across to safety they were forced to land frequently, exposing themselves to the dangers of a marauding Granpa Chook. Though the odds were rather better for them, there were hundreds of them and only one Granpa Chook, while it was the other way around with the two of us.

We seemed to have arrived early and so I made for my secret mango tree, which grew on the other side of the playground. Leaving my suitcase at its base, I climbed into its dark, comforting canopy of leaves. Granpa Chook, taking a run-up and flapping his wings furiously, flew up and perched on a branch beside me, swaying and wobbling and making a lot of unnecessary noise and fuss.

I carefully explained the situation to him. He just sat there and tossed his silly cock's comb and squawked a lot. I tried to impress on him that this was the big time, that things were different here to down on the farm. I must say that any chicken who could outsmart Inkosi-Inkosikazi's cooking pot and get the better of his magic circle had to be a real professional, so I didn't lecture him too much. Granpa Chook was a survivor; how fortunate I was to have him as my friend.

After a while we left the mango tree, and skirting the edge of the playground we made our way to the side of the hostel which contained the small kids' dormitory. It looked out onto a run-down citrus orchard of old, almost leafless grapefruit trees. Half a dozen cassia trees had seeded themselves over the years and their bright yellow blossom brought the dying orchard back to life. The ground was covered with khaki weed and black jack which reached to my shoulder. No one ever came here. It was the ideal place for Granpa Chook to stay while I reported to Mevrou.

Deep inside the orchard I set about making a small clearing amongst the rank-smelling weed and in the process unearthed a large white cutworm with a grey head and a yellow band around its neck. Granpa Chook thought all his Christmases had come at once, and with a sharp squawk he had the plump grub in his beak. You could see the progress of that worm as it made a bulge going down his long, naked neck.

The clearing complete, I drew a circle on the ground and he settled politely down into it. It still annoyed me a bit that he refused to go through the whole magic rigmarole, but what's the use, you can't go arguing with a chicken, can you?

I found Mevrou in the wash house folding blankets. She looked at me with distaste and pointed to a tin bucket which stood beside the mangle. 'Your rubber sheet is in that bucket, take it,' she said.

I tried not to sound scared. 'I . . . I am cured, Mevrou,' I stammered.

'Ha! Your *oupa*'s beatings are better than mine then, ja?'

I stood with my head bowed, the way you were supposed to in the presence of Mevrou. 'No, Mevrou, your beatings are the best . . . better than my granpa's. It just happened, I just stopped doing it.'

'My sjambok will be lonely.' Mevrou always called the bamboo cane she carried her sjambok. She handed me a coarse towel and a blanket. 'You are too early, there is no lunch, the other children will be here not till this afternoon.' The blanket smelt of camphor balls and with the familiar smell the old fear returned and with it came doubt that perhaps I wasn't cured of my bed-wetting habit.

I dropped my blanket and towel off in the small kids' dormitory and returned to Granpa Chook. The absence of lunch didn't bother me. Nanny had packed two large sweet potatoes in my suitcase and I now planned to share one of these with Granpa Chook.

As I approached the abandoned orchard I could hear a fearful squawking coming from Granpa Chook. Suddenly he rose from above the weeds, his short wings beating the air. I lost sight of him again as he plunged back into the undergrowth. Up he came again, neck arched, legs stretched with talons wide. Down again, the weeds shaking wildly where he landed. This time he didn't come up and he had stopped squawking, though the khaki weed continued to shake where he'd disappeared. My heart beat wildly. Something had got Granpa Chook. A weasel or a feral cat? It was my fault, I'd left him helpless in the magic circle.

I stumbled blindly towards the tiny clearing where I'd left him, khaki weed and black jack lashing out at me, holding me back. Granpa Chook stood inside the circle; held firmly in his beak was a three-foot grass snake. With a vigorous shake of his head and a snip of his powerful beak he removed the head from the snake and, to my astonishment, swallowed it. The snake's head went down in the same way as the fat cutworm had done. Unaware that the show was over, the snake's brilliant green body continued to wriggle wildly in the weeds.

The toughest damn chicken in the whole world tossed his head and gave me a beady wink. I could see he was pretty pleased with himself. I'll tell you something, I don't blame him, how can you go wrong with a friend like him at your side?

The snake had ceased to wriggle, and picking it up I hung it from a branch of a cassia tree growing only a few feet from the window nearest my bed in the little kids' dormitory. Now there were two hatless snakes in the world and I was involved with both of them.

The afternoon gradually filled with the cacophony of returning kids. I could hear them as they dumped their blankets and suitcases in the dormitory and rushed out to play. Granpa Chook and I spent the afternoon making his shelter from bits of corrugated iron I found among the weeds. He seemed to like his new home, scratching for worms where I'd pulled up the weeds. He would be safe and dry when it rained.

By the time the wash-up bell went at a quarter to five, I was a bit of a mess from all the weeding and building. I left Granpa Chook for the night scratching happily away in his new home and washed under a little-used tap on the side of the building facing the orchard. By the time the supper bell went the late afternoon sun had dried me and I was good as new. I waited until the last possible moment before slipping into the dining hall to take my place at the bottom table where the little kids sat.

Shortly after lights out that night I was summoned to appear before the Judge and the jury. It was a full moon again, just like the very first time. But also a moon like the one that rose above the waterfalls in the dreamtime when, as a young warrior, I had conquered my fears.

The Judge, seated cross-legged on a bed, was even bigger than I remembered. He wore only pyjama pants, and now sported a crude tattoo high up on his left arm. Cicatrisation wasn't new to me, African women do it to their faces all the time, though I had not seen a tattoo on white skin before. Reddish-pink skin still puckered along the edges of the crude blue lines which crossed at the centre like two headless snakes wriggling across each other.

Absently rubbing his tattoo, the Judge shook his head slowly as he looked at me. 'You are a fool, a *blêrrie* fool to have come back, Pisskop.' A small lump of snot in his left nostril pumped up and down as he breathed.

'You have marks like a Kaffir woman on your arm,' I heard myself saying.

The Judge's eyes seemed to pop out of his head. He snorted in amazement and the snolly-bomb shot out of his nostril and landed on my face. His hand followed a split second later. I felt an explosion in my head as I was knocked to the floor.

I got to my feet. Stars, just like in the comic books, were dancing in a red sky in front of my eyes and there was a ringing noise in my ears. But I wasn't crying. I cursed my stupidity, the holidays had blunted my sense of survival; adapt, blend, become part of the landscape, develop a camouflage, be a rock or a leaf or a stick insect, try in every way to be an Afrikaner. The jury was silent, struck dumb by my audacity. A warm trickle of blood ran from my nose, across my lips and down my chin.

The Judge grabbed me by the front of my pyjamas and pulled me up to his face, lifting me so that I stood on the very tips of my toes. 'This sign means death and destruction to all Rooineks. And you, Pisskop, are going to be the first.' He released me and I stumbled backwards but managed to stay on my feet.

'Yes, sir,' I said, my voice barely audible.

'This is a swastika, man! Do you know what that is?'

'N . . . no, sir.'

'God has sent us this sign from Adolf Hitler who will deliver the Afrikaner people from the hated English!'

I could see the jury was deeply impressed and I was too.

The Judge turned to address the jury, prodding at the swastika.

'We must all swear a blood oath to Adolf Hitler,' he said solemnly. The jury crowded around his bed, their eyes shining with excitement.

'I will swear too,' I said hopefully. The blood was still running from my nose and some had dripped to the floor.

'Don't be fuckin' stupid! Pisskop, you *are* the English.' The Judge stood upright on the bed and held his arm aloft at an angle, with his fingers straight and pointing to the ceiling. 'In the name of Adolf Hitler we will march every Rooinek bastard into the sea.'

I had never been to the sea but I knew it would be a long march all right. 'The blood oath! The blood oath!' the jury chanted.

'Come here, Pisskop,' the Judge commanded. I stepped over to his bed. 'Look up, man.' I looked up at him as he stood high above me on the bed. He wiped his forefinger under my nose and then he pushed me so that I sat down hard on the floor. He held up his finger, my blood on its tip shining in the moonlight.

'We will swear this oath with the blood of a Rooinek!' he announced solemnly. Two members of the jury lifted me to my feet while the others crowded around me, sticking their pudgy fingers into the blood running from my nose. The supply wasn't coming fast enough and one boy tweeked my nose to increase the flow.

This seemed to cause it to stop altogether, so that the last two members were forced to dab their fingers into the drops of blood on the floor.

The Judge, wiping the blood on his finger across the swastika, instructed the jury to do the same. Soon the swastika on his arm was almost totally concealed. 'Death to all Englishmen in South Africa, the fatherland,' the Judge cried, raising his arm once more.

'Death to all Englishmen in South Africa, the fatherland!' the jury chorused.

The Judge looked down at me. 'We won't kill you tonight, Pisskop. But when Hitler comes your days are numbered, you hear?'

'Yes, sir, when will that be, sir?' I asked.

'Soon!' He stepped from the bed, and placing his huge hand over the top of my head he turned me towards the dormitory door and gave me a swift kick up the bum which sent me sprawling headlong across the polished floor. I could smell the wax polish on the floorboards and then I got to my feet and ran.

Back in my own dormitory the little kids leapt out of bed, crowding around me, demanding to know what had happened. Too upset to mind my tongue, I sniffed out the story of the swastika and the blood oath and my threatened demise upon the arrival of Hitler.

An eight-year-old named Danie Coetzee shook his head solemnly.

'Pisskop, you are in deep shit, man,' he said.

'Who is this person called Adolf Hitler who is coming to get Pisskop?' a fellow we called 'Flap-lips' de Jaager asked.

It was apparent nobody knew the answer until Danie Coetzee said, 'He's probably the new headmaster.'

There had been some talk among the kids the previous term about the headmaster and his 'drinking problem'. I had wondered at the time what a drinking problem was. Obviously it was something pretty bad or the huge, morose man we all feared wouldn't be leaving.

One of the kids started to chant softly: 'Pisskop's in trouble. . . Pisskop's in trouble. . .' The others quickly took up the chant which grew louder and louder. I placed my hands over my ears to try to stop it.

'Still!' The dormitory rang to the command. Mevrou stood at the doorway, her huge body filling the door frame.

'We was just talking, Mevrou,' Danie Coetzee said. As the oldest of the small kids he assumed the position of spokesman.

'You know that talking after lights out is verboten, Coetzee.'

Danie Coetzee was left standing at the end of my bed as the others tiptoed back to their beds. 'Ja, Mevrou. Sorry, Mevrou.' His voice sounded small and afraid.

'Bend over the bed, man,' Mevrou instructed. The cane cut through the air in a blur as she planted it into the seat of Coetzee's pyjamas. He let out a fearful yelp, and holding his bum with both hands hopped up and down. Without further ado, Mevrou left the dormitory.

For a moment there wasn't a sound and then Danie Coetzee, his voice on the edge of tears, blurted out, 'You will pay for this you *blêrrie* pisskop Rooinek!'

I waited until everyone was asleep and then crept quietly to the window. The full moon brought a soft sheen to the leaves of the grapefruit trees which seemed to shimmer in the ghosted light. Granpa Chook's headless snake made a silver loop in the moonlight, a beautiful and unexpected decoration on the branch of the cassia tree. 'I didn't cry. They'll never make me cry again!' I said to the moon. Then I returned to my bed. It was the loneliest moment that had ever been.

Granpa Chook's cover was blown the following morning. Like all kaffir chickens he was an early riser. Before even the six o'clock wake-up bell went, the whole dormitory had awakened to his raucous crowing. I awoke, startled out of a deep sleep, to see him perched on the window sill nearest my bed, his long scrawny neck stretched in a mighty rendition of cock-a-doodle-doooo! Then he cocked his head to one side, gave a tiny squawk and, from the window, flew onto my iron bed head. Stretching his long neck towards me, almost to the point of losing his balance, he gave my ear a gentle peck.

The kids raced from their beds to surround me. 'It's an old kaffir chicken come to visit Pisskop,' Flap-lips de Jaager yelled excitedly.

Granpa Chook, imperious on the bed head, fixed them with a beady stare. 'He is mine,' I said defiantly, 'he is my friend.'

Well! You should have heard them carry on. Danie Coetzee, temporarily forgetting his revenge for the caning the previous night, chortled: 'Don't be stupid, man, nobody has a kaffir chicken for a friend!'

'I do, he can do tricks and everything.'

'No he can't! He's a dumb kaffir chicken. Wait till the Judge hears about Pisskop's new friend,' Flap-lips de Jaager volunteered and everyone laughed.

The wake-up bell went, which meant Mevrou would arrive in a minute or two, and so we all scrambled back into bed to await her permission to get up. I barely had time to push Granpa Chook through the window into the orchard and climb back into bed when her huge form loomed through the door.

Mevrou paced the length of the dormitory, her sjambok hanging from a loop on the black leather belt of her dark blue uniform. She stopped as she reached my bed, whipped off the blanket and examined the dry mattress.

'Humph!' she snorted, dropping the blanket onto the floor. I jumped from my bed and stood beside it. She ignored me and turned slowly to address the dormitory. 'I am warning you, *kinders,* if I hear you talking after lights out again, my sjambok will also talk to all of you, you hear?'

'Ja, Mevrou,' we chorused.

Suddenly her eyes grew large and seemed almost to pop out of her head: 'Pisskop! There is chicken shit on your pillow!'

I looked down at my pillow in horror: deposited neatly between two lines of its mattress-ticking cover, Granpa Chook had left his green and white calling card.

'Explain, man!' Mevrou roared.

No explanation but the truth was possible. Shaking with terror I told her about Granpa Chook.

Mevrou glowered at me, and undoing the buckle of her leather belt she slipped the cane from it. 'Pisskop, I think you are sick in the head, like your poor mother. First you come here and you piss in your bed every night. Then you come back and you fill it with chicken shit!' She pointed to the end of the bed where Danie Coetzee had taken his medicine the previous night. 'Bend over,' she commanded.

She blasted me four strokes of the sjambok. Biting back the tears, I forced myself not to grab my bum by clamping my hands tightly between my thighs and hunching my shoulders. This also seemed to stop me shaking.

What a shit of a day already!

'Clean up your pillow and bring this devil's chicken to the kitchen door after breakfast, you hear?' At the door she turned and faced us: 'Go to the showers now,' she commanded.

Granpa Chook and I were in a terrible jam, all right. After breakfast I slipped out of the hostel to find him. He was still in the old orchard clucking and scratching around looking for worms. I produced a slice of bread which I'd saved at breakfast, and while breaking it up into bits small enough for him to swallow explained the latest disaster to him. So much for my resolution not to cry, I could feel the tears running down my cheeks.

After Granpa Chook had had his breakfast I picked him up and, fighting my way through the khaki weed and black jack, I took him to the edge of the orchard to a low corrugated iron fence which marked the hostel boundary. Standing on tiptoe I looked over the fence. My heart gave a leap; in the distance I could see three kaffir huts with smoke rising from a fire, for sure they'd keep kaffir chickens and Granpa Chook could board with them.

Considerably cheered, I explained this new plan to Granpa Chook and then pushed him over the fence. There is a blurred distinction between imagination and reality in a five-year-old child and the new plan, once imagined, was immediately achieved.

Granpa Chook, though, had other ideas. With an indignant squawk and a flap of his wings he was back on my side of the fence. We pantomimed for the next few minutes: over the fence I'd put him and back he'd come. Finally it became clear that the toughest damn chicken in the whole wide world had no intention of deserting his friend, even if his own life was at stake.

We waited at the kitchen door for about ten minutes before Mevrou appeared. 'So this is the chicken that shits in your bed, Pisskop?'

'It wasn't on purpose, Mevrou. He's very clean and very clever too.'

'Look who talks of clean! A chicken is a chicken. Who ever heard of a clever chicken?'

'Look, Mevrou, I'll show you.' I quickly drew a circle in the dust and Granpa Chook immediately hopped into it and settled down as though he were laying an egg, which he couldn't, of course. 'He'll stay in that circle until I say to come out,' I said.

For a moment Mevrou looked impressed and then she suddenly scowled. 'This is just some dumb thing kaffir chickens do that white chickens don't,' she said smugly.

'No, Mevrou!' I begged. 'He can do lots of other things too!'

I made Granpa Chook hop around the perimeter of the circle on one leg going 'squawk' with every hop. I showed her how he would fly onto my shoulder and, at my command, peck my ear.

This last trick signalled the end of Mevrou's patience. 'Your hair will be full of lice, you stupid boy!' she screamed. Just inside the kitchen door stood a butcher's block with a large cleaver resting on it. 'Give me that filthy, lice-ridden, bed-shitting, kaffir chicken!' she yelled, grabbing the cleaver.

Two cockroaches resting under the cleaver on the block raced up the back of Mevrou's hand. She let out an almighty scream, dropping the cleaver and frantically flapping both arms. One cockroach dropped to the floor, while the other ran up her arm and disappeared down her bodice.

With a delighted squawk, Granpa Chook came charging into the kitchen and scooped up the cockroach frantically crossing the kitchen floor. Mevrou was waving her arms, her bosoms jiggling up and down. She made little gasping noises as though she was struggling to get a scream out as she danced from one foot to the other in extreme agitation. The second cockroach fell from under her skirt and made for a crack in the polished cement floor. But Granpa Chook was too fast for it and had it in a trice.

Mevrou had turned a deep crimson and her head seemed to vibrate from the shock. 'It's orright, Mevrou, the other one fell out and Granpa Chook got it,' I said, pointing to Granpa Chook strutting around looking very pleased with himself.

I rushed to fetch a kitchen chair and Mevrou plopped down into it like an overripe watermelon. Taking a dishcloth from a drying rack beside the huge black woodburning stove, I began to fan her the way I had seen Nanny do when my mother had one of her turns.

I became aware of a dripping sound coming from under the rattan seat of the chair and realised in alarm that Mevrou had pissed her pants. I think she must have been too upset to notice it herself. I wondered how many strokes pissing your pants would earn in her book. When she had recovered somewhat she pointed a trembling finger at Granpa Chook.

'You are right, Pisskop. That is a good chicken. He can stay. But he has to earn his keep,' she gasped. Then she seemed to become aware of what had happened beneath the chair. 'Go now,' she said, and grabbing the cloth from my hand she pointed to the door.

And that's how Granpa Chook came to do kitchen duty. Every day after breakfast he checked every last corner in the hostel kitchen for creepy-crawlies of every description. The toughest damn chicken in the world had survived, he had beaten the executor by adapting perfectly and we were safely together again.

The weeks and then a couple of months went by. I had become slave to the Judge. In return for being at his constant beck and call, I was more or less left to my own devices. The odd cuff behind the head or a rude push from an older kid was about all I had to endure. Things were pretty good, really. If the Judge needed me he would simply put two fingers to his mouth and give one of his piercing whistles, and Granpa Chook and I would come running.

Granpa Chook was now under the protection of Mevrou, although he still needed to be constantly on the alert. Farm kids just can't help chucking stones at kaffir chickens. He would cluck around the playground during lessons, hunting for grubs. The moment the recess bell went he would come charging over to my classroom, skidding to a halt in the dust, cackling his anxiety to be with me again.

No class existed for my age and so I had been placed with the seven-year-old kids, all of whom were still learning to read. I had been reading in English for at least a year so that the switch to reading Afrikaans wasn't difficult, and I was soon the best in the class. Yet I quickly realised that survival means never being best at anything except being best at nothing, and I soon learned to minimise my reading skills, appearing to pause and stumble over words which were perfectly clear to me.

Mediocrity is the best camouflage known to man. Our teacher, Miss du Plessis, wasn't anxious for a five-year-old Rooinek to shine in a class of knot-headed Boers. She was happy enough to put my poor results down to my inability to grasp the subtlety of the Afrikaans language as well as being the youngest in class, whereas I already spoke Zulu and Shangaan and, like most small kids, found learning a new language simple enough.

It became increasingly hard for the other kids to think of me as being different when no visible or audible differences separated us. Except, of course, for my hatless snake; but even this, like a kid with a birthmark or a little finger missing, started to go unnoticed. I was becoming the perfect stick insect.

And then on September 3rd, 1939, Neville Chamberlain finally and sadly concluded that Herr Hitler was not a gentleman, not to be trusted and not open to negotiation. That Britain, having let Czechoslovakia down thoroughly, couldn't face the embarrassment of doing the same thing to Poland and so found it necessary to declare war on Germany. The new headmaster had arrived.

At lunch in the hostel dining hall, the old headmaster with the drinking problem addressed us. He stood, swaying slightly, both hands holding the edge of the table. Then, picking up a knife, he thumped it on the table with the handle. 'Silence!' he roared. Whereupon Miss du Plessis, lips pursed, rose quickly and left through the swinging doors. The old headmaster seemed not to notice, dropping the knife onto the table he started to talk in a very loud voice, as though he were addressing hundreds of people: 'Today, England has declared war on Germany!' He paused to gauge the effect of his words on us. There was no reaction except for a low murmur from where the senior boys sat. 'Do you know what this means, man?' Not waiting for an answer he continued, 'It means freedom! Freedom and liberty for our beloved fatherland! Adolf Hitler will destroy the cursed English and remove the yoke of oppression placed on the Afrikaner nation by these *uitlanders* who burn down homes and imprison Boer women and children in concentration camps where twenty-six thousand died of starvation, dysentery and black-water fever!'

The headmaster made it sound as though it was all happening at that very moment in South Africa. I suddenly realised that this was what had really happened to my mother. She had been mistaken for a Boer woman and put in a concentration camp.

The headmaster took a couple of steps back from the table and then lurched forward again, his spit-flecked mouth worked silently, as though he were trying to say something but it wouldn't come out. Instead he raised his arm in the same way the Judge had done in the dormitory. 'Heil Hitler!' he blurted out at last.

Just then the doors burst open and Mevrou entered the dining room; through the briefly open doors we could see Miss du Plessis standing in the hallway biting her knuckles. Mevrou marched up to the headmaster, and taking him firmly by the elbow she led him quickly from the dining hall.

'Heil Hitler!' he shouted back at us as he passed through the swing doors.

We sat there bewildered. Then the Judge jumped to his feet and stepped up onto the bench on his side of the top table. He rolled the sleeve of his shirt up over the top of his shoulder so we could all see the crude blue crossed and angled lines of his swastika tattoo.

'Adolf Hitler is the King of Germany and God has sent him to take South Africa back from the English and give it to us.' He jabbed at the swastika on his arm. 'This is his sign . . . the swastika, the swastika will make us free again.' His right hand shot up in the same salute the headmaster had given moments before. 'Heil Hitler!' he cried.

We all jumped to our feet and, thrusting our arms out in the manner of his own, yelled, 'Heil Hitler!'

It was all very exciting. To think that this man, Adolf Hitler, who was going to save us all from the accursed English, was going to be our new headmaster!

Then, slowly at first, the words of the Judge on the first night back at school began to form in my mind, gathered momentum, and then roared into my consciousness.

'Don't be stupid! Pisskop, you *are* the fuckin' English!'

The long march to the sea had begun.

Flap-lips de Jaager at our table just kept on shouting 'Heil Hitler' and soon everyone was chanting it louder and louder. A piercing whistle from the Judge finally stopped them.

'Some of us have sworn a blood oath to Adolf Hitler and the time has now come to march the Rooineks into the sea. After school we will meet behind the shit houses for a council of war!'

I don't suppose any of us had much idea of where the sea was supposed to be, somewhere across the Lebombo Mountains and probably over the Limpopo River. Whichever direction, it was a long, long way away. The long march to the sea would be a pretty serious undertaking and I could understand why it would take some planning.

The dining room buzzed with excitement and the Judge held up his hand to silence us. Then he pointed directly at me. 'Pisskop, you are our first prisoner of war!' He brought his fingers together and raised his arm higher. 'Heil Hitler!' he shouted.

We all jumped up again, but the two kids on either side of me pushed me back into my seat. 'Heil Hitler!' the rest of the dining hall chorused back.

It was the most exciting day in the school's history, although my own prospects looked pretty bleak. What was certain was that Granpa Chook and I were living on borrowed time and needed to make some pretty urgent escape plans. I was in despair. Even if I did know how to get home, which I didn't, how far could a little kid and a chicken travel without being spotted by the enemy?

That afternoon in class Miss du Plessis, who seemed even more upset than usual, rapped my knuckles sharply on two occasions with her eighteen-inch ruler. In the end she grew totally exasperated when, deep into my escape plans, I simply didn't hear her ask what three times four came to.

'*Domkop*! You will have to stay in after school!' The idea was impossible. Granpa Chook and I had to escape before the council of war met behind the shit houses.

'Please, miss! I'm sorry, miss. It won't happen again, miss,' I begged. In a desperate attempt to make amends I blew my camouflage. I recited the nine times table, then the ten, eleven and twelve. I had carefully concealed my knowledge of anything beyond the four times table and, what's more, we hadn't even reached the eleven and twelve times tables in class. The effect was profound. By the time I had almost completed the twelve times table, which I'd learned from the back of the Judge's arithmetic book, Miss du Plessis was consumed by anger.

'Twelve times twelve is, ah . . . one hundred and . . . er, forty-four,' I announced, my voice faltering as I perceived the extent of her indignation.

'You wicked, rotten, lying, cheating child!' she screamed, raising her steel-edged ruler. The blows rained down on me though, in her agitation, her aim was wild and I took most of them on my arms and shoulders. One swipe got through my guard and the thin metal strip in the ruler sliced into the top of my ear. I dropped my guard and grabbed at my ear which was stinging like billy-o. The warm blood started to run through my fingers and down my arm.

The sight of the blood snapped Miss du Plessis out of her frenzy. She looked down at me and brought her hand to her mouth. Then she screamed and fell dead at my feet.

The shock of seeing Miss du Plessis drop dead at my feet was so great that I was unable to move. The blood dripped from my ear onto her spotless white blouse until a crimson blot the size of my fist stained the area just above her heart.

'Cripes! You've broken her heart and killed her,' I heard Flap-lips de Jaager say as he ran from the classroom. All the others followed, screaming as they fought each other to vacate the scene of the crime. I just stood there, unable to think, the blood leaking from my head.

I was unaware of anyone entering the room until a huge hand lifted me and hurled me across the classroom where I landed against the wall. I was too stunned to hurt and sat there propped up by the wall like a discarded rag doll. Mr Stoffel, the master who taught the Judge's class, was on his knees bending over Miss du Plessis and shaking her by the shoulder. His eyes grew wide as he observed the blood on her blouse. 'Shit, he's killed her!' I heard him say.

Just then Miss du Plessis opened her eyes and sat up like Lazarus. Then she looked down and saw her bloodstained blouse and with a soft sigh she passed out again. Mr Stoffel slapped her cheeks and she opened her eyes and sat up. 'Oh, oh, what have I done!' she sobbed.

Quite suddenly the classroom grew very still and dark, like a cloud passing over the sun. I could dimly see Mr Stoffel coming towards me, his long, hairy arms flapping at his sides as though in slow motion, his shape wavy at the edges. I tried to cover my face but my arms refused to lift from my lap.

'Look what happens when you forget your camouflage, Pisskop,' I observed to myself. Then I must have passed out.

I awoke in my bed in the small kids' dormitory, but before I'd opened my eyes I could smell Mevrou at my side. She must have seen the flicker of my eyelids. 'Are you awake, Pisskop?' she asked, not unkindly.

'Ja, Mevrou.' I was back in the real world and I quickly gathered my mental camouflage about me. My head was swathed in a thick crêpe bandage and I was wearing my pyjamas. My head didn't hurt a bit but my shoulder ached where I'd landed against the wall.

'Now listen to me, Pisskop.' There was a note of urgency in Mevrou's voice. 'When the doctor comes you must tell him you fell out of a tree, you hear?'

'Ja, Mevrou.'

'What tree did you fall out of, Pisskop?' she asked.

'There was no tree, Mevrou.' I had fallen at once for the trick.

'Domkop!' she shouted. 'Wash out your ears. What did I just tell you, man?'

'It was the mango tree, the big one next to the playground,' I corrected.

'Ja, that's good, the mango tree.' She rose from the chair beside my bed. 'You have a good memory when you try, Pisskop. Remember to tell the doctor when he comes.'

No sooner had she left than I leapt from the bed and ran to the window where I whistled for Granpa Chook. In a few moments he appeared, clucking and beady-eyed as ever as he came to rest on the window sill beside me.

'Granpa Chook, we're in a lot of trouble,' I told him and explained about the arrival any day now of Adolf Hitler who was coming to march us into the sea. 'Can you swim?' I asked him. Granpa Chook was so amazing that it wouldn't have surprised me if he turned out to be the only chicken in the world who could swim.

'Squawk!' he replied, which could have meant he could or he couldn't, who's to say? Granpa Chook wasn't always easy to understand.

We could hear voices coming towards the dormitory so I quickly pushed Granpa Chook back into the orchard and jumped into bed.

To my joy Mevrou entered with Dr Henny. He sat on my bed and unwound the bandage around my head. 'What's the matter, son? You look pretty done in.'

Even if Dr Henny wasn't a Rooinek I knew he was on my side, and I longed to burst into tears and tell him all my troubles. But I had already blown my camouflage once that day with near disastrous results. A bandaged ear and a sore shoulder weren't too bad a result for having been unforgivably stupid. Next time I might not be so lucky. Choking back the tears I told him how I had fallen from the big old mango tree next to the playground.

I must have laid it on a bit thick because he turned to Mevrou and in Afrikaans he said: 'Hmm, except for the cut between the ear and the skull there are no contusions or abrasions, are you quite sure this child fell from a tree?'

'The other children saw it happen, Doctor. There is no doubt.' Mevrou said this with such conviction that I began to wonder myself. I realised that Dr Henny's line of questioning could only mean trouble for me.

'It's true, sir. That's what happened, I fell out of the tree and hurt my shoulder against the wall.'

Dr Henny didn't seem to notice that I'd replied in Afrikaans. 'The wall? What wall?'

Fear showed for a moment in Mevrou's eyes but she quickly recovered. 'The child doesn't speak Afrikaans very well, he means the ground.'

'Ja, the ground,' I added, my camouflage damn nearly blown sky high.

Dr Henny looked puzzled. 'Okay, let's look at your shoulder, then.' He rotated my shoulder clockwise. 'That hurt? Tell me when it hurts.' I shook my head. He moved it the opposite way with the same result. Then he lifted it upwards and I winced. 'That's sore, hey?' I nodded. 'Well it's not dislocated anyway.' He checked my heart and chest and my back with his stethoscope which was cold against my skin. 'Seems fine. We'll just put in a couple of little stitches and you'll be right as rain,' he said in English.

'Can I go home please?'

'No need for that, old son. You'll be brand new tomorrow.' He dug into his bag and produced a yellow sucker. 'Here, this will make you feel better, you get stuck into that while I fix up these stitches.'

He must have seen the look on my face. 'Ja, it's going to hurt a bit, but you're not going to cry on me now, are you?'

'He's a brave boy, Doctor,' Mevrou said, relaxed now that the truth had remained concealed.

'Well done,' Henny said, dabbing my stiches with mercurochrome, 'no need for a bandage, we'll be back in a week to remove the stitches.' He turned to Mevrou, 'Let me know if he complains of backache.' He took a second sucker from his bag and handed it to me. 'That's for being extra brave.'

'Thank you, sir. Doctor Henny, are you English?' I asked, taking the second sucker.

His expression changed and I could see that he was upset. 'We are all South Africans, son. Don't let anyone tell you otherwise.' He spoke with a quiet vehemence, then repeated: 'Don't let anyone ever tell you anything else!'

I had certainly had better days, but a two-sucker day doesn't come along very often so it wasn't all bad.

Despite my prisoner of war status, the kids were pretty good for the next few days. My stitches made me a hero in the small kids' dormitory and even Maatie de Jaager kept his loose mouth buttoned for a change.

We had a new teacher, Mrs Gerber, who turned out to be the wife of the Government vet who had once come out to the farm to check Granpa's black Orpingtons for Newcastle's disease. Mrs Gerber wasn't tetchy and I don't think she even knew I was a Rooinek. She wasn't a real teacher so she was quite nice.

There was a rumour going around that Miss du Plessis had suffered a nervous breakdown. I knew of course that I was to blame and it struck me with dismay that I had probably been the direct cause of my mother's nervous breakdown as well. I must be a nervous breakdown type of person. First my mother, now Miss du Plessis and, while I hadn't given Mevrou one yet, I had caused her to piss in her pants, which was probably the next best thing.

Granpa Chook and I discussed our predicament at some length but were unable to reach a useful conclusion. After all, Granpa Chook was a kaffir chicken and they don't have such a good life. One minute you're walking along scratching about and the next you're dinner for a jackal or a python, or bubbling away in a three-legged cast-iron cooking pot. Granpa Chook, a proven survivor, worked on the principle that if anything bad could happen it would. A five-year-old isn't much of a pessimist, though we agreed that one thing was for sure, something pretty bad was bound to happen.

THREE

The night after I had my stitches out I was summoned to appear before the Judge and jury.

The Judge had been quite nice to me over the previous week and, because of my sore shoulder, hadn't required that I carry his books to school each day. In fact, because Miss du Plessis was generally disliked, I'd become a bit of a hero.

But Rooineks in this part of the world are not designed to be permanent heroes. I knew it would soon come to an end: when the stitches were out, my temporary reprieve would be over. So, here I was again, being marched straight into another calamity.

'Stand to attention, prisoner Pisskop,' the Judge snarled.

I drew myself up, my arms ramrods at my side. 'Bring your stupid legs together, man!' one of the jury shouted.

'Name?'

I looked confused, everyone knew my name?

'What is your name, Pisskop?' the Judge asked again.

'Pisskop?' I ventured, still not certain what he meant.

'What does your name mean?'

Again I looked querulous. 'That I piss my bed?'

'Ja, and chickens shit in it as well! What is a Rooinek?'

'I am English.'

'Yes I know, man! But how do you know you're a Rooinek?'

'I . . . I just know, sir.'

The Judge shook his head and gave a deep sigh. 'Come here. Come closer, man.'

I stepped forward to stand directly in front of where he sat cross-legged on his bed. The Judge's arm came up and my hand flew up to protect my face, but instead of hitting me he pulled at the cord of my pyjama pants which collapsed round my ankles.

'Your blêrrie snake has no hat on its head, domkop! That's how you know you're English! Understand?'

'Yes, sir.' I bent down to pull my pyjama pants back up.

'Don't!' I jumped back to attention. 'What am I, Pisskop?' the Judge demanded.

'A Boer, sir?'

'Yes, and what is a Boer?'

'An Afrikaner, sir.'

'Yes, of course . . . but what else?'

'A Boer has a hat on his snake.' Why, when He has made all white people look alike, had God given the English snakes without a hat? It seemed terribly unfair. My camouflage was perfect except for this one little thing.

'Tonight you will learn to march. We must get you ready for your march into the sea.' The Judge pointed to the corridor between the beds and gave me a push. I tripped over my pyjama pants and fell to the floor. One of the jury reached down and pulled the pants away from my ankles. I rose bare-arsed and looked uncertainly at the Judge. 'March!' he commanded, pointing down the corridor between the beds once more. I started to march, swinging my arms high. *'Links, regs, links, regs, halt!'* he bawled. Then again: 'Left, right, left, right, halt! Which is your left foot, prisoner Pisskop?' I had no idea but pointed to a foot. 'Domkop! Don't you even know your left from your right?'

'No, sir,' I said, feeling stupid. But I did now, the left side was where my shoulder hurt.

'Every day after school you will march around the playground for five thousand steps, you hear?' I nodded. 'You will count backwards from five thousand until you get to number one.'

I couldn't believe my luck, no one had laid a hand on me. I retrieved my pyjama pants and scurried back along the dark passage to my dormitory.

Being a prisoner of war and learning how to march wasn't such a bad thing. I had nothing to do after school anyway. But I must admit, counting backwards from five thousand isn't much of a way to pass the time. It's impossible anyway, your thoughts wander and before you know it you're all jumbled up and have to start all over again. I learned to mumble a number if anyone came close, but mostly I did the Judge's homework in my head. Carrying his books from school, I would memorise his arithmetic lesson and then I would work the equations out in my head as I marched along. If things got a bit complicated, I'd make sure nobody was looking and I'd work out a more complex sum using a stick in the dirt. It got so I couldn't wait to see what he'd done in class each day.

The Judge was an awful domkop. In the mornings carrying his books to school I'd check his homework. It was always a mess and mostly all wrong. I began to despair for him and for myself as well; you see, he could only leave the school if the work he did during the year gave him a pass mark. So far, he didn't have a hope. If he failed I'd have him for another year. That is, if Hitler hadn't come by then to march me away.

Escape seemed impossible, so I'd have to think of something else. Over a period of several marching afternoons a plan began to form. The something else, when it finally emerged, was breathtakingly simple though fraught with danger. For the next two days I thought of little else. If I blew my camouflage and helped the Judge with his homework so that he would pass, would he not be forced to spare Granpa Chook and me if Adolf Hitler arrived before the end of term?

I must say I was worried. Every time I had blown my camouflage disaster had followed. Finally, after a long talk with Granpa Chook, we agreed it was a chance worth taking.

After breakfast the following morning, when I was folding the Judge's blanket and arranging his towel over his bed rail, I broached the subject. He was sitting on a bed licking his pencil and trying to do some last-minute arithmetic.

'Can I help you, sir?' My heart thumped like a donkey engine, though I was surprised how steady my voice sounded.

'Push off, Pisskop. Can't you see I'm busy, man.' The Judge was doing the fractions I'd done in my head the previous afternoon and getting them hopelessly wrong.

Gulping down my fear I said, 'What happens if you don't pass at the end of the year?' The Judge looked at me, I could see the thought wasn't new to him. He reached out and grabbed me by the shirtfront.

'If I don't pass, I'll kill you first and then I'll run away!'

I took my courage in both hands. 'I . . . I can help you, sir,' I stammered.

The Judge released me and went back to chewing his pencil, his brow furrowed as he squinted at the page of equations. He appeared not to have heard me. I pointed to the equation he'd just completed. 'That's wrong. The answer is seven-ninths.' I moved my finger quickly. 'Four-fifths, six-eighths, nine-tenths, five-sevenths . . . ' I paused as he grabbed my hand and looked up at me, open-mouthed.

'Where did you learn to do this, man?'

I shrugged, 'It's just easy for me, that's all.' I hoped he couldn't sense how scared I was.

A look of cunning came into his eyes. He released my hand and handed me the book and the pencil. 'Just write the answers very softly and I'll copy them, you hear?'

The camouflage was intact and I'd moved up into the next evolutionary stage. From knowing to hide my brains I had now learned to use them. Granpa Chook and I were one step further away from the sea.

But I had already experienced the consequences of revealing too much too soon. I knew if a domkop like the Judge went from bottom to the top of his class overnight, Mr Stoffel would soon smell a rat. Telling the Judge he was a duffer was more than my life was worth. Besides, I was beginning to understand how manipulation can be an important weapon in the armoury of the small and weak.

'We have a problem,' I said to the Judge.

'What problem, man? I don't see a problem. You just write in the answers very soft, that's all.'

'Judge, you're a very clever fellow.'

'Ja, that's right. So?'

'So arithmetic doesn't interest you, does it? I mean, if it did you could do it,' I snapped my fingers, 'just like that!'

'Ja, if I wanted to I could. Only little kids like you are interested in all that shit!'

I could see this conclusion pleased him and I grew bolder. 'So you can't just get ten out of ten today when yesterday you only got two sums right out of ten. Mr Stoffel will know there's some monkey business going on.'

The Judge looked worried. 'You mean, you're not going to help me?'

'Of course I am. But you will get better a little bit each week and you'll tell Mr Stoffel that you suddenly got the hang of doing sums.'

The Judge looked relieved and then grinned slyly. *'Jy is 'n slimmetjie,* Pisskop,' he said.

The Judge had called me clever. Me! Pisskop! Rooinek and possessor of a hatless snake! It was the greatest compliment of my life and I was beside myself with pride.

But before the Judge could notice the effect of his words on me, I quickly resumed my obsequious manner. The thrill of the compliment had almost caused me to forget my other anxiety.

'What will happen if Adolf Hitler comes before the end of term?' I asked, my heart beating overtime.

The Judge looked at me blankly, then suddenly grinned, understanding the reason for my question. 'Okay, man, you got me there. I will say nothing until I've passed at the end of the year.' He shook his head and gave me a look not entirely without sympathy. 'I'm sorry, Pisskop, after that I will have to tell him about you. You must be punished for killing twenty-six thousand Boer women and children. You and your stupid kaffir chicken are dead meat when he comes. But I'll tell you something, I give you my word as a Boer, if I pass in sums, I swear on a stack of Bibles not to tell Adolf Hitler until next term.'

The Judge, his brow furrowed as though he were doing the calculations himself, started to copy over the answers I had written in his exercise book.

I had won; my plan had worked. I could hardly believe my ears. Granpa Chook and I were safe for the remainder of the term.

The Judge had come to the end of his copying. I had never seen him quite so happy, not even when he was Heil Hitlering all over the place. I saw my opportunity and, taking a sharp inward breath, said quickly, 'It will be difficult to march every afternoon and still do your homework, sir.'

The inside of my head filled with a zinging sound. Had I gone too far? I'd won the battle and here I was risking all on a minor skirmish. Marching around wasn't so bad. Quite fun really. What if he realised I used the time to do his homework anyway?

The Judge sniffed and wiped his nose on the back of his hand. 'Orright, no more marching. But you do my homework, you hear? If I catch you and that kaffir chicken messing around, you'll do twice as much marching as before. You are both prisoners of war and you better not forget it, man.'

Victory was mine a second time. My first conscious efforts at manipulation had been successful. It was a heady feeling as Granpa Chook and I followed the Judge to school that morning.

One thing is certain in life. Just when things are going well, soon after they are certain to go wrong. It's just the way things are meant to be.

Mrs Gerber told us that day in class, there had been an outbreak of Newcastle's disease on a chicken farm near Merensky Dam. Her husband, the vet, had left to visit all the surrounding farms.

Even the youngest kids know what havoc a disease of any kind can cause with poultry or livestock. Of course, rinderpest and foot-and-mouth disease amongst the cattle were the worst, but every farm keeps at least fifty chickens for eggs, so Mrs Gerber's news was met with consternation. My mother had once said that if my granpa lost all his black Orpingtons it would break his heart.

It was pretty depressing to think of my mother with her nervous breakdown in an English concentration camp knitting jumpers with funny sleeves. Knitting away with all the Boer mothers and children as she waited to starve to death or die of blackwater fever. Meanwhile, back on the farm, there was poor old Granpa slowly dying of a broken heart. That was, if Adolf Hitler didn't arrive first. If he did, I knew Granpa wouldn't even have the strength to make escape plans or drive the Model A and then what would become of me?

Maybe I could live with Nanny in Zululand? This thought cheered me up a lot. Adolf Hitler would never look for a small English person in the middle of Zululand. Inkosi-Inkosikazi would hide me with a magic spell and they wouldn't have a hope. As for Granpa Chook, Adolf Hitler would never be able to tell an English-speaking chicken apart from all the other kaffir chickens. I decided right there and then, when I got back to the farm I would put this excellent plan to Nanny.

From what we could gather from the Judge, who was allowed to listen to the news on Mr Stoffel's wireless on Saturday nights, the war was going pretty badly for the English. Adolf Hitler had taken Poland, which I took to be a place somewhere in South Africa, like Zululand, but where the Po tribe lived. The Judge made it sound as though Adolf Hitler could be expected any day now in our neck of the woods.

I had no idea that South Africa was on England's side, from where I sat the English were most definitely the local enemy. While I knew myself to be English, I regarded this as my misfortune, like being born into a poor and degenerate family.

Most of my information came from the regular war councils the Judge held behind the school shit houses. All the senior hostel boys were stormtroopers and Danie Coetzee, as head of the small kids' dormitory, was also allowed to attend. As the official prisoners of war, Granpa Chook and I were dragged along for the purposes of interrogation and torture.

I was blindfolded and tied to the trunk of a jacaranda tree with a rope around my chest and waist, leaving my arms and legs free. This was because two of the main tortures required my hands to be free.

Most torture sessions began with the iron bar which was known as 'Chinese torture' after the make of the Judge's big, cheap pocket watch, one of his most treasured possessions. I was required to hold the bar out in front of me while he timed each session, so that I would have to hold the bar up longer than the previous time before dropping it. My times were duly recorded by a kid called Boetie Van der Merwe, who was known in the Nazi Party as Stormtrooper, Timekeeper and Tallyman.

Van der Merwe was very proud of his job and would remind me at every opportunity of the minimum time allocated for the next Chinese torture session. If I failed to better my previous time I got a severe cuff from the Judge and the six stormtroopers whose turn it was to beat me up.

The second main torture which required my hands be free was referred to as 'shooting practice'. Every stormtrooper carried a catapult as his deadly weapon. Farm kids all have catapults for shooting birds and grow very skilled at using them. While they were not allowed to be worn openly, all the senior boys had one stashed away and they would wear these around their necks at Nazi Party meetings.

For shooting practice I was required to stretch my arms out on either side of me with my palms open and turned upwards. An empty jam tin was placed on either hand and each of the stormtroopers was allowed two shots to try to knock the tins down. The six best results for the day earned the right to beat me up on the next occasion it became necessary. As usual, Boetie Van der Merwe was the tallyman.

I must say this for those Nazis, while they hit the tins from twenty feet often enough, only once did I collect a stone which thudded into the butt of my hand. Lucky it was my left hand as I was unable to use it for several days.

Granpa Chook would fly up onto a branch of the jacaranda where he would keep a beady eye on the proceedings. He was known to the Nazi Party as Prisoner of War Kaffir Chicken Rooinek. There isn't too much interrogation and torture you can do to a chicken. As Mevrou's leading kitchen insect exterminator, Granpa Chook was pretty safe. Tough as the Judge was, he wasn't willing to take Mevrou on.

He would look up at Granpa Chook and say menacingly, 'Your time will come, Prisoner of War Kaffir Chicken Rooinek, don't think we've forgotten about you, you hear?'

I was constantly fearful for Granpa Chook but there wasn't much I could do about it. Like me, he was a prisoner of war. Together we just had to hope for the best and try to muddle through. Besides, Granpa Chook had it easy up there in the jacaranda tree while I was the one who suffered at ground level.

The Nazi Party sessions were held twice a week. Although they would leave me trembling for hours afterwards, the physical damage wasn't too bad. I only got hit if I dropped the iron bar too soon and in one or two other conditions, like when the Judge got very excited or I failed to answer one of his ranting questions fast enough for his liking.

'What is your mother, Pisskop?'

'A whore, sir!' I had no idea what a whore was, but I knew it was the answer he wanted.

'Who does she sleep with?'

'Kaffirs, sir.'

'Ag sis man! Dirty, stinking Kaffirs!' the rest of the Nazis would chorus, groaning and sticking their tongues out and clasping their hands to their throats pretending to vomit.

Even the smallest farm kid knows about animal sex, though it never occurred to me that humans performed the same function. I would wonder why this particular answer was so insulting. After all, Nanny had slept with me on her sleeping mat at the foot of my bed all my life and to the Nazis she was a Kaffir.

'What are you, Pisskop?'

'A piece of shit!' I would respond.

'Not shit! Dog shit!' they would all chorus back.

You can get used to anything, I discovered. They expected me to make the mistake so that they could all pantomime back. Halfway through the interrogation I would be blindfolded. Then, often in the middle of an interrogation, someone would throw a bucket of water over me. Knowing it might come but not knowing when, meant that I would get an awful shock. The imagination is always the best torturer.

Or they would release half a dozen red ants down my trousers and watch me frantically trying to find them as the ants bit painfully into my scrotum and the soft inner parts of my legs. If I tore my blindfold away it would mean a double clout from every member of the Party. I soon learnt that a red ant tends to bite only once if you leave it alone. But, let me tell you something, that one bite isn't a very nice experience.

If some new trick, like the red ants, worked, they would congratulate each other loudly and yell with laughter as my legs pumped up and down and my hands searched frantically in my khaki shorts to rid myself of the marauding ants.

The Judge encouraged new insults and tortures, but he ruled out any torture that left obvious bruises. For instance, Chinese burns were allowed but pinching was out. As the last term wore on, their limited minds ran out of ideas, and as I knew all the answers to all the dumb questions and had admitted to everything they accused me of while happily accepting all their insults, the proceedings quietened down a lot. I have found in life that everything, no matter how bad, comes to an end.

One thing got to all of them more than anything else. They couldn't make me cry. Even the Judge, with all the fear he could provoke, could not make me cry. I suspect they even began to admire me a bit. Many of them had little brothers of my age at home and they knew how easy it is for a five-year-old to cry. In fact I had turned six but nobody had told me, so in my head I was still five.

Not being able to cry was the hardest part for me as well. Crying can be a good camouflage. In truth, my willpower had very little to do with my resolve never to cry, I had learned a special trick and, in the process, had somehow lost the knack of turning on the tap.

What they didn't know was that behind the blindfold I had learned to be in two places at once. I could easily answer their stupid questions, while with another part of my mind I would visit Inkosi-Inkosikazi. Down there in the night country I was safe from the stormtroopers who were unable to harm me or make me cry.

As they tied the dirty piece of rag over my eyes, I would take three deep breaths. Immediately I would hear Inkosi-Inkosikazi's voice, soft as distant thunder: 'You are standing on the rock above the highest waterfall, a young warrior who has killed his first lion and is thus worthy to fight in the impi of Shaka, the greatest warrior king of all.'

I stood in the moonlight on the rock above the three waterfalls. Far below I could see the ten stones wet and glistening and the white water as it crashed through the narrow gorge beyond. I knew then that the person on the outside was only a shell, a presence to be seen and provoked. Inside was the real me, where my tears joined the tears of all the sad people to form the three waterfalls in the night country.

The last term of the year had come to an end, only one more day remained, just one more interrogation, then freedom.

The Judge had pleased Mr Stoffel with his efforts in the final term and his poor performance earlier in the year had been forgotten. He was top of his class by the time term ended. Mr Stoffel would hold him up as an example and I think he also liked to take a bit of the credit. The Judge had been considered a hopeless case and now he was the star performer. The Judge showed me his report card which said, in black and white, that he had passed. He had come to accept his brilliance and expected the compliments of his fellow Party members. Not only was he tough but he was also smart, it was a most satisfactory situation.

Therefore I had no reason to expect anything but a light going over at the last interrogation and torture session before the Judge would disappear from my life forever. After all he owed me something, and as Adolf Hitler, despite his smashing victory at a place called Dunkirk, hadn't arrived yet he hadn't been compromised one bit.

Prisoners of War Pisskop and Kaffir Chicken Rooinek were marched off to the jacaranda tree for the last time under the Nazi leadership of the Judge. This time I was blindfolded immediately as I was tied to the tree in the usual manner. I could hear Granpa Chook squawking away in the branches above me. I was about to visit the night country when the Judge's voice rang out harshly.

'This is the last time, English bastard!'

With a sudden certainty I knew today would be different. That, in his mind, the Judge owed me nothing. The bad times were back. I tried to get down to the safety of the night country, but the fear rose in me like a Vesuvius spewing vomit and I was unable to detach myself from it.

'Today, Englishman, you eat shit.' His use of the word 'Englishman' rather than the familiar, almost friendly Rooinek added greatly to his menace.

'Hold your hands out in front of you.' I could hear him sniff as I held my hands out in front of me, palms upwards. He grabbed my arms about the wrists and held them so tightly I couldn't move them. 'Bring it here, Stormtrooper Van der Merwe,' I heard him say.

A soft object was dropped first into one hand and then into the other. 'Close your hands, bastard,' the Judge commanded.

The pain in my wrists was almost unbearable. Slowly I closed my hands. 'Take his blindfold off,' the Judge commanded again. The rest of the Nazis had grown very quiet and one of them unknotted the blindfold. I blinked at the sudden light. My nose as well as my eyes had been covered by the blindfold and even before I'd looked down a terrible smell rose up at me. My hands were sticky and I opened them to see that they contained two squashed human turds.

The Judge released my wrists. 'Now, lick your fingers,' he demanded.

I stood with my hands held out in front of me, not knowing what to do.

'I am going to count to three, if you haven't licked your fingers I'm going to knock your blêrrie head off, you shit house!' The Judge stood pop-eyed in front of me and I could see he was trembling.

I was too deeply shocked to react. I think I would have eaten the shit when the message finally made it through my disconnected brain. But at that moment all the wires were fusing.

'Een . . . twee . . . drie!' he counted. The Judge reached three and I remained with my hands held out in front of me, quaking with terror. He made a gurgling sort of animal sound deep in his throat, then, grabbing my wrists, he forced my hands into my mouth. My teeth were clamped shut in fear, and the shit was rubbed all over my lips and teeth and the rest of my face. Some of it must have got onto the Judge's hand because he released my wrists and wiped it through my closely cropped hair.

Then he grabbed the tree trunk about two feet above my head, his body straddled over mine. First he tried to shake the tree. Then he began beating at it with his clenched fists. Suddenly he threw his head back so that he was looking directly upwards into the tree.

'Heil Hitler!' he screamed.

In the tree high above the Judge Granpa Chook's anus opened, and from it dropped a perfect bomb of green and white chicken shit straight into the Judge's open mouth.

Granpa Chook had waited until the last day of term to give his opinion of the Nazi Party. As usual it was short, accurate and to the point.

The Judge spat furiously, bent double, racing round in circles clutching his throat and stomach, hawking and spitting and then finally throwing up. He raced for the tap and filled his mouth and spat out about six times. Then he stuck his index finger into his mouth like a toothbrush and rubbed his teeth and gums, took more water and spat and spat.

'Run, Granpa Chook! Run, man, run!' I screamed up into the tree.

But Granpa Chook had done enough running for one old kaffir chicken. Sitting squawking up there amongst the purple jacaranda blossom he sounded as though he was laughing his scraggy old head off.

'Please run, Granpa Chook, please, please run! The bastard will kill you!' I screamed, oblivious to the shit on my face and m my hair.

Granpa Chook hopped onto a lower branch and then, to my horror, flew onto my shoulder and gave my ear one of his famous Granpa Chook kisses. I grabbed him, intending to throw him on his way, but as I lifted him from my shoulder there was an explosion of feathers in my face. Granpa Chook let out a fearful squawk as he was blasted from my hands and fell to the ground. The Judge stood a few feet away, his empty catapult dangling in his left hand.

'Run, Granpa Chook, run for your life!' I pleaded.

Granpa Chook tried to get up from where he had landed but the stone from the Judge's powerful catapult had broken his ribcage. He made several more attempts, each time falling back onto his wing. I think he knew it was useless. After a while he just sat there, looked up at me and said 'squawk!'

Danie Coetzee ran over and grabbed Granpa Chook. I managed to kick him once, but then he held Granpa Chook triumphantly upside down by his legs. Granpa Chook beat his wings furiously, the pain must have been terrible. Quite suddenly he stopped and I thought he must be dead. But then I saw his bright, beady eye trying to find me from his upside down position.

'No blêrrie kaffir chicken shits on me! Hang him up by the legs next to Pisskop,' the Judge commanded. He was still doing little dry spits and wiping his mouth on the back of his hand. Two stormtroopers slung a piece of rope over a branch and Granpa Chook soon hung upside down just beyond my reach and at about the level of my head.

'Please, sir. I will do anything! Anything you ever ask! Anything you want! Please don't kill Granpa Chook!'

The Judge, his eyes cruel, bent down and looked into my face. 'Now we'll see who'll cry,' he grinned.

I was seized by panic. 'Kill me!' I begged. 'Please kill me. But don't kill Granpa Chook!'

The Judge butted me on the forehead with the heel of his hand and my head slammed against the trunk of the jacaranda, leaving me dazed. 'Ag, shit!' he exclaimed, some of the shit on my face had rubbed off onto his hand. Then he wiped his hand in my hair once again.

'You're shit and your fuckin' kaffir chicken is shit. Did you see what he did to me? Me, Jaapie Botha! That fuckin' chicken shit in my mouth!'

Still dazed, I tried another desperate tack. 'I'll tell Mevrou!' I shouted, trying to sound threatening.

'*Mevrou kan gaan kak!*' (Mevrou can go to shit!) The Judge spat on the ground, this time with a proper, not a chicken-shit spit. He turned to the stormtroopers. 'Prisoner of War Kaffir Chicken Rooinek will be executed, two shots each!' He moved to take his place in the shooting line as the rest of the stormtroopers loaded up their catapults.

I sloughed the last of my camouflage. 'I'll tell Mr Stoffel about how I did your arithmetic for you!' I screamed at the Judge.

I heard the soft 'pfflifft' of his catapult at the same time as I felt the stone slam into my stomach. The pain was terrible, it seemed to be happening in slow motion as though the stone had a life of its own, gnawing at my gut, burning and squirming through my intestines and into my back. A vicious, determined, alive, eyeless thing. The shock to my system was enormous, my eyes bugged out of my head and my tongue poked out in involuntary surprise.

'Fire!' A series of dull plops tore into the fragile bones of Granpa Chook's breast. The first stones had set the rope swinging, but the stormtroopers were expert shots and their second shots also tore into the funny old body of that upside-down chicken. Spots of blood dropped into the dry dust and among the fallen jacaranda blossoms, the rope swinging so that no two drops landed in the same place. Granpa Chook, the toughest damn chicken in the whole world, was dead.

A tiny feather drifted towards me, it was one of the soft downy ones which grew at the very top of Granpa Chook's scrawny legs. It stuck to a piece of shit in my face. The Judge walked over and untied the rope from around my waist and I dropped to my haunches at his feet. He placed his bare foot on my shoulder.

'What are you, Englishman?'

'Dog shit, sir.'

'Look at me when you say it!' he barked.

Slowly I looked up at the giant with his foot resting on my shoulder. High above him I could see a milky moon hanging in the afternoon sky. We had got so close, Granpa Chook and I had got so close to making it through to the end, just a few more hours.

I spat at him, 'You're dog shit! Your ma is a whore!'

He pushed violently downwards with his foot, sending me sprawling. Then he let out a howl, a mixture of anger and anguish. 'Why don't you cry, you fuckin' bastard!' he sobbed and started to kick blindly at me.

The stormtroopers rushed to restrain him, pulling him from me. The Judge allowed himself to be led away and we were left alone behind the shit houses under a white moon set in a flawless blue sky.

I untied the broken body of Granpa Chook and we sat under the jacaranda tree and I stroked his bloody feathers. No more gentle African dawn folding back the night, no more early cock-a-doodle-doo to tell me you are there, my loved and faithful chicken friend. Who will peck my ear? Who will be my friend? I sobbed and sobbed and sobbed. The great drought was over, the inside man was out, the rains had come to Zululand.

After a long, long while, when the crying was all out of me and the loneliness bird had entered to build a nest of stones in the hollow place inside of me, I carried Granpa Chook to the orchard and laid him in the place I had made for him to keep him from the rain. Then I climbed through the window into the dormitory to fetch my new red jumper, the one my mother had knitted in the concentration camp and Nanny had fixed.

I gathered as many rocks as I could find and then I pulled my red jumper over Granpa Chook's body, his wings poked out of the arm holes and his long neck stuck out of the head part and his feet poked out of the bottom.

He looked the best I'd ever seen him. I took the jam tin I had used for his water and, in about five minutes, I'd collected twenty little green grasshoppers, which are the very best chicken scoff there is. I placed the tin beside his body so that he'd have a special treat on the way to heaven. Finally I covered his body with the stones.

South Africa's first victim in the war against Adolf Hitler was safe at last.

I sat there on my haunches beside the pile of stones as the afternoon sun began to set. Now the sun was passing beyond Zululand, even past the land of the Swazi and now it leaves the Shangaan and the royal kraal of Modjadji, the rain queen, to be cooled in the great, dark water beyond.

The first bell for supper rang and I moved to the tap and began to wash the blood and shit from my hands and face and hair.

Deep inside me the loneliness bird sat on its crude stone nest and laid a large and very heavy stone egg.

The bell for supper sounded. The last supper. Everything comes to an end. Tomorrow I would be going home for Christmas and Nanny. Wonderful, soft, warm Nanny.

But life doesn't work that way. I, most of all, should have known this. At supper Boetie Van der Merwe told me Mevrou wanted to see me in the dispensary. 'If you tell about this afternoon, we'll kill you,' he hissed. I wasn't frightened, I knew a proper ending when I saw one.

Only hours remained before my liberation, nothing the Judge, Mevrou and, for the moment anyway, Adolf Hitler could do would alter that. Soon I would be returning to my quiet backwater.

I didn't know then that what seemed like the end was only the beginning. All children are flotsam driven by the ebb and flow of adult lives. Unbeknownst to me the tide had turned and I was being swept out to sea.

FOUR

At the end of supper, after Mr Stoffel had read the Bible lesson and concluded evening prayers, I waited for Mevrou outside the dispensary. She arrived a short time later. 'Kom!' Mevrou said as she brushed past me. I entered and waited with my hands behind my back, my head bowed in the customary manner.

'Why is there blood on your shirt, Pisskop?'

I looked down at my shirt which was stained with Granpa Chook's blood and a biggish spot where the stone had torn into me.

Mevrou sighed and sat down heavily on a bentwood chair painted the same light green as the dispensary walls. 'Take off your shirt,' she commanded.

I hurriedly removed my shirt and Mevrou made a cursory examination of my stomach. 'Ag, is that all?' She prodded at the wound the stone had made and I flinched involuntarily.

'Please, Mevrou, I fell on a rock.' Mevrou removed the cork from a large bottle of iodine and upended it onto a wad of cotton wool.

'Yes, I can see that.' She dabbed at my wound and the iodine stung like billy-o and I winced and hopped up and down in dismay, wringing my hands to stop the burning pain. 'Come, that's not enough.' She upended the bottle once again and dabbed hard at my tummy. This time I knew what to expect and, gritting my teeth and closing my eyes tightly, I managed to hold back most of the pain. 'You can't go getting blood poisoning on the train,' she said, tossing the wad on the table. She retrieved the cork and pushed it back into the bottle.

'What train, Mevrou?' I asked, confused.

'Your oupa called long distance on the telephone from a *dorp* in the Eastern Transvaal called Barberton. You are not going back to the farm. He says Newcastle's disease has made him kill all his chickens and he has sold the farm to a Mevrou Vorster.'

'What's my granpa doing in this town called Barberton, Mevrou?'

My head was swimming, my whole world was coming apart at the seams. If Granpa had sold the farm to fat Mrs Vorster and was making telephone calls from some strange town in the Eastern Transvaal, where was Nanny? Without Granpa Chook and Nanny, life was not possible.

'I'm not a mind reader. Maybe he got work in this place.' She reached into her bag and held up an envelope. 'In here is the ticket. Tomorrow night you will catch the train to Barberton. Two days and two nights. I will take you to the train.' She dismissed me with a wave of the envelope.

I turned to go, and as I reached the door Mevrou called me back. 'You can't take the chicken, you hear?' She looked at me smugly. 'South African Railways won't let you take a kaffir chicken, not even in the goods van.' She seemed pleased with this thought. 'I will take the chicken, he will earn his keep even if he is only a kaffir chicken.'

'He is dead, Mevrou. A dog ate him today.' I managed somehow to keep the tears out of my voice.

'That is a shame, he was good in the kitchen.' She rose from her chair with a sigh, fanning herself with the letter. 'I'm telling you, man, a kaffir chicken is no different from a Kaffir. Just when you think you can trust them, they go and let you down.'

I had never owned a pair of shoes. At that time, in the Northern Transvaal, a farm kid only got boots if he had rich parents or if he had turned thirteen. That's when the Old Testament says a boy becomes a man. A pair of khaki shorts, a shirt and a jumper when it was cold was all you got. Underpants hadn't been invented. Even if they had been, Boer kids wouldn't have worn them. More expense for what?

The day after Granpa Chook's funeral was the last day of term. Everyone was up and packed long before breakfast. After breakfast Mevrou summoned me to the dispensary to tell me that after lunch we would be going into town to buy a pair of tackies for me at Harry Crown's shop.

'What are tackies, Mevrou?'

'Domkop! Tackies are shoes made of only canvas with rubber bottoms. Don't you know anything? Make sure you have clean feet or we will be shamed in front of the Jew.'

From my secret mango tree, I watched the kids leave the hostel. Parents arrived in old pick-up trucks and mule carts. Some kids left on donkeys brought to the school by a farm servant. I watched as the Judge left in a mule cart. He made the black servant sit on the tailboard, then he jumped up into the driver's seat, took up the reins and the whip and set off at a furious pace, whipping at the mules and making the whip crack like a rifle shot. I breathed a huge sigh of relief. As my mother used to say, 'Good riddance to bad rubbish.'

Finally everyone had gone and I climbed down from the mango tree and crossed the school playground. It wasn't the same without Granpa Chook. The sun felt the same. The little green grasshoppers still couldn't make it across the playground in one hit. The day moon, made of skimmed milk, still hung in the cloudless morning sky. But it wasn't ever going to be the same again. I saved the need to grieve for a later time. I had enough on my mind with the prospect of going to town to buy a pair of shoes and catching the train. I'd never owned a pair of shoes and I'd never been on a train, never even seen a real train. Two nevers in one day is enough to fill anyone's mind.

After a lunch of bread and jam with a mug of sweet tea, I hurried to meet Mevrou in the dispensary, stopping only long enough to give my feet and legs a good scrub like Mevrou said. The same shower which had been dripping that first night when I thought I was in a slaughter house was still sounding drip, drip, drip, like a metronome. Funny how little kids can get things mixed up like that. It all seemed such a long time ago; I sure had been a baby then.

I had been waiting at the dispensary a few minutes when Mevrou arrived. She was wearing a shapeless floral cotton dress and a funny old black straw hat with two cherries on it. A third wire stem stuck up where a cherry had once been. In her town clothes she looked not unlike fat old Mrs Vorster, except younger and with a moustache.

The town I knew to be about two miles from the school. 'Maybe we could visit the railway station as well as Harry Crown's shop?' I suggested tentatively.

'It is enough that I do this for you, Pisskop. What do you want? Blood from a stone? Tonight I must do it all over again for you. There is nothing at the station to see, only sleeping Kaffirs waiting for the train.'

For the remainder of the journey we said nothing. Mevrou walked three paces ahead of me all the way to town. Her huge shape sort of rocked along, stopping every once in a while to catch her breath. The early afternoon sun beat down on us. By the time we arrived Mevrou was very hot and bothered, and her special smell was worse than ever.

Harry Crown's shop was closed and nothing much seemed to be happening in the main street. Mevrou took a large red *doek* from her basket and proceeded to wipe her face. 'Everyone is still having their lunch, we must wait,' she explained. With great effort she climbed the five steps up to the stoep of the shop and sat down on a bench beside the padlocked door. 'Go and find a tap and wash your feet,' she panted.

I crossed the street to the garage which had a sign which read Atlantic Service Station. It had two pumps outside a small office and workshop bay. Just inside the bay was a tap. The whole place smelt of oil and grease. I washed my feet and walked back across the road on my heels so as not to dirty my feet. Half a dozen Africans were asleep at the far end of the verandah where there was a second entrance to the shop. Above this entrance was written 'Blacks only'. I wondered briefly why whites were not allowed to enter.

Flies, flying heavy in the heat, settled on sleeping eyes and every now and again a desultory black hand would come up and brush at them, its owner seemingly still asleep.

One black man with his left eye missing remained awake and sat with his back against the shop wall. His cupped hands and mouth concealed a Jew's harp which twanged an urgent rhythm.

'The Jew is late, who does he think he is?' Mevrou said impatiently. She half turned and addressed the African playing the Jew's harp. 'Hey, Kaffir! Where is the baas?'

The black man jumped to his feet, removing the tiny harp and placing it in the pocket of his ragged pants. He said nothing, not understanding Afrikaans.

'Do you work here?' I asked him in Shangaan.

'No, small baas, I also, I am waiting. The big baas for the shop will be here soon I think. When the hooter goes for the saw mill he will surely come.'

'He doesn't work for Mr Crown, Mevrou.'

Just then a hooter sounded. We were familiar with the saw mill hooter, which blew at one o'clock and again at two.

Almost on the dot a big, black Chevrolet drove up and parked outside the shop.. It was the most beautiful car I had ever seen. I had never imagined a motor car could be as shiny and powerful. The man inside it revved the engine before he cut the ignition and it roared as though alive. Obviously being a Jew was a very profitable business. Maybe I could be one when I grew up.

Harry Crown was a fat man in his late fifties. He wore his trousers high so that his entire tummy and most of his chest were covered with trouser top, held up by a pair of bright red braces. His white open-neck cotton shirt seemed to extend no more than eight inches from his collar before it was swallowed by his trousers. He was almost completely bald and when he smiled he showed two gold front teeth.

'A thousand apologies, Mevrou. Have you been waiting long?' he said, making a fuss of unlocking the padlocked doors to the shop.

'Ag, it was nothing. Not even a few minutes,' Mevrou said, all smiles for the fat, bald man.

In the part boarded off for white customers, two large ceiling fans whirred softly overhead and the shop was dark and cool. Mevrou heaved herself gratefully onto a chair beside the counter and Harry Crown poured her a cup of coffee from a pot he removed from a small hotplate on a shelf behind the counter.

'What can I do for you, Mevrou?' he asked, then turning to me he bowed slightly. 'And for you, Mister?' he said solemnly.

I was not used to jocularity so, not knowing what to do, I dropped my eyes to avoid his gaze.

Observing my shyness he turned from me to a large glass jar on the counter and from it produced a raspberry sucker, its ruby head wrapped in Cellophane. He held the sucker out for me to take. I looked at Mevrou who took a polite sip from her coffee cup and then nodded. I took the delicious prize and put it into my shirt pocket.

'Thank you, Meneer,' I said softly.

'Ag, eat it now, boy. When we have finished business you can have another one.' He paused. 'A green one maybe, huh?' He turned to Mevrou. 'I have had this shop for thirty years and I can tell you with

God's certainty that children like raspberry first and green second. If I know nothing for certain in this life, of this one thing I am sure.' He snapped his braces with his thumbs and gave a loud, happy snort.

I had never met a man who laughed and carried on like this and I felt intimidated, so I left the raspberry sucker in my pocket where I hoped it was safe.

'What is your name, boy?' Harry Crown asked.

'Pisskop, sir,' I replied.

Harry Crown's shiny bald head jerked back and he looked down at me in consternation. 'Pisskop? Pisskop! This is a name for a nice boy?' he asked in alarm. 'Who calls you this name?'

Mevrou interrupted sharply. 'Never mind his name, what have you got in tackies? The boy must have some tackies. He is going on the train alone tonight to his oupa in Barberton.'

Turning momentarily to acknowledge he had heard her, Harry Crown turned back to me and gave a low whistle. 'Barberton eh? That is in the lowveld in the Eastern Transvaal. Easy two days away in the train, a long journey alone for a small boy.' He had moved around from behind the counter and was looking at my feet. 'We have nothing so small, Mevrou. I don't have much call for tackies. The Boere round here don't play much tennis.' He chortled loudly at his own joke, which was completely lost on Mevrou and me.

'Show me what you got, Mr Crown. His oupa did not send enough money for boots, only tackies.'

'It makes no difference, boots, smoots, tackies, smackies, the boy's foot is too small.' He moved back behind the counter where he pulled a battered cardboard box from the shelf. From it he withdrew a pair of dark brown canvas shoes.

'Let the boy try them,' Mevrou said.

'It is useless, Mevrou. These tackies are four sizes too big for him. It is a miracle I have these, but they are too big already.'

'The boy will grow,' Mevrou said, a trifle impatiently.

'Ja certainly, Mevrou. Maybe in five or six years they will fit him like a glove. In the meantime they will fit him like the clown in a circus.' He slapped his stomach. 'Very amusing,' he said to himself in English.

'We will try them on. With newspaper we can fix them.'

'Mevrou, with the whole *Zoutpansberg Gazette* we couldn't stuff these tackies to fit. He has very small feet for a Boer child.'

'He is not a Boer child. He is a Rooinek!' Mevrou said, suddenly angry. She put the cup of coffee down on the counter, and leaning over grabbed the tackies and turned to me. 'Put your foot up here on my lap, child,' she ordered.

The first tackie slipped around my foot without touching the sides. With my heel on Mevrou's lap the canvas shoe seemed to reach almost up to my chin.

Mevrou pulled the laces tightly until the eyelets overlapped. 'Now the other one,' she said.

I stood there, rooted to the floor, not daring to move and not knowing what to do next. The tackies seemed to extend twice the distance of my feet.

'Walk, child,' Mevrou commanded.

I took a tentative step forward and the left tackie stayed behind on the floor, though I managed to drag the right one forward by not lifting my foot.

'Bring some paper.' Mevrou cunningly fashioned two little boats from strips of newspaper. She then put the paper boats in the tackies and instructed me to insert my feet into them and tied the laces. This time they fitted snug as a bug in a rug. Though I must say they felt very strange and when I walked they made a phlifft-floft sound where the tackies bent at the end of my toes.

I had never felt as grand in all my life. 'We will take them,' Mevrou announced triumphantly. She reached into her handbag for her purse.

Harry Crown sighed. 'Those tackies are no good, Mevrou.'

If Mevrou had had her sjambok she would have made fat old Harry Crown bend over the counter and she would have given him six of the best.

'How much?' she said curtly, her lips pursed.

'Half a crown, for you only two shillings,' Harry Crown said, adjusting the price automatically, his heart obviously not in the sale.

I tugged at the end of a lace and to my relief the bow collapsed. I did the same for the second tackie then slipped ever so carefully out of the newspaper boats and handed the tackies to Harry Crown.

'You poor little bugger,' he said in English. He slipped the tackies back into the soft brown cardboard box and when he saw Mevrou wasn't looking, quickly put two green and two red suckers into the box and handed it to me. 'I wish you health to wear them,' Harry Crown said in English. Speaking out of the corner of his mouth he added, 'Can she understand English?'

Not daring to reply, I shook my head almost imperceptibly, indicating no.

'Inside is for the journey, green and red, the best! Believe me, I know. So long, Peekay.' He patted me on the shoulder. His eyes widened and drawing up to his full height, his hands clasped over his belly, gold teeth flashing, he grinned. 'Maybe the tackies don't fit, but I think your new name fits perfect. Peekay! Ja, that is a nice name for a brave person who is travelling by himself to the lowveld to meet his granpa.

Mevrou, who was practically snorting with rage, threw two shillings on the counter and marched out of the shop. I followed along with the precious box of loot under my arm. At the door I turned to say goodbye to Harry Crown.

'Goodbye, sir!' I said in English. The two English words sounded strangely out of place, like a language newly learned.

Mevrou turned furiously. Grabbing me by the ear, she hissed, 'Do not talk to that . . . that dirty Jew in the accursed language. You will hear from my sjambok when we get home!'

'Ouch! You have my sore ear, Mevrou.' I knew immediately she'd feel guilty grabbing me by my recently damaged ear, even though it was completely healed.

Mevrou let go of my ear as though it were a red-hot poker. You've got to be quick on your feet in this world if you want to survive. Though, once you know the rules, it is not too hard to play the game.

Mevrou stormed ahead and I fell some five paces behind her. After I'd given her what I hoped was enough guilt for her to withdraw the promised thrashing, I dropped back another fifteen paces and took the raspberry sucker out of my pocket. Taking off the Cellophane wrapper I licked the tiny bits of crimson sugar crystal which had stuck to it before throwing it away. I then settled down to suck my way back to the hostel.

I was right about the sjambok, which was not mentioned on our return. I spent the remainder of the afternoon putting more stones on Granpa Chook's grave and making a border around the pile of rocks with white pebbles which took ages to collect from all around the place. I must say, the toughest damn chicken in the whole world had a very impressive grave, a stone cairn which would probably last forever, hidden by successive generations of khaki weed and blackjack.

The cook boy had packed me a big brown paper bag of sandwiches for the train journey. We left the hostel about five o'clock to catch the seven o'clock train. My suitcase, though large, contained very few things. Two shirts, two pairs of khaki shorts, my pyjamas, the four suckers which I'd hidden in a pair of shorts and my new tackies with the paper boats in them. There was plenty of room for the sandwiches. While the suitcase banged against my knees, it wasn't really heavy and besides, with all the iron bar torture sessions, my muscles were pretty big. Mevrou was completely puffed out from making two trips into town in one day, and with the suitcase banging against my knees it took us almost an hour to get to the station.

The station turned out to be a raised platform about thirty yards long upon which sat a building with two doors facing the railway line. On one door Station Master was written and to the right of this door was a window. Above the window it read Tickets. On the remaining door it said Waiting Room. Outside the station master's office there were three truck tyres painted white and in the middle of these grew red cannas, their long, flat leaves dusty and shredded with the blooms equally torn and bedraggled looking. Mevrou seemed to know the station master. He opened the locked waiting room for us and brought her a cup of coffee in a big white cup with SAR monogrammed on it.

'Don't worry, Hoppie Groenewald is the guard on this train, he will take good care of the boy.' He turned to acknowledge me for the first time. 'He is champion of the railways, you know. That Hoppie,' the station master grinned at the thought, 'he laughs all the time, but if you get into a fight, I'm telling you, man, you better pray he's on your side!'

I wondered what a champion of the railways was, but I clearly understood, and greatly liked, the idea of having someone on my side who was good in a fight. My life seemed to be made for trouble and it would make a nice change to have a champion of the railways beside me when the next lot hit, as was bound to happen.

Sometimes the slightest things change the directions of our lives, the merest breath of a circumstance, a random moment that connects like a meteorite striking the earth. Lives have swivelled and changed direction on the strength of a chance remark. Hoppie Groenewald was to prove to be a passing mentor who would set the next seventeen years of my life on an irrevocable course. He would do so in little more than a day and a night.

'The boy is a Rooinek and also too small to fight yet,' Mevrou said, as though it were only a matter of time before my bad English blood would turn nasty. She produced a ticket from an envelope and inserted a large safety pin into the hole at one end. 'Come here, child.' She pinned the ticket to my shirt pocket. 'Listen carefully to me now, man, this ticket will take you to Barberton but your oupa only sent enough money for one breakfast and one lunch and one supper on the train. Tonight you eat only one sandwich, you hear?' I nodded. 'Tomorrow for breakfast another one and for lunch the last one. Then you can eat on the train. Do you understand now?'

'Ja, Mevrou, for the next three meals I eat the sandwiches.'

'No, man! That's not what I said. For tonight and for breakfast tomorrow and lunch tomorrow. And also eat the meat first because the jam will keep the bread soft for tomorrow. Do you hear?'

'Ja, Mevrou.'

She took out a small square of white cloth about the size of a lady's hanky and placed it on her lap. In the centre she placed a shilling.

'Watch carefully now, Pisskop. I am putting this shilling in here and tying it so.' She brought the two opposite corners together and tied them over the shilling and then did the same with the remaining two. She took a second large safety pin from her handbag, then, pushing the doek with the shilling into the pocket of my khaki shorts, she pinned it to the lining.

'Now listen good. It is for an emergency. Only if you have to can you use some of it. But you must tie up the change like I just showed you and put it back in your pocket with the safety pin. If you don't need it you must give it to your oupa, it is his change.'

The station master entered and told us that the train was on time and we had five minutes.

'Quick, man, get your tackies,' Mevrou said, giving me a push towards the suitcase.

I was seized by a sudden panic. What if I opened my suitcase and she saw my suckers? I placed the case flat on the floor and opened it so the lid was between Mevrou and me, preventing her from seeing inside. Just as well, a green sucker had worked out of its hiding place in my shorts and my heart went thump. Phew! I removed the tackies and quickly snapped the case shut. I slipped each foot carefully into a paper boat and Mevrou tied the laces. I tried desperately to memorise how she did this but wasn't sure I had the idea.

'Please, Mevrou, will you teach me how to tie the laces so I can take my tackies off in the train?'

Mevrou looked up, alarmed. 'You must not take your tackies off until you get to Barberton. If you lose them your oupa will think I stole the money he sent. You keep them on, do you hear me now?'

The train could be heard a long way off and we left the waiting room to watch it coming in. Real walking in my tackies was difficult and very different from the three or four tentative steps I had taken in Harry Crown's shop. I stumbled several times as I went phlifft-floft, phlifft-floft from the waiting room to the edge of the platform. Bits of newspaper crept up past my ankles and I had to stop and press them back in.

With a deafening choof of steam, immediately followed by two short sharp hisses and a screeching sound of metal rubbing on metal, the huge train pulled into the station, and carriage after carriage of black people went by. They were laughing and sticking their heads out of windows and having themselves a proper good time. Finally the last two carriages and the goods van came to a halt neatly lined up with the platform. The two end carriages read South African Railways First Class and Second Class respectively. I had seen pictures of trains of course, and sometimes at night as I lay in the small kids' dormitory I had heard a train whistle carried in the wind, the beautiful sound of going to faraway places away from the hostel, Mevrou, the Judge and his Nazi stormtroopers. But I must say I wasn't prepared for anything quite as big and black and blustering with steam, smoke, fire, brass pipes and hissing pistons.

Africans appeared as if from nowhere. They carried bundles on their heads which they handed up through the third-class carriage windows to the passengers inside and then climbed aboard laughing with the excitement of it all. From inside the carriages came song and more laughter and a great deal of shouting and good-natured banter. I knew at once that I would like trains.

The guard leapt down onto the platform carrying a canvas bag with Mail stamped on the outside. He handed it to the station master who gave him an identical bag in return.

The station master introduced the guard to Mevrou. 'This is Hoppie Groenewald, he is guard and conductor until you get to Gravelotte. He will look after the boy.'

Hoppie Groenewald grinned down at me and tipped his navy blue guard's cap to Mevrou. 'No worries, Mevrou, I will look after him until

Gravelotte. Then I will hand him over to Pik Botha who will take him through to Kaapmuiden.' He opened the door of the second-class carriage and put my suitcase into the train and indicated that I should enter. The three steps up into the carriage were fairly high and I put my tackied foot on the bottom step. As I put my weight on the step the toe of the tacky buckled and I fell on my bum on the platform. Wearing shoes was a much trickier business than I had first supposed. A bit distressed, I wondered how adults seemed to manage so easily. I tried to get up but the tackies were too big and I couldn't get a proper grip on the loose gravel which covered the platform.

'Get up, man!' Mevrou said, visibly annoyed. She shook her head, 'For God's sake! Even now you make trouble for me.'

Hoppie Groenewald put the canvas mail bag on the platform, and bending down he grabbed me under the armpits and hoisted me high into the air and through the door to land inside the carriage.

'No worries, little brother, I too have fallen up those *verdomde* steps many a time. I, who am a guard and soon to be a conductor, and who should know better.'

He retrieved the mail bag and put it next to my suitcase. Then he hopped up the steps without even looking and unhooked a neatly rolled green flag from above the door of the carriage. He unfurled the flag and absently pulled at a chain attached to a button on his navy serge waistcoat and withdrew a large silver whistle from his fob pocket.

'Watch the Kaffirs get a fright,' he said with a grin. He showed me how to hold onto the handrail inside the door and lean out of the carriage so I could see down the full length of the train to the third-class carriages. He then jumped back onto the platform and began to wave the flag, giving a long blast on his whistle.

You should have seen the kerfuffle. Africans who had left the train to stretch their legs or have a pee scrambled frantically to get through the doors of the carriages as the train began slowly to move, laughing and yelling and climbing on top of each other. Hoppie Groenewald gave two more short blasts on his whistle and hopped aboard the train.

'Goodbye, Mevrou. Thank you,' I shouted, waving at her.

'Keep your tackies on, you hear!' Mevrou shouted back.

It was a dry-eyed farewell on both sides. I ardently hoped the Rooinek and Mevrou would never have to see each other again.

Hoppie Groenewald closed the carriage door as the train began to gather momentum. He quickly refurled the flag and clicked it back into its holder next to a red one above the door. Then he picked up my suitcase and opened the door to the nearest compartment.

The train was moving along smoothly now and I enjoyed the comforting, predictable clickity-clack, clickity-clack of the carriage wheels.

The empty compartment had two bright green leather seats facing each other, each seat big enough for three adults. A small table, which I was later to discover turned into a wash basin, was positioned between the two windows. The rest of the compartment seemed to be panelled in highly varnished wood and immediately above each green leather seat was a glass frame about ten inches high running the length of the seats. Inside the frames were lots of photographs. It was all very posh. Before it got completely dark, Hoppie Groenewald turned on the compartment lights and all seemed very cosy . . . just like the beginning of a proper adventure.

'It's all yours until we get to Tzaneen. After that who knows. No worries, Hoppie will take good care of you.' He looked down at my tackies, bits of newspaper were sticking out of the sides and up past my ankles.

'The old cow can't get you now, take them off,' the guard said. I tugged the canvas shoes off. My feet were hot and uncomfortable and had turned black from the newsprint rubbing off on them. It felt delicious to squiggle my toes again. Hoppie Groenewald stuck his hand out. 'Shake a paw. You know my name but I haven't had the pleasure.'

I'd already thought about what Harry Crown had said and had decided to take his advice and call myself Peekay. 'Peekay,' I said tentatively. I pronounced it in English, the way Harry Crown had, so it sounded like a proper name.

I suddenly felt new and clean. Nobody ever again would know that I had been called Pisskop. Granpa Chook was dead and so was Pisskop. The first two South African casualties in the Second World War.

'All the best, Peekay. We will be pals.' He took his cap off and put it on my head. I wondered if he was a Nazi. He didn't seem to know I was English, so why tempt fate?

'Thank you for taking care of me, Mr Groenewald,' I said politely and handed him back his cap.

'Ag man, just call me Hoppie.' He grinned as he replaced his cap.

Hoppie left to check the tickets in the African carriages but promised he would return soon.

It was almost totally dark outside, as I sat alone in a lighted room, flying through the African night, clickity-clack, clickity-clack. I had defeated the Judge and his Nazi stormtroopers, survived Mevrou and I had grown up and changed my name, clickity-clack, clickity-clack.

Opening my suitcase I took out one of Harry Crown's green suckers. Carefully removing the Cellophane wrapper I licked the bits of green sugar that had stuck to it. The faint taste of lime transferred to my tongue, sweet promise of the main event when I began on the sucker itself.

Harry Crown was right of course, the green ones were a very close second to the raspberry. I examined the photographs above the seats, sepia-toned pictures of a flat mountain with a streak of white cloud resting just above it. The caption underneath read, 'World famous Table Mountain wearing its renowned tablecloth'. All there was was a big white cloud above it but I couldn't see a renowned tablecloth. Another showed a big city seen from the air with the caption, 'Cape Town, home of the famous Cape Doctor'. I wondered what the doctor had done to be famous and rich enough to own a big town for his home. He must have been richer even than Harry Crown. Years later I discovered that the Cape Doctor was a wind which blew in early spring to clean out the flu germs and general accumulated nasties that had gathered during the winter. Another photograph of Table Mountain was captioned 'Truly one of the world's natural wonders'. The last picture showed a big white house and it said, 'Groot Constantia's famed and spacious cellars, the home of superb wine'.

'Well,' I thought, 'this will be a pretty good journey if we visit all those places!' I decided I'd ask Hoppie about them when he came back.

Hoppie returned after what seemed ages but probably wasn't very long. On a train, with the darkness galloping past, time seemed to disappear, the clickity-clack of the wheels on the track gobbled up the minutes.

He plonked himself wearily on the seat opposite me. 'Sis, man, those Kaffirs stink!' he declared, then gave me a big grin and a light playful punch to the point of my chin. 'When we get to Tzaneen in an hour we'll have some dinner. We stop for forty-five minutes to take on coal and water and there's a cafe across the road from the station. From Tzaneen I'm only the guard and another conductor takes over. What's your favourite food, Peekay?'

'Sweet potatoes,' I answered.

'Sweet potatoes, maybe and maybe not, I've never asked for sweet potatoes at that cafe. How about a mixed grill. A two-bob special, heh?'

'I've only got a shilling and it's for emergencies. Is a mixed grill an emergency?' I asked.

Hoppie laughed. 'For me it is. Tonight I'm paying, old mate. The mixed grills are on me.'

I didn't want to ask him what a grill was and how it was mixed so I asked him about the pictures on the wall. 'When are we going to see Table-Mountain-one-of-the-natural-wonders-of-the-world?'

'Huh, come again?'

I pointed to the picture above his head. 'When do we go there?'

Hoppie turned around to look at the picture, but he didn't laugh when he worked out what I was talking about. 'It's just stupid pictures showing where South African Railways go, but we are not going there, Peekay.' He started to study all the pictures as if he'd noticed them for the first time.

'I almost went to Cape Town last year to fight in the finals but I was beaten in the Northern Transvaal championships. Split decision, but the referee gave it to the fighter from Pretoria. I'm telling you, man, I beat the bastard fair and square. It was close, I've got to admit that, but I knew all the time I had him on points.'

I listened, astonished. What on earth was he talking about?

Hoppie looked me straight in the eyes. 'You're almost looking at the railways boxing champion of the Transvaal, you know.' He brought his finger and thumb together in front of my face. 'That close and I would of been in the National Railway Boxing Championships in Cape Town.'

'What's a boxing champion?' I asked.

It was Hoppie's turn to look astonished. 'What a domkop you are, Peekay. Don't you know what boxing is?'

'No, sir.' I dropped my eyes, ashamed of my ignorance.

Hoppie Groenewald put his hand under my chin and lifted my head up. 'It's nothing to be ashamed of. There comes a time in everything when you don't know something.' He grinned. 'Okay, man, settle down, make yourself at home, we're in for a long talk.'

'Wait a minute, Hoppie,' I said excitedly. I clicked open my suitcase. 'Green or red?' I asked, taking out a sucker of each colour. I had decided that I would have one sucker in the morning and one at night, that way they would last me the whole journey. But a friend like this doesn't come along every day and I hadn't heard a good story since Nanny.

'You choose first, Peekay. What's your favourite?'

'No, you choose, Hoppie. You're the one who is going to tell the story so you get first choice,' I said with great generosity.

'Green,' he said. 'I like green, my mother had green eyes.' He took the green sucker and I put the raspberry one back and clicked the suitcase shut.

'I've just had one,' I said, grateful that I had two of the best raspberry ones left for the next two days.

'We will share then,' he said, 'you lick first because I'm going to be too busy doing the talking.' He watched me as I unwrapped the Cellophane and licked it clean. 'When I was your age I used to do the same.' He looked at his watch. 'One hour to Tzaneen, just about time for a boxing lecture and maybe even a demonstration.'

I settled back happily into the corner of the large green leather seat and proceeded to lick the sucker. One and a half suckers in less than an hour was an all-time happiness and having a real friend was another. What an adventure this was turning out to be.

'Boxing is the greatest sport in the world,' Hoppie began, 'even greater than rugby.' He looked up, ready to defend this last statement if necessary, but saw that I was prepared to accept his premise. 'The art of self-defence is the greatest art of all and boxing is the greatest art of self-defence. Take me, a natural welterweight, there isn't any man I have to be afraid of, not even a big animal like a front-row forward. I'm fast and I can hit hard and in a street fight a little bloke like me can take on any big gorilla.' He jabbed once or twice into the air in front of him to demonstrate his lightning speed.

'How little can beat how big?' I asked, getting excited.

'Big as anything, man. If you've got the speed to move and can throw a big punch as you're moving away. Timing, speed and footwork, in boxing they are everything. To be a welterweight is perfect. Not too big to be slow, not too small to lack a punch. A welterweight is the perfect fighter, I'm telling you for sure, man!' Hoppie's eyes were shining with conviction.

I stood up on the seat and lifted my hand about another eight inches above my head. Which, of course, was about the height of the Judge. 'A little kid like me and a big kid, big as this?'

Hoppie paused for a moment; he seemed to be thinking. 'Ja, now you see with small kids it's a bit different. Small kids don't have the punch. Maybe they're fast enough to stay out of the way. but one stray punch from a big gorilla and it's all over, man. Kids are best to fight in their own division.' He looked at me. 'Who you want to fight, hey? What big kid gave you a bad time? Just you tell me, Peekay, and he'll have to reckon with Hoppie Groenewald. I'm telling you, man, nobody hurts a friend of mine.'

'Just some boys at school,' I replied, delighted that even though this was the wrong place and time, I now had someone strong in the world who was on my side. I wanted to tell him about the Judge and his Nazi stormtroopers, but I wasn't prepared to go the whole way. Hoppie Groenewald didn't know I was a Rooinek and he might think differently if he found out.

'Well, you just tell them next time they'll have to reckon with me,' Hoppie growled.

'It is all over now,' I said, handing him the sucker.

He took the sucker and started to lick it absently. 'Peekay, take my advice. When you get to Barberton, find someone who can teach you to box.' He looked at me, squinting slightly. 'I can see you could be a good boxer, your arms are strong for a little bloke. Hey, stand up again, let me see your legs.'

I stood up on the seat. 'Not bad, Peekay, nice light legs, you could have speed. With a boxer speed is everything. Hit and move. Hit and move, one two one, a left and a left again and a right.' He was sparring in the air, throwing lightning punches at an invisible foe. It was scary and exciting at the same time.

'Wait here,' he said suddenly and left the compartment. He returned in a couple of minutes carrying a pair of funny-looking leather gloves.

'These are boxing gloves, Peekay. These are the equalisers, when you can use them well you need fear no man. In the goods van I have a speed-ball, tomorrow I will show you how to use it.' He slipped the huge gloves over my hands which disappeared into the gloves halfway up to my elbows. 'Feels good, hey?' he said, tying the laces.

My hands in the gloves were just as lost as my feet had felt in the tackies when Mevrou first made me put them on. Only this was different. The gloves felt like old friends, big yes, and very clumsy, but not strangers.

'C'mon kid, hit me,' Hoppie said, sticking out his jaw. I took a jab at him and his head moved away so my glove simply whizzed through the air. 'Again, hit me again.' I pulled my arm back and let go with a terrible punch which landed flush on his chin. Hoppie fell back into the leather seat opposite me, groaning and holding his jaw. 'Holy macaroni! You're a killer. A natural-born fighter. You sure planted one on me, man.' He sat up rubbing his jaw and I began to laugh. 'That's the way, little *boetie,* I was beginning to wonder if you knew how to laugh,' he said with a big grin.

And then I started to cry, not blubbing, just tears that wouldn't stop rolling down my cheeks. Hoppie Groenewald picked me up and put me on his lap and I put my arms with the boxing gloves around his neck and buried my head in his blue serge waistcoat. The heavy chain that held the whistle was cool against my face.

'Sometimes it is good to cry,' he said softly. 'Sometimes you fight better when you've had a good cry. Now tell old Hoppie what's the matter.'

I couldn't tell him of course. It was a dumb thing to cry like that, but it was as far as I was prepared to go. I got off his lap. 'It's nothing, honest,' I said, going to sit on my side of the compartment.

Hoppie picked up the sucker which he'd put on the table before we had started to spar and held it out to me. 'You finish it. It will spoil my appetite for my mixed grill. You're still going to have a mixed grill with me, aren't you? I mean, I'm paying and all that.'

I reached for the sucker but the gloves were still on my hands and we laughed together at the joke. He pulled the gloves off and handed it to me.

'No worries, Peekay. When you grow up you'll be the best damn welterweight in South Africa and nobody . . . and I mean no-bod-ee, will give Kid Peekay any crapola. I'm telling you, man.'

When we reached Tzaneen, Hoppie pulled down a bunk concealed in the wall above my head which, to my amazement, turned out to be a proper bed with blankets and sheets. From a slot behind the bunk he took out a pillow with a pillow slip, and a small towel. He then put my suitcase on the bed to reserve it, in case other folk came into the compartment at Tzaneen.

Taking me by the hand, we crossed the station platform which looked much like the one from which we had left, only the platform was longer and the buildings bigger. Opposite the station was a lighted building with a big glass window on which Railway Café was written. Inside were lots of little tables and chairs. Several people were seated, eating and drinking coffee. There seemed to be a lot of smoke in the room.

A pretty young lady behind the counter looked up as we entered and gave Hoppie a big smile. 'Well, well, look who's here. If it isn't Kid Louis, champion of the railways,' she announced. An older woman came out of the back. Wiping her hands on her apron, she came up to Hoppie and he gave her a big hug.

'Your cheeky daughter is already giving me a hard time, *ounooi,*' Hoppie said. 'She needs to go three rounds in the ring with Hoppie Groenewald and then we'll see who's laughing.' He was grinning from ear to ear.

'So when's your next fight, champ?' the lady behind the counter asked.

'Tomorrow night at the railway club in Gravelotte, a light-heavy from the mines. It's the big time for me at last.' Hoppie smiled.

The pretty young lady giggled. 'Put two bob on the other bloke for me.' One or two of the other customers also laughed, but in a good-natured way. The older woman was clearing a table for us and fussing around Hoppie. He turned towards me, and taking my hand held my arm aloft. 'Hello everyone, I want you to meet Kid Peekay, the next welter-weight contender,' he said, keeping his voice serious. I dropped my eyes, not knowing what to do.

'Enough of your nonsense, Hoppie Groenewald. Come sit now or you will not be fed before the train leaves,' the older woman fussed.

The pretty young woman smiled at me. 'How would the contender like a strawberry milkshake?' she asked.

I looked at Hoppie. 'What's a milkshake, please, Hoppie?'

'A milkshake is heaven,' he said. 'Make that two, you lazy frump.' He turned to the older woman who was still fussing about. 'Two super-duper mixed grills please, *ounooi*. Me and my partner here are starving.'

Hoppie was right again, a strawberry milkshake is heaven. When the mixed grill arrived I couldn't believe my own eyes. Chop, steak, sausage, bacon, liver, chips, a fried egg and tomato. What a blow-out! I had never eaten a meal as grand and was quite unable to finish it. Hoppie helped himself to the remaining food on my plate, although I slurped the milk-shake, in its aluminium shaker, right down to the last gurgling drop.

The pretty lady came over and sat with us and Hoppie seemed to like her a lot. Her name was Anna and her lips were very shiny and red. The clock above the counter read ten o'clock. It was set into a picture of a beautiful lady in a long white nightdress that clung to her body. She too had very red lips and was smoking a cigarette; the smoke from the cigarette curled up on to the face of the clock where it turned into running writing. The running writing said 'C to C for satisfaction.' I had never been up as late as this before and my eyelids felt as though they were made of lead.

The next thing I remembered was Hoppie tucking me into my bunk between the nice clean, cool sheets and the pillow that smelt of starch. 'Sleep sweet, old mate,' I heard him say.

The last thing I remembered before I fell asleep again was the deep, comforting feeling of my hands in the boxing gloves. 'The equalisers,' Hoppie had called them. Peekay had found the equalisers.

FIVE

I woke up early and lay in my bunk listening to the clickity-clack of the rails. Outside in the dawn light lay the grey savannah grasslands; an occasional baobab stood hugely sentinel against the smudged blue sky with the darker blue of the Murchison range just beginning to break out of the flat horizon. The door of the compartment slid open and Hoppie, dressed only in his white shirt and pants with his braces looped and hanging from his waist, came in carrying a steaming mug of coffee.

'Did you sleep good, Peekay?' He handed me the mug of coffee.

'Ja, thanks, Hoppie. I'm sorry I couldn't stay awake.'

'No worries, little boetie, there comes a time for all of us when you can't get up out of your corner.'

I didn't understand the boxing parlance but it didn't seem to matter. To my amazement Hoppie then lifted the top of the small compartment table to reveal a wash basin underneath. He turned on the taps and hot water came out of one and cold out of the other. He kept running his fingers through the water until he said the temperature was 'just right'.

'When you've had your coffee you can have a nice wash and then I'll take you to breakfast,' he said.

'It's okay, Hoppie, I have my breakfast in my suitcase,' I said hastily.

Hoppie looked at me with a grin. 'Humph, this I got to see. In your suitcase you have a stove and a frying pan and butter and eggs and bacon and sausages and tomato and toast and jam and coffee?' He gave a low whistle. 'That's a magic suitcase you've got there, Peekay.'

'Mevrou gave me sandwiches for the first three meals because my oupa didn't send enough money. Only last night we had a mixed grill when I should have eaten the meat one,' I said in a hectic tumbling out of words.

Hoppie stood for a moment looking out of the carriage window, he seemed to be talking to himself. 'Sandwiches, eh? I hate sandwiches. By now the bread is all turned up in the corners and the jam has come through the middle of the bread. I bet it's peach jam. They always have blêrrie peach jam.' He turned to address me directly, 'Where are these sandwiches?' I pointed to my suitcase on the seat below my bunk. He stooped down and clicked it open and from the case removed the brown paper package tied with coarse string.

'As your manager, it is my solemn duty to inspect your breakfast.

Fighters have to be very careful about the things they eat, you know.' He unwrapped the parcel, splotches of grease had stained the brown paper. He was right, the bread had curled up at the corners. He removed the slice of bread uppermost on the first sandwich and sniffed the thin brown slices of meat, then he replaced the slice. He dug down to the bottom two sandwiches; the jam had oozed through the middle of the brown bread while the outside edges had curled inwards dry and hard.

'Peach!' Hoppie said triumphantly. 'Always peach!' He looked up at me, his eyes expressionless. 'I have sad news for you, Peekay. These sandwiches have died a horrible death, most likely from a disease they caught in an institution. We must get rid of them immediately before we catch it ourselves.' With that, he slid down the window of the compartment and hurled the sandwiches into the passing landscape. 'First-class fighters eat first-class food. Hurry up and have a wash, Peekay, I'm starving and breakfast comes with the compliments of South African Railways.'

I flung the blanket and sheet back to get down from my bunk and looked down at my headless snake in horror. Hoppie had removed my pants before putting me to bed. My heart pounded. Maybe it had been dark and he hadn't noticed I was a Rooinek. If he found out, everything was spoiled, just when I was having the greatest adventure of my life.

'C'mon, Peekay, we haven't got all day you know.' Hoppie pulled his braces over his shoulders.

'I am still full from the mixed grill last night, Hoppie, I can't eat another thing, man.' I quickly pulled the blanket back over me.

'Hey, you're talking to me, man, Hoppie Groenewald. Who you trying to bluff?' He took a step nearer to the bunk and ripped the blanket and sheet off me in one swift movement. My hatless snake was exposed, not six inches from his face. I cupped my hands over it but it was too late, I knew that he knew.

'I'm not the next welterweight contender, Mr Groenewald, I'm just a verdomde Rooinek,' I said, my voice breaking as I fought to hold back my tears. It always happens, just when things are perfect, down comes the retribution.

Hoppie stood quietly in front of me, saying nothing until his silence forced me to raise my downcast eyes and look at him. His eyes were sad, he shook his head as he spoke. 'That's why you're going to be the next champ, Peekay, you've got the reason.' He paused and smiled. 'I didn't tell you before, man. You know that bloke who beat me for the title in Pretoria? Well he was English, a Rooinek like you. He had this left hook, every time it connected it was like a goods train had shunted into me.' Hoppie brought his arms up and lifted me out of the bunk and put me gently down beside the wash basin. 'But I think you're going to be even better than him, little boetie. C'mon, wash up and let's go eat, man.'

I can tell you things were looking up all right. Hoppie took me through to the dining car which had a snowy tablecloth on every table, silver knives and forks and starched linen napkins folded to look like dunces' caps. Even the coffee came in a silver pot with SAR in running writing on one side and SAS done the same way on the other. A man dressed not unlike Hoppie, but without a cap and with a napkin draped across his arm, said good morning and showed us to a small table. He asked Hoppie if it was true that the light-heavy whom he was to fight that night had a total of twenty-seven fights with seventeen knockouts to his credit . . . a real brawler?

Hoppie said you couldn't believe everything you heard, especially in a railway dining car. That it was the first he'd heard of it. Then he shrugged his shoulders and grinned. 'First he's got to catch me, man.' He asked him about something called odds and the man said two to one on the big bloke. Hoppie laughed and gave the man ten bob and the man wrote something in a small book.

The man left and soon returned with toast and two huge plates of bacon and eggs and sausages and tomato, just the way Hoppie said it would happen. I decided that when I grew up the railways were most definitely for me.

'Are you frightened about tonight?' I asked Hoppie. Although I couldn't imagine him being frightened of anything, I wanted him to know I was on his side. He had told me how it was with a light-heavy, and it was obvious the man he was going to fight was to him just as big as the Judge was to me.

Hoppie looked at me for a moment and then washed the sausage he was chewing down with a gulp of coffee. 'It's good to be a little frightened. It's good to respect your opponent. It keeps you sharp. In the fight game, the head rules the heart. But in the end the heart is the boss,' he said, tapping his heart with the handle of his fork. I noticed he held his fork in the wrong hand and he later explained: a left-handed fighter is called a southpaw. 'Being a southpaw helps when you're fighting a big gorilla like the guy tonight. Everything is coming at him the wrong way round. It cuts down his reach, you can get in closer. A straight left becomes a right jab and that leaves him open for a left hook.'

Hoppie might as well have been speaking Chinese, but it didn't matter: like the feel of my hands in the gloves, the language felt right. A right cross, a left hook, a jab, an uppercut, a straight left. The words and the terms had a direction, they meant business. A set of words that could be turned into action. 'You work it like a piston, with me it's the right, you keep it coming all night into the face until you close his eye, then he tries to defend what he can't see and in goes the left, pow, pow, pow all night until the other eye starts to close. Then whammo! The left uppercut. In a southpaw that's where the knock-out lives.'

'Do you think I can do it, Hoppie?' I was desperate for his confidence in me.

'Piece sa cake, Peekay. I already told you, man. You're a natural.' Hoppie's words were like seed pods with wings. They flew straight out of his mouth and into my head where they germinated in the rich, fertile, receptive soil of my mind.

The remainder of the morning was taken up with Hoppie writing up some books in the guard's van where he had a bunk, table and wash basin and a cupboard all to himself. Attached to a hook in the ceiling was a thing he called a speedball, for sharpening your punching. I was too short to reach it but Hoppie punched it so fast he made it almost disappear. I was beginning to like the whole idea of this boxing business.

Hoppie explained that at Gravelotte the train had to take on antimony from the mines. There would be a nine-hour stop before the train left for Kaapmuiden at eleven o'clock that night. 'No worries, little boetie. You will be my guest at the fight and then I will put you back on the train.'

At lunch my eyes nearly popped out of my head. We sat down at the same table as before and the man who had been at breakfast, whose name turned out to be Gert, brought Hoppie a huge steak and me a little one.

'Compliments of the cook, Hoppie. The cook's got his whole week's pay down on an odds-on bet with four miners. He says it's rump steak, red in the middle to make you a mean bugger.' Gert laughed. 'I reckon his wife is going to be the mean bugger if you don't win.'

Hoppie squinted up at Gert. 'I get my head knocked in, the cook loses his money, but the man who keeps the book always wins, eh Gert?'

Gert looked indignant. 'Not always, Hoppie. I dropped a bundle when you lost to that blêrrie Rooinek in Pretoria.'

'My heart bleeds for you, man, fifteen fights, fourteen wins and you've always given my opponents the better odds. Christ, I've made you rich!' Hoppie said and began to tuck into his steak.

At breakfast we had been in too early to see many other passengers, but at lunch the dining compartment was full and everyone was talking about the fight. Gert was moving from table to table, and in between serving was taking ten-shilling and pound notes from passengers and writing it down in his book.

Hoppie looked up at me, the handle of his fork resting on the table with a piece of red meat spiked on the end. 'You a betting man, Peekay?'

I looked at him confused. 'What's a betting man, Hoppie?'

Hoppie laughed. 'Mostly a blêrrie fool, little boetie.' Then he explained about betting. He signalled for Gert to come over. 'What odds will you give the next welterweight contender?' he asked, pointing to me.

Gert asked me how much I had.

'One shilling,' I said nervously.

'Ten to one,' Gert said, 'that's the best I can do.'

'Is this an emergency?' I asked, fearful for Granpa's shilling.

'At ten to one? I'll say so!' Hoppie answered.

It took positively ages to get the safety pin inside my pocket loose and then to undo the doek Granpa's shilling had been tied into. I handed Gert the shilling and he wrote something down again in his little book. Hoppie saw the anxiety on my face. It wasn't really my shilling and he knew it.

'Sometimes in life doing what we shouldn't do is the emergency, Peekay,' he said.

We arrived in Gravelotte at two-thirty on the dot. The heat of the day was at its most intense and the vapoured light shimmered along the railway tracks. Hoppie said the temperature was one hundred and eight degrees and tonight would be a sweat bath. There were lots of rails in what Hoppie called the shunting yards and our train was moved off the main track into a siding.

'This is where I got my shunting ticket. When the ore comes in from Consolidated Murchison and you got to put together a train in this kind of heat, I'm telling you, Peekay, you know you're alive, man,' Hoppie said, pointing to a little shunting engine moving ore trucks around.

We crossed the tracks and walked through the railway workshops where they were working on a train. The men stopped and talked to Hoppie and wished him luck and said they'd be there tonight, no way they were going to work overtime. The temperature inside the corrugated-iron workshops seemed worse than outside and most of the men wore only khaki shorts and boots, their bodies shining from grease and sweat. Hoppie called them 'Grease Monkeys' and said they were the salt of the earth.

We arrived at the railway mess where Hoppie lived. We had a shower and Hoppie opened a brown envelope which a mess servant brought to him when we arrived. He read the letter inside for a long time and then, without a word, put it into the top drawer of the small dressing table in his room. He said it was best to keep my old clothes on because we would have another shower before the fight and I could put a clean shirt and pants on then.

'We are going shopping, little boetie, and then to the railway club to meet my seconds and have a good look over the big gorilla I'm fighting tonight. Bring your tackies, Peekay, I have an idea.'

We set off with my tackies under my arm. The main street was only a few hundred yards from the mess and there didn't seem to be too much happening. Every time a truck passed it sent up a cloud of dust, and by the time we got to the shop Hoppie was looking for, I could taste the dust in my mouth and my eyes were smarting. It sure was hot.

The shop we entered had written above the door, G. Patel & Son, General Merchants. On its verandah were bags of mealie meal and red beans and bundles of pickaxes, a complete plough and a dozen four-gallon tins of Vacuum Oil paraffin. Inside it was dark and hot and there was a peculiar smell quite unlike anything I had previously experienced.

'It smells funny in here, Hoppie.'

'It's coolie stuff they burn, man, it's called incense.'

A young woman dressed in bright swirls of almost diaphanous cloth came out of the back of the shop. She was a mid-brown colour, her straight black hair was parted in the middle and a long plait hung over her shoulder almost to her waist. Her eyes were large and dark and very beautiful. On the centre of her forehead was painted a red dot.

Hoppie nudged me with his elbow. 'Give me your tackies, Peekay,' he whispered. I handed him the two brown canvas shoes which had endured no more than twenty or so steps and showed no sign of wear.

'Good afternoon, Meneer, I can help you please?' she said to Hoppie.

Hoppie did not return her greeting and I could tell from the way he looked at her that she was somehow not equal. I thought only Kaffirs were not equal, so it came as quite a surprise that this beautiful lady was not also. 'Tackies, you got tackies?' he demanded.

The lady looked down at the tackies Hoppie was holding. 'Only white and black, not brown like this.'

'You got a size for the boy?' Hoppie said curtly. The lady leaned over and looked at my feet and went to the other end of the counter. She brought a whole lot of tackies tied together in a bundle back with her. She unpicked a pair and handed them to Hoppie, who said, 'Try them on, Peekay. Make sure they fit, you hear?'

I slipped into the tackies which were white and looked splendid. They fitted perfectly. 'Tie the laces,' Hoppie instructed.

'I can't, Hoppie. Mevrou didn't show me how.' The beautiful dark lady came around the counter, went down on her haunches and started to tie the laces. Her coal black hair was oiled and the path down the centre of her head was straight as an arrow. When she had finished tying the laces she tested the front of the tackies with the ball of her thumb, pressing down onto my toes, then she looked up at me and smiled. I couldn't believe my own eyes, she had a diamond set into the middle of one tooth!

She turned to look up at Hoppie. 'They fit good,' she said.

Hoppie waited until she was back behind the counter. 'Okay, now we make a swap. Those tackies for these tackies.' He placed my old tackies in front of her.

The lady stood looking at Harry Crown's tackies and then shook her head slowly. 'I cannot do this,' she said quietly.

Hoppie leaned his elbows on the counter so he was looking directly into her eyes. His back was straight, his jaw jutted out and his head was held high, his whole body seemed to be threatening her. He allowed his silence to take effect, forcing her to speak again.

'These are not the same, where did you buy these tackies ?' She picked up one and examined the sole, then she turned towards the door behind the counter and said something in a strange language. In a few moments we were joined by a man with the same straight black hair and brown skin but dressed in a shirt and pants just like everyone else. The lady handed the tacky to the man, speaking again in the strange language. He seemed much older than her, old enough to be her father. The man turned to Hoppie.

'We cannot make a change, this tacky is not the same. See here is the brand, made in China.' He tapped the sole of the tacky with his forefinger. Then he walked over to the bundle on the counter and pulled one tacky loose from the pile. 'See, by golly, here is altogether another brand

and not from China, this time made in Japan. That is a different place you see, this is a different tacky. You did not buy this tacky from Patel & Son. You must pay me three shilling.'

Hoppie appeared not to have heard, and leaning over the counter he tapped the man on the shoulder. 'Outside it says Patel & Son, this is your daughter but where is your son, Patel ? '

Patel's face lost its aggrieved look. 'My son is very-very clever. A very-very clever student who is studying at University of Bombay. Every month we are sending him money and he is sending us letters. Soon he will be returning BA and we will be most overjoyed on his returnings.'

'Sixpence and these tackies, Patel. I can't be fairer than that, man,' Hoppie said emphatically. Patel bent and twisted the tacky in his hand, a sour look appearing on his face.

'One shilling,' he said suddenly.

'Sixpence,' Hoppie said again. Patel shook his head.

'Too much I am losing,' he said.

Hoppie looked at him. 'Patel, this is my last and final offer and only if the boy gets a *bansela,* I'll give you another tickey, take it or leave it, man!' Patel shook his head and clucked his tongue and finally nodded. Hoppie took the ninepence out of his pocket and put it on the counter. The beautiful lady held out a yellow sucker.

'Here is your bansela,' she said with a smile and I caught another glimpse of the diamond. I thanked her for the sucker, wondering what yellow tasted like. I still had one red one and with this one I would have two for the fight tonight.

'Thank you, Hoppie,' I said, looking down proudly at my new white tackies. I can tell you they looked good and I could walk in them just like that.

'Better take them off, Peekay. If you're going to be in my corner tonight we don't want you wearing dirty tackies, man,' Hoppie said with a grin. I took the tackies off and Hoppie tied the laces in a knot and hung them around my neck. I turned to thank Patel. He seemed to have become very excited and was pointing to Hoppie.

'Meneer Kid Louis, I am very-very honoured to meet you! All week, my golly, I am hearing about you and the fisticuffs business. This morning only, the telephone from my brother in Mica and my brother in Letsitele is ringing for placing a wager. My goodness gracious, now I am meeting the person myself!'

Hoppie laughed. 'Bet the ninepence you rooked out of me on me and it will pay for your son's education, Patel.'

'No, no, we are doing much, much better. Ten pounds we are wagering on Kid Louis.'

'Holy shit! Ten pounds! That's twice as much as I win if I win.'

Patel proffered the ninepence he had been holding. 'Please take it back, Meneer Kid Louis, it will bring very-very bad luck if I am keeping this money.'

Hoppie shrugged and pointed to me. 'Give it to the next welterweight contender.'

'You are a boxer also?'

I nodded gravely, in my head it seemed almost true. Patel dug into his pocket and produced a handful of change, he dropped the ninepence amongst the coins and selected a shilling. 'Here is for you a shilling,' he said fearfully. Turning to Hoppie he said: 'Please, you must be fighting very-very hard tonight.'

Hoppie grinned at him. 'You don't know what you just did, Patel, but it is a very good omen.'

'Thank you, Mr Patel,' I said, my hand closing around the silver coin. Granpa's change was safe again and I must say it was a load off my mind.

As we left the shop Hoppie gave me a bump with his elbow. 'You're a funny little bugger, Peekay. You don't call a blêrrie coolie "Mister". A coolie is not a Kaffir because he is clever and he will cheat you any time he can. But a coolie is still not a white man!'

'That lady had a diamond in her tooth, Hoppie.'

'Yeah, the bastards have got lots of money all right. You never see a poor *charah*. Behind the shop is probably a big V8 Pontiac.'

'What if she swallows it?'

'What?'

'The diamond . . . if it comes loose or something?'

Hoppie laughed. 'They'd be sifting through kak for days!'

We stopped at a café and Hoppie bought two bottles of red stuff. The old lady behind the counter took them out of an ice box, opened them, popped a sort of pipe only made of paper into the tops and handed them to us. I watched to see how Hoppie did it and then I did it too. Tiny bubbles ran up the bottle and went up my nose and it tasted wonderful. On the side were the words American Cream Soda. The stuff was like a raspberry sucker, only different. It was the first bottled soft drink I had ever tasted.

We arrived at the railway club just before five o'clock. The club manager, who came onto the verandah to meet us, said the temperature was still in the high nineties, the rains were overdue and there was already severe drought in the Kruger National Park at the far end of the Murchison range.

The club was cool with polished red cement floors and large ceiling fans. The manager told us the boys from the mine had already arrived and the railway boys, including Hoppie's seconds, were with them in the billiard room having a few beers. Hoppie took my hand and we followed the manager into the billiard room.

The room contained three large tables covered in green stuff on which were lots of pretty coloured balls. Men with long sticks were knocking the balls together all over the place. In the far corner some twenty or so men were seated at a long table covered in aeroplane cloth on which were lots of brown bottles. They all stopped talking as we walked in. Two of them put down their glasses, rose from the table and came towards us smiling. Hoppie shook them by the hand and seemed very happy to see them. He turned to me and said: 'Peekay, this is Nels and Bokkie. Nels, Bokkie, this is Peekay, the next welterweight contender.' Both men grinned and said hello and I said hello back. We walked over to the group of men who had remained sitting around the long table.

Bokkie cleared his throat and put his hand on Hoppie's shoulder. He was a big man with a huge round tummy, and a very red face with a flat nose that appeared to have been broken several times. I noticed that Hoppie was staring at a man who was sitting at the table with a jug of beer in front of him. The man was looking straight back at Hoppie, and their eyes were locked together for a long time. Hoppie was still holding my hand and although his grip didn't seem to increase I could feel the sudden tension. At last the man grinned and dropped his eyes and reached out for his glass.

'Gentlemen,' Bokkie said, 'this is Kid Louis, the next welterweight champion of the South African Railways.' The men at the side of the table nearest to us all cheered and whistled, and a man on the other side of the table stood up and pointed to the man Hoppie and I had been staring at.

'This is Jackhammer Smit. Stand up, Jackhammer, where's your manners, man?' he grinned. The miners surrounding Jackhammer whistled and cheered just as the railway men had done a moment before. Jackhammer rose slowly to his feet. He was a giant of a man with his head completely shaved. Hoppie's grip tightened around my fingers momentarily and then relaxed again. 'This is one big gorilla, Peekay,' he said out of the corner of his mouth. Jackhammer took a couple of steps towards us. His heavy eyebrows were like dark awnings above coal-black eyes. A growth of several days made a bluish stubble over his chin and gave him a permanently angry look. His nose was almost as flat as Bokkie's and one ear looked mashed.

Hoppie stuck his hand out but the big man didn't take it. The men all fell silent. Jackhammer Smit put his hands on his hips, and tilting his head back slightly he looked down at Hoppie and me with eyes of anthracite and doom. Then he turned back to the miners. 'Which of the two midgets do I fight?' The miners broke up and beat the surface of the table and whistled. Jackhammer Smit turned back to face us. 'Kid Louis, huh? Tell me, man, what's a Boer fighter doing with a Kaffir name? Shit man, you should be ashamed of yourself. Kid Louis? I don't usually fight kids and I don't fight *Kaffirboeties,* but tonight I'm going to make an exception.' He laughed. 'You the exception, railway man. Every time I hit you you're going to think a bloody train shunted into you!' He turned and grinned at the seated miners who shouted and cheered again, then he walked the two steps back to his chair where he slumped down and took a deep drink from the jug of beer.

Hoppie was breathing hard beside me but quickly calmed down as the men turned to see his reaction to Jackhammer's taunts. He grinned and shrugged his shoulders. 'All I can say is, I'm lucky I'm not fighting your mouth, which is a super heavyweight.'

Jackhammer exploded and sprayed beer all over the railway men who were seated opposite him. 'Come, Peekay, let's get going, man,' Hoppie said, moving towards the door to the cheers, whistles and claps of the railway men.

Bokkie and Nels followed quickly. Hoppie turned at the door. 'Keep him sober, gentlemen, I don't want people to think I beat him 'cause he was drunk!'

Jackhammer Smit half rose in his chair as if to come after us. 'You fucking midget, I'll kill you!' he shouted.

'You done good,' Bokkie said, 'it will take the bastard two rounds just to get over his anger.' He then told Hoppie to get some rest, that they'd pick us up at the mess at seven-fifteen to drive to the rugby field where the ring had been set up. 'People are coming from all over the district and from Letsitele and Mica, and even as far as Hoedspruit and Tzaneen. I'm telling you, man, there's big money on this fight, those miners like a bet.'

'No worries,' Hoppie said. 'See you at quarter past seven.'

We walked the short distance to the railway mess. The sun had not yet set over the Murchison range and the day baked on, hot as ever. 'If it stays hot then that changes the odds.' Hoppie squinted up into a sky the colour of pewter, his hand cupped above his eyebrow. 'I think it's going to be a bastard of a night, Peekay. A real Gravelotte night, hot as hell.'

When we got to the mess Hoppie told me his plan. 'First we have a shower, then we lie down, but here's the plan, Peekay, every ten minutes you bring me a mug of water. Even if I say "no more", even if I beg you, you still bring me a glass every ten minutes, you understand?'

'Ja, Hoppie, I understand,' I replied, pleased that I was playing a part in getting him ready. Hoppie took his railway timekeeper from one of the fob pockets of his blue serge waistcoat hanging up behind the door.

'Every ten minutes, you hear! And you make me drink it, okay little boetie?'

'I promise, Hoppie,' I said solemnly as he began to undress for his shower.

The window of Hoppie's room was wide open and a ceiling fan moved slowly above us. Hoppie lay on the bed wearing only an old pair of khaki shorts. I sat on the cool cement floor with my back against the wall, the big railway timekeeper in my hands. In almost no time at all Hoppie's body was wet with perspiration and after a while even the sheet was wet. Every ten minutes I went through to the bathroom and brought him a mug of water. After five mugfuls Hoppie turned to me, still on the bed resting on his elbow.

'It's an old trick I read about in *Ring* magazine. Joe Louis was fighting Jack Sharkey. Anyway, it was hot as hell, just like tonight. Joe's manager made him drink water all afternoon just like us. To cut a long story short, by the eighth round the fight was still pretty even. Then Sharkey started to run out of steam in the tremendous heat. You see, Peekay, the fight was in the open just like tonight and these huge lights were burning down into the ring, the temperature was over one hundred degrees. In a fifteen-round fight a man can lose two pints of water just sweating and if he can't get it back, I'm telling you, man, he is in big trouble. I dunno just how it works but you can store water up just like a camel sort of, that's what Joe did and he's the heavyweight champion of the world now.'

'What did Mr Jackhammer mean when he said you were a Kaffir-lover, Hoppie?'

'Ag, man, take no notice of that big gorilla, Peekay. He's just trying to put me off my stride for tonight. You see Joe Louis is a black man. Not a Kaffir like our Kaffirs, black yes, but not stupid and dirty and ignorant. He is what you call a negro, that's different, man. He's sort of a white man with a black skin, black on the top, white underneath. But that big gorilla is too stupid to know the difference.'

It was all very complicated, beautiful ladies with skin like honey who were not as good as us and black men who were white men underneath and as good as us. The world sure was a complicated place where people were concerned.

'I've got a nanny just like Joe Louis,' I said to Hoppie as I rose to get his sixth mug of water.

Hoppie laughed. 'In that case I'm glad I'm not fighting your nanny tonight, Peekay.'

After a while Hoppie rose from the bed and went to a small dresser and returned with a mouth organ. For a while we sat there and he played *Boeremusiek* on the mouth organ. He was very good and the tappy country music seemed to cheer him up.

'A mouth organ is a man's best friend, Peekay. You can slip it in your pocket and when you're sad it will make you happy. When you're happy it can make you want to dance. If you have a mouth organ in your pocket you'll never starve for company or a good meal. You should try it, it's a certain cure for loneliness.'

Just then we heard the sound of a piece of steel being hit against another. 'Time for your dinner,' Hoppie said, slipping on a pair of shoes without socks and putting on an old shirt.

Dinner at the railway mess was pretty good. I had roast beef and mashed potatoes and beans and tinned peaches and custard. Hoppie had nothing except another glass of water. Other diners crowded round our table and wished Hoppie luck and joked a bit, and he introduced me to some of them as the next contender. They all told him they had their money on him and how Jackhammer Smit was weak down below. They almost all said things like, 'Box him, Hoppie. Stay away from him, wear him out. They say he's carrying a lot of flab, go for the belly, man. You can hit him all night in the head, but his belly is his weakness.' When they had left

Hoppie said they were nice blokes but if he listened to them he'd be a dead man.

'You know why he's called Jackhammer, Peekay?'

'What's a jackhammer, Hoppie?'

'A jackhammer is used in the mines to drill into rock, it weighs one hundred and thirty pounds. Two Kaffirs work a jackhammer, one holds the end and the other the middle as they drill into the sides of a mine shaft. I'm telling you, it's blêrrie hard work for two big Kaffirs. Well, Smit is called Jackhammer because, if he wants, he can hold a jackhammer in place on his own pushing against it with his stomach and holding it in both hands. What do you think that would do to his stomach muscles? I'm telling you, hitting that big gorilla in the solar plexus all night would be like fighting a brick wall.'

'I know,' I said excitedly, 'you keep it coming all night into the face until you close his eye, then he tries to defend against what he can't see and in goes the left, pow, pow, pow until the other eye starts to close. Then whammo!'

Hoppie rose from the table and looked down at me in surprise. 'Where did you hear that?' he exclaimed.

'You told me, Hoppie. It's right, isn't it? That's what you're going to do, isn't it?'

'Shhhhh . . . you'll tell everyone my fight plan, Peekay! My, my, you're the clever one,' he said as I followed him from the dining hall.

'You didn't say what happened to Jack Sharkey?'

'Who?'

'In the heat when Joe Louis fought him and drank all the water?'

'Oh, Joe knocked him out, I forget what round.'

Bokkie and Nels picked us up in a one-ton truck which had South African Railways, Gravelotte painted on the door. Nels and I sat in the back and Hoppie sat in the front with Bokkie. In the back with me was a small suitcase Hoppie had packed with his boxing boots and red pants made of a lovely shiny material and a blue dressing gown. Hoppie was very proud of his gown and he had held it up to show me the 'Kid Louis' embroidered in running writing on the back.

'You know the lady in the cafe in Tzaneen, the young one?'

'The pretty one?' I asked, knowing all along whom he meant.

'Ja, she's really pretty, isn't she? Well, she done this with her own hands.'

'Is she your *nooi*? Are you going to marry her, Hoppie?'

'Ag man, with the war and all that, who knows.' He had walked over to the dressing table and taken the brown envelope from the top drawer. He tapped the corner of the envelope into the palm of his open hand. 'These are my call-up papers. They were waiting for me when we got in today. I have to go and fight in the war, Peekay. A man can't go asking someone to marry him and then go off to a war, it's not fair.'

I was stunned. How could Hoppie be as nice as he was and fight for

Adolf Hitler? If he had got his call-up papers that must mean that Adolf Hitler had arrived and Hoppie would join the Judge in the army that was going to march all the Rooineks, including me, into the sea.

'Has Hitler arrived already?' I asked in a fearful voice.

'No, thank God,' Hoppie said absently, 'we're going to have to fight the bastard before he gets here.' He looked up and must have seen the distress on my face. 'What's the matter, little boetie?'

I told Hoppie about Hitler coming and marching all the Rooineks right over the Lebombo mountains into the sea and how happy all the Afrikaners would be because the Rooineks had killed twenty-six thousand women and children with blackwater fever and dysentery.

Hoppie came over to me and, kneeling down so that his head was almost the same height as my own, he clasped me to his chest. 'You poor little bastard.' He held me tight and safe. Then he took me by the shoulders and held me at arm's length, looking me straight in the eyes. 'I'm not going to say the English haven't got a lot to answer for, Peekay, because they have, but that's past history, man. You can't go feeding your hate on the past, it's not natural. Hitler is a bad, bad man and we've got to go and fight him so you can grow up and be welterweight champion of the world. But first we've got to go and fight the big gorilla who called me a Kaffir-lover. I tell you what, we'll use Jackhammer Smit as a warm-up for that bastard Hitler. Okay by you?'

We had a good laugh and he told me to hurry up and put my tackies on and he'd show me how to tie the laces like a fighter.

The sudden sound of a motor horn outside made Hoppie jump up. He put the dressing gown in the suitcase with his other things. 'Let's go, champ, that's Bokkie and Nels.'

'Wait a minute, Hoppie. I nearly forgot my suckers.' I hurriedly retrieved them from my suitcase.

SIX

The rugby field was on the edge of town, down a dusty road. By the time we arrived I could taste the dust in my mouth. We parked the ute with all the other cars and trucks under a stand of large old blue gums, their palomino trunks shredded with strips of grey bark. In the centre of the football field the men from the railway workshop had built a boxing ring that stood about four feet from the ground. The miners, who were responsible for the electrics, had rigged two huge lights on wire which stretched from four poles, each one set into the ground some ten feet from each corner of the ring.

Huge tin shades were fitted over the lights and in the gathering dusk the light spilled down so that it was like daylight in the ring. Hundreds of moths and flying insects spun and danced about the lights, tiny planets orbiting erratically around two brilliant artificial suns. The stands, which were really a series of stepped or tiered benches each about twenty feet long and twelve high, were arranged in a large circle around the ring. It meant everyone had a ringside seat. There looked to be about two thousand men packing the stands, while underneath them, looking through the legs of the seated whites, the Africans stood or crouched, trying to get a view of the ring as best they could.

Bokkie and Nels led us to a large tent, on the side flaps of which was stencilled Property of Murchison Consolidated Mines Limited. We entered to find Jackhammer Smit, his seconds and four other men, three of them ordinary size and one of them not much bigger than me. Hoppie whispered that they were the judges and that, 'the dwarf is the referee'. I was fascinated by the tiny little man with the large bald head. 'He may look silly, man. But take it from me, he knows his onions,' Hoppie confided.

Jackhammer Smit had already changed into black shiny boxing shorts and soft black boxing boots. In the confines of the tent, lit by two hurricane lamps which cast a bluish light, he seemed bigger than ever. As we'd entered he'd turned to talk to one of his seconds. My heart sank, Hoppie was right, I had seen his stomach muscles as he had turned, they looked like plaited rope and his shoulders seemed to loom over the smaller men.

'This is one big sonofabitch, Peekay,' Hoppie said. 'Moses was still blubbing in the bullrushes the last time he weighed in as a light-heavy.' He clipped open his small suitcase, and taking off his shorts and shirt he quickly slipped on a jock strap. He looked tough, tightly put together, good knotting around the shoulders and tapered to the waist, his legs slight but strong. He slipped on his shiny red shorts and sat down on the grass of the tent floor to put on his socks and boxing boots.

Jackhammer Smit now stood in the opposite corner of the tent facing us, with the light behind him. He looked black and huge and he kept banging his right fist into the palm of his left hand. It was like a metronome, a solid, regular smacking sound that seemed to fill the tent.

The referee, who only came halfway up Jackhammer Smit's legs, called the two boxers together. I wondered if all dwarfs had such deep voices. He asked them if they wanted to glove up in the tent or in the ring.

'In the ring,' Hoppie said quickly.

'What's blêrrie wrong with right here, man?' Jackhammer shot back.

'It's all part of the show, brother,' Hoppie said with a grin, 'some of the folk have come a long way.'

'Ja, man, to see a short fight. Putting on the blêrrie gloves is going to take longer than the fucking fight.'

'Now, boys, take it easy.' The referee pointed to a fairly large cardboard box. 'Them's the gloves, ten-ounce Everlasts from Solly Goldman's gym in Jo'burg, specially sent, man,' he said with obvious pride.

Bokkie walked over to the box and took the two pairs of gloves out, and moving over to Smit's seconds he offered both sets to them. They each took a pair, examined and kneaded them between their knees before making a choice. The gloves were shiny black; they caught the light from the hurricane lamp and, even empty, they looked full of action.

Bokkie held the gloves out for Hoppie to inspect. 'Nice gloves, not too light,' he said softly.

'No worries.' Hoppie put a towel around his neck and then slipped into his dressing gown. Bokkie slung the gloves around Hoppie's neck. 'Let's kick the dust,' Hoppie said, moving towards the open tent flap.

Suddenly Jackhammer barked, 'What you say, Groenewald, okay by you, winner takes all?'

Hoppie turned slowly to look at the big man. 'I wouldn't do that to you, Smit, what would you do for hospital expenses?' He took my hand.

'That kid of yours is gunna to be a fucking orphan by the time I'm through with you t'night, you nigger lover,' Jackhammer yelled at Hoppie's departing back.

Hoppie squeezed my hand and laughed softly. 'I reckon that was worth at least another two rounds, Peekay.' Pausing in the dark outside the tent, he took me by the shoulders. 'Never forget, Peekay, sometimes, very occasionally, you do your best boxing with your mouth.'

A small corridor intersected the stands on either side of the brilliantly lit ring by which the patrons and the fighters entered. It at once became obvious that one semicircle contained only miners while the other only railway men, while smiling, excited African faces under the stands peered through gaps between the legs of the whites. I had never been at a large gathering of people before and the tension in the crowd was quite frightening. I held onto Nels' hand tightly as he took me to the top tier of a stand and handed me over into the care of Big Hettie.

Big Hettie seemed to be the only lady at the fight. She was the cook at the railway mess and Hoppie had introduced us earlier at dinner. Big Hettie had given me a second helping of peaches with custard and Hoppie had said that I had better eat it even if I was full because Big Hettie was a genuine heavyweight who could take on two drunken railwaymen with one arm behind her back.

Big Hettie patted the place beside her. 'Come sit here, Peekay. You and me is in this together. If that big baboon hurts Kid Louis we'll go in and finish off the big bugger ourselves,' she said, rocking with laughter.

Hoppie was seated on a small stool in the corner of the ring with Bokkie standing over him bandaging his hands. When Jackhammer Smit entered, he didn't look up. Jackhammer paused in the middle of the ring and cocked two fingers in Hoppie's direction, much to the delight of the miners who were cheering him like mad.

'Ho, ho, ho, have we got a fight on our hands!' Big Hettie said gleefully. Then she rose from her seat and in a voice that carried right over the ring she yelled, 'I'll give you two fingers, you big baboon, right up the arse!'

It was almost totally dark. The sound of a woman's voice was unexpected and for a split second the stands were hushed, and then both sides convulsed with laughter.

Big Hettie sat down again. Reaching into a large basket at her side she brought out a half-jack of brandy. She popped the cork from the slim, flat bottle and took a long swig, grimacing as she withdrew it from her lips as though it was really nasty *muti*. 'That will fix the big ape,' she said, thumping the cork back into the half-jack with the flat of her hand.

The fighters had both been gloved up and while Hoppie remained seated on the tiny stool, Jackhammer Smit continued to stand, looking big and hard as a mountain. While my faith and my love was invested in my beloved friend, I'd been around long enough to know the realities of big versus small. Big, it seemed to me, always finished on top, and my heart was filled with fear for my new-found friend.

'My God! Look at that sparrow fart!' Big Hettie exclaimed, pointing to the tiny referee. 'How the devil is he going to keep them men apart?'

'Hoppie says he knows his onions, Mevrou Hettie,' I ventured.

Jackhammer Smit began to shuffle around the ring throwing imaginary punches. He seemed to be increasing in size by the minute, while Hoppie, seated on his stool, looked like a small frog crouched in the corner of the ring. Nels was putting Vaseline over Hoppie's eyebrows while Bokkie seemed to be giving him some last-minute instructions.

The tiny referee said something and the seconds left the ring and the fighters moved to the centre. The crowd grew suddenly still. Standing between the two men with his head thrown right back, the referee looked up at them and said something. They both nodded and touched gloves lightly and then turned and walked back to their corners. The crowd began to cheer like mad. The referee held his hands up, turning slowly in a circle to hush the crowd, his head only just showing above the top rope of the ring. Soon a three-quarter moon, on the wane, would rise over the Murchison range, though as yet the night was matt black with only a sharp square of brilliant light etching out the ring with the three men in it. It was as though the two fighters and the dwarf stood alone, watched by an audience of a million stars.

The referee addressed the stilled crowd, his surprisingly deep voice carrying easily to where we sat. '*Dames en Here*, tonight we are witnessing the great biblical drama of David and Goliath.' He paused for his words to take effect.

'Weeping Jesus! Sparrow Fart's going to give us a Bible lesson,' Big Hettie hissed at no one in particular. She took a quick swig from the half-jack as the referee continued.

'Will history repeat itself? Will David once again defeat Goliath?' The railwaymen went wild and the miners hissed and booed. The referee held his hands up for silence. 'Or will Goliath have his revenge?' The miners cheered like mad and this time it was the railwaymen who booed and hissed.

The little man held up his hands again and the audience calmed down.

'Introducing in the blue corner, weighing two hundred and five pounds and hailing from Murchison Consolidated Mines, the ex-light-heavyweight champion of the Northern Transvaal, Jackhammer Smit. Twenty-two fights, eleven knockouts, eleven losses on points, a fighter with an even stevens record in the ring. Ladies and gentlemen, put your hands together for Jackhammer Smit!' The miners cheered and whistled.

'What's eleven losses on points mean, Mevrou Hettie?' I asked urgently.

'It means he's a pug, a one-punch Johnny, a slugger,' she said, taking another swig and wiping the top of the bottle with the palm of her hand. 'It means he's no boxer.'

The referee turned to indicate Hoppie who raised his hands to acknowledge the crowd. 'In the red corner, weighing one hundred and forty-five pounds, from Gravelotte, Kid Louis of the South African Railways, Northern Transvaal welterweight champion and the recent losing contender for the Transvaal title; fifteen fights, fourteen wins, eight knockouts, one loss.' He cleared his throat before continuing, 'Let me remind you that the fighter he narrowly lost to on points in Pretoria went on to win the South African title in Cape Town.' He raised his voice slightly. 'Let's hear it for the one and only Kid Louis!' It was our turn to cheer until the referee orchestrated us back to silence. Hoppie had once again calmly seated himself on the tiny stool, while Jackhammer Smit was snorting and throwing punches at an imaginary opponent, soon to become Hoppie.

'This is a fifteen-round contest, may the best man win.' The referee had already assumed the authority of the fight and he didn't look small any more. It was clear the crowd accepted him. He moved to the edge of the ring where the light spilled sufficiently to show three men seated at a small table. 'Ready, judges?' They nodded and he turned to the two fighters. 'At the sound of the bell come out fighting, gentlemen.'

Out of the darkness the bell sounded for round one.

Hoppie jumped from the stool as Nels pulled it out of the ring and Jackhammer Smit stormed towards him. In the oppressive heat the air was as still as a dead man's breath and the big boxer's torso was already glistening with sweat. I had earlier unwrapped my first sucker, as usual licking the clear Cellophane clean. It was the yellow one the beautiful Indian lady with the diamond in her tooth had given me, and the wrapper tasted vaguely of pineapple, only even sweeter than a real pineapple.

Hoppie danced around the big man and Jackhammer Smit let go two left jabs and a right uppercut, all of which missed Hoppie by a mile. He followed with a straight left which Hoppie caught neatly in his glove as he was going away. Hoppie feinted to the right as Jackhammer tried to catch him with two left jabs, then he stepped in under the last jab and peppered Jackhammer's face with a two-handed attack. Two lefts, then two stabbing rights to the head. The blows were lightning fast; Hoppie had moved out of reach by the time Jackhammer Smit could bring his gloves back into position in front of his face. Hoppie continued to back-pedal most of the time, making Smit chase him around the ring. Occasionally he darted in with a flurry of blows to the head and then danced out of range again. Jackhammer came doggedly after him, trying to get set for a big punch, but Hoppie was content to land a quick left and a right and then move quickly out of harm's way. The first round saw him land a dozen good punches, most of them just above Jackhammer's left eye, while the big man only managed a long straight left that caught Hoppie on the shoulder as the welterweight was moving away.

It was clear that Jackhammer Smit was having trouble with the southpaw and was showing his frustration. The bell went for the end of the first round and the fighters returned to their corners. This time, like Hoppie, Jackhammer sat down, breathing heavily. He drank deeply, straight from a bottle of water one of his seconds held up to his mouth. The other second sponged him, dried him and smeared Vaseline above his left eye.

Hoppie looked composed, breathing lightly. He drank from a bottle with a tiny bent pipe coming out of it, rinsing his mouth and spitting the water back into a bucket Bokkie held for him. Nels was massaging his shoulders and Hoppie was nodding his head at something Bokkie was saying.

'Is Hoppie winning, Mevrou Hettie?' I asked anxiously.

'It's early times yet, Peekay. In the early rounds the Kid will be too fast for the big guy, but one thing's for sure, Hoppie's punches are too short to hurt Smit.'

The bell went for round two, a round much the same as round one except that Jackhammer Smit landed three punches to Hoppie's head, all of them glancing blows, but each time the miners went wild. After the second round a red blotch began to appear above Jackhammer's left eye. The next three rounds saw Hoppie leading Smit all around the ring making him throw punches that nearly always missed and then darting in with a quick flurry of blows before bouncing back out of harm's way.

The bell went for the sixth round and Jackhammer shuffled to the centre of the ring, his gloves rotating slowly in front of his chest. He was getting the hang of the southpaw and was going to make Hoppie take the fight to where he stood rooted to the centre of the ring.

Jackhammer dropped his gloves, leaving his head a clear target, knowing he could take anything Hoppie dished out. Hoppie was forced to move in close enough for Smit to hit him in the gut and around the kidneys. In this way Hoppie had to take a couple of vicious blows to the body every time he moved in to hit the spot above Jackhammer's left eye. Jackhammer gave a grunt as he drove a left or a right into Hoppie's body and the crowd responded as one man with an exclamation of pain. By the end of the sixth Jackhammer's left eye was almost closed but deep red welts showed on Hoppie's ribs where Jackhammer had caught him. Both men were breathing hard as they returned to their corners.

'It's not looking good for the Kid. The big ape has found his mark and he's going to wear him down with body punches. You could of fooled me, he got more brains than I would have given him credit for,' Big Hettie said. She didn't show any emotion, appraising the progress of the fight as though she were simply an informed, though disinterested, bystander.

'Don't let him have brains, Mevrou Hettie. Brains is one thing you've got to have to win,' I said in anguish. Big Hettie was fanning herself with a brightly coloured Chinese paper fan, the perspiration running down the sides of her face and neck. 'He hits awful hard, Peekay,' she said absently.

The bell went for the seventh and Jackhammer shuffled back to the centre of the ring. The heat was plainly telling on him and his gloves were held even lower than before. This left enough of his body exposed for Hoppie to hit him at long range, getting a lot more power behind his punches. The left eye was closed and Hoppie was beginning to work on the right, jabbing straight lefts right on the button every time. Near the end of the round he attempted a right-cross to Jackhammer's jaw just as the big man had moved back slightly to throw a punch. Hoppie missed with the right and was thrown slightly off balance as Smit followed through with an uppercut that caught the smaller man under the heart. You could hear his grunt as the punch landed and Hoppie's legs buckled under him as he toppled to the canvas.

'Oh, shit! One-punch Johnny has found the punch. Goliath wins in seven,' Big Hettie said in dismay as the miners went wild. The tiny referee was standing over Hoppie and yelling at Jackhammer Smit to get into a neutral corner, but the big man just stood there his chest heaving, waiting for Hoppie to rise so that he could finish him off. The referee wouldn't start the count and precious seconds passed as the big man stood belligerently over the fallen welterweight. Jackhammer's seconds were screaming at him to move away and when finally he did so a good thirty seconds had passed.

The referee started to put in the count. Hoppie rose onto one knee and waited until the count of eight before rising and getting to his feet. The referee signalled for the fight to continue and Jackhammer Smit lumbered across the ring to finish Hoppie off. The almost forty-second respite had been enough to stave off disaster and Hoppie simply kept out of harm's way as Jackhammer, energy leaking out of him with every assault, kept charging at him like an angry bull. The bell went just as Hoppie landed a hard left uppercut to Jackhammer's eye when the big man tried another desperate charge.

'Dammit, Peekay! That was lucky. Thank the Lord Jesus, Sparrow Fart knows the blêrrie rules, the Kid was out for a ten count for sure.' Big Hettie removed a dishtowel that covered the basket and mopped her face and bosom. 'Smit's just another stupid Boer after all. All balls and no brains. Hoppie can thank his lucky stars for that.'

In all the excitement I had bitten the sucker clean off its stick and crunched it to bits, shortening its life by at least half an hour. I ran my tongue around the inside of my mouth, seeking the last of the pineappley taste. It could be a long time before another one came my way. Big Hettie took a Thermos flask from the basket and, using the silver lid which was shaped like a cup, poured it full of hot, sweet, milky coffee and handed it to me. Then she opened a large cake tin and handed me a huge slice of chocolate cake. My eyes nearly stood out on stalks, this was going to be a night to remember all right. If Hoppie, beloved Hoppie, could just keep away from the big gorilla. The way he danced around the big man, seeming only to get out of the way of a punch at the last second, reminded me of how Granpa Chook used to dodge when stones were thrown at him. I only hoped that Hoppie had the same survival instinct. For an instant I grew sad. In the end even Granpa Chook's highly developed sense of survival couldn't save him, the big gorilla finally got him.

The eighth round saw another change in the fight. Jackhammer Smit had chased Hoppie too hard and too long. The gorilla's great strength had been sapped by the heat and he was down to barely a shuffle, both eyes nearly closed. Hoppie was hitting him almost at will and Jackhammer pulled the smaller man into a clinch whenever he could, causing the tiny referee to stand on the tips of his toes and pull at his massive arms, yelling 'Break!' at the top of his voice.

The ninth and the tenth rounds were much of the same but Hoppie didn't seem to have the punch to put Jackhammer away. Early in the eleventh Smit managed to get Hoppie into yet another clinch, leaning heavily on the smaller man. As the referee moved in to break them up, Jackhammer Smit stepped backwards into him, sending the tiny referee arse over tip to the floor. Still holding Hoppie, Smit headbutted him viciously. On the railway side of the ring we saw the incident clearly, but all the miners, like the ref, saw was Hoppie's legs buckle and the welter-weight crash to the floor as Jackhammer Smit broke out of the clinch.

This time Smit moved quickly to the neutral corner and the referee, bouncing to his feet like a rubber ball, started to count Hoppie out.

Pandemonium broke loose. The railwaymen, shouting 'Foul!' began to come down from the stands shaking their fists. At the count of six the bell went for the end of the round and Bokkie and Nels rushed into the ring to help a dazed and wobbly Hoppie to his corner.

A score of railwaymen had reached the ring and were shouting abuse at Jackhammer. The miners were yelling and coming down from their stands and, I'm telling you, the whole scene was a proper kerfuffle.

Jackhammer sat in his corner vomiting into a bucket, and Bokkie and Nels were frantically trying to bring Hoppie around, holding a small bottle under his nose. I had begun to cry and Big Hettie drew me into her bosom while hurling abuse at Jackhammer Smit. 'You bastard, you dirty bastard, come into my kitchen tomorrow and I'll de-knacker you, you sonofabitch!' she screamed.

I could hear her heart going boom, boom, boom and the smell of brandy on her breath was overpowering. I can tell you, I stopped crying quick smart, her arm was pinning me to her heaving bosom so tightly that I was beginning to feel faint. Thank God she released me so she could stand up and shake her fist.

Several fights had started around the base of the ring and the judges' table had been overturned. The referee stood in the centre of the ring, his hands raised, his head shining like a beacon. He didn't move and this seemed to have a calming effect on the crowd. Others rushed in to stop the ringside brawling, pulling their mates away. Not until there was complete silence did the referee indicate that both fighters should come to the centre of the ring. Hoppie, meanwhile, seemed fully recovered while Jackhammer, huge chest still heaving and both eyes puffed-up slits, looked a mess. The referee took Hoppie's arm and raised it as high as he was able. 'Kid Louis on a foul in the eleventh,' he shouted.

The railwaymen went wild with excitement while the miners started to come down from their stands again. 'Shit, it's going to be on for-one-and-all,' Big Hettie said.

Hoppie jerked his arm away and started an animated argument with the ref, pointing his glove at the near-blind Jackhammer. Finally the referee held his hands up for silence. 'The fight goes on!' he shouted and both boxers moved back to their corners. The bell began to clang repeatedly and in a short while the ringside fighting stopped and the men, walking backwards still shaking their fists at each other, returned to their seats.

'That Hoppie Groenewald is mad as a meat axe,' Big Hettie declared. 'He had the blêrrie fight won and he wants to start all over again!' She wiped away a tear with the dishcloth. 'Jesus, Peekay, he has guts, that one is a real Irishman!'

Ten minutes passed before the bell went for round twelve, by which time Hoppie was good as gold and Jackhammer's seconds, in between his bouts of vomiting, had managed to half open his left eye. The closed lids of his right eye extended beyond his brow so that he was forced to hunt Hoppie with only half a left eye.

It was no contest. Hoppie darted in and slammed two quick left jabs straight into the half-open eye and closed it again. The rest of the round was a shambles, with Jackhammer simply covering his face with his gloves and Hoppie boring into his body. The years behind a jackhammer were counting and Jackhammer Smit simply leaned on the ropes and took everything Hoppie could throw at him. He grunted as Hoppie ripped a blow under his heart and Jackhammer opened his gloves in a reflex action. Hoppie saw the opening and moved in with a perfect left uppercut that landed flush on Jackhammer's jaw. The big man sank to the canvas just as the bell went for the end of the round.

Hoppie's shoulders sagged as he walked back to his corner. It was clear to us all that he was exhausted, fighting more by instinct than by conscious will. Jackhammer's seconds climbed into the ring and helped him to his feet, leading the almost blind fighter to his corner.

'Sweet Jesus, they gotta throw in the towel!' Big Hettie said in elation. 'Hoppie's got it on a TKO.' My heart was pounding fiercely. It seemed certain now that small could beat big, all it took was brains and skill and heart and a plan. A perfect plan.

But we were wrong. The bell went for the thirteenth and Jackhammer Smit rose slowly to his feet, half-dragging himself into the centre of the ring. Hoppie, too exhausted to gain much from the rest between rounds, was also clearly spent. He hadn't expected Jackhammer Smit to come out for the thirteenth and his extreme fatigue sapped his will to continue. It was as though both moved towards the other in a dream. Hoppie landed a straight left into Jackhammer's face, starting his nose bleeding again. He followed this with several more blows to the head but his punches lacked strength and Jackhammer, unable to reply, his pride keeping him on his feet, absorbed the extra punishment. He managed to get Hoppie into a clinch, leaning hard on the smaller man in an attempt to sap what strength was left. When the referee shouted at the two men to break he pushed at Hoppie and at the same time hit him with a round arm blow to the head that carried absolutely no authority as a punch. To our consternation and the tremendous surprise of the miners, Hoppie went down. He rose instantly to one knee, his right hand on the deck to steady him. Jackhammer, sensing from the roar of the crowd that his opponent was down, dropped his gloves and moved forward. Through his bloodied fog he may not have seen the punch coming at him. The left from Hoppie came all the way from the deck with the full weight of his body to drive the blow straight to the point of Jackhammer Smit's jaw. The giant wobbled for a split second then crashed unconscious to the canvas.

'Timber!' Big Hettie screamed as the crowd went berserk. I had just witnessed the final move in a perfectly wrought plan where small defeats big. First with the head and then with the heart. To the very end Hoppie had been thinking. I had learned the most important rule in winning . . . keep thinking.

For a moment Hoppie stood over the unconscious body of his opponent, then he brought his glove up in an unmistakable salute to Jackhammer Smit. He moved slowly to a neutral corner and the referee commenced to count. At the count of ten Jackhammer Smit still hadn't moved. Hoppie moved over to his corner and then, turning to us, he held his arms up in victory. His legs were wobbling as Nels pushed the stool into the corner for him to sit down.

In my excitement I was jumping up and down and yelling my head off. It was the greatest moment of my life. I had hope. I had witnessed small triumph over big. I was not powerless. Big Hettie grabbed me and held me high above her head. In the bright moonlight we must have stood out clearly. Hoppie stood up unsteadily and, grinning, he waved one glove in our direction.

Jackhammer had been helped to his feet by his seconds and was standing in the centre of the ring supported by them as the referee called Hoppie over. Holding Hoppie's hand up in victory he shouted, 'The good book tells the truth, little David has done it again! The winner by a knockout in the thirteenth round, Kid Louis!' The railwaymen cheered their heads off and the miners clapped sportingly and people started to leave the stands.

As the boxers left the ring, Jackhammer still supported by his seconds, Gert, the waiter who took bets in the dining car on the train, entered the ring and began to settle bets. It had been a tremendous fight and even the miners seemed happy enough and would stay for the *braaivleis* and *tiekiedraai* afterwards.

It took four big railwaymen to get Big Hettie down from the top of the stand where we had been sitting. She had finished one half-jack of brandy and was well into the next and so was in no state to make it to the bottom on her own.

'We showed 'em. Our boy sure socked the bejesus out of the big Palooka! Jaysus, Peekay, what a fight, heh ? A darlin' boy with the heart of a lion.' Big Hettie was speaking in a soft accented English, which came as a surprise. 'Oops!' she said as she nearly missed her step and fell heavily against two of her helpers who were laughing almost fit to burst.

We walked over to the ring where Gert was paying out. Big Hettie had one hand resting on my shoulder as though I were a sort of human walking stick. 'I always speak the Irish tongue when I've had toomush brandy. Me darlin' father, God rest his soul, he used to say, "M'dear, only the Irish tongue is made smooth enough fer a dacent drinkin' man when he's had a few." And he was right, you cannot get properly sozzled speaking the verdomde taal!'

I said nothing. Hoppie must have told Big Hettie I was a Rooinek, but I wasn't taking any chances and my camouflage remained intact. I saw no point in letting her know there was an enemy or even a friend in her midst.

At the ringside the men were lining up to be paid. As we drew closer Big Hettie, reverting back to Afrikaans, shouted at Gert, 'You good-for-nothing *skelm!* Where's my fiver?' Speaking Afrikaans seemed to have an immediate sobering effect on her. She moved imperiously to the head of the queue where Gert took five one-pound notes from his satchel and handed them down to her.

'Thank you for your business, Hettie,' Gert said politely.

Big Hettie squinted up at him, 'And don't you forget our little business either, my boy. Three cases of Crown Lager for the mess tomorrow night. Bring them early so I can put them on ice.'

'You said only two,' Gert whined.

'The Afrikaner in me said two, but it was such a good fight, the Irish in me says three. You won big anyway, the odds were against Hoppie Groenewald winning.'

'Scheesh! I didn't win so big, there was a last-minute rush to bet on Hoppie.'

'Pig's arse! You won't eat steak till next Christmas if it isn't three cases for my boys.' By this time Big Hettie seemed completely sober.

'A man might as well not make book with you around, Hettie.' Gert grinned and turned back to his other customers.

Hoppie came out of the tent just as we reached it and was immediately surrounded by railwaymen. He looked perfect, except for a large piece of sticking plaster over his left eye where Jackhammer Smit had butted him. Well, not absolutely perfect, in the light you could see his right eye was swollen and was turning a deep purple colour.

Bokkie and Nels were with him. Neither could stop talking and throwing punches in the air and replaying the fight. I was too small to see Hoppie as more and more railwaymen crowded around him. Big Hettie grabbed me and lofted me into the air. 'Make way for the next contender,' I heard Hoppie shout. Hands grabbed hold of me and carried me over the heads of the men to where he stood.

Hoppie pulled me close to him and put his hand around my shoulder. 'We showed the big gorilla, heh, Peekay?'

'Ja, Hoppie.' I was suddenly a bit tearful. 'Small can beat big if you have a plan.'

Hoppie laughed. 'I'm telling you, man, I nearly thought the plan wasn't going to work tonight.'

'I'll never forget, first with the head and then with the heart.' I hugged him around the top of the legs. Hoppie rubbed his hand through my hair.

The last time someone had done this, it was to rub shit into my head. Now it felt warm and safe.

It was almost three hours before the train was due to leave and most of the crowd had stayed behind to meet their wives after the fight at the tiekiedraai dance. Miners and railwaymen, as well as the passengers travelling on, all mixed together, the animosity during the fight forgotten. Only the Africans went home because they didn't have passes and wouldn't have been allowed to stay anyway.

With a slice of Big Hettie's chocolate cake already in me I could scarcely manage two sausages and a chop. I even left some meat on the chop which I gave to a passing dog, who must have thought it was Christmas because, from then on, she stayed with me. She was a nice old bitch, although she looked a bit worn out from having puppies and her teats hung almost to the ground. She walked slowly, like old bitches do, and after a while I felt we'd always known each other. One ear was torn and her left eye drooped, probably from a fight or something. She was a nice yellow colour with a brown patch on her bum.

It had been a long day and I was beginning to feel tired. I'd never been up this late when I was happy. Hoppie found me and the dog sitting against a big gum tree nodding off. Picking me up, he carried me to the utility. I was too tired to notice if the old yellow bitch followed us.

Big Hettie was sitting in the back of the truck, her huge body almost filling it. She had a fresh half-jack and was using it to conduct herself in song, 'When Irish eyes are smilin' sure it's like the mornin' breeeeze!' I was amazed at her raucous sound. I had never before encountered a woman who couldn't sing.

'Shhh! Hettie, the next contender wants to sleep,' Hoppie said.

Big Hettie stopped, the brandy bottle poised mid-stroke. 'Me darlin' boy, come and give Hettie a big kiss.' It was the last thing I remember. Big Hettie was speaking Irish again. I guess she must have gone back to being drunk.

SEVEN

I woke at dawn to the by now familiar clickity-clack of the carriage wheels. From the colour of the light coming through the compartment window I could see it was the time Granpa Chook would come to the dormitory window and crow his silly old neck off. I supposed he had conditioned me to waking at first light.

The light which fled past the compartment window was still soft with a greyish tint; soon the sun would come and polish it till it shone. The landscape had changed in a subtle way. Yesterday's rolling grassland was now broken by an occasional koppie, rocky outcrops with clumps of dark green bush, each no more than a hundred feet high. Flat-topped fever trees were more frequent and in the far distance a sharp line of mountains brushed the horizon in a wet, watercolour purple. We were coming into the true lowveld.

I sat up and became aware of a note pinned to the front of my shirt. I undid the safety pin to find a piece of paper with a ten-shilling note attached to it. I was a bit stunned. I'd never handled a banknote and it was difficult to imagine it belonged to me. If one sucker cost a penny, I could buy one hundred and twenty suckers with this ten shillings. On the piece of paper was a carefully printed note from Hoppie.

Dear Peekay,

Here is the money you won. We sure showed that big gorilla who was the boss. Small can beat big. But remember, you have to have a plan - like when I hit Jackhammer Smit the knock-out punch when he thought I was down for the count. Ha, ha. Remember always, first with the head and then with the heart. Without both, I'm telling you, plans are useless!

Remember, you are the next contender. Good luck, little boetie.

Your friend in boxing and always,

Hoppie Groenewald

PS Say always to yourself, First with the head and then with the heart, that's how a man stays ahead from the start. H. G.

I was distressed at having left the best friend after Granpa Chook and Nanny that I had ever had, without so much as a goodbye. Hoppie had passed briefly through my life, like a train passing in the night, I had known him a little over twenty-four hours, yet he had managed to change my life. He had given me the power of one, one idea, one heart, one mind, one plan, one determination. Hoppie had sensed my need to grow, my need to be assured that the world around me had not been specially arranged to bring about my undoing. He gave me a defence system and with it he gave me hope.

In the early morning the clickity-clack of the carriage wheels sounded sharper and louder as though racing towards the light. It was only by concentrating hard that I could hear the cadence of someone breathing, first an inhalation, deep and mournful, then complete silence for a few moments and then a powerful whistling sound as a great volume of air was exhaled. At first I thought it might be a part of the train. After all, I was not much of an expert on trains.

But then I began to suspect that the whistling sound had something to do with the smell in the compartment. It was so severe I had to cover my nose with my sheet. Holding my nose, I peered over the edge of the bunk. In the bunk below me lay Big Hettie still fully dressed. She was heaving in her sleep like a beached sperm whale. With every intake of air her bosom and stomach rose almost to touch the bottom of my bunk. Wow! Kapow! What a stink! Her arm was stretched out with her hand planted firmly on the carpet, acting as a prop to prevent her from tumbling to the floor.

On the bunk directly opposite her was a smallish suitcase and a very large square wicker picnic hamper. Big Hettie and I had the compartment to ourselves. Which was just as well as Big Hettie's brandy breath filled it and I knew that if I remained in my bunk I was done for. I moved to the bottom of my bunk and managed to push the compartment window down. Sitting as close to the window as possible I gulped at the fresh air flying past. Then, withdrawing my head when my nose was almost frozen, I removed the doek from my pocket and carefully folding Hoppie's note and the ten-shilling banknote together I tied them into the corner with Granpa's shilling. Then I pinned the doek back into my pocket, feeling dangerously rich.

Dangling from my bunk I managed to swing clear of Big Hettie's body to land with a soft thud on the floor. My heart beat wildly at the thought of waking her up, but it soon became apparent that she was pretty fast asleep. The door to the compartment was open just a crack, and using both hands I slid it open just enough to squeeze through into the corridor. The corridor window almost directly opposite was half-open, and by standing on my toes I could get my nose into the fresh air.

I stood there watching the early morning folding back. It can be very cold in the lowveld before the sun rises and without a blanket I soon began to shiver. I tried to ignore the cold, concentrating on the clickity-clack of the carriage wheels. I became aware that the clickity-clack was talking to me: *Mix-the-head with-the-heart you're-ahead from-the-start. Mix-the-head with-the-heart you're-ahead from-the-start* the wheels chanted until my head began to pound with the rhythm. It was becoming the plan I would follow for the remainder of my life; it was to become the secret ingredient in the power of one.

It grew too cold to stand there in the corridor with the window open, so I made my way down to the end of the carriage and sat on the lavatory with the door closed. Then I felt like having a piss and I did that and pulled a lever at the side of the toilet and a trap door at the bottom of the toilet bowl opened directly onto the tracks. The noise of the wheels rose up at me and you could see a blur of gravel and a flash of sleepers as the train whizzed over them. I stood there with my hand on the lever; since the episode with the Judge I had thought a bit about shit. At the hostel we did it in tins which would be taken away every week, and empty ones that smelt of disinfectant put in their place. I often wondered where they took all the stuff. At least now I knew what the railways did with theirs.

It grew too cold even in the lavatory and so I made my way back to the compartment. As I slid back the door, I saw that a calamity had befallen Big Hettie. The arm that had propped her up all night had finally collapsed and she lay with the top half of her massive body on the floor while her legs remained on the bunk. The skirt of her dress had ridden up to cover her face. With each intake of breath, it was sucked tightly against her face and with every exhalation it billowed out like the collar on a frill-necked lizard. Her huge legs, bluish-white and laced with varicose veins, stuck out of an enormous pair of shiny pink bloomers, the elastic ends of which reached down to just above her knees. She appeared to be carrying most of her weight on her neck and shoulders, and I observed that her face was growing increasingly flushed and tiny bubbles were forming at the corners of her mouth. I tried to wake her by shaking her as hard as I could. 'Wake up, Mevrou Hettie,' I begged, but she just grunted and inhaled, was silent and exhaled with a whistle of stale air and a short snort which brought on the bubbles. I soon realised that she couldn't remain half in and half out of the bunk in such a topsy-turvy position, but lifting her back onto it was plainly beyond me.

I climbed over her body and onto her bunk. Using all my strength and by propping my legs against the walls of the compartment, I managed to push both her legs off the bunk so that they landed on the compartment floor with a great plop I was sure would wake her. Her huge body now filled every inch of floor space between the bunks as neatly as if she had been canned in a sardine factory in Portugal, but she did not wake. The bright red colour soon left her face and while she continued to whistle she did not snort, which I took as a good sign. Soon even the bubbles stopped.

I climbed onto her tummy and managed to pull a blanket off her bunk. I pulled her dress down and covered her with the blanket and, with some difficulty, managed to get a cushion under her head. She gave a soft sigh and then let go a huge burp which was damn nearly the end of me. Boy, did she stink!

The blanket wasn't big enough to cover her entirely. It fell like a small blue tent, covering her bosom and tummy and reaching to the top of her legs. The Big Hettie tent was pitched right in the middle of the compartment, inhaling and exhaling and whistling away.

I wrapped myself in the remaining blanket and sat with my nose at the open compartment window. There was simply nothing else I could think to do. The sun was coming up over the distant Lebombo mountains and the African veld sparkled as though it were contained in a crystal goblet.

There was a sudden rattle at the door and a single sharp word, 'Conductor!' whereupon the door slid open to reveal a slight man in a navy serge uniform just like Hoppie's. Only this man looked very neat and his boots shone like a mirror. Around the edge of the elliptical blue and white enamel badge on his cap it read, South African Railways – Suid Afrikaanse Spoorweë, but unlike Hoppie's which had the word Guard written across the centre, this badge read Conductor. I don't suppose it is important to know what a badge says, but when you're small and on your own, you've got to gather all the information you can, as fast as you can. Good camouflage depends on this.

The man at the compartment door wore a thin black moustache which looked as though it had been drawn on with a school crayon. His bleak expression suggested someone already soured by the burdens of life. He looked down at the Big Hettie tent with her head only inches from his polished boots.

'What's going on here, man?' he demanded.

'Mevrou Hettie fell off the bunk, Meneer,' I answered in a frightened voice.

'Why me? Why always me? Why always Pik Botha? Why not somebody else? What have I ever done to anyone?' He looked directly at me. 'Does she belong to you?' he asked in an accusing voice. Before I was able to reply he put a finger and thumb to his furrowed brow and with a wince corrected himself. 'No, of course not. That is Big Hettie.' He gasped as the realisation hit him fully. 'My God! Big Hettie is on my train!' He sounded as if he were about to cry. 'What am I going to do, man!' he wailed.

'I, I don't know, Meneer. She was just here when I woke up.'

Pik Botha sniffed, jerking his head back. 'Well, I'm telling you now, man, she can't stay like this!' He looked down in distaste at the slumbering woman, then stuck his hand into the compartment, leaning slightly over Big Hettie. 'Where's your ticket? Give it here, boy,' he said.

'I have it here, Meneer.' I hurriedly fumbled with the safety pin where Hoppie had pinned my ticket to the clean shirt I had changed into for the fight.

'Bring it here, man, I can't climb over this dead cow to get it.' I crawled along the bunk and, by stretching out my arm as far as I could, managed to reach his hand.

'This ticket is not clipped,' he said accusingly. 'You got on this train who knows where? I'm not a mind reader, this ticket is not clipped, man!'

'I didn't know I had to give it to be clipped, Meneer,' I said, suddenly fearful.

'It's that verdomde Hoppie Groenewald! He did this on purpose to make work for me. Not clipping tickets is an offence. Just because he is going into the army he thinks he can go around not clipping tickets. Who does he think he is, man? What do you think would happen if we all went around not clipping tickets?'

'Please, Meneer, Hoppie clipped everybody's ticket. He only forgot mine, that's the honest truth, honest!' I pleaded, frantic that Hoppie would get into trouble on my behalf.

'Humph! It wouldn't surprise me to find that that one lets dirty Kaffirs ride for nothing and then does bad things to their women. He is not a married man, you know. First I lose one pound ten shillings betting on that big ape from the mines and now that one who calls himself after a nigger boxer goes around not clipping people's tickets.' He paused and cleared his throat. 'I'm afraid it is my duty to report this,' he said, his lips drawn thinly so that his crayon moustache stretched in a dead straight line across his upper lip.

'Please, Meneer, he hates Kaffirs just like you. Please don't report him.'

'It's all right for you. You're his friend, you'll say anything.' He paused as though thinking. 'Orright, I'm a fair man, you can ask anybody about that. But mark my word. Next time that Hoppie Groenewald is going to be in a lot of trouble or my name is not Pik Botha.' He withdrew a pair of clippers from his waistcoat pocket and clipped my ticket.

'Thank you, Meneer Botha, you are a very kind man.'

'Too kind for my own good, boy! If you help others all you get is a kick in the face. But I am a born-again Christian and not a vengeful type. The Bible says, "Vengeance is mine, sayeth the Lord", but sometimes, I'm telling you,' he nudged Big Hettie with the toe of his shiny boot, 'the cross the Lord expects me to carry is very heavy, man.' He gave Big Hettie several more quick nudges with his boot. 'Wake up, you old cow! This compartment is the property of the South African Railways and it says in the rules, no passenger shall decamp on the floor of the carriages. Wake up! You are officially breaking the rules lying there like a dead cow.

Snort, sigh, breath in, silence, breath out, whistle, snort, was all he got back.

'Come, boy, I will take you to breakfast, your ticket says you get breakfast.'

Breakfast was another feast of bacon and eggs with toast, jam and coffee. It was too early for the other passengers and a waiter called Hennie Venter served us. He was pleased as punch with himself because he had won five pounds on the fight. Forgetting what he had said to me about losing one pound ten, Pik Botha proceeded to give him a long lecture on the sin of fighting and the even greater evil of gambling. He ended by asking Hennie if he was ashamed and ready to repent.

Hennie put down a plate of fresh toast covered with a linen napkin to keep it warm. 'No, Meneer Botha, gambling is only a sin if you lose because you didn't back your own kind, but bet on the other side.' He lifted the silver coffee pot and commenced to fill the conductor's cup.

'Hmmph! He's only a grade two railwayman and look how cheeky he is already, young people don't know their place any more. Bring more coffee, man, can't you see this pot is cold?' Pik Botha cried.

We returned to the compartment to find Big Hettie still whistling and snorting away. Pik Botha, a little mellowed from breakfast, did not prod her with the toe of his shiny boot. 'She's not a true Afrikaner, you know. Her father was an Irishman who was too fond of the bottle, drink is a sin that is passed on. The Bible says the sins of the fathers shall be passed unto the third and fourth generation.' Now he gave Big Hettie a nudge. 'Here lies a good example of God's terrible vengeance.'

'Balls!' Big Hettie said suddenly, opening one eye and looking backwards up at us. 'Pig's arse! You are a miserable Bible-bashing, two-faced bastard, Pik Botha. You probably already had a good look up my dress heh? Get me up, you self-righteous little shit! Get me up at once!'

'I did not! How could I? A person would have to climb over you to get such a look, and you have also a blanket over you,' Pik Botha whined.

'Mother-of-Jesus! My head hurts. I must have water, my mouth tastes like the splashboard of an Indian lavatory in the mango season.'

'Thou shalt not take the name of the Lord thy God in vain,' Pik Botha spluttered.

Big Hettie ignored him. 'I must have a glass of water, Peekay, or I shall die.'

'I will have to climb over you, Mevrou Hettie. The glass and the wash basin are on the other side.'

'Climb over, darling. Take also the blanket off me, I am burning up.' I climbed over Big Hettie, and when I got to the empty bunk I pulled the blanket off her. Crawling to the end of the bunk, I removed a glass from the chrome metal loop where it rested on the wall, and lifting the lid off the washbasin I half filled the glass with water. I had to sit on Hettie's chest to give it to her and she drank greedily. She had three half-glasses full before she'd had enough. 'Thank you, darling,' she smiled, 'you've saved my life for sure.'

'The wages of sin is death!' Pik Botha spat out.

Half turning her head towards him, Big Hettie said, 'Oh my God, to think I may die on the floor of a second-class compartment of the South African Railways under the incompetent management of that snivelling arsehole, Pik Botha.' She paused for a moment. 'Who, by the way, calls himself a man and then bets against his fellow railwayman in boxing matches!'

'It's a free world! How was I to know that big ape had a glass jaw?' he protested in his whining voice.

'Glass jaw! What do you mean, glass jaw? Glass jaw my arse! Hoppie Groenewald knocked him out fair and square!' Big Hettie's face had turned purple with indignation and her head bobbed up and down on the pillow. 'Oh, oh, my head, get me a wet towel, Peekay, I think it's going to explode.'

I scrambled over to the basin, and removing the hand towel from where it was hanging at the side of the basin, I rinsed it in cold water.

'Wring it out well, you hear,' Pik Botha shouted, 'I can't have wet towels. These towels are the property of South African Railways and you are supposed to use them for drying yourself, not for wetting yourself.'

'Ja, Meneer Botha,' I replied. I was suddenly grateful for the Judge's iron-bar torture because I was able to wring the small towel out quite well. I sat on Hettie's chest, and folding the wet towel to the right size I laid it across her forehead.

'*Dankie, liefling,*' she said. She half turned her head again to Pik Botha. 'So? Have you thought of a plan to get me up, domkop?'

'Please do not talk to me like this, Hettie. I am a grade one conductor with seventeen years' service in the railways. This whole train is under my command and all the people in it must do as I say. I demand more respect!' Pik Botha seemed on the verge of tears. 'I will have to get first inside the compartment and that is impossible without climbing over you.'

'Well take your boots off first.'

Pik Botha crouched down in the corridor and began to untie the laces of his boots. From where I sat I could see him pull off his boots and line them up against the outside wall of the compartment, toes pointing into the corridor.

He stretched his leg over Big Hettie's body in an attempt to reach the bunk without having to climb over her. His toes inside a well-darned black sock were wiggling like a pig's snout, trying to find the edge of the bunk. A larger man with longer legs might have made it, but Pik Botha's exploring big toe was well short of its mark. 'It's not possible, Hettie,' he said mournfully.

'Do it backwards, stupid! Come in backwards with your legs first.'

With his hands flat on the corridor floor, Pik Botha edged into the compartment backwards. He placed one foot on one of Big Hettie's breasts, then he followed with the other. He inched his way over her belly until he was obliged to put both his hands on her shoulders, his head only inches from her face. Big Hettie suddenly let go an enormous burp. The blast of foul air took all the strength out of Pik Botha's arms and he collapsed into the mountain of flesh below him.

Big Hettie let out a gasp. 'Excuse me!' she said, then she began to giggle, wobbling like a jelly mountain. 'Oh Christ! Oh Jesus! Ha . . . ha . . . ha, hee, hee, hee, Lord have mercy, hee, hee . . . ha . . . ha . . . ha, are you trying to love me . . . hee, hee, or help me? Tee, hee, hee . . . ha . . . ha . .

. ha . . . snort, ha . . . hee, hee, either way you're doing . . . hee . . . hee . . . a terrible job!' Big Hettie gave two more snorts and her head fell back onto the pillow exhausted. 'Oh, oh, I'm dying,' she moaned, and lifting the arm that pinned Pik Botha down she wiped away her tears. Sensing freedom, Pik Botha pushed off Big Hettie's shoulders with both hands and raised his torso. He managed to get his hands around the raised edge of the bunk on either side of Big Hettie, and inserted one foot between Big Hettie's calves while the other foot rested on the edge of the bunk.

Panting furiously he raised himself to a standing position. 'God will punish you for this. "He who plucks one hair from the head of a child of mine, it is as though he doeth this to me, thus sayeth the Lord".' Pik Botha was shaking his finger at Big Hettie and panting away like the old yellow bitch I had met the previous night.

'Keep your preaching for the next prayer meeting at the Apostolic Faith Mission, you miserable little shit house. Here, give me your hand.' Big Hettie stretched her arm out, offering her hand to Pik Botha. He shied away in alarm. 'Grab it dammit, man!'

'No damn fear, you'll only pull me back again,' Pik Botha said in terror.

'Do not flatter yourself, man. Use both hands, I can't stay like this all day unless you can cut a hole in the floor,' she threatened.

That was enough to spur him to action. He grabbed Big Hettie around the wrist with both hands while she grabbed onto his arm with her own hand. Grimacing with the effort, he started to pull. Big Hettie's freed shoulder wobbled a little in response but no other part moved. 'Pull, man!' she shouted, but soon it was obvious that nothing was going to happen. 'Give Tarzan here a hand, Peekay. Show him what a real man can do,' she said in some despair.

There wasn't any space to stand so I sat astride Big Hettie's hips, my feet not quite reaching the edge of the bunk on either side. The idea was to get Big Hettie's torso into an upright position, which might then enable us to get under her arms from the back to lift her up. I grabbed her around the wrists with both hands which failed to meet, but nevertheless gave me quite a good grip. Pik Botha was forced to bend over so that he could grab Big Hettie higher up her arm. 'Now get your backs into it, men. I'm going to count to three, on three give it all you've got, you hear? One, two, three!' We both pulled with all our might. After about five minutes of repeating such efforts she hadn't budged an inch.

'It's no use,' Pik Botha gasped. We were all beginning to realise that we were in a real pickle. The effort to co-operate had cost Big Hettie dearly and she lay there panting in a lather of sweat, her face as red as an old turkey cock's. Pik Botha stood with one foot still balanced on the edge of the bunk and the other inserted between Big Hettie's calves, wiping his sweaty hands on the shiny backside of his navy serge pants. He had taken off his jacket and thrown it on the top bunk. On his silver tie clip 'Witnessing for the Lord' was written. I wondered briefly what it meant.

'One last try. Just one more go. This time it will work for sure,' Big

Hettie panted, her voice not sounding too hopeful. She made me clasp my hands together and she then grabbed me around both wrists, thus allowing Pik Botha to get a better two-handed grip around her wrists. He had also managed to get his bum up against the washbasin which gave him a much better pulling purchase.

'One, two, three. Pull!' Big Hettie commanded. We both pulled like mad, Pik Botha grunting with effort behind me. Big Hettie's way of holding me wasn't such a good idea, her hands were wet with perspiration and I could feel my own hands beginning to slip from her grasp. Suddenly they squeezed out like a wet pumpkin pip and I was catapulted violently backwards, the back of my head slamming hard into Pik Botha's crotch. He gave a loud scream and both his hands shot down between his legs.

Despite her discomfort, Big Hettie let out a scream of delight. 'You've knackered him, boy!' she roared. 'You've taken what was left of his manhood!' Her laughter filled the compartment, causing her great body to shake up and down.

'Coffee! Coffee! Early morning coffee!' It was Hennie Venter, the waiter from breakfast, doing the morning wake-up call. He paused at the open door of our compartment. 'Coffee?' he asked, starting to bring the tray down from his shoulder. His eyes widened in disbelief as he observed Big Hettie pumping up and down with laughter and Pik Botha moaning and clutching his genitals. He only just managed to lower the tray to the corridor floor before he burst into laughter. 'Pik Botha! You dirty old bastard! Sis, man! The door is not even closed.'

The sudden appearance of the waiter seemed to bring Big Hettie around. 'Hennie Venter, not a moment too soon!' she declared.

Hennie, convulsed with laughter, appeared not to hear her. 'A cup of coffee, Mevrou?' he asked and then burst into renewed laughter.

They calmed down and with some difficulty Hennie Venter managed to pull the still groaning Pik Botha over Big Hettie's body and through the compartment door. He stood in the corridor almost doubled up, his face as white as a ghost. He winced, sucking the air through his brown teeth, as he bent down further to recover his boots.

I bundled up his coat and threw it over to Hennie Venter who draped it over the hapless Pik Botha's shoulder. With one hand carrying his boots and the other clutching his waterworks, he hobbled away down the corridor towards the guard's van.

Hennie Venter turned out to be the practical sort. He made me fetch a second pillow which he added to the first one to prop Big Hettie's head up as far as she could go. He even managed to get her to drink a cup of coffee by herself. He inspected the situation carefully and then announced that there was no way of lifting Big Hettie without first removing the lower bunks.

'Sorry, Hettie,' he said, shaking his head, 'we're going to have to wait until we get to Kaapmuiden.' He started to pour Hettie another cup of coffee.

'No damn fear!' she said quickly. 'Unless you want to cut a blêrrie hole in the floor.'

Hennie Venter scratched his head, giving Big Hettie a quizzical look. 'What the hell are you doing on this train, anyway?'

Big Hettie half turned to look backwards and up at him, her mouth in a pout of annoyance. 'Do you think for one moment that I would let this poor child travel all the way to Kaapmuiden on his own?' she asked.

Hennie Venter persisted. 'You were also a little drunk, maybe?'

'Pissed as a newt, drunk as a skunk,' she giggled. 'What a fight it was eh, Hennie?'

'You can say that again, Hettie,' Hennie said happily. 'I won two weeks' wages with a ten bob bet. *Magtig*! What a fighter that Hoppie Groenewald is. A real white man!'

Big Hettie looked up at me sheepishly. 'I came to look after you, Peekay.' She grinned suddenly. 'Anyway, man, let's make the most of a bad situation, heh? I always say, if you can't change things then you have to make sure you're riding on the front elephant and not walking with the poor people at the back. It's time for breakfast and I must say I'm starving.' She looked back at Hennie Venter. 'Off you go, you skelm, six sausages, six rashers of bacon, nice 'n' crisp mind, five hard-boiled eggs to constipate me and half a loaf of toast cut thick with lots of butter. No more coffee, you know what coffee does to a person, I'm going to have to cross my legs as it is. For Peekay, the same only half.'

'Nee, nee, Mevrou Hettie, I have already had breakfast,' I protested.

'Nonsense, child, you are no bigger than a sparrow. What will your mama say if I hand you over like this? We must feed you up and that's all there is to it.'

Hennie Venter left us to fetch breakfast and I imagined Big Hettie feeding me up in the next eight hours so that I arrived in Barberton as big as, if not bigger than, the Judge. There my granpa would be, looking around for a real skinny kid to get off the train, and there I'd be, big as the Judge. What a nasty shock he would get! 'I already ate a whole plate of things, Mevrou Hettie,' I said again.

'Never mind, Peekay, a little more never hurt. You've got to be like the Bushmen in the Kalahari desert, they eat as much as they can get in the good times till their bottoms stick out like their stomachs. Then when the bad times come they live off their own fat.' She chuckled softly, 'I reckon a person like me could go a whole year, or even more, living off their own fat, but you, my poor little blossom, I doubt if you'll get to Kaapmuiden.'

Hennie Venter returned with a large tray of food which he carefully balanced on Big Hettie's stomach. He left us to serve breakfast to the other passengers in the dining car, closing the door behind him and promising to return later.

The tray went up and down as Big Hettie breathed. She could only see what to take from a plate on a down breath, for on an up breath the tray raised above her eye level. I managed to eat one more sausage. Big Hettie didn't seem to notice and polished off my breakfast as well. Though when she finished she said, 'You'll never get to play rugby for the Springboks if you eat like a bird, Peekay.'

'That's okay, Mevrou Hettie,' I answered, 'I'm going to be a welter-weight, which is not so big.'

She seemed amused. 'Just like that good for nothing, Hoppie Groenewald, huh? Well you could do worse, I suppose. Not a bad bone in his body that one. He could have made it big time but he doesn't hate. Not even Kaffirs, which isn't natural.'

I was shocked. Hoppie hadn't said anything to me about the necessity of hate. Was this something he had neglected to tell me?

'How do you learn to hate, Mevrou Hettie?' I was fearful that it might prove to be something beyond the ability of a five-, really six-year-old. Perhaps that's why Hoppie hadn't mentioned this hate business. But hadn't he said I was a natural? If I was a natural, then I would be able to learn it for sure.

'The killer instinct, he hasn't got the killer instinct. You can tell when a fighter's got it. It's proper hate, like the Boere hate the Rooineks. It has to be blind hate like that, them or us, him or me, nothing less. Hoppie Groenewald just never learned to hate.'

'Then I will learn to hate also,' I said with conviction.

Big Hettie rocked with laughter. 'Plenty of time for that, Peekay. Better still to concentrate on love, there is already too much hate in this land of ours. This country has been starved of love too long.'

I wasn't listening, my mind was busy with the need to learn to hate. 'Didn't Hoppie hate Jackhammer Smit?'

'That was pride, Hoppie has plenty of that. And courage and even brains.' Big Hettie suddenly sensed my anxiety. 'Look here, man, maybe that's enough.' She chuckled softly, 'He sure out-foxed that big ape, Smit!'

I cast my mind back to when I had done the Judge's homework, just like that! I had no doubt I had brains. But during the torture sessions I hadn't shown any pride and precious little courage, although I had to admit to myself I wasn't at all sure what pride meant. Maybe I was fatally flawed? Only brains and nothing to go with them?

'How do you learn to have pride and courage, Mevrou Hettie?'

'My goodness me, we are full of questions, Peekay. Now let me see.' She thought for a few moments and then replied, 'Pride is holding your head up when everyone around you has theirs bowed. Courage is what makes you do it.' She looked up to see the confusion in my face. 'Never mind, Peekay, the understanding will come suddenly when you need it.'

I wasn't at all sure about that. Big Hettie's advice seemed downright stupid to me. I knew already that camouflage was the only way, that bowing your head with the rest was the best way to survive. Take the incident with Miss du Plessis, hadn't I raised my head then and she damn near cut it off? And Granpa Chook, if he hadn't shat in the Judge's mouth, we'd still be together. There were no two ways about it, when you stood out in the crowd, trouble was sure to follow.

Maybe there was something more to understand, the world of grown-ups seemed very complicated. I was good at remembering things, so I tucked Big Hettie's words away. Some day they might make sense.

Nanny was the only grown-up I knew who answered questions properly and she wasn't really a grown-up because she was a nanny. When you asked her a thing she would answer with a story or a song and when she hadn't an answer she would say, 'That is a matter for later finding out.' She was always right, sooner or later the answer would come from somewhere. It seemed to me that white people grown-ups always had to have an answer on the spot. Like Pik Botha, they lived most of their lives being miserable and asking, 'Why me?' all the time. Nanny would say, 'Sadness has a season and will pass.' Then she would laugh and hug me and say, 'But it isn't the season for sadness yet.'

I kept wetting the towel for Big Hettie and got her two Aspros from her handbag. She told me to scrounge around because she might have some peppermints in there. I found half a packet, and she said, 'Give me a couple and try one yourself, Peekay.'

I took two large round white peppermints out of the pack and put them in her hand and popped a third into my mouth. At first nothing. Then, pow! I lasted about two good sucks and then spat the peppermint into my hand, it was like swallowing fire! I watched Big Hettie suck away happily. Talk about courage! But I must say those peppermints cleaned up her breath a treat.

Big Hettie and I just lay there, she on the floor and me on the bunk. She talked about her life, which seemed to have been quite a good one, but with some sadness also. Mostly she talked about men.

'Men, Peekay, are a good woman's downfall. Most of them are rotten but you've got to have them anyway. Without a man a woman's life is more rotten than with one. It's no use pretending you don't care, that you're stronger than a man. Because even if it is true, it means nothing except loneliness. Men are pigs who sleep with Kaffir women, and get drunk and beat you up. But a good beating never hurt and sometimes it's the only way those stupid men can show you they love you. It's stupid, heh?'

I tried to imagine a man beating up Big Hettie. 'My granpa couldn't beat up a flea,' I said, trying to comfort her. Big Hettie stood six foot seven inches and weighed nobody knows how much. Even the Judge with all his stormtroopers couldn't get the better of her.

'Once I loved this little flyweight,' she continued. 'That's how I learned about boxing, Peekay. It was during the great depression and you couldn't find work nowhere, man. Me and that little flyweight, we used to travel all over the Transvaal and once to the Orange Free State to fight. There was never another flyweight to fight, the Boere like to see the bigger men and so he always had to fight way out of his division. A middleweight usually. If he was lucky he'd get a welterweight, but it didn't happen very often.

'That little flyweight of mine was game and he loved to fight, but you can't give away that much weight and he used to take some terrible poundings and nearly always lost. Afterwards I'd patch him up and he'd make me talk to him about the fight. Blow by blow, where he was good and where he went wrong. I'd tell him how he was always winning, which was true, he'd be a mile ahead on points and then the big ape he was fighting would catch him a lucky shot and put him away. And he used to look at me and say, "Next time, Hettie, you'll see, I'll win for sure."

'And then we would buy a bottle of cheap brandy and drive out of the town we were in and sit in the back of the Model T and get drunk. When he was drunk it was his turn to replay the fight, only he'd get it all mixed up in his head and he'd think he was still in the fight and I was his opponent and he'd beat the shit out of me. And I always let him, because he had to have some wins for his pride.

'Then when I had taken a beating and he had counted me out, we would drink some more and replay the fight again, which this time he won fair and square. We would then find some nice place behind some bushes, and take our blankets and make love. I'm telling you, Peekay, most men can't get it up when they're drunk, but not my flyweight, he could go all night. What a man he was. They were good times. Oh, oh, such good times.'

Big Hettie's story worried me no end. Here it seemed big always beat small, except in a set-up. 'Hoppie was smaller than Jackhammer Smit and he beat him fair and square.' I said, somewhat defensively.

'Ja, that is true, Hoppie has brains. My flyweight had mashed potato for brains. But I loved that little fleabite until the day he died from taking on one big ape too many.' Big Hettie's eyes welled with tears. 'He was coming out for the sixth round when he staggered and fell. The crowd booed and booed, but he never faked anything in his life and I knew something terrible had happened. He had a brain haemorrhage, just like that. I carried him out of the hall in my arms and we sat on the grass outside in the fresh air with lots of stupid people in a circle looking down at us. But I didn't see any of them, just my darling little flyweight. And then he died right there in my arms.' Big Hettie was sobbing softly.

'Don't cry, Mevrou Hettie, please don't cry.' I quoted Nanny, 'Sadness has a season and will pass.'

She stopped sobbing after a while and dabbed at her eyes with the damp towel. 'He was the best. The very best of men.' She said it so softly I knew she was speaking to herself.

We talked about this and that deep into the hot morning. Big Hettie did most of the chatting as I had developed into a listener. Once I had been a regular chatterbox but school had changed all that. A person of my status was not expected to talk much and, besides, listening is a good camouflage. I soon discovered that it is also an art. You learn not simply to listen to what people say. It's what people don't say that is important. If you listen hard enough you can hear the most amazing things going on behind the speaker's voice. Quite often there is a regular conniption going on. It takes years to make a good translation of this secondary soundtrack and as a small child I could only define it as friendly or otherwise. For camouflage reasons this is often sufficient.

Around noon Hettie dozed off; this time her breathing was much better. Outside the compartment window the bushveld baked in the hot sun. The sunlight flattened the country in the foreground and smudged the horizon in a haze of heat. It is a time when the cicadas become so active that they fill the flat, hot space with a sound so constant it sings like silence in the brain. While I couldn't hear them for the clickity-clack of the carriage wheels I knew they were out there, brushing the heat into their green membraned wings, energising after the long sleep when their pupae lay buried in the dark earth, sometimes for years, until a conjunction of the moon and the right soil temperature creates the moment to emerge and once again fill the noon space.

In the heat the compartment seemed to float, lifting off the silver rails and moving through time and space. Through hours and days and weeks and years, off the blue planet, past the moon and the sun, into centuries and millenniums and aeons. Skirting planets, weaving through the stars. Coming finally to a black hole in space, further even than the mind can think, beyond even the curve of infinity and the silver cord which rings the cosmos. There I would remain safely hidden until I could grow up to be welterweight champion of the world.

'Are you asleep, Peekay?' I opened my eyes to see Big Hettie looking at me. 'A glass of water if you please.' She ran her tongue over her dry lips and removed the towel from her forehead. She handed me the towel and I gave her the glass of water which she gulped greedily. She handed the glass back and I refilled it. 'You're one in a thousand, Peekay,' she said gratefully.

I wet the towel, folded it and placed it over her head. 'One in maybe even a million,' she sighed. I could see she was restless and kept licking her lips. 'What's for lunch, do you think?'

'Meneer Venter hasn't been yet, Mevrou Hettie,' I answered.

'Ag man, I didn't mean that lunch. A person can't eat a train lunch. Breakfast is tolerable, lunch unbearable and dinner unthinkable. Open up my hamper, Peekay, and let a person hear what is inside.' She laughed. 'I'll tell you something, I wasn't concentrating too well when I packed it last night.'

I withdrew the slim bamboo rod threaded through the wicker and opened the large basket. Inside was enough food to feed an army. 'Tell me what we got in there, darling,' Big Hettie said anxiously.

'Two roasted chickens, nearly a full leg of mutton, some corned beef, three mangoes, lots of cold potatoes and sweet potatoes too, two oranges and there is also a big tin.'

'Thank the Lord I brought the tin,' Big Hettie said with obvious relief. 'Open it, Peekay. Quick, man, open the tin!' I was surprised at the urgency in her voice. I lifted the large round tin out of the hamper and, clamping it between my knees, struggled to remove the lid. It came away suddenly, sending me sprawling backwards on the bunk, and the tin slid over the edge of the bunk, spilling half of a large chocolate cake onto Big Hettie's stomach. In two swift movements her arm rose and fell, the edge of her hand sliced through the thick layer of deep brown chocolate icing rending the cake into two large pieces. She had started to pant and her eyes were glazed as she crammed her mouth full of cake. She grunted and snorted and even moaned as she demolished the first hunk, and then reached greedily for the second. Her face was covered with chocolate icing. Stuffing the last bits into her mouth she sucked at her fingers as a small child might, two at a time. Then she plopped her thumb in and out of her mouth several times and ran her hand across her bosom, her fingers moving like a fat spider hunting for any cake she might have missed. She looked up at me and I dropped my gaze, ashamed and frightened, though at the same time I instinctively knew I was watching a sickness or a sadness or even both.

When she had finished Big Hettie was in a lather of sweat, the front of her dress soaked in perspiration, covered with cake crumbs and stained with chocolate icing. She used the damp towel to wipe her face and then lay there panting heavily, her eyes closed. I watched as tears ran down the side of her face, but she said nothing for a long while.

When she had recovered her breath she opened her eyes, which were red and looked puffy. 'I am sorry, Peekay. I am very, very sorry,' she said, her voice almost a whisper.

'It is nothing, Mevrou Hettie, it was only that you were hungry. Chocolate cake makes me feel like that all the time.'

'I'm sorry I ate all the cake, Peekay. But now you get first pick of everything!'

It had been a long time since I had been given first pick of anything and I laughed. 'There is enough for the whole train in here, Mevrou Hettie. I will have cold roast potatoes, after that sweet potatoes, they are my two favourites.'

'And maybe a nice piece of chicken, heh?'

Granpa Chook's death was still much too close to me. The prospect of eating one of his distant relatives, even if this chicken hadn't been a proper chicken person or even a kaffir chicken like Granpa Chook, was impossible to contemplate. Biting into a delicious golden potato, I shook my head.

'To be a welterweight you must eat properly, Peekay. Meat will make you strong. Some mutton perhaps?' she said coaxingly.

When pressed by my mother to have a second helping, my granpa used to say: 'A cow has eight stomachs but I, alas, have one. A cow must keep on chewing but I, my dear, am done.' I swallowed the potato and recited this to Big Hettie. It was bound, I felt, to cheer her up.

Instead she started to cry again.

'I'm sorry, Mevrou Hettie, I'm very sorry, I didn't mean to make you cry again, it is only a silly thing my granpa says to my ma just to tease her.'

Big Hettie sniffed, blew her nose and wiped her eyes. A piece of chocolate icing from the cloth smeared on the bridge of her nose. 'It is not you, liefling. It's old Hettie. She's the one I'm crying for.' She smiled weakly through the tears. 'What the hell, Peekay, what do you say?' she sniffed. 'Might as well die eating as starving, pass me that leg of mutton, my good man!'

I handed her the leg of mutton, one half of which had been sliced away almost to the bone. Resting the big end on her chest, she commenced to happily tear away at the meat on the bone while I demolished a large sweet potato and a mango.

When she had finished the bone had been picked almost clean. To my surprise, she asked me to tear up one of the chickens and place the pieces on her stomach, also to put the slices of corned beef with it. She tore at the chicken as though she were starving, even crunching some of the softer bones. The chicken and the corned beef were soon demolished and with a soft sigh she wiped the grease and sweat from her face. Using the cake tin, I gathered up the chicken bones scattered over the area of her stomach and tipped them out of the window.

I then washed the mango from my face and hands, and set to work, soaking and squeezing out the only remaining towel. This I handed to Big Hettie and retrieved the old one which I washed with a bit of soap, rinsed and hung over the compartment window sill to dry. I had seen Dum and Dee*, our kitchen maids, do the same thing with the wiping up cloths at home after dinner, so I knew I was doing it right. Only they used to hang the cloths from a small line at the side of the big black wood stove so the dry cloths always smelt a little of soup.

Big Hettie put the new cloth, wet as it was, over the front of her dress. 'It's so nice and cool and the heat of my body will soon dry it,' she said, but I knew it was an attempt to hide the chocolate and grease stains. I thought about having to wash Big Hettie's dress. It would take all day and would need a basin as big as a small dam.

There was a sudden rattle as the compartment door slid open and Hennie Venter appeared. 'I'm sorry I've been so long, Hettie, but Pik Botha says he can't walk and is sulking in the guard van, and I have had to do conductor duty because Van Leemin the guard is drunk again. But also I have had to serve lunch,' he finished in an apologetic voice.

'What's for lunch?' Big Hettie asked.

Hennie seemed surprised at the question. 'Beef stew with mashed potato and peas like always.'

'Keep it! The boy and me would rather starve than eat that pig's swill,' she said haughtily.

'Banana custard for pudding today.' Hennie said enticingly.

'Ummph, and tastes like what comes out of a baby's bum,' Big Hettie said scornfully.

'Well, if you don't want any help I'll kick the dust.' Hennie looked over at the open hamper and winked at me. 'I'm sorry you two decided to starve, are you sure there is nothing I can do for you?'

'You can get me off this blêrrie floor, man!' Hettie said in a forlorn voice.

The waiter clucked his tongue sympathetically. 'Soon, Hettie. We get to Kaapmuiden in two hours. There they will know what to do.'

Hoppie had explained to me that from Kaapmuiden I would have to take the branch line to Barberton, a further three hours journey 'in a real little coffee pot', he had said. He had told me the story of a washerwoman with a huge pile of freshly ironed washing on her head who was walking along the railway line when the Barberton train drew up beside her. The driver had leaned out of the train and invited her to jump aboard into the Kaffir carriage. 'No thank you, baas,' she had replied, 'today I am in a terrible big hurry.' It was a funny story when Hoppie told it, but I knew it wasn't true because no white train driver would ever think to offer a Kaffir woman a ride in his train.

The afternoon was still and hot and it was nearly four o'clock when we arrived in Kaapmuiden. The train pulled slowly, shyly into the busy junction, the way trains do when they arrive in places where there are other trains. Kaapmuiden served as the rail link between the Northern and Southern Transvaal and the Mozambique seaport of Lourenço Marques and so was full of its own self-importance.

The station was all huff and puff, busier even than Gravelotte, with engines shunting, trucks banging, clanging and coupling on lines criss-crossing everywhere like neatly arranged spaghetti. Our train drew slowly into the main platform and with a final screech of metal on metal, drew to a standstill.

'What do I do now please, Mevrou Hettie?' I enquired nervously. I had put on my tackies, even though I knew I was to change trains and wouldn't arrive in Barberton until well into the evening. At the beginning of my journey the original over-sized tackies had been a banal signal of the end of the Judge, his stormtroopers, the hostel and Mevrou; a grotesque chapter in my life. Equally this second pair, fitted to my feet so perfectly by the beautiful Indian lady, seemed to symbolise the unknown. Sometimes we live a lifetime in two days. The two days between the first tackies and the snugly fitting ones I now wore were the beginning of the end of my small childhood, a bridge of time that would shape my life to come.

'We must wait here, Peekay. Hennie Venter will bring some men to help me and then I will put you on the train to Barberton. There is plenty of time, your train leaves at six o'clock.' Big Hettie was obviously in great discomfort and, now that relief from her ordeal was at hand, her great body had started to tremble with shock.

I watched from our compartment window as our carriage was uncoupled and, with much fuss, shunted into a small siding where a gang of men were waiting. Among them was Hennie Venter. As we came to a halt, he stuck his head through the open window.

'Nearly over, Hettie, we'll soon have you back on your feet,' he said cheerfully.

I passed all our stuff through the window and then, rather than clamber over Big Hettie again, I came through the window myself, jumping the short distance onto the siding. It was nice to be standing in the sun again. Two of the men climbed through the window onto one of the bunks. Using monkey wrenches, they managed to loosen the bolts attaching the bunk to the compartment wall. Then they slung ropes around both ends of the bunk, secured them to the one above and removed the bolts so the bunk was held suspended away from Big Hettie. Climbing onto the top bunk, they were able to lift the suspended one sufficiently for two men, crouching in the doorway of the compartment, to lift Big Hettie into a sitting position. The four men then tried to raise her to a standing position, but her weight was too much for them and she seemed unable to use her legs. Big Hettie was plainly in some distress and her face was very red. After a while it became plain that the whole ordeal was too much for her and she was too exhausted and too weak to stand up. She simply sat on the floor of the compartment, flushed and panting, her back propped up by a mound of pillows. A huge, sadly battered rag doll.

The men left to fetch a block and tackle. I returned to the compartment and sat on the bunk next to Big Hettie. Hennie Venter remained outside looking into the compartment, his arms resting on the window sill.

Big Hettie's breathing was becoming more laboured as she asked Hennie Venter to go to her hamper which now rested on the platform outside and take the remaining chicken and potatoes and fruit from it, pack them into the cake tin and put it into my suitcase. He nodded and left the window.

'It will be late before you get to Barberton, liefling. What will your oupa think of me if you have had no supper?' she panted, her hand clutching at her left breast.

I was too polite to tell Big Hettie that eating chicken was no longer my speciality. Instead I thanked her and then asked, 'Will you not be coming to the train like you said, Mevrou Hettie?'

She said nothing for a long while as though she were trying to gather up enough strength to speak without gasping. 'I think it is the final round coming up for me, Peekay. I have a terrible pain.' The colour had drained from her face and her lips had turned blue. Her left hand was kneading her left breast.

I scrambled over to the window. Hennie Venter had opened my suitcase and was putting the big cake tin into it. 'Meneer Venter! Come quick, Mevrou Hettie is sick!' I yelled.

I turned back to look at Big Hettie. Her voice was hardly more than a whisper. 'Hold my hand, Peekay,' she gasped. I moved back along the bunk and she took my hand into her own. Her grasp was weak, as though no strength remained in her.

'I don't think I can come out for the next round, liefling.' The words were sandwiched between sighs, quite different from the windy breathing of the morning.

Hennie Venter stuck his head through the window. 'Oh my God! I'll fetch the doctor.' I could hear his boots scrunching on the gravel as he started to run.

'Please don't die, Mevrou Hettie,' I begged, suddenly very afraid.

'Ag, Peekay, it has not been much of a life since my flyweight left me, it's not so much to give up.' She turned to look at me and a tear squeezed out of the corner of her eye and rolled in slow motion down her cheek. 'Peekay, you will be a great welterweight, I know it. You have pride and courage. Remember I told you about pride and courage?'

'Pride is holding your head up when everyone around you has theirs bowed. Courage is what makes you do it,' I repeated, my lips trembling.

'You will be a great fighter, I know it,' she whispered. Big Hettie gave a little jerk and the pressure on my hand increased momentarily. Then her huge hand opened and she slid back into the pillows. For such a big, loud woman it was such a small, quiet death.

I started to cry. It wasn't a pain like Granpa Chook, it was a sadness. Even then I instinctively understood that the blithe spirit is rare among humans and that, for the period of an evening and a day, I had been with a part of the human condition at its best.

After a while I could hear the men returning with the block and tackle. They were laughing and chatting as men do when they are having a bit of a holiday from routine. Big Hettie could be moved now.

EIGHT

It was just after ten in the evening when the train puffed into Barberton station. The conductor woke me before we were due to arrive. My head was dizzy with sleep and mussed up with the events of the day.

Hennie had put me on the train, his mood a mixture of concern for me and the need to get back to the action, where he was such an important cog in the sad machinery of the day. 'You eat something, you hear. Here's a tickey to buy a cool drink,' he said handing me a tiny silver coin.

'I have money, Meneer Venter.'

But he insisted I take the threepenny bit. 'Go on, take it, take it, it is only a blêrrie tickey!' he blustered.

Fortunately he didn't have to hang around too long, we had only just made it to the Barberton train in time. As we departed with a great chuffing sound that seemed too big for the little coffee-pot engine, Hennie shouted: 'I will tell Hoppie Groenewald you behaved like a proper Boer, a real white man!'

I climbed down the steps of the carriage onto the gravel platform of Barberton station, struggling with my suitcase which had now become quite heavy with Big Hettie's tin. I had left its contents untouched, too tired and bewildered to eat. The platform was crowded with people hurrying up and down, heads jerking this way and that, greeting each other and generally carrying on the way people do when a train arrives. My granpa didn't seem to be amongst them. I decided to sit on my suitcase and wait, too tired to think of anything else I might do. I must have been crying without knowing it, maybe it was just from being tired or something. I had been in worse jams than this one, and I expected any moment that I would hear my nanny's big laugh followed by a series of tut-tuts as she swept me into her apron. That's when everything would be all right again.

A lady was approaching, although I could only see her dimly through my tears. She bent down beside me and crushed me to her bony bosom. 'My darling, my poor darling,' she wept, 'everything will be the same again, I promise.'

My mother was here! She was alive. Thin as ever, but not dead from dysentery and blackwater fever.

Yet I think we both knew everything would never be the same again.

'Where is my nanny?' I asked, rubbing the tears from my eyes.

'Come darling, Pastor Mulvery is waiting in his car to take us home to your granpa. What a big boy you are now that you are six, much too big for a nanny!'

The hollow feeling inside me had begun to grow and I could hear the loneliness birds cackling away, their oily wings flapping gleefully as they sat on their dark stone nests.

Clearing her throat and reaching for my suitcase, my mother straightened up. 'Come darling, Pastor Mulvery is going to take us home to your grandfather.'

Her remark about my not needing a nanny now that I was six struck me so forcibly that it felt like one of the Judge's clouts across the mouth. My nanny, my darling beloved nanny was gone and I was six. The two pieces of information tumbled around in my head like two dogs tearing at each other as they fought, rolling over in the dust.

My mother had taken my hand and was leading me to a big grey Plymouth parked under a street lamp beside a peppercorn tree. A fat, balding man stepped out of the car as we approached. His top teeth jutted out at an angle, and peeped out from under his lip as though looking to see if the coast were clear so that they might escape. Pastor Mulvery seemed aware of this and he smiled in a quick flash so as not to allow his teeth to make a dash for it. He reached for my suitcase, taking it from my mother. 'Praise the Lord, sister, He has delivered the boy safely to His loved ones.' His voice was as soft and high-pitched as a woman's.

'Yes, praise His precious name,' my mother replied. I had never heard her talk like this before. It was quite obvious to me that the concentration camp must have had something to do with it. My finely tuned ear could hear all sorts of crazy bits and pieces going on behind her words.

Pastor Mulvery stuck his hand out. 'Welcome, son. The Lord has answered our prayers and brought you home safely.' I took his hand which was warm and slightly damp.

'Thank you, sir,' I said, my voice hardly above a whisper. It felt strange to be speaking in English. I climbed into the back seat of the car next to my mother. All the loneliness birds had become one big loneliness bird on a big stone nest, and I could feel the heaviness of the stone egg as it hatched inside me.

Granpa Chook was dead, Hoppie had to go and fight Adolf Hitler and maybe he would never come back again, Big Hettie was dead and now my beloved nanny was gone. Like Pik Botha, my mother seemed to have entered into a very peculiar relationship with the Lord that was bound to create problems. My life was a mess.

We drove through the town which had street lights and tarred roads. It was late and only a few cars buzzed down the wide main street. We passed a square filled with big old flamboyant trees. The street was lined with shops one after the other, McClymonts, Gentleman's Outfitters, J. W. Winter, Chemist, The Savoy Café, Barberton Hardware Company. We turned up one street and passed a grand building called the Impala Hotel which had big wide steps and seemed to have lots of people in it. The sound of a concertina could be heard as Pastor Mulvery slowed the Plymouth down to a crawl.

'The devil is busy tonight, sister. We must pray for their souls, pray that they may see the glory that is Him and be granted everlasting life,' he said in his girlish voice.

My mother sighed. 'There is so much to be done before He comes again and takes us to His glory.' She turned to me. 'We have a lovely Sunday school at the Apostolic Faith Mission, you are not too young to meet the Lord, to be born again, my boy. The Lord has a special place in His heart for His precious children.'

'Hallelujah, praise His precious name, we go to meet Him!' Pastor Mulvery said.

'Can we meet Him tomorrow please? I am too tired tonight,' I asked.

They both laughed and I felt better. The laugh that rang from my mother was the old familiar one, the concentration camp hadn't stolen it. 'We're going straight home, darling, you must be completely exhausted,' she said gently.

I had almost dropped my camouflage, but now it was back again. Big Hettie had said Pik was a born-again Christian and also that he belonged to the Apostolic Faith Mission. Her tone had implied that both situations left a great deal to be desired. How had my mother come to this? Who was this strange man with escaping teeth? What was this new language and who exactly was the Lord?

I had seen my return to Granpa and to Nanny first as a means of urgent escape from Adolf Hitler and then, when Hoppie had calmed my fear of his imminent arrival, the continuation of my earlier life on the farm. Living in a small town hadn't meant anything to me. Living with silly old Granpa and beautiful Nanny had meant everything. My mother had been a nice part of a previous existence, though not an essential one; she was a frail and nervous woman, and Nanny had taken up the caring, laughing, scolding and soothing role mothers play in other cultures. My mother suffered a lot from headaches. In the morning when I was required to do a reading lesson and had come to sit on the cool, polished red cement verandah next to her favourite bentwood rocking chair eager to show her my progress, she would often say: 'Not today, darling, I have a splitting headache.'

I would find Nanny and I would read my book to her, and then she would bring a copy of *Outspan*, a magazine that used to come once a month, and she would point to pictures that showed women doing things, and I would read what it said about the pictures and translate them into Zulu. Her mouth would fall open and she would groan in amazement at the goings on. 'Oh, oh, oh, I think it is very hard to be a white woman,' she would sigh, clapping her hands.

I guessed that was why my mother was always getting splitting headaches, because she was a white woman and, like Nanny said, it was a very hard thing to be.

We drew up beside a house which sat no more than twenty feet from the road. A low stone wall marked the front garden and steps led up to the stoep which ran the full width of the house. The place was only dimly lit by a distant street lamp so that further details were impossible to make out in the ghoulish darkness. Two squares of filtered orange light, each from a window in a separate part of the house, glowed through drawn curtains, shedding no real light but giving the house two eyes. The front door made a nose and the steps to it a mouth. Even in the dark it didn't seem to be an unfriendly sort of place. Behind the funny face would be my scraggy old granpa and he would tell about Nanny.

Pastor Mulvery said he wouldn't come in, and he praised the Lord again for my delivery into the bosom of my loved ones and said that I would be a fine addition to the Lord's little congregation at the Apostolic Faith Mission Sunday school. My mother also praised His precious name and it was becoming very apparent to me that the Lord was a pretty important person around these parts.

We watched the red brake lights of the big Plymouth twinkle and then disappear down a dip in the road, for we seemed to be on the top of a rise. 'What a precious man,' my mother sighed.

Lugging my case in front of me with both hands I followed her up the dark steps. Her shoes made a hollow sound on the wooden verandah and the screen door squeaked loudly on its heavy snap-back hinges. She propped it open with the toe of her brown brogue and opened the front door. Sharp light spilled over us and down the front steps, grateful to escape the restrictions of the small square room.

This room, at least, was not much altered from the dark little parlour on the farm. The same heavy, overstuffed lounge and three high-backed armchairs in faded brocade, with polished arms and ball and claw legs of dark lacquered wood, the backs of the lounge and chairs scolloped by antimacassars, took up most of the room. The glass bookcase still contained the red and gold leather-bound set of the complete works of Charles Dickens and the two large blue and gold volumes of *The Invasion of the Crimea*. The old grandfather clock stood in a new position beside a door leading out of the room into another part of the house, and it was nice to see the steady old brass pendulum swinging away quietly in its glass-fronted cabinet. On one wall was my granpa's stuffed Kudu head, the horns of the giant antelope brushing the ceiling. Above and on either side of the glass bookcase hung two narrow oil paintings, one showing a scarlet and the other an almost identical yellow long-stemmed rose. Both pictures were framed in the same flat brown varnished frames and were the work of my grandmother who had died giving birth to my mother. The paintings had been rendered on sheets of tin and the paint had flecked in parts leaving dull pewter-coloured spots where the backgrounds of salmon and green had lifted. Alone on one wall was a hand-coloured steel engraving in a heavy walnut frame showing hundreds of Zulu dead and a handful of Welsh soldiers standing over them with bayonets fixed. They stood proud, looking towards heaven, each with a boot and putteed leg resting on the body of a near-naked savage. I had always thought how very clean and smart they still looked after having fought at close quarters with the Zulu hordes all night, each soldier seemingly responsible, if you counted the bodies and the soldiers in the picture, for the death of fifty-two Zulus. The caption under the painting, etched in a mechanical copperplate, read: The morning after the massacre. British honour is restored at Rorke's Drift, January, 1879. Brave men all.

The tired old zebra skin which, along with everything else, I had known all my life, covered the floor, and the ball and claw legs of the lounge suite had been placed over the spots where they had worn the hair off the hide in their previous parlour existence. The only change in the room, for even the worn red velvet curtains had come along, was a small, round-shouldered wireless in brown bakelite which rested on the top of the bookcase where the gramophone had previously stood.

Perhaps only the outside of things had changed and the inside, like this room, largely remained the same. For a moment my spirits lifted. Just then my granpa walked into the room, tall and straight as a bluegum pole. His pipe was hooked over the brown tobacco stain on the corner of his bottom lip and he stood framed by the doorway, his baggy khaki pants tied up as ever with a piece of rope, his shirtsleeves rolled up to below the elbow on his collarless shirt. He looked unchanged. He took two puffs from his pipe so that the smoke whirled around his untidy mop of white hair and curled past his long nose. 'There's a good lad,' he said. His pale blue eyes shone wet, and he blinked quickly as he looked down at me. The smoke cleared around his head as he raised his arms slightly and spread his hands palms upwards as though to indicate the room and the house and the predicament all in one sad gesture of apology.

'Newcastle's disease, they had to kill all the Orpingtons,' he said.

'They killed Granpa Chook,' I said softly.

My mother put her hand on my shoulder and moved me past my granpa. 'That's right, darling, they killed all Granpa's chooks. Come along now, it's way past your bedtime.'

I hadn't meant to say anything about Granpa Chook. My granpa, after all, had never known him. It just came out. One chicken thing on top of another chicken thing. He had been enormously fond of those black Orpingtons. Even Nanny had said they must be Zulu birds because they stood so black and strong, and the roosters were like elegantly feathered Zulu generals. She had never commented on Granpa Chook's motley appearance. While Nanny had never seen him at the height of his powers, like Inkosi-Inkosikazi she knew him to be different, an exception, a magic chicken of great power who had been conjured up by the old monkey to watch over me. Only on one occasion had she ventured the opinion that it was just like the old wizard to choose a lowly kaffir chicken and a

Shangaan at that, when, to her mind, he could have dignified the relationship with one of Granpa's magnificent black Orpington roosters. If a chicken was to become home to the soul of a great warrior, why then could he not be an exemplary example of chickenhood? She had tut-tutted for a while and then, shaking her bandanna'd head, said: 'Who can know the way of a snake on a steep rock?' Whatever that was supposed to mean.

Nanny. Where was she now? Was she dead? Tomorrow I must speak urgently to my granpa. For, while grown-ups never talk to small kids about death, my granpa would tell me for sure. I would ask him when I returned his shilling to him in the morning.

I awakened early as always, and padded softly through the sleeping house to find myself in the kitchen. The black cast-iron stove was smaller than the one on the farm and, to my surprise, when I spit-licked my finger before dabbing it on one of the hot plates, it was cold. On the farm it had never been allowed to go out. The two little orphan kitchen maids Dee and Dum had slept on mats in the kitchen and it had been their job to stoke the embers back to life if the stove showed any signs of going out. This kitchen smelt vaguely of carbolic soap and disinfectant and I missed the warm smell of humans, coffee beans and the aroma of the huge old cast-iron soup pot which plopped and steamed on the back of the stove in a never-ending cycle of new soup bones added and old ones taken out. In the country food is a continuous preoccupation, not simply a pause to refuel. Country people know the sweat that goes into an ear of corn, a pail of milk, a churn of butter, bread warm from the oven and the eggs and bacon which sizzle in the breakfast frying pan. Food is hard earned and requires the proper degree of respect. This stove was bare but for the presence of a large blue and white speckled enamel kettle which looked new and temporary.

The doorway from the kitchen led out onto a wide back stoep which, unlike the front of the house, was level with the ground and looked out into a very large and well tended garden. The fragrance of hundreds of rose blossoms filled the crisp dawn air and I observed that stone terraces, planted with rose bushes, stretched up and away from me. Each terrace ended in a series of six steps and at the top of each set of steps an arbour of climbing roses bent over the pathway. Blossoms of white, pink, yellow and orange, each arboured trellis a different colour, cascaded to the ground in colourful loops. The path running up the centre of the garden looked like the sort of tunnel Alice might well have found in Wonderland. Six huge old trees, of kinds I had not seen before, were planted one to each terrace. It was a well-settled garden and I wondered how it came to be Granpa's. Nothing on the farm had ever seemed to be well settled except the bits which had broken down forever.

I now saw that our house was situated a little way up a large hill, which accounted for the steps in the front and the terraces behind. Beyond a dark line of mulberry trees at the far end of the garden and a stone wall enclosure which stretched halfway across the last terrace, the hill of virgin rock and bush rose up steeply. It wasn't an unfriendly-looking hill and its slopes were dotted with aloe, each tall, shaggy plant carrying a candelabra of fiery, poker-like blossoms. A crown of rounded boulders clustered, like currants on a cupcake, at its very top.

As I walked up the path, I saw that each terrace carried beds of roses set into neatly trimmed lawns, though the last terrace was different. On one side it contained the stone wall enclosure too tall for me to see over; on the other it was planted with hundreds of freshly grafted rose stock behind which, acting as a windbreak, stood the line of mulberry trees.

Except for the strange and beautiful trees and whatever might lie behind the stone wall, no plants other than roses appeared to grow in this very tidy garden. Only the fences on either side testified to the sub-tropical climate. Quince and guava, lemon, orange, avocado, pawpaw, mango and pomegranate mixed with Pride of India, poinsettia, hibiscus and, covering a large dead tree, a brilliant shower of bougainvillaea. At the base of the trees grew hydrangea, agapanthus, and red and pink canna. It was as though the local trees and plants had come to gawk at the elegant rose garden. They stood on the edges of the garden like colourful country hicks, jostling and pushing each other, too polite to intrude any further.

I decided to explore behind the stone wall a little later and ducked under the canopy of dark mulberry leaves. The ground under the trees had been completely shaded from the sun and was bare, slightly damp and covered with fallen fruit. As I walked the moist berries squashed underfoot, staining the skin between my toes a deep purple. I hadn't eaten since lunch with Big Hettie the previous day, and I began to feast hungrily on the luscious berries. The plumpest, purplest of them broke away from their tiny slender stalks at the slightest touch. Soon the palms of my hands were stained purple and my lips must have been the same from cramming the delicious berries into my mouth. Above me the birds, feeding on the berries, squabbled and chirped their heads off, the leaves and smaller branches shaking with their carry-on.

Emerging from the line of mulberry trees clear of the garden, the first of the aloe plants stood almost at my feet, its spikes of orange blossom tinged with yellow two feet above my head. In front of me, stretching upwards to the sky, the African hillside rose unchanged, while behind me, embroidered on its lap, tizzy and sentimental as a painting on a chocolate box, lay the rose garden.

Without thinking I had started to climb, skirting the rocks and the dark patches of scrub and thorn bush. In half an hour I had reached the summit and scrambling to the top of a huge, weather-rounded boulder I looked about. Behind me the hills tumbled on, accumulating height as they gathered momentum until, in the far distance, they became proper mountains. Far to my left an aerial cableway strung across the foothills into the mountains remained motionless, work had not yet started for the day. Below me, cradled in the foothills, lay the small town. It looked out across a vast and beautiful valley which stretched thirty miles over the lowveld to a slash of deep purple on the pale skyline, an escarpment which rose two thousand feet to the grasslands of the highveld.

It was the most beautiful place I had ever seen. The sun had just risen and was not yet warm enough to lap the dew from the grass, but it was sharp enough to polish the air. I could see the world below me but the world below could not see me. I had found my private place; how much better, it seemed to me, than the old mango tree beside the hostel playground. Above me, flying no higher than a small boy's kite, a sparrowhawk circled, searching the quilted backyards below for a mother hen careless enough to let one of her plump chicks stray beyond hasty recovery to the safety of her broody undercarriage. Death, in a vortex of feathered air, was about to strike out of a sharp blue early morning sky.

Chimneys were beginning to smoke as domestic servants arrived from the black shanty town hidden behind a buttress of one of the foothills to make the white man's breakfast. The sound of roosters, spasmodic when I had started my climb, now gathered chorus and became more strident and urgent as they sensed the town start to wake. Part of the town was still in the shadow cast by the hills, but I could see it was criss-crossed with jacaranda-lined streets. My eyes followed a long line of purple which led beyond the houses clustered on the edge of the town to a square of dark buildings surrounded by a high wall perhaps a mile into the valley. The walls facing me stood some three storeys high and were studded with at least a hundred and fifty tiny dark windows all of the same size. The buildings, too, were built in a square around a centre quadrangle of hard, brown earth. On each corner of the outside wall was a neat little tower capped with a pyramid of corrugated iron which glinted in the early morning sun. I had never seen a prison, nor had I even imagined one, but there is a race memory in man which instinctively knows of these things. The architecture of misery has an unmistakable look and feel about it.

My granpa, who was an early riser, would be out and about soon, and it took no more than twenty minutes to clamber down the hill, back under the green canopy of mulberry trees and into the rose garden. He was cutting away at the arbour on the third terrace, snipping and then pulling a long strand of roses from the overhang and dropping it on a heap on the pathway. He looked up as I approached down the corridor of roses.

'Morning, lad. Been exploring, have you?' He snipped at another string of roses and pulled it away from the trellis. 'Mrs Butt is an untidy old lady, if you let her have her way and don't trim her pretty locks, she's apt to get out of control,' he announced cheerfully. I said nothing. Much of what my granpa said was to himself and asking questions was no use. I was soon to learn the names of every rose in the garden and Mrs Butt, it turned out, was the name of this particular cascade of tiny pink roses.

I pulled the lining of my shorts' pocket inside out and carefully unclipped the large safety pin which held Mevrou's doek. Crouching on the ground at the old man's feet, I unknotted the grubby cloth to reveal Granpa's shilling, the threepenny bit Hennie had given me on my departure from Kaapmuiden and my folded ten-shilling note. I removed Granpa's shilling and once again knotted the cloth and pinned it back into the pocket lining of my trousers. 'This is your change from the tackies, Granpa,' I said, rising and holding the gleaming shilling out to him. He paused, holding the secateurs like a sword above his head. 'Here, take it, it's your shilling, isn't it,' I repeated. He reached down for the coin and dropped it into the pocket of his khaki trousers. 'There's a good lad, that will buy me tobacco for a week.' I thought he sounded quite pleased so I took a deep breath and came out with it.

'Granpa, where's Nanny?' He had moved back to the roses, and now he turned slowly and looked down at me. Then he walked the few paces to the steps leading up to the terrace and slowly sat down on the top step.

'Sit down, lad.' He patted the space beside him on the step. I walked over and sat down beside him. He removed his pipe from his pocket, tapped it gently on the step below him and a plug of ash fell from the pipe. He blew through the pipe twice before taking his tobacco pouch from his pocket and refilling it. My granpa was not one for hurrying things so I waited with my hands cupped under my chin. Lighting a wax match on his thigh, he started at last to stoke up, puffing away at the pipe until the blue tobacco smoke swirled about his head. For a long time we sat there, my granpa looking out at nothing, his pipe making a gurgly noise when he drew on it, and me looking at the roof of the house which had once been painted but now only had patches of faded red clinging to the rusted corrugated iron. Coming up the hill in front of the house I could hear a truck, its low gear rasping in the struggle to get up the hill, then a pause as it reached the top and slipped into a higher gear, relieved the climb was over.

'Life is all beginnings and ends. Nothing stays the same, lad,' my granpa said at last. Then he puffed at his pipe and seemed to be examining his fingernails which were broken and dirty from gardening. 'Parting, losing the thing we love the most, that's the whole business of life, that's what it's mostly about.'

Shit, I know that already, I thought to myself. Then my heart sank. Was he trying to tell me Nanny was dead?

He was doing his looking-into-nothing trick again and his pipe had gone out. 'She was a soft and gentle woman. Africa was much too harsh a place for such a trembling little sparrow.' With this he struck another match and touched it to his pipe. Puff, puff, swirl, swirl, puff, puff, gurgle, but he did not continue. While it didn't sound a bit like big, fat Nanny, my granpa was always a bit vague about people and the sentiment seemed appropriate enough, so I waited patiently for him to continue. Taking his pipe from his mouth, he used it to indicate the rose garden around us. 'I built it and planned it for her; the roses, to a rosebud, were the ones which grew in her father's vicarage in her Yorkshire village, the trees too, elm and oak, spruce and walnut.' He replaced the pipe in his mouth, but it had gone out again and he had to light it a third time. This time he cupped his hands around the bowl and gave it a really good stoking up so that at one stage his head disappeared completely behind the clouds of blue smoke. I had already observed that my granpa could waste a great deal of time with his pipe when he didn't want to give my mother an answer or needed time to think. So I waited and thought it best to say nothing, though none of it made sense. Nanny, who discussed everything with me, had never once talked about the roses in the farm garden, and I knew for a fact that she came from a village in Zululand near the Tugela river. While she had often talked about the crops and the song of the wind in the green corn, of pumpkins ripening in the sun which were as big as a chief's beer pots, and of the sweet *tsamma* melons which grew wild near the banks of the river, she had never, even once, mentioned anything about roses to me.

After another long while of looking into nothing my granpa continued. 'When she died giving birth to your mother, I couldn't stay on here in her rose garden.' He looked down at me as though seeking my approval. 'Sometimes it's best just to walk away from your memories, just put one memory in front of the other and walk them right out of your head.'

I was beginning to realise that Nanny had nothing to do with my granpa's conversation.

'Her brother Richard had come out from England to try to cure his arthritis and decided to stay on. A grand lad, Richard, and a good rose man. In thirty years he hadn't changed a thing. When the roses grew old he replaced them with their own kind.' He pointed to a standard rose on the terrace below him. From it rose two perfect long-stemmed blossoms, the edges of their delicate orange petals tipped with red. 'I'll vouch that is the only Imperial Sunset left in Africa,' he said with deep satisfaction. He tapped the bowl of his pipe on the step until the smoking ash fell from it. Then, picking up the garden shears where they lay on the step below, he rose and turned to look about him. 'Now Dick's dead I've come home to her rose garden. The pain is gone but the roses, the sweet Yorkshire roses, not a day older, bloom forever on.'

They were the most words I could recall having come from my granpa in one sitting. While he hadn't answered my urgent questions about Nanny, I could see that he had said something out loud that must have been bouncing around in his head for a long time.

'There's a good lad, off you go and play now.' He moved over to resume the tidying up of old Mrs Butt. I rose from the steps and started to walk towards the house. Smoke was coming from the chimney and breakfast couldn't be too far away. The clicking of the shears suddenly ceased. 'Lad!' he called after me. I turned to look at him, his shaggy old head was almost touching the canopy of roses covering the arbour. 'You must ask your mother about your nanny, it's got something to do with that damn fool religion she's caught up in.'

Imagine my delight when I walked into the kitchen to find our two little kitchen maids Dee and Dum. They saw me enter and with a squeal of pleasure rushed over to embrace me, each of them holding a hand and dancing me around the kitchen. 'You have grown. Your hair is still shaved. We must wash your clothes. Your mouth is stained from the fruit. You must eat. We will look after you now that Nanny has gone. Yes, yes, we will be your nanny, we have learned all the songs.' The two little girls were beside themselves with joy. It felt good, so very good to have them with me. While they had only been on the periphery of my life with Nanny, who had scolded them constantly and called them silly, empty-headed Shangaan girls but loved them anyway, I now realised how important they were to my past. They were continuity in a world that had been shattered and changed and was still changing. Now that my mother was following the Lord and could no longer be relied upon, my granpa and the two girls were my only constants.

'Me, Dum,' one of them said in English, tapping her chest with one hand while covering her mouth with the other to hide her giggle.

'Me, Dee,' the second one echoed, the whites of her eyes showing her delight as they lit up her small black face. They were identical twins and were reminding me of the names I had given them when I was much smaller. It had started as Tweedle Dum and Tweedle Dee and had simply become Dum and Dee. I laughed as they showed off their English.

The room smelt of fresh coffee and Dee moved over to a tall, brown enamel coffee pot on the back of the stove, and Dum brought a mug and placed it on the table together with a hard rusk and then walked over to a coolbox on the stoep for a jug of milk. She returned with the milk and Dee poured the fresh coffee into the cup, both of them concentrating on their tasks, silent for the time being. Placing the pot back on the stove, Dee ladled two carefully measured spoons of sugar into the mug of steaming coffee, using the same spoon to stir it. It was a labour of love, an expression of their devotion. Dum brought me a *riempie* stool and placed it in the middle of the kitchen. I sat down and Dee placed the mug on the floor between my legs so that I could sit on the little rawhide chair and dunk the rock-hard rusk into it just the way I had always done on the farm. The two girls then sat on the polished cement floor in front of me, their legs tucked away under their skirts.

On the farm they had simply worn a single length of thin cotton cloth wrapped around their bodies and tied over one shoulder. Their wrists and ankles had been banded in bangles of copper and brass wire which jingled as they walked. Now these rings were gone and over their slim, pre-pubescent twelve-year-old bodies they wore identical sleeveless shifts of striped navy mattress cotton which reached almost to their ankles.

While I dunked and sipped at my coffee we chatted away in Shangaan. They asked me about the night water and I told them that Inkosi-Inkosikazi's magic had worked and the problem was solved. They clucked and sighed about this for a while and we then talked about the crops and about the men who came in a big truck and lit a huge bonfire and killed and burned all the black chickens. The smell of burning feathers and roasted chickens had lingered for three days, but no one was allowed to eat the meat. Such a waste had never been seen before. How my granpa had sat on the stoep at the farm for a day and a night, watching the fire die down to nothing, silently puffing at his pipe, leaving the food brought to him and letting the coffee beside him grow cold.

At last we reached silence, for the subject of Nanny had been standing on the edge of the conversation waiting to be introduced all along and they knew it could no longer be delayed.

'Where is she who is Nanny?' I asked at last, putting it in the formal manner so they could not avoid the question. Both girls lowered their heads and brought their hands up to cover their mouths.

'Ah, ah, ah!' they shook their heads slowly.

'Who forbids the answering?'

'We may not say,' Dee volunteered, and they both let out a miserable sigh.

'Is it the mistress?' I asked, already knowing the answer. Both looked up at me pleadingly, tears in their eyes.

'She is much changed since she has returned,' Dum said.

'She has made us take off our bangles of womanhood and these dresses make our bodies very hot,' Dee added with a sad little sniff. Both rose from the floor and moved over to the stove where they stood with their backs to me, sobbing.

'I will ask her myself,' I said, sounding more brave than I felt inside. 'At least tell me, is she who is Nanny alive?' They both turned to face me, relieved that there was something they could say without betraying my mother's instructions.

'She is alive!' they exclaimed together, their eyes wide. Using their knuckles to smudge away their tears they smiled at me, once again happy that they could bring me some good news.

'We will make hot water and wash you.' Dum reached down beside the stove for an empty four-gallon paraffin tin from which the top had been cut, the edges hammered flat and a wire handle added, to turn it into a container for hot water.

'See, the water comes to us along an iron snake which comes into the house,' Dee said, moving over to the sink and turning on the tap.

'I am too old to be washed by silly girls,' I said indignantly. 'Put on the water and I will bath myself.' Apart from wiping my face and hands with a damp flannel, my mother had let me climb into bed without washing, and I hadn't really washed since the shower with Hoppie at Gravelotte.

The girls showed me a small room leading off the back stoep in which stood an old tin bath. Carrying the four-gallon paraffin tin between them, they poured the scalding water into the bath. Then they fought over who should turn on the cold tap positioned over the tub. Dum won and Dee, pretending to sulk, left the bathroom. She returned shortly with a freshly washed shirt and pair of khaki shorts. I ordered them both to leave the room. Giggling their heads off, they bumped and jostled each other out of the small, dark bathroom.

That was a bath and a half, I can tell you. It soaked a lot of misery away. The thought that Nanny was still alive cheered me considerably and made the task of asking my mother about her a lot easier.

After breakfast my mother retired to her sewing room and several people turned up to see her. They were women from the town and I could hear her talking to them about clothes. When I questioned the maids about this, they said, 'The missus has become a maker of garments for other missus who come all the time to be fitted.' On the farm my mother had often been busy making things on her Singer machine, and had always made my granpa's and my clothes. Now she seemed to be doing it for other people as well.

Apart from a garden boy who came in to help my granpa, Dum and Dee were our only servants. They cleaned, scrubbed, polished, did the washing and prepared most of the food, though my mother did the cooking and the general bossing around like always. The maids slept in a small room built onto the garden shed behind the enclosed stone wall, which also housed the kitchen garden and an empty fowl run, the thought of chickens being too much for my granpa to contemplate.

At the time I was not concerned about how we lived, though later I was to realise that making enough to get by was a pretty precarious business in the little household. My granpa sold young rose trees and my mother worked all day and sometimes long into the night as a dressmaker. Between making dresses and serving the Lord she didn't have much time for anything else.

I whiled away the morning and after lunch gathered up enough courage to venture into my mother's sewing room. She had a new Singer machine with an electric foot treadle. It wasn't like the old one where you had to treadle it up and down to make it work. You simply put your foot on the little electric footrest and the sewing machine hummed away stitching happily. Dee had given me a cup of tea to take in to my mother and I had hardly spilled any by the time I handed it to her.

My mother had looked up and smiled as I entered. 'I was just thinking to myself, I would die for a cup of tea, and here you are,' she said as I gave her the cup. She poured the spilt tea in the saucer back into the cup and then took a sip, closing her eyes. 'Heaven, it's pure heaven, there's nothing like a good cup of tea.' She sounded just like she used to before she went away. For a moment I thought all the carry-on with Pastor Mulvery was exaggerated in my mind because I knew I had been very tired. I sat on one of the chairs and waited. 'Come in for a bit of a chat, have you? You must have so much to tell me about your school and the nice little friends you made.' She leaned over and kissed me on the top of the head. 'I tell you what. Tonight, after supper, when your grandfather listens to the wireless, we'll sit in the kitchen and have a good old chin-wag. You can tell me all about it. I'm dying to hear, really. Granpa tells me fat old Mevrou Vorster who we sold the farm to says you speak Afrikaans like a Boer. I suppose that's nice, dear, though thank goodness you won't need to talk it in this town. Dr Henny wrote to say you'd got into some sort of scrape with your ear. Is that all right now?' I nodded and she continued, 'I'm better now, quite better. The Lord reached down and touched me and I was healed. It is a glorious experience when you walk in the light of the Lord.' She stopped and took a sip from her cup.

'Mother, where is Nanny?' I asked, unable to contain myself any longer. There was a long pause and my mother took another sip and looked down into her lap.

Finally she looked up at me and said sweetly, 'Why, darling, your nanny has gone back to Zululand.'

'Did you send her there, Mother?' My voice was on the edge of tears.

'I prayed and the Lord told me. He guided me in my decision.' She put down her cup and fed a piece of material under the needle, brought the tension foot down onto it and, feeding the cloth skilfully through her fingers, zizzed away with the electric motor. Then, with a deep sigh, she stopped. Lifting the tension foot, she snipped the cotton thread and looked down at me. 'I tried to bring her to the Lord but she hardened her heart against Him.' She looked up at the ceiling as though asking for confirmation. 'I can't tell you the nights I spent on my knees asking for guidance.' She looked down at me again, and pursing her lips threw her head back. 'Your nanny would not remove her heathen charms and amulets and she insisted on wearing her bangles and ankle rings. I prayed and prayed, and then the Lord sent me a sign I was looking for. Your grandfather told me about the visit of that awful old witchdoctor and that it had been at your nanny's instigation.' Her face grew angry, 'That disgusting, filthy, evil old man was tampering with the mind of my five-year-old son! God is not mocked! How could I let a black heathen woman riddled with superstition bring up my only son?' She picked up her cup and took a polite sip. 'Your nanny was possessed by the devil,' she said finally, satisfied the discussion was over.

I tried very hard not to cry. Inside me the loneliness birds were laying eggs thirteen to the dozen. Forcing back the tears, I got down from my chair and stood looking directly at my mother. 'The Lord is a shithead!' I shouted and rushed from the room.

I ran through the Alice in Wonderland tunnels and under the mulberry trees to the freedom of the hill, my sobs making it difficult to climb. At last I reached the safety of the large boulder and allowed myself a good bawl.

The fierce afternoon sun beat down, and below me the town baked in the heat. When was it all going to stop? Was life about losing the things we love the most, as my granpa had said? Couldn't things just stay the same for a little while until I grew up and understood the way they worked? Why did you have to wear camouflage all the time? The only person I had ever known who didn't need any camouflage was Nanny. She laughed and cried and wondered and loved, and never told a thing the way it wasn't. I would write her a letter and send her my ten-shilling note, then she would know I loved her. Granpa would know how to do that.

As I sat on the rock high on my hill, and as the sun began to set over the bushveld, I grew up. Just like that. The loneliness birds stopped laying stone eggs, they rose from their stone nests and flapped away on their ugly wings and the eggs they left behind crumbled into dust. A fierce, howling wind came along and blew the dust away until I was empty inside.

I knew they would be back, but that, for the moment, I was alone. That I had permission from myself to love whomsoever I wished. The cords which bound me to the past had been severed. The emptiness was a new kind of loneliness, a free kind of loneliness. Not the kind which laid stone eggs deep inside of you until you filled up with heaviness and despair. I knew that when the bone-beaked birds returned I would be in control, master of loneliness and no longer its servant.

You may ask how a six-year-old could think like this. I can only answer that one did.

NINE

'It is a fine sunset, ja? Always here is the best place.' I looked behind me, and there was a tall, thin man, taller, much taller and perhaps even thinner than my granpa. He wore a battered old bush hat and his snowy hair hung down to the top of his shoulders. His face was clean shaven, wrinkled and deeply tanned, while his eyes were an intense blue and seemed too young for his face. He wore khaki overalls without a shirt and his arms and chest were also tanned. The legs of his overalls, beginning just below the knees, were swirled in puttees which wound down into socks rolled over the tops of a pair of stout hiking boots. Strapped to his back was a large canvas bag from which, rising three feet into the air directly behind his head, was a cactus, spines of long, dangerous thorns protruding from its dark green skin. Cupped in his left hand he held a curious-looking camera which appeared to be secured by a leather strap about his neck.

'You must excuse me, please, I have taken your picture. At other times I would not do such a thing. It is not polite. It was your expression. Ja, it is always the expression that is important. Without expression the human being is just a lump of meat. You have some problems I think, ja?'

At the sound of his voice I had stood up hastily and now faced him a little sheepishly, looking down at him from the rock, a good six feet higher than where he stood. He made a gesture at me and the rock and even at the sky beyond.

'I shall call it Boy on a Rock.' He paused and cocked his head slightly to one side. 'I think this is a good name. I have your permission, yes?' I nodded and he seemed pleased. Dropping the camera so that it hung around his neck, he extended his right hand up towards me. He was much too far away for our hands to meet but I stuck mine out too and we both shook the air in front of us. This seemed to be a perfectly satisfactory introduction. 'Von Vollensteen, Professor Von Vollensteen.' He withdrew his hand and gave me a stiff little bow from the waist.

'Peekay,' I said, withdrawing my hand at the same time as he dropped his. His friendliness was infectious and no hint of condescension showed in his manner. Best of all, I could hear nothing going on behind the scenes.

'Peekay? P-e-e-k-a-y, I like this name, it has a proper sound. I think a name like this would be good for a musician.' He squinted up at me, thinking, then took a sharp intake of breath as though he had reached an important decision. 'I think we can be friends, Peekay,' he said.

'Why aren't the thorns from that cactus sticking into your back?' The canvas bag was much too lightly constructed to protect him from the vicious three-inch thorns.

'Ha! This is a goot question, Peekay. I will give you one chance to think of the answer, then you must pay a forfeit.'

'You first took off all the thorns on the part that's in the bag.'

'Ja, this is possible, also a very goot answer,' he shook his head slowly, 'but not true. Peekay, I am sorry to say you owe me a forfeit and then you must try again for the answer.' He stroked his chin. 'Now let me see ... Ja! I know what we shall do. You must put your hands like so,' he placed his hands on his hips, 'at once we will stand on one leg and say, "No matter what has happened bad, today I'm finished from being sad. Absoloodle!" '

I stood on the rock, balanced on one leg with my hands on my hips, but each time I tried to say the words the laughter would bubble from me and I'd lose my balance. Soon we were both laughing fit to burst. Me on the rock and Professor Von Vollensteen dancing below me on the ground, slapping his thighs, the cactus clinging like a green papoose to his back. I could get the first part all right, but the 'Absoloodle!' at the end proved too much and I would topple, overcome by mirth.

Spent with laughter, Professor Von Vollensteen finally sat down, and taking a large red bandanna from the pocket of his overalls, wiped his eyes. 'My English is not so goot, ja?' He beckoned me to come down and sit beside him. 'Come, no more forfeiting, too dangerous, perhaps I die laughing next time. Come, Peekay, I will show you the secret.' He jerked his thumb over his shoulder indicating the cactus. 'But first you must introduce yourself to my prickly green friend who has a free ride on my back.'

I scrambled down from the rock and came to stand beside him. 'Peekay, this is *Euphorbia grandicornis,* he is a very shy cactus and very hard to find in these parts.'

'Hello,' I said to the cactus, not quite knowing what else to say.

'Goot, now you have been introduced you can see why Mr *Euphorbia grandicornis* does not scratch my back.' I walked behind him and looked into the canvas bag. Inside was a small collapsible shovel and the roots of the cactus were swaddled in hessian and tied with coarse string. The part of the bag resting on Professor Von Vollensteen's back was made of leather too thick for the long thorns to penetrate. 'Not so stupid, ha?' he said with a grin.

'Aaw! If you'd given me another chance I would've got it,' I said, immediately convincing myself that this was so.

'Ja, for sure! It is always easy to be a schmarty pantz when you know already the trick.'

'Honest, Mr Professor Von Vollensteen, I think I could've known the answer,' I protested, anxious now to impress him.

'Okay! Then I give you one chance more. A professor is not a mister but a mister can be a professor. Answer me that, Mister Schmarty Pantz?'

I sat down on a small rock trying to work this out, my heart sank, for I knew almost immediately he had the better of me. I had simply thought his first name, like Peekay, was a little unusual. I had never heard of anyone called Professor, but then I was also the first Peekay I knew of, so who was I to judge?

'I give up, sir,' I said, feeling rather foolish. 'What is a professor?' He had removed the canvas bag from his back and once again held the camera cupped in his hands.

'Peekay, you are a genius my friend! Look what we find under this rock where you are sitting. This is *Aloe microsfigma*!' I rose from the rock and joined him on his knees looking underneath it. A small cluster of tiny spotted aloes, each not much bigger than a two-shilling piece grew in the grass at the base of the rock. Even at close quarters they would have been hard to see and to an untrained eye almost impossible. The old man brushed the grass out of the way, and lying flat on his tummy he focused the camera on the tiny succulents. Behind him the sunset bathed the plants in a red glow. 'The light is perfect but I must work quick.' His hands, fumbling with the camera, were shaking with excitement. Finally he clicked the shot and got slowly back to his knees. Removing a Joseph Rogers from the pocket of his overalls, he used the small knife to separate four of the aloes, leaving twice as many behind. He held the tiny plants in his hand for me to see. *'Wunderbar,* Peekay, small but so perfect, a good omen for our friendship.'

I must say I was not too impressed but I was glad that he was happy. 'You haven't said what a professor is.'

He wrapped the tiny aloes in his bandanna and placed them carefully into his canvas bag which he then slung back over his shoulders. 'Ja, I like that, you have good concentration, Peekay. What is a professor? That is a goot question.' He stood looking at the dying sun. 'A professor is a person who drinks too much whisky and once plays goot Beethoven and Brahms and Mozart, and even sometimes when it was not serious, Chopin. Such a person who could command respect in Vienna, Leipzig, Warsaw and Budapest and also, ja, once in London.' His shoulders sagged visibly. 'A professor is also some person who cannot any more command respect from little girls who play not even schopstics goot.'

I could see his previous mood of elation had changed and there was a strange conversation going on in his head. But then, just as suddenly, his eyes regained their sparkle. 'A professor is a teacher, Peekay. I have the honour to be a teacher of music.' He put his hand on my shoulder. It was the first time he had touched me and the gesture was unthinking and friendly, like another kid might hold you when you are playing. 'You can call me Doc. You see I am also Doctor of Music, it is all the same thing. I am too old and you are too young for Mister this or Professor that. You and me will not hide behind such a small importance. Just Peekay and Doc. I think this is a goot plan?'

I nodded agreement, though I was too shy to say the word out loud. He seemed to sense my reluctance. 'What is my name, Peekay?' he asked casually.

'Doc,' I replied shyly. Hoppie was the only other adult with whom I had been on such familiar terms and I found it a little frightening.

'One hundred per cent! For this I give you eleven out of ten. Absoloodle!' he said and we both started to laugh.

The sun sets quickly in the bushveld and we hurried down the hill, small rocks rolling ahead of us as we raced to beat the dark. Below us the first lights were coming on, the chimneys were beginning to smoke as tired servants prepared supper for their white mistresses before washing the dishes and going home to the native location.

'So it is you who live now in the English rose garden,' Doc said when we reached the dark line of mulberry trees. 'Soon I will show you my cactus garden.' While it was too dark to see his face, I sensed his smile. 'We will meet again, my goot friend Peekay.' He touched me lightly and I watched his tall, shambling figure with the *Euphorbia grandicornis* sticking up beyond his head moving into the gathering darkness.

'Good night, Doc!' I said, and then on a whim shouted, '*Euphorbia grandicornis* and *Aloe microsfigma*!'

The old man turned in the dark, 'Magnificent, Peekay. Absoloodle!'

Euphorbia grandicornis, I rolled the name around in my head. Such a posh name for a silly old cactus with thorns. I wondered briefly how it might sound as a name for a fighter, but almost immediately rejected it. *Euphorbia grandicornis* was no name for the next welterweight champion of the world.

When I entered the kitchen, Dum and Dee averted their eyes and Dee said, 'The missus wants to see you, *Inkosikaan*.' She looked at me distressed. Dum walked over and reached out and touched me.

'We have put some food under your bed in the pot for night water,' she whispered, and they clutched each other and whimpered in their anxiety that they might be discovered.

I knocked on the door of my mother's sewing room. 'Come in,' she said and looked up as I entered. Then she bent over her sewing machine and put her foot down on the motor and sewed away for quite a while.

Of course, she did not know she was dealing with a veteran of interrogation and punishment and, since I had suddenly grown up on the hill, I was uncrackable. A real hard case.

After a while she stopped, and taking off her glasses she rubbed the top of her nose with her forefinger and thumb and gave a deep sigh. 'You have hurt me and you have hurt the Lord very deeply,' she said at last. 'Don't you know the Lord loves you?' She didn't wait for my answer. 'The gospel says, whosoever harms a hair upon the head of one of my little ones, harmeth me also.'

I had heard the same thing said by Pik Botha, which just about confirmed everything I thought about the Lord. Pik Botha and my mother and Pastor Mulvery were all working for the same person.

My mother continued, 'When I had my quiet time with the Lord this afternoon, He spoke to me. You will not get a beating, but He is not mocked and you will go to your room at once without your supper.'

'Yes, Mother,' I said and turned to go.

'Just a moment! You have not apologised to me for your behaviour.' Her eyes were suddenly sharp with anger.

I hung my head just like I used to do with Mevrou. 'I'm sorry, Mother,' I said.

'Not sorry enough, if you ask me. Do you think it's easy for me trying to make ends meet? I'm not supposed to get tired. I'm only your mother, the dog's body about the place. All you care about is that black woman, that stinking black Zulu woman!' She suddenly lost her anger and her eyes filled with the tears of self-pity. Grabbing the dress she had been sewing she held it up to her eyes, her thin shoulders shaking, and began to sob. 'I don't think I can take much more, first your grandfather and then those two in the kitchen and now you!' She looked up at me, her pretty face distorted and ugly from crying. Then, with a sudden little wail, she once again buried her head in the dress and started to sob hysterically.

I felt enormously relieved. This was much more like my old mother. She was having one of her turns, and I knew exactly what to do. 'I'll make you a nice cup of tea and an Aspro, and then you must have a good lie down,' I said and left the room.

Dum and Dee were delighted that I hadn't received a beating and hurriedly made me a pot of tea and then turned it around and around on the kitchen table to make it brew quickly. Dee handed me two Aspros from a big bottle kept in a cupboard above the sink and I put them in my pocket, for I was afraid that if I put them on the saucer I'd slop tea over them.

My mother was sitting at the machine unpicking stitches as I entered the sewing room. Her eyes were red from crying but otherwise she seemed quite composed. I put the cup of tea down carefully on the table next to the machine and fished in my pocket for the Aspros which I placed next to the cup. 'Thank you,' she said in a tight voice, not looking up at me. 'Now go straight to your room, you may not come out until morning.'

It was light punishment, I had expected far worse. In the chamberpot Dum and Dee had left three cold sausages, two big roast potatoes and a couple of mandarins, a proper feast. There wasn't much else to do but go to sleep after that. It had been a long day and a very good one. The loneliness birds had flown away, and I had grown up and made a new friend called Doc and had learned several new things. *Euphorbia grandicornis* was an ugly green cactus with long, dangerous looking thorns, *Aloe microsfigma* was a tiny, spotted aloe which liked to hide under rocks and a professor was a teacher who taught music. Also, there was a rose called Mrs Butt and another called Imperial Sunset.

Tomorrow I would write a letter to Nanny and send her my ten shillings. She would like that and she would know that somebody loved her. I fell asleep thinking about how big the hole would have to be to bury Big Hettie in, about Hoppie fighting Adolf Hitler, which would probably be an easier fight than the one against Jackhammer Smit, and how I was going to become welterweight champion of the world.

Two days later I was sitting on the front stoep watching army trucks passing the front door, for I had discovered that an army camp was being set up in the valley about three miles out of town. The big khaki Bedford, Chevrolet and Ford trucks, their backs covered with canvas tarpaulin canopies, had been passing for two days. Some contained soldiers who sat in the back carrying .303 rifles. But mostly they carried tents and timber and other things needed for building an army camp.

My granpa, when he heard the news on the wireless, had said it was typical of the army big-wigs, putting a military camp at the end of a branch line, which couldn't move troops out fast enough to anywhere, least of all to Lourenço Marques, where the Portuguese couldn't be relied on to maintain their neutrality for one moment.

My Adolf Hitler fears returned immediately. Lourenço Marques, I discovered, was no more than eighty miles away if they came through Swaziland. I was glad that my granpa had Nanny's address in Zululand and that I had sent her off a postal order for my ten shillings, my love in a letter and a photograph taken much earlier showing her holding me. If she couldn't get somebody to read the letter, she'd know it was from me and my original escape plan would still be intact.

I was also glad the army was so close at hand. Lourenço Marques, the nearest seaport, was obviously where Adolf Hitler planned to march all the Rooineks from these parts into the sea. Even an army at the end of a branch line was better than no army at all.

My mother added that Lourenço Marques was probably seething with German spies at this very moment, and they were probably using code words on Radio Lourenço Marques to relay messages to the Boer Nazis who were plotting to tear down the country from within. I thought about the Judge and Mr Stoffel and how they always listened to the wireless. When my granpa said that was a lot of poppycock, I was not so sure.

I thought about these things as I watched a convoy of one hundred and five army trucks go by, the biggest yet by far, so I didn't notice Doc coming up the hill until he almost reached the gate.

'Goot morning, Peekay.' He was dressed in a white linen suit and wore a panama hat, so that I hardly recognised him. He carried a string bag and a silver-handled walking stick, and under one arm was a large manila envelope.

'Good morning, Doc,' I said, jumping to my feet. I found it a little strange to say his name out loud, though in my head I'd said it a thousand times.

'I can come in, ja?' I hurried down the steps to open the gate. 'This is an official visit, Peekay, I have come to see your mother.'

I felt stupidly disappointed. I hadn't known he knew my mother. I followed him up the steps. 'You will introduce us please,' he said as we reached the verandah.

Unreasonably pleased that I was his first friend, I opened the front door and led him into the parlour. Visitors to the farm had been infrequent but the routine was unerring. First you sat people down and then you gave them coffee and cake. I asked Doc to sit down and he did so but not before he had stood in the centre of the zebra skin and slowly turned around taking the room in. When he reached the grandfather clock he paused and said, 'English, London, about 1680, a very good piece.' He took a gold Hunter from his fob pocket, and snapping it open examined it briefly. 'Four minutes a month,' he said, returning the watch to his pocket. I was amazed he should know how much our grandfather clock lost, for he was right. I thought perhaps my granpa had told him.

'Do you know my granpa?' I asked Doc.

'I have not yet had this pleasure but it will be okay, we are both men of thorns, with me the cactus, with him the rose. The English and the Germans are not so far apart. It will be all right, you will see.' He said this just as I was about to leave the room to get Dum and Dee to bring coffee and cake.

I was dumbfounded, Professor Von Vollensteen was a German! What should I do? My grandfather had gone to the library in town to change his books, that was one good thing anyway. You never knew what he might do coming face to face with a German, although even against Doc I didn't fancy his chances. I decided to say nothing to my mother, she might have a conniption on the spot.

Dum and Dee had somehow known we had a guest and were putting out the tea things and half a canary cake on a plate. I could hear the sewing machine zizzing away as I walked over to the far side of the house to tell my mother she had a guest. I knocked before opening the door.

'There is someone to see you, Mother,' I shouted over the sound of the whirring machine. She stopped sewing and looked up.

'Tell her to come in, darling, it must be Mrs Cameron about her skirt.'

'It is Professor Von Vollensteen. He wants to see you,' I said in a low voice.

'Professor whom?' she asked, removing her glasses and looking directly at me.

'He is a teacher, a teacher of music,' I said urgently in an attempt to hide my confusion. She rose to her feet and patted her hair and reached for her bag. From it she took a compact and, looking into the tiny mirror on the inside flap of the bag, hurriedly powdered her nose.

'Well he can't teach music here, we haven't got that sort of money,' she said, putting the pad back into the compact and snapping it shut. I followed behind her, not at all sure of the reception Doc would get.

But my mother was country-bred and all visitors were treated courteously no matter what their purpose. Doc rose from the lounge as she entered and extended his hand. 'Madame,' he said, bowing slightly, 'Professor Karl Von Vollensteen.'

My mother extended her hand and Doc took it lightly and bowed over it bringing his heels together. 'Please sit down, professor, will you take coffee with us?' She reached no higher than his waist and when he sat down her head was level with his.

'You are very kind, madame. Today we have two things.' He reached into the string bag at his feet and produced a jam tin which held a small plant. The plant had only two leaves which stuck straight up out of the tin and were tinged with pink around the edges. They looked exactly like two light green rabbit ears. 'Allow me please to introduce *Kalanchoe thyrsiflora,* quite rare in these parts, often mistaken for a plant, but I assure you, madame, a true cactus.' Doc handed the jam tin to my mother who remarked that she couldn't possibly remember the name and laughed her nervous laugh. 'Ja, it is a difficult name but, if you wish, you may just call it Rabbit Ears,' Doc said charitably, though he somehow left the impression that the little cactus was demeaned by such a common name.

Dum and Dee entered, Dee carrying a tray with cups and cake, and Dum carrying the china coffee pot we used for visitors. Dee set the tray on the traymobile and carefully wheeled it over to my mother who sent her back to fetch a knife for the cake. Dum, keeping her back straight and her arm rigid, bent her knees almost to the ground so she could put the coffee pot down on the traymobile without any possibility of spilling it. Dum, too, was sent back to the kitchen, for the coffee strainer.

'You can tell them a hundred times over, it's useless. I don't know what goes on inside their heads,' my mother sighed, putting the tiny plant on the shelf under the traymobile. I had been standing beside her chair and now she turned to me. 'Run along now.'

Doc looked up. 'With your permission, madame, I would like for Peekay to stay please?'

'Who?' my mother said.

'Your son, madame, I would much like him to stay.'

My mother turned to me. 'What on earth have you been telling the professor? Who is Peekay?'

'It's my new name. I, I haven't told you about it yet,' I said, flustered. My mother laughed, but I knew she was annoyed.

'Why, you have a perfectly good name, my dear.' She gave me a funny look, then turned to Doc. 'Of course he may stay, but I'm afraid our family never had much of an ear for music and lessons would be much too expensive.'

Without looking at Dee and Dum, who had re-entered the room and now stood beside her, she held her hand out for the knife and strainer and dismissed them with an impatient flick of her head.

'I am most grateful, madame.' My mother lifted the coffee pot. 'Black only, no sugar,' Doc said, leaning forward in anticipation.

My mother poured his coffee. 'A nice piece of cake, professor?' Doc put his hand up in refusal. 'Thank you,' he said. It was a speech habit I was going to find hard to get used to, saying, 'Thank you,' when he meant, 'No thank you,' and clearly my mother misunderstood him for she placed a piece of the canary cake on a sideplate and handed it to him with his coffee. He accepted the cake without further protest.

Doc put the coffee and cake on the zebra hide between his legs and picked up the manila envelope. 'And so now we have the second thing.' His eyes sparkled as he handed the envelope to my mother.

'Goodness, what can it be?' she said, pulling out the tucked-in flap of the large brown envelope. She withdrew the largest photograph I had ever seen which, to my amazement, turned out to be me sitting on the rock on top of the hill. 'Goodness gracious!' My mother stared at it, momentarily lost for words. The photograph showed every detail, even the lichen on the rock, more clearly than any I had seen before. Shafts of sunlight shining through a silver-edged cloud seemed to be directed straight at the rock on which I sat. My body, half in shadow, appeared to be as one with the rock. I didn't know it at the time, but it was an extraordinary picture. At last my mother spoke. 'Wherever did you take this? It is so sad! Why did you take a picture of him when he was looking sad?'

Doc rubbed his chin, it was plainly not the comment he expected and he needed a moment to think about the answer. Ignoring the first question he leaned forward as he answered the second. 'Ja, this is so. Only one great picture shows a man when he smiles. Frans Hals, *Laughing Cavalier,* early seventeenth century.' He pointed at the grandfather clock. 'Around that time they make this clock also. The smile, madame, is used by humans to hide the truth, the artist is only interested to reveal the truth.' He leaned back, clearly satisfied with his reply.

'Goodness, professor, all that is much too deep for simple country people like us. He's only a very little boy, you know? I prefer him to smile.'

'Of course! But sadness, like understanding, comes early in life for some. It is part of intelligence.'

My mother's back stiffened. 'You seem to know a lot about my son, professor. I can't imagine how, he has only been home from boarding school for three days.'

Doc clapped his hands gleefully. 'Boarding school! Ha, that explains I think everything. For a boy like this, boarding school is a prison, ja?'

My mother was beginning to show her impatience, her fingers tapped steadily on the arms of the chair, a sure sign that things were not going well. 'We had no choice in the matter, professor. I was ill. One does the best one can under the circumstances.' She looked into her lap, her coffee untouched.

Doc suddenly seemed to realise that he had gone too far. 'Forgive me, madame.' He leaned forward. 'It is not said to make you angry. Your son is a gifted child. I don't know where, I don't know how. I only pray it is music. Today I have come to ask you, please madame, let me teach him?' He had spoken to my mother softly and with great charm, and I could feel her relax as his voice stroked her ego.

'Humpf! I must say you seem to know more about him than his mother. I can't see how he is any different to any other child of his age,' she said huffily, though I could tell this was just a pretence and that she was secretly pleased by the compliment. My mother was a proud woman and didn't expect charity from anyone. 'It is out of the question. Piano lessons don't grow on trees, professor.'

'Ja, that is true. But, I think, maybe on cactus plants.' Doc's deep blue eyes showed his amusement. 'For two years I have searched for the *Aloe microsfigma*, from here, zere, everywhere. Then, poof! Just by sitting on a rock, *Aloe microsfigma* comes. The boy is a genius. Absoloodle!'

'Whatever can you be talking about, professor? What have you two been up to?' Whereas before she had been angry, now she was plainly charmed by him.

'Madame, we met on the mountain top with only the face of God above us, the picture will capture the moment forever,' he shrugged his scrawny shoulders. 'It was destiny, the new cactus man has come.'

My mother seemed unsure how to take this. 'I am a born-again Christian, professor, God's name is only used in praise in this house,' she said, mostly to cover her confusion but also as a caution to Doc not to assume an over-familiar manner with the Almighty.

'God and I have no quarrels, madame. The Almighty conceived the cactus plant. If God would choose a plant to represent him, I think he would choose of all plants the cactus. The cactus has all the blessings he tried, but mostly failed, to give to man. Let me tell you how. It has humility but it is not submissive. It grows where no other plant will grow. It does not complain when the sun bakes its back, or the wind tears it from the cliff or drowns it in the dry sand of the desert or when it is thirsty. When the rains come it stores water for the hard times to come. In good times and in bad it will still flower. It protects itself against danger, but it harms no other plant. It adapts perfectly to almost any environment. It has patience and enjoys solitude. In Mexico there is a cactus that flowers only once every hundred years and at night. This is saintliness of an extraordinary kind, would you not agree? The cactus has properties that heal the wounds of men, and from it come potions that can make man touch the face of God or stare into the mouth of hell. It is the plant of patience and solitude, love and madness, ugliness and beauty, toughness and gentleness. Of all plants surely God made the cactus in his own image? It has my enduring respect and is my passion.' He paused and pointed to the little green plant in the jam tin. '*Kalanchoe thyrsiflora,* such a shy little lady. Two years I search to find her, now she grows happily in my cactus garden where her big ears listen to all the gossip.'

'I'm sure that's all very nice, professor, but what does it all mean?' my mother said. I could see she was confused, not knowing whether, in the end, Doc had praised or blasphemed God.

'My eyes are not so goot. If the boy will come with me to collect cactus specimens, I will teach him music. It is a fine plan, ja? Cactus for Mozart!'

My mother looked pleased, as though a new thought had come into her head. 'His grandmother was very creative, an artist you know. But I don't know if there were any musicians in the family, perhaps Dad will know.' She pointed to the two rose pictures on either side of the bookcase. 'Her work,' she said modestly, 'she only ever painted roses.'

Doc did not turn to look at the pictures. 'When I came in I saw them already, very goot.'

The idea of a musician in the family was clearly to my mother's liking. The Boers are a naturally musical people, and any excuse for a gathering brought out the concertinas and guitars and even an occasional violin. In my mother's eyes it was their sole redeeming feature. The idea of a son who played the piano, let alone classical music, was a social triumph of the sort she had never expected to come her way. Even in this largely English-speaking town, a classical piano player in the family was a social equaliser almost as good as money.

I was to learn that the Apostolic Faith Mission, who believed in being born again, baptism by immersion, the gift of speaking in tongues and faith healing, was deemed pretty low on the social scale. Barberton was not the sort of town which encouraged the crying out in prayer or sudden spontaneous religious combustion from the floor of a charismatic church. My mother was constantly fighting the need to remain loyal to the Lord and his religiously garrulous congregation while at the same time aspiring to the ranks of 'nice people'.

Old Pisskop at the piano promised to be the major instrument in balancing the family social scales. The bargain was struck just as Mrs Cameron arrived for her fitting. In return for trekking around the hills as Doc's constant companion, I would receive free piano lessons. I had to work very hard on my camouflage to contain my delight. While I had no concept of what it meant to be musical, from the very beginning pitch and harmony had been a part of my life with Nanny.

The long summer months were spent mostly with Doc, climbing the hills around Barberton. Often we would venture into the dark *kloofs* where the hills formed deep creases at the start of the true mountains. These green, moist gullies of treefern and tall old yellow wood trees, the branches draped with beard lichen and the vines of wild grape, made a cool, dark contrast to the barren, sun-baked hills of aloe, thorn scrub, rock and coarse grass.

Occasionally, we saw a lone ironwood tree rising magnificently above the canopy. These relics had escaped the axes of the miners who had roamed these hills fifty years before in search of gold. The mountains were dotted with shafts sunk into the hills and mountainside, dark pits and passages supported by timber which, before it was consigned to the tunnels, may have stood for a thousand years.

Doc taught me the names of the flowering plants. The sugarbush with its splashy white blossoms. A patch of brilliant orange-red seen in the distance usually meant wild pomegranate. I learned to differentiate between species of tree fuchsia, to stop and crush the leaves of the camphor bush and breathe its beautiful aromatic smell. I recognised the pale yellow blossoms of wild gardenia and the blooms of the water alder. Monkey rope strung from tall trees draped with club moss was given names such as: traveller's joy, lemon capers, climbing saffron, milk rope and David's roots. Nothing escaped Doc's curiosity and he taught me the priceless lesson of identification. Soon trees and leaves, bush, vine and lichen began to assemble in my mind in a schematic order as he explained the nature of the ecosystems of bush and kloof and high mountain.

'Everything fits, Peekay. Nothing is unexplained. Nature is a chain reaction. One thing follows the other, everything is dependent on something else. The smallest is as important as the largest. See,' he would say, pointing to a tiny vine curled around a sapling, 'that is a stinkwood sapling which can grow thirty metres, but the vine will win and the tree will be choked to death long before it will ever see the sky.'

He would often use an analogy from nature. 'Ja, Peekay, always in life an idea starts small, it is only a sapling idea, but the vines will come and they will try to choke your idea so it cannot grow and it will die, and you will never know you had a big idea, an idea so big it could have grown thirty metres through the dark canopy of leaves and touched the face of the sky.' He looked at me and continued, 'The vines are people who are afraid of originality, of new thinking; most people you encounter will be vines, when you are a young plant they are very dangerous.' His piercing blue eyes looked into mine. 'Always listen to yourself, Peekay. It is better to be wrong than simply to follow convention. If you are wrong, no matter, you have learned something and you will grow stronger. If you are right you have taken another step towards a fulfilling life.' He would sigh and squint at me. 'Experts, what did I tell you about experts, Peekay?'

'You can't always go by expert opinion. A chicken, if you ask a chicken, should be stuffed with grasshoppers, mealies and worms.' Even after repeating it a hundred times I still thought it was funny.

Or Doc would show me how a small lick of water trickling from a rock face would, drop by drop, gather round its wet apron, fern and then scrub and later trees and vines until the kloof became an interdependent network of plant, insect, bird and animal life. 'Always you should go to the source, to the face of the rock, to the beginning. The more you know, the more you can control your destiny. Man is the only animal who can store knowledge outside his body. This has made him greater than the creatures around him. Everything has happened before; if you know what comes before then you know what happens now. Your brain, Peekay, has two functions; it is a place for original thought, but also it is a reference library; use it to tell you where to look and then you will have for yourself all the brains that have ever been.'

Doc never talked down. Much of what he said would take me years to understand, but I soaked it up nevertheless, storing it in my awkward young mind where it could mature and later come back to me. He taught me to read for meaning and information, to make margin notes and to follow these up with trips to the Barberton library where Mrs Boxall would give a great sigh when the two of us walked in. 'Here come the messpots!' She claimed she had to spend hours erasing the pencilled margin notes in the books we borrowed. Doc once insisted they made the books more valuable and Mrs Boxall arched an eyebrow, 'Written in German and in Kindergarten, Professor?'

Doc shrugged, looking up from his book and removing his gold-rimmed reading glasses. 'Kindergarten, that also is written in German, Madame Boxall.'

But I don't think Mrs Boxall really minded. The books on birds and insects and plants were seldom borrowed by anyone else and, besides, as most of the books in the natural history section had once belonged to him, Doc adopted a proprietorial attitude towards the town library. Over the years his tiny cottage had become too small to contain them all and they had been bequeathed to the library which now acted, in Doc's mind anyway, as a bibliographical outpost to his cottage. Doc also taught me Latin roots so I was no longer forced to resort to memory alone, and the botanical names of plants began to make sense to me.

We climbed the high *kranses* and the crags in search of cactus and succulents. Towards the end of summer, on the side of a mountain scarred by loose grey shale and tufts of coarse brown grass, I stumbled on *Aloe brevifolia,* a tiny thorny aloe.

Doc was overjoyed. 'Gold! Absolute gold!' He jumped into the air and, upon landing, missed his footing on the shaley surface and fell arse over tip down the mountain, coming to a halt just short of a two-hundred-foot drop. He climbed gingerly back, hands bleeding from clutching at the sharp shale, a sheepish grin on his weather-beaten face. But the triumph of the rare find still showed in his excited eyes. 'Brevifolia in these parts, so high, impossible! You are a genius, Peekay. Absoloodle!'

It was the find of the summer and, to Doc, worth all the weary hours spent on the hills and in the mountains. We recorded the find with the camera and removed six of the tiny plants, leaving double that number clinging precariously to the inhospitable mountainside.

Like me, Doc was an early riser, so just after dawn all that summer he gave me piano lessons. 'In one year we will tell, but it is not so important. To love music is everything. First I will teach you to love music, after this slowly we shall learn to play.'

I was anxious to please Doc and worked hard, but I suspect he knew almost from the outset that I wouldn't prove an especially gifted musician. My progress, while superior to that of the small girls he was obliged to teach for a living, indicated a very modest talent. In the years that followed, it was enough to fool my mother and all the big-bosomed matriarchs who ruled the town's important families. At concerts which, I hasten to add, were not in my honour, I represented the cultured element and they would applaud me deliberately and loudly.

These occasions, which occurred in the spring and autumn, made my mother very proud, though they also represented a compromise with the Lord. Concerts were the devil's work and very much against the Lord's teaching. They were just the sort of thing which, like money-lending, the Lord had clearly condemned when he castigated the Pharisees and Saducees in the temple of Jerusalem. She justified my participation and her attendance by pointing out, to herself mostly, that many of the great classical musicians wrote music for the church.

The Lord's will was equally explicit on drinking and smoking, the bioscope and dancing, except ballet. Ballet was another of the items cherished by the lavender-scented ladies from the town's upper-echelon families, and the ballet performance usually preceded my piano recital. Together they made up the cultural component of the twice-yearly concert. Chopin, by yours truly, and Tchaikovsky's Dance of the Swans by gramophone record, danced to by six-year-old neophytes in white tutus and duckbilled headdresses made of paper mâché.

We were the cultural meat in a popular sandwich otherwise liberally filled with amateur vaudeville acts, solo songs of an Irish nature, single or combined concertina, piano accordion and guitar renditions of well-known Afrikaans folk songs usually performed by the Afrikaner warders from the prison. To redress the racial balance, a Gilbert and Sullivan male quartet would generally follow. One English comic opera song was reckoned by the concert committee to equate roughly with a dozen Afrikaans folk songs no matter how pleasingly syncopated, harmonised, toe tappin' and hand clappin' they might prove to be.

The concert would always end with the All Saints Anglican church choir singing 'White Cliffs of Dover' with the audience joining in. To show the Rooinek majority where their unspoken loyalty lay, the warders and their families would leave the town hall prior to the mass rendition of 'White Cliffs'. This would be accompanied by some booing and catcalls from less well-bred members of the remaining audience.

Germany had covertly helped the Boers during the Boer War. Apart from arms and ammunition sold for profit, she had donated food and medical supplies and had even sent medical orderlies and doctors to the harassed Boers who, due to the British scorched-earth policy, were dying less from the aim of the British Lee-Metfords than from a land which could no longer feed them. To the Boers, Germany was an old and trusted friend in a country where a contract was a handshake and declared friendship a bond that continued beyond the grave. Anti-semitism in the

Dutch Reformed Church, where Jews were thought of as Christ-killers, had always existed and the concept of the superiority of some races over others was never for one moment in doubt. In this context, to many Boers Adolf Hitler was only doing his job and, to some minds, doing it damn well.

After the warders and other Nazi-sympathisers had walked out, the remainder of the audience would stand up, lock arms and sing 'White Cliffs of Dover' at least twice to confirm doubly their love for a Britain facing her darkest hour. To bring the concert to a tearful close the concert party, with warders and other Afrikaners missing, would gather on the stage, each of us holding a long-stemmed rose delivered earlier by me as a sign of our family's inherent good breeding. With the misty-eyed audience fresh from the mawkishly sentimental journey to a country most of us would never see, we stood to rigid attention while a scratchy 78 r.p.m. rendered 'God Save the King'. Whereupon the cast hurled the long-stemmed roses into the audience.

My granpa, my mother and I then walked home, having politely refused the Mayor's invitation to the traditional post-concert party for the cast at the Phoenix Hotel. Worldly parties typified by one such as this, where drinking, smoking and dancing took place, were pretty high up on the Lord's banned list.

The next issue of the *Goldfields News* would report the concert with the warder walkout splashed across the front page. Tongues wagged for days. Important people suggested the military be brought in to wipe out this nest of Nazi vipers or that the prison be moved to Nelspruit, an Afrikaans town forty miles away, where most of the prisoners probably came from in the first place.

My granpa, with his experience in fighting the Boers, had once been canvassed for his opinion by Mr Hankin, the editor of the *Goldfields News.* But they didn't print what he said. What he said was: 'I spent most of the Boer War shitting my breeches as a stretcher bearer. The only thing those buggers do better than music is shoot. Without them the concert wouldn't be worth a cardboard boot.'

Maybe Mr Hankin thought his newspaper gave the family enough publicity, because he never again asked my granpa for his opinion on anything, even though the prison warders did the same thing at every concert for the duration of the war. Mrs Boxall, who was the town's correspondent on matters cultural, could always be relied on to devote most of her column, 'Clippings from a Cultured Garden by Fiona Boxall', to my performance. For days after it appeared my mother was in a state of dazed euphoria and I was conscripted to deliver a bunch of roses to the library twice a week for a month.

In the process of keeping faith with my mother, Doc instilled in me an abiding love for music. What my clumsy hands could never play I could hear quite clearly in my head. A love of music was, among his many gifts to me, perhaps the most important of them all, and he continued to teach me even after his calm and gentle life was thrown into turmoil, and the joy of being alone with him on the high cliffs and kranses was stolen from my childhood.

TEN

I had been enrolled at the local school when the new term began at the end of January. Six was the starting age for Grade One, but after a few days it was clear that my year spent in a mixed-age class at boarding school had put me well ahead of the rest of the kids. I was pushed up to Grade Three where I easily held my own against kids two years older than me. Doing the Judge's arithmetic, my early grounding in reading, a comprehensive understanding of Afrikaans in a classroom of English-speaking kids coming without enthusiasm to the language for the first time, and Doc's demand from our first day that I write up my field notes all gave me a hugely unfair advantage. I might possibly have been elevated even further but for the embarrassment it would have caused.

I quickly earned a reputation, rather unjustly, for being clever. Doc had persuaded me to drop my camouflage and not to play dumb. 'To be smart is nót a sin. But to be smart and not use it, that, Peekay, is a sin. Absoloodle!' I had needed little encouragement. Under his direction my mind was constantly hungry, and I soon found the school work tedious and simplistic. Doc became my real teacher and school was simply time spent between eight and one o'clock when I would rush from the classroom to his cottage hidden in the cactus garden.

His thorny garden was a never-ending source of delight. It was half an acre on the more or less flat top of a small hill which overlooked the town and valley. A ten-minute climb to solitude, up a little dirt and rock road that led nowhere else. His cactus garden may well have been the best private collection of cacti and succulents in the world. I, who grew to be an expert on cacti, have never seen a better one.

Doc's cottage had three rooms and a lean-to kitchen. The three rooms were called the music room, the book room and the whisky room. Each having its specified purpose, music, study and drinking himself to sleep. For in all things, even in drunkenness, Doc had a tidy mind.

In the first year we spent together I never once witnessed him drunk, though when I arrived just after dawn for my music lesson I often had to wake him, whereupon he would stumble outside to retch and cough. Then he would come to sit beside the Steinway, his blue eyes red-rimmed and dulled from the previous night's whisky, his long fingers wrapped around the enamel mug of bitter black coffee I had made him on the

Primus. Doc never talked about drinking. All he would sometimes say as I set my music out on the big Steinway was, 'Pianissimo, Peekay, the wolves were howling in my head last night.' I would look through my music for something soft and easy on the nerves. Perhaps this is why, as I grew older and more proficient, I seemed more attracted to playing Chopin. There is a great deal less fortissimo in a Chopin *étude* than in Liszt or Brahms, and Doc's early morning hangovers may, over that first year, have somehow inclined me to softer music.

It was the cactus garden which testified to 'his problem with Doctor Bottle', as my mother would call any person who ever held strong drink to their lips. Bordering both sides of the path for a hundred yards through the cactus garden were embedded Johnny Walker bottles, their square bases shining in the sun like parallel silver snakes winding around the cactus and aloe and blazing orange and pink portulaca. Each bottle represented an attempt to obviate some private torture. Doc made no apology for his drinking. He seldom even mentioned it and when he did it was always blamed quietly and politely on the wolves, which I imagined slavering away, great red tongues lolling, gnashing teeth chomping up Doc's brains.

It was at sunset on a Saturday afternoon late in January 1941, a little more than a year after Doc and I had first met on the hill behind the rose garden. We'd spent the day in the hills and had almost arrived back at Doc's cottage. We'd found a patch of *Senecio serpens* high up in a dry kloof, growing over the tailings of an old digging. It was a nice find although blue chalksticks, as they are commonly called, are not too rare unless they flower in an unusual colour. We had decided to plant them in the cactus garden and wait until they flowered again. That was the magic of the cactus garden, some succulents can play dumb; a common blue chalkstick can turn from a Cinderella into a princess in front of your very eyes. I was the first to notice the army van with the white-stencilled Military Police on its hood. The van was parked directly in front of the whisky bottle path which led to the cottage, hidden from view amongst the tall cactus. Two men leaned against the front mudguard smoking, their red-banded khaki caps resting on the hood of the van which had been turned to face down the hill. Doc was explaining the differences between the genus *Senecio serpens* and the lighter-coloured *Glottiphyllum uncatum,* banging his long hiking stick into the ground as he walked and getting generally excited as he did when his mind was absorbed in esoteric botanical detail.

The two men saw us approach, and dropping their cigarettes ground them underfoot. Clearing their throats almost simultaneously, they reached for their caps, carefully placed them back on their heads the way men do when they are about to undertake an unpleasant duty. Both wore khaki bush shirts, shorts, brown boots, puttees and khaki stockings, though one of them wore the polished Sam Browne belt of an officer while the other, a sergeant, wore a white webbing one. The officer stepped right in front of Doc who stopped and looked up in surprise. Doc was taller than the officer by at least a foot, so the military man was obliged to look up at him. He had a thin black pencil moustache just like Pik Botha, and although he was not standing to attention his body seemed permanently rigid. From the top pocket of his tunic he removed a piece of paper which he held up.

'Good afternoon, sir. You are Karl Von Vollensteen, Professor Karl Von Vollensteen?' he asked in a sententious voice.

'Ja, this is me,' Doc said, surprised that anyone would question so obvious a fact.

The officer cleared his throat and proceeded to read from the paper he held in front of him. 'Under the Aliens Act of 1939 and by the authority vested in me by the Provost Marshal of the South African Armed Forces, I arrest you. You are charged with conspiracy to undermine the security of a nation at war.' He handed the paper to Doc. 'You will have to come with me, sir. The civilian police, under the direction of military security, will search your premises and you will be detained at Barberton prison until your case can be heard.'

To my surprise Doc made no protest. His face was sad as he looked down at the officer and handed him back the piece of paper without even glancing at it. He raised his head to look over the officer and past where the sergeant was standing next to the van, his gaze following the line of the cactus garden. He turned slowly, his eyes filled with pain, taking in the hills, the marvellous aloe-dotted hills, his garden of Eden for twenty years in the Africa he so savagely loved. Finally he turned to look over the town, across the valley to the sun beginning to dip behind the escarpment.

'The stupidity. Already the stupidity begins again,' he said softly, then turning to me he patted my shoulder. 'You must plant the *Senecio serpens* to get the morning sun, they like that.' He removed his bush hat and absent-mindedly put it on the roof of the van. He got his red bandanna from his overalls and slowly wiped his face and sniffed into it and pushed his nose around before returning it to the pocket of his overalls. Then he lifted his bush hat from the roof of the van and put it on my head. I looked up at him in surprise, Doc didn't play that sort of childish game. But his eyes were sad and his voice soft, barely above a whisper. 'So, now you are the boss of the cactus garden, Peekay.' I wanted to cry and I think Doc wanted to as well. But we didn't. We both knew enough not to show our feelings in front of the military.

Turning to the officer, Doc said, 'You will please allow me first to shave and change my clothes. A man must go to prison in his best clothes.'

The officer rolled his eyes heavenwards. From the number of cigarette butts on the ground they had been waiting for some time and he obviously wanted to get going. 'Orright, professor, but make it snappy.' Turning to the sergeant in an official manner he rapped, 'Sergeant! Escort the prisoner to his house for kit change and ablutions.'

We walked slowly down the whisky bottle path and Doc dropped his canvas shoulder bag on the open verandah. I followed him into the dark little cottage. 'Do not light the lamps, Peekay, the light is soft and we will soon be gone.' I followed him to the lean-to kitchen where he placed an enamel basin on the hard earth floor and poured water into it from a jug. I took the jug and refilled it from the rainwater tank behind the cottage. Doc's cottage, isolated from the town by the small hill, had no running water. He stripped down in the lean-to kitchen and using a *loofah* washed himself from head to toe. I brought him the fresh jug of water and, stepping out of the lean-to into the garden, he stood beside a tall cactus and poured it over his head, giving the cactus the benefit of the overflow. Then he wiped himself briskly with an almost threadbare towel. He was brown all over, for we often lay on a rock in the hills to sun ourselves after a swim in a mountain creek. His thin body was hard and sinewy, and the snowy-white hair on his chest seemed incongruous. I had seen my granpa nude and while he too was a thin man, he didn't have the same hard-as-nails look.

The sergeant had grown impatient waiting around the kitchen and had wandered into the music room where he was playing chopsticks on the Steinway. Doc seemed not to hear as he shaved carefully, stropping his cut-throat razor for ages until it was perfect. Then he dressed slowly in his white linen suit and black boots. Finally he placed a spare shirt and his shaving things in a sugar bag, and walking through to the book room he selected a large book from the very top shelf of one of the bookshelves which he had constructed from bricks and pineboard planks. 'Put it also in the bag, Peekay.' I took the large leather-bound volume from him and looked at the spine. It was an old book whose maroon leather binding was scuffed and mottled with rough brown leather spots showing through the once smooth and polished cover. The title embossed on the spine was hard to read as the gold had mostly worn away leaving only the pale embossing. It read, *'Cactaceae. Afrika und Amerika. K. J. Von Vollensteen.'* I opened the heavy book to find that it was written in German. I walked into the whisky room where Doc had left the sugar bag, and using the edge of the blanket on the small, hard bed I wiped the dust from the cover of the book and put it in the bag. On the packing case dresser next to the bed was half a bottle of Johnny Walker and this too I put in the bag. Then heaving it over my shoulder I joined Doc who was standing at the front door. He removed his panama hat from a hook on the wall and picked up his silver-handled walking stick leaning in the corner behind the door. 'We are ready, sir,' he said, turning slowly to the sergeant a few feet away in the music room.

The sergeant rose from the piano stool. 'That's a blêrrie good peeana you got there, professor. Once in the bioscope I saw this fillim star dance on the top of a peeana just like this one, only it was all white. I think it was Greeta Garbo but I'm not sure.' He took a last look around the cottage, 'Okay man, let's go.' He took the sugar bag from my shoulder and looked into it. 'Hey, what's this? You can't take whisky where you going, are you stupid or something?' I started to apologise, but he checked me with his hand and grinned. 'If you like we can have a quick spot now, *oubaas?'* he said to Doc. 'Who knows when you'll get another chance hey?' He gave him a conspiratorial wink and uncorked the bottle. Raising it to his lips, he took a long drag of whisky. He winced as he withdrew the bottle from his mouth, then wiped his mouth with the back of his hand and the top of the bottle with the palm of his hand. 'Lekker, man, that's blêrrie good whisky! No use leaving it lying around hey?' He handed the bottle to Doc who raised his hand in refusal. 'C'mon don't be stupid, man. It's going to be a long time between drinks, better make the most of it.' He held it towards Doc after taking another long swig. In two goes he had reduced the whisky to less than a quarter of a bottle. Doc took the bottle of Johnny Walker and held it briefly to his lips without opening his mouth before handing it back. The sergeant shrugged. 'Suit yourself, man, all the more for me, it's blêrrie good whisky. Who knows ? Tomorrow maybe we're all dead.' He took another long swig and walked over to the piano. 'In this fillim this man was playing the peeana like at a funeral, then a drunk tipped some whisky on it and suddenly it was playing like mad.' He tipped the remaining whisky over the keys of the Steinway. Doc, who had been standing passively waiting, seemed to come alive. He raised his stick and rushed at the sergeant.

'*Schweinhund* Do not defile the instrument of Beethoven, Brahms, Bach and Liszt!' He brought his cane down hard onto the sergeant's wrist and the bottle fell from his hand to smash on the cement floor. Gripping his wrist, the sergeant danced in agony amongst the broken glass. Doc, using the sleeve of his linen jacket, ran his arms across the keys in an attempt to wipe them and sent the piano into a glissando. Then he turned and walked towards the front door.

'You fucking Nazi bastard!' the sergeant yelled. I hurried after Doc and he caught up with us on the path outside the cottage. 'I'll show you, you child fucker!' He was trying to remove a pair of handcuffs from his belt as he ran. 'Stop! You're under military arrest!' But Doc, his head held high, simply continued down the path towards the van. The sergeant grabbed Doc's arm and clicked a handcuff around his compliant wrist. Doc seemed hardly to notice and just kept walking, obliging the sergeant to hang onto the other handcuff as though he were being dragged along like a prisoner. He took a swinging kick at Doc, knocking his legs from under him and bringing the old man to his knees on the path. In his fury and humiliation he aimed a second kick just as, screaming, I flung myself at his legs. The army boot intended for Doc's ribs caught me under the chin, knocking me unconscious.

I awoke in Barberton Hospital with a man in a white coat shining a torch into my eyes. My head was ringing as though voices came from the other end of a long tunnel. 'Well, thank God for that, he's regained consciousness,' I heard him say.

'Thank you, Jesus,' I heard my mother say in a weepy voice. I looked around to see her seated at the side of the bed. She looked pale and worried and her hair hung in wisps around her eyes for she had come out without her hat and still wore her pink sewing smock. My granpa was also there, sitting on a chair at the opposite side of the bed. I tried to talk but found it impossible and my jaw hurt like billy-o. I managed a weak grunt without opening my mouth, but that was all. My mouth tasted of blood and, running my swollen tongue around my palate, I realised that several of my teeth were missing.

The doctor spoke to me. 'Now son, I want you to tell me how many fingers I'm holding up in front of you.' He held up two and I held up two fingers. 'Again.' He held up four fingers and I too held up four. He repeated this with several combinations before he finally said, 'Well, that's something anyway, he doesn't appear to have concussion. We'll have to X-ray the jaw, though I think it's probably broken.' He turned to my mother and granpa. 'The boy is in a lot of pain, we'll be taking him into theatre almost immediately, we may need to wire his jaw and there are several broken teeth which we will have to clean up. He'll be sedated when he comes out so there isn't any point in your staying.'

They both rose and my mother leaned over and kissed me on the forehead. 'We'll see you tomorrow morning, darling. You be a brave boy now!' My granpa touched me lightly on the shoulder. 'There's a good lad,' he said.

I watched them leave the emergency ward where I appeared to be the only emergency, as the other three beds were unoccupied. My jaw ached a great deal and, while I think I may have been crying, I only recall being terribly concerned for Doc.

It turned out my jaw had been broken. They wired the top jaw to the bottom one in the closed mouth position so I was unable to talk. I couldn't enquire about him. Adults decide what they want kids to know and all my mother would say when she came to visit was, 'You've had a terrible shock, darling, you mustn't think about what happened.'

In fact, that was all I could think about. Doc was the most important person in my life and the thought of him lying in a dark cell probably dying was almost unbearable. I managed to communicate to a junior nurse called Marie, who had taken to calling me her little *skattebol,* that I wanted paper and a pencil. She brought a pad and a pencil and in running writing I wrote, 'What's happened to Professor Von Vollensteen?' She read the note and her eyes grew large.

'Ag no, man! Sister says we can't tell you nothing.' She held out her hand for the pad and pencil but I quickly tucked it under the quilt. 'Give it to me back! Please, I'll get into trouble with Sister!' I shook my head, which hurt. 'I'll tell on you, you hear!' But I knew she wouldn't. I felt less vulnerable with the pad and pencil beside me. I tore a single sheet from the small pad and brought it out from under the bedclothes. Placing it on the cabinet beside my bed, I leaned over and wrote, 'My name is not skattebol, it is PEEKAY.' I didn't much like the endearment as I didn't see myself as a fluffy ball which is a name you give to really small kids. I tore the bit I'd written on from the sheet of paper and handed it to her. She read it slowly then walked to the end of the bed.

'That's not what it says here,' Marie said, looking down at the progress chart which hung from the foot of the bed. 'Don't you know your proper name then?' she teased. 'It's wrong,' I scribbled, tearing off a second note and holding it out to her. 'Sis, man! You don't even know your own name. I never heard of a name like Peekay, where'd you get a silly name like that?' On the remaining scrap of paper I wrote, 'I just got it.'

Marie took a sharp breath. 'Anyway, it's a rotten name for a hero who tackled a German spy when he was trying to escape.' Her eyes grew big again and she moved her spotty face close to mine. 'It says in the paper you even may be going to get a medal!' She drew back suddenly, alarmed that she'd told me too much. 'Don't you tell Sister I told you, you hear.' She brought a finger up to her lips, 'I promise I'll call you Peekay if you promise to stay *stom*.' I nodded my head, though I wondered how she thought I could tell anyone. The tears began to roll down my cheeks. I hadn't wanted them to, they just came because of the news about Doc. I could hear his voice when the officer had handed him the piece of paper. 'The stupidity. Already the stupidity begins again.'

'Don't cry, Peekay. Sister'll know I told you if you cry,' Marie said, distressed. I knuckled the tears from my eyes and then she bathed my face with a wet flannel. 'I don't really think Peekay is a silly name,' she said gently. 'Who showed you how to write so good? I went to school up to fourteen and even I can't write so good as you.'

After three days alone in the ward I was moved onto the verandah where there were eight beds all occupied. Except for the fact that I still couldn't talk, I was much better. I had walked into the ward with the sister and, with the exception of two old men who were asleep, all the others had applauded and said things like, 'Well done, son!' One man said that I was a proper patriot. As soon as Sister left the ward I wrote on a piece of paper as big as I could, 'What happened to Professor Von Vollensteen?' I jumped out of bed and took it over to the bed nearest me and gave it to the man in it. He read it and handed it back to me.

'You mean the German spy? Sorry, son, we're not supposed to tell you,' he winked at the others, 'we got strict orders.' The others all nodded. 'Mind you, you're a brave little bugger, I have to say that for you.' The other men seemed to agree with him.

My mother came to the hospital in the mornings when Pastor Mulvery was able to bring her. She sat with me while he went around the hospital to witness for the Lord. But first he came in to see me, and he'd flash his lightning smile which prevented his two front teeth from escaping and held my hand in his damp, warm grasp for ages until it felt as though it wanted to jump out of his soft grip and run away and hide. In his soft woman's voice he said, 'We're all praying that this terrible ordeal will make you accept Jesus into your heart.' Then, still holding my hand, he knelt beside the bed and my mother also knelt on the other side, and Pastor Mulvery would pray out aloud. When he prayed his voice rose even higher and he became quite excited.

He would start with a few random 'Hallelujahs' and my mother would respond with 'Praise His name! Praise His precious name!' And Pastor Mulvery would say, 'Lord, we are gathered here in Your precious name to pray for this poor child.' 'Amen,' my mother would say. 'In his terrible affliction, show him the path to salvation. Oh precious Redeemer who died on the cross so we might be free.' 'Hallelujah, praise the Lord,' my mother would answer. 'Son, open your heart to Jesus, accept Him into your life. Lord, do not condemn him to the terrible fires of hell, grant him everlasting life with your glorious salvation.' 'Hallelujah, blessed be His name!' 'Bring your sin to Jesus, son, lay it at His feet so that He may grant you His precious redemption. Precious Jesus, answer our prayers, open his young heart, let him see you in all your glory. Lord, we pray for this child's soul, we earnestly beseech you to bring him from darkness to the light, from the inky black of the stone tomb on Golgotha into the glorious morning of the resurrection of our sweet Jesus Christ!' 'Yes Jesus! Precious Jesus!' my mother would be saying on her side of the bed. And so it would go every morning.

Not long after I'd first met Doc, we were sitting on our rock on the hill behind the rose garden and I had asked him why I was a sinner and what I had done to be condemned to eternal hell fire unless I was born again.

He sat for a long time looking over the valley and then he said, 'Peekay, God is too busy making the sun come up and go down and watching so the moon floats just right in the sky to be concerned with such rubbish. Only man wants always God should be there to condemn this one and save that one. Always it is man who wants to make heaven and hell. God is too busy training the bees to make honey and every morning opening up all the new flowers for business.' He paused and smiled. 'In Mexico there is a cactus that even sometimes you would think God forgets. But no my friend, this is not so. On a full moon in the desert every one hundred years he remembers and he opens up a single flower to bloom. And if you should be there and you see this beautiful cactus blossom painted silver by the moon and laughing up at the stars, this, Peekay, is heaven.' He looked at me, his deep blue eyes sharp and penetrating. 'This is the faith in God the cactus has.' We had sat for a while before he spoke again. 'It is better just to get on with the business of living and minding your own business and maybe, if God likes the way you do things, he may just let you flower for a day or a night. But don't go pestering and begging and telling Him all your stupid little sins, that way you will spoil His day. Absoloodle.'

I still sometimes got a bit scared about going to hell and I used to think quite a lot about being born again. But my heart didn't want to open up and receive the Lord. All the people I knew who had opened up their hearts to Jesus struck me as a pretty pathetic lot, not bad, not good, just nothing. I couldn't afford to be just nothing when I was aiming to be the welterweight champion of the world. I guess my mother was right when she said if I kept rejecting the Lord and hardening my heart one day He might just go away and leave me to it. That's what must have happened because after a while it got a lot easier and I didn't worry as much. I decided I liked Doc's God a lot more than my mother's and Pastor Mulvery's and Pik Botha's and all the people who loved Jesus at the Apostolic Faith Mission. Jesus, who was God's dearly beloved son, seemed to be in charge of things there. He seemed to be very keen on saving souls and had actually died for their sins, but I couldn't help feeling it may have been a bit of a waste. Still, they seemed pretty grateful because they spoke a lot more about Jesus than about God. Jesus was definitely number one at the Apostolic Faith Mission.

Later I was to learn that there was a third party involved called the Holy Ghost who spoke in tongues of invisible fire and he gave people a thing called 'the gift of tongues'. When he did this, people would jump up in prayer meetings and wave their arms around and shake a lot with their eyes closed. They never seemed to bump into anything either, it was quite uncanny. And they'd babble away and sing, using strange words. I'd try to do it afterwards but it never sounded right. It was a gift all right.

A visiting pastor from the Assembly of God Church in America told us once when we were having a revival week that he had definite proof that a woman who had never been out of her small town in America spoke in Swahili when the Holy Ghost entered into her. There was a missionary from Africa who understood Swahili present in the same small church in America and she'd understood every word. He didn't tell us what she said, but he said there were lots of cases like this and that he'd personally witnessed quite a few. I had listened from then on but nobody in the Apostolic Faith Mission ever spoke Zulu or Shangaan. Maybe Zulu and Shangaan weren't exotic enough for the Holy Ghost. I wondered what was so special about Swahili.

Pastor Mulvery got up from beside the hospital bed and gave me a flash smile and said that Jesus loved me anyway. Then he trotted off with the Bible under one arm and a handful of tracts to visit all the other patients, and my mother called him a precious man and stayed with me.

After I got the pad I wrote her a long note asking her about Doc. She took it and without reading it, asked, 'Is this about the Professor?' Her lips were drawn tight as I nodded. Then she scrunched the note in her hand. 'I don't want you ever to mention his name again, do you hear? He is an evil man who used you to cover up the terrible things he was doing and then he nearly killed you.' There were sudden tears in her eyes. 'The doctor says, if he had caught you on the side of the head he would have killed you! Another three inches and you would have been dead. You've been through a terrible experience and I've prayed and prayed the Lord will make you forget it so you are not scarred for life.' She wiped her eyes and blew her nose.

'No! No!' I forced myself to say. What came out was sort of two squeaks from the back of my throat which forced their way past my bruised and swollen tongue and out of my clamped mouth. I started to cry silently without wanting to in front of my mother. They were blaming Doc for what had happened to me and I was the only one who knew the truth and I couldn't help him. It was my fault anyway. If I hadn't put the bottle of Johnny Walker in his sugar bag this never would have happened. Doc, whom I loved so dearly, had become another Pisskop victim. This time it was much worse than a nervous breakdown.

My mother had stopped sniffing when she saw my tears. 'You poor little mite, you've been through a terrible time. We'll never talk about it again. Mrs Boxall from the library has asked to come and see you but the doctor and I have agreed that you're not well enough to have visitors.' She opened her bag and withdrew a green folded card. 'Now I have some good news for you. Your report card came and you came first in your class. Your granpa and I are very proud of you.' She beamed at me, her tears forgotten. 'They've put you up another two classes, you're going to be in with the ten-year-olds. Fancy that, seven and in with the ten-year-olds!' She handed the report card to me and through my tears I took it and tore it into four pieces. For a long time my mother said nothing, looking down at the pieces of green cardboard in my lap. Finally she gave a deep sigh. I hated her sighs the most because they made me feel terribly guilty. 'The Lord has blessed you with a good brain. I pray every day that you will take Him into your heart and use your fine mind to glorify His precious name.' She gathered the pieces up and dropped them into her handbag, giving me a sort of squiffy smile. 'I'm sure it can be mended, you are just not your old cheerful self at present, are you?' But her eyes weren't smiling as she spoke.

That afternoon I wrote a note to Mrs Boxall at the library. All it said was, 'Please come! In the afternoon,' and I signed it. I also wrote a note for Marie asking her if she would take the note to Mrs Boxall at the Barberton public library. Marie had switched mid-week to night duty and came on at six p.m. with our dinner. I handed her the note. She read it and quickly hid it in the pocket of her white starched junior nurse's uniform. She picked up my dinner tray from the trolley and brought it over to me.

'I'll only do it if it's got nothing to do with that spy,' she whispered as she put my tray down in front of me. I handed her the second note. She gave me a suspicious look as she took it. 'I got to read it first before I say I'll do it.' She read the note and seemed assured by its contents. 'I've got my day off tomorrow, I'll do it then. Now promise you'll eat your pumpkin, you left it last night and also your peas.' She seated herself on the side of the bed and, taking up a teaspoon, she filled it with pumpkin and put it through the hole in the corner of my mouth. I had lost four top and bottom teeth on the same side where the sergeant's boot had landed, and Marie called it my 'feeding hole'. She was the best of anyone at getting the mashed food they were beginning to give me through the hole without making my gums bleed.

I spent the rest of the evening writing for Mrs Boxall a long, detailed description of what had happened. Doc, when I presented him with my botanical notes, would always stress that a botanist is concerned with detail. 'Observation is what makes a scientist,' he said. 'It is only by seeing things in minute detail that we learn their secrets. Others can walk past a plant for a whole life and never even notice the colour of its blossoms, but the botanist knows every beat of its heart and turning of petal.' And so I wrote it all down just the way it happened, even the swear-words, and then I hid the three sheets of paper in my pillowslip. Mrs Boxall came the very next afternoon. In her string bag she carried a new *William* book by Richmal Crompton, a book called *Flowers from the banks of the Zambesi* by Revd William Barton of the London Missionary Society and three copies of *National Geographic.* 'You are such a precocious child, Peekay, I hope they suit your catholic taste.' Like Doc, Mrs Boxall never talked down to me. With the result that I didn't always understand her and wondered what the Catholics might have to do with my taste.

I withdrew my notes from inside the pillow and handed them to Mrs Boxall. 'Well now, pray, what have we here?' she said, taking the three pages and reaching into her bag for her glasses. She read for a long time and then read the three pages again before looking up at me. 'Remarkable! You are a remarkable child. This comes just in time. A military court is being convened next week and things are looking pretty grim for our professor, my dear. The whole jolly town is up in arms about him. People are seeing Jerries in their chamberpots.' She chuckled at her own joke. 'I tried to see him in prison but those dreadful Boers said only authorised people could see him. If a librarian isn't an authorised person then who is, I ask you? But the stupid warder at the gate wouldn't budge. I've started a petition in the library but so far I only have twelve signatures and three of them are Boers, and we all know where their sympathies lie, do we not? That dreadful little man, Georgie Hankin, has threatened to say some perfectly ghastly things about me in *Goldfields News* and has told me privately that, if I persist, he can't have a Nazi-sympathiser writing a column in his newspaper. Honestly, you'd think it was *The Times* of London the way he carries on about that dreadful little rag!' She paused, dug once more into her string bag and withdrew a copy of the *Goldfields News.* Taking up almost half the front page was Doc's picture of me sitting on the rock. Above the picture in huge black letters it said, THE BOY HE TRIED TO KILL! Just above the headline and below the masthead was written Special Spy Edition. Under the picture the caption read, Like Abraham's biblical sacrifice of Isaac, the innocent boy waits on the rock. No doubt Georgie Hankin, who as usual had it all wrong, saw this as his finest professional hour.

Doc's arrest had occurred just in time for the weekly edition which appeared on a Monday. It carried the original news of the arrest and this special two-page mid-week edition, using precious rationed newsprint, was an attempt by Mr Hankin to achieve immortality in his profession. The reason Mrs Boxall hadn't been able to visit me was because Dr Simpson, in resisting Georgie and his photographer's attempts to come and see me, had banned all visitors. She was surprised that I hadn't seen the earlier paper and promised to bring it the following afternoon, though as a trained librarian she had little trouble verbally reproducing the essence and the flavour of Monday's big story.

The essence of the story reported in the *News* was that the Provost officer and his sergeant had waited most of the afternoon for Doc to arrive. When he appeared with a small boy in tow, he was in a dishevelled state and it was obvious to the two military policemen that he had been drinking. The sergeant, on the orders of the officer, escorted him back to his cottage to allow him to clean up. Whereupon, when his back was turned, Doc attacked the sergeant with a heavy metal-topped walking stick and attempted to run for the hills. It was pointed out that Doc knew the hills well and would easily be able to conceal himself indefinitely in one of the hundreds of disused mine shafts dotted all through the mountains. He would then make his way across the mountains to Lourenço Marques, the nearest neutral territory.

The story had gone on to say that the sergeant was stunned from the blows he had received and it looked as though Doc would make good his escape had it not been for me who had bravely tackled him. Hearing my scream, the officer had rushed down the path just in time to see Doc take a vicious kick at my head. The officer arrested the suspected spy at the point of his pistol.

The editorial went on to point out that Doc was a noted photographer, and that under the guise of photographing cactus he had undoubtedly taken pictures of likely enemy landing places and established landmarks and mine shafts for storing food and weapons for enemy spies infiltrating South Africa from Portuguese territory. The paper pointed out that there were no pictures to be found of such places, confirming that they had already reached the enemy and that no clever spy would leave such incriminating evidence around. Fortuitously, inside the expensive German Leica camera the spy had used that very afternoon was exposed film of a hole in the mountainside, with the ore tailings dug from the mine heaped directly outside the shaft making it an ideal defensive position. In Doc's notepad had been found a compass bearing and exact location of the disused mine. There had also been several pictures of a succulent, which proved how cunning and careful to cover up Doc had been.

The picture was, of course, the site where we had found *Senecio serpens,* the blue chalksticks. The remainder of the exposed pictures on Doc's film had been of the succulent. Doc, as he had taught me to do, always established the location of a find, the direction of the prevailing winds, by studying the bush and larger plants in the immediate area, the soil conditions and the surrounding rock types.

To the rumour-happy folk of Barberton it was all very feasible and few of them paused long enough to examine the evidence or to question the town's fifteen-year relationship with Doc. Mrs Boxall said people were going around saying, 'Once a Jerry always a Jerry!' satisfied that this covered a multitude of sins. 'Goodness, Peekay, I'd suspect my dear old father before I'd suspect the professor. He doesn't have a patriotic bone in his body unless it's for Africa and has something to do with cactus.' She folded my notes carefully and placed them in her handbag. 'Oh dear, I nearly forgot, I brought you a bag of gob-stoppers. Oh my goodness!' she said in an alarmed voice. 'I'd quite forgotten about your jaw, what an idiot I am.' She dropped the rock-hard candy into her bag and clipped it shut and leaned over and touched me on the chin. 'Chin up, old chap, we've got all the evidence we need to get our mutual friend out of trouble. I'll get back tomorrow with the news.' She was gone, her sensible brogue shoes clattering on the polished cement floor, her back straight as a ramrod and her bobbed head held high. I could hear her still clattering down the verandah long after she was out of sight.

For the first time in a week I felt happy. Mrs Boxall was not the sort to be trifled with and I had every confidence that she'd sort things out. She was Doc's friend and mine as well and, as Doc had so often said, 'This woman, she is not a fool, Peekay.'

But I didn't see Mrs Boxall the next day. Somehow my mother had heard of her visit and had seen Dr Simpson who brought down a ban on visitors again. I had begun to make semi-intelligent sounds through my wired jaw and Marie, after a few trial sessions, had little trouble understanding me. She said she had a little brother who was a bit wonky in the head and I sounded a lot like him, which made it easy for her to understand me. It was nice to talk to someone again and it was Marie who told me about my mother's visit to Dr Simpson which she overheard while she was in the dispensary. My mother said nothing to me the morning after she had visited the doctor and I was once again cut off without any news. Marie also told me that I would be going home on Tuesday and she was quite sad about it. She was fifteen years old and came from a farm in the valley. She only got one weekend a month off to go home. She lived in the nurses' home while all the other juniors lived in town. She wasn't very pretty or very clever and she had pimples, which she called her 'terrible spots', so she didn't have any friends. I told her I was her friend and if she liked she could come into the hills with me. She seemed a bit worried about that and said girls weren't supposed to go climbing hills, but she'd like to come anyway.

On the Monday evening she came into the ward and put a large brown paper bag on the bed. She brought a finger to her lips, signalling for me to say nothing. 'Mrs Boxall brought it to the nurses' home, she says it's the latest on you know what,' she whispered, thrilled to be a part of the conspiracy but also frightened. Though later when she was feeding me, she said, 'I did nothing wrong, did I? I just brought in this brown paper packet, that's all. It's only polite to do people a favour, isn't it?'

I had looked into the paper bag which, at first glance, seemed to contain nothing but bananas, but under the bananas was a tightly folded newspaper and a letter from Mrs Boxall. After lights out I stuffed both into my pyjama jacket and walked down the corridor to the lavatories. Taking the letter out, I began to read. It was written in Mrs Boxall's neat librarian's hand.

Dear Peekay,

Much news from the war zone. I have been to see Mr Andrews. He is the lawyer who comes into the library and only takes out books on birds. He read your notes and he said, 'By Jove! This places a different complexion on everything.' He seemed very hopeful that he could get to the military judge when he arrives from Pretoria next Wednesday. He agrees with me your notes are excellent. 'Too good,' he said 'who will believe a seven-year-old can express himself in such detail?'

Well, my dear, that's the problem he thinks we may have. He knows about your inability to speak. But he's hit on a clever plan. He wants you to take an intelligence test, a written test in front of the judge so the judge can make up his own mind. Mr Andrews has been to see your mother but she won't hear of your having anything to do with the case. But she did say she'd pray about it so all is not lost. It's a bit of a problem really, but we're not beaten yet. I'm sure God is on our side and not on the side of Georgie Hankin or the military. British justice will come through in the end, even if we have to write personally to Mr Winston Churchill.

Can you come and see me when you get out of hospital? Keep your chin up!

Yours sincerely,
Fiona Boxall
Librarian

I wondered what sort of test the judge would give me. What if I failed and let Doc down? What if the Lord didn't give my mother permission for me to see the judge?

But the Lord, with a little help from Mr Andrews who came from one of the oldest and most important families in town, came out in favour of my being a witness at the hearing. The lawyer had pointed out that it was very much in my mother's interests to clear our family name as the prattle tongues in town might well accuse her of neglect for having allowed me to roam the hills with a German spy.

I was released from hospital on Tuesday and on the following morning Mrs Boxall called round in Charlie, her little Austin Seven, to pick me up and take me down to the magistrates' court where the military tribunal was to be held. Mr Andrews was waiting for us and so, to my surprise, was Marie.

'She seems to be the only one who can understand you, Peekay, so we've brought her along as interpreter. It was my idea and a good one, even if I say so myself,' Mrs Boxall declared. Marie was dressed in a freshly starched nurse's uniform and looked even more scared than I felt.

Mr Andrews left us and we had to wait a long while, sitting on a bench in the waiting room. Finally, he came back and said the judge would see us privately in the magistrates' chambers and, depending on how things went, I wouldn't be required as a witness.

None of this made very much sense to me but we had to walk down a long corridor of cork lino that smelt of floor wax. A lady with a trolley full of teacups went rattling past us and she stared at me. I was not yet used to people seeing me with my jaw wired up. I looked into every open door in the hope that I might see Doc. We finally reached a door with Magistrate in gold lettering on a square of polished wood screwed to the door. Mr Andrews knocked on it softly and a voice said 'Come!' and we followed him in. Sitting behind a desk was a man wearing a proper uniform with tie and polished leather Sam Browne belt. He stood up when we entered, and I could see he wore long pants and a revolver at his side. Mr Andrews introduced him to us as Colonel de Villiers. There were four chairs arranged in front of the desk and we all sat down. My notes were on the desk on top of a file that was tied with purple tape. Colonel de Villiers put on a pair of gold-rimmed spectacles which slid down his nose as he looked up, so he looked over the top of them as he spoke.

'Well now, young man, Mr Andrews here tells me that you are bright enough to have written these notes.' he tapped my notes with his forefinger. 'How old are you?'

'Seven, sir,' I rasped at the back of my throat. The colonel, Mr Andrews and Mrs Boxall turned to look at Marie. Her mouth opened but nothing came out. Her whole face appeared to be frozen in terror, then two big tears squeezed out of her eyes. She tried again but still nothing came out. I held up seven fingers to the colonel who looked stern and cleared his throat.

'I see, seven. Well, you write very well for a seven-year-old. I think someone must have helped you, don't you?' I looked at Marie who was sniffing into a hankie Mrs Boxall had handed her. I shook my head. 'Umph!' the colonel grunted and looked at Mr Andrews. 'These alleged swear-words the sergeant is claimed to have said, they would seem an unlikely part of the vocabulary of a seven-year-old child who, you tell me, has a religious background. I am also a little surprised at his knowledge of Latin, *Senecio serpens* and *Glottiphyllum uncatum* seem a little esoteric for a small boy who, I imagine, like all small boys, is more interested in getting his mouth around a sucker than a Latin noun.'

Mrs Boxall said, 'The professor is an amateur botanist of considerable ability and the child has been trained by him to take punctilious notes. Besides, he has almost perfect recall.'

'Hmm . . . a bit too perfect if you ask me, madam,' the colonel said, as though talking to himself. I could see Mrs Boxall bristle.

'He did it all himself, I seen him do it in the hospital,' Marie said suddenly, her voice quaking with terror.

'Well that's one good thing, little Miss Florence Nightingale has found her voice,' the colonel said. 'Perhaps we can get on with the interview now?' He turned to me. 'Son, I want you to tell me the whole story again, just as it happened.' I repeated the story although Marie had no chance of pronouncing the Latin names of the two succulents which I then referred to as 'blue chalksticks and another succulent genus which I can write for you, if you want?' The colonel pushed a piece of paper across the desk and I wrote the Latin names on it. 'Extraordinary, it seems I owe you an apology, madam,' he said, dipping his head at Mrs Boxall. When we got to the swear-words Marie refused to say them. 'Please, sir, I can't say them words, I've never said words like that in my whole life,' she said fearfully but with absolute resolve.

The colonel would cut in every once in a while and ask me questions such as, 'What was the colour of the sergeant's cap and belt?' They were all questions which involved some minor piece of detailing, but I had no trouble answering them.

When I was finished, he told Marie that she had done an excellent job and she blushed crimson and the pimples stood out on her face. Then he turned to Mr Andrews.

'The child's statement coincides almost precisely with that of the prisoner. We have already determined that neither has been in a position to compare notes nor to have a third party co-ordinate a defence. Mrs Boxall did try to see him but was not allowed to do so. The prisoner has been visited and interviewed only by military personnel, and I am satisfied that the incident took place as the boy has alleged. I am quite sure the court will find for the defendant in all matters except one. I will ask that the charges of assault to a minor and attempted escape be withdrawn. Quite obviously the striking of the Provost sergeant was under severe emotional provocation and the court is likely to look upon it as such. Both the army and the prison reports state that the prisoner smelt heavily of whisky but we can quite easily ascertain whether his coat sleeve is stained.'

He pulled at the purple tape on the file and opened it up. Inside were two folded copies of the *Goldfields News,* the picture of me sitting on the rock, and a number of Doc's other photographs and also one of his small spiral-bound notepads. The colonel held up one of the newspapers. 'Really, this kind of hysterical nonsense makes it very difficult for us. The trial of aliens is distressing enough without having the general population turning the butcher, the baker and the music maker into enemies of the State. The only charge Professor Von Vollensteen faces is a technical one, that of not having registered as an alien.' He rose from his chair and smiled briefly at me. 'I only wish I could be here to have a chat with you when your jaw is better, young man. I am also beginning to form a healthy respect for the teachings of your professor.' He shook Mrs Boxall and Mr Andrews by the hand and said something privately to him, then Mr Andrews hustled us out of the room.

When we got back to the waiting room Mr Hankin of the *Goldfields News* was waiting. Mr Andrews spoke to him and he nodded towards the colonel's office. Mr Hankin rose and walked towards the office. 'I think Mr Hankin's career as a spy catcher is about to come to a sticky end,' Mrs Boxall said to me and then started to laugh. 'We won, Peekay, we won!' she said triumphantly.

But we hadn't won. While Doc was acquitted of all the charges just as the colonel said he would be, he was charged with being an unregistered alien and the court ordered him to be detained in a concentration camp for the duration of the war. The *Goldfields News* headline read, NO SPY BUT STILL A GERMAN! It was a year before Mrs Boxall agreed to resume her column, 'Clippings from a Cultured Garden by Fiona Boxall'.

ELEVEN

Doc was to be kept in custody at the Barberton prison until arrangements could be made to send him to a concentration camp somewhere in the highveld. Two days after Doc had been sentenced I went to the library to take a bunch of roses from my mother to Mrs Boxall. Mr Andrews had explained to my mother how my evidence had saved Doc from a severe sentence, one that might well have killed a man of his age. He had also persuaded her that we had nothing to be ashamed of and that he only wished his two sons, now at boarding school in Johannesburg, had had the benefit of a man as remarkable as the professor. My mother decided that the Lord had guided her in the matter and that His will had been quite clearly wrought through me. The roses to Mrs Boxall were her sign that the librarian's trespass into the hospital to see me had been forgiven.

Mrs Boxall seemed excited when she saw me come through the door. 'I'm so fearfully glad you came, Peekay, I have a letter for you.' I handed her the roses. 'How very nice of your mother.' She placed them on the book-sorting table and withdrew into her tiny office to return with a small blue envelope which she handed to me. The envelope was sealed and I opened it carefully pulling back the flap at the back, the glue giving way reluctantly. 'Do hurry, Peekay, I can't bear the suspense,' Mrs Boxall said, looking over my shoulder. I withdrew a single sheet of cheap exercise paper and opened it. Doc's neat hand covered the page. 'Oh dear, I'm such an awful nosy parker! May I read it with you?' Besides Hoppie's note, it was the only letter I had ever received and the first one sealed in an envelope. I would have preferred to read it alone but of course I couldn't possibly say so and I nodded my agreement.

Dear Peekay,

What a mess we are in. Me in this place where they tear down a man's dignity and you with a broken jaw. But things could be worse. I could be a black man and that would be trouble and half. Absolute.

I have been placed under open arrest, it means I can go anywhere in the prison grounds and my cell is not locked. Best of all, it means I can have visitors. Will you come and see me?

Ask Mrs Boxall to telephone the people here and make arrangements. There is also good news about the Steinway. The Kommandant is going to allow me to have it in the prison hall. This is good news, ja?

I do not think of myself as a German. What is a German? To say a man is a German what is that? Does it tell you if he is a good man? Or a bad man? No, my friend, it tells you nothing about a man to say he is German. A man must think what he is inside. What he is on the outside, how can this matter?

Also, because I am German, I am well treated by the warders. This also is stupid. Have you planted the Senecio serpens? *No of course not, I am getting old and think only of my own welfare. Perhaps Mrs Boxall will take the books in the cottage and put them in the library? In the meantime I am treated well and whisky is getting easier not to have. Please come soon.*

Your friend, Doc.

'We will call the prison at once,' Mrs Boxall said, inviting me into her office.

The superintendent of Barberton prison, Kommandant Jaapie Van Zyl, told Mrs Boxall that Colonel de Villiers had said Professor Von Vollensteen should be allowed access to the boy within the normal rules of the prison. He added that he had heard of my bravery and wanted to meet me himself. That if Mrs Boxall cared to have me bring Doc library books this would be permitted. The professor was a musician and a scholar and Barberton prison was honoured to have him.

Mrs Boxall selected three botanical books she knew to be among Doc's favourites and I set out with a note from her to visit Doc in prison.

I arrived at the gates of the prison which were made of wrought iron and locked with a huge chain and padlock. It was the biggest lock I had ever seen, nearly twice the size of a grown-up's hand. I wondered how big the key would have to be to open it. The gate seemed about twelve feet high and along the top there were pipes welded every two feet or so. They were about three feet long, bent inward at a thirty-degree slant threaded with strands of barbed wire six inches apart and set into huge blocks of blue granite. Without thinking I identified the components of the rock, mainly felspar and quartz, quarried in the Barberton district, so in addition it contained a fair amount of mica. After a year with Doc it had become second nature to identify almost anything that didn't move and I was an expert at the geology of the district.

I decided that escape from inside the wall would be impossible. Set high up to the side of the gate was a church bell and from it, hanging almost to the ground, was a rope. A sign fixed onto the wall said, Ring for attention. My heart beat wildly as I tugged on the rope and the noise from the bell seemed deafening as it cracked the silence. Almost immediately, a warder carrying a rifle slung over his shoulder came out of the guard house some twenty feet from the gate and walked towards me. His highly polished black boots made a scrunching sound on the white gravel driveway. I handed my note to him through the bars of the gate and he opened it suspiciously. He looked at the note for a bit and then looked up at me.

'*Praat jy* Afrikaans?' he asked.

I nodded my head, indicating to him that I understood Afrikaans. The swelling in my tongue had subsided and while my voice had very little volume and sounded a bit gravelly I could talk quite clearly through my wired-up mouth. The young guard looked relieved and started to talk in Afrikaans. He asked me to read the note as he didn't have much English, coming from the North Western Transvaal where only the taal is spoken. 'It says that I am here to visit Professor Von Vollensteen and have permission from Kommandant Van Zyl,' I told him.

'I will get on the telephone and ask. Better wait here, you hear.' He walked over to the guard house and I could see him talking on the phone. He was quite young and looked nervous. Finally he replaced the receiver and stuck his head out of the door. 'Kom!' he beckoned to me. But the gate was locked and he shook his head in exasperation and disappeared to return with a very large key on a huge ring. To my surprise the gates opened smoothly and closed with a clang as he locked them behind me.

The young warder told me to report to the office in the administration block and pointed it out to me. '*Totsiens* and thanks for reading the note, you are a good *kêrel,*' he said.

The area between the gate and the administration block was completely bare. Lawn stretched from either side of the gravel driveway for about five feet and thereafter the square turned into a parade ground of sun-hardened red clay. The strip of living green on either side of the pathway was a brilliant though incongruous contrast to the baked earth of the parade ground and the dead blue-grey walls and buildings. I could see a warder's head in the window of a little tower built onto and jutting out from the wall. There was a stretch of walkway for fifty feet on either side of the tower. Two guards with rifles slung over their shoulders paced up and down this walkway. I seemed to be the only person on the ground below them and I wondered how, on my way out, they'd know I wasn't a prisoner trying to escape. Maybe they'd give me a white flag to carry or something.

It was one of the longest walks of my life. I could sense the oppression of the place, the terrible silence. Without trees, no cicadas hummed the air to life. No birds punctuated the stillness. My bare feet on the gravel made an exaggerated sound. There were tiny dark windows arranged three storeys high. Each was divided by two vertical steel bars. I imagined hundreds of eyes hungrily devouring my freedom as they watched from the prison darkness.

The door of the administration block was open, and after hesitating I put my head around it. Inside was a small hallway that had the same wax polish smell of the magistrates' courts. Three benches, arranged like church pews, filled half the hallway and there was a window with bars set into a wall. Through the bars I could see an office. I walked into the hallway and sat on the front bench and waited.

I don't know how long I sat there, but it seemed to be a very long time. I could see two men in uniform pass the grille window occasionally, but they never looked out. I could hear them talking on the phone. After I'd been there for ages and ages I heard the voice of a man on the phone behind the grille, he was shouting in Afrikaans and seemed very angry.

'He hasn't arrived, you domkop! Are you sure you directed him to this building? We can't have a blêrrie kid walking around the prison. It's been almost half an hour and there's no sign of him. We'll have to look for him now and it's all your blêrrie fault!' I could hear the receiver being slammed back into its cradle. 'Kom!' I heard the voice say to someone else and a moment later a door opened and a big man followed by another big man who looked younger than the first one came out.

The big man saw me as he entered the hallway. 'Jesus Christ! Where have you been?' he shouted at me.

'I been here, I been here all the time, Meneer,' I rasped.

'Well, why didn't you make yourself known then?' he asked in a slightly mollified voice, possibly because he had noticed my wired jaw.

I pointed to the two notices on the wall behind the benches. 'It says on that notice, Wait here and on that other one it says, Silence,' I replied fearfully.

The younger of the two men suddenly laughed. 'I think the kid won the first round, lieutenant,' he said.

'Okay, man, I admit you got me there fair and square,' the older one chuckled. 'Kom, we must take down your name and things.'

They led me into the office and after taking my name, address and age the older one made a phone call and asked to speak to the Kommandant. Then he put the phone down. 'The Kommandant wants to see you but he's doing an inspection now, we have to wait twenty minutes.' He turned to the younger warder. 'Klipkop, get Peekay here a cup of tea and a biscuit.' I wondered how someone could be called 'Klipkop'. In Afrikaans it means stone head. But when I looked at the tall, blond man, his rawboned features looked as though they could well have been carved out of stone.

Klipkop rose and held out his hand. 'Seeing we're going to be here for a while we might as well introduce ourselves. Oudendaal, Johannes Oudendaal,' he said formally in the Afrikaans manner, giving his surname first, then repeating it attached to his Christian name. 'This is Lieutenant Smit.' He indicated the older warder, who stretched out his hand without looking at me and I took it briefly, blushing with embarrassment. I wondered whether Captain Smit was related to Jackhammer Smit, maybe his brother? But I didn't have the courage to ask. After all, Smit is a pretty common Afrikaans name. If he was, I hoped he was a better type than the miner. 'Come, I'll show you where we make tea,' Klipkop said. 'There's a Kaffir who makes it but if we want a cup in between we make it ourselves, it's very handy. Every week we put in a shilling for milk and sugar and biscuits, but the authorities supply tea. You got to watch the Kaffir, or the black bastard pinches everything. I'm telling you, man, this place is full of thieves.'

I followed him into a small kitchen behind the office and he put water into an electric jug and plugged it in. 'Peekay, that's a name I haven't heard before.'

'It's just a name I gave myself. Now it's my real name,' I said.

'Ja, I know man, it's the same with me. They call me Klipkop because I box and can take any amount of head punches. Now I sometimes find it hard to remember my born name.'

For a moment I was stunned. 'You box?' I asked.

'Ag ja, man. In this place if you want to get on you have to box, but I like it anyway. On the weekend we travel all over the place to fight, it's much better than rugby, man.' He took three mugs down from a cupboard above the small sink. 'Lieutenant Smit is the boxing coach, he used to be a heavyweight.' He paused as he spooned a heaped tablespoon full of tea from a much used tea caddy into the pot. 'But all the easy stuff is over now, man. Next month I have my first professional fight. There's good money in the fight game. I've got a nooi in Sabie and we're thinking of getting married.' He poured the water from the electric jug into the tin teapot and then stirred it with the tablespoon before placing the lid on the pot. 'Do you box, Peekay?' He asked the question to be polite and did not expect my reaction.

My heart was pounding as I spoke. 'No, but can you teach me please, Meneer Oudendaal?'

He looked at me in surprise and must have seen the pleading in my eyes. 'First your jaw has got to get better, but I think you're a bit young anyway. Lieutenant Smit teaches also the warders' kids but I think the youngest in the junior squad is already ten years.'

'I can be ten. I'm ten in class already. I could be ten in boxing easily and my jaw will be better in eight weeks,' I begged.

'Hey, whoa! Not so fast! Ten is ten. On the form we wrote you were seven years old only.'

'If you fight first with the head and then with the heart, you can be ten years old,' I said.

'Magtig, you're a hard one to understand, Peekay. You'll have to ask Lieutenant Smit, he's the boss. But if you ask me, I don't think you've got a snowball's hope in hell.'

'Will you at least ask him for me?' I rasped. The excitement made me over-project so that my throat was strained.

'I'll ask him, man, but I already told you what he'll say.' He picked up the pot and poured tea into the three enamel mugs, added milk, three teaspoons of sugar and stirred them all. He went to the cupboard and took out a tin and prised it open. 'That blêrrie Kaffir! We had nearly a quarter of a packet of Marie biscuits in here, now they all gone. It's time that black bastard went back into a work gang. Take your cup and bring the milk, Peekay. If you come again, next time we'll have biscuits.'

'Please, Meneer Oudendaal, you won't forget to ask the lieutenant? You see, I've got to start boxing because I have to become the welterweight champion of the world.'

I said it without thinking. It was more a thought expressed aloud than a statement. Klipkop whistled. 'Well you're right, man, with an ambition like that you've got to get started early.' He paused, two steaming cups in one hand, the teapot with the sugar bowl balanced where the teapot lid would normally have been in the other. 'Me, I'll be happy if I can beat the lieutenant's brother in Nelspruit next month.' He turned and looked over his shoulder at me. 'You can call me Klipkop if you like, I won't mind, man.'

I followed him back into the office where Lieutenant Smit was working on some papers. Klipkop put a mug of tea down in front of him. 'Peekay wants to ask you something, lieutenant,' he said and turned to me. 'Ask him, man.'

Lieutenant Smit hadn't looked up from his papers but he gave a short grunt. 'Please, sir, will you teach me how to box?' I asked, my voice down to a tiny squeak.

He still didn't look at me but instead lifted the tea to his lips, and first blowing the steam from the surface took a sip from the mug. 'You are too young, Peekay. In three years come back, then we will see.' He was taller than me even when he was sitting down and now he looked down at me. 'We read about you in the paper. You have lots of guts, that's a good start but you are not even big for seven like a Boer kid.' He ruffled my hair. 'Soon you will be ten, just you watch.'

At that moment an African came into the room. He was quite old and looked very thin, wearing the coarse knee-length grey canvas pants and shirt of a prisoner. In his hand he held the teapot lid. 'I have come to make tea, baas, but the pot she is not here,' he said slowly in Afrikaans. He stood with his head bowed. In two bounds Klipkop had reached him, and grabbing him by the front of his canvas shirt he lifted the African off his feet and gave him a tremendous swipe across the face. The blow landed with a loud, flat sound and the black man's face seemed to squash in slow motion as Klipkop's huge hand landed on the side of his nose and mouth. Klipkop released his grip and the man fell at his feet, whimpering.

'You black bastard! You stole the Marie biscuits. Not just one, you piece of dog shit, you stole them all!' He gave him a kick in the rump.

'No baas! Please baas! I not stole biscuit. I good boy baas,' the old man pleaded and still holding the teapot lid he locked his free arm around Klipkop's ankles.

The warder turned to Lieutenant Smit. 'Please, Lieutenant, can't we transfer this black bastard to the stone quarry? First he steals sugar, now the Marie biscuits.' He looked down at the whimpering African at his feet. Blood from the prisoner's nose had dripped onto the shiny toe of his boot. Klipkop kicked him loose, sending the black man flying against the wall where he hit the back of his head with a thud, the teapot lid clattering to the floor at his side. 'He's bleeding on me, the filthy black shit house is bleeding all over my boots!' He thrust one foot towards the dazed African slumped against the wall. 'Lick it off, Kaffir, make quick!' The stunned man bent over the proffered boot and licked the blood from the toe cap, then, without being told, did the same with the other boot, at the same time holding his hand up to his nose to prevent further blood spilling on the warder's boots. 'Now wipe your filthy black spit off my boots, you black bastard, I don't want foot and mouth disease!' Lieutenant Smit, who hadn't even looked up, grinned at the joke. The African removed his canvas shirt, and trying to sniff back the blood commenced to wipe Klipkop's boots with it. 'On the floor also,' the warder said, pointing to several scarlet drops of blood on the floor. The black man wiped the drops of blood from the green linoleum floor. 'Now get up and clear out, you bastard!' The African scrambled to his feet and Klipkop gave him a flying kick which sent him sprawling again. Crawling on all fours, his shirt clutched in one hand, the black prisoner fled from the room.

Klipkop examined his hand. 'They got heads made of blêrrie cannon balls.' He grinned. 'I'm learning, man, notice I didn't hit him this time with my fist.' He turned to me. 'Always remember, when you hit a Kaffir stay away from his head. You can break your fist on their heads, just like that. Hit him in the face, that's orright, but never on the head, man.' He made a fist and rubbed it into the palm of his hand. 'I got a big fight coming up, I can't afford a broken fist from a stinking Kaffir's head.'

Lieutenant Smit hadn't said a word. He took another sip from his tea. 'We can't send him to the quarry, man. He's had rheumatic fever, he'd die in a week. Besides he is the first Kaffir we've had who can make proper coffee and tea.' He pointed at the cup in front of him. 'Not like this shit. I told you not to stir it and to warm the pot first.' He turned to look at Klipkop, with just the hint of a smile on his face. 'Next time, man, ask before you hit. I ate the blêrrie Marie biscuits, I never had breakfast this morning so I ate them.'

Klipkop's mouth fell open and then he grinned. 'Okay, so I hit him because he steals the sugar, what's the difference?'

The phone rang and Lieutenant Smit picked it up and listened for a moment. 'Right,' he said into the receiver and replaced it. He turned to me. 'The Kommandant is back, come on, son.'

Grabbing Mrs Boxall's books I followed the lieutenant up a set of stairs to the second floor. We entered a small outer office where a lady sat behind a desk typing on a big black machine which had Remington Corona in gold letters on its back. 'Go right in, Lieutenant Smit, the Kommandant is waiting for you,' she said, smiling at me.

We entered a large office, dark brown and filled with dead animals. A kudu head was mounted directly behind the Kommandant's desk with a sable antelope head beside it, the elegant curved horns touching the wall. There were gemsbok and eland heads to complete the display of larger antelope and next to them, in a cluster of five heads, were the smaller variety of buck: grey duiker, klipspringer, steenbok, reebok and springbok. I turned to face the wall behind me, for it too was covered in trophies. This time a large black-maned lion looked down at me, mouth in the full roar position. Next to it were a leopard and a cheetah. All the carnivores were on one side of the door while on the other were their most common prey, a zebra and a black wildebeest. Below these, fixed to brackets on the wall, were a Boer Mauser and a British Lee-Metford. Immediately below these two Boer War rifles was a long-shafted Zulu throwing assegai. The rest of the wall space was taken up with small framed pictures, mostly of hunting parties standing over dead animals.

The room was furnished with two heavy leather club chairs and a large matching sofa, and on the polished floorboards were a zebra and a lion skin. Directly behind the Kommandant's head and below the kudu and sable antelope hung two large portraits. One was of King George and the other of President Paul Kruger, the last president of the defeated Boer Republic. The picture of the Boer president was in an elegant oval walnut frame. King George looked to be the sort of official photograph in a cheap gilt frame issued to public institutions and requiring mandatory display.

Kommandant Van Zyl rose from behind his desk, which was really a large ball and claw dining room table with a sheet of glass covering its surface. There was nothing on the table except the pad on which he appeared to be writing, his fountain pen and an ashtray.

'Good morning, Smit. Sit down, please.' He turned to look down at me. 'So this is the boy, eh?' He walked out from behind his desk and stuck out a huge hand. 'Good morning, Peekay.' He was even bigger than Lieutenant Smit and his tummy stuck out in front of him even more than Harry Crown's. Like the Lieutenant and Klipkop, he wore the grey military-style uniform of a prison warder. The only differences were four stars and a crown on his shoulder tabs and a small tab of blue velvet inserted into the top of his lapels. I shook his hand shyly, not quite knowing what to say.

'Sit, son.' He pointed to the remaining leather chair. I pushed myself up into the large chair. By sitting on the edge I could make my feet almost reach the ground. Kommandant Van Zyl sat down heavily on the sofa.

'So, you want to see our professor?'

I nodded my head, 'Yes please, sir.'

The Kommandant adjusted himself on the sofa, his body soaking up most of it. 'The law says he must be detained and I must follow the law, but inside this place, *I* am the law. In here he can come and go as he pleases provided he stays within the gates. Also he can have visitors in official visiting hours.' He looked at me and smiled. 'I have decided to make an exception in your case. You can come any time you want, only not

Sundays,' he paused and looked at me again, 'how do you like that, hey? Two old *maats* together again.'

'Thank you, Meneer Van Zyl,' I said.

'Ag man it's nothing.' He looked at Lieutenant Smit as though he felt the need to explain his decision. 'A friendship between a man and a boy is not a thing to be broken. This boy has no father, I know what that is like, man. My father died with the Carolina burghers at Spion Kop when I was the same age.'

'Yessir,' Lieutenant Smit said, looking down at his hands which were crossed in his lap.

'Make out a permanent pass for the boy so he can come any time except Sunday, you hear?'

'Ja, Kommandant.' Smit looked at the larger man. 'What about the professor's peeano?'

Kommandant Van Zyl slapped his hand on his thigh. 'I clean forgot. Thank you, Smit.' He turned to me. 'We are going to let the professor have his peeano here, there are already many musicians amongst us. Everybody thinks Boere are not cultured, but I'm telling you man, when it comes to music we leave everyone for dead. For us it is an honour to have a man such as him in our prison community. Magtig! A real professor of music, here, in Barberton prison. *Wonderlik*!'

'Thank you for letting me come to see him, Meneer.'

'The boy has nice manners. I like that,' he said to Lieutenant Smit. 'It's nothing. You can come any time, you hear.' He hesitated for a moment. 'Peekay, we need just a small favour. On Monday, about one o'clock, we will be having a nice little surprise for the town folk in the market square. I already telephoned the mayor but I can't trust him to tell people. Will you inform Mrs Boxall who telephoned about you and who, I understand, is also a friend of the professor? Ask her to tell everyone, you hear.' I nodded and he seemed pleased. 'Dankie, Peekay, I think we will like each other a lot. Now Lieutenant Smit is going to take you to see the professor. I see you have some books for him.' He stretched his hand out. 'Show me.' I jumped down from the big chair and handed the books to him. He opened the top one and leafed through it for a few moments. 'Plants, I don't know much about plants. Animals, that's my speciality, you can ask me anything about animals, you name it,' he brought his hands up as though he were squinting down the barrel of a rifle, pulled an imaginary trigger and made a small explosive sound, 'I've shot it.' He lowered the imaginary rifle and grinned at me. He had two gold teeth. 'I love wild animals,' he said. His hands returned to the books which he handed back to me, and his face wore a look of benign satisfaction as he scanned the trophies around the walls.

Lieutenant Smit cleared his throat loudly and the Kommandant turned back to us. 'Well it's been nice to meet you, Peekay.' He patted me briefly on the shoulder. 'If you want anything you just come and see me, you hear?'

It was like the time I had to decide whether to offer to do the Judge's arithmetic. Like then, I was doing pretty well. Why risk it? If I got on the wrong side of the lieutenant, I stood to lose everything, even the chance of becoming a boxer once I turned ten.

'Please, Meneer Van Zyl. Could I learn to box here?'

The Kommandant had already risen from the sofa, preparing to dismiss us. 'You want to box?' he looked at me. 'That's the lieutenant's department.'

'I already told the boy he must wait until he is ten, then maybe,' Smit said, trying not to sound terse.

'When you're seven it's a long time to wait till you're ten. That's nearly half your life,' the Kommandant said.

'We train at five-thirty in the morning. Unless he lived here, how could he get here?'

'I will get here, I promise. I will never miss, not even once. Please, Meneer Smit?'

Lieutenant Smit looked down at his boots for a long time. 'We can try when your jaw is fixed. But I must have a note from your mother to say it's okay to teach you.' He looked up, appealing directly to the Kommandant. 'He is too small, Kommandant.'

'He will grow, Smit; as I recall you and your younger brother started very young. Is he still fighting?'

'Yes, sir, his next fight is against Oudendaal.'

'That's right, the Lowveld heavyweight title next Saturday, you must get me tickets, lieutenant.'

'Yessir, your secretary has them, sir.'

Kommandant Van Zyl ushered us to the door. 'All the best, Peekay.'

When we reached the bottom of the stairs Smit stopped, and getting down on his haunches he grabbed me by the front of the shirt. He had said nothing when we left the Kommandant's office, but I was too good at listening to silence not to know I was in real trouble. I closed my eyes, waiting for the clout across the head that must inevitably come. I hadn't been hit for a year except for a few hidings from my mother which you couldn't really call hidings after what I'd been through. But the memory of a skull-stunning blow across the head was still very much a part of my experience. To my surprise the blow didn't come and I opened my eyes again to look straight into Lieutenant Smit's angry face. 'I'm telling you flat, don't do that to me again, you hear? When I tell you something I mean it, man!' He shook me hard, expecting me to cry; instead I held his gaze. 'Who you looking at? You trying to be cheeky?'

'Please, Meneer, I saw your brother fight in Gravelotte last year. That's when I decided.'

A look of amazement crossed Smit's face. 'You were there? *Wragdig*? You saw that fight?'

I nodded. 'He fought Hoppie Groenewald . . . Kid Louis,' I corrected. Lieutenant Smit released his grip on the front of my shirt.

'I was there also. Magtig! That was a fight and a half. You saw it? Honest?' He rose from his haunches and suddenly his eyes grew wide. 'The kid with Hoppie Groenewald! I remember now. We thought you was his kid.'

We had reached the office again. Klipkop was on the floor doing push-ups and broke his sequence and stood up rather foolishly as we entered. 'You know the fight in Gravelotte my brother had against Groenewald the welterweight last year?' Klipkop nodded. 'Peekay saw that fight, he is a personal friend of Groenewald.'

The warder laughed. 'I lost a fiver on that fight. Who would have expected a welter to beat a light-heavy?'

'I'm telling you, Groenewald isn't just an ordinary welter. You mark my words, if he comes out of this war he's going to be South African champ, you can put money on it,' Smit said. 'He'd take you with one arm behind his back, man.'

Klipkop grinned, 'That'll be the frosty Friday. No way, man! I'm going to do the same to your brother on Saturday as he did.'

'Don't be so blêrrie sure of yourself, Oudendaal. Jackhammer Smit is no pushover, this time he'll be fit. Don't count your blêrrie chickens before they hatch!'

Smit turned to me suddenly. 'Okay, I changed my mind, you on the squad. But no fighting for two years, you hear? Just training and learning your punches and technique, you understand me?'

I nodded, overjoyed. My eyes brimmed with tears. I had taken the first step to becoming the welterweight champion of the world.

'Klipkop, take Peekay to see the professor. I'll make a phone call and you can meet him in the warders' mess.' He turned to me. 'Come back when you're finished and I'll have your permanent pass ready for you.'

We left the administration block and passed through another building. 'This is the gymnasium for the prison officers,' Klipkop said. We walked over to the punching bag and the boxing ring set up at one end of the large room. Large leather balls lay on the floor and Klipkop bent down and scooped one up in his hand. 'Here, Peekay, hold on to this.' I put both my hands out and he flipped the ball lightly into them and suddenly I was sitting on the floor with Klipkop laughing over me. 'It's a medicine ball and it weighs fifteen pounds. When you can throw one of these over my head you'll be strong enough to begin to box.' I got up, feeling very foolish, then I bent down and tried to pick the large brown leather ball up. Using all my strength I managed to lift it but was happy to let it drop again. 'Not bad, Peekay,' Klipkop said with a grin. We were standing next to the ring and I liked the smell of the canvas and the sweat. I wondered how I could possibly wait two years before I climbed into the ring to face a real opponent.

We left the gymnasium and crossed the huge indoor courtyard, an area half the size of a football field which I had seen from the top of the hill on my first morning in Barberton. The prison blocks rose up on every side of the square where two old lags were raking its neat gravel surface so all the tiny rake lines ran diagonally across the quad. 'It's Friday, diagonal lines. I like Monday best when they make a big star in the middle,' Klipkop said. I wasn't sure what he meant but I was soon to learn that each day had a different rake pattern. It was how the prisoners knew what day of the week it was.

'Where are all the prisoners, Klipkop?' I asked. The two old lags doing the raking were the only humans I had seen since leaving the administration building.

'Ag man, they're all out in work gangs. Most work on farms, some at the quarries and some at the saw mills at Francinos Rust. The people who hire them must call for their gangs at four o'clock in the morning and they got to be back here by six o'clock at night. What you see around here in the day time is just old lags, too old to work hard like that black bastard who makes our tea. Also the murderers, they not allowed to come out of their cells, even to eat. But we don't keep them long, man. It's not good to have murderers around, the other Kaffir prisoners get very restless.' He grinned, 'The warders don't like them around also, so we hang them jolly quick smart, I'm telling you.'

'What about the white prisoners, do they also work in the gangs?'

Klipkop looked surprised. 'No blêrrie fear! Gangs is not a white man's work. Mostly white men are only here in transit to Pretoria. They don't have to work so hard, because they not here for long. If they real hard cases, like that guy who murdered his wife and three children in Noordkaap, we just locked him up till the district judge sentenced him, then we put him on the train to Pretoria. If you lucky you get sent along as a guard, you get a day off in Pretoria and ten and sixpence expenses.'

We had crossed the gravel quad and passed though a narrow archway which led to the back of the prison. A long corrugated-iron shed stretched from the main building and smoke rose from three chimneys along its length. 'Kitchens. The warders' mess is on the other side,' Klipkop said.

Doc was overjoyed to see me and he hugged me and patted me on the head and his sharp blue eyes went watery. 'Now I see you I can sleep again. Let me see your jaw? Tut-tut-tut, I wish only I could have taken the kick, then you would be okay. Yes, I think so? Peekay, why are the peace lovers always the first to suffer in the war? Can you talk?' I had never seen him so worked up and his words tumbled out so that I had no chance of getting a word in.

'My jaw is not so bad. They are going to take the wire out in six weeks, maybe even four, but I have learned to talk with my mouth shut.'

Doc laughed. 'You and I, Peekay, even when they cement our mouths, we find a way to talk.' He was still patting me on the head as though to reassure himself that it was really me.

I handed him the books from Mrs Boxall and he held them briefly before putting them on the table beside him. 'She is a goot woman, not so stupid either. You and she, Peekay, eleven out of ten for brains. Absolute. Also Mr Andrews. I do not think they would listen to a poor old German professor of music on his own. German measles was in the air and only you and Mrs Boxall don't catch a big dose, ja?' He chuckled at his sad little joke.

'I can come and visit you as much as I like,' I said happily.

Doc looked bemused. 'Without the hills it will not be the same, what can I teach you here, my friend?'

'Lots of things, like out of books and things. And I could go into the mountains and find things and bring them here and then we could talk about them.'

Doc gave me one of his proper grins. 'You are right, Peekay. A man is only free when he is free in his heart. We will be friends like always. Absoloodle. But also one more thing, they are going to let me have the Steinway here. You can continue your lessons. You must tell your mother this, I think she will be happy. On Monday they are letting me come with them to get it. If they move it wrong it can be damaged. I will see my cactus garden one last time. Maybe also you can be there, Peekay?'

Dr Simpson had said that another week's recuperation was in order. My granpa had given me a big wink and said, 'Who are we to argue?'

'I'll be waiting for you, I've already planted the *Senecio serpens,* just like you said, facing east.'

Doc looked pleased, but then a worried expression crossed his face. 'Peekay, on Monday is happening a stupid thing. It is not my decision, but please you must trust me, that is why I want you to be there. I think Kommandant Van Zyl wants to be a schmarty pantz with some people in this town. I am too old for such silly games, you will help me, please?'

'Kommandant Van Zyl said I was to tell Mrs Boxall everyone has to be in the market square at one o'clock, but he didn't say what it was all about.'

Just then Klipkop emerged from the door leading to the kitchen carrying a small plate of roast potatoes. 'Here, have some,' he said offering me the plate. I pointed to my wired mouth and he laughed, 'Sorry man, I clean forgot.' He offered the plate to Doc who shook his head.

'Monday, Peekay. Be so kind as to be at the cactus garden at twelve o'clock, then I will explain. Also, tomorrow maybe find for me Beethoven Symphony Number Five, you will see on the cover is printed my name and Berlin 1925. Inside I have marked the score. That is the one I want.' I knew where to look, for the music Doc played only to himself was kept under the seat of his own piano stool. I found it strange that he would ask me to find it. After all he knew perfectly well where it was. 'Peekay, put what's above the score in my water flask, the key for the piano stool lid you will find under the pot on the stoep where grows the *Aloe saponarie.*' He said all this in a perfectly straight voice in English. Klipkop appeared either not to understand or to be disinterested. I looked quizzically at Doc but he put his forefinger to his lips and indicated the warder with his eyes.

A hooter sounded somewhere in the prison. 'Lunchtime, Peekay, we must get back to the lieutenant and the professor must go to lunch.' Klipkop pushed the last potato into his mouth. 'You can stay if you want and have lunch with the prison warders.'

'I have to get home for lunch, thank you, Mr Oudendaal. What is the time, please?'

'That was the twelve o'clock hooter. Just call me Klipkop, okay?' I nodded, I was becoming accustomed to calling adults by their Christian names. I would have to run all the way home as my mother would expect me back from the library by now. I wasn't at all sure how she would take the news of my potential comings and goings to the Barberton prison, nor how I would break the news to her. This more immediate preoccupation made me forget Doc's curious instructions.

After Sunday school the next day I went to the cactus garden. Dum and Dee had the afternoon off on Sundays and had excitedly agreed to come with me to clean things up a bit for Doc's return the following day. They took brooms and feather dusters and other cleaning things in two galvanised iron buckets which they carried on their heads, chatting away happily about how they would clean my friend's house like it had never been cleaned before. There wasn't much they could do on their half-day off as they hadn't yet learned to speak Swazi. While I didn't think of it at the time, they must have felt isolated from their own kind. On the farm they had been at the centre of things. Quite important really, by comparison with the farm workers, certainly a notch up the social ladder. Here they were two lonely little girls who, outside our home, could make no contact and who knew no other people. We were their family and they were as cloistered as nuns in a convent.

When we arrived at the cactus garden they set to, delighted that they owned every inch of the task without supervision from anyone. I went straight to the large terracotta pot on the stoep of Doc's cottage where *Aloe saponarie*, also known as Soap Aloe, was growing. It has spots of lighter green and rust on its thick leaves.

It was with some difficulty that I pushed the large terracotta pot aside to reveal the key to Doc's piano stool. I hurried to the stool and opened it. The recess was almost a foot deep and it was packed with sheets of music and handwritten music manuscripts. There was also a bunch of programmes tied with tape, though at the time I didn't know what they were. The top one had Doc's name on it and the rest were written in German. I dug down quite deeply into the manuscripts and sheet music without finding Beethoven's Fifth Symphony. Then, lifting another batch of paper, I revealed a bottle of Johnny Walker Scotch. I lifted the bottle and directly under it was the piece of music for which Doc had asked.

On Friday afternoon after lunch I had gone to see Mrs Boxall in the library to give her the Kommandant's message.

'Whatever do you think they're up to, Peekay?' she had said, a worried look on her face. 'Do you think it has anything to do with the professor?'

'I don't think so. At twelve o'clock they are going to fetch the Steinway and take it to the prison. Doc asked me to be there to help him.'

'My God! He's going to give a concert! The professor is going to give a concert in the market square. How thrilling, how perfectly thrilling!' I had never seen her so excited.

It was suddenly also clear to me. 'I don't think he's very happy about it. He said Mr Van Zyl was trying to be a smarty pants with the people of the town. That he would need my help.'

Mrs Boxall, in her excitement, appeared not to have heard me. 'I once checked up on our professor, he turned out to be terribly famous.' Her eyes shone. 'There's something dark and very mysterious about it all, if you ask me. Why would a famous European pianist give it all up and bury himself in a tiny dorp in Africa where he lives on the smell of an oil rag giving lessons to little girls?'

'I think he just likes collecting things like cactus and aloes and climbing in the mountains,' I said, though she didn't appear to be listening. She had her elbow on the desk, chin cupped in her hand, and was obviously deep in thought.

'Peekay, did he ask you to do anything? I mean when he said he needed your help?'

'He asked me to get out Beethoven's Fifth Symphony with his name on it and Berlin on the cover.'

'Hip hip hooray! Jolly good show! Beethoven, eh? What a treat we're in for. I heard the Fifth for the first time when I was a gal and we'd travelled up to London to hear the brilliant young Artur Rubinstein play at the Albert Hall.' Mrs Boxall clasped her hands and looked up at the ceiling fan turning fitfully above her head. 'Oh bliss! Oh blissful bliss! '

'He also said I must put what is above the sheet music into his water flask.'

'Whatever can he mean?' she said absently. It was obvious her mind was on Doc's concert in the market square and her duty as the town's cultural representative was clear. This was no time to attempt to solve one of Doc's conundrums. 'Peekay, you'll have to excuse me, my dear. I think we're going to have to close early today. I have such a lot of phoning to do. One o'clock, are you sure that's the time Mr Van Zyl said?' I nodded and prepared to leave. 'You will thank your dear mother for my lovely roses. I shall write her a nice note next week.' She had already started her telephoning and as I went out of the door of the library I heard her say, 'Barbara, you'll never guess!'

Now I stood holding Doc's music, staring down at the bottle of Johnny Walker. Doc only ever drank in his room, why would he keep a bottle in his piano stool? If Klipkop hadn't walked in at the moment he was about to tell me, everything would have been clear. I reached into my pocket for Doc's note and read it again, maybe there was a clue I'd missed. I kept coming back to the last words, . . . *and whisky is getting easier not to have.* Had I been older it wouldn't have been a puzzle at all, but seven-year-olds are not very good at puzzles and usually know nothing about the drinking habits of grown-ups.

I wasn't at all sure I was doing the right thing but the bottle was directly above the musical score Doc wanted and it was the only item in the piano stool which you could pour into a water flask. I was more than a little conscious that when I had last interfered with Doc's whisky, the repercussions had been enormous. I took the water flask and the bottle of Johnny Walker into the cactus garden where I dug a hole in the ground and planted the flask with its neck protruding. I must say it was a good plan and I spilled hardly any. After that I planted the bottle upside down. It was to be the last Johnny Walker bottle to be planted in Doc's cactus garden.

I returned the flask to the piano stool, placing Doc's musical score over it. Then I locked the seat and put the key in my pocket.

I was waiting at Doc's cottage by nine a.m. on Monday morning. Dee and Dum had cleaned everything and the place was spotless. The Steinway shone like a mirror, from a fresh coat of beeswax. The girls had spent an hour cleaning the whisky from the keys. Seated on the two piano stools, they had giggled fit to burst at the cacophony they made. I don't believe they'd ever had a more enjoyable afternoon. They continued to clean Doc's cottage every Sunday afternoon for the next four years, until I'm sure they believed it was their sabbatical home.

I passed the time waiting for Doc separating succulents and generally clearing weeds from a small part of the garden. After a couple of hours I heard the low whine of a truck and the less agonised sound of a light van as they made their way up the steep road to the cottage.

The black prison flat-top was a Diamond T. The van, coming along behind it, waited a little way down the road while the truck turned to face downhill again. On the back were six black prisoners and two warders carrying rifles. The driver and third warder sat in front. I recognised one of the warders as the young one who had let me into the prison on the previous Friday and I said hello. He jumped down from the back of the truck and stuck his hand out. 'Gert Marais, *hoe gaan dit?*' I shook his hand and replied that I was well and, in the Afrikaans manner, enquired formally about his health. Just then the van drew up and I could see that Klipkop was driving and Lieutenant Smit was beside him. They stopped in front of the lorry and Klipkop jumped out. Walking to the rear of the van he unlocked it. To my surprise Doc stepped out. He was dressed in a clean white shirt, blue tie and his white linen suit. The place where his knee had torn through the trouser leg when the sergeant's kick brought him to the ground had been mended, the suit had been washed and pressed and his boots shone. I had never seen him looking so posh. Lieutenant Smit and Klipkop both greeted me like an old friend.

I could see Doc was agitated and when Klipkop and Lieutenant Smit moved towards the house he turned to me urgently. 'We must talk,

Peekay, today is a very difficult thing for me to do.' We followed the two warders into the cottage and Doc pointed to the Steinway and the stool. He was too preoccupied to notice the clean up and while I felt a little disappointed I said nothing.

Cleanliness wasn't something I regarded too highly myself. Two of the other warders came in, leaving Gert and one other warder to mind the prisoners. Together with Doc they discussed how the Steinway might be safely moved.

Klipkop went to call the prisoners in and Doc turned to Lieutenant Smit and asked if he could go and look at his garden, as he couldn't bear to see the piano being moved. Smit laughed and added that it was necessary to have a warder along. 'I know Gert Marais. Can he come please?' I asked. Lieutenant Smit shrugged his shoulders and signalled for Gert to come with us.

'I can't have you two escaping into the hills, now can I?' he said jokingly. But I was to learn that Lieutenant Smit was a careful man and liked to play things by the book. Gert couldn't speak English which meant Doc and I could talk without the danger of being overheard.

We walked in the garden, following the Johnny Walker bottles as they meandered through the tall cactus and aloe. For a long time Doc said nothing, stopping to look at plants and bending down to examine succulents which grew close to the ground. It was as though he was trying to memorise the garden, to etch it on a plate in his mind so the memory of it would sustain him in his prison cell. At last we stopped and sat on a natural outcrop of red rock with our backs to the town below and looking up into the hills. Gert stood some little way away chewing a piece of grass, his rifle slung carelessly over his shoulder. He seemed happy to be away from his superiors.

Finally Doc started to talk. 'Peekay, these domkopfs want I should do a recital in the town today. I have not played a concert since sixteen years, now I must play again. Peekay, I cannot do this, but I must.'

I looked up at Doc and I could see that he was terribly distressed. 'You don't have to, Doc. They can't force you!' I said defiantly but without too much conviction. My short experience with authority of any kind had shown me that they always won, they could always force you.

Doc turned to look at me. 'Peekay, I love you more than my life. If I don't play today they will not let you come to see me.' I could feel the despair in his voice as he continued softly, 'I do not think I could bear that.' I hugged him and he patted my head and we sat there and looked at the hills dotted with the aloes in bloom and at the blue and purple mountains beyond them. At last he spoke again. 'It was in Berlin in 1925. I had been ill for some months and I was coming back to the concert circuit with a concert at the Berlin Opera House. I had chosen to play –' he turned to me – 'the score you found in my piano stool. Beethoven's Symphony Number Five is great music but it is kind to a good musician, the great master was a piano player himself and it is not full of clever tricks or passages which try to be schmarty pantz with the piano player. That night I played the great master goot, better than ever until the third movement. Suddenly, who knows from where it comes, comes panic. In my fingers comes panic, in my head comes panic and in my heart comes panic. Thirty years of discipline were not enough. The panic swallowed me and I could not play this music I have played maybe a thousand times when I practise and forty times in concert. Nothing. It was all gone. Just the coughing in the crowd, then the murmuring, then the booing, then the concert master leading me from the stage.' Doc sat, his head bowed, his hands loosely on his knees. 'I have never played in front of an audience again, not since this time in Berlin. Every night for sixteen years I have played the music, the same music and always in the third movement it is the same, the music in my fingers and my head and my heart will not proceed. It is then the wolves howl in my head and only whisky will make them quiet again. Today, in one hour, I must play that music again. I must face the audience or, my friend, I lose you.

I cannot pretend to have understood the depth of Doc's personal dilemma. I was too young, too inexperienced to understand his pain and humiliation. But I knew he was hurting inside and I knew there was nothing I could do to stop it. 'I will be there with you, Doc. I will turn the pages for you.'

Doc took out his bandanna and blew his nose. 'You are goot friend, Peekay.' He gave one of his old chuckles and rubbed a hand through my hair and then examined one of my hands. My kneecaps and hands were dirty from weeding between the cactus. 'Better wash in the tank if you are going to be my partner, we must look our best. Ja, this is true, the audience has been waiting sixteen years.' He rose and took me by the hand. 'Come, Peekay, we go now.'

On the journey into town Doc and I sat in the front of the van with Lieutenant Smit. Klipkop drove the truck while Gert sat in the back of the van. The Steinway had been loaded onto the flat-top and roped. Even so, five prisoners were arranged around it to hold it firmly in place on pain of death, while one sat with Doc's piano stool between his legs.

About half a mile from the market square the Diamond T stopped and the two warders herded the six blacks off the truck. One of them climbed back on while the other started to march the prisoners out of town towards the prison. We entered the top of Crown Street about three hundred yards from the market square. The main street was deserted, as quiet as a Sunday afternoon. 'Jesus Christ, I hope this doesn't backfire on the Kommandant,' Lieutenant Smit said, almost as though speaking to himself. We had been travelling behind the truck and now we moved ahead of it. I noticed all the shops were closed, even Goodhead's Bottle Store and the Savoy Café, which never closed for lunch. We turned the corner into the square and my mouth dropped open.

The market square was packed with hundreds of people who had started to cheer as they saw us. A warder signalled us to a space which had been kept clear under a large flamboyant tree. Lieutenant Smit told Gert to stay with the van but not to show his rifle. Then he jumped out and, walking in front of the Diamond T, he guided it into a roped-off section in the centre of the square.

Several warders scrambled up a stepladder onto the flat-top and untied the ropes securing the Steinway. One placed Doc's piano stool in place while another, an electrician from the prison, rigged up a microphone.

The moment we saw the crowd, Doc began to shake. I was half sitting on his knee and I could feel him quivering. 'Peekay, did you do what I said about the water flask?' he asked in a tight voice.

'It is in the piano stool, Doc.'

'Peekay, you must take it and when I ask, you must hand it to me, you understand?' I nodded.

When we drew to a halt under the large flamboyant tree the Kommandant was waiting for us. He opened the van door and Doc got out, very unsteady on his feet.

Kommandant Van Zyl took him by the elbow and held him firmly. 'Now then, Professor, remember you are a German, a member of a glorious fighting race. We of the South African Prison Service are on your side, you must show these Rooineks what is real culture, man!'

Doc looked round fearfully to see if I was by his side. 'Do not forget the flask, Peekay,' he said. We walked to the centre of the square, Doc holding tightly onto my hand and being steadied by the Kommandant.

The excitement of the crowd could be felt around us. Nothing like this had happened on a dull Monday since war was declared. We reached the flat-top to find that some twenty rows of chairs had been placed behind the ropes on either side of it. The chairs must have come out of the shops and offices, for no two matched, but they formed a ringside audience of the best people in town. Mrs Boxall was in the front row. She was dressed in her best hat and gloves as were most of the other town matrons considered of social rank. At the back end of the lorry, in three rows of identical chairs, sat the prison warders and their wives, the men in uniform and the women wearing their Sunday best. It was obvious they were very pleased with themselves.

Doc had pulled himself together a little by the time we reached the truck and he and I climbed the stepladder onto the flat-top without assistance.

The Kommandant, helped up by Klipkop, climbed the stepladder onto the flat-top. Klipkop then walked over to the microphone. 'Testing one, two, three, four,' his voice boomed from the four corners of the market square. Satisfied, he climbed down again to join Lieutenant Smit on the ground. The Kommandant moved over and stood in front of the microphone.

'Dames en Here, ladies and gentlemen,' he began. But from then on he spoke in English. 'As you all know from reading the newspaper, there has been a very big fuss made about one of our most distinguished citizens,

Professor Karl Von Vollensteen, a professor of music from across the seas. The good professor, who has lived in this town for fifteen years and has taught many of your young daughters to play the peeano, was born in Germany. It is for this alone that he is being put under my custody.' Several pockets of people in the crowd had started to boo and someone shouted, 'Once a Jerry, always a Jerry!' which brought about a little spasmodic laughter and clapping. The Kommandant held up his hand. 'I am a Boer, not a Britisher. We Boers know what it is like to be robbed of our rights!'

Considerably more booing started and the same voice in the crowd shouted, 'Put a sock in it, Jaapie!'

The Kommandant, as though replying to the heckler, continued. 'No it is true, I must say it, you took our freedom and now you are taking the professor's!'

This time the booing started in earnest and suddenly Mr O'Grady-Smith, the mayor, stood up and shouted up at the Kommandant, 'Get on with it, man, or we'll have a riot.'

The Kommandant turned angrily on the mayor, oblivious of the microphone in front of him. 'Don't you blêrrie tell me to get on with it! Jes because you the mayor of this dorp you think you can boss people around, hey?'

The booing stopped, for Mr O'Grady-Smith was no more popular than the Kommandant. He was also a very fat man and at least ten inches shorter than the Kommandant. He strode from his seat, and with the help of a couple of town councillors mounted the stepladder and walked over to the microphone. Standing on tiptoes he shouted into the loudspeaker, 'It's high time we moved the jail and the nest of Nazis who run it out of Barberton. This town is loyal to King George and the British Empire. God save the King!'

Most of the crowd clapped and cheered and whistled, and Mr O'Grady-Smith turned and looked up at the Kommandant, a smug, self-righteous expression on his face.

From where I stood next to Doc on the flat-top I could see about a dozen men making their way through the crowd towards us. 'Some men are coming,' I said to Lieutenant Smit, who was now standing beside the stepladder with Klipkop to discourage any further townsfolk from emulating the mayor. They quickly mounted the flat-top, pulled up the ladder and placed the microphone next to the Steinway so that the bottom half of the flat-top was clear. Without any ceremony, the mayor and the Kommandant were hastily pushed to the top end to stand beside the seated Doc and me.

There was a good ten feet between the truck and the first row of seats behind the ropes. This was to allow the more important citizens a clear view of Doc at the piano. The attackers crossed this strip of no man's land and swarmed onto the back of the flat-top. Lieutenant Smit and Klipkop held the high ground which evened things out considerably while the other warders took the clearing between the lorry and the seats. The flat-top and the apron around it were filled with fighting men and the screams of the ladies as they tried to back away from the brawl. The Kommandant ventured out from behind the Steinway and received a punch on the nose. Fat Mr O'Grady-Smith was crouched on all fours halfway under the piano, trying to look invisible.

Only Mrs Boxall stood her ground and was waving desperately in our direction and, I suddenly realised, at me. 'Jump down, Peekay, run for it, jump, jump!' she screamed.

Just then Doc tugged me on the sleeve. 'The flask, Peekay.' His hand was outstretched. I handed the flask of whisky to him and he unscrewed the cap and took a slug and handed it back to me. 'When I make my head like so, you must turn the page.' He turned to the score in front of him and paged quickly to the beginning of the fortissimo movement, which in Beethoven's Fifth occurs at the end of the second movement. Then he started to play. The microphone had been knocked down and its head now rested over the upright section of the piano. It picked up the music, which now thundered across the square.

Almost immediately the crowd grew quiet, and the fighting stopped. The flat-top cleared and the men around the apron slipped back into the crowd. The mayor squeezed out from under the Steinway, he and the Kommandant were helped down the replaced stepladder. Even the sobbing ladies soon grew quiet.

On and on Doc played, through the second into the third movement and, hardly pausing, into the fourth, his head nodding every time he wanted the page turned. It was a faultless performance as he brought the recital to a thunderous close.

Intellectually the audience had probably understood very little of it. It was not, after all, their kind of music. But emotionally they would remember Doc's performance for the rest of their lives. Mrs Boxall was weeping and clutching her hands to her breast, and the other ladies also pretended to be swept away with it all.

Lieutenant Smit shouted at several of the warders who began to clear a way for the truck. Lifting the microphone off the back, he shouted for Klipkop to get into the truck and drive away, then he jumped into the passenger side of the cabin as the big Diamond T started to move. Doc, who had been bowing to the crowd, fell back onto his seat. With a flourish of the keyboard he began to play Beethoven's Moonlight Sonata.

I had never seen him so happy. He played all the way back to the prison, not stopping when we got to the gates and reaching the final bars as we drew up outside the administration building. Then he took a long swig from the flask and rose from the piano and looked out over the prison walls to his beloved hills.

I quickly opened the piano stool and put the flask into it together with the score. I locked it and slipped the key into my pocket.

Doc rubbed his hand through my hair. 'No more wolves. Absoloodle,' he said quietly, and then he looked up at the hills again.

TWELVE

Dee or Dum woke me up at a quarter to five every morning with coffee and a rusk. Shortly after five I strapped my leather book bag to my shoulders and was off at a trot to the prison some three miles down the road.

I was let in the gates without equivocation, as regular as the milkman and just as harmless. The guards, with an hour and a half to go before the nightshift ended, waved from the walkway on the wall. They were weary from the boredom of guard duty, and I was the first tangible sign after the grey dawn that the long night was almost over.

I learned that the greatest camouflage of all is consistency. If you do something often enough and at the same time in the same way, you become invisible. One of the shadows. Every recidivist knows this. In prison, to be successful, plans have to be laid long term. Habits have to be established little by little, each day or week or month or even year, a minute progression towards the ultimate goal. When a routine is finally set, authorities no longer see it for what it is, a deception; but accept it for what it isn't, an authorised routine. The prisoner enjoys the advantage over his keeper of continuity. Warders change, get promoted, move elsewhere. But old lags, those prisoners who remain inside with long sentences, have the advantage of time to plan. In prison, the old lag is the real authority. The warder unwittingly depends on the old lags to run the prison system, for it is they who restrain the younger prisoners who lack the patience to go along with the system or who see violence as the only solution to getting what they want. A prison without this secondary system of authority can be a dangerous and unpredictable place.

I found myself a part of this shadow world, brought into it with great patience over a long period by an old, toothless lag known as Geel Piet. Translated from Afrikaans, his name simply meant Yellow Peter. In fact, it was more than simply a name. Geel Piet was a half-caste, or a Cape Coloured, neither black nor white, treated as a black man but aspiring in his soul to be a white one. Geel Piet was the limbo man of Africa, despised by both sides. He was also a recidivist, an incorrigible criminal who freely admitted that it was hopeless for him on the outside. Geel Piet was the old lag who exerted the most influence in the shadow world of the prison.

My prison day began in the gymnasium at five-thirty a.m. where the boxing squad, under the direction of Lieutenant Smit, assembled for callisthenics. There were twenty of us altogether and this included four other kids between eleven and fifteen. Seniority went by weight, with Klipkop, who had defeated Jackhammer Smit on points over ten rounds and was now the Lowveld heavyweight champion, the most senior, down to myself at the very bottom of the ladder.

Lieutenant Smit stood in the boxing ring with a whistle in his mouth and to a series of whistles we would perform a routine of exercises familiar to everyone. These were interspersed with push-ups and sit-ups at any interval Lieutenant Smit wanted them. Each session of push-ups and sit-ups was of longer duration than the previous one. Lieutenant Smit was a big believer in push-ups to strengthen the arms and the shoulders, and sit-ups to strengthen the gut muscles. He also liked fighters, and contended that the Boer made a better fighter than boxer and that most prison warders were naturally aggressive and better equipped to be fighters. He said toughness and determination overcame skill in the ring. The boxers from Barberton prison were known throughout the Lowveld and as far as Pietersburg and Pretoria as tough men to take on.

Lieutenant Smit was true to his word and for the first two years he would not allow me to step into the ring. 'When you can throw a medicine ball over Klipkop's head, then you will be ready,' he said. The first of my goals was set, and for the fifteen minutes after callisthenics, when all the other boxers were paired off with sparring partners, I worked until I could no longer lift my arms.

After a five-minute shower I reported to the prison hall for my piano lesson with Doc, and at seven-thirty we would both go into breakfast at the warders' mess.

Doc had a special status in the prison. While he lived in a cell, he could come and go as he pleased, he ate in the warders' mess, and wasn't required to do any special work. 'You just play the peeano, professor,' Kommandant Van Zyl had said, 'that's your job, you hear?'

Doc often wandered into the gymnasium to watch the squad going through its paces. He knew that I yearned to box, to stand up against another person in the ring. While he made it clear that he didn't understand why I should have such a need, he respected my ambition and soothed my impatience with musical analogies. 'In music you must first do the exercises, always first the exercises. If you do the exercises goot then you have the foundations. You cannot build a good musician on a bad foundation. I think with this boxing business it is the same. Ja, I think this is true. '

And so I did all the things required of a boxer and practised on the punching bag until the whole armoury of punches was as familiar to me as the piano scales. That old punching bag took a terrible hiding on a daily basis over those first two years. I would imagine it cowering as it saw me approach, sometimes even whimpering. 'Not too many of those deadly uppercuts today, Peekay!' Or, 'Oh no! Not the right cross. I can't take any more right crosses.' I'm telling you, man, that big old punching bag learned to respect me all right.

But it was the speedball which I grew to love. Gert, the young warder who spoke no English, was also on the boxing squad and we'd become firm friends. He'd modified an old punching ball in the prison workshop so that it stood low enough for me to reach.

I can remember the first day when, after many weeks of practice on the speedball, I achieved a continuity of rhythm, the ball a blur in front of my boxing gloves. I imagine Fred Astaire or Bojangles must have felt the same way when they got their first complete tapdance sequence from their taps.

After several weeks Lieutenant Smit walked over to watch me. My heart pounded as I concentrated on keeping the speedball flurried, a blurred, rhythmic tat-tat-tat-tat of leather on leather. 'You're fast, Peekay. That's good,' he said and then walked away. Two years later when I mastered a difficult passage in a Chopin prelude, the thrill was minor compared to Lieutenant Smit's praise. They had been the first words he had specifically directed at me in the six months I had been on his squad.

Doc's Steinway was kept in the prison hall, a fairly large room with a sprung wooden floor used mostly for tiekiedraai dancing and other events in the lives of prison officers and their families. There was also an upright French Mignon piano, for Doc's Steinway was not to be used except to play classical music. This was an express order from Kommandant Van Zyl, who pointed out that a peeano of such superior qualities should not be expected to play tiekiedraai or to accompany the banjo or accordion. Naturally his wishes were respected and the Steinway became a symbol of something very superior which, in the eyes of the prison officers and their families, elevated them and gave them a special social status. Doc and I, the only two people who played on the Steinway, were included in this status. While my own playing was elementary and far from competent, it was respected as proper music and was referred to as my gift. The fact that the great German professor of music gave me lessons was the only confirmation needed that I must be a budding genius. Doc was kind enough never to contradict this opinion. While being the most honest person I have ever known, he was not a fool. He quickly learned that every small advantage in the prison system was mental capital in the bank, but it was a shame that his brilliance as a teacher was wasted on such inferior clay.

I visited the cactus garden most days on my return from school, and every Sunday after church I went with Dee and Dum to clean Doc's cottage and work in the garden. Doc and I discussed the progress of the cactus garden in detail from a chart prepared by him of every succulent and cactus species in the garden. Considering there were several thousand, it was an intellectual task of some brilliance. In correcting the chart, which took me some weeks, I found that he had only made eleven errors. Taking a small patch of garden at a time from the chart, I reported on its progress. Doc made notes on the comings and goings of blossoms and instructed me when to thin or separate plants. The separated plants I put in a hessian bag and brought it to the prison where Doc had started a second cactus garden. Sometimes insects ate a cactus bloom and I'd capture a specimen in a matchbox and bring it to Doc for identification. If it was within my capacity to do anything about them, he instructed me in their elimination. This was rare. Doc believed all creatures had a place in the system and, in the end, everything sorted itself out. It was only when an insect appeared in such numbers that it was likely to disrupt the ecology of the garden that he instructed me to act. He would liken this to a locust plague which, though a natural thing, was a riotous act of nature which should be contained. In these cases he supplied the know-how, Mrs Boxall or my granpa supplied the materials and Dee and Dum supplied the labour. Usually the enemy was overcome. The girls saw this as part of their Sunday outing and took great pride in their work. They enjoyed the business of working with the soil, though I dare say so much effort on something as silly as a cactus must have left them bemused.

Marie, the little nurse from the hospital, had been invited home soon after my jaw incident and had become firm friends with my mother. She loved needlework and would sit for hours chatting away to my mother and doing buttonholes and making shoulder pads and bits and pieces. It seemed certain she would soon fall into the clutches of the Lord.

Being a farm girl she understood Dee and Dum and to my surprise only bossed them about a little. She taught them to cook a number of new dishes, including pumpkin scones and cornbread, and they soon became my favourites. I took her to see Doc's cottage one Sunday afternoon; the two black girls were silent for most of the way. When we arrived at the cottage, Marie started to tell them what to do; their faces grew longer and longer as the afternoon progressed. At last even I saw the mistake I had made, and Marie, much to the delight of Dee and Dum, wasn't invited again. I think they both liked Marie a lot, but there are certain things between women that musn't be tampered with. Doc's house wasn't his any more, it belonged to Dee and Dum, and Marie's imperious instructions were those of an intruder, or even a guest who had forgotten her manners.

Marie brought sweet potatoes for me from her farm, and fresh eggs, sometimes even a leg of pork, a churn of farm butter or several pounds of home-cured bacon. She always brought a large bunch of cured tobacco leaf for my granpa. He smoked a Rhodesian blend called African Drum and hated the sharp, raw, unblended tobacco from Marie's farm, though he was much too polite to tell her. He would hang it by the stems from the ceiling of the garden shed. Occasionally he added a couple of large leaves to a forty-four-gallon drum filled with rainwater which stood directly outside the shed. The tobacco-infused water was used for aphids on the roses. But the water required only a tincture of tobacco, and the supply hanging from the ceiling grew alarmingly. Eventually it was to become one of the most important factors in my rise within the prison system.

For the first year Geel Piet, the half-caste, was a part of morning piano practice, for he was always in the hall on his knees, polishing the floor. After a short while he became entirely invisible, a shadow in the background who greeted Doc and myself with, '*Goeie Môre, Baas en Klein Baas.*' He followed this with a toothless smile and then a soft cackle as though the day was perfect and he couldn't think of any place he'd rather be. Doc, who was no racist and I, who had mixed with servants all my life, both returned his greeting. It was forbidden to talk to any of the non-European prisoners and our careless replies must have been a great encouragement to the old man.

Geel Piet was small and battered-looking. His left eye hung lower than his right and the bottom eyelid drooped, showing more of the eye than one would normally see. Both eyes were permanently bloodshot and somewhat weepy. His nose had been completely flattened and his deep yellow face was criss-crossed with scars. A section of his bottom lip had been cut away, leaving a purple wedge of scar tissue to droop in a line of permanent disappointment from the corner of his mouth. He stood around five foot two inches on his buckled legs, for they were more than simply bandy, the result of having been broken several times and no doubt carelessly mended. Had he been able to straighten them he might well have been four or five inches taller. In the process of surviving, Geel Piet had achieved an outward appearance which would have made it near impossible for him to last for very long outside the jail system. He had worn out his luck in the outside world, if indeed he'd ever had any. Born in District Six, the notorious coloured township in Cape Town, Geel Piet had been in and out of jail for forty of his fifty-five years. He took pride in the fact that he knew the working, at an intimate level, of every major prison in South Africa, and he was the grandmaster in the art of camouflage. Should a warder beat him for whatever imagined reason, Geel Piet bore no animosity, no hate. He had long since transcended both, and regarded a beating as self-inflicted because it resulted from some piece of carelessness. Geel Piet had no sense of morality, no sense of right or wrong. He existed for only one reason, to survive the system and to beat it, to gain more from it than he was entitled to. He had long since realised that, for him anyway, freedom was an illusion. He had accumulated years of sentences, he wasn't quite sure or no longer cared how many, and was realist enough to know that he was unlikely to survive the system at his age and with his deteriorating health.

After all the years of incarceration he was a polished performer, no less a maestro at his profession than Doc was at his. Perhaps more so, for as a procurer Geel Piet was a genius.

Geel Piet ran the prison black market, in tobacco, sugar, salt and *dagga* (cannabis). In the end, he controlled the mail coming and going from the prison and thus the money brought in. He also had an encyclopaedic knowledge of boxing and a rare gift for spotting errors of style and weakness in performance. My desire to become a boxer was all too apparent, but it is a sixth sense to men who have to survive on their wits, and who have to sniff the air before every move and wager everything on a chance observation or a cunning guess, that told him I was an easy mark.

It took just over a year for Geel Piet to ingratiate himself to the point where I would unknowingly begin to serve him. Our entire relationship was built upon small conversations eked out over weeks until an understanding formed which eventually led to the conspiracy which made me present him with a leaf of tobacco.

I had been culling a patch of *Euphorbia pseudocactus,* a cactus-like plant which grows close to the ground and is extremely thorny. It has a habit of spreading quickly under ideal conditions and it had started to invade territory in the cactus garden which didn't rightly belong to it. Because of the thorns I had put Doc's cutting in a galvanised bucket which I'd brought from the garden shed at home. Almost without thinking I had lined the bottom of the bucket with a large tobacco leaf which was covered by the thorny cactus for Doc's prison garden. Something must have made me do it: perhaps Geel Piet, somehow, with his patience and snatches of seemingly unconnected dialogue. Tobacco is, after all, the greatest luxury and the most essential commodity in the prison system. With the war on, the normal shortage behind the walls had become severe, so that it was more highly prized than ever.

I was never searched as I entered the prison, although on this particular day, carrying a bucket rather than a bag, a mildly curious guard wanted to know what was in the bucket and had come over to take a look. In fact I had not been worried, having entirely forgotten about the tobacco leaf. 'Funny how he likes all these ugly plants, hey?' the guard said, for Doc's cactus garden was directly outside the warders' mess and was the butt of many a joke, most of them about cactus being just the sort of plant for a prison. 'If the prisoners revolt we'll all hide in the professor's garden, those blêrrie Kaffirs wouldn't be game to try to get us out.'

I had taken the bucket through to the hall after the squad workout and as usual Geel Piet, who was becoming more and more useful and who, over the ensuing year would assume the place of personal servant to Doc, took the bucket with the cuttings to Doc's garden. He had returned with it, his permanently broken face wreathed with smiles. 'I will help you to be a great boxer,' he simply said. And that was how it all got started.

I broached the subject of the tobacco to my granpa when I returned home that afternoon after school. I did not really think about the moral issue involved. After a year of going in and out of the prison each weekday I had come to understand the system. Morality was suspended, war existed between two sides and even aged eight I could see the odds were heavily biased towards one of them. The prison warders were an extension of the kids at the hostel: a brutal force confronting a defenceless one where crimes supposed or otherwise were being paid for. The idea of committing further petty crime in this sort of atmosphere and being brutally, often savagely punished, was bizarre and quite unreal. Doc and I were not a part of either side; we were an audience who would, from time to time, make a decision to enter the play. While we couldn't change the plot, we could relieve the actors of their tedium.

My granpa was generally suspicious of unquestioning moral rectitude, preferring to judge each item as it came to him; as prepared to have Inkosi-Inkosikazi cure his gallstones as he was to give the Boers credit for being musicians and good shots. We sat on one of the steps leading up to a terrace. Between much tamping, tapping and lighting of pipe and staring into the distance over the paint-faded and rust-stained roof, and after ascertaining that I was never searched, he decided that the prisoners should have the tobacco.

'Poor black buggers, it's worse for them than it was in England in the seventeenth century. Most of them are in for crimes that deserve no more than a tongue lashing.'

He was wrong. Barberton was a heavy-security prison and most of the prisoners, except for the politicals, had committed crimes that were worthy of formal punishment in any society. It was the administration of the prisoner's life that was the real crime, and it was not unusual for a prisoner to be beaten to death for a comparatively minor infringement of prison rules. Such occasions were discussed among the warders quietly, almost secretly, but with an inner glee.

I think my granpa was partly influenced by the thought that the mounting stock of tobacco leaves from Marie's farm would start to dissipate and that in some small way he too was fighting the sort of injustice he abhorred. He carefully instructed me in the use of tobacco-infused water for insect control, and gave me a note to Doc explaining how it was done. The plan was for Doc to set up his own drum beside the cactus garden and infuse it with two tobacco leaves at rare intervals. In the event of a single load of tobacco entering the prison being discovered, Doc, a non-smoker, could quite easily explain its destination.

Doc had requested to remain in Barberton prison rather than be transported to an internment camp in the Highveld. The thought of being away from his beloved mountains, his cactus garden and his piano, was more than he could bear, and I'm sure our friendship also played a large part in his reluctance to leave Barberton. Kommandant Van Zyl, who had come to regard Doc as the personal property of the prison and a constant thorn in the side of the English-speaking town, was more than happy to co-operate. I think in the end the military authorities must have given up trying to extricate him from the civil prison system, and Doc spent the remainder of the war under the benign supervision of the Kommandant.

Of course, Doc was co-conspirator in what became a sophisticated smuggling system. Being in the prison constantly he was there when the work gangs returned at night and left again at dawn. He was forced to see an aspect of Africa he had never witnessed. Doc was a man who preferred not to take sides in any issue other than one of the intellect. Rather than face the dilemma of black and white confrontation and the pre-ordained decision of white superiority, he had chosen to avoid it altogether by not having servants or any dependence on Black Africa. But he was also a compassionate and fair-minded man and the unthinking brutality of the warders offended him deeply. Both of us lacked the wisdom or the knowledge of the baser side of men, though I probably had more experience of this than Doc did. We saw the brutality around us not as a matter of taking an emotional side, or of good versus evil, but as the nature of evil itself, where good and bad do not come into play. We were simply intellectually forced to take the side of the prisoners. Man brutalised thinks only of his survival. Geel Piet was as ruthless as his oppressors and of necessity a great deal more cunning. The power the tobacco and the other things which later came into the prison gave him was enormous, and he used it to ensure his own survival and to serve his own ends as ruthlessly and as carelessly as the warders used their superiority.

As it turned out he spoke English passably, but had chosen Afrikaans to make his mark with me, knowing that Doc would then not be in a position to understand what he was saying and therefore to see through his long and carefully planned campaign. His next conquest after me was to be Doc. He became the perfect servant to him, a humble man who strove to anticipate Doc's every need while never intruding into the world Doc and I shared as expatriates of an orderly social environment.

Geel Piet successfully contrived to get into the gymnasium while the squad was working out. At first he was a familiar shadow, hardly noticed, polishing the floor or cleaning the windows. Then gradually over a year he became the laundry boy, picking up the sweaty shorts and jockstraps and the boxing boots in the shower room and returning them the next day freshly laundered and polished. By the time I could throw a medicine ball over Klipkop's head, Geel Piet had established himself as an authority on boxing. The lieutenant gave him the job of supervising the progress of the kids in the squad, only occasionally taking over when he felt it necessary to establish his superiority by deliberately contradicting an instruction from Geel Piet to one of us.

The standard of the young boxers improved measurably under Geel Piet's direction for, despite his background, the old lag was a maker of boxers. When he hadn't been in prison he'd worked in gymnasiums, and somewhere in the dim past had been the coloured lightweight champion of the Cape Province. He had a way of teaching kids that made even the Boer kids respect him, though at first it was only their fear of Lieutenant Smit that prevented them from refusing to be coached by a blêrrie yellow Kaffir.

From the first day Lieutenant Smit agreed that I could begin to box I was under Geel Piet's direction and he treated me like new clay. From day one Geel Piet concentrated on defence. 'If a man can't hit you, he can't hurt you,' he'd say. 'The boxer who takes chances gets hit and gets hurt. Box, never fight, fighting is for heavyweights and domkops.'

It wasn't what I had been waiting for two years to learn. But Doc persuaded me Geel Piet was right, and the logic, even to an eight-year-old, was irrefutable.

It was some weeks before I was allowed to get into the ring with an eleven-year-old from the squad. The boy's nickname was Snotnose, Snotnose Bronkhorst, because there was always a snolly bomb hovering from one or both of his nostrils. He was a big kid and a bully but he had only been with the squad for a few weeks and he lacked any real know-how. He had pushed me away from the punching ball, and I had tripped over a rubber mat and fallen. Picking myself up I had squared up to him, when Lieutenant Smit, seeming not to have noticed the incident, said he wanted to see us in the ring. My heart thumped as I realised that the moment had come.

We climbed into the ring and it was Hoppie and Jackhammer Smit all over again, in size if not in skill. But to my satisfaction I had absorbed a great deal over the past two years and even more over the six weeks Geel Piet had been coaching me. Snotnose chased me all over the ring, taking wild swipes, any of which, had they landed, would have lifted me over the ropes. Over a period of three minutes I managed to make him miss with every blow while never even looking like landing one myself. After three minutes Lieutenant Smit blew his whistle for the sparring session to stop.

I noticed for the first time that most of the squad had gathered around the ring and when the whistle blew they all clapped. It was one of the great moments of my life.

Peekay had completed his two-year apprenticeship. From now on it was all the way to the welterweight championship of the world.

I turned to walk to my corner before climbing out of the ring, and sensing something was wrong I ducked just as a huge fist whistled through the air where my head had been a second before. Without thinking I brought my right up in an uppercut, using all the weight of my body behind the blow. It caught Snotnose Bronkhorst in the centre of the solar plexus and I could feel my glove sinking deep into the relaxed muscles of his stomach, forcing the air from his ribcage. He staggered for a moment and then, clutching his stomach, crumpled in agony onto the canvas, the wind completely knocked out of him. The cheers and laughter from the ringside bewildered me. Looking over the heads of the squad I saw Geel Piet, unseen by any of them, dancing a jig in the background, his toothless mouth and funny lip stretched wide in uncontained delight.

Throwing caution to the winds he yelled, 'We have one, we have a boxer!' The coloured man's intrusion into the general hilarity caused a sudden silence around the ring.

Lieutenant Smit advanced slowly towards Geel Piet. With a sudden explosion Smit's fist slammed into his face. The little man dropped to the floor, blood spurting from his flattened nose.

'When I want an opinion from a fucking Kaffir on who is a boxer around here, I'll ask for it, you hear?' Then, absently massaging the knuckles of his right hand, Smit turned back to the squad. 'But the yellow bastard is right,' he said. 'Get into the showers now, make haste. Bronkhorst, you are a domkop,' he added as Snotnose rose shakily to his feet.

I was still standing in the ring, a little bewildered at the fracas I had caused. I watched Geel Piet crab-crawl along the gym floor, making for the doorway. When he reached it he got unsteadily to his feet and looked directly at me. Then he grinned, and without raising his hands gave a furtive thumbs-up sign, a movement so slight it would have gone unnoticed to a casual observer. To my amazement, the expression on his battered face was one of happiness.

On my way to school that morning Snotnose Bronkhorst sprang from behind a tree and gave me a proper hiding, although I managed to get him with a right cross that snapped his head back as well as a solid uppercut in the balls which made him release me so that I could run for it.

It had been my experience that the Snotnoses of this world were a plentiful breed and I thought it might be a good idea to learn street fighting as well as boxing. Geel Piet, I felt sure, would show me how to fight dirty as well.

But I was wrong. Perhaps I was the first human clay Geel Piet had been responsible for shaping into a boxer, but it was more likely pride; he was a purist and he knew the corruption that turns a boxer into a fighter and a fighter into a street brawler.

'Small boss, if I teach you these things a street fighter knows, you will lose your speed and you will lose your caution, and when you lose your caution you will lose your skill.' His face split into a grotesque smile. 'It will take longer to win as a boxer, but you will stay pretty.'

I was disappointed. Being tough was one of the ambitions I had set for myself. Being pretty certainly wasn't on my list of priorities! How could you be tough if you had to bob in and out like a blowfly? 'Please, Geel Piet,' I begged, 'just teach me one really rotten dirty trick.' After some days of nagging he agreed.

'If I teach you one, then you must promise not to ask again, you hear?'

'It's got to be a proper one, the worst in the book, you've got to promise that too?'

'Okay man, I will teach you the Sailor's Salute. It is the best dirty trick there is. But you got to know timing also to get it right. A boxer can know this trick and still be a boxer.'

'Promise it's the worst one of all?'

'Ja, man, I'm telling you for sure. It is so rotten the police use it all the time so they can say in the charge book they never laid hands on you. Its other name besides the Sailor's Salute is the Liverpool Kiss.' He held the flat of his hand three inches from his brow and with a short, lightning-fast jerk of his head his forehead smacked loudly onto the hand. 'Only you do this against the other person's head, like so.' He drew me towards him and in slow motion demonstrated the head-to-head blow. Even in slow motion he nearly took my head off and my eyes filled with tears. It was the head butt Jackhammer Smit had used to floor Hoppie, and now I knew why Hoppie had gone down so suddenly.

'Do it to me also,' Geel Piet said, patting his forehead with the butt of his hand. I did so and received a second severe blow to the head. I was beginning to have misgivings about street fighting. It sure wasn't like fighting a punching bag.

But over the next few weeks I perfected the Liverpool Kiss. The quick grab of the punchbag and a lightning butt to the imagined head of an opponent. Every now and again Geel Piet allowed me to practise on him and he grinned when I got it right. 'Once you got it, you got it for life. But only use it quick and as a surprise. If you get it right you kiss your opponent to sleep with just one little tap, no problems, man.'

School had one disadvantage. I was two classes higher than my age group and so friends were hard to make. The kids of my own age thought of me as a sort of freak and in fact, with my early school background and now my prison experience, I was a lot tougher than any of them. Doc and the jaw incident had made me somewhat of a celebrity but I kept mostly to myself, being a shy kid and the smallest in my class. I acquired a reputation for superiority without having to earn it and so was left pretty much alone. I wasn't aggressive, and when a challenge came from a boy called John Hopkins and his partner Geoffrey Scruby, supposedly the two toughest kids in my class, I tried to avoid the fight they demanded, mostly because I was arrogant enough to believe that my status as future world welterweight champion made it inappropriate for me to be a street fighter. The Judge and even the jury had been so much tougher than these two that it never occurred to me actually to be frightened of them. The English-speaking kids at school had no idea of my boxing or prison background, as the small contingent of Afrikaans kids in the school seldom mixed with the English and almost never spoke with them, other than to challenge them to fight. The two ten-year-olds badgered me for some days and so I took the problem to Geel Piet, who immediately understood my dilemma.

'Small boss, it is always like this. This is what you must do. You must make them feel you are scared. Tell them, no way man. Tell them you don't want to fight. Let them get more and more cheeky, more and more brave. Even let them push you around. But always make sure this happens when everyone is watching. Then after a few days they will demand to fight you and they will name a time and a place. Try to look scared when you agree. You understand?' Geel Piet held me by the shoulders and looked me straight in the eyes. 'More fights are lost by underestimating your opponent than by any other way. Always remember, small baas, surprise is everything.'

It happened just as he said, a constant badgering during break, then a few pushes in front of everyone. Protests from me that I didn't want to fight. Finally a demand that I be behind the bioscope after school where I could choose either of them to fight.

When I got to the small yard behind the town cinema where all the official school fights took place, it was packed, with at least fifty kids crowded around John Hopkins and Geoffrey Scruby. All of them were English-speaking with the exception of Snotnose Bronkhorst, who had somehow got wind of the fight. To my surprise he stepped up to me and said in Afrikaans, 'I'm here to be your second, these are all Rooineks, you can never tell what they'll do.'

I looked at him in surprise. 'I'm also a Rooinek.'

'Yes I know man, but you're a Boer Rooinek, that's different.'

I elected to fight Hopkins who seemed delighted as he was the bigger of my two tormentors and had not expected to be chosen.

The kids formed a ring and Snotnose, who didn't know a lot of English, simply said, 'Okay! Make quiet! Fight!'

Hopkins threw a haymaker at me and missed by miles and I landed a hard blow to his ribs. He looked surprised and shook his head and came rushing in again swinging at my head. I ducked in under his punch and caught him hard on the nose. He stopped dead in his tracks and brought his hand up to his face. I hit him with a left and then a right to the solar plexus and to my astonishment he started to cry.

'All over!' Snotnose held up my hand as Hopkins, sniffing and thoroughly humbled, walked back into the crowd. I pointed to Geoffrey Scruby. 'Your turn now, Scruby,' I said, feeling a rush of adrenalin as I saw his fear.

'I'm sorry, Peekay,' he said softly. I had won. Just as Geel Piet said. Suddenly the crowd loved me. And I liked the feeling a lot.

Then Snotnose stepped up.

'Does any of you blêrrie Rooineks want to fight him?' he asked. There was complete silence and nobody stirred, not even the bigger kids. 'You're all yellow, you hear!' he snarled, then he turned slowly and looked at me with a grin on his face. I grinned back. He seemed an unlikely ally but he had stood by me. 'Okay then, I will,' he said. There was a murmur of apprehension through the crowd. They were clearly shocked at the idea, I must say I was pretty shocked myself.

'It's not fair. You're much bigger than him,' Geoffrey Scruby said. 'And older,' someone else shouted.

'Shurrup, man, or I fight you.' Snotnose walked up to Scruby and stabbed him in the chest with his forefinger. Then he turned and squared up to me.

It had been four months since we'd first met in the ring and he'd learned a fair bit about boxing in the meantime. I tried to stay out of his way, dancing around him, making him miss. But he hit me a couple of times and it hurt like blazes. I was connecting more often than he was, aiming my blows carefully, but I knew it was only a matter of time. *First with your head then with your heart, first with your head then with your heart*, Hoppie's words drummed through my brain as I tried to stay alive. Snotnose had tried to come in close on one or two occasions, but soon learned that this evened things up. At close range I was much the better boxer. So he stood his distance and picked his shots, knowing that a big punch had to get through sooner or later. All I could do was to try to make him miss. The kids, now on my side, were yelling their heads off trying to reach me with their encouragment. But I think they all knew the Boer was too tough and that the outcome was inevitable.

'Come closer, Boer bastard. Are you scared or something?' I taunted. Snotnose stopped in his tracks and his eyes grew wide. With a roar of indignation he bore down on me. I stepped aside at the last second and he missed knocking me over. As he turned to come back at me his head was lowered so it was on a level with mine. He had his back to the bioscope wall and I had mine to the crowd. I stepped in, and using both hands grabbed him by the shirtfront and gave him a perfectly timed Liverpool Kiss. The blow was so perfect I felt nothing. Snotnose simply sat on his bum, completely dazed. He just sat there in the dirt quite unable to comprehend what had happened. The crowd hadn't seen it either. They were behind me and my hands flying up to grab his shirtfront must have looked like a two-fisted attack. Forever afterwards it was retold that way; 'Then Peekay said, "Come closer, you Boer bastard," and with two dazzling punches to the jaw he knocked Snotnose Bronkhorst out.'

To my surprise Snotnose started to sniff and then got up unsteadily and made his way through the crowd and down the side of the building. He stopped halfway down the alley and shouted in Afrikaans, 'I'll get you back for this, you Rooinek bastard!' The English kids jeered as he walked away, but I knew better. One doesn't allow a Boer to lose face and expect to get away with it. Though, to my amazement, even Snotnose came to believe that he had been punched.

After the fight with Hopkins and Snotnose Bronkhorst my status at school improved immeasurably. While there were no more than sixty Afrikaans pupils, the sons and daughters of Noordkaap miners, farmers, men who worked in the saw mills at Francinos Rust and the warders' kids, they tended to be bigger than the English kids and much more aggressive. Most of the English boys had at some time or another suffered at the hands of one of the Boers. I was seen as being the one kid who had successfully fought back and won. A single victorious ship on an ocean of defeat.

Occasionally a Boer boy of roughly my size would cross the lines to challenge me and after school the back of the bioscope building would be packed with kids. The Boer kids on one side and the English on the other with my opponent and myself sandwiched in between. The prison guys formed a clique of their own, not sure where they belonged but seemingly glad when I won. Geel Piet was a good coach and, as I was never matched with one of the prison kids, my superior boxing skill allowed me to win. Whereupon a bigger Boer kid would challenge one of the English boys of roughly the same size and usually manage to beat him, which restored the racial status quo.

The prison kids explained that it was acceptable to be beaten by me as I was a sort of honorary Boer who spoke the taal and was also one of them. That came first. Even Snotnose left me alone unless we were sparring in the gym when he would go all out to try and hurt me.

This position of semi-neutrality had a great many advantages. In times of war there always has to be a go-between, someone whom both sides are prepared to trust. I was accepted by everyone as a brain and so I ended up doing the negotiation between the Boers and the English, often sorting out differences, arranging sides for rugby or *kleilat,* marble contests and *bok-bok,* an exceedingly rough game based on strength and endurance which the Boers, despite having fewer boys to choose from, usually won.

With some forty kids of my own age I was now undisputed leader, a situation I must confess I found to my liking. Being somebody after being nobody for so long was a heady experience but I also found it, on occasion, a bit onerous. Fights had to be settled, bullying stopped and the small kids set straight when they did things wrong. And then there was the tobacco crisis.

The tobacco crop on Marie's farm failed. This left a period of three months when the curing shed was empty. Marie kept apologising for this, as though it were somehow her fault; the more my granpa protested that he didn't mind the more guilty she seemed to become. By this time Geel Piet had become undisputed quartermaster for the prison. To tobacco we had added sugar, salt and a letter-writing business which was getting news in and out of the prison to and from all over South Africa. Postal orders would come in from outside contacts. Prisoners would order sugar, salt and tobacco, and Geel Piet would add thirty per cent to the groceries and charge threepence a cigarette. Tobacco was by far the greatest luxury because it was rationed due to the war. It was, of course, unavailable to the casual purchaser and impossible for an eight-year-old to buy under any circumstances. The little I brought in leaf form was carefully rolled into slim cigarettes. A single cigarette in a week of hard labour was a luxury beyond the imagination of the average prisoner. Somehow I understood how such a small thing as a cigarette, a tablespoon of sugar or a teaspoon of salt made the difference between hope and despair. A prisoner with a cigarette safely stashed in a used .303 cartridge case up his anus considered himself rich. These cartridge cases were highly prized; they were after all, in conjunction with his anus, the only private storage space a prisoner had. We kids gathered them from the rifle range at the army camp and they were the only item which Geel Piet actually gave away; as the prisoner's pantry they were essential to his business.

Letters were becoming a big thing at the prison and Doc wrote most of them as Geel Piet dictated to him. The little man could remember the contents of entire letters, together with the addresses of a dozen or more black prisoners at a time. Doc would write them at night. He would then write out a sheet of music theory for my homework and attach the letters to the back of it. Any search would have quickly revealed them but Doc was not a naturally cunning man and I think in his mind he regarded my music book as somehow, like the Steinway, above the possibility of question.

The letters were much of a muchness, men not accustomed to writing are apt, in any language, to reduce their words to simple formalities such as telling their families they were all right and enquiring after the health and welfare of the wife and kids, all the small, important human things that make us all, in the end, exactly the same. Some would include a request for money, although most knew this to be impossible and were too proud to impose such a burden on their families. It was not unusual for a family not to know that a husband had been arrested or where he was detained. He had simply disappeared and was often sent to a prison some distance from the place of his arrest. To trace him without the co-operation of the police was nearly impossible and so the letters provided a vital link in the spiritual welfare of the prisoners.

Mrs Boxall acted as postmistress and I must say she ran a pretty slick operation. The letters would be dropped in after school. Using the large square stamp used for marking the inside covers of books and which said: BARBERTON MUNICIPAL LIBRARY, de Villiers St, Barberton, we stamped a blank envelope, attached a postage stamp to it and included it in the original letter with instructions to the receiver to use it as the return envelope. We also wrote the name of the sender on the inside of the return envelope. This was done because we often received letters which started, *Dear Husband* and carried no other identification. Finally Mrs Boxall or I would address the outgoing envelope and send it off.

She explained these elaborate precautions to me. 'The world is full of sticky beaks. If we get a lot of letters addressed to the library in primitive handwriting, the postmaster just might smell a rat. I've been sending out overdue notices to country members for years which include return addressed envelopes using the library rubber stamp, so he won't suspect a thing.' And he didn't. The system worked perfectly and returned letters were taken into the prison and locked away in Doc's piano stool, to which only he and I had a key, though I'm sure Geel Piet could have picked the lock any time he chose to do so.

The money prisoners received from outside was generally in the form of a postal order for two shillings. As all incoming mail was opened by Mrs Boxall, she cashed the postal orders and put the money back into the envelopes and wrote the names of the recipients on the front. I pasted the envelope back together using the large pot of library glue and a slip of rice paper to cover the slit where the envelope had been carefully opened using Mrs Boxall's letter knife. The knife had a handle striped red and white like a barber's pole, and on the blade on one side was written, Have you written to your sweetheart? and on the other, A souvenir from Brighton 1924. I used to wonder who had Mrs Boxall for a sweetheart, but I think I already knew it was nobody.

And so a regular mail system in and out of the prison was established with Mrs Boxall cheerfully paying for the stamps and stationery. She would often sit and read a letter to one of the prisoners from a wife, written by someone who could write in English, and as she read it to me the tears would roll down her cheeks. The letters were mostly three or four lines, often in a huge, uncontrolled childlike hand.

My Husband Mafuni Tokasi,

How are you? The children are well. We have no money only this. The baas says we must go from this place. There is no work and no food. The youngest is now two years. He looks same like you. We have no other place to go.

Your wife Buyani

A postal order for two shillings in the letter meant that the whole family might not have eaten for two days or more. Mrs Boxall would wipe her eyes and say her conscience was quite clear and even if she was arrested she knew she was jolly well doing the right thing. She badgered friends and people coming into the library for clothes and these she sent off to needy families, even sometimes sending off a postal order of her own to a prisoner's family. She referred to prisoners as 'Innocents, the meat in the ghastly sandwich between an uncaring society and a vengeful State'. Her code for these families simply became the word 'sandwich'. 'We need more clothes for the sandwiches,' or 'Here's a poor sandwich for whom we'll have to find half a crown.' She kept a forty-four-gallon drum in the library which had a six-inch wide slot running almost the width of its lid like a huge money box. On the side was written: Cast-off clothes for the Sandwich Fund. People would bring lots of stuff and no one ever asked what the Sandwich Fund was.

'People feel they ought to know, so they don't dare ask,' she would say. She once told me that the sandwich was named after the Earl of Sandwich, who was a terrible gambler and because he was always so busy gambling he had no time to take meals. To overcome the problem his butler had made him two hunks of bread with something in between them. These were the first sandwiches. 'If anyone ever asks we'll say it's the famous Earl of Sandwich Fund for the poor. That ought to shut them up, don't you think, Peekay?'

Eventually someone must have asked, because the Earl of Sandwich Fund became the most social of all the war effort funds in Barberton. Even more important than knitting socks for prisoners of war. At the Easter and Christmas fête held in Coronation Park, Mrs Boxall and I ran a sandwich stand where cakes and other delicacies donated by the town's leading families were sold. My mother sent pumpkin scones baked by Dee and Dum who were also allowed to work on the stand. Mother made two identical pinnies and caps for them and they worked from dawn until dusk laying out cakes on the trestle tables and cutting and buttering bread and making sandwiches.

Because I was on the boxing squad and regarded as one of the prison kids, the wives of the warders baked for days for the sandwich stand and gloated when their cakes and cookies were the first to go. Boer baking was generally superior to that of the town's leading socialites. The rather snobbish Earl of Sandwich Fund sandwich stand earned enough to pay for the entire mailing system and to send money and clothing to a great many destitute families.

When the tobacco crisis came we solved it through the Earl of Sandwich Fund. Mrs Boxall sent a note to the headmaster of our school requesting that children bring in cigarette butts from home. She even managed to get the butts from the sergeants' mess at the army camp. Everyone assumed the re-cycled tobacco was going to the prisoners of war as Mrs Boxall simply referred to them as prisoners. Some kids brought half-packets of unsmoked cigarettes from a parent's precious ration, a sacrifice to the war effort. I took half a packet of smokes to Geel Piet, who thought all his Christmases had come at once. The bags of butts were taken to Doc's cottage where Dee and Dum, their noses masked by a dish towel, spent Sunday afternoon shredding the week's tobacco supply. Geel Piet never had it so good. When the new crop came from Marie's farm, it was with some dismay that he was forced to switch back to straight tobacco leaf.

What I didn't know was that little by little the prisoners had pieced it all together and I had been given the credit for everything. I was enormously surprised, when one day I passed a gang of prisoners who were digging a large flower bed in the Town Hall gardens, to hear the chanter who was calling the rhythm so the picks all rose in unison and fell together, change his song at my approach.

'See who comes towards us now,' he sang. 'Tell us, tell us,' the rest of the work gang chanted back. 'It is he who is called the Tadpole Angel,' the leader sang. 'We salute him, we salute him,' they chorused.

I glanced around me to see whom they were singing about, but there was no one to be seen. The warder, who recognised me, obviously didn't know Zulu. He called out to me, 'How things going, man?' and I replied, 'Very good, thanks.' The warder, who was bored, obviously wanted me to stop for a chat.

'He who is a mighty fighter and friend of the yellow man,' the leader continued. 'The Tadpole Angel, the Tadpole Angel,' the chorus replied, their picks lifting on the first Tadpole Angel and coming down on the second. I realised with a shock that they were talking about me.

'I hear the lieutenant is going to let you fight in the under-twelve division in the Lowveld Championships in Nelspruit this weekend.'

'Ja, I'll be the smallest, but he thinks I'll be okay.'

'We thank him for the tobacco, the sugar and the salt and for the letters and the things he sends to our people far away.' 'From our hearts, from our hearts,' came the chorus.

'Nine is not very old, man, eleven can be blêrrie big with a Boer kid.'

I shrugged my shoulders. 'I am ten in two weeks.' I was trying to hide my embarrassment at the salutation going on around us.

'Ja, man, and the kid you fight will be most likely twelve in two weeks,' he said gloomily.

'I have to go, I'm late for the library.' I wanted only to get away from the chanting of the prison gang.

'You'll be okay, man, I seen you sparring, you fast as buggery.' He looked at me closely and grinned, 'You is a funny bloke, Peekay. Now why you blushing like mad suddenly, hey?'

'He is the sweet water we drink and the dark clouds that come at last to break the drought,' the leader sang. Up came the picks, 'Tadpole Angel.' Down they went in perfect unison, 'Tadpole Angel. We salute him, we salute him.' I started to run towards the library and broke out in a sweat, my embarrassment consuming me.

I tackled Geel Piet about the matter the next morning and he admitted that this was my name. 'It is a great compliment, small baas. For them you are a true angel.'

Doc was listening, as Geel Piet and I now spoke in English when we were with him. 'Ja, and for you we are all angels, Geel Piet.' He chuckled. 'You are a rich man I think, ja?'

Geel Piet made no attempt to deny it. 'Big baas, it is always like so in a prison. If I am discovered I will be killed, so I must have something for risking my life. Thirty per cent is not so much, in Pretoria and Johannesburg it is fifty per cent, in Robben Island and Pollsmoor it is sixty per cent.'

'I think you are a skelm, Geel Piet, but we will say no more.' Doc, like Mrs Boxall, had come to realise how important the letters were and how the small amount of contraband made life bearable for men who were shown no compassion and whose diet of mealie meal and a watery stew of mostly cabbage and carrots, with an occasional bit of gristle floating on the surface, was only just sufficient to sustain them though not sufficient for the brutally hard work on the farms or the saw mills or the granite quarries. He had also come to accept the role Geel Piet played in the distribution system, knowing that without it chaos would ensue. 'Inside all people there is love, also the need to take care of the other man who is his brother. Inside everyone is a savage, but there is also happening tenderness and compassion.' Doc sighed and took out his bandanna and wiped his face as though trying to wipe the prison atmosphere from his skin. 'When man is brutalised in such a place like this, always he is looking for small signs. The smallest sign that someone is worried for him is like a fire on the dark mountain. When a man knows somebody cares he keeps some small place, a corner maybe of his soul clean and lit.'

While the food allocated for each prisoner was insufficient to keep a man doing hard physical labour, whoever hired a gang was expected to supply a meal at noon. It was this meal which kept the prisoners alive, for the regulations required it to be a vegetable and meat stew consisting of eight ounces of meat per prisoner and a pound of cooked mealie pap. I sometimes heard the warders discuss a scam whereby they tried to get a contractor to cut the rations in half, pay the warder ten shillings and save himself ten shillings. This only worked when gangs were hired for short periods, otherwise the men soon grew too weak to work. It was a big risk. Lieutenant Smit rotated warders so they had a different gang each week and couldn't set up a scam. The prison authorities depended on this one good meal a day from outside so they could cut rations on the inside. Although, I must say, Geel Piet told me this story and so it is not necessarily the entire truth. If a warder was caught in a scam he was not only dismissed but drafted into the army. Nobody in the boxing squad ever tried a scam, they were all Lieutenant Smit's men and, even more than the good musicians, were considered special, seldom having to go out with gangs and mostly getting guard duty on the day shift.

While no more than a quarter of the prisoners were Zulus, they held the highest status in the prison. Work songs were mostly composed in Zulu, and it was always a Zulu who called the time and set the working pace. Zulu is a poetic language and while many songs are traditional, the ability to create spontaneous new lyrics to capture a recent incident or pass information on was almost always handled by a Zulu prisoner whose gift for poetry was greatly respected.

Even among the old lags this method of passing on information was used. When a warder spoke an African language in this part of the world it was seldom Zulu, more likely to be Shona, Shangaan or Swazi, and even these would only be spoken by warders who came from farms. Townsfolk do not learn an indigenous African language other than Afrikaans and sometimes a language developed for use in the mines, known as Fanagalo, which is a mixture of several African languages as well as Afrikaans and English.

I asked Geel Piet why the word 'Angel' was prefaced with the word 'Tadpole'. At first he seemed not to know, or at least pretended not to, but I understood enough of Zulu naming to know that nothing is accidental and a name is chosen carefully so that it is a good description of status or of some characteristic which unmistakably belongs to the recipient.

For instance, Klipkop did not know that his nickname was 'Donkey Prick'. This came about from his habit of using a long rubber truncheon which he used with the least excuse. Most warders used their fists on prisoners. Their logic for doing so was quite simple, punishment administered with the fist was unofficial or, as the warders called it, friendly persuasion, while the truncheon was used when reports needed to be made. Klipkop was the exception, as heavyweight champion of the Lowveld he had to take good care of his hands, so he took to using the donkey prick for casual punishment. As he was also complaints officer it didn't much matter. 'A man like me can't afford to break a pinkie or something on some stinking black bastard's kop,' he would explain defensively, for even outside the prison a man was expected to use his fists on a Kaffir, reserving the sjambok for serious misdemeanours.

I recall walking down a long winding passage in the interior of the prison administration building where half a dozen old lags could always be found on their knees, their kneecaps swathed in polish rags, as they shone an already immaculate corridor floor. Long before we even sighted them I could hear one of them sing out, 'Work hard and keep your heads down, Donkey Prick is coming,' and back would come the chorus, 'Donkey Prick, Donkey Prick.' As we passed, each prisoner would stop polishing briefly, and bringing his hands together in a gesture of humility would smile and say, 'Good morning baas, good morning small baas.'

Knowing there was some reason for 'Tadpole' before 'Angel' I persisted in questioning Geel Piet about it. 'It is like this, small baas. The professor is known as Amasele (the Frog), because he plays his peeano at night when the prison is quiet. To the Zulus the frog makes always the loudest music at night, much louder than the cricket or the owl. So it is simple, you see. You are the small boy of the frog, which makes you a Tadpole.' It was a perfect piece of Zulu naming logic.

THIRTEEN

While Geel Piet was growing rich and even seemed to be getting a little pot belly, he had also become indispensable to the boxing squad. He maintained the gym, organised the laundry and even had the blue and yellow boxing singlets and white trunks made in the prison workshop. But most importantly his knowledge of boxing was encyclopaedic and he was a demanding and resourceful coach. The squad kids had been turned into clever boxers, our natural aggression combined with real skill. From the under fifteen division down to the under twelve, the Barberton Blues hadn't lost a fight in two years.

How I got my first real fight was a matter of sheer luck. The championships in Nelspruit were in early August, only days before my tenth birthday, and I had tried to persuade anyone who would listen that ten was almost eleven and that one year wasn't much to have to forfeit. But Lieutenant Smit wasn't the sort of man who changed his mind and nobody, least of all me, was willing to petition him on my behalf. In fact the two under twelves, Snotnose Bronkhorst and Fonnie Kruger, were almost twelve and therefore two years my senior, and being Boer kids were much bigger.

Geel Piet claimed he saw intelligence and speed in me that more than made up for my lack of size. He was a fanatic about footwork. 'You must learn to box with your feet, small baas. A good boxer is like a dancer, he is still pretty to watch even if you look only at his feet.' He taught me how to position myself so the full weight of my body was thrown behind a punch and, despite my size and my speed, my punches were capable of gaining respect from a bigger opponent. 'If they do not respect your punch they simply keep going until they knock you down, man. A boxer must have respect.'

I longed to have a real fight against an unknown opponent. In two years I had never missed a day of boxing and I had worked with all my heart and soul for the moment when I could climb into a boxing ring with real people watching and an opponent whose every blow, unlike those of my sparring partners, could not be anticipated.

On the Monday of the week of the championships Snotnose didn't turn up at the gym. After the session Lieutenant Smit called Geel Piet over and they talked earnestly for quite a time, every so often looking in my direction. Finally Geel Piet came over to me. He was trying hard to keep the smile off his face. 'Ag man, I'm a heppy man today, small baas. You want to know why?'

'They going to let you out of jail?' I said.

He laughed, 'No, never no more. I'm heppy here, man. I got my own stable of boxers, I got a good scam going. I will die heppy in this place.'

'What then?'

He bent down so his face was only inches from my own. His breath smelt foul. 'You got your first fight, man! Small baas, Bronkhorst he is sick with the yellow disease, you got his place.'

I couldn't believe my ears. Snotnose had jaundice which had been going around the school. I went to hug Geel Piet, but he quickly sidestepped. 'No, no small baas, the lieutenant will come over and beat me.' He grinned. 'Today this black bastard is too heppy to have his nose busted. Better go over quick, man, and thank the lieutenant. Make quick or maybe he changes his mind, hey?'

I ran over to where Lieutenant Smit was talking to Klipkop, and stood and waited. They ignored me for a long time and then the lieutenant said in a brusque voice, 'What is it, Peekay?'

'Thank you for the fight, Lieutenant Smit,' I stammered. 'I will try my hardest.'

He massaged his knuckles. 'That won't be enough, you're going to get your head knocked in, but it will do you good. Nobody should win their first fight.' He turned and walked away.

Geel Piet told me to bring my tackies in the next morning so they could be properly cleaned for me to wear at the fight. Using a piece of string he measured my chest and my waist. When I got home after school I told Dee and Dum my tackies should be put next to my school satchel so I wouldn't forget them, as Geel Piet needed to clean them. Dum got up quietly from where she was sitting on the floor at my feet while I drank a cup of coffee. She returned a few moments later with my tackies. They had been scrubbed and were spotless. 'Who does this yellow man think he is?' she asked. 'Does he think we let our baas go around in dirty things?' She and Dee were clearly hurt. I had to go to some lengths to explain that Geel Piet did all the things for the boxers and that now I was one of the squad he would do the same for me. 'He will not wash your clothes or clean your tackies,' Dee said. 'It is a woman's work and we will look after the clothes of him who belongs to our own *kraal*,' Dum added.

I wasn't at all sure how my mother would take the news of my inclusion in the squad. Boxing was never mentioned, and as far as she was concerned my early morning journey to the jail was in order to take piano lessons. She had been very busy of late with a commission from a Johannesburg shop to make three ball gowns and her Singer machine could be heard whirring away late at night. I knocked and entered the sewing room. It seemed full of a plum-coloured taffeta evening gown which was almost finished. My mother rose and held it against her body and she looked just how I imagined Cinderella must have looked when she went to the ball. The neckline plunged in a deep vee-line and the sleeves were puffed. The skirt billowed from the narrow waist and, as she moved, the taffeta caught the light and rustled in a most expensive and provocative way.

'Such an extravagance, I can't imagine where they found the material for this in the middle of the war.' She kicked at the skirt and it billowed out to reveal a second layer of net in a peacock blue.

'You look beautiful,' I said, not thinking to flatter her.

My mother laughed, and reaching for a cloth-padded hanger proceeded to hang the dress up on a rod protruding from the wall. Even away from her body the dress had a life of its own, filling the small sewing room with glamour. 'That's the trouble with the things of the devil, they are often sorely tempting and very pretty,' she said with a sigh.

I had forgotten for a moment that dances were very high on the Lord's banned list. My heart sank. If dancing was frowned upon by the Lord, what would he think of a boxing match? I immediately consoled myself with the knowledge that, as far as I knew, God was a man, and therefore He'd obviously like boxing a lot better than dancing.

'You've come about the boxing, haven't you?' my mother said, resuming her seat at the sewing machine.

'Yes, Mother.' I was unable to conceal the surprise in my voice.

'Yes well, Lieutenant Smit, a very nice man, came to see me this morning, though I'm not at all sure I liked what he had to say. I've spoken to your grandfather about it and I made it the subject of my quiet time with the Lord after lunch. I have to tell you He gave me no clear guidance on the matter, though your grandfather seems to think it can't do you any harm.' Her head jerked back in a sudden gesture of annoyance. 'Oh, how I do wish you'd stick to the piano. It's quite clearly the Lord's wish that you do so or He wouldn't have made it possible for you to learn under such trying circumstances. Lieutenant Smit seems to think you have a natural talent as a boxer which is more than the professor has admitted about your music.'

'Doc has said my Chopin is coming along extra good,' I said, mimicking him ever so slightly.

My mother was sewing a press stud onto what looked like a cummerbund for the taffeta dress, and she now looked up at me. 'I do wish you wouldn't call him by that silly name. Heaven knows this town has few enough nice people and, after all, he is a real professor of music and merits your respect. His being German is simply unfortunate. I suppose we'd all talk German with a funny accent if Hitler won the war. You'll have to sleep on Friday afternoon if you're going to be up that late on Saturday night.'

I jumped with joy. 'Thank you, thank you, thank you,' I cried and gave her a hug and a kiss.

'I'm not at all sure the Lord approves,' she said, but I could see she was glad I kissed her. 'Run along now.'

On Friday morning, after callisthenics, Lieutenant Smit called us all together around the ring. 'I want to tell you first a few things,' he said. He turned to the five kids standing to one side with Geel Piet. 'The rules for under fifteen says, you get knocked down, you out. No use getting up, man, you finished and *klaar.* So don't get knocked down, hey.' He indicated Klipkop who was standing on his right. 'Sergeant Oudendaal is a semi-pro so is not allowed to fight, so Gert will fight in the heavyweight division and Sergeant Oudendaal and me will be your seconds. You do as you told, man, and no monkey business, you hear? Don't go thinking you know better. You all know the rules, the most clean blows landed wins, that's how Geel Piet here taught you. The rest of you in the weight divisions just fight your normal fight, if you need to change tactics I'll tell you, man.' He was turning to leave the ring when his eye caught something at his feet. He stooped down and picked up a small blue singlet, on the front of which in yellow were the letters BB, standing for Barberton Blues. He turned the singlet around to face us; on the back, written in neat cut-out letters, we saw PEEKAY. 'Welcome, Peekay,' he said and everyone clapped. 'Welcome to the Barberton Blues.' There was a roaring in my head and my throat ached as I choked back the tears. Lieutenant Smit bent down again and picked up a pair of blue shorts with a yellow stripe down the side, and bundling the shorts and singlet together he threw them at me. They parted company in mid-air and my left hand shot out to grab the singlet while my right fetched the shorts out of the air. 'The little bugger is fast and uses both hands well. I only wish he carried another fifteen pounds,' he said as he climbed from the ring.

I showed Doc my singlet and shorts and he seemed very pleased for me, and I told him about the three rounds. 'Do you think you can go three rounds with Mr Chopin, Peekay?' he asked. I nodded, determined to show Doc that his precious music was not taking a backseat, although I suspect he knew that my mind was more on staying on my feet and not getting knocked down than on the *étude* with which I was trying to come to grips. Out of the corner of my eye I saw Geel Piet enter. I knew that if he wanted to he would come in unnoticed, that he had worked out the exact angle to enter so he was seen without disturbing anyone. It was unusual for him to come into the hall at this time. I always put the day's mail in the piano seat and later, when he came in to polish the Steinway, he would retrieve it. We had decided the three of us should never be seen together near the postbox. I glanced over to where he stood pretending to clean a window, a bucket at his feet. Finally Doc noticed him and raised his hand for me to stop.

'You must not come when we practise, that is the rule,' he admonished. The battered little man quickly picked up the bucket and trotted towards us. Doc looked annoyed. 'What is it?'

'Please, baas, it is very important, baas.' Geel Piet put down the bucket and withdrew a parcel wrapped in a piece of cloth. 'The people have put money together and in the bootmaker's we have made for the small baas a present.' He opened the cloth to reveal a pair of boxing boots. I gasped. They were beautiful, the black leather brought to a soft sheen and the soles the bluish white of raw new leather. 'It is from all the people, a present for the Onoshobishobi Ingelosi, it is from all of us so you will fight a mighty fight tomorrow, small baas.'

I leapt from the piano stool, unable to contain my delight. 'It is why I asked you for the tackies, small boss.' He gave me a big, toothless smile. 'It was to know the size.'

I quickly pulled my school boots off and put the boxing boots on. The leather was soft and pliant, and the boots felt light as a feather and fitted perfectly. 'Geel Piet, they are the nicest present anyone ever gave me, honest.'

'They are from all the people, it is their way to thank you.'

Without warning he dropped to his knees, and using the cloth in which the boxing boots had been wrapped he started to polish the floor around my feet. Some instinct in him which never rested had sensed danger. A good five seconds elapsed before the warder actually stood at the entrance to the hall.

He was a new sergeant whom we'd only met once in the mess. His name was Borman and he had been transferred down to the Lowveld from Pretoria Central because of his wife's asthma.

He stood, one hand holding the door frame. 'Professor, the Kommandant wants to see you, report to administration after breakfast you hear?' He turned to go, then caught sight of Geel Piet. 'Kom hier, Kaffir!' he rapped.

The little man jumped up and ran across the hall. 'Ja baas, I come baas,' he cried.

'What you doing in this place?' the warder demanded.

Doc bent down and picked up one of my school boots. 'The boy got some kak on his boots, he come to clean them.' He appeared to be scrutinising the sole of one of my boots. 'Ja this is so,' Doc said, waving the boot at the warder and then pointing to where Geel Piet had been cleaning the floor. 'Also some was on the floor when he walked in.'

Sergeant Borman grinned. 'Next time make the black bastard lick it clean, he is used to eating shit.' He turned to Geel Piet, 'That's right isn't it, Kaffir? You all eat each other's shit, don't you?'

Geel Piet had his head bowed and was standing to attention, though his thin, bandy legs, crossed with scars and blobbed with black scar tissue from past bush sores, didn't actually come together at the knees. 'No, baas,' he said softly. There was no fear in his voice, only a sort of resignation. He seemed to know what would happen next.

The warder reached out and grabbed him by his canvas shirt. 'When I say so, you say yes, understand? Now, do you eat shit, Kaffir?'

'Yes, baas,' Geel Piet replied.

'Loud! Say it loud, you shit-eating bastard!'

'YES, BAAS!'

'Yes, baas what?'

'Yes, baas, we eat each other's shit!'

The sergeant from Pretoria turned to us. 'There you are, Professor. I told you they eat each other's shit. Next time make him lick it up, it will be a proper treat for him.' He turned and walked away.

Geel Piet came padding over to us, his bare feet making hardly any sound on the sprung wooden floor. 'Thank you, big baas,' he said with a grin. 'He is right, man, in prison we all eat shit.' He turned to me as he picked up the bucket. 'Your feet, small baas, box with your feet, punch clean so it is a scoring shot. No clinches, that way a bigger boxer can push you over. Good luck, small baas, the people are with you.'

'Thank you, Geel Piet, tell the people I thank them.'

'Ag man, it is nothing, the people love you, you are fighting for them.' He was gone.

Doc cleared his throat to break the silence. 'Maybe now we can play Chopin, yes?'

I gave him a big hug. 'That sure was quick thinking, Doc.'

He chuckled. 'Not so bad for a brokink-down old piano player, ja?' He frowned suddenly. 'I wonder what wants the Kommandant?'

We were to leave for Nelspruit, a distance of some forty miles, at eight a.m. the following morning. Though I avoided having to rest on Friday afternoon, I had been ordered to bed at six o'clock. I woke as usual just before dawn and lay in bed trying to imagine the day ahead. What if I was beaten first off? How would I hide my despair? With seven Eastern Transvaal teams competing, I had to win twice to get to the final. I had never boxed six rounds in my life, and even if I got through them I would have to box another three in the finals! What if I lost concentration and the other kid pushed me over? Even if I was winning, I'd lose because I'd hit the canvas!

I couldn't stand the 'What ifs' any longer, and I quickly got out of bed and dressed and ran through the garden. In a little more than ten minutes I was on top of the hill sitting on our rock.

It was early spring and the dawn wind was cold, I shivered a little as I watched the light bleed into the valley and merge with the darkened town below me, smudging the darkness until the roofs and streets and trees were rubbed clean. The jacaranda trees were not yet in bloom but patches of bright red from spring-flowering flamboyant trees already dotted the town. I tried to think how Granpa Chook would have looked at the situation. He would have taken things in his stride, just like any other day. While Granpa Chook was a less important mentor now, he remained a sort of checkpoint in my life. A reference on how to behave in a tight spot. I thought of Hoppie too. If only Hoppie could have been there to see me. 'First with your head and then with your heart, Peekay.' I could almost hear his cheerful and reassuring voice.

After a while I felt much calmer. I made my way back down the hill as the sun began to rise. Some of the aloes, mostly the taller *Aloe ferox*, were showing early bloom. I watched as a ray of sunlight caught a tiny jewelled honeysucker as it hovered around a spray of orange aloe blossom. Its long hooked needle beak probed for nectar, the tiny bird's wings beating so fast they held it suspended in one spot, too fast even to make a blur in the surrounding air. I imagined being able to punch that fast, my opponent retelling the fight to someone else. 'I was still thinking about throwing a right when the welterweight champion of the world hit me three hundred times on the chin.' Even to me it sounded improbable.

When I got back to the house Dee and Dum had prepared breakfast, brown kaffircorn porridge, fried eggs and bacon. On the kitchen table stood my school lunch tin. After their day spent as purveyors of sandwiches to the Earl of Sandwich Fund at the Easter fete they regarded themselves as world authorities on the sandwich, and my school lunch was always a bit of a surprise. Grated carrot and jam was one of the combinations that would crop up once in a while, or avocado pear and peanut butter. I had drawn the line at onion and papaya, and gooseberry jam and Marmite was another variety struck off their culinary repertoire.

I wondered briefly what they'd packed to sustain me, hopefully for nine rounds of boxing, but refrained from looking. Until, unable to contain themselves, they opened the tin to show me six pumpkin scones neatly wrapped in greaseproof paper. 'We baked them last night, your favourite!' Dum said and I could see they were both very pleased with themselves.

I packed all my stuff into my school satchel, including my beautiful boxing boots which Dee had given another polish, even though they were spotless. At half-past seven I had already said my farewells to my granpa and my mother, and was sitting on the front wall waiting for the blue prison light utility which was to pick me up. I could have gone to the prison but Gert said, 'No problems, it's only a few minutes out of our way, save the energy for the ring!' Gert wasn't like the other warders. Indeed all the kids thought he was the best thing since sliced bread. He liked to help people and he once told me he only hit Kaffirs if they really did wrong. 'A Kaffir hurts also, maybe not like a white man, 'cause they more like monkeys, but they hurt also when you hit them.'

After breakfast when I had gone to bid my granpa goodbye I put the question to him about being knocked down so that even if I was winning the fight I would lose it. The usual tamping and puffing and lighting up took place. Finally, squinting into a haze of blue smoke he answered.

'I think you'd best do what I did in the Boer War.'

'What was that?' I asked anxiously.

'Why lad, run away as much as possible.'

That was the trouble with my granpa, the advice he gave when you needed it most wasn't always very useful.

I saw the blue prison ute coming up the hill with Gert at the wheel. Next to him someone sat reading a newspaper, I couldn't see who it was.

Gert stopped outside the gate. 'Jump in the back with the other kids, Peekay,' he said cheerfully. I climbed into the back of the ute, helped by one of the others. It was an exciting business all right as Gert changed gears and we pulled away. A fourteen-year-old called Bokkie de Beer was in charge and he told me no one was allowed to stand up. All the other kids were giggling and splurting into their hands as they looked at me.

'What's so funny?' I shouted above the sound of the wind and the roar of the engine. Bokkie de Beer pointed to the rear window of the driver's cabin. I followed his hand and there, framed in the window, wearing his unmistakable panama hat, was the back of Doc's head. I couldn't believe my eyes and all the kids fell about laughing at my astonishment. I just couldn't believe my good fortune.

It was the first time since my arrival by train three years earlier that I had left the small town. It was a perfectly clear, early spring morning as we travelled across the valley towards a row of distant hills. The thornveld and the flat-topped acacia had already broken into electric green leaf. In a month they would be a mass of tiny pom-poms that turned the valley into a sea of yellow and pink.

The road from Barberton was tarred all the way and by nine-thirty we'd reached Nelspruit. My wind-blown skin felt tight around the eyes and cheeks, and I was glad to get out of the back of the ute when we drew to a halt in a parking lot behind the town hall. I rushed to Doc's side to open the door for him. His blue eyes were shining and I think he was almost as excited as I was.

'We are together outside again, Peekay. It is goot, ja? Absoloodle.'

'How did you escape?' I asked clumsily.

He chuckled. 'With the permission of the Kommandant. That's what he wished to see me about after breakfast yesterday.' He saw me frown; we both knew the way of the prison system where nothing is given unless something is taken in return. Doc shrugged. 'It is not so much he wants. He wants only I should play a little Chopin when the brigadier comes from Pretoria next month.'

I knew how Doc felt about playing in public. He refused to play at any of the town concerts and had long since retired as a musician. While he overcame his fear when he triumphed at the Beethoven lunchtime recital in the market square, Doc was a perfectionist and it gave him great pain not to meet the standards he demanded for himself. When I told him Mrs Boxall had said there was no one in Barberton who didn't think he was the greatest pianist they had ever heard, he had replied, 'You must thank Madame Boxall for her kindness, but I am too old and too weak to inflict badly played Beethoven and Mozart on myself.'

'You should have said no!' I said.

'Tch-tch, Peekay, then I would not see you in your debut. One day I will say, I was there when the welterweight champion of the world made his boxing début. Absoloodle!'

'You still shouldn't have.'

'Beethoven yes, Mozart yes, Brahms yes, but Chopin I can still play enough not to tear myself to little bits. I will play Chopin to this Mr Brigadier. That is not so hard, ja.'

We entered the Town Hall through a back door and walked down a corridor until we reached a room which said Barberton *Bloue* on a piece of paper stuck on the door. The room smelt of dust and sweat, even though nobody had changed yet. Lieutenant Smit was standing against the far wall and next to him stood Klipkop.

'This is where you will change today, but not all at once, hey?' The room tittered. 'This morning are the preliminary fights for the kids and this afternoon for the weight divisions. Tonight, starting six o'clock, the finals. Nobody leaves the town hall and if I catch anyone drinking a beer, I'm warning you now, there'll be trouble. We come here to win and that is what we going to do! Okay, so what's our motto?'

'One for all and all for one,' we all shouted. Doc put his hand on my shoulder and I felt very proud. 'I wish Geel Piet was with us,' I whispered. The room emptied and Klipkop shouted for the kids to stay behind. Doc, who was in charge of first aid, left to fetch the towels and the first-aid kit from the parking lot but promised to be right back.

Klipkop grinned. 'Today, man, I'm Geel Piet.'

'Does that mean we can hit you and you can't hit back?' Bokkie de Beer said cheekily, and we all laughed.

Klipkop smiled. 'I will look after you and the lieutenant and me will be your seconds. You can all get changed now and I'll fetch you in fifteen minutes. Don't nobody go nowhere, you hear?'

I found a corner and took my boots from my book satchel and put them on first. All the kids crowded around. 'Where'd you get those, man?' Bokkie de Beer exclaimed. I had been too excited to think up an explanation.

'My, my granpa made them,' I stammered.

'Boy, you lucky having a bootmaker for your granpa,' Fonnie Kruger said.

'Well, he's not really a bootmaker, more a sort of gardener.'

'Well, he's blêrrie clever, that's all I can say,' Bokkie de Beer said enviously and the other kids seemed to agree with him.

I rolled my grey school socks down so they made a collar just above the boots. Then I put my lovely blue singlet on and the blue boxing shorts with the yellow stripe down the side. Geel Piet had sized the waist perfectly but the length was wishful thinking. The bottoms of the shorts went way past my knees. When I stood up the other four kids broke up. Maatie Snyman and Nels Stekhoven even rolled on the floor. I guess I must have looked pretty funny with my sparrow legs sticking out, but I also felt terribly proud.

Fonnie Kruger and myself were the first of the Barberton Blues to fight as we were in the under twelves, the most junior division. We waited for Klipkop and followed him into the Town Hall. Kids from other major towns in the Eastern Transvaal were standing in groups with adults, and they too were changed and ready. I looked around wondering whom among them I would have to fight.

Doc entered the hall and moved over to me. We sat on two chairs, slightly away, but within easy beckoning distance from the others. Doc held my hand and I think he was more nervous than I was. He had taken out his bandanna and was wiping his brow. 'I think examinations in the conservatorium in Leipzig, when I was so big as you, was not so bad as this, ja. Absoloodle.'

'I'll be okay, Doc. I'll dance and everything, just like Geel Piet says. Lieutenant Smit says I'm blêrrie fast, you'll see they won't hit me, for sure.'

'It's nice of you to say this, Peekay. But what happens when comes one big Boer and connects?'

I grinned, trying to make him feel better. I repeated Hoppie's comment. 'Ag man, the bigger they are the harder they fall.' I felt pretty corny saying it and I knew now why Hoppie had said it to me. He must have felt pretty corny too.

Doc groaned and buried his head in his red bandanna. 'Peekay, I want you should be very careful. In that ring are not nice people.' Just then Klipkop called me over and Doc squeezed my hand. 'You must use your feet to run away, Peekay. In my head I can hear only Wagner. No Mozart, only Wagner.'

Klipkop and Lieutenant Smit were standing with a large bald man with a big tummy who wore long white pants and a white singlet. A few feet from them stood two adults and a kid. The kid was quite a bit bigger than me though not as big as Snotnose. He wore a red singlet and in white on the front was the word Sabie. That was the town where Klipkop had his nooi, to whom he had recently become engaged.

The big man in the singlet looked at me and then at Lieutenant Smit. 'He is not very big. Are you sure you want him to fight?'

The lieutenant nodded. 'It will be good for him.'

The big man looked at the boy from Sabie and then looked doubtfully back at me. He turned to Lieutenant Smit. 'His opponent is eight inches taller and has probably got five inches more reach, man.'

'If I think he's getting hurt I'll pull him out.'

'I blêrrie well hope you know what you doing, man,' the big man said, shaking his head. The two men from Sabie were grinning and I could hear what they were saying inside their heads. They were glad their kid was going to get an easy fight first up.

Klipkop turned to me. 'This is Meneer de Klerk, Peekay. He is the referee and also the judge. He just came down from Pretoria last night.'

'Good morning, Meneer,' I said, sticking out my hand. The referee took it and shook it lightly.

'You got nice manners, son,' he said. Behind his back I could see one of the men pushing the kid from Sabie so he would do the same thing.

Meneer de Klerk turned and indicated a large wooden crate on the floor below the boxing ring. Inside the crate were at least fifty pairs of boxing gloves. 'I want ten-ounce gloves. I don't want to see no kid hurt. Pick your gloves and then show them to me, you understand.'

'We got our own gloves,' Lieutenant Smit said.

'Then bring them, let me see.'

'Us also,' said one of the men from Sabie and stepped forward holding out a pair of gloves.

Meneer de Klerk examined both sets of gloves and declared them suitable. 'Okay, glove up. We on in five minutes.' He turned to a man sitting at a table directly beside the ring. 'Five minutes, you hear?' The man nodded and consulted a large pocket watch in front of him. He also had a bell and was obviously the timekeeper.

Klipkop and Lieutenant Smit both worked on lacing me up. I felt very important as neither of them had ever actually supervised any aspect of my boxing before.

'Remember, Peekay, boxing is a percentage game. Just make sure you hit him clean and more times than he hits you. No clinches, in clinches he can throw you off your feet. Stay out of the corners, stay off the ropes.'

The man at the table rang the bell and we walked over to the ring. Klipkop helped me through the ropes, and then he and the lieutenant climbed in after me. There was a proper stool in the corner and Lieutenant Smit told me to sit on it. I felt a bit silly because the kid from Sabie was standing up and punching into the air, and I was sitting like a little kid on a chamberpot.

'Right! Both in the middle,' Meneer de Klerk called and climbed into the ring. 'What's your names?'

'Du Toit, Meneer.'

'Peekay, Meneer.'

'I want a clean fight, you hear? No clinches. When I say break, you break. No hitting below the waist or behind the head. One knock down and the fight is over. You understand, Peekay? Du Toit?'

'Ja, Meneer,' we both said.

'Right, when you hear the bell you come into the centre of the ring, touch gloves and start boxing. Good luck.'

I walked back to my corner and on Lieutenant Smit's instructions sat down. Because it was the first fight of the day, all the teams were gathered around the ring and there were even some people from the town watching. It was my first boxing crowd and my heart was beating. Du Toit was standing in his corner and he too was looking around. I don't think either of us wanted to make eye contact. Seen from my stool he seemed very big, but I had waited too long for this moment to be afraid.

The bell rang. 'Box him, Peekay, you hear,' Klipkop said as I jumped from the stool.

We touched gloves in the middle of the ring, and as he pulled away I darted in and snapped a left and a right to Du Toit's jaw. His eyes widened in surprise. I could see that the punches hadn't hurt him, but nevertheless my early aggression had caught him unawares and he looked surprised.

He was a good boxer and didn't lose his composure but circled around me. He threw a straight left which went over my shoulder and flew past my ear. I went in under the arm with a quick uppercut and caught him hard in the ribs. I heard him wince so I knew I'd hit him hard. He caught me with a right on the shoulder and spun me around. I anticipated the left coming at me and ducked under it and got another good body blow on exactly the same spot as before. His arms wrapped around me and I was in a clinch, which I wasn't supposed to be in. I hit him furiously in the ribs with both hands, but my blows were too close to be effective and I knew he could hold me as long as he liked.

'Break!' I heard the ref say, and as Du Toit's arms slackened I got right out of the way. For the rest of the round I let him chase me. I was much the faster boxer and had much better foot work. Towards the end of the round I could see by the way he set his feet which punch was going to come next. Just as the bell went I got inside with a short right and clipped him neatly on the point of the chin.

I had heard nothing during the fight and now realised that the crowd was making quite a noise, and that my name was being shouted in encouragement. At the end of the round there was a lot of clapping and one or two whistles.

'You done good, Peekay,' Klipkop said. Lieutenant Smit wiped my face with a towel. 'He's missing with the right cross, but not by much. Watch it, man. If that kid finds his range he's going to hurt you bad. Keep your chin buried in your shoulder, that way if he gets one through you'll take most of it on the shoulder.'

The bell went for the second round and I let Du Toit chase me around the ring. I think he must have been told to try to get me into a corner because he would work me carefully towards one but at the last moment I'd feint left and duck out right, and his right cross would miss by miles. But then I did it once too often and he caught me with a left uppercut in the gut and had it not been for the ropes behind me I might have gone down. He knew he'd hurt me and in his anxiety to capitalise was telegraphing his blows, trying for the big hit. All I could do was duck until I could use my feet to get out of trouble.

To my surprise, in the second half of the round he seemed to be tiring. He'd thrown a lot of punches, most of them landing on my gloves, though he did hit me a good body blow that hurt like hell. I began to move in quickly and pick him off. Towards the end of the round the crowd was beginning to laugh as I seemed to be able to hit him almost at will. A look of desperation had crept onto his face. I don't think I was hurting him much but I was making him very tired and very frustrated, just the way Geel Piet had said it must be done. The bell went and I was sure I had won the round.

'You don't have to hit him again to win,' Lieutenant Smit said. 'Just stay out of his way, you hear? Just counter punch, no attack. You going to win this clear, man, unless he cops you a lucky one.'

'You do like the lieutenant says, Peekay. You just stay out of trouble,' Klipkop added with a grin.

The bell went for the final round and we went into the centre of the ring and touched gloves. Du Toit must have had instructions to nail me because he kept rushing me, throwing wild punches. I'd nail him with a straight left or a right hook as he passed, but I was careful not to get set to throw a big punch. The crowd was laughing as I made him miss and I was beginning to feel pretty good. I had out-boxed him and hadn't been hurt, the bell would go any moment and I'd won. The right cross came at me and I couldn't move out of the way. It smashed into my shoulder and into my face and I felt as though I had walked into a telegraph pole. I felt myself going and grabbed at the ropes behind me to stop myself falling. The next blow came but I managed to get my head out of the way, then Du Toit threw another right and it just grazed my face. But my legs felt okay and my head had cleared. I ducked under a straight right and danced out of the way just as the bell went.

'Phew!'

Doc was at the ringside jumping up and down. 'Eleven out of ten. Absoloodle!' he yelled at me. It was the happiest moment of my life.

I had started to move back to my corner when Meneer de Klerk called us both into the centre of the ring. We shook hands and I thanked Du Toit for the fight but I think he knew he'd lost as his eyes brimmed with tears and he didn't reply. 'You got nice manners, you been taught right, Peekay,' Meneer de Klerk said again. Then he took us both by the hand and said: 'The winner three rounds to nothing is Gentleman Peekay!' He held my hand up, and the crowd clapped and laughed at my new name. The Barberton Blues all yelled and whistled.

'That was good,' Lieutenant Smit said. 'But it's early times, you were lucky, man, you got a palooka. When I tell you to stay out of the way you stay out of the way, you hear? That right cross nearly brained you, man. Two like that early in the next bout and we throw in the towel, you understand!'

I nodded, and tried to look contrite. As Klipkop pulled the big mitts off my hands I suddenly felt light, as though I was going to float away. It was a wonderful feeling. It was the power of one stirring in me. Nothing Lieutenant Smit said could dampen my spirits. I jumped down from the ring feeling ten feet tall.

Doc gave me a big hug, and then he held both my hands and we did a little jig which made me feel a bit silly but he was very happy. 'Peekay, I am very proud today! Absoloodle!' Then he stopped and reached into his pocket for his red bandanna and sniffed into it. He looked up, his blue eyes all watery. 'Such a dancer, already. Absoloodle.' I had never heard him say so many absoloodles before.

Fonnie Kruger won his fight against a kid from Boxburg and so did

Maatie Snyman in the under thirteens, Nels Stekhoven in the under fourteens and Bokkie de Beer in the under fifteens. I'm telling you, we were a pretty proud lot in the Barberton Blues, every one of us had advanced to the semis. Fonnie Kruger and I were both in the under twelve division; if we got through the semis we'd be in the final together. But our hopes were soon dashed. There was a kid from Lydenburg called Kroon who was the biggest eleven-year-old I had ever seen. He was at least a foot higher than me and twice as wide. He wasn't a boxer, but he polished off a kid from Nelspruit in the first round when he sat him on the canvas after about one minute. We instantly dubbed him Killer Kroon. We all got scared just looking at him and Bokkie said he was glad he was fighting in the under fifteen division and not in the under twelve.

Fonnie Kruger got Killer Kroon in the semis and managed to go one round before he was sat on his pants, seconds after the second round had begun. I think he was glad that it was all over. Killer Kroon had closed his right eye. 'It's like boxing a blêrrie gorilla,' he said when he climbed down from the ring.

Just before lunch I entered the ring again to fight a kid from Kaapmuiden. He was a square-built, nuggety sort of bloke and very strong around the shoulders but not a lot taller than me. It was the first time I had stood up to another boxer whose chin level wasn't above my head. It was a good fight and my speed saved me from taking the weight of his blows. He hit hard and straight, but I was able to move away as the punch came so the sting had gone out of it. Nevertheless he landed quite a lot of punches and was scoring well. Before the final round began Lieutenant Smit wiped my face.

'You're not doing enough to make certain of this fight. Watch his straight left, he keeps dropping his right glove after he's thrown the left. Get in under the blow and work him with both hands to the body. I want to make certain you got enough points.'

We touched gloves for the final round and Lieutenant Smit was quite right. The kid, whose name was Geldenhuis, threw his left and then curiously dropped his right. I went in underneath and got five or six good blows to the body before he pushed me away. The final bell went and the crowd chanted, 'Gentleman Peekay! Gentleman Peekay!' They were all Afrikaners and the English word obviously amused them. I thanked Geldenhuis who also thanked me. Then Meneer de Klerk announced for the second time that day, 'The winner in two out of three rounds, Gentleman Peekay!' The crowd laughed and clapped, and the Barberton Blues went wild.

Doc could hardly contain himself. 'Not even one scratch, black eyes not even one. Perfect, you should play Chopin so good as this, ja?' He laughed and handed me a towel. 'Lieutenant Smit says you must have a shower and change into your clothes again. Tonight, six o'clock we fight again.' He suddenly grew serious. 'Peekay, in the finals is a big Boer, you must dance very goot, in him is too much Wagner. You must box like a Mozart piano concerto, fast and light with perfect timing, ja?'

Doc found a small antechamber leading off the corridor in which there was a leather couch. After lunch he made me lie down. I was anxious to watch the adult preliminary fights and succumbed with ill grace. Despite the heat he threw a prison blanket over me, and to my surprise I fell asleep. It was five o'clock when he came to fetch me and I felt a little stiff and sore. He made me have a warm shower before I changed into my boxing things again. By the time we got back into the Town Hall it was almost six o'clock and the preliminaries were over. Bokkie de Beer said five of the Barberton Blues were through to the finals, including Gert who had had an easy and a hard fight, but was okay. That made nine of the fourteen Barberton Blues in the finals. I went over to Gert to congratulate him and he seemed pleased.

'Ag it wasn't too hard, Peekay. I think I got lucky. But like you, man, I got a Boer in the finals that's as big as a mountain, a super heavyweight. He won both his fights on knockouts in the first.'

'You got the speed, speed is everything,' I quoted Geel Piet.

'Not if he gets me in a corner,' Gert said solemnly.

'Then stay out of corners, man!' I said flippantly, but the advice was meant as much for myself as it was for him.

'You on soon, I've got my money on you, Peekay. You can do it, I'm telling you.' But I could hear him talking in his head and he was very, very worried about me.

Fonnie Kruger came over and said that Lieutenant Smit wanted me.

Lieutenant Smit and Klipkop were in earnest conversation with Meneer de Klerk and seemed not to notice my arrival. I stood and waited for them.

'The Boer kid has thirty, maybe forty pounds on yours. I don't like it. I don't like it one bit,' the referee was saying, shaking his head.

'You saw him in the other two fights. He hardly got touched, our kid's a good boxer,' Klipkop said.

'He's better than that. He's the best I've seen in a long time. But he's a midget compared to Kroon. Kroon dropped both his opponents in the first. That's a bad kid. I work with young boxers every day, I'm telling you, this kid is not a sportsman.' Meneer de Klerk threw his hands open in a gesture of reconciliation. 'There's plenty of time, he's only ten. Let the boy grow a bit, wait till next year. He's champion material, too good to spoil with a mismatch.'

I could see a hesitant look cross Lieutenant Smit's face. The voices going on inside his head were confused. My heart was going boom, boom, boom and I couldn't swallow; there was a huge aching lump in my throat. Then he cocked his head and squinted at the bald referee. 'I make you this promise, Meneer de Klerk. If my boy even looks like being hurt we throw in the towel. You don't know Peekay. That kid has worked three years for this fight. In three years he hasn't missed one training session. For two years he just fought the bag and the ball. I can't pull him out without giving him a chance.'

'I'll give him one round, Smit. If he even looks like being hit in the first round I'm giving the fight to Kroon on a TKO, you understand?'

Lieutenant Smit nodded his head, 'Ja, okay, you the ref, man.' He turned and saw me and I grinned at him as though to indicate I'd just arrived. They had to give me a go. I had to fight Kroon. Kroon was no bigger to me than Jackhammer Smit was to Hoppie. I could take him, I knew I could take him. 'We got to glove up now, Peekay,' Lieutenant Smit said as he took a glove from Klipkop and slipped it over my left hand.

I climbed into the ring and sat on the little stool and Killer Kroon also sat on his. When he sat down he didn't look as though he was on the potty. He stared directly at me. Shit, he was big! He had a grin on his face and I could hear his conversation to himself, 'I'm going to knock this little bugger out first round.'

'You got to catch me first, you bastard,' I said to myself. But I could feel his hugeness growing and beginning to fill the ring.

With the arrival of the townspeople for the finals, the Town Hall was at least half full. I had looked down on a bigger crowd when I played Chopin at the Barberton concert, but a boxing crowd is different, much more raw or something. I remembered Doc's words, 'You must box like a Mozart piano concerto.' In my head I could hear the way Doc would play a Mozart concerto, no arpeggio, fast and straight, the timing perfect. It made sense to box Killer Kroon in the same way.

'Never mind his head, Peekay. You just keep landing them to the body. Quick punches in and out with both hands. Scoring shots. Stay out of reach and don't let him get you against the ropes, not even once. You box him in the middle of the ring. Make him work, make him chase you all the time, you hear?'

I listened to them carefully, but I knew the real answer came from Geel Piet. That I had to box with my feet. I had no idea what sort of a boxer Killer Kroon was. His first opponent had lasted less than a minute and Fonnie went down a few seconds into the second round but had spent all of the first back-pedalling.

As I just sat there waiting, Kroon stared at me with an evil grin, and I began to feel very small and a little bewildered. The feeling of being in front of the Judge came back to me, and the ring became the dormitory and the audience the jury.

I closed my eyes and counted from ten to one. I stood on a rock just below the full moon, the roar of the falls in my ears. The river and the gorge and the African veld stretched out below me in the silver light. I was a young Zulu warrior who had killed his first lion and I could feel the lionskin skirt around my hips, the tail of the lion wrapped around my waist. I took a deep breath and jumped the first of the falls into a pool lashed with white spray and thunder, rose to the surface and was swept to the rim of the second, plunged downwards and rose again to be swept to the edge of the third pool where I fell again, rising to the surface at the bottom of the falls where the water danced with silver and the first of the stepping stones shone wet in the moonlight. I crossed the ten stones to the other side, and opened my eyes and looked directly at Kroon. Killer Kroon saw something in my eyes which made him turn away and not look at me again.

The referee called us up, and taking us by the wrists he held our hands in the air, introducing me first. 'On my left, Dames and Here . . . Gentleman Peekay of the Barberton Blues.' The crowd gave me a big hand, although this was mixed with laughter as they saw my size next to Killer Kroon. 'On my right, from Lydenburg, Martinus Kroon.' The crowd had already chosen sides and with the exception of the Lydenburg squad the clapping was only polite. I went back and sat on my stool. It was the first fight of the finals and anticipation made the crowd enthusiastic even though it was the most junior fight of the night.

The bell went for the first round and I sprang from my stool while Killer Kroon got up slowly, almost disdainfully. We moved to the centre of the ring, and he threw a left at my head which only came up to below his shoulder. I could see it coming for miles and let it pass my ear. He followed with a right and I ducked under the punch. It was almost the same opening Du Toit had used and I followed it the same way with a left and a right under Kroon's heart. I got some body behind the two punches which I drove in hard but he didn't even seem to notice. I danced quickly out of the way and a clumsy uppercut with his left missed my chin by six inches. The crowd winced at the ferocity of the punch even though it was all show and no blow.

I stayed in the centre of the ring, moving around Kroon who threw four more punches and missed. He threw another right which parted my hair but the punch was too hard, throwing him off balance. I moved in fast and hit the same spot under the heart with a left and right combination which I repeated. Four good short punches with plenty of shoulder behind them. But I'd been too greedy getting the extra two punches home. His huge arms locked around me and, lifting me bodily, he threw me away from him. I was sent spinning across the ring, my legs working like pistons to keep me on my feet. I bounced into the ropes, and grabbed the middle one with both arms to steady myself. I was wide open as the straight right came at me. It should have been an uppercut. I was against the ropes and would not have been able to move out of the way of a punch coming up at me. To put everything he had into the punch, Killer Kroon had pulled his shoulder back just a fraction too far. It allowed me a split second to move my head to the right. Instead of sending me bye-bye-birdie, the blow caught my ear and it felt like a branding iron had been pushed into the side of my head. But I'd taken worse from the Judge, and I feinted left and moved off the ropes under his right arm. He turned quickly but my feet were already in position and he walked into a perfectly timed right cross, coming at him with the full weight of my body behind it. The punch had landed flush on the point of his chin and his head snapped back. I knew I had hurt him. It was the best punch I had ever thrown by far. Gert said later, had I been nearer to Killer Kroon's size, he'd have been out for a week.

Kroon shook his head in bewilderment. He was hurt and he was mad and he came looking for me. I stayed out of his way, taking a straight left on the shoulder moving away, and managed two more good punches to the spot under his heart when he telegraphed another right cross. The spot under his heart had developed a red patch. The bell went for the end of round one, and as I returned to my corner I could see a grin on Meneer de Klerk's face.

Doc was standing outside the ring in my corner as Lieutenant Smit and Klipkop climbed in to attend to me. He had his bandanna in both hands and was twisting it round and round with the tears falling down his cheeks.

'You done good,' Klipkop said with a huge grin. Lieutenant Smit said nothing at first but smeared Vaseline over the ear where Kroon had glanced his big hit off me. He covered my good ear with his hand.

'Can you hear me, Peekay?' He spoke from the side I'd been hit.

'Ja, lieutenant, I hear you good,' I replied.

'If a thick ear is all we get out of this fight we'll be blêrrie lucky.' He turned to Klipkop. 'Give him another half-glass of water. Rinse only, don't swallow.' He looked directly at me. 'Now listen good, Peekay. It looks like this gorilla's only got four punches. Straight right, straight left, right cross and left uppercut. He's a fighter and he's never needed any more than those; every one is a good punch and he throws them well except the left uppercut is a bit clumsy, and he tries to hit too hard with the right cross so you can see it coming. You done good to move under it and hit him under the heart. That's a damn good punch. He's very strong but if you can get in enough of those they're going to count in the end and you'll slow him down for the third. Keep moving, you must keep moving, you hear? Make him work, he's not as fit as you, make him work and keep hitting him on that spot under the heart, okay?'

I had never heard Lieutenant Smit talk so fast, and listening to what he wasn't saying I could see he now thought I had a chance. 'No more attack, counter punch, you hear? Only counter punch.' I nodded and the bell went for the second round.

Kroon came storming out of his corner and I could see from the look in his eyes that he wanted to finish the fight. For the first half of the round I ducked and weaved and back-pedalled and moved him around. He must have thrown fifty punches without landing even one. The crowd was beginning to laugh as he repeatedly missed and he was becoming frustrated. Towards the second half of the round he slowed down just a little and his right cross wasn't coming quite so fast. He was breathing heavily and to my surprise I could smell his sweat. A kid's sweat doesn't smell until he's about Bokkie de Beer's size, but I could smell Killer Kroon's sweat all right, plain as anything. I moved up a little closer and started coming in under the right cross again, to land on the same spot under the heart time and time again. I couldn't believe his lack of imagination. The right cross came at me regular as clockwork, and I moved under it and landed two and sometimes four punches to the spot under his heart. His breathing was getting heavier and heavier and he grunted as I landed a left and a right, and I realised that my punches to the heart were beginning to hurt him. I was getting pretty tired myself when the bell sounded for the end of the second round.

The crowd stood and clapped. As I returned to my corner I looked towards Doc. He had the bandanna in his mouth and was chewing on it.

'He's going to try and finish you this round, Peekay. You got both rounds, you miles ahead on points. He is going to try to put you down.' Lieutenant Smit's usually calm voice was gone and he was breathing hard. 'Stay away, man. I don't care if you don't land a blêrrie punch, just run away, keep clear, you hear? Keep clear, you got this fight won. Magtig! You boxing good!' His eyes were shining as he spoke.

The bell for the final round went and we met in the centre of the ring and touched gloves. Killer Kroon was still breathing hard and his chest was heaving. As we moved away he said, 'I'm going to kill you, you blêrrie Rooinek.'

Geel Piet said you always had to answer back, so they know you're not afraid. 'Come and get me, you Boer bastard!' I shot back at him. He rushed at me and I stepped aside but his swinging arm caught me as he passed and knocked me off my feet. It wasn't a punch, it was the inside of his arm, but it sat me down. I couldn't believe it had happened. One knockdown and you lose the fight! I had lost the fight! I had opened my mouth to talk, lost my concentration and lost the fight! I couldn't believe it was me sitting on the canvas. There was a roaring in my ears and a terrible despair in my heart.

'No knockdown, continue to box!' I heard Meneer de Klerk shout as though in a dream. I was coming to my feet but it felt as though I was underwater. The thought of defeat had drowned my senses. Killer Kroon rushed in and that clumsy left uppercut just missed my chin. This time he should have used the right cross as I couldn't move upwards to my feet and sideways at the same time. A right cross would have caught me flush on the chin and finished me for keeps. Instead I simply moved my head backwards and the uppercut whizzed safely past the point of my chin. I was back on my toes and dancing out of reach, moving around him. The stupid bastard couldn't box for toffee. No way was he going to get a second chance at me.

I was making him miss pretty easily and began to realise that there was something wrong with him. His breath was coming in rasps and his chest was heaving, his punches had lost their zing. I moved up and hit him as hard as I could with a two-fisted attack to the spot under his heart and his hands fell to his sides. His gloves came around my waist but there was hardly any strength left in him and he leaned heavily on me, his gloves working up and down my waist. The thumb of his glove must have caught the elastic band of my boxing shorts for they slipped neatly over my hips and fell to my ankles. I didn't know what to do. I couldn't step backwards for fear of falling, anyway his arms and weight made it impossible to move. So I just stood there and hit him again and again as he draped his arms over me, my bare arse pointed at the crowd. Then he gave me a last desperate push and I tripped over the shorts caught around my ankles and fell down. I tried to pull my pants up with my boxing gloves but without success. The crowd was convulsed with laughter and Killer Kroon was standing over me with his hands on his knees, head hanging. He was rasping and wheezing and trying to take in air.

'No knockdown!' Meneer de Klerk shouted. 'Get back to your corner, Kroon!' He grabbed me by the wrist and jerked me to my feet and then pulled my pants up. I had been covering my snake with my gloves. In those days nobody wore underpants and I was bare-arsed and fancy free in front of everyone. But I didn't care a damn, the only thing that mattered was Killer Kroon in the ring with me. I would have fought him with no clothes on if necessary. Meneer de Klerk wiped my gloves on his pants. 'Box on,' he said. I turned to face Killer Kroon's corner. He was standing with his back to me and his chest was still heaving. Suddenly a towel lofted over his head and landed at my feet. I couldn't believe my eyes. Kroon's corner was throwing in the towel, the fight was over! Meneer de Klerk moved quickly over to me, and with a huge grin on his face held my hand aloft. 'Winner on a technical knockout, Gentleman Peekay!' he announced. The crowd stood up for the second time and shouted and cheered, and Lieutenant Smit and Klipkop jumped into the ring. Klipkop lifted me up and held me high above his shoulders and turned around in the ring and everyone went wild.

Meneer de Klerk had moved over to Kroon's corner, and now he came back to the centre of the ring and held his hand up for silence. The timekeeper rang his bell until the crowd quietened down. Klipkop put me down again. 'The Lydenburg squad want me to say that Martinus Kroon retired because of an asthma attack.' A section of the crowd started to boo and there was general laughter. 'More like a Rooinek attack!' someone shouted. The bald referee held up his hand once more. 'I just want you to know that I had the fight scored two rounds to none for Gentleman Peekay and I also had him ahead on points in the third round. The technical knockout stands. Let me tell you something, this boy is going to be a great boxer, just remember where you saw him first.' The crowd whistled and stomped and cheered again, and Lieutenant Smit held my hand up and then we left the ring. Doc was crying and I had to sit down and hold his hand for a bit, and then we went together to the showers. But first Doc and I shared the last two pumpkin scones.

'I think Geel Piet and the people will be very happy tonight,' Doc said as he handed me a towel. 'I go to get you a soft drink? What colour do you want?'

'But we haven't got any money,' I said.

'That's what you think, Mister Schmarty Pantz!' Doc fished into the pocket of his white linen suit and produced two half-crowns.

'Five shillings! Where'd you get that?' I said in amazement.

He grinned slyly. 'I am making this bet with a nice man from Lydenburg.'

'A bet! You bet on me? What if I'd lost? If I'd lost you couldn't have paid him!'

Doc dropped the coins back into his coat pocket with a clink and then scratched his nose with his forefinger. 'You couldn't lose, you was playing Mozart,' he said.

I asked for an American cream soda. It was the drink Hoppie had bought me in the café at Gravelotte after we'd changed the tackies at the Patels' shop, and it was still my favourite. It was also the closest I could come to sharing my win with Hoppie. If Geel Piet and Hoppie could have been there, everything would have been perfect. Not that it wasn't perfect. But more perfect.

FOURTEEN

By the time we got to the last fight of the evening, the Barberton Blues had won five of the eight finals and only the heavyweight division remained. Naturally it was the event from which the crowd expected the most and they were not disappointed. Gert was matched with a giant of a man called Potgieter, a railway fettler from Kaapmuiden who was six foot seven and a half and weighed two hundred and eighty-nine pounds. Gert was no lightweight and at six foot one he weighed two hundred and twenty.

Potgieter was a better boxer than he first appeared and in the first round he had Gert hanging on twice, but Gert won the round by landing more clean punches. In the heavyweight division a knockdown did not mean the end of the fight and in the second round Potgieter, way behind on points, connected with an uppercut under the heart which doubled Gert up like a collapsed mattress before he dropped to the canvas. The bell went at the count of five but it looked all over for him anyway.

To our surprise he came out for the final round and started hitting Potgieter almost at will. The big man knew he was behind on points so he dropped his defence, confident he could take anything Gert dished out. Gert dished out plenty and there was blood all over the giant's face and one eye was completely closed. He smiled throughout the fight, a grotesque, dangerous-looking smile from a mouth that was missing the front teeth. Gert's straight left and right were working like pistons into a face that was moving relentlessly forward. Potgieter chopped his way to within range of Gert and finally managed to trap him in a corner. The uppercut seemed to be in slow motion as it caught Gert on the point of the jaw. The warder was out cold even before his legs had started to buckle and we thought he'd been killed. The referee counted him out, and Klipkop and Lieutenant Smit lifted him unconscious from the floor and carried him to his corner. Gert had, as usual, fought with too much heart and not enough head. If only he had known about Mozart.

It was after ten o'clock when we left Nelspruit. We kids huddled together in the back of the utility, sharing two rough prison blankets. The indigo night was pricked with sharp cold stars. We'd spent what energy remained in lavish praise of each other and of the glorious Barberton Blues, and now we were silent and sleepy. Klipkop drove this time, as Gert was not in such good shape and had gone home in the thirty-nine Chevy with Lieutenant Smit.

Bokkie, Fonnie, Nels and Maatie were soon sleeping fitfully. Jolts woke them momentarily, their dulled eyes opening for a minute before heavy lids shut them down again. I was enormously tired as well, but couldn't doze off. In my mind each of my three fights kept repeating themselves. I played them back in sequence as though they were scenes on a loop of film which I was able to edit in my imagination, snipping here, joining there, remaking the fights, seeing them in my mind as they should have been.

I didn't know it then, but this ability totally to recall a fight scenario made me a lot more dangerous when I met an opponent for the second time. In the years ahead I also taught myself to fight as a southpaw, so I could switch if necessary in the middle of a fight, as though it were entirely natural for me to do so.

It was nearly midnight when the ute stopped outside our house. Everything was in darkness. I crept around the back because the kitchen door was never locked. A candle stub burned on the kitchen table and on the floor, each rolled in a blanket, lay Dum and Dee. I tried to tiptoe past but they both shot up into sitting positions, like Egyptian mummies suddenly come to life, the whites of their eyes showing big with alarm.

They were overjoyed at my return and switched on the light to examine me. They burst into tears when they saw my swollen ear and it took some effort to calm them. When I told them that I had won, they showed only polite joy. They clucked and tut-tutted like a pair of old *abafazi* around a cooking pot and declared they'd be up at dawn to look for poultice weed against the horrible bruises which were undoubtedly concealing themselves all over my body. Despite my protests, for I was almost too tired to stand up, Dum sat me down and washed my face, hands and feet with water from a kettle kept warm on the stove. Dee dried me on a coarse towel and at last I was allowed to totter off to bed.

At Sunday school the next morning Pastor Mulvery noticed my fat ear and gave me a lightning on/off smile showing his escape-attempting front teeth. 'Have you been listening to the devil again, Peekay?' He hee-hawed quite a lot over his clever joke and no doubt repeated it to the Lord later. He always said you had to tell the Lord everything.

I remained unsaved, unborn again, despite the fact that I was officially slated in the minds of every lady in the church as my mother's special prayer burden. I guess if they'd known what was going on in the prison they'd have mounted a whole revival campaign to try and bring me to the Lord. Once I asked in Sunday school if black was equal with white in heaven. The Sunday school teacher, a lady with big breasts and a sharp nose named Mrs Kostler who looked like a fat pigeon, stopped in mid-reply and sent one of the other kids to look for Pastor Mulvery.

'Not exactly, but not exactly not,' Pastor Mulvery said, and then thumbing through Mrs Kostler's Bible he read, ' "In my father's house are many mansions, I go to prepare a place for you".' He put the Bible aside. 'Many mansions is the Lord's way of saying that He loves all of mankind but that He recognises there are differences, like black and white. So He has a place for black angels and another place for white angels,' he said smugly. I could see he was pretty pleased with his reply.

A girl called Zoe Prinsloo asked, 'Does that mean we don't have to have dirty Kaffirs in our mansion?'

'Ag man, Zoe,' Mrs Kostler cried, 'in heaven nobody is dirty, you hear, not even Kaffirs!'

'Will they still work for us?' I asked.

Mrs Kostler looked to Pastor Mulvery for a reply. 'Of course not, nobody works in heaven,' he said, a little impatiently.

'If nobody is dirty and nobody works in heaven, and black and white are equal, why then can't they live in the same place as us?'

Pastor Mulvery gave a deep sigh. 'Because they are black and it wouldn't be right, that's all. The Lord knows more about such things than we do, man. We mustn't question the wisdom of the Lord. When you are born again you'll understand His infinite wisdom and you won't ask such silly questions.' I knew Mrs Kostler would report all this back at the next ladies' prayer meeting and I'd have to face another session with my mother. It wasn't easy being a sinner.

She would send me to my room, and come and sit on my bed and sigh quite a lot. Then she would say, 'I'm very disappointed in you, son-boy. Mrs Kostler says that you were questioning the word of God. Why do you mock the Lord so? You are not too young for His wrath. "I am not mocked," sayeth the Lord. I pray for your precious soul every day, but you harden your heart and one day the Lord will not proffer up unto you His mercy and His everlasting forgiveness, and you will be damned.' She would sigh a few more times. It was the sighs that got to me. I couldn't bear to think I was hurting her so much. But I didn't really know how to stop either. It was natural for me to ask questions. Doc demanded them, had trained my mind to search for truth. To confront that which lacked logic or offended common sense was as natural for me as climbing trees. I was a sleuth in search of the truth and once on the track of biblical malpractice I found it impossible to let a contradiction pass or an assumption go unquestioned.

I would ask for forgiveness and agree to apologise to Mrs Kostler or whoever at the Apostolic Faith Mission I might have offended. But it was never enough. My mother demanded an orgy of confession. She wanted me to renounce my sins, retract my point of view and go down on my knees and beg forgiveness from the Lord. I couldn't do it and so I compounded her disappointment in me.

So she would make me stay in my room and go without supper instead.

I kept a stick of *biltong* under my mattress for these occasions. Marie often brought these hard sticks of dried game home from the farm and Dee and Dum and I, being the only ones without false teeth, were the only ones who could eat it. I would sit in bed reading, cutting off delicious slivers of sun-dried venison with my Joseph Rogers pocket knife. It was Doc's really, but I was minding it for him while he was in prison.

Marie had surrendered to the army of the Lord and in some measure made up for my recalcitrance. Creating born-again Christians for Pentecostals was like scalp-hunting for Red Indians. Occasionally there was a really big coup, when a well-known drunk or fornicator or even a three-pack-a-day cigarette smoker was brought trembling to his knees before the Lord. This person then testified in front of the congregation. I'm telling you, some of these past sinners washed in the blood of the Lamb really got carried away when the congregation started to respond. When the halleluja-ing and praise the Lord-ing and spontaneous bursting into song and clapping of hands and sighs of joy were going on, the convert would be crying and sniffing and having a really good time telling about all his really bad deeds. Every time the testimony got really juicy, a silence fell on the congregation as they soaked up the last drop of vicarious sin. I have to admit, it was pretty impressive when a repentant drunk was saved. One day you would have to cross the road so as not to go near him and the next, after he was born again, he was called brother, shaken warmly by the hand and loved by everybody. I guess the Lord has to be given credit for that.

But sometimes being born again didn't last and the person who used to be loved was said to have backslid. Backsliding was the worst thing that could happen in the Apostolic Faith Mission. It meant all the spontaneous love had been wasted and that the devil had won. Mind you, this was generally seen as a temporary setback. To the Pentecostals the things of the flesh, tempting as they might be, didn't compensate for the promise of everlasting life. Once you were born again and then became a backslider you challenged this premise, and jeopardised the whole glorious presumption of pay now play later. The born-again Christians were all working very hard for their segregated mansions in heaven.

I think I instinctively recognised winners and losers and it seemed to me the members of the Apostolic Faith Mission were to be found more often on the losers' side of life. This was a situation which they seemed to enjoy. 'Blessed are the poor, for they shall see the kingdom of God.' A converted drunk or a sinner who admitted to adultery was such an obvious loser that he just naturally belonged. Backsliding was therefore not easily accepted and a lot of work went into bringing the lost child back to the Lord. The stakes were pretty high. In return for bringing a really lost soul to the Lord you gained a fair amount of real estate in the sky, according to Pastor Mulvery. At least a two-storey mansion set back from the street with trees and green lawns where the soft breezes carried the glissando of harps. Which was a damn sight better than the crackle of hell and the dreadful moans of the everlastingly condemned.

For the drunks who were smart enough to become born again and then backslide, the Apostolic Faith Mission served as a sort of drying-out clinic where love and reassurance, fresh clothes and a new start could be found from time to time. Really juicy backsliding testimonies filled the church and gave everyone present a precious time with the Lord and Pastor Mulvery a bigger collection plate. Church members put a lot more work and enthusiasm into a bad sinner than someone like Marie who came to them meek as a lamb without any spiritual blemishes, hardly worth a spontaneous halleluja and certainly not worth a good public weep to the glory of the Lord.

Marie's spiritual moment of glory came later when she testified in front of the congregation and told how she had brought an eighty-nine-year-old Boer to the Lord on his death-bed. How he had been afraid to die and when she had brought him to Christ he had closed his eyes and with a soft sigh gone to meet his maker.

I had privately thought this an almost perfect solution. The old man had spent his life as a sinner and then, at the last possible moment, was snatched from the jaws of hell by a pimply-faced girl whose heart was filled with love and compassion. I wondered briefly whether this entitled him to a full heavenly mansion or maybe just the garden shed at the bottom of Marie's garden? Anyway, she got a terrific response from the congregation. Snatching lost souls from the brink of the fiery furnace was pretty high on the list of important conversions and it immediately altered her previous status of sweet girl to that of a capable and resourceful soldier in the army of the Lord.

Like me, Dum and Dee were holding out, although to them the whole business was a bit confusing and their true status was never really known. They had been semi-ordered to be born again by my mother and naturally they had complied. My mother gave them a Shangaan Bible but it was left to me to teach them to read it, and we had concentrated more on the Old Testament where the stories of the warriors, drought and famine were much more to their liking. Their favourite was the one about Ruth in the cornfield trying to find enough corn to feed her family after the harvesters had been through the fields. The concept of a white man coming along and forgiving everyone's sins and then getting nailed to a post for his trouble, to Dum and Dee seemed a highly unlikely story. As Dum pointed out, white men never forgive sins, they only punish you for them, especially if you are black. To accept the black man's sins and agree to be responsible and even crucified for them only proved he must have been crazy. Dee then asked, if he'd already done the dying for black people's sins, why was the white man always punishing the black man? I was prepared to agree she had a point and as I also found the miracles very suspect, we just naturally stayed with the Old Testament, which had witchdoctors like Elijah and great leader kings like Moses and fierce and independent generals like Joshua. A book like this made sense, and posed all the problems and terrors their own legends told about.

My mother claimed Dee and Dum, along with Marie, on her personal born-again list. There were others, for on Wednesday afternoons she stopped sewing and headed for the hospital with a marked Bible and a bagful of tracts. The tracts had headings such as Sinner snatched from certain hellfire and The man who talked to God about sin and Salvation: God's precious promise. The one she claimed was the big artillery in the hospital environment was called Hell is one mortal blink away. She had taken Pastor Mulvery's place after I was released from hospital, and from time to time found worthy sinners lurking behind starched sheets. They were usually fraught with the anxiety of fresh stitches from a hysterectomy or a gall-bladder operation and ripe for the softening-up process. My mother began by enquiring about the operation. She was an expert, perhaps even the world champion, on operations. She seemed to have undergone all the major operations a woman can expect and a few others on the side just to round out her experience. At the drop of a medical complaint she could detail every phase of an operation from the first tiny suspicious pangs of pain to the post-operative depression. My gift for recalling every detail of a fight must have come from her, for she could do the same with operations, even the bits when she was under anaesthetic.

Having determined how long the sinner was likely to be in hospital and therefore how captive as an audience, the spiritual ear-bashing began; Marie did the follow-up work for the Lord, keeping the sinner Christwise until the next Wednesday visit. They shared the souls they saved and often witnessed together at the Sunday morning meeting where they basked in the warmth of the spiritual love they received from the congregation. The Lord had a couple of stormtroopers in them, all right. Pastor Mulvery used to refer to them as 'the sisters of redemption', adding that the Lord had touched them in a special way.

Marie was still very conscious of her pimples. One day my mother said enough was enough, if the Lord cared about every sparrow that fell, then surely he cared equally about Marie's pimples. The two of them went down on their knees and exhorted the Lord to cast out the pimple demon. To my complete surprise He did. Within a year Marie's face was as smooth as a baby's bottom, and she turned out to be quite pretty underneath. That was a mighty testimony session, with Marie crying and ruining her new-found prettiness, and my mother telling the dramatic story of the Lord's wonderful pimple cure. Pastor Mulvery did a neat little summary afterwards by saying the Lord's rewards are not only in heaven where the big pay-out takes place but also on earth as instanced by the demise of Marie's pimples. My mother's faith and her work with Marie for the Lord had been rewarded personally by Him.

When I first told Doc about the concerted prayer campaign for the removal of Marie's pimples, he suggested that I advise her to eat lots of salad, no fat and lean meat only twice a week. Marie tried it, found she liked it better than the stodgy hospital food, and kept to this diet fairly diligently. When I told him of the cure through prayer he declared that some things were too mysterious for words. I thought about it a little more and finally made the connection between the diet and the cure, and

I asked him why he hadn't pointed out the possibility of the change in diet making the difference.

'Peekay,' he said, 'in this world are very few things made from logic alone. It is illogical for a man to be too logical. Some things we must just let stand. The mystery is more important than any possible explanation.' He paused for a moment and tapped his fingers on the edge of the keyboard. 'The searcher after truth must search with humanity. Ruthless logic is the sign of a limited mind. The truth can only add to the sum of what you know, while a harmless mystery left unexplored often adds to the meaning of life. When a truth is not so important, it is better left as a mystery.' It was an answer which left me confused for some years, for Doc worshipped the truth and had always demanded it between us at any cost.

Geel Piet had not expected me to win through to the finals in Nelspruit. The most he had hoped for was a berth in the semis. His delight at the Monday morning training session knew no bounds. 'The people are very happy. I'm telling you, since we heard the news they have talked about nothing else, man. The Zulus say you are surely a Zulu chief disguised as a white man, for only a Zulu can fight with this much courage.' He laughed. 'When we heard the news, everybody who had a *stompie* smoked it and the warders could not stop the people singing in the night.'

In fact, one of the warders told Doc and me at breakfast on Monday morning that there had been a strange feeling in the prison on Saturday night and they had alerted off-duty men to be on standby. He said that at about seven o'clock, before any of the warders knew the results, one of the old lags told him I had won. He had only officially been told after midnight,. when the news came from the warder on duty at the gates within minutes of the return of Lieutenant Smit to the prison. 'Wragdig, man. Kaffirs are funny that way. Sometimes they just know things without the telephone or anything. I seen it before in Pollsmoor when a prisoner is going to be hanged. The decision is made not even in the jail but they know even before the instructions come to the Kommandant. An old lag once told me they send out their combined energy to find out. I dunno how it works, man, but I'm telling you they blêrrie well know.'

At my piano lesson on Monday, Doc found an excuse for Geel Piet to come into the hall and I played back the three fights blow by blow to him. He nearly died laughing when I told him about my pants falling down. I added that I would get my mother to shorten them and tighten the elastic around the waist. It was Geel Piet who cottoned on to why Killer Kroon had the asthma attack.

'He is not used to boxing three rounds hard. Probably he never even boxed three rounds before, because he always got a TKO decision like the first two fights. Then you come along and he has to chase you all over the place, man, and you keep hitting him under the heart. So what do you think happens? He has to breathe harder and harder, man, and the strain brings on his asthma attack. I had an aunty in Cape Town who couldn't even climb some steps without getting an asthma attack. I'm telling you, it's the truth, man. You found his weakness and you attacked it.' He smiled, 'Hey man, blêrrie lucky he had a bad left hook. When you came in under his right cross he could've done some real damage with a good left hook.'

That morning Lieutenant Smit had made a short speech to us all. 'I'm proud of you all, you hear? Not one boxer let us down, even those of you who lost, you fought good.' He turned to Klipkop. 'Wait until that Potgieter turns professional, man, I'm telling you, you in for a lot of trouble.'

'Let him come,' Klipkop mumbled.

'Gert, you done good. You hit him maybe ten times for every one time he hit you but two hundred and twenty pounds isn't two hundred and eighty pounds. That big ape belongs in the jungle.' We all laughed and then he said, 'I left the smallest for last. The under twelve finals was the best boxing match I have ever seen.' Fonnie Kruger punched me in the ribs and I didn't know how to stop my face burning. 'No, honest man, if you all want a lesson in boxing then watch Peekay.' He paused and looked directly at Geel Piet standing twenty paces behind us. 'Geel Piet, you just a yellow Kaffir, but I got to hand it to you, you a good coach.'

We all looked round to see Geel Piet cover his face with both hands and dance from one foot to another as though he were standing on hot coals.

'Don't think you can get cheeky now, you hear?' Lieutenant Smit said. But there was a hint of amusement in his voice.

Geel Piet pulled his hands down over his face as though wiping away the expression concealed under them. 'No, baas, thank you, baas. This yellow Kaffir is a very happy man, baas.'

The prison photographer came into the gym and Lieutenant Smit announced we were going to have our picture taken but not our fingerprints. We all laughed and the photographer lined us up, fussing around until he had got it just right. There was an explosion of light as he took the picture, and then he said he wanted to take another for luck. Lieutenant Smit looked about him as Doc entered the hall. 'Come Professor, come stand here,' he invited and then to everyone's surprise he beckoned to Geel Piet. 'You too, Kaffir,' he said gruffly.

Klipkop stepped out of the photographer's former arrangement. 'No way, man! I'm not having my photo taken with a blêrrie Kaffir!'

Lieutenant Smit brought his hand up to his mouth and blew a couple of breathy notes down the centre of his closed fist. 'That's okay, Sergeant Oudendaal,' he said pleasantly. 'Anybody else also want to step out?'

Geel Piet stepped out of where he was standing on the edge of the group. 'I am too ugly for a heppy snap, baas,' he grinned.

'Get back, Kaffir!' Lieutenant Smit commanded.

Geel Piet returned to the edge of the group, whereupon the remainder of the adult boxers stepped out of the group with the exception of Gert, then Bokkie de Beer moved away followed by the other kids. I could see they were real scared. Only Doc, Gert, Geel Piet and myself were left when Lieutenant Smit stepped back into the picture. 'Okay man, take the snap!' he commanded.

The photograph captured the exact moment when I understood with conviction that racism is a primary force of evil designed to destroy good men.

We were all given a large ten by eight inch photograph of the Barberton Blues and the photographer gave Doc, Gert and me a copy of the second photograph. The lieutenant refused his copy which I begged from the photographer and gave to Geel Piet privately. He kept it in the piano stool and looked at it every day when he collected the prisoners' mail.

Some weeks later Lieutenant Smit was promoted to captain and some people even started to talk about him as the next Kommandant. He called me aside after training session one morning and asked if I would return the second photo and get Doc's copy back as well. I had no option but to obey, and Gert did the same. Lieutenant Smit tore them up but forgot about the extra copy. He obtained the plate from the prison photographer and destroyed this also. A man cannot be careful enough about his career and the second photograph had been aberrant to his normal behaviour. He had no intention of living to regret it.

Between Doc and Mrs Boxall, my education was in fairly safe hands. Mrs Boxall consulted with Doc by note and they decided on my serious reading. She was the expert on English literature and he on the sciences, music and Latin. The Barberton library, apart from containing Doc's own botanical collection, had also been the recipient of two surprisingly good private collections, and Mrs Boxall said it was choked with intellectual goodies for a growing mind. Both Doc and Mrs Boxall were natural teachers and enthusiasts who never lost patience when my young mind couldn't keep up. Doc set exams and Mrs Boxall conducted them in the library. I had an exam on Tuesday and Friday every week and I grew to love this time spent with Mrs Boxall, who often violently disagreed with a conclusion reached by Doc. I was the carrier of debate notes and some of the intellectual arguments went on for weeks at a time. I was never excluded, and I learned the value of debate and of having a point of view I was prepared to defend.

The three of us had been playing chess for some time. Doc and Mrs Boxall each had a board and Gert had made one more, turning the chess figures on the lathe in the prison workshop and doing the wood inlay for the board by hand. It was not as good as Doc's ivory set but Doc said it was very well made and original. The two boards were set up, one with my game and the other with Mrs Boxall's. Every morning I gave Doc Mrs Boxall's move and he positioned it on the board and made his reply which I took back to her. We set ten minutes aside at the end of the lesson to play. At first that was enough for Doc to beat me but as the months and years went by, a game would often last a week.

I had never beaten Doc in four years, and in two years Mrs Boxall only managed it once. It was the game the Russian Lenchinakov played when he beat the American Arnold Green in 1931 and she had studied it for three weeks. Even so she was lucky to pull it off. On her eighth move Doc realised she wasn't playing her usual game. 'Ask Madame Boxall who is playing for her this game?' he instructed me. But it was already too late, he had walked into an audacious trap set so early in the game that he had not suspected she was capable of such a move.

When I brought her the news that Doc had conceded the game she jumped up from behind her desk and rubbed her hands gleefully together, a huge grin on her face. 'By golly, it feels dashed good to beat the pompous old Teuton,' she exclaimed. 'Tell him not to be a bad sport, all's fair in love and war!'

Two of me were emerging, a small boy approaching eleven who climbed trees, used a catapult, drove a billycart and led an eager gang in *kleilat* and other games against the Afrikaner kids, and a somewhat precocious child who often left the teachers at school in despair, unable to cope with my answers or even tolerate the fact that I was already well in advance of anything they had to teach. They simply awarded me first place in class every term and got on with the business of teaching the other kids.

In my tenth year a new teacher, Miss Bornstein, arrived at the school. She taught the senior class, getting them ready for the emotional leap into high school and while I was still two classes below the seniors she had summoned me to her classroom after school one Friday afternoon.

'Hello, Peekay, come in,' she said as I knocked on the door. She was seated at her table reading a book.

'Good afternoon, miss,' I said, entering a little fearfully. She looked up and smiled, and my head began to zing as though I'd been clocked a straight right between the eyes by Snotnose. Miss Bornstein was the most beautiful person I had ever seen. She had long black hair and the biggest green eyes you've ever seen and a large mouth that shone with red lipstick. Her skin was lightly tanned and without a single blemish. At ten you are not supposed to be sexually attracted, but every nerve in my body cried out to be a closer part of this beautiful woman. She was dazzling and when she smiled her teeth were even and perfectly white. Except for the fact that she was not as willowy as the C to C cigarette lady painted on the clockface of the railway cafe in Tzaneen, she could have been the living version.

'They tell me you're rather clever, Peekay.'

'No miss,' I said without false modesty. Despite the fact that I was accepted as the brightest child in the school, both Doc and Mrs Boxall had been careful to disabuse me of such a notion. 'Cleverness is a false presumption,' Doc had explained. 'It is like being a natural skater, you are so busy doing tricks to impress that you do not see where the thin ice is and before you know, poof! You are in deep, ice-cold water frozen like a dead herring. Intelligence is a harder gift, for this you must work, you must practise it, challenge it and maybe towards the end of your life you will master it. Cleverness is the shadow whereas intelligence is the substance.'

Miss Bornstein tried me on Latin vocabulary and then on my Latin verbs. It was pretty simple stuff but as Latin was only taught in high school in South Africa she seemed impressed. She then made me sit at a desk and handed me the book she had been reading. 'Do as many of these as you can in ten minutes,' she instructed.

The book had thirty pages, and was full of little drawings and sentences with missing words and trick questions where you had to pick the answer from several choices. It was like old homework for me. This was Doc's personal territory and he had a great many books on logic and thinking, as he would call it, out of the square. Miss Bornstein's book was for beginners and I finished the whole thing in under five minutes.

I had to wait while she marked the answers. After the first page she looked up and chewed on the end of her pencil, and then tapped it against her beautiful white teeth, her long, polished red nails holding the pencil lightly so that it bounced making a rat-tat-tat-tat sound. Then, using it to point at me, she said, 'I wouldn't say you were stupid, Peekay.' She turned to the last page and marked it, I guess because the book was supposed to go from easy to hard. She looked up again. 'No, I wouldn't say that at all.'

After that she made me read a book out loud and do a writing test, and then she opened her suitcase, brought out a chess board and set it up. 'You open,' she said. I used one of Doc's favourite openings and she whistled through her teeth as she studied it. After an hour I conceded the game. Doc said it was the thing to do when you were going to stalemate anyway. It made your opponent less wary and therefore gave you an advantage next time. 'But only do this in a friendly match,' he cautioned. 'Chess is war and in war nothing can be predicted except death.'

Miss Bornstein looked up at me, a flicker of annoyance crossing her face. 'Don't ever do that again!' she said. 'When I play chess I'm your opponent and not to be patronised like some silly woman!'

I blushed furiously. 'I'm sorry, miss,' I said, mortified and wondering what the word meant.

'Miss Bornstein please, Peekay. "Miss" sounds just like any other kid who doesn't know any better. Samantha Bornstein. You may call me Sam in private, if you like. I think you and I are going to see quite a lot of each other.'

The idea of calling this beautiful creature by her Christian name was unthinkable. And by a boy's name, a common boy's name like Sam, plainly impossible.

Miss Bornstein thanked me for coming and said that on Monday I was to report to her class. 'Though I can't for the life of me think what we're going to do with you, but at least you'll make a worthy chess opponent,' she said, with a throatiness in her voice that made my chest feel tight.

I told Doc about the whole incident on Monday morning and at the end he asked two questions. 'Tell me, Peekay, how bad in love are you?'

I told him that I didn't know much about love but it was like being hit in the head with a really good punch.

'I think maybe you in love bad, Peekay. About women I don't know so much, but I know this, I think it is not so smart to tell Madame Boxall. I will think about this. Maybe Geel Piet can help also?' We left it at that for the time being.

'Next question, please! Madame Bornstein, she plays chess maybe better than Madame Boxall?'

I told Doc that Miss Bornstein was a good chess player and had I not used one of his sneakiest openings she would most likely have beaten me. 'She's much more cunning than Mrs Boxall,' I concluded.

'Hurrumph! Cunning? This is goot,' he grunted and opened the book at my music lesson. At the end of the practice he handed me a hastily scrawled note. 'Please, with my compliments, to give this to your Madame Bornstein and tomorrow you bring the reply if you please.' I knew better than to open the note.

'Please, Doc, don't tell her I'm in love with her,' I pleaded.

Doc looked askance. 'This I would never do, Peekay. Absoloodle. To be in love is a very private business.'

With Lieutenant Smit's promotion to captain, Sergeant Borman became the new lieutenant. This was not a popular promotion, though it was not unexpected. Borman had been sucking up to the Kommandant ever since he'd come down from Pretoria. He let it be known that his wife's asthma had curtailed a promising career at Pretoria Central, where to survive a warder had to be tougher and smarter than the hard case rapists, grievous bodily harms, thugs, thieves and con merchants. A sergeant under these conditions, he hinted, was easily the equivalent of lieutenant in a small-time prison such as Barberton. He demonstrated at every opportunity that he was tougher and harder than any of the other warders. A glance as he passed was sufficient to get him going.

'Who you looking at, Kaffir? You trying to be cheeky, hey?'

'No baas, no inkosi, I not cheeky, I not look.'

'Don't tell me you not cheeky. I know what you thinking, Kaffir! On the outside you all gentle Jesus and on the inside you a black devil, you hear.'

'No, inkosi. Inside same like outside.'

'That will be the blêrrie day, Kaffir. Come here. Come!' The prisoner would hasten towards Borman and stand head bowed to ragged attention. 'Look me straight in the eyes, Kaffir.'

'No baas. I not look you.'

'Look, you black bastard! When I tell you to look, you look, you hear?' The prisoner would lift terror-stricken eyes to meet those of the sergeant. 'Ja, it's true, man, inside is filth.' He would hit the African with a hard punch into the gut, doubling him over. 'Stand up, you black bastard, we got to get the filth out, we-got-to-get-it out!' He would hit the prisoner again and again in the same spot. 'Vomit out the filth, make clean inside!'

Most Africans from the Lowveld have weak stomachs from having been infected with Bilharzia. The larvae, found in river water, enter the system through the skin and eventually attack the liver and the kidneys. Three or four hard punches in the gut will generally cause severe vomiting and great pain.

Borman would look at the vomit on the floor and over the prisoner's hands as the man tried physically to hold back the contents of his gut. 'Ag sis! Now look what you done now! Why did you make dirty on the nice clean floor?' The donkey prick would come down hard across the prisoner's neck. 'Because you a fucking animal, that's why.' He would continue to hit the prisoner until the prisoner collapsed.

Making an unnecessary mess was a major prison offence and entitled a warder to use the donkey prick in an official capacity. Borman took great pride in the fact that he could legitimise an interrogation within three or four minutes from the time he started to taunt a prisoner. The English equivalent of the name the prisoners gave him was, 'Shit for Brains'. When he was anywhere near you would hear the chant go out, 'Move away, move away, here comes Shit for Brains. Here comes he whose mother threw away her child, kept the placenta, and called it Shit for Brains.'

Lieutenant Borman was too old to belong to the boxing squad, but he often talked big about the fighter he had once been. Gert said that a man who talks about how tough he is, is probably yellow. But, while the warders didn't like Borman, they respected him for being a professional. He spoke Fanagalo pretty well and since most prisoners learn to speak this African lingua franca, he used the African way of frightening the soul with word pictures. It was not uncommon for a prisoner to be reduced by him to a state of abject terror without physical torture. If there was any trouble in the prison, the Kommandant soon learned to put Sergeant Borman in charge. It was this facility to terrorise the prisoners, both physically and mentally, that had made him the Kommandant's choice to take over when Lieutenant Smit was promoted.

Lieutenant Borman deeply resented the freedom Geel Piet had achieved in the gymnasium under Captain Smit. 'Give a lag a blêrrie pinkie and before you know it they eaten your whole hand off up your shoulder,' he would insist. Geel Piet was careful to keep out of his way. When Borman entered the gym, unless he was in the ring actually coaching one of the kids, Geel Piet would quietly slip away. Lieutenant Borman's eyes would follow him as he crept out. 'He will get me. One day, for sure, he will get me. All I can say is I hope I come out the other side alive,' the battered little coloured man confided in me.

Captain Smit would watch Geel Piet leave the gymnasium when Borman entered, but he remained silent. Borman was not overly impressed with Doc or myself. He saw the unholy alliance of Doc, Geel Piet and myself as a basic breakdown of the system. Because he was a professional, he was quick to realise that such a break in the normal discipline of the prison could lead to other things. As a sergeant his influence did not carry to the Kommandant. But as a lieutenant his power increased enormously.

Had it not been for the Kommandant's desire to keep Doc sweet for the bi-annual visit of the inspector of prisons, Lieutenant Borman would almost certainly have had his way and our freedom within the prison would have been severely curtailed.

The Kommandant was a man who saw things in simple terms. Doc at his Steinway was the cultural component of the Inspector's visit. A braaivleis and tiekiedraai, the fun; a boxing and shooting match, the physical; showing the Kommandant as a man of culture who was nevertheless a fun-loving disciplinarian. He had no intention of allowing Lieutenant Borman to disrupt his careful plan. Nevertheless, it was apparent to us that Borman was patient and relentless, determined to find something which would lead to our destruction.

The war in Europe was rapidly drawing to a close. The Allies had crossed the Rhine and were moving towards Berlin. Doc was terribly excited. After four years' incarceration he had a deep need for the soft green hills, the wind-swept mountains and the wooded kloofs. We would talk about walking all the way to saddle-back mountain on the border of Swaziland and tears would come into his eyes. It was as though, now that the prisoner years were almost over, he dared to think for the first time of freedom. He would look over the prison walls to the green hills beyond and his voice would tremble. 'The years of hate are nearly over, it is soon time to love again, time to climb high with the sun on the back until a person can reach up and touch nearly the sky.'

Doc's second book on the cacti of Southern Africa had been written while he was in prison. This one was in English, each page edited by Mrs Boxall who in the end had come to confess that there was more to the jolly old cactus than she could possibly have imagined. Doc now talked of making the photographic plates and Mrs Boxall went to see Jimmy Winter at the chemist to get him to put aside one spool of precious rationed film each month until she had three dozen waiting for Doc on his release. Jimmy Winter was an artist who, when he wasn't running his chemist shop, loved to paint the hills. Before Doc went to prison he would sometimes come across him in some lonely spot high up on a mountain top painting away.

By the time the Allies had crossed the Rhine, precious few music lessons were taking place. We spent most of the hour discussing our plans for Doc's release. He made me describe the cactus garden and the rate of growth of each plant and he talked happily about the extensions he would need to accommodate the stuff we would find waiting for us in the hills. Also, all the photos we needed for his book.

Like me, Miss Bornstein had never managed to beat Doc at chess. So she introduced her grandfather, Mr Isaac Bornstein, who was referred to as Old Mr Bornstein. Old Mr Bornstein turned out to be a match for Doc and the two of them were having a mighty go at each other, with Doc clucking and shaking his head as he read Old Mr Bornstein's latest move. 'Such a German, but very clever, ja this move is goot.' He would move over to the board which rested on top of the upright piano, make Old Mr Bornstein's move and think for a while and then make his own. '. . . But not so clever as me, Mr Schmarty Pantz Isaac!'

To Doc's surprise Mrs Boxall had accepted Miss Bornstein quite happily and the two of them were really making a go of the Sandwich Fund, which was sending out weekly bundles to prisoners' families, as well as food parcels. They discussed the time when, with the war over, it would be necessary to come clean, but decided the end of the war wouldn't bring about the end of human need and they'd find some excuse to continue.

Doc, Geel Piet and I had discussed the matter of my love for Miss Bornstein and, I must say, neither of them was a lot of help. Between the three of us we knew very little about women. Geel Piet never had a mother, or at least he could never remember having one. His aunty, the one with asthma who couldn't climb up steps, had taken him in with her nine kids, and then when she got sick and couldn't manage he had gone to an orphanage and at the age of ten had been thrown onto the streets.

Doc had been a bachelor, though evidently not a very promiscuous one. He spoke with horror of the big-bosomed Frauleins who demanded to see him after concerts and came to the conservatorium with invitations to dinner or afternoon tea. Sometimes, when they were very persistent and he could no longer politely refuse, he went, only to find his hostess, with a very revealing *décolletage,* the only other guest. These moments of terror had scared him off women, seemingly forever.

Geel Piet was quick to point out that his adult experience with women was entirely inappropriate and had no relevance to my predicament. The two of them finally decided that regular bunches of roses from my granpa's garden was all that was needed. The rest would take care of itself.

I was not quite sure what the rest was. 'I think maybe just let the roses do the talking, Peekay,' Doc advised and Geel Piet had added that he'd heard somewhere that lots of roses sent to a lady always did the trick. I wondered for some time what the trick was until Bokkie de Beer told me. I was unable to imagine myself doing the trick with Miss Bornstein.

Mr Isaac offered to motor out to the prison to visit Doc, but this had been turned down by Doc who wouldn't even let Mrs Boxall come to see him. Doc was a proud man and he was determined to meet his peers on equal terms. The prison put him at a distinct disadvantage and made him an object of sympathy. He could not bear such an idea. But now that the war was drawing to a close he talked often of visiting Herr Isaac, which was his name for Mr Isaac, and of the grand games of chess which awaited the two of them.

Mr Isaac Bornstein had arrived from Germany in 1936. He had escaped the Holocaust and had come to live with his family. Miss Bornstein's father had come to South Africa as a young man in 1918. The Bornsteins were the only Jews in Barberton where he was in partnership with Mr Andrews as the town's only firm of solicitors. Miss Bornstein, who had been lecturing at the university in Johannesburg, had returned home because her mother was dying of cancer.

I heard all this from Mrs Boxall who, it turned out, had known Miss Bornstein 'since she was a gel' and didn't mind at all when she discovered I was in love with her. 'She'll make someone a fine wife and if she's prepared to wait until after you're the world champion, then the two of you will make a fine couple.' Mrs Boxall knew that nothing, not even marriage to Miss Bornstein, was allowed to stand in the way of my being welterweight champion of the world. In the meantime I started the barrage of roses, which my granpa would select for me each Friday.

To my surprise my granpa seemed much more informed on the subject of being in love than Doc and Geel Piet, and he examined me closely on the quality of my love. His had been of the highest quality involving the building of an entire rose garden with roses and even trees imported from England. When I said that I was not prepared to give up being world welterweight champion for Miss Bornstein, amid a lot of tapping and tamping and staring into space over the rusty roof, he announced that the quality of my love was certainly worth a dozen long-stemmed roses a week but fell short of a whole garden. I accepted this verdict although I knew it was impossible to love anybody more than I loved Miss Bornstein.

The Kommandant had long since accepted that Hitler wasn't going to win the war and together with most of the warders had joined the Nelspruit chapter of the Oxwagon Guard, a neo-Nazi group dedicated to the restoration of independence for the Afrikaner people. The Oxwagon Guard was very similar to the Ku Klux Klan only it included the English in with Jews and Kaffirs as the corrupters of pure Afrikanerdom. The war had helped them to grow into a powerful secret society which would one day become the covert rulers of South Africa and the major influence in declaring it a republic. I heard all this from Snotnose whose father was a member. He went away on weekends to a training camp where they sat around a big bonfire and sang songs and plotted the downfall of the Smuts government. He also told me that the Kommandant was only a *veldkornet* and that Lieutenant Borman was the boss of the Barberton chapter. During the day the Kommandant could do anything he liked to Lieutenant Borman but at night, outside the prison, the warder from Pretoria was the boss. His wife didn't have asthma at all. Lieutenant Borman had been sent down from Pretoria by 'them' to get the Oxwagon Guard started. Bokkie de Beer said all this was true and that he'd swear it on a stack of Bibles. He'd heard his ma and pa talking about it in the kitchen at home when he was supposed to be asleep.

I could understand their hatred for the English and the Kaffirs. After all there were those twenty-six thousand women and children still to pay for. And Boers just hate Kaffirs anyway. Dingane, the King of the Zulus, had murdered Piet Retief and all his men after he'd given his word he wouldn't. So there was that to pay for as well. But why the Jews? I hadn't heard of any nasty business between the Jews and the Boers, and no one I asked seemed to have either. I'd only known two Jews in my whole life, I was in love with one of them and Harry Crown was the other. I even decided that when I grew up, I'd be a Jew. At one stage I thought that maybe I had been left on the doorstep as a baby by a wandering Jew, and my mother had found me and decided not to tell me. This, I felt certain, explained my headless snake and the absence of a father. But when I asked my mother she seemed pretty shocked at the idea and told me that the Lord was not at all pleased with the Jews. That they had been scattered to the four corners of the earth because they hadn't recognised Him when He came along and had nailed Him to the cross. She was quite adamant that I hadn't been found on the doorstep and that my circumcision was a simple matter of hygiene.

I'd read about circumcision in the Bible; when King Herod heard about Jesus being born he sent his soldiers to kill all the babies who were circumcised. When I asked in Sunday school what being circumcised meant, Mrs Kostler pouted and replied that it wasn't something I should know about at my age.

'But it's in the Bible, so it can't be nasty, can it?' I protested. So, as usual, she sent me to Pastor Mulvery who agreed that I should wait to find out. It was Geel Piet who finally told me, at the same time pointing out in the showers that I was in fact circumcised. It was then that my Jewish theory started to develop. If it hadn't been for the fact that my mother was a born-again Christian and couldn't tell a lie, I'm not so sure I would have believed her rather pathetic explanation about hygiene. Perhaps she asked the Lord for special permission to tell a lie so as not to hurt my feelings.

Snotnose couldn't tell me why the Oxwagon Guard hated the Jews, but Bokkie de Beer said it was because they killed Jesus. Well, all I could think was the Boers had mighty long memories and it was news to me that the Boers were around at the time of Jesus. But then my mother told me the Lord also allowed people to be born-again in other churches, except in the Catholic Church, which was the instrument of the devil. She said there were even born-again Christians in the Dutch Reformed Church. This immediately explained everything. The Boers had simply gone along with the rest of Christianity in condemning the Jews by adding a hate straight from the Bible to the existing hate for the English and the Kaffirs. That way they were bound to get the Lord on their side. It was a neat trick all right, but I for one wasn't falling for it. Quite plainly the Oxwagon Guard was the next threat now that Adolf Hitler had been disposed of, or nearly anyway. News of Germany's imminent collapse was coming through on the wireless daily.

The Kommandant promised Doc he would be released the day peace was declared in Europe, whether his papers were in order or not. We were already into the first days of summer, and Doc and I had talked about being out of prison in time for the firebells, the exquisite little orange lilies no bigger than a two-shilling piece, flecked with specks of pure gold, which bloomed throughout the hills and mountains after the bushfires. Doc was disappointed when the firebells came and went, and VE day had not arrived.

We had already arranged for a new depository for the tobacco leaves, sugar and salt and, of course, the precious mail. These were placed in a watering can made of a four-gallon paraffin tin which had been fashioned originally for Doc's cactus garden. The homemade watering can had been doctored by Geel Piet. A false bottom had been inserted leaving a space which was cunningly fitted with a lid to look like the real bottom. Filled with water the homemade watering can looked perfectly normal, and would even work if it became necessary to appear to be watering plants. It was left standing in Doc's cactus garden and on my way to breakfast I would simply pass through the garden and put the mail and whatever I'd brought into the false bottom of the can. It was natural enough for me to go to the warders' mess via Doc's cactus garden as I often brought new plants for the garden. The warders almost never came this way and habitually used the passage in the interior of the building to get to the mess. We had been using this method for some months as the idea was to make it routine before Doc left and the piano stool with him. The Kommandant understood Doc's need for his cactus garden and decided it would remain as a memorial to Doc's stay, also allowing that Geel Piet could maintain it. As I would be continuing on with the boxing squad, the new system was nicely designed to work without Doc.

The writing of the letters proved to be a more difficult task. Geel Piet wrote with great difficulty at a very elementary level. Without Doc to take dictation, the prisoners would be unable to get messages to their families and contacts. This was solved when Geel Piet and I approached Captain Smit to ask if, for half an hour after boxing, I could give Geel Piet a lesson to improve his reading and writing. Captain Smit was reluctant to agree at first but finally gave his consent.

A strange relationship had grown up between the captain and the little coloured man. They only spoke to each other on the subject of boxing and Captain Smit would occasionally belittle a suggestion from Geel Piet to one of the boxers, but you could see that he respected Geel Piet's judgement and it was only to show who was the boss of the boxing squad. In the months which followed my win against Killer Kroon I continued to enter the ring against bigger, stronger and older opponents, yet had never lost a fight. Captain Smit saw in me the consummate skill Geel Piet had as a coach and secretly admired him for it.

I knew this because Bokkie de Beer said Captain Smit had told his pa that I would be the South African champion one day, '. . . because, man, he is getting the right coaching from the very beginning.'

Under the guise of learning how to read and write, Geel Piet would stare into a school book and dictate the prisoners' letters to me. His facility for remembering names and addresses was quite remarkable. He claimed it was easy for him, he could remember the names of the horses and their odds for every Johannesburg maiden handicap since 1918.

We had the new system up and running well before VE day and, while it wasn't quite as foolproof or as convenient as the piano stool, it worked well enough. Geel Piet was too old a lag not to maintain absolute caution and he would never let me get careless or less mindful of the risks involved. For instance, on rainy days I would bring nothing to the prison as the idea of my taking the outside path in the rain to the warders' mess rather than through the interior passage would seem both silly and, to an alert warder like Borman, suspicious. Nor would the drops be made every day or on the same days. Geel Piet was smart enough to know that little boys are not consistent and so he created this random pattern for my drops even allowing that on some dry days I would take the interior passage to the mess as well. While the system was clumsy and not as convenient as the old one, it was very fortunate that Doc was smart enough to initiate it some time before he left.

One morning, shortly after he had been promoted to lieutenant, Borman wandered into the hall while we were practising. This was simply not done. The Kommandant's orders were that we should not be disturbed during our morning session, two geniuses at work, so to speak. Lieutenant Borman walked over to us, his boots making a hollow sound on the sprung floor. I continued to play until his footsteps ceased as he came to a halt just behind me.

'Good morning, Lieutenant Borman,' we both said together.

'Morning,' Borman said in a superior and disinterested way. He was carrying a cane not unlike the one Mevrou had carried and with it he tapped the leg of the piano stool. 'Stan' up, man,' he said to me. I rose, and he bent down on his knees and with his index finger and thumb stretched he measured the width of the seat. 'A bit deep, hey, maybe something lives inside this seat?' He got down on all fours and put his head under the seat. 'Maybe a false bottom, hey?' He tapped the bottom of the piano stool which gave off a hollow sound. 'Very inter-res-ting, very clever too.' Doc rose from his stool, inserted the key into my stool and raised the lid. Lieutenant Borman started to rise. Halfway up he could see that the seat was filled with sheets of music. Remaining in a crouched position he stared at Doc and me for what seemed like a long time. 'You think this is funny, hey? You think this is playing a funny joke on a person?'

'No, Lieutenant,' Doc said, his voice surprisingly even. 'I think only you should ask before you look. Inside lives only Klavier Meister Chopin.' He opened the lid of his own stool, 'And here lives also Herr Beethoven,

Brahms, Mozart and Bach, and maybe are visiting also some others, perhaps Haydn, Liszt and Tchaikovsky, but not Strauss, definitely not Strauss. Like you, my dear Lieutenant, Strauss is not welcome when I am teaching.'

Lieutenant Borman rose to his full height. He was a big man with a roll of gut just beginning to spill over his belt, and was used to looking down at people, but Doc's six foot seven left him five inches short as the two men stared at each other. The lieutenant was the first to drop his eyes from the gaze of Doc's incredibly steady blue eyes. He laid the cane on top of the Steinway and hitched his pants up. 'You think I don't blêrrie know things is going on? You think I'm a blêrrie fool or something, hey? I got time. I got plenty of time, you hear?' He picked up the cane then brought it up fast and down hard against the open lid of my piano stool, the blow knocking the lid back into place. The sound of the cane against the leather top echoed through the hall. He turned slowly to face Doc again, pointed the cane at Doc so that it touched him lightly on the breast bone as though it were a rapier. 'Next time you try to be cheeky you come off secon' bes'. I'm telling you now, you kraut bastard, I'm finish an' klaar with you both!' He turned and stormed out, his heavy military boots crashing and echoing through the empty hall.

'Phew!' I sighed as I closed the lid of Doc's piano stool and sat down weakly on my own. Doc also sat down, reached over to the Chopin Nocturne No. 5 in F sharp major on the Steinway music rack and commenced to fan himself with it. He was silent for a while, seemingly lost in thought, then said softly, 'Soon come the hills and the mountains.'

FIFTEEN

We were reasonably safe for the month after the piano stool incident as the inspector of prisons was due to arrive and Lieutenant Borman had the job of seeing that the place was spick and span, with fresh whitewash everywhere you looked. Much to Doc's annoyance even the stones bordering his cactus garden were whitewashed. He was prepared to accept whisky bottles outlining his paths but painting real stones seemed to him an insult against nature. Fresh gravel was brought into the inner courtyard together with several loads of finely crushed iron pyrites and mica with which a large letter 'B' was formed in the centre. The darker colour and sheen from the mica and pyrites mix made the letter shimmer against the almost white gravel. The 'B' of course stood for Barberton. This was the lieutenant's idea and he spent hours supervising the old lags sweeping and raking, until it was perfect. I must hand it to him, it did look very nice. Gert said the Kommandant was particularly pleased and Borman was up to his eyeballs in his good books. The prison corridors smelt of polish and the cells of Jeyes Fluid disinfectant. Window-ledges were painted prison blue and everywhere you went smelt of new paint. But it was done early so the smell would have gone by the time the brigadier arrived. New canvas uniforms were issued to the old lags to be worn only during the visit. This was because they were doing all the painting and cleaning, and their old patched and worn uniforms had paint on them and would give the game away. The Kommandant wanted the brigadier to think that everything was normal and that he could have popped in any old time and found things just the same. After the inspection, the lags handed back their new uniforms and wore their old patched and worn clothes until they finally fell apart.

Captain Smit had arranged the usual boxing exhibition and for weeks the Kommandant spent most of his mornings, as he did before every inspection, practising his pistol shooting on the pistol range behind the warders' mess.

The rapidly approaching VE day was a matter of concern to the Kommandant. If it arrived before the brigadier's visit then the truly cultural part of the programme would disappear with the release of Doc. He had tried to elicit a promise from Doc that, should this occur, he would return to the prison and play for the inspector. But Doc had not spent over four years in prison for nothing and he had learned the rules of prison life where everything is in return for something else. The *Goldfields News* had already printed a picture of the Kommandant above a piece by him saying that Doc was in prison because he was a German and that the moment Germany surrendered Doc would be released. The Kommandant couldn't go back on his word without losing face. This he would not allow to happen. Doc's price for staying over, if necessary, caused an uproar among the warders but as far as the Kommandant was concerned no price was too high for a smooth visit. Doc asked if he could give a concert for all the prisoners.

On Sundays, being God's day, the prisoners did not go out in work gangs. Instead they were locked in their cells and fifty at a time were allowed in the exercise pen, a high-walled enclosure of brick and cement about the size of two tennis courts. This was done tribe by tribe, each tribal group allotted ninety minutes. First the Zulus, followed by the Swazis, then the Ndebele, Sotho and Tsonga. The Boers had long understood the antipathy each tribe has for the other, and by keeping the tribes separated in prison they maintained the traditional tensions between them. This was thought to lessen the chances of a mass uprising or a prison strike.

Doc told me how each Sunday he would take a position in the guard tower overlooking the exercise pen to listen to them. Each tribe would use much of the ninety minutes allotted to them singing together, and he soon learned which tribal song each tribe liked best. He had written out the music for it, and then he had composed a piano concerto which represented, in melody terms, each of these songs. Doc said that he had never heard such magnificent harmony. Most of the songs were very beautiful and even though he did not understand the words, he could hear in them the people's longing for their homes, their people, the comfort of their fires, and the lowing of the cattle in the evening. He would sigh and say that his concerto could never capture the beauty of the original voices. He called it 'Concerto of the Great Southland'. It was this which he hoped to play to all the prisoners as his tribute to them before he left the prison.

The idea was for Doc to play the concerto through first, each movement in effect being one or more of a particular tribe's songs. Then on the second time through the tribe whose movement it was would sing the song to Doc's accompaniment on the Steinway. In this way each of the tribes represented in the prison would participate in the concert.

Once the Kommandant had agreed that the concert could go ahead, a great deal had to be done. No rehearsal was possible of course, but through Geel Piet each of the tribes was told which song was needed and the exact time it should take to sing. At night Doc would play the various songs fortissimo with all the hall windows open so the sound carried to the cell blocks. The warders claimed you could hear the cockroaches scratching as the prisoners strained to hear the music.

Because Doc would be at the piano, he decided I should conduct. This I would do in the simplest possible sense, signalling the piano breaks and the pianissimo as well as the fortissimo to the choir. After some weeks I was quite good at taking my directions from Doc and we went through the concerto during morning practice until I knew what every shake and nod of his head meant. Geel Piet had also taken basic instructions back to the prisoners so supposedly they knew what my hand signals would mean. Had Doc proposed that I assume the role of conductor in front of a white audience I could not have done so, but such is the nature of white supremacy in South Africa that I thought little of standing up in front of three hundred and fifty black prisoners and directing them.

Geel Piet informed me of the mounting excitement among the inmates. For several weeks the warders had an easy time, they simply had to threaten an inmate with non-attendance at the concert to get him to comply with any instruction. When the news spread that the Tadpole Angel would be directing the people in the singing *indaba*, it was immediately assumed the concert had a mystical significance and I had chosen this time to meet all of the people. Work time was used as practice, and farmers and the people at the saw mills who hired gangs spoke of singing from dawn until dusk. Even the dreaded quarries rang with the songs of the tribal work gangs. Concerto of the Great Southland was being wrought into being, a musical jigsaw where, on the big night, all the pieces would be brought together under the magic spell cast by the Tadpole Angel.

Lieutenant Borman had tried his best to prevent the concert from taking place, but Captain Smit seemed to have decided that it was a good idea, perhaps for no other reason than that the concert was opposed by Lieutenant Borman. The two men had never liked each other and Captain Smit, who was not a member of the Oxwagon Guard, was said to have been bitterly opposed to the elevation of Borman to lieutenant.

The concert was to take place on the parade ground, and a special platform had been built in the carpentry shop to raise the Steinway above the level of the prisoners. It was proposed that each tribe would form a semicircle around the platform with ten feet separating each group. Two warders carrying sjamboks would be stationed in this corridor to stop any monkey business. A double shift issued with extra ammunition would be on guard duty on the walkways along the wall, and throughout the concert spotlights would be trained on the prisoners.

The concert was scheduled for Monday May 7th, 1945 and all the warders had been placed on full alert. Prisoners were never paraded at night and rumours were rife of tribal fights and vendettas being settled in the dark, as well as of an attempted prison break by the Zulus. The warders, whipped up by Lieutenant Borman, grew increasingly edgy as the concert night drew closer.

Lieutenant Borman had taken to wearing a Sam Browne belt across his shoulder with a revolver with its holster unclipped on his hip, and he lost no opportunity of telling anyone who was prepared to listen that trouble, more trouble than any of the warders could handle, was on its way. 'Give a black prisoner a pinkie and he eats your whole arm off at the shoulder, I'm telling you, man.' He said it so often that it became a joke around the prison and some of the warders started to refer to him behind his back as Pinkie Borman. He even tried to have the concert aborted at the last minute, claiming that it was against prison regulations to assemble more than fifty prisoners in one place at the same time. Captain Smit had demanded that he show him the standing instructions but he couldn't find them, claiming he knew them from Pretoria.

It was difficult to get my mother to agree to me staying up late for the concert. After consulting the Lord and receiving a note from Miss Bornstein which assured her that my school career would not be affected by one late night during the week she gave her permission.

Doc asked me how I would be dressed as conductor. The choice was limited: khaki shirts and shorts, and a pair of black boots with plain grey school socks were the entire contents of my wardrobe. Then Geel Piet suggested that I should be dressed in my boxing uniform, wearing the boots the people had made for me. Doc thought this was a splendid idea and I must say I quite liked it myself. Doc decided it would be awkward for me to wear boxing gloves as it would make it difficult for me to conduct. Geel Piet seemed disappointed and later came back with the suggestion that I should wear gloves and then just before the concert proper began, remove them. He seemed awfully keen on the idea and assured me that it wouldn't be showing off one little bit.

Thus, on the night of the concert, all the myths Geel Piet had so carefully nurtured among the prisoners about the Tadpole Angel would harmonise in my appearance as their leader, uniting all the tribes in the great singing indaba.

In any other society Geel Piet would have been a great promoter. He knew how to set the warp so as to weave a complex pattern which appealed to the imagination of the people. The Tadpole Angel would appear to the people dressed as a great fighter who would lead them in their tribal songs, crossing over the barriers of race and tribe. Was he not already a slayer of giants? Was he not the spirit of the great chief who bound Zulu with the Swazi and the Ndebele and the Tsonga and the Sotho so that they all sat on one mat in a great singing indaba? The one who touched the pencil and letters went out to the families of the people and returned with news of loved ones, who caused children to be warm in winter and wives to have dresses and food for hungry infants? Did he not bring tobacco and sugar and salt into the prison, making it disappear when he entered and reappear when there was no risk? How otherwise could he do this thing for four years without being caught by the Boers?

As with Mrs Boxall's Earl of Sandwich Fund, Doc's wonderful Concerto of the Great Southland was appropriated by the prisoners as being my work and my doing. Geel Piet's clever entrepreneurial mind had seen that it would be more appropriate if it was presented in this way.

The night of Doc's concert arrived. The moment I passed through the gates I knew something in the prison was different. The feeling of despair was not in the air. The sad chattering which was in my mind the instant I stepped within the prison grounds had ceased. The thoughts of the people were calm. I felt a thrill of excitement. Tonight was going to be special.

A full moon had risen just above the dark shadow of the hills behind the prison walls and the parade ground was flooded with moonlight. Doc's Steinway stood sharply outlined on the platform with its top already propped up. The scene had a silence of its own, like looking into a Dali painting. I stood for a moment, for even at my age with my limited grasp of logistics and the law of human probability, this concert seemed a remarkable thing.

As I stood looking at the Steinway etched in the moonlight, the floodlights, bright and sudden as a burst from a welding gun, came on. When my eyes had adjusted to the harsh, raw light I could see that around the platform in a semi-circle on the hard ground, whitewashed lines denoted the area for each tribe. A dozen warders carrying sjamboks came out of the main building and walked towards the piano, their boots making a scrunching sound on the gravel footpath.

I crossed the parade ground, entered a side door and made my way to the hall where Doc would be waiting for me. He was sitting at the Mignon upright, absently tapping at the keys. He looked up as I entered. 'Geel Piet is late, he should be already here now,' he said, his voice tetchy. Doc had grown very reliant on Geel Piet and he regarded him as an essential part of the entire operation. Without him working with the prisoners, a concert still fraught with the potential for unrehearsed disaster would have had no chance of succeeding.

'He'll be here any minute, you'll see,' I said to cheer him up. 'I'll save time and go and get my gloves.' I hurried from the hall and walked down the passageway towards the gym. An old lag was coming towards me carrying a two-gallon coffee pot, another followed him with a tray of mugs and a tin of brown sugar. They were taking coffee to the warders on duty in the parade ground. 'Have you seen Geel Piet?' I asked one. I spoke in Shangaan for I could see from the cicatrisation on his cheeks that he was of the Tsonga tribe. 'No baas, we have not seen this one,' he said humbly. As I departed I heard him say to the lag behind him, 'See how the Tadpole Angel speaks the languages of all the tribes, is he not the chosen leader of the people?'

When I reached the gymnasium I switched on the lights in the gym and the shower room. The lights above the boxing ring were on the wall opposite and the ring was in semi-darkness, but there was enough light for me to see into the box containing the boxing gloves and I quickly selected one of two pairs I liked to use. I went to the showers where I undressed and put on my boxing singlet, shorts, socks and boots. Then I loosely tied the laces of the gloves together and slung them around my neck for Doc to lace up for me later.

I returned to find Doc still alone in the hall, the expression of concern showing clearly on his face as he absent-mindedly gloved me up. 'It is too late to wait longer, we must go now, I will tell Geel Piet I am very cross because this happens.'

The door I'd used to enter the building couldn't be opened from the inside, so we left the hall and walked down the long passage into the main administration building which led out to the parade ground. We passed through the small hallway where I had first entered the prison four years earlier. The lights were out in what was then Lieutenant Smit's office but which was now occupied by Lieutenant Borman. I allowed Doc to walk ahead, and moved over to the service window and peered for a moment into the darkened office. In the half-light I could see where Klipkop sat and next to him the larger desk which was Lieutenant Borman's. My eyes wandered around the room and stopped when they rested on a thin strip of light showing under the door of the interrogation room which led off from the main office. The door must have been slightly ajar, because I heard the unmistakable thud of a blow and a sudden sharp groan such as men make when they receive a hard punch to the solar plexus. It was not an unusual occurrence but it seemed inappropriate on this full moon night of the playing of the Concerto of the Great Southland.

The prisoners were already seated in their marked off sections when we arrived, the warders walking up and down the corridors striking their sjamboks against the sides of their legs and looking business-like. The prisoners avoided looking at them, almost as though they were not there. Talking was not allowed, but as we passed I could see the people smiling and a low murmur swept over the seated prisoners as Doc and I stepped onto the platform.

The Kommandant arrived shortly after us and stood on the platform to address the prisoners. Lieutenant Borman was to have done the translation into Fanagalo but appeared not to have arrived. The Kommandant was clearly annoyed by this and after a few minutes during which he looked at his watch repeatedly, he started to speak in Afrikaans.

'Listen to me, you hear,' he said and I quickly translated into Zulu. He looked surprised. 'Can you translate, Peekay?' I nodded. 'Okay, then I will speak and stop after every sentence so you can translate.'

The Kommandant was uncomfortable talking to the prisoners, and he spoke too loudly and too harshly. 'This concert is a gift to you all from the professor who is not a dirty criminal like all of you, you hear! I don't know why an important person like him wants to make a concert for Kaffirs, not only Kaffirs, but criminals as well. But that's what he wants so you got it because I am a man of my word. I just want you to know it won't happen again and I don't want any trouble, you hear, you just listen to the peeano and you sing, then we march you back to your cells.' He turned to me, snorting nervously through his nostrils. 'That's all. You tell them what I said now.'

I said the Kommandant welcomed them and that the professor welcomed them and thanked them for coming to his great singing indaba. He hoped that they would sing each tribe better than the other so they would be proud. They should watch my hands, and I took my boxing gloves off to demonstrate the hand movements. When I had finished the sea of faces in front of me were smiling fit to burst and then spontaneously they started to clap. 'You done a good job, Peekay,' the Kommandant said, pleased at this spontaneous response to his speech.

Doc played the Concerto for the Great Southland through entirely and the prisoners listened quietly with nods of approval as they heard the melodies of their own tribal songs. At the end they all clapped furiously.

I then stood up and showed them how I would bring each tribe into their part and stop them by fading their voices out or simply ending a song or a passage with a downward stroke of the hands, a slicing gesture. I asked them to raise their hands if they understood and a sea of hands rose.

Doc played the prelude which was a musical medley of each of the melodies and then I brought in the Sotho singers. Their voices melded into the night as though they had caused the early summer air to vibrate with a deep harmony before they broke into song. It was the most beautiful male singing I had ever heard. They seemed instinctively to understand what was required of them and followed every gesture as though anticipating it. They were followed by the Ndebele who carried a more strident melody and whose voices rose deep and true, repeating the thread of the song carried by a single high-pitched male voice, chasing the single voice, sometimes even catching it to surround it and nourish it with beautiful harmony before allowing it to escape once more to carry the song forward again. The Swazis followed as beautiful as any, then the Shangaan. Each tribe sounded different, seemingly building on the tribe before, each separated by a common refrain which was hauntingly African and seemed somehow to be a mixture of all. The Zulus took the last part which rose in power and majesty as they sang the victory song of the great Shaka, using the flats of their hands to bang on the ground as the mighty Zulu impi had done with their feet, until the parade ground appeared to shake. The other tribes soon got the rhythm and they too hit the ground to add to the effect. The concerto lasted for half an hour, the last part being the by now familiar refrain which all the tribes hummed in a glorious finale. Never had a composer's work had a stranger debut and never a greater one. Eventually the composition would be played by philharmonic and symphony orchestras around the world, accompanied by some of the world's most famous choirs, but it would never sound better than it did under the African moon in the prison yard when three hundred and fifty black inmates lost themselves in their pride and love for their tribal lands.

Doc rose from the Steinway and turned to the mass of black faces. He was crying unashamedly and fumbling for his bandanna, and many of the Africans were weeping with him. Then without warning came a roar of approval from the people that would have been impossible to stop. Doc would later tell me that it was the greatest moment of his life, but what they were saying was 'Onoshobishobi Ingelosi! Onoshobishobi Ingelosi!' Tadpole Angel! Tadpole Angel! chanted over and over again.

The Kommandant looked worried and some of the warders had started to slap the sjamboks against the ground. Onoshobishobi Ingelosi! Onoshobishobi Ingelosi! Doc had risen from his seat to take a bow and I jumped up onto it and started to wave my hands to indicate that the chanting must stop. Almost instantly there was silence. Doc looked up surprised, not sure what had happened. I said, 'The great music wizard and I thank the people for singing, you are all men who tonight have brought honour to your tribes and you have brought great honour also to the great musical wizard and to me.' I would have lacked the maturity to make such a speech in English but the African tongue is gracious and by its very nature fits such words easily. 'You must go quietly now in the names of your wives and your children, for the Boers grow restless.' My voice was a thin piping sound in the night.

Suddenly a shower of stars sprayed across the sky above the town and then another and another, single red and green stars that burst high, cascades that danced in the heavens. The prisoners looked up in awe, some even covering their heads against the magic. A warder came hurrying up to the Kommandant, whispered in his ear and the Kommandant turned towards Doc and then extended his hand. 'You are free to go, Professor. The war in Europe is over. The Germans have surrendered.' He pointed in the direction of the town. 'See the fireworks, the blêrrie Rooineks are already celebrating.' A final cascade of stars burst against the dark sky and the black men cried out in awe; they had never seen such a happening before.

Was this not the final sign? Even the heavens spoke for the Tadpole Angel, spoke for all to see. The myth of the Tadpole Angel was complete. Now it could only grow and shape as legends are wont to do. Nothing I would ever do could change things. I had crossed the line to where only the greatest of the medicine men have ever been, perhaps even further, for not even the greatest were known by all the tribes and honoured by all of the people. I had become a myth.

Each tribe rose when they were commanded to do so and marched silently away until the parade ground was empty but for the guards who manned the walls, and the Kommandant.

'Magtig! I have never seen such a thing in all my life, man,' the Kommandant said, shaking his head. He turned to Doc, 'Your music was beautiful, man, the most beautiful I have ever heard and such singing we will never hear again. Peekay, some day you will make a great Kommandant. I have never seen such command of black men. It is as though you are some kind of witchdoctor, hey?'

Quite suddenly there was a single voice in the night as though from the direction of the gymnasium, 'Onoshobishobi Ingelosi!' I heard it just the once and the sad voices in my head began chattering; the trouble in this place had returned.

Doc was overwhelmed by the news of the German surrender and the excitement of the concert, and he sat on the piano stool for a long time sniffling into his bandanna. The Kommandant bade us goodnight and the floodlights had once more been switched off so that the moon, which had risen high in the sky, ruled the night again. Then I remembered Geel Piet. I turned to Doc who looked up at me at the same time, we were thinking the same thing.

'Geel Piet never came. I cannot understand it. He would not have stayed away,' Doc said. I could see he felt guilty for not having thought about his absence sooner.

There was a scrunch of footsteps on gravel and soon Gert appeared out of the darkness. 'Captain Smit says it's late and school tomorrow, so I must drive you home now, Peekay.'

I was surprised, for I had expected to walk home as always. 'I'll go and get changed and take the gloves back,' I said, and I left Doc sitting on the piano stool, staring at his hands.

'It was a wonderful concert, Professor,' I heard Gert say in his halting English as I ran into the dark towards the gymnasium. I entered the side door to the gym and switched on the light, moving past the wooden horse and the medicine balls, and giving the punching bag a straight left and a right hook. The big wooden box in which we kept the gloves was just to the side of the ring. I had tied the laces of my gloves together after the concert and had strung them around my neck as before. I secretly felt this made me seem more like a fighter. Now I took the gloves off and threw them towards the box from halfway across the gym. It was almost a good shot with one glove landing inside the wooden box while the other hung over the rim. I moved over to drop the glove in and suddenly, with a certainty I knew always to trust, became aware that something was terribly wrong. I ran over to the wall opposite and turned the ring light on. For a split second the sudden blaze of light blinded me; then I saw the body in the centre of the ring.

Geel Piet lay face down, as though he had fallen, his arms stretched out to either side of him. His head lay in a pool of blood where he had haemorrhaged from the nose and mouth. Without thinking I jumped into the ring screaming, although I could hear no sound coming from me. I fell to my knees beside him and started to shake him, then I rose and took him by one of his arms and tried to pull him to his feet. I began bawling at him, 'Get up, please get up! If you'll get up you'll be alive again!' But the little yellow man's body just flopped at the end of his arm and his head bounced in the pool of blood which splattered in an explosion of colour around his face. Inside me the loneliness bird cackled: 'He's dead . . . he's dead! He'll never be alive again!' I kept pulling him and trying to make him come alive. 'Please Geel Piet! Please get up, if you can get up you'll be alive again! It's true! I promise it's true! Please!'

There was a trail of blood as I pulled him across the ring. And then I saw that in his other hand he held the picture of Captain Smit, Doc, Gert, myself and himself. The corner of the photograph covering Captain Smit's head was soaked in blood. I dropped his hand and fell over his body and sobbed and sobbed. Then I felt myself being lifted from Geel Piet's body by Captain Smit, who held me like a baby in his arms and rocked me as I sobbed uncontrollably into his chest. 'Shhhh, don't cry, champ, don't cry,' he whispered as he rocked and rocked me. 'Shhhh. I will avenge you, this I promise. Don't cry, champ, don't cry, little brother.'

The festivities in honour of the inspector of prisons were held on the following Saturday night. Doc tried to get out of playing; the death of Geel Piet had upset him dreadfully and the idea of returning to the prison, even for the concert, filled him with apprehension. The Kommandant didn't quite see it the same way, Geel Piet was simply another Kaffir. 'No man! Fair is fair! I gave you your Kaffir concert, now I want my brigadier concert! I'm a fair man, and I kept my word. I let you leave the prison the morning after Germany surrendered. A man's word is his word.'

Doc's return to his cottage had been an emotional business. Dee and Dum had scrubbed and polished and his home had never been as clean and neat. Gert dropped Doc at the bottom of the hill as the roadway to the cottage had eroded over the four years he'd been away and it wasn't a good idea to try to drive to the top. Gert reported the road would not allow the truck to return the Steinway; the very next day Klipkop sent a prison gang to repair the road. They worked on it furiously so that it would be ready on the day after the concert for the piano to be returned.

Doc had mentioned on his way home that his first job would be to extend the cactus garden. Gert told Captain Smit who instructed the warder ganger that, after they'd completed the road repairs, the work gang should construct the new terraces Doc required.

Mrs Boxall had ordered groceries from H. C. Duncan, the town's leading grocery shop, and had made sure that the municipal ratcatcher had been up to the cottage to check the outside lavatory hole to see that no snakes or anything else had made their home down there in the past four years. He had dropped a bucket of chlorine pellets down the hole and for the first week you had to hold your nose against the sharp fumes when you entered. When Dee and Dum unpacked the box of groceries from H. C. Duncan they found that Mrs Boxall had included a parcel of her own which contained one of those really soft rolls of toilet paper. Goodness knows where she found it, because only the hard kind had been available since the war. Dee and Dum held the roll against their cheeks and exclaimed at its softness, marvelling that paper such as this could be used for such a silly purpose. I must say they had a point. Doc would have agreed, for he only ever used the *Goldfields News.*

Mrs Boxall also gave me a bottle of Johnny Walker for Doc which she said Mr Goodhead of the Barberton Bottle Store had been fearfully sweet and let her have. After my jaw incident and all the mentions I'd heard of the demon drink down at the Apostolic Faith Mission I wasn't at all sure that Mrs Boxall was doing the right thing. I carried the whisky up to the cottage convinced that at any moment the Lord might send a bolt of lightning out of the clear blue sky to strike the bottle from my hand and possibly take me along with it. If God could part the Red Sea then striking a bottle of Johnny Walker with a bolt from the blue seemed like a simple enough thing for Him to do.

For several weeks before Doc's release Mrs Boxall had been sending the boy from the library to the cottage with his bike basket filled with Doc's books. She referred to these books as not really the town's property but simply 'borrowed for the duration'. When Doc returned to his cottage on the morning after the people's concert he found it exactly as it had been some four years before, with only the Steinway missing. He told me some weeks later that he sat down on the stoep and wept and wept because his friends had all been so lovely to him.

After school on the first day of Doc's freedom I found him in his cactus garden cutting a dead trunk from a patch of halfmens; their proper name is *Pachypodium namaquanum* and they stand about seven feet tall and look like large, prickly elephant trunks sticking out of the ground.

I made coffee and we sat on the stoep for a while. Neither of us had mentioned Geel Piet, both unwilling to share our individual grief. After a while Doc brought up the loss by saying, 'No more letters for the people. No more anything.' Then we talked about the garden for a while and Doc pointed to an overgrown hedge of krans aloe which he had originally used as a windbreak and which was now beginning to intrude into the garden. 'We are being invaded by *Aloe arborescens.* I will attack soon, ja in one week.' I could see he loved the idea of making plans again, of being free to decide the divisions of the days and the weeks ahead.

He rose from his stool to refill his coffee mug and groaned. I looked up in alarm to see him trying to conceal his pain with a smile. 'Ja, I am a domkopf, Peekay. This morning I climb the hill to our rock but such a small climb has made me very stiff. It is four years since, and my muscles are soft and my lungs soon grow tired. It will take maybe a month, maybe more before we can go into the hills again.' He walked stiffly towards the kitchen where I had left the coffee pot, and for the first time I saw that Doc had become an old man.

He spent most of Thursday and all of Friday in the cactus garden, content to be on his own. He planned an excursion to visit Mrs Boxall at the library on Saturday morning, the day after school broke up for the June holidays and the day of the Kommandant's concert. He had instructed me to ask her if this would be convenient. Mrs Boxall was in quite a tizz when I told her that Doc would be coming to see her. I also told my granpa of Doc's visit to the library and early on Saturday morning he cut two dozen long-stemmed pink and red roses for Doc to give to Mrs Boxall. 'He can't go giving her a bunch of cactus flowers now, can he?' he declared a little smugly. My granpa was a rose man and saw no virtue whatsoever in a cactus garden.

We arrived at the library just as the clock on the magistrate's court tower struck nine. The library was closed and the library boy was sitting on the step outside. 'The missus, she be come soon,' he said. Doc started to stride up and down the footpath, stopping to hook his finger into the front of his celluloid collar and to clear his throat. Then I saw Charlie, Mrs Boxall's little navy blue Austin Seven, coming down the road towards us. It was making a dreadful racket and was obviously quite sick but Doc seemed not to hear it approaching. 'Here she comes!' I yelled, and thrust the bunch of roses at him. He jumped visibly and grabbed the flowers with both hands. Charlie lurched to a halt outside the library and the engine died with a clunking sound. Mrs Boxall stuck her head out of the window and spoke to me.

'Come along, Peekay, give a gel a hand, there's a good chap,' she said cheerily. In my anxiety for Doc I didn't move immediately. 'Come along, Peekay, open the door, you're not a Boer you know.' I hurried to open the door of the Austin. 'Now that the war is over we can all go back to having nice manners,' Mrs Boxall said, stepping out of Charlie. I realised she was grateful for the opportunity to chide me so as to cover the first few moments of her reunion with Doc. She looked up at Doc and gave him her best smile. Doc thrust the roses at her. 'And here's the man with the nicest manners of all,' she said, burying her nose into the pink and red blossoms and breathing deeply. 'There's nothing quite as charming as roses, don't you think?' She cradled them in her arm like the Queen and stretched her hand out towards Doc. 'Roses say so much without having to say anything at all.' Doc immediately clicked his heels together, almost knocking himself over in the process, then he bowed stiffly and, taking her hand, lifted it high above her head and kissed it lightly.

'Madame Boxall,' he said.

'Oh dear, I have missed you, Professor. It is so very nice to have you back.' I thought for a moment that she might cry, but instead she buried her head in the roses again and then looked up brightly. 'A cup of tea for Peekay and me and for you, Professor, I have some fresh ground Kenya coffee. Peekay, bring my basket from Charlie.' She handed the roses back to Doc and reached into her handbag for the keys to the library. 'I've baked a lovely Madeira cake, it's in the tin beside the basket, do be sure to bring it along, Peekay.'

Once we were inside it was like old times. The four and a bit years slipped away and it was the same old Doc and Mrs Boxall. Doc spoke with some consternation of the prospect of returning to the prison that evening to fulfil his obligation to play for the brigadier and Mrs Boxall volunteered to drive us over. Doc, to my enormous surprise, then suggested that she might like to attend the concert and she seemed thrilled at the idea. We phoned Captain Smit who said that Mrs Boxall was most welcome, that any friend of Doc's was a friend of his.

We then talked for the first time about Geel Piet. Mrs Boxall had never met him but he was almost as real to her as he had been to Doc and me.

Doc lamented the fact that the Sandwich Fund was effectively finished and to our surprise Mrs Boxall would hear of no such thing. 'Just a temporary hiccup, we can't have Geel Piet thinking we're a bunch of milk sops. I have a plan.' She gazed at us steadily. 'I'm not prepared to reveal it yet, not even to the two of you. But I can tell you this much. I had proposed taking the train to Pretoria but now, by golly, Pretoria seems to have come to us.' She wore one of her tough expressions and so we didn't question her any further. 'It's my plan and, if it doesn't work, then only I shall look a proper idiot,' she declared.

On the night of Geel Piet's death, Captain Smit had led me sobbing and hiccuping to the blue prison Plymouth, where Gert was waiting to drive me home. He had told me that I needed a break from training and was not to return to the prison until the boxing exhibition for the brigadier on Saturday night. It was a nice holiday but, as prospective welterweight champion of the world, it worried me that I wasn't in training. It hadn't yet occurred to me that I would return to a boxing squad that was now without Geel Piet, and that from now on I would simply be the most junior boxer under Captain Smit's concerned but preoccupied care.

On Saturday night Mrs Boxall picked us up at the bottom of Doc's road. Even though the road was now in splendid repair Charlie, in his present state of health, was not considered capable of climbing it. We arrived at the prison just before seven o'clock and made our way to the hall. Doc's piano recital was to be the first item of the evening: it was the cultural part, it was thought best to get it over with while everyone was still well behaved. After that, the audience would go through into the gym for the boxing exhibition and then back to the hall for the tiekiedraai dancing and braaivlies. The air smelt smoky from the braaivleis fires which had been lit on the parade ground immediately outside the hall. Someone was already playing a piano accordion in the dark, his swaying torso silhouetted by the light from one of the fires.

Mrs Boxall, Doc and I found three seats in the front row so that Doc could get to the Steinway easily. I hadn't seen Gert since he had driven me home four days before and he now made a special point of coming over to me. I excused myself and we moved off into the corner for a chat. Gert told me again how sorry he was about Geel Piet and how it wasn't the same without him on the boxing squad.

'Man, I don't understand, he was only a Kaffir but I miss him a lot,' he confided. He also told me that the brigadier's inspection was an all-time success and that Lieutenant Borman was up to his eyeballs in the Kommandant's good books right up until late that afternoon.

'What happened this afternoon?' I asked, delighted at the suggestion that Lieutenant Borman might have fallen from grace.

'The brigadier stood up and said to us all that he had never seen a prison in better shape. But that also Pretoria had heard of the Kaffir concert.' He paused and his eyes grew wide, 'I'm telling you man, we knew who had told them about it and we thought we were in a lot of trouble.'

He shook his head from side to side. 'But it wasn't like that at all. The brigadier said that it was a piece of proper prison reform and that Barberton led the way and the Kommandant was to be congratulated. Not only were the prison buildings and grounds immaculate and the discipline first class, but also prison reform was taking place that was an example to the rest of the country. You should have seen Pinkie Borman's face, man, he was furious. I nearly wet my pants. Everyone was looking at him with this big smile on their faces, even the Kommandant.'

Snotnose came over and said Doc wanted me. Gert told me he'd see me later in the gym. Doc had decided to play Chopin's Nocturne No. 5, the same piece I had so unsuccessfully been coming to grips with for some weeks. I knew the music well enough to turn the pages for him and that's why he had sent for me. Doc had agreed to play two pieces for the concert. When I had enquired about the second piece he had said it was to be a surprise and that after the Chopin nocturne I was to return to my seat beside Mrs Boxall.

The hall was almost full, and the warders and their wives and guests from the town had all taken their seats when the Kommandant walked to the front of the hall and stood beside the Steinway.

'Dames and Here,' he began, 'it gives me much pleasure to welcome you all to this concert in honour of our good friend Brigadier Joubert, Transvaal Inspector of Prisons. The brigadier this very afternoon said nice things about Barberton prison and I just want to say to all my men that I am proud of you. Now it is our turn to say nice things about the brigadier who is a good *kêrel* and also a good revolver shot as some of us saw at the pistol range this afternoon. We thank him for his visit and,' the Kommandant grinned, 'for going so easy on us.' The audience laughed and he continued, 'No, seriously man, it is men like Brigadier Joubert who make the South African Prison Service a place where good men can hold their heads up high.' He paused and seemed to be examining the large gold signet ring on his hand before looking up again. 'The concert we held for the black prisoners last week, the brigadier was kind enough to say, was a good example of prison reform. It was just a little idea I had and it worked. But the brigadier is a man of *big* ideas that work, a big man who gives us inspiration and strength to continue.' I could feel Mrs Boxall's arm trembling against my own and I turned to see her trying very hard not to laugh. 'He is a man of the Church, a God-fearing man and a man dedicated to the prison service.' The audience broke out in spontaneous applause and the Kommandant let it go on for a moment before holding his hand up. 'He is also a cultured man, which brings me to our first item on the programme for tonight.' He cleared his throat and looked around. 'All of you know that we have had in this prison as our guest,' one or two titters issued from the audience and the Kommandant went on, 'no, I mean it, man, as our honoured guest for the past four years, a man who is a musical genius. This is the last time we will hear him play for us. Last week he helped us with the prisoners' concert and tonight he is giving a personal one just for us in Brigadier Joubert's honour. I ask you now to welcome Professor Von Vollensteen.' Doc rose and did a small bow to the audience and gave me a nod, and with the applause continuing we moved over to the Steinway.

Doc lost no time getting started and the Kommandant was still on his way to his seat when the first notes of the Chopin nocturne filled the hall. At first the music was wonderfully relaxed, deceptively simple and straightforward and then, as the recital continued, the melody line became more and more ornamental.

Doc's finger technique was remarkable as the delicate filigree writing for the right hand came into play. In the middle section the music became more and more complex, fast and urgent, leading to a long crescendo and frenzied climax where Doc could shake his head a lot and bang furiously at the keys which he knew the audience would like. The nocturne ended with an elegant descent in steps towards a rustling, almost muted final chord.

Doc had chosen well. Chopin's Nocturne No. 5 is not difficult music to understand and it is very beautiful. The audience stood up, clapped and seemed very pleased. Doc rose and took a bow, and nodded for me to return to my seat next to Mrs Boxall. Then he removed several sheets of music from inside his piano stool and fixed them carefully to the music rack. He turned to the audience and cleared his throat.

'Ladies and gentlemen, tonight I would like to dedicate this next piece of music, which I have played once only before, to a friend, a very good friend. I have named this music by his name and it is for him. I give you, "Requiem for Geel Piet"!'

Without further ado Doc sat down at the Steinway and commenced to play the Concerto of the Great Southland which he had now renamed. The melodies of the tribal songs seemed to take over the hall, as the Ndebele song followed the Sotho with its more strident rhythm, Doc's left hand taking the part of the solo high-pitched voice and the right chasing it as the singers themselves had done. The Swazi melody followed and then the Shangaan, each separated by the haunting refrain that carried a hint of each, yet acted to lead away from the one and into the other. Finally came the victory song of the great Shaka and the Steinway seemed to build the drama of the magnificent Zulu impi, the chords crashing as they marched into battle. The requiem closed with a muted and very beautiful compilation of the songs of the tribes. The music seemed to swell as all around us from the cells beyond the hall the voices came as the tribes completed the requiem. Geel Piet, who had had no tribe, whose blood was the mixture of all the people of Southern Africa – the white tribe, the Bushman, the Hottentot, the Cape Malay and the black tribal blood of Africa itself – was celebrated in death by all the tribes. He was the new man of Southern Africa, the result of three hundred years of torture, treachery, racism and slaughter in the name of one colour or another.

There was a special kind of silence as the performance ended. To our own was joined the silence of the listeners beyond the hall. We had all been a part of the lament for Africa. Requiem for Geel Piet was a lament for all of us, the tears shed for South Africa itself.

During the applause Brigadier Joubert, the Inspector of Prisons, rose from his seat and moved to the front of the hall. He raised his hands for silence and the hall grew quiet again. Taking a khaki handkerchief from his trouser pocket he slowly wiped his eyes and began to speak very emotionally.

'Tonight, dames and here, we have heard a work of true genius. Whoever this Geel Piet was, we know from his name that he was an Afrikaner who is honoured by this music. He was also the spirit of Africa and as Afrikaners we should all honour him and his death.' He folded the handkerchief neatly and put it back into the pocket of his tunic. 'All I can say is that he must have been a great man for the professor to write a piece of music just for him. I now ask you all to stand and to bring your hands together once again for the professor.' I saw that Captain Smit had a big smile on his face and was clapping madly. Even the Kommandant seemed to have decided to ignore the irony, he was clapping for all he was worth. I think he must have seen a colonel's insignia on the lapels of his uniform in the very near future.

Doc stood with his head bowed throughout the brigadier's speech and I could see that he had his bandanna out and was doing one of his sniffs into it. I knew he was crying for Geel Piet. But I also knew Geel Piet would have found this moment very funny.

'Ag, man,' he would have said, 'why must a man always wait until he is dead for such a clever joke to heppen?'

Then the warders, wives and guests moved into the gym to watch the boxing exhibition. The chairs were being cleared from the hall to get ready for the Boere music and tiekiedraai which, with the braaivleis, were the highlight of the evening.

Captain Smit had worked out a routine for the boxing exhibition which was pretty clever. All the boxers were seated in a row facing the ring and he was in the ring with a whistle round his neck, acting as referee. When the audience had filled the gym he blew his whistle and I climbed into the ring with Snotnose. We shook hands and Captain Smit blew his whistle again and Snotnose and I started to box. The idea was that after every round, one of the boxers would step down and another would replace him. As the youngest I stepped out first and Fonnie Kruger came in and boxed the next round with Snotnose. Then Maatie Snyman replaced Snotnose and fought Fonnie, and then Fonnie stepped down and Nels Stekhoven came in, and so on right up to the heavyweights, where Klipkop fought Gert, and then as a joke I stepped in and fought the final round with Klipkop. It was a good way to entertain the crowd, as every boxer ended up fighting someone lighter and heavier than himself, and we fought as hard as we could to give them a good show. It all went like clockwork and not a word was spoken by Captain Smit who just blew his whistle to start and stop a round. When I stepped into the ring with Klipkop the crowd cheered like mad and someone said, 'Murder da bum, Peekay!' and everybody laughed. I danced around Klipkop and gave him a terrible time, punching him in the solar plexus. He also attempted to take my head off with huge uppercuts, always missing by a mile. The crowd enjoyed it a lot, and finally Captain Smit blew his whistle and held my hand up and there was a lot of cheering.

Afterwards, as the crowd was leaving, I went over to Doc and Mrs Boxall to tell them that I had to change and would see them at the braaivleis. Mrs Boxall said that she wanted to have a word with the inspector chappie and that she'd be obliged if Doc would go with her for moral support, so they'd see me later. As I turned to go she called me back.

'Peekay, I must say I've never been too keen on your boxing. But you do seem to be rather good at it and I do believe you will be a welter-weight champion of the world some day. Jolly well done is all I can say!'

'A champion already. Absoloodle!' Doc added.

We were all in the showers changing when Klipkop came in. 'Captain Smit wants you all to come back into the gym when you finished. Make quick, you must all be there in the next ten minutes. When you get into the gym the lights will be off. Only the lights above the ring will be on.' He had changed hurriedly as he spoke, and now he fumbled with his shirt buttons and then sat down and pulled on his socks and shoes. 'Sit in the dark and be very quiet. Not near the door but on the far side of the ring, you hear?' We all nodded and he hurried from the room.

We hadn't been seated long in the darkened gym when one of the double doors opened spilling a shaft of light from the passage into the gymnasium. Caught in the light were Captain Smit, Klipkop and, standing between them, Lieutenant Borman. The door swung back into place and we could only dimly see the three men walking towards the ring while they would not have been able to see us. Then they appeared suddenly in the circle of light illuminating the ring.

'Climb in, Borman, up into the ring,' Captain Smit said.

'What you doing man, what's happening?' we heard Lieutenant Borman say.

'Just climb in, we'll tell you in a minute. Everything will be made clear in a minute,' Captain Smit said. Borman climbed up into the ring and Captain Smit and Klipkop followed. A pair of boxing gloves hung from the posts of each of the two boxers' corners and in one of the neutral corners lay what appeared to be a piece of rolled up canvas. Like Captain Smit, Lieutenant Borman was wearing civilian clothes, an open neck shirt and long pants. Captain Smit leaned into the ropes and removed his shoes, leaving his socks on.

'Take off your shoes, please, Lieutenant,' Klipkop said politely.

'Hey man, what's going on here?' Borman said, with just a hint of apprehension in his voice. 'I'm not going to fight, man. I don't want to fight nobody. What's going on?'

'Take off your shoes, please Lieutenant,' Klipkop repeated. Captain Smit picked up his shoes and placed them neatly beside a corner post.

'I got no quarrel with you, Smit. I never done anything personally to you. Why do you want to fight me?'

'Take off your shoes or am I going to have to take them off for you, Lieutenant?' Klipkop asked calmly.

'Keep you hands off me, you hear,' Borman snarled. 'I am your superior, Oudendaal! You show me respect or you on report, you hear?' He seemed to gain courage from the sound of his voice, shaking his finger as he shouted at Klipkop. Klipkop sighed, shook his head slowly and started to move towards Lieutenant Borman. Borman hurriedly pulled one shoe off and dropped it on the canvas, then removed the other and placed them both in the neutral corner right next to the rolled up piece of canvas.

From the moment Captain Smit had stepped into the ring he had remained silent, and I could sense this was beginning to unnerve Borman. Klipkop lifted the gloves from the post nearest to the lieutenant and walked over to him.

'Give me your hand, please sir,' he said in a matter of fact sort of voice.

Lieutenant Borman immediately folded his arms, tucking his hands under his armpits. 'No man! No way! You can't make me fight, man. Let Smit tell me first what I done.' Captain Smit had retrieved the gloves in his corner; placing one between his legs, he slipped his hand into the other. 'Jus' tell me, you hear!' Borman shouted. Captain Smit looked up from the glove straight at Borman. Keeping his eyes fixed on the lieutenant he slowly pulled the glove from his fist and dropped it, then opened his knees so that the second glove also fell onto the canvas. He walked over to the neutral corner and picked up the object lying there. We could now see, for sure, that it was a roll of canvas. He held the roll up to his chin so that it unrolled. My heart gave an enormous leap. The canvas sheet Captain Smit was holding was covered with dry blood. Borman pulled back in horror but then, as quickly, recovered himself.

'What's this, man? I never saw that before in my whole life.'

Captain Smit said nothing but began to roll the canvas up again. I had been terrified, when I climbed into the ring earlier, that I might see signs of Geel Piet's blood, but the old canvas had been removed and the ring re-covered. The sight of Captain Smit holding part of the old blood-stained canvas brought back the shock I had felt, and without realising it I began to sob. Suddenly a large hard hand covered my mouth, and Gert's arm came around my shoulder and drew me into him.

Captain Smit put the canvas back in the corner and retrieved the boxing gloves. Klipkop pulled Borman's arms open and slipped his gloves on. This time the lieutenant made no move to stop Klipkop who laced up the gloves.

'I don't know what you talking about, you hear! I swear I was at home the night the Kaffir died. I can prove it! I had to go home because my wife had an asthma attack. Everybody saw I wasn't at the Kaffir concert. That's because I was at home. I got called on the telephone, my wife had a bad attack and I had to go home. You're mad, I'm telling you, you mad, I never done it. I never killed that Kaffir!'

Klipkop finished tying Captain Smit's gloves and he walked to the centre of the ring. 'No butting, no kicking, fight like a man,' Klipkop said, and climbed out of the ring leaving Smit and Borman to fight.

Captain Smit started across the ring towards Lieutenant Borman, but Borman held up his glove open-handed. 'Look. I admit I phoned Pretoria about the Kaffir concert, I admit that. Orright you got me on that. I thought I was right, I done my duty, that's all. You can't blame me for that. I done what I thought was right.'

Captain Smit brushed the open glove aside with a left and drove a hard right into the soft roll of gut that spilt over Borman's belt. The lieutenant doubled up, clasping at his stomach with both hands trying to catch his breath. Smit stood over him waiting. Without warning, Borman suddenly smashed his gloved fist into Captain Smit's balls. The captain staggered back, grabbing at his genitals, and then he sank to his knees. Borman was on him in a flash, and catching him on the side of the jaw he sent Captain Smit crashing to the canvas. Borman shouted, 'You Kaffirboetie, you nigger lover, don't fuck with me you hear, man!' He kicked Captain Smit in the ribs just as Klipkop, who had climbed back into the ring, reached him and brought his arms around him. But Borman's blood was up, he was a big man, and he jerked free just as Captain Smit was attempting to rise. He caught Smit another solid blow to the side of the head, putting him back on the canvas. Klipkop tried to hold Lieutenant Borman again.

'I killed the bastard, you hear!' Borman shouted. 'I killed that yellow nigger. He wouldn't tell me who gave him the letters, who brought the letters in. I caught him red-handed, two letters, man, red-handed! Two fucking letters in his pocket. He wouldn't tell me. I broke every bone in his face. I jammed the fucking donkey prick up his arse till he shit his entrails, but he wouldn't tell me! The black bastard wouldn't talk!' There were flecks of foam at the corners of Borman's mouth and he began to sob.

Captain Smit had dragged himself to his feet and stood facing Borman, who was no longer trying to get out of the bear hug Klipkop held him in. Bringing his gloves up, Smit signalled to Borman to come and fight. Klipkop released his grip and Borman rushed at Smit, walking into a straight left from Smit that stopped him in his tracks. Borman charged in again and Captain Smit stopped him again, repeating the straight left into the face. It was obvious that Borman had never been a boxer. A trickle of blood ran from his nose and he brought his arm up to wipe it. A smear of blood covered the top of his arm and he stared down in horror at it. 'Shit, I'm bleeding!' he cried. 'Jesus Christ, I'm bleeding!'

Then Captain Smit stepped up and smashed his glove into Borman's face. The blow seemed to flatten Borman's nose and he dropped to the canvas. Covering his face with his gloves, he wailed, 'Don't hit me, please don't hit me!'

Captain Smit signalled to Klipkop to get Borman back onto his feet. Klipkop got his arms under Borman's armpits but the man refused to get up. The blood from his nose had stained his white shirt and his eyes were wide with terror. Klipkop let him go and he dropped to the ground; then, crawling on all fours towards Captain Smit, Borman held Smit around the legs. 'Please don't hit me, Captain. I don't understand, why you doing this to me? It was only a Kaffir, a dirty stinking yellow man, why you hitting a white man over a Kaffir?'

Captain Smit kicked his legs free of Borman's embrace. 'You can't even fight, you low bastard. You can't even stand up and fight like a man!' It was the first time Smit had spoken since they'd entered the ring. He turned and extended his hands to Klipkop who unlaced and removed the gloves. Then Smit went over to the neutral corner, picked up the canvas roll and unrolled it beside the sobbing officer. Klipkop grabbed Borman by the legs and Captain Smit grabbed him around the wrists, and they lifted him and placed him on the blood-stained canvas and rolled it around him. 'This Kaffir's blood will haunt you till you die,' Captain Smit said. He picked up his shoes and then he and Klipkop climbed from the ring. Klipkop moved over to the wall and reaching for the switch plunged the gymnasium into darkness.

In the darkness from the direction of the swing doors there came a sudden shout, '*Abantu bingelela Onoshobishobi Ingelosi*!' The people salute the Tadpole Angel! The door opened slightly and in the shaft of light it threw we saw a black figure slip quickly out of the gymnasium. The people knew. The curse was fixed. Lieutenant Borman was dead meat.

When I got outside, the tiekiedraai dancing was already going full swing with someone on the Mignon hammering out the Boeremusiek accompanied by the man with the piano accordion and a banjo player. Outside, on the parade ground, warders and their wives stood around the barbecue fires now burnt down to glowing embers, home-made sausages known as *boerewors* were held over the fires and the sizzle of the fat dropping from the sausage skins made the embers flare in the dark.

Doc and Mrs Boxall were nowhere to be seen. I watched the guy beating the Mignon half to death, thankful he wasn't using Doc's Steinway, when I felt a tap on my shoulder. 'Howzit?' It was Gert. 'How you getting home?' he enquired. 'Maybe I can borrow the Plymouth and take you all.' I explained that Mrs Boxall had brought us in her old crock which made a fearful racket and I was doubtful that it had long to live. 'You know where the professor and that lady is don't you?' Not waiting for my reply, he said: 'I seen them going into the administration building with the brigadier and the Kommandant.'

Gert was amazing like that; he always seemed to know what was going on. 'Maybe the professor will get a medal or something for the Kaffir concert.' Then he giggled, 'Jesus! I hope the brigadier never finds out that Geel Piet was only a broken down old lag.' He punched me lightly on the shoulder, 'Sorry man, about shutting your mouth back there.' I hung my head, the memory of the blood-stained canvas still too sharp in my mind for me to chance looking at him.

'You did right,' I said softly.

'So long, Peekay, I'd better kick the dust,' Gert said.

At last Doc and Mrs Boxall came out. I ran up to them and I could see Mrs Boxall was excited.

'By Jove, Peekay, miracles will never cease. I do believe we've done it!' she exclaimed.

'Done what?' I asked.

'Have done what?' she corrected automatically. 'We have been given permission to start a letter-writing service. Isn't that simply grand news? The brigadier says that every prisoner may send and receive one letter a month. It's the first time it has happened in South Africa and it's going on trial for six months.' She grabbed me by the hand and Doc by the other and we danced around in a circle to the sound of the tiekiedraai music coming from the hall. 'You're going to be needed because you speak three African languages as well as English and Afrikaans. Every Sunday morning after church we'll come out for two hours and take dictation from the prisoners. I say, it's a real victory for the forces of good. The brigadier was most impressed when I told him that it would be done under the auspices of the Earl of Sandwich Fund,' she stopped, puffed from the dancing, and then giggled. 'The Kommandant assured the brigadier that the Earl of Sandwich Fund was a very respected organisation with worldwide contacts and that all the warders' wives baked for it at the Christmas and Easter show.' We all started to laugh. Doc finally said, 'Madame Boxall, you are absoloodle the best. For this I give you eleven out of ten.'

She did a small curtsey. 'Why thank you, kind sir!' She gave Doc one of her extra special smiles. We hung around for a while longer just so we wouldn't seem rude and finally made our way to the car. As we approached we could hear soft grunting sounds and then we saw that a pair of boots was sticking out from under Charlie. Gert got up sheepishly and wiped his grease-blackened hands on the sides of his khaki shorts. He bowed awkwardly to Mrs Boxall.

'Does Mevrou speak Afrikaans?' he asked me.

I shook my head. 'I'll translate, if you like?'

Gert nodded. 'Tell her she's got more power now, you only had three cylinders firing,' he spoke fast, swallowing his words as he fought his shyness, 'but you still got a bad knock in the diff.' He turned to Mrs Boxall. 'If you can get it here tomorrow, maybe just after you been to church, I'll borrow the Plymouth and drive you home, and I'll fix the car up for you.' I introduced Gert to Mrs Boxall and translated what he'd said. Mrs Boxall was very grateful and called Gert 'A dear, sweet boy,' which I didn't translate but I think he understood because he seemed very embarrassed.

'Oh dear, I have no idea what a knock in the diff is. Is it something very bad?'

'It's the differential, I think it's pretty bad,' I replied without consulting Gert.

Pulling up his socks which were already pulled up Gert stammered, 'Good night, Missis,' in English and then walked quickly away into the dark.

We zoomed away and Mrs Boxall had no trouble driving up the Sheba road hill. The difference in Charlie was amazing now that we were driving on all cylinders. We dropped Doc off at the bottom of his hill. I think the new four-cylinder Charlie could've made it easily but Mrs Boxall had never been invited by Doc to his cottage, and she said as she drove me home 'This wasn't the right time' – whatever that was supposed to mean.

SIXTEEN

Mrs Boxall promised to talk to my mother about the new letter-writing arrangements in the prison. These were to take place on a Sunday morning and I had some real doubts about being allowed to partake in them. Sundays were difficult for me; it was a day filled with taboos, beginning with Sunday school and church in the morning and ending with evening service, which consisted of a short message from Pastor Mulvery, and then 'a precious time', when the congregation witnessed for the Lord. I wasn't allowed to do anything except the Lord's work on a Sunday, but as I wasn't a born-again Christian any of the Lord's work I might do, like reading the Shangaan Bible to Dee and Dum, wasn't creating any bricks for my mansion in the sky. Reading the Bible was regarded as the most superior type of work for the Lord. I was required to read three pages of the New Testament every day and ten pages on Sunday, and I did my compulsory Sunday reading during Pastor Mulvery's Message from the Lord. You'd think if something was called a Message from the Lord, it would be a proper message, such as you might give to a person. But Pastor Mulvery's messages rambled all over the place threading bits of the scripture together and frequently leading to wildly unusual conclusions which tended to prove Pastor Mulvery was right while all the gospel scholars since St Paul were wrong. He would call the Catholic Church the 'Catlicks' and they were his special target. He would go to endless trouble to demonstrate that the Catlicks had perverted the Word of God. He would point out that the Latin scholars who had translated the St James version into English from an original Catlick translation had not understood the original Greek translation of the original Hebrew. As Pastor Mulvery knew no Latin and no Greek and certainly no Hebrew, and never gave examples of the corrupted Words of God in Latin or Greek so that I could at least check his accuracy with Doc, he was able to build some pretty impressive arguments against the perfidy of the Catholic Church. I can tell you one thing, you wouldn't have wanted to be a Catlick on a Sunday evening service with Pastor Mulvery delivering one of his messages.

Because reading the Bible on Sunday didn't count for my heavenly brick account, I was expected to find other kinds of good deed stuff. Each Sunday evening my mother would question me closely about this.

Sometimes I really had to scrape the bottom of the barrel for things to claim, like praying for Hitler. Which I hadn't done of course, but it sounded good and was unusual enough to throw my mother off the scent.

In fact, praying for Hitler created a real crisis at that evening's debate. Marie, who was always there for supper on Sundays, said praying for Hitler wasn't valid coming from me, as it was a case of one sinner praying for another. My mother then debated with her as to whether a sinner praying for a sinner was an okay idea. My granpa said he thought it was time he was excused from the table so that he could go to his room and pray for fewer debates of this sort. My mother then said, as it was Sunday, she was not going to tell him how rude and hurtful his remark had been.

So getting to the prison for two hours every Sunday to take dictation wasn't simply a question of Mrs Boxall asking my mother. A great deal of toing and froing to the Lord would have to take place and my fear was that the Lord was going to be hard put to see that taking dictation from a bunch of criminals was the very best possible use of my indentured Sabbath.

My fears proved to be correct and the scheme had to be delayed a month while my mother and the Lord came to grips with the small print. A major investigation such as this one would begin by looking for a precedent in the Bible. In this regard I scored a direct hit when I pointed out that St Paul, in his Epistles, had written from prison in Rome. This was just the sort of material my mother liked to take with her when she had a chat with the Lord and so I expected an early reply from Him. My granpa said later that my St Paul research was a stroke of genius. But, it turned out, the Lord wasn't all that satisfied because Paul was a born-again Christian, personally converted on the road to Damascus, and he was in prison under an unjust Roman regime. The prisoners in Barberton prison were criminals being punished by a just regime. The point here was that Paul was doing the Lord's work while I was potentially aiding the devil writing letters from hardened criminals, bound to be up to no good, spreading a network of subterfuge and intrigue throughout South Africa.

To my wife, Umbela,

I send you greetings in my shame. Who is putting food in the mouth of our children? It is hard in this place, but one day I will come to you again. The work is hard but I am strong, I will live to see you again.

Your husband,
Mfulu

I wasn't able to tell my mother how innocent the letters really were because she didn't know about the previous letters or the tobacco, sugar and salt. So for the next week I read the New Testament like mad. There had to be something in there to help me. Pastor Mulvery was always taking bits and pieces of disconnected scripture and putting them together to mean just about anything; surely I could do the same.

I took the problem to Doc but for once he wasn't much help. He pointed out that according to the great German Lutheran scholars the prison writings of St Paul probably took place about AD 63. Which was nice to know, but no help whatsoever.

Doc's mind was far too logical for this kind of thing so I took the problem to my granpa who, after my telling opening move with St Paul, seemed anxious to see that the debate was conducted fairly. We sat on the steps of one of the rose terraces, my granpa tapping and tamping and lighting and staring squinty-eyed through the blue tobacco smoke over the rusty roof into the pale blue beyond. After a long time he said, 'All I know about the Bible is that wherever it goes there's trouble. The only time I ever heard of it being useful was when a stretcher bearer I was with at the battle of Dundee told me that he'd once gotten hit by a Mauser bullet in the heart, only he was carrying a Bible in his tunic pocket and the Bible saved his life. He told me that ever since he'd always carried a Bible into battle with him and he felt perfectly safe because God was in his breast pocket. We were out looking for a sergeant of the Worcesters and three troopers who were wounded while out on a reconnaissance and were said to be holed up in a dry *donga*. In truth I think my partner felt perfectly safe because the Boer Mausers were estimated by the British artillery to be accurate to 800 yards and we were at least 1,200 yards from enemy lines. Alas, nobody bothered to tell the Boers about the shortcomings of their brand new German rifle and a Mauser bullet hit him straight between the eyes.' He puffed at his pipe. 'Which goes to prove, you can always depend on British army information not to be accurate, the Boers to be deadly accurate, the Bible to be good for matters of the heart but hopeless for those of the head and finally, that God is in nobody's pocket.' He seemed very pleased with this neat summary which nevertheless wasn't a scrap of help to me.

However, on Sunday night three weeks after Mrs Boxall had first approached my mother, my granpa elected to play a part in the supper debate. My mother opened by saying the Lord was 'sorely troubled' over the whole issue which had 'weighed heavily upon her'. She liked to use words like 'sorely troubled' and 'weighed heavily' in her debates and I knew they impressed the pants off Marie.

Marie's cousin had lost her husband in a shooting accident leaving her with a small child. My mother had comforted Marie by saying that she would ask the Lord to 'bind up the wounds of her heart and pour in the balm of His comfort. That He would be Husband to the widow and Father to the orphan.' Marie sniffed a bit and said they were the most beautiful words she had ever heard.

My granpa cleared his throat. 'Were there not a couple of chaps who were crucified on either side of Christ, thorough scallywags as I recall?'

'The Word refers to them as thieves who were crucified beside the

Lord, though I don't see that they have anything whatsoever to do with the matter,' my mother replied, her irritation thinly disguised. 'I do not recall it saying in the Bible that they wrote home from jail.' I knew that my granpa's opinions on biblical matters, coming as they did from a sinner who had steadfastly refused to accept Christ into his life, were not very highly regarded.

'I seem to remember that Christ forgave one of them, promising him a berth in heaven right there on the spot. Or am I mistaken?'

'Goodness! The Lord does not promise people "berths" in heaven,' my mother said sharply. ' "Verily I say unto you, today shalt thou be with me in paradise" is what the Lord said.'

'It seems to me, from that remark, that Christ has no objections to convicted felons entering the kingdom of God,' he declared.

'Of course he doesn't! That's the whole point. Jesus was sent to save the most miserable sinners amongst us. His compassion is for all of us, His love everlasting and His understanding infinite. Seek His forgiveness and you're saved. You're no longer a murderer or a thief, you're one of the Lord's precious redeemed. The thief on the cross beside Him was saved when he confessed his sins, he was washed by the blood of the Lamb.'

'Hallelujah, praise His precious name,' Marie offered absently.

'And the prisoners here in Barberton. Like Him, could they also be saved?'

'You know as well as I do they could,' my mother said primly.

'How?'

'By accepting Christ into their lives, by renouncing the devil and. . . ' my mother stopped and looked straight at my granpa. 'You know very well how.'

'Oh I see. You are going to make it possible?'

'Well, no. The Anglicans and the Dutch Reformed have got the prison ministry and they do absolutely nothing. It's iniquitous. We've prayed a great deal about this, prayed that the Lord would make it possible for the Assembly of God missionaries to have the prison concession so that they can spread His precious word and bring the gospel to those poor unfortunate sinners.'

'Has it not occurred to you that the Lord may have answered your prayers?' my granpa asked.

'What on earth are you talking about?'

'Well, if the lad has direct access to the prisoners, could he not distribute tracts and that sort of thing?'

It was a master stroke. In return for being allowed to take dictation on Sunday at the prison, I was required to take gospel tracts in Sotho and Zulu from the Assembly of God missionaries and give one to each prisoner after he had dictated his letter to me. My mother and Marie had scored another major triumph, first the hospital and now the prison; they were earning recognition as a couple of hardcore fighters in the Lord's army.

What's more, my time on a Sunday was counted as first-class work for the Lord.

I don't exactly know how it happened but I did it just the once, then it suddenly got done all the time. One of the prisoners had said that tobacco was sorely missed, and the next week I cut a piece of tobacco leaf exactly the same size as a tract and slipped it inside one. The next thing I knew Dee and Dum were slipping these neatly cut squares of tobacco leaf into every tract, and I would take a whole bunch with me and sort them into their four African languages, and put the various piles in the drawer of the desk at which I sat, leaving an 'innocent' pile of Sotho tracts in front of me on the desk. After one of the people had dictated his letter to me I would hand him a tract from the drawer. This was Doc's idea and on two occasions the warder who attended the letter-writing sessions absently picked up a tract, looked at it in a cursory manner and then returned it to the pile on the desk.

Letter-writing suddenly became very popular and those of the people who didn't have anyone to write to would ask me to write to King Georgie. When I asked them what they wanted to say to the King of England it was almost always the same thing.

Dear King Georgie,

The people are happy because you are our great king. I send greetings to the great warrior across the water.

Daniel Mafutu

After a while a letter to King George was simply a euphemism for a tract. One tract and contents made two cigarettes and were an unimagined luxury. Not only had the Tadpole Angel contrived to continue the supply of tobacco into the prison, but the people no longer had to pay for it and it came together with paper to roll it in. For a generation afterwards, cigarettes in South African prisons were known as 'King Georgies' and some old lags still use this expression today. And of course the mystique which surrounded the Tadpole Angel continued to grow; nothing, it seemed, was impossible for him. More importantly for the Kommandant, the letter-writing experiment proved to be a huge success and, before the summer was over, he had been made a full colonel and also received a commendation from Pretoria for his work in prison reform. The Assembly of God missionaries kept up the supply of tracts and even had them translated into Swazi and Shangaan. When I told Doc that King Georgies now came in Swazi and Shangaan he smiled and said, 'God's ways are mysterious, Peekay. I think because the people cannot read they now send smoke signals up to God.'

It was not long after Geel Piet's death when Lieutenant Borman started to complain of piles. 'Now I'm in administration I sit too much,' he'd say to any person who'd listen. 'I can't eat steak, it hurts too much passing through, man, there's even blood in my shit.' It was true he seemed to be losing weight and Captain Smit advised him to see a doctor. 'It's only piles, my old man was a train driver, he had the same thing.' His wife sewed a special cushion for him which he brought to work and sometimes he'd walk around carrying the cushion in case he suddenly had to sit somewhere.

'It's God's justice,' Gert confided to me, 'Geel Piet wasn't the only one he's used the donkey prick on.' He giggled, 'I hope the bugger can't sit for six months!'

No one said anything but you could see it in their eyes, those of us who had been in the gym that night all knew Borman was under a curse.

Geel Piet had once told me how prisoners could think so hard that, collectively, they could make things happen. Like when they knew I had beaten Killer Kroon hours before anyone brought the official news of my win. How they always knew when there was to be a hanging minutes after a judge had issued the warrant, sometimes hundreds of miles from the location of the prison where the hanging was to take place.

'Ja, it is true, small boss, I have seen it heppen lots of times,' Geel Piet had said gravely. 'Sometimes, when there is enough hate, this thinking can kill. The people will think some person to death. Such a death is always long and hard, because the thinking takes place over a long time. It is the hate; when it boils up there is no stopping it, the person will die because there is no *muti* you can take to stop this hating thing.'

Anyone who is born in rural Africa is superstitious and the warders, who were mostly backwoodsmen, were particularly so. We all watched Borman as he started to shrink. His extended gut remained but everywhere else the flesh started to fall off him. He seemed to age in front of our eyes and the thinner he became the more vicious he was with the prisoners.

Another prisoner died mysteriously and after a short enquiry Borman was put on a charge and suspended from duty pending the enquiry. Shortly afterwards he experienced a severe rectal haemorrhage and was rushed to Barberton hospital where the surgeon, in an attempt to stop the bleeding caused by a rupture to the wall of the bowel, packed his rectum with giant cotton swabs – a procedure known to be about as excruciatingly painful as it is possible to experience. The doctor's cursory examination revealed the presence of a fungating growth.

Within weeks of leaving prison Doc was fit enough again to head for the hills and we would climb away from the town at first light every Saturday morning. We'd breakfast on hard boiled eggs and yesterday's bread with a thermos of sweet, milky coffee high up on a ridge somewhere or beside a stream. Sometimes we'd make for Lamati Falls, a smallish waterfall ten miles into the hills and we'd wait for the morning sun to whiten the water where it crashed into a deep pool which stayed icy cold throughout the year. Doc was like a small boy; the years seemed to fall away from him as we scampered up the sides of mountains or slid down into deep tropical kloofs, where giant tree ferns and the canopy of yellow-wood turned the brilliant sunlight into twilight, and where the soil was moist and smelt both of decay and new life at the same time.

Doc was busy taking the photographs for his new book and sometimes we'd hunt all day for a single perfect specimen. It was good to be working with Doc again. He was an exacting task master who, when we found a specimen to his liking, demanded to know the soil types and the shales, the rocks and the other botanical plants which grew within a radius of fifty feet, the direction of the wind and the hours of sunlight the cactus or aloe he was photographing would receive. Some days we'd communicate all day in Latin and in this way Doc gentled me into Ovid, Cicero, Caesar's Conquest of Gaul, and Virgil. Mrs Boxall countered this with the English poets. Wordsworth, Masefield and Keats were her favourites, with Byron, Tennyson and Walter de la Mare, if not her favourites, a matter of essential education for a gentleman. I asked Doc about German poets and he replied that Goethe was the only one in his opinion who could be considered worthy, but that personally he found him a terrible bore and that the Germans put all their poetry into music. He declared I should study the English for their poetry and the Germans for their music.

It was a lopsided sort of a catch-as-catch-can education, added to by Miss Bornstein who had been busy preparing me for a scholarship to a posh private school in Johannesburg. An education well beyond my mother's income as a dressmaker. I was not yet twelve, the minimum required age for entry into a secondary school, and I had languished in standard six for three years during which Miss Bornstein had privately educated me in 'all those things there's never time to learn at school'.

A month before my twelfth birthday I sat for the scholarship exam to the Prince of Wales School, and at the end of the term to my absolute mortification Mr Davis, the headmaster of Barberton school, announced that I had received the highest scholarship marks this school had ever given and that I would be starting as a boarder at the commencement of the first term in 1946. Doc, Mrs Boxall and Miss Bornstein had trained me well, if sometimes a little erratically. I was to find at the Prince of Wales School my knowledge in some things exceeded that of the senior forms and even the masters themselves, while in others I was no better than the brighter chaps in my form. But above all things I had been taught to read for pleasure and for meaning, as both Doc and Mrs Boxall demanded that I exercise my critical faculties in everything I did. At twelve I had already known how to think for at least four years. In teaching me independence of thought they had given me the greatest gift an adult can give to a child, besides love, and they had given me that also.

And so the last summer of my childhood came to an end. I also sat for the Royal College of Music Advanced Exams and passed, although my marks weren't spectacular. I think this was as much as Doc expected from me. He knew I had no special gift for music and what I achieved had been simply out of love for him. For his part he had fulfilled his contract with my mother, for whom my passing the exam was confirmation of my genius. In my mother's mind I had become the logical successor to the young Artur Rubinstein, and it was one of the major disappointments in her life that at boarding school I would elect to play in the jazz band. Jazz was the devil's music and another indication to her that I had hardened my heart against the Lord.

Before Geel Piet died he had been teaching me how to put an eight-punch combination together. I worked solidly all summer on this combination and at the championships held in Boksburg I retained the under twelve title, though this time without effort, even stopping a bigger kid in the second round on a TKO. Killer Kroon had not entered the championship even though he would have been in the division above.

Everyone, even Doc, seemed pleased that I had won a scholarship to the Prince of Wales School in Johannesburg, though I think he was trying very hard to be brave about the break-up in our partnership. Writing for the *Goldfields News,* Mrs Boxall really went to town in her column, 'Clippings from a Cultured Garden', writing about the town's *budding* intellect and its *finest flower* which turned out to be me. News of my pass in the Royal College of Music exams had me declared a *blossoming* musician. In the Afrikaans section of the paper my name appeared as the winner of the Eastern Transvaal under-twelve boxing title. My mother declared, 'Our cup runneth over!' but if I would accept the Lord into my heart her joy would be a hundredfold what she was feeling now. But I could see she was pleased, especially when she started to receive invitations to tea from the town's most important families and her dressmaking business picked up so much that she only had time to accept the juiciest invitations.

I kept my apprehension about returning to boarding school to myself; it seemed I would once again be the youngest kid in the school, though this aspect anyway now left me unconcerned. If they had a Judge at the Prince of Wales School, all I could say was he'd better be able to box. In fact, the only question I asked about the school was about boxing. The reply came back that boxing was a school sport and the boxers were under the instruction of Mr Darby White, ex-cruiserweight champion of the British Army.

The final crisis of that last summer of childhood came when the clothing list arrived from the Prince of Wales School. As she read it the tears started to roll down my mother's cheeks. Marie was there on her afternoon off from the hospital so it must have been a Wednesday. My mother read the list aloud. 'Six white shirts with detachable starched collars, long sleeve. Three pairs of long grey flannel trousers (see swatch attached). Six pairs grey school socks, long. One school blazer (see melton sample attached), school blazers or blazer pocket badge and school ties obtainable from John Orrs, 129 Eloff St, Johannesburg. One grey V-neck jersey, long sleeves. Shoes, with school uniform, brown. Shoes, Sunday, black. Blue serge Sunday suit, long trousers.'

'We don't have the money, we simply don't have the money,' she kept repeating.

'Ag man, jong, where's your faith?' Marie said indignantly, not impressed by my mother's tears. 'The Lord will supply everything, just you see. We going to pray right now, go down on our knees and give the precious Lord Jesus Peekay's order. C'mon let's do it now!'

My granpa rose from the table and excused himself but I was obliged to kneel with Marie and my mother. Marie must have reasoned that, as a heathen, my prayers wouldn't have too much impact, because she took the clothing list from my mother and handed it to me. 'We going to pray out loud to the Lord, it's always best when you need something bad to pray out loud. When I tell you, you read out the list, okay?'

I nodded, grateful that I wouldn't have to pray out loud.

'Precious Lord Jesus, we got a real problem this time,' Marie began.

'Praise the Lord, praise His precious name,' my mother said.

'You know how clever Peekay is and how he has won a thing to go to a posh school in Johannesburg for nothing.'

'Precious Saviour, hear Thy humble servants' my mother said, attempting to bring a bit of tone into the whole affair.

'Well we got lots of trouble, man, I mean Lord,' Marie continued, 'the clothing list arrived today and it broke our hearts.'

'Precious Jesus! Blood of the Lamb!'

'The cupboard is bare, there are no clothes for school hanging up in it. What we need, Lord Jesus, Peekay is going to say right now, so please listen good and you talk up, Peekay, so the Lord can hear, you hear? He's going to tell you now, Lord,' Marie prayed, cueing me in.

I must say I'd never been quite as close as this to the Lord before and I was quite nervous. 'Ah, er . . . six white shirts with detachable starched collars, long sleeve,' I read. 'Three pairs of grey flannel trousers (see swatch attached).'

'Show Him the swatch, man,' Marie whispered urgently. I didn't know quite what to do so I held the swatch of grey flannel up to the ceiling. After a few moments, when I reasoned the Lord had had a good enough look, I continued, 'Six pairs of grey school woollen socks, long.'

'Only three pairs, man! What about the three pairs you already got for school here?' Marie said in a stage whisper.

'Oh,' I said. 'Only three pairs, please.' My mother had stopped punctuating Marie's remarks and I looked at her. At first I thought she was crying, her face was all squished up and she was holding her hand across her mouth. Then I realised that she was desperately trying not to laugh. I started to giggle.

Without opening her eyes Marie admonished me. 'Peekay, stop it! God will punish you! It's hard enough asking the Lord for you, you not even being born again an' all that! But if you laugh we got no chance.' Her voice became conciliatory. 'Sorry, Lord, he didn't mean it, you got my word for it, it won't happen again. Go on, start reading again, the Lord hasn't got all day you know!'

I went on reading the list and also showed the Lord the swatch of green melton blazer cloth. When I got to the bit about school badges being obtainable from John Orrs, 129 Eloff Street, Johannesburg, Marie whispered again.

'You don't need to give Him the address, He knows where it is.' I finally got to the blue serge suit. 'That's his Sunday suit for going to church, Lord,' she said, to remind the Lord that I was still within his grasp every Sunday. My mother threw in a few more, 'Praise the Lord, praise His precious names' and the request for the contents of my clothing list was over. The rest was now up to the Precious Redeemer.

Marie's eyes blazed with faith and I could see she was pretty pleased with the way she had asserted herself. There was absolutely no doubt in her mind that the Lord would provide. My mother also seemed considerably cheered up and called for Dum to make tea. I must confess, not being a Christian, I didn't share their confidence. There seemed to me to be a whole heap of clothes in that list and all I had was three pairs of grey socks, two pairs of gym pants and the tackies. These latter items had appeared in a separate list titled 'Sport and Recreation', which included two rugby jerseys, house and school colours, rugby socks, rugby boots, white cricket shirt and shorts Form one and two, cricket longs Form three onwards. The optional section on this list included cricket boots and white cricket sweater with school colours. It seemed an amazing collection of clothes for one person.

I mentioned the clothing crisis to Doc. Not that he could have helped. Doc, at best, lived hand to mouth with just enough over for an occasional book and film for his Leica camera. But he mentioned it to Mrs Boxall and Mrs Boxall mentioned it to Miss Bornstein, and the two women went into action.

Miss Bornstein called me over at the end of class and asked me to copy out the clothing list. I did so and handed it over to her. She read it for a moment. 'What about these swatches, can you get the grey and the green swatch, Peekay? Even if you cut off a little, it's absolutely necessary for me to have them.' I promised to get hold of the swatches somehow, feeling pleased that the matter of my school clothes wasn't singularly in the Lord's hands any longer.

'We don't have very much money,' I said, for the first time in my life realising that money was important. I knew we were poor but it hadn't seemed to matter much. I'd had the occasional penny to spend on nigger balls, large black and extraordinarily hard balls that sucked down into layer after layer of different colours and which would last a good two hours in the mouth. My friends were generous with their sweets so I'd never really felt poor or needed money. I always somehow managed to save up four shillings for Christmas and old Mr McClymont at the drapery shop would give me four ladies' hankies and a man's one as well as a bandanna for Doc. The ladies' hankies would go to my mother, Mrs Boxall and Dee and Dum while the man's was for my granpa. They always looked surprised when they got them, but I don't suppose they were. The only alternative to a handkerchief was a cake of Knights Castile soap and I couldn't see the value in something that wore out after a few baths. When they went to clean Doc's cottage on a Sunday Dee and Dum spread their hankies carefully over the top of their heads in the African fashion. They could never understand why white people would blow the stuff from their noses into such a pretty piece of cloth. Sunday at Doc's cottage was their big outing and they liked to look pretty. When they got there they removed the hankies of course, but they never once used them for blowing into. I think they liked their hankies better than anyone, although I know Doc liked his bandanna which was always a red one.

'There are lots of ways to skin a cat,' Miss Bornstein said. 'This town isn't going to let its *enfant terrible* go to boarding school looking like a ragamuffin.'

Between Miss Bornstein and Mrs Boxall the cloth for my trousers and blazer and blue serge suit just appeared, though I expect old Mr McClymont had a hand in it somewhere. Then Miss Bornstein sprung her surprise. Old Mr Bornstein, who had become Doc's formidable opponent at chess, had been a tailor in Germany. He would cut the cloth and do the hand work if my mother would do the machine work. The suit was easy because 'a suit is a suit, already' but we needed a blazer to make sure that mine was cut and tailored in the same way as those purchased from John Orrs, 129 Eloff St, Johannesburg. Miss Bornstein said children tend to pick on you if you're different and it was important to get everything just right. Mrs Andrews had sent two of her sons to the Prince of Wales School and she still had a school blazer which she gave to Mrs Boxall. Old Mr Bornstein took it apart to see how it was made and did a whole lot of tut-tutting about the poor workmanship. He then cut the blazer to my size and as the badge, which was three ostrich feathers sticking out of a crown, was almost new he cut it carefully around the edges and sewed it onto my new blazer so well that you would have needed a magnifying glass to see where he'd done it. Mrs Boxall sent to Johannesburg for two red, white and green striped school ties which were her special present. All my shirts were cut from a pair of cotton poplin sheets Miss Bornstein said her mother had never used. Old Mr Bornstein knew just how to make the collars so that the starch collars donated by old Mr McClymont fitted perfectly. Marie and her mother knitted me three pairs of socks for Christmas. Only the brown and black shoes remained, and at the prison Christmas party for all the warders Captain Smit handed me a large parcel from the boxing squad. Inside were a pair of new brown shoes and a pair of black ones, and a brand new pair of boxing boots. 'Magtig, Peekay, we are all proud of you going to that posh Rooinek school in Johannesburg, just don't get all high and mighty on us all of a sudden when you get back, heh.' Everyone laughed and cheered and I felt the sorrow of leaving people I loved. Even old Snotnose had become a good friend over the years and I would miss them all a lot. The Kommandant stood up and recounted the first day he'd met me and said that I had proved that English and Afrikaner were one people, South Africans. That perhaps with my generation the bitterness would pass. He said I was a leader of men and that even the prisoners respected me for my letter-writing. There was some more clapping and, shaking at the knees, I thanked them all. I can't remember what I said but I promised I would never forget them and I never have.

Only one more incident is worth recording in that long, last summer of childhood. My mother and Marie had already testified to the congregation about the Lord's miraculous answer to their prayers. Only the requested V-neck long sleeve mid-grey jersey was missing from my kit but, as it was summer in Johannesburg, my mother knew that the Lord would provide in time for winter. Which He did. Four knitted jerseys were pushed into her hands by separate dear, sweet, Christian ladies less than a fortnight later.

On the same night my mother and Marie also testified that the Lord had once again blessed their work in the hospital. For several weeks they had worked for the salvation of a dear man who was dying of cancer of the rectum – a man still in the prime of his life, struck down by this terrible disease. They told how they had testified to him and had seen him wrestle with the devil, how they had wept for him and pleaded with him to take the Lord Jesus into his heart and how finally, after a massive rectal haemorrhage and with the hours running out, Lieutenant Borman had surrendered his life to the Lord Jesus and had gone to meet His Saviour in paradise.

Lieutenant Borman died knowing what it felt like to have a donkey prick jammed up your arse until your entrails spill out.

SEVENTEEN

It wasn't until I went to boarding school the second time that I learned that survival is a matter of actively making the system work for you rather than attempting merely to survive it.

My partner from the very first day at school was Hymie Levy. Hymie was Jewish of course, which was a very rare occurrence at the Prince of Wales School.

I was wrestling my heavy suitcase off the train at Johannesburg Central Railway Station when he walked towards me.

'Hey you, stop! If you want to build muscles take a Charles Atlas course.' He signalled for the black porter to take my suitcase. 'Howzit? I'm the token Jew. Who are you ?'

'Thanks, my name's Peekay,' I said, proffering my hand.

He took it almost absently. 'Hymie ... Hymie Levy, what's your first name, Peekay?'

'It's just Peekay, first and second,' I replied.

Hymie stopped in his tracks. 'Just one name, you're not bullshitting me now are you?'

'Ja, that's right, just one.'

Hymie seemed to be thinking as we continued together down the platform. 'I like that, no complications. Me, I've got the whole catastrophe, Hymie, Solomon, Levy; you can't get more kosher than that, kings and priests, not bad insurance for a kid whose parents escaped the Holocaust by pretending they were Roman Catholics.'

I had no idea what he was talking about but he seemed a nice sort of a chap. All the Jews I'd ever known were pretty nice. Harry Crown and old Mr Bornstein and of course Miss Bornstein. It seemed a pleasant coincidence that the first kid I should meet from the Prince of Wales School was a Jew.

We were supposed to meet the school sergeant at the station and I was glad to have someone who was so obviously confident along with me. We heard him before we actually saw him. 'Prince of Wales new boys over here! Ahaaat the double!'

'Christ, Peekay, look at that!' Hymie said pointing to a large man wearing a scarlet tunic. Despite ourselves we straightened up a bit and Hymie ran a comb through his dark, brylcreemed hair which was swept up in the pompadour style of the time and ended in a ducktail at the back.

As we drew nearer we could see four other kids who had formed a line in front of the big man who stood to rigid attention, his pace stick clasped under his armpit. The top half of his face was hidden from view under the shiny black peak of a red-banded guardsmans' cap. The only thing that protruded from under the peak was a large waxed moustache. On the right sleeve of his military tunic were three gold sergeant's stripes above which sat a brass crown. His trousers were of black serge with a red stripe running down the sides of each leg leading directly to a pair of highly polished black boots which appeared to be rooted to the platform. A white shirt with celluloid collar and black tie completed his uniform.

Hymie tipped the porter who added our suitcases to a pile already stacked on the platform and we joined the four other boys to stand, more or less at attention, in front of the school sergeant.

I was tired and, except for cleaning my teeth and splashing the gritty feel of the train journey from my face, I hadn't washed since the morning of the previous day. The Barberton train had left at four o'clock that afternoon, its single school carriage pulled by the coffee pot to Kaapmuiden, where it was shunted onto the school train which would travel through the night to Pretoria and Johannesburg. Several other Barberton boys and girls went to school in Pretoria, while one boy wore the navy blue blazer of St Johns College and another the black and white stripes of Jeppe High, both Johannesburg schools. I was the only one going to the Prince of Wales and, I must say, I had felt constrained and thoroughly out of place in long pants, starched collar, blazer, tie and a strange straw hat called a boater.

It was a big send-off, much bigger than anyone had expected. Of course my mother, Granpa, Marie and Dee and Dum were there, also Doc and Mrs Boxall, Miss Bornstein and old Mr Bornstein and all the kids from the boxing squad, who clapped and howled and whistled when they saw me in my uniform. Snotnose and Bokkie pretended to fall on the ground they were laughing so much, in particular at my straw boater. Gert finally had to tell them to behave, but I could see he also thought I looked pretty funny in my fancy Rooinek school clothes. But the really big surprise came when a prison truck arrived and from it climbed the prison brass band. They set up their stands in the middle of the platform and commenced to play.

'It's the Kommandant's idea, Peekay,' Captain Smit said. 'He wanted to give you a big send off. You know, man, he is very proud of you.' He paused for a moment, 'So am I. I got money on it, you going to be the welterweight champion of the world one day. Don't let that Rooinek school change that, you hear?' He gave me a playful punch on the shoulder. 'You're a proper Boer, little boetie, we all counting a lot on you.'

At last the guard blew his all-aboard whistle and I said goodbye to everyone and climbed into the carriage. Dee and Dum and Marie were all having a bit of a sniffle and my mother would have too if she hadn't thought she ought to set an example for Marie. Doc was burying his nose in his red bandanna and pushing it all over the place. When the guard blew his final whistle and the band struck up with 'Now is the hour for us to say goodbye' nearly everyone started to blub and I was pretty choked up myself.

I recalled how I had last boarded a train to leave a part of my life behind me, how I had fallen over with my clown tackies stuffed with newspaper, and how Hoppie Groenewald had dusted me down and lifted me up the steps, explaining how he too was always falling down the stupid things. 'No worries, little boetie, Hoppie Groenewald will look after you.'

Now here I was, dressed in a starched collar, hand-tailored blazer, long pants and highly polished shoes. Gert had shown me how to polish boots prison-style until you could see your face in them. The coffee pot's chuffa-chuffchuffing drowned the band, and then the farewell party soon grew so small I could hardly make out Dee and Dum still waving. I looked up to see the hills and in particular the hill behind the rose garden where I had met Doc the day I had gone to grieve for the loss of Nanny. I was once again alone in a railway compartment headed for a new adventure.

After the train left Kaapmuiden I lay awake for a long time in the top bunk of my compartment listening to the wheels saying 'First-with-the-head-and-then-with-the-heart. First-with-the-head-and-then-with-the-heart.' It was as though Hoppie was coming with me on this second train ride into manhood. The night rushed past the window, black light broken only occasionally by a pinpoint as we roared past a cooking fire in an African village.

Every once in a while the train would whistle at something in the dark and I knew the sound would carry for miles across the veld. 'First-with-the-head-and-then-with-the-heart. First-with-the-head-and-then-with-the-heart.' The hectic clickity-clack finally put me to sleep.

Now we were standing in front of this huge old soldier who looked like a recruiting poster for the Great War. With his pacing stick still held under his arm he removed a small spiral-bound note pad from the top lefthand pocket of his tunic and flicked it open. Pulling his head back and squinting down his nose, he looked at each of us in turn. I wondered why he didn't simply lift the peak of his cap so that he could see properly.

'Righto then, my name is Bolter, Mr Bolter to Mrs Bolter if there was a Mrs Bolter which there ain't, thank Gawd! Sarge to you lot. Answer your names as I call them out!' He shouted this information at us as though he were addressing the entire length of the platform. I could see that the five guys around me were just as scared as I was. He glanced down at the pad in his hand. 'De la Cour!' A pale looking kid with curly blond hair stuck his hand up in the air. 'Not your hand, lad! You only raise your hand when you want a pee! Present Sarge! Or just, Sarge!'

'Present, Sarge,' De la Cour said softly.

'Look lively now, lad. Put some Marmite into it!' He glanced briefly at his note pad. 'Atherton!'

'Present, sir!' the kid next to me shouted so that we all jumped.

'Don't call me sir!'

'Present, Sarge,' the blond boy with pale blue eyes said, this time more quietly.

'Atherton? You have a brother at school, in forty-three?'

'My cousin, sir,' Atherton replied.

'Sarge! When I want to be a gentleman I'll bloody well tell you. It's obvious, Atherton, all the brains in your family went to your cousin.'

'Yes, Sarge,' Atherton said, his face a deep beetroot.

'Best fly-half in the school's history, got his colours in form four, let's hope you follow in his footsteps, Mr Atherton. If you do I shall forgive you this one indiscretion. Now look sharp, lad.'

Sergeant Major Bolter consulted the tiny notepad once again. 'Peekay!'

'Present, Sarge!'

'Peekay? No initial, just Peekay? What sort of a name is that, pray tell?'

'It's what I've almost always been called, Sarge.'

'Well I'm afraid that won't do, it's not Christian, lad. A gentleman always has two names at the very least. That is if he isn't a lord. You're not a lord or a duke, are you?'

'No, Sarge. It's just my name. Miss Bornstein wrote to the school and explained.'

Sergeant Major Bolter sighed deeply and bowed slightly towards me with a pretend smile on his face. 'Oh she did, did she now? Well that's settled then, isn't it? I mean if Miss Bornstein asked, we can't quibble over a small matter like a gentleman's Christian name and surname being the one and the same, can we?'

'I'm not a gentleman either, Sarge,' I said, my voice trembling slightly. I knew I was in trouble but I thought it might be best to clear up any misconceptions in one hit. The kids around me giggled with the exception of Hymie who gave me a light nudge with his elbow.

The sergeant major's moustaches seemed visibly to bristle as he drew himself up to his full height. 'I'm the only one around here who's allowed not to be a gentleman, lad,' he announced, as though the subject was closed to further discussion.

'Ryder!' A boy with dark hair and piercing blue eyes jumped to a sort of attention.

'Present, Sarge! It's Cunningham-Ryder, Sarge, with a hyphen.'

Sarge looked at him and gave a meaningful sigh. 'And, Mr Cunningham-Ryder with an 'ifin, do we have a Christian name to go with our double-barrelled moniker?'

'Yes, Sarge. George Andrew Sebastian, Sarge.'

'Well now, that's more like it, ain't it, lads? Cunningham-Ryder has three Christian names and two surnames and Peekay here has none. What do you say to that?' The relief I felt at being passed over was short-lived, the bastard was going to have another go.

Levy gave me a small dig with his elbow. 'Perhaps Cunningham-Ryder can give Peekay one of his names, Sarge?' he said. We all turned to look at him, stunned at his audacity.

'What's your name, lad?' Sergeant Major Bolter asked softly, which did nothing to conceal the terrible menace in his voice.

'Levy, Sarge. Hymie Levy, and I'm not a gentleman or a Christian. I'm a Jew. My dad had to pull all sorts of strings to get me in.' He wore an ingenuous expression as he looked directly at the sergeant major.

We all fought back our laughter, but to our surprise Bolter didn't explode. Turning to his notepad, he said, 'Levy, here at the Prince of Wales School everyone is a Christian and a gentleman and that includes both you and Mr Peekay.' He glanced up. 'Johnson!' We all looked over at a small freckle-faced boy with red hair who stood next to Levy with his mouth slightly open. 'Johnson!' Sarge repeated, raising his voice several decibels. The kid with the open mouth had to be Johnson; he was the only as yet un-named one among us, but he remained silent, his terror-stricken gaze fixed on the large man. With a sort of stop-start jerky movement he raised his hand.

'Do we want to do wee-wee, lad?' I could see Sarge was growing impatient with us all.

'No, sir,' Johnson gulped the words out.

'Do not call me sir, you piss-wit!' Sergeant Major Bolter yelled and several people walking along the platform stopped to stare at him. And that's how 'Pissy' Johnson came to get his nickname.

I was enormously impressed with Levy. I had never met a Jewish person my age or someone who couldn't become a Christian even had he wanted to. I knew instantly I liked him. As it transpired Hymie Levy was to become my closest friend, while Paul Atherton, Pissy Johnson and 'Cunning-Spider', which is how Cunningham-Ryder was to become known, were the group with whom I mostly went around.

The school charabanc driven by Sarge had taken us through the sky-scrapered streets out through a place called Hillbrow where we followed a tram down into increasingly quieter suburbs. We left the tram at its terminal and drove into a leafy suburb named Houghton where the houses, set in perfectly manicured lawns and brilliant gardens, were bigger than any I had ever seen. The top of the charabanc brushed against the cool dark oak trees that lined the quiet streets. We passed an occasional nanny wheeling a baby carriage with large wheels that even sported springs. All the nannies wore identical black dresses with a starched white pinny and all the baby carriages seemed to have come from the same factory. I wasn't much for symbols, my life had somehow contrived to be a mixture of people so that social status meant very little to me. Nevertheless I sensed that I was entering a new kind of world with a different set of rules.

We turned into a gateway, through a huge open gate with the crown and three ostrich feathers outlined in its wrought-iron design, and continued down a roadway bordered on each side by giant English oaks. On the way to Wellington House, one of the three boarders' houses at the Prince of Wales School, we passed an emerald green cricket pitch with a rotating hose chit-chit-chittering a jet of water in a large circle around the pitch. On the far boundary, neatly enclosed by a white picket fence, stood a small white pavilion, behind it grew another row of giant oaks and beyond them rose several sets of rugby posts, still further yet the neo-gothic clock tower of the main school rose above the trees. It seemed the perfect place for a posh school but I was not at all sure that it was the perfect place for the future welterweight champion of the world.

Hymie Levy had seated himself beside me on the ride to school and had set about explaining his theory of survival. We were, he decided, odd-bods, he a Jew and me with only one name. Odd-bods, he asserted, were always singled out by plebeians, the worst kind of which were middle-class, Anglo-South African Protestants, who undoubtedly made up the remainder of the school. I wasn't quite sure whether belonging to the Apostolic Faith Mission qualified me as a Protestant but I had to agree with him that my background was probably different from that of the other guys in the bus. From my previous bout of boarding school I had already learned that being different doesn't pay off. This time I was determined to enter the school environment on my own terms. There wasn't too much I was frightened of and I was fairly confident that I could compete intellectually. It was time to remove my camouflage; all my life I had let others provide for me and, while I loved the people who had nurtured and built me intellectually, I felt that emotionally it was time to provide for myself. Everyone on the intellectual side of my life seemed to agree that an exclusive private school education was what I needed, while those on the physical side, mainly the boxing squad, were more than a little dubious about an elitist Rooinek school education. I had been torn between the two, never clearly deciding who I was, changing my camouflage to suit. I had accepted an education at an elitist boarding school while at the same time nurturing my ambition to become the welterweight champion of the world. It didn't take too many brains to figure out that world champion boxers are not spawned within a system designed to educate upper middle-class Christian gentlemen.

I placed less importance on my intelligence than on my prowess as a boxer. If the Prince of Wales School tried to disabuse me of my ambition to be the welterweight champion of the world, then the intellectual nourishment it might furnish as compensation would not be sufficient incentive for me to remain. But I wasn't about to let this happen. No more camouflage for Peekay, I would simply be the best. I hadn't discussed this with either Doc or Miss Bornstein. I was on my own again and I had to do my own thinking, so when Hymie started on about beating the system I knew immediately what he was on about.

He passed me a stick of spearmint and commenced talking again. 'Now my theory is that to beat any system you have to know it intimately. Rebellion is senseless and being pointedly different only leads to persecution; the only way to control any system is from inside it the way the Jews have always done.'

'It didn't seem to help them with Hitler,' I said. I didn't know much about the Jews in Nazi Germany but Miss Bornstein had told me a little and had added that Old Mr Bornstein actually felt guilty for escaping the Holocaust.

'A-ha, that was different. Hitler's Nazi party presented an impossible problem for the Jews of Germany. After all, you can't undermine a system from within when you're excluded from it in the first place, can you?'

Hymie's point was not well made. I was to learn that he was obsessed with the Holocaust, that it sometimes clouded his otherwise excellent judgement. I could never quite understand why he possessed this obsession; his parents had escaped from Warsaw before the Jews were incarcerated in the ghetto or were even unduly persecuted. Hymie had never known any real racial prejudice, yet he had a strong sense of alienation as well as, it seemed to me at times, of guilt.

Doc had taught me well and I wasn't about to let Hymie get away with a cheap shot like that.

'Every system tends to be mutually exclusive; they're all about keeping someone or something out; by keeping the Jews out of the Nazi party Hitler was acting typically. No system wants to be undermined or abused and therefore it is constantly on guard to exclude those who would destroy it. If, as you say, it is a common Jewish tactic to invade from within then this should have been possible even with the Nazi party. We have to conclude that the Jews failed to defeat Hitler, failed to defeat the system and as a consequence paid a terrible price. It wasn't an exception at all.'

Hymie grinned. 'Hey! You can think. I'm not used to that in a goy. Here, shake a paw.'

I allowed the compliment and shook his hand, although I wasn't quite sure what he meant. 'What's a goy?'

'A Christian, a gentile. Hey, can we be friends, I mean proper friends, Peekay?'

'Sure,' I said, not really meaning it.

'You see, you're different. I know that now. And I'm certainly different. I always have been, but being a Jew at a school like this makes me even more so. I reckon we'll need each other.'

'What for? You mean to beat the system?'

'No, no, to use it. I've got a hunch we'll be a terrific combo.'

I wasn't sure he was right. I still had a problem. While I had all the physical and intellectual equipment needed to succeed within the system, I lacked one thing. Money. The only way I could succeed without money was by being a loner. Friendship with this particular tribe of Christian gentlemen required resources. You were expected to pay your way. The only other way was by ingratiation, but I was damned if that was ever going to happen to me again. Pisskop was still the dark shadow of Peekay, still alive in my mind; come what may, I would never again stoop to conquer.

Added to this was the fact that I was basically a loner. Other than Doc, and when I was small, Granpa Chook, I'd never been in the position of having a partner and I'd never really had a best friend who was my own age. Having an immediate friend in this strange new environment sounded nice, but it also made me feel vulnerable.

'Have you honest and truly only got one name?' Hymie asked suddenly.

'Well sort of, you see I've only ever used one name. One name is me.'

'They won't let you get away with it you know, the system can't handle things like that.'

'It's just going to have to,' I replied, sounding a lot braver than I really was. I longed suddenly to ask Doc what he would advise under the circumstances, though I already knew the answer. He would simply have said that a man has the right to any name he wants to give himself; if a man is saddled with a name he didn't choose, how can he possibly be free for the rest of his life? 'We got to be who we got to be, absoloodle!' he'd conclude after we had carefully and fully discussed the matter. Doc was not a man to make compromises on important issues such as determining who a person really is in his own mind.

'I bet you're good at sport. Me, I'm rotten,' Hymie said.

'I'm okay.'

'What's your best sport,' Hymie asked, humouring me, 'rugby?'

'No, I box.'

Hymie jerked back in his seat, plainly shocked. 'You what!'

'I'm a boxer.'

'Yeah, that's what I thought you said. Why man, that's positively Neanderthal.'

'You could get badly hurt saying that to the wrong boxer,' I grinned.

Hymie reeled back in mock terror, 'Careful, man, in a Court of Law a boxer's hands are considered lethal weapons.' He was suddenly serious again. 'I tell you what. I'm a gambler and you're a boxer, that's yet another reason why you and I have to stick together, Peekay.'

'What do you gamble on?' I asked.

Hymie sighed. 'I'm a Jew. People expect Jews to be good with money. So what do Jews do? They oblige. My old man is filthy rich and he'll give me all the money I need. But that's the very problem, you see. I have to make my own; it's an intellectual thing not a greedy thing. I'm not really a gambler, gamblers are stupid; making money is simply a way of keeping myself mentally fit. Can you understand that?'

'No.'

'Are you rich, Peekay? I mean your parents?'

'Hell no, I won a scholarship here. My mum's a dressmaker.'

'Well, that's why you don't understand. For me money is like boxing is for you; it's my way of getting even with the world. For a rich Jew money is a weapon; unless I know how to make it on my own I will be defenceless.'

I was suddenly fascinated. It wasn't that Hymie's philosophy was the antithesis of all I'd been taught, although I knew the Lord was against money and definitely in favour of the poor. It was just that, well, Doc and Mrs Boxall, or even Miss Bornstein, had never mentioned money or its importance in the scheme of things. I'd been forced into thinking about money for the first time when the list for my school clothes had arrived, and I had already worked out that not having any at a boarding school for the sons of the rich was pretty well going to shape my school career.

'Are you very good at making money?' I asked Hymie.

'About as good as you are at boxing,' he replied.

'You've got yourself a partner, Hymie. Money is something I have to learn about.'

Hymie grinned, 'It's a deal, Peekay. I had a feeling you were a bloody good boxer.'

I was by nature a fairly quiet sort of a guy and had no trouble getting on with things. As a new boy I was at the bottom of the heap but was fortunate enough to be selected as the fag for the head of the house, Fred Cooper, who was also the second prefect of the entire school and the captain of the First XV Rugby. This immediately gave me some extra status amongst the other new boys all of whom, like me, were allocated to a school or house prefect.

Fagging was hard work and we were on standby for the school and house prefects from first bell at six a.m. until lights out at nine-thirty. No chore was thought too menial, and a prefect had only to yell from his study and all the fags within hearing distance would have to come running. Last new boy to arrive did the chore. In addition to this, each fag had a list of duties he was obliged to perform for his personal prefect. He made his bed, shone his shoes, cadet and rugby boots, washed his rugby togs or during the summer blancoed his cricket boots, and if he was an officer in the cadet corps polished his Sam Browne and brasses, laid out his clothes, tidied his study, ran his messages and made trips to the tuck shop on his behalf.

The first tanning I received was for scooping the tiniest dab of cream off the top of a cream bun I was delivering to Fred Cooper. At least it started with the tiniest scoop and then, in an attempt to smooth the scooped part, I took one or two more small scoops on the end of my finger. By the time I arrived at Fred Cooper's study, the bun looked somewhat rearranged.

'You rotten little bugger! You've been norking my cream bun,' Cooper yelled at me.

'My hand slipped over it and I had to lick it off sort of, sir,' I explained, not quite willing to tell an outright lie.

'Shit! Did you lick my bloody bun, Peekay?'

'No, sir, just my hand.'

'Close the door, boy. We have an excellent way to train slippery hands.' Cooper reached for the cane which hung behind the door. 'How many times do you reckon it slipped?' he asked.

'Not many, sir,' I said fearfully.

'Not many is once or twice or three times, tell me, man?'

'Once?' I said hopefully.

'Right, bend down.' I bent down holding my knees and proffering my arse. Whack! 'That's one for your slippery hand.' Whack! 'That's one for your slippery tongue.' Whack! 'And that's one for your poor memory.' Cooper returned the cane to the back of the door and pointed to the cream bun on his desk. 'Eat it! And go and get me another one with your own money.'

I stood looking at the cream bun with its shiny brown top and cream-filled centre. This was my first major crisis. 'I . . . I don't have any money, sir.'

Cooper turned back to his book. 'Use those slippery fingers of yours to find some,' he said, dismissing me.

I left his study holding the offending cream bun gingerly in my hand. Pocket money was drawn every Wednesday after lunch and every Saturday morning, but as I hadn't been given any for the term, the fact that it was Tuesday meant two things: none of the other fags would have any money this late in the week and even if I could borrow some I had no possibility of paying it back.

My arse stung like hell, but I hardly noticed it in my anxiety. Hymie Levy was waiting at the end of the corridor which led to the sixth form studies.

'Christ, Peekay, I could hear it from here, that bastard sure blasted your arse!'

'I'm in deep shit,' I told him. 'I've got to buy Cooper another cream bun and I haven't got any money.'

Hymie shrugged, 'Easy man, I'll give it to you.' Then he pointed to the bun in my hand, 'What's that? That's a cream bun!'

I explained to him what had happened. 'Sorry, but I can only accept a loan if you'll let me do something to pay it off,' I added.

'Don't be stupid, Peekay. Pay me tomorrow after pocket money.'

It was the first time I had had to admit that I had no money whatsoever.

'You mean nothing? No money at all?' Hymie was clearly astonished. He dug into the change pocket of his grey flannels and produced a two-shilling piece. 'Here, take it, you can pay me back when you leave school.'

'Bullshit, Hymie, that's in five years.'

Hymie grinned, 'I'm a Jew, remember, we're supposed never to forget.'

'You're also a pain in the arse, Levy. Keep your two bob, I only need threepence anyway. Bugger it! I'll go and throw myself on Cooper's mercy.'

'What, and get your bum blasted again? Give us that bun. Here, hold this.' He carefully lifted the top half of the bun and handed it to me. Then, using his forefinger, he spread the cream from the centre of the botton half of the bun to the edges, piling the cream high on the edges. He held out his hand for the top and replaced it onto the bottom half, squeezing lightly with his forefinger and thumb to force both halves together. As he did this the cream squirted out of the sides as natural looking as you please. He handed the fully restored cream bun back to me, a satisfied grin on his mug.

'Gee thanks, Hymie. I owe you man,' I said, relief flooding over me.

'Don't thank me, Peekay. It took two thousand years of persecution by bastards like Cooper to make me smart; I really ought to thank him.'

It was the first time we'd beaten the system, although of course it was Hymie who had really done so. After I'd given Cooper his 'new' bun, we retired behind the bogs and laughed our heads off. Then Hymie took out his miniature chess set and we battled it out for the next hour. We were evenly matched players; his cunning was matched by my years of memorising all Doc's games plus my having a reasonable grasp of the niceties of the game. We were in the school first chess team right from the start, which wasn't earth-shattering news; the Christian gentlemen were not exactly breaking down the doors to join the chess club.

Boxing presented a problem. It wasn't a major sport at school and therefore not compulsory. Only about twenty boys out of the six hundred in the school took part. Darby White, the gym master and ex light-heavyweight champion of the British Army, had turned six of these twenty into a fairly good boxing team, although I soon learned that we only boxed the Afrikaans schools as the other English schools didn't go in for boxing. No other boxer in the school of any weight had been trained as well as I had been or came close to my skill. Sarge was also very keen on boxing and he and Darby White would work the squad together. While the school team was said to be game, morale was pretty low when I arrived. The school had won only six individual bouts in five years and none in the past two years, let alone a boxing match. The red, white and green ribbon, which were the school colours and which had been tied around the handle of a massive wooden spoon and hung from one of the beams in the gym, were beginning to fade, the spoon having been in permanent residence with the Prince of Wales School so long.

Darby White would sometimes look up at it a little wistfully and say, 'I don't expect ever to win the schools trophy but I'd just like to lose that dirty great wooden ladle for just one year.'

I told Hymie about this and he immediately became interested. Hymie's interest in sports was zero, but he couldn't resist an intellectual challenge. 'How good are the other chaps in the squad?' he asked. I was forced to admit that they were pretty average. The kids in the prison squad back home could have taken them with one arm tied behind their backs. 'How good a coach is Darby White?' Darby White wasn't Geel Piet but he knew his boxing and he was certainly as good as Captain Smit.

'I think he's lost his enthusiasm, but he seems to know his onions,' I replied.

'You need a manager and I know just the chap,' Hymie said. That was the nice part about Hymie, he never bragged but he was absolutely certain of his superiority. It crapped a lot of people off, but Hymie had prepared himself for a life where the slings and arrows were fairly frequent and he didn't seem to give a damn whether or not he was liked. 'Persecution is the major reason for a Jew to exist. If it didn't happen we'd soon be as intellectually inferior as you lot,' he'd say.

I asked Hymie how he proposed to turn possibly the weakest school boxing team in the world into a winning combination. He looked at me and for once the slightly cynical grin left the corners of his mouth. 'We need only one winner for a start. One guy you can rely on to win. The rest is easy, the rest is only good management. When men can be made to hope, then they can be made to win.' He placed his hands one on each of my shoulders. 'How many fights have you won in the ring, Peekay?'

'Thirty-four,' I replied.

'How many have you lost?'

'Well . . . none,' I said, a little embarrassed.

'You'll do nicely. There's nothing a gambler likes better than a certainty.'

'This is the Highveld; the standard is much higher than in the Lowveld where I've done all my boxing. Sooner or later every boxer gets beaten.'

'Sure, sure, but let's do all we can to delay that moment as long as possible. Peekay, I smell money in that boxing team.'

'You mean by becoming an integral part of the system, me boxing and you managing, and then making it work for us?'

'I love a fast learner,' Hymie said.

When Darby White and Sarge saw me work out I could see they were enormously impressed. 'Where'd you learn to box, son?' Darby White asked.

Without thinking I answered, 'In prison, sir.'

It was a reply Darby White would never grow tired of recounting. To my often acute embarrassment it became his favourite boxing story and given the slightest opportunity, he'd recount it to the coaches from the other schools.

Sarge was second in command of the boxing squad and acted with Darby White as a second or alone when Darby was refereeing a fight. As a young guardsman with the Coldstream Guards he'd been quite a useful amateur in his day. Later he'd worked as a second under the famous English trainer Dutch Holland of the Thomas à Becket Gymnasium in south London. Dutch Holland was the best cut-man in England and Sarge claimed to have learned the art of stemming an eye bleed from him. A cut eye would usually stop a fight in school boxing, which wasn't always fair as the better boxer could lose on a TKO when he was ahead on points.

Sarge could work miracles with a cut-stick, cotton wool swabs, adrenalin and vaseline. In fact, his special skill as a cut-man was one of the weapons Hymie was to use in his campaign to lift the boxing squad out of last place in the schools competition.

Hymie had himself elected as the manager of the boxing squad by the simple expedient of volunteering for the job. No first form boy had previously held this job. The managers of the various major sports, cricket, rugby, swimming, shooting and, of course, boxing were invariably chosen from fifth form boys who, while not being sportsmen, were known to be brains; hence these positions came to be known as 'swot spots' and the fifth form boy honoured with a swot spot would invariably become a school prefect in the year following.

However, the swot spot for boxing had become a school joke and was therefore seen as not worthy of a brain. It was considered extremely poor form to apply for it, and Darby White had for the past four years rejected the few applicants on the basis of them not being known brains and therefore simple opportunists. In putting his case for the swot spot in boxing, Hymie pointed out to Darby White that as he was in the school senior chess team he qualified in the brain department and besides, with a first former in the job, Darby could look forward to five years of continuity, with all the advantages of long-term planning.

Hymie's arguments were persuasive. The most telling of them being that we couldn't do any worse than we were doing, so Darby might as well give him a go. Darby White only jingled his balls in his white duck trousers furiously for about two minutes before agreeing. Darby was quite unable to make a decision of any sort without putting both hands into his trouser pockets and giving his balls a tumble, the longer the process the more complicated the decision.

My first fight was as a flyweight, although at one hundred and two pounds I was a very light one and would be fighting a kid who weighed nearly ten pounds more than me. It took place in the school gymnasium a month after the term had begun. Home matches drew little attention from anyone at the school. School spirit did not extend to boxing; it was a recognised fact that we always lost and only the boxing squad and first form boarders, conscripted to watch, would be present to see the tripe walloped out of the Prince of Wales team. These one-sided bouts were privately referred to as 'two-fisted attacks from the hairy backs'. As in: 'Another seven to zero two-fisted attack from the hairy backs.' The malevolence between Afrikaans and English-speaking South Africans continued unabated, with the English still feeling mightily superior. The fact that only Afrikaans schools boxed was further reason to dismiss the boxing team as being somewhat *déclassé* and not worthy of the finer traditions of the school. Darby White in his white ducks and singlet, with his belly spilling over the old tie which held his trousers up, and Sarge in his jazzy hotel doorman's uniform and silly pace stick, were looked upon as a comic opera team by the remainder of the mortar and gowned teaching staff. Nothing was ever said, but you simply knew that those who laboured in the field were not equal to those who laboured in the mind.

While only the handful of Prince of Wales kids attended that first fight the gym was packed with kids from the opposition school, an Afrikaans high school named Helpmekaar, which translated into English means Help each other. Helpmekaar enjoyed a huge reputation in all sport except cricket. Its boxing team was said to be the best in South Africa and had won the South African schools Boxing Championships the year before.

At one hundred and eleven pounds the kid I was fighting was just one pound short of being a bantamweight. I didn't mind as I was used to fighting guys heavier and bigger than me, and had fought tougher looking kids than him before. But Hymie was concerned; this was the first time we were going into business together and at the weigh-in he'd looked worried.

'Ten pounds is a lot to give away, this Geldenhuis guy is supposed to be shit hot.'

'C'mon, Hymie, he's a new boy just like us, how would they know? How's the book going?'

'Great, that's the problem. I've been taking bets in the toilet from the Helpmekaar chaps all night and I've got you at ten to one against four to one on Geldenhuis, and they're falling over themselves to bet on their man.'

'That's great, did you tell the first form boarders to bet on me?'

'Ja, they're all pretty excited, but their bets aren't anywhere near enough to cover us if Geldenhuis wins. Christ, Peekay, I must be mad. It's not having all the facts that's pissing me off. We have no form on Geldenhuis, none on you for that matter, we're making book in the dark, that's just plain dumb.'

'We've got to start somewhere. Let's start by trusting each other.'

'No offence, Peekay, but next time first the facts and then the trust.' It was perhaps the most important thing Hymie ever said to me. Hymie was the supreme example of Hoppie's dictum: First with the head and then with the heart. It was to be the basis of our business operations from that time on.

Geldenhuis was solidly built around the shoulders and I knew I'd have to stay away from his right, which he kept throwing straight from the shoulder as he shadow boxed while waiting for the fight to begin.

Geel Piet had warned me that some boxers throw shadow punches before a fight to deceive their opponent into thinking they lead with a left or a right when in actual fact it's the other way around. The idea is to surprise your opponent in the first few seconds and so unsettle him. I studied the big kid and decided there wasn't any subterfuge in his shadow boxing, he was much too confident to bother with any tricks. His leading hand was the left and I noticed he held his right too low, leaving his jaw unprotected. His slightly more open stance suggested that he saw himself as a fighter. In which case he would come out hard and fast hoping to nail me early with a good punch.

For my part I would always 'just sit on the pot', as Geel Piet called sitting quietly on the tiny three-legged corner stool waiting for the fight to begin. 'Tell them nothing, jong,' he had said, 'just sit and watch, watch very carefully. I'm telling you, man, you can tell a lot about a boxer even before he throws a punch, if you watch him carefully.'

The bell for the first round went and after we'd touched gloves the Helpmekaar kid came at me fast. He was hard eyed and I could sense he planned to make short work of the fight. I saw the first straight left coming from a mile off and allowed it to miss the side of my head by a fraction. A near miss with the leading hand often gives a boxer the confidence to try again immediately with a similar punch, thrown even harder than the first it invariably throws the boxer slightly off balance. The second straight left came right on time and as it whistled past my ear his right dropped to the level of his chest leaving his head wide open. I stepped in and with my body slightly turned to maximise the power, the right hook I threw landed flush on the point of his chin. He was already off balance, moving into my punch, and he hit the canvas hard, sprawling on his back. While the blow carried all my strength behind it, it was also a perfectly timed punch and a gasp went up from the Helpmekaar crowd while a wild cheer rose from our first form boarders.

The kid on the canvas sat up as the ref began to count. There was no way I could have knocked him out but he was clearly shaken. Young guys are too proud to stay down for the compulsory eight count and he jumped to his feet glowering at me. The surprise had been on the other foot and I now expected him to move around me for a while, waiting for a chance to use his superior strength to nail me with a few solid blows to the head. First you're going to have to catch me you Boer bastard, I thought. The referee went through the compulsory eight count, then wiped his gloves and told us to box on.

I was so obviously lighter than the other kid and now, looking into his eyes, I suddenly realised that he had regarded the blow as a fluke and had no intention of boxing smart. He moved straight at me again with his right still held too low. He was telegraphing the punch to come by watching the point of my chin. Christ, he's going to try the left lead again. As Geel Piet would say, 'Some fighters you can read better than a book but, ag man, the story has no blêrrie imagination.'

The straight left came hard and missed, merely flicking my ear. I brought my right across his left and hit him on the side of the jaw, only just missing the point. I followed with a left hook into his solar plexus and he sat down hard, the seat of his pants seeming to bounce as he hit the canvas. I cursed myself, you don't get too many chances for a really good right cross in a fight and I hadn't set myself correctly. Nevertheless it was a good punch and the left had dug in just below the ribs where it really hurts.

Geldenhuis was strong and game and was back onto his feet in a second. He waited for the compulsory eight, and as the ref wiped his gloves he warned him that one more knock down meant the fight was over. I knew I'd have to be lucky to get a third crack at him and decided it was time to box, to wear him down jab, jab, jab, waiting for the chance to come under his left lead to land a series of solid punches under his heart. That way, if he wasn't enormously fit, I'd sap his stamina to give me another crack at him in the third and final round. The bell rang for the end of the round and I returned to my corner to find Darby and Sarge grinning from ear to ear.

In the second round I simply boxed him. His style was exuberant and I waited for him to grow impatient as I kept him at his distance with constant jabs to the face. Towards the end of the round he must have realised that the fight was slipping away and he seemed determined to knock me down, even if it meant taking a couple of punches on the way. He came at me with both hands swinging. I think he expected me to move away so that he could nail me in a corner. But I stood my ground and hit him with a straight left which pushed him back against the ropes. I followed in with Geel Piet's eight-punch combination, two good scoring shots to the head one of which opened a cut above his eye, the next bang on the nose, one more into the cut and the rest neatly placed under his heart. To my surprise, when the bell went for the end of round two, the Helpmekaar guys gave me a round of applause.

Geldenhuis didn't come out for the third round. The referee had examined the cut above his eye and stopped the fight. I'd won on a TKO, the first win for the Prince of Wales School in two years.

It didn't seem to matter that we lost the other seven fights, though all had lasted the distance. The boxing squad, generally outclassed, hadn't fought with such spirit and determination for years. Sarge was walking around flashing his mouth full of gold teeth and saying in a whisper that carried for yards, 'Bloody marvellous, that ought to show those bloody Boers who's boss.' You'd have thought we had won the match.

The boxing coach from Helpmekaar came over and patted me on the back. 'Who taught you to box, son?' he said in English.

'I learned in Barberton, Meneer,' I replied in Afrikaans.

He looked suddenly smug. 'Magtig. I knew you were too good for an Englishman! I've never seen a kid your age throw an eight-punch combination. Come to think of it, I've never seen any kid throw an eight-punch combination. Who taught you to box, man?'

'Meneer Geel Piet,' I replied.

'Well I wish we had him at Helpmekaar, that's all I can say, man.'

'I don't really think you would have wanted him,' I replied, but he seemed not to hear me.

'You're an Afrikaner, what are you doing in a school like this ?' Without waiting for my answer he continued, 'Listen, we could arrange for you to come to Helpmekaar, you'd be with your own people; we can organise a boarding scholarship.'

'I'm English. A Rooinek,' I said quietly. For the first time in my life I felt enormously proud about something. Perhaps it was wrong to be proud, but I'd waited a long time to come to terms with being a Rooinek.

The coach from Helpmekaar looked at me for what seemed like a long time. 'Well you don't box like an Englishman. Don't desert your own kind, son. Englishmen don't talk Afrikaans the way you do; I know, I'm a language teacher as well as a boxing coach.'

'I am English,' I replied in English, 'honestly, sir.'

'Well, Englishman, I doubt that there's a kid in your weight division anywhere in South Africa who could beat you, that is, if this Rooinek school doesn't bugger you up.'

He turned away abruptly, walked over to where Darby White was standing juggling his balls and looking pleased with himself. I could see they were both looking at me and Darby White had a proprietorial grin on his face.

I felt a hand on my shoulder and I turned to see the big kid I'd fought. He wore a large pink elastoplast patch over his left eyebrow. 'Howzit?' He stuck his hand out. 'Jannie Geldenhuis. No hard feelings, okay? You won fair and square, man,' he said in English with a thick Afrikaans accent.

'Thanks for the fight,' I replied in Afrikaans as I shook his hand.

He grinned and seemed pleased that I'd replied in Afrikaans. 'Ag man, I don't think I even hit you once, I've never done that before. It'll teach me a blêrrie good lesson; you looked such a little bugger, I thought I had an easy fight on my hands.'

I smiled at him. 'You're such a big bastard I thought I was going to get a hiding.' Gert had always said that a man should be magnanimous in victory and Jannie Geldenhuis seemed like a nice bloke.

'Ja, that was the blêrrie trouble, man, so did I.' He grinned again. 'Just you wait, man, I'll get you back on the rugby field, what possie you play?'

'Scrum-half. By the way, my name's Peekay.'

'Ja, I already know. Me too, I'm also a scrum-half. *Alles van die beste,* Peekay.' He turned to go and then turned back and rubbed the point of his jaw. 'Jesus, you hit me a beauty in the beginning of the first round!' Then he went to join his school mates.

'Ja, so long, Jannie,' I said, pleased it had ended this well.

Hymie walked up just as Geldenhuis departed. 'Howzit? What did the hairy back want, your autograph?'

'Nothing. He just said no hard feelings, he'd see me on the rugger field.'

Hymie grinned, 'I'll say no hard feelings, we're rich!' He frowned suddenly, 'but we've still got to hate the bastards.'

'Shit, Hymie, not after it's over!' I said grinning.

'It may only have been a boxing match to you!' Hymie pointed to the wooden spoon hanging from the beam above our heads. 'To me it's the beginning of getting rid of that! We can only do that by learning to hate.'

I sighed. 'Hymie, you've got to learn there are good Boers and bad Boers, just like everyone else. You can't just lump them all together.'

'The only good Boer is a dead Boer!' Hymie snorted.

'The only good Kaffir is a dead Kaffir is where that came from,' I said, chiding him for his lack of originality.

'Yeah, them too,' he added ruefully.

'Christ, Hymie, you're a Jew! How can you say things like that?'

Hymie laughed, 'I'm a very complicated Jew,' he said. 'Peekay, if we're going to win against those Boers we've got to learn to hate them. Don't you even understand the fundamentals?'

'Bullshit!'

'Yeah, it is. You're right, it is bullshit.' He looked at me and grinned again, 'But for Christ's sake, don't tell the others; we've got them thinking they can win, that the enemy isn't invincible.'

He was the only one on the boxing squad who hadn't congratulated me and I wondered why. I was to learn that Hymie was the world's best persuader, he could pump courage and spirit into a dejected boxer, soothe his battered ego and recover his self-esteem. Hymie smoothed words on and gently massaged them in as though they were a magic balm. But he only used them this way for a pre-determined purpose and only with people he considered less than his equal. A light pat on the back was all I ever got. Hymie considered me his equal and he allowed me to share his superior intellect, which was usually two or three jumps ahead of anyone else.

'Well tell me?'

'Tell you what?' Hymie asked.

'How much? How much did we make?'

Hymie grinned, 'Enough for you to buy Cooper several hundred cream buns if you ever have to again. I reckon we'll get a fiver out of it each.'

'Jesus, Hymie, that's wonderful!'

'It's only the beginning, Peekay. This time we gambled and won. Next time you fight we're going to know the form. We're going to know everything it is possible to know about your opponent. Every time he scratches his bum we're going to analyse why. The making of money should never be left to chance.'

After my solo victory against Helpmekaar, Atherton, Cunning-Spider and Pissy Johnson immediately joined the boxing squad, along with twelve of the other new boys. It soon became apparent that Pissy Johnson was totally unco-ordinated and would never make a boxer, but Atherton and Cunning-Spider were natural athletes and quickly caught on. Hymie called the new boys 'the Wooden Spoon Goons', swore us all into an elaborate brotherhood and elected himself President for Life and me Captain.

Hymie knew the value of a little mystique, the initiation into the Wooden Spoon Goons involved the exchange of everyone's blood except his own. He swore each of us into the brotherhood and then instructed me to swear him in as President for Life. He had personally composed the protocol for the ceremony and when his turn came he handed me a slip of paper to read which went like this: '*Do you, Hymie Solomon Levy, solemnly agree to fight with all your wit and skill and nerve to restore The Prince of Wales School to its former boxing glory*?' This came as somewhat of a surprise to all of us as we had no idea there had been any former glory to restore us to.

'I do,' Hymie said.

'*Do you agree to act selflessly without thought of personal glory or gain as the President for Life of the Wooden Spoon Goons*?' I wondered how he managed to reconcile this with our business arrangements.

'This I do solemnly declare to do,' Hymie said in an impressive flourish of grammatical construction.

'*In consideration for so doing and in the year nineteen hundred and forty-six in the reign of His Gracious Majesty King George the Sixth, I, Peekay, Captain of The Wooden Spoon Goons, declare Hymie Solomon Levy, President for Life.*'

Hymie had confided to me in a rare moment of introspection that in naming him his parents had thrown the whole bloody Polish ghetto at him. 'Why couldn't they have given me just one Goy name, like Derek or Brian or Arthur or something?' It was the only time I ever heard him question his Jewishness.

Later, as we were walking back to Wellington, I ribbed him about the restoring us to our former glory bit in the swearing in ceremony and also mentioned the no personal gain clause in his oath as President for Life.

Hymie stopped and turned to face me. With an exaggerated sigh, as though he had seriously come to doubt my sagacity, he said, 'For Chrissake, Peekay, don't you read history? It doesn't matter how much of a crap-up a country makes, by the time it gets into history it's been turned into glorious tradition. It's the same with an institution; you can't go having the school losing on its boxing team generation after generation, history simply doesn't allow for that sort of truth. Of course we've got a glorious tradition, because if we haven't we have now and as Wooden Spoon Goons we're going to have to restore the Prince of Wales to its former glory, whatever the fuck happened in real life.'

'Wow!' as Doc would say. 'No doubtski aboutski, Hymie Levy was the absoloodle best!'

'As for the personal gain, our primary purpose is to restore the school to its former boxing glory; there is no thought of not doing so if we can't make a quid out of it. That's what I mean by no thought of gain. We are not creating a business situation, we are merely exploiting one. Not to do so would be tantamount to sheer neglect, almost criminal if you ask me.'

There had been one strange happening at that first fight against Helpmekaar. Sarge had approached Darby White just before the fight to say that about a dozen blacks, all very neatly dressed and very clean, were standing outside the gymnasium and wanted permission to come in and watch. Darby, with much juggling of his balls, was reluctant. If they were caught on the streets without a note from their employers they would violate the Pass laws which put a nine o'clock curfew on all Africans. He didn't want to have a run-in with what he referred to as 'the constabulary', which if you have ever had any dealings with the South African Police Force is a very benign way of describing one of the toughest paramilitary forces in the world.

However, all the blacks showed him notes from their respective employers and he finally allowed them to stand by the door with Old Jimbo, the boot boy from School House who hadn't missed a fight at the school for twenty years. The boxing coach from Helpmekaar came over and protested and to our surprise Darby replied that the boys, like Old Jimbo, were school servants and welcome to stay.

My fight was first, and after I had been given the decision over Jannie Geldenhuis and the excitement had died down a bit, I looked up towards the door. Except for Old Jimbo and a very tall man, the Africans were no longer there. Upon seeing me looking in his direction the tall black man raised his hand in a clenched fist. 'Onoshobishobi Ingelosi!' he shouted and was gone.

'What the hell was that all about?' Sarge said, looking up from cutting the tape on my gloves. 'Sounded like some sorta war cry. Ungrateful blighters, they've all gone 'ome after the first fight.'

It was the first appearance of the people.

At first my black fan club, as it was to become known, was only a dozen or so but when the venue permitted it, it would grow to several hundred and later a great deal more than that. The legend of the Tadpole Angel was spreading.

After a few weeks, it became obvious that my identity had somehow been revealed to the school servants through the same weird osmosis in Africa that makes news penetrate prison walls, travel over mountains and into the townships until it becomes a part of the very air itself. And so a subtle change began to take place. The best cuts of meat appeared on the juniors' table and seconds were always brought first to where I sat. I found that my chores had been taken over. I would go to Fred Cooper's locker to get his rugby gear out for washing or his cricket boots for cleaning, only to find that they'd been done. His Sam Browne and brasses always shone like a mirror and even the laces in his rugby boots were washed. Only the morning chores, such as making Cooper's bed, were left to me, as there were no dormitory servants around first thing in the morning. My own gear was always spotless and back in my locker clean or polished by the time we got back to Wellington from the main school each day for lunch. On one occasion my football jersey had been ripped, I had made a hopeless job attempting to repair it and it concerned me greatly. I knew with certainty that my mother could not afford to replace it. I arrived back at Wellington for lunch to find that it had been neatly machine-darned, washed and ironed and was as good as new.

I spoke often to the school servants in their own languages but they never for one moment admitted to anything. They had heard the legend, knew the myth and had simply reacted without needing direction from anyone. In fact, I knew there would be no interested party looking after me, no concerned group of ex-prisoners. Africans don't work like that, each simply acted out his feelings, responding to what he or she felt. The legend of Onoshobishobi Ingelosi was sufficient in itself; it fed off my presence and not because of anything I would consciously do. In fact, despite my desire to do so, there was nothing I could do to stop it. My boxing was the needed proof of my status as a warrior and the fact that I only fought the hated Boer, yet another.

As is so often the case with a legend, every incident has two possible interpretations, the plausible and the one which is moulded to suit the making of the myth. Man is a romantic at heart and will always put aside dull, plodding reason for the excitement of an enigma. As Doc had pointed out, mystery, not logic, is what gives us hope and keeps us believing in a force greater than our own insignificance.

The boarders put my privileged position down to my near fraternal attitude to the school servants, which nicely explained their anxiety to help me. I was, I was beginning to understand, a natural leader and leaders, I have found, need never explain. In fact the less they explain the more desirable they become as leaders. Except to Doc, I had never been given to explaining myself and this was taken as strength by those who followed me. In truth, my reluctance to share my feelings was born out of my fear as a small child when I had been the only Rooinek in the foreign land of Afrikanerdom. I had survived by passing as unnoticed as possible, by anticipating the next move against me, by being prepared when the shit hit the fan to take it in my stride, pretending not to be hurt or humiliated. I had learned early that silence is better than sycophancy, that silence breeds guilt in other people. That it is fun to persecute a pig because it squeals, no fun at all to beat an animal which does not cry out. I had long since built the walls around my ego which only the most persistent person would ever manage to climb.

EIGHTEEN

I was the youngest kid in the first form but, what with one thing and another, I was clearly seen to have a bright future at the Prince of Wales School. My boxing win had made me a hero amongst the first form boarders who, elated by the financial gain from betting on me, had become devoted fans and who now exaggerated the fight in their constant retelling of it to any of the day boys who cared to listen. The next two matches had been away from the school and these I had also won, and the boarders had once again shared in the spoils. Although we didn't have enough information on the two boxers I fought, my opponents were comparatively easy and as both had been beaten by Geldenhuis we took the chance of giving the Afrikaans punters more than attractive odds to back their own fighter, with the result that we turned both matches into nice little earners.

The retelling of these two fights, by Hymie in particular, made them out to be gladiatorial bouts which made the first fight against Jannie Geldenhuis seem like a kissing match. By the time the next home match took place there was standing room only in the school gym and the fifty or so Africans who had turned up were obliged to watch the fight through the large bay windows.

To the delight of the school crowd, I won what turned out to be an easy fight. The other kid was very aggressive, prepared to take any sort of punishment to get a punch in. He was said to have won his first three fights inside the distance. But he came at me wide open on three occasions in the first round and I sat him on his pants in the middle of the ring three times. Three knockdowns was all it took to win a fight. The school was further vindicated when our light-heavyweight, Danny Polkinhorne, won on points in a brawling but thrilling three rounder.

Hymie and I had started a register on every boxer the school fought against, in every weight division. I would sit with him during a fight and describe the opponent fighting one of our boxers. I would talk about his footwork and his style, his weaknesses or strengths in ring craft, and his personality in the ring. I would point out those boxers who dominated the space they boxed in as if they owned the ring, and those who seemed to be fighting in borrowed space. We would separate the stand-up fighters from the boxers. We would note those who cut easily around the eyes.

Hymie would jot down every punch thrown in a fight, how many and what they were. Our notes would end with my summary of the entire fight and of the boxer, noting the punches he liked to throw the most and how many he threw during a fight. Boxers were obliged to weigh in before stepping into the ring, and Hymie would record their fighting weight and compare it with the next time they fought. We kept all these records in a big leather-bound accounting book, on the cover of which was embossed in gold: *Levy's Carpet Emporium, 126 Church Street, Pretoria. 'Carpet fit for a Prince'.* In this book, written in Hymie's neat, already mature handwriting, we would add to a boxer's profile every time he fought against the Prince of Wales School.

In a remarkably short time Hymie began to grasp the niceties of boxing. While I could remember the most minute details of almost every fighter, Hymie quickly developed the ability to anticipate with uncanny precision the way a boxer would fight the next time he appeared in the ring. He had an unerring instinct for a boxer's weakness and so we were able to prepare our own boxers to fight an opponent to exploit these. Of course, it also allowed us to set the odds on a fight with a high degree of success. Business was booming, for while the Prince of Wales boxers were still regular losers, the odds we offered meant our losses were well contained and that after a short while we could usually depend on one or two wins to pick up the big money.

After the first year when we had boxed every school twice and I was still unbeaten, it became difficult to get a bet against me. The Afrikaans kids weren't fools and we were forced to offer more and more attractive odds on my opponent to the point where we were taking unnecessary risks and it was beginning to put me under pressure. In a fight against Geldenhuis towards the end of the second year where the odds were twenty to one on Geldenhuis beating me, I only narrowly won on points.

The Afrikaners had wised up. Profits were down. With our juniors beginning to win they could no longer hedge their bets against me by taking shorter odds on some of the other fighters. Hymie decided it was time to quit the bookmaking business.

'It's time to get out, Peekay. There are two important rules of business, knowing when to get in and when to get out. Of the two, knowing when to get out is the most important. We've got bigger fish to fry.'

I'd enjoyed two years of regular pocket money and I didn't relish the prospect of being broke again. 'These fish we are going to fry, what are they?'

'I'm buggered if I know,' Hymie said, 'but something will come along, business is simply a matter of opportunity and money. If you've got the capital, sure as tomorrow is Tuesday, an opportunity will come along.'

We'd built up a considerable bank over the first two years, fifty per cent of everything we made went into our capital which was earning interest in the Yeoville branch of Barclays Bank.

That's when I had the idea. 'Hymie, we've got fifty quid in the bank and we're getting two and a half per cent on our money, which isn't very much. I mean one pound ten a year, it's nice but it isn't world shattering.'

Hymie laughed, 'There was a time not so long ago. . .'

I cut in, 'Yeah, I know, one pound ten was a lot of money, more than I'd ever owned. But listen, pocket money's on Wednesday and Saturday, by Tuesday and Friday everyone's broke.'

We were sitting on a bench under the oak trees bordering the cricket field and Hymie jumped up in alarm. I could see he was upset and he leaned over me and gripped the back of the bench on either side of me. 'Peekay, are you crazy! Don't you understand? I'm the token Jew around here! What the fuck do you think the Christian gentlemen are going to say? A money lender! Me? Christ Peekay, the whole purpose of my education at this goy school is so that sort of stigma can be removed from my Jewishness. I'm here for the politics and the polish. I've already had several hundred years training in usury!'

'That's all the banks do, isn't it?' I replied. 'If you want a loan from a bank you've got to go cap in hand and they don't even have to earn it in the first place; people just give it to them for a lousy two and a half per cent interest and they then turn around and lend it for seven per cent, that's nearly two hundred per cent profit. That isn't usury?'

'Peekay, you don't understand; when the banks do it it's business, when a Jew does it, it's exploitation!'

'I see, so a Jew can't own a bank?'

'Of course he can. Rothschild, one of the world's most famous banks, is owned by a Jewish family; the Rothschilds are one of France's and England's most respected families.'

'Yeah, I know,' I said, 'they started in Frankfurt-on-Main in Germany towards the end of the eighteenth century as money lenders!'

'Christ, Peekay, I don't need to do this; there are other ways to make a quid, you'll see.' Hymie was clearly distressed. 'In the meantime you can borrow from our capital for pocket money.'

'You don't need to do this, but I do. I'm not going to use our capital, I can earn my own way. I'm sorry if I've hurt your sensibilities, Hymie, but I've climbed into the ring twenty-five times in the last two years to support our book-making business, it's your turn now.'

Hymie released the bench and straightened up, clasping his hands behind his back as though he was preparing to give me a lecture.

'Do you know why I really came to the Prince of Wales School, Peekay?' He didn't wait for my answer before continuing. 'Let me tell you. When the Prince of Wales, I mean the then future King, came to Pretoria there was a reception held for him by the Red Cross. My old man supplied the red carpet for the occasion. The deal was free carpet for an invitation. He stood in line and the Prince shook his hand. He never quite got over it. It was as though he'd touched the face of the Almighty. He'd made it. He'd reached the social pinnacle. He was a gentleman at last. A gentleman with a heavy Polish accent, but a gentleman no less. He bought his own carpet back from the Red Cross for a huge sum and carpeted the lounge room at home. I don't think one day of my life went by without at least one mention of the fucking carpet: "A Prince already, with his own feet walked on zat carpet my boy!"' Hymie mimicked. 'Then he read in the paper that there was a Prince of Wales school in Johannesburg and that the Prince was to lay a wreath at the school's war memorial. He decided that if he had a son he would bring him up as the perfect English gentleman... correction, perfect Jewish English gentleman. This school and Oxford to follow, is going to make me the first "respectable" Jew in our family since Moses bawled in the bullrushes. I'll tell you something, Peekay, if he had had to carpet every classroom, all three boarders houses and the school quad to get me in here he'd have thought it was a bargain.'

'What you're saying is that by becoming money lenders we fuck up everything?'

Hymie grinned, 'Yup! That's about it.'

'Well then we'll call it a bank. Look, Hymie, it meets every criterion we've established for a business. There is a known need for our services. The risk factor is small and easy to control; our creditors can hardly default can they? We don't have to borrow capital and the profits are reasonable and regular. As Doc would say: "No doubtski aboutski," it's perfect and it's honest. . . well sort of.'

'What will you do if I say, no?' Hymie asked.

'I'd find it very difficult to come to terms with your answer. Now let me tell *you* a story. The guy who taught me boxing was a Cape Coloured and by any standards a bad bastard. He'd spent more time in prison than out on the street. He was the worst kind of recidivist. By any standards the scum of society. He lied, cheated and robbed. He'd also been beaten up more times than you and I have had hot breakfasts. He was the ultimate loser. That's how the world saw him. That's how they judged him.'

'You're talking about Geel Piet, aren't you?' Hymie said.

'Ja, well Geel Piet was just about the best friend I ever had. He died for me. A warder named Borman rammed a two-foot baton up his arse until he haemorrhaged to death. Geel Piet could have saved himself simply by confessing that it was me who smuggled the prisoners' mail into the prison. But he didn't. I didn't see him as any of the things he was supposed to be. I saw him as one of the best human beings I am ever likely to know. Christ, Hymie, it's not what a man does, it's what a man is that counts!'

We called it the Boarders' Bank, but it simply became known as the Bank and was an immediate success. Interest was at ten per cent per week and loans were never extended beyond a fortnight. Which was long enough for any kid to write home for money if he got himself into a financial fix. In the four years we remained at school we didn't incur a single bad debt. The funny thing was that not only the boarders but also the day boys regarded the Bank as a valued institution. Moreover, Hymie's antecedents never entered into it, although the Bank formed the basis of some of his more spectacular future financial ploys. I could say *our* spectacular successes, but Hymie was the real wizard and I remained the sorcerer's apprentice. The Bank also formed the basis for my pocket money; a source of great personal pride to me. I'd solved the major emotional problem confronting my school career and, unencumbered with money problems, was now free to forge ahead.

By the time we had reached Form three, the younger boxers were beginning to win on a regular basis and Atherton and Cunning-Spider had each won six of their last seven fights, Atherton as a lightweight and Cunning-Spider as a light-welterweight. Hymie's Wooden Spoon Goons were building a reputation and gaining a whole heap of respect from the Afrikaans schools. The Prince of Wales School was no longer a joke and the Boer War was often won by the English these days. That was the year we finally lost the wooden spoon and the faded green, red and dirty white ribbon was removed and replaced with the colours of another school. Hymie had achieved his first objective which he told the Wooden Spoon Goons was only, 'A small pimple on the great hairy arse of my ambition for the gentlemen Christian boxers.'

In the three years it took to lose the wooden spoon, I earned an exaggerated reputation as a boxer amongst the Afrikaans schools on the Witwatersrand. I started to fill out and by the time I was fourteen I was fighting as a bantamweight. Every fight, at school or away, was attracting the people. A match a hundred miles by bus or train from the school would attract just as many Africans as one at home where the boxing bouts had been moved away from the gym to the school hall. Here the Africans were allowed to sit at the very back of the hall separated from the whites by a wide corridor. During the summer it was popular to have the boxing out of doors, usually with the ring set up on a rugby field. At these times the blacks would be allowed to watch the fights, even those held at the most racist Afrikaans schools, where they were kept well separated from the white spectators. It was at one of these out of town Afrikaans schools that I first heard the word 'apartheid' used to describe the place where the black spectators were allowed to sit and I have often since wondered if I had witnessed the first use of a word which would become universal as an expression of oppression.

The boxing matches at these outdoor venues usually started at six just as the sun was beginning to set and were all over by eight when it was still light enough on the Highveld not to need lights over the ring. It was at another of these outdoor fights that we invented the famous 'sunblinder'. The Prince of Wales boxer simply used the ring so that his opponent could be turned to face into the setting sun which would momentarily blind him. The idea was to work an opponent round and then time a punch just as the hapless boxer moved into the direct line of the late afternoon sun. If a boxer was clever enough on his feet this simple expedient could be made to work half a dozen times during a fight, often earning the extra points required to get the decision. The gentlemen Christians had no compunction about doing this to their opponents; after all this was the Boer War and no quarter was given or expected. Hymie got the idea from a movie he had seen which showed how the Battle of Britain Spitfires had come out of the sun to pounce on unsuspecting German aircraft.

The people would watch the fights in silence until it was my turn to fight and then invariably a soft, almost imperceptible hum would begin, growing in volume and, in the African manner, always in perfect harmony. Then a leader would take up a chant which might go something like this: 'He is the chief who comes in our dreamtime, the caster of spells and the bringer of wisdom.'

'Onoshobishobi Ingelosi!' the people would chorus in reply.

'He can dance in the dew without leaving footprints and stalk the wind until it howls to be free.'

'Onoshobishobi Ingelosi!'

'His blows are like the summer thunder and his lightning strikes his foes!'

'Onoshobishobi Ingelosi!'

'For cunning he matches the thin moon and for wisdom the full, for is he not Lord of the dark and the light, the day and the night?'

'Onoshobishobi Ingelosi! Onoshobishobi Ingelosi!'

'He will win for the people, he will win for all the people, in all the tribes, the people are all his people!'

'He will win, he will win, he will win for the people, Onoshobishobi Ingelosi! Onoshobishobi Ingelosi! Onoshobishobi Ingelosi!!'

Once the fight started there would be not a sound from the black spectators and after I had won the tall black man who had been present at my first fight in the school gym would raise his hand in the fisted salute. 'Onoshobishobi Ingelosi!' he would shout and the blacks would silently leave. I was later to hear that the absolute silence during a fight was so they could not be accused of barracking for me and in so doing incur the wrath of my opponent's people, and thus be banned from attending. In fact the absolute silence from the African stands was uncanny and made a contribution to unnerving my opponents.

Hymie was quick to realise the potential of the black audience and in return for admitting them to the boxing matches at the Prince of Wales School they were required to sing. This was thought no hardship, as most Africans love to sing and soon a tradition was born. Hymie also persuaded Darby White to move my fight up so that I was higher on the bill. This meant that the black audience would be able to stay as late as possible while still allowing them time to be home by nine o'clock curfew.

Parents and members of the public began to attend these summer evening fights and the Afrikaans schools were forced to do the same as us to attract white spectators. The fights became popular events, with the

African singing a big drawcard leading, as it did, to what was soon regarded as the feature of the entertainment, the chant that preceded my bout.

It is an indication of the enormous dichotomy between white and black that for the first three years no white spectator bothered to ask for a translation of what was being said in the chants. People seemed intrigued by the fact that a small white boy had gathered a huge black following but they simply put this down to my skill as a boxer. The presumption of the white man knows no bounds in Africa. The full story would never come out but somewhere along the line the words Onoshobishobi Ingelosi were translated to mean Tadpole Angel.

The Tadpole Angel quickly became my fighting name among the whites and also, to my extreme mortification, with the kids in the Afrikaans schools. Translated into English it was a dumb name and my embarrassment increased when it was further modified by an anti-following of Afrikaners who referred to me as 'little angel' and even sometimes as 'Mama's little angel.'

Though not large in number, I was conscious of this very vocal group who, like the much larger group of blacks, attended every fight, but who came in the hope that Mama's little angel, the *Kaffirboetie,* would come to a sticky end at the hands of one of their own kind.

By contrast, the people saw the name in only one light. I was fighting for them against the Boer. The tangible evidence of the enemy in the form of the dissident group of Afrikaners only served to increase their fervour. Their numbers multiplied each week and their chants grew more elaborate and beautiful. In fairness it must be said there were whites who were on my side, adult Afrikaners who loved to see me box and didn't give a damn about my being a Rooinek.

The fact that I hadn't been beaten wasn't as big a deal as it may seem; there were several kids from other schools who enjoyed unblemished records.

My mind was permanently focussed on a single fixed point, the welterweight championship of the world. I thought about it so often, reaffirmed my determination so frequently, that hardly an hour of my life passed when it wasn't in my thoughts. To lose a fight would be a backward step, a hair-line crack in my armour. The only way it was going to happen was for me to come up against a boxer who was a helluva lot better than me. Not just more talented but also a lot better trained.

While I told myself that each win was a small deposit on the ultimate ownership of the world welterweight crown, the enormous need in me to win touched on a whole heap of other responses a fourteen year old can't really work out. It had something to do with rejecting the Lord, with my mother, the Judge, being surrounded by guys who came from wealthy homes, even my headless snake. While I didn't think of it as camouflage, I now know that it was, that I kept myself protected by being out in front. Too far in front to be an easy mark.

Doc and Mrs Boxall had taught me to think. Mrs Boxall in the general sense and Doc in the particular. Doc's life was a constant pre-occupation with minutiae, his eye sought always what lay hidden yet was important, he knew that nature guards her secrets jealously, that acute observation begins with a questioning mind. 'Always to ask questions, ja this is so, maybe the answers come slow, but always they are coming if you wait with your head and your eyes.'

Geel Piet taught me to anticipate the problems likely to occur in any situation and to review the answers to them long before disaster struck. His mind was a network of emergency plans. While small boys are not natural pessimists, he nevertheless taught me the value of a routine which, when practised a thousand times, becomes an automatic reaction to a crisis.

Over all this lay Hoppie's dictum: *First with the head and then with the heart:* Winning was something you worked at intellectually, emotion clouds the mind and is its natural enemy. This made for a loneliness which often left me aching to share an emotion but equally afraid that if I did so I would reveal a weakness which could later be used against me. Only Doc was allowed to know all of me with nothing held back.

But even Doc was lost to me when sex lightning struck and puberty arrived in a surge of lust. The superior equipment my mentors had given me and which I had unknowingly used so effectively to perfect my camouflage was suddenly useless. Nothing I had been taught prepared me for the onset of my sexual drive. I found myself more completely a loner than ever, but this time I was trying to keep the lid on an emotional cauldron that threatened to boil over and drown me.

I woke each morning with a rigid tent pole which, in the school tradition, I took to the showers, using my erection as a hook over which to drape my towel. While I joined in with the general hilarity at those of us who had been struck by sex lightning, I knew I was faking it. Buried deep where I hoped he would never surface lay Pisskop and his hatless snake and, while circumcision was too common among the guys at the Prince of Wales to cause embarrassment, my dick was the part of my anatomy that had started all my problems and now it was behaving in a manner over which I had absolutely no control.

Sex had never been discussed at home but among the guys in the boxing squad it was referred to as 'doing it'. Snotnose was said to be *almost* doing it to Sophie Smit, Captain Smit's daughter, having given her tits a feel-up in the dark at a Saturday matinee and, it was hinted, a feel *down there,* as well.

I knew enough about the ways of the Lord to know that if I should find myself in the fortunate position of being able to do it to Sophie, I would be committing a mortal sin. Though I freely admit, even in my pubescent state with my brains turned to meat loaf, I was aware that the chances of my achieving a supine Sophie were just about non-existent, I knew that the Lord, heavily backed by my mother, wasn't the sort of person who settled for innocence by omission. My case was hopeless. Even for a sinner I was sinning at an alarming rate. Not only in my head but also behind a closed toilet door where I actively fantasised *doing it* to Sophie Smit.

The fact that I wasn't a proper born-again Christian somehow made it more important that I practise restraint. It became a test of character which I was failing on a daily, sometimes twice daily, not to mention nightly basis. I tried to keep it down to a minimum, promising myself after each time it happened that I was definitely cured, and this had been the last time my fingers would play a tune on the pork flute. Ha, ha . . . some last time! No matter how hard I tried to reform my wicked ways and to concentrate on other things my tent pole would erect at the most awkward times and I would need to sneak off to seek relief.

The trouble was that Hymie seemed not to have been struck by sex lightning at all. He talked dirty in the usual schoolboy way, though never in the same explicit terms as the constantly randy group around him. Not that I was among these big mouth fantasisers, my sex life was clandestine, a furtive business. But what the others claimed out loud they'd like to do with the Vargas girls in *Esquire* magazine was simply a paraphrase of what I felt myself. Cunning-Spider, Paul Atherton and Pissy Johnson were also sex struck though, I felt certain, not as badly as me. Hymie on the other hand seemed to sail through puberty like a bloody eunuch.

I don't want to go on about it; but it was an awkward enough time and, because it disrupted the carefully constructed pattern of my existence, it forced me to think about other aspects of my life.

Hitherto I had never questioned the motives of the adults around me, nor had I felt any reason to question the conventional wisdom they assumed was correct for me. Now I was beginning to see that the plans for my future were being largely made by other people. That in return for being allowed to dream my boxing dream, I was allowing others to map the road ahead for me. I was perceived as a winner and everyone likes to help a winner. I could sense that I was clever enough to win most of the glittering prizes yet to come and this would inevitably lead to a life of privilege, to doors being opened, barriers lowered, places made for me as I was passed from hand to hand among the rich and the privileged until I melded perfectly, indistinguishable from those few who, in the white man's Africa, have so much power over the many who have none.

Doc had taught me the value of being the odd man out. The man assumes the role of the loner, the thinker and the searching spirit who calls the privileged and the powerful to task. The power of one was the courage to remain separate, to think through to the truth and not to be beguiled by convention or the plausible arguments of those who expect to maintain power, whatever the cost.

At fourteen I had no hope of seeing things quite as clearly as this, but I instinctively understood that power is beguiling and man does not lightly give it up. To maintain it he will bend the truth and warp his values. I was a child of Africa, a white child to be sure, but nevertheless Africa's child.

The black breasts which had suckled me, and the dark hands which had bathed and rocked me, left me with a burden of obligation to resist the white power which would be the ultimate gift from those who now trained me.

I saw this same sense of aloneness in Hymie. I sensed his Jewish alienation and I understood the intelligent, clear-eyed pessimism that seemed a part of everything he did. He had inherited loneliness. Despite his need for me, he knew himself ultimately to be on his own. Though we never spoke of it, our friendship was forged on this common knowledge. We had instinctively come together to learn, each from the other, those lessons we needed to use the power within us effectively, to think and act differently from those around us.

To win took on a new meaning. It was still part of my fierce-eyed determination to become the welterweight champion of the world, but in the years to follow winning would become the ultimate camouflage as I trained to be a spiritual terrorist. To achieve this new and barely understood aim, I had to appear to be damn near perfect in everything I did even at the risk of appearing to be a bit of a pain.

Each week I received a letter from Doc, Mrs Boxall and Miss Bornstein. While I wrote home fairly regularly, I think my mother must have been too busy sewing to write very often. Sometimes on the bottom of Doc's letters would appear two inky thumb prints under which Doc would write in his small neat hand, *From Dee and Dum who ask who is washing your clothes and baking rusks for your coffee in the morning?* Dee and Dum continued to make the sojourn to Doc's cottage for the weekly clean-up and he had grown very fond of them. Doc's letters were about the hills and his beloved cacti, and while I had continued my piano under the instruction of the school music master, he never mentioned music in his letters. I think Doc knew I was destined for other things. Mrs Boxall would write all the town gossip, and she said that the Assemblies of God had supplied two young missionaries who could speak four African languages between them to take on the prison letters. She was still in charge, determined that God would not be allowed to interfere with the perfectly lovely business of writing a letter to your loved ones. In one of her letters she had added that the people sadly missed King Georgie and that letter-writing had fallen off a fair bit after I had left.

The Earl of Sandwich Fund had started to spread and Mrs Boxall was elected chairwoman of seven different groups which had started prison rehabilitation work among black prisoners in South Africa. Many of these early members of the Sandwich Fund were to become the leaders of the Black Sash movement, a movement among South African women which started in the mid-fifties to protest against apartheid and injustice against the black people. It continues as one of the few voices of freedom coming out of this sad land; a voice muted from protest against a regime afraid to hear the just and anguished cries of the people.

Miss Bornstein was determined to develop my intellect and insisted on knowing in some detail exactly which books we were reading, maths we were doing and, in fact, everything. I had written to her about Hymie and she included him in her letters which would consist mostly of pages and pages of questions and discussion points. Finally she would always include in her weekly letter a chess move for each of us from old Mr Bornstein who in the six years we were at school we never managed to beat.

Hymie would groan loudly when the weekly letter arrived plump with questions. He'd hold his hands to the side of his face and rock in an exaggerated manner. 'Oy veh!' he'd say, imitating his granma, 'the only reason I elected to come to this institution for Christian gentlemen was to get away from Jewish women, now I'm at fucking correspondence school with one!' But Miss Bornstein had a way, even at long distance, of involving one's pride and the interest she stimulated in her letters put Hymie and myself far ahead of anyone else in the A class at school.

Hymie was the first to use what became a famous expression throughout the school. We were in 'Mango' Cobett's history class and Mango, an asinine man who taught with a very highbrow bias and was a dreadful snob, was talking about the Crimean War and the Charge of the Light Brigade. Mango carried the nickname because he had an oval-shaped head with fine blond hair which clung to his skull and a sharp blond goatee, the whole assemblage resembled a well-sucked mango pip. Though South African born, he was an avowed anglophile and spoke in a dewy-eyed manner about the bravery of Lord Cardigan in the Charge of the Light Brigade.

From the back of the class where we both sat Hymie interjected, 'According to Miss Bornstein, he demonstrated a lamentable lack of control over the French; he also lacked common sense and a sense of responsibility to his men, sir.'

There was a stunned silence, Mango's mouth was half open and he could hardly believe his ears.

'According to Miss Bornstein, Lord Raglan was also completely out of his depth, in fact, a bumbling old fool,' Hymie added.

Mango Cobett finally regained his voice. 'According to whom, Levy?'

'According to Miss Bornstein of the famous Jewish correspondence school, sir,' I interjected. The classroom broke into an uproar.

'Shut up! Everyone shut up at once!' Mango Cobett yelled. The classroom quickly murmured down into silence. Both Hymie and myself were known as brains and Mango wasn't game enough simply to punish us with a couple of hours' detention without first asserting his superior historical perspective.

'I was unaware that the Jews played a part in the Crimean War. I take it your Miss Bornstein is a history scholar of some distinction, perhaps a better source than *The Invasion of the Crimea* by A. W. Kinglake.' He picked up one of the books which lay on the desk in front of him and held it high, squinting slightly as he read the spine. 'William Blackwood and Sons, Edinburgh and London, 1864. I'd say that was from the horse's mouth, wouldn't you?'

'More like the horse's arse, sir,' Hymie quipped, and the classroom broke up again.

Kinglake's *Invasion of the Crimea* was one of the volumes my granpa had at home along with the complete works of Charles Dickens and I'd read both volumes of Kinglake's account when I was eight. According to Miss Bornstein, Kinglake's account was remarkable but she had also read the Russian and French accounts, and now felt the official British version was heavily jingoistic and apt to blame the French and the Turks while allowing that Lord Raglan, the British Commander in Chief, though competent was somewhat inexperienced in asserting Lord Cardigan to be a man of great sagacity and leadership skills. Miss Bornstein, Hymie and I had been conducting an involved correspondence on the very volumes Mango was quoting from.

'According to Miss Bornstein, A. W. Kinglake was commissioned by the War Office to write the series, which was never a good start. The book has been republished several times and the 1864 version, slightly amended, was the fourth edition. More appeared after the first Boer War when the Transvaal had regained its independence, previously having been shamefully annexed by Britain after gold had fortuitously been discovered. The history was meant to remind the British of their recent glorious past so that they wouldn't dwell too heavily on the trouncing they'd received from a handful of determined farmers who aimed straight and didn't form into a square to fight. According to Miss Bornstein it is rather long on glory and somewhat short on the true facts. The volumes were republished again, just two years before the declaration of the second Boer War. They were, of course, ideally timed and put the British public in the mood for another territorial rape and pillage in the name of Queen and Empire.' Hymie had exactly quoted a passage in one of Miss Bornstein's letters; it was word perfect, even comma perfect.

Mango Cobett's usually deathly pale face had flushed a dark red. 'Are you challenging the integrity of one of the finest historians to come out of the British Isles, Levy?'

'No, sir,' Hymie said. 'Miss Bornstein is.' The class broke into spontaneous laughter again.

'Shut up! Shut up!' Mango yelled. 'I've heard enough!' The class settled down and a flushed Mango Cobett commenced to walk up and down the length of the classroom. 'The Battle of Alma, the first in the Crimea, where the British took the Russian General Menshikov head on, Russians 9,000 dead, British 2,000! Those, gentlemen, are the facts.'

I jumped in. 'According to Miss Bornstein, Lord Raglan lost control of the Battle of Alma almost from the moment it started. He set the frontal attack and then lost control while the French climbed the steep cliffs near the mouth of the river and outflanked Menshikov with very few casualties.'

'Nine thousand Russians, two thousand British!' Mango said emphatically.

'Two thousand dead in three hours!' I retaliated. 'The French lost less than two hundred men.'

'The Russians were peasants without any training and fought in dense columns. Menshikov had scrambled eggs for brains,' Hymie said, to the delight of the classroom.

Mango Cobett pressed on. 'The Battle of Inkerman, Russians 11,000 dead, the British 2,640!' He leaned on the figure forty to emphasize his exact knowledge of the numbers involved.

'According to Miss Bornstein, Lord Raglan exercised no influence on the course of the fighting. The Battle of Inkerman was called the "Soldiers' Battle" because units were committed to the battle piecemeal and the soldiers had to work it out for themselves,' Hymie replied.

'The Russians on the other hand were commanded by General Russian eggs himself,' I said smugly, causing the class to laugh once more.

'That will be enough, Peekay,' Mango said, not too happy about arguing on two fronts. 'We have one more battle to go, the Redan.'

'Ah, the Redan! According to Miss Bornstein . . .'

'Quiet, Levy!' Mango demanded. 'The Russian losses are not known but are thought to be twice that of the British.'

'The British lost five thousand men at the Redan, and again Lord Raglan lost control of the battle,' I said, determined that he should not be allowed to cover up the British losses.

'Lord Raglan was a very sick man and died of cholera ten days after the Redan. He can't be entirely blamed for the huge losses,' Mango retorted.

'You've missed the Charge of the Light Brigade, sir,' Hymie said with a grin.

'Ah yes, Lord Cardigan's Light Brigade, a mistake, a question of a misunderstanding and an ill-drafted order.'

'And under pig's-trotters-for-brains Lord Cardigan, seven hundred mounted troopers charged into the valley of death and four hundred died!'

'I don't like your attitude, Levy. Lord Cardigan was a member of the British aristocracy and is not subject to schoolboy humour. While we're on the subject, Peekay, Menshikov was a respected Russian general and also above your puerile wit. You will both see me outside the masters' common room at the conclusion of school. Your attitude to this history lesson has been reprehensible to say the least.' The bell went for recess and the colour drained back out of Mango Cobett's face. As we were leaving the class he had one last jibe. 'Let me assure you both, England did not conquer half the known world including this country because she placed stupid commanders in the field.'

'According to Miss Bornstein. . .' we both began, and Hymie finished . . . 'that's not true.'

The expression was born. From that moment on, any boy in the Prince of Wales School who disagreed with a statement made by a master would signal his disagreement by prefacing it with, 'According to Miss Bornstein. . .' It caused so much exasperation amongst the teaching staff that it was eventually taken to the head, St John Burnham MA (Oxon), known as Singe 'n Burn, who prided himself on being a liberal educationalist. To the mortification of the masters and in particular Mr Hemming the senior English master, Singe 'n Burn declared the expression, 'a legitimate paraphrase for a dissenting opinion.' And so the expression, 'According to Miss Bornstein,' was officially written into the school vocabulary.

We arrived outside the masters' common room just after three o'clock armed with Miss Bornstein's two letters on the subject of the Crimean War. But Mango refused to continue the argument and simply gave us two hours of detention and a two thousand word essay to write on the Crimean War. He added that the next indiscretion would result in a visit to the head.

Hymie said in disgust, 'I told you history was all bullshit. There goes another generation of Christian gentlemen school boys who will grow up to believe the Charge of the Light Brigade was one of England's finest hours.'

'But it was,' I said.

'It was what?' Hymie said, not sure he'd heard me correctly.

'It was one of England's finest hours. What's important is not whether you win or lose but how you play the game.'

'Bullshit! If the Jews had played that game we'd have been extinct fifteen hundred years ago.'

'You have to be a Christian gentleman to understand,' I kidded him.

'Do me a favour, Peekay, don't just read history, feel it. Try to imagine being an ordinary guy on a half-starved horse, your regiment decimated by cholera, you've got a lance in your hand and are looking into the barrels of the Russian artillery holding the Vorontsov Ridge at Balaclava. Do you know why the English managed to conquer half the globe? Because they were so bloody stupid! Some half-witted lord jumped up in a general's uniform would simply advance on a position and expend men; he didn't care, they were only yeomen and slum slush, cannon fodder. He just kept sending them in and so help me they kept on going, until eventually he won. You call that bravery? I call that two things, murder and stupidity. The generals murdered their men and the men were too stupid to resist.'

'And too brave, it wasn't just stupidity.'

Hymie ignored my interjection. 'History makes it all okay. History forgets the vomit and the shit, the blood and the horses with their guts blown away, the cries of men as they shit their pants and drowned in their own blood. The Charge of the Light Brigade is celebrated because it was the most obviously stupid, most spectacularly stupid, most stupendously stupid sacrifice of men until the brilliant British generals finally topped it for sheer cold-blooded slaughter in the trenches in Flanders and on the cliffs above Gallipoli.'

Hymie changed course suddenly. 'Hitler murdered six million Jews. He had to round them up and rail them to the death camps and the world wept for man's inhumanity to man. But underneath it all there is the feeling that the Jews should have fought, should have resisted, should have died defending their kith and kin, should have died like men. All the women and children and the cobblers and tailors and small shopkeepers who believed that they were Germans and Poles and Hungarians, who believed passionately in logic and order, in Kant and Spinoza, and in minding their own business and never getting involved and most of all, in never volunteering to be stupid, should have turned into a fighting machine that takes pride in dying.

'Because they didn't go chasing a piece of coloured bunting around the place, history may yet judge them cowards.' Hymie sniffed and wiped his nose across the back of his hand. I had never seen him quite as upset and angry before.

'When a British general looking for a new swatch of ribbon for his chest sent men into battle in the eighteenth and nineteenth centuries and then again in the Great War Englishmen volunteered to go. They actually handed themselves over into his care and in return for their trust he was just as careless with their lives as the Jew-killers of Auschwitz, Dachau, Treblinka, Belsen and the other death camps were with the lives of my kind. But when it was all over, the world, or the English-speaking world anyway, cheered their Christian gentlemen heads off. More tradition had been made, more regimental bunting to hang in St Paul's and Westminster Abbey. More bullshit.' He sniffed again and grabbed me by the shoulder.

'You know something, Peekay? History stinks and it's bastards like Mango Cobett who add to the putrefaction by believing the crap that's written. Take my word for it, in another thirty years the Germans will claim that only a handful of SS caused the Holocaust unbeknownst to the good burghers who stayed at home and knitted socks for Jewish prisoners of war.'

To Mango Cobett's credit, the detention essays Hymie and I wrote on the Crimean War shared the history prize that year. Miss Bornstein's evidence was too conclusive.

With her weekly letters, some of them up to twenty pages, Miss Bornstein had the happy knack of instigating a line of reasoning which would stimulate us both. We'd rush to the school library to follow its course. By the time we were in form three we were fairly skilled researchers and were given permission to spend Wednesday afternoons at the Johannesburg Public Library.

Form three was a big year for us. It was the year the boxing team lost the wooden spoon and also the year we published, with the help of a typist and the Gestetner machine in Hymie's father's carpet emporium, *The Miss Bornstein School of Correspondence Notes. Results fully guaranteed or your money back. Peekay & H. S. Levy. 5/-.* There were two books, one for Form one and the other for Form two.

Hymie and I had argued furiously about the price. Five shillings was outrageous when a science textbook cost only two shillings.

'If we charge what it appears to be worth we'd be lucky to get sixpence,' he admitted. 'Good business is when people perceive something to be valuable, and the best way to encourage this perception is by guiding their thinking.'

'You mean by charging outrageously?'

'Now wait a mo, Peekay, that's not quite fair. Value for money is when the customer is satisfied that he has made the right purchase decision. Or do you disagree?'

I was forced to agree. 'Well then, what are we promising with the *Miss Bornstein School of Correspondence Notes,* for Forms one and two?'

'The promise is on the cover, but the bloody promise holds good whether we charge them sixpence or ten bob.'

'Not so. A five bob price tag means at least two things: that the information in the notes is important and rare and that by following it, success is guaranteed. The second promise is convenience; all the information they need is between two covers, they don't have to *schlep* through a dozen textbooks, the authors have done all the mental legwork for them. If we charged them sixpence they wouldn't value the book and so it wouldn't work for them.'

'Shouldn't we dress them up a bit? For two bob a copy we could probably afford to have them printed with a hard cover. At least that way the value would be perceived to be better?'

Hymie looked at me in astonishment. 'Peekay, are you mad? Do you want to kill the business in one year?'

'What do you mean?'

Hymie picked up a copy of our textbook and holding it by one corner he shook it violently. The staples in the centre margin gave way and the pages flew apart.

'There you are, look at that! They're rubbish, we'll never get away with this,' I protested.

'Bullshit, they're perfect, they'll only just hang together for one year. If we have them properly printed and bound the guys will sell them at the end of the year to the incoming form. Where would our business be then?'

Hymie was right, despite the price there wasn't a kid in either form who didn't purchase a copy and no one asked to have their money refunded. We were a good business combination with the added advantage of being generally popular; in particular, my ability in the boxing ring and, to a lesser degree, on the rugby field created quite a large following among my peers. Doing business with the Bank when you were broke became the norm for both day boys and boarders, so that every time we went out into another business venture the reception we got was usually pretty good. We referred to this accumulation of goodwill as our 'Image', a word I discovered in an American book on business practice and which had not then gained the currency it enjoys today.

I must say, while Mango Cobett was a bit of a buffoon and a terrible snob, Singe 'n Burn, the head, had taken care to staff the school with liberal thinkers. He was less interested in turning out what he referred to as 'the private school product' than he was in encouraging individuals to emerge. He would refer to his idealised person as a Renaissance man. A boy who delighted in learning for its own sake, the inspired amateur in the gifts of the body and the spirit. The complete man, superior by virtue of his curiosity and the careful nurturing and harvesting of his gifts. A man who was modest and unassuming because he had no need to hide his thoughts or his deeds from others, nor had he the need to seek their approval.

Singe 'n Burn was an Englishman coming to the end of what is usually referred to as a distinguished career. To parents he represented all the values of the English Public School system, coming as he did from Winchester where he had been a senior housemaster. For the board of governors he epitomised a system of privilege which they held in great esteem and desired him to emulate as faithfully as possible.

In his twenty years as headmaster of the Prince of Wales School Singe 'n Burn never quite came to terms with the wealthy South African schoolboy. In a curious way the boys shared the belief in their social superiority with their English public school counterparts, though perhaps the basis for this superiority was different.

In the first instance, like all white South Africans, English and Afrikaans, they believed that God had ordained their superiority as white men. To this was added their proxy Englishness and their absolute belief in the right of wealth and privilege. Perhaps, after all, not so different from their English cousins.

Singe 'n Burn's pupils came to him with minds already narrowed, bigots with their dislike and distrust of the Afrikaner intact. Among them was the unspoken belief that they were the intellectually and culturally superior of South Africa's two white tribes. To this was added their spoken belief that they were of a higher species than the blacks. This corruption of the spirit had taken place in the cradle and the task of driving the racist out of the boy was fruitless. St John Burnham was forced to take in largely shallow minds to be fattened with sufficient information to pass the matriculation exams. Alas, the potential for a Renaissance man to emerge from this intellectual scrubland was severely limited.

Yet for twenty years Singe 'n Burn had kept his dream alive. While most of the boys from the Prince of Wales School were interchangeable with the product of any of the private schools in South Africa, that is, equipped for a society where money and social position were important, he kept for himself just six boys each year. They were the raw material for his Renaissance men, a handful of brilliant boys who were known as St

John's People, pronounced 'Sinjun's People'. These boys were selected in Form three for special tuition under the direction of Singe 'n Burn, who elected to neglect the many for the precious few. Sinjun's People were the roses amongst the tangle-weed and the school's considerable reputation as a nursery for the country's future leaders had been built on these half-dozen carefully nurtured young minds brought to flower in Sinjun's hot-house.

Brains alone did not qualify a boy to be one of Sinjun's People, though intellect played a significant part in the training to come. 'It is the spirit of the boy, an unselfconscious ability to maintain his status among his peers while remaining true to himself in his beliefs, opinions and actions,' is how Singe 'n Burn would explain it at the first headmaster's assembly at the beginning of each year.

There was always a great deal of speculation in Form three and, indeed, among the rest of the school when the election of Sinjun's People took place just prior to the Easter break.

I had prepared myself in my old way for a disappointment, and had I not been among the chosen six it would have hurt my pride enormously but I knew I would survive. The betting on me being included was pretty high. But I didn't share this general confidence, not for reasons of false modesty, but because of my boxing. While the boxing team had given the school a new status, compared to cricket and rugby it was a sport of small importance. Several of the masters considered it unsuitable for a school of our reputation, and but for Darby and Sarge it would probably have been phased out. I had maintained my position as one of the brains of the school but had never left any doubt that boxing came first in my immediate ambitions. I was certain this would count against me. In my final interview with Singe 'n Burn he had noted that my boxing appeared to come first, ahead of my competence as a musician and as a promising young scholar. 'Your boxing? Is this an obsession with you, Peekay? Where do you propose to take your skill? I must say it seems an unlikely future pastime for a gentleman, even though Lord Byron was said to have been a talented boxer.' When I replied that I intended to be the welterweight champion of the world his eyebrows had shot up and he had looked at me over his steel-rimmed spectacles. 'Hmm,' was all he said by way of reply.

Hymie was also among the fifteen candidates to be interviewed by the head. While he was regarded as a powerful intellect Hymie was generally thought to be too brash, and was therefore regarded by most of the schoolboy punters as being a long shot. When I queried him on his interview with Singe 'n Burn, he seemed reluctant to talk about it and so I didn't question him any further.

Sinjun's People were traditionally selected in order of merit, and this provided Hymie with a business opportunity that was to be one of our greatest successes. Apart from doing some of the legwork and sharing in the considerable profit, I played no part in its formation. We called it

'Levy's Remarkable Multiple of One Hundred'. As a punter you could bet two ways, by paying a shilling you could nominate any three successful candidates from the list of fifteen finalists, regardless of order. The winners, for there were certain to be more than one, to share a pot of thirty pounds. Or if you took two bets or more you qualified to enter Levy's Remarkable Multiple of One Hundred which carried a prize of one hundred pounds and required only two successes, the names of the boys in first and second place on the Sinjun's People list.

It was clever stuff; every boy believed he knew at least three certainties and so had an excellent chance to share in the thirty-pound pot. Most punters couldn't resist doubling their bets for a crack at the big money, one hundred pounds if there was only one winner and a guaranteed twenty quid if there were more. Many of the kids, in particular day boys, put ten shillings and a pound on in an effort to get as many combinations right as possible. Even in this haven for little rich boys, a hundred quid represented a fortune. There wasn't a kid in the school who didn't have at least two bets going.

We set up office in the main school bogs for an hour before school and at lunch break every day for a week before the final selection of Sinjun's People. The queue outside the toilet stretched well into the playground and anyone observing the toilets must have wondered whether an outbreak of the runs had struck the school.

Hymie took the money while I acted as pencil man, the guy who wrote down the bets. Tension was high on the last day before the following morning assembly when Sinjun's People were announced. The excitement had helped a little to quell my fears for us both. Hymie, by his own admission, considered himself a doubtful candidate. 'Shit, Peekay, it's obvious, I'm too much of a gunslinger and not enough of a poet to please Singe 'n Burn.' Privately I agreed; his wheeler-dealer reputation and my boxing preference counted heavily against us. In Hymie's case the betting showed this; not once did his name appear in the one/two combination whereas mine did so frequently.

We'd taken bets totalling a staggering one hundred and ninety pounds; win or lose we'd made a neat profit of sixty quid. We'd worked out the odds on someone taking out Levy's Remarkable Multiple of One Hundred and they were small but certainly not impossible, whereas we knew we'd have several winners in the thirty-pound pot. A perfect scam and good business to boot. A guaranteed profit, a number of satisfied winners and the chance to make a huge profit in the event of Levy's Remarkable Multiple of One Hundred not having to pay out. You had to hand it to Hymie, it was copybook stuff.

I could hear my heart beating furiously as I stood next to Hymie in headmaster's assembly the following morning. The hymn chosen before morning prayer was, 'O God Our Help in Ages Past', a favourite, although today it seemed to go on for about twenty minutes. The prayer which followed was a long-winded affair about humility in honour and fortitude in times of disappointment. It had obviously been carefully chosen by Singe 'n Burn for the occasion. Then followed a host of trivial school housekeeping notes, including an admonition to stay away from the swimming pool which was being emptied for repainting over the Easter break, and an aside about more boys signing up for their beginner's life-saving certificate.

At last Singe 'n Burn cleared his throat for the major business of the day. Standing on the platform in a black gown with purple lining, he had removed his mortarboard so that the light caught his snowy white hair. At a time when short back and sides was the national norm his hair fell almost to his shoulders and a pair of steel-rimmed spectacles sat on the end of his long, impressive nose. St John Burnham MA (Oxon) was the most headmasterly looking headmaster I have ever seen, better even than anything out of a Billy Bunter comic.

The entire school was deadly quiet. Apart from the fifteen candidates, there wasn't a boy present who didn't have money resting on the outcome of the next few minutes. Singe 'n Burn cleared his throat and began.

'Each year the school council allows me a very special personal indulgence. I am allowed to choose from the third form those half dozen boys who will become Sinjun's People.' He paused to look up into the stained glass windows at the rear of the hall, as though asking for divine guidance. 'Now, you will all know that I do not take this task lightly. It is, after all, as much a sadness as it is a celebration, for while six are to be chosen, nine who have made it to the finals will be asked to step aside. It is these nine good men and true who make my task an almost impossible one. After all, who is to say I'm right? I feel sure someone else, choosing in my place, might select six boys equally equipped and talented, though different to those I have chosen. All the candidates this year were exceptional young men, all deserve to be included, but alas, there are only six places. My congratulations to you all and a word of solace for those of you who do not become Sinjun's People.' He paused and directed our attention to the 1929 Scroll of Honour painted in gold leaf on a panel in the centre left-hand side of the hall. 'The name at the very top of that 1929 Scroll of Honour belongs to the present South African High Commissioner to London, a brilliant diplomat and scholar and the youngest man ever to hold this position. I shouldn't be at all surprised if some day he becomes our Prime Minister.' He paused again to gain maximum effect for the words to follow. 'This brilliant boy was not elected in his day to be among Sinjun's People.' His eyes seemed to travel across each row as he looked down at us over the tops of his spectacles. 'I had intended to read Rudyard Kipling's great poem "If" to you at this juncture but was reminded that it is a part of your English curriculum this term and therefore well known to you all. I shall spare you a repeat performance. Let me conclude by saying, in my experience the glittering prizes in life come more to those who persevere despite setback and disappointment than they do to the exceptionally gifted who, with the confidence of the talents bestowed upon them, often pursue the tasks leading to success with less determination.' He paused and from inside his gown he produced a sheet of paper.

'The following boys from the third form have been chosen to be Sinjun's People for the remainder of their tenure at the Prince of Wales School. My congratulations to you all.' He glanced down at the piece of paper he was holding and commenced to read: 'Levy H. S., Lyell H. R., Quigley B. J., Minnaar J. R. . . .' I had punched Hymie in the ribs when his name came up, but now I could feel my face burning and a huge lump grew in my throat. I was sure I would suffocate. . . 'Eliastam P. J.,' the head paused to clear his throat and then looked up over the assembled boys. Time hung like cobwebs in the air and the paper he'd been holding seemed etched like a white tombstone floating in space.

'And Peekay,' he said finally.

I felt weak in the legs and it took all my strength of will not to start crying on the spot. I had made it. I was the sixth part of Sinjun's People.

Atherton, Cunning-Spider, Pissy Johnson, Hymie and I celebrated by feasting on Perk's pies, cream buns and Pepsi-Cola all that afternoon before Atherton, Cunning-Spider and Pissy Johnson had to leave for the four o'clock roll call. Sinjun's People were not required to attend roll call and as they left playfully cursing us we looked suitably upset, though secretly we felt enormously privileged.

Nine punters had won on the first bet sharing the thirty-pound pot between them. There were no winners on the second bet. Hymie himself had been the wild card, and while some of the punters might have selected him for inclusion in their first bet, none had thought to place him first or second in Levy's Remarkable Multiple of One Hundred. The fact that my name had appeared most often in either the first or second slot meant that most of the bets were not even close. We had cleared one hundred and sixty pounds on the deal.

After the others had left for roll call I turned to Hymie. 'Okay, smartarse, how did you do it?' I said, delicately licking the excess cream squirting from the side of my last cream bun.

'How did I do what?' Hymie said dreamily, upending a Pepsi into his mouth in an attempt to hide his grin.

'You know what I'm talking about! You knew from the betting that your chances of being selected in the number one spot were considered zero. Even I wouldn't have put you there. With you in the number one spot we had to win the big money. How did you do it?'

He removed the Pepsi from his mouth and placed it on the floor beside him. 'It was partly luck, but mostly my usual good judgement,' he said in his unassuming way.

'Christ you're a humble bastard, Levy! Okay, tell me the good judgement part first.'

'Well I guess we should have been happy with a sixty quid profit, with a reasonable chance of winning the big money as well. But there was still an element of luck involved. I had somehow to work out a way whereby the betting was completely honest, but the punter's chance of winning was cut down and ours increased.'

'You greedy bugger, Levy.'

'No, not greedy, I just don't like to gamble, but I do like to win and to win you have to make the odds negligible. Now, you take the horses. There are roughly fifteen horses in a race and over the whole of last year I analysed the results of every race run at Turfontein racecourse. In that entire time the first and second favourites won in correct sequence one hundred and four times in eight hundred and thirty-two races, that means the bookmaker has eight chances of winning to one of losing. That's good, but not good enough.'

'Yeah, sure, but we had sixty quid marked off for a profit anyway. That's a damn good week's work.'

'I know, but the whole thing lacked intellectual excitement. It didn't depend on my wits.'

'Hymie, you can't have it both ways. You want a totally safe scam but you still want to get an intellectual kick from winning.'

'That's what I've told you before. With a Jew making money for its own sake, it is a matter of intellectual survival.'

'Okay, I accept that; so tell me, man, how did you fix it?'

'Fix it!' Hymie exploded. 'Are you calling me a cheat?'

His outburst was totally unexpected and I was shocked. 'Ferchrissake, Hymie, you know what I mean,' I said quickly, trying to hide my embarrassment.

Hymie sighed, 'In the end it's always the same, the Gentile believes the dirty Jew is cheating, that's right isn't it?'

'Bullshit, Hymie! That's not what I meant, I'm truly sorry. You know how I feel about you.'

Hymie held my gaze for a long time. 'Yeah, I do,' he said with a grin, 'but thanks for saying it anyway.'

'Well go on,' I said, greatly relieved and anxious to leave the incident and continue the conversation.

Hymie continued. 'It does rather seem like a fix, doesn't it? But all I did was tamper a little with human nature.'

'You'll have to explain that.'

'Well, when you told me about your interview with Singe 'n Burn. . . how he had questioned you about your boxing.'

'I don't understand. What had that to do with setting up the Multiple of One Hundred bet?'

'Well, you know my theory of a winner. Find one winner and you can build everything around him? Well, you've always been my one winner and with the strong likelihood of your placing in the number one slot for Sinjun's People, Levy's Remarkable Multiple of One Hundred would have been much too risky. It meant the punter had only to get one more correct name to win.'

'But I told you the boxing issue might have eliminated me all together.'

'Not a chance, old buddy! There was never any chance that you wouldn't be chosen, but I was willing to bet that Singe 'n Burn wouldn't be able to resist the temptation to give you your first tutorial.'

'My first tutorial?'

'Christ, Peekay, sometimes you're thick. Singe 'n Burn is a self-confessed liberal thinker, deeply suspicious of the obsessive personality. That's the whole point of his Renaissance man, moderation in all things even in moderation. He was signalling his disapproval by placing you in sixth possie.'

'Jesus, Hymie, you took the trouble to think all that out?'

'Thinking is never any trouble, you should try it sometime.' He grinned suddenly, 'Besides, I might have been wrong, Singe 'n Burn might have just dropped you one slot and you'd still be up there in one of the top two positions. I had to put us completely out of danger. I had to get myself chosen, not just chosen, but elected to the number one slot. You see, even if you were in the number two position and as a rank outsider, a non-contender, and I was in the number one slot, that would make it impossible for anyone to get a correct sequence. Nobody in his right mind would combine a hundred to one shot in with a certainty when both places counted together for the win.'

'You've got me. How the hell did you make it happen?'

'Well, I'd figured out how Singe 'n Burn was going to react with you and when you know the man you know the thought process. The opposite to an obsessive personality, in this case yours about boxing, is a well-adjusted one. The epitome of a well-adjusted personality is modesty and a willingness to sacrifice your own ambition for the greater good of the whole. What was it that Christ said? "No greater love hath a man than he lay down his life for a friend".' Hymie gave a little laugh, 'So when Singe 'n Burn discovered personal sacrifice together with generosity of spirit to be a fundamental part of my character, I knew I had the number one possie in the bag.'

'And just how did you prove this to him? I mean, those two personality traits are not exactly obvious in you,' I added with a tinge of sarcasm.

Hymie turned to me, an embarrassed look on his face. 'I don't think you're going to like this next bit much. We were talking about the importance of friendship and I brought up my friendship with you. Singe 'n Burn then asked me about your obsession with boxing.' He paused, 'Are you sure you want me to go on?'

'I think I know where this is leading, but I can't stop it now, go on.'

'Well, I told him about your childhood, your last boarding school, the prison, although I promise I didn't tell him about the Tadpole Angel, just Geel Piet and the boxing, just some of the stuff you told me.'

'Jesus, Hymie, that was confidential.'

'Yeah, I know, I mean I knew it was, but you'd never actually told me not to tell anyone.' Hymie paused, 'Christ, Peekay, you've got nothing to be ashamed of.'

'I've never been ashamed of anything in my life, except when I was made to feel that way the first time I went to boarding school. It's . . . well, it's just that I don't want any Christian gentleman feeling sorry for me because my mum hasn't two bob to her name.'

Hymie jumped to his feet and grabbed me by my blazer lapels. 'You bloody fool! They'd do anything to be like you. So would I. To have done the things you've done, led the life you've led. Believe me, being rich in a Jewish household isn't a lot of fun. Everything is overdone. Too much love, too much money, too much food, too much care, too much reminding you that you're different, that you're Jewish. I've been bored since I was five years old! Bored by the predictability of being born into a wealthy middle-class Jewish home. You can have my twelve bedrooms and six bathrooms. I'll swap you my old man's five cars and three chauffeurs for a fortnight with Doc.'

I suddenly realised that I was making far more of a meal over his indiscretion with my past than he had made when he thought I had accused him of cheating.

'Okay, we're quits, you smooth-talking bastard,' I said, grinning. 'Now, get on with the story. How, for instance, did telling him all this, talk him into giving you the number one spot?'

'I simply told him that I was a Jew, which I suppose he knew already but it didn't hurt to remind him. That my father was enormously rich. That I had enjoyed and would continue to enjoy every possible privilege. That I would be sent to Oxford where I would read law and well blah, blah, blah. The future for me was all sewn up.'

'So?'

'This is the worst part. I told him that if I was selected to Sinjun's People and you were not, that I wished to forfeit my spot in your favour.' He looked at me querulously, waiting for my anger.

I was silent. I knew with a sudden certainty that Hymie, after hearing the results of my interview with Singe 'n Burn, had grown concerned that my boxing obsession would eliminate me from Sinjun's People. That he'd ridden to the rescue, prepared to sacrifice any chances he might have had to ensure my inclusion. In the process he had read Singe 'n Burn brilliantly and had capitalised handsomely on the situation.

'You'd have done that anyway, wouldn't you? You'd have been prepared to give up your chances even if the scam hadn't been there.'

'Hell no! No bloody fear!' he said in alarm. 'Christ, Peekay, it's a dog-eat-dog world; where would the Jews be if all of a sudden they started making sacrifices for the bloody Christians!'

'Thanks, Hymie,' I said.

'Don't insult my intelligence, Peekay. If you're trying to tell me I wasn't doing all this for mercenary motives I resent it. Don't you think I'm capable of thinking up a ploy as good as this one turned out to be?'

'On the contrary, you had it figured out so that whatever happened you influenced the game.'

Hymie blushed, which I'd never seen him do before. 'No point in leaving things to chance; much too risky,' he said with a deprecating grin.

'Christ, the number one spot always belonged to you anyway.'

'You're right,' he said. 'Look, why don't we take a tenner each for the holidays?' He handed me a ten-pound note. 'I'll put the rest in the bank. I've got big plans for next term we'll talk about after the holidays.'

NINETEEN

Going home at the end of each term was like sloughing a skin. The joy of a small town lies in its unchanging nature. Except for Doc, Mrs Boxall, Miss Bornstein, old Mr Bornstein, the guys at the prison and of course, my mother, Granpa, Marie and especially Dum and Dee, people would look up when you entered a shop and enquire casually, 'Goodness, hols again, Peekay? How's life in the big city? Are you playing in the Easter concert? What can I do for you?' They'd say this almost in one breath, not because they were bored and felt compelled to be polite, but mostly because time has a sameness in a small town, which the coming and going of people doesn't disturb. I liked the idea of nothing ever changing in Barberton, it gave me a sense of belonging. Now that the war was over and the military camp no longer a part of the town's economy, Barberton settled back into its favourite old scuffed leather armchair and went to sleep again. Even the prison warders seemed to fit into the community more easily and for the last two concerts they had remained while 'God save the King' was played, though Mrs Boxall reported that they still protested in their own way by not standing to attention. This made Mr Hankin, of the *Goldfields News* mad as usual, but it rated a paragraph, not a leader or the entire editorial like the good old days.

Mrs Boxall had become a firm favourite at the prison. The Kommandant, who had become a colonel because of Doc's concert, decided he liked prison reform and had allowed her to start a Sunday morning school for the prisoners. She had negotiated with the Kommandant to reward progress with King Georgies. The Pentecostal missionaries, who had agreed to do the teaching in return for a fifteen-minute sermon every Sunday, disagreed violently with the distribution of tobacco to students who excelled. Their God was neither a consumer of strong drink nor a user of tobacco. They were forced to conclude that God worked in mysterious ways when attendance and scholastic effort increased markedly with the introduction of King Georgies as an incentive. A prisoner would study for every limited moment he had during the week for the reward of one cigarette. With the result that many blacks left prison able to read, write and do simple arithmetic. Mr Bornstein, Miss Bornstein's father, had converted the Earl of Sandwich Fund into the Sandwich Foundation and already one little old lady had left it a bequest of two thousand pounds. The letter-writing sessions still continued, and during the holidays I'd take over from the missionaries and Marie's father's tobacco leaf would once again be fitted into the folds of the tracts and given out with every letter. In fact during every school holiday letters to King George, which of course we never posted, became very popular again. The Tadpole Angel was back in town and Gert used to swear that trouble in the prison was almost non-existent during these periods.

Gert, with encouragement from Mrs Boxall, had tackled English and now spoke it fairly well. He'd become very attached to Doc and Mrs Boxall and made sure that the repairs around Doc's cottage or Mrs Boxall's house were done and that Charlie's motor was kept going. Every time I'd get home it would be the same thing, 'I'm telling you, man, only chewing gum and axle grease is holding that old *tjorrie* together; one day I'm just going to have to take it to a cliff top, say a prayer and push it over. Only it won't be able to make it up the hill in the first place!' But under Gert's concerned and tender care Charlie kept going.

Klipkop had been transferred to Pretoria and Gert, to his enormous surprise, had been given the job of assistant to Captain Smit. As a consequence he had earned his corporal's stripes. He was now the prison heavyweight and would be fighting for the vacant title at the next championships. The giant Potgieter, who had continued to beat Gert in the final of the two subsequent championships after Gert's original defeat in Nelspruit, had turned professional.

The Lowveld Championships had been expanded and were now known as the Eastern Transvaal Championships, bringing in some of the bigger towns and making it tougher for the Barberton Blues. As they always occurred during the December school holidays, it was important to Captain Smit that I take part as a member of the Blues.

Regular boxing against the Afrikaans schools during term had made me a much better boxer, although I personally longed for the magic of Geel Piet, who knew how to make me think better in the ring. Whereas Darby White and Sarge, like Captain Smit, were honest carpenters, Geel Piet had been an artist and I missed his uncanny understanding of how to exploit my personality in the ring.

I felt I wasn't growing as a boxer. Yehudi Menuhin once said that playing the violin is like singing through your limbs; Geel Piet had had the ability to make boxing seem the same, each punch the result of perfect timing, continuity, controlled emotion and intelligence. If I was to become the welterweight champion of the world, I knew I'd soon have to find a coach who thought beyond schoolboy boxing.

The holidays were packed. I'd be at the prison at five-thirty a.m. for boxing, and Captain Smit would make me go three rounds with two of the other kids. Mostly with Snotnose and Jaapie, both heavier than me but really the only two boxers who could box well enough to push me. Both would itch to have a go, both were fighters in the Smit tradition, and both were very tough. It called for all my ringcraft to stay out of trouble. Halfway through the second round, Captain Smit would blow his whistle and one of them would step down and the other come in. This meant each of them only boxed one and a half rounds and so they'd go flat out, prepared to take a few punches to get a good one in. Captain Smit was convinced that it was the only way to increase my speed and keep me sharp.

After an hour and a half in the prison gym I'd head for Doc's cottage, where either Dee or Dum, who took it turn about, would have delivered breakfast. By the time I arrived at eight, the coffee would be made and a loaf of fresh bread would be on the table, together with eggs and bacon, plopping away on the back of the stove waiting for me to arrive. Doc was, after all, still a German and he expected me to be exactly on egg-and-bacon time. The girls loved the holidays and they'd spoil me rotten, with baking and fussing and generally cooking up a storm. Doc always claimed he put on several pounds when I was around.

Doc and I would sit outside on his stoep for breakfast and we'd plan the weekend hike. This usually meant repeating an old trail. Doc would bring out his notepad and we'd discuss the last time we'd done the planned walk, which might have been five years before. We'd discuss every specimen we'd found then and sometimes even leave the table to check the progress of some long forgotten succulent we had collected. Doc was still tied to the Steinway and his little girl students during the week, so our long walks had to take place over the weekend. Though I'm sure, after a while, he'd have had it no other way; the planning and the discussion over his notes became just as important to him as the excursions themselves. At nine he'd give me a piano lesson, shaking his head at the bad habits I'd acquired under the direction of Mr Mollip, the Prince of Wales School music master. 'This Mr Muddleup, you are sure he teaches pianoforte?' he would say, shaking his head. 'I think maybe the banjo yes?' He would spend the rest of the holidays getting me back into some sort of musical shape.

The first time I played St Louis blues for Doc I had expected to shock him out of his pants. In fact it was meant as a joke. Instead he nodded quietly. 'Ja, that is goot.' I turned to look at him in surprise. 'But to play black, the music must come from your soul not out from your head, Peekay.' He indicated that I should rise from the piano stool, and seated in my place he played the piece in the same haunting way as Hymie's seventy-eight of Errol Garner.

'Bloody hell, Doc, where'd you learn to do that!' It was the first time I'd sworn in Doc's presence but he seemed not to notice. 'Okey-dokey, Mr Schmarty-Pantz, who is a person called W. C. Handy?'

'He sounds like a lavatory brush,' I said flippantly.

'Mr W. C. Handy wrote this music, and now you want to play it without heart and even without knowing who is the composer! Would you do this to Beethoven or Bach? No, I think not. But now Mr Schmarty-Pantz thinks to play the black man's music is easy.'

'Sorry, Doc, it was only a joke. I only wanted to shock you.'

'Then to shock me you must play me bad music, not play me good music badly,' he said softly.

I was the one who had been shocked and Doc had in the process taught me once again to do my research and my thinking before I did my judging. 'Where'd you learn to play like that, Doc?'

Doc laughed. 'So long ago, ja, when I wrote my first book on cactus in North America, I was in New Orleans. I had no money so I played fifteen minutes classical every night in a fancy cathouse, the Golden Slipper. Ja, this is the name of that place. After I play comes every night a jazz band and soon we talk and so on and so forth, and they think the German professor is very funny, but not my music. The rich people who come to this cathouse, they don't understand Mr Beethoven and Chopin and Brahms. But the black men, they understood. I teach them a little of this and a little of that, and they teach me a little of that and a little of this'; he touched the keys and played a couple of bars of blues music. 'It was here I meet Mr W. C. Handy and later also Mr Willie Smith?'

'You met Willie Smith!' I yelled at him. '*The* Willie Smith?'

'Ja, I think there is only one.'

'Doc, please, please teach me how to play jazz piano.'

Doc laughed, and affecting his version of an American accent replied, 'Not on your sweet-tootin' nelly, Peekay.'

'Please, Doc!'

He shook his head. 'I cannot teach you what I cannot feel. Peekay, you must understand this. It is not possible for a man to touch the heart of the negro man's music when he cannot feel it through his fingers.'

Doc had just explained to me why I would never amount to much musically. What Geel Piet knew I had as a boxer, Doc knew I lacked as a musician.

I would leave Doc at eleven o'clock and by a quarter past I had arrived at Miss Bornstein's house. Mr Bornstein who, as I mentioned before, was a lawyer in partnership with Mr Andrews, had a big white double-storey house designed in the Cape Dutch style. A huge bougainvillaea creeper cascaded purple blooms over one side of the house, its mass of purple blossom stark and beautiful against the wall so gleaming white that it hurt to look at it in the near noon sun. The next impression the eye met was of the sweeping lawns which smelt of cut grass and never seemed to lose their wet green look even in the late summer when every other lawn seemed strawed and faded from the heat. There were other things in the garden, trees and tropical shrubs and a bed of deep red canna. And of course all the usual junk like roses and things. But all I seem to remember is the dramatic splash of the deep purple bougainvillea against the blinding white of the house, the green, perfectly manicured lawns and the chit-chit-chit of the hose spitting stingy jets of water somewhere in the garden.

I'd spend the first half-hour or less, depending only on whether I could hold out that long, playing a game of chess with old Mr Bornstein. He would always checkmate me with the same words: 'Not so shameful. Tomorrow maybe, if God spares us, you will win.' God spared us but I never won.

A houseboy in a white starched coat would then bring me a glass of milk and two chocolate biscuits, my favourite. Then the lesson would begin. We'd work until two o'clock when the same boy brought in a jug of orange juice and a plate of polony and tomato sandwiches, also my favourite.

Miss Bornstein was determined that I should win a Rhodes scholarship and go to Oxford, and the work we did was far in excess of anything I needed to know to pass my matriculation. With her pushing me, particularly in Latin and Greek, by weekly letter and during the school holidays and with the tuition reserved for Sinjun's People, I was probably getting as fine an education as it was possible for anyone of my age to absorb.

After orange juice and sandwiches I was free. Some days I'd spend the afternoon with Mrs Boxall or help Granpa in the garden or play a little snooker down at the Impala Hotel with John Hopkins and Geoffrey Scruby and some of the other guys all of whom, like me, were going to boarding school. They'd drink a couple of beers and smoke a little, and we'd all generally act a bit tough with each other, though I was always in training and neither smoked nor drank.

I was beginning to understand how intellect separates men. For common ground we would talk rugby and cricket and girls. Daily we destroyed the reputations of the girls who'd been in class with us in primary school and who were now supposedly screwing like rattlesnakes. We never quite worked out with whom; it was always supposed to be someone older than ourselves, like Paul Everingham and Bob Goodhead who were in Form six at Jeppe High and who both had their school colours for rugby and cricket.

Puberty had taken a fierce and urgent grip on all of us so that the fantasy of fucking was never more than an unuttered sentence away. But my mind, when it wasn't on sex, was different. I guess it had always been, but now the dichotomy was beginning to show. I didn't feel superior, there was nothing to be superior about; my mind simply seemed to gaze over different intellectual landscapes. I dare say had I not been a boxer and rugby player and greatly respected for the former, the rest of the chaps in Barberton would have dismissed me as a brain and a bit of a loner.

I found Doc, Mrs Boxall, Miss Bornstein and old Mr Bornstein a source of stimulation, but the adult mind had lost much of its craziness, its zany quality, and I missed the verbal jousting that Hymie supplied in our day-to-day relationship at school. In fact, when I got back to school after the holidays, it would take me a couple of days to get my verbal riposte sharp and my timing right again.

'Christ, Peekay, your brain's addled by too much deep and meaningful discussion about the weather and the crops and whether the locusts will come again this year!' Hymie would tease. Atherton, Pissy and Cunning-

Spider also shared an intelligence which would readily mix into a really good verbal over an abstract point simply for the love of argument itself.

Hymie would contend that anything, no matter how banal, could be raised to the level of intelligent debate if the minds which attended to it were good enough. He told the story of the little cobbler in a shtetl in Russia who was spreading honey on a piece of bread when the bread fell to the floor. To his amazement the bread fell right side up. 'How can this be?' he said, and with the slice of bread in his hand he ran to consult the rabbi and the village elders. 'We are Jews in Russia; how can it be that I spread honey on my bread and when it fell to the floor it landed right side up? Since when did luck such as this come to a Jew?' The rabbi and the elders pondered the point for several days, consulting the Torah frequently. Finally they called the little cobbler to the synagogue. The rabbi pronounced the verdict, 'The answer my boy is quite clear, you honeyed your bread on the wrong side.'

We had all cawed and moaned at the story but Hymie, as usual, had made his point; good conversational debate was an end in itself and talking for the love of conversation is what makes us human.

That Easter holiday Doc and I had planned an overnight hike to a waterfall we knew about some twelve miles past Saddleback Pass. As waterfalls go it wasn't a major one but it tumbled down through an area of rainforest which, in our only previous visit, we'd come across too late to explore properly. The cliffs rising above the forest looked interesting and Doc was sure we'd find succulents and several species of dwarf aloe in the rocky crags and ledges. I had been concerned when Doc had suggested the hike; it was a good twenty miles across the mountains and Doc was over eighty. Just how far over no one knew and, while he was as lean as a twist of liquorice and tough as a mountain goat, it was a hard day's march by any standards, and in the notes he had made on our previous trip nearly eight years earlier, he'd noted that the hike had been an exhausting one.

He had answered my protests with typical Doc logic. 'Peekay, if not now it will be never again. Our work here is unfinished, the topography; see I have made a drawing here in my notes, suggests limestone in the cliffs. If this is true it is rare, almost impossible, some geological freak happening maybe?'

Doc knew he'd stirred my need for adventure, and the prospect of finding something that shouldn't be there allowed me to brush my concern aside and agree that we should undertake the trip.

Doc had managed to postpone his little girls for Friday and we set out at dawn with our blanket rolls, billy cans and enough food for two days, as well as a hurricane lamp, Doc's eight-battery Eveready torch, rope, a small hammer and a dozen homemade metal spikes hooked at the ends to secure the rope if necessary. Gert had made these for Doc in the prison metal shop soon after he'd left prison and they'd been invaluable for scrambling up rock faces now that Doc wasn't as young a mountain goat as he pretended to be.

By the time the sun rose over the escarpment and filled the de Kaap Valley, we had climbed the foothills and were into the mountains proper. The aloe and thorn scrub were replaced by scree and tussock grass, turning to rocky crags where the wind can be cold even on a hot day. We often saw an eagle high above us seemingly drifting without purpose, carried by the currents of air. With a stop for lunch of cheese and cream crackers, washed down by a billy of sweet black tea, we crossed Saddleback Pass in the early afternoon and started the climb down the other side. By late afternoon we'd reached the peculiar formation of mountain cliffs rising above the deep kloof of rainforest Doc had noted in his diary.

We made camp beside a mountain brook flowing from the waterfall which dropped like a bridal veil down the far edge of the cliffs above us. I had chosen our campsite on the edge of the rainforest where an overhanging rock protected us from the wind. It can get bitterly cold during the night in the mountains and we set about collecting firewood before we lost the light. High above us we first heard and then saw a troop of baboons climbing the strange cliff face and running along the white ledges eroded into the face of the rock. Their urgent barking echoed down into the kloof where we'd made our camp.

Doc put his field glasses onto the cliff. 'It's too much shadow now, but I think tomorrow we find up there for sure something.'

Darkness comes quickly in the mountains and less than an hour after we'd arrived the sun had set, throwing the deep kloof into shadow. Even though there was still some light I got the fire for supper going, the dry branches crackling and popping with plenty of smoke to ward off the mosquitoes which always seem to come from nowhere moments after sunset. I set about making our supper while Doc washed at the stream. Chopping an onion and two tomatoes into a billy can, I then upended a can of bully beef into the billy, mashing it all together with my hunting knife, ready for when the fire would glow down so that it would cook slowly. I'd already trapped two large sweet potatoes under the unmade fire so that we'd be able to pluck them out of the cooking embers later for dessert. The rainforest grew dark first, the clear outlines of the giant tree ferns smudged and then blackened into darkness while high up in a yellow wood tree a couple of green loeries called out one last time before they called it a day. Next the valley on the edge of the forest where we'd camped dimmed down for the night, closing out the light, blurring rock and bush and tree. Finally the sky on the high ridge above us pulled a dark sheet over us and pinned it with stars. The distant sound of falling water from the falls seemed to emphasise the silence. Doc spoke quietly in the night. 'No one has written a great symphony or even a concerto about Africa. Why is this so?'

He hadn't expected an answer and I waited for him to continue.

'The music of Africa is too wild, too free, too accustomed to death for romance. Africa is too crude a stage for the small scratching of the violin, too majestic for the piano. Africa is only right for drums. The drum carries its rhythm but does not steal its music. Timpani is the background, the music of Africa is in the voices of the people. They are its instruments, more subtle, more beautiful, infinitely more noble than the scratching, thumping, banging and blowing of brass and wind and vellum, strings and keyboard.'

'What about Requiem for Geel Piet?' I asked.

Doc chuckled. 'For twenty years I have tried to compose ten or even five minutes of music, good music for the great Southland. And then, after twenty years of failure, I find it in the chain gangs, in the rhythm of a pick and the sweat of black backs, and the vicious crack of the sjambok and the almost noiseless thud of the donkey prick. The voice music is not the keening of despair but the expression of a certainty that Africa will live and the spirit will survive brutality. The music of Africa is in the soul and its instruments are in the voices of its people. Such a domkop, Peekay. All the time it is waiting absoloodle under my long German nose. Requiem for Geel Piet is not my music, it is the music of the people. The necklace is only mine because I strung the beads.'

I handed Doc a steaming plate of bully beef. Then, using a short stick, I rolled the two sweet potatoes from the embers to cool a little for later. We ate in silence. Doc never took food for granted and would chew for ages before swallowing. I added a couple of logs to build the fire up again and then walked down to the stream to wash the plates and fill the billy.

After I'd made coffee and poured a tablespoon of condensed milk into the tin mug just the way Doc liked it, I placed the steaming cup next to him and sliced open his sweet potato. Steam rose from its fat, succulent belly and to this too I added condensed milk as a special treat. The mosquitoes, kept at bay by the early smoke from the fire, were out in force again. I rubbed Citronella oil over my arms and legs and handed the bottle to Doc. The oil smelt pretty bad, but it was a damn sight better than being bitten half to death. We'd been going since four-fifteen in the morning and were exhausted. Too tired to wash the mugs, I wrapped myself in my blanket. Checking first to see that Doc lay well clear of the fire, I curled up under the overhang of the rock so that my blanket wouldn't be wet with dew in the morning, and went to sleep.

I awoke at dawn, and keeping my blanket wrapped around me I built the fire up again. The valley was shrouded in mist and the rainforest which began not twenty yards from our camp site was invisible. Minutes after the sun hit the valley the mist would vanish, but until it did the cold would remain. My hands were freezing as I filled the billy from the stream for coffee. Doc was snoring again, tightly wrapped in his blanket, and I let him sleep on until I'd made his coffee and blown a generous tablespoon's worth of condensed milk into it. I did the same for myself and the steaming mug soon warmed my hands. I didn't wake Doc; I knew the smell of the fresh-brewed coffee would do that for me. Doc loved coffee more than I think he loved his cactus garden and almost as much as Beethoven and J. S. Bach. Pretty soon his nostrils began to twitch, and grunting to himself he sat up in the blanket and knuckled his eyes open. High up through the mist we could hear the barking of the baboons; the sun must have reached them and they were moving on.

Doc gripped the mug I gave him in both hands, then looking up in the direction of the cliffs invisible above him in the mist he said, 'Today will be different, Peekay.' The barking of the baboons echoed down the misty valley. 'Ja, for sure and absoloodle, today we find something.' Taking a careful sip of coffee, 'I hope you sleep good, Peekay?' he asked.

I cooked two sausages and a couple of rashers of bacon, and then split the sausages down the centre and laid them on two slices of bread, topped them with bacon and sandwiched them with two more thick slices of bread. I handed one of the crude sandwiches to Doc and ate the other myself, holding it to my mouth with both hands.

While we were having a second cup of coffee the sun was beginning to dazzle its way through the mist and seemingly in minutes the valley was filled with sunshine. A few patches of mist hung near the floor of the rainforest, but they too were soon gone. Above us the strange-looking cliffs looked less foreboding in the bright morning light and I scanned them to see how we might set about the climb.

In a mist-shrouded landscape, sounds are always exaggerated. Now, with the mist gone, the morning settled down into all its reassuring components, the chatter of birds, running water, the urgent whirr of a grasshopper and in fact the generally busy noises of the mountain day coming fully to life. I walked over to a small clump of bushes and was in the half squat position with my pants around my ankles when two plump bush partridges whirred from the underbrush directly beside me. I rose, my pants still around my ankles, and squinting down the barrel of an imaginary shotgun, I let them have it, first with the left and then pulling carefully around to get the second bird with the right barrel. I then watched, laughing, as they disappeared like a couple of hurricane fighters over a small ridge beyond me.

After washing I cleaned up camp and stowed our stuff under the overhanging rock, sprinkling our blanket rolls with Citronella oil. If anything approached, particularly a scorpion looking for a nice warm place to nestle, the unfamiliar smell of the oil would drive it away.

Doc slung the rope around his neck and hung his eight-battery Eveready torch from his belt. I took a small climber's rucksack with water bottle, trowel for digging footholds, hammer, metal spikes, paraffin lamp and Doc's field glasses. The climb didn't look too bad, buttresses of rock led to long ridges eroded into the face of the rock, as though the cliff face itself were made from a composition of hard and soft rock. It was these seemingly soft, white striations of rock which had first caught Doc's interest and which he was pretty sure would be dolomite or some sort of limestone. The torch and the paraffin lamp were a giveaway. Doc, always a romantic, was hoping we'd find a cave in the cliff face, a prospect which naturally appealed to me enormously.

We climbed for an hour, the going not too hard. Doc, despite his age, was a skilled mountaineer who took no chances and whereas I might have made it to the first ridge of eroded rock perhaps a hundred foot from the ground in half the time it took us, our progress was sure and the way back carefully mapped out in our minds. Getting down a steep face can often be more difficult than getting up it. The first ridge of eroded rock proved Doc's theory to be right, the material was dolomite which had been worn away by tens of thousands of years of wind and rain to make deep ledges with overhangs cut into the cliff face. We followed the ledge until we found a way back onto the cliff face, and continued to climb. It took us another hour to get another hundred feet up the cliff to yet another ledge. This one, more exposed to the wind, had been cut deeper into the rock and we could smell where the baboons had settled for the night. Another fifty feet up the face and we came to a third ridge, deeper yet again. Walking along this ridge we found it gouged deeper and deeper into the cliff face until it came to a sudden end. We'd reached a blind alley; there seemed to be no way of getting back onto the face so that we could climb higher.

By now we'd been going almost three hours and the sun, beating onto the face of the cliff, was hot. Doc's khaki shirt was wet with perspiration and I suggested we sit down for a drink and a rest. The ridge we were sitting on was, I judged, about a hundred feet from the top of the cliff but it appeared impossible to go any further. Down below us we could see the canopy of the rainforest, with one old yellow-wood tree, its branches stretching clear to the sky fifty feet above the canopy of the forest and no more than a hundred feet below where we were sitting. Doc said it could well be a thousand years old. The cliff face was shaped in a wide arc and on our right, about a hundred feet below us, the waterfall gushed from the rock face, more a fine, misty spray than a gush really, but sufficient to feed the stream we'd camped beside.

Doc took his notebook from the rucksack and turned to a crude sketch he'd made of the cliff from the ground level the previous afternoon. 'Ja, we are sitting now in the deepest ledge, above is harder rock and not so deep striations.' He sighed, clearly puzzled. Doc didn't like to be wrong about his observations which he would only have permitted himself to voice after a great deal of careful consideration. 'Well Peekay, we found dolomite and also there is water, but no cave. This is very strange. You can see the waterfall comes straight from the cliff, the stream must run deep inside the face of the cliff. There should be caves. Ja, this is so, absoloodle.'

I walked back to the wall at the end of the ledge and peeked over the edge, hoping to find a small ledge which would take us further across the face. About three feet below me a small ridge of rock, no more than six inches wide, ran for two or three yards and then took a slight turn so I was unable to see whether it continued. I swung my body over the edge of the ledge, dangling my feet until they reached the narrow ridge of rock. With my stomach against the cliff I edged my way along it. I'd hardly moved more than three feet when I found myself looking directly into a hole in the cliff, about two feet wide and three feet high. I was able to look some ten feet down the tunnel before it turned to darkness. It was quite clearly an entrance to a cave, and not simply a tunnel worn into the rock. A fire bush grew from a crack in the rock to the right of the opening to conceal it from being seen from below. Suddenly a bat flew out of the tunnel, blurred past me, and I heard the unmistakable squeak of bats deep in the rock face. I was certain I had found a cave.

'I've found it! We've found our cave!' I yelled. My voice, hugely magnified, echoed down the valley. It would take very little effort to lift myself up into the hole, but holes have a habit of containing surprises infinitely worse than a few hundred harmless bats. So I edged back to where Doc was waiting. Helping me back up onto the ledge, Doc too was excited. 'So, I am right, Peekay,' he said triumphantly. I explained that if we could secure a rope handrail it would be possible for him to follow me into the cave.

We discussed a way of doing this for some time. Then, hammering a couple of spikes into the floor of the ledge, we secured one end of the rope through the eyes of the spikes, both of us pulling on the rope to make sure the spikes were firmly bedded into the rock. Next we tied the rope to my waist and I tucked three spikes, the hammer and Doc's torch into the back of my belt where I could reach back and get them comfortably. Doc paid out the rope as I slid backwards, down onto the thin lip of rock below the ledge. Had I fallen it was unlikely Doc would have been able to haul me back again but I was very sure on my feet and unconcerned by heights. In less than thirty seconds I was in front of the cave entrance. I lifted myself through the hole with comparative ease and commenced to crawl along the narrow tunnel which continued in a slightly upward direction for about twenty feet then widened out. I untied the rope from around my waist and removed the long silver torch from my belt. The daylight had disappeared by the time I'd crawled to the end of the tunnel so I switched on the powerful Eveready to find that the tunnel led into a cave which appeared to be about fifteen feet long and equally wide, while being high enough for me to stand upright.

The cave smelt powerfully of baboons and bats. As I played the torch around the walls I could see hundreds of bats hanging from the roof and the walls. I returned down the narrow passage to the cliff face, and sticking my head out yelled at Doc that I'd found a big cave. My voice echoed down the valley as the barking of the baboons had done the previous evening and again that morning.

'It's not too hard, Doc. I'll hammer a couple of spikes into the tunnel wall and tie the rope and you can use it as a handrail to come across.' I set about this task, drawing the rope tight so that it made a firm handrail from the ledge into the mouth of the tunnel. Doc was a fearless old coot and dropping himself backwards onto the rock ridge and holding the rope he quickly edged across the cliff face to the mouth of the tunnel. I pulled him in and now he was lying on his belly looking into the dark tunnel.

'Wunderbar, Peekay, a cave. How big? A big one, yes?' he panted.

'You'll have to crawl, it's slightly upwards. Follow the torch, it's only about twenty feet in.'

The cave was not high enough for Doc to stand upright so he squatted holding the torch while I lit the hurricane lamp which he'd brought with him in the rucksack strapped to his back.

I placed the lamp in the middle of the cave where it threw a dim but adequate light and Doc started to examine the walls with the torch beam.

The floor was covered with bat shit. 'It should smell worse than this.' Doc took out a box of matches and struck one on the side of his pants. The match flared, momentarily lighting his face. 'A wind! In here is a wind, from some place else there is coming a wind.' Doc was right, the flame from the match was flickering and then went out. He shone his torch into the left corner of the cave where a sharp buttress of rock protruded. The torch light played on the rock and as Doc swept the beam to the top of the buttress the light disappeared into a void. We realised that there was an opening beyond it from which came the unmistakable sound of water dripping. We both moved round the back of the rock to discover the opening about four feet above the ground which reached to the ceiling. Doc lit the opening for me to scramble through and he passed the lantern to me and then the torch before following. As he dropped to the ground I swung the powerful torch into the black void.

'Holy Molenski!' The torch showed a huge chamber, from the floor and the ceiling of which grew stalactites and stalagmites. The roof of the cave must have been at least forty feet high and the snowy white calcareous structures falling from it, some of which had reached the ground, looked like an illustration from a child's fairy tale. Pools of infinitely still water on parts of the cave floor mirrored the grotesque shapes, creating an enchanted world which appeared to be carved in crystal.

I handed the torch back to Doc and took up the lantern as we moved forward to explore. Doc kept stopping to train his torch on one or another of the beautiful crystal columns. 'Absoloodle, absoloodle wunderbar!' he kept repeating. It was certainly the most amazing natural phenomenon I had ever witnessed and I followed Doc as we explored the huge chamber. We found several fissures in the walls, none of which were wide enough to climb through; we traced the source of the water to a point high in the ceiling from which a constant drip of water fell. Doc pointed out that this drip was too rapid for the formation of stalactites. The gradual movement of water seeping through rock collects a load of calcium carbonate, when it finally squeezes through to the ceiling of the cave and reaches the air it sheds its load of calcium carbonate and an infinitely small part of a stalactite is formed. Each drop adds its minute contribution. He pointed to a massive stalactite to our right. 'Perhaps three hundred thousand years, maybe more.' Doc's voice was filled with awe. On the far wall, some sixty feet into the cave, a ledge of rock protruded about fifteen feet from the floor. Above it hung huge spikes of stalactite and clumps of glittering crystals, while directly under the ledge, like grotesque legs to a giant table, stalagmites had grown. A buttress of crystal stalagmite had grown to the one side of the platform to resemble steps leading up to it, so the entire effect was like a magnificent slab held high by crystal shafts with huge spikes of crystallised light suspended above it.

'Look, Doc, it's like Merlin's altar in the crystal cave!'

Doc sucked in his breath, 'Ja, in such a place went Merlin for sure.' He pointed to the throne, 'To lie on this altar and in a hundred and fifty thousand years maybe the body would be a part of this cave. A part of the crystal cave of Africa. Imagine only this, Peekay.'

I grinned, 'Can you hold off for a while, please Doc, I still need you here.' The thought of Doc dying had never entered my head. I often thought of him growing old, unable to do the things we'd done in the past; but I never thought of him as disappearing, not being there, not being a part of my life. I understood death, it happened at any time. It was a brutal accident like the death of Granpa Chook or Geel Piet, or Big Hettie's flyweight. Even Big Hettie's death could be explained in that she was freakishly big and thus fell into the category of unexpected death. Doc did not fall into any of the criteria I had set aside in my mind for death. Doc was calm, and reason and order and the kind of death I knew had no part in the expectations for our relationship.

He had walked ahead up to the crystal-like speleothems which formed the steps to the platform. Climbing these, his boots made a scrunching noise on the hard calcium deposits, and soon he stood on the platform. Suddenly, without warning, he squatted and then stretched out full length, so his body was lost from my sight.

'Ah, come on, Doc! That's not funny,' I said, suddenly a little scared. Doc's torch shone upwards, lighting the stalactites falling from the ceiling above him so that they looked like crystal bolts of lightning frozen in place above him. It was the most frightening and magnificent effect I have ever seen.

Doc's voice came back to me, sounding serene. 'It is beautiful, Peekay, we must never tell any person about the crystal cave of Africa.'

'C'mon, Doc, you're giving me the creeps,' I answered, not fully taking in what he had said.

Doc stood up, shining the torch straight into my eyes so that I was blinded by the light. 'You must promise me, Peekay. It is very important. You must promise, please?' He withdrew the torch from my face and in the fuzziness the temporary blinding had created he looked just like Merlin, standing between huge spikes of crystal on the platform ten feet above me.

'Doc, please come down. I promise, now please come down.'

'Ja, I come. Remember you have promised, Peekay.' He made his way down from the platform carefully and I ran to give him a hand. He was breathing heavily, and as I helped him down I could feel the excitement in the old man.

We made our way back to the bat cave and Doc shone the Eveready back into the chamber. 'Peekay, we have found a place in Africa no man has ever seen, the purest magic cave, the crystal cave of Africa.'

'Come on, Doc, let's skedaddle, what's the time?' He fished into his trouser pocket for his hunter and shone the torch on its face. 'Half clock ten,' he said. Doc always told the time in this funny manner.

'We've got to go. If we get back to camp by noon it'll be dark by the time we get home.' Fortunately most of the way home was downhill and we knew we would gain a couple of hours on the way back. I calculated it would be around eight that evening before we would be home. Walking the foothills in the dark wouldn't be much fun and Doc would be exhausted. My anxiety to get going had taken the edge off my excitement. Doc grabbed me by the arm; he was still shaking. 'Remember, Peekay, this is our cave; the crystal cave belongs only to you and to me.'

'Okay, Doc, I promise. I already promised. Now let's get the hell out of here.' It wasn't at all like Doc to be so insistent, anyway he knew he could trust me implicitly. The cave had had a tremendous effect on him and I knew he'd want us to come back, though I doubted that he'd be able to make such a tough climb for much longer. I'd cut the rope we'd taken into the cave but had left the rope handrail intact for Doc to use getting out. Once we were back on the ledge I began to retrieve the two metal spikes, as we'd already lost two by having to leave them embedded in the tunnel wall.

'No, leave them, Peekay,' Doc said suddenly, 'there is no time.' It was unlike Doc, who was always very careful about equipment. We'd account for everything before moving on from a camp site or where we had been collecting specimens. It was the first time he had ever been devious and I realised how emotionally charged he had become over the crystal cave; the old bugger was determined to come back.

We arrived back in the foothills above the town just as a giant moon was coming up over the escarpment, flooding the de Kaap Valley in silver light. It was a full moon again and that was always a difficult time for me. It had been a full moon when Granpa Chook died and while the memory of that funny old rooster had dimmed, when the moon was full memories came galloping through the silver night to sadden me. It had also been a full moon when Geel Piet had died.

I was right, this would be the last big trek with Doc, who was at the point of collapse by the time we finally reached his cottage. I laid him on top of his bed and removed his boots. He had two large blisters, one under each big toe, so I threaded a needle and cotton and ran a loop of cotton through each blister which I then tied, leaving them overnight to drain the fluid. It was a technique Doc had shown me years before and I knew that by morning the blisters would have flattened and there would be no pain. I washed his face and put Vaseline over a cut under his eye and threw an army blanket over him. He was a tough old blighter and in the morning I was pretty sure he'd be okay.

'Ours. The crystal cave. Africa. You, me, Peekay,' he mumbled and then seemed to drift off into sleep. I waited until his breathing was deep and even before leaving for home. On the way the moon was so bright that one could see the purple blossom of the jacaranda trees. I was saddened at the thought of never again being with him in the high mountains. Each time I came back from school Doc seemed a little more frail. We had found the crystal cave of Africa but would I see it only once? Perhaps I would return, perhaps not. When you share things, as Doc and I had done, somehow it seemed wrong to halve the secret by returning alone. I thought of the rope rotting and perhaps in a hundred years they'd find the holes where the spikes had long since rusted out and observe the rust stains in the dolomite. They'd search and find minute metal fragments which they'd analyse, and then propound all sorts of theories that would have nothing to do with a six foot seven inch German professor of music and the future welterweight boxing champion of the world.

TWENTY

The second term of Form three began with a new aspect of school life. Singe 'n Burn's tutorials three times a week were quite unlike school. We talked for an hour and from it would come at least three hours of reading and preparation for the next tutorial. The headmaster had a wide grasp of subjects and he was quick to discover where a boy's special aptitudes lay. These he would cultivate carefully while at the same time balancing the mental menu with the discipline of tackling subjects which, though less interesting, he thought essential to a well-rounded education. Sinjun's People seldom met as a group and once chosen they were never mentioned again in the activity of the Prince of Wales School. No attempt was ever made to make any one of us seem special or especially important, although a powerful struggle between the six took place in the normal course of school, with each one of Sinjun's People competing fiercely in the classroom for honours. All this, combined with boxing and rugby football, left me very little time to myself.

Hymie had also revealed his big plan. By now he was so intimately involved with me as a boxer as well as a friend that he acted quite unself-consciously as my manager. In two and a bit years Hymie had acquired a remarkable expertise on boxing, and he too was aware that we'd reached the limitations of both Darby White and Sarge and needed to take the next step in my training.

'Who's the best professional boxing trainer in South Africa?' he'd asked one afternoon shortly after our return to school.

'You already know the answer to that; Solly Goldman.'

'Well, I went to see him during the holidays. We're working out for him when he gets back from a trip to England in six weeks. If he likes what he sees, he'll take you on.'

'Jesus, Hymie, that's wonderful! How'd you get him to agree? Solly Goldman only handles professionals.'

For once Hymie wasn't ready with a flip answer. He looked down at the back of his hands as he answered. 'We're going to pay him. We've got enough money in the bank to pay him for a year then we'll think of something else.' Hymie looked up at me. 'Now I know what you're going to say; but as far as I'm concerned my money is yours, you'd do the same for me.'

'It's not on, Hymie. Thank you, but it's simply not on. There are two reasons. The first you already know about, no hand-outs, not under any circumstances, friendship notwithstanding. The second is more practical, that's our business capital; the first rule of business is never to eat into your capital, you above all people know that!'

'Look, we'd still keep the Bank. I can borrow money from my old man to keep the float going. You don't have to take a hand-out. You can buy back your share of the float capital from the profits and you can take a salary as pocket money; you'll see, it will work out.'

'Hymie, there's nothing in the world I want more than Solly Goldman's expertise, but I can't do it. It's got something to do with an incident in my life when I was five years old and I've promised myself I would never again forfeit my independence, never again find myself in a position where I wasn't in control of my life.'

Hymie looked hurt and I couldn't blame him; in a sense I was rejecting his friendship and his trust. But the wounds entrenched by the Judge and the Nazi stormtroopers had left adhesions on my psyche as a constant reminder to me that I was on my own.

'Okay, Peekay, have it your way, man.' Then Hymie grinned. 'If I think up a scam and your share makes enough money to pay Goldman, will you be in it?'

I grinned, relieved that he had accepted my objection. 'That's business, that's different! But only if I play my part and the whole thing's kosher.'

'Shake a paw, partner,' Hymie grinned. 'This one is going to be an intellectual masterpiece!'

Atherton, Cunning-Spider and I had been a combination on the rugby field from Form one. I was a natural scrum-half with Atherton, following in the footsteps of his famous cousin, developing into a brilliant fly-half, while Cunning Spider was a centre with a lot of style. Hugh Lyell and Jean Minnaar, both Sinjun's People, were also on the team. While I was still technically under fourteen I elected to play in the under fifteen team to keep the combination together. Pissy Johnson, who seemed to grow bigger every term, was a front row forward and, of course, Hymie only became interested because most of the Wooden Spoon Goons were in the team. The under fifteen team in any school is the nursery for the first fifteen and so the players in it are always carefully watched by the rugby masters who regarded this particular team as one with great promise.

Hymie, as usual, analysed the teams against whom we played and, like his boxing notes, we had a pretty good idea of their game plan and capability before taking the field against them.

As he had done in his swot spot in boxing, Hymie made us think and behave like winners. 'Winners make their own luck but winners are also lucky,' he said.

In the under thirteens and fourteens, when we had played Helpmekaar, the Afrikaans school where I had boxed my first bout to beat Jannie

Geldenhuis, the much bigger Helpmekaar forwards had made mincemeat of us and the stronger, bigger backs had run us off our feet. Geldenhuis, playing scrum-half opposite me, had thoroughly enjoyed his revenge on each of these four occasions. In the last under fourteen match there they'd beaten us narrowly and as we left the field he'd given me an unnecessarily patronising pat on the back. 'In the ring is one thing, on the rugby field is another. Rugby is more important than boxing, man.' We'd met five times in the ring and while he was always a tough opponent, on each occasion I'd beaten him; he had a right to try and get even. We would play each school twice during a season and so in our personal score it was me with five boxing wins, Helpmekaar four rugby wins. Hymie, in particular, was anxious to change these rugby statistics when we met in the under fifteens. While the Helpmekaar team were still bigger than we were, things had evened out a bit in size. Hymie was convinced we could beat them. 'Look at the statistics, Peekay. In the under thirteens they beat us twenty to nil and again fifteen nil; last year it was nine nil and ten three and we scored a try to two free kicks and a drop goal. Statistically we have to take them this year.'

I had my doubts. Helpmekaar with four wins to their credit in the preceding two years had a right to be confident. 'Hymie, they're Boers, they'd rather die than lose to an English school; it's not simply a matter of statistics!'

'Ja, I know, that's what we're going to have to fix.'

On the Wednesday afternoon two weeks prior to the match, when we were meant to be studying at the Johannesburg library, Hymie drew me aside. 'Will you come to Helpmekaar with me this afternoon to see Jannie Geldenhuis, don't ask any questions, just say, yes . . . it's important.'

Sitting on the top deck of the Parktown bus he outlined his plan. 'There are nearly twelve hundred kids at Helpmekaar and six hundred at our school. If we can get most of them to place a bet on Helpmekaar winning against our under fifteens we could really clean up; we'd have your Solly Goldman money.'

'Christ, Hymie, we're back to straight gambling! You're crazy, this isn't like those first boxing matches when we took a few bets in the toilet before the fight. There I was a surprise factor in that scam; the punters from the other schools didn't know we had a boxer who could fight. This is just the opposite; they know how good we are and what's more we've never beaten them! This whole thing contradicts our business philosophy.'

'You know what your problem is, Peekay? You worry too much.'

'With you as a friend, that's hardly bloody surprising. I hope you've got a plan?'

Hymie opened his hands expansively. 'Does a bird fly? Of course I've got a plan, but I may have to tapdance a little when we get there so please excuse me if I don't explain it to you in detail. But I promise you our business philosophy is intact.'

'Hymie, listen! Picking up a dozen punters in the shit house is one thing; taking on a whole bloody Afrikaans school is another. You don't know these buggers like I do; these guys don't gamble, the Afrikaans are very religious, you know.'

'Greed, my dear Peekay, transcends religion. Did not the Roman soldiers gamble for Christ's garments at Golgotha? Besides, when those Helpmekaar guys see the odds I'm offering, their little Boer hands won't be able to get a kitchen knife to their money boxes fast enough.'

'Hymie, I hope this whole thing's kosher. If it turns out to be a con and they find out, we're dead meat!' Hymie had taught us all the Jewish word 'kosher' and it had become the generic term for something being legitimate.

Hymie smiled. 'I've racked my brains; in fact I'm rather ashamed of myself but, even with my considerable intellect, there is no way of ensuring the outcome other than to pay them off, which is patently impossible. We simply have to beat them on the day. Believe me, it's as kosher as my granma's chicken soup.' He turned to me and gave me his most disarming smile. 'Peekay, I know you've got a considerable rep with these Boers, no way I'm going to spoil that. You're the only Rooinek Christian gentleman they respect,' he paused. 'Just get it into your head that we can beat the bastards!'

'I hope you didn't mean you'd pay them off if you could find a way?'

'No, of course not, I was only kidding. The nicest part of a scam is the brains part. Anyone can learn to cheat.'

We reached the top of the hill and arrived at the Helpmekaar gates just as school was getting out. A sea of brown blazers piped with yellow braid engulfed our two green ones. Remarks were flying left, right and centre and things were getting decidedly uncomfortable.

'What now?' I whispered to Hymie.

We just wait here, you'll see,' he replied.

Just then a voice cut through the sea of brown blazers, 'Peekay, howzit?' It was Jannie Geldenhuis. 'Sorry I'm late, man, I had to see one of the masters. Come with me.' He extended his hand in the Boer manner and we shook it in turn, and then followed him through the gates.

'Magtig, I thought we were going to be lynched,' I said to Jannie in Afrikaans.

'No way, man, they all know you here, you a sort of hero.'

We had reached the school toilets where a couple of guys about our own age were having a quiet smoke. Jannie asked them politely to leave and they kicked at the ground with the toe cap of their shoes, then deciding to obey, killed their cigarettes by pinching the heads off and put the unused stompies in their blazer pockets for use later.

Hymie said he'd accept odds of three to one on the Prince of Wales School winning.

Geldenhuis gasped. 'You're crazy, man! We already beat you four games to nil!'

'Those are the odds,' Hymie said quietly.

'That's blêrrie terrific for the punters,' Geldenhuis said, 'but what about us? We . . . you'll be cleaned out! Fifteen per cent of nothing is nothing, and I'll end up with my arse kicked by twelve hundred bloody angry Helpmekaar punters.'

Geldenhuis was not just a pretty face, I observed. Hymie'd gone crackers! Helpmekaar had to be favoured to win. Three to one odds was suicide.

'Okay, Geldenhuis . . . Peekay and I will give you a written guarantee that we'll honour our debts if the Prince of Wales loses.' He reached into the inside pocket of his blazer and handed me a square of folded paper. I opened it to see that it was a guarantee by the Bank to pay in the event of a Helpmekaar win. There was a place at the bottom for two signatures. Hymie had already signed as one of them.

'Sign it and give it to him,' Hymie said casually.

I made a rough calculation in my head. Assuming two thirds of the punters bet against us at an average of two shillings a bet, we stood to lose around three hundred and seventy pounds. If we sold the Bank to a syndicate and our rights to the famous *Miss Bornstein School of Correspondence Notes,* and took all our savings, we could just make it.

I breathed a sigh of relief; if it had been more than our total assets I would have had to turn Hymie down in front of Geldenhuis, causing us both no end of embarrassment. I borrowed Hymie's Parker 51 and holding the guarantee against the toilet wall I signed it. But I can tell you I was not happy; Hymie Solomon Levy was going to be in a lot of shit when we were alone again.

Geldenhuis took the guarantee from me, read it and pulled out a small leather wallet from his pocket. As he opened it to stow the guarantee I noticed it contained no money.

'Okay, Geldenhuis, twenty per cent of the winnings or fifty quid now, it's your choice,' Hymie said.

Like me before Hymie had entered my life, Jannie Geldenhuis had probably never seen a ten-pound note in his life, much less fifty. Eight pounds a week was the average white workers' wage; Helpmekaar was not a private school and his parents were probably battling to make ends meet.

Hymie had read his man correctly. 'I'll take the fifty pounds now,' Geldenhuis said.

Jannie Geldenhuis must have believed we couldn't win; Hymie was offering him fifty quid against a potential of seventy-five.

Hymie pulled out his wallet and opened it. 'Just a second!' Geldenhuis said suddenly. He withdrew his wallet again and took the guarantee from it and proffered it to Hymie. 'I got a condition of my own; without it we got no deal, man.'

We both looked at Geldenhuis with surprise. 'What's the condition, Jannie?' I asked.

'Well, first of all, I'm only agreeing to set up the Helpmekaar side of the betting because you're in this, Peekay.' He jabbed his finger in Hymie's direction. 'I don't do business with a Jewboy!'

'Hey, now wait a minute!' I was suddenly angry, 'Hymie and I are in this together, no Hymie, no deal!' I turned to Hymie, 'C'mon, let's piss off.'

Hymie put his hand up in a conciliatory manner. 'Now hang on a sec. Take it easy. We're a partnership; if Jannie here wants to deal with you that's fine.' He had moved so as to unsight Geldenhuis and gave me a knowing wink, then turned again so that Geldenhuis could see him and removed five ten-pound notes from his wallet. 'Here, Peekay, you pay the man.'

Before I could take the money, Geldenhuis said, 'That's not the condition.' The beginnings of a smile played at the corners of his mouth.

I was still angry. 'So what's the condition, Geldenhuis?'

'Fight me!'

He must have seen the surprise in my face. 'What here? Now?'

'I just turned featherweight, you still easy a bantamweight; I want a last chance to get even.'

'And if he says no?' Hymie asked.

Still looking directly at me Geldenhuis said: 'No deal! You can stick your fifty quid up your Jewboy arse! What do you reckon, Peekay? Box me three rounds here in the gym?'

'Christ, and to think I liked you, Geldenhuis. You're on! But I haven't got any gear.'

'I already thought of that, I got stuff for you.' Geldenhuis paused and then shrugged his shoulders, 'Hey, no hard feelings, man. You a Rooinek, I'm a Boer, I won't be happy till I beat you,' he said simply.

'You may be a long time unhappy, man! Where do I change?'

'Who's going to referee?' Hymie asked.

Jannie Geldenhuis pointed to Witwatersrand University campus which was only a couple of hundred yards from the school. 'We got a guy from Wits just in case you said yes.'

Geldenhuis put the guarantee back into his wallet and I turned to follow him out of the toilets, but Hymie stood his ground.

'Just a moment, Geldenhuis!'

We turned to face Hymie who held the five ten-pound notes up in his hand, just the hint of a smile played over his face.

'I bet you fifty quid Peekay smacks your arse!'

Geldenhuis stood, his arms held stiffly as though at attention, he was rigid with anger. Hymie had outfoxed him and avenged himself at the same time.

'You got your bet, Jew!' he spat.

Geldenhuis took us over to the shower block and pointed to a brown paper bag on a bench. 'Everything's there, I'll see you in the gym.' He turned and walked away, presumably to change elsewhere.

'Christ, what a turn up for the books,' Hymie said.

The gear fitted well enough and the boxing boots were nicely worn. We left the showers and walked down a long corridor towards the gym. I entered ahead of Hymie. Suddenly the hall resounded with clapping and whistling, it was packed to the rafters with Helpmekaar guys.

'Holy shit!' I exclaimed, turning to Hymie.

Hymie glanced at the grinning faces looking at us. 'Keep calm, pretend you're not surprised; we don't want him to have the psychological advantage.' Hymie, as usual, was thinking on his feet. We climbed up into the ring and Hymie gloved me up. Geldenhuis was already in his corner throwing punches into the air. As usual I sat on the pot and waited.

The referee, a chap in his mid-twenties, called us into the centre of the ring. 'Okay, boxers, shake hands! Break when I say break. A knockdown takes a compulsory count of eight and I don't start counting until you're in a neutral corner. Three warnings on a foul and the fight goes against you.'

Neither of us were listening to him. 'This time I get you Rooinek,' Jannie Geldenhuis said out of the corner of his mouth.

'This fight comes to you with the compliments of the Jewboy, Boer bastard!' I spat back.

'Ready, timekeeper? Seconds out of the ring!' The bell went and we danced towards each other. I could see Geldenhuis meant business; he had five defeats to avenge and his eyes were hard. Fighting in the enemy camp in front of a hostile crowd I wasn't about to let him have the satisfaction. He was a naturally aggressive fighter and I wasn't going to give him the opportunity of landing a few good punches early so I spent the first half of round one on the back foot using the ring and staying clear of the ropes. Later Hymie told me the Helpmekaar kids were yelling their heads off but it was as though I was fighting in a vacuum, my concentration was complete. Geldenhuis threw a lot of leather but most of it landed on my arms and gloves, though he did score with two punches: a beautiful uppercut as he caught me briefly on the ropes and a right under the heart. Both punches hurt like hell. It was sheer luck that I hadn't had any lunch. Sinjun had had me for a tutorial which had gone on an extra half hour and so I'd missed lunch. I was willing to bet Geldenhuis hadn't eaten since morning.

I caught Geldenhuis a beautiful punch on the jaw which stopped him in his tracks. He had come at me with a careless left lead and I brought my right hand across his lead to hit him hard on the side of the jaw. Jannie was a sucker for repeating a mistake and later in the round he led again with a sloppy left. This time I came under the blow and caught him with everything I had under the heart. I could see his eyes boggle and he staggered back into the ropes where I hit him with a left-right combination in the gut, expecting his gloves to open so that I could get an uppercut to the jaw. Instead, anticipating the uppercut, he defended his head, leaving his gut exposed. In went the Geel Piet eight-punch combination and he grabbed at the ropes just as the bell went. The first round was mine.

Hymie had noticed the same thing as I had. Geldenhuis had developed a peculiar habit; in order to set himself for a left hook, he held his right elbow high, opening up his rib cage, and I'd given him a lot of punishment in the area right under the heart. The eight-punch combo was just what I needed to soften him up for later in the fight. As Geel Piet would say, 'If you hit them enough in between the heart and the belt the legs will soon melt.'

To my surprise, in the second round he continued to be the aggressor. I'd never seen him fight better. His punches were crisp and finding their mark disconcertingly often. In the middle of the round I changed to a southpaw stance. This confused him enough to get me through the round with no more punishment. And while I'd put a lot of hard work into his body he'd won the round, I felt sure. When a fighter gets set and is able to move his opponent into the corners, he can do a lot of harm and look very good.

I hated to lose the second round, it gives your opponent the psychological advantage, knowing he's going into the last round with his tail up. Besides, it gives the referee a chance to call a draw if the final round isn't convincing. The extra weight Jannie had gained had increased his strength and he had seemed to take in his stride the punishment I'd given him.

Jannie knew he had to make the final round look good, and I knew I had to make it look great. As a fighter he had the edge over a boxer; the aggressor moving relentlessly forward is a crowd pleaser and a partisan crowd is apt to forget the winner is the guy who lands the most clean punches. I hoped the ref was good enough to call it correctly but with a home crowd like this a close decision in my favour would get us lynched.

Jannie began the final round by circling me, boxing clever. I had switched back from a southpaw stance and he was no match for me as a boxer, provided I stayed in the centre of the ring and off the ropes. I held him off easily enough. He kept moving in close, trying to throw the left hook to the head, the punch he'd decided would take me out. I could have kept him off with a straight right, just jabbing away and scoring, but I felt I was fast enough to keep my head out of the way of his vicious left hook which, every time he threw it, lifted his right elbow and made a delicious target for me to plant a hard left uppercut under his heart. To a percentage boxer like me this was money in the bank.

Geldenhuis threw another hard left hook which caught me a glancing blow on the side of the head. I didn't even have to look, the right elbow would be way up in the air and I drove a left hook in as hard as I could. The light suddenly left his eyes; Geel Piet was right as usual, his head had gone.

I changed onto the front foot and into attack. The sudden onslaught caught Geldenhuis completely by surprise and gaps in his defence opened up everywhere. His concept of me as a boxer who worked mostly off the back foot was so completely fixed in his mind that he was unable to respond to the fighter who now brought the fight to him, hitting him seemingly at will. He dropped his defences as he reached out too soon for a clinch and I caught him on the point of the jaw with a right cross which knocked him into the ropes, leaving his midriff exposed as his hands shot up into the air. I moved in with another of Geel Piet's eight-punch combinations, all of them clean, hard punches even though they were thrown at short range. He pulled me into a clinch and the ref separated us. I'd taken the stuffing out of him and thirty seconds later he missed with a right and the left that followed, and I hit him with the best punch I had thrown in my life, a right uppercut which packed everything I had behind it and caught him perfectly under the point of the chin.

It was the first absolute knockout I'd ever achieved. Jannie Geldenhuis went down like a sack of potatoes and lay sprawled on the canvas. I retired quickly to a neutral corner; while he hadn't moved I fully expected him to take the eight count before getting up. The ref stood over him counting; at seven Geldenhuis managed to get up onto his elbow but that was all. At ten he slumped back onto the canvas.

The ref moved over and held my hand up. The audience was clearly stunned. After their initial shock, and as Jannie got to his feet, they stood up and gave me a really big round of applause. Hymie jumped into the ring and held my arm up again, which was unnecessary. Jannie Geldenhuis helped by his seconds climbed through the ropes without coming over.

I grinned. 'Christ Hymie, what a preliminary for getting the punters ready to bet on a game of rugby.'

'Couldn't be better if I'd set it up myself,' he said.

We climbed from the ropes and the Helpmekaar chaps made way for us as we walked towards the door. 'Promise me something, Hymie.'

'Yeah, sure, what is it?'

'Promise me you didn't set this all up?'

'Are you crazy! What about that anti-semitic bastard?'

'You got your revenge; that was the quickest fifty quid anybody ever had.' We had reached the privacy of the showers and Hymie started to giggle. Soon we were thumping each other on the back and howling with laughter.

On the way back in the bus I turned to Hymie. 'You haven't answered my question.'

'What question?'

'Was today a set-up?'

Hymie looked down at his hands, 'Technically no. But when you bring the right elements together you're entitled to expect a predictable outcome.'

'I ought to bust your teeth, Hymie Solomon Levy! I ought to do it right now!'

We repeated the attractive odds at the Prince of Wales and as we had expected the gentlemen Christians bet heavily on Helpmekaar to win. School spirit was one thing but money was quite another. Only the

Wellington House boarders, Darby and Sarge and the under fifteen team itself bet on the Prince of Wales School. Setting the odds up as he had done had the result of inspiring the under fifteens enormously. The David and Goliath syndrome was operating, Hymie's psychology was perfect; by the day of the game we really thought we could win. At Helpmekaar it was hoped it would have a different effect, for while the Afrikaans punters bet heavily on their team to win, the team itself should have felt a little uneasy. Why would we make the Prince of Wales School the favourite, when virtually the same team we were fielding had been beaten on four previous occasions? Like ours, their team contained a number of boxers in its ranks and they'd seen how we had improved out of sight in the ring, to the point where we had drawn the last boxing tournament with them. If we could do it in boxing. . . ? Hymie and I were known not to be fools.

Hymie's poison, we hoped, was working.

Despite being only an under fifteens match, the game drew the biggest crowd of the season. The punters from both schools were out in full and Hymie was still taking bets when the two teams were lined up on the field. He had even got the school pipe major to play 'Scotland the Brave' out in the middle before we ran on. It was grand stuff.

The ref blew his whistle and Atherton kicked off, a short kick which landed in the middle of their forwards. Pissy Johnson, by some miracle, got there first and bowled over the Helpmekaar forward who caught the ball. A loose scrum formed but the ball wouldn't come out and the ref blew his whistle for a set scrum.

It was our loose head and, despite a big push from Helpmekaar, the ball came to me quite cleanly. We were halfway between the halfway mark and their twenty-five and Atherton was standing almost on the halfway line directly behind me. I knew he was going to go for the drop kick which, even for him, seemed a bit ambitious. I flipped the ball back at him as their flankers broke away and seemingly with time to spare he put the ball straight through the posts for four points. It was the best drop kick I had ever seen from him and it set the tone of the match.

Shortly afterwards we scored a converted try and just before half-time they landed a free kick. At half-time it was nine three, but their heavier pack was taking its toll and we were exhausted.

In the second half they closed down the game and eventually scored by pushing our lighter pack over the line. It was nine to eight with ten minutes to go and I could see our forwards were dead on their feet. It was just a matter of time before they scored. Somehow we hung on, tackling everything in sight.

Hymie had the pipe major on the sideline and he was blasting away, but we were too tired to care or even hear him. Geldenhuis had given me a torrid time and was over-anxious to get at me. On two occasions during these last minutes of the game when they were camped on our line I'd dummied a pass from the scrum and his over-eagerness to get to me put him off-side and gave us a free kick. These two relieving kicks alone may well have saved us.

With two minutes to go we packed down for a scrum on our five-yard line. It was our loose head but they were pushing us hard towards the line. Somehow we managed to ruck the ball. I dummied a pass to our full-back and Geldenhuis hesitated for a fraction of a second, enough time for me to move down the blind side. I drew their wing and passed to Atherton who'd come round with me. He cut inside, drew their fly-half and kicked the ball across field towards the far corner posts. Lyell, our right winger, beat the full-back to the ball and scored in the corner. The Prince of Wales School went berserk, despite the fact that they'd all lost their money. Atherton failed to convert the try but we'd won twelve to eight.

When all the bets were counted and we'd paid the faithful handful who'd bet against Helpmekaar, we were left with four hundred and eighty-seven pounds, fifteen shillings and sixpence. Of the eighteen hundred kids in the two schools almost every one of them had a bet on the outcome. It was the mightiest scam of all time and my share paid Solly Goldman for the next three and a half years.

Hymie broke out a fiver for a party in the team dressing room and sent Geldenhuis and the Helpmekaar team a case of Pepsi and four dozen cream buns. He opened a cream bun and placed a tenner in it, and put it on top of the pile of buns going to the Helpmekaar dressing room. 'That will teach the hairy back to do business with a Jewboy,' he laughed.

The Solly Goldman Gym in Sauer Street was just like any gym you've read about. It smelt of sweat, chalk, liniment and hope. Solly ran his gym colour-blind, the way gyms are run the world over. His only concession to apartheid was a locker room for non-Europeans. The rest depended on your skill as a boxer. The Johannesburg police turned a blind eye to Solly's personal race integration programme. The police commissioner, Kruger, was a boxing man, and to boxing men black isn't black in the ring. Too many great black boxers existed in the world and a man jabbing a pair of twelve ounce gloves into your face wasn't a dirty Kaffir; he was a boxer, if only for the duration of the fight.

While a number of amateurs worked out in the gym, none of them was instructed by Solly, who had his work cut out handling the pros. Boxing was becoming a big-time sport in the African townships surrounding Johannesburg, and Solly had a regular stable of black fighters he trained in return for a percentage of the purse. Black and white boxers were not allowed to fight in public for the same title but they'd spar together and sometimes the sparring would get out of hand when a white or a black guy, but it was mostly the white boxers, decided to have a go. Solly would let it go for a couple of rounds, particularly when it looked as though the white man was getting a bit of a drubbing.

The first time Hymie and I appeared, Solly put me in with a young pro bantamweight who hadn't been out of the amateur ranks very long. After two rounds he stopped the sparring session.

'Who taught you to box, Peekay?'

I told him about Geel Piet without giving him the exact details.

'Next time you see him, my boy, you give him my compliments.'

'He's dead, Solly.'

Solly cocked his bald head to one side. 'Well he didn't die in vain, my son, he's given you an almost perfect grounding; you use the ring like a wizard.'

'Thank you,' I said, not quite knowing what else to say. Solly Goldman was the best and I found his over-generous compliments unnerving.

'Thank me later, my boy, there's a lot of work to get through. You need a little more starch in your left hand and your right is no great shakes niver. Like all amateurs you're looking for points, you hold your hands too bleedin' high. You're fast enough to drop 'em a little and give yourself more punching power. We'll get you onto weights and build up your upper body. It would also be very comforting indeed to know you also packed a good left right combination. Before I'm through with you, my son, you're going to be the only amateur boxer in South Africa who can put a thirteen-punch combo together. That's the show stopper, that's the one man band that starts with a bleedin' mouf organ and ends with a big bass drum.'

I was amazed that Solly Goldman, a cockney Jew from London, could read so much into my boxing after watching me for only two rounds. But he was true to his word. By the Christmas holidays I was a vastly improved boxer with a lot more power in both hands. We fought as usual in the Eastern Transvaal Championships that December and Captain Smit couldn't believe the difference. The championships were in Barberton and it seemed the whole town turned out to see me box. My mother stayed at home but my granpa had a ringside seat with Doc, Mrs Boxall, Miss Bornstein and old Mr Bornstein. Miss Bornstein told me later that old Mr Bornstein winced every time I threw a punch, while Doc, by now a seasoned campaigner, pretended to take it all in his stride.

I was awarded the trophy for best boxer in the tournament, and afterwards my granpa and I walked home while Mrs Boxall drove Doc to his cottage. We reached the front gate and my granpa patted me on the shoulder. 'I've never been so proud in my life, son,' he said and then, to cover his embarrassment, reached into his white linen jacket for his pipe.

I had been home a week. The train from Johannesburg arrived at Nelspruit at nine a.m. on the previous Saturday morning. Usually I would then go on to Kaapmuiden and wait until mid-afternoon for the coffee pot to Barberton which would crawl exhausted into town about eight in the evening. But to my delight Gert was waiting for me at Nelspruit.

'Ag man, we had to put in some papers here about a white drunk and disorderly who attacked a prison gang with a pick handle so Captain Smit said take the car and pick up Peekay at the same time.' He extended his hand, 'How goes it, man?'

On the road back to Barberton, Gert told me that Doc had been in a storm in the hills and had caught pneumonia and spent a week in hospital. 'He's looking old, Peekay. I reckon he'll be making his peace pretty soon.'

I was stunned. 'He's a tough old bugger; he'll be okay I'm telling you,' I said, more to give myself comfort than as a reply.

'Ja, he's tough all right, but the old bugger must be eighty-five, maybe more; he can't last forever, man.'

'Well, he's still climbing into the hills, that's something at least.'

'Not since he was sick; he talks about it, about when you get back, but I dunno, man, I reckon he's finish and klaar. I told him I'll send a gang any time to work in the cactus garden but he says he can still manage. But I dunno, man.'

I said nothing. A huge lump grew in my throat and the road in front of me blurred. The thought of Doc not being there when I returned home from school was too distressing even to contemplate.

'Those two abafazi at your house look after him like he's a chief. They spend all their spare time over at his place and they bring food every day, and now they even shave him.'

Doc was the most independent person I'd ever known and I knew at once that Gert wasn't imagining things. If Dee and Dum had to shave him his hands must have become very shaky.

I had bought Dee and Dum a Singer hand machine and they'd turned their sewing into a regular little business making cotton shifts for many of the local house-servants. My mother and Marie had shown them how to cut out, and how to make buttonholes and hem by hand, and they were going great guns. I had learned by accident that Dee and Dum were using their small earnings from sewing to look after Doc who could no longer take in his little girls for music lessons. When I could after that, I would send them money for him. The Bank was a regular source of income and I could generally manage a pound a week, and what with one or two other scams Hymie and I had going, between the girls and me, Doc was okay.

Realising that my mother would expect me home on the coffee pot, I asked Gert to drop me off at the bottom of Doc's road. Hiding my suitcase under some bushes I climbed up to the cottage. He was sitting in the shade on the stoep in his favourite riempie chair and I thought he must be asleep. But he looked up and saw me approaching, and rose from his chair a little stiffly, one hand on the small of his back. His six foot seven frame almost touched the rafters of the verandah and he seemed to be swaying slightly as his arms went out to me. I ran up to him and he put his hands on my shoulders, and then I could no longer contain myself and I grabbed him fiercely.

'Please, Doc, please don't die,' I sobbed.

Doc and I seldom showed emotion, our love each for the other was so fierce that it burned like a flame inside of us. But now I was suddenly overcome, Gert's conversation on the way over, mixed with the emotion of seeing him standing with his arms outstretched to me, frail as a wisp of smoke, was too much.

His hand came round and patted me on the back. 'Absoloodle! We have no time to die, Peekay, the hills are still green and waiting; it is not yet time for the crystal cave of Africa.'

I pulled away from him and he sat down in his chair. Still sniffing I wiped my eyes with the back of my hand. 'You've been sick, Doc. Gert told me you've been sick.'

'Just a bad cold, Peekay. It was nothing.'

'It was pneumonia!'

'Ja this is true, but some pneumonia is big, some is small; this was a *piccaninny*, a very small pneumonia for sure and absoloodle.' He rose again from the chair. 'Come I make coffee, Peekay.'

'Marie will tell me how bad it was.'

Doc threw up his hands. 'Marie! Such a person! "Professor you must give your life to Jesus, there is not much time. You must choose between the eternal damnation of hellfire or the love of Jesus Christ." I think maybe I stay a little longer here, miss, I say to this Marie. I think she was quite a lot disappointed. Ja, I think so,' Doc said, chuckling as he poured a mug of strong black coffee for me, holding the coffee pot in both hands to stop himself shaking.

We sat on the verandah sipping our coffee in big tin mugs, Doc's only half-full so that he wouldn't spill it. He was up to all his tricks to hide his frailty. We said very little. I could see Doc was happy I was back and I felt I would give him strength. We talked about the crystal cave of Africa, which Doc now regarded as our greatest discovery.

'It is good we are together again, Peekay. On Christmas Day I will be eighty-seven years old.'

'Doc, you've got to live until I'm welterweight champion of the world; you've got to make it until you're at least ninety-four or five!'

Doc chuckled at the urgency in my voice and rose slowly from his chair. 'Come, I show you *Pachypodium namaquanum*. It grows so big, maybe we have the world champion here also.'

As we walked together into the cactus garden, Doc still tall and straight as *Pachypodium namaquanum* himself, there seemed to be a little more spring in his step. 'Next week we will go into the mountains, Peekay, it has been too long.'

We did, mostly skirting the foothills and taking the easy paths, but Doc seemed to gain strength and was much better by the time I returned to school in mid-January.

TWENTY-ONE

Nineteen-forty-eight was a great year in South Africa's history. Princess Elizabeth had recently toured and we'd all stood beside the road and waved flags, and caught a glimpse of our future Queen as she rode past in a long, black, open Rolls-Royce.

It was the year South Africa got white bread, an event which excited a lot more people than catching a glimpse of the future Queen of England.

History will tell of how the election of the Nationalist Party, who still hold power in South Africa forty years later, was the turning point when the Afrikaner once again became the dominant force in the country. History is bound to treat this event with great pontification, showing how the struggle between the two white tribes of Africa reached its climax. In fact the turning point came, not because of an ideological clash between white and white, but because the Nationalists promised to bring back white bread to replace the healthier wholewheat loaf which had been introduced during the war. An already overfed white minority elected to vote on its stomach. Within a week of being elected, the Nationalists kept their promise and white South Africans derived great satisfaction from knowing that for once they had a new government which kept its word. Meanwhile, the black South Africans prepared to bend their backs to the sjambok and for the invention of a new game where they voluntarily fell on their heads from the third storey of police headquarters to the pavement below. It was curious that the whites, renowned for their sporting prowess, never learned how to play this game and there isn't a single instance of a white South African becoming proficient at it. Nobody ever got their Springbok blazer for this new national game, even though a lot of very good heads played it with great courage.

Hymie, in a grim pun, said the election of the Nationalists to power was one of the crummiest moments in the history of any people.

Nineteen-forty-eight was the year South Africa lost all hope of joining the brotherhood of man. Yet the black man held his humiliation and his anger at bay. It was not until 1952, four years later, that Chief Lutuli of the African Congress and his counterpart, Dr Monty Naicker of the Indian Congress, led the black and coloured people in the first defiance campaign where the words, 'Mayibuye Afrika!' became the cry of the black man asking for an equal share of justice and dignity for himself and his family.

Private schools have a habit of carrying on regardless, oblivious of social or political change. Had it not been for a boxing incident which led to the establishment of a Saturday night school for Africans, the Prince of Wales School would certainly have remained smugly wrapped in its cocoon of privilege and white supremacy.

The incident happened during the ten-day Easter break in 1949. Hymie's parents decided to spend the Jewish Passover with relatives in Durban. Hymie elected to stay home and invited me to spend the short holidays with him. I wrote to Mrs Boxall who wrote back to say Doc was well, so I agreed. The cook and the rest of the staff would take care of us and one of the chauffeurs would drive us the forty miles from Pretoria to Johannesburg every day to work out in Solly Goldman's gym.

Solly protested but we insisted he be paid extra for the holidays. Hymie's entrepreneurial sense extended to all things. He'd go to Barclays Bank in Yeoville on Saturday morning and demand a brand new five-pound note. Keeping it unfolded he'd place it beside the week's entry in a large leather-bound ledger. On Sunday morning, after I'd worked out we'd go into Solly's ramshackle office and Hymie would open the ledger where he had written in his neat, precise hand: *Paid to S. Goldman five pounds for services rendered*. He would make Solly sign the ledger and remove the five-pound note from the page. Then they'd shake hands solemnly like a couple of little old men, whereupon Solly would get his revenge by stuffing the pristine five-pound note carelessly into the back pocket of his dirty grey flannels.

Solly was a very natty street dresser but in the gym he always wore a sweatshirt and the same old grey flannels, tied around the waist with a frayed brown striped tie.

'Why do you go to all that trouble when he just shoves it into his back pocket?' I once asked Hymie.

'So he'll stick it carelessly into his back pocket. Every week my stupid ritual and his defiance reminds him not to take us for granted. Every time he sticks it into his back pocket like that I know he won't.'

On the third day of the Easter holidays Solly asked whether he could see Hymie and me in his office. He pointed to two old cane upright chairs and, pushing a pile of papers out of the way, sat on the corner of a desk covered to a depth of six inches in evenly distributed paper. In addition to boxing bills, unopened letters and general paper clutter, there was a bronze cup about ten inches high green with verdigris, a telephone and a large desk blotter added to the mess. The telephone sat on top of the desk blotter which was covered with coffee rings and hundreds of names and numbers. If anyone had ever replaced the top layer of blotting paper Solly's gym would have ground to a halt.

'You've had an offer of a fight for Peekay in Sophiatown next Saturday night. It's not my decision, mind, but it can't do the lad no 'arm.'

'Sophiatown! You mean the black township?'

'Yeah, I'll admit it's a bit unusual; it's a young black bantam who's just turned pro.'

'Solly, are you crazy? Peekay's an amateur, he can't fight a pro!'

'The black kid's not from up here, he isn't registered in the Transvaal yet. Technically he's an amateur here. Anyway, if the fight takes place in a native township, who the hell's going to know?'

'You should know better than that, Solly.'

Ignoring Hymie's remark, Solly appealed directly to me, 'This fight would do you a lot of good, sharpen you up nicely for the South African Schools Championships an' all.'

'Christ, Solly, you're off your rocker!' Hymie continued. 'You find a professional bantamweight, probably in his twenties, and you want to put him against Peekay who's fifteen years old?'

'That's just the point, my son. Peekay wouldn't be mismatched, the black kid is only just sixteen. Three professional fights. Would I mismatch Peekay? Don't insult my intelligence.'

'Hey, hang on, wait a minute both of you.' I turned to Solly, 'There's more to this isn't there? First we're fighting a black man in a black township, that's not allowed for a start; then an amateur is fighting a pro . . .'

'An unregistered pro,' Solly interjected.

'You haven't answered my question, Solly,' I repeated.

'It's not what you're thinking, Peekay, there's no money in it; there would be no purse for the fight.'

'What about the book?' Hymie asked.

'No betting niver, Gawd's onna!' Solly folded his hands on the desk in front of him and stared down at the untidy blotter.

'We're waiting, Solly,' Hymie said.

'It's Nguni, he wants the fight . . . Mr Nguni.'

'Who's he when he's at home?' I asked.

'He's a black fight promoter. Owns the game in the black townships.'

'So what's that to us?' I asked.

Solly looked up at me. 'He reckons if 'e was to match you with this Mandoma bloke it would be a t'riffic fight, that's all.'

'If you'll come clean with the real reason you want this fight we could discuss it. What is it, Solly?' I asked again.

Solly threw his hands up. 'Okay, it's business. Mr Nguni brings in the blacks, I train 'em, we share in the action. When you've got fifteen per cent of fifty black fighters on the black township circuit it's a nice little earner. I don't honestly know why 'e wants this fight. I admit it don't make a lotta sense.'

Hymie spoke as though he was thinking aloud. 'The black guy is squeezing you and now you're putting the hard word on us. I can understand that. But even if he is making book, and you say he isn't, that's not a big enough reason. He could lose his boxing promoter's licence if he got caught.'

'Hymie's right, Solly. There has to be a better reason. Nguni is either a fool or he's taking an enormous risk for a reason we don't know about. Either way, we wouldn't want to get involved. By the way this Mandoma, is he a Zulu? I had a nanny named Mandoma.'

'Buggered if I know; until they earn me a quid they're just black monkeys wearing boxing gloves,' Solly said absently.

Hymie's chauffeur was waiting in the Buick which was parked on a vacant lot a block away. As we walked to the car Hymie kept shaking his head. 'I don't get it; this Nguni guy would have to be crazy to take the risk of putting on a fight between a nigger pro and an amateur white guy in a black township. The cops would have him on about ten counts. I mean what's the angle? A fifteen-year-old schoolboy boxer and a sixteen-year-old black bantamweight is not exactly big time, even in a black township.'

'You haven't figured it out have you?' I said quietly.

'No, not yet, but I will.'

'Don't bother, it's got something to do with the people.'

Hymie spun around and grabbed me, 'You're right, Peekay. The Tadpole Angel!'

We turned into the vacant lot to find the Buick shining like a great black beetle among the cut down forty-four gallon drums half filled with solid tar, piles of bricks and the accumulated debris that seems to furnish vacant city blocks. The chauffeur was talking with a tall, well-dressed African and stepped forward as he saw us approaching.

'Well, we're going to know what the scam is in about thirty seconds. Look who's here, Hymie.' The tall black man straightened slightly as we came up. He was the tall African who always led the people in the chant to the Tadpole Angel.

'This man he want speak you, baas,' the chauffeur said to me.

'I see you,' I said in Zulu to the African who towered above me.

'I see you, Inkosi,' he replied and shook my extended hand lightly, barely touching it. Politeness required that we talk about other things before coming to the reason he wanted to speak to me. This is the Zulu way.

'The weather has been hot and the rains have not come; where I come from the crops will be thirsty.'

'It is so also in my place; the herd boys will need to drive the cattle far from the kraal to find grazing and the river will be dry but for a few water-holes.'

'What's he saying?' Hymie chipped in.

'Nothing yet, we're still talking about the weather.'

'Your kraal is a far place from here?'

'Many, many miles, Inkosi, my kraal is near Ulundi in Zululand.' The royal homesteads of three out of the four great Zulu kings, Dingane, Mpande and Cetshwayo, had been near Ulundi and the chances were that the tall man in front of me was a high-born Zulu.

'It is a long way from your wives and children; it is not good to be away from them.'

'It is the custom, Inkosi. For the white man's pound the black man must leave his family. These are hard times and I have few cattle and land.'

The time had come to introduce myself. 'I am Peekay,' I said softly, extending my hand for a second time.

'I know this, Inkosi. I am Nguni.' We shook hands a second time; this time first in the conventional manner and then by slipping the hand over the corresponding thumb to grip it in a kind of salute which is a traditional African handshake.

'I see you, Nguni.'

'I see you, Peekay.' It was audacious of Nguni to call me by my name but I didn't mind. I felt as though he had known me a long time anyway.

'Is it about the business of the boxing in Sophiatown?'

'It is so,' Nguni confirmed softly.

'Can we speak in English so my friend can share this talk?'

Nguni laughed, showing a brilliant smile. 'My English she is not so good,' he said in English.

Nguni's English turned out to be very good and Hymie seemed relieved that he could share in the conversation.

'It's about the Sophiatown business,' I said to him.

'Ask him, no wait on, I'll ask him myself . . .'

'Hymie, this is Mr Nguni,' I turned to Nguni. 'This is my best friend, Hymie Levy.'

'How do you do,' Nguni said to Hymie, instinctively not extending his hand but bowing his head slightly instead.

'Howzit!' Hymie said, not yet used to the idea of meeting a black man on equal terms. 'Why did you ask Mr Goldman if you could arrange a fight with Peekay?'

Nguni looked surprised. 'It is always so in boxing, to ask the trainer?'

'I'm the manager, it is me you have to ask.'

Nguni threw back his head and laughed. 'We knew this thing, but also if your trainer he say this thing cannot happen I do not think you will listen?'

'What did you offer him to make him agree?'

'It is not necessary; he has boxing business same like me.'

'How many boxers have you got, Mr Nguni?'

'All,' Nguni replied simply.

'You're not bullshitting me, you control all township boxers?'

Nguni turned to me and said in Zulu, 'Your friend has no respect, Inkosi.'

'I apologise for him, Nguni. He acts only like a white man from the city.' I turned to Hymie. 'Turn it up.'

Hymie shook his head. 'Sorry, Mr Nguni, no hard feelings hey? This fight you want . . . it's just that it doesn't bloody well make sense.'

Nguni turned to me and spoke in Zulu. 'I will have to explain it in Zulu; this man I think he does not understand the ways of the people.'

'Mr Nguni's going to explain the reason to me in Zulu, it's evidently pretty complicated,' I said to Hymie.

'You are Onoshobishobi Ingelosi,' Nguni began, 'this is very powerful among the people. The people see you box only against the Boer and always you are winning also. The people think you are a great chief of their tribe, the Sotho think this, the Shangaan think this, the Zulu also, all the people,' he paused, 'I think this also. It is witnessed that you can make the stars fall from the heavens.'

'It is not true, Nguni. I am not a chief of the people,' I said quickly.

'Who is to say what is true and what is not true. The people know these things; it is not for you to say, Inkosi.'

'It's about the Tadpole Angel, we were right,' I said to Hymie.

'There is a woman who has thrown the bones and made a fire to read the smoke,' Nguni said suddenly. 'The bones say Onoshobishobi Ingelosi who is a chief must fight him who is also a chief among the people.'

'A witchdoctor? She said this?'

'This is so, Inkosi.'

'This chief. Who is this chief I must fight?'

'He is the great great grandson of Cetshwayo.'

'Pssh! Many such Zulus exist. Cetshwayo has surely many, many great great grandsons.'

'He is the one,' Nguni said quietly. The Zulus do not inherit titles but it is known who has the blood. 'One day he will be a chief.'

'Why is it necessary to fight this person who will one day be a chief?'

'The people must see if the spirit is still with you. You are a man now; the people knew the spirit of a great chief was in the small one, but now they must know if it is still in the man.'

'You mean if I lose to him who will be a chief, then I will no longer be Onoshobishobi Ingelosi?'

'This is so, Inkosi. The woman says this is in the bones and in the smoke.'

'Then I will lose,' I said suddenly. 'That way the legend will be dead.'

Nguni shrugged his shoulders. 'It is not for me to say, Inkosi. You will only lose if you are not Onoshobishobi Ingelosi.'

'But if you can arrange the fight it will be good for you as a promoter?'

Nguni looked down at the palms of his open hands which were almost yellow, the colour of Sunlight soap. 'This is true but it is expected I should do this thing. Have I not led the people to all your fights?'

'This is true, you are the one,' I said, ashamed of myself.

'Then you will fight?'

'First we must talk to Hymie, he is my brother in this matter.'

'I understand, it is right that it should be so.'

Hymie was clearly impatient to get a translation and when I told him what had been said he shook his head. 'Christ, it's witchcraft, Peekay. This is 1949!'

'Ja, I know, but it might as well be 1849. Some things don't change.'

'So what do we do?' he asked.

'We fight, we have no choice.'

'I don't understand? Why?'

'It's difficult for you, but the people believe in the Tadpole Angel. I've never said this before, but it's a symbol, a symbol of hope. There is a story amongst all the tribes that a chief will rise who is not of them but who will unite them against the oppressors.'

'It is so, Mr Levy,' Nguni said.

'And this is the test to see if you're kosher?'

I laughed despite myself. 'Hymie, I didn't start this, it just happened. I don't want it any more than you. If the young Zulu chief Mandoma gives me a hiding, it's all over. But I can't walk away without the fight; that would make a fool of the people all these years. I couldn't do that.'

'What a shit of a possie to be in, but it's not a good enough reason to throw the fight.'

'You know me better than that, Hymie.' I turned to Nguni and offered him my hand, 'Mr Nguni, tell the people I will fight this one who will be a chief.'

'I will tell the people,' he said.

I set about preparing for the fight with Mandoma the Zulu bantamweight with all the vigour and purpose I could command. While I longed to be rid of the concept involving the Tadpole Angel it was quite impossible for me to bring myself to the point where I would throw the fight. I had steeled myself to win so often that, in my mind, a single loss in the ring would have meant that I would not become the welterweight champion of the world. A childish concept perhaps, but nonetheless one which was bound with steel wire through my resolve. I had even taught myself never to consider the consequences of losing a fight. Too much cross-referencing of consequence robs the will of its single-minded concentration to win. While this fanatical resolve never to be beaten may have been a sign of immaturity, the sophistication I brought to the task of winning I was to see adopted by sports psychiatrists throughout the world in later years. The mental exercises adopted, first behind the Iron Curtain and then worldwide, in an attempt to win that endless cold war called the Olympic Games or any of the other master race events, were all familiar to me.

The greatest difficulty confronting me with the Mandoma fight was information. We knew nothing about the Zulu bantamweight. I always felt awkward going into a fight with an unknown opponent. It was like entering a dark room having been told to beware of the trap doors. If you know everything there is to know about an opponent your mind will do the fighting for you, triggering the body mechanism to do the things it needs to do a fraction faster. It is this fraction that makes for a winner.

The power of one is above all things the power to believe in yourself, often well beyond any latent ability you may have previously demonstrated. The mind is the athlete; the body is simply the means it uses to run faster or longer, jump higher, shoot straighter, kick better, swim harder, hit further or box better. Hoppie's dictum to me: 'First with the head and then with heart' was more than simply mixing brains with guts. It meant thinking well beyond the powers of normal concentration and then daring your courage to follow your thoughts.

Saturday arrived. The fight was to take place in a ring set up in an African school soccer field in Sophiatown. We arrived about four-thirty on the outskirts where Mr Nguni was waiting for us.

The roads were dusty and it had been a hot day. Dust clung to the whitewashed walls of shanties and shops and everywhere there were advertising signs, for Gold Seal Cooking Lard, Blue Light Paraffin, Primus Stoves, Drum Tobacco and Sunlight Soap. There were a few trucks on the road and we saw one native taxi and several buses crowded to the point of bulging, though hundreds of people were on bicycles. The chauffeur kept an almost constant hand on the horn, which only seemed to add to the sense of excitement. As we drew closer to the school, people were lining the dusty narrow streets which seemed to weave haphazardly in among shanties built from every conceivable kind of material. Mr Nguni requested I turn my window down so the people could see me. Blushing, I complied. 'You are very famous in this place, Peekay. The people have come for many, many miles to see you.'

'Why are they all women and children?' Hymie asked.

'It is the men who will see the fight. The women they have come to see the Onoshobishobi Ingelosi.'

'Christ, I had no idea. You're more famous than Johnny Ralph, Peekay.' Johnny Ralph was the reigning heavyweight champion of South Africa and a household name among whites.

Mr Nguni laughed. 'Johnny Ralph, they do not know who is this boxer in Sophiatown.'

'Mr Nguni,' I said, 'you must tell the people I am not a chief. I have no power. You must tell them that the Onoshobishobi Ingelosi is only a name, a name I was given at the prison in Barberton. It was for nothing.'

Mr Nguni turned to me in the back seat. He was clearly shocked. 'I cannot do this thing, Inkosi. It is not for me to say who is Onoshobishobi Ingelosi. Tonight we will see, we cannot change this thing, it is in the bones and in the smoke.' He turned back to the chauffeur to give a direction.

'Shit! He believes it himself,' Hymie said out of the corner of his mouth.

We turned into the school grounds and were met by a sea of Africans. The Buick was forced to inch its way through the crowd. It was an hour and a half before the fight and the soccer ground was totally full, with only a narrow aisle leading to the ring in the centre. There must have been ten thousand spectators with more pouring through the school gates.

'I thought you said it would be a fight in a school,' Hymie said to Mr Nguni. 'I thought you meant a school hall or something. The whole of Africa has come to see the bloody fight! What if there's trouble, a riot or something?'

'No, no! No trouble here, Mr Levy. The woman, she will speak to the people.'

'You mean the witchdoctor?' I asked.

'It is she, Peekay, she will speak to the people.'

Hymie grinned nervously, 'It's got to be the first time a witch-doctor has ever announced a fight. Are you sure you've told me everything there is to know about you, Peekay?'

I grabbed him by the shirtfront, 'Don't *you* start now!'

We were taken to a shower block to change. Solly Goldman was waiting for us. 'They're doing it kosher orright; they've got Natkin Patel, the Indian referee from Durban to handle the fight. Blimey! 'Ave you seen the crowd?'

I changed and we walked along to the school hall for the weigh-in. Hymie looked at the scales; they'd been borrowed from a local trader and were the kind on which bags of mealie meal are usually weighed. 'What's the bloody difference; we're going to fight him anyway, even if he's over the limit,' Hymie said.

'It is very important, Mr Levy. The people must know everything is correct,' Mr Nguni said.

Standing in the middle of the school hall beside the scales were a dozen or so Africans all neatly dressed in suits and ties. Though the suit parts were not always of the same parentage, they were clean and pressed. Standing to one side was Gideon Mandoma, the Zulu bantamweight I was to fight.

I broke away from Solly and Hymie, and walked over to him and extended my hand. 'I see you, Gideon Mandoma,' I said in Zulu.

Gideon Mandoma took my hand, barely shaking it. He did not look up as he replied, 'I see you, Peekay.'

'I hear you come from the Tugela River Valley. It is where my nanny came from when I was a small infant; her name was Mary Mandoma, was she from the same chief's kraal perhaps?'

Gideon Mandoma looked up at me, his eyes wide, a shocked expression on his face. 'The one you are asking about is my mother. She is dead now five years.' He pointed a finger at me. 'You are the one of the night water?'

It was my turn to be shocked. I stood in front of the Zulu fighter completely stunned. I was going to fight Nanny's son, the infant she had had to leave to look after me. It was I who had stolen the milk from her breasts when she had been hired to be first my wet nurse and then my nanny.

Gideon was the first to recover. 'They say you are a chief, but must prove you have the spirit of Onoshobishobi Ingelosi. I know I am a chief and have the spirit of Cetshwayo and before that of Mpande, Dingane and even of Shaka the king of all the kings.' His eyes grew suddenly hard. He had waited a long time and now he would fight the one who had taken his mother from him so that he had not known her until he was six years old. It was not meant to be like this, but for him there was now an added reason to win. To the Zulu there is no such thing as coincidence. I knew this would be a certain and powerful sign for him. Gideon Mandoma had a reason greater than my own to win. For the first time in my boxing career I was afraid. I knew Mandoma could beat me.

We weighed in, in front of Solly, Mr Nguni, Natkin Patel the Indian referee and the other Africans. Both of us made it into the bantamweight limit, though I had five pounds to spare and Gideon was right on the limit.

The sun was setting as we walked out to the ring and already the air smelt of wood smoke and coal fires. It was still bloody hot and I'd been drinking water all day. I wondered about Mandoma; if he'd been right on the limit he'd have stayed off liquids, and we were fighting a six rounder, my first ever. It was the compromise Solly had reached with Mr Nguni, the difference between the three rounds of an amateur fight and the ten of a professional. It struck me that if I could keep him moving around the ring, the black fighter might just dehydrate enough to weaken in the last two rounds.

An old woman wearing a tired looking fur coat over a shapeless dress was haranguing the crowd from the ring. Her high-pitched voice carried to where we were standing on the steps of the school building. As she came to the end of her talk the crowd responded in thunderous applause. Two men entered the ring and lifted her, and two others standing outside the ring took her from them.

'It is time. We must go now, please,' Mr Nguni said, and he led us down the narrow human corridor to the ring, following a rubber electrical cord which connected with a microphone. Gideon Mandoma and his seconds had preceded us by a few yards and the whole football field thundered to the roar of the crowd. We entered the ring almost together, though from opposite sides, and the human roar increased. Hymie and Solly were my seconds and Hymie moved over to the black fighter's corner to check the glove-up, while a large Zulu in a mismatched suit with the jacket straining at its single brown button came over to do the same for us. I could feel the sweat running down from my armpits as Solly taped my hands and gloved me up.

Mr Nguni held his arms up and slowly the crowd grew silent. The microphone on a stand had been lifted into the ring and his voice echoed around the field as he addressed the crowd. First he introduced the referee, pointing out that he was an Indian who had come from Durban especially for the fight. The point of his neutrality was not lost on the crowd who gave Natkin Patel a big hand.

Mr Nguni then told the crowd that they all knew why this fight had been arranged. It was not for him to talk about it any more. The talking would now be between the two spirits and the stronger would win, and the people would know what they could think. The crowd was completely hushed as he spoke. He then introduced Gideon Mandoma who, arms held high, moved to the centre of the ring to huge applause. Mr Nguni held his hands up for silence and then asked the crowd to sing 'Nkosi Sikelel' i Afrika', the African national anthem.

Ten thousand voices sang in perfect harmony and I shall forever remember the beauty of the moment. The yearning and love Africans put into this anthem is a hugely emotional experience. I was hard put to keep my concentration. Gideon Mandoma had the perfect reason to win the fight and now had been given the greatest inspiration any boxer ever had.

I was having trouble keeping the steel trap in my mind closed. Images of Nanny swept through my head. A sweet, dark woman who gave me unstintingly of her love, who never once mentioned the child torn from her when her breasts were still firm with milk. Gideon Mandoma had a right to hate me and hate is a good friend in a fight.

Next Mr Nguni called me to the centre of the ring and, to my surprise, the applause was just as thunderous. As I stood there he began the chant of the Tadpole Angel, his voice ringing out to the silent crowd. When it came time to respond with the chorus 'Onoshobishobi Ingelosi . . . shobi . . . shobi . . . Ingelosi', ten thousand voices rolled like thunder. I stood in the centre of the ring, the tears rolling down my cheeks. It was perhaps the greatest single moment of my life. The people wanted to know. This was not a fight between black and white, it was a testing of the spirit, the spirit of Africa itself. Two kids, not fully grown, on a hot summer evening that smelt of wood smoke and sweat, would decide if there was hope for white and black and coloured, for the people of the great Southland.

'Mayibuye Afrika!' Mr Nguni shouted.

'Mayibuye Afrika! Afrika! Afrika! Come back, Africa! Come back, Africa!' the crowd thundered back.

Handing the microphone carefully through the ropes, Mr Nguni left the ring and Natkin Patel called us over. He had deep pock marks over his face which was almost precisely the colour of good curry, silly as that comparison sounds. His steel-grey hair was brylcreemed flat across his head, the parting absolutely straight with not a single hair crossing the shiny road of his scalp. He was dressed in a white shirt, cream flannels and white tackies, and looked more like a cricketer than a boxing referee. We both looked down at the ground as he spoke.

'You are listening to me, please. When I am shouting break you must break, at once. When a knockdown is coming I am counting to eight, then I wipe your gloves also and then you continue. No heads, no elbows, you must fight clean or, by golly, I am giving you penalty points. Good luck, boys.' He patted us both lightly on the shoulders. 'Shake hands; when the bell is sounding please to come out fighting.' Our gloves touched lightly though neither of us looked at the other.

I walked back to my corner and sat down. The bell rang. 'Go get him, Peekay,' I heard Hymie say as he pulled the stool out of my corner. I jumped up towards a blur of brown coming towards me across the ring.

Mandoma was coming at me fast, throwing everything. His punches landed on my arms and my gloves, he had come at me so quickly that he was able to keep me in my corner and I was forced to pull him into a clinch. The ref called for us to break as I managed to swing him around; the sun was in a perfect position, low and dying fast. He turned right into it, blinded for the split second it took for me to put a hard straight left bang on the nose. It was a good punch and a trickle of blood ran from one nostril. I would be bloody lucky to pull that stunt again, the sun wouldn't last more than another round and he'd probably wised up already. Mandoma was enormously aggressive, prepared to waste a dozen blows to break through my defence. Towards the end of the first round he caught me under the heart and I thought I was gone. He packed a left hook like a charging rhino. I was keeping him away by jabbing my left at him. They were all scoring shots but none of them were hurting him. The bastard was terribly strong. I spent the first round looking for bad habits, but apart from the fact that he was throwing too much leather it was going to be difficult to fight him on the backfoot. The bell went for the end of round one and already I was sweating profusely.

'Take a look at Mandoma, he's leaking,' Hymie said.

'Christ he hits hard, I'm going to have to keep him moving, keep him off balance.'

'Only for the first four rounds. Look at him.' Hymie was right; Mandoma was in a lather of sweat and with the sun so low it seemed even hotter than before.

'Watch and see if he drinks in round four,' I said to Solly as the bell went for round two.

'Just box him, my son, keep him moving, coming to you,' Solly said quietly.

Mandoma came at me just as hard in the second round, and while I took most of his punches on the gloves and arms, I realised that if he kept it up like this he'd hurt my arms and weaken me that way. I needed to make him miss more but he was fast as blazes and I had all my work cut out staying out of his way. I landed enough good punches to be ahead on points at the end of the second round, but there wasn't much in it and I was using every bit of ringcraft I knew to stay out of trouble.

We came out for the third and again he came at me with the leading hand and crossed over with a right hook that caught me on the side of the jaw. Quite suddenly I was on the canvas, sprawling on my back. I could see two of Mandoma as he retired to the neutral corner and then the ref began to count. I knew I'd been hit hard but felt nothing; my head was ringing and I was using all my concentration to hear the count. At six my eyes suddenly cleared and at eight I was back on my feet. It had been a beautiful punch and I knew I couldn't take too many others like it and survive. Patel wiped my gloves and made me count the three fingers he held up to me, and then six. It was all valuable time and my head had stopped ringing. Finally, he told us to box on.

Mandoma was after blood and came in too fast and carelessly. This alone saved me. If he'd waited to get set for another big punch he would have taken me. He wanted the knockout and his eyes were telegraphing his punches. Halfway through the round I was feeling strong again and I began to work to the old plan. Ignoring his head I went for the body, under the heart, in the soft area under the rib cage and into the solar plexus. He'd throw a wild left hook or a right uppercut and I'd follow in with two or three hard blows to the spot. Nothing fancy, but I could feel my knuckles digging deep. If I could stay away from the big punch and if he kept sending me a letter every time he prepared to throw a punch, I'd eventually get him. I'd been in against fighters most of my life. Mandoma had a bigger punch than any I'd been in the ring with before and he was bloody fast. But I thought he was becoming predictable as most fighters do.

Had it been the usual three round fight the decision may well have gone to Mandoma. By the fourth round he had started to slow down. He'd been chasing me for three rounds and throwing a lot of leather; the heat had to get to him. But he hadn't taken water, just rinsing and spitting. So I kept going low and hard, and toward the end of the fourth round I heard him grunt as I got three solid punches home. It was beginning to go like clockwork. Mandoma pulled me into a clinch and on the break hit me with a beautiful left lead. I thought I'd run into a train. I went down, my arse actually bouncing on the canvas. I couldn't believe it; I shook my head but it wouldn't clear. At the count of eight I was only just able to stand. Mandoma had me; one half-decent punch and I was history.

The ref asked me if I was allright and when I nodded he wiped my gloves and told me to box on, this time not asking for a concussion count. I knew I had to hang on until the end of the round. Patel wouldn't stand for more than two knockdowns. That is, if I could have gotten up a third time. 'Dance, klein baas, your feet, you must dance, only your feet can keep you out of trouble,' I could hear Geel Piet clear as anything. To my enormous relief the bell went for the end of the fourth.

'He's got a huge punch in both hands, lad, but he's slowing. I want you to box him close so he can't put a big one in; keep working at his body, he has to be feeling it.'

'You could have fooled me,' I panted. But my strength was coming back. I rinsed and spat, the water cool and delicious to my mouth.

'Christ, he's taking water!' Hymie said. 'The bastard's taking water!'

The first twenty seconds of the fifth round were the hardest yet. Mandoma threw everything at me, but I wove and ducked, back-pedalled and kept out of the way. He threw a left lead and I crossed over with a right, catching him under the eye and opening it up. His nose was still bleeding and while I hadn't hit him much in the head, I'd kept the nose bleeding with a regular jab right on the button. Nothing influences a referee more than a liberal splash of blood. Mandoma threw another left hook, telegraphing it from a yard away, and I moved in and had him on the ropes with an orthodox straight left followed by a straight right to the head. Two copybook punches which, when timed correctly, carry a lot of zap.

The black fighter's hands came up to defend his head, and I moved in close as his gut area opened up and in went a Geel Piet eight, right where the water he had swallowed would be. I knew the pain and the nausea would be terrible and he gave a loud gasp as the flurry of punches went home, and tried to chop my gloves away with his own. I was ready with a right hook which caught him flush on the jaw, coming up with all my strength behind it. While his punches had bounced me off my feet, mine bounced him hard against the ropes and then he sank to his knees, both his gloves resting on the canvas. Blood from his nose dripped onto the grey canvas as I retired to a neutral corner.

At eight he rose, but I could see he felt bad and I moved in and began to pick him off. I could have come in swinging and tried to finish him, but a fighter like Mandoma digs deep for his courage and can always find that one last big punch. I was almost certain that he was a spent force and wouldn't recover between rounds fast enough. I'd get him in the final round. The bell went and I got to my corner to be met by Hymie and Solly, both shouting at me.

'Ferchrissake, why didn't you finish him off,' Hymie screamed. 'His gut, his gut is gone; you could have taken him, now he's got bleedin' time to recover,' Solly said.

'He only needs one more big punch and he can take me out,' I protested. I was following a Geel Piet plan and not a Solly Goldman plan. Geel Piet would have wanted me to box him off his feet, not punch him. 'You must always go safety first, klein baas, box, box, box, never fight.'

Solly regained his composure. 'You're right, son. I'm glad one of us is still thinking.' Whether he believed it or not, he knew he had to restore my concentration and was aware that in his excitement he'd acted foolishly.

The bell went for the final round. Mandoma, desperate for strength, had taken water again. For the first minute of the last round he came hard, but his timing was out and he wasn't putting his punches together properly. I stayed away from him, flicking lightly at his cut eye, keeping the blood coming, waiting for the chance to move in. He hit me with a right cross which, had it come earlier in the fight, would have put me down. Now it lacked authority. It was time to move in. I worked him into his own corner and went to work under his heart. Three solid punches before he managed to pull me into a clinch. He was too spent to stay out of trouble. After each break I'd move him back into a corner and set to work on his body. I couldn't believe he could still be standing. I'd never hit anyone as often or as hard. But the bastard wouldn't go down. I had to put him on the canvas again. I started to hit the black fighter hard on the nose, and his gloves went up and opened him up down below. The Geel Piet eight became the Solly Goldman thirteen, the first time I had ever got a thirteen combination together perfectly. Mandoma gave a sort of a gurgle and then a sigh and fell. He was totally exhausted; his eyes were open looking at me but his body could no longer respond and he was unable to get his head off the canvas. He'd been boxed off his feet. His heart hadn't died; it just couldn't hold him up on its own. Mandoma was the greatest natural fighter I had ever seen.

I had never been as exhausted in my life. Not only had I never boxed six rounds before, I'd never taken as much punishment. I tried to walk with dignity to the neutral corner as Natkin Patel started to count Mandoma out.

For the first time in the fight I heard the crowd, who were going absolutely wild.

'Onoshobishobi . . . shobi . . . shobi . . . Ingelosi!' the chorus rolled like thunder across the football field. On and on it went until the microphone was pushed back into the ring and Gideon Mandoma's seconds had helped him to his corner. I walked over to see if he was all right and to shake his hand.

'You are the great chief, you are him who is Onoshobishobi Ingelosi,' Mandoma said, and standing on still trembling legs he held up my hand. The crowd went wild.

'It is you who are a chief, your spirit is still with you; we will be brothers, Gideon Mandoma.'

'I see you, Peekay. We have taken the milk from the same mother's breast, we are brothers.' I held up his hand and the crowd roared their applause.

Mr Nguni was back at the microphone and after some trouble got the crowd to quieten down. I had returned to my corner and was sitting on the pot while Solly was rubbing me down and Hymie held a fresh towel to drape over me.

'We have seen what we have seen. You must all go to your homes, tell the people that the spirit within the Onoshobishobi Ingelosi lives also in the man. You have seen it with your own eyes and it is so,' he said simply. He turned and called Gideon Mandoma and me over and we stood next to him with our arms around each other. 'We have seen the spirits fight, in this we are all brothers,' Mr Nguni said and the roar of the black crowd closed the proceedings.

I touched Gideon on the shoulder and returned to my corner. It was just beginning to move into darker twilight and the smell of wood smoke and coal fires came to me again. In the distance a train whistled, cutting through the hubbub of the departing crowd. All around us black faces were grinning and some would stretch out and touch me lightly as though I were a talisman. But most looked at me and I could see that they believed. The legend was cast deeper and would spread further. I wondered if it would ever end. I suddenly realised that every bone in my body felt as though it had been broken.

With my arm around Hymie's shoulders for support we walked through the corridor of black bodies on our way back to the school. Black hands touched me, wiping sweat from my body and wiping it onto their faces.

'There you are, what did I tell you, lads, didn't I say it would be a t'riffic fight?' Solly said as we entered the school. 'Blimey! Twice there I thought you was gone, my son. It's good to know you can take a punch. Lemme tell you, I never seen an amateur throw a perfect thirteen-punch combination before. It was worth comin' just for that.'

'Cut it out, Solly, can't you see Peekay's hurting?' Hymie cut in.

'Not as much as the swartzer, my boy,' Solly said.

When we got to the shower block I sat down and started to cry. It was as though I saw the years ahead. The pain in my body had somehow sharpened the focus of my mind. I saw South Africa. I saw what would come. Something had happened to me; Hymie was talking but it was as though his voice were in an echo chamber. No, not an echo chamber; in the crystal cave of Africa. His voice echoed across the tops of the rainforest, down the valley just as the barking baboons had done. 'I've found it, Doc. I've found the power of one!' Hymie's voice was saying. The cave about me was shining crystal, the crystal became my pain and the pain sharpened as the light grew more intense. My concentration focused down to a pinpoint. The sadness I felt was overwhelming; sadness for the great Southland. In the whiteness, in the light, was a sound, as if the light and the sound were one. It was the great drum and the voices of the people. They came together as an echo. 'Mayibuye Afrika! Afrika! Afrika!' Come back, Africa! Africa! Africa! My life, whatever it was to become, was bound to this thing; there was no escaping it, I was a part of the crystal cave of Africa. And in the pain and confusion I wept, I could see only destruction and confusion and the drum beat; boom, boom, boom, and the light began to fade and Doc entered the cave, his hair white as snow, tall as ever, 'You must try, Peekay. You must try. Absoloodle!'

Hymie put his arm around me. 'There's more to this Onoshobishobi Ingelosi than I know about, isn't there, Peekay?'

'Christ, I dunno. I just don't know,' I sobbed.

'Don't worry, Peekay, no one can hurt you. No bastard can hurt you while I'm alive!'

'Doc's dead!' I heard my voice saying as though it were totally divorced from my body.

That evening when we returned to Hymie's place in Pretoria there was a message to call Mrs Boxall.

'Peekay, we have sad news, the professor has disappeared! Gert, and all the warders not on duty, and half the men in town are in the hills looking for him, but he's been gone two days. Now they say there's little chance of finding him alive!' Her voice faltered and then broke as she began to sob. The line from Barberton was crackling, fading in and out, and Mrs Boxall's sobs grew and receded. 'Please come home, Peekay, please come quickly; you're sure to find him, you went to so many places together,' she wept.

Hymie forced me to sleep. 'We'll wake you at two a.m. and a chauffeur can drive you the two hundred miles to Barberton; you'll arrive by sun-up.'

I knew where to find Doc. I knew that somehow he had done the impossible and had reached the crystal cave of Africa. Doc would be Iying on the platform, his arms across his chest. In one hundred thousand years people would find the cave again and would climb up to the magic platform and they'd say, 'What a strange coincidence, that looks just like the shape of a man made of crystal. A very tall, thin man.' And then I cried myself to sleep.

TWENTY-TWO

No one, not even I, knew Doc's religion, but after a week where I had visited all our old haunts (except one) with various teams of men, it was decided that a church ceremony should take place. Marie came forward and claimed that Doc had found Christ while he was in hospital with pneumonia and my mother was ecstatic. Pastor Mulvery claimed the right to hold a burial service sans Doc's mortal remains. I didn't protest. Marie had convinced herself that Doc had said yes to Jesus and she had notched him up as one of her most important salvations. I don't think Doc would have minded too much; besides, his love for the great Southland was complete in the most beautiful eternity he could conceive of, not dust and ashes but a wonderful pagan burial that would make him a living part of his beloved Africa. His spirit would dwell in the crystal cave of Africa looking out across the rainforest down the misty valley and over distant mountains which smudged blue as a child's crayon drawing.

Doc's death left me completely numb. I went through the motions but it was as though I had lost my centre of gravity. Everything seemed topsy-turvy; people would speak to me but I wouldn't hear them. Their mouths opened like goldfish in a bowl, but nothing came out. Their movements seemed exaggerated as though by walking up to me they were growing bigger from the same spot, their feet not moving but their bodies just elasticising cartoon-like to where I stood. The pain was all inside, deep and dull, and I knew it was this that made me feel numb. I felt I would never be quite the same again, that I could never love as much again. I kept telling myself that I knew Doc was going to die, that Doc had been telling me himself for months, but I knew nothing about this sort of death. Death was violent and ugly like Granpa Chook and Geel Piet, or even macabre like Big Hettie. Death, as I had come to know it in Africa had no gently slipping awayness about it, no dignity. And so I felt Doc had cheated, he'd just gone, he'd disappeared, he had made death happen rather than have it happen. I felt cheated, even angry. Why hadn't he waited for me? Why hadn't he told me so that I could have taken him to the crystal cave? But secretly I knew that I couldn't have done it; I would have clung to the last thread of life in him. I also knew that he would have known this. But it didn't help the numbness. It didn't take away the need, the dull permanent ache under my heart on the exact spot where you work on another boxer till he runs out of steam. That was it precisely: the bell had gone but I couldn't find the strength and the will to come out for the next round on my own.

Pastor Mulvery said a lot of things about it being the end of Doc's travail and his vale of tears. He had called Doc a great piano player and gardener. 'The Lord Jesus has given our beloved professor a garden in heaven filled with the fragrance of pansies and sweet peas where he can play his music for a choir of angels.'

The regulars in the congregation must have thought it was one of his better descriptions of the born-again hereafter and they peppered Pastor Mulvery's eulogy with 'Praise the Lord' and 'Blessed be His glorious name'. I heard it all, but it didn't make any sense; it had nothing to do with Doc. Absoloodle not.

'Oh, dear, oh goodness, dearie me. Our dear, dear professor would most certainly have chosen eternal hellfire in preference to an eternity spent in a bed of pansies and sweet peas, playing for a choir of angels,' said Mrs Boxall, having been exposed to Pastor Mulvery and the workings of the Apostolic Faith Mission for the first time.

The aloe was in bloom on the hillside above the rose garden and early on the day of the service I had climbed to our rock and cried for a while until the sun came up over the valley. On the way down I gathered several candelabra of aloe blossom which I put in a large copper vase I found in the back room of the church. When I entered the church later to attend the funeral it had been removed and an arrangement of pink and orange gladioli had been put in its place.

Even old Mr Bornstein, wearing a hat throughout, attended the service with Miss Bornstein. Miss Bornstein's shiny lipstick and long red nails looked strangely out of place in a church which taught that make-up of any sort, except for face powder, was a sin. I once heard long painted nails described by a lady witnessing for the Lord as the devil's talons dripping with the blood of sinners. Miss Bornstein looked beautiful among the scrubbed, plain-faced women, with their greying hair pulled back and held by cheap celluloid clips, their hats stuck with sprigs of linen flowers, some small attempt at adornment. I could see them stealing glances at her, at her perfect complexion, magnificent shining, almost purple black hair, green eyes and brilliant sinful lips and nails. They would spit it all back in righteous vituperation when next they gaggled around a cup of tea to tell each other they had seen sin in the flesh, the devil himself sitting among them.

Outside the church after the service, as there was no Doc in a coffin to look solemn about, the regulars were able to congratulate Marie for her spectacular conversion. Even my mother got a bit of gratuitous praise for her original foresight in bringing Doc into focus as a potential candidate for salvation.

All the warders who knew Doc, including Captain Smit and the Kommandant, came to pay their respects. Afterwards Captain Smit invited me back to the prison where the boxing team was having a wake. This turned out to be a jolly affair, more like a braaivleis and singsong, and I tried hard to be cheerful, for I suspect it was held as a gesture and as a bit of a cheer-up for me. Doc would have approved much more of this than of the sanctimonious burial service.

Gert took me to one side. When I'd arrived back to help in the search for Doc, I'd taken over from him. He had barely slept for three days and had been exhausted. 'Tell me, man, how come we never found him? You know every place he went.'

'Ja, it's funny that, but you know Doc, Gert. He probably had a place in an old mine shaft that only he knew about, some place he found years ago before he met me.'

Gert looked at me directly. 'No man, no way. You and him was too close. I reckon you know but, ag man, you right, I wouldn't tell also if it was me.' Gert was a naturally quiet person who didn't miss much; he'd just been promoted to sergeant and everyone said he was going places.

Doc left everything he owned to me, including the Steinway. He left a small insurance policy worth about twenty pounds to Dee and Dum. My mother had the Steinway moved to the lounge at home where it practically filled the room so that the two chairs which matched the sofa had to be put on the back verandah. A jolly good idea because that's where everyone sat anyway. Except for church ladies and town people coming for fittings, we never had proper visitors of the kind that got sat uncomfortably in the front room, so the back stoep was perfect for the old ball and claw brocade chairs, which after forty years of being stuck in the parlour saw some real 'bottom work' at last.

At first I think my granpa was a bit hurt about the banished chairs. His beautiful wife, for whom the rose garden had been created, had originally bought the furniture. But by the time I was back for the holidays again one of the chairs was permanently claimed as his and had several small burn holes in the upholstery where bits of glowing tobacco ash had fallen from the bowl of his pipe to burn through the faded brocade.

Doc's cottage was well away from any other European houses on a small *koppie,* and his will read to me by young Mr Bornstein showed that he owned the whole of the small hill. I moved Dee and Dum in as caretakers, although it was really intended as their home. The tiny three-room cottage with lean-to kitchen was a veritable mansion after the small brick room next to the rose nursery which they had shared. They had both been terribly distressed at Doc's death. Doc had asked them to pack food for three days and not to speak to anyone about his departure. When he hadn't returned on the fourth day Dee had gone to see Mrs Boxall who had raised the alarm. True to her word, Dee had simply told Mrs Boxall that Doc hadn't returned from the hills the previous evening as his bed had not been slept in and the ash in the tiny potbelly stove was cold. They had both confessed to me about Doc requesting food for three days, which meant that when Mrs Boxall had called me, Doc had actually been gone four days. When I had known with absolute certainty after the fight with Gideon Mandoma that Doc was dead, he had been out three days. It would have taken him two days to reach the crystal cave of Africa, whereupon he would have rested and then, some time on the third day, climbed the cliff. Doc was a methodical man; he would have planned everything meticulously to the last ounce of his energy. Marie told me that while he was in hospital he had complained each night of being unable to sleep and they had given him a sleeping pill. Doc would never have taken a pill, which he termed 'putting bad chemicals in the blood'. I knew that he would now have the sleeping pills with him. Doc never did anything carelessly and he wasn't going to be any different in planning his death.

It was Dee and Dum keeping faith with Doc which prevented the search parties from going further into the hills. In one day a frail old man recovering from pneumonia could not have travelled far into the foothills, least of all across the Saddleback Range. I knew Doc better than that; he would have planned it, knowing his chances for success.

I waited until the day before I was due to return to school and the furore of Doc's death was beginning to die down a little so that I would be allowed to go into the hills alone. Telling my mother at supper the previous evening that I was going for a last ramble in memory of Doc, I left home before dawn. I knew there was still something Doc needed; if it had not been so he would have left some sort of message for me. Together with Dee and Dum, I searched the cottage and the cactus garden in vain. Doc wanted me to perform some last duty, I felt quite sure about this; and, in any case, I needed to perform some sort of ritual of my own to mark Doc's passing. I packed a can of sardines, a couple of oranges and filled my old school lunch tin with a tomato, two boiled eggs and a couple of leftover cold potatoes and, with a bottle of water and a torch, I set off. To avoid suspicion I didn't take rope as I was certain I could climb the cliff without it.

Pausing only at sunrise to drink and to eat a potato, by mid-morning I had arrived at our old campsite on the edge of the rainforest. Above me the cliff loomed, now suddenly meaning so much more to me. Doc, as I had expected, had used the site again. There had been no rain for the last ten days and the ash in the fire hole I'd dug was still fresh and powdery. To make certain, I went to the spot where I had buried our rubbish and dug it up. Sure enough a second bully beef tin and the wrapping from a packet of Bakers Pretty Polly Crackers had been added. Doc loved the dry, tasteless crackers and always bought the same brand.

Half an hour later I was standing on the shelf which led to the cave. At first there seemed to be no sign of Doc having been there and my heart beat furiously. What if Doc hadn't made it? What if he had fallen trying to scale the cliff and lay somewhere in the thick rainforest which grew at its base? I fought back the panic, for I knew I would have to find him and somehow get him up the cliff and into the cave and onto the platform. A task which would take me two days, if I could achieve it at all.

I also knew that if Doc lay in the crystal cave of Africa he would not have wanted me to enter. Doc was a man of great sensitivity and the idea of subjecting me to the sight of his corpse on the platform would be unthinkable. He would have left me instructions outside the cave, in daylight; that's where his message would be. I began to search the shelf inch by inch. Doc had trained me to observe and I knew he would expect me to make the kind of detailed examination of the shelf which would be beyond the casual searcher so that if he had hidden something it would not be apparent to any but a trained eye.

I searched for half an hour but the limestone shelf had been worn out of the cliff face by a hundred thousand years of wind, rain and water erosion, the hollowed-out shelf was smooth and regular and there were no cracks in the dolomitic rock. I began to doubt. Doc might have intended to leave me a message but been on the point of collapse when he finally made it up to the shelf, saving every ounce of strength for the task of reaching the platform.

And then I saw it. A dark stripe of some sort of mineral sediment, long since dry, had stained a small part of the shelf. I ran my hand over the stained rock and received a sudden sharp prick. I pulled my hand back and looked at it; a tiny drop of blood formed on my palm. Sticking out of the middle of the dark patch no more than an eighth of an inch, was the point of the blade of Doc's Joseph Rogers pocket knife.

Doc had discovered that the dark sedimented patch was softer than the rock surrounding it and he had gouged a hole into the centre of it using the pocket knife. He had then mixed the sand which came out of the hole with a little water from his water bottle and, first inserting the knife with the tip of the blade only just showing, he had repacked the granules of sand to mend invisibly where he had buried the knife.

It was typical of Doc; he trusted his training of me so much that he knew he could make the hiding place difficult for others to find, and that I would find it. I scraped the dirt away from the point of the blade and dislodged the small knife. Around its handle, tied with cotton thread, was a note.

The hole appeared deeper than I had first suspected, deeper and wider, and behind the knife was Doc's gold hunter. With the tip of the knife I pulled the fob chain out and then the beautiful old gold pocket watch. I stuffed the watch and chain into my trouser pocket and with clumsy, trembling hands picked at the cotton thread tying the note to the black bone handle of the knife.

It was a page torn from one of Doc's small field notepads and margin to margin from the top to the bottom of one side of the page were musical notes, minute in size but exact, a precisely written piece of music. I turned the page. In Doc's neat handwriting was a short note centred on the page.

My dear Peekay,

In all the world no man has such a friend as you. Last night is come some music to my head, when it is coming I know it is time for me to go. Maybe, who can say, it is the music for Africa? Maybe only it is my music to you? Not so good as Mozart, never like Mr Beethoven or like Mr Brahms, but maybe better than a Chopin nocturne. Such a little piece of music for such a long life. I am such a domkopf. But not such a domkopf that I don't let you be my friend. For this I am having eleven out of ten. I must go into the crystal cave of Africa now. You must not follow until it is your time also. Maybe in one hundred thousand years we will meet again.

Goodbye, Mr Schmarty Pantz welterweight champion of the world.

Your friend,
Doc

I had done my crying for Doc and the note gave me comfort. Doc was safe and where he wanted to be, and his secret would be kept forever. I entered the tunnel leading to the outer cave. Testing the rope handrail we'd built for Doc's entry to the cave the first time, I found it still strong. He would not have had a great deal of difficulty getting into the narrow entrance. It took me only a few minutes to work the steel hook out of the tunnel wall and to remove the rope.

I returned to the cliff shelf and removed the second spike and put the two spikes and the rope into my rucksack. In a very few years the small holes the spikes had made would be eroded from the rock face, leaving no trace of man. Only the baboons or an occasional leopard would visit the outer cave, but neither would enter the dark, damp inner crystal cave of Africa. Doc would be safe for the hundred thousand years it would take to turn him into crystal, forever a part of Africa.

I was home again just as the moon was rising over the valley. The pain, the deep dull pain under my heart had lifted. Sadness remained, but I was now proud that Doc had achieved what he wanted to do. And we would always be bound together; he was very much a part of me. He had found a small, frightened and confused little boy and had given him confidence and music and learning and a love for Africa, and taught me not to fear things. Now I didn't know where the boy began and Doc ended. I had been given all the gifts he had. Now that Doc was resting right I knew we could never be separated from each other.

The coffee pot left at four the next day to connect with the all-night sleeper from Kaapmuiden to Johannesburg. That last morning at home I walked into the front room and opened the Steinway and started to practise Doc's music, which I'd earlier transcribed onto three sheets of music manuscript. After I picked at the notes for an hour, the melody began to form. It was a nocturne with a recurring musical phrase running through it. Very beautiful, it was unmistakably African, with a sadness and yearning for something that seems to be in the music of all of the people. The musical phrasing and the recurring melody were somehow familiar, like something I'd heard in a dream or the dreamtime or which simply races unknown through your blood. And then I realised what it was. It was the chant to the Tadpole Angel.

I stopped bewildered. Doc had never heard the chant which had started only after I had gone to boarding school. I played the music again; it was no coincidence, the chant was clearly a part of the music, it ran through the nocturne repeating itself in a dozen variations but always there: clear, unmistakable, wild, beautiful. Onoshobishobi Ingelosi . . . shobi . . . shobi . . . Ingelosi, the piano notes enunciated as clearly as if the people themselves were singing it.

It was getting late and it was time to say my goodbyes to Mrs Boxall, old Mr Bornstein and Miss Bornstein. Gert had promised to pick me up and run us down to the station in the prison's new Chevy which meant my mother and my granpa didn't have to rely on Pastor Mulvery, whose anxious-to-escape front teeth and unctuous presence I found increasingly depressing, and I was glad that he wouldn't add to the awkwardness I always felt at departures.

I put Doc's music between the pages of a slim volume of poetry by Wilfred Owen which Mrs Boxall had given me. 'Not as soppy as Rupert Brooke, but a better war poet I feel sure,' she had said.

Leaving home with the knowledge that when I returned it would be to a place which no longer meant Doc, made this parting almost unbearably sad for me. My mother tried to chat brightly, but she wasn't much of a bright chatterer and my granpa just tapped and tamped and puffed and turned and looked up at the mountains and said, 'The cumulus nimbus is building up, could be a storm tonight, just as the Frensman are in loose bud.' Frensman was a deep red long-stemmed rose and unless the petals were still in tight bud the storm would damage them. Gert, who at the best of times didn't have too much small talk, added to my sense of foreboding and made the waiting for the coffee pot to pull out almost unbearably long. I put my hand into the pocket of a new pair of grey flannel slacks, made for me by old Mr Bornstein, and took out Doc's hunter. I was about to click it open when I was conscious of my stupidity and quickly slipped the beautiful old watch back into my pocket. My haste in doing so immediately pointed to my guilt. I thought I might have escaped detection but after a couple of minutes, when my mother had turned to talk to my granpa, Gert whispered, 'So you found him, hey? I'm blêrrie glad, Peekay.' I ignored his remark, pretending not to hear him, and I knew Gert would remain silent.

A whistle warned of our departure and the small crowd on the platform became animated, as happens when an over-extended farewell is suddenly terminated. It occurred in our group too, each of us secretly glad that the waiting was over. 'Look after yourself, son boy,' my mother said, offering the side of her powdered cheek.

'There's a good lad,' puff, puff, my granpa shook my hand. As I looked into his face I realised that his blue eyes had become a little rheumy and that the skin around his cheeks and mouth stretched tightly, as happens with thin men when they begin to grow old.

Gert gripped my hand in the traditional excessively firm Afrikaner manner. 'All the best, Peekay, see you in July, man.' He jumped into a boxing stance; it was a small physical joke to hide his awkwardness. 'Keep your hands up, you hear.' He grinned and leaned forward so that only I could hear, 'No more fighting Kaffirs you hear, their heads is too hard, man.'

The coffee pot gave a blast of steam whistle, loud enough to belong to a much bigger, more important train. The people in the third-class Blacks Only carriage yelled and screamed with delight, five or six heads and a dozen arms to each carriage window waving bandannas and generally making the most of the farewell occasion, as the little train slowly left the platform. I continued to wave until the train had passed the long bend which took the platform from sight. With a conscious sigh of relief I leaned back into the green leather seat. I knew I'd have the compartment to myself until Kaapmuiden, and I cherished the idea of being on my own. It had been a long week since I had fought Gideon Mandoma.

Hymie was full of news when we got back to school. He'd worked out a formal business arrangement with Mr Nguni and now there were twenty young black boxers training at Solly's gym, as well as three black boxing officials who would be trained in the handling of boxers and would eventually sit for their referee's tickets.

Gideon Mandoma and three other young fighters were separated from the other blacks to do their workouts with me on Wednesday afternoons and before church on Sunday mornings. Gideon soon became more than just a good sparring partner. He laughed a lot and had a quick wit which delighted me. His English wasn't strong and at first we mostly spoke in Zulu, until after a workout some three weeks into the term he patted me on the shoulder with his glove, 'No more Zulu. Peekay, your Zulu comes from my mother's breast; now my English must come from your fists. You must teach me English.' He propped and slowly stroked his hair in a backward movement the way Hymie would do it, lightly touching it as though preening in front of a mirror. 'I have one good English word from Hymie.' He mimicked the way Hymie spat words out: 'Cheeky bloody Kaffir!' Gideon threw back his head and laughed happily. 'This English I understand very good.'

It was then that I hit on the idea. 'We're going to start a school for Solly's black boxers,' I announced to Hymie on the tram back to school after training.

'Christ, Peekay, isn't that going a bit far? Educate the black bastards and before you know where you are they'll want to take over the country.'

'It's as much theirs as it is ours. More actually,' I said, surprised at his outburst.

'You're perfectly right, but can't we let them take a little longer to find out? Keep the buggers in the dark as long as possible?'

'Hymie, what are you saying? I thought you were a liberal thinker?'

Hymie laughed. 'First and foremost I'm a pragmatist but there's bound to be a quid in it somewhere, although I'm buggered if I can see where. How do you propose going about it; integrate the Prince of Wales School?'

'C'mon, Hymie, take this seriously. If we go to Singe 'n Burn and put it to him as two Renaissance men and give him a whole line of bullshit about liberalism blah, blah, blah, I'm sure he'll be in it. We could have the black school in one of the classrooms on a Saturday night.'

'Already I like it! One lesson a week shouldn't pose too much of a threat to white civilisation as we know it on the southern tip of Africa.'

'Well, what do you reckon?'

'Offhand I can't think of a way to make any money out of it but as Karl Marx, or was it Christ, said: "Man does not live by bread alone". Okay, whatever you say.'

'Great! Because you have to open the subject with Singe 'n Burn by telling him that as a Jew you know what it's like to be an oppressed people.'

Hymie thought for a moment. 'Fine, nothing to it, I simply go in and ask Singe 'n Burn to open a black school in this citadel of white privilege, pointing out to him that as an expertly oppressed person for roughly nineteen hundred years . . .'

'Good, I'll make an appointment to see him after school tomorrow.'

Singe 'n Burn proved more difficult than we had anticipated. He was not at all sure of the attitude the Nationalist government might take to one of the country's most famous English-speaking private schools becoming the cradle of black adult learning.

There were, of course, black schools and some very good ones. But most Africans left school before they reached high school and a great many more after only two or three years of the most basic education. Some, perhaps a majority, never made it to school at all. If, in later years, they wished to learn to read and write, then no adult school facilities existed for them.

We seemed to have reached a stalemate, with Singe 'n Burn promising to put the issue to the school governors, where it was almost certain to be defeated. Their idea of Christian gentlemen did not include the brotherhood of man, if it meant lowering the colour bar.

Our arguments had been sound but our politics naive. In South Africa, when a black skin is involved, politics and social justice have very little in common.

'We've been a couple of schmucks to think he'd buy it straight off like that; we're going to have to make the bastard feel guilty, it always works with a Renaissance man,' Hymie said. We were sitting in the prefects' common room which was seldom used by the other prefects after school and was a nice private place to talk or work.

'I thought we'd already made him feel guilty?'

'Guilty in the mind, intellectual guilt yes. But guilty so it hurts inside, that's different. Jews are expert at soul guilt. Let me illustrate what I mean. Until we fought in Sophiatown, the only black people I knew well were Mary, our cook, and Jefferson, the butler. And, of course, the various other nameless servants who pretended to work around the place. The afternoon of the fight was the first time I had ever been close to African people. I mean actually experienced them as people, not just servants or faithful family retainers, but as people with problems. I mean just like other ordinary people. I haven't told you before, but the effect was shattering. I found myself liking them. More than that, I understood for the very first time how the persecuted Jew must have felt. When they sang for you, not just for Gideon, that was understandable, but for you also, the generosity of spirit made me ashamed of my white skin. That's the sort of guilt I mean.'

'Christ, Hymie, you didn't tell me any of this.'

'So what's to tell? You can't tell it, you have to feel it. That's what Singe 'n Burn needs. He needs to feel not what he is denying but whom he is denying. We're going to introduce him to Gideon.'

'You had ten thousand Africans singing Sikelel' i Afrika to experience; do you think Gideon can convince him on his own? He's the only tone-deaf Zulu ever born.' It was true, Gideon had a singing voice like a rusty rasp on hardwood.

'No, of course not. But by the time we're finished with that cheeky black bastard he's going to sound like Othello.'

Hymie and I composed a speech for Gideon Mandoma which, I must say, was pretty terrific. The idea was that Gideon would learn it in Zulu and I'd translate it into English as though hearing it for the first time. Singe 'n Burn would be so knocked out by the language, the poetry and the brilliance that he would realise the black man was not just a hewer of wood and a drawer of water, nor even a noble savage, but someone who had all the brilliant potential even to become one of Sinjun's People.

We trained Gideon in the speech and, dressed in a white shirt, neatly patched pair of pants from an old suit and with his old black shoes shining, we presented ourselves at Singe 'n Burn's study. I must say he was very gracious and we all sat in his big old leather armchairs and Miss Perkins, his secretary, brought us tea and Marie biscuits. We'd anticipated the offer of tea and had practised Gideon in the balancing of a cup on his knee so he looked pretty suave and at home. But I knew on the inside he'd be all tom-toms and flutter.

I explained to Singe 'n Burn that Gideon's English wasn't sufficiently fluent for him to conduct a conversation and that I would act as interpreter. I think the fact that one of Sinjun's People could conduct the interview in Zulu impressed the old boy no end.

Gideon, as we had rehearsed it, began in English. His beautiful white teeth flashing in one of his best smiles: 'Excuse for my English, sir, she is not so good for tell this thing in my heart.'

The head nodded sympathetically. I could see the plan beginning to work already. Gideon cleared his throat and then began in Zulu. After each carefully rehearsed sentence I translated in my best voice, keeping it low and dramatic.

'I do not come from a nation of slaves, but I have been made a slave. I come from a people who are brave men, but I am made to weep. I, who am to become a chief, have become what no man ought to be, a man without rights and without a future.' I paused dramatically before continuing, 'I am seventeen summers; I have killed a lion and sat on the mat of the high chief, but I have been given my place. That place is not a seat at the white man's table, and that place is not a voice in the white man's indaba.' I could see Singe 'n Burn was beginning to feel uncomfortable. He wouldn't know what hit him by the time we were through. Talk about guilt, old Singe hadn't seen anything yet.

To my surprise Gideon suddenly stopped following the script. 'My bondage is not of the white man's making. My bondage is not forced upon me by the white man's sjambok. My bondage is in my own brain. Here in my head I carry the Zulu pride of my ancestors but I also carry no learning. My stupidity is my bondage; it is the instrument of the black man's misery and despair. If the white man would give me his rights and the same voice, I would not be able to use them, I would still be in bondage. I would still be a servant, a black Kaffir, an inferior human, because I would not know how to use these rights, how to make my voice felt amongst the people. Please, sir, my mind cries for knowledge. I wish to cup knowledge in my hand and drink it as one drinks water by the side of a stream. I am naked without knowledge. I am a nothing without learning. Please, sir, give me this knowledge, give me this learning, so that I too can be a man.'

Gideon's words had been so easily put that I had no trouble making an almost perfect translation and his flow was hardly interrupted. The tears rolled down his cheeks and he made no effort to wipe them away. I realised suddenly that for a Zulu to cry is a great shame, but he couldn't wipe away his tears with the cup and saucer balanced on his knee. I leaned forward and removed the cup and looked over at Hymie, not daring to look at Singe 'n Burn. I could see Hymie was annoyed that I'd removed Gideon's cup; the tears were the best part, the clincher. Othello had nothing on Hymie's cheeky black bastard.

'The tears are not for myself, they are for the people, Inkosi,' Gideon said softly, wiping them away with the back of his hand. I sneaked a look at Singe 'n Burn and saw his eyes had grown misty and he too was struggling with his emotions.

'Remarkable, quite remarkable.' Then turning to Hymie and me, he said: 'This young man shall have his school and I charge you both to give of your best.'

We'd won! Singe 'n Burn, the senior housemaster from Winchester School and trustee of the great private school tradition to the colonies, Renaissance man and liberal thinker, had been made to touch the heart and feel the soul of black Africa.

Hymie was the first to react. 'Can the school supply exercise books and stationery, sir?' Singe 'n Burn nodded.

'See Miss Perkins for a stationery authority, Levy. Your students must be properly equipped.'

'Thank you, sir,' I said then turned to Gideon to tell him the news. Gideon broke into a giant smile.

'Many boy, same like me, we thank you, Inkosi.' Singe 'n Burn acknowledged Gideon with a nod of his head. It was plain he was enchanted with the young Zulu chief.

The school began with the black boxers from Solly's gym its only pupils. Within a month, local chauffeurs, cooks and houseboys had swelled the ranks and Pissy Johnson, Cunning-Spider and Atherton, as well as two guys from School House who could speak Sotho, were roped in to teach on Saturday nights.

Even before the head's agreement we had despatched a long letter to Miss Bornstein asking her how we should best go about teaching language and numbers to adult Africans. She had responded with a superb set of teaching notes and several textbooks which enabled Hymie and me to prepare a complete curriculum which I was able to translate into Sotho, Zulu and Shangaan as well as Fanagalo.

With Singe 'n Burn's approval we also set about teaching the curriculum to the newly elected Sinjun's People so that the night school could be carried on after Hymie and I matriculated at the end of the year.

After only a few weeks the results were astonishing. Students, loaded down with homework after Saturday night's four-hour teaching session, would return with everything done, anxious for more. Word of the school spread among the Prince of Wales School boys and soon collections of nursery rhymes, primers and all sorts of textbooks were brought in and we had more volunteers than we could cope with. Then Hymie, loath to waste any free resource, hit on a one-to-one teaching method where every black student had a personal white tutor. All our black students would be taught collectively in the school hall for the first hour after which they would break away into a corner of a classroom with their personal tutors. Every tutor worked to a set of notes supplied by us and was required to stick to Miss Bornstein's outlines.

Progress was much faster than it would have been for any white students in a conventional classroom situation. Hymie, not content with our first curriculum, worked and worked on the notes, ironing out the errors and getting them perfect.

Some four months later we were visited by a reporter and photographer from the *Rand Daily Mail* and in the following Wednesday morning edition we had a full page write-up, which also contained a picture of Hymie, Gideon and me.

The article, very exaggerated, told a cocked-up version of the fight I had with Gideon and how Hymie and I had opened a school for boxers which continued to grow, giving the impression we had become a major black education resource. It was full of inaccuracies but nevertheless it caused some real excitement in the school. Singe 'n Burn called Hymie and me into his study and admonished us for not checking with him before speaking to a reporter. He suggested it was altogether a rather silly thing to have done in the light of the political situation, where black schools were forbidden in white urban areas.

Coming out of the head's office, Hymie shrugged his shoulders. 'Any publicity is good publicity, I guess.'

'I hope you're right, I reckon we goofed.'

'Yeah, so do I,' he said softly.

The following Saturday night the police raided us. The doors of the hall were suddenly blocked by khaki uniformed police both white and African. A police lieutenant wearing a Sam Browne belt and a holstered revolver jumped up onto the stage and blew his whistle loudly.

'This is a police raid, everybody remain seated and nobody will get hurt, you hear!' He stood on the stage, his legs apart, with his hand on his revolver holster as though daring one of us to move. 'Who is in charge here?'

'*Ons is*,' I said in Afrikaans, indicating Hymie and myself.

The police officer continued in English. 'Why is there no adult in charge?'

'The class is run by the boys,' I said.

'You mean white kids teach these blêrrie Kaffirs?'

'That's right.' I was beginning to gain courage after my initial surprise.

'Ag sis, man, are you telling me you teaching blêrrie stinking Kaffirs their ABC's? Don't you have anything better to do with your time on a Saturday night?'

'Have you got a search warrant?' Hymie asked.

'Who're you, man?' the policeman asked.

'You answer my question first,' Hymie said in an even voice.

'Hey, you being cheeky?'

'He merely asked if you have a search warrant, officer,' I said. The policeman suddenly realised that we were not intimidated. In fact he was wrong; we were both scared to death.

'And what if I heven't?' he challenged.

'Then you're trespassing and I must ask you to leave at once,' I said.

'You're only a blêrrie kid, who you think you talking to, hey?'

'If you haven't got a warrant to enter this school then piss off!' Hymie spat at the officer.

To my surprise the police officer suddenly grinned. Then stroking his nose with his forefinger and thumb he said, 'You're the Jewboy, hey.' He turned towards me. 'And you the boxer who fights Kaffirs.' He pointed at the Africans seated silently in front of us. 'Let me see the Kaffir you fought, man.'

Without being asked to do so Gideon rose from his chair. 'Come here, Joe Louis, come and stand next to the Jewboy and the Kaffirboetie.'

The officer called a black policeman over from the doorway, and as he waited for him to come onto the stage, he undid the shiny brass button holding the flap of his khaki tunic pocket and withdrew a piece of paper which he extended in our direction. 'Here, Jewboy, read it for yourself.' Hymie moved over and accepted the paper which was obviously a warrant to enter and search the premises. The lieutenant turned to the black policeman at his side. 'Tell the black bastards that they must all show their pass books and a pass from their employer to stay out after nine o'clock curfew.'

I turned to the white policeman. 'It isn't nine o'clock yet, Lieutenant. No one's broken curfew.'

He grinned. 'Ja I know, man, but it will be when I'm finished here and any black bastard without a pass is arrested.'

'This warrant is for St Johns College,' Hymie said suddenly. 'Look, see it says St Johns College, Houghton. That's the school about a mile down the road!'

'Don't play silly-buggers with me, you hear? Or you three will spend the night in a cell down at Central.'

Hymie walked over to the white police officer. 'Read it for yourself. It says St Johns College, Houghton. That's not us. Now will you kindly leave!'

'This is the right place, this is the place in the newspaper, I'm telling you, man! St Johns, that school, does it also teach Kaffirs?' I could see he was suddenly confused.

'You'll have to ask them that yourself, officer,' I said, not trusting myself to look at Hymie.

The police officer folded the warrant and put it back in his pocket. 'I should arrest you for obstructing the police in their duty; you know it's only a technical error, man. They got it wrong when they was looking on the map. This is the school, I'm telling you!'

'That's not what it says on your piece of paper. I really must ask you to leave, officer,' Hymie said, playing the situation for all it was worth.

'Okay, Jewboy, but don't think you seen the last of me. I know a comminist when I see one.' He pointed to me. 'You too, you and your Kaffir friend. I can smell a comminist a mile off.'

He left with his men and we could hear their boots on the cobblestones as they crossed the school quad.

'Holy Molenski! That was close,' I said. 'What happens now?'

Gideon grinned, a lopsided sort of smile, 'I think it is finish . . . the school is finish.'

'Not on your fucking life!' Hymie said. 'I'll get my old man's lawyers if they try doing that again.'

Gideon gave a wry laugh. 'You will be safe but we will go to jail, it is always like so. You are very clever and the magic of the Onoshobishobi Ingelosi is make the change for the school name on the paper. But the police they are bad people; they will not give up so easy, but also I think the big baas for headmaster he will make finish with this school.'

'Over our dead bodies,' Hymie said. 'I'm telling you, he'll fight for the night school.'

But he didn't. The next Monday the two of us were called to Singe 'n Burn's office to be confronted by an officer of the South African police force.

'This is Captain Swanepoel of the Johannesburg Central Police Station; he wishes to ask you a few questions,' Singe 'n Burn said sternly. 'It seems your report to me on the weekend doesn't quite correspond with the one submitted by the police officer who attended your class on Saturday night. I urge you to tell the complete truth to Captain Swanepoel.'

'We told you precisely what happened, sir,' I said to the head.

'With respect, the officer in charge of the visit is trained to report correctly; you can take my word for that,' the police captain said.

'Well then, in that case there will be no difference in our versions, Captain Swanepoel. I mean if we both told the truth,' Hymie said softly.

'The truth? What is the truth? In my experience the truth goes out the window when emotions come in. Emotions always tell a story different; you take my word for that, Headmaster,' Captain Swanepoel replied.

'Captain, both these boys have been trained to observe a situation with some dispassion, even though it be one in which they are involved.'

'Ja, I mean no disrespect, Headmaster, but I must take the written evidence of an adult police officer against two young boys who were very excited at the time.'

'Perhaps Captain Swanepoel can tell us where our evidence differs, sir?' I asked.

'Well, yes, of course.' The head cleared his throat. 'According to Captain Swanepoel you did not co-operate with the officer in charge of the visit and you were abusive in the extreme.'

'We were not given the opportunity to co-operate, sir. The officer was both abusive and bullying; and referred to me as a Kaffirboetie, Levy as the Jewboy, and to Gideon Mandoma as a blêrrie stinking Kaffir.' I looked up to see the beginnings of a smirk on Captain Swanepoel's face.

'This is not possible, a police officer of the South African Police Force is trained to be respectful to the public,' he turned to Singe 'n Burn. 'People make things up all the time, things the police are supposed to say.'

'Are you calling us liars, Captain?' I said.

Swanepoel ignored my question. 'It says here that you used abusive language to the officer in charge of the investigation ?'

'Yes, I told him to piss off,' Hymie said, 'but you have yet to answer Peekay's question, Captain.'

'I will answer it later, son, don't you worry about that,' Swanepoel shot back. 'Is what you said not abusive language?'

'Levy was extremely provoked and as the officer had no right to be on the premises the remark was not unjustified, sir,' I replied.

'I didn't ask you and he didn't answer my question.' He pointed his finger at Hymie. 'I'm asking you again, is what you said not abusive language?'

'Put like that, yes, but. . .'

'No but, man, you admit you were abusive to the officer then?'

'I admit I told him to piss off, Captain,' Hymie replied.

'Then we are in agreement. The first fact we challenge turns out to be correct; why must I not believe this report is a correct statement of what happened?'

'I say, that's not fair rules of debate, Captain Swanepoel,' Singe 'n Burn demanded.

Captain Swanepoel turned to face the headmaster. 'I am a police officer, not a school teacher; I look at the evidence, I do not play games.'

'We have forty-two Africans as well as our own chaps who will confirm what we've said,' I protested. I'd heard the warders interrogate prisoners and they would use the same technique as Swanepoel was now using on us.

'Ah yes, forty-two hostile witnesses. Africans do not have the same idea about truth as a white man. As for the other white boys, we are reluctant to take evidence from juveniles.'

'You still haven't answered my question, Captain,' Hymie said, his teeth clenched.

'You know something, son, sooner or later your type of person comes before the police again. I will remember your face.'

'*Please*! Answer our question, sir!' Hymie shouted.

Swanepoel laughed, 'When we meet again, I will answer it then, you hear?'

'What happens to this report, Captain Swanepoel?' Singe 'n Burn asked.

The police captain sighed. 'Because of the technical error in the search warrant I must very reluctantly withdraw this report.'

'May I please have it, Captain Swanepoel?' I asked.

Swanepoel laughed again. 'The South African Police do not give souvenirs; if you want some souvenirs, go to the Easter show.'

'I'm delighted to hear that's the last of it,' Singe 'n Burn said, obviously relieved.

'No, Headmaster, it is only the beginning. You can consider yourself very lucky we got the wrong school name on the search warrant because today I have come here as a friend. If we come again next Saturday night and we find that this wonderful school you have here is teaching black communists then we will be forced to make some very unfortunate conclusions.'

'I really do protest, sir!' Singe 'n Burn was suddenly angry.

Captain Swanepoel grinned. 'These days it is not very hard to find a black communist.' He looked at Hymie. 'Or even a white one,' then at me, 'even more than one. When blacks want suddenly to have education you can take it from me, they up to no good; somebody else or something else is behind it.'

'Are you telling us to close down the night school, Captain?'

'Headmaster, the law in this matter is not clear yet, but teaching black people in a white school will not be allowed in the new Group Areas Act. You can see my position, Headmaster. I must tell you also my duty in this matter is very clear. Next time we will not make a mistake with the search warrant. And when we come we will find something.' He paused and looked again at us, 'We always find something.'

He rose and extended his hand to Singe 'n Burn. The headmaster did not take it; instead he gripped the side of his desk and leaned forward slightly. 'We will not be intimidated by the police, Captain Swanepoel. We have not broken the law and as far as I know this is still a free and democratic country.'

Captain Swanepoel shrugged and stooped down to retrieve his cap from the floor by his chair. 'I am sorry you will not co-operate with the police, sir.' He adjusted his cap, then turned back to face the headmaster, touching the peak lightly in a casual salute. 'Good afternoon, sir.' Without a look at Hymie or me he turned and left, closing the door quietly behind him.

'Shit, what now?' Hymie said under his breath.

'What was that, Levy?'

'Nothing, sir.'

The light from the window backlit Singe 'n Burn's snowy hair and he looked frail as he continued to grip the desk, swaying slightly as though the motion kept him from disintegrating into a million tiny bits which would silently float away on the dusty beam of sunlight.

'Bravo, sir,' Hymie said.

He shook his head slowly, 'We are beaten.'

'But you just said . . . ?'

'Sheer bravado, my boy. We will have your school on Saturday and Captain Swanepoel will officially raid the Prince of Wales School, after which the board of governors will meet and their conclusion is foregone.' He looked up. 'Nevertheless, we will open next Saturday evening, a Pyrrhic victory to be sure, but there is an important principle at stake.'

We left the head's office in a thorough downer. 'Fuck the Pyrrhic victory, the principle and the principal as well!' Hymie exploded, once we were out of earshot.

'We'll have to let Gideon and the other boxers know. It's only fair that they decide for themselves whether they'll come.'

'Yeah, I suppose,' Hymie said morosely. 'What about the others?'

'Forget it, they won't come. Last Saturday was enough; there's no principle involved for them, just another opportunity taken away, another door closed. They spend their lives being screwed by the system. Would you turn up if you knew you were almost certain to be arrested, thrown in jail, lose your job and be branded as a communist?'

'I'm beginning to realise how lucky I am to have a white skin.' Hymie was taking it worse than I was. I had been around this kind of intimidation all my life and I knew Captain Swanepoel could have been a lot more difficult had he chosen to be.

'What are we going to do, Peekay?'

I laughed, 'You really are a city slicker aren't you, you still think the police are there to protect you from the big bad wolf? After Saturday night this whole scenario was predictable. The Nationalists don't see it as a kindergarten for adult blacks, to them we are starting a black revolution in the heartland of white privilege.'

'You can't be serious. Our dumb school for boxers and house boys?'

'From little acorns mighty oak trees grow. The Nats are not stupid. You should know. The Jews made that mistake before with the Nazis; they thought of them as a bunch of thugs whom they could buy off. Have you seen the educational qualifications the Nationalist government has for its cabinet? It's probably the best educated cabinet in the world. Racism does not diminish with brains; it's a disease, a sickness, it may incubate in ignorance but it doesn't necessarily disappear with the gaining of wisdom!'

'Are you telling me you knew all along this was going to happen?'

'No, of course not. I thought we had a chance; you were right to be somewhat cynical at the beginning, but it was worth a try.'

'But just now in the head's office ... you seemed so disappointed?'

'Christ, Hymie, I'm not saying I wanted it to happen! I was angry and bitterly disappointed. Disappointed that I was right.'

'You're a complicated bastard, Peekay. I'm supposed to be the realist in this partnership. What do we do now?'

'Well Saturday's out for a start; no point in putting the boxers in jeopardy, not for a Pyrrhic victory anyway.'

'Well, at least we can teach them after boxing.'

'No way. That Swanepoel bastard will be watching us like a hawk.'

'I feel so bloody helpless.' Hymie looked at me and shrugged, 'You know, before our visit to Sophiatown I couldn't have given a damn. Yeah, sure, I'd probably have gone along with you on the school, like you've gone along with me on some of our scams. But after the fight, seeing those people, it's different somehow. I begin to have a concept of the people, of what it means to be oppressed, of what it must have meant to be a Jew in Hitler's Germany.' It was the first time I'd seen Hymie confused. He'd come up against something that couldn't be resolved with money or influence. 'It was such a small thing they wanted and we failed. I mean, those poor blighters wanted so badly to learn, just to read and write and do a few sums. It was the least we could do.' Hymie was almost crying from rage.

'So, that's what we're going to continue to do. I didn't spend four years with Geel Piet without learning how to beat the system.'

'What do you mean, Peekay?'

'Correspondence school. Miss Bornstein's Correspondence School!'

'Peekay! You're a genius! We've already got the whole course in three African languages, as well as Fanagalo. It's in the bag, old chap; we'll guinea-pig the whole thing. We'll make it free for the class who have just been expelled, then with Mr Nguni's help and for a small sum, yet to be determined, we'll sell a correspondence course for blacks throughout South Africa. We'll even send one to Captain Swanepoel and tell him to jam it up his arse so that every time he farts he sounds intelligent!'

Miss Bornstein's Correspondence School would one day become the biggest of its kind in the southern hemisphere, with Miss Bornstein as actual principal. Mr Nguni simply let it be known that the course came from the Tadpole Angel who wanted the people to take pride in learning to read and write and do sums. It would turn out to be one of the more important elements in his financial and political empire in the years to come.

TWENTY-THREE

Nineteen-fifty-one was the year I won the South African Schools featherweight title, and the Prince of Wales School won the schools championship for the third year running. Darby and Sarge were heroes and both had become welcome members of the masters' common room. Success of any sort seems to break down social barriers. We all sat for our matriculation, although a first-class pass for Sinjun's People was a foregone conclusion. Atherton was selected for the South African schoolboy rugby team to tour Argentina and Cunning-Spider had made it into the Transvaal Schools cricket team. Pissy Johnson, with a lot of coaching from Hymie and me, felt confident that he'd get the marks in his matric to study medicine. He had become an expert at fixing cuts in the ring and from this small beginning his ambition to be a doctor had blossomed.

I had, by all accounts, a brilliant school career, getting my colours in rugby and three times for boxing as well as being head prefect and a company commander in the school cadet corps. While my music hadn't really progressed, I was still by school standards considered amongst the more superior musicians.

In Sinjun's terms, I was well on my way to being a Renaissance man. In my own terms I felt less successful. I had survived the system but that was in many ways the problem. I seemed to be losing control of my own life, forfeiting my individuality for the glittering prizes and the accolades of my peers. The need to win had become everything, the head had become more important than the heart; Hoppie's advice had worked too well.

I had supported myself at school with the Bank and the various scams Hymie and I had developed. But what had been intellectual amusement for Hymie was deadly serious for me. I needed the money not only to survive but as a means of dignity. Hymie and I had become inseparable friends and with the death of Doc he was certainly the most important person in my life. But I knew deep down that Hymie had been chosen because he could help me survive the system. I was a user. It had become a habit; winner that I seemed to be, I had become a mental mendicant.

I was conscious also of the price I paid. That in return, people took strength from me. Hymie, Miss Bornstein, Mrs Boxall all needed me as a focal point. I was required to perform for them in return for their unstinting help and love. The concept of the Tadpole Angel which I had tried to set aside would not leave me. After the Mandoma fight the black crowds at my boxing matches had become enormous and at the South African Schools Championships the police had been called to disperse the chanting crowd outside the Johannesburg Drill Hall. I knew that eventually something more was expected of me. All my life I'd been pushed around. By the Judge. By the Lord. By the concept of the Tadpole Angel. In my own way I had fought and in return had been given Doc and Hoppie and Geel Piet as my mentors. The point of all this was difficult to understand. Perhaps, after all, life is like this. But I felt that I needed to take one independent action that would put my life back under my own control. It was as though I needed to lose but hadn't developed the mechanism to do so. I only had one problem with this; I hadn't any idea how to go about doing so.

The only totally independent thing in my life was my ambition to become the welterweight champion of the world. It was the only thing that couldn't be manipulated. I either had it in me or I hadn't. It was the thing those who loved me, with the exception of Captain Smit and Gert, couldn't understand. It was the one thing in my life that seemed to make sense to me. In this single action there was no corruption of the spirit.

In the last week of term Singe 'n Burn accompanied me to my interview with the Rhodes scholarship board. I had sat for two scholarships. One to Witwatersrand University and another to the University of Stellenbosch, an Afrikaans-speaking university with a brilliant law school. But, more than anything, I wanted to go to Oxford. I felt I was unlikely to compromise this desire, come what may. Hymie's family had already agreed to pay for me to go, but even as a loan I found this unacceptable. Unacceptable to me, to the memory of Doc, to Mrs Boxall, Miss Bornstein, Captain Smit, Gert, Hoppie Groenewald, Big Hettie and, most of all, to Geel Piet, who had never in his life experienced a hand extended to him in help.

Even my mother, convinced that the temporal things of life were secondary and who had given the Lord the entire credit for making my education possible, had sat behind a sewing machine from dawn until dusk to support me as much as she was able.

I was a man now; I was through with taking. I felt the rest was up to me. If I didn't know what the next step in my life was to be, I felt that I might set it in motion by acting independently of the help that was always so generously extended to me by others.

Hymie, the gambler and businessman, reckoned the odds on my winning one of three Rhodes Scholarships for South Africa were less than even. As the time for my interview grew close he grew more and more distraught. He sensed my need to act independently and that to some large degree the Rhodes Scholarship would achieve this aim. At the same time he wanted to cushion me from the disappointment if I lost. It was not unknown, but highly unusual to be awarded a Rhodes Scholarship straight from school. Rhodes scholars were almost always chosen after an initial degree at university, when the student had already confirmed a brilliant school career with an equally brilliant first degree taken in conjunction with a sporting and cultural contribution in the university environment.

'Christ, Peekay, in my old man's terms the fees to Oxford are petty cash. We'd be together like always, and come back home and eventually open a practice together. You can start looking after the people and I'll make us a squillion dollars. It's all so easy. Why do you have to make it so bloody difficult?'

'Well, for a start I'm going to be welterweight champion of the world. If I took your dad's money, I'd have to use all my time to justify it at university.'

'You don't have to justify it, you can do both!' Hymie yelled.

'You know me better than that. Let me tell you something stupid, Hymie. If I had to choose between becoming welterweight champion of the world and taking a law degree at Oxford, the boxing would win.'

He looked stunned. 'Why? You're not the sort of guy who wants to be famous that way. In fact, you're exactly the opposite.'

'It's got to do with something which happened when I was very young. I can't explain it; it's just got to be that way.'

'Peekay, the money you'll make as a professional, even a world champion, will be nothing compared to the two of us together in a law practice.'

'It's not something I can explain. I've worked for this since I was six. It has nothing to do with the importance of being the welterweight champion of the world.' I chuckled inwardly. How the hell could I explain to him that I was doing it, in part, for a dead chicken!

'Look, Peekay, you're only just a lightweight; it will be two, maybe three years before you become a welterweight. You can take your degree, or a good part of it anyway, and then go on with your boxing career. I'll help you. We'll even make a lot of dough out of it.'

The interview with the selection board was a fairly harrowing experience, the first hour taken up with the board talking to Singe 'n Burn while I cooled my heels in the waiting room of University House. The waiting was the worst part. The selection committee was comprised of three fairly elderly men who simply started to chat with me. One of them, a thin man with round steel-rimmed glasses which slid down to the tip of his very long nose and whose hair was parted precisely in the middle and slicked down with brilliantine, looked like Ichabod Crane. He peered at me over the top of his glasses and quoted the first line of three verses from Ovid, then asked me to complete them. I had to laugh, it was stuff I'd learned from Doc when I was nine.

'Not bad, not at all bad, only one small mistake.'

'Please, sir, I disagree,' I replied, my heart in my mouth. The three poems had been among Doc's favourites and I knew them intimately. I was certain I'd not made a mistake.

'Bravo, young man!' Ichabod said. 'You're quite correct and, besides, you had the courage to say so.' He pulled his glasses back to the top of his nose and wrote something down on a tablet of lined bright yellow paper.

The three examiners looked positively musty with learning and not at all like sporting types. But, after they'd chatted to me seemingly about this and that, they fixed on my boxing. Why, they wanted to know, was I obsessed with boxing? My submission showed me to be a brilliant student, a very talented musician, a good rugby player and a brilliant boxer. One of them read from the submission, 'Has the ambition to become a professional boxer and to win the welterweight championship of the world!' I could see he was quite taken aback.

'Surely a boy of your obvious intelligence, or according to your headmaster, brilliance, must see that a vocation as a professional pugilist is not compatible with reading law at Oxford?'

'Lord Byron was a pugilist, sir. No one doubted his intellectual integrity,' I answered. He grunted and wrote something down on the pad in front of him. Ichabod Crane had a slight smile on his face.

'Ah, I do not recall whether Byron was an Oxford man!' he said, which caused his two colleagues to laugh.

'Your point is well made, Mr . . . er, Peekay, but as I recall he was an amateur.'

'There is considerable evidence that he fought on occasions for a wager which today would make him a professional, sir.'

'Be that as it may, a small wager on the side amongst friends is hardly the same thing, is it?'

'No, sir,' I replied, unwilling to press my luck any further by pointing out that quite large sums of money were involved.

At the end of the interview I was asked to wait with Singe 'n Burn in the waiting room. The head seemed even more nervous than me and made me repeat every word of the interview. When I got to the bit about Byron he was delighted. 'Excellent!' he said, clapping his hands, but then when I told him about Byron fighting for a wager and the somewhat brusque reply I had received, he frowned. 'That's Lewis of Natal University, a man who doesn't care to be contradicted.' When I concluded my account he simply said, 'Well done, Peekay, you have acquitted yourself well.'

We were then ushered back in, and it was Ichabod Crane who announced that I had been listed in the last five candidates and would be required to sit for the Oxford University entrance examinations.

'The Prince of Wales School which you attend has an enviable reputation, and if you are an example of its product, the least I can say for myself and my colleagues, is that we have been impressed.' They then stood up and shook hands with us both.

Singe 'n Burn was elated, we were over the major hurdle. They had taken my schoolboy candidature seriously. Several days later I sat with Hymie for the Oxford University entrance examinations the results of which would be announced before the Rhodes Scholarships.

I arrived home for the Christmas holidays to find my picture was on the front page of the Goldfields News. Mr Hankin, frustrated newspaperman to the last, had used the picture Doc had taken of me sitting on our rock the first day we had met on the hill behind the rose garden. Despite the fact that everyone in town knew who I was, above it a banner headline read: BOY ON A ROCK FOR OXFORD! I recalled with a touch of bitterness the stupid old fart's last use of this picture on the front page, when he accused Doc of being a Nazi spy and of breaking my jaw.

I found myself a local hero once again. As far as the town was concerned my elevation to Rhodes Scholarship status was all over bar the shouting. In the month it took for the results of the Oxford entrance examinations to come through, Miss Bornstein became a nervous wreck.

Down at the prison they were much more impressed with Solly's thirteen-punch combination. If they could have chosen between a scholarship to Oxford, a place they'd never heard of anyway, or a thirteen combo, there is little doubt they'd have plumped for the latter. Once again I won the Eastern Transvaal featherweight title and also best boxer of the championships. With this, my fourth successive win, Captain Smit, in what he later described as one of the great moments in his life, was able to claim the trophy permanently for the Barberton Blues.

My examination results arrived in late January and stated that I had received a distinction in all subjects. Miss Bornstein was beside herself and it was such big news around the place that old Mr Bornstein contrived to lose the first ever game of chess to me while denying hotly that he had purposely done so. Four days later a letter arrived from the Rhodes scholarship committee.

Dear Mr 'Peekay',

On behalf of the selection committee for Rhodes Scholarships for the year 1951, we regret to inform you that your application has been unsuccessful.

I have been asked by the selection committee to commend you for the manner in which you conducted yourself during your interview and for the results you achieved in the required examination.

It is the earnest opinion of the committee that, having completed your first degree, you should apply again.

Yours faithfully,
L. J. Fisher
Secretary to the Committee

The people around me had become accustomed to my winning; it was a habit they shared, an indulgence they took for granted. I could see they were shocked and bitterly disappointed that, having done their part, I had somehow failed them. Miss Bornstein and Mrs Boxall were distraught beyond belief, having quickly convinced themselves of some sort of plot. My mother, after shedding a few tears, soon concluded that the Lord had decided it was not His will for me and that, if only I would accept Him into my heart and into my life, His purpose for me would become clear. Two days later she announced at the dinner table that the Lord had guided her quite clearly and that I should give up boxing as it displeased Him. When I had done so, I would be guided in the Lord's special plans for me.

When I replied that boxing was too important to me, she had burst into sudden tears. 'That is the devil in you talking, God is not mocked!' she shouted, leaving the table with her face buried in her table napkin.

'There, there. There's a good lad,' my granpa soothed.

The following day a letter arrived from Singe 'n Burn in which he said that he was confident I would ride through the disappointment and that I had the internal fortitude to grow stronger from the experience. He added that the true Renaissance man accepted defeat as the ingredient which made eventual success worth striving for, blah, blah, blah. He then added that he had received a letter from Professor Stonehouse of Witwatersrand University who, it turned out, was Ichabod Crane. In it Stonehouse had remarked that the committee had been visited by a Captain Swanepoel who had not been complimentary about the school and its activities, and in particular my implication in these activities. He wanted to assure Singe 'n Burn that should he hear otherwise, this involvement by the police did not affect his judgement nor did it, he felt sure, affect that of his colleagues. Stonehouse concluded by saying that my application for a scholarship to Witwatersrand had been accepted and that he hoped the headmaster would be able to influence me to accept.

The following week the second scholarship, to Stellenbosch, was confirmed and I received an invitation to apply to Natal University. But I knew, in the minds of those who loved me, that this would be accepting the crumbs from the rich man's table. They were emotionally involved with Oxford and no other place, no matter how grand, would have satisfied their expectations for me and rewarded them for the parts they had played.

Only my granpa seemed unconcerned. He'd said nothing when the letter from the committee had arrived, except of course, 'There's a good lad.' I found him later in the garden grafting rose stock and we sat out of the blazing December sun in the dark shade of one of the big old English oaks. As usual he took ten minutes to tap and tamp and strike and eventually puff up a blue haze around his head. I'd given him a tin of Erinmore which I'd bought in Johannesburg and the honey-treated tobacco smoke smelt delicious as it swirled around his head.

'My brother Arthur went to Oxford, he was the clever one in our family. Like you he won scholarships, first to grammar school and then to Oxford.' He puffed and looked over the roof which still hadn't been painted. 'In my time not too many grammar school boys made it through to the dreaming spires of Oxford and Cambridge.'

'What happened to him, Granpa?'

The old man puffed at his pipe and stared out into space for ages, puff,

puff, puff. 'I don't know what went wrong, lad. He rose to be Lord Chief Justice of Appeal and was completely crippled by arthritis by the time he was forty. A miserable life really; made a lot of money and a lot of misery for himself and everyone else. According to my sister Jessie, he died rich and lonely.' He puffed on his pipe a little longer. 'Funny thing about Arthur, he never could get things in their right perspective.'

Hymie had sent a telegram every week demanding to know if the results had come out and asking me to phone him, reverse charges, when they did. I called him from Mrs Boxall's office in the library.

'Hard luck, Peekay, so close, so bloody close!' There was a click on the phone and then a woman's voice. 'Operator here, please do not swear on the public telephone,' the phone clicked again. 'Christ! Who was that?' Hymie said on the other end. The phone clicked again and went dead. I dialled the exchange.

'Operator, I was cut off.'

'Peekay, this is Doris Engelbrecht!' Doris was a woman in her mid-twenties, a Marie 'tonsillectomy' convert who now taught Sunday school at the Apostolic Faith Mission. 'I am supposed to cut off calls that contain obscene language. Your party in Pretoria used filthy language and has taken the Lord's name in vain. I can't allow it on the public telephone even if he is paying reverse charges.'

'I'm sorry, Doris, he just talks like that, he means no harm, it's just his way.'

'Ag sis, Peekay, how can you know such a person? You who are so clever and all, and whose mother is a very high up born-again Christian?'

'Doris, you're not supposed to be listening; telephone calls are meant to be private.'

'It says in the book I must not allow people to use obscene language on the telephone. How can I not allow them when I don't hear them?'

There seemed to be no ready answer to this. 'Doris, if you get me my party in Pretoria, I'll tell him not to use bad language.'

'Tell him also to wash his mouth out with Lifebuoy soap!' Doris said.

The phone rang a couple of minutes later. I grabbed it and before Hymie could speak said, 'Watch your mouth, Levy. Doris the born-again Christian is monitoring you.'

There was only the slightest pause on the phone. 'What's your favourite chocolates, Doris?' Hymie asked. There was silence on the other end. 'Black Magic or one of those big three-pound boxes with the picture of an English cottage on the outside showing all the flowers in the garden, you know, with a big pink ribbon?' The silence continued. 'I just want to say I'm sorry for my language; language like that can upset certain parties.'

Doris's voice cut in sharply. 'Tell the party on the other end I will not be tempted by the devil, Peekay!'

'Ag man, Doris, my friend has a chocolate factory; it is just a way of saying sorry,' I coaxed.

'A box so big you can't pick it up with one hand, Doris,' Hymie said.

'The box with the garden and the pink ribbon, then,' Doris piped in a small voice.

'Okay, then you've got to promise not to listen any more, Doris,' I said.

'Only if you promise on the Lord's name that your friend won't swear some more,' she said, a trace of warning still in her voice.

'Thanks, Doris,' we both said. The phone clicked and Doris was gone.

'For Christ's sake, don't forget to send the chocolates, Hymie. I've got to live in this town.'

'Is it safe to talk now?' Hymie said.

'Of course! You have the word of a born-again Christian!'

'No I won't forget; we keep a roomful of obscenely large boxes of chocolate at the carpet emporium. My dad calls them his "sweeteners"; every customer gets a box when a salesman determines it's time to close the sale. My dad claims his entire carpet empire is built on chocolate.' Hymie laughed, 'He even calls the salesmen his chocolate soldiers!'

His voice changed abruptly. 'The offer still stands, old mate. You don't have to take the money, it's just a loan. Now that you've passed the Oxford entrance examination and all.'

'Hymie, we've been through that! You promised you wouldn't bring it up again.'

'Cripes, Peekay, what are you going to do?'

I told him about the three scholarships I'd been offered and the paragraph in the letter which encouraged me to apply again when I had obtained my first degree.

Hymie was silent for a moment. 'Got it! We'll go together to whatever university you choose and then we'll take the last two years at Oxford. You're only just seventeen and I'm just eighteen, we've got lots of time!'

It was my turn to be silent. 'You've forgotten one thing,' I said finally.

Hymie was quick as a flash. 'Of course I haven't; we'll go to Witwatersrand and Solly can continue to train you, and the old combo will stay together.'

'It sounds great, Hymie, but you've already been accepted for Oxford. This doesn't fit in at all with your plans.'

'Plans! Plans are meant to be broken. This is a much better idea.'

But I knew it wasn't.

'Let me think, Hymie. I just need a few days to think things out.' I knew quite suddenly that I would have to visit the crystal cave of Africa, that I had to 'speak' with Doc. Doc was still a very real part of my life and I had come to think of the crystal cave of Africa as the place I would be closest to him.

'Call me, reverse charge, in a week; you promise now. So long, Peekay.'

The next morning I packed a rucksack and left before dawn for the cave. By mid-morning I had climbed to the shelf next to the cave. I had no desire to enter. Doc's spirit was everywhere. I was as close as I needed to be.

The shelf faced west and caught the late afternoon sun so that now I sat in shadow, the smooth dolomite surface still cold from the night. I closed my eyes as Inkosi-Inkosikazi had shown me how to do so many years ago.

Now there came the sudden roar of water in my head and then I saw the three waterfalls. I was standing again in the moonlight on an outcrop of rock directly above the falling water. Far below me the river rushed, tumbling into a narrow gorge. Just before the river entered the gorge an apron of green water spread from the base of the last of the falls and across its centre, a small boy's jump separating them, were the ten black stepping stones, their smooth wet surfaces only inches above the swirling current.

I took a deep breath and launched myself from the rock; the cool air mixed with spray rushed past my face. I hit the pool at the bottom of the first waterfall, the sound of the splash drowned in the roar of the water. I surfaced to be swept over the second of the falls and then again over the third, landing in the deep pool of swirling green water. I fought my way to the surface and struck out towards the first of the black stones. Pulling myself up onto it, I hurriedly jumped from one stone to another, finally leaping for the pebbly beach beyond. I felt my toes and the ball of my foot touch the smooth round river pebbles, and as I landed I found myself inside the crystal cave of Africa.

The cave was illuminated as though by soft sunlight and I had no trouble seeing around me. It was more magnificent than I had ever imagined, the stalactites suspended in every imaginable colour, some hanging thirty feet from the ceiling. I walked towards Doc's platform skirting the mirror-still pools of water reflecting the grotesque and beautiful stone icicles. A ray of sunlight, as sharply defined as if it were painted in a Raphael sky-scape, fell onto the platform. I looked up to see a perfectly round hole in the ceiling through which the sun shone as though predestined for this precise hour of this precise day. The beam of light shone through the crystalline structures above the platform and spilt down the steps leading up to it. Slowly I climbed the rough, natural steps until finally, standing on the top step, I looked down onto the platform where Doc lay at my feet.

Doc lay as I had imagined he would, fingers extended, arms bent at the elbows and crossed at the wrists across his breast, his legs straight, like the effigy of a medieval knight at rest on a gothic tomb in a quiet corner of a great cathedral. He was made of pure crystal, the soft sunlight reflected from the effigy dancing at the edges. Doc's sculptured face was surrounded by burnished light.

I told him of my fear of losing control of my destiny, how, because I had camouflaged myself so well, I seemed now to be shaped and directed too much by the needs of others. How the power of one within me was being dissipated even though their purposes for me were not corrupt or ill-intentioned. On the contrary, their deeds came swaddled in the innocence of love. I was becoming powerless as those around me plundered my spirit with the gift of themselves.

It was as though there was a voice inside me explaining me to myself; I had become an expert at camouflage. My precocity allowed me, chameleon-like, to be to each what they required me to be. To Doc a companion, to Mrs Boxall an enchantment, to the people a champion, to Captain Smit a fulfilment, to Miss Bornstein a bright lint in a dull warp, to Hymie a foil, to Singe 'n Burn a product and to my peers an idealised schoolboy, a winner and a great guy.

I was a poor boy among rich ones and in my mind the status they gained by the simple expedient of being wealthy was only leavened by my superior performance in every other expectation. I had come to identify with my camouflage to the point where the masquerade became more important than the truth. While this posturing was so finely tuned it was no longer deliberate, it had nevertheless been born out of a compulsion to hide. As a small child I had discovered that only two places are available to those who wish to remain concealed. The choices are to be a non-entity or an exception. You either disappear into a plebeian background or move forward to where most others fear to follow.

My camouflage, begun so many years before under the persecution of the Judge, was now threatening to become the complete man. It was time to slough the mottled and cunningly contrived outer skin to emerge as myself, to face the risk of exposure, to regain the power of one. I had reached the point where to find myself was essential.

I was not conscious of how long I had been sitting cross-legged on the shelf but slowly my eyes focused and the soft blur of blue in front of them sharpened into the mountains to the west. In the rainforest below me I heard the cry of a red loerie. My legs were stiff and my ankles sore where they had been crossed. I felt an overwhelming sense of freedom . . . the same sense of being free that I had felt when the big, black, hissing train had pulled out of the platform, away from the hostel, Mevrou and the Judge. When Hoppie had sat opposite me and we had first shared an adventure and a green sucker between us.

I had come back from the dreamtime in the crystal cave of Africa with a certainty that I would be tested once more before the power of one would become mine alone. When my destiny would be in my own hands.

I continued to sit completely still as Doc had taught me to do when observing any living thing. 'Still like rock, Peekay, past the itch and the scratch and the pain, where the concentration sees with a diamond-sharp light.' And so I sat perfectly still, emerging slowly from the cocoon of the trance I had been in. In my mind I asked Doc for a sign.

At that moment, sitting still as a rock on the shelf directly outside the crystal cave of Africa, I had no doubts, nor was I troubled by the intellectual absurdity of the request for a sign, a confirmation in a physical sense of the message I felt so clearly within me.

At first it was hardly a movement at all, less even than the flicker of an eyelid, a slight blurring of light. Then the head of the black mamba rose above the edge of the shelf two feet from where I sat. Its flat anthracite head froze inches above the shelf. Its forked tongue, as though possessing a life of its own, flicked and trembled the air for vibrations. The huge snake rose, periscoping above the shelf, moving forward until its head was no more than six inches from my face. I could see its eyes, black tektites without movement set above jaws of injected death. Its head moved in slow motion from side to side, sweeping across my sightline. If it struck I would have fifteen minutes to live . . . enough time to enter the cave and lie beside Doc before my nervous system collapsed. The mamba's head moved below my line of sight and then came to rest on the toe of my boot. I could feel the pressure of its body as it slid over the boot and along the shelf to disappear over the cliff's far edge. The snake could only have come out of the cave. Doc had sent me a sign. I knew what I was required to do.

Slowly the numbness left my body and I felt the rush of adrenalin as it hit my bloodstream, leaving me trembling. I waited until the shaking had ceased before I dropped down to the tiny ledge and worked my body flat against the cliff wall until I stood facing into the opening to the cave. The floor of the tunnel leading to the cave was covered with sand worn from the walls by the erosion of the wind. I could clearly see where the snake had entered and then returned, no doubt having fed on the hapless bats asleep inside. Doc had sent me the sign I wanted.

I carefully worked my way back to the ledge, shouldered my small rucksack and started to climb down the cliff. The snake was unlikely to be on my path. Fat from eating bats, it would find a place to sleep under the safety of a rock where it was unlikely to be disturbed.

Once I had recovered from my fear, I found the snake an entirely appropriate, even perhaps a magnificent symbol. The black mamba, the most deadly snake in the world, takes one partner for life. If its partner is killed the second snake will often wait for the killer to return, prepared to die in order to take revenge. Not naturally aggressive, it will nevertheless defend its young, raising itself onto the last few inches of its tail and striking sideways in a whipping action. As most humans instinctively raise their arms in panic to defend their eyes the mamba fangs most often strike into the top of the upper arm. The journey to the heart is swift and the outcome deadly certain.

There was a great deal of consternation from everyone concerned when I announced that I wanted to take a year off between school and university, and that I would go up to Northern Rhodesia to work in the copper mines. It was as though all who loved me, even the boxers, felt that if I broke the continuity of my life, the spell which bound our relationship would be broken.

Gert's brother had visited him at Christmas from the Copperbelt and had talked of the shortage of white labour in the mines of both the Copperbelt and the Congo. The Korean War had just started and copper prices had soared. He told of diamond drillers making two hundred pounds a week and young grizzly men making a hundred after they were paid their copper bonus.

Northern Rhodesia was a British colony across the Zambesi; it was far away from the people who held me so dearly within the thrall of their ambitions. It was away from the legend of the Tadpole Angel. It was even away from boxing. I saw it as an opportunity to come to terms with myself and to build my body to the size of a welterweight. The hard underground work would toughen me, while twelve months away from the ring would do me no harm. I had been boxing since I was seven years old and had fought one hundred and sixteen amateur fights. My instincts, which always served me well, told me it was time for a rest.

Gert's brother, Danie, worked as a diamond driller, the elite corps among the Copperbelt miners. Most of the diamond drillers were Afrikaners from Johannesburg attracted by the huge copper bonus white mine workers were being paid. They were so named because the cutting edge of the drill bits were studded with industrial quality diamonds to make them hard enough to cut through the rock. Danie worked in a mine near Ndda, in the centre of the Copperbelt. He said he could get me a job as a grizzly man at the Rhoan Antelope Mine owned by Anglo American in the small mining town of Luanshya. A grizzly man worked with high explosives and was the next highest paid job in the mine.

The four-day trip by train left South Africa at Beitbridge and travelled across Southern Rhodesia to Victoria Falls where I crossed the Zambesi into Northern Rhodesia. Southern Rhodesia is not unlike the Eastern and Northern Transvaal but across the great Zambesi the country changes to flat grassland and equatorial forest. The trees which covered vast areas of the country were unlike any I had seen before, for they carried their autumnal colouring all through summer. Leaves of brilliant reds and yellows and even mauves and purple, all the colours expected of a northern hemisphere autumn. A passenger who sat beside me told me of giant edible mushrooms that appear in the forest overnight and grow two feet tall with a canopy three feet across. A mushroom weighing thirty pounds. I'd been around long enough not to take everything I heard as gospel, but in the months to come I would see Africans selling these huge mushrooms at the side of the road, simply cutting off the amount the purchaser required. Giant, brilliantly coloured moths with a wingspan ten inches across also bred on the wet, leafy floor of the forest.

Northern Rhodesia felt different and the Africans, like most from central Africa, were truly black, their faces seemingly flatter and their build smaller than the lighter milk chocolate brown of the Zulu or the Shangaan. They spoke Swahili, and it was with some consternation that I realised it was a language I did not speak and that I was cut off from the African people for the first time in my life. In the mines they talked a language known as Ki-swahili which was not unlike Fanagalo, but like all languages designed for a working purpose, it was limited and stunted. Africans raw from their villages in the bush were recruited to the mines where they were taught this mine language so that they could take instructions from their white bosses and, in many cases, talk to each other.

A work gang often contained black miners from half a dozen different tribes, each with a different language.

At four o'clock in the afternoon on the fourth day we finally pulled into the sleepy town of Ndola. Ndola was really only a small community made up of miners' families and tradespeople who lived off the giant copper mines. The remainder of the town's people were British colonial service administration officers and their families. It made for an uneasy white dichotomy. The mining families seldom mixed socially with the civil service families established at a separate end of the town. Ndola was thirty miles or so from Luanshya but the end of the railroad as far as passenger trains were concerned.

Gert's brother met me at the station where the air was filled with the babble of confused and frightened blacks. White mine officers feigned indifference while blue uniformed black mine policemen filled with self-importance and professional impatience herded and pushed hundreds of Africans from the train. Too late now to turn back, they had been harvested from the bush like wild tsamma melons.

For the past two days and nights the train had stopped at small sidings with no more than a tin shed and a small clearing to separate them from the rest of the bush. Here small groups of perhaps a dozen Africans wrapped in blankets would be herded onto the train by a black recruiting officer. The whites of their eyes showed their fear and confusion as they were bundled aboard the hissing, steam-belching monster, jeered at by those who had earlier been gathered up and who were by now, with arms resting casually on the sills of carriage windows, accustomed to the clickity-clack of momentum and the wonderment of the snake which runs on an iron road.

Now they were almost at the end of their journey. I watched as the black mine police tried to get them roughly into line. They came only because drought and a great locust plague had destroyed their crops and the grazing for their cattle. Driven from their villages as indentured labour for the mines, they would work for a year so they could send money to keep their starving women and children alive. The fear these poor creatures felt the first time they were plummeted into the bowels of the earth was a source of great mirth to the initiated black miners as well as to many of the whites.

Gert's brother noticed me looking at the poor buggers. 'Ag man, they like a monkey when they first come. They can't even climb a ladder and when you show them a mirror they go almost white when they see the big ape looking back at them. It's very funny man, I'm telling you.' He picked up my suitcase and I followed him over to a green Bedford utility. 'I just come off shift so I'll drive you to Luanshya. I telephoned the mess there yesterday and they know you coming. Tomorrow you got to report to the mine recruiting office for a medical and then you go sign on for the School of Mines for three months. I got to warn you, man, they got a Welsh bastard there called Thomas; watch out for him. If you get out of the School of Mines and get your blasting licence you go onto grizzlies for six months, three if you lucky. But the money is good.'

'Why only six months or even three?' I asked as we pulled out of the station.

'I didn't want to tell you before, but if you on grizzlies much longer the odds is cut down.'

'The odds?'

'Ja man, the odds of getting badly injured or killed.' Gert laughed. 'They don't pay you that kind of money for nothing, you know.'

'Does everyone go onto grizzlies?'

'Ja, all the young guys; if you over twenty-two your reactions not fast enough. Only young guys are fast enough or,' he grinned, 'mad enough to do it!'

'Christ, it doesn't look as though I've got a lot of choice!'

Gert's brother laughed again. 'None. All young guys got to be grizzly men, nobody else will do it. On the Rand it's not even allowed. Moving ore through a grizzly is the best way, but it's also the most dangerous. The miner's union on the Rand won't have a bar of it and grizzlies are banned anywhere in South Africa, but here in Northern Rhodesia they don't care, man. As long as they get the muck out they happy.' He paused as he made a turn, heading the ute onto a corrugated dirt road leading out of town. 'But you make blêrrie good money and if you careful you'll be orright.'

I laughed. 'Don't worry, Danie, I'll be bloody careful!'

He looked at me, his hands vibrating on the steering wheel as we hit a particularly badly rutted strip. 'That's the blêrrie trouble, a grizzly man comes on night shift, eleven to seven; he got the job to pull all the ore out of a stope. That's my job as a diamond driller; I drill the stope all day and you got to pull the muck out through the grizzly at night. If you too careful and you don't get enough muck through the grizzly so I got an empty stope to work with, you in a lot of trouble man!' He gave me a knowing grin. 'You do that a few times and you can collect your ticket. The diamond driller is king and you fuck up his stope you don't work in the mines no more, man.'

I remained silent. I hadn't any idea what he was talking about, but I gathered that whatever a grizzly man did he was under all sorts of pressure. And pressure creates accidents.

'That's one good thing about Thomas in the school of mines; he makes things so blêrrie bad in your training that, if you make it and get your blasting licence, you got a good chance of staying alive on a grizzly.'

Danie left me at the mine mess where I had a room reserved for a month before I moved into a hut of my own in one of the single men's compounds surrounding the mess.

'I'll try to visit sometimes, you hear. But up here it's not so easy; each mining town is on its own, and you will work night shift and me always day so it's no use for me to come over. If it gets very bad you can call me.'

He scribbled the name of his mine and a phone number on a piece of paper. 'Just leave a message for me at the mine office; I'll come as soon as I can.' He extended his hand. He was a big bloke, six foot two or three and he had the usual Afrikaner gorilla grip.

I thanked him for his help. 'Ag man, Peekay, any friend of my little boetie is a friend of mine. Gert says you a real man and will one day be world champion; I'm glad to help.' He paused. 'There's boxing up here also, but nobody as good as you. Some of the Kaffirs is okay, they will be quite good to practise on; these blêrrie apes has got heads so hard they'd wear out a diamond drill. So long, Peekay, all the best, hey.' I watched as the ute accelerated, skidding its wheels before moving away in a cloud of dust.

Apart from the smelter and the mine administration offices the small mining town of Luanshya consisted of two parts. The town itself, which contained the married mine officials and their families, school teachers, shop owners, and colonial administration, most of whom were police, and a quite separate area for single men of several hundred small circular huts known by the South African term 'rondavels'.

Each of these rondavels had a corrugated iron roof and walls and floor of cement. A square flyscreen verandah, six feet wide and fifteen feet in length, was attached to each hut. While this stoep was a flimsy affair intended to keep mosquitoes out and let a breeze in, the door to the hut was made of sheet iron, almost impossible to break down if locked from the inside. Two small windows on either side of the hut were barred. There was nothing friendly or homely about these huts except perhaps for a large ceiling fan which sometimes, on a blazing hot day after a nightshift working a grizzly, stirred the air enough to induce a fitful sleep.

The rondavel contained a bed and mattress, a wardrobe, a table and two chairs. In the centre of this untidy army of huts was the mess, where for a few pounds a month you ate. The block I was to live in contained men from forty-two countries, many of whom had a dubious past and a doubtful future in the country from which they originated. While there were a few grizzly men like myself, young guys who were fast and fit enough to work the tungsten steel grizzly bars without killing themselves, most of the miners were in their thirties, some even older. They were without exception tough, hard men who had come for the money. Few were traditional miners; many were drunks and criminals, some of them ex-Nazis on the run, some mercenaries who had just kept moving when the war ended, waiting for another to happen though not prepared to don a uniform for formal affairs such as the one gathering momentum in Korea. Some were card sharps, con men and thieves who, while working in the mines in order to remain in town, had come for the after-hours action.

I learned that the normal courtesies did not apply, and not to ask a man where he came from or to inquire into his past. He might tell you when he became soulfully or sentimentally drunk, but most of the crud, as the compound men were called by the town's people, had learned to keep their mouths shut, drunk or sober. I also quickly learned to keep my hut shut on a Saturday night, when the week after I'd been allocated one I narrowly avoided being pack raped. In a town with no women, other than a handful of married dames, a seventeen-year-old boy was a grand sexual opportunity for a drunken group of Germans, Russians, French Algerians and Slavs. Had I not been rescued by Rasputin, a giant Georgian who almost never spoke, I would have been bum bait for sure. While the town itself was policed, the crud compound was on mine property and largely left alone unless a stabbing took place or a drunken brawl got out of hand.

Every six weeks a Belgian DC-3 would land on the small airstrip a mile out of town near number nine shaft. To the cheers of the waiting crud it would disgorge twenty-five whores from Brussels via the Belgian Congo where they had already spent a lucrative week in the copper mines of Katanga province. A couple of weeks on their backs would set them up for a year at home. Indeed many of them were young housewives putting together the deposit for a home or shop girls earning a dowry. Europe was short of men and a girl had to have a little more than a respectable background if she hoped to marry. Two easily explained weeks away on holiday and a pair of constantly opening legs was all it took to consolidate a proposal for marriage with the deposit, ostensibly from the bride's parents, on a nice little cottage in the suburbs of Antwerp. Some of the ladies were professional whores, because that's what some of the crud wanted. A good whore knows how to get drunk with a man, give him what he wants and rob him of a week's wages without disturbing his anonymity or touching his heart. A man on the run finds compassion or love or even pretended innocence his greatest source of emotional danger.

The crud would wait from dawn on the day the whore flight came in, chaffing each other about getting the fresh meat and the prettiest women, cursing the bloody frog crud across the Congo border for having first go, telling each other that it was a well-established fact that frog crud have tiny pricks and that's why the women went there first. They would tell each other with winks and guffaws that, had it been the other way around, the bloody frogs would have ended up getting it for nothing because the whores wouldn't have known they'd been on the job. The whores were known as French letters because the frog crud had first dipped their pens in and then sent them by airmail across the border. The Congo miners were a mixed lot just like the Copperbelt, though the majority were Belgian who spoke French. But the distinction escaped most of the crud. 'If he speaks French he's a frog. So who's going to argue?'

My new life began in the School of Mines, a school conducted mostly underground on day shift at number nine shaft which stood on the edge of town. It was run by two large Welshmen who, it was claimed, played together in the front row for Cardiff before the war. Dai Thomas and Gareth Jones were a remarkable duo with Thomas working underground with the class and Jones, an ex-school teacher and the mine technical officer, taking the two-hour theoretical class before our eight-hour underground shift began.

The combination was worked to extract the maximum agony out of the three months spent in their care. Jones would feed Thomas the weaknesses of each member of the class and Thomas would exploit these for all he was worth when we arrived underground. They saw themselves as being in the practical business of showing men how to stay alive underground and they damn near killed them in the process.

At seventeen I was the youngest and also physically the smallest of as tough a collection of reluctant students as ever assembled to learn anything. We had all come for the money and not for the career, but the Northern Rhodesian Department of Mines required that all miners obtain their blasting licence, a process which required that we learn not only how to use dynamite but that we were trained as lashers, timber men, drillers and pipe fitters. The first two months were physically the hardest of my life. At one hundred and thirty pounds I was not designed for the kind of work required. This was not South Africa and Thomas demanded that the men under him do all the work normally done by African miners. The back-breaking labour of drilling and lashing a freshly blasted haulage could bring grown men to total exhaustion and, many a time, to the point of mutiny. Thomas was remorseless. Lashing was the process of removing blasted rock by hand and shovel and loading it into underground trucks. This we performed six hours a day, every day for the first month, often in narrow haulages a thousand feet underground in temperatures of a hundred degrees. The eight-hour underground shift allowed half an hour for lunch and a five-minute water break every hour. Years of boxing had conditioned my arms and upper body and I quickly learned the rhythm of working a blunt-nosed, long-handled miner's shovel. But by the end of the shift I was buckling at the knees and blubbing from exhaustion. Thomas heckled the men with invective, constantly trying to provoke a fight, trying to make a man lose his head and have a go at him. One or two tried and apart from receiving a thrashing were expelled from the school, their chance at the big money gone forever. I longed to take Thomas on. No one knew I was a boxer and when I was not too exhausted and could dream a little, I fantasised about him throwing punches at me, missing hopelessly and finally falling exhausted on the ground having been made a monkey of in front of the crud. In my daydream I would leave him grovelling on the ground while I quietly picked up my long-handled shovel and continued lashing the end without saying a word. Just the knowledge that I could probably manage to do this in real life kept me going when he baited me, sometimes without let-up for an hour at a time.

'Okay shit for brains, you're so fucking smart, how much gelignite is required to blast a twelve hole end?' In the first week I had read the textbooks Gareth Jones had issued to us from cover to cover, and Thomas soon discovered I knew the answers to the simple questions he threw at us when we went underground each day. He didn't like a smartarse in his class and seemed determined to get me. He would ask questions which appeared in the books weeks ahead of our learning them, but I usually knew the answer. The rest of the crud were not known for their brains and reading isn't generally a strong point among such men. I knew I couldn't goof the answer just to satisfy Thomas's need to put me in my place. The crud derived enormous pleasure from my getting the answers right and therefore, in their minds, getting the better of Thomas.

'Six foot drills or nine, sir?' I'd ask.

'You being a smartarse, boyo?'

'No sir, but it would make a difference wouldn't it?'

'Of course, you half-wit, of course it would make a difference!'

'Well, that's why I asked, Mr Thomas.'

Caught in his own verbal trap, Thomas would answer angrily, 'We don't use too many nine-foot Jackhammer drills, now do we?'

'If the rock is a bit cakey we do, sir,' I answered.

Thomas would jump up in glee. 'There's precious little cakey rock in a fucking copper mine, boyo!'

'In that case eighteen pounds, sir,' I would answer smoothly. The men around me would wear smiles as big as water melon slices.

'Correct!' Thomas would yell. 'But don't you be a smartarse with me, boyo, or you'll be lashing ends until your arms fall off and you have to use your shoulder stumps to pick your nose.'

'Yes, sir,' I'd say, but I knew he would have the last say, moving me over to a badly blasted end where the ore had broken in large lumps too big for a shovel so that I had to break and lift the rock all day until I collapsed from exhaustion.

'No malingering, boyo, back on the job in five minutes or you're fined a quid.' In the School of Mines we were paid a token salary which just covered the cost of the hut and our mess bill with a couple of quid over for essentials. If, by the end of the month, you were down five pounds it made things tough.

I told myself that nothing Thomas said or did could wear me down. I convinced myself that the hard work was why I'd come, and indeed, after two months in the School of Mines my body had never been harder and I knew the muscle bulk would soon begin to follow. While I kept a speed-ball and a punching bag in my hut where it wouldn't be noticed and worked out every day with weights in the club gym as well as doing five or six miles of road work three times a week, I made no attempt to join the boxing club.

Sport was the one thing both miners and good citizens shared and the club, heavily subsidised by the mines, was the social centre of the small town. The club affected all the traditions and mannerly ways anglophile institutions of this sort demand from lower middle-class members who find themselves fortuitously thrust into the upper echelons of a colonial backwater society, and it solved the problem of having to accommodate the multi-national crud by building a separate bar for them. This was in a separate building from the club, with its own entrance where men could come without being seen by the town establishment, mine officials and the more acceptable of the miners' families.

The crud bar, as it was known, contained a fifty-foot bar counter, cement floor and white lavatory tiles six feet up the walls. It also featured swing doors like a Western saloon. The bar room itself was empty and permitted standing room only. Outside was a beer garden with a hundred tables or so, each one sporting a permanent tin umbrella welded into the centre of a steel table which, in turn, was bolted onto the painted green cement yard. The chairs too were made of steel, their legs permanently bolted to the cement. Each table and six chairs were painted a different colour so that from a distance it all looked very gay. Above the tables, suspended like tall washing lines, were strings of coloured lights which at night gave a weird sort of green and mauve cast to everything.

Three barmen, all Germans, all called Fritz and all fat, worked the bar like an ordinance office. Each Fritz operated his third of the bar, and behind him was a complete stock of liquor and a cash register. He never left his own territory to pour a drink, draw a beer or make change. Each Fritz was known by a number, Fritz One, Fritz Two and Fritz Three. Each had a crud following whom he came to regard as regular to his part of the bar. The Fritzs boasted there wasn't a drink in the world they didn't have or couldn't make. But mostly they served brandy, beer, rum and vodka, in that order. If you did your drinking standing in the bar you could get your liquor served by the measure and your beer by the glass. But if you wished to sit outside, you got a jug of beer or bought a full bottle of spirits, unless you wanted to keep fighting your way back into the bar for single serves. No Fritz was ever known to move from behind the long bar. The crud bar stayed open from seven a.m. until midnight when one Fritz would hose it out, removing at the same time the crud too inebriated to leave on their own.

During the day, until three o'clock when the day shift ended, the three Fritz wives, each one as big as her husband, worked the crud bar. They were known as Mrs Fritz collectively and remained un-numbered. Husband and wife, it seemed, never got together and it was a source of constant wonder among the crud that the Fritzs between them boasted fifteen fat blond children. The joke going around was that when the Fritzs left the crud bar they were going to buy the whole red light district in Hamburg.

At the end of three months, only eleven of the eighteen men who joined the School of Mines with me remained. We were eligible to take our blasting licence, choosing either the international or Northern Rhodesian version. Thomas, in a rare show of kindness, suggested that I sit for the international, as he hadn't had a student pass the international in seven years.

'If you pass you'll be the youngest ever, which would be a feather in Mr Jones' cap, and I might even take a pat on the back myself, boyo.' The rugby season had begun and Thomas had discovered, too late to be of any use to me, that I could play and in the trials looked like I could make the first team of which he and Jones were selectors.

The examination was held at the office of the Department of Mines in Ndola. It consisted of a half-hour written examination and an hour of verbals. This was because many of the men were not much good at writing but could answer most of the questions put to them directly.

Most of the guys with me were frightened to the point of paralysis. If you failed you returned to the school for another month, and failure after that and you were out of the mines. I had been coaching them for the last month and had come to be known as Professor Peekay. On the bus into Ndola I fired endless questions at them.

All but a huge Boer from the Orange Free State obtained their blasting licence. The Boer, a likeable enough bloke but thick as mahogany, was out forever, but cheered himself up with the knowledge that he had been accepted as a stoker on the Northern Rhodesian Railways. Thomas and Jones had followed us to Ndola by car and after the morning's examination we'd all repaired to Ndola's only hotel, where just about everyone got very drunk and ended up telling Thomas what a good old bastard he was. I had passed the international licence and must have consumed a gallon of lemon squash just responding to the toasts the men kept proposing to Thomas, Jones and Professor Peekay. The more drunk they became the more effusive, until towards the end Thomas had become a certain candidate for sainthood, and they all swore that they would protect me against all comers and that there was nothing I couldn't ask them for.

My life as a grizzly man commenced the next day when I went underground for the first time on my own, on the eleven to seven shift.

The workings of a grizzly need to be briefly explained. Imagine if you will, a funnel pointing downwards towards the ground. The top bit of the funnel before it narrows down to the spout is the stope, which is, in fact, a huge underground hole. The spout from it is used for getting the rock, blasted off the sides of the hole, out of the hole. This spout is sixty feet long and leads directly to a main haulage. The bottom of the funnel spout is fitted with a steel door worked with compressed air. Halfway down it, that is thirty foot from the main haulage and the same distance from the beginning of the stope, a set of six tungsten steel bars are fitted across the funnel spout with a narrow walkway cut sideways into the rock leading to it. These six tungsten bars are known as a grizzly. The reason for this name being that tungsten bars were made in Canada, hence 'grizzly bars'. The ore drilled and blasted from the sides of the stope by the diamond drillers is funnelled down the spout at the bottom of the stope and comes rushing down, with the smaller bits falling through the grizzly bars, filling the bottom half of the funnel spout. The bigger bits fall onto the bars and need to be blasted through them into a suitable size for loading onto the trucks in the main haulage. Underground trains pull up to the compressed air door, and operators standing on the main haulage open the door at the end of the funnel and fill the trucks with ore. It's really a very simple operation but also a very dangerous one. The grizzly man works the bars which are directly under the mouth of the stope which is capable of disgorging rocks the size of small motor cars without warning.

The grizzly man works in the dark; his miner's lamp attached to his hard hat with the battery clipped to his webbing belt is the only source of light. He has five Africans to help him lash the rock through the grizzly bars and to prepare mud for the explosives. Occasionally he will get the muck flowing from the stope and it will continue to run all night, with only an occasional blast or a little work on the bars with long crowbars to keep it going. But mostly it's gut-wrenching work laying charges and working ore through the bars, sometimes as many as forty or fifty blasts a night until a powder headache caused by the sweet, sickly smelling gelignite sticks threatens to tear your head off your shoulders. Only diamond drillers, who use more gelignite than grizzly men, get worse powder headaches, sometimes being reduced to a state of unconsciousness or temporary insanity by the terrible pain.

A grizzly man works on the actual bars which are about six inches thick and two feet apart. Safety rules require that he be attached to a twenty-foot chain which clips to the back of his webbing belt. But the chain, like so many safety procedures, is a Catch 22. If he slips and falls through the bars into the bottom half of the funnel his back will snap like a piece of celery as his fall is broken by the chain some fifteen feet below the bars. If he doesn't break his back and the muck starts to run, the ore coming through the bars would tear him into mince. A good grizzly man takes his chances on the bars without a safety chain and learns, even in the dark, to be as agile as a monkey, jumping from bar to bar all night carrying a five-foot steel crowbar in his hands.

Grizzly men always work the same grizzly, knowing their lives depend on their intimate knowledge of the character of the stope and the funnel. Each grizzly has a personality of its own and a good grizzly man can read his grizzly as though his mind is tuned into the very rock it's made from. A slight leaking of pebble in a hang-up and he knows to run for safety as a hundred tons of rock is about to come down directly over his head. The wrong pitch in an echo from the stope and he knows a single rock may come hurtling through to smash him off the bars. His reactions are as fine-tuned as those of a top racing car driver, and his adrenalin pumps all night. At the end of a shift a grizzly man will have lost four or five pounds in weight and will be in a state of total exhaustion. At the end of three months he is taken off grizzlies for a spell of two months, before he is allowed to return. While the money was enormous, most grizzly men elected not to return and took a lower-paid job as a pipe fitter, timber man or ganger.

One particular job on the grizzly led to the final unnerving of even the most courageous of men. Some time during most shifts and often three or four times, the rock would become blocked at the mouth of the stope. That is, at the very top of the funnel some thirty feet above the grizzly bars. In mining terms this was known as a hang-up or a bunch of grapes. Rocks of every size jammed the mouth of the stope. The safety procedure required to dislodge the rock and get the stope flowing again was to make up a parcel of gelignite. This is then tied to the end of a thirty-foot bamboo pole. The sticks of explosive are then wrapped with cordtex, which is explosive made into a cord which looks like white electrical flex. The idea is to push the parcel of gelignite against the rocks jamming the mouth of the stope, then to light the fuse attached to the end of the cordtex which has been trailed from the parcel of gelignite to the level of the grizzly. Whereupon, if you're very lucky, the blast against the hang-up hopefully dislodges the rocks, causing the mouth of the stope to open again and the muck to flow.

But life on a grizzly isn't meant to be easy, and dynamite or gelignite, when it is not sealed with a mud pack, blasts outwards away from the rock, taking the line of least resistance. Blasting a hang-up with the bamboo pole technique is seldom successful. The pressure on the grizzly man is enormous; he must get the muck flowing and, using the bamboo pole technique he could blast away unsuccessfully all night. He is paid by the truck load, and if he doesn't empty his stope the diamond driller will lose his day shift, which often results in a grizzly man losing a couple of teeth. Apart from all this the grizzly man's pride is involved. A grizzly man who leaves a grizzly hung up is the lowest form of life in a mine. As Thomas would say, 'It's just not fuckin' done, boyo!'

After unsuccessfully trying to bring a hang-up down with a bamboo pole bomb, the grizzly man fills the front of his thick woollen miner's shirt with mud and a gelignite bomb strung with cordtex, and scales the sheer face of the funnel until he reaches the hang-up. This is the dangerous part; if the hang-up comes down while he is fixing the explosive against it, the grizzly man is dead, thrown sixty feet down through the bars to be buried under fifty tons of rock. Fighting the panic of being totally committed with nowhere to go, you find a jamming point between the rocks and insert the gelignite bomb. Then you wind the cordtex around it and let enough cordtex fall to the grizzly below so that you can attach a fuse to it. Finally you seal the bomb with mud to make it airtight so that the blast will go inwards into the rock. Having set it and packed it you then have to come down again, each precarious step up and down the sheer face of the funnel a gamble that the hang-up will hold. Back at the grizzly level you connect the cordtex to a fuse, signal the African to blow the warning hooter, light the fuse with a cheesa stick, a flare the size of a thick pencil which, once lit, cannot be extinguished. Then you have thirty seconds to retire into the safety tunnel before the blast goes off.

If the hang-up still doesn't come down you are forced up again, aware that with the added blast it could be teetering and on the point of crashing down. You soon learn to make only one trip up the funnel laying several blasts across the face of the hang-up and stringing them together with cordtex. This means you spend ten or fifteen minutes up against the hang-up with each second increasing the tension and the danger. But this way, when the four or five bombs go off simultaneously, you have a good chance of bringing the hang-up down. It all depends on nerve . . . yours. If you have the nerve to stay up the funnel for fifteen or twenty minutes, carefully laying a blast pattern and sealing each bomb with mud, it takes a very big hang-up to defeat you. In the year I was to work grizzlies, five of the twenty grizzly men working the mine were killed when a hang-up gave way while they were up the funnel laying charges against it.

Mine rules did not permit grizzly men to climb up into the mouth of the stope; caught doing it meant instant dismissal. But because you were forced to at least twice during a shift, the shift boss would stay away from the grizzly levels so that he wouldn't catch you. Everyone's copper bonus depended on the grizzly man getting the ore out of the stope. No shift boss would police the rules when he knew that the bamboo pole technique was so ineffectual that a hang-up might remain all night and not a ton of ore would be moved out of the stope.

When I wasn't shitting myself I took a perverse pride in being a successful grizzly man. I was the youngest in the mine with one of the best ore tallies. The diamond driller who worked the stope above my grizzly was an Afrikaner called Botha whom I never met as he worked day shift and I worked nights. The diamond drillers were the underground elite and never spoke to the grizzly men personally; the work was too dangerous and a driller didn't want the responsibility of knowing who was working his stope. But if you kept your ore tally up and his stope empty, he would send you a case of brandy at the end of each month.

A case of brandy from your diamond driller was the badge of honour every grizzly man worked for; in the crazy crud world of the Central African copper mines it became an approbation even more important than money.

I gave the brandy to Rasputin, the giant Georgian who lived in the hut next to me. Rasputin worked as a timber man on the same night shift as I did and we cycled to number seven shaft about three miles out of town where we both worked. From the night he had saved my rear end virginity, we had been friends, our friendship based less on words than on the things we shared. Rasputin spoke very little English and rather than learn any more he simply didn't talk. He'd sit on my stoep or I on his, and we'd play chess. He was a good enough player to keep me interested and if I lost concentration he would sometimes take a game. Often we would simply sit and I would read a book or he'd play his collection of Tchaikovsky symphonies and concertos on his new portable record player. He never played anything but Tchaikovsky and would sit with a huge block of native timber in one hand and a kindling axe in the other, and without ever releasing the block of wood he would chip away until three hours later it became a perfect ball. Rasputin was almost as tall as Doc had been but he was twice as broad, even bigger than the Afrikaners, and the axe would have weighed five pounds. The act of carving the block of wood into a ball was one which took almost unimaginable strength. When Rasputin wasn't carving a ball he was sharpening the axe. He would work away to the music, going through the entire repertoire of concertos and of the three symphonies. Sometimes silent tears would roll down his cheeks and spill into his shaggy beard. These he never bothered to wipe away, but he simply continued to carve at the block of wood, occasionally putting down the axe long enough to pick up a tin mug filled with VSOP brandy which he would half-empty in one gulp and then refill to the brim. When Tchaikovsky came to an end, which meant sitting through all three of his piano concertos and his violin concerto and at least three symphonies, mostly his number one in G minor, two in C minor and always ending with his sixth, the grand and brilliant Pathètique, a bottle of Botha's brandy would be empty and the wooden ball would be complete.

Rasputin would carefully pack away the record player, dust the records and slip them into their jackets, and lay them on top of a towel in an old suitcase. Then he would take the wooden ball and add it to a pile on the floor inside his hut. There must have been six or seven hundred of these about the size of a bowling ball, stacked in separate heaps of about one hundred each, one ball added each day. Some of the older ones had turned a lovely silver grey colour and others bore beautiful markings from the native timber he used. Each ball was identically sized and beautifully made; you could pick up two, carved months apart, and their perfect roundness and size were so close the eye couldn't pick out the difference, each ball a testimony to his enormous skill and strength. His hut smelled of the sap of young timber, not unlike the smell of a forest. Rasputin would step into his hut and take a deep breath, inhaling the sappy odour of the uncured native timber.

'Smell like Roosha, Peekay.' I often wondered if in his native Russia he had once lived among the birch forests of the Taiga, but I could think of no way of asking him.

I became fascinated by the beautifully carved balls and found that I could hold the axe in position to work a piece of wood for no more than three minutes before the hand holding the wood would no longer function and the pain in my right wrist from holding the axe became unbearable. I realised that the exercise involved would strengthen my arms, wrists and even my hands for boxing, so I purchased a smaller and lighter axe and Rasputin sharpened it for me until it was like a razor. The idea that I wished to emulate him gave the huge bear of a man great pleasure. We'd sit on his verandah whittling away, listening to Mr Tchaikovsky, Rasputin drinking brandy and shedding tears which fell like drops of liquid silver down his cheeks to disappear into his huge black beard.

Eventually I worked out that the wooden balls were Rasputin's calendar, one ball for each day he had spent in the mines. By my reckoning he had been there about three years.

We would meet after our shift came up at seven a.m. and cycle back to the mess for breakfast. Rasputin would always be showered and waiting for me as my cage came up from underground; somehow he managed to finish his shift early and get up to the surface before the grizzly men.

'Much muck move, Peekay. You good boy,' he would say without fail as I stepped out of the cage. Then he would take my miner's lamp from me and put it on charge in the battery room so that I could go straight to the shaft office, check my ore tally, sign off and quickly get to the showers. When I emerged from the change rooms twenty minutes later he would be standing outside in the morning sunlight with my bicycle, ready for a quick getaway.

I'd been off grizzlies for only a week after having done my three months, when the mine captain called me into his office and asked me to volunteer to go back on. I was supposed to be rested with a main haulage job such as bossing a gang of lashers but three grizzly men had been badly injured and the mine had no replacements coming out of the School of Mines. The incentive was to double my copper bonus for the period I was back on grizzlies. It seems Botha the diamond driller had been screaming about the new grizzly man on his stope and wanted me back. The money and the compliment were too much for me. Youth has a strong sense of its own immortality and I was no different from most. I found myself back at my grizzly platform for another three months. At the end of the month two cases of brandy arrived from Botha which made Rasputin completely independent of the crud bar. He was so proud of me he started to cry.

Lashing a case of brandy to the carrier on each of our bikes we pushed them the three miles to town, the twenty-four bottles in each case clinking merrily as we steered the bikes over the corrugated dirt road. When we arrived at the crud compound he put the cases in his hut and emerged moments later carrying an ancient twelve-bore shotgun.

'Tonight Rooshan stew!' he announced. Rasputin's rabbit stew was his highest compliment and I must say it really was delicious, a thick broth flavoured with strange herbs he gathered in the wild and delicious chunks of pink rabbit meat served with tiny whole onions and potatoes. I watched as he headed for the bush, not even waiting to have his breakfast at the mess.

I rose at four in the afternoon as usual. From Rasputin's hut came the delicious smell of the rabbit stew. I knew he would call me at about five-thirty to eat and so I headed off to the shower block to do my ablutions. We would eat and then attend a movie at the club. It was Wednesday night and Wednesday was always a Western. Rasputin loved Westerns with a passion. We would arrive early and sit in the front row, Rasputin with a bottle of brandy and his mug, ready to shout and scream and wave his fists at the baddies on the screen. He would weep when the hero was in a tight spot about to be burnt by Indian braves or tortured by malicious outlaws. Finally, when the film reached its climax and the hero emerged unscathed and triumphant with the girl, he would stand up and bang his mug against the empty brandy bottle and shout his approbation in Russian. Nobody seemed to mind. Rasputin was a part of the Wednesday Western and he'd always buy sweets and ice cream at the interval for all the kids. It became a tradition to yell and scream and pretend to cry at all the places Rasputin did and a grand time was had by all.

At five-thirty I heard his bellow, 'Peekay, you come!'

Rasputin had placed two bowls on the table and beside them were two large spoons. Arranged in a jam tin in the centre of the table were wild flowers he had gathered when he was out rabbit-hunting and beside the flowers rested a round loaf of fresh bread. The flowers were a nice homely touch and the stew in a large pot on his single electric burner smelt wonderful. Rasputin poured it straight from the pot into the bowls; the delicious broth came steaming up at me. He dipped into the pot with a fork, stabbing chunks of pink rabbit meat and placing them in my bowl. Finally he produced a bottle of lemonade for me and, filling his tin mug with brandy, we tucked in, tearing huge hunks of bread from the loaf and slurping hungrily at the delicious stew. Neither of us said a word until it was all eaten and we'd had a second helping.

'Russian stew very delicious, Rasputin,' I said finally, rubbing my tummy to emphasise my satisfaction.

Rasputin looked pleased, even a little embarrassed at the compliment. He rose from the table, and walking over to the wardrobe withdrew from it the ancient twelve-bore shotgun. Pretending to aim at an imaginary rabbit in the distance he squinted down the barrel. 'Ho, ho, Peekay, rabbit go meow meow, me go boom boom, rabbit kaput!' he laughed uproariously and put the shotgun back into his cupboard.

I had never eaten a cat before but I knew there was no way I would be able to refuse Rasputin next time he paid me his supreme compliment and went rabbit-hunting again. I quietly prayed that I wouldn't do anything in the future that would please him too much. I wondered silently which of the town families was wondering what had happened to their cat.

TWENTY-FOUR

It is the human experience, particularly true of the young, that all routine no matter how bizarre soon becomes normal procedure. Just as the survivors of the Nazi concentration camps talk of the routines imposed and followed which measured the days of horror until they seemed the normal passages of life, working a grizzly became a job as unexceptional as any other. Boldness, at first a stranger to be treated with caution, soon becomes a friend, then partner and finally is taken for granted, as is the daily relationship between two married people.

There comes a stage when the nervous system adjusts to accommodate the new environment, in which a former state of anxiety becomes one of calm, and situations which formerly brought a rush of adrenalin through the blood leave it calmly going about the business of supplying the heart.

A good grizzly man attracts a good black gang. Africans straight from the bush instinctively understand the group security a confident leader brings. As the months went by and my grizzly remained accident-free and I unscathed, those blacks who worked regularly with me would seldom stay away sick, preferring to shiver through a bout of malaria rather than to take a chance of losing their place to another black anxious to work in a *juju*, or mystically protected gang.

When a grizzly man blew himself up it was not unusual for him to take his number one boy with him. The number one is the most experienced mine boy in the gang, usually a second timer. Better paid than the rest of the crew, he acts as black leader as well as right-hand man to the grizzly man. It is he who handles the charges and prepares the mud packs to bed down the explosives. If an accident occurs he is generally working close to his grizzly man. Knowing this, a good grizzly man will generally dismiss his number one to the safety shaft, to man the blast warning siren before he lights the fuse, and a good number one will repay his grizzly man by building the mystique of the grizzly man in the eyes of the bush Africans who make up the rest of the gang.

Once a gang has been associated with an accident on the grizzly level, they become bad juju in their own eyes and in the eyes of the other black miners. It was inconceivable to these primitive bush Africans that a superior white man should die and that a thoroughly expendable black one should live. The gods had, quite obviously, made a mistake. The 'stick lightning' had been meant for them; the mark of death was upon them if they remained in the mines.

Black miners did not understand or believe in the concept of increasing odds and would have been quite unable to grasp the simple logic which dictated that the longer I remained working grizzlies the more likely I was to come unstuck. The superstition which held them to me is understandable in a simple mind; the fact that I began to half believe it was not.

With the exception of a week's break after my first three months on grizzlies, I had been working for nine months. While I knew that simply by requesting to do so I could be relieved, I hung on. Botha's two cases of the best South African brandy continued to arrive for Rasputin at the end of every month and the fact that the ore tally pulled from my grizzly almost always headed the night's tally list did important things for my ego, though I would probably not have admitted this even to myself. Even in this unlikely environment I still hadn't conquered the need to be the best. Though the odds had grown well beyond simple foolishness, I convinced myself that my brains (ha-ha) were the difference, that I knew how to survive a grizzly because I could read it better and was less likely to make emotional decisions under pressure. Which was, of course, a load of codswallop.

I had reached the point where Fats Greer, who drove the number seven shaft hoist and who also acted as the mine's part-time insurance agent refused to give me cover. 'For fuck's sake, Peekay, the all-time record for a grizzly stand is eleven months and the bastard who had it is pushing up daisies. Stop being a smartarse.

But I was through doing what other people wanted and I told myself that if the copper bonus held and I could stay on grizzlies for a year I would have earned enough to put myself through Oxford. No more emotional handouts for me. I could pay my own way! My whole life had been a testament to using the human resources around me, to winning against the odds. If I understood the system as I felt I did, I was no longer willing to pay the emotional price it demanded from me. If this was only in my own mind, well, every man is an island and at the same time also Robinson Crusoe; you're on your own and must learn to fend for yourself. The year of despair I had spent as a five-year-old, in the hands of the Judge, had tainted everything I had subsequently done. My childlike notion of camouflage to avoid being emotionally besieged had persisted. In my mind, although I'm certain at the time I would not have been able to articulate the idea, the mines represented a return to fear of that first boarding school. But this time it was I who would win. The grizzly I worked would be the Judge, but this time I would not be broken. I had come to the mines to find out who the hell I really was.

It is curious that in the retelling of a dangerous situation the explanation is often made to include a premonition of the disaster. Whereas, in truth, most accidents strike like a viper of lightning from an apparently clear blue sky. It is as though human beings like to pump up the importance of a near escape or even a catastrophe by placing the hand of destiny at the helm of calamity.

The day before the grizzly got me I dreamed I was bent over a routine charge to light the fuse. A normal length of fuse is designed to take two minutes to reach the dynamite charge but for a routine explosion of rock resting on the grizzly bars a good grizzly man will cut the fuse to a burn-through of thirty seconds, which is enough time to get into the safety shaft. During a single underground shift on a hard night when the muck refuses to run, a grizzly man can make forty or fifty separate rock blasts. With a saving of ninety seconds for most of these he can easily cull an extra hour's tally from the shift. In ore terms this can make a considerable difference to the night's final tally.

In my dream I held the lighted cheesa stick to the fuse, waiting for the familiar kick of sparks to indicate that it was alight. But the fuse turned instead into the black mamba of the crystal cave of Africa; it rose as it had done outside the cave, its head weaving and its darting tongue becoming the spluttering sparks of the lighted fuse. Mesmerised, I was unable to move until I realised it was too late. I jabbed the cheesa stick at the head of the snake as it struck. The lighted stick of sulphur blended with the explosion as I was blown to smithereens.

I awoke, my heart pounding furiously. Grizzly men often talked of the dreams: 'When the dreams come it's time to quit.' I had not dreamed before and now I was afraid; the grizzlies had started to invade my subconscious. That night I told the shift boss I wanted off and gave him a week's notice. He didn't question me but simply nodded and said, 'You earned it, Peekay, we'll give you a soft option, maybe lashing on a main haulage hey?' I thanked him but he suddenly looked alarmed. 'Shit! Who's going to tell Botha; he thinks you're Jesus Christ.' He grinned. 'Someone else can tell the sonovabitch, that's the day shift's job.' While I had received two cases of brandy regularly for the past five months, I had not met Botha. As I mentioned, it was a tradition that a diamond driller and his grizzly man didn't meet. Nobody seemed to know quite why this was, but like most time-worn behaviour it had turned into a superstition and both men would go to some pains never to meet while they worked in conjunction with each other.

'Rasputin will miss the brandy,' I said, conscious that now that I had made the decision to quit, a weight had lifted from my mind.

The shift boss laughed. 'You can bloody well tell him that!' Rasputin was the best timber man in the mine, but the scourge of shift bosses whom he wouldn't allow near his work site when he was building a bulk-end or timbering a new haulage. But they had all come to accept Rasputin; what he did, he did well, without taking unnecessary chances with his gang. That was the first rule of mining; the rest was simply the niceties of deferring to authority, a concept the huge Georgian seemed not to understand.

There was nothing exceptional about the first part of the shift following my talk with the shift boss. I stopped to rest my gang as usual between three and four in the morning, the time known everywhere men work underground as 'dead man's hour'. It is the time when the human pulse is said to regulate by running slow and the circadian rhythm to falter. It is the time, old timers insist, when the bad accidents happen. To work through dead man's hour would be sorely to tempt fate. While we are meant to be rational humans there lurks in each of us a covert superstition which probably began when man worshipped rocks and trees; and which we ignore at our own peril. For the grizzly man, better the hour saved by cutting fuses short than one used when death stalks the dark underground tunnels at the same time every night.

At four-fifteen I completed laying the mud pack over a routine charge, cutting the fuse short as usual. I had inserted it under the mud-covered gelignite and took the lighted cheesa stick from the number one boy, whom I called Elijah because he liked to light the cheesa stick himself, forfeiting his chance to retire to the safety of the escape shaft. He waited with me until the fuse began to splutter. With the cheesa stick Elijah handed me I touched the notched and splayed end I'd cut to reveal the granules of black gunpowder which ran through the body of the fuse. Nothing happened. No flare as the gunpowder caught, no familiar splutter as it tore down the centre of the fuse. Even before I could question the reason, the vision of the black mamba filled my mind's eye, 'Christ! It can't be. It's a running fuse!' A running fuse is when a fuse burns inwards and appears from the outside to be inert while in fact it is moving just as quickly towards the charge of gelignite. It is extremely rare; most grizzly men have never seen one or, if they have, haven't lived to tell the story.

I grabbed Elijah by his shirt collar and propelled him towards the safety shaft, tackling him the last few feet into the shaft as I dived for safety a split second before the charge went off. The explosion roared fifteen feet from where we lay. Had the snake not returned to me in my dream I might have persisted with the shortened fuse. Three seconds longer and Elijah of the burning bush and I would have been history.

Rising to his knees and dusting his hands on the seat of his trousers, Elijah started to babble with excitement as the rest of the gang came running towards us. He told them how a devil fuse which did not light had set off the charge, but how I had known of its magic and thwarted its evil intention by pulling him to safety. The gang listened with open-mouthed astonishment. Then each in turn came over to me and touched my arm, dropping their eyes as they did so. Once again I had confirmed my magical status; was this not yet more proof that their collective safety was assured? The Tadpole Angel was back at work again.

I am forced to admit, I too felt hugely elated by the experience, enchanted with the meaning of the dream. I kept asking myself whether I would otherwise have recognised a running fuse? It was a mining occurrence so rare Thomas hadn't even mentioned its possibility in the School of Mines. I had seen it noted briefly before being dismissed as extremely unusual in one of the numerous textbooks we'd been issued, a textbook possibly only I, amongst the class, would have taken the trouble to read.

Instead of seeing the near disaster as a real life warning, I became so elated I decided to withdraw my notice to quit grizzlies. I felt a tremendous sense of my own destiny, of the rightness of the path I had chosen. I had gambled and won, my slate was wiped clean, the accident designed to happen had been thwarted, the original odds were once again restored. I would see this old bitch grizzly through until the fifteenth of February, one week over eleven months, to the day. Screw Fats Greer, I'd make it a new record.

I admit to the unsoundness of my reasoning, but it wasn't all stupidity. The pay for a soft option job on a main haulage was less than half the amount I was receiving each month working a grizzly. With my double copper bonus as well as my tally bonus I could add another forty per cent to this as well. Giving all this up would mean staying on at the mines another three months and by doing so missing the commencement term at Oxford.

Feeling good all over, I walked up to the grizzly, and standing on the bars shone my lamp up at the hang-up which had developed at the mouth of the stope. It looked unsafe, a bunch of grapes where the loosening of one small rock might bring the lot down. Fifty tons of rock could be held suspended above my head by a mere pebble. The old bitch was playing with me, teasing me, my ears strained to hear her talk . . . a creak, a moan, the echoed clatter of a single pebble . . . so I might read the constraint of the rock avalanche poised above my head.

It came at last, the sudden sharp, erratic clatter of a single rock as it broke free from the hang-up to ricochet against the steeply funnelled rock sides leading from the stope. One, two, it would take three bounces before landing on the grizzly bar furthest from where I stood. My intimate, almost instinctive knowledge brought about from working more than two thousand hours on this one grizzly told me the rock was about the size of a large grapefruit and that it almost certainly preceded the collapse of the hang-up.

I moved fast, leaping instinctively across the bars towards the protection of the safety shaft. Above me the hang-up groaned momentarily, a second or two's warning before the roaring avalanche followed. My feet had already left the bars in the final leap to safety when the single rock hit the grizzly and, bouncing erratically off the tungsten steel bar, flew through the air to hit me in the stomach.

The roar of the rock breaking free reached my ears before I was knocked unconscious through the bars, to fall sixty feet down the almost empty shaft.

The fall should have killed me. The ten tons of rock which followed me through the bars should also have done so. I had been unconscious the moment the rock struck me and had fallen through the bars like a sack of potatoes, bouncing against one wall of the down shaft. My hard hat had miraculously stayed on and prevented my head from being smashed in as I landed in about three feet of fine shale at the bottom of the grizzly. The shale had been the result of the huge rock I had blasted through the bars with the running fuse. I had been conscious at the time of using too much gelignite but the grizzly shaft below the bars had been empty and a good grizzly man tries to put a buffer of fine shale against the pneumatic steel doors to protect them from the effect of bigger rocks smashing against them. I had landed in this soft bed of shale and sand, my body rolling and finally wedging under a narrow shelf of rock where the side of the shaft had been carelessly blasted. Ten tons of rock from the hang-up had followed me through the bars, covering my body and building up over me though, miraculously, in pieces big enough to allow some air to reach me.

I lay unconscious under the shelf, covered by several tons of rock. What happened over the next seven hours I have pieced together from talking with my gang and the rescue team.

Elijah was shocked beyond belief. His elation of a few minutes before had turned to complete dismay. Yet he hadn't panicked and had sounded the blast warning hooter ... five prolonged blasts each interspersed with fifteen seconds of silence, then a minute break and a repeat of the same pattern three times. There was no mistaking the disaster message. The rest of the gang huddled together in the safety shaft, too shocked to respond, their lives suddenly shattered with the certainty in their minds of their own death should they remain even to help with the rescue. For them their luck had run out, their white talisman was dead. It was time to get to the surface, hand in the copper discs which hung around their necks and get back to the jungle where in the bright tropical sunlight it was more difficult for death, which saw better in the dark, to find them.

Rasputin, working on the main haulage half a mile away, was the first white man to hear the disaster warning. He sent his number one boy to alert the underground shift boss, and he headed for my grizzly. Frantic with concern he nevertheless loaded an empty truck with bulkhead timber and instructed his gang to push it to the area of the accident. If it was a grizzly disaster, Rasputin knew the huge slabs of native timber would be needed for any rescue attempt.

News of a disaster in the mines spreads seemingly by osmosis. Grizzly men who were working the sixteen hundred feet level with me would close down their grizzlies and bring their gangs in to help. I'd done it myself on three occasions and I knew what it was like when the rescue crews finally pulled the smashed and broken, even sometimes the separated parts of a body from the blood splattered rock and placed it in a canvas body bag. I had even seen blood leaking from the pneumatic doors closing the bottom of a grizzly shaft and had waited the six hours it had taken finally to get to the body which lay only a few feet away, as I did now.

It was an unspoken rule that the grizzly men helped in any rescue attempt. They were the personal witnesses to the death with which they had learned to live every time they climbed the sixty feet of vertical ladder shaft to a grizzly level. The generally unsuccessful rescue attempt was a grim ritual they felt forced to play a part in, out of respect for a dead brother.

Rescue procedure is dictated by the environment. A stope and the grizzly below it are a live thing and have to be silenced before a rescue attempt can be made. The shaft directly above the grizzly bars has to be timbered up, the old bitch silenced. Huge bulkend timbers, capable of holding back rocks crashing from the stope, were used for this task. Shoring up the grizzly shaft was in itself a dangerous task, particularly as timbermen are not adept at reading a grizzly. The job was complicated by the twenty tons or so of rock which rested on the bars when the hang-up had come down. This would need to be manhandled into the air escape and safety shaft, while the pieces too large to lift would remain on the bars where they acted as some sort of protection should the bulkend timbers give way.

It was Rasputin's task to build the bulkhead that shored up the shaft above the grizzly. The ten foot by ten inch raw native timber slabs, known as ten-by-tens, weighed well over three hundred pounds each and had to be manually pulled up the sixty-foot entry shaft to the grizzly level. By the time the rescue crew arrived from the surface, the giant Georgian had already exhausted his own crew and the crews from the three other grizzlies were working turnabout to haul the heavy raw timber.

Rasputin worked in a cold, controlled fury, though with no unnecessary movement or wasted energy, speaking quietly to the blacks to keep them from panic; he'd even managed to get my crew back to work. He knew that rescue was a long process made dangerous by hastily contrived directions and the terrible infection of fear. From the grizzly level he directed the removal of the manageable rock which lay on the tungsten bars. When the rescue captain arrived on the grizzly level, panting from the exertion of climbing the ladders up the entry shaft, Rasputin was waiting for him at the top.

'No come here, Peekay he mine, I fix!' He glared at the rescue captain, opening and closing his huge fists.

The light from the captain's white hat shone into Rasputin's eyes and held the fury and cold determination. Rasputin was taking no chances; handing the rescue operation over to the mine captain wasn't going to happen. 'Okay, Ruski, I'll send a rigger and an electrician up to give you lights and a rock hoist; you just carry on.'

'You send Zoran the Croat, I work him.' He turned back to the grizzly. Later the rescue captain, a man named McCormack, a decent sort of guy and a very experienced miner, would tell how he knew, looking into the crazed eyes of the Russian, that the giant would have snapped his neck like a chicken bone and thrown him back down the entry shaft had he taken a step towards the grizzly. He felt a lot better about not examining the accident site when the electrician returned after setting up the lights to report that the rescue was futile; there was absolutely no chance of my having survived.

Rasputin had allowed the rigger, a Yugoslav simply known as Zoran, to remain and had demanded that his own gang, only just rested from hauling timbers, be sent up to him. Maintaining his furious though measured pace, he timbered up the shaft above the grizzly. Three hours passed before it was safe to enter the shaft where I lay buried.

Rasputin, his woollen miner's vest and the shirt over it soaked with perspiration, paused only briefly to drink a canteen of water before allowing himself to be lowered by the hoist the Yugo had rigged to the rock covering me nearly fifty feet below. Working with great grunts he started to fill the hoist basket, giving a short, sharp whistle each time the basket was ready to be hauled up.

With Rasputin safely down the shaft McCormack and the remainder of the rescue crew, together with the three grizzly men, had crowded into the grizzly area. The white men worked with the blacks to empty the basket and pass the rock along fire-bucket style to the air escape shaft. The Russian's work proved to be a model rescue operation and McCormack set up the oxygen tent and the transfusion apparatus he knew the mine medic would want when eventually he arrived.

McCormack would have liked to have sent an African down every ten minutes, about the time it took to exhaust a man lifting rocks, some of which weighed as much as fifty pounds. But he knew Rasputin would not allow this. An African careless or inexperienced might cause a rock slide, impacting the rock which lay over me even further. Until he actually lifted my body and held my chest to his ear, Rasputin was not going to accept my death.

Men, especially miners, who live in the constant shadow of death do not stand mute-voiced and solemn for hours at the scene of an accident. The look one sees on the gawking faces of people surrounding a road accident victim is not the same as the one worn by miners. Miners carry their grief in an outwardly matter of fact way, each man a silent repository of his own feelings, each grizzly man knowing his name may well be on the next card in a stacked deck.

Mick Spilleen, known of course, as Mickey Spillane, an illiterate Irishman who had been in the School of Mines with me and who had only just volunteered to come back onto grizzlies in an attempt to pay his gambling debts, was the first to start the betting. 'The Ruski won't make it, I'm tellin' you now, lads.'

'I reckon he will, man,' someone else said, probably Van Wyck the Afrikaner. Suddenly every one was in on the betting. Even Elijah, who had refused to leave the grizzly level when my gang had been relieved, was allowed to put five pounds, a week's wages, on the Russian getting to my body before he collapsed. Mickey then offered odds of fifty to one on my being alive and this time only the little African took the bet, putting another week's wages on the talisman who had kept them all alive over almost nine months. Most of the men bet against Rasputin lasting the distance and the bets between the dozen or so whites present amounted to nearly two thousand pounds. When, years later, I told Hymie of the incident, asking him how he would have bet, he had laughed, 'The Irishman was right; only I'd have offered two hundred to one against your making it. But I would have shortened the odds on the Russian.'

Rasputin's tremendous energy was beginning to give out. He was digging deep for the strength to keep going, his breathing laboured and rasping. When the basket was filled he could no longer summon up the breath to whistle. Zoran, watching from the top, would start to lift the basket, whereupon the giant would stoop down, his huge hands raw and bleeding, clasping his knees. Once he threw up, and once he removed his torn shirt and miner's vest and, tearing strips from the shirt, bound his bloody hands. But always as the bucket lowered he was ready to start loading again. Several of the men had offered to replace him but he'd simply shaken his head. 'Nyet, nyet!' he gasped. Soon the flinted edges of the broken rock he was lifting cut into his chest and stomach. His dirt-covered torso, caught in the light from the single electric bulb burning directly above him, glistened with blood and raw exposed flesh, his stomach muscles pumping red. The men above watched fascinated, waiting for the moment when the giant would collapse.

'He's done for, I'm tellin' you now; half a ton more and he's history,' Mickey whispered, even though there was no chance of the Russian hearing him or even understanding his heavy brogue. What they were witnessing was a great feat of strength and they told each other they would one day tell their grandchildren of this night.

It must have been about this time when Rasputin heard me groan, though how he would have done so over his rasping breath was a miracle. He gave a sharp agonised cry and threw himself at the rock in the area from which the sound had come. No longer bothering about the basket he tore the rock aside, frantically stacking it behind him. He worked, 'possessed by the devil himself', Mickey later claimed. Rasputin was finding strength to continue from beyond the realm of normal human consciousness, his breath coming in short animal snorts, like a pig sniffing for truffles. The blood streamed from his chest and stomach, soaking the top of his pants down to the knees while the ragged bandages were ripped from hands reduced to raw slabs of meat.

When he finally reached me, wedged miraculously under the narrow though protective ledge, my body was soaked in blood, as it turned out, from large sections of skin which had been removed in the fall. Rasputin lifted my unconscious body to his chest and placed his ear to my heart.

'Peekay he live!' he wailed. Slowly he sunk to the ground, his legs no longer able to hold him.

We sat in a nest of rock like the one the loneliness bird laid deep inside me, my head resting in the giant's blood-soaked lap. He'd severed his index finger at the first knuckle and as he tenderly stroked my forehead the blood from the stump ran down my brow and filled the cups made by my closed eyes. The hollows soon filled, then ran from the overflowing bowl down my cheeks. Rasputin tried to stop the flow, wiping at it with the stump of his severed finger, unaware of the real source of the blood. 'Peekay! Rasputin find Peekay; Rasputin make rabbit stew,' he sobbed.

Later Mickey Spillane would claim that when they got to us there were tears of real blood coming from the giant's eyes, but by that time he was already dead.

I spent a week in hospital, most of it being treated for shock. The skin had been scraped from a large part of my body and I was badly bruised, but not a single bone was broken. When I regained consciousness and heard of Rasputin's death I wept and then begged that they delay the burial until I could attend his funeral. In a hot climate in a town without a mortuary it wasn't possible and the huge Georgian had been buried for three days when they released me from the cottage hospital. While I looked a mess with both eyes blackened and the skin on each side of my face purple with scab, I was in excellent shape. My first task was to go to the general store in Luanshya and order a tombstone for Rasputin, a black granite slab which would have to come from Bulawayo more than six hundred miles to the south and would take several weeks. On it would be written simply *RASPUTIN, maker of excellent rabbit stew, who gave his life for his friend.* I then went to the small cemetery where he lay under a mound of red clay. On top of the clay was a single wreath of battered gladioli. We were almost at the beginning of the rainy season and it had rained a little the previous night and the heavy drops of tropical rain had kicked up the red clay so that the pink and orange petals, opaque from being wet, were stained with mud. Rasputin loved wild flowers as Doc had loved aloe: why is it that the ubiquitous gladioli always crowds everything else out? I dropped painfully to my haunches as the scab on the side of my leg stretched, and read the mud-splashed card on the wreath. *RIP. The management, Rhoan Antelope Mine.* That was all. I had taken Rasputin's old shotgun with me and now I rose, and lifting the old gun to my shoulder I fired both barrels over his grave. It was a pointless gesture, I guess, and the kick of the gun into my bruised shoulder made me hop around in pain. But it was just the sort of thing which could happen in a Wednesday matinee Western and of which I could see Rasputin thoroughly approving.

The following day I returned to the grave, having loaded all Rasputin's wooden balls into the back of a borrowed utility. With a long-handled lasher's shovel I flattened the mound and buried the shotgun next to him; then I built a pyramid over the grave using all the wooden balls. When I was finished it stood five foot tall. Taking careful measurements I had the welding shop at number nine shaft make me a pyramid-shaped containing frame with small bars running parallel every four inches across the sides, so that the balls, while being clearly seen, could not be removed. The metal frame was completed in two days and together with the help of Zoran the Yugo I rigged a hoist over Rasputin's grave and dropped it neatly over the wooden balls, seating the corners into a cement footing.

It made a very impressive tombstone and when his headstone arrived Rasputin's grave would be the pride of the tiny cemetery.

Together with Zoran, who could speak a little Russian, we went through Rasputin's papers. There wasn't very much to tell of his past; Norwegian seaman's papers bearing his name, a Russian passport and his discharge papers from the Russian navy which indicated he'd been a stoker. Finally we found a sheet of paper on which a woman's name, similar to the one in his passport, was written. It was followed by an address in Russia. Zoran had said that a slight difference in surname was common in Russia and I gathered he meant that this was a feminine version of the male surname. Rasputin's bank account came to nearly seven thousand pounds and I arranged to send this to the name on the slip of paper, after taking Zoran with me and convincing the district magistrate that this was Rasputin's closest kin. A wife, a sister or a mother? But at least someone, somewhere, other than me, who would remember him for the good fortune he had brought them.

I had been visited in hospital by Fats Greer, the part-time insurance agent. He pushed a piece of paper in front of me. 'Sign here, Peekay,' he said, his pudgy finger indicating a blank line on the sheet of paper. I signed. 'I need two cheques for twenty pounds each, don't date them.' To my surprise he produced my cheque book. 'Elijah, your number one boy, delivered your *chorla* bag to the mine captain after your accident. I took the liberty of using the keys in it.' I nodded still a bit dazed and not really knowing what was happening; as far as I knew he had refused to cover me for the last two months on grizzlies. I signed the cheques and asked him what it was all about. 'I'll tell you when you feel a little better.' He grinned, 'The crazy Ruski gave you more than his life, son.' A week later I was to learn that Rasputin had a long-standing insurance policy with Fats Greer for a thousand pounds and had made me the benefactor. Fats also handed me a cheque for five hundred pounds, 'What's this for?'

'Your accident compo,' he replied. 'Check your cheque butts, you never missed a premium.' He walked away whistling to himself.

It meant that I had no need to return to the mines for a further three months. As Solly Goldman would have put it, 'You're home and hosed, my son!' With the money I had saved and Rasputin's legacy I had sufficient funds for three years at Oxford. I also had enough left over to travel to London once a week for training by the famous Dutch Holland. Holland didn't usually take amateurs but Hymie had sweet-talked him into allowing me to show my stuff. If he liked what he saw, he'd take me into the professional ranks under his care.

I had three weeks' sick leave after coming out of hospital and I knew that the best way to get rid of my bruises was to work my body. I put in a lot of road. I also rigged an extra heavy homemade canvas punchbag the mine sailmaker had made for me, hanging it from a rafter Zoran had reinforced on the verandah of my rondavel. Beside it hung the speedball and the lighter punching bag I had brought from South Africa and on which I had worked out every day I had been at the mines.

Speed was something I couldn't afford to lose and while the work in the mines had built up my body so that I was by now almost a welterweight, I didn't want to forgo speed for the extra power I had gained. The year away from boxing had been good for me. While I hadn't talked about it to anyone even in the letters I wrote, the flame that lit my ambition to be welterweight champion of the world burned as fiercely as ever and had never left me for even one single moment of any one day.

In fact, when I regained consciousness in the hospital I thought that I had been fighting for the world championship and that I had been knocked out. The disappointment I felt was enormous, and when I was fully conscious and aware of what had happened I comforted myself with the knowledge that I now knew what it felt like to lose the world championship; it now only remained for me to experience winning it.

I sweated out the aches and pains over three hard training sessions a day. Within a fortnight the scabs were beginning to flake off, leaving large blotches of new pink skin all over my body which made me look a little like an albino who'd been passed backwards through a meatgrinder. My head had also been shaved to get at a cut on my skull which had turned out to be pretty superficial and had only required five stitches. As Solly Goldman would say, I looked a proper Charlie. The mine required that I complete a final shift, though not on a grizzly, so that I could sign all my papers and be passed as completely fit again. This was so that I couldn't sue them at some later date for some real or imagined after-effect.

I spent the last week of my sick leave writing home, to Miss Bornstein and Mrs Boxall and of course to Hymie who had written to me weekly from Oxford. I also wrote to Gert and to Gideon Mandoma who was already beginning to write quite well himself. Finally I wrote to Singe 'n Burn whose retirement from the Prince of Wales School coincided almost exactly with my own from the mines. They had all written regularly with Miss Bornstein and Mrs Boxall keeping up with Hymie and Singe 'n Burn, to my constant surprise, wrote every six weeks or so. After his initial disappointment over my refusal to take a scholarship to a South African university he had become imbued with the idea that I should make it to Oxford under my own steam and had arranged for me to be accepted at Magdalen College with Hymie. I knew this final letter telling them all that I'd made it would be a big event for them. I was back on track and all would be forgiven. The prodigal son had returned. I even wondered if old Mr Bornstein might let me win another game of chess.

There had been almost a full case of brandy left in Rasputin's hut and I decided to take it up to the crud bar on the Saturday before my final work day on Monday. I left it this late, not wishing to be seen much in public. I was quite well known around town because I played scrum-half for the Luanshya rugby team and had been selected on three occasions to play for the Copperbelt. It embarrassed me to be made a fuss of and so I kept pretty much to myself.

I intended to go to the crud bar just after three o'clock when Fritz One, Two and Three came on duty. The idea of going earlier when the Mrs Fritzs were doing the morning shift and being fussed over by the three fat fraus was too much to contemplate.

I planned to ask Fritz whoever to raffle off the case of brandy and to use the proceeds to buy ice cream for the kids at the Wednesday matinee in memory of Rasputin. I figured the brandy would more than likely raise enough money to pay for ice cream for several weeks. It was something I felt sure Rasputin would have liked.

I had attended the last two Wednesday matinees, sitting in the same place Rasputin and I had sat. The kids had come in as usual and sat all around me. I groaned and moaned and shouted and generally carried on a treat in all the places the big Russian would have done. At first the kids did not respond but I persisted and soon they fell into the familiar mood and we all had a good time. Except at the end of the first Wednesday I began to cry which had spoilt it a bit for them. As usual during interval I bought ice creams all round and the kids went along with the new game, knowing full well what I was attempting to do. When, at the third Wednesday matinee after Rasputin's death, I told them I would be leaving, two small boys had approached me.

'Don't you worry about Ruski's grave and the wooden balls and all, we'll look after them for you, Peekay,' the larger of the two assured me.

'Yes, for ever and ever!' the smaller added.

Rasputin's affairs were finally in the only hands he would have personally trusted. 'You'll have to paint the metal pyramid frame every year or it will rust away after a while,' I said.

'What colour?' the bigger one asked.

'Red, of course!' the smaller answered.

'Yes, red, that would do nicely,' I said.

'You see, I told you! Russians like red,' the small boy said in triumph.

I lugged the case of brandy up to the crud bar. It was early yet and only a handful of men were there. On the few occasions I had been in the bar I had done my drinking with Fritz Three and I now walked over to his section of the long bar and explained my purpose.

'Ja, for sure, we do this, but you must make ze book,' Fritz Three replied emphatically, as though the idea had been his all along. Without my asking he made up a large lemon squash with soda and a dash of bitters the way I liked it.

'No, no, I don't want to bet, just a raffle, Fritz Three.'

'Ja raffle! You make ze book, come I show you.' He raised the bar panel to let me in behind the bar, and lifting the case of brandy he indicated that I should follow him into a back room which turned out to be an office. From a drawer he withdrew a staple gun, a roll of adding machine paper about two inches wide, an old Croxley fountain pen repaired with an inky piece of sticking plaster, scissors, an ink pad and rubber stamp. Working quickly he cut off a four-inch length of paper and wrote the number one at each end of the strip, doing this until he had twenty slips of paper marked from one to twenty which he then stamped on the right-hand side with the rubber stamp which read Luanshya Club and stapled the opposite end to make a neat little book of raffle tickets.

'Now we have one raffle book, ja? You make like this for five hundred tickets . . . Okey dokey?' I nodded and then told him that I wanted to buy two more bottles of brandy to complete the case. 'No, Fritz buy!' he said, jabbing his finger at his chest. 'Ruski he my fren.' He left me in the office and returned to his bar.

I worked happily making tickets for an hour or so, creating a sophisticated version by using a large pin to punch a perforation line down the centre of each book I completed so the bit the customer retained could be parted easily. The noise in the bar grew steadily as more and more men came in. Making the raffle tickets was routine work and I was soon lost in thought, oblivious to the noise outside.

A soft, though urgent whistle cut through my day-dreaming. I looked up to see the large shape of Fritz Three filling the doorway. I was immediately aware that there was silence in the crud bar.

The fat German seemed agitated, his mouth working wordlessly and one hand hooking the air in an urgent gesture for me to approach.

'What's wrong, Fritz?' He winced at the sound of my voice.

'Shh! You will be quiet please, we have here some trouble, ja.' I rose and walked quietly towards him. 'Botha! Botha, the diamond driller, he got powder headache and he go mad.' He stabbed his forefinger over his shoulder. 'If he find you he vill kill you!' he whispered hoarsely.

'Shit Fritz, Botha's my diamond driller, he wouldn't hurt me,' I whispered back.

Fritz Three grabbed me by the shirtfront. 'He does this before. All men must bugger off from crud bar when Botha drink the brandy, until he is kaput and falls on the floor. Ja, this is when I call the hospital. If he catch you, he kill you, Peekay.' He pointed to the window. 'Please you will jump now.'

I moved over to the window and attempted to open it, but it had been nailed shut. Suddenly the snake was back in my mind's eye, its diamond-shaped head with tiny darting tongue flicking faster than I could blink. I turned back at the sound of a cry of panic from Fritz Three to see his fat body jerked backwards into the bar beyond. A huge man, almost the size of Rasputin, rushed forward crashing his forehead against the top of the doorway. He let out a roar of astonished pain and blood ran from his head as he stooped to enter. His eyes were puffed and swollen and shot with blood. From his nostrils ran a thick trickle of yellow mucus.

'*Kom hier jou fokker*!' he roared as he came at me with both hands, bending forward slightly as though he were about to catch a trapped rabbit.

'It's me, Botha! It's Peekay, your grizzly man!' I shouted back at him.

The huge man seemed not to hear me. 'I kill you! I kill you, you bastard!' His sleeves were rolled up almost to the top of the shoulder in the Afrikaans manner and as he lunged at me I saw the tattoo.

Under normal circumstances I would have easily avoided his clumsy lunge but the shock of recognition caused me to freeze on the spot. Tattooed high up on Botha's left arm was a jagged, badly etched swastika. I had seen this tattoo before . . . on the Judge.

Botha, the Judge now grown into a crazed giant of a man, grabbed my shirtfront with one massive hand, and with the other he grabbed the back of my belt. He lifted me from the ground and moving through the door he threw me over the long bar into the bar room beyond.

I landed on all fours, but managed to break my fall with the butt of both hands. An anger so cold and fierce possessed me that I felt my mind would have to be torn from it, like a finger torn from dry ice. My concentration was so complete that the edges of the room disappeared and the huge form of the Judge as he climbed over the bar came into such sharp focus that, at ten feet, I could see the individual hairs on his day-old stubble.

'First with the head and then with the heart, that way small can beat big.' It was Hoppie's voice that I heard in my head and my resolve became a solid force, a pure, clean feeling, totally controlled by my head.

'Jaapie Botha come! Come, man, come, I've been waiting for you for most of my life.' There was a menacing growl in my voice I had not heard there before.

Fritz Three, back behind the safety of the long bar, screamed at me. 'He been sniff gelignite, he crazy! Run, Peekay. That Boer kill you!'

The Judge dropped from the bar and with an angry roar charged towards me. A powder headache as severe as his could cause temporary insanity and I knew he was capable of killing. I stepped to the side and hit him with a left uppercut hard on the nose, seating the punch deep, aware that the crude explosion of pain into the swollen sinus tissue would be devastating. A man my size. would certainly have passed out from the blow. Bellowing like a wounded animal, the Judge turned to face me again, blood and mucus running from his nose.

I had waited a long time for this moment; I knew exactly what to do. The Judge was the bull and I was the matador; it was I who would shape the fight. I knew suddenly that all of Geel Piet's footwork had been designed for this moment; it was time for the 'klein baas' to dance.

The Judge was a man of around twenty-five but he had already let himself go around the middle and his brandy gut hung over his belt. Years of working on a farm and then in the mines had built up his bulk and he was probably at the height of his physical strength. But, looking at him, I knew his condition was poor. With his sinuses already severely blocked I would try to work on his mouth. If I could make him swallow enough blood as well as lead him into frequent charges, he'd soon be winded. My hands were strong from carving Rasputin's balls and the skin and knuckles were hardened from the canvas punching bag I had worked with my bare fists. The Judge charged repeatedly and each time he came at me I stepped in with a lightning punch and hit him on the nose or in the mouth. Soon he was spitting a lot of blood, his chest heaving deeply as he tried to regain his breath. The salty blood would be mixing with the brandy in his stomach by now. Later I would put a Geel Piet eight right into the nexus of the solar plexus, where all the nerve ends came together.

He was beginning to move more slowly, trying to get me into a corner where he could crush me. I let him work me until he had my back right into the corner then I lifted my hands up as if I was going to plead for mercy. His punch came from ten miles away, I ducked and weaved out of the corner as his huge fist smashed into the wall. His knuckles split, the bones in his wrist smashing through the skin, splattering blood all over the tiles as his wrist and hand broke.

The cold rage inside me cocooned me into a circle of concentration, centred on the Judge and myself. Like a Goya painting, only the action in the centre mattered; the rest was blurred peripheral belonging to another place and another time. I was unaware that the space behind the bar had filled, a couple of hundred miners were standing three deep along the sixty-foot counter. The Judge turned suddenly and lumbered towards the bar. Men pushed back in fear and collided with shelves and bottles of spirit which rained down on them. The Judge grabbed a half empty bottle of brandy from the counter which no one had thought to remove. He smashed it on the edge of the bar, sending a spray of brandy into his face, some of it going into his eyes and blinding him. The Geel Piet eight went into the blinded man's gut and I finished it off with an uppercut into his pulped and smashed nose. By the time he swung the broken bottle I was clear again.

The Judge, as though in slow motion, fell to his knees and threw up onto the floor. The fight had been going nearly twenty minutes and I hadn't said a word, my fury concentrated in both my hands. My knuckles were raw and bleeding from hitting him, but I felt nothing.

As he sat there in his own vomit a small child's voice cried out from somewhere deep inside my body, 'You killed Granpa Chook!'

The Judge rose slowly to his feet using the broken bottle to push himself up off the floor. His face was a bloody mess, blood dripped from his broken hand and wrist, the front of his shirt stuck to his chest and stomach, soaked with brandy, blood and vomit. He lifted his head and looked up at me, through his broken lips he whispered the single word, 'Pisskop.' Using his remaining strength he hurled the broken bottle at me missing me by several inches. His useless broken hand and wrist hung at his side and he swayed unsteadily on his feet. The Solly Goldman thirteen went in, each punch deep and hard into the Judge's gut. The hurl of vomit travelled three feet before it splashed to the floor as the Judge collapsed unconscious.

My head exploded. The roar in my head was all white light. It was time for the heart. I was onto his body in a flash, straddling his torso. The snot and blood ran from his nose as his head rested on his right arm just above the broken wrist. His left arm with the swastika tattoo faced me. I was unaware of having gone to my shorts but Doc's Joseph Rogers pocket knife was open in my hand, the blade small but razor sharp. It struck high up on the arm where the mamba strikes and sliced through the epidermis above the ragged swastika, the blade cutting a square about four inches across and three down, then I crossed the square from corner to corner to make an X in a cross of St Andrew and then again from centre to centre to make the cross of St George, cutting deep almost to the muscle. The blood, before it started to run down his arm, made a perfect Union Jack. Across the jagged blue lines of the swastika I cut P. K. Then, smearing my hand into the mess on his shirtfront, I rubbed it into the Union Jack and into the initials, knowing it would set up a massive infection and cause the keloid to build up on the arm. Nothing would ever remove the wide band of scar tissue which would form to make up the flag and the initials which cancelled the swastika. I wiped my hands and the blade of Doc's knife on the back of the Judge's shirt and rose to my feet. Closing the blade of Doc's Joseph Rogers I returned it to the pocket of my blood-splattered shorts. 'Rasputin thanks you for the brandy, Botha,' I said, suddenly calm.

I became aware of the men behind the bar. They hadn't moved and were silent, their eyes following me, as I walked slowly towards the Western style saloon doors and then out of the crud bar. Outside, high above me, a full moon, pale as skimmed milk, floated in a day sky. I felt clean, all the bone-beaked loneliness birds banished, their rocky nests turned to river stones. Cool, clear water bubbled over them, streams in the desert.

TANDIA

For Damon Courtenay, my son. Who through all the bad years never once asked, 'Why me?'

Together since the world began, the madman and the lover.
Discovered by Allied troops written on a latrine wall at Dachau.

ACKNOWLEDGEMENTS

Writing is one of the lonely things we do, yet every writer needs friends who help in little ways and big. This second book has been very difficult as, I am told, second books are meant to be. My thanks to my wife, Benita, who did the continuity reading and who wasn't afraid to tell me when she thought it wasn't working; Owen Denmeade, who waited every fortnight for the next chapter and helped in a hundred different ways; Alex Hamill and my agency George Patterson, who again made things easier in the balance between a working writer and a writer who also works.

In South Africa those people who helped generously with time and information: Lynette McGuire, who so very competently checked my facts and who did the political and historical research and much more; Dr Louis and Justine Rapeport; Leigh Voight; Jorgen Schaderburg, whose photography for *Drum* magazine gave me the mood and tense of the time in which I write; T. P. Naidoo for his insights into the Durban Indian community in the fifties and Mrs Mayat for the same; Shaun Rack, whose unshakeable belief in his sad country helped temper my pen.

In America: Louis H. Holt of Reno, Nevada; the poet Tenbroek Patterson in Cambridge, Mass.

In London: Prof. Louis Ecksteen of the S.A. Embassy; M. M. Dube of the Swaziland High Commission; Mic Cheetham, my agent, who works quietly behind the scenes.

In Australia: Jill Hickson, my agent, who has done so very much to ensure my success as a writer; Prof. Brent Waters; Dr Irwin Light; Erica Light; Chig Chignall; Ray Black; Alan Barry; Julie Quinlivan, who designed the dust jacket; Giles Hugo, Sharon Dunn and Heidi Smith.

Also, those writers too numerous to mention from whom I have borrowed facts and insights on and into South Africa.

Finally, Laura Longrigg my London editor, who made the rough passages smooth in more than one way.

BOOK ONE

ONE

On the morning she was raped Tandia had risen just before dawn and come back to the graveside to pay her proper respects to Patel. Someone had been there before her. She looked at the grass around the grave but only her own footprints showed on its wet, dew-frosted surface. They must have come last night.

Tandia had been the last to leave the funeral on the previous evening, just a little after sunset when the cicadas in the dusty mimosa trees around the cemetery had suddenly shut down. She'd watched the two black grave-diggers working to fill the hole. As they sliced their long-handled shovels into the red clay they chanted a soft urgent rhythm. When they'd heaped the soil high enough and patted it down and rounded it properly, one of them, using the back of his shovel, drove a crude wooden cross into the comfortable looking mound of soil. They departed still singing softly, shovels across their sweat-wet shoulders, their diminishing shapes outlined against the red sun.

Tandia had arranged all the wreaths over the bare mound of earth. Directly under the wooden cross she'd placed a large bunch of Easter lilies wrapped in cellophane. The card, pinned to the broad satin ribbon, read: 'REST IN PEACE, PATEL. POLICE BOYS BOXING CLUB'.

Now, someone had moved the Easter lilies to the side to make a place at the foot of the cross for a small Indian oil lamp with a bright blue flame that burned perfectly still, as though frozen in the pewter light. Beside it stood a tiny brass vase from which burned four sticks of incense, and around the cross hung a bright garland of miniature orange and yellow marigolds.

Tandia watched as tiny puffs of grey smoke broke away from the sticks. The incense made a warm smell in the dawn air, a little bit of home comfort for Natkin Patel, South Africa's best-known Indian boxing referee, who had been born a Hindu and who died a Christian.

Tandia wondered about the appearance of the Indian stuff on Patel's grave. Was Patel already a Christian when he had put his curry sausage into her black mother? Or did it happen only after she was born? Which God was going to punish him for bringing a bastard mixed-race child into the world? Do you suppose the Gods keep score? When you turn your back on one God and choose another, does the old God demand vengeance? Or would the Lord Krishna, Patel's old God, be satisfied with a garland of miniature marigolds, four sticks of incense burning in a cheap brass vase and a lighted oil lamp? A careful person like Patel would not have wanted to take any chances. For damn sure, he would have decided it couldn't hurt to leave both gates to paradise a little open. That was Patel all right. He'd always liked to make arrangements a long way ahead.

Patel would have liked the funeral. Quite a lot of white people came. Also, of course, important leaders of the Durban Indian community. Because he was Church of England, which is a pretty rare thing to be when you are a South African Indian, and because he was well respected by the police, they had given permission for his lying-in to take place at Kruger's Funeral Parlour.

Kruger said he was prepared to make this concession for a boxing referee and coach who, even if he was an Indian, was greatly respected and a good type of man. Nevertheless, allowing a dead Indian to be laid out for inspection in a whites-only funeral parlour was a very brave and honourable thing for him to do. To show their appreciation, Mrs Patel and the two boys, Teddy and Billy, had asked Kruger, along with Captain Vermaak, president of the Police Boys' Boxing Club, to be pall bearers.

Lying in the small funeral parlour in his expensive stinkwood coffin, arms crossed, eyes closed, his curry-coloured skin with its tiny indented smallpox scars losing its sheen, Patel looked different. It was his hair; it was no longer parted the way he always wore it, pasted down with Brylcreem so that the roadway down the centre of the scalp was precise, not a single hair trespassing to the other side. Kruger, who should have known better, had parted Patel's hair with a side parting. Patel looked like a stranger.

Patel was Tandia's only loved one. If you could call him that. He hadn't even touched her since she was six years old. She knew that as a baby he'd loved her, she knew that for sure. Now, before he was dead that is, she didn't think so. Maybe he just felt guilty. Although guilty was perhaps the wrong word. More like ashamed. Ashamed that a person like him had sunk so low as to do it to a kaffir woman. She loved him anyway.

Tandia had always thought the time would come when he'd love her again. When she was grown up, after she'd done all the things he wanted her to do, then there would be a reconciliation. He would recognise that he had a clever daughter as well as two fat legitimate sons who were, anyway, a load of rubbish. It wasn't fair! Patel just wasn't the sort who would go and drop dead on a person. Especially in the boxing ring with white people standing all around. He would rather die than have a thing like that happen to him.

The morning of his death, when he'd appeared at the back steps for his boots, he'd been his usual self, the smooth skin on his forehead glowing, his hair oiled and parted perfectly in the middle, the pleats in his gaberdine trousers sharp as a knife and his heavily starched white shirt crackling as he pulled his boots on. That morning he'd been a million miles from being dead.

Yesterday, after the first few Indians had gone into the funeral parlour they came back out into the bright sunshine, but instead of saying nothing, like people do at such times, everyone was whispering about the wrong parting of Patel's hair. 'What can you expect? Isn't that typical of the whites to bugger up an important thing like a person's hair!' Of course the whisper didn't get to where Mr Kruger was standing under a big old fig tree with all the other white people from the boxing club.

Tandia waited until the last mourner had come out of the parlour. She stood beside the coffin and looked furtively up at the white funeral attendant in the frock coat and cravat who stood watch beside Patel's dead body. He was young and fat and his face was covered in acne scars and purplish bumps where the acne still bothered him. He didn't look too dangerous; still, you never knew with those young white guys. What if she acted brave as anything?

Just the thought of going up to this oozy white person made Tandia's mouth go dry. If Patel was alive he would have been able to do it. He was always boasting that he was well known in white circles. As a small child Tandia had thought he said white *circus.* For years she imagined Patel was some sort of performer, an acrobat or something. But now there was nobody who would be game enough to take the matter up with Mr Kruger. She'd watched the Indian mourners as they came out of the little chapel; one thing was for sure, none of them was going to make a fuss about Patel's hair.

Tandia moved up to the fat white man in the frock coat. 'Excuse me, *meneer.*'

'Can I help you?' She was surprised he spoke English; she'd expected him to be an Afrikaner.

Despite her boldness, the dryness in Tandia's mouth stopped her next words. She had first to work her tongue around the top of her mouth before she spoke again. 'Excuse me, sir, you combed his hair all wrong. It should be parted down the middle.'

There was a moment's silence as the attendant looked at Patel and then back at Tandia. 'That's not my job.' He turned and, pointing to heavy red velvet drapes that hung from the ceiling to the floor and formed the rear wall of the chapel, he added, 'The corpses, I mean the passed-away persons, they all done by Mr Kruger, the boss. I just stand by the coffin, you understand?' He leant forward, his voice almost a whisper. 'I'm just here in case someone gets hysterical and flings themselves on the body.' His voice was surprisingly high and whiney, and he was plainly as intimidated by these surroundings as Tandia. 'Please don't make trouble, this is the first time I done this job.' He shrugged his shoulders and the nape of his frock coat rose up to his ears and then fell back again. 'That's why Mr Kruger gave me only a coolie funeral.'

Tandia smiled up at him. He was a dumbbell but she sensed he meant no harm and this gave her the confidence she needed to continue. 'Tell me, please, have you got a comb?'

'Yes, of course.' The big man brought his hands up and patted both sides of his breast frantically, producing a small black comb from his top left pocket. The movement was amazingly quick for such a big, slow-thinking man.

Struggling to remain calm, Tandia said, 'Perhaps, maybe you could comb my father's hair with a middle parting?' She smiled. 'Please, so he dies happy?'

'No way!' He pulled back in alarm. 'No, man, I can't do that. I don't do the touching. I don't touch no stiffs, I can't do what you asking me. No bladdy way!'

Tandia snatched the comb from his hand and quickly combed Natkin Patel's stiff hair over his eyes. Swallowing her panic, she said to herself, 'Please God forgive me, I'm only doing this so he dies happy, he was a very proud man!' She drew the small comb down the centre of the cold scalp; it was like parting a doll's hair on a papier-mâché head. But Patel's hair had been lacquered to keep it in place. 'Please God, make it lie down!' she pleaded. Frantic, she flung the comb down on his chest and used the palms of her hands to smooth the hair down on either side of his skull. Patel's head was icy cold to her touch and she gave a short, involuntary shiver. It still wasn't perfect, but it looked okay, much more like the real Patel; like he'd been asleep and mussed it up a bit.

The white man at her side cleared his throat. 'Come, hurry up, *jong.* I got to close the lid now.'

Tandia nodded. 'Thank you, sir, he can rest in peace now.'

Reaching behind a vase of gladioli he brought out a large screwdriver. 'Ag, man, he's dead anyway, I don't see what his hair has got to do with anything.' From his trouser pocket he produced a large brass screw and, closing the lid of the coffin, he inserted the screw into the keyhole of the brass locking-plate and screwed it shut. Tandia remembered she'd left his comb resting on Patel's beautifully starched shirtfront. It was too late to rescue it and she hoped the attendant wouldn't remember. It was a cheap comb anyway; for sixpence you could buy one like it anywhere.

The funeral parlour attendant replaced the screwdriver and moved over to the rear wall of the chapel where he pulled open the drapes to reveal a large, round-shouldered radiogram. He pushed a small lever on the turntable and the record arm rose. Removing the record and blowing on it quickly, he flipped it onto the reverse side and re-positioned it. Then he pushed down on the lever again and the arm rose slowly, swung above the turning record and plunged downwards. With a slight crackle of static, the needle came to rest in a groove and almost immediately the strains of a Bach funeral cantata filled the small room. The big man rolled his eyes and let out a huge sigh of relief. In his anxiety to get his routine right he appeared to have forgotten about Tandia. He jerked the curtain together and moved hurriedly towards the closed chapel doors, pausing only to adjust his coat, pulling simultaneously at both sides of his lapels. Taking a deep breath, he straightened up, lifted his chin and swung the doors inwards so that the organ music could escape into the sunshine.

Tandia slipped quietly behind the curtain where she watched as the light flooded into the dark funeral parlour. She could see Teddy and Billy, the two Patel boys, coming up the steps followed by Kruger and Captain Vermaak. Behind them came four Indian friends of Patel. They all had their hands clasped as they walked over to Patel's coffin and took up their positions. The organ music rose to a crescendo and Kruger nodded to the attendant who, in turn, nodded back to the pall bearers who hoisted Patel's stinkwood coffin onto their shoulders and carried it slowly back towards the door. Billy and Teddy on either side at the front led the coffin out and the attendant, looking pleased that he'd pulled it all off successfully, brought up the rear.

Tandia forbade herself to cry at the funeral. Crying was the biggest mistake she could make in front of Mrs Patel. If Mrs Patel saw her crying she knew what she'd be thinking. 'That coloured bitch is trying to show more grief than his proper family!' By closely observing the business of death, her mind stayed busy and she was able to push her sorrow aside by crowding it with detail.

Tandia often did this. When a thing got too hard to bear or if it began to crowd her emotionally, she would do what she thought of as '*thinking a thing inside out*'.

When, for instance, they started to throw handfuls of earth over Patel's coffin it was such a personal and private thing to do that her grief threatened to overwhelm her. She wanted to rush forward and put her own handful of red clay over Patel, to stand over his grave and weep for him. But she dared not move forward. She hadn't been invited to the funeral and she had fully expected Mrs Patel or Billy or Teddy to send her home when she turned up at the parlour. Now she crowded in the details, the droning on of the minister, all the dust-to-dust and ashes-to-ashes stuff, people fidgeting, the Indian guests awkward when the Bible was being read. She watched from the very edge of the mourners, too far away to see into the open hole and positioned so as not to be seen by Mrs Patel or her two fat sons, who were having a really good time sniffling and blowing into their hankies, which was a big, fat laugh, because everyone knew they hated Patel. He wanted them to be boxers but they'd both turned out soft and fat and scared of their own shadows.

Anyone watching the funeral would have picked her out quite easily. At nearly sixteen she was tall and slim for her age and was becoming everything Patel had said she would be. Tandia was not aware of her beauty. Her green eyes, small, straight Indian nose, skin the colour of bluegum honey, beautiful bone structure, full lips and close-cropped peppercorn hair were a cultural corruption, an act of sin. To see her extraordinary beauty you needed eyes that made no racial judgement and there were few of those in South Africa.

Tandia had no guidance into womanhood. It arrived shortly before her thirteenth birthday, one cold June morning three years earlier, when she had awakened and discovered blood. She was terrified. Unable to confide in anyone, she bathed herself and afterwards used an old blouse to make a crude pad before pulling on her school bloomers. That night and for the two following she lay in her dark little shed weeping until she fell asleep exhausted. When she rose at dawn to set and start the kitchen stove she wrapped the blood-spotted rag in a scrap of newspaper and burnt it.

Then the bleeding stopped and that part of her seemed normal again. Two months later the bleeding returned. She felt a terrible despair. Was it the kaffir in her which had caused some dreadful disease? She was going to bleed to death!

Tandia decided to kill herself first. She would take the bus to the beach and just walk into the sea and then keep walking. It was the best thing to do. If Patel knew she had inherited a disease from her black mother's side she felt sure he would no longer keep her or pay for her schooling.

Tandia had decided to do it on the weekend after she'd finished at Patel's printing shop where she worked every Saturday. She would go home to Booth Street as usual and prepare the Patels' dinner. That would leave her plenty of time before eleven o'clock curfew to take the bus to the beach and hide some place. After curfew it would be quiet, she would wait until the police van had driven up and down the beach to see if any blacks were on the streets, then she would do it. It would definitely be best to die on a Saturday night because on Sunday she had a half-day off and Mrs Patel got Patel's breakfast and so nobody would miss her, not even at lunchtime, because on Sundays Mrs Patel always visited the home of either Teddy or Billy in Clairwood and Patel spent the day at the boxing club..

When they returned in the evening to discover she hadn't prepared the evening meal or even cleaned the house, that was the first time she'd be missed. Which gave her plenty of time to drown, be washed out to sea and never found again.

Maybe they'd even be a little sorry about losing her. She didn't care about Mrs Patel, but she wanted Patel to be sorry. She wanted him to mourn her just a little bit.

Tandia quite liked the idea of simply disappearing off the face of the earth. Though having to die in order to do so seemed unfair.

By Friday however the bleeding had stopped again. Hope springs eternal and it seemed silly to kill herself when maybe she was cured. Tandia's next period occurred on a Monday and was over before Saturday. Once again she was saved from the watery deep.

Tandia began to wonder about the disease. She could honestly say she felt no ill effects from it, in fact, after each time, she seemed if anything to feel better. Her breasts had begun to swell noticeably and her hips didn't seem to jut out as much either. But she had to face reality, for you couldn't get to be thirteen in a place like Cato Manor and not know that there were diseases black women got *down there*, horrible diseases that a person could pass on to someone else and which would eventually kill them as well.

It briefly occurred to Tandia to try to see Dr Rabin, who was a much-loved young white doctor who came even at night for coloureds and blacks and had once come when Patel's pleurisy turned into pneumonia. Except for smallpox and polio vaccinations, which had taken place at school, Tandia had never been near a doctor. Now, having convinced herself that the bleeding was something she had inherited from the black part of her, she became obsessed with hiding it from Patel or anyone who might know the family, even Dr Rabin.

The Thursday her period came back Tandia was locked in the school lavatories when she overheard a conversation between Maree Ratchee and Fatima Suluman, two fifth-form seniors.

'I wish I could get out of stupid basketball tomorrow, there's a Rasheed Mantella film on at the Odeon in Victoria Street,' she heard Fatima say.

'Ag, man, do what I did, tell Miss you got your periods.'

'God, I'm dumb! I should have thought of that!' There was a pause and Fatima's voice brightened. 'It's not too late, I'll tell her they just came!'

'Better be careful, she takes the date down so next time she knows if you lying.'

'But it's true, I really have got my periods, but, to tell you the honest truth I don't bleed very much. I could play if I wanted to.'

'You're lucky, man. I bleed a lot every month and feel lousy,' Maree replied as the two girls left the lavatory block.

Tandia felt quite dizzy. *Period* was a word she'd vaguely heard before from the other girls, always accompanied by giggles, but until this moment it had never occurred to her that it had anything to do with her own condition.

After school that day Tandia waited outside the gates until Fatima Suluman appeared. Nervous, she fell into step beside the bigger girl. At first Fatima appeared not to notice her. It was not unusual for one of the brats to get a crush on a senior and she wasn't going to encourage the little coloured girl.

While Tandia wasn't exactly ostracised by the girls at the school, for the most part their friendliness ended at the school gates. This wasn't so much a thing decided by the girls themselves as by their parents, several of whom had written to the headmistress suggesting that Durban Indian Girls' High was exclusively for Indian girls and that didn't, as far as they understood, include people of mixed race. The headmistress, who was not easily pushed around, and who knew Patel, ignored their letters.

'Fatima, can I ask you a question, please?' Tandia said at last.

'Ja, of course.' She sensed the anxiety in the smaller girl's voice but she was also keen to get rid of Tandia before they reached the bus stop. She didn't want to have to sit with her all the way to Victoria Street where she got off.

'When you bleed every month. Can you tell me about that, please?'

Fatima stopped, taken by surprise. She looked around quickly to see if anyone else had heard, then she turned to Tandia. 'Shhh! Don't talk about such things! Somebody might hear you, jong!'

Tandia's eyes filled with tears, 'Sorry, Fatima, but it's . . . it's happening to me also! I don't know what to do!'

Fatima put her arm around the smaller girl, drawing her into her ample waist. 'C'mon then, stop crying, what's the matter? Tell me, what is it, Tandia?'

The feel of the bigger girl's arm around her was almost more than Tandia could bear. It was the first time in years that someone had touched her to comfort her and she desperately wanted to remain in Fatima's embrace. 'C'mon, it's only your silly periods!' Fatima said gently.

Sniffing, Tandia pulled away. 'I heard you in the lavs today, you were with, with, Maree Ratchee. You said . . .' Tandia let out a sudden sob, 'you said you bleed every month also!'

Fatima took Tandia's hand and together they retraced their steps towards the school gate. She heard the bus arrive and pull to a halt at the bus stop. She'd be late for her afternoon job at the Goodwill Lounge. Never mind, the little kid needed her. 'Listen, we'll go back and sit on a bench in the playground and talk, heh? I'll tell you everything. Don't worry, it's just stuff that happens when you start to become a woman.'

The following morning Fatima found Tandia before school assembly and told her to meet her at the lavs at lunch. At the break Fatima led Tandia into one of the toilets and, opening a brown paper bag, she pulled out a dozen small squares of towelling about the size of a bathroom flannel, an elastic loop large enough to slip around Tandia's waist, and two good-sized safety pins. She quickly showed her how to fashion a snug pad to contain her bleeding and how to attach it with the pins to the loop around her waist.

It was the nicest thing Tandia could ever remember anyone doing for her. Fatima replaced everything in the paper bag and handed it to Tandia who, quite unable to speak, was trying hard to hold back the tears. Fatima closed the door slowly. 'See ya later, alligator!' she said and was gone.

Tandia latched the lavatory door where she remained for the rest of her lunch break. At first she cried a bit, hugging the brown paper bag to her chest. Then she put the bag on the floor between her legs and hugged herself again, but this time she smiled. She was happy that her childhood was coming to an end and that she had started to become a woman. It meant she was getting closer to the time when Patel would love her again.

Fatima had said after your periods a woman could have a baby. Tandia thought about it being possible for her to have a baby. Not that she would ever have a baby. No man would ever want to marry her anyway. But she didn't care about that. She was glad about that. She shuddered at the thought. Ag, sies! No man was ever going to touch her, put his sausage in her like Patel had done to her mother. Never, never, never! The end of recess bell rang and she picked up the paper bag and ran happily from the toilet block.

Now, three years later, she stood at Patel's graveside just as dawn was breaking. In Tandia's mind she came to have a good talk to him. It had almost been dark by the time she'd completed decorating his grave with the wreaths the previous evening and she hadn't been able to say goodbye properly. She had planned a conversation which she could never have hoped to have with him while he had been alive. But overnight, as she lay in her iron cot in the shed, his death had built a bridge, a place to cross so that she could reach him. In death Patel became the father he had never been in life.

Earlier, as she made her way to the cemetery, she had even tried using the various words for father in her mind. She'd tried the three conventional versions, throwing back her head and saying them out loud, testing them out on the stars in the pre-dawn sky. 'Father!' It sounded awfully posh. Patel was definitely not a 'Father'. 'Dad?' Could she ever have a relationship as casual as such a marvellous, warm, taken-for-granted word? She tried the third, 'Daddy'. She liked it best because it was so patently a contradiction of the relationship she had had with Patel. Except for when she was very small, when she would sit on his knee and he would absently stroke her tiny shoulder and talk to people about her green eyes. At that time the word had been possible and now that Patel was dead she wanted it returned to her.

But Natkin Patel the small printing shop owner, first-class Indian person, illegitimate curry sausage user, policeman's friend, who was well known in white circles, was still too soon buried for any of these names to work very well.

Tandia's final image of Patel was him sitting on the steps of the back *stoep* not even acknowledging her as she handed him the boots she'd carefully polished. But she knew time and several visits to the cemetery would soften the hard edges of the reality. She would now have someone to whom she could talk, with whom she could share her loneliness, and onto whom she could focus her abundant but unrequited love.

The curious invention of making Patel alive now that he was dead so pleased Tandia that she had momentarily postponed the fear she felt at the prospect of being thrown out on the street when she returned home at sunrise. But now that fear returned. If, as she had decided, she would use Patel's graveside for really important conversations, none was more important than the one she brought with her on this first cold dawn morning.

Tandia finally came to grips with the thing on her mind. The thing she wakened to every day of her life as long as she could remember. The thing she never said aloud, but was now going to ask Patel here in the Indian cemetery with the dew clouding the cellophane wrappings around the Easter lilies and with the pungent smell of the incense filling the air.

In the Indian Christian cemetery there was plenty of room between the graves for patches of grass, dandelion and blackjack to grow. Not many Indians died Christians, so you could pick and choose your spot. Mrs Patel chose a lot about fifteen feet from a grave which boasted a six-foot marble cross and belonged to T. W. Nepul, who had been a wealthy merchant and important spokesman for the Durban Indian community. It was said also that he had been a personal friend of General Smuts. She liked the idea of her own husband being close to a bit of gratuitous wealth and prestige. If a person could pick any spot in the graveyard, as Patel himself would have said, 'Dammit, man, it doesn't do any harm to be always with the best people.'

'What am I?' Tandia began. 'Am I Indian? Or am I a kaffir?' She talked directly to the mound of earth at her feet. 'Please, Patel, what will I do now, you must tell me, please?'

She paused as though waiting for him to answer; then she continued. 'Do you think because I'm mixed race I'm a coloured? I don't want to be a coloured. Also, not a black person. Patel, can I please be an Indian when I grow up? Mrs Patel doesn't like me. When she throws me out and I have to get a passbook from the police, can I tell them I am your daughter, that I'm an Indian girl?'

With Patel's death Tandia knew things were going to be very difficult for her. When she got back to the house in Booth Street she expected no mercy from Mrs Patel. Would she simply send her packing? Kick her out of the only home she had ever known, the dark little corrugated-iron shed in the back yard? In her imagination Tandia could hear the old woman's voice. 'Go on, *voetsak*! Take your things and get out of my house!' Surely she wouldn't do that? She must give her a chance to find a job first!

Mrs Patel was an ignorant woman. She couldn't read or write and hadn't taken up Christianity like her husband. Her own religion commanded absolute obedience to Patel, but she had been deeply disturbed by his change of faith. The Patel caste is a religious one. Other castes may change, could change, but not a Patel. It was a hugely offensive thing to have done to his caste. Especially as Patel's religious zeal was shown to be less one of burning faith than of a desire to achieve assimilation into the European genre. Being a Hindu required her to forgive him everything, even sleeping with a black woman. Now, with Patel dead, the hackles of fidelity and obedience were undone; now she was in control.

From the very beginning Mrs Patel couldn't do anything about the black child her husband had spawned. Natkin Patel wanted his bastard daughter and he seemed to feel an attachment to the plump honey-skinned baby that he'd never felt for his two sons.

'See,' he said, picking her up, 'the skin is soft like velvet, darker, maybe a little darker, but not so black as a kaffir. I'm telling you, man, this one is lucky, bladdy lucky. Look! Green eyes! An Indian and a kaffir mix and, goodness me, out come green eyes!'

Patel was a good cut-man in the ring and so fancied himself a bit medically minded. 'How can it be? You mix a black with an Indian; one thing is certain . . .' he paused for effect, 'all dark eyes, every bugger has dark eyes. Tell me, hey? Where have you seen a green-eyed kaffir or an Indian? 'I'm telling you, not even so many white people have green eyes.' He absent-mindedly stroked the baby. 'Usually with kaffirs you get gene swamp.' 'Gene swamp' was Patel's very own expression; he'd invented it to explain why mixed marriages between blacks and whites didn't work. 'The ugliness of the kaffir comes out and nothing good of the white or the Indian is left.' He bounced Tandia on his knee. 'But not this one, hey? I'm telling you something for nothing, except for her hair, which I got to admit is a kaffir's hair, this one is going to be very, very pretty.'

Mrs Patel said nothing, her humiliation greater than she believed she could bear. Patel wasn't even ashamed! He talked openly to people about his bastard daughter. It wasn't respectful. It wasn't fair. She'd done her job as a good wife and given him two sons to look after his old age and no silly daughters to bleed him dry with wedding dowries, and in return he insulted her name and her race.

She would suck her dislike for Tandia through her gold teeth. 'Sies, man, how could you love that?' At least she didn't have to have his shame in the house. Tandia lived in the corrugated-iron shed in the back with her kaffir mother. When Tandia was five her mother died quite suddenly. Her death came as somewhat of a surprise to the neighbourhood, for she was a robust and happy woman who performed the task of servant to the Patel household with cheerfulness and energy.

Nobody knew about the poisoning of Tandia's mother, but then again, everybody knew. The police, of course, treated it just like another dead black person. It happened all the time. Maybe even some money changed hands? Patel was well known in boxing circles, white boxing circles, where the police were very big. He could easily have paid someone not to look too closely.

Tandia had grown up with the story of her mother's death. It remained street gossip for years, and there was no doubt in her mind that Mrs Patel had been responsible. She had no evidence to prove it, but she knew the woman's hate was big enough.

The hurt at being hated so much by Mrs Patel had only been bearable when Tandia took it out of herself and turned it inside out, turned Mrs Patel into an ignorant but honest and jealous woman who had been cheated by her husband.

Deep in thought, Tandia was unaware of the two men creeping up behind her in the cemetery. She sensed their presence too late. Her left arm was grabbed from behind and twisted painfully behind her back.

'Don't struggle, kaffir, or I break your bladdy arm, you hear?'

She felt the cold metal of the handcuff as it snapped around her wrist. Her free arm was pulled behind her and the second metal bracelet snapped onto it. She didn't scream at first, her shock was too great. But then it came, the pitch so high its beginning was silent, a rasp of cold air pulled into her epiglottis. The scream cut across the misty, dew-soaked cemetery; it may even have reached half a mile away to where the cement-block houses of the new Indian township began. But it had no second breath, no second pull of fright. A hard hand slammed across her mouth, the signet ring striking her front teeth. Her head pushed downwards, they raced towards the headstone, the force of the man propelling her impossible to resist. Instinctively she brought her shoulder around to take the brunt of the crash as her slim body slammed into the cold marble cross.

The grip on her mouth and neck loosened and then her attacker released her altogether. Her knees buckled and she started to fall. A hand grabbed the chain connecting her handcuffs and broke her fall, allowing her to sink to her knees. She didn't feel the metal band being loosened from her left wrist and was barely conscious of her arms being brought around the base of the cross and of the handcuff snapping around her wrist again. Her attacker stood directly behind her, working purposefully.

'That's right, kaffir, in the doggy position, you people like that, hey?' He gave two sharp barks, 'Woof woof!' Tandia heard a short laugh and for the first time became aware that a second man was present. The cotton shift she was wearing was bunched and a hand pulled at her bloomers. It was the feeling of the elastic pulling over her thighs that brought her back to her senses. She kicked out with her left foot and connected with the squatting policeman's thigh, knocking him over.

'Fok! The black bitch has dirtied my uniform!' He reached out and, grabbing her ankle, jerked her leg straight. With her knees no longer supporting her, Tandia crashed onto her stomach. Straddling her the policeman pulled her bloomers down. Then he brought his hands under her hips and jerked her back to her former kneeling position. He was a strong man, but now he panted slightly from the effort and he spoke in short, sharp bursts. 'You dirty my nice clean uniform, hey. I got to teach you some manners, man. Kicking with your dirty kaffir feet. That's not nice, you hear!'

Tandia heard the click of his belt buckle. 'Don't move. You hear? Stay jus' like that.' His voice was steadier now, more confident. She heard the second man laugh. 'Take your boots off, man, your trousers won't go over your boots, *domkop*!' The man behind her gave a grunt, then another as the second boot came away; then came his voice again, light, almost flippant. 'First you got to learn not to kick your betters!' She felt the sting of the leather belt even before her mind registered its sound on her buttocks. The belt came down twice more, each lash followed by a grunt from the policeman. Tandia screamed; the pain was terrible. 'Coming, ready or not!' She felt his hands on either side of her thighs pull her back up, then a brutal thrust and a sharp pain. She gasped and let out another scream. The policeman slipped one hand around her waist holding her hard against him and clamped the other over her mouth. His grip was too tight for her to bite his fleshy, nicotine-smelling palm.

'Jesus, a virgin! The-black-bitch-is-a-fucking-virgin!' The repeated force of the body slamming into her was synchronised with his voice. She fought for breath, snorting through her nostrils. Nothing else mattered, not the pain, nothing; he was suffocating her and she was fighting to get enough air to stay alive.

Suddenly, the hand over her mouth relaxed and the grotesque presence dismounted. Tandia remained very still. Panting, but very still, her eyes tightly closed. She was aware, for the first time, of the taste of blood in her mouth. It was the only thing that seemed real. She held on to it. The salty, normal taste of blood kept her from passing out. Would they kill her? Not if she didn't look. Not if they knew she hadn't seen their faces. Tandia, who had so often wondered whether her life was worth anything, suddenly knew she wanted to live.

'Hey, Geldenhuis? C'mon, your turn. Nice tight pussy. A very recent virgin. Guaranteed only one owner!'

'Don't use my name in front of the kaffir girl! I don't fuck kaffirs.'

There was a moment's pause. 'Ja, is that so? How come then, you always like to watch?'

'C'mon, hurry up, jong, it's already half past six. We got to report.' Nervous anger strained the second man's voice. 'We only came to pay our respects to old Patel!'

The policeman who had raped her was breathing less heavily now, aware perhaps that he had upset his superior. He changed the subject: 'What's going to happen about your title fight with Gideon Mandoma now Patel's dead?'

Geldenhuis didn't answer. '*Kom! Maak gou, jong!* It's nearly bladdy sunrise!'

Tandia felt the sudden downward pressure of a boot in the small of her back. 'Nice one! Her black arse looks like a hot cross bun.' She lay absolutely still, the gravel chips cut into her stomach and her arms pulled painfully as the handcuffs looped around the cross held her rigid. Her shift remained bunched above her waist. Tandia kept her eyes tightly shut even after she heard the soft click of the key and felt the handcuffs removed from her wrists.

She lay there as though dead, not a muscle moving. Inside her head she screamed, '*Please God, don't let them kill me!*'

Tandia felt the sudden downward pressure of the boot again, this time on the base of her neck. 'Don't open your eyes, kaffir, not for a long time, not for ten minutes, you hear?' It was the voice of the second man, the one called Geldenhuis. The pressure increased and her head was pushed into the ground. 'Hey! You! Kaffir! I asked you, do you hear?'

'Yes, *baas*,' she sobbed.

The boot twisted into her neck, sending a sharp stab of pain down her spine. '*Ja dankie, baas!*' the voice demanded. She felt his hand tug at her shift and pull it down over her thighs.

'Yes, thank you, baas,' Tandia whimpered.

'You report this you dead meat!'

Tandia lay there for a long time. The sun came up and took the morning cold away but she kept her eyes shut. She was a kaffir, that at least had been decided.

Tandia opened one eye. It focussed on a willy wagtail sitting on a half-fallen tombstone ten feet from where she lay. Cut into the pocked cement tombstone she read the words, 'Dearly beloved', but the remainder of the writing on the lopsided tombstone was covered with dry lichen. The willy's tail was going up and down, regular as a metronome. A tiny breeze caught and ruffled the white feathers on its breast. It cocked its head slightly and looked at her without curiosity. Then it flew away and rested on the temporary wooden cross on Patel's grave. But it didn't stay long; its tail only went up and down three or four times before it took off again. Maybe because of the incense? Can birds smell? Tandia didn't know.

All the tears, the bitter child tears were over. The white man had decided for her. She was a stinking black kaffir who had had her buttocks parted by a white man's hands.

Tandia's world crumbled. The small amount of self-esteem she had harvested out of her childhood had come from her efforts at school. Now, with Patel dead, there would be no more school. She had been crushed, she was suddenly no better than the lowest black person. A stinking, dirty kaffir!

Tandia lay very still and let the hate come in. Let the hate spread, enter her salty, blood-rinsed mouth and creep down her dry throat and into her chest and down, down, down, to congeal in her stomach so that she thought for a moment she would vomit. She gulped, but she held the hate down. She held it until it spread throughout her whole body. And then, only then, when she knew it would never leave her, Tandia allowed herself to weep again.

This time it was a cry that started on the surface like a child crying and then burned deeper and deeper so that it ended up a whimper, hardly a cry at all. It was only then, when the crying was leached out of her, that the fear came, it rose up in her breast until she could contain it no longer. 'Patel!' she screamed. 'Why did you have to die!' At almost sixteen, life as a kaffir had begun for Tandia.

TWO

Tandia arrived back at Booth Street before Mrs Patel had risen. She moved painfully over to the yard tap and washed the red cemetery clay from her feet and legs. Then she filled a four-gallon paraffin tin bucket and carried it into the shed where she poured the cold water into a large white enamel basin. She undressed slowly, pulling the cotton shift carefully over her bruised body. With a cloth she rinsed in the bucket she wiped as much of the blood away as she could see before she squatted in the basin to bathe. The skin around her wrists had been rubbed away and in some places the handcuffs had cut deeply into the flesh so that each time she put her hands into the basin the water around her wrists stained pink. The cruel welts made by the policeman's belt still burned her buttocks and when she wiped tenderly over them there was blood on the cloth, although whether from the welts or from the other place you couldn't be certain.

Up to this moment Tandia's life had been a dichotomy, a two-person affair. She would return home from school and take off her white blouse and gym frock, her short white socks and shiny black shoes, and change into a servant's cotton shift and blue beret. Then she'd wash and hang out her school uniform to dry; later, before she went to bed, she would starch and iron it when she did Patel's shirts. This personal task completed, she would change from a bright little Indian schoolgirl into the Patels' black servant. It was an emotional journey Tandia made every day of her life and one which she walked with a terrible loneliness.

As a child she had cried the loneliness out of her system as she lay in the dark on a coir mattress in the hot shed. She could remember thinking that even the rats that scurried across the corrugated-iron roof above her head had mothers and fathers. She only had Patel whom she was allowed to call Patel, and not 'baas', like a kaffir, but not daddy either, like a proper daughter.

Her bath completed, Tandia wrapped her towel around her torso and dragged the basin which was almost two feet in diameter to the doorway, tipping its contents into the dusty back yard. The water splashed, runneled and rushed for a few feet before being sucked into the dry earth. Moments later only a damp stain showed where it had been, and that too would soon disappear, baked dry in the hot mid-October sun.

Tandia returned the basin to its place under her iron cot, and she applied a damp cloth to her swollen eyes and mouth. Then she dressed slowly, not only because of the pain but also because she sensed that the ritual of changing from servant to schoolgirl, a moment which every school morning of her life she had cherished, might be coming to an end. Her blouse crackled with the starch, just the way Patel's shirts did, and the freshly washed and ironed gym frock fell neatly on her trim body. Her back hurt as she bent down to put on her white socks and tie the laces of her brightly polished shoes. She would say nothing of her early morning graveside visit to say goodbye to Patel. If she told the old woman anything it would only give her yet another reason to throw her onto the street. 'Please God, let her tell me I can stay,' Tandia prayed. 'I'll do anything, anything she says. Just let me stay and finish school next year.'

Just as she did every day Tandia crossed the yard and climbed the steps onto the stoep and entered the kitchen to make breakfast. The old woman was sitting at the kitchen table shelling peas. She was wearing her deep purple sari, always a bad sign; purple was a colour that made Mrs Patel very cranky. Shelling peas was Tandia's work and her heart sank.

'Good morning Mrs Patel,' she said brightly as she reached behind the door for the apron she wore to protect her school uniform. Then she crossed the kitchen, tying the apron as she walked toward the stove to fetch the kettle for morning cha.

'Where you think you going, hey?' Mrs Patel did not look up as she spoke so she didn't see Tandia replace the kettle and, turning from the stove, lower her head and clasp her hands in fear. Nor did she wait for Tandia's reply. She had rehearsed her speech a dozen times and she wanted it to come out just the way she had thought it. 'You think we got money for school now that Mr Patel is dead, you think that?'

She looked up for the first time, her eyes shining with malice. 'You mad, you hear! You nothing but a stinking kaffir. Go! Get out of my house. You got one hour, then you out. Get out of that school uniform, it's mine now, you hear?' She paused, sucking air through her gold teeth. 'You a dirty kaffir going to an Indian school. You who is not even a Hindu!' Her body juddered at the ecstasy of the moment for which she had waited so long. 'What do you think the mothers of the Indian girls think of me, hey? "That Mrs Patel from Booth Street,"' she mimicked, '"she sends her husband's kaffir bastard to a good Indian school!"' She paused to catch her breath. 'I waited a long time, now it's my turn!' Rising from the kitchen chair she pointed to the kitchen door. 'Get out of my house, kaffir!' Lifting the white enamel colander from the table she hurled it at Tandia. The colander hit Tandia's shoulder and fell to the cement floor, clattering amongst the bouncing, scattering, gleefully escaping peas.

Tandia looked up at the old woman. The blow from the dish hadn't hurt her, but somehow its impact had strengthened her nerve, so that she now stood her ground. Yesterday she would have fled in tears. But a lot had happened since yesterday. She had grown up and learned the true meaning of hate. Not the soulful badly-done-by kind of hate she had nursed in childhood nor the deep resentment she felt for the old lady, but a new kind which burned inside her guts so fiercely it felt as though it was stripping away the lining of her stomach. She had also learned the power of a naked threat. The power contained in the voice of a policeman called Geldenhuis when he said, 'You report this and you dead meat!'

Tandia looked up at the old woman, with the new hate and the power she now borrowed from the memory of the policeman's voice. Her voice was even and she spoke slowly. 'One day I am going to get even, I don't care how long it takes.' She paused. 'For my mother and for me also. I swear it on my mother's grave!' She pointed at Mrs Patel. 'You better pray to Arthie Paraschatie to protect you, because one day, sure as God, I'm coming back to get you!'

At the mention of Arthie Paraschatie, the Hindu Mother of God, Mrs Patel drew back. 'My sons will beat you, you hear! Do not come back to this house. You stay away, or I call the police!'

Tandia picked up the colander and, taking it by the handles, she placed it upside down over the old lady's head and patted it twice. 'Goodbye, you old witch! Good riddance to bad rubbish!' Whereupon she turned and walked from the kitchen.

No sooner had she got to the back yard than her newly gained courage collapsed. She thought of rushing back to ask forgiveness from the old woman, beg a little time, a few days to get a pass and find somewhere she could live. But she knew it was useless; even this would be denied her by the triumphant old bitch. She wiped her tears and entered the shed and pulled the large enamel basin out from under the cot.

Tandia knew enough to realise that her life, despite Mrs Patel, despite the loneliness, had been a fortunate one by the standards of a great many Indian and coloured families and almost all the urban black ones. Natkin Patel had been, by Durban Indian standards, a wealthy man and he had used his wealth and position to give her a chance in life.

She had expected Mrs Patel to send her packing and after Patel's funeral she'd worked out a plan. She had five pounds exactly, an amount that had taken her nearly ten years to save. She would take the bus to Clairwood; blacks as well as Indians lived there. At Clairwood or perhaps Jacobs, she would find a nice clean black family with whom she could board. Her five pounds would buy her food and board for six weeks and leave enough over for train fares so she could go in to town to look for a job. She would be sure to find a job of some sort in that time. She could clean, cook – Indian food anyway – wash and iron and work a sewing machine, so she could work as a housemaid or she might even get a job as a junior clerk or a sales assistant in an Indian shop in Victoria Street. She spoke both Tamil and Hindi as well as Zulu and, of course, Afrikaans and English, so that should help a lot. Before she had fallen asleep the night before, Tandia had decided that she wasn't entirely helpless and that when she got settled she'd complete her matriculation at night school or by correspondence school.

But now, back in the tin shed, a terrible fear struck her and Tandia started to cry again. She had used the last scrap of her courage in the kitchen with the old lady; she had no more left as she began to pack her things into the basin. Her stomach churned and she realised she hadn't eaten since lunch the previous day when the old lady had locked the house up to go to the funeral and removed the key from its usual hiding place under a loose brick in the back wall. Tandia packed her school books first, then leaving one cotton shift on the bed she rolled the other two up and placed them in the basin. Mrs Patel hadn't said anything about shoes so, technically, she was entitled to take them. She left them on but removed her blouse, gym frock and school beret and hung them together with her spare blouse on a wire hanger which she then hung on a nail protruding from one of the two wooden roof beams a foot above her head.

It didn't take long to pack away the fifteen years of her life. She had accumulated almost nothing of personal value other than a few trinkets, ribbons and bits and pieces which were all contained in a biscuit tin. The last thing she packed was a small kewpie doll someone had given Patel for her when she was a small child. The paintwork on its face had almost totally rubbed off and only a suggestion remained of the doll's large, wide-open painted blue eyes and red bow lips. She'd named the doll Apple Sammy, although she'd long since forgotten why she'd given it a boy's name or even such a silly one. The worn but much loved little doll had rested on her bed for as long as she could remember and now she hugged it briefly, wrapped it carefully in the third cotton shift and put it into the basin. She now set the basin into the centre of a square of cheesecloth and, in the African style, drew the corners over the top and knotted them.

Tandia, an African of very recent persuasion, did not know how to hoist the basin onto her head and walk away, straight-backed and proud with her hips and arms swinging free. She managed to carry the basin out of the shed into the yard where she set it down. It was much too heavy to continue to carry in her arms, and she quickly decided she would have to fashion a head cloth and rest the basin on it, keeping it steady by holding on to either side.

Tandia returned to the shed to fetch the blue servant's beret for this purpose. As she entered she was struck by the sight of her gym frock and blouse and her school beret hanging from the hook. Through her teary eyes it looked as though she herself was hanging from the nail. The shock she felt caused her hiccups to stop and a surge of anger overcame her. She reached out and lifted the kerosene lamp from the shelf above her iron bed and, removing the fluted glass from the kerosene bowl, she unscrewed the wick and sprinkled methylated spirits over her school uniform. The duality of her life was over.

Tandia carried the paraffin-soaked gym frock, blouse and school beret out into the yard and hung them from the clothes line. Lighting the end of the paraffin-soaked wick from the lamp, she set her school uniform alight. She waited long enough to make sure the flame from the wick had caught; then, on a sudden impulse, she retrieved her school beret and replaced it on the burning hanger with her blue servant's one. Quickly she pulled the paraffin-splashed beret over her hair. Then crouching down on her haunches with her back held straight she carefully lifted the basin onto her head and rising slowly to a standing position walked out of the back gate without looking back.

Tandia had only gone a few yards down the alley when she heard the old woman screaming blue murder. 'Fire! Fire! My house is on fire! Come quick, she's burning down my house! Somebody, come quick!'

'See ya later alligator!' Tandia shouted back to her. She knew the washing line was well away from anything and that there was no possible chance of the house or anything else other than her past life catching alight, and for a moment she enjoyed the old woman's distress. But suddenly that petty victory tasted bitter in her mouth and she knew she had made a devastating mistake.

The bus stop was no more than half a mile from Booth Street but it took Tandia almost fifteen minutes to approach it. The large enamel basin was balanced precariously on her head and her neck and back hurt but she was too concerned with getting it to the bus stop to let the pain intrude. A hundred yards from the deserted stop she saw the bus approaching. Tandia started to trot awkwardly towards it but soon realised that she would be unable to cover the distance in time. She stopped and freed one hand from the rim of the basin to signal the Indian driver to stop. Running late for school, she'd done the same thing a hundred times before and she recognised the driver as someone who had often stopped for her. But now he looked blandly back at the young black girl with a large basin on her head and the big Leyland bus roared past her in a cloud of dust.

Dismayed, Tandia turned suddenly in the direction of the departing bus and the basin slipped and toppled to the road. Her books and belongings broke through the cheesecloth covering and scattered across the roadway. A *bakkie* following closely behind the bus caught the biscuit tin with all her precious bits and pieces and squashed it flat under its rear tyre; another wheel caught two of her textbooks. The driver gave a short impatient honk on his horn and accelerated away.

Tandia was too spent for tears. She began to gather her things together. It seemed impossible to her that it was only just approaching nine o'clock in the morning. She was beyond thinking rationally, simply holding on to the single idea that she must take the bus to Clairwood and find somewhere to stay.

On her haunches on the side of the road, she placed the last of her books back into the now chipped and slightly misshapen basin. Cocooned in her misery, she wasn't aware of an approaching vehicle until she heard the sudden scrunch of its front tyres. She looked up as the van slowed beside her and its passenger door swung open. A pair of black boots landed on the road even before the *kwela-kwela* had come to a complete stop.

The policeman leaned down, and jerked Tandia sharply to her feet. Tandia cried out in pain as the black policeman gripped her lacerated wrists. 'What is your name?' he demanded. Tandia stared dumbly back at him, her mouth slightly open, unaware of the tears running down her face. The policeman must have felt a wetness in the palm of his right hand for he suddenly released his grip and looked down. The sight of the blood on his hand seemed to make him even more angry. With a look of contempt he reached out and wiped his hand on the front of her shift allowing it to come to rest between her small breasts. Whereupon he gave her a sharp, impatient push and swiped her across the top of her head, removing her beret which fell onto the roadway. 'What is your name, *umFazi*?'

The driver of the police van, a white officer, leaned across. 'Hey, you kaffir! Is your name Patel? Tandia Patel?'

Tandia, her fear and confusion showing, nodded dumbly. The police officer glanced at his wristwatch. 'You don't look like a kaffir, more like a coloured. How come you got the same name as the complainant, she said you was a black person.' He didn't wait for her reply. 'Anyway, whatever you are, you under arrest, you hear?' He jerked his head, indicating the black policeman. 'Arrest her, but make quick, it's already long past nine o'clock, we supposed to knock off an hour ago, now I got to write up a fokking charge sheet.'

For the second time that day Tandia felt a pair of cold handcuffs close around her wrists. The black man now seemed oblivious to the condition of her wrists and snapped the handcuffs firmly shut. He appeared not to notice as Tandia winced from the pain. Pointing to the back of the van he gave her a sharp shove between her shoulder blades. Despite her terror Tandia could think only of her books.

'Bring my things, please,' she said in Zulu. The black policeman ignored her and hastily unlocked the padlock on the van door and swung the van doors open. He gave her a perfunctory push. Tandia, desperate for her books, resisted. 'My basin, you must bring my basin!' she begged. The black man pushed her harder this time and unable to grasp onto anything she fell over the tailgate.

'Get in before I hurt you!' he hissed. 'Can't you see the baas is in a hurry?' Then he turned to retrieve the battered basin.

'Fok! Make quick, jong!' the white officer shouted from the front of the van.

The policeman hurriedly slid the heavy basin into the back of the van and slammed the two doors shut. The police van had already started to move when she heard the clunk as the passenger door closed.

At first the interior of the van seemed completely dark and Tandia lay on the floor until her eyes adjusted. Then she crawled awkwardly on her elbows and knees towards the basin. Her knees hurt and she began to feel the loss of circulation in her hands because of the handcuffs. A narrow bench ran the length of each side of the van and Tandia used the one nearest to the basin to pull herself up onto her haunches; then she pushed her back against the bench so that she could maintain her balance as the van jolted and picked its way along the rutted township road. A sudden jerk of the van sent her sprawling. She regained her balance with difficulty and managed to pull herself up onto the bench where she was able to look directly down into the basin. The cover had been torn from her Latin primer and her algebra textbook was broken in half, but her other books seemed intact. She looked to see if her brown school beret was in the basin but it wasn't. It had been left on the roadside together with the squashed biscuit tin. With her beret the last of Tandia's self-esteem was gone.

Tandia's arrest had happened so unexpectedly she hadn't really connected it to a cause. Now she realised that Mrs Patel must have called the police. The stupid, ignorant old woman had accused her of trying to burn the house down. Tandia began to sob. Her small, sweet, innocent revenge was going to send her to prison where no one would find her and she was certain to die.

As she sobbed she felt herself grow angry, stupidly angry at Natkin Patel for dropping dead without warning her. One minute he was there in all his shiny, clean self-importance, the next he was gone before she got her proper chance in life.

Tandia's ego was too fragile to carry her anger for Patel for long. Now her despair turned inwards onto herself. She had been stupid to burn her gym frock. Childishly stupid. She had allowed her emotions to show, had put them on display and they had been used against her. Through her despair came the tremulous conviction that she would never again allow her emotions to be the mistress of her actions.

By the time the police van drew up behind the Cato Manor police station Tandia had regained her composure somewhat. She waited in the back of the stationary van for what seemed like an age before she heard the bolt slide open and the double doors of the paddy wagon opened to reveal the black constable again.

Tandia was led into the charge room to find the police officer who had driven the van seated at a small table opposite which stood a smaller chair. It reminded Tandia of a classroom chair, a thought which somehow increased her anxiety. Resting on the table was a typewriter, patches of wear showing through its black paint.

The white policeman looked up from the report he appeared to be reading and followed Tandia with his eyes as the black man instructed her to stand beside the chair. Then he removed her handcuffs and quickly left the room.

Tandia had never ached as much in her life and despite the intimidating chair and her sore bottom, she longed to sit down. The white officer dropped his gaze again and continued to read. She clasped her hands behind her back and surreptitiously attempted to rub the circulation back into them.

Finally the white officer glanced up at her and then back at the paper in his hand. 'Can you write your name?' he asked in Afrikaans.

'Ja, meneer,' Tandia replied. The policeman looked up in surprise. He had probably expected her to call him 'baas', or even to deny any knowledge of the *taal*.

He placed the document on the table facing Tandia, opened it and indicated a place at the bottom of the third page. Then he reached into the pocket of his khaki tunic and withdrew a blue Croxley fountain pen. 'Then sign,' he instructed, holding the pen out for Tandia. Tandia reached out to take the pen but the circulation had not yet fully returned to her hand and, unable to grasp it, she dropped it to the table. A momentary flash of anger showed in the white man's eyes but he quickly concealed it and gave a sigh of impatience. 'No funny buggers, you hear? Jus' sign the charge sheet.'

Tandia felt a lump in her throat as she tried to speak. Finally in a small, frightened voice she managed to ask, 'What does it say, meneer? Can I read it please?'

The police officer snatched the report from the table. Pushing his chair back he began to fan himself with it. 'It's just an ordinary charge report, you sign it now, okay?' He kept his voice low as he half rose from the chair and leaned forward to place the report back on the table in front of her, but the threat in it was unmistakable.

Tandia swallowed hard, moving her tongue across the roof of her mouth to get her saliva working. 'Please, meneer, I must read it,' she said in a barely audible voice.

This time the policeman sprang from his chair and grabbing the report he thrust it at Tandia so that the paper was only inches from her face. 'What's that you saying, kaffir?' He pulled the paper back from her face and began to jab at it with his right index finger. 'We got all your paticklers here! You trying to be cheeky, hey? You charged with arson, you hear? You know what is arson? You tried to burn down the house of your employer! That's a very serious offence!'

His hand opened suddenly and he smacked Tandia hard across the face. The small chair toppled as she staggered backwards trying to maintain her balance. 'Don't fok with me, kaffir! You sign, jong, or you in the deep shit, you hear?'

He dropped the sheet of paper at her feet and lowered himself back onto his chair. 'Pick it up!' He pointed at the fallen chair. Sobbing, Tandia righted the chair; she was still seeing stars from his blow. 'The paper also!' he shouted.

She felt faint and could barely see it on the floor. Her hands shook so violently she had to make several attempts to grip the edge of the charge sheet. She held it out to the policeman who snatched it from her and dropped it onto the table. Then he picked up the pen. To Tandia's surprise he now spoke softly. 'C'mon, man, now sign. It's late, I want to go home, I'm already an hour and a half late, I want to go home and have my breakfast.'

Tandia burst into tears. The police officer leapt from his chair and struck her a violent blow on the side of her face knocking her over and sending her sprawling across the polished cement floor.

Seemingly in an instant, he was at her side. 'Fok you, kaffir! Get up!' He bent down and grabbed her arm and pulled, but Tandia resisted and the white man released his grip on her bleeding wrist. 'Fok! Get up! I haven't got all day!' It was then that she noticed the dirt on his trousers, a soil mark just above his knees where she had kicked him in the cemetery. A moment later he drove his boot into her kidneys. Tandia screamed then gave a low moan and passed out.

She came to as she was being dragged by two black policemen along a long corridor. Tandia tasted blood and she tasted the hate and she kept her eyes tightly closed. They came to a halt and she was lowered to the floor. Her face still stung from the violent slap she had received and the polished cement floor was cool on her bruised cheek. She heard the slight rattle of keys and the sigh of a heavy door opening, then she was picked up again and lowered to the floor of the cell.

Long after she'd heard the clunk of the door closing and the rattle of the keys as she was locked in, Tandia continued to lie with her cheek pressed against the cool cement floor of the dark cell. She was like one of those stick insects that continues to play dead long after its attacker has lost interest in it. Eventually she opened her eyes, raised herself to a sitting position and looked around the small cell. It contained a bench which ran the length of one wall. A toilet bucket sat in one corner smelling sharply of disinfectant. On the floor beside the bucket lay a single scrap of newspaper. A light bulb, protected by a cover made of heavy wire mesh, was set into the ceiling at least twelve feet above her. The light was off and the only light coming into the cell was from a small barred window about ten feet from the floor. The effect was like being thrown into an empty well or a dark pit.

Tandia rose and sat on the bench. The fact that she was alone and the shouting had stopped was an enormous relief, but she was too numbed to think. She vaguely sensed that it was a useless pursuit anyway. The act of thinking suggests there are choices and she was beginning to realise that for a black person the choices are almost non-existent.

Tandia wondered briefly about the welfare of her basin, though now it seemed to represent a life which had been taken from her. The idea that she could educate herself in an environment where mere survival took all the energy she possessed suddenly seemed ridiculous. After the events of the past few hours Tandia was prepared to give up even before she got started.

After a while, when she had become accustomed to the dark cell,

Tandia lay down on the bench and gazed up at the square of light coming through the window. Beyond it she could see a patch of blue sky and, just cutting into the frame, the white crescent of a day moon.

She must have dozed off for a while, for she was startled to hear the key in the door. It opened only slightly and she heard the scrape of a tin plate as it was pushed into the cell. Tandia waited until the key had been turned and removed from the lock before moving to the doorway. Two hunks of white bread and a tin mug of cold black tea rested on the plate. The bread was stale but not too bad when she washed it down with the bitter-tasting tea.

Having eaten for the first time since noon the previous day Tandia felt stronger. She looked up through the small window to find that the day moon had disappeared and the sky seemed a lighter blue. It was past noon, she thought. The bread and tea must have been lunch.

But Tandia was wrong. She had slept most of the day and it was now five in the evening. She was not to know that the meal she had just eaten was all she was entitled to receive over a twenty-four-hour period. A district police station is not equipped with cooking facilities and besides, any policeman will tell you, a hungry kaffir is a more co-operative one.

The sleep had stiffened her and she became aware of just how badly she hurt. The pain seemed to have seeped into her bones and into her spirit and she felt utterly miserable. Now, having eaten, her bowels needed to work and she was forced to use the sharp-smelling bucket in the corner. She used up the small square of newspaper, praying that she would not need to go again.

Hitching up her bloomers, she felt the small knotted square of cloth pinned inside them, which contained her money – the five one-pound notes which made up her lifetime savings. Tandia felt a sudden surge of hope: she would offer to pay for the gym frock, to compensate Mrs Patel. Then maybe they would just give her a beating and not send her to gaol. After what she had been through she could take the *sjambok.* In the end it would be a small price to pay for her freedom and she knew that rather than go to gaol, she would take any punishment, no matter how severe.

Hope is a flame that kindles new expectations by grasping at passing straws. The food and the sleep allowed Tandia to hope just a little. She had a chance if she could stay out of prison.

The blue framed square of light above her head began to darken and the cell was in almost total darkness before the lone ceiling light came on. The weak bulb made the cell no brighter than it had been during the day, but the absence of the comforting square of sky at the window made Tandia's new-found optimism soon collapse. Her bruised little body was hurting all over and no matter how she sat or lay she was in pain.

There was a sudden rattle at the door followed by the sound of a woman swearing in a mixture of Zulu and English. Then followed a sharp expletive from a male voice. The cell door swung open and a black woman was pushed in and the door closed behind her. The woman appeared not to have seen Tandia, imagining herself alone in the cell. She leaned with her back against the heavy door, swaying slightly, obviously drunk, her chin resting on her large breast. She wore a half-smile and her nose was bleeding slightly. She sniffed and then wiped her nose by running the top of her index finger past both nostrils, across the back of her hand and back again pulling the blood and mucus back into her nose. Then she examined the blood on her hand, brought her hand to her mouth and slowly, like a cat licking its fur, she licked the blood clean, starting at the tip of her index finger and working back across her hand.

The woman was perhaps in her mid twenties, broad-hipped and with a bottom that protruded enormously in the short, tight knitted skirt she wore. Tandia, who had grown accustomed to the dim light, could see her quite clearly. She had a broad, almost flat face and she wore bright red lipstick which gave her thick lips an added fleshiness so they looked like raw meat. The trickle of blood had reappeared at both nostrils and added to her carnivorous appearance. To Tandia, she looked as though she was getting ready to eat somebody.

The woman, bringing both her hands up to her mouth, suddenly retched. Half-stooped, she lurched over to the bucket in the corner and threw up. The sour smell of stomach-fermented kaffir beer filled the cell. The woman was sick three more times, the noise of her spitting and hawking filling the small cell. Finally she turned from the bucket and straightened up. She was panting from the effort of throwing up and her carnivorous lipstick was now smeared across her face. Steadying herself by placing her hand on the wall, she wiped her eyes with her free hand and looked about her. It was then that she saw a frightened Tandia hunched in the darkest corner of the cell.

'Shit! Who you?' She wasn't really asking a question and her flat gaze was not in the least curious. She withdrew her hand from the wall which caused her to lurch slightly forward. 'Don't fuck with me, you hear!' Her words seemed to upset her balance and she fell two steps backwards until her shoulders bumped into the wall, whereupon she gave a soft groan and slid slowly to the floor beside the bucket, one fat arm coming to rest inside it. In moments she began to snore. The tight skirt had ridden up her thighs and Tandia now saw that she wore nothing underneath.

Tandia didn't know what to do. She sat in the dark corner, one arm drawing her legs up against her chest, the fist of her free hand in her mouth in an attempt to hold back the panic she felt rising within her. After a while her breathing calmed a little. What should she do? If she took the woman's arm out of the shit bucket she was fearful that she might wake and beat her up. Her sense of survival told her to leave things as they were and her sensibilities, already deeply offended, told her that she could not do so, that the mess in the bucket was in part her doing.

Tandia waited until she was sure the woman was not likely to wake from her drunken sleep and crept over to the bucket. The woman's hand rested on the bottom, covered in shit and vomit. Gagging as she lifted the arm out of the mess, she rested it on the floor beside her and carefully removed the *doek* the woman wore tied around her head. Using the head cloth she wiped the foul-smelling hand and arm clean. Tandia's heart leapt with fear as the woman gave a sudden groan, sighed deeply and, lifting her arm, dropped it back in the bucket. Tandia pulled back in horror; the stench was overpowering. She began to cry softly.

After a while she dried her tears. She was crying too much. Crying was an indulgence she would have to learn to do without. She now realised that the woman had passed out and was unlikely to be roused, so she moved over to her again. Once again she removed the woman's hand from the slop bucket and wiped it as clean as she was able, using the now soiled doek. Then she dragged the unconscious woman clear so that she lay on her side with her lipstick-smeared cheek against the cement floor. This seemed to stop her snoring.

Several hours seemed to pass in the stinking cell and Tandia, when she felt she could bear it no longer, would concentrate on the tiny window until she could make out the pinprick of stars in the tiny square of darkness. She imagined how fresh and clean it was out there with the stars, how some of the air from the space surrounding them was finding its way into her miserable cell. She was not sleepy and her body ached in even more places when she lay down. Besides, the idea that the woman might wake while she was asleep made her fearful of closing her eyes even as she sat. She conjugated the verb 'lacrimare', 'to cry', in imperfect, future, future perfect and past perfect. Patel had always stressed that she must be good at Latin; he dreamed that she would go on to become a lawyer. She went on to irregular verbs with funny endings and then recited her personal and relative pronouns. 'Qui, quae, quo, quod,' she whispered to herself. It was strangely comforting to be using her mind and she challenged herself to remember Book Four of Virgil's *Aeneid*, especially the part where Aeneas enters the underworld and finds himself in the Elysian Fields. That was her set text in the end-of-year Latin exam, which she would now never take.

It must have been quite late when Tandia heard the rattle of the key in the door of the cell. A black constable appeared and without even glancing at the sleeping woman beckoned Tandia to come out of the cell. He was a much older man than the policeman who had arrested her earlier in the day. 'Down there, but wait first.' He spoke quietly and locked the cell door as Tandia waited for him. The light in the corridor was much brighter than in the cell and she held her wrists out to him for the handcuffs. He looked at her swollen and cut wrists and then up at her face. The expression in his eyes was not unkind and he shook his head once and clicked his tongue in sympathy. Then he pointed down the corridor and nodded for her to start walking. 'Go to the end of the passage, the last door on the left.'

Tandia's rubber-soled school shoes made almost no sound on the cement, but when the policeman turned to follow her the metal tips on the heel and toe caps of his boots sent a clicking metallic sound racing down ahead of her to the end of the passageway.

Tandia turned at the last door on the left and found herself back in the charge room. She hesitated at the door and waited for the black constable to catch up. Seated on the table, with his legs swinging over the side, was a white policeman she had not seen before. She felt enormous relief that it wasn't the same police officer who had so intimidated her when she had been brought in.

The man seated on the table didn't look up. But, aware that she stood at the door, he pointed to the larger of the two chairs, the one which had been previously used by the other policeman. The white officer sat on the end of the table and Tandia was brought to the chair by the black constable. 'Sit.' He indicated the chair beside her.

'Ja, sit, please,' the white officer added quietly. Tandia, as though afraid to make the slightest sound, lowered herself slowly into the same chair used by her white tormentor of the morning. She noted that the seated police officer held the charge sheet in his right hand and that the typewriter still stood at the opposite end of the table from where he sat. Apart from the three words, the white police officer remained silent, swinging his legs and blowing a tuneless whistle. Not as much a whistle as the controlled breathiness a person affects when they appear lost in their own thoughts. Tandia grew more and more apprehensive as she waited. The black constable had taken up a position at the door with his legs apart and his hands clasped behind his back. He seemed relaxed and uninterested, his eyes turned downwards.

After a while Tandia, who had kept her eyes downcast, ventured a glance at the white man seated on the table. He was small for a policeman. She was used to thinking of size in the boxing parlance used by Natkin Patel, and she judged him to be a welterweight. Tandia was used to the policemen around Cato Manor where white police sergeants were generally much older men. This one wore a crew cut with a clipped, blond moustache and seemed to be in his early twenties. His nose had been broken more than once which gave his boyish face a slightly romantic appearance. He looked clean and tough sitting there looking down at the floor. He turned suddenly and looked at her and before she dropped her gaze she saw his eyes. They were very pale blue, like a favourite blue cotton shirt that has been washed a thousand times. His eyes didn't look tough at all and Tandia's heart skipped a beat. Perhaps it wasn't going to be like the other one.

'You see this?' he said, lifting what looked like the charge sheet Tandia had refused to sign earlier. Tandia nodded, afraid to speak. Then he brought his free hand up and tore the sheet of paper in two. At the sound of the paper tearing, Tandia looked up in surprise. He placed the two pieces together and tore them down the centre once again. Then he dropped the pieces on the floor under his feet. 'You Patel's daughter, aren't you?' He didn't wait for her confirmation before continuing. 'He was a good guy. A bladdy good ref, even a good coach.' He paused, thinking for a moment, 'Ja, I can say it for sure, when it came to boxing, he really knew his onions.' He glanced up at Tandia, the beginnings of a smile on his face, 'You his daughter, hey. Maybe he was a Indian, but sometimes you've got to make exceptions, Patel was a good guy.' He paused, 'Ja, he was definitely a good guy.' Unlike the previous police officer he spoke in English, though it was at once obvious he was an Afrikaner. He glanced up at Tandia quickly and then back at the floor. 'Ag jong, I suppose you people also got feelings, I'm sorry about his death, you hear?' Then he added again, 'He was a okay guy.'

Tandia sat looking down at her hands. 'Please, sir, I will pay back the money for the gym frock, I have enough money!' She was surprised at her own audacity.

The policeman's pale blue eyes seemed to stare at something beyond her, as though he saw things in the air behind her back. 'Ag, that!' He pointed to the scraps of paper on the floor. 'That's all finish and *klaar*.'

Tandia's green eyes were questioning and she was very close to tears. Before she could speak he shrugged and then added, 'It's the least we can do. Boxing's like that, sometimes there's no colour bar. In boxing Patel was a real white man.'

'Thank you, sir,' Tandia said quietly, and then added, 'Am I free to go now?'

The policeman seemed not to hear and turned his torso slightly to face her. He wore a boyish grin as he spoke. 'Lucky you didn't sign the charge sheet this morning hey? Once you sign, there's no turning back, proceedings have to happen, you got to go in front of the magistrate.' He glanced abruptly at his watch and then turned and looked towards the door and nodded. 'You go out there now, I'm telling you, jong, you'll be back here quick smart. It's nearly twelve o'clock in the night and you haven't got a pass.' He grinned. 'A police patrol would pick you up in no time flat. Better you stay here tonight hey?'

Tandia looked up at him fearfully, her heart beating wildly. 'Please, sir, do not take me back to that cell, there is a woman there!'

The white sergeant turned and looked enquiringly at the black constable at the door. 'A shebeen prostitute, she is drunk, sir,' the black man answered.

The sergeant turned back to Tandia. 'Ja, I know what you mean.' He looked up at Tandia suddenly. 'This gym frock, the one you burned. What school was that?'

'Durban Indian Girls' High School, sir,' Tandia replied. She looked up at the policeman, 'I will pay for it, for everything.'

The white policeman gave a low whistle as though he was impressed. 'Ja, I already heard of that school. That's the one down at Brighton le Sands.' He paused. 'I'm not from Durban myself you understand.' He said this as though to indicate that he was superior to the local police product. 'I come from Jo'burg, they don't have such a thing as a Indian private school in Johannesburg. There are not so many rich Indians there, because, you see, we got the Jews.' He gave a short, bitter snort. 'The Jews are even better at rooking the public than the coolies.'

'Yes, sir,' Tandia said softly.

'An' now you not going there no more, hey?'

'No, sir.'

'At this school, do the girls talk about . . . you know, sex?'

Tandia looked up, shocked. 'No, sir! Never, sir! On my word of honour!' She was aware of her sudden outburst and lowered her voice. 'It is forbidden, sir.'

The police officer's eyes resumed their faraway look, but his voice was suddenly hard. 'Has a man ever done it to you?'

The shock of the question caused Tandia to gasp. She could feel the panic beginning to suffocate her and she was breathing hard, her face deeply flushed.

The black policeman's voice speaking in Zulu came suddenly from the direction of the door. 'You do not have to answer that, umFazi. Do not answer him, it is better you start to cry.'

The white policeman turned furiously to the door. His look was met by the impassive face of the black constable. 'Hey, jong, what did you say to her?'

The black policeman looked directly back at the white man. 'I said she must be quick and answer the questions, sir.'

Tandia began to sob. Quiet little sobs which shook her shoulders and could barely be heard. 'Listen, you black bastard, when I want you to speak, I'll ask, you hear?' the white officer snapped.

The black policeman pulled himself to attention, 'Yes, sir!' he replied in an automatic way. His eyes held steady as he met the white sergeant's angry glare.

The white policeman turned away. 'Cheeky bladdy kaffir,' he said as though to himself. Then he called, 'Okay, take her back to the cell. I can't interrogate a subject who is crying.' He jumped from the table and started towards the door.

Tandia rose from her chair quickly, 'Please, sir. You said I was free, sir!' she cried, beginning to follow after him across the room.

The white policeman whirled around to face her. 'Who said that?' he cried angrily. He turned back to the constable at the door. 'Did I say that?' He turned again, pointing an accusing finger at Tandia. 'Did I say this black person was free?' Tandia was unable to meet his gaze and lowered her eyes. 'You won't answer my questions. That is not co-operating with the police. Now, all of a sudden you want to go free. I am a police officer and I am asking you questions in the course of my duty. You refuse to answer!' His pale blue eyes were flecked with cold, bright anger and a small muscle in the left side of his cheek jerked suddenly.

'No, sir, I have not done this thing. I am a good girl, sir,' Tandia burst out.

'You are lying!' The white man shouted, pointing to the smaller of the two chairs. 'Sit there!'

Tandia sat down and covered her face with her hands, trying hard to stifle her sobbing.

The black constable took a step towards her. 'I will take her back to the cell now, sergeant?'

'I thought I told you to mind your own bladdy business, constable? You speak again, you on report, you hear?' He turned to Tandia. 'I haven't got all night to waste. I asked you nicely, now I'm going to ask you one more time. Have you had sexual intercourse with a man?'

Tandia pulled her hands away from her face. 'I was raped! This morning I was raped!' she sobbed.

The white officer allowed Tandia to cry for a few moments. He walked back to the table and lifted himself back onto it. This time he sat directly in front of her. Tandia's eyes were level with the table top, so now when she raised them she looked directly into the white man's crotch. Seated like this, his presence was hugely threatening; his legs swung casually, one on either side of the small chair, seeming to trap her between them.

Tandia tried to sniff away her tears and suddenly started to hiccup. The white police officer called over to the constable, 'Hey, Matembu. That's your name, isn't it? Bring some water, make quick!'

The black policeman left the room and returned shortly with a tin mug of water. The sergeant took it from him and held the mug out to Tandia. 'Here, take it, drink, you'll feel better.' His voice was conciliatory. She took the mug from him and holding her nose she drank deeply until the mug was empty. In order to avoid his crotch and look into his face she was forced to pull her head back.

'Thank you, sir,' she said in a voice barely above a whisper. She put the mug down beside her chair.

'It works with me like that also, funny, isn't it?' the police officer said in a friendly voice.

Tandia nodded dumbly, then she sniffed and knuckled her tears away. Her nose was running and she didn't know what to do about it. The white policeman turned to the constable once again. 'Go in the lavatory, bring some paper,' he ordered.

The black policeman returned and placed a roll of lavatory paper on the end of the table. 'Take it,' the white policeman said, 'blow your nose.'

Tandia was obliged to rise from the small chair and reach past the white officer to get the roll. As she did so his legs closed around her thighs just for a moment then he released her again. It was a crude, intimate gesture yet so quick that she wondered for a second whether it had happened at all. Her heart beat wildly as she sat back in the small chair. Eyes lowered, she unwound a length of toilet paper, tore it off the roll and proceeded to wipe her nose and then blow it hard. The paper was hard and unyielding, not suitable for the task she was using it for. Having cleared her nose somewhat Tandia was forced to hold the sticky mess in her closed hand.

The police sergeant leaned backwards on his hands opening his crotch even further. 'Did you report this rape to the police?' he asked.

'No, sir,' Tandia replied softly.

'And where did this rape take place, and what time also?'

Tandia spoke in small sobs. 'This morning. About six o'clock. At the Indian cemetery. Where, where . . . they buried Mr Patel!'

'The person who you said raped you. Can you describe this man to me?'

'There were two of them, but I did not see them,' Tandia sniffed.

The sergeant raised his eyebrows, his voice affecting surprise. 'Now all of a sudden it's two men, hey! Two men raped you, but you didn't see them? How can this be? It is already light by six o'clock?'

'From behind, they grabbed me from behind. Only one raped me.' Tandia shuddered involuntarily.

The sergeant leaned forward and folded his arms across his chest, rocking slightly. 'This is a very curious business. They raped you in broad daylight, or one of them did anyway, and you didn't see them?'

'He told me to shut my eyes. Also the other one said if I opened my eyes he would kill me. I was very afraid!' How could she tell him that they had been policemen? He wouldn't believe her and any chance she had of getting off would be destroyed forever.

'And you didn't report this to the police?'

'No, no sir.'

'Why not? Don't you know it is against the law not to report a crime?'

'I was too afraid, sir,' Tandia replied softly.

'Afraid? All of a sudden you're afraid of the police? Innocent people got no reason to be afraid of the police. You prefer a rapist to a member of the Sou' African police force?'

'No, sir. I was very frightened, sir. I didn't know what to do, I didn't want to make any more trouble!'

'Oh, I see, you were already in trouble. What trouble is this? Tell me. What sort of trouble were you already in?'

'About Patel. Mrs Patel was going to kick me out.' Tandia whimpered, looking up and appealing to him with her eyes. 'She hates me.'

There was a long pause as the policeman appeared to be thinking. When at length he spoke there was a hard edge to his voice. 'I think you lying, you hear? You lying to me, jong.'

Tandia looked up in alarm. 'No, sir! It is true! I will swear on the Bible!'

The white man had the distant look in his eyes again, as though he could read things dancing in the air. When at last he spoke his voice was quiet. 'You a whore. A black whore who does it for money in the cemetery. Sies, man. Did you do it in the cemetery next to the grave where your father was buried?'

'No, no!' Tandia cried. And then she froze and her eyes widened in alarm. It had taken all this time to sink in. The voice, the frightening voice after the boot had rested on her neck as she lay at the foot of the marble cross, it belonged to the one in the graveyard who had been called Geldenhuis. It was Geldenhuis who was questioning her.

Tandia knew she was utterly and devastatingly beaten, that if she admitted she knew him she wouldn't leave the police station alive.

Geldenhuis changed tack suddenly. 'This money, you said you had to pay for a new gym frock? Where did you get this money?'

'It was mine, sir. I saved it for ten years.'

His voice suddenly boomed above her. 'You got this money from being a prostitute! You went to the coolie cemetery before school, most likely lots of times, and you did it there! You think I am stupid or something?'

'No, sir. It's not true, sir.'

'What is true and what is not true is not for you or me to say, it is only for the magistrate to decide. Where is this five pounds?' he said suddenly.

'I have it here,' Tandia whimpered.

The policeman stretched out his hand, 'Give it here,' he demanded.

Tandia knew she was badly trapped. 'I cannot show it to you, sir,' she whispered.

'You have this money concealed on your person, but you cannot produce it? Let me ask you a question. If you went to the lavatory, could you produce it then?'

Tandia said nothing.

'I see, the police know about these things. It is called a body search. Do you know who keeps their money in such a place?'

Again Tandia remained silent.

'Whores! That is the place prostitutes keep their money!'

'It is not what you think!' Tandia blurted out. She was distressed beyond tears. Geldenhuis had completely broken through her defences. If she took the money out of her bloomers right there in front of him, it would prove very little except that she was brazen enough to lift her skirt and put her hand down her pants. In his eyes this would only condemn her further. Tandia turned to look towards the black constable, but he immediately averted his eyes. She was beyond his help.

Geldenhuis lowered himself from the table and walked round to sit on the chair opposite her and called for the black constable to place the typewriter in front of him.

From a drawer in the table he removed a charge sheet and rolled it into the typewriter. He typed 'PATEL, Tandia', deliberately, using only two fingers, stopping when he had completed the two words. He then looked up casually at Tandia. 'Your address, what is your address?' he demanded.

'I have no address, sir,' Tandia replied.

'Vagrant,' the sergeant said, typing out the word slowly using only one finger to select each letter. 'No fixed address,' he said again deliberately pecking out the words on the typewriter. Then he looked up, leaned forward and placed his elbows on the table. 'Do you know what I'm doing?' he asked.

As he typed Tandia had torn off a length of toilet paper and blown her nose and attempted to wipe her tears. Her eyes were red-rimmed and swollen and her pretty little face was bruised and sore. She nodded her head in reply to Geldenhuis.

'I'm charging you with a one seven five, soliciting in a public place.' He shook his head as though regretting the need for what he was doing. 'It's so easy, you know. All you got to do is tell me the truth and you can go.' He cleared his throat, 'Look at me please,' he instructed. Tandia looked up at Geldenhuis across the table. He smiled and spread his hands and turned his palms upwards. 'Just tell me you did it in the cemetery and got paid for it, that's all. I'm a man of my word, just say, "Yes. Yes I did it, sergeant," and we won't lay a charge, you hear. You can leave the station with no police record. You know what it means to have a police record, don't you?'

Tandia's hands were on her lap curled around several messy scrunched balls of toilet paper and now she fixed her eyes on her clenched fists and remained silent. If she told a lie and said she was a whore, she was free, her life could begin again. If she maintained her innocence who was going to believe her? Who would believe that over ten years she had saved every penny, tickey and sixpence she had earned at Patel's printing shop, for getting the lunches for the men or running an errand or writing a letter for someone who couldn't write until she had five pounds of her own? If she admitted the truth, that it was two policeman who had raped her and that Geldenhuis was one of them she would not be alive for long, that was for sure. She was conscious of the white man looking down at her, fixing her with his pale eyes, eyes which she now perceived as more deadly than a snake. Tandia raised her head slowly until she looked directly at Geldenhuis. 'I will say it,' she said, and began to weep softly.

'No, man, saying it is not enough. I will write it down and then you will sign it, you hear?' Geldenhuis tried hard to conceal the triumph in his voice. He had broken her. He felt his erection grow almost to the point of release. Maybe she was only a schoolgirl but she wasn't stupid. What he had done required skill, real brains. He had won. It was better even than boxing.

Tandia knew she was hopelessly trapped. The last time she had refused to sign she had been hit and kicked unconscious and thrown into that foul-smelling cell. The thought of what Geldenhuis would do to her if she withheld her signature was almost more than she could bear.

This time the keys rattled along at a fair pace. He stopped once near the end. 'What is your Christian name, Matembu?' he asked the black policeman at the door.

The black constable straightened up. 'My name is Joshua, sir.'

Geldenhuis typed and removed the paper from the typewriter. He handed it to Tandia across the table. 'You read it first, then you sign it,' he said lightly.

Tandia, her hands shaking visibly, started to read the confession.

I, Tandia Patel, whose signature appears below, do knowingly and freely admit, in the presence of Sergeant J. T. Geldenhuis, a police officer stationed at the Cato Manor Police Station, that I did solicit for the purposes of sexual intercourse, two male persons unknown to me in the location of the Clairwood Indian Cemetery at approximately 6 a.m. on the 17th day of October 1952. And I further state that I did perform sexual intercourse with one of these men in return for the payment of the sum of five shillings.

Signed: (Miss) ....
Tandia Patel. Date: ....
Witness: (Sergeant) ....
Jannie Teunis Geldenhuis
Witness: (Constable) ....
Joshua Matembu

As Tandia read the piece Geldenhuis had written she couldn't think beyond the fact that it spelled freedom. She had been raped, violated and beaten. She was exhausted and humiliated and her body ached from the beating it had taken over the past eighteen hours. The niceties of moral rectitude taught so steadfastly at Durban Indian Girls' High School had no validity in her present circumstances. A refusal to sign the confession would do nothing for her self-respect nor did it even serve the useful purpose of adding to her hate. She became aware of Geldenhuis staring at her and when she had finished reading she looked up into his pale blue eyes. 'I will sign it,' she whispered again.

Geldenhuis said nothing. He was in control of himself again. He merely handed her his expensive fountain pen. Tandia's chair was too low for her to sign the paper while seated. She released the sticky balls of toilet paper in her hand and dropped them beside her chair and wiped her hand surreptitiously on the back of her shift. Then she rose and, crouching over the table, shakily signed the confession.

Tandia remained standing as Geldenhuis reached over and lifted the paper. He drew it towards him as though he was going to kiss it, but instead, he blew briefly on Tandia's signature and then waved it in the air. He then took the pen and signed the document himself. He called over to the black policeman, 'Hey, Matembu, come and sign your name.'

The black constable walked reluctantly over to the table. 'I not want sign this paper, sir. This bad paper.'

The white sergeant didn't look up. 'Sign it, man, you a material witness,' he said impatiently.

'This paper, sir, it not for charge sheet. I do not want sign this paper,' Matembu persisted.

Geldenhuis shot from his chair, 'I'm not bladdy asking you, I'm telling you! It's a fucking order, you hear!' He proffered his pen and moved Tandia's confession over to the edge of the table where the black man stood.

The black policeman took the pen and slowly signed his name and returned the pen to the sergeant. 'I will get her things, sir. The umFazi has a basin. I will get the keys from the desk sergeant, sir?'

'Ja, orright, also a police car, tell the sergeant I need a police car for only one hour.'

The black man turned to go and then turned to Geldenhuis. 'It is very, very late, sir. I must ask the desk sergeant for a police pass if the umFazi is going to be released on the street tonight.'

'Just get her things, you hear? She will not need a pass.' Geldenhuis folded Tandia's confession carefully. The black policeman looked hesitant. 'I'm telling you, man, she won't need a pass!'

'Please, sir, I have signed the paper. You said you would let me go if I signed that paper,' Tandia begged.

Geldenhuis stood with his hands on his hips. 'Where would you go? You have nowhere to go.' He glanced at his watch. 'It is one o'clock in the night, there are bad people out there.' He undid the button on the right breast pocket of his tunic and took out his wallet, then he carefully slipped the folded confession into it. 'I will keep this, you hear? I can use it any time I want, you understand? Any time. It is a legal document.' He spoke quietly with no threat in his voice, which, to Tandia, now seemed more threatening than had he shouted at her.

Geldenhuis placed the wallet back in the pocket of his khaki tunic and fastened the polished button. 'Sit,' he commanded, indicating the bigger chair once again. 'Sit, I want to have a nice little talk with you.'

Tandia did as she was told. She was filled with despair. She'd signed his paper and now he wasn't going to let her go. Or was he? He'd asked Matembu to get her things but he wouldn't authorise a late-night pass. Geldenhuis again sat sideways on the table, one elbow resting on the typewriter. He was relaxed, even friendly. 'You know something, Tandia?' It was the first time he had used her name in conversation. 'You are what in the police we call a *swart slimmetjie*, a clever black. And your kind, the *swart slimmetjie*, your kind we hate the most. You got a bit of education, you too smart for your own bladdy good. If I let you just walk out the station tonight, I'm telling you, jong, you'll be back in no time flat.'

'No, sir, I won't be back. I do not ever want to see this place ever again!'

Geldenhuis sighed, as though he was trying to explain something to a backward child. 'Ag, ja, man, you can try, but I'm telling you, it will be no good. No matter how hard you try, we will bring you back. We keep our eye on all the clever ones. You see, sooner or later they join the ANC. I'm telling you, jong, a black kaffir with an education is a dangerous person in the hands of the ANC.'

Tandia looked down into her lap, afraid to meet his eyes, the blue eyes that saw everything.

Geldenhuis tapped the wallet in his breast pocket. 'Now you know why I got this piece of paper. That's one reason.' He paused and then said,

'Look at me.' Tandia lifted her frightened gaze to his face. 'I want to help you. You want to know why because?' Tandia did not reply and once again lowered her eyes. 'Look at me, dammit,' Geldenhuis rapped. Then, as suddenly he smiled again. 'Natkin Patel showed me a lot of things that made me a better boxer.' He paused and brought one leg up so that his heel rested on the edge of the table, his hands capping his knee. 'Do you know about boxing?'

'Only a little bit,' Tandia sniffed. Geldenhuis nodded and continued, 'Next month I fight a Zulu boxer called Mandoma. He fights in the Transvaal and he's very good. Patel trained me for this fight which is for the South African professional welterweight title. He has seen Mandoma fight lots of times and he thinks I can beat him. I think so also.' Geldenhuis stopped talking and seemed to be lost in his own thoughts.

Tandia knew what Geldenhuis was talking about. Some years previously Patel had been called up to Johannesburg to referee a fight which took place in Sophiatown under unusual circumstances between Gideon Mandoma and a white schoolboy. Though both fighters were only in their teens at the time, Natkin had been impressed with what he saw. From that point on he had followed Mandoma's career in the ring.

If Patel had been helping to prepare Geldenhuis for a fight with Mandoma, Tandia thought, then the white policeman must be a very classy fighter. What's more, he had the hate. Patel always said that to be a champion, a boxer has to have the hate. Tandia knew at first hand that Geldenhuis had the hate.

Geldenhuis spoke at last. 'You see, I owe Patel. So I will help you. I will pay my debt, you hear?'

'Thank you, sir,' Tandia said, trying to conceal the fright in her voice. She wanted nothing more from the monster who sat on the table beside her. No matter how dangerous it was outside on the streets, it was better than being in this room with this white man who totally controlled her.

'I will help you, and you can help the police. Would you like to help the police?'

Tandia did not reply and Geldenhuis took her silence to mean that she would co-operate. 'You see, if you help the police, then you safe, as a *swart slimmetjie*, you safe.' He grinned suddenly. 'You on our side, man!'

Tandia waited for the trap to close. 'What must I do, sir?' she asked in an uncertain voice.

'Ag, easy stuff. I will take you to this place where you can stay. They will give you work also. It is a woman who owes me a favour.'

Tandia sensed the plan Geldenhuis had hatched in his head was important to him and she grew a little bolder. 'What must I do for the police at this place?'

'People will come. Sometimes Indian people, rich Indian people. Sometimes white people. Also important rich ones. You will watch and you will learn who they are and you will tell me what they do and say.'

'What kind of place is this place?'

'Ag, you know, it is place where they have women, where men go sometimes.'

The trap had been sprung! Geldenhuis was going to find her a place in a brothel. Tandia looked up at the white man, her distress plain. The police sergeant had a smile on his face and he absently tapped the outline of his wallet in the breast pocket of his tunic.

He jumped from the table and straightened the tunic of his uniform by pulling it down first from the front and then the back and smoothing the waist with his palms. 'I will speak to my friend.' He beckoned to Tandia. 'Come, I must take your fingerprints and then we go hey?'

THREE

The clock on the charge office wall showed a quarter to two when Tandia finally lifted the large basin to her head and started to walk out of the Cato Manor Police Station. She kept her eyes downcast and followed Geldenhuis out into the dark street. As she passed through the door the black constable whispered, '*Hamba khashle, intkhosatana*, go well, young lady.'

'C'mon! I haven't got all bladdy night!' Geldenhuis called. Tandia walked slowly towards the police car. He stood beside the open boot and indicated she should put the basin in and then slammed it shut. 'Climb in the back, be quick!' he snapped, the authority now back in his voice.

Tandia's relief at leaving was so great that she hardly noticed which way Geldenhuis drove. They seemed to drive for some time through the dark streets of the township and then onto a tarred road with street lights. It was not until they reached the lighted street that he spoke to her again.

'I can't take you to the place where this woman is, so I'm taking you to the train station. There are no more trains tonight but you must wait there.' He offered no further explanation and shortly afterwards they drove up to the Cato Manor railway station. 'Wait in the car,' he said and then walked up the steps into the stationmaster's office.

He returned quite soon with a sleepy looking railway official and told Tandia to get out of the car. The man from the railway was the first person other than policemen Tandia had seen in what seemed to her like a lifetime. To Tandia he represented the normal world she had once known and she immediately felt more secure. The official wasn't wearing the coat of his blue serge uniform, his waistcoat was unbuttoned and his tie knot pulled down, which made him look friendlier. A bluish rash of stubble covered his jowls and he scratched at his crotch absently as though he was not yet properly awake.

In a manner common to South African whites, Geldenhuis spoke to the railway official as though Tandia wasn't present. 'Look, man, I want you to let this girl sit on a bench until the first train.' He paused. 'By the way, when is that?'

The railway official automatically reached for his pocket watch. Forgetting that his waistcoat was unbuttoned he dug his thumb and forefinger into the roll of fat where his fob pocket ought to have been. 'Ten minutes to five,' he said automatically, looking down into his empty hand.

'Ja, okay, she will be gone before then.'

The railway official looked at Tandia for the first time. 'Has she got a pass?' He pointed at her and turned to Geldenhuis. 'She looks like she's been in a fight. She's not a *tsotsi*'s girl is she?' The idea of her being a street hooligan's woman seemed to wake him up and he wagged the finger at Tandia. 'I don't want any trouble from a bladdy coloured or kaffir gang, you hear?'

'No, man, no trouble,' Geldenhuis said impatiently, 'Jus' let her sit on a bench, okay, hey?'

The railway man shrugged. 'Ja, if she's got a pass it's okay by me.'

Geldenhuis clicked his tongue. 'No, man, she hasn't got a pass! I just want her to sit on a bench until some people come.'

'You better give me your name and your phone number in case some other police come,' said the stationmaster.

Geldenhuis wrote down his phone number and name and, tearing the page from a small spiral notepad, handed it to the official who turned and walked away without bidding him goodnight.

Geldenhuis turned to Tandia. 'Don't try and leave here; you haven't got a night pass, and if some other police pick you up you'll be charged and go to the lock-up for six days. Just stay here on a bench, okay?'

Tandia nodded; the thought of being apprehended again terrified her. Geldenhuis opened the boot and she lifted the basin to her head. Very little strength remained in her beaten body and she rose slowly to an upright position. 'Can I go now please, sir?' she whispered.

'Ja, go!'

Tandia walked up the station steps into the building. 'Hey!' Geldenhuis called. The heavy basin on her head caused Tandia to turn slowly to face him. If he called her back again she knew she would surely faint. He stood with his elbow resting on the top of the open driver's door.

'Yes, sir?' it was hardly a whisper and the white policeman would have had difficulty even detecting the movement of her lips.

Geldenhuis patted the breast pocket of his uniform and grinned. 'Jus' remember, jong, in the eyes of the law you nothing but a whore!'

Tandia turned and walked into the station building where she found a bench on the platform stencilled 'Non-Whites.' She pushed the basin under the bench and sat down on the deserted platform. She was unutterably tired but the joy of having finally escaped Geldenhuis overcame her weariness for a moment and she impulsively rose from the bench and pulled the basin out from under it.

The two cotton shifts into which Apple Sammy, Tandia's kewpie doll, had been wrapped hadn't come undone when the basin had toppled to the road. Now she removed the doll and examined it. Apple Sammy had large, ingenuous dark-blue eyes which had faded somewhat and the once bright rose rouge on his cheeks was now only faintly discernible, but he seemed no worse for wear. Tandia adjusted the doll's legs and pulled at his tiny pink organza skirt.

Tandia sat with the small doll clutched tightly to her chest and started to rock. She was too tired to try to think about what might happen next. Weariness overcame her and despite her fear of being accosted on the lonely platform, she fell asleep.

Tandia wakened slowly. Her body ached terribly but her head, which also hurt, rested against a warm, wonderful softness. She felt herself cradled, as though she was being held in a comforting embrace. The experience was so unfamiliar that, at first, she believed herself to be dreaming. To add to the dreaming quality, a sweet-smelling perfume reached her nostrils. Slowly, tentatively, she opened her eyes.

'Shhh, *skatterbol*,' she heard a woman's voice say softly.

Tandia looked down. She still clutched Apple Sammy to her chest. She tried to sit up but the arm around her held her firmly. Frightened, she looked up into the caramel-coloured face of a very big and smiling woman with the longest false eyelashes she had ever seen.

The woman wore an outrageously large purple hat decorated with pink ostrich feathers. Her pink satin dress stretched tightly over her enormous bosom, at the same time allowing a large amount of warm caramel flesh to spill out of its deeply plunging neckline so that her breasts looked as though they were trying to escape. The effect the woman created was of richness, and the strong, sweet-smelling perfume which Tandia now realised belonged to her, added to the opulent effect.

'Don't be frightened, baby, I ain't going to hurt you none.' The words were clipped and staccato and sounded American. 'Name's Mama Tequila, pleased ter . . . meet'cha.' She offered her right hand for Tandia to shake.

'Hi,' Tandia whispered, barely touching the hand with its long, shiny red nails.

'What's your name, honey?'

'Tandia,' she cleared her throat, 'Tandia Patel.'

'Tandia, that's a real swell name. You got no place to go? That's it, huh? You little orphan Annie sittin' on your fanny?' Mama Tequila had the raspy voice of a heavy smoker and now she laughed uproariously at her own joke, interjecting her laughter with a fit of coughing. She stopped laughing abruptly and reached into her handbag, a large purple leather affair that matched her hat. From it she withdrew a silver cigarette case. 'Smoke, honey?'

Tandia, who was completely overwhelmed by the presence of this large woman, shook her head.

Mama Tequila helped herself to a cigarette, closed the case and tapped the tobacco end on its silver lid. She returned the case to her bag and then dug around in it to produce a regulation American army Zippo lighter. She flicked it alight and held it to the end of the cigarette, squinting through the smoke as she drew in and then exhaled. Then she slipped the cover back over the Zippo and returned it to her handbag. She spoke with the cigarette between her lips. 'It ain't pretty like everything else, but it sure lights every time. I kind of like pretty things, but a pretty lighter that don't work is like a pretty woman that don't work.' She withdrew the cork tip from her lips. 'Ain't no good to nobody, leastways herself!' She chuckled, 'I bet you like pretty things too, hey honey?'

Tandia didn't answer. She wanted to pinch herself to make sure she wasn't dreaming; nothing like this monstrous pink creature had ever happened to her before.

'Sure you do, you a very pretty girl, pretty girls got to have pretty things, or they die!' She shook her head slowly as though talking to herself. 'There is plenty of time to be ugly.' She turned and looked directly at Tandia. 'You got to use pretty, while you got pretty, honey, that the rule of womankind!'

Mama Tequila started to chuckle again, her breasts heaving. 'You see this big, hip-pie-pot-to-mass, honey? Well, once upon a time, I was just as pretty and dainty as you, baby.' She seemed to find this particularly funny, her laughter disappearing finally into a wheeze until she grew quite red in the face and started to cough. She threw the cigarette to the ground and bending forward brought both her hands up to cover her mouth. Tandia knew she ought to pat her on the back but she hesitated. She had never deliberately touched an adult female person before and now the idea frightened her.

Mama Tequila glanced at her briefly between a spasm of coughing. Her eyes were teary from the coughing and her mascara had started to run; she seemed to be appealing for her help. Tandia took a deep breath and started to slap the large woman on her back. To her surprise Mama Tequila ceased coughing almost immediately. In a voice drawn thin after the paroxysm of coughing she said, 'Ain't nutting but coffin nails, them damned cigarillos!'

She straightened up, dug into her handbag and produced an absurdly small lace handkerchief with which she wiped her eyes, then she held it to her nose and blew. She found a compact in her bag and proceeded to repair her make-up. Returning the make-up to her bag, she turned to Tandia, her face serious for a moment. 'This ain't no place for a couple of high-class ladies, honey,' she rasped.

Tandia instinctively liked the big woman. She wanted to go with her but her escape from Geldenhuis was still too recent. The idea of being tied to another human being she didn't know and whose motives she couldn't begin to discern, frightened her. 'Where we going to?' Instinctively she picked up Apple Sammy from her lap and clutched the doll to her chest.

Mama Tequila didn't answer her directly. Instead she looked hard into Tandia's eyes. 'Look, kid, you a mess. You been beat up bad.' She touched Tandia's face gently. 'Look what them mothers did to you!' She reached out and removed Apple Sammy from Tandia's grasp and placed the kewpie doll on her lap. Then she took both Tandia's arms, and drew them gently towards her. When she spoke again the toughness had gone from her voice.

'You poor baby, them wrists, they are bad. We got to clean you up, honey. We leave you like this you going to have yourself a pair of permanent bracelets.'

Mama Tequila placed Tandia's hands back on her lap one on either side of Apple Sammy. Then she rose slowly from the bench and began to tug at her skirt, pulling the tight satin back down to her knees. She adjusted her hat in an imaginary mirror, her hands fluttering around its rim, a small tug here and a little pat there, like two busy brown spiders, the ends of their fat legs dipped in brilliant scarlet.

She took a few steps towards the entrance of the station, and pushing two fingers into her mouth she let go a piercing whistle. She turned to Tandia. 'C'mon, kid, let's kick the dust, we're going home to Bluey Jay.'

In what seemed like a matter of moments a tall, very black man appeared. His head was completely shaved and a jagged scar ran diagonally across the top of his shiny scalp to just above his left eyebrow. It looked as though the skull had been cracked open and then clamped until it grew back together again. The eye directly under the scar was only half open, a condition which seemed permanent as the skin around the eye was puckered like the top of a leather drawstring purse. The tall black man smiled as he approached Mama Tequila and Tandia noticed that his two front teeth were missing but the incisors on either side had each been filed to a point and were made of gold.

'This is Edward, King George, Juicey Fruit Mambo, honey. He is my driver. Just call him Juicey Fruit Mambo. Never mind your basin, he'll bring it.' Mama Tequila started to walk away. 'Now you just follow me, baby,' she called; she seemed to alternate the two endearments 'honey' and 'baby' as though she hadn't quite decided which suited Tandia best, though 'baby' seemed to be winning.

Juicey Fruit Mambo grinned at Tandia. He reminded Tandia of a horror story she'd read as a small girl in a book she'd borrowed from the school library. It had been entitled 'Doctor Weirdwolfe's Tales of the Supernatural'. The scariest story in the book was about a monster named the Master of Evil who lived in the *under-world* with a huge and grotesque wet nurse who cared for the monster children of his victims. They all lived in a giant tent made from the membraned wings of vampire bats, surrounded by a garden of carnivorous plants that fed on birds and bats and flying insects, reaching up on coiled stems to snatch them from the very air itself. The Master of Evil would come up into the *above-world* through the foul-smelling city sewers, into the dark, cold, misty streets where he would waylay young women returning from the tavern at night, biting them on the right breast with his two gold incisors so that nine months later they gave birth to boy monsters.

From infancy these children were unable to bear bright light and screamed until they were placed into a dark cupboard, where they would lie quietly all day. But when night came, especially when it was a full moon, they would howl like wolves. Each year, on St Crispin's day, the children born to the Master of Evil were put out into the icy streets to die. Mysteriously, by morning there was never any sign of them. People claimed they had been gathered up by the Master of Evil who would take them back to his terrible wet nurse, who fed the children on blood from her breasts.

Then, when they were grown up, the Master of Evil would file and cap their teeth with gold like his own and send them out to hunt alone in the dark alleys in the *above-world*. The story ended with the warning that, at that very moment, in the city where the reader dwelt, lurking in the foul-smelling sewers was a Master of Evil waiting to sink his golden incisors into young women returning from the taverns late at night.

It was quite a silly story really, but Tandia could recall being very frightened that such a dreadful creature was waiting in the dark sewers under Durban. The road outside Patel's house was the only paved one in the township and thus contained a stormwater drain, from which the Master of Evil might appear at any moment, within yards of where Tandia lay in the iron shed in the back yard.

Juicey Fruit Mambo bent from the waist and scooped up Tandia's basin. He held it in front of him as though it was a tray filled with precious things charged especially to his care. Tandia thanked him softly and, picking up Apple Sammy from the bench, she followed the large, pink woman out of the station building.

Directly below the steps, where Geldenhuis had parked the police car, now stood a large black motor with its engine running and its back door open. Mama Tequila stood at the car door and waited for Tandia to reach her before she got in. She patted the seat beside her. 'Come, baby, you're safe in Mama's big, black, shiny Packard limousine. Come sit here with Mama, honey.'

The back of the car smelt of expensive leather, not unlike Patel's boots when they were new. Tandia sat wide-eyed and nervous on the edge of the back seat with her hands tightly gripping the seat in front of her. Mama Tequila took Apple Sammy from Tandia's lap and placed the doll between the two of them. 'She a proper lady riding in a limousine now, honey,' she said and then, as though to demonstrate how a proper lady sat, she closed her eyes and fell back into the soft leather, exhausted.

Tandia heard the slam of the boot closing and moments later Juicey Fruit opened the driver's door and slid behind the wheel. 'Home to Bluey Jay,' Mama Tequila instructed wearily without opening her eyes, 'We gonna take Miss Tandia here into our everlovin' care.'

The big car climbed away from the flats of Cato Manor station towards the Berea, away from the poorer parts of the city into the heights above Durban where the posh white people lived, a part of town where

Africans, Indians or coloureds weren't allowed to live even if they had all the money in the world.

Soon they left the big walled houses and leafy streets of the Berea behind and drove down dark avenues of gum trees. The white bark on their perfectly straight trunks ghosted as the headlights caught and then lost them again. Once in a while they'd pass the shadowy outline of a house set back from the road and then they left the bluegums and for a short while they drove along the open highway on the road to Pietermaritzburg. Juicey Fruit Mambo finally slowed the Packard and turned into a small dirt road.

The way was no more than a farm road, rutted and uneven in places so that Juicey Fruit Mambo seldom took the Packard out of low gear. Half a mile or so up this road he stopped at an imposing set of double wrought-iron gates set between two large white painted cement pillars. It was bright moonlight and it was easy to see that not even a wire strand fence attached to either side of the brilliant white gateposts. In fact, these posts were not white at all, but a violent pink in the light of day; now, caught in the bright headlights of the car they looked dazzling white.

Juicey Fruit Mambo tapped the horn once sharply, even though a small boy of about eight years old holding a hurricane lamp was hurrying down the long curved driveway towards the gate. The boy was almost immediately followed by an old Zulu running on spindly buckled legs who carried a *knopkierie* and a short *asegai* in one hand and with the other held up his ragged khaki shorts to prevent them from falling down.

The boy placed the hurricane lamp on the side of the driveway and swung the gates open just as the Zulu came to a panting halt and stood to attention at the side of the driveway. Still clutching his pants he gave Juicey Fruit Mambo and his passengers a toothless smile and saluted, touching the large wooden knob of his fighting stick and the blade of his spear lightly to his grizzled head.

Juicey Fruit Mambo laughed. 'Go back to sleep, old man. Go back and dream of a hundred cattle and five fat-buttocked wives all of dem young with sweet milk in their breasts.' Pointing to the small boy, he added, 'Dis brave warrior will guard us well tonight, see, it is a miracle, his pants stay up on their own. So he has both hands free to fight de evil *skokiaan*.' He reached out and patted the small boy on the head and then pointed to the full moon which frosted the surrounding trees and silvered the surrounding landscape with a light almost as clear as day. 'Tonight, God has supplied de light. Do not insult him with your little lantern. If I had a newspaper and, if I could read, I would read by the light. Dere are no shadows in such a night to conceal danger. Is it too much to ask that you can walk by it?' He slipped the car into gear and moved into the long driveway leading to the house.

Around a curve the lights of the Packard revealed a large mansion resting amongst several very big trees. The house was in darkness except for a solitary light which burned a dim welcome inside the arched doorway.

The driveway led directly past the front of the house and Juicey Fruit Mambo continued past the front door and around the far side of the house. Caught in the headlights, Tandia observed what appeared to be a row of outhouses. Juicey Fruit Mambo drove past these to the very end and turned the Packard into a lean-to garage.

Mama Tequila, who had remained with her eyes closed even at the gate, now opened them as Juicey Fruit Mambo switched off the ignition. 'Welcome to Bluey Jay, honey,' she said wearily.

Juicey Fruit Mambo opened the rear door on Tandia's side. The very first sounds she heard as she stepped from the car were the croaking of a frog and the electric singing of crickets. Holding Apple Sammy tightly she stood waiting, sensing the alien space around her. The air was cool and she could smell the slightly damp earth at her feet and the cudlike odour of the grass. It made her think of Patel in his cold grave and she shuddered involuntarily. A sudden breeze arose and sent the leaves of the large trees around the house roaring. Just as suddenly the breeze stopped and after barely a moment of silence the frog and the crickets took up again. The sky, almost pewter in the moonlight, showed a few of the brighter stars and through the branches of a giant old wild fig tree she could see the speckled light of the moon. Tandia had never been in the country before and she found it frightening and very strange. Never mind the Master of Evil lurking in the city sewers, some very strange things could happen in all this space and loneliness, she thought.

'Come, baby, it's late, we got to clean you up some and put you to bed.' Mama Tequila took Tandia by the elbow and they followed Juicey Fruit Mambo, who'd raced ahead to open the door and turn on a light in the small scullery which served as the back entrance to the house and which led directly through to a large kitchen.

Tandia walked slightly ahead of Mama Tequila as they entered the door, which was only just large enough for the big woman to fit through. She went into the room, brightly lit by four lights which ran down the centre of the ceiling. Taking up the middle part of the room was a huge, scrubbed-pine table above which, from a large circle of iron suspended on heavy chains, hung all manner of pots and pans. A huge cream AGA cooker with two giant covered hotplates sat in a whitewashed alcove. The walls of the kitchen consisted of wooden shiplapped cupboards of a soft yellow wood which stretched up from the floor to a ceiling turned a deep honey colour from a couple of generations of cooking vapours. The room was scrubbed and spotless and smelt of a mixture of blue carbolic soap, floor wax and linseed oil, with just a hint of ground coffee and yesterday's stock-pot added. Its red painted cement floor was waxed and shining. To one side, though commanding a clear view of the entire room, stood a very large leather club chair with a coffee table beside it, on which stood a black bakelite telephone.

Juicey Fruit Mambo pulled a chair from the table and indicated to Tandia that she should sit. Tandia lowered her aching and exhausted body into the chair. She gave a small sigh and rested her arms on the table and, still clutching Apple Sammy in one hand, she placed her head in the crease of her right arm. Within seconds she was asleep. Apple Sammy fell from her grasp and clattered to the floor. Juicey Fruit Mambo, without bending his knees, scooped up the little doll and placed it back on the table. Then he lifted Tandia carefully into an upright sitting position, placed his ear to her chest and pulled one of her eyelids up to examine her eye.

'I do not think she will wake up tonight,' he said as he rearranged Tandia's arms carefully on the table, making sure that her wrists were not pressured. Then he lowered her head to rest on the upper part of her right arm once again.

Mama Tequila came over to the table to look at Tandia. She spoke quietly in Zulu to the tall African. 'This one is a great prize; you must take good care of her.' She turned and walked slowly towards the large armchair.

'I hear you, Mama Tequila,' Juicey Fruit Mambo replied softly, his expression serious. 'She is like a young tsamma melon ready to be picked. I think, for the white man, this one, she is very beautiful?'

Mama Tequila gave a soft sigh, but made no reply as she shifted her huge weight down onto the leather armchair. A slow protesting 'pffft' of air escaped from the leather upholstery.

'I will make coffee and bring you some Cape brandy?'

'No, first you must wash the girl and bandage her. Put her in Hester's room for tonight. She's gone to the Drakensberg with her Boer from the Free State.' Mama Tequila fanned herself absently with a Japanese fan. The design on the fan showed a demure little geisha girl peeping from behind a fan of her own. 'Also, the way she walked, I think she been raped. Make sure she's clean at the back and is not hurt in the front.'

Juicey Fruit Mambo lifted Tandia's limp form from the chair and carried her from the room. Mama Tequila reached into her bag and found a cork-tip, but after taking only a couple of puffs she ground it impatiently in the ashtray beside her and reached for the telephone, which she placed on her lap. She dialled a number and sighed heavily as she waited for someone to pick up at the other end. 'Cato Manor *Polise Stasie*,' a sleepy voice answered.

'Sergeant, you the best, you hear! This little baby, she the greatest po-ten-shal I ever did see!' Mama Tequila gushed.

Geldenhuis switched to English. 'Ag, it's you, Mama Tequila. Every-thing is all right then?'

'You done me a good turn, Sergeant,' Mama Tequila paused for effect. 'My mama always told me, "Child, one good turn deserve another."' She waited for the policeman to make his demand.

'Not now. Some other time. I'll let you know,' Geldenhuis said.

Mama Tequila grimaced in annoyance. She liked things clean-cut, that way you knew where you stood. She chuckled. 'Your pleasure is my pleasure, Sergeant. You come any time, you hear?'

'Ja, okay, so long, Mama Tequila.'

She heard the click as he replaced the receiver. A lot of cops came to Bluey Jay. The law of the one-eyed snake was stronger than the Immorality Act forbidding sex between whites and coloured or black people, but she always felt uncomfortable when Geldenhuis arrived. He would sit in the small parlour bar and sip a beer and talk to the girls but he'd never partake, never leave the bar and slip quietly upstairs with one of them to return, in the timeless brothel tradition, half an hour later to slip into his seat unseen and unseeing as if nothing had happened.

There was something wrong with that one. By this she didn't mean that Geldenhuis was a corrupt young cop. Mama Tequila was completely resigned to that. After all, if there were no bad cops she wouldn't be in business, or at the very least, business would be a damn sight harder. It was more than that, and she wondered if it had been him who had raped the girl. She made a mental note to get to know Geldenhuis better. Until you knew a man's special weakness, that thing which would indict him in his own eyes, you were vulnerable. She was smart enough to know that the old-fashioned type of policeman, the good old guys who came for an occasional quickie and who you paid with a fiver every week and threw in a few quid as an annual donation to the Police Boys' Boxing Club, were on the way out. The Geldenhuis era had arrived.

FOUR

Tandia could hear Hester coming down the upstairs corridor. Hester wore scuffs which slapped against the back of her heel and then hard against the polished yellowwood floor boards. 'Hey, Tandia, guess what!'

Tandia raised her pen from her work. It was simply amazing how Hester could get noise, even a sort of rhythm, out of wearing a pair of scuffs. All the girls wore them when they were not working but Hester's scuffs went 'slap, schliptt, slap, schliptt, slap, schliptt!' 'How does she do that?' she thought. Though she had to admit it was typical of Hester, who did everything loudly and with drama. Hester was a noise factory. She just couldn't help herself. She even slept loudly, for she suffered from nasal polyps and snored so badly that Mama Tequila had given her the room at the end of the corridor with the bathroom in between it and the others.

Mama Tequila had also stopped booking her out on dirty forty-eights. Too many customers were returning her to Bluey Jay after one night demanding their money back. None of her clients ever complained that Hester didn't deliver. She delivered all right! That was part of the problem. Hester was so good at her job that she quickly exhausted even the most virile of her mostly middle-aged clients, who, attempting to renew their vigour with a couple of hours' shut-eye, would find themselves trapped in a room where the very walls seemed to vibrate with Hester's bronchial sonority.

Only the big Boer from the Free State didn't seem to mind. He'd get completely blotto on VSOP Cape brandy and then he'd giggle and take Hester into his arms, arms which were burnt a deep bronze from where the line of his short sleeves ended. 'Come, my little beauty, let me grow some grass between your two beautiful dark hills,' he would say, burying his great ginger beard between Hester's big brown boobs. 'Together we'll snore the night into little pieces smaller than matchsticks.'

With a sigh Tandia replaced the cap on her Croxley fountain pen. Hester's arrival always demanded her full attention. It was the end of her school work for the moment.

Hester's long pink fingernails appeared around the door. They were followed almost immediately by her head. Hester was a back-slidden Pentecostal and she would explain that the Lord didn't mind pink nails, pink nails were all right, almost natural; it was the long, shiny red ones like Sarah's that He was very against.

'Hey, Tandia, listen to this!' She walked over to where Tandia sat at the little table that served as desk. 'You going to get some new school uniforms, man. It's true! Only just now I heard Mama T calling on the telephone to Sonny Vindoo.'

'Sonny who?' Tandia was delighted at the prospect of the uniforms.

'Vindoo, he's the Indian tailor who makes us special things sometimes, when Mama T wants to put on a bit of a show for an important new client.' Hester brought the tips of the fingers of both hands to her lips and her eyes grew large. 'They pink!'

'What's pink?'

'The school uniforms, they going to be pink, God's honour!'

Tandia buried her face in her hands as Hester continued, 'You know how she's mad about pink? I'm telling you, jong, Mama T is having pink gym frocks made. I heard her tell Sonny Vindoo to find three pairs of pink stockings and a pink beret also.' Hester put her hand on Tandia's shoulder. 'I swear on my mother's grave, it's true!'

'She can't do that! They won't allow it. The colour is brown. The colour for Durban Indian Girls' High School is dark brown!'

'I dunno about that, jong. All I can say is I heard her clear as anything.' Hester put her fist up to her ear and brought her hand onto her ample dark bosom the way Mama Tequila did when she made a phone call; then she started to mimic Mama Tequila. 'Listen, Mr Dine-o-mite, I want you should go to John Orrs. Tell them Mama Tequila she want seven yards pink gaberdine. Okay, lover? Also four yards pink cotton poplin. Nice, you hear? Pretty rose pink.'

Sonny Vindoo liked to be paid in kind, so Mama Tequila maintained her customer persona when she talked to him. The little Indian tailor looked a little like Mahatma Gandhi and affected a dhoti and round steel-rimmed glasses to emphasise the likeness. The very first time he had done any work for Mama Tequila he'd handed her an invoice on which he had written in his neat, clerical hand:

For services rendered please render the services of:
1 only Blonde Bombshell.

Which is how Sonny Vindoo got his name, Mr Dine-o-mite, and at the same time got Sarah chosen for him, the frizzy, ginger-headed Sarah being the closest the Bluey Jay establishment could get to a blonde at the time.

Hester could mimic Mama Tequila down pat and despite her concern, Tandia was forced to laugh. But then she looked worried again. 'Oh no! What am I going to do?'

Tandia, who had never spent a day of her life in bed, woke very late on the Saturday after she'd been rescued by Mama Tequila. She felt too weak too move; her whole body seemed to be burning and her mouth was dry. She ran her tongue over her lips which were cracked and swollen. Her eyes had difficulty adjusting to her surroundings; the room hummed and seemed to spin slowly above her head, and the air around her had a fractured luminosity, like used cellophane paper. Slowly the humming ceased and the room grew steady but the cellophane nature of the air persisted so she could not very clearly make out the tall, dark shape standing quietly beside her bed.

Juicey Fruit Mambo smiled his sharp, golden-toothed smile and Tandia, feverish and disorientated, screamed and then began to sob. It was the Master of Evil from the underworld and he was going to bite her with his golden teeth. 'Don't bite me! Please don't bite me! Please, please! I don't want to have your baby!'

Juicey Fruit Mambo bent over her and placed his hand on her shoulder and Tandia became hysterical and tried to beat him off with her fists. The shock of finding herself confronted by the Master of Evil lent her strength. She rose up and, standing on the bed, beat frantically at the black man's chest. He brought his arms around her and held her tightly until what little strength she had gained from the sudden shock had spent itself. Exhausted, Tandia wept against his chest, blood running from her lip where she'd bitten it. Finally she lost even the strength to weep.

'Shhhh! Missy Tandia, no more now, you heah? I am not bite you. Shhhh! You very sick but not to die, I tink. No more for you cry, Missy Tandia.' After a while he laid her head gently back onto her pillow where Tandia, her eyes red from weeping but still bright with fever, stared up at him in catatonic terror.

Mama Tequila heard Tandia screaming but her progress up the stairs was painfully slow, although she was hurrying and was panting fiercely as she came through the door. 'Jesus! What happened?'

Juicey Fruit Mambo shook his head slowly, then he brought the palm of his hand against his forehead and wiped across it, flicking the imaginary sweat from his brow. 'She has the hot sickness, madam,' he explained.

'Go get some ice from the bar fridge. Also a towel. Quick, man!' Mama Tequila lowered her body onto the side of the bed and lifted Tandia's unresisting form from the pillow and held her tightly to her bosom.

To Tandia, in her state of confusion, Mama Tequila was almost as great a shock as finding the Master of Evil hovering over her. She was wearing a huge pale pink silk kimono which was embroidered in the elaborate oriental fashion with brilliantly coloured roses, peonies, hummingbirds and butterflies. To Tandia in her state of confusion she looked like a garden dancing in the air with a grotesque disembodied head floating above it.

Tandia believed that she was beyond help. She had been carried to the underworld by the Master of Evil who had bitten her, not only on the chest but all over, so that now her body hurt terribly. Too weak to resist or even to sob, she lay helpless against Mama Tequila's heaving breasts as the huge woman rocked her, making soft shhhing sounds.

After a while, when Tandia's breathing had grown more steady, Mama Tequila laid her back on the bed. Tandia felt sure she was about to die. Horrible as this seemed, it was strangely painless and an end which she welcomed. Patel would never forgive her if she had the Master of Evil's baby. She must die! It was very important! He wouldn't love her if she didn't die to save his fragile ego from destruction. A man like him who was known in the best white circus.

Juicey Fruit Mambo returned with a small enamel basin filled with water into which he had placed a couple of trays of ice cubes; a small towel was also draped over one arm. He placed the basin beside the bed and dug into his trouser pockets to produce a bottle of pills. Then he rinsed the towel, wrung it out to make a small square parcel of it, and placed it against Tandia's fevered brow.

'Hold her head up,' Mama Tequila said, shaking two small pink pills from the bottle. Juicey Fruit Mambo lifted Tandia's head from the cushion and Mama Tequila slipped two tablets into her mouth. The pills tasted bitter and Tandia swallowed eagerly from the glass of water Juicey Fruit handed her, drinking its contents down completely. 'She is thirsty, I will bring some more,' he said, and left the room.

The effect of the barbiturate soon sent Tandia to sleep and it was late in the evening when she wakened again. The fever in her still raged and she could hear someone singing, 'Lay that pistol down, babe . . . lay that pistol down!' It seemed to be coming from a long way away and she opened her eyes slowly. 'Pistol packin' Mama . . .' The electric light was on in the room and this time Dr Louis Rabin was at her side. Tandia knew then that Patel knew. Knew for sure!

'I'll give her a shot of Pen-G to fight the infection. Her pulse is very slow, which is probably from the shock; she is undoubtedly somewhat traumatised.' He didn't speak again for some time, his finger touching her lightly in various parts of her burning body. 'Hmm, from the contusions this little lady has been through a bad time.'

Then what seemed like ages later she heard his voice again, as though he was speaking in an echo chamber. 'Now Tandia, I'm going to roll you over, I'm going to give you an injection in your bottom. It's not very nice, I know. But it will fix you. So you be a brave girl now, you hear?'

She felt his cool, strong hands on her hot skin as he rolled her onto her side, then a sudden jab of pain from the needle, followed almost immediately by a slow, welling, almost unbearable pain as Dr Louis Rabin pressed down on the plunger and ran the dose of penicillin into her system.

Tandia started to cry again. The injection seemed to exacerbate all the other pains in her body. Patel knew about the monster baby, that's why he had called Dr Louis Rabin. 'I don't want to have the baby!' she sobbed, 'Please, Patel, it wasn't my fault! Please, please, I didn't do it!'

Dr Louis looked at Mama Tequila. 'What's this about a baby?'

Mama shrugged her shoulders. 'I think she was raped, doctor.' She turned to Juicey Fruit Mambo who nodded his head to verify her opinion.

Doctor Rabin spun round to look at the tall black man. 'You? You raped her?'

A look of astonishment crossed Juicey Fruit Mambo's face, then he shook his head and laughed grimly. 'No, doctor, I cannot do dis ting.'

'He's impotent,' Mama Tequila said quietly. 'We got a tip-off from the police and found her on a bench on the railway station very early this morning.' She pointed to Tandia's bandaged wrists. 'Han'cuffs done that. I think the police probably raped her.'

'Did she tell you that?'

Mama Tequila sighed, 'No, doctor.'

Doctor Louis started to unwind the bandage on Tandia's right wrist. 'Then let's not go around accusing people before we know, hey.' He removed the last of the bandage and gently lifted the boracic lint Juicey Fruit had placed around her wrist. What he saw caused him to give a low, spontaneous whistle. 'Not good. You're right, these lacerations could have been made by handcuffs.'

Juicey Fruit Mambo spoke quietly, 'I am sure, doctor.' He held both his arms together, wrists upwards, both his hands balled into a fist which he held out for Dr Louis to see. A deep welt of shiny scar tissue slightly less than a quarter of an inch thick made a complete bangle around both wrists. It was almost as though the scar had been carefully and deliberately fashioned. He laughed bitterly, 'I know dis ting, doctor. Same like me, she has the bracelets. I tink dis is a *bansella* for the black people from de policeman.'

Mama Tequila could smell trouble. Dr Louis wasn't afraid to take on the police on behalf of any of his patients. He wasn't scared of anyone; a man like that could make a lot of trouble for a person.

The doctor had removed the bandage and liniment from Tandia's other wrist and was probing the deep wound softly with the pad of his forefinger. 'You are right, doctor,' Mama Tequila offered, 'we don't know for sure, do we? Maybe a rope could have done this also? There are many, many bad people around these days.' She looked up at Juicey Fruit Mambo and shook her head almost imperceptibly, indicating that he shouldn't interfere again. He sniffed and pulled at the top of his nose with his forefinger and thumb and then rubbed his hand twice across his mouth as though trying to remove from his lips any further chance of spontaneous comment.

'There is too much police brutality these days. Mama Tequila, if you want to press charges I'll testify that, in my opinion, these lacerations were as a direct result of the overzealous use of a pair of police handcuffs.'

Mama Tequila brought her hand up to her breast, trying hard to conceal her shock at the suggestion. 'No charges, doctor! You must understand, we want no trouble with the police in this place. Juicey Fruit Mambo will take good care of her wrists.'

'Oh yes, of course, it was the police who told you where to find her,' Dr Louis said.

He turned to Juicey Fruit Mambo. 'You've done a good job, the wounds are nice and clean.' He liked to explain things. 'She has good skin, I don't think she will scar too badly.' He brought out his bag and producing a small pad started to write. He wrote for some time, filling several pages.

The coloured woman and the black man waited silently until Mama Tequila could no longer contain herself. 'That is a very long prescription, doctor?'

Doctor Louis, 'Ag, man, just notes, you never know when such notes can come in handy.' He resumed writing but shortly afterwards came to an end. He flipped back to the first page. 'Mama Tequila, do you know who this young girl is?'

Mama Tequila shook her head, 'Only her name, doctor. Her name is Tandia Patel.' She was annoyed that Dr Louis had chosen to make notes but she could think of no way of preventing him.

Dr Louis wrote Tandia's name and surname on the top of the pad. 'Ja, I thought so. Her father was a patient of mine. He dropped dead three days ago of a sudden heart attack in the middle of refereeing a boxing match.' He smiled, 'She is his *love* child, you know.'

Mama Tequila sniffed. Was there no end to this man's naivety? She was still annoyed that he'd made the notes and she answered testily, 'I too am such a love child, doctor. South Africa is full of these love children. A white man grabs a black woman and for a few shillings they do it in the bushes because she is too afraid to say "no baas" or she needs the money so her children can eat. You call this a *love* child? What must I say, doctor?'

'Ja, I know, it's easy for me to talk, but Patel was different. He didn't throw her away, he brought her up and gave her a proper education. Only the other day he was telling me she's got one more year to matric. I'm telling you, Mama Tequila, this is a very bright girl.' He paused and rubbed his chin, 'I'm damn sure she doesn't belong in a place like this.'

Behind the doctor Mama Tequila could see Juicey Fruit Mambo shaking his head sadly. 'You mean just the stupid ones belong in a whorehouse, doctor?' she said.

Dr Louis Rabin kept his head lowered and looked into his cupped hands. 'If I sounded patronising you must forgive me. But please, listen to me for just a moment. How many bastard children created between black and white manage to get a proper education? Tell me, Mama Tequila, when did you leave school? Standard five perhaps? Just before high school?'

'Standard two,' Mama Tequila said defiantly. 'I learned to read and write and do some sums.' It was enough.

The doctor turned to Juicey Fruit Mambo, 'And you, boy?'

Juicey Fruit Mambo's head shot up. 'I am not boy, doctor, I am a man, same like you!' Then, just as quickly, he looked down contritely, adopting the practised mendacity that the African learns to use before authority. The defiance was absent from his voice. 'I am not go to the school, doctor.'

Dr Louis flushed deeply but chose to ignore Juicey Fruit Mambo's admonishment. 'There you are! You see now what I mean?' He turned to look at the large woman. 'Standard two only and you are even more lucky than some. Here you've got one of your own kind, a young coloured girl who has not even a year to go for her matric. Someone who, I'm telling you, could go far. How can you put her on her back to work for you? I'm asking you truly now, explain to me how could you do a thing like that?'

Mama Tequila started to giggle, then stopped abruptly when she realised, following Juicey Fruit Mambo's outburst, that her laughter would be seen by Dr Louis as a further put-down. 'Doctor, you a good man and I respec' you, you know that. All the coloured people respec' you. But now you got to lissen to me, you hear? You sit in your consulting rooms and the black people come and the coloured people come and even some white people, they come also. And the black man and the coloured look at the whites and think, "See, we also, we can have the best doctor, just like the white man!" When you give them medicine they pay just like the white man. But you know something, doctor? In the township hospital there are two black doctors and three coloured, also some Indian doctors. For much less money, sometimes even for nothing, they can see these doctors. Why do they come to you?'

Dr Louis Rabin opened his mouth to attempt to answer but Mama Tequila held up her hand. 'No, please, doctor, I'm telling you, you don't know the answer. I will tell you. You see, you a white man, no matter how clever the coloured doctor or the black doctor, even if they just as clever as you, they not.' She dug her finger in under her left breast to indicate her heart and made a twisting motion. 'They know in here, in their hearts, the white doctor is better. When my girls get sick and I call you, they know Mama Tequila loves them.'

'That's not true, Mama Tequila, a medical degree is the same for everyone!'

'Ja, but it doesn't work like that. The coloured doctor can take out your appendix just the same as you, but he can't take out a building licence to live in a big house in the Berea just like you. No, man! Who does he think he is? All of a sudden the cheeky kaffir thinks just because he a doctor, he also a white man!' She paused. 'And us too! The coloured and the black people, we also believe he is just a bladdy kaffir in a white coat, or just a dirty coloured or bladdy coolie who is trying to be something he can't ever be. Tell me, doctor. Except now he gets maybe more money, how does all that white education help a coloured doctor or lawyer or teacher?'

Dr Louis sighed. 'Look, Mama Tequila, I'm a Jew. The Jews have been persecuted for hundreds of years. My family fled from Poland; my father, even today, hardly speaks English. Believe me, when we came here we had nothing, we were poor, poor as black people.' Dr Louis lowered his voice for emphasis and wagged a finger. 'But always! Always the Jews have understood one thing,' he smacked his fist into the open palm of his left hand. 'Education! Education is everything! But it takes money to be educated.' He smiled, pleased with himself. 'So to answer your question, to make money is very important.'

Mama Tequila threw back her head and laughed uproariously. 'You dead right about that, doctor.' She cleared her throat suddenly. 'Only one thing is different. If you had left Poland and you come here and you had a black face, what would have happened then?'

Dr Louis winced. 'I think I'm beginning to understand, Mama Tequila,' he said quietly.

The big woman laughed. Then she changed the subject abruptly. 'So tell me, to become a doctor takes how long, please?'

Dr Louis was still smarting from her rebuke. 'Six years, then two years' internship. Why do you ask?'

Mama Tequila looked down at Tandia, who from time to time still tossed feverishly, though she appeared to be asleep again. Juicey Fruit Mambo was holding a cold towel to her head.

'You see this little girl, doctor? You right about her, this one, she's special, number one.' Mama Tequila paused for emphasis. 'Doctor, I've got people who come here to Bluey Jay, important, high-up people, white men, some even politicians, lawyers and magistrates, one is even a judge. These people will pay very, very, well for this one if I train her right. On her back this clever little skatterbol can make more money in the next eight years than your kaffir doctor or coloured lawyer will make in his lifetime!'

She pointed a long varnished nail at the doctor. 'I don't want to talk dirty in front of a doctor, but we coloured ladies, we got a saying: "The best brains a pretty coloured lady got is between her legs!"'

Dr Louis laughed in spite of himself. 'You don't leave me with too many answers,' he said finally.

'Come, we have some coffee, hey? Sarah made some *koeksisters* this morning before she went to Mass. If I tell her you came and didn't eat some she will be very unhappy.'

Juicey Fruit Mambo had remained behind with Tandia. He didn't know what had gotten into him. Almost from the moment he had set eyes on her he had felt differently about the young girl who lay tossing and turning in Hester's bed. It wasn't love. He felt a kind of kinetic energy in her presence as though he was connected to her by some form of invisible cord. He could feel the burning of her fever on his own flesh and sense the little girl's despair as though it was his own. Juicey Fruit didn't bother to examine these feelings. In such things his African culture, depending on your viewpoint, was either too primitive or too sophisticated. He simply decided that it was henceforth his job to care for Tandia, that the rest of his life would be taken up with this task.

Juicey Fruit Mambo had been with Mama Tequila for three years. He too had been a gift from the police. They'd stuck a cattle prod up his arse and burned him, so that he was no longer a man, whereupon they'd dropped him head first down a stairwell so that when he landed two floors below his brains had bubbled through his broken skull for all to see.

He had refused to die in the wretched cell into which they'd thrown him. In the two days of delirium which followed, the deep cuts to his handcuffed wrists were created, which were to earn him his permanent bracelets. Reluctantly the police were forced to cart him off to a black hospital. For, while his broken skull could easily be explained as attempted suicide, the terrible lacerations to his wrists were plainly the result of police brutality, something the coroner would be obliged to include in his report. When, five months later, he was released from hospital, the so-called terrorist gang of which Juicey Fruit Mambo was supposed to have been a member, had been acquitted by the courts for lack of any reasonable evidence.

The police had made a real botch-up of the whole affair and the newspapers had been quick to point this out. Anxious not to attract any further publicity they'd taken Juicey Fruit Mambo to Mama Tequila so that if he tried to make a fuss, he would be immediately compromised by reason of working in a brothel.

But Juicey Fruit Mambo hadn't made a fuss. He had the rest of his life to get even. The hate in him for the white man was a hot, palpable thing he carried with him every day of his life.

Mama Tequila poured a large cup of black coffee for Dr Louis and, without asking, she added four teaspoons of sugar and stirred. It wasn't the way he usually drank his coffee, but it was the way she believed he did and after a few times it was pointless to bring it up. She handed him the cup. 'Okay, doctor, what must I do to get those notes you made, hey?'

Dr Louis looked into his coffee. 'You already know that.'

Mama Tequila said nothing. How could a man be so smart and so stupid at the same time? 'The price, it is too high, doctor.'

'Just one year, until she matriculates. Then she can make up her own mind. Let her finish her education, Mama Tequila.'

'What must I do with an educated whore? Who's going to pay?' Mama Tequila asked roughly, but she could feel the better part of her nature beginning to win. This worried her somewhat; in her experience conscience made a lousy bookkeeper. 'I run a good house, doctor, this isn't a bladdy boarding school!'

'I tell you what. I'll throw in twelve visits free of charge to you or any of your girls for the remainder of the year if you promise not to put her to your kind of work until she matriculates. How's that?'

It was a generous offer; coming out to Bluey Jay in the middle of the night was a big sacrifice for any doctor, let alone a white one, to make for a sick whore. Mama Tequila lifted her coffee cup to her lips and blew the steam from the top; then she took a tiny ladylike sip and looked at Dr Louis out of the corner of her eye. 'Twelve visits, no time limit, maybe it takes two years, maybe even more.'

'Ja, that's okay by me.'

'Starting tonight?'

Dr Louis grinned, 'Ja, what's the difference?'

'Just one more thing, doctor. Tandia is going to this big school to learn how to be clever, but there is things she got to learn here also.'

'What kind of things?' Dr Louis asked suspiciously.

'Ag, I can't explain, tricks of the trade. She got to make herself useful. There is all sorts of things a person on the game has to know.'

'A person on the game? I thought we decided she wasn't going to do that?'

'Ja, of course, but she like an apprentice. I got a big establishment to run, doctor.'

'Can she learn these things standing up?' Dr Louis asked.

Mama Tequila laughed, but looked hurt. 'We already shook hands, doctor. You got my word, the girl is safe with me until she finish her school, then she can decide what part of her body her brain is in.' Mama Tequila raised an eyebrow. 'If she got any brains left from all that education, she not going to need too many to work that out, also!'

Dr Louis pushed his chair back from the table and extended his hand. 'I'm proud of you, Mama Tequila.'

Taking the doctor's hand, Mama Tequila grinned. 'I'm telling you, doctor, I'm getting too soft in my old age. C'mon, hand over, where's the bladdy notes?'

Mama Tequila was as good as her word. With Tandia standing by, she called the headmistress of Durban Indian Girls' High School posing as Tandia's auntie. The headmistress declared herself annoyed at Tandia's absence. 'I know there have been extenuating circumstances and we do commiserate, but Tandia has been away for nearly three weeks. I'm sure I don't need to point out to you that a small note from her aunt dropped in the mail with an explanation was all that was required.'

'Her daddy, you know, Patel the famous boxing coach he dropped dead all of a sudden, it made her very sad, Mrs . . .?'

'Miss Naidoo!' Tandia said in a loud whisper.

'. . . Miss Naidoo. You see, it made her sick and everything,' Mama Tequila continued.

'I'm sorry the child has not been well, but we do expect common courtesy, Mrs . . .'

'Mama Tequila!' To Mama Tequila she didn't sound sorry at all.

'Will she be sitting for the end-of-year exams, Mrs Tekella?'

'Yes, I suppose, the doctor says one more week, is that orright?' Mama

Tequila was not often intimidated, but she didn't seem to be able to get the hang of this stuck-up individual who was Tandia's headmistress. One thing was for sure, this one wouldn't know how to run a brothel if her bladdy life depended on it. All the clients would leave their trousers behind and run for the hills!

She had thought about adopting her Mae West persona, but as she generally used it only on her clients, she was glad now that she'd kept it straight. An American auntie from the deep South would have seemed an improbable relation for a schoolgirl who was the love child of an Indian and a Bantu.

'We begin exams in a week. Tandia will have missed all her preparation classes.'

'That's orright, Miss, don't worry, she's clever as anything. If you want her Monday she'll be there for sure, I guarantee it!' Mama Tequila was beginning to regain her usual composure and now she adopted what she considered was a snooty voice. 'My chauffeur will drop her off in a Packard personal.'

If Miss Naidoo had felt herself put in her place her voice gave no sign that this was so. 'She will need to bring a doctor's note when she returns. Goodbye, Mrs Tekella!'

Mama Tequila felt the receiver go dead in her ear. She turned to see Tandia with her fist in her mouth in an attempt to stifle her giggles. She had been able to hear the headmistress's shrill voice almost as clearly as if she had the receiver to her ear and, as far as she was concerned, Mama Tequila had come out quits, even ahead if you counted the bit about the car. Nobody in the history of the world had ever done that with Miss Naidoo before.

'Humph! This Miss Naidoo, she needs a man real bad, Tandy. I'm telling you, she one mixed-up lady, that one. What kind of car she got?'

Tandia looked at her in surprise. 'She hasn't got a car, Mama T.'

Mama Tequila clicked her tongue. 'She hasn't got a car and she hasn't got a man, tell me, has she got lots of pretty dresses and rings and things?'

Tandia laughed. Laughter was happening to her a lot lately. 'I think she's only got four dresses, they all nearly the same, not pretty at all and she never wears any jewellery, only a watch.'

'So tell me, why is she so stuck up, then?'

'Ag, headmistresses are like that, Mama T. She hasn't got time for a man or for riding around in a big car or looking pretty and wearing jewels. A person has got to work very hard and be very clever to have her job.'

'I see, if you very clever and you get a big education and you work very hard, you get this job?'

Tandia nodded. 'Ja, but also, you got to be lucky. There's not so many jobs high up like that for women.'

Mama Tequila put her arm around Tandia's shoulder and drew her into her bosom. 'Okay, skatterbol, if you want you can go back to this school. But I'm telling you something for nothing, this woman can't teach you anything that's going to help you, man, I think maybe it's all a big waste of brains!'

The pink school outfit was Mama Tequila's idea of sticking it right up Miss Naidoo. When she returned, Tandia was going to be the best-dressed, prettiest girl in the whole school.

Every time she thought about the pink gymfrock Tandia nearly died of embarrassment. How was she possibly going to tell Mama T? She'd begged Hester to tell her, but there was a darker side of Mama Tequila's nature and she took it badly when one of her projects was thwarted. Hester wasn't game to incur Mama Tequila's wrath on her behalf. In her world you looked after yourself first. It wasn't unkindness, it was instinct, like breathing, and her instincts had served her well in the past.

Tandia also now understood why Juicey Fruit Mambo had been grinning his head off for the last couple of days. He was happy for the surprise coming her way.

The next day was the Saturday before her return to school on Monday. At six o'clock sharp Mama Tequila reached into her small sequinned evening bag and produced a large brass key to unlock the door to her private salon. She was dressed to the nines; Saturday night was a big night at Bluey Jay, not as posh as a Friday, but bigger and much, much noisier. The bulk of the Saturday night trade were men who came off the whalers and deep-sea fishing trawlers that used Durban as their home port.

After three months at sea chasing the giant sperm whale their wages were burning a hole in their pockets and that wasn't the only thing that was overheated in their trousers. You could always tell the young men off the whalers or the big commercial fishing trawlers; they were scrubbed nearly raw in the attempt to eliminate the smell of fish or whale oil from the pores of their skin. They wore their sports jackets and ties awkwardly and constantly pulled at the collar buttons of their shirts, lifting their chins slightly and moving their heads from side to side.

Saturday night at Bluey Jay was fun for one and all. The pianola in the guest salon ran hot with honky-tonk and *tickie-draai*. A girl could expect to turn a dozen tricks before the boys, their pockets lighter and with three months of wildly imagined promiscuity tapped and emptied in almost as many minutes, were shooed off the premises into taxis waiting to take them back to their cheap billets in town.

Now, an hour before the first of the Saturday night crowd would begin to appear, Mama Tequila entered her private salon and gazed with deep satisfaction at the magnificent room that never failed to convince her that God was on the side of the honest brothel-keeper. She wore a full-length pink crushed-velvet gown, pink high-heel shoes studded with rhinestones with a pink taffeta turban on her head. To top it all off she carried a large pink ostrich feather fan. She crossed the room as regally as the queen she was and sat on a high-backed Victorian chair of monstrous proportions which was covered in a watered taffeta of deep purple.

Bluey Jay had been the home of an Irish Australian jockey named Bluey

J. McCorkindale, who had come out with the New South Wales Light Horse during the Boer War and had stayed on. As a talented young jockey well schooled in the rough and tumble of Sydney's Randwick and Rose Hill racecourses he'd ridden a few winners for Barney Barnato, the diamond and gold multi-millionaire, and had soon put together enough to start his own stud farm. Barney Barnato and Solly Joel, Barney's almost equally wealthy partner, had put their bloodstock with him. A third share in a stallion named Blue Jay, foaled from the great Irish stallion, Mount Joy, and the American mare, Miss Scarlet, had made McCorkindale wealthy enough. The stallion became the greatest money-earner in the history of the South African turf and Bluey's winnings, invested with advice from his two racing partners, had done the rest and put him into the truly rich class.

The little Australian jockey had then gone over to Sydney to look for a bride to bring back with him. Instead he returned to South Africa with a house. A three-storey Victorian mansion of Sydney sandstone, a triumph of the stonemason's art, with wide verandas running top and bottom around the house, decorated with magnificent traditional ornate wrought-iron railings and posts. With seventeen bedrooms, five bathrooms and with its several reception rooms and two salons it seemed just the house for a sporting man like Bluey J. McCorkindale, who was the fifth son of a drunken Irish strapper and who had been brought up in a three-room worker's cottage in the dockside suburb of Woolloomooloo and who, at eight years old, had started work as a stable boy.

Bluey J. had ordered the house to be dismantled stone by stone, right down to the last velvet curtain and solid brass curtain ring, packed in trunks and crates and shipped in carefully marked sections to Durban where it had risen again. Bluey J. McCorkindale had made only one concession to his adopted land; he had ordered the floors to be made of African yellowwood.

The salon and the shining yellow floors were Mama Tequila's special joy. She had come upon the mansion when, in a post-war return to Christian values, Durban's police commissioner, Kommandant Vermaak, had decided that the waterside brothels, which had done such a sterling job of rest and recreation for troops and sailors during the war, had to go. Mama Tequila, who owned two of these BB-TM ('Biff! Bang! Thank you, ma'am!') sex emporiums, was not displeased with the Kommandant's zeal.

She'd made a fortune during the war but now the quick-sex business had fallen on hard times. All her life as a working girl and later as a madam, Mama Tequila had dreamed of owning a brothel like one she had once seen in a movie set in turn-of-the-century New Orleans. She wanted a brothel that catered for the carriage trade, people with money and manners and political clout. A house with nice girls who knew their trade and didn't smoke *boom* or drink neat Cape brandy.

Mama Tequila had been raised in the slums of Cape Town's District Six and she'd learned, very early in life, that a man's snake wasn't like everybody said, colourblind. The white snakes liked to creep into black holes and the black ones into white. She'd also learned that coloured girls were the perfect compromise; they could pass, in most instances, for white with black snakes and for black with white ones. For it was the minds of the snakes that got a vicarious pleasure out of colour; the snakes themselves with their single blind eye, seldom stopped to compare skin tones.

When she found Bluey Jay on thirty acres of rolling green hills within half an hour's drive of Durban she'd known at once that there was a God in heaven. For the outside of the house, somewhat in need of repair, was almost a direct replica of the one in the movie. Inside nothing had been touched since the time of Bluey Jay himself. Whilst the drapes were faded and worn and the upholstery on the Edwardian couches and formal chairs and the Persian carpets were almost threadbare and some of the furniture was badly in need of french polishing and restoration, it was all there. Mama Tequila could hardly believe her eyes.

All it needed was money to restore it and Mama Tequila had plenty of that. She had found a Mr Leonard Polkinghorne, a highbrow Englishman who wore detachable starched collars and who had once worked as an assistant curator at the Victoria and Albert in London, and was now head curator of the Pietermaritzburg museum. Leonard Polkinghorne was an expert on Victorian and Edwardian decor and she assigned him the task of returning the formal rooms in Bluey Jay to their former glory.

'Nothing changed, you understand, Mr Lennie, just exactly the same as before, only everything pink.' Mama Tequila couldn't bring herself to pronounce his surname, which seemed to her amazingly apt for the restoration of a house intended as a brothel and was yet another sign from God that she was doing the right thing.

'Mr Lennie, do you know what kind of place is this?' Mama Tequila asked when she took him out to show him the property. Leonard Polkinghome looked at the scaffolded Bluey Jay and then back at Mama Tequila who sighed and said carefully, 'Mr Lennie, this is going to be a place where you come when you are tired of your wife.'

'Ah, I see, a rest home! That's perfectlay splendid, I'm perfectlay happy to be associated with a rest home.' Leonard Polkinghorne was very big on the word 'perfectly' which he pronounced in this funny way.

Mama Tequila sighed again; this was one dumb person orright. 'Ja, but more like an *excitement* than a rest, Mr Lennie.'

A slow grin spread over Leonard Polkinghorne's face and his eyes grew wide. 'I say! You don't mean?' Mama Tequila nodded her head. 'Yes you do! By jove, a brothel! How perfectlay marvellous!'

The one-eyed snake strikes again! Mama Tequila thought happily. 'The best, Mr Lennie, the best whorehouse in the world and also, when you and I finish with it, the prettiest.'

The restoration of Bluey Jay outside and inside, and including electricity and new plumbing, had taken a sizeable bite out of Mama Tequila's wartime fortune, but Mr Lennie's fee wasn't one of her expenses. He elected to take his retainer in what he referred to as 'dalliance time'. Mama Tequila, happy to oblige, carefully worked out the total amount owed to him in hours. It was an agreement which Mr Lennie said suited him 'absolutely perfectlay', and which eventually took a great deal of the starch out of his collar. At Bluey Jay he was known to the girls as 'Mr Perfect Lay'.

All the girls had been told to appear at a quarter past six in the salon and they now stood around Mama Tequila's chair 'oohing' and 'aahing' her dress.

'Jesus, Mary, Mother of God! Have mercy on a poor working girl, Mama T! How much time am I going to have to give to Mr Dine-o-mite for this beautiful creation!' Sarah cupped her hands over her face and groaned in mock agony.

'Talking of Mr Dine-o-mite, he gonna be here soon,' Mama Tequila chuckled, 'but he just come to make a delivery.'

Juicey Fruit Mambo, dressed in a white tuxedo jacket, black stovepipe trousers, white shirt and pink bow tie, walked into the salon carrying a small scolloped silver tray on which rested nine tiny glasses of sherry and one of green chartreuse. There were eight working girls at Bluey Jay, not counting Tandia, and Juicey Fruit now dispensed a glass to each of them as well as to Mama Tequila. Finally he placed the glass of green chartreuse on an occasional table to await the arrival of Sonny Vindoo. He returned moments later with a glass of lemonade, which he handed to Tandia.

Mama Tequila, who had missed the fact that Tandia hadn't been served a glass of sherry, now noticed the lemonade. 'Juicey Fruit Mambo, I do declare! You go back now and bring Miss Tandia a glass of sweet sherry like everybody else! She a working girl too, you know.' She fanned herself lazily with the ostrich feather fan.

Juicey Fruit was not happy as he accepted the glass of lemonade back from Tandia and left the room. He returned in a few minutes with a single glass of sherry in the centre of the tray. Tandia took up the tiny glass. She had never tasted alcohol and she was actually quite frightened at the prospect; she imagined all sorts of things happening to her which would be quite beyond her control.

This was the first time she had been in this magnificent room with its rich cedar panelling and beautiful pink velvet curtains which fell from scolloped velvet pelmets above two large windows, to the floor sixteen feet below. The break-front covered an entire wall and was filled with dark green morocco leather volumes, the titles embossed in gold on the spine of each book. On the three remaining walls were four large portraits of pretty ladies dressed in the silks and satins of Edwardian England, the decolletage of each allowing a provocative display of creamy bosom. Several pink chaises longues and formal chairs, small tables and pink Persian carpets seemed to be arranged or scattered haphazardly around the room, and the beautiful yellowwood floor, where it showed in places not covered by carpets, kicked back the light from a huge crystal chandelier that cascaded from the centre of an ornate plaster-moulded ceiling composed of garlands of fruit and flowers, onto which clung a heavenly host of fat cherubs. Above the pink marble fireplace was a huge pink ceramic bowl of peonies. To give the beautiful room a final touch of distinction, to the side of the window furthermost from where Mama Tequila sat was a pink grand piano. (It was in fact a pianola but Tandia had no way of knowing this.) The room had a warm, flushed presence and Tandia had never seen anything as breathtakingly beautiful in her life.

Mama Tequila raised her glass, which looked like a topaz-coloured bauble in her enormous hand. 'Welcome, Tandia to Mama Tequila's salon. You is now one of us, a working girl, only perhaps your work is a bit different. Tonight and from now on you only got one name, you hear? You Miss Tandy, jes' like Miss Hester, Miss Sarah, Miss Jasmine.' As Mama Tequila spoke a girl's name, the girl in question would empty the glass of sherry in her hand. 'Miss Colleen, Miss Hettie, Miss Doreen, Miss Johanna and Miss Marie. Now it your turn, Miss Tandy, you and me, we drink to your success, to Bluey Jay and to old Mama Tequila.' She lifted the glass above her head.

'Welcome to Bluey Jay, Miss Tandy!' all the girls chorussed as Tandia threw back her head and screwed her eyes up tightly in anticipation of a foul-tasting liquid. To her surprise she tasted only the slightly bitter taste of cold tea. She opened her eyes, her surprise showing.

'Hey, man, we got to watch this one, she likes it!' Hester squealed and the large room filled with the laughter of the Bluey Jay girls. It was the first time in her life Tandia had ever belonged to anything or anyone other than Patel. Despite the fact that Juicey Fruit Mambo had substituted cold tea for her sherry she felt a warm glow inside her. A thing which glowed between the chest and the pit of her stomach but also seemed to include her heart, it was a feeling which made her want to cry and laugh at the same time.

Juicey Fruit Mambo entered the room to collect the glasses. When he reached Tandia he grinned and as he took her glass he whispered, 'Dis skokiaan not for you, Miss Tandy, you must be very, very strong for the learning.'

The girls crowded around Tandia offering their congratulations and welcoming her to their society. In a few moments Juicey Fruit Mambo was back and he whispered into Mama Tequila's ear. She nodded and he left the salon again. Mama Tequila clapped her hands for silence and pointed to the door. All eyes turned as in walked Sonny Vindoo, carrying a large flat brown paper parcel on outstretched hands. 'Greetings and felicitations to the Madam Mama Tequila and her very, very beautiful girls and double greetings to Miss Tandy!'

He turned and bowed to Tandia, jerking his head forward in an almost military fashion, whereupon his glasses slid off his nose and landed on the parcel. The effect on Mr Dine-o-mite of losing his eyes was instant. Still holding the parcel he turned completely around twice and then headed blindly off in the direction of the grand piano. Without his spectacles Sonny Vindoo seemed unable to speak, and it was the light of the setting sun coming through the window beside the piano that attracted him. Tandia ran quickly ahead of him and grabbing his glasses from where they had landed on top of the parcel she slipped them onto the bridge of his nose and around his ears. The effect was equally instant. Mr Vindoo stopped on the spot and his voice returned, 'My goodness gracious me, you are a very, very kind young lady, Miss Tandy.' He turned to face Mama Tequila again. 'Your instructions, Madam, obeyed to the very last letter, everything in order, shipshape and Bristol style.'

'Honey, you got da verbal diarrhoea tonight, that for sure! Come now, give Mama Tequila that parcel. If you gone and done like I say,' she winked at Sarah, 'Miss Sarah, she in big trouble next Wednesday!'

Sonny Vindoo giggled and shook his head. 'You are talking about naughty-naughty time! That Sonny Vindoo is not this Sonny Vindoo. This Indian gentleman of very excellent morals who is standing here and who has even met the great Mahatma Gandhi himself, is very, very pure in his thoughts. It is the other one, the one who is coming up with a very excellent transcendental meditation plan!'

'Come again, Mr Dine-o-mite, what this transil-meddle jazz?' Mama Tequila asked.

'This is a very clever idea invented by an Indian holy man. You are closing your eyes and you thinking only very pure and excellent thoughts and next thing, by golly, you are travelling anywhere you want to go, sitting even in Buckingham Palace taking cha with Her Majesty Queen Elizabeth!'

He smiled and looked around at the girls, who were giggling politely behind their hands. Only Hester laughed aloud. To emphasise his point the little Indian tailor removed one hand from the parcel and wagged his finger at Mama Tequila. 'Only, I am not using it like this to have cha with the Queen. I am sitting in the back of the Chevrolet like a proper nabob and I am saying to Abdulla, "Abdulla, it is Wednesday". Then I am closing my eyes and thinking very hard with all my might about this very beautiful establishment,' he stepped forward and placed the brown parcel on Mama Tequila's lap and then, stepping back, spread his hand wide. 'That is why, when I am here, I am not here!'

'My God, I'm being fucked by a ghost!' Sarah yelled in mock consternation.

The room rocked with laughter and Tandia had never enjoyed herself so much. She'd forgotten for a moment about the gym frock, but now Mama Tequila, still giggling, began to open the parcel on her lap. 'Tandia, come here, baby,' she beckoned. The girls all crowded round to look. Only Hester remained slightly to one side, silent for once in her life. The crackle of the paper seemed to take an eternity and then Mama Tequila withdrew a bright pink gymslip. She held it up and the slip fell over her knees. 'My, that pretty! What you say, baby?' The girls all oohed and aahed and Tandia, despite her dismay, managed to smile. Mama Tequila handed the gym frock to her and delved back into the parcel. 'That ain't all, baby!' She produced a blouse and a pair of pink woollen stockings and a bright pink beret. 'You gonna be the prettiest li'l girl that school did ever see!'

Tandia burst into tears. Despite the terrible embarrassment the pink garments represented for her, she was loved. They cared, all of them, they cared about her, Tandia Patel. She wouldn't think of Monday, only about now, about the warmth and the love surrounding her. She handed the clothes to Hester and embraced Mama Tequila, her tears making dark, wet stains on the woman's pink gown. Then she turned to confront a grinning Sonny Vindoo. She hugged him as well. 'Thank you, Mr Vindoo, my clothes are very lovely,' she said tearfully.

'Miss Tandy, I am hearing you are going to Durban Indian Girls' High School, a very excellent institution. My daughter, she is married now, she went to this school, where she is getting first-class honours in her matriculation!'

Mama Tequila once again clapped her hands to gain attention, for Juicey Fruit had entered and nodded to her from the door. 'Hey-ho! Party time, darlings! The fine young men from them boats they here already in the other salon! Oh, ho! Let the business of Bluey Jay begin! Them honky-tonk fisherman boys they gonna die 'less they get their snake medicine tonight!'

She turned to Tandia. 'Miss Tandy, you be nice now and show Mr Dine-o-mite out the back door.' She turned to Sonny Vindoo, her eyes wide. 'Unless of course, he want to tran-sil-meddle-tate hisself back into the loving arms of Mrs Vindoo!'

Tandia woke early on Monday morning. Outside her window the bush doves were cooing in the wild fig trees, and although it was only a few minutes past five, the sun was already up. In the distance she could hear a couple of cockerels crowing. A soft breeze billowed the terylene curtains in her bedroom, carrying with it just a hint of wood smoke from the African *kraal* down by the river. It was a perfect early November morning and it had all the makings of a perfectly ghastly day for Tandia.

She had slept fitfully, the matter of Mama Tequila's pink school uniform never quite leaving even her subconscious. In the month since Patel's death much had changed for her. She found herself increasingly gregarious in the company of the girls and a special friendship with Juicey Fruit Mambo was rapidly developing. She felt entirely safe with him around her, a new feeling for her, and one which she found simply wonderful. With Juicey Fruit Mambo it was the way she had always believed it might become with Patel. But she was still a shy, frightened little girl and today the best friend in the world couldn't help her, she was on her own. Juicey Fruit Mambo would drive her to the school gates and from that moment on she was alone. She cringed inwardly as she thought about it. She was going to be the laughing stock of the whole school and she had no doubt she would be held up to ridicule in assembly by Miss Naidoo.

Tandia went down the hall to the bathroom to shower and to clean her teeth. After she'd completed her toilet she returned down the quiet passage, the smooth, polished yellowwood floors cool on her bare feet. Her own room was on the furthest end of the long corridor and she had to pass the rooms of all the sleeping girls except Hester. As she walked past the door to Sarah's room she noticed that it was slightly ajar and she moved over to close it. Mama Tequila, for reasons she had never explained, insisted that the girls sleep with their bedroom doors closed. Tandia's hand was on the door knob and, on a sudden impulse, she opened Sarah's door a little further. The room smelled of cigarettes and slightly stale perfume; on the dresser beside the bed was an empty half-jack of brandy and a used glass. Sarah was naked, lying on her side facing the door, her sheet kicked into a crumpled heap at the end of the divan bed. Tandia started to withdraw in embarrassment but then held still. There was something vulnerable about the way Sarah lay, she had her knees tucked up and she sucked on her thumb like a child. In repose her scrubbed face, small round breasts and slender shoulders made her look younger than she was.

Sarah suddenly opened her eyes, seemingly from a deep sleep. She showed no surprise whatsoever at Tandia's presence in the room. She turned over and reached for the Wesclock which rested on the floor beside the bed. 'Christ, Tandy, it's only a quarter to six, go back to bed, it's still night time.' She sat up and reached for the sheet, pulled it up over her body and rolled over in bed, turning her back to Tandia.

'I couldn't sleep, I'm used to getting up early.' She turned to go but suddenly blurted out, 'Sarah, what am I going to do!'

Sarah groaned and turned back to face her, 'What's the matter with you kid, can't a person get some sleep around here?' Tandy flushed and started to apologise, backing out of the door. 'I'm only playing, jong. Come and sit here,' Sarah said, patting the divan beside her.

Tandia walked over and sat down on the edge of the bed as Sarah propped herself up onto one elbow. 'C'mon, kid, you better tell me, are you in trouble or something?'

'It's Monday, Sarah, I've got to go back to school today!'

'So? You got new everything, you should be very excited, you a very lucky girl, what Mama T did was nice.'

'Sarah, the school colours are brown! A brown gymslip and white blouse. Mama Tequila has made everything in pink!'

'You mean you the only one in the whole school with a pink uniform? Why didn't you tell Mama T?'

Tandia shook her head. 'I wasn't supposed to know, it was a surprise, remember? Sarah, what am I going to do?'

Sarah looked at Tandia. School carried no cherished memories for her, she had left at eleven and her impression of her time there was one of constant harassment, punishment and humiliation. 'Simple, man, don't go. Wait till Juicey Fruit drives away and then don't go in. Go to the bioscope, there's a good picture at the Odeon, Fred Astaire and Ginger Rogers, they got a ten o'clock matinee.' She reached for her bag on the dresser beside the bed. 'Here, I'll give you some money.'

'But Sarah, I want to finish school. Mama T said I could do that. They all going to laugh their heads off, all the girls and the teachers too. Miss Naidoo is going to send me home, and then what?'

Sarah sat up in the bed and took Tandia into her arms. 'Come now, Tandy, it's not so bad, sticks and stones can break your bones but words can never harm you.' Tandia had wrapped a towel around her when she'd come from the bathroom and her shoulders were bare. 'Sometimes it's good to be different, Tandy.' Sarah kissed Tandia gently on the top of the shoulder and then as gently on the neck. 'When you on the game, being different is normal.' Her hand pulled at the folded towel between Tandia's small, firm breasts and opened it up. Tandia's heart was pounding. Sarah's hands seemed to be melting her body as though years of tension were being run through her caressing hands. Tandia had never felt like this before, it was as though her body had grown another dimension, had become another place. Sarah's tongue was caressing her neck and then moved downwards to her breast, 'Sshhh! don't say anything, Tandy, everything will be orright.'

For a long time afterwards Tandia lay in Sarah's arms, her body filled with the warmth of loving. Even after her breathing had quietened down she wanted to lie there long enough to be able to fold her feeling into an emotional envelope she could store in her subconscious against hard times.

Sarah stirred. 'Go now, Tandy, when they laugh at you in school, jus' remember, you a proper woman now, you know things they don't know, they can't do nothing to hurt you, they all stupid girls in their brown gymslips, you hear?'

Juicey Fruit was waiting for her in the kitchen and when she arrived he sat her down at the head of the table and placed a plate of steaming mealiemeal porridge in front of her, pushing the milk jug and the sugar closer to it, fussing like an old umFazi. Next he brought Tandia two pieces of already buttered toast.

'Thank you, Juicey Fruit Mambo.' Tandia was not used to being waited upon.

'You very beautiful today, Missy Tandy.'

Tandia was unable to look Juicey Fruit Mambo in the eye lest she betray her feeling about the bright pink gymslip. 'You too, Juicey Fruit Mambo.'

Juicey Fruit had on a pink shirt and a red bow tie and he wore two gold sleeve bands just above the elbows. The creases in his black trousers were perfect and his black shoes were highly polished. He was obviously pleased that Tandia had noticed his careful colour co-ordination and his gold incisor teeth shone as he smiled at her. 'Mama T she give to me dis shirt, long, long time ago, it is very beautiful I tink.'

They left Bluey Jay at half past seven. Tandia was very quiet sitting next to Juicey Fruit Mambo in the front of the Packard. He had tried to make her sit in the back but she had protested which, in the end, seemed to please him. As they were coming down from the Berea towards the port Juicey Fruit Mambo glanced at her. 'Missy Tandia, why for you are not happy for going to school?'

Tandia bit her lip, but a tear ran down her cheek as she stared resolutely through the windscreen. 'Juicey Fruit Mambo, he also very sad when you not happy today.' He glanced at her. 'Why you cry, Missy Tandy?'

Tandia could contain herself no longer. 'Ag, Juicey Fruit Mambo, you can't understand this thing. In the school the clothes the girls must wear is brown,' she plucked at her gymfrock. 'Like this but only brown.'

'But pink more pretty than brown?'

'Ja, I know, but they don't allow it. I'm going to get into terrible trouble and everyone will laugh at me!' She covered her face with her hands.

Juicey Fruit Mambo drew the car to a halt at the kerb. 'Missy Tandy, Mama Tequila she spend much, much money for dis clothes for your school. Dey not laugh for dis clothes, Missy Tandy. Dis clothes is for new!'

Tandia realised that he was deeply worried by her distress but was quite unable to comprehend the significance the colour of her gymslip and blouse had. 'You are right,' she said. 'Come now, we must go or I'll be late.'

Juicey Fruit Mambo pulled away from the kerb; he knew the matter remained unresolved, there were some things about women which he could never hope to understand, and it was better not to try. He guided the big Packard smoothly through the narrow back streets and finally turned into Prichard Street, drawing up outside the school gates. He suddenly saw what Tandia had meant. Hundreds of girls were milling around the playground and moving through the gates; all wore identical clothes, a brown gymslip, white blouse, short white socks, brown shoes and a brown beret. He put the car into gear and started to turn the steering wheel so when a gap in the traffic arrived he could move off. He had no idea what to do except he knew he couldn't leave Tandia to go in alone in her pink uniform.

'What you doing, Juicey Fruit Mambo? I must get out here.'

'No, Missy Tandy . . .' His voice was cut short by an urgent banging on the window on Tandia's side of the car. They both turned to see Sonny Vindoo looking at them. He carried a big brown package under his arm and indicated that Tandia should roll down the window.

'Nearly I am missing you! Let me get in the back.' He opened the back door of the Packard and jumped in. 'My very clever son, University of Bombay, B.A. Degree honours, businessman and also photographer, his business is in Pickering Street, it is two minutes, no more, we must go there now.' He passed the parcel over the back of the front seat to Tandia, 'Open please!' he said happily, leaning forward to look over her shoulder.

Juicey Fruit swung into the traffic as Tandia pulled the string which held the large flat parcel together. The parcel contained a new brown gymslip, white blouse and a slightly worn brown beret. Sonny Vindoo giggled. 'I make these for you, Miss Tandy and also, the beret, which I am not making, it is left over from my daughter when she attended this excellent school.'

Tandia burst into tears. 'Please, please, no time for tears now, must change blinking, jolly quick!' He turned to Juicey Fruit Mambo. 'You must turn here, see the shop, "Singer & Necchi Sewing Centre".'

'I know this place, baas,' Juicey Fruit Mambo said. He had a huge grin on his face and his gold incisors flashed as he shared in Tandia's happiness.

The car drew to a halt outside a small shop. On either side of the doorway were display windows; on the one appeared the Singer Sewing Machine logo and on the other the Necchi. Painted under each imprimatur were the words, 'Sole Agency'. Several sewing machines of each brand were displayed in their respective windows. In the centre of each window set on a small easel was a large photograph. On one rested a portrait of a prosperous-looking Indian man hand-tinted in the old-fashioned manner, while on the other was a full-length colour photograph of a bridal couple. Above the door was a third sign which read: 'Jamal Vindoo – Photographer, Wedding and Family Portraits. Colour or Hand-Tinted. Apply Rear of Building.' An arrow pointed away from the door to a small lane running down the side of the building. It was a nice tidy little shop.

Sonny Vindoo jumped from the back of the car and hoisted up his dhoti. 'Come, Miss Tandy, hurry please!'

Tandia gathered up the parcel on her lap, got out of the car and followed Sonny Vindoo up the front steps of the shop. A young man appeared at the doorway but the little Indian pushed him aside. 'Good mornings later, Jamal!' Sonny Vindoo shouted. 'To the change room!' Tandia smiled through her tears at Jamal, whom she took to be Sonny Vindoo's Bombay-educated son, and who stood aside as she followed Sonny Vindoo into a shop which was filled with the whirring of sewing machines. At their entrance, several woman seated at the machines ceased sewing and looked up from their work. Sonny Vindoo crossed the room making for a bright orange floral curtain which hung across one corner. As he reached the curtain he held it apart. 'In here, Miss Tandy, I am waiting outside, doing guard duty.' He scowled through his steel-rimmed spectacles at the grinning seamstresses as though to indicate to them that he would not tolerate any interference or even comment.

Tandia found herself in a small store room filled with bolts of men's suiting and bright lengths of dress material. There was just enough room for her to stand.

'Thank you, thank you, Mr Vindoo!'

'No time for thank yous! You must hurry now, please. Any minute the school bell is clanking, then, my goodness, where shall we be then? We shall be up the bloomin Khyber Pass!' Sonny Vindoo fussed and drew the curtain back across the doorway.

Tandia changed quickly. There were no white socks included in the parcel, but she regarded this as a small matter. She couldn't take the grin off her face, she was saved! Mr Dine-o-mite had ridden to the rescue and at the same time had allowed Mama Tequila to save face.

She emerged from behind the curtains looking just like any other Durban Indian High School girl. Over her arm she carried her pink outfit. Even her socks looked no worse than as if they'd been accidentally left to soak in a bucket with some red garment which had run.

Sonny Vindoo looked her up and down admiringly and silently congratulated himself. 'Not so pretty as before, but I think you are feeling much better, hey, Miss Tandy? It is a very great pity we do not have time for Jamal to take your photograph!'

Tandia bent down impulsively and kissed the little man. He'd come out without shaving and the white stubble on his cheek felt like sandpaper against her lips. Kissing anyone was something she could not previously have imagined herself capable of doing, but after Sarah's room this morning everything was changed; she was loved and a woman now, and different.

Like Sonny Vindoo on a Wednesday evening, Miss Tandy was a different Tandia Patel. 'Mr Vindoo, I will pay you back, I swear it!' She sighed and grinned and wanted to hug him again and again.

'It is my great personal pleasure,' Sonny Vindoo said and then, glancing at his watch, added in a panic, 'Come, come, we must hurry like blazes!' as he made for the door of the shop. 'Farewells later!' he yelled at Jamal as he disappeared into the bright sunlight outside.

Juicey Fruit Mambo was seated behind the wheel of the Packard, the engine of the big car running and the door on Tandia's side open for her to jump in for a quick getaway. Parked directly behind him was Abdulla in Sonny Vindoo's Chevrolet, who had tran-sil-meddle-tated from nowhere.

FIVE

Living in a brothel soon became a normal way of life for Tandia. Bluey Jay represented a grand step up for her; the dark little shed with its earth floor and constant smell of paraffin from the lamp which had been her only source of light at night was replaced by her own brightly-lit room with its divan bed and chenille bedspread, dresser, wardrobe and small painted table and chair where she did her homework. From her window she looked out into the branches of a huge old wild fig tree which had stood for a hundred years before Bluey Jay was built. One branch grew so close she could have climbed out onto it, and looking through its leaves seen the glint of the river bordering Mama Tequila's property and the five grass huts of the small African village resting beside it.

After her recovery Tandia often walked through the hills surrounding Bluey Jay with Juicey Fruit Mambo. At first she had been appalled by the open space and the vast domed sky above her. Even the soft rustle of wind through the tall summer grass made her nervous, and the sudden blurr and whirr of a covey of quail rising in front of her would send her terrified into the arms of Juicey Fruit Mambo. Juicey Fruit Mambo, who came from a Zulu village close to the high mountains of the Drakensberg, was patient with her and tried hard not to laugh at her city ways. He told himself that he too could remember when, as a country boy, he had first seen the city with its hard, square surfaces; even the trees along the roads stood in circles cut from the concrete hardness and the air came down from the same blueness he had always known but seemed stale and stifling, and the people around him had lost the calmness in their faces. It had been as daunting to him as the countryside now seemed to Tandia. After a while he would see that she was gaining confidence and would jump from one rock to another or stoop to pick a flower or ask him the name of a bird which sang in the green kloofs of tree fern and monkey vine that grew in the creases and folds of the foothills.

Mama Tequila, despite her seemingly benign exterior, ran a strictly ordered establishment where the rules were disobeyed at one's own risk. As she well knew, girls who make their living on their backs have a tendency towards indulgence in food, wine, pills and Mary Jane, which was her name for *boom* or marijuana. Mama Tequila needed her girls alive and kicking when they turned a trick and the 'trick zombies' who worked the dockside BB-TMs were not a part of Bluey Jay. To work for Mama Tequila a girl had to be able to please a man, not simply with her body, but with her entire presence.

At eleven o'clock every Sunday morning all the girls would meet in the kitchen for brunch. It was Josie the cook's day off, and Mama Tequila took pride in serving the repast herself.

She would be up quite early on a Sunday morning baking bread and scones so that Bluey Jay on the sabbath always smelled of furniture polish, fresh-baked bread and brewed coffee. Her speciality was the omelette, and she would prepare her mixture in advance, thickening it with fresh cream and dusting it with finely chopped parsley. Then she'd carefully remove the rind and cut out the white strips of fat from the crispy bacon which she served with her eggs.

Mama Tequila might have been fat herself, but she knew that a good brothel can afford only one fat ride. In the case of Bluey Jay this was Hester, who, anyway, was more plump than fat and whose diet Mama Tequila watched like a hawk.

Mama Tequila called these Sunday morning meetings, 'chew the fat chats', an expression which might have spilled over from her Mae West pose into her everyday language. Chew the fat chats were as close to democracy as Bluey Jay came. It was at these times that the girls could discuss the house with Mama Tequila, bring out any problems they might have with a regular client, or ask her considerable advice on the ways of mice and men.

Mama Tequila had been blessed with a limited talent as a singer and in her youth when she wasn't at the bioscope picking up what she thought of as Black American language, she used to sit around in bars waiting for a singing gig. She liked to dance and she liked a drink and she was just sufficiently light-skinned to pass for white in a nightclub. She also discovered before she was Tandia's age that men couldn't keep their hands off her. The rest, as they say in the classics, just came naturally and she was retired as a chanteuse and on the game full time before she was nineteen.

There was very little Mama Tequila didn't know about men and nothing about them that she trusted, unless it was the wilfulness of their one-eyed snakes. She'd had a hundred or more affairs with men in her life and none of them had turned out well. Mama Tequila knew how to make money out of men but men always seemed to end up making a monkey out of her.

At sixty-five she'd given up hope of being loved without being robbed and purchased Bluey Jay. The year she'd taken off to repair and restore the beautiful old house had seen her also fall in love again, this time with the thing she had created. Now, five years later, she was running the prettiest and, some said, the best whorehouse in the Southern Hemisphere.

On Sunday mornings Tandia often rose early to help Mama Tequila in the kitchen. At Bluey Jay everyone worked for their living and this included Tandia. Mama Tequila kept her promise to Dr Louis and Tandia was kept on her feet at all times doing her share to keep the house running smoothly.

Juicey Fruit picked Tandia up from school at three o'clock and they were back at Bluey Jay by a quarter to four. She was then allowed an hour or so for homework. At five o'clock she took over from Josie the cook or one of the girls as room maid. She would replace the bottom sheet and clean the wash basin, placing fresh towels beside it after each client. Tandia would work from five in the evening until half past nine, when she was packed off to bed and the other girls took over as room maids again until one in the morning, when the house closed.

On Saturdays, Bluey Jay only opened at half past six in the evening and Tandia was required to work through until closing. With the boys from the boats invading Bluey Jay, the joint would be jumping from early evening, and every hand was needed. Two coloured women also came out from Durban around five and worked with Tandia to keep the linen changed and the rooms clean. After Bluey Jay had closed down for the night, the two ladies would sleep in the servants' quarters at the back of the house and Juicey Fruit Mambo would take them back to town on Sunday morning when he drove Sarah to early Mass.

The chew the fat chats had made Tandia an expert in the theory of how to make a man happy, and Mama Tequila referred to her as the 'wise young virgin'. Mama Tequila saw no point in not exposing her to the finer details of the game. Tandia was a coloured girl, though a very clever one, and the more she knew about life, the better she might be at surviving it. The life of a high class whore for a girl with a coloured skin was a damn sight better than most and Tandia had the looks and brains to go right to the top. Mama Tequila had very little time for dumb, lazy women and she demanded the highest standards from the eight she employed at Bluey Jay. 'Whores with a future' was how she described them.

Hester liked the idea of being a whore with a future. She was a backslidden Pentecostal and it worried her a lot. Before she became a whore she'd worked in a fish factory, scaling and filleting fish and packing the fillets into trays of crushed ice. She had suffered from permanent chilblains and it was here, in the freezing fish hall standing up to her ankles in water, where she had first developed nasal polyps.

For her efforts Hester had earned five pounds a week with overtime. The only thing she had going for her was her skill with a filleting knife and the fact that God loved her; as a born-again Christian she was absolutely, positively guaranteed a place in heaven.

It was an evangelical chorus much favoured by Pastor Mulvery, the new preacher at the Assembly of God mission hall she attended that finally decided her destiny.

I will make you fishers of men,
fishers of men,
fishers of men.

I will make you fishers of men,
if you only follow me!

Hester finally realised in the middle of singing this dumb chorus one Sunday morning that Jesus Christ had recruited mostly fishermen as his disciples. Which meant that somewhere on the shores of Galilee there had to be a fish factory where they dumped their catch for girls like her to clean and pack. Working in a fish factory with Jesus Christ as the foreman wasn't Hester's idea of heaven and so she'd become a whore, which seemed much the more intelligent option when you had enormous boobs which even the pastor couldn't take his eyes off during prayer meetings. She'd open her eyes in the middle of all the 'Hallelujahs' and 'Praise the Lords' and see him looking straight at them, his eyes almost standing out on stalks! So when Mama Tequila described Hester as a whore with a future, she liked it a lot.

Hester wasn't surprised or even cynical when Pastor Mulvery had turned up one day at Bluey Jay, ostensibly to witness to the girls, but after half an hour with Mama Tequila he'd paid his money and had his way with Hester. After which he'd asked her to pray with him, saying he'd ask God in His infinite mercy to forgive them both because, 'We know'd not what we were doing.' The Bible didn't say anything about Jesus doing anything for the girls who worked in the fish factory on the shores of Galilee, but now it seemed, all of a sudden, He was walking around forgiving whores all over the place. She felt grateful to Pastor Mulvery, with his sticking-out buck teeth which had trouble sucking on her big boobs, for pointing this out to her.

Sometimes the chew the fat chats would get quite specific. One Sunday morning, a month or so after Tandia arrived at Bluey Jay and after she had started school again, Sarah asked a question about fellatio. 'Mama T, last week old Coetzee, you know, the magistrate from Pinetown? He couldn't get it up, too much brandy, so I tried to give him a number three, but it was hopeless. It just keeps hanging there like a old piece of *biltong*!'

Even though the girls had all laughed, this was serious business. Mama Tequila guaranteed satisfaction and it meant Sarah would have to give him a free session next time he came.

Mama Tequila rose slowly and waddled over to one of the shiplapped kitchen cupboards. From her apron she took the large bunch of keys which she carried about her person at all times. Selecting a small key, she unlocked the cupboard and withdrew the chamois leather drawstring bag which contained Herman the Hottentot.

Herman the Hottentot was an eight-inch, beautifully carved, wooden penis standing at full erection. The carving, complete with testicles, was of sneezewood, a handsome, finely grained rose-red wood darkening to golden brown with a beautiful satin lustre. The detail was meticulous and the piece was much, much better than a simple pornographic curio. It also looked to be fairly old and someone, not Mama Tequila, had bored a hole into its flattened back and glued into it a one-inch piece of pine dowelling to act as a hand grip.

In fact, Herman the Hottentot, so purposefully carved, would have made an awkward dildo. But for Mama Tequila's purposes it was ideal.

The girls were all seated at the breakfast table with Mama Tequila at the top in her specially reinforced bentwood chair. Now she held Herman the Hottentot up and demonstrated with the tips of her fingers how to begin the massage and then, bringing the carving to her lips, she showed how the stimulation was completed with the lips and the mouth.

She placed Herman the Hottentot back on the table in front of her. 'You can do it perfect, but sometimes you going nowhere, man, the one-eyed snake is fast asleep. You can feel and kiss and stroke and suck, but you won't make that old one-eyed snake stand up. So you got to tell it a story where it is the hero.' Mama Tequila paused. 'You see, the mind makes the best erections. If you can get the mind on your side, then nearly always, the one-eyed snake will open his eye and stand to attention. In a case like magistrate Coetzee, you have to talk dirty, but not filthy, you hear? For Coetzee, who is Dutch Reformed Church, dirty is okay, he can understand dirty, but filthy reminds him you a whore. He a magistrate, he don't like that!'

'Mama T, how do you know the difference between dirty and filthy?' Hester asked. 'I always thought they the same thing? With the Pentecostals they all banned, even saying "hell" and "dammit", they not allowed.'

Mama Tequila shook her head. 'Ag, never mind that, Hester, language is a wonderful thing, you can play with it, get it just right, like a acrobat on the high wire in the circus, balanced just perfect. If you got the right words, I'm telling you, you can get a man like old Coetzee to stand up every time!'

The girls all stopped eating. This was always the best part of a chew the fat chat. When Mama T got going there was nobody on the game who was better. Now looking over at Tandia she said, 'Make some more coffee please, skatterbol.' Tandia rose from the table as Mama Tequila took a cork-tip out of her silver cigarette case and lit it with her Zippo. 'Here the words you going to say,' she drew on her cigarette and the lighted end glowed brightly as she inhaled deeply; then with her head thrown back she exhaled a surprising amount of the smoke up towards the ceiling where the big fan caught it and dispersed it over the room.

'When you begin, you speak very slow, you hear? Like you a clairvoyant or something. Coetzee, you a naughty boy! I seen you, I seen you looking at her, the little kaffir girl. You hiding behind this big rock, I seen you, man, hiding there where the kaffir women come to wash themselves. This little kaffir girl, she maybe thirteen, fourteen, the same age as you, but she very mature, a woman already. The water on her, it makes her black skin shine and her bottom is nice and tight and round and firm, hey? Her legs is long and her little boobies, they perfect, turned up and big enough for only one handful. She is washing herself and the soap and her hands as they go all over her body, they your hands, man! You can feel they your hands. Her hands go between her legs. Her bottom, it moves round slowly as she washes there. She is a kaffir, a dirty kaffir, who you not allowed to touch. But your snake inside your pants, this snake doesn't know this. No, man! No way this snake knows. It wants to touch, there is a place it wants to go.' Mama Tequila picked up Herman the Hottentot and allowed her fingers to do wondrous things to it, demonstrating what they should be doing while the words were weaving their way into the mind of Coetzee the magistrate. The girls watched, completely fascinated as Mama Tequila continued her verbal titillation. 'Now all the other women, they go away, only the one your snake wants, she stays, the forbidden fruit is alone in the hot sun and cool water. The water she splashes over her body rinses away the soap. Then she sits down in the river and goes under and then stands up, her beautiful black body shining with the water running off her. She begins to come out, her feet are splashing in the shallow water now. She walks towards the big rock, her hips slow, nice, to where you are hiding. She lies down, right there on the warm river sand next to the rock. She lies there with her wet, shining black body and she closes her eyes. You take off your short pants and your snake is free, strong, standing up, a white man's big strong . . .' Mama Tequila laughed suddenly and almost simultaneously the girls around the table let out a surprised sigh.

'Ag, damn!' Hester cried, dismayed that she wasn't going to hear the end.

Mama Tequila chuckled, 'Then, Sarah, if old Coetzee is not the most *upstanding* citizen you ever seen, then you better call the ambulance, you hear? Because for damn sure, he's dead!'

The girls all laughed and clapped. 'That was a good one, Mama T,' Sarah said, and they all nodded agreement. Mama Tequila was the best teacher; they all felt warm and needed and very superior. They were whores with a future.

Mama Tequila turned to see what Tandia was doing with the coffee. She was nowhere to be seen and Sarah jumped up and ran towards the big AGA stove. Tandia was pressed up against her corner of the alcove biting her hand, the tears running down the cheeks, her shoulders heaving with the effort to contain her emotion. Blood ran from the corner of her mouth where she had bitten into her hand.

'Oh my God!' Sarah stretched out her arms and bent down to embrace Tandia. She took the little girl in her arms and started to rock her. 'Shhh! Don't cry, Tandy. It's only pretend, don't cry, skatterbol, no one can hurt you, you hear? You safe here.'

The girls had all risen from the table and crowded around the cooking alcove. 'Let her go!' It was Mama Tequila's voice. Confused, Sarah looked up first at Mama Tequila and then back to Tandia. 'Leave her, you hear!'

She turned to the girls. 'Out! Go to your rooms! You too Sarah, go now, jong, before I lose my temper.'

Sarah released Tandia, propping her up against the split logs stacked against the rear wall of the alcove. '*Maak gou*,' Mama Tequila said in Afrikaans, a language she rarely spoke and only when she was upset. Sarah rose quickly and left the room, following the other girls out.

Mama Tequila remained standing for perhaps fifteen minutes until Tandia began to calm down. 'Go to the table, Miss Tandy!' she ordered, turning slowly and moving across the room to the big club chair.

Tandia rose and, sniffing, sat at the table. Mama Tequila held a cork-tip in her hand which she now fed slowly into her mouth and lit with the Zippo. She withdrew the cigarette and pushed the smoke out lazily. 'Why you crying, Miss Tandy?'

'You, you know why, M . . . mama T,' Tandia sobbed.

When Mama Tequila spoke again her voice was sharp. 'Now you listen to me, you little shit!' She lowered her voice as Tandia looked up at her in tearful alarm. 'You listen good, you hear? You can leave today, take your basin and pack your things.' She reached for her bag on the small table and started to rummage through it until she found her purse. She opened the clip and removed five crumpled one-pound notes which she flung down onto the floor in front of her. 'Take it, it's the five pounds we took out of your pants when you came here. Before tonight you out, gone from this place, you understand!'

Tandia's world collapsed about her. She'd only heard half of Mama Tequila's titillation talk to the girls when she found herself back in the cemetery talking to the dead Patel and then it all happened again, the handcuffs and the marble cross and the big, hard white man inside her! 'Please Mama T, let me stay! Please! I will do anything. Anything you want, jus' let me stay here, I beg you Mama T!'

Mama Tequila looked at Tandia and began to talk softly. 'You not special, Miss Tandy, you dirt. You nothing. You know why? Because you a coloured person who is sorry for herself. Inside you like a white person, inside you rotten white meat, you got a white heart. You think something bad happened to you? *Wragtig*, I'm telling you, you don't know what bad is! Rape! Rape is nothing, you hear? When Sarah was six her daddy raped her, when she was eleven he threw her out the house because he was puffing his *slang* into her baby sister. At thirteen she a whore already, already working on the streets. But she's not sorry for herself, all the others is the same, some of my girls are worse even than that!'

'Please forgive me, Mama T, I swear on my mother's grave, it will never happen again. Please, I won't feel sorry for myself ever again, just let me stay!'

'Miss Tandy, this a whorehouse! The business we got here is to fuck men.' She pointed at Herman the Hottentot. 'Around here that is the boss. Hester and Sarah and Jasmine and Colleen and Hettie, Doreen, Johanna an' Marie, they all got one job, to make him happy. But they my whores, you hear? What happened before is over, finish and klaar, a white person can cry about yesterday, they got that luxury; for a coloured person there is no yesterday, you got to use all your courage and your strength to stay alive for today. You waste it on yesterday, you a dead kaffir. You understan' what I'm saying, girl?'

Tandia nodded, then sniffed and wiped her nostrils with the back of her hand. There was blood on her hand where she'd bitten herself and now the blood smeared over her face. She was just like the woman, the black shebeen whore at the police station. 'Yes, I will try, Mama T.'

'Try is not enough, Miss Tandy. If you going to be a whore, you going to be a whore with a future. If you going to be a lawyer they going to try to kill you. And they not going to rest until they got you on the slab, the mortuary, a dead kaffir lawyer! You got to make yourself so when they stick the knife into your heart the blade break. When they get another one, it break also! And another and another. Then maybe you can have a future too!'

Tandia's voice was hardly a whisper. 'Please Mama T let me stay?'

'Miss Tandy, this the first and last time, you hear?'

Tandia rose from her chair and rushed over to Mama Tequila and hugged her. 'Thank you, Mama T, I will not let you down.'

Mama Tequila patted Tandia on the back and then pushed her away, but she did so gently and Tandia knew she'd been saved. 'Go now, you can tell everyone they can come out of their rooms.'

Tandia was walking towards the kitchen door to leave when Mama Tequila called her back. 'No more what you doing with Sarah. No more, you hear?'

'Yes, Mama T,' Tandia whispered.

The hot coastal summer passed for Tandia as she entered her final year at high school. Except for Sundays, when she and Juicey Fruit Mambo would head for the high mountains, her time was taken up with work at Bluey Jay or school work.

Tandia had been brought down to solid ground with a terrible thump after the Herman the Hottentot incident. She was smart enough to realise that she would be required to adapt absolutely to the environment of Bluey Jay, that Mama Tequila would tolerate nothing less. Her quiet, shy ways would have to go. At sixteen Tandia had spent the larger part of her waking hours by herself, if not always physically, certainly in her head. The habit of going for long periods without talking was inappropriate at Bluey Jay, which was a rowdy, aggressive place, loud with vulgar laughter and sudden melodramatic tears.

To Tandia's astonishment the girls all seemed to cry for the wrong reasons. Never for the past which had been steeped with misery, but over such dumb things as a quarrel about whose turn it was to do something in the kitchen or simply because two of them were wearing the same colour gown or stayed too long in the bathroom, silly stuff which Tandia couldn't imagine even getting upset about.

Mama Tequila worked her hard but Tandia didn't mind; she'd always worked hard and now she learned to do with less sleep. She'd never been a big sleeper; her early childhood terror as she lay alone in the shed at the house in Booth Road had conditioned her. She began to find ways to be indispensable at Bluey Jay, not simply as a room maid but in a number of other chores as well. At first she had to practise laughing when one of the girls said something funny, but after a while she found that buried all these years inside her was lots of bubbling laughter. Driven at first, by the circumstances surrounding her, to seem gregarious and happy rather than naturally quiet and timid, Tandia now found that she was posing less and that laughter and involvement was coming naturally to her. At sixteen her body had suddenly shaped into its female lines. Curves which had been threatening to arrive seemed to wait almost precisely for her sixteenth birthday. Then they shaped her torso and rounded her hips into a tight lithe woman's shape. Her legs, always unusually long, now seemed to fit her body naturally. Each day she seemed to grow more beautiful. The girls at Bluey Jay had all been picked by Mama Tequila because of their looks. But they all understood that Tandia wasn't of the same clay. With her green eyes and perfect skin, she was destined to be a beautiful woman. They cherished this thought among themselves; Tandia was going to be too beautiful to ignore, even in South Africa.

For her part, Tandia carried her beauty with a naturalness and lack of affectation that endeared her to them all. She simply saw it as a contribution to the atmosphere at Bluey Jay, an abstracted thing which she could use to full effect in her new environment.

From Juicey Fruit Mambo she learned to run the bar and from Mama Tequila she learned how to hustle customers. A shilling glass of Scotch was five shillings at Bluey Jay and Tandia could convert it into a double and look abject at her mistake, making such a beautiful mess of trying to pour the extra Scotch back into the bottle that a customer would beg her to stop and be happy to pay ten shillings for his drink. She could water drinks perfectly for drunks and, if they were sufficiently drunk, get them onto cold tea without them knowing the difference. While the kaffir with the gold teeth had to be watched like a hawk, no customer ever thought of Tandia cheating them. At first Tandia was simply the late afternoon barmaid relief for Juicey Fruit Mambo, but after just a few weeks Mama Tequila announced at a chew the fat chat that Tandia had achieved solo status in the saloon bar.

It happened one Sunday morning when Tandia, like all the other girls, had appeared in her chenille dressing-gown in the kitchen. It was unusual for Tandia to be dressed this way, but Mama Tequila hadn't remarked on it. Tandia was usually up hours before the rest of them, dressed and doing her homework and already in the kitchen to help when she appeared to cook breakfast. Mama Tequila made a mental note to take her temperature after the session. Tandia up this late and still not dressed was obviously not well and she knew, since the day of the Herman the Hottentot affair, Tandia would rather die than complain of not being well.

Her announcement that Tandia was to be allowed the third billet in the bar was a singular honour. The girls showed their delight by getting up from their chairs and crowding around her.

Tandia flushed with pleasure. She loved the important feeling working behind the bar counter gave her, and to be put on an even footing with Juicey Fruit Mambo and Mama Tequila as custodian of the saloon bar was an unexpected honour. She'd been up and about since dawn, and now she stood up. Closing her eyes briefly and taking a deep breath to contain her terror she allowed the dressing-gown to slip from her shoulders. She stood before them in her pink gymslip and stockings, standing on her toes to simulate the effect high heels would give her. She had taken eight inches off the skirt of her gymslip and the tops of her stockings could just be seen held with the pink ribbons of her suspenders. Her blouse was unbuttoned to show the curve of her breasts and she held herself in a provocative pose, her body slightly turned with her hands on her hips and her left shoulder thrust forward. Six months previously she might have looked like a young girl playing at being a femme fatale, but now she was provocatively sexy. Mama Tequila who seldom showed surprise at anything drew back and then burst into applause. Unthinking, she slipped into her American vernacular, 'Baby, you just the sexiest thing I ever did see!' she said, with obvious admiration. The girls all clapped and laughed and Marie ran from the room and appeared a few minutes later with a new pair of white high-heeled shoes which she made Tandia put on. It was the biggest move Tandia had ever made on her own and it felt good.

Mama Tequila made Tandia practise walking in the pumps. She was stiff for days afterwards but Tandia knew the effect was worth it and she could hardly wait to return from school the next day and to appear in her new guise in the saloon bar.

Tandia had such a natural sweet innocence about her that the effect she had on customers was doubled. She was totally desirable and totally unattainable at the same time. The combination made her a formidable attraction behind the bar. For Mama Tequila made it known that, under no circumstances, was Tandia for sale. If anything this increased her desirability to the Bluey Jay regulars.

With Tandia at the bar, customers not only increased but stayed longer and spent more. Just in case a customer lost the urge to use the upstairs services of the house or was drinking too slowly, Mama Tequila would give Tandia a signal by placing her hand over her glass. Tandia would wait until the customer was ready to order again.

'Same again, Miss Tandy.'

Tandia would pretend not to understand the request and her eyes would grow big. She'd put her hands on her waist and lean back slightly with her left shoulder thrown forward, the way Mama Tequila had taught her. 'Oh, sir, not the same again! Last week was good, Jasmine says you were so very good and very nice to her also. But you can't have the same again!' Tandia would take a deep breath and giggle, 'So! This week we have a special treat for you! Doreen is going to take you today and she has some lovely, lovely surprises for you.'

Tandia was never explicit nor did she talk dirty. She was becoming an actress who worked with body language and with her eyes. Words could only have cheapened the merchandise she had for sale at Bluey Jay. Tandia understood when Mama Tequila said that a whorehouse was a theatre of the mind, and she intended to be the perfect understudy to the leading lady.

The client would laugh. 'That's not what I meant, Miss Tandy. Give me another drink.'

'Certainly, sir, what will it be? Another lager? It will be waiting for you, a big cold glass with the foam running down the side, just how you like it. Because you going to need a long, cold beer when Miss Doreen is finished with you, believe me!'

'That child, ain't she the limit!' Mama Tequila would shake her head and chuckle. 'Mister you take no notice dat little hustler! Miss Tandy you give the gentleman guest another beer before I take the strap to you, you heah?' The customers would wince at the sudden vision of someone taking the strap to Tandia. Mama Tequila would turn to the customer. 'I ain't saying she's not right, that Miss Doreen, she special, she the best, but she expensive.' Mama Tequila would lean over and whisper into his ear, 'For five pound she do anything, you hear? Anything you want!'

At that moment Doreen would walk into the bar, signalled by a buzzer under the bar counter. Mama Tequila would say, 'Miss Doreen I want you to be nice to our gentleman guest.' She would roll her eyes. 'Real nice. He deserve the best you got, Miss Doreen, the best he ever had, you hear?'

SIX

Shortly after its win in the 1953 elections, the Nationalist government formed a covert police squad in all major cities whose job it was to track down the subversive elements in the urban black, coloured and Indian communities. To cover their activity, but also because the government saw a connection between the two, they were given the public brief of enforcing the Immorality Act. Both these aims, covert and otherwise, suited the career aspirations of Geldenhuis perfectly. He applied and was accepted into the special police unit known simply as the Special Branch, though the unit was popularly referred to as the Spy and Thigh Squad, which later became abbreviated to its acronym, SAT.

The appointment of Geldenhuis to SAT was his biggest career move yet. Meanwhile Tandia, the black *slimmetjie* whom, as a type, Geldenhuis so despised, had all but completed her secondary school education and aspired to enter university to read law. Geldenhuis too had been busy during the year, learning the Zulu language – a facility which in the years to come would make him a formidable interrogator.

He knew instinctively that future personal power lay in exploiting the Immorality Act, that the sexual apartheid of South Africa combined all the ingredients for achieving that power. Geldenhuis saw a situation where a white official – in his imagination this was always a magistrate or person capable of influencing the affairs of apartheid – was sexually compromised by ruthless black activists seeking to subvert the system. He was convinced that sex would become the major weapon the terrorists would use to undermine the infrastructure of apartheid, and he set about building a reputation for himself as the guardian of white morality. He made frequent arrests, mostly on the waterfront where the hapless 'trick zombies' worked, bagging a mixture of customers: foreign sailors, white kids drunk and derring-do on a Saturday night out, fishermen and whalers and the general human flotsam of port life together with an occasional solid citizen, a minor public servant or a small shopkeeper. It was these *respectable* arrests which soon earned Geldenhuis a big reputation. The newspapers played them up and in the process destroyed the lives of a lot of little people and their families, while at the same time pandering to the righteous indignation of the 'thou shalt not commit adultery' segment of the white, Calvinist public, who saw adultery committed with a black or coloured person as the most venal of all possible crimes: a triple whammy which, in some minds, transcended even murder.

Durban became one of the first cities openly to establish an Immorality Squad, and in less than a year it was being led by Detective Sergeant Geldenhuis. His appointment was a popular one; not only was he a diligent and persistent law officer but he had also recently gained some public notoriety by beating a black fighter named Gideon Mandoma. The twelve-round championship fight had resulted in a bitterly disputed verdict and Geldenhuis had taken the South African welterweight boxing title.

Then Jamal Singh had been arrested. The Singh case had attracted widespread publicity, doing more to damage South Africa in the eyes of the world than anything previously perpetrated in the name of apartheid. The government and the Dutch Reformed Church saw it as the price to be paid for moral rectitude in a world which was clearly controlled outside of South Africa by the Jews and the Communists. Geldenhuis had hidden in the boot of Singh's car as the Indian businessman had driven off to keep an assignation with a white prostitute and had photographed Jamal Singh and his sex partner *in flagrante delicto* in the back seat of Singh's olive-brown Chevrolet. The barrister appearing for Singh had asked how Detective Sergeant Geldenhuis had known his client's designation. Geldenhuis had replied that it had been a matter of diligent detective work. Asked to explain this further, he had admitted to concealing himself in the boot of the car on several occasions. At the conclusion of the trial, which became known as the 'Cop in the Boot' trial, Jamal Singh had been sentenced to five years in prison. Geldenhuis had received a letter from the Minister for Justice, commending him for his diligence as an officer of the law and for his outstanding example as a member of the Afrikaner race.

It was this letter which, seated at the bar counter at Bluey Jay, he now showed to Mama Tequila, with Tandia in attendance behind the bar. Tandia remained terrified of Geldenhuis who had been coming to Bluey Jay fairly regularly over the period she had been with Mama Tequila. She had told her about Geldenhuis wanting her to spy for him and, to her surprise, Mama Tequila had laughed.

'Rule number one, Tandy, nobody has a name in a brothel. If a customer says his name is Pinocchio, next time he comes in you say, "Good evening Mr Pinocchio". If the police show you a picture of this guy you shake your head, you never seen him in your life before. That the one rule cannot be broken in a place like this.'

Geldenhuis had tried on several occasions to get information from Tandia but she had simply invoked rule number one and smiled, though she'd quaked in her boots, saying she didn't know the identity of any of the people who came. After a while he stopped asking.

Tandia was quite unable to explain to herself why she felt guilty when Geldenhuis appeared; guilty at having been raped. The totally irrational response that she was at fault, that somehow she had done something to have caused it to happen, refused to go away. Sometimes the memory of it struck her like a blow to the head, a physical thing she could feel. Then she would crawl up into a ball and try to think it away, wash it out of her system with tears that squeezed to the surface like shards of glass. Rape was not only a thing of the mind, an imagined hand which held her heart like an unforgiving sponge and squeezed until she felt the muscle and the sinew and the blood vessels popping out between her fingers as though, at any moment, it would split from the pressure and allow the life to explode out of her. It was also a great heaviness in her gut as though her stomach contained two large round river stones submerged in black bile which made her feel nauseous and too weary to rise from her bed. This second feeling was her fear, the never-ending malignant fear. It would come upon her the moment she set eyes on Geldenhuis.

While some of the policemen were still regular customers, this was less and less true as the Immorality Act took effect. A police officer in the Transvaal had been given a four-year prison sentence on a morals charge and now, with the formation of SAT Squad, the code of honour which existed between policemen had been largely eliminated. No officer in the force was safe any longer.

Mama Tequila didn't use her American persona with the police, for they were strictly about business: the business of survival. She'd been in business long before the Immorality Act and her connections with the Durban police force and judiciary went back a long way to friendlier times when a policeman could remove his khaki uniform and have a little bit of fun for a change.

Mama Tequila wasn't silly enough to trust the police, even in the good old days, and the huge old safe at Bluey Jay contained at least one ten-by-eight, black-and-white photograph of each of her customers caught in a compromising position. Some of these photographs had turned brown with age and were mostly of policemen who had used her services when she ran her dockside BB-TMs. There was only one exception: Geldenhuis. Much as Mama Tequila had tried to suggest to him that a bounty of golden flesh was available to him at no charge, Geldenhuis had never used the services at Bluey Jay.

'That's a very nice letter, you can't get more high up than that.' Mama Tequila proffered the letter to Tandia but Geldenhuis snatched it from her hands.

'Ag, it's nothing, I jus' got lucky.' He folded the letter and returned it to his wallet. He laughed suddenly. 'You know what I told Jamal Singh, I said to him, "You stupid bastard, if your want a stray fuck why didn't you call me!" But then I looked in his eyes and I knew all of a sudden that what he wanted was a white woman, it had to be a white woman. Sies, man! What a disgusting bastard! What could I do? I had to arrest him.'

'You mean you was lying in that car boot just to warn him and then give him my address?' The sarcasm was apparent in Mama Tequila's voice.

Geldenhuis flushed and picked up his beer and took a sip to regain his composure. 'Of course not, man. We knew he was doing it, that was one thing we knew for sure, but catching him, that was another thing! Always he would slip the police tail. I had to do something, man. You never know how many white women a bastard like that will do it to if you don't catch him and put him in gaol.'

'Detective Sergeant, I been a whore a long time. I been a owner of a whorehouse also a long time. A black whore, a coloured whore, a white whore, they all the same. A whore is a whore! What make you think a white one is better than a black one? Their pussy, it work just the same.'

'Ja, I see what you mean, Mama Tequila,' Geldenhuis said politely, 'but you got to understand, when a Indian wants to do it to a white person it's a political thing. "Look!" he's saying, "I'm just as bladdy good as you, I can screw your woman just like you."'

Mama Tequila kept the smile on her face, though Tandia could see that the back of her neck had gone a crimson colour, a sure sign she was very angry. 'I jus' got one word to say, Detective Sergeant. Bullshit!'

For a moment Tandia thought she'd heard Mama Tequila incorrectly. Geldenhuis's blue eyes had assumed the dreamy, faraway quality she recalled from the interrogation room and she knew she'd heard correctly. It made her fear rise up and threaten to choke her. Her hand shot up involuntarily and gripped her throat in alarm. She was afraid to look at Geldenhuis, for she knew instinctively he would never forgive Mama Tequila's insult. But when he spoke his voice was perfectly controlled. 'You a coloured person, I don't expect you to understand.' Then he took up his beer. Holding the glass up in front of him as though he were about to propose a toast, he threw back his head and drained it, wiping the flecked foam from his mouth with the back of his hand. 'I need to see you privately, Mama Tequila.' He looked momentarily at Tandia and then turned back to Mama Tequila. 'Is there somewhere else we can go?'

Mama Tequila returned to the bar about half an hour later. 'Give me a double brandy, Tandy.' Tandia reached for the VSOP bottle and measured the brandy into a small balloon glass. It was unusual for Mama Tequila to drink during the afternoon; she usually had her first snort around six.

Mama Tequila took the glass and raised it to her lips, taking a slug straight down so that half the brandy in the balloon disappeared. She grimaced as she placed the glass back on the bar. 'Miss Tandy, we got troubles!' she said.

'What sort of troubles, Mama T?'

Mama Tequila looked up at Tandia, her eyes slits of polished anthracite buried in a bed of mascara and false eyelashes. 'Whores' troubles, Miss Tandy. Geldenhuis wants you!'

It was Wednesday in the longest week of Tandia's life. Wednesday afternoons, from after lunch until five, Mama Tequila called 'Pay and Lay Day'. It was the time at Bluey Jay she kept for the cops, all of whom were required to arrive strictly by appointment and on time.

The procedure was simple. One cop in and one cop out. The first police officer at Bluey Jay would drive his car to the back of the big old house, the next to the front. When the second arrived the first was already waiting in his car and when the second had been taken indoors the first drove off. This way Mama Tequila could pay off and if necessary accommodate six dishonest policemen in one afternoon.

On this Wednesday there would be only Geldenhuis. Much to Mama Tequila's annoyance he had insisted he be the only person at Bluey Jay that day. All the girls had been given the afternoon off to do their Christmas shopping in Durban and had left before lunch in the Packard. Packed like herrings in a tin, with a scrunch of skidding back tyres on the gravel and squeals of laughter, Juicey Fruit Mambo roared off with Mama Tequila's entire sex inventory. By half past one he had returned and waited at the cattle gate for Geldenhuis to arrive.

Geldenhuis arrived at Bluey Jay a little after two and apologised to Mama Tequila who met him at the door. 'Sorry, Mama Tequila, but that cheeky bladdy kaffir of yours stopped me at the cattle gate and had a look in the boot! I don't know what he expects to find there.'

Mama Tequila laughed. 'A policeman, maybe?' Despite himself, Geldenhuis grinned. Then he abruptly cleared his throat. 'We alone here, hey?'

She nodded. 'Josie, she's the cook, I told her not to come today. The black servants all gone home to their kraal and the girls in Durban doing Christmas shopping. Only you and me and Miss Tandy, ja and of course, Juicey Fruit Mambo, who will stay at the gate until you come out again.'

Geldenhuis pushed past Mama Tequila further into the hall. 'I think I'll jus' take a look myself. Do you mind?'

Mama Tequila spread her hands. 'Help yourself, we got nothing to hide here, Sergeant.'

'*Detective* Sergeant,' Geldenhuis corrected, grinning. 'You don't get it for nothing, you know. Stay in the bar, okay? I just want to have a quick deck for myself.'

'Miss Tandy will also be in the bar when you get back,' Mama Tequila called after him. In her eight years at Bluey Jay her authority had been absolute and now, for the first time, she felt like an alien. It was like being back in a BB-TM during wartime when the military or naval police would just walk in and open doors and walk out again without even giving her the time of day. People like that had no respect.

Mama Tequila wasn't a woman who put a lot of trust in life; she knew that in the process of living it you did more picking yourself up and dusting yourself off than tapdancing. She had long since discovered it didn't do to harbour grudges. The world was full of bastards and hating them was a time-consuming and poorly paid business. But there had to be exceptions, and Geldenhuis was developing in her mind as one of them.

The spoiling of Tandia by him upset her greatly, although she wasn't prepared to admit this, even to herself.

The moment Mama Tequila had mentioned Geldenhuis's desire for her, Tandia had begun to shake. She had placed the glass she'd been polishing onto the counter where it rattled momentarily as its base landed imprecisely, her shaking hand misjudging its surface. 'Please Mama Tequila, don't make me do it, not to him! Anyone, even old Coetzee or Mr Perfect Lay! Please! I beg you!' A darkness had formed inside her head and around her eyes and she had gripped the edge of the bar counter so her knees wouldn't collapse under her.

Mama Tequila had taken the bottle of Cape brandy from the counter and, picking up the glass, she had poured a dash of brandy into it. 'Here, drink. Drink all of it.' Tandia had taken the glass and swallowed the brandy. The shock to her system had been enormous as the fiery liquor hit her throat. 'Come sit here, Miss Tandy,' Mama Tequila had said, patting the bar stool next to her. Tandia, her eyes watering from the effect of the brandy, had lifted the bar counter and come to sit beside Mama Tequila.

The large woman had lifted her brandy balloon. 'Time's come, baby. Them's the breaks. I kept my word to Dr Louis. Now you finished school you owe me, you hear?'

Tandia hadn't tried to protest as she fought to conceal her fear. Mama Tequila had taken her hand. 'Tandy, sometimes we got to do things we don't like. That goes for everyone, but most of all for women and even more, most of all, for coloured women. When you live in the white man's world that the rules. It's no use crying, no use saying it's unfair, because you wasting your time. Okay, so you got to learn the rules better, you got to be more clever than they are. You got to be better than the white man at being a bastard. You hear what I say, child?'

Tandia had nodded. The burning sensation of the brandy had left a warm glow in her stomach. 'Mama T, I'd rather fuck a dog!' she said fiercely.

Mama Tequila's head had jerked back in astonishment. She had never heard Tandia use a coarse word. She had stared at her in amazement; then her face had broken into a huge smile. 'Miss Tandy, so would I, baby! But sometimes you got to fuck the dog shit instead!'

Mama Tequila had kept Tandia busy in the bar until late the previous night. Mr Dine-o-mite and the Singh brothers, cousins of the famous Jamal Singh, and a friend were the other regulars that night. With them they had brought two Indian businessmen from the Transvaal who, apart from going upstairs for a while, spent the evening marvelling at the beautiful old house and happily paying for double Scotches. Around eleven, when the two Transvaal wallahs were too drunk to make much sense and one of them complained of having his Scotch watered, Mama Tequila looked suitably shocked and used this as an excuse to send them all packing. The Singh brothers apologised profusely, insisting on paying for four extra Scotches to make up for the bad form of their Transvaal friends and leaving a ten-bob tip for Tandia. A little after eleven o'clock that night Mama Tequila closed Bluey Jay down for the night and Tandia was free to go to her own room.

Tandia found herself running down the corridor as she drew closer to her room. The panic, kept at bay all evening, was rising up in her like a dark presence. There was no escaping, she would have to sleep with Geldenhuis, and she was about to drown in the misery of this thing inside her. She closed the door behind her and rushed to the window, sure that she was about to suffocate. At the window she took great gulps of night air until after a while the feeling in her settled down to the old heaviness, the great big round stones in her belly.

Tandia stood by the window. Outside the night was silver, like the first night she'd arrived at Bluey Jay; and once again the moon was full and she could see it through the leaves of the wild fig tree. The room in the early December heat was warm and a mosquito buzzed around her head. She let it be; mosquitoes, for some reason, never bit her. The ache inside her was so intense it seemed to swell outwards, filling the room. A wave of panic swept over her and she found herself on the window sill and in a single step outwards into space she had climbed onto the huge old branch that grew right up to it. The moment she found herself in the tree she felt a strange relief overcome her. She was alone in a secret place, and with the leaves concealing her from the rest of the world the moonlight turned the space around her into a cocoon of silver. Tandia sat there in her own space unable to cry. In the early hours of the morning she crept back into her small room and collapsed on the bed where she rolled herself up into a ball and clutched Apple Sammy to her breast, sleeping fitfully until she was wakened by a wood pigeon calling in the branches of the fig tree.

Geldenhuis came back into the bar and sat on a stool at the far end of the bar, nearest the door. 'Howzit, Tandia?' he said casually. Then he turned his attention to Mama Tequila. 'I never realised it was such a big house and also so posh. I never been in a nicer place than this. I reckon B. J. Vorster himself wouldn't have a better house. A beer please, Tandia.'

'Detective Sergeant, you know better. It's Miss Tandy, that how all the girls is addressed in this place.' Tandia froze. Mama Tequila was treating her exactly like one of the girls, like a whore.

'Ag, man, with us it's different. We know each other from old times, hey Tandia?'

Tandia placed a glass of lager on the bar in front of him, not responding to his question.

'All the same, that the way we do it here. If you want to use this house you got to understand the rules.'

Geldenhuis laughed. 'Okay, you win.' He reached for the beer in front of him and, lifting it up, downed the entire glass in one go.

'Would you like another beer, Detective Sergeant Geldenhuis?' Tandia asked softly.

'No, man, I'm in training. One beer a day, that's all I'm allowed.'

Mama Tequila clapped her hands. 'We got a special treat for you, Detective Sergeant, you and Miss Tandy. You've got the Jade Room, a very beautiful room, all green, everything in it is green to go with Miss Tandy's dress and also her eyes.'

Tandia was dressed in one of Marie's green satin dresses that went to just below the knees. The thin shoulder straps set off her shoulders and the curve of her breasts. Mama Tequila had made her wear lipstick and a little eyeshadow, and it made her look more grown up. Tandia was utterly desirable and Mama Tequila had never seen her look more beautiful. 'May God forgive me,' she thought.

'Not the green room. I don't like green!' Geldenhuis said suddenly.

'But we made it ready.' Mama Tequila smiled. 'This is my house, Detective Sergeant Geldenhuis. We like to give our guests the best. I insist you take the Jade Room.'

Geldenhuis turned on Mama Tequila. His eyes narrowed. 'I wasn't born yesterday, you know! Not the bladdy Jade Room, you hear?'

Mama Tequila looked contrite as she fanned herself. 'I'm sorry, Detective Sergeant, we like things to be nice. Perhaps the Pink? The Pink Room, it's very nice also.'

'Ja, okay, the Pink is orright.' To conceal his anger he turned to Tandia and attempted a smile. 'Come, show me where is the Pink Room, Tandia.'

Mama Tequila raised her glass to her lips. '*Miss Tandy*,' she said softly, as though speaking to herself.

Geldenhuis followed Tandia up the wide sweeping staircase which led to the client wing of the big old house. Her heart was beating furiously, but somehow the fact that Geldenhuis seemed to be making no attempt to be nice made it easier. She would just lie still and think about being up in the branches of the wild fig tree in the moonlight, floating inside the silver cocoon, hidden even from herself. Mama Tequila had given her a tube of lubricant gel. 'You use this, Tandy, and breathe hard you hear, hard as anything!' She had demonstrated, bringing her voice up to a series of sobbing gasps. 'Then they think you liking it and it's over quickly.'

They entered the Pink Room, the pride of the brothel. It was a room designed for dalliance but not one in which to spend too much time. The pinkness overwhelmed a person as an aphid might feel finding itself suddenly thrust deep into the petals of an overblown rose. To compound the incarnadine feel of the room, a strip of mirror about three feet wide and six long was fixed to the ceiling so that the entire room was reproduced in its reflection. In the very centre of the mirror was a small circle of clear glass no more than three inches in diameter. Looking directly into the mirror with the myriad details of the room reflected into it made it impossible to see the circle, but fixed neatly into it was the lens of a reflex camera.

'This a very nice room, better than the green one, I think,' Geldenhuis said, standing in the centre of the room with his hands on his hips and looking about him in a proprietorial manner. 'Why did the old cow want us to have the green one?'

'The Jade Room, it is also nice,' Tandia said, starting to remove the satin bedspread. She folded the spread neatly and looked down at the pink satin sheets which fitted perfectly without a wrinkle, precisely turned over at the top. Geldenhuis crossed the room and entered the small shower recess. She could hear him pull back the pink plastic shower curtain. When he entered again he'd removed his tie, and unclipped his Sam Browne belt and police revolver, which he now placed on the vanity table beside the bed.

Tandia kicked off her high heels. She wasn't wearing stockings and only wore a pair of panties under Marie's dress. She moved over to where Geldenhuis stood and started to undo the brass buttons on his tunic.

The sequence of a seduction was familiar to Tandia, as it had been discussed often enough at the chew the fat chats. Tandia removed Geldenhuis's khaki tunic and placed it on a hanger in the wardrobe; then she returned and unbuttoned his shirt. Geldenhuis had started by putting his hands around her tiny waist but now he put both his hands on her bottom, one on each buttock, and began to massage. Tandia knew she was supposed to gyrate her hips and move in closer to him, pretending to be sexy, but she couldn't do it. She peeled his shirt over his shoulders and waited for him to remove his hands from her bottom so that she could slip the sleeves away from his arms. But he let the shirt hang from his waist and continued to pummel her bottom. 'C'mon, Tandia, be a little responsive, man. I like you, I want you to like me also.'

'Let me take your shirt off, Detective Sergeant.'

Geldenhuis removed his hands and pulled the sleeves away from his arms. He quickly moved towards the wardrobe to hang his shirt up. 'You can call me Jannie when we like this, you hear?' Tandia nodded her head. Geldenhuis stood in his pants and boots with his torso bare. He was a medium-sized man and he carried no fat. The muscles on his stomach were clearly defined above a trim waist, and his torso widened out into big, well-muscled shoulders. In boxer's terms he looked like a puncher, as though he might carry a knockout in both hands, a left-right combination which could put an opponent flat on his seat with a look of surprise on his face.

'So far so good,' Tandia thought to herself, knowing that the hard part was yet to come. She moved back to stand in front of Geldenhuis and, as his hands went out to hold her, she knelt down on the carpet in front of him and started to undo his bootlaces. She worked the laces very loose so that the boots would come away easily. Then she removed his boots and socks and placed them beside the bed the way she had been shown.

Still on her knees Tandia undid the flybuttons on Geldenhuis's trousers and then unclipped the waistband. Hooking her thumbs into each side of the waistband she pulled downwards until her thumbs included the elastic band of his underpants. Then in a single movement she pulled both garments down to his ankles. She waited, her eyes downcast, while he stepped out of them. Tandia was terrified of raising her eyes, as she knew she eventually must do. She had never seen an erection other than the one represented by Herman the Hottentot. Mama Tequila had explained that the next bit was essential. 'Tandy, some men, they not clean, they got things, maybe a little sore or something, even very small it dangerous, you hear.' She had picked up Herman the Hottentot and showed Tandia where to look. Then she had placed her forefinger and thumb around the base and run them firmly along the satin-smooth length of sneezewood to the carved bulbous tip. 'You do like this, you milk it and watch. If a drop comes out that clear like water you okay, but if it milky, even a little bit cloudy, you finish and klaar with this man, you hear?' Tandia was now aware that to make this examination she must pretend to 'fondle' Geldenhuis, to pretend she was indulging in foreplay, and she knew suddenly that this was something she simply couldn't do.

Instead, averting her gaze, she half-turned as she rose, so that by the time she stood erect she had her back to Geldenhuis. She brought her hands around and unhooked her dress at the back and pulled down the zipper to reveal the curve of her beautiful back. Then she pulled her dress down over her thighs and, taking her panties with her, she stepped out of Marie's dress.

Tandia now stood completely nude with her back to Geldenhuis, terrified to turn around. She could sense him moving towards her and her heart beat furiously.

'*Magtig!* You're beautiful!' she heard him say and then, almost in slow motion, the nightmare of the cemetery started all over again. Geldenhuis reached out and grabbed his tie from the vanity table. With his free hand he gripped her by the back of the neck and pushed her hard so that she fell sprawling across the bed on her stomach. Then he grabbed her arms and brought them behind her back, tying them together at the wrists using his necktie.

'Don't shout, you hear! If you shout or scream, I promise I'll kill you!' Tandia's hands were securely tied and she felt his hand press down into the small of her back as it pinned her down. She turned her head to see him again reach towards the vanity table beside the bed and withdraw his service revolver from its holster. 'Lie very still or you a dead kaffir, you hear?' Tandia was close to fainting with terror when she felt the sudden cold of the barrel between the crease of her buttocks. She jerked involuntarily. 'Lie still, dammit!' The cold steel worked closer in, then she felt a terrible searing pain as the barrel was pushed into her anus. She gasped and then screamed. But Geldenhuis anticipated her and slammed his cupped hand across her mouth, cutting the scream short. He jerked her head back and held her. 'You scream just once more and I pull the trigger you black bitch!' He held her head pulled back until she was forced to relax and then he took his hand from her mouth and allowed her head to collapse back onto the bed. The barrel hadn't moved and, apart from the pain, she felt as though she was about to become incontinent.

When Geldenhuis spoke again his voice was calm. It was the same reasonable tone she remembered from the interrogation room of the Cato Manor police station. 'What's this I hear about going to the university, hey? I thought we talked about that? Remember? When I told you we don't like *swart slimmetjies.* Clever kaffirs just make trouble. Why do you want to make trouble for me, Tandia? Why, hey? I told you I was your friend. But now, all of a sudden, now you want to go to the university to study law? That's a very dangerous precedent. I don't think we can allow such a dangerous precedent.' He was exerting a steady downward pressure on the revolver so, as he talked, the barrel moved further and further inwards. 'In fact, I can definitely say, we not going to allow this precedent.' She heard Geldenhuis sigh heavily. 'Tandia, you make me sad, you hear? First you break your promise to me. I ask you to tell me the names of people who come here, but you never did that. Now you want to go to the university, when already I told you I don't like *swart slimmetjies*!' She felt the downward pressure of the barrel; the pain was making it hard for her to concentrate. 'I think maybe I wasting my time on you, I should just pull the trigger now and shoot the shit out of you.' He laughed, 'What you say, hey? What's another dead kaffir anyway?'

Tandia lay very still. She never doubted for a moment that he would kill her if he chose to do so. The pain had now become a deep throb and she knew she must be bleeding. Her fear completely enveloped her, like a soldier on the battlefield pretending to be dead as the enemy passed by. The rhythm of his legs against her increased and, rather than hear him, she sensed that he was breathing harder. She gasped as the revolver was painfully and suddenly withdrawn and she heard the soft clunk as it landed on the carpet. 'Turn over!' Geldenhuis demanded. Terrified, Tandia turned onto her back. Geldenhuis stood over her. His blue eyes, sharp and angry, seemed to pierce directly into her like the pin-sharp pain of a sunspot focussed on skin through a magnifying glass. His left hand held his erection arrogantly and his right rested on his waist. Suddenly his mouth shaped into a snarl and his hand shot out and grabbed her hair, jerking her into an upright position.

'Suck!'

Somewhere, deep down in a long, dark corridor of her soul, Tandia heard a silent scream. Her mouth opened and took him in and her teeth bit down as hard as she possibly could.

Tandia heard a scream and felt a stunning blow to the side of her head. The scream and the blow mixed so that the man's scream and the pain to her head became one, a misted crimson thing that rang sharply like the sing of electricity through wire. As Geldenhuis struck her she must have released her grip on him, for, clutching at his scrotum, he reeled backwards, tripped and fell, hitting his head against the side of the vanity table. This undoubtedly saved Tandia's life. Geldenhuis was a boxer who was used to taking a punch and the blow to the back of his head was only sufficient to slow him down for the few seconds it took Juicey Fruit Mambo to cross the room. Geldenhuis, intent on killing Tandia, didn't see him coming. His hands closed around the gun just as the African loomed over him. He heard the sudden snarl of an animal coming in for the kill and saw a glint of gold teeth as he felt himself being lifted above the black man's head. He fired at precisely the same moment as his body smashed against the wall.

Juicey Fruit Mambo, tears streaming down his big, ugly face, bent over the bed, lifted the unconscious Tandia into his arms and carried her from the room. 'It all right, Missy Tandy, I come for you, Edward King George Juicey Fruit Mambo, he look after you now, he be warrior for you, always.' The huge black man wasn't even aware of the blood dripping from his ear where the bullet from Geldenhuis's gun had sliced off the lobe neat as anything.

SEVEN

Detective Sergeant Geldenhuis had been admitted to the exclusive Bayview Private Clinic built on the heights of the Berea overlooking the wide sweep of the bay and the city below. Mama Tequila had paid for a private room for him and, despite all the windows being open, the oppressive humidity beat the best efforts of the electric fan, which swung in a wide arc above the policeman's bed. Small beads of sweat showed on her upper lip as she fanned herself. It was going to be another stinker, and she yearned for the cooler months of July and August when the air was light and clear and the sun was warm on a person's back.

It was six in the morning and Mama Tequila was bored. She'd been waiting since dawn. Now she looked around for the hundredth time at the details of the room. Why always white? she asked herself. Why not pink? Pink would cheer a person up, make them feel better when they just had a big op. If she ever built a hospital it would be pink and then everyone in it would be a lot happier.

But she was forced to admit it was unlikely, whatever the colours of the wall or the sheets, that Geldenhuis was going to be happy when he regained consciousness. Lying there with a tube up his nose he looked a proper mess. His head was bandaged, his shoulder strapped and his arm was in a sling, the arm fractured and the collarbone broken when Juicey Fruit Mambo had smashed the policeman's body against the bedroom wall. But, of course, the real damage was the secret concealed below the starched sheet covering him from the waist down.

The cover-up was simple enough and it would hold up well if Geldenhuis agreed to co-operate, which Mama Tequila felt confident he would do. Juicey Fruit Mambo had been a different matter. He had pronounced himself anxious to see that the policeman bastard bled until he croaked. At first there was no way he was about to leave Tandia and drive Geldenhuis to where Dr Louis could operate. He only agreed to go after Mama Tequila had convinced him that the bleeding from her anus was reasonably superficial and that her face, though badly swollen, was not permanently damaged; and that besides, if she didn't get Geldenhuis to the hospital, Tandia was as good as dead anyway. But he went only on the condition that Dr Louis came back to Bluey Jay to look at Tandia.

Mama Tequila, afraid, with some justification, that the big Zulu might kill the police officer on the way to the hospital had gone with him. She also needed to get Dr Louis to co-operate with the motor accident story. Half a mile or so from Bluey Jay, she had picked the spot for the accident to be faked. Juicey Fruit Mambo had driven a hundred yards or so further on to where the road took a sudden turn around a stand of tall old blue gum trees and announced it as perfect. The police car would appear to have missed the turn and skidded off the road into one of the big trees.

Before they left, Mama Tequila had inserted a small sterile sea sponge into Tandia's rear and, despite the hot afternoon, wrapped her in a warm eiderdown. Then she had given Tandia an Amatyl tablet, hoping to calm her down sufficiently to make her sleep. She'd previously given her a stiff brandy and the combination of brandy and bromide had made Tandia groggy even before Mama Tequila left with Juicey Fruit Mambo for the hospital.

Jamal Vindoo, who had been concealed in the attic with his Leica, was the only other person left at Bluey Jay that afternoon, but Mama Tequila ruled out the possibility of his staying with Tandia. She had immediately sent him back to Durban on his motorbike with his precious spools of film and a set of instructions on what she wanted done with them. His role as photographer might just prove to be the salvation of the whole situation. She'd heard Jamal roar off on his BSA and had prayed silently, '*Please* God don't let there be a fuck-up with them photos!'

Tandia would be alone at Bluey Jay for the next two and a bit hours until either they returned from the hospital or the girls arrived by taxi from town. Juicey Fruit Mambo had suggested they take Tandia to the hospital, but Mama Tequila had also vetoed this idea. Tandia was coloured and would not be admitted, so that Dr Louis would have to examine her in the Packard. Besides, it would look far too suspicious and raise needless questions.

In her own mind, Mama Tequila had no choice. The police officer automatically qualified over Tandia for treatment. It was a matter of common sense and she wasn't about to let her heart rule her head in such a fundamental and important matter. Even if Tandia's injuries had been worse than those of the police officer, so that by leaving her behind it may have meant that Tandia would die, Mama Tequila's options remained the same. In the end Tandia was just another kaffir girl. On the other hand, the death of a white police officer in a brothel, in particular the leader of SAT, would destroy them all. Mama Tequila was prepared to sacrifice a dozen Tandias rather than to have that happen.

After Juicey Fruit Mambo had dropped Geldenhuis and Mama Tequila off at the hospital and returned to stage the accident, she confessed the entire story to Dr Louis. 'Doctor, I should have listened to you,' she said in conclusion. 'God is punishing me. I promised you I wouldn't put the child to work on her back until she finish school. I done that, Doctor. I kept my word to you! But when Detective Sergeant Geldenhuis came along, what could I do? It was blackmail, doctor. What could I have done? You tell me.'

Dr Louis patted the big woman on the shoulder. 'Mama Tequila, I'm a doctor not a priest. You did what you had to do. I'm not saying it's nice, but then who am I to say? Just the other day a patient of mine, a Jew who was in Treblinka concentration camp during the war, told me how the guilt is eating him up alive, how in the concentration camp he was what they called a Kapo, a Jew who was a policeman of his own people. He told me how he had condemned hundreds of his fellow Jews to death just so he could stay alive himself.' Dr Louis sighed. 'We are all guilty, we all do things that destroy others.'

Mama Tequila was greatly heartened by Dr Louis's observations. Her conscience wasn't in the least bit concerned nor was her soul tainted with the slightest sense of guilt. Whores are whores and life wasn't meant to be easy. If you played on the street sooner or later you got run over by the garbage truck. But the nice, safe, white Jewish conscience of Dr Louis meant he was going to cover for her. He'd as much as said so. All she had to do was push the advantage home.

Her eyes were downcast, her false eyelashes brushing her cheeks. 'I give you my word, doctor, God's honour, on my mother's grave, Tandia will never work in my house again! Never, you hear?' Mama Tequila raised her eyes slowly. It seemed to Dr Louis that the wetness of a tear made her coal-black eyes shine between the two broad strips of mascara, but he couldn't be absolutely sure.

'That's good, Mama Tequila. I am very fond of Tandia and she is going to be in a great deal of pain. I will go out to see her just as soon as I have finished with the barbarian policeman.'

'How long will that be, doctor?' Mama Tequila asked.

Dr Louis shook his head. 'It will be late, I'm afraid.

'You see, it's a big operation. He needs a general anaesthetic, maybe three hours. What has happened is very serious. I only hope I can patch him up.' His face was serious. 'The chances, well, I've got to tell you right now, they're not good.'

'You mean he could, you know, lose it?'

'Ja, that's possible, but I don't think so. A human bite is notoriously poisonous. Sepsis will undoubtedly occur. He will be in a great deal of pain for a very long time, but the bite is quite near the top, so we'll hope for the best, hey?' Dr Louis was off again explaining everything in detail. If I can stem the arterial bleeding and if the urethra is not badly crushed, that's the pipe where he urinates, we may still end up with something that dangles.' He shook his head. 'But I don't think it will give him much pleasure to look at again or even to use.'

Mama Tequila was genuinely shocked. 'What do you mean, doctor? You mean, he can't make love no more . . . ever?'

'Well, ja, perhaps even that. It's not so much the scar tissue and the damaged arteries that will inhibit some of the blood from getting through, the psychological damage to his self-esteem will be enormous. This, on its own, is capable of causing erectile failure.'

Despite her anxiety, a slow smile spread over Mama Tequila's face and she clapped her hands in delight. '*Wragtig!* There is a God in heaven! You mean you can fix him up so he can do it, but really he can't, because he too ashamed of his one-eyed snake?' She giggled gleefully. 'Just wait till Juicey Fruit Mambo hears about this!'

A nurse came over and told Dr Louis it was time to scrub up. Mama Tequila held onto his arm. 'Please, doctor, you must let me see him first when he wakes up. I beg you, I must be the first to see him, even before the police. It is very important.'

'I understand, Mama Tequila. I'll drop out to Bluey Jay to take a look at Tandia Patel after I've finished here. I'll let you know then when it will be okay to see the patient. You might as well go home now, it won't be tonight, that's for sure.'

Juicey Fruit Mambo returned to fetch Mama Tequila and he drove her to Pickering Street. They pulled up outside the sewing-machine shop and he helped Mama Tequila out of the back of the car. 'Don't wait here, come back for me in half an hour, you hear?' He watched as she walked slowly down the side passage to the back of the shop, and when a strip of light appeared as the door was opened, he drove off.

Jamal Vindoo was a handsome young man with a complexion the colour of crystallised honey. He appeared to be in his mid twenties and had grown a Clark Gable moustache, perhaps to give his boyish good looks a little more maturity or because he thought it would make him more attractive to the girls. Clark Gable moustaches were all the rage with the young guys at Bombay University where he had studied, to his father's immense pride.

He ushered Mama Tequila into a small reception area which contained two wicker chairs and a small wicker couch, on which were fitted cushions of bright Indian cotton. A matching wicker coffee table, draped with an elaborately embroidered shawl, took up the remainder of the space. Standing in the centre of the table was a brass vase which contained a dozen or so brightly coloured yellow, pink and red paper roses and a round brass ashtray. On a small shelf on the wall furthermost from the door burned the *Deepam*, or God lamp; placed beside it, in a miniature brass vase, burned a single stick of incense.

To anyone entering the room there was no hint that it was a photography studio. The only picture on the wall was a large oval walnut frame which contained an old-fashioned hand tinted photograph of a much younger Mr Dine-o-mite, who looked sternly out into the world through his pebble, steel-rimmed glasses, wearing his best Mahatma Gandhi lookalike expression.

'Sit, please.' Jamal Vindoo casually indicated a chair and then, realising Mama Tequila's size, moved his hand to denote the wicker couch. 'May I bring you some refreshment, some cha perhaps, Pepsi?'

Mama Tequila shook her head and got straight down to business. 'Sit, Mr Vindoo. Look, I want to thank you again for coming. The man who does it other times is in hospital with pneumonia.' It seemed appropriate to exaggerate the previous photographer's bout of 'flu. 'You did me a big favour; you came, no questions asked, I liked that!' She looked at him, her face grim. 'What you saw today is very serious. If it got out what happened, I'm telling you, man, they throw us into jail and they throw away the bladdy key!' With a groan she eased herself down into the wicker couch and, opening her handbag, produced her silver cigarette case and Zippo, which she placed on the coffee table beside the ashtray.

Jamal Vindoo looked hurt. 'You can trust me implicitly in this matter. I am a very discreet person, Madam Tequila.'

'Not Madam! In my profession that mean something else. Mama, Mama Tequila.' The words 'discreet' and 'implicitly' grated on Mama Tequila; so did the young Indian's carefully modulated stuck-up accent. She sighed heavily. 'In my experience, *trust* is always a matter of how much money. *Discreet*, that a question of how much more.' She dug into her handbag and produced an envelope which she held out to him. 'In here is fifty pounds.'

Jamal Vindoo took the envelope, and as he did so he bowed his head. 'You are very generous, Mama Tequila. I will fetch the prints.' He started to walk towards the door leading to the interior of the studio, and stepped through a curtained doorway leading to an interior room. A few moments later Jamal Vindoo returned with a large manila envelope which he handed to Mama Tequila.

Mama Tequila looked up at the young man. 'In here is everything I asked for?'

Jamal Vindoo nodded. He stood over her with both hands in his trouser pockets, jiggling his goolies. 'Sure, two ten-by-eights and three five-by-four prints of everything, just as you asked.'

Mama Tequila withdrew a fat pile of photographs. The young Indian photographer had been away from Bluey Jay less than four hours and he must have worked hard to get the prints ready. She was pleased with what she saw. The photographs were well contrasted and perfectly in focus. In some he had used a zoom lens with devastating effect. Mama Tequila's heart thumped as she looked at his work. For the first time she understood clearly what had happened, from the moment Tandia had stepped out of her dress with her back turned to Geldenhuis to the arrival of Juicey Fruit Mambo.

She halted momentarily when she came to the first shot where Tandia stood naked. The photograph framed Tandia's body perfectly, with only Geldenhuis's hand and part of his arm reaching out into the picture. To Mama Tequila, Tandia was simply and utterly exquisite.

Jamal Vindoo had felt the same way. Tandia's beauty had left him devastated from the moment the solution in the developing tray brought her into being. He was aware of his hand shaking as he washed the print and pegged it to the drying line. With this picture alone he had disobeyed Mama Tequila's orders and had printed two ten-by-eights for himself.

The light kicking back from the overhead mirror moulded Tandia's body perfectly and he told himself, as a professional photographer, it was his duty to keep these prints for his portfolio. Besides, without the police officer, whose name he didn't know, the picture was not incriminating. There could be no possible harm in owning it. Despite Tandia's apparent vocation, the young girl with the beautiful sad expression held such great emotional appeal for him that he knew he would not be able to rest until he got to know her.

'Where are the negatives?' Mama Tequila asked.

His hands still in his pockets, Jamal Vindoo shrugged. 'You asked only for the prints. A photographer always keeps his negatives.'

There was a pause. 'I see,' Mama Tequila said. Then she looked up at him smiling. 'How much?'

Jamal too smiled. This was turning out much easier than he'd expected. 'Negatives are a photographer's bread and butter. People re-order, sometimes years later.' His right eyebrow was slightly arched. 'You never know who or where these orders will come from, do you?'

Mama Tequila made a note to get to know him better. He was clever and he was corrupt. It was a combination she understood and generally found to be useful in a young man. 'Okay, sonny, let's talk!' She smiled, then pointed to the oval picture on the wall. 'Your daddy has told me how proud he is of you, Jamal. He tells me you the first one in his family, even if you could go back three hundred years, even more, who has been to the university. *Magtig!* He thinks the sun and also the moon shine out of your backside!'

Jamal Vindoo looked slightly uncomfortable as he too looked up at the picture of his father. 'He is a good man, even, in his own way, an *éminence grise*.'

'You can say that again! *Eminence* is right. Only the other day I heard they going to make him a member of the Indian Academy! This is a very big exclusive honour for a man who didn't go even to high school.'

'Yes, he's delighted, election to the Academy is very important to him.'

'Not only him, man! Only very high-up Indians are on that thing.' Mama Tequila paused, 'Your father, he is more than a good man, you hear? More, much more! Your father is a man a person can trust!' She produced a small handkerchief from her bag and, sighing, dabbed at the corners of her eyes. She replaced the hanky and withdrew an envelope which she offered to the young Indian photographer. 'Here, open it, see what is inside.'

Jamal Vindoo took the envelope while Mama Tequila returned to scrummaging in her bag. The photograph he withdrew from the envelope lacked the quality of his own work but the subject and detail was unmistakable. It showed Mr Dine-o-mite in the nude, his small body and spindly legs no bigger than those of a prepubescent boy. He still wore his steel-rimmed glasses and his face carried a slightly bemused expression as Sarah knelt in front of him, enclosing him.

'Ag, here it is!' Mama Tequila exclaimed as she produced a second envelope. 'The negative!' She removed the negative and held it up for him to see, then she replaced it in the envelope.

Without a word Jamal rose and, placing the picture he held back into its envelope, he put it into his shirt pocket and disappeared through the curtained doorway. He returned a minute or two later carrying a second envelope which he dropped on Mama Tequila's lap.

Mama Tequila looked up and smiled, fanning herself with the envelope containing the negative of Jamal's daddy. The young photographer now stood in front of her, a surly expression on his handsome young face, his hand arrogantly proffered, ready to take the envelope she held.

Mama Tequila continued to fan herself with it, seemingly unaware of his open hand. Jamal felt his hand grow heavy, as though it suddenly contained too much blood. Every muscle in his body strained to snatch the envelope but he lacked the courage to do so. Mama Tequila held her small smile and he found himself mesmerised, quite unable to act. He bit down hard on his back teeth to prevent himself from crying out in frustration.

Still smiling, Mama Tequila put the envelope he had given her into her bag. Then, to Jamal's consternation, she also replaced the envelope containing the negative. This was too much for the young Indian. 'That negative belongs to me now!' he expostulated.

Mama Tequila reached forward and withdrew a cork-tip from the silver case and, squinting, lit it with her Zippo. Inhaling deeply, she rested back into the wicker couch and blew a cloud of blue smoke into the young man's crutch. Finally she looked up at him. 'Negatives are a madam's bread and butter.' She arched her eyebrow slightly, imitating his own earlier expression. 'You never know when and how you going to need them, do you?'

When Jamal Vindoo hadn't snatched the envelope from her hand, Mama Tequila knew she'd broken him. She picked up her silver cigarette case and thumbed it open, offering it to Jamal. 'Cigarette?'

The young photographer bent down gratefully and took a cigarette from the silver case, lighting it from the Zippo Mama Tequila held. Then he moved over to sit in the wicker chair nearest to her.

Mama Tequila's voice was businesslike. 'Your pictures are good, man. I can use you. Ten pounds with the negative. That for every client.' She drew on her cigarette, then exhaled. 'What do you say, Mr Photographer?'

Jamal Vindoo suddenly burst into laughter. Bending forward he stubbed his cigarette into the brass ashtray. 'You know something? I don't even smoke!' he exclaimed. Turning to her he extended his hand. 'You got a deal, Mama Tequila, but only if I get that negative of my father!'

Mama Tequila rose slowly. 'I'll do better than that, my boy.' She plucked a paper rose from the brass vase on the table and held it to the God lamp on the wall. The crinkly paper flared and blazed. Taking the envelope from her bag, she held the corner to the blazing rose, and finally, when the flames threatened to burn her fingers, she dropped what remained of it into the brass ashtray. She added the wire stem of the spent rose to the ashtray and withdrew a second, which she now lit. 'Here, give me that photo of your daddy.' She held her hand out and Jamal Vindoo hastily withdrew the photograph from his shirt pocket and handed it to her. Mama Tequila touched it to the burning rose and waited until it was well alight before she added it to the ashtray. With a melodramatic sigh, she said, 'There you are, finish and klaar! No more bad luck for someone who is nearly, almost, but now definitely going to be a member of the Indian Academy of South Africa!'

Jamal Vindoo rose from his chair and extended his hand. 'Mama Tequila, I have acted in a churlish and reprehensible manner, I apologise.'

Mama Tequila grinned and before shaking his hand she placed the second spent rose into the ashtray. 'First apologise for the dirty language, jong! What means *churlish* and *reprehensible*, also, I know what means *éminence*, but what means *éminence grease*?'

Jamal laughed, embarrassed. 'It means a person of great respect who has grey hair.'

'Ja that is a good way to think of your daddy,' Mama Tequila said, gathering up her cigarette case and Zippo and moving towards the door. 'Thank you, Jamal, it was a pleasure to do business with you, you hear?'

Mama Tequila and Juicey Fruit Mambo returned to Bluey Jay to find that Dr Louis had just arrived and was attending to Tandia. He had given her a local anaesthetic and was making a proctoscopic examination. The area was badly swollen and while the muscle hadn't been torn she required quite a bit of sewing up. The effects of the barbiturate had largely worn off and Tandia was awake and in a lot of pain when he arrived. The needle he used for the anaesthetic needed to be inserted in several places and Tandia, biting into the soft part of her thumb, drew blood trying to refrain from screaming. Now, as he stitched her, Dr Louis said, 'Tandia, you're going to be extremely sore for the next couple of weeks and must go on a diet of soft food only. I will treat the infection with sulphur drugs and you must rest for at least a week. You can't go to school until you can sit down again.'

Tears ran down Tandia's cheeks as she spoke. 'When will that be, Dr Louis?'

Dr Louis stroked her brow. 'No use going for a couple of weeks, I'd say.' He touched the cheekbone just below her left eye. 'Anyway, my girl, you're going to have a doosey of a black eye, you don't want to go to school wearing a shiner like this, do you?'

'We're doing our matriculation trials, I can't miss them!' Tandia's consternation was obvious.

'Look, I'll come every day and help you with your Latin and science. I think I'm still good for those. Maybe maths also. The rest is just silly stuff you can study on your own.' Dr Louis withdrew two small bottles. He held up the first. 'These, they're called Amatyl, you take one at night before you go to sleep for the next week.' He held up the second bottle. 'These are painkillers, you take two every four hours.' He was about to put the pills on the table beside her when Juicey Fruit Mambo's hand appeared and took the bottles from him.

Dr Louis turned in surprise. He had been aware that Mama Tequila had entered the room while he had been examining Tandia but he hadn't seen the black man enter and stand quietly beside the window directly behind him.

Juicey Fruit Mambo sensed what Dr Louis was thinking. 'I been nurse aide one time, I will look after Missy Tandy, doctor.' He grinned. 'I hear also for de food, only soft, very soft. I will make for her.'

Dr Louis turned back to Mama Tequila. 'I will come every day for the next week or so.' He saw Mama Tequila's expression and put his hand up. 'Don't worry, no fee. You pay for the barbarian in hospital, I'll take care of Tandia.' He placed his hand on Tandia's shoulder. 'It's going to be a bit painful when the anaesthetic wears off but Juicey Fruit Mambo will give you a pill. You've had a hard time, but you're going to be all right. I'll come and see you tomorrow. Goodbye, Tandia.' He rose and gathered his stethoscope and other belongings from the bed and placed them in his bag.

'Is he, you know, is he going to die, Doctor?' Tandia asked fearfully.

Dr Louis laughed. 'No fear! But he's going to be a very sick policeman for a while.'

'I'm sorry, I didn't mean it! I tried to do what Mama Tequila said. I don't know how it happened. Will they throw me in jail?' she sobbed.

Dr Louis took Tandia into his arms. 'Sssh! Tandia, take it easy, hey? Nothing is going to happen to you. You go to sleep now. In the morning it will be all right, you'll see.' He lowered Tandia onto the bed and pulled the eiderdown over her. 'You poor little bugger,' he said softly as he rose and moved to the door.

'Thank you, doctor, thank you for coming to see me.'

Dr Louis stood at the door. 'You couldn't do me a favour could you, Tandia?' He didn't wait for her to reply. 'You couldn't get a first-class matric and then study law and then take on the barbarians in Pretoria and beat the bastards hollow, could you?'

Tandia nodded through her tears. 'Ja, doctor, I promise,' she said, her voice barely above a whisper.

Dr Louis waited for Mama Tequila to pass through the door before he shut it quietly behind him, leaving Juicey Fruit Mambo with Tandia.

'Is she going to be truly orright, doctor?' Mama Tequila asked as they walked down the yellowwood corridor.

'Ja, physically, yes, the revolver did surprisingly little damage. It is more the shock than the physical aspect which concerns me. The body can heal but the mind takes a lot longer. That's why I will come every day for the next week. She will be very depressed. It is important to keep her mind on other things.'

Mama Tequila felt reassured by his words. Mental anxiety was the prostitute's lot in life. You learned to cope, to bury the hurt and the fear so deep that you sometimes found it difficult to find. It was better to be hard. It was best to get that over with when you were young.

At the top of the stairs they found Jasmine waiting. 'How is she, doctor?' she asked shyly. Jasmine was a Cape Malay and a favourite among the girls, quiet as a mouse.

'You can go in, sit with her if you like. She's a bit upset now, but she's going to be all right,' Dr Louis said.

Mama Tequila glanced at her watch. The little prostitute reacted immediately. 'Sarah said it was okay, Mama Tequila? We only got five clients, she said I could come?'

'Ja, okay, but not too long, you hear.' She looked at her watch again. 'It could get busy before midnight. Juicey Fruit Mambo is also with Tandia. Tell him he must go and help Sarah in the bar.'

'Yes, Mama T. Goodnight, doctor,' Jasmine said, hurrying away.

Jasmine opened the door to Tandia's room quietly. Tandia was lying on her side with her back to the door and Juicey Fruit Mambo stood to attention at the foot of her bed. The huge black man held his hands clasped in front of him and slow tears rolled down his cheeks. There was absolute silence in the room and he seemed not to notice Jasmine's entrance until she walked over to him and took his arm. Standing on tiptoe, she whispered Mama Tequila's instructions. Juicey Fruit Mambo nodded and walked from the room, making no attempt to stem his tears.

Jasmine let herself down carefully onto the bed and placed her hand on Tandia's shoulder. After a while she began to hum an old slave lullaby her grandmother had sung to her as a child. The words finally broke free from the hum, sad and sweet and low and comforting . . .

Slaap Piccaninny
Die vee's in die kraal
Almal my skapies
en bokkies . . .
More vroeg kry jy
van soet pap en maal
en'n paar spier-wit sokkies . . .
Doo Doo . . . !
Doo Doo . . . !

Although it was only a song about a small herd boy who, having put the sheep and goats away for the night, could dream of a breakfast of sweet porridge and a pair of snowy white socks, it carried with it a great yearning for freedom and a cry for the beloved country. A silly little lullaby that contained all the love of the coloured people for their land and their place in it. A song of the twilight people, the words washed in the tears of the forgotten tribe.

Geldenhuis stirred. Even before he sensed the pain in his groin he felt the rawness in his throat and then, as though it was moving up slowly from somewhere deep inside of him, the pain arrived. It pushed remorselessly to the forefront of his consciousness until he could feel the sweat of it break out on his forehead and the sharp singing of it in his head as the pain buzzed him, roaring through his body. A glass of water was held to his mouth and he gulped at it greedily. 'Not too much, you'll vomit.' The glass was pulled away and the cool water down his throat seemed to evaporate in seconds as the furnace of pain burned through every nerve and muscle and sinew in his body. He thought he could hear himself crying, but he wasn't sure. Maybe it was someone else, someone in another room. The pain was beyond crying. Crying wouldn't help it. It was beyond the simple business of anguish or the false hope of a scream. It ate at him, it had huge jaws which tore at his flesh, like a pack of hyenas tearing at a carcass in the dark. A dark night. No moon. Just the tearing of flesh and the crunching of bones somewhere out there in the darkness. He felt a stab of cold on his arm, a small square of ice that burned, not like the other, but a pain no less, then a stab, everything exaggerated, everything bigger than him, bigger than he could possibly bear. A mountain of pain sat between his legs; then the relief as the morphine struck his brain and took hold of his body and blanketed down his pain, patting it into place, leaving him gasping with sweat-soaked relief.

'The kaffir! The fokking kaffir with the gold teeth! I'll kill the black bastard!' These were the first words that came from his mouth. Then he lay still for a long time, panting, his chest heaving. Outside, in the tropical garden, the birds filled the air with morning sound.

'Water, someone give me some water,' Geldenhuis croaked. The nurse had left with the hypodermic needle in a small, kidney-shaped metal dish covered with a white napkin. Mama Tequila rose from her chair and held the glass to his lips. Geldenhuis drank deeply and she took a chance and let him drink the glass down. This seemed to make him feel a little better and he opened his eyes. At first they remained blank, then the sense appeared in them, like a pebble plopped into still water. 'Mama Tequila? Where am I?'

'Lie still, you a very sick person, Detective Sergeant.' Geldenhuis tried to move his head but the pain cut through the effects of the morphine. He stared helplessly at Mama Tequila.

'What happened? Where is this place?' He seemed overcome by the effort to talk and closed his eyes again.

'You had a bad accident, Detective Sergeant. Listen very carefully, don't say nothing, you hear? Jus' listen. You were going to see a farmer by the name of Van Jaarsveld, remember? He lives about two miles before Bluey

Jay.' After the long wait for him to regain consciousness, when she had rehearsed the story a hundred times, Mama Tequila was now only too anxious to get the story out. 'His wife, she phoned you, her husband been having it off with the kaffir girl servant.' Mama Tequila dug into her handbag and produced a note. 'I wrote it all down here, everything, just like it happened.' She held it open in front of Geldenhuis. 'Open your eyes, man, you got to read it!'

Geldenhuis hadn't indicated that he'd heard a word but now he opened his eyes and started to read the note, reading a few lines then closing his eyes and then having another go, until he nodded his head imperceptibly. 'Read it again, sergeant! It very important. You have to tell this to the police when they come!'

'More water!' Geldenhuis croaked. Mama Tequila poured a fresh glass from the water jug beside his bed and again he drank the whole glass down. His eyes were bright, almost as though he was in a fever. 'You lying, you hear, I remember everything, now! You fokked, you hear? You finish and klaar!' The anger showed clearly in the policeman's face as his mind started to rebuild the incident at Bluey Jay.

'Please, Detective Sergeant, I beg you!' Mama Tequila held the piece of paper in front of him again. 'Read it, this is what happened, I'm telling you, it's the only way! I'm begging you, on my bended knees, Detective Sergeant Geldenhuis!'

Geldenhuis closed his eyes when Mama Tequila placed the note in front of him. Now he opened them again. 'I swear it, I'm going to kill you and that black bitch who bit me . . . and the kaffir! The kaffir with the gold teeth! You all dead, you all fokking dead kaffirs, you hear!' He closed his eyes again and lay still, panting from the effort of his outburst.

'Open you eyes, Detective Sergeant Geldenhuis,' Mama Tequila said softly. Geldenhuis opened his eyes and the shock of what he saw pulled his body rigid. The pain cut through the effects of the morphine and he nearly passed out. Mama Tequila held a ten-by-eight print of him standing behind Tandia, the snout of his police revolver pushed deeply into her while his left hand held his erection. In the photograph he was grinning, and every detail, the blood running down the inside of Tandia's thigh, even the chamber of the revolver showed clearly in the picture. Geldenhuis closed his eyes and two large tears ran down his cheeks.

'Okay! Now fok off you black bitch!'

'No, sergeant, not before you read the note one more time!' Mama Tequila held it open again in front of him. Then, when he'd nodded, she folded it and put it into her handbag. 'I will pay for you while you here. You got a broken pelvis also, that what Dr Louis Rabin going to say,' she pointed to the sheet covering his waist, 'to explain what happened down there. You can't be moved, you hear? Not for a long time. The doctor, he will see the police when they come. You can't have no visitors today, you too sick.' The big woman rose stiffly from the chair beside him and gave a big sigh as she moved from the room. She wasn't stupid and she knew enough about men like Geldenhuis to know that the nightmare had only just begun.

On her way out she stopped to see the night sister. 'Please, sister, you have got perhaps a favourite charity?' She opened her purse and took from it two five-pound notes. 'I want to show my very sincere appreciation. As you can see I am a very small person who is not possible to see in a place like this so early in the morning?'

The sister smiled. 'You don't need to do this. Dr Rabin already told us you weren't here this morning.'

'No, take it, please!' Mama Tequila pressed the notes into the woman's hand.

'Thank you! I will use this money for the African baby clinic I run in Clairwood every Saturday.'

Mama Tequila laughed. 'Ag, babies! In my line of work, sister, that a dirty word!' She turned and walked slowly down the corridor and into the sunlight where Juicey Fruit Mambo, polishing the bonnet of the Packard, waited for her.

'Edward King George Juicey Fruit Mambo, I think we going to be okay.' She paused and sank back into the soft leather of the Packard's rear seat, closing her eyes. 'For the time being, anyway.'

'I think you very, very clever madam, madam!' Juicey Fruit Mambo announced as he switched on the ignition and turned the big car into the hospital driveway. The Packard's tyres scrunched on the gravel as they drove past a long bed of scarlet canna under a blaze of flamboyant trees. Sitting opposite the road as they turned out of the gate were two grey rhesus monkeys. 'I think that policeman he got friends who come to visit,' Juicey Fruit Mambo giggled. But Mama Tequila didn't hear him, she was already asleep.

Any half-decent police enquiry would have shot holes through the accident staged to explain Geldenhuis's injuries. After all, most arrangements contrived in a crisis fall apart on closer examination. But it wasn't in the interests of the SAT Squad to dig too deeply. Geldenhuis had corroborated the evidence Mama Tequila and Juicey Fruit Mambo had given the investigating sergeant, who wasn't trying to be Sherlock Holmes anyway.

Old Coetzee, who was the magistrate appointed to preside at the routine enquiry, saw no reason to ask a whole bunch of awkward questions. He ruled that the accident was due to the driver's failure to correct his steering while attempting to avoid an animal crossing the road.

Of course there were rumours, but these were dismissed by most solid burghers as too bizarre and silly to entertain. The 'cop in the boot' was a hero as well as a clean-cut, upright boxing type. Geldenhuis's 'broken pelvis' mended in about three months, which meant his return fight with Gideon Mandoma had to be cancelled. It wouldn't take place for twelve months or so now, the time it would take his bones to knit properly and for him to get back into fighting trim.

In mid January, when Geldenhuis was only halfway through his recovery, the matriculation results came out. Tandia achieved a first-class matric with distinctions in four subjects and a high distinction in Latin.

Tandia called Dr Louis Rabin and Sonny Vindoo when she obtained her results and, in her mind, there now remained only one more thing to do. After lunch that afternoon she persuaded Juicey Fruit Mambo to drive her in the Packard to the Christian Indian cemetery where Patel was buried. Going back was a difficult thing for her to do and for a while she simply sat in the car outside the little graveyard, trying to summon up enough courage to enter.

From where she sat she could see over the wrought-iron fence; the tall marble cross to which she had been handcuffed still stood there. Strangely, she could barely remember the policeman who had raped her. It was the dark spectre of Geldenhuis who lurked in the shadows of her consciousness. This was where it had all started, where the nightmare had begun. Her fear of Geldenhuis had never really left her; it would come out of the blue like a punch in the belly, or lurk like a grey shadow at the edge of her mind. Sometimes it was the first thing to happen when she awakened. At other times it arrived suddenly, striking at her when she was reading a book. Then again, it came like a slap in the face when she was cooking or making a bed or warming a brandy glass for a client in the bar. It was always with her, a little bit or a lot. The only place it didn't seem to come was when she climbed out onto the branch of the old wild fig tree at night and sat in her silver cocoon. The fearful presence of Geldenhuis hadn't found her there, didn't seem to know about this place or couldn't come through her bedroom window.

Juicey Fruit Mambo, sensing Tandia's melancholy, climbed from behind the wheel and went to sit in the back of the car. 'I am very tired today, Miss Tandy. Last night de frogs dey make many, many noise outside my house by the river!' Juicey Fruit Mambo had his own room in the outbuildings behind Bluey Jay but preferred to live in the kraal with his adoring gang of kids. Now he crossed his arms and with a deep sigh closed his eyes. In a matter of seconds he commenced to perform an exaggerated pantomime of feigned sleep, so much so that his pretend snores softened the edge of Tandia's anxiety and gave her the courage to leave the safety of the car and enter the gates of the cemetery.

In the fifteen months since Tandia had left him, Patel's grave had changed. The rounded mound had been flattened and a carpet of untidy grass and dandelion weed now covered the red clay. An ostentatious polished black basalt tombstone had replaced the wooden cross. To Tandia the makeshift wooden cross had seemed more appropriate to the business of death. There seemed to be something slightly obscene about a squared-off block of hard polished granite planted above the slow and natural decay of dust to dust.

Tandia read the inscription on the black tombstone.

Natkin Patel.
Born 6th January 1898,
died 14th October 1952.
Boxing promoter and businessman,
beloved daddy of Billy and Teddy,
husband of Injira Patel.

'And father of Tandia Patel, who just got a first-class matric, hooray!' Tandia was suddenly no longer afraid. 'We did it, Patel! Four distinctions and a high distinction in Latin! What do you think of that, Mr Boxing Promoter! Mr Well Known in White Circus!' She laughed happily. 'What do you think of that, hey, Dad, Daddy, Pa, Pop?' She used all the pronouns together and they fitted perfectly, natural as anything. Patel had come back to her, he loved her again, that was for sure!

EIGHT

Tandia had grown to understand a lot more about life and the way she fitted into it in the fifteen months she'd been at Bluey Jay. Her final year at school had shown a remarkable change in her. Though still a loner, she was now prepared to assert herself, and she discovered in the process that the other girls would defer to her if she pressed an issue or suggested an opinion. Her very separateness was the strength they now perceived in her. She was no longer seen as a lonely little girl, but as someone who seemed to fill the space around her, content with her own presence, independent and confident.

In fact, Tandia's aloneness and independence had always been a part of her. Parted from her mother when she was no more than a toddler, being alone had become the state of mind in which she existed. She was skilled in the art of the camouflage, giving out only sufficient of herself to fulfil whatever role she was obliged to play.

With Patel she had been expected to perform two roles, one as servant and the other as revenge on his two fat-headed sons. Maid and schoolgirl. Useful to him as a general factotum and reward for his ego. She had played both roles well. At home she had been eager to please and had never complained or shirked her work. At school she had been the quiet-as-a-mouse outsider, the little girl who didn't quite belong, but who worked well enough and hard enough not to be noticed. Tandia had performed these ordinary parts so well that she had become all but invisible, the role of servant to the Patel household and that of Patel's ego-boosting bastard schoolgirl daughter substituting for a life which, in her mind, she had postponed until she grew up.

But at Bluey Jay it was different. Now she knew herself to be ready at last to grow up. The obligations of her childhood were over. She existed for herself alone. Sitting in her silver cocoon in the branches of the old wild fig tree, she would look through the canopy of leaves up at the night sky until she found a single star which by a careful framing of leaf and branch she could isolate, so it appeared to shine alone in the firmament, a single pinpoint of light in an eternity of space. Tandia would imagine herself as the star, absolutely alone in the firmament, destined to be a sufficiency in herself.

Because she was surrounded by girls who thought of little else but physical attraction, she began to see herself in these terms as well, and the constant claims of envy at her looks from the other girls led her to understand that she was beautiful. This was really the first thing she owned by herself, without an obligation to someone else. She began to understand the difference in the way men looked at her, began to sense the power which lay within her. If she was beautiful, that was power; if she was intelligent, that too was power. Both used together suggested ambitions which each on their own could not achieve. If she added to this the camouflage she was already skilled at employing, she had the key to surviving. But it was a key which also opened lonely, empty places in her personality.

At Bluey Jay Tandia now learned how to adapt to her environment so that she could not only survive it, but use it for her benefit. She could hide behind other people's perceptions of her while remaining true to a personality which grew from her aloneness, her fears and, increasingly, from an aching need within her to be loved.

Tandia had had no love experience. Love for her had always been a matter of seeking approbation. If you pleased someone enough they would love you in return. Now, she knew this to be naive. She sensed that love was something else, without knowing how to go about discovering what it was. Even her loving of Sarah, her first touching-with-the-fingertips love, she now knew to have been a sisterly act and a physical gratification for Sarah – no more. Except for the very first time, Sarah had made no attempt to comfort her or to chase away the dark shadows. She had seemed unable to share in a secret intimacy of silences understood and of loving whispers sucked into the pores of her being like warm sunshine. Sarah was a working girl who had scraped herself off the pavement too often in life to venture beyond the emotional possibilities of simple sexual gratification.

Not long after Mama Tequila had terminated Tandia's liaison with Sarah, Tandia came to see clearly that the act of becoming physically attached to someone at Bluey Jay would rob her of the power she had as a beautiful woman. Her expectation of sex with a man in the loving sense, the way she heard the girls talk about in a yearning, sighing way, was deeply, if not permanently, buried by her fear and guilt.

Sex was a commodity which surrounded them all. It was the stock on the shelves of the shop in which they worked. Tandia saw that what was on sale to clients at Bluey Jay was not what she wanted or needed or expected to have. It was not a path along which she was likely to find the kind of love she needed. There was no morality involved in this decision; the luxury of a moral stand in a whorehouse was understandably not available to her. The love she hoped for, but never expected to find, had no physical aspect and so she didn't know if she'd even recognise it, should it ever come within her reach. And so Tandia put it aside. She would survive without whatever it was she knew to be missing in her personality. Someone who knew her well might simply conclude that she lacked an understanding of love, that it was an experience she had never felt, so that she was unable to love in the all-consuming and selfless sense. But then, of course, there was nobody who knew her remotely well enough to draw any such conclusion.

Prior to her brutalisation by Geldenhuis, Tandia had accepted Mama Tequila's right to work her on her back after she had completed high school. She had even thought of it as a perfectly legitimate way to earn sufficient money to pay her way through university. But after her experience with Geldenhuis she knew that, come what may, she could not be turned into a working girl. Not by anyone, not for anything. Tandia knew that the instinct which had made her bite Geldenhuis would assert itself again. It was the first time she had tasted hate and she now knew she could live with it. She understood fear and she now understood hate. She could exercise charm and power over those around her; this would have to be enough to survive in the hostile grown-up world she found herself in.

Dr Louis sought Tandia out whenever he visited Bluey Jay. He had become very attached to her and would encourage her by talking dreamily of her prospects. 'Tandia, you're the first of a new breed, the new Africa. The brain hasn't been called grey matter for nothing, you know! It has no colour bar. When your kind have shown the barbarians in Pretoria that you are intellectually just as sound, just as good as they are, they can no longer call you savages. One day we will have a new class system in South Africa, like the rest of the civilised world! A system based on a person's ability. You, my dear, will be one of the beautiful new South Africans.'

But one of the barbarians in Pretoria, the Minister, among other things, of Bantu Education, Doctor Hendrik Verwoerd, was taking no such chances. Not too long after Dr Louis had his dream, Verwoerd invented a new little kink in the Bantu educational system: 'The Bantu is inferior! Science has proved his brain size is smaller than the whites. Therefore they cannot hope to compete with the white man!' To prove this, the all-white parliament passed the Bantu Education Act. It forbade the Bantu people from learning the same subjects at the same level as the white student and set up a separate curriculum which educated the blacks and the coloureds to virtual serfdom.

'Nice one, Verwoerd!' the white part of the nation cried in appreciation and tucked him into their minds as a future prime minister.

Girls were taught Domestic Science, a euphemism for washing and ironing, cooking and other domestic chores. They were taught arithmetic, but only sufficient to count the change when the missus sent them to the shops. Boys became carpenters and builders and all the other manual labour niceties which involve dirt, sweat and broken bones and which allow an overclass to be supported by an underclass of skilful hewers of wood and careful wielders of water.

In one hit, Doctor Verwoerd, one day to be the chief white honcho, the Prime Minister of South Africa, had smashed the Aristotelian concept that the mind shall decide the priorities for mankind and be the arena in which equality is decided.

The black people, trying to reach for the stars, were being educated with their faces pushed into the dirt. Skin tone was winning over grey matter. Dr Louis's barbarians were in full cry.

Dr Louis would hold Tandia's hand, as though she was a person he liked a lot. He was so genuine in his enthusiasm for his lovely dream that Tandia began to believe it too, if only for the hour he would spend with her going over her essays and cluck-clucking over her Latin tenses.

He was a Latin nut and was probably responsible for Tandia's high distinction in the subject. Over the months of her final year at high school he had often visited Tandia to work with her on her Latin and maths, and over the cramming weeks before her matriculation he would come almost every day. He was the first person she had called after receiving her matriculation results. Sonny Vindoo was second. 'Jolly, very good show, Miss Tandy, we are having a very big celebration and I am awarding you a new dress, any colour, any style, any material your very superior mind desires!'

Tandia's relationship with Mama Tequila was a curious one. She admired the fat woman greatly and saw in her some of the things she was beginning to understand about herself. Tandia instinctively knew that Mama Tequila had hidden her own feelings so deeply and so long ago that she would not know where to find them even if she ever did need to use them again. The apparent dichotomy in her persona was perfectly predicated so she could function with the very minimum of emotional energy. She was a clown to her clients and a business person who saw her working girls as a commodity she referred to as whore, in the same way as a draper might refer to cloth or a sheep farmer to wool. On the flip side of the Mama Tequila coin was a woman who ran a stable of whores for profit. The only emotional energy she spent with them was in order to make them better at making money. The working girls gave her credit for kindness and personal attention to their needs which Tandia could see was seldom justified. They praised her frequently and boosted the old woman's ego so that they could feel themselves needed and loved. Tandia, at sixteen, was perhaps too harsh a judge, but you grow up pretty quickly in a brothel, and she soon learned to look for the motive when Mama Tequila appeared to show someone a kindness or took the trouble to talk one of the girls out of a misery. It was rare that she couldn't find one. Mama Tequila was as much a part of Tandia's education into grown-up life as Dr Louis or Sonny Vindoo. The only difference was that she trusted the two men but not, for a single moment, the old woman.

And so goodness and badness arrived together in Tandia's life. By watching Mama Tequila cover her every move with deception and blackmail, Tandia learned a great deal about the principles of fighting and surviving the unjust systems of the white man. Tandia's beautiful green eyes were becoming less and less wide-eyed as she grew to understand the price of freedom for the underclass in South Africa.

Sonny Vindoo would often speak to her of Mahatma Gandhi, how he had come to South Africa to challenge the precepts of apartheid with the absolute logic of a fine legal mind; how, with ruthless authority and undeniable credentials, he presented to his opponents in the South African government under Jan Christiaan Smuts the absurdity of the concept of racial inferiority based on colour or creed. 'Miss Tandy, evil can withstand truth for a very, very long time. Evil is a very clever bugger, but in the end, truth, you can be sure, will prevail.' He would look directly at her through his pebble glasses: 'British Justice, my dear, it will win the day.' He said this in such a way that Tandia imagined British Justice as a troop of cavalry, a cloud of dust on the horizon, riding to the rescue of the coloureds and blacks of Africa. The fact that British Justice had hitherto shown very little truth and almost no equality for the black man, nor had it shown any inclination to lead the race relations of South Africa from darkness into the light, didn't seem to concern Sonny Vindoo in the least. He and Dr Louis were on the same side against the overwhelming forces of evil. They were both soft men in the hard fight which lay ahead. Tandia loved them dearly, but she knew, in the end, South Africa would need the hard-as-diamonds Juicey Fruit Mambos to rise up and crush the oppressor more than it would need the strawberry mousse of white liberalism. Truth and justice had failed to appear when needed and so had no further part to play in the settlement of the scores. She had felt the cold, remorseless steel and the ripping, cuffing, sliding of a gun barrel inside her. She knew what it was going to take to win.

It was a long way to have travelled in fifteen months, and as Tandia left Patel's grave with its obscene new headstone, she wondered when she would return again. On a sudden impulse she tried to close the cast-iron gate that led into the cemetery but it sagged on its hinges; weed and grass had grown around its base, holding it firmly in place. Patel's influence was not over yet.

When Tandia reached the Packard, Juicey Fruit Mambo was now genuinely asleep in the back seat. She shook him awake. 'Come on, Juicey Fruit Mambo, we have to get the pies and sausage rolls for tonight.'

That night at Bluey Jay there was to be a party. From the end of the second week in January to the first Monday in February Mama Tequila closed Bluey Jay. With lots of money in their pockets, the working girls all went on holiday.

The party was held on the Friday prior to the Sunday when they left, and always began in the same way. Juicey Fruit Mambo would serve them all a glass of champagne, French no less, and Mama Tequila would make her speech.

This year her evening dress hugged her figure so tightly that it looked like a series of undulations laminated in scarlet velvet. The hemline and the plunging breastline were trimmed with pink ostrich feathers and she wore an elaborate Indian-style turban of the same material, with three pink ostrich feathers pluming towards the ceiling. From toe to top of ostrich feathers she stood seven feet tall and was undoubtedly the most imposing presence in the salon which included the grand piano with its tummy open, festooned with pink-and-white balloons. Mama Tequila's fingers were encrusted with diamonds and a two-inch diamond choker around her neck flashed a distress beacon every time she moved her head.

The girls all gathered around her holding their champagne glasses. They too wore evening dresses. Tandia wore a simple peacock-blue shantung sheaf which fitted her figure closely and was cut high in the Chinese cheongsam style to reveal almost the full length of her left leg as she walked. It had been a Christmas gift from Sonny Vindoo, who had been back twice to make sure it fitted perfectly. Sarah and Hester, in a rare collaboration between Catholic and Pentecostal, had paid for her high heels, which they'd had covered with the same shantung so as to match her gown. Standing in the circle with the other girls, waiting for Mama Tequila to start the pre-holiday proceedings, she looked simply ravishing.

The painters, carpenters and plumbers, under the supervision of Mr Perfect Lay, who drove down from Pietermaritzburg twice a week to supervise them, were due to start work on the following Monday, after the drapes and the carpets had been removed for cleaning and the upholsterer had checked the couches and chairs for repairs. Mama Tequila liked Bluey Jay to commence business each year looking and feeling brand new, a house refreshed. The night when the girls kissed the working year goodbye was known as Frog Friday.

The rules for Frog Friday were simple: the girls could drink as much as they liked, get as drunk as they liked and, in the morning, sleep as long as they liked. All day Sunday, taxis would arrive from town to take them to Durban Central to catch their trains to wherever they were going. It was a day of kissing and crying, of sudden panics, things packed, unpacked, decided upon, decided against, outfits changed, changed again and then returned to the original. The best part of the working girl's holiday might well have been the excitement of getting ready to leave.

Mama Tequila held her glass above her head. 'Okay, man, let us begin. A toast to us all and also to Bluey Jay!'

'Us and Bluey Jay!' the girls all chorused.

'And Juicey Fruit Mambo!' Tandia added.

They all turned to see Juicey Fruit standing behind them in his tuxedo and pink bow tie. He was shaking his head, suddenly embarrassed by the attention.

'Juicey Fruit, where's your glass?' Jasmine said. Putting down her own, she hurried over and, taking up a champagne glass, filled it. When she handed it to Juicey Fruit Mambo, he shuffled his feet and smiled and looked acutely ill at ease.

'A toast to Edward King George Juicey Fruit Mambo, the pride of Zululand!' Mama Tequila shouted.

'The pride of Zululand!' they all joined in.

Juicey Fruit Mambo lifted the wide-rimmed glass and, opening his huge mouth like Bluto in a Popeye cartoon, managed to empty the entire glass down his throat without it ever touching his lips. The girls all clapped and Juicey Fruit grinned, his two gold incisors shining.

'So now, we here again to begin another Frog Friday. One more year has passed and we still here, we still the best whorehouse in the world!' Mama Tequila appeared to glance behind her to the entrance to her salon, as though she expected someone to appear. 'You hear that, Mr Minister for Injustice! We still here and we going strong, man, like the bladdy blue train!'

'I'll drink to that!' Sarah shouted, and upended her glass.

'Me also!' Hester echoed, and did the same thing.

'Yeah!' the girls all shouted, throwing their heads back and emptying their glasses.

'Keep the champagne coming, Juicey Fruit Mambo,' Mama Tequila ordered. 'But seriously, my dears, let me say a few things I got on my mind before you's all get sozzled, hey?'

They all quietened down and Mama Tequila waited until Juicey Fruit Mambo had refilled her glass before continuing. 'Firstly I got to say you all good whores. The best! I couldn't ask for better. Except for Tandy. Jesus! She never going to make a whore, I'm telling you that, for sure!' They all laughed, and Tandia blushed violently.

'She got too much brains to be a whore, Mama T!' Doreen laughed. 'You can't have no whore speaking Latin and algebra!'

'Ag man, you mad! Algebra is not a language!' Marie said. 'It's like doing sums, only harder, stuff like A plus B equals something else you never heard of to the square root, jong!'

'A plus B equals Tandia never going to be a square root!' Mama Tequila cackled and the room broke up again. 'Now shurrup everybody! I haven't said nothing of what I'm going to say to you yet!' She emptied her glass again and turned, waving it. 'Where's that cheeky bladdy kaffir?' she said, joking. 'Juicey Fruit Mambo, a person could die of thirst around here. Keep the champagne coming, you hear!' The big black man, laughing at the insult, hurried over and filled Mama Tequila's glass. Mama Tequila took the bottle from his hands. 'You see what it says on this bottle? Veuve Clicquot. You know what means that in frog language? It means the Widow Clicquot. I'm telling you, man, that Mrs Veuve Clicquot that some dame! Her husband passes away (God rest his soul), next thing you know she's having a party with her own name on the champagne. Now that class, you hear! In any book, that first class! That the kind of woman whose champagne we like to drink.'

Mama Tequila was getting pretty tipsy, which meant she'd been toasting the Widow Clicquot all afternoon. 'Okay, okay, listen, ladies! On Sunday you all going far and wide to have a damn good holiday. You got a hand-bag full of money and you all got a good time to give away for free,' she burped. 'Now, that the first thing I want to talk about. Don't give no free pussy to no one, you hear! You want to know why? Okay, I'll tell you why. A whore got to have some respect for herself.' She looked around the room, her glance seeming to take in each of the girls. 'And don't give it to a bright boy or a jazz man and also no coloured who wear a big fedora and drive a convertible because, man, you know where they been and it isn't where you want to go, which is straight to Dr "VD" Suluman when you get back.' Mama Tequila stretched her forefinger and thumb wide. 'Which is a needle this long in your bum every day for a week! That all I want to say on the question of loving. So now you can have some more champagne and . . .' She turned to Juicey Fruit Mambo. 'Go see if the big surprise arrive yet.'

The girls were surprised. Mama Tequila's Frog Friday wasn't a party in the traditional sense with proper men. If a person wasn't one of the girls at Bluey Jay and didn't get drunk it could be pretty boring really. But, for the eight working girls at Bluey Jay, it was an occasion buoyed up by the prospect of going on holidays and this, along with the French champagne, was enough to get the party going. But this year things had been different.

The Geldenhuis incident with Tandia had left them all fearful in the weeks leading up to Frog Friday and had dampened down much of the anticipation the girls felt about the end of the working year. It wasn't something they spoke about much, even to each other. It was something they felt, a dark, private shadow which hung over their future. Bluey Jay was a way of life, but also it was a tenure which promised to lead to a normal life with a man and kids and a home of their own. Each of them had a dream and Tandia, because of what she'd done to Geldenhuis, had put this dream in jeopardy. They felt angry and betrayed, not really as much by Tandia but more by Mama Tequila herself. Mama Tequila had seen the opportunity to compromise Geldenhuis, which was fine and all right, but she'd risked them all in the process by using a person any of the girls could have told her was not up to the task.

For her part Mama Tequila was aware of this. She accepted that she'd played it the wrong way. She'd been too anxious to compromise the policeman, to get enough dirt on him to ensure her own survival. There were other ways open to her. A quiet word in the Detective Sergeant's ear by Dr Louis, for she still had his examination notes from when Tandia had come to Bluey Jay, would probably have discouraged him, for a while anyway.

Geldenhuis had too much to lose. He was a local hero, a national sporting identity and a police officer who had been brought to the favourable attention of the Minister of Justice. His career was on the up and up; all he had to do was keep his nose clean and, sooner rather than later, he'd find himself in Pretoria hitting the big time.

It wouldn't have taken a lot of pressure to keep him at arm's length. But Mama Tequila couldn't resist nailing him once and for all. She didn't like him and had stupidly allowed this to be a factor in her decision to sacrifice

Tandia. Now she'd have to be very careful with the girls or her mistake could destroy her. With the amended Immorality Act three years in existence prostitution had been driven underground; the girls in it were mostly black crud or lazy white sluts who were badly trained with a booze problem, or a pill or hashish habit, or all three. She knew her chances of recruiting a new line-up such as the present one at Bluey Jay was virtually impossible.

Every year at Christmas Mama Tequila handed them their post office books with the money they'd made for the year. Every year on their return from holidays she started a new book for each of them. Now she had nothing with which to hold them; they were all fully paid up. Whores are naturally superstitious, and, if they thought their luck had run out at Bluey Jay, they might just call it a day and stay away. Sarah would stay, of course, because she was being trained to run the house. But then, on the other hand, if she felt there might be no house to run, she too might not return.

Johanna, a girl from a small country town in the Northern Transvaal, who normally didn't say very much and just got on with her job, brought all their fears into the open. 'Maybe I'm stupid, jong, but I'm not so stupid I don't know that what happened to Geldenhuis isn't finish! That bastard is a Boer and a policeman; that's the worst combo there is! I'm telling you, man, our troubles, they just beginning!'

Mama Tequila knew she was going to have to turn on one hell of a party to win back her authority so they would trust her sufficiently to return after the holidays.

'Sarah done a poem!' Doreen shouted. She was a girl who had started life, like Jasmine, in the slums of Cape Town's District Six, and she was notorious at Bluey Jay for the fact that she couldn't hold her liquor. She was already quite tipsy.

'On the peeano!' Doreen added, and Hettie and Colleen rushed over to the grand piano. Removing the balloons from its interior, they gave each of the girls several balloons to hold and closed the lid. Sarah sat down on the piano stool, removed her high heels and then, helped by Heffie and Colleen, climbed onto the top of the grand. She fumbled in the bodice of her gown for a moment and produced a small sheet of folded paper from her bra.

'Juicey Fruit Mambo! More frog juice for the poet!' Mama Tequila demanded. But the huge black man appeared to have left the room. Hester picked up the bottle of champagne.

'Hey! Where's my glass?' Sarah asked.

Jasmine handed Sarah's glass to Hester who filled it and passed it up to her. Sarah held the glass out in front of her slightly above her eyeline.

'I dedicate this noble poem to Mama Tequila and all the working girls and also Juicey Fruit Mambo!' She smiled, 'And, oh yes! To the best lover in South Africa, the one and only, transil-meddle-tated, Mr Dine-o-mite!' They all cheered and sipped from their glasses.

Sarah took a generous gulp of champagne and handed her glass to Jasmine. 'But the main person I dedicate my poem to is Tandy.' She looked around at all the girls and at Mama Tequila.

That one will one day make a bladdy good madam, Mama Tequila thought to herself.

Sarah continued. 'We very proud today with what you done, Tandy, being in the paper and all with top marks in everything, Latin and algebra and hard stuff like that. I'm telling you, to know a person like you, with so much brains a person's head could burst, is a very big honour.'

Tandia buried her head in Jasmine's shoulder, totally embarrassed by the sudden attention. 'But being clever an' all, that's one thing, but being brave that a altogether different thing.' Sarah paused and looked around at them all again in a melodramatic fashion. She was a little tipsy, but so were they all and her longish pauses didn't seem to worry them. 'Tandy done the bravest thing I ever heard of in my whole life as a working girl. Something we all thought about lots of times before, when some bastard is giving a person a bad time. So here is my poem,' she said finally. Holding the scrap of paper almost at arm's length, Sarah cleared her throat and commenced to read.

Roses are red
Violets is blue
Geldenhuis was bit
So now he can't screw!

The laughter started slowly in Mama Tequila and built like a rumbling volcano, shaking her to the foundation, gushing from her, a veritable explosion of mirth. 'Ho . . . ho . . . ho . . . hee . . . hee . . . hee, snort-snort, hee-hee-hee . . . Oh my God! Ho . . . ho . . . hee-hee-hee . . .' Juicey Fruit rushed to support her as her knees gave way, but still she laughed, a massive scarlet chortling blancmange of heaving mirth. The girls came to help her as Tandia pushed the piano stool under Mama Tequila's bottom to take her sagging weight.

It was the sort of laughter they all needed. And Tandia knew that she too was expected to laugh. Sarah had, after all, done it for her. Tandia was not unaware of the unspoken disapproval of the working girls, and Sarah's poem had been a gift of generosity. The Geldenhuis incident had been with them all. Now, at last, it was out, brought to the surface by a silly, childish little poem which had somehow made it all warm and safe again.

Mama Tequila knew that she couldn't have asked for anything better, and she now realised how much strain she herself had been under. It was good to laugh and she let it all roll out of her. At last she was sufficiently in possession of herself to talk, but she was afraid that if she spoke in her natural voice her emotion might show, so she slipped into client vernacular. 'Sarah, honey, you the best, you hear? You da poet lorrikeet!' She started to chuckle softly. 'Say it again, Sarah, do it one more time, baby!'

Sarah held the poem out and started to read again, but before she had completed the first line Mama Tequila was off again. The poem was a trigger all right! She raised her arms above her head to clap her hands together and suddenly her red velvet gown split from under the armpit down to her thighs. This caused fresh gales of laughter. 'Ho . . . ho . . . ho . . . hee . . . hee-hee, I think I going to wet my pants! Sarah, Mr Dine-o-mite, he ain't going to get no pussy for this dress, you hear?'

Frog Friday, despite the anxiety they had felt leading up to it, was showing all the signs of being an all-time success. Hester and Marie, each taking an arm, led Mama Tequila across the room towards the door. As they reached the entrance to the salon Juicey Fruit Mambo appeared. 'It is all ready, madam,' he said.

Mama Tequila turned back into the room and addressed the girls. 'Go now into the other salon, everyone! In there is my big going-away surprise!' Turning to Hester and Marie she said, 'You too, darlings! Juicey Fruit Mambo will help me to my room. Go on, go now, enjoy your party. Hurry, jong. If you get there fast you can take first pick!'

Hester's scream of delight as she entered the client salon made all the other girls come running. Standing around the room were eight of the best built hunks of super manhood she'd ever laid her eyes on. Their arms bulged and their pectoral muscles smashed aside the buttons on their shirts to reveal chests and stomach muscles a girl could die for. Hester, with four or five of Madam Veuve Clicquot's special thigh-warming tonics under her belt, was willing to commit suicide on the spot. She grabbed at the biggest, horniest man she could see. Doreen did the same and soon every man in the room had a girl draped on his arm. This was Mama Tequila's special treat: beautiful, taut, young coloured men who looked like Adonis to make up for all the wheezing and burping, the pot bellies and the limp little willies they'd had to coax to life during the year. Or, as Hester had once said, 'Some, they an insult to a one-eyed snake, man! They just blind worms with a swollen head!'

Tandia, for whom no man had been allocated, walked over to the pianola and, sitting down, started to pedal it. Most of the tunes were well-known *boere musiek* numbers, old favourites that caused the feet to tap and the blood to rise. In about five minutes flat the place was jumping.

Juicey Fruit Mambo dispensed beer from bottles buried in tin tubs of crushed ice, and the two coloured women from Durban appeared from the kitchen carrying pies and sausage rolls and an assortment of good things men like to eat: sausages and chops and big, juicy steaks. The girls were swung and danced and picked up and fussed over until the shirts of the men clung to their massive chests. Sarah removed the shirt of her partner and the other girls soon followed suit. It was a sweating, laughing, dancing, hugging, swinging, lifting party and Marie told Hettie she thought she'd passed away and woken up in heaven.

And then Johanna got the gramophone going and the lights dimmed and the night softened to Nat King Cole's 'Mona Lisa' and the couples drew closer, chest and breast and breathing heavier as Frank Sinatra stroked them with 'Bewitched, Bothered and Bewildered' and 'The Lady is a Tramp'. One by one, they danced off the floor and up the blackwood stairway, each girl with a man in tow and a lot of loving mischief on her mind. The beautiful young man carrying Jasmine up the stairs stopped halfway and said, 'Man, if I die now, I'll kill myself!'

As parties go, there have been bigger parties, louder and more colourful ones with live music and more spectacular entertainment, certainly more drunken parties or parties for more important people, but Frog Friday 1954 was, in its own small way, one of which the human race had a right to be proud. No one threw up or grew violent or felt left out or unrequited. At two a.m., Juicey Fruit Mambo knocked on the various doors to tell the boys their taxis were waiting. They appeared soon afterwards and each wore a smile and a stunned look in his eyes.

As for the girls? The widow Clicquot could not have done a better job. Everything the French sailor had told Mama Tequila about her champagne proved to be true. Mama Tequila's eight working girls had been transil-meddle-tated right into heaven.

But all this happened long after Tandia had been replaced at the piano pedal by one of the coloured ladies from Durban. Halfway through the evening, after the men had all eaten, Juicey Fruit Mambo handed over the task of serving drinks to the other one and left the party. Some twenty minutes later he returned to tell Tandia she was required in Mama Tequila's salon.

'What is it, Juicey Fruit Mambo?'

He grinned, his gold incisors gleaming. 'I think you be very, very happy, Missy Tandy, big *indaba* for you!' he giggled, but would say no more.

Tandia stopped in the girls' waiting room and patted her face with a towel and added a touch of lipstick. She couldn't imagine what Mama Tequila might want. Frog Friday had been the biggest day of her life, the day she matriculated with honours and, in her mind, started her life properly and truly. From now on she was beautiful and brand new, no longer the daughter of Natkin Patel, known in the best white circus, but Tandia Patel, a black *slimmetjie* who was her very own person. And for just a moment, as she opened the door to Mama Tequila's salon, she wasn't scared at all.

She was surprised and delighted to see Dr Louis and Sonny Vindoo. Her surprise was even greater when she recognized the round, squat shape of Old Coetzee with his puffy eyes and whisky nose, his untidy suit jacket open as usual, showing his waistcoat with his gold watch chain looped across his big belly. With him stood a very tall, thin man in a dark suit with perfectly round glasses which sat halfway down his long, sharp nose. His steel-grey hair, plastered down with hair oil, was parted down the centre just the way Patel had worn his. His narrow face had a disappearing chin and it looked as though he didn't laugh a lot. In his dark grey serge suit and white shirt he needed only to stand on one leg and he would have been Icabod Crane.

Sonny Vindoo rushed to welcome her. 'My dear, dear, Tandia, how very beautiful you are looking!' He giggled, 'I must be having the name of your dressmaker at once, my goodness, yes!'

Old Coetzee pulled himself up to his full height which wasn't much bigger than five foot six inches. '*Magtig!* You are a pretty girl, man!' he said, to Mama Tequila's surprise. He was an important, upstanding Afrikaner and she couldn't remember ever hearing a Boer paying a compliment such as this to a coloured person. What a waste, Mama Tequila sighed; she would be worth a king's ransom if she worked on her back.

'Please, everybody sit!' Mama Tequila indicated the comfortable high-backed Victorian armchairs which had been drawn into a semicircle round a low coffee table with ball-and-claw legs. 'Juicey Fruit Mambo will bring drinks.'

'You must come and meet Professor Ryder, the head of the Law School at Natal University,' Sonny Vindoo said. 'And, of course already you are knowing Magistrate Coetzee.'

'Howzit, Tandia,' Dr Louis called, using the casual slang expression to ease her nerves.

'Good evening, Magistrate Coetzee, good evening, Dr Louis,' Tandia said politely, trying hard not to sound nervous. Her heart was thumping. The thin man, who looked like one of the marabou storks Juicey Fruit Mambo had once identified for her on a walk along the river, was from the university.

In her pink gymslip behind the bar it was easy to know the role she was required to play. She was Miss Tandy with the beautiful smile who kept the drinks coming, the shy, ingenuous part of a double act with Mama Tequila. But what was she here? What was expected of her? She knew instinctively that she was required to impress Professor Ryder, who didn't look like the sort of man who was going to be a pushover charmwise. There could only be one reason why Sonny Vindoo and Dr Louis were here, though how Old Coetzee fitted in she couldn't imagine. He'd paid her a compliment, which was a very strange thing for a man like him to do.

In her mind she saw him standing to rigid attention, the top part of him fully dressed right down to his watch chain, but with his trousers around his ankles. Across his left shoulder was the old Boer Mauser that usually hung on the wall directly above the blackwood stairs. Sarah knelt on the floor in front of him.

Sarah had accidentally come upon the solution to Old Coetzee's erectile problem when he'd taken down the old rifle and, with tears in his brandy-bright eyes, stroked it lovingly. 'Miss Sarah, this is a Mauser 8mm carbine, it's what nearly beat the *verdoemde rooinekke* in the Boer War! This is the rifle that defended the *republiek*! I worship this rifle! With five thousand more Boers on horseback and this carbine, I'm telling you man, Queen

Victoria would be crying tears in her English teapot and *Oom Paul* would still be president of the *republiek*!'

Sarah couldn't be sure about Queen Victoria but she knew for sure Oom Paul, the first president of the Transvaal Republic, had been dead for more than fifty years. 'That's very nice, Magistrate Coetzee, if you want you can bring it with you,' Sarah suggested, in an attempt to coax the old bugger into the pink room so that she could begin the arduous task of bringing him to gratification. Old Coetzee lumbered after Sarah, following her into the room like an excited schoolboy.

Thinking only to amuse him Sarah had commanded, 'General Coetzee, Commander of the Boer Republican Army, friend of President Oom Paul Kruger himself, stand to attention!' To Sarah's surprise Coetzee had immediately shouldered the old German rifle and stood to rigid attention beside the bed. Sarah was not one to miss an opportunity and she'd quickly slipped her hands under his waistcoat and undone his belt and trousers, pulling them down to his ankles. 'Watch careful as anything, you hear? The British are everywhere, jong!' she commanded him. Old Coetzee's eyes darted around the room as Sarah went to work on him. Occasionally, he'd remove the Mauser from his shoulder and fire an imaginary shot. 'Got him, got the *verdoemde rooinek* right between the eyes!' he shouted quickly, working the bolt action of the old rifle to eject the imaginary cartridge case before placing it back over his shoulder. In a surprisingly short time, Old Coetzee had risen to the occasion and before you could say, 'God save the Boer Republic!', she'd finished him off with French.

As Mama Tequila and the other three men sat down, Tandia extended her hand to Professor Ryder. 'How do you do, sir.' It was a brave thing to do; coloured girls don't shake hands with important white people who might think they were cheeky or trying to be the same as a white or something. Immediately he'd released her hand she began to worry.

But Professor Ryder didn't seem to mind. He sat down and crossed his long legs and looked at Tandia over the top of his glasses, which appeared to have slipped halfway down his long nose. 'Dr Rabin tells me you know your Latin, Tandia. Certainly a high distinction in your matriculation exam is very commendable.' He cleared his throat, reached up and brought his glasses back to rest on the bridge of his nose. 'We'll begin with something simple, okay? I want you to conjugate a few curly irregular verbs. The future perfect tense of the verb "to use", if you please?'

Ah!, thought Tandia, he's like Dr Louis, always a puzzle, trying to trick me with a deponent verb, passive in form but active in meaning. She had learned from Mama Tequila the value of a little drama, and now she gave the lanky professor a dazzling smile where he might have expected a serious schoolgirl demeanour. '*Usus ero, usus eris, usus erit. Usi erimus, usi eritis, usi erunt*,' she said, to Dr Louis's obvious relief.

'Very good Tandia.' The professor appeared to be thinking. 'What about the perfect tense in the subjunctive?'

Tandia completed this request as effortlessly as the first. '*Usus sim, usus sis, usus sit. Usi simus, Usi sitis, usi sint.*'

Professor Ryder grinned. 'That's the easy bit over. Now let's try you on Virgil's *Aeneid*, the fourth part.'

Tandia could feel the blood rising into her face and her mouth was suddenly dry. She regretted her previous aplomb. Virgil's Aeneid IV was Dr Louis's territory and, to please him, she'd studied the Latin poet more diligently than she was required to do at school, even after a while getting to quite like him. But she wasn't sure what the professor would expect from her.

'*Dulces exuviae, dum fata deusque sinebant, accipite hanc animam, meque his exsolvite curis*; "sweet relics, sweet so long as God and Destiny allowed, now receive my soul and free me from this suffering",' Professor Ryder recited, making each word sound as though it was delivered from a lectern.

The relief Tandia felt was palpable. She knew this passage was part of the Queen of Carthage's death soliloquy. She knew the two lines that followed, and quoted them in a quiet but firm voice which belied the terror she felt. '*Vixi, et, quem dederat cursum fortuna, peregi; et nunc magna mei sub terras ibit imago*. "I have lived the life and finished the course Fortune has allotted me. Now my wraith shall pass in state to the world below." '

The professor followed with another passage from Aeneid IV. It was one of Dr Louis's favourites and she had no trouble completing it.

'Very good! "*Hunc ego Diti sacrum iussa fero, teque isto corpore solvo*," ' Ryder quoted, his voice deep and over-projected; he seemed to be enjoying himself and Tandia was beginning to feel embarrassed. It was gobbledy-gook to Sonny Vindoo and Mama Tequila, and probably to Old Coetzee as well.

Tandia knew that these were the last lines of Book IV but she didn't know them nearly as well as the other two passages. Her mind went blank. It was a four-line stanza and the last lines had simply disappeared from her memory. 'Ah . . . ah . . .' She looked at Dr Louis, who seemed to be urging her on with his eyes, the fingers of both his hands spread wide.

'It is my favourite, man! Don't finish it, Tandia, let me please. *Omnis et una dilapsus calor, atque in ventos vita recessit*; "At once all the warmth fell away and the life passed into the moving air." '

'My goodness me, that was very well done!' Sonny Vindoo said, clapping his hands in applause. 'Miss Tandy could perhaps complete it prettier, but I'm telling you, no better!'

Professor Ryder laughed. 'We shall never know! You have some very good friends, Tandia Patel. Did you know that?'

'No, sir . . . yes, sir! I mean, I don't know, sir.' Tandia looked up at Professor Ryder and he could see she was very close to tears, the strain of his examination clearly showing. 'Please, sir, I mean, Professor, please let me go to your university? I will work hard, I will do anything!'

'Ja, I can tell you that true, Professor. Tandy can cook and clean and you can ask her anything, she knows it right off, anything you want to know. The hardest stuff you can think, she knows it already,' Mama Tequila tapped her head, 'it right here inside her *kop*!'

'Ja, she's very clever, the most clever you can find anywhere, but I think there are some other problems, hey, Professor?' Sonny Vindoo had sensed that Ryder was troubled and that he had hoped to gain a slight advantage by compromising Tandia with his impromptu examination.

'No problems! She will pay, we don't want no charity, you hear!' Mama Tequila's voice was indignant.

'That's not the question, Madam Tequila,' Professor Ryder said. 'The girl's marks are sufficient to get her a scholarship to our university college for non-whites, I'm sure I can help her there, though I regret there is no law faculty. Perhaps Fort Hare?' He paused and clasped his hands together in front of him. 'It's . . . well frankly, it's just damned awkward in my own faculty!'

'You mean because Tandia's a coloured?' Doctor Louis asked quietly.

Ryder looked uncomfortable and glanced at Tandia. 'Perhaps Tandia should leave the room?'

'No, Professor, she a big girl, leaving this room not going to change her colour!' Mama Tequila said.

'I wasn't simply referring to the student's colour. There are other complications. She's a female, and well, er . . . law for a woman?' Mama Tequila's outburst had added to his obvious discomfort. Tandia could sense he was beginning to wonder how he'd been persuaded to come to Bluey Jay in the first place.

'Okay, let me say something!' It was Old Coetzee who spoke. 'In this room is Mr Vindoo, he's an Indian and Mama Tequila who is a coloured person and Dr Louis who is a Jew and you, Professor, who are a Britisher and me, I am a Boer, an Afrikaner, but, in the end, we are all South Africans, you hear.'

Just then Juicey Fruit Mambo entered carrying a tray with ice, water and two decanters, one of Scotch and the other brandy. He'd also opened a bottle of coca-cola and added it with a glass to the tray for Tandia. He placed the tray down on a small coffee table and, as quietly as he'd entered he turned and walked back towards the door, giving Tandia a quick, encouraging flash of the gold incisors as he left. Old Coetzee pointed to the departing black man, 'And the Bantu, we like to forget the Bantu, who are also South African, not just Zulu or N'debele, Sotho or Shangaan or Pondo, but just as much, maybe even more, South Africans than us.'

Tandia moved over to the tray and started to pour drinks for everyone. She knew all their preferences, except that of Professor Ryder. She placed her hand on the Scotch bottle and he nodded, then on the water jug and he shook his head and pointed to the ice tray. Hiding behind the bottle of coke she found the tiny glass containing green chartreuse which Juicey Fruit Mambo had poured ready for Sonny Vindoo.

Tandia had remained standing when Mama Tequila and the men sat down and, although it wasn't as bad, her mind recalled the time at Cato Manor police station after she'd been arrested and she had been made to stand while the policeman interrogated her. She didn't have the courage to sit down, thinking that she might look too forward, a cheeky bladdy kaffir should she do so, now the drink tray saved what was beginning to develop into an embarrassing situation for her.

Old Coetzee continued. 'We all got one thing else in common.' He paused, accepting a brandy from Tandia. 'Hate! We all hate each other!'

'Oh, I say, is that quite fair?' Professor Ryder exclaimed. 'I think you're probably quite a nice chap for a magistrate and a Boer,' he laughed.

Old Coetzee held up his hand. It was obvious he wanted to be taken seriously. 'No, please! Let me talk, man. This country is not built on understanding or compassion or the mutual co-operation of its people. It is stitched together with the needle of hate and the thread of fear. The Afrikaner hates the Englishman, but both are also South Africans. The English South African calls the Afrikaner a "hairy back" and hates him back. The Indians, who came out here as indentured labour, they are hated by the blacks. This hate is encouraged by the white man, just like the white man encourages the various native tribes to hate each other. It creates a buffer zone of hate. A safety zone built on hate. If one kaffir tribe hates another one, the Zulu the Sotho and so on, and they all hate the Indian, then the white administration, people like me, we can control and direct the hate!'

Old Coetzee held his brandy balloon up and moved it in a slow arc, taking them all in and stopping at Mama Tequila. 'Then there are the coloureds, the children of the white man's guilt! They remind us every day that we are not invincible and superior, but weak and human.' He paused. 'So they are hated by everyone the most of all!' Old Coetzee brought the glass to his lips, emptying almost half before he put it down again. 'Hate, fear and greed! These are the components on which South African society is based!'

There was silence in the room. It was a startling admission, but hugely more so coming from the Afrikaner magistrate who was meant to uphold the sacred concept of apartheid.

Finally, Sonny Vindoo spoke up. 'Tonight, Magistrate Coetzee, I will go home a very, very happy man! I'm telling you now, I'm not thinking I will ever in the whole of my life hear a Afrikaner say these things!'

Old Coetzee smiled. 'I am a Boer, you must understand. What I think and what I say and what I do, they not always the same thing. You have just heard me thinking aloud; you must not judge me by my thoughts.'

Professor Ryder leaned forward. 'What are you saying, Magistrate Coetzee? That the Afrikaner is maintaining a position he doesn't feel?'

'Ag, there you go, you see! You English, you make everything seem like it's truth or lies. I didn't say what I feel, man. I said what I think! That is not the same thing.'

'Surely it is difficult, if we're thinking in terms of a lifestyle, a philosophy, to separate the two. We feel so we think?' Dr Louis said.

'For the Jew yes, in particular, the Jew! The Jew is firstly an intellectual and a rationalist. For a thousand years he is persecuted and still he looks for reason. Spinoza, Maimonides, Erasmus, Kant, Marx! In every humble shetl the rabbi and the elders are the seekers of truth and the law, the translators of hot grassroots feelings into cool intellectual reasoning.

'But my people, the volk, they are not thinkers. They feel and they act. They have won the right to this land with their blood! First from the black man, then twice they fought the Englishman for it. They lost it to the verdoemde rooinekke; their women and children died like flies in the British concentration camps. These feeling, ignorant *boere*, who were very proud men, swore a sacred oath on the graves of their women and children. They made a covenant with God that they would remain true to themselves as a people. *Heren volk!* God's people in the land God gave them! They swore they would win back this land and keep it forever.' Old Coetzee had become quite worked up. He removed a kerchief from his trouser pocket and wiped his brow. The room was silent, embarrassed by the Afrikaner's outburst.

When Old Coetzee resumed, his voice was surprisingly calm. 'There was only one weapon left to this pathetic, defeated, ignorant bunch of farmers with their ragged, sweat-stained clothes and their half-starved bodies. These men knew they had not been defeated by the Lee Metfords of the English marksmen, who were a joke, but by the cruel scorched-earth policy of the British. Their fields were burned, their homes razed to the ground, their women and children herded into captivity, where twenty-seven thousand died of dysentery, blackwater fever and God knows what else. Their sad-faced, barefoot children and their calm, resourceful wives, the guerilla widows who had kept vigil on the lonely farms, had been destroyed. These women had stoically endured all, had waited in fear for the men they loved to come home, a fleeting shadow in the night, often after months away on commando, only a single night, from moon rise to break of cold dawn across the pale veld. Who saw him leave again, a memory of muffled hooves in the misty morning light. A man who had come and gone and in the haste of rumbled loving, fierce touching and urgent need, brought only more aching loneliness and despair. These women, clutching their ragged children, watched as the hated rooinek soldiers razed their homes and torched their fields. The British might just as well have gunned them down in their farmhouses. It would have been a better way for them to die than in the mud and squalor of rat-infested, disease-ridden concentration camps.

'And so the *volk* bent down and picked up the only weapon left to them. They picked up hate and they sharpened it and kept it bright and waited for Jehovah, the God of vengeance, to give them their day of reckoning. In 1948 when the Nationalists came to power, God had been merciful, the day of vengeance had arrived.'

Professor Ryder cleared his throat. 'Surely, Magistrate Coetzee, all this is a little simplistic? After all we're a complex, modern society in a very sophisticated world. For God's sake, man! We are halfway through the twentieth century!'

'That's where you're wrong, Professor!' Old Coetzee replied. 'Hate and fear doesn't work like that. It doesn't die out just because you're in a sophisticated, or so-called sophisticated society. Hitler came to power in the most sophisticated society in Europe and the weapon he used was hate! He slaughtered six million of Dr Rabin's people with hate!' He turned to Dr Louis. 'Dr Rabin, you mark my words, now the Jews are in Palestine, their time for hate has come.' Coetzee took a sip of brandy and leaned back in his chair. 'Is the Jew going to hold Israel with reason and intelligence or with feeling? The Jew has come home to the promised land. How is the Jew going to hold his land? Let me tell you, man. He will hold it with feeling. He will die for it. He will learn to hate for it!'

Dr Louis had heard enough. 'Magistrate Coetzee, the Jews have been put in an impossible position. They believe they have come home. They believe Israel is the birthright of every Jew. "Next year in Israel", these have been the last words spoken in prayer every Friday at Shabbas for nearly two thousand years. Now the Jew has come home to a small piece of barren earth surrounded by his enemies!'

'And South Africa? Is this not the same? Inside are a black people who believe their land has been taken. Outside we are also surrounded by black nations who are our enemies. Are we not a minority, a small white minority, who have nowhere else to go? For the Jew it is a new thing to be a nation, a thing of ten years only; for us it is three hundred years. Like you Jews, we Afrikaners believe this is the promised land, this is our birthright. If we share our power we will lose it. So we hold it with the gun and we hold it with hate and finally, we hold it with fear! Hate and fear for those who would rise up to destroy us.'

'And greed? Before, you said greed, Magistrate Coetzee,' Sonny Vindoo added softly.

Tandia was exhilarated by the conversation. She had never heard anything like it. Never heard the position of the white man and, in particular, the Boer put so perfectly. For the first time in her life she could see where she fitted. To her surprise she wasn't angry or embittered. Both these reactions now seemed to her to be self-destructive, almost naive. She could feel the hate she knew she carried in her heart grow sharper. It had a point. A direction. Old Coetzee had explained to her what a powerful weapon it could become.

'Ah, greed! Let me tell you about greed, meneer Vindoo. Greed is the gift of the British to South Africa.' Old Coetzee was enjoying himself. 'When gold was discovered in the Transvaal Republic greed, not hate or fear, greed took over. I'm not saying the Boer wasn't greedy also, when he fought and took the black man's land; in today's terms that is also greed. But it was also the way of Africa. Shaka and Cetewayo, the great Zulu conquerors, did the same to the tribes they destroyed. But gold! The discovery of gold, that was a different kind of greed. Gold built a new lifestyle based on greed: of having more than you need, of having more than the seasons brought a man or the droughts denied him, of having power. It brought migration, people from Britain and Europe. The Afrikaner watched as the Britisher and the Jew got the gold and he saw how the European mind cared no more for the black man's welfare than the Boer did. In fact, you may say less. With the old system of paternalism there was some understanding between the white man and the black. Then the men of gold brought the black man into his mines, put a pickaxe in his hands, broke his black back with work and paid him a pittance in wages. He turned the rural economy into a city-based one where the black man was totally dependent for his very existence on the white capitalist mines. The men of gold shared nothing and gave nothing back. It was a system based entirely on white greed and black labour. He learned that he who pays, says. Money is power. So he learned the ways of capitalist greed also and he added them to his hate and his fear.'

As Tandia brought him a second Scotch, Professor Ryder rose from his chair. He took the glass from her absently. 'Magistrate Coetzee, I am, I must say, enormously impressed by your perspicacity.' He paused, preparing to make his point. 'But I must insist, you have missed the central point, the simple question of biology. My people have been in Natal for a hundred and ten years, ever since the 1840 settlers. We, the British South Africans, realised just like the Boer South Africans that miscegenation was not the way to go forward, that the mix of black and white didn't advance the noble savage or appreciate the white man. In fact the opposite was true . . .' He stopped suddenly and coloured violently, turning to look at Mama Tequila. 'I do apologise, Mama Tequila, what I have just said must seem unforgivable to you. I beg your forgiveness, I apologise.'

Mama Tequila laughed. 'What are you apologising for, Professor? Embarrassing me? Or for telling what you think is the truth?'

'Well, er . . .'

But Mama Tequila continued. 'I am a coloured person, that not a person in South Africa. A black is a person, and a white is a person. But I am a non-person. For the Afrikaner I am his guilt. He calls me a *Hotnot*, because he says I'm from the Bushman and the Hottentot, or a Cape Malay or even round here in Durban, a Mauritian coloured or a *Maasbieker*, who is a coloured person who supposed to come from Mozambique. Always I am something else from somewhere else, not what happened when his daddy or his *oupa* lay down with a black kaffir girl when the *ounooi* has gone to visit her sister in another *dorp*.

'For the Englishman I am an inferior non-person, a mistake for which he thinks only the Afrikaner is responsible, a *boere* bastard! How come there are four million non-people like me in this country, answer for me that, hey? I'm telling you something, Professor, I am the result of the hate and the fear and the greed Magistrate Coetzee just talked about. Three hundred years of hate and fear. So what am l? I'm going to tell you now! You the Britisher! You the Afrikaner! You the Jew! You the Indian! You know what I am. I am the child of South Africa. Not the non-person, the *real* person! You hear, I, me, this person who is sitting in this big chair, Sophie Van der Merwe, born in District Six on August 28, 1889, in Cape Town. I am the only *real* South African!' Mama Tequila was crying quietly. Her tears, gathering mascara on the way, ran black down her rouged cheeks. Professor Ryder sat down abruptly, as though he had been filled with air and now was suddenly and unexpectedly deflated.

Sonny Vindoo got up from his chair and moved over to join Tandia, who ran over to comfort Mama Tequila. 'Please, take no notice, I am just a stupid old woman, a *hout kop*,' she sniffed. 'Tandia, more brandy for Magistrate Coetzee, also Scotch for the doctor and the professor.'

'No, no I'm fine,' Dr Louis said, placing his hand over his glass.

'Go sit, Sonny,' Mama Tequila said, pushing the little Indian gently from her. She smiled through her tears. 'I don't know from where comes these stupid words, I am jus' a old coloured woman who doesn't know no better, man! Now it my turn to apologise, Professor.'

Old Coetzee rose from his chair a little unsteady on his feet, but when he spoke his voice was quiet and reasoned. 'What we have just heard, maybe it will not change any of us. I am a Boer, an Afrikaner, my mind says one thing, my heart says altogether another thing. We, *die volk*, we a stubborn people, a stupid people of the heart. I don't think we will ever learn this simple lesson.'

He polished off the remainder of the brandy and handed his glass to Tandia, indicating with his open palms that he did not require a refill.

Mama Tequila, who had recovered from her lapse, hoped to hell he would remember Sarah was not available tonight and would go home quietly.

The magistrate removed his gold hunter from his fob pocket and glanced down at it. 'Professor, it is getting late and you are our guest, so I will spare you further rhetoric. It is a strange little fraternity here tonight, very unexpected, hey? I'm sure you will appreciate that what has been said in this room is private. How is it that a man can go his whole life and never sit down and talk in a group such as this one? The true terror of apartheid is that it separates our minds, we do not know each other's thoughts. We all have too much to lose by loose talk. But I just got this one more thing to say. It concerns Tandia Patel, who as you can see is a coloured person. A non-person just like Mama Tequila. She is also a *real* child of South Africa and I must add, as an old man of course, if all our children were as beautiful we would be the best-looking race of people on earth.'

Tandia felt herself blushing violently. Old Coetzee continued. 'Today, out of a possible five hundred marks in five subjects in her matriculation exams, Tandia Patel obtained four hundred and eighty-one! Is this a non-mind in a non-person? Is this the inferior result of miscegenation? Or do you have a place in the Law faculty of your university for a beautiful, intelligent, real child of South Africa?'

Tandia could feel her heart pounding and her head seemed to fill with blood. She burned fiercely; then she grew as suddenly cold. She tried to hold herself rigid, but she seemed to have no control, and her entire body trembled as the professor spoke.

'Tandia Patel will be the first coloured female student to read Law at Natal University, that is my promise,' Professor Ryder said quietly.

Tandia brought her hands up to her face and burst into tears. She wasn't prepared for this moment. Her upbringing contained nothing in it which told her how to react. She panicked and turning on her heels rushed for the doorway. Pushing blindly through the door, she found herself in Juicey Fruit Mambo's arms. 'Oh, oh, Patel, daddy! I been accepted in the best white circus!' she wept.

The huge black man picked her up, his gold incisors flashing, and his smile seemed to disappear past his shot-away earlobe. 'Edward King George Juicey Fruit Mambo, we very happy for going to the university, Miss Tandy! We very smart combo, for sure!' He laughed, swinging her around again. 'Me, myself, I am cleaning for dat classroom and you, you learning to be big, big lawyer for de people so de white policeman he be very, very afraid!'

NINE

Maybe there is some connection between repressive regimes and good roads? The road from Johannesburg to Durban is claimed to be equal to any in the world, including the autobahns built by Adolf Hitler and the autostrada constructed in Italy by Mussolini. As roads go, this one is wide, fast and well made, with long perfectly flat grey stretches. There is a popular notion that parts of it are designed so that Sabre jets can land on it when the black revolution comes.

The journey in the big Packard promised to take just over five hours of fairly sedate Juicey Fruit Mambo driving. Mama Tequila with Tandia in tow was headed for Sophiatown to visit her sister Flo, or Madam Flame Flo as she was known by the *majietas* and the bright boys of Kofifi, the other name by which this rag-tag, multiracial community was known. Madam Flame Flo was the biggest shebeen queen in Sophiatown, a well-known figure who had resided there since the mid thirties.

In this little Chicago with its unpaved, dirty alleys and roadways delineated by leaning fences, ruts and puddles, the good mixed in almost equal proportions with the bad. There were some rich people, but they were overwhelmed by the poor; and as for the middle class, they were simply those families who ate three times a day.

In Sophiatown there were stone walls topped with glass built by the wealthy to keep out the marauding poor, but these most often acted as the one sturdy wall to the shanties of beaten tin and scraps of timber which were abutted to them. In this thoroughly mixed community there were no nature strips or carefully manicured lawns to create a no-man's-land separating the haves from the have nots. No municipal laws called for segregation by colour, income or status, so Sophiatown became more a conglomeration of ways to live than the result of town planning.

The township paid almost no taxes and in return received very little help. The utilities were almost non-existent, and electricity was a status symbol. Most families lived and died by lamp and candlelight. A toilet was usually a pit in the ground topped with a small movable outhouse of corrugated iron with a crude seat built into it. In the summer the sides were too hot to touch and hundreds of bluebottles filled the interior. You could hear and smell the presence of a *kakhuis* long before you arrived at it.

The sprawling 'Blackopolis', as the newspapermen called it, was also the biggest pain in the arse the Nationalist government had on its racist agenda. There were also other, smaller pimples on the backside of apartheid: Alexandra to the north, Orlando township to the south-west and, of course, Cape Town's ancient and venerable District Six, a slum which had existed for nearly two hundred years. But none was thought quite as important to cauterise from the body of the Nationalist state than was Sophiatown. Blacks from every tribe, as well as those who had been Kofifi-born and claimed no tribe at all, coloureds, Indians, Chinese and whites, lived together and had done so for well over thirty years. Racial harmony was not what the government were about and they had no intention of allowing an example of it to continue.

In fairness, the word 'harmony' was a description ill suited to the goings-on in Kofifi. Sophiatown was an untidy drawer which had jammed and refused to close in the neatly arranged filing cabinets of Johannesburg, where every class and colour knew its proper place. But Sophiatown was also the last living demonstration of the thing Old Coetzee had spoken about in Mama Tequila's salon, where people put aside their differences and had a shot at living together as human beings. Another name for it was hope.

Madam Flame Flo had started making her fortune almost immediately after arriving in Sophiatown from the Cape. She had been a good-looking woman of twenty-five, with an almost pure white, blue-eyed bastard baby and no real prospects ahead of her.

Fortune had smiled on Flo Van der Merwe from the very beginning. At the bus station on her way to Sophiatown she had sat down beside a diminutive coloured man who took a shine to her blue-eyed baby daughter and who introducted himself as Geel Piet, which simply meant Yellow Peter. Flo was to learn that names were important in Sophiatown; but only the very rich and the law abiding, both of whom were in limited supply, called themselves by their real names.

Geel Piet, who claimed to have been a professional boxer and from the look of his face must have been a very bad one, turned out to have made a vocation of having his bones broken in just about every prison in South Africa. It was difficult to tell his age. His body seemed to bear witness to a series of unfortunate happenings more than to an ageing process. It was as though he'd been poorly constructed in the first place, had been broken regularly over his adult years and on each occasion been badly mended.

Geel Piet had tagged along with the slim woman with the flaming henna-dyed hair and her chubby fair-skinned baby, promising to help her find accommodation. True to his word, he found her a place to live. A friend of a friend had a small, dark room for rent with a communal tap and a pit-toilet shared by several houses in the vicinity. The room was at the top end of Good Street, Sophiatown's major and most notorious thoroughfare. It had seemed to Flo an exciting and rather frightening place to live after the quieter streets of Cape Town's District Six.

After settling her in, Geel Piet had stolen five pounds from her handbag, her entire stake for a new life in the big city. He had returned just after eleven o'clock curfew that night with an armful of groceries, handing the destitute and distressed young mother twenty pounds. Geel Piet was a racing man extraordinaire and had brought home two winners at Turffontein racetrack that afternoon.

Geel Piet didn't stay in Sophiatown long. Over the ten years that followed, he used to visit Madam Flame Flo occasionally, always between bouts in prison. Even after she had become rich and a famous figure in Sophiatown, she never turned him away. Perhaps the only clean sheets and soft bed Geel Piet ever knew were in the spare bedroom of her large house. In her mind he'd laid the foundation for her fortune and Madam Flame Flo wasn't a fair-weather friend, the sort of person to forget a thing like that.

On the morning following her arrival in Sophiatown, Geel Piet had shown Flo how to brew a concoction which he'd learned to make in Barberton Gaol, a small but notoriously brutal and greatly feared prison in the Eastern Transvaal. The home-made liquor consisted of yeast, a quantity of the small-seeded brown maize known as kaffir-corn, brown sugar and the coarse brown bread the natives ate. It was all mixed together in a four-gallon paraffin tin filled with water and allowed to stand overnight. The result was a pungent brew with a real wallop! Flo had named it Barberton and dispensed it in jam tins at a nice profit to the Saturday-night Good Street crowd.

Over the years many shebeen queens had produced their own liquor, but Flo's special brand of Barberton was never seriously challenged. Some people said that her secret ingredient was arsenic, others claimed it was cyanide pinched from the gold refinery at Modderfontein, others that it was the rainwater she used from her big round tank. Madam Flame Flo never told, and in a country where liquor was forbidden to blacks (except for the sour, fermented porridge-like kaffir beer served in government drinking compounds), she became a very rich and even, in her own way, powerful woman.

In 1945 Madam Flame Flo had heard of Geel Piet's death at the hands of a warder named Kronkie in the very same Barberton prison from which her famous concoction was derived. She had ordered a polished granite tombstone on which she'd inscribed:

GEEL PIET
We drink to
his
sacred memory.
DIED 1945

She'd loaded the headstone onto the back of a bakkie, driven the three hundred and forty miles to the tiny mountain town of Barberton, and arrived at the notorious prison. There she had demanded to see where Geel Piet had been buried.

At first the Kommandant had refused to take her seriously. 'Hey, jong, he was just a *boesman* who died. We just dug a hole and put him in. *Dood vlies is dood vlies*! Dead meat is dead meat. Who you think he was, Jesus Christ in disguise?'

But Madam Flame Flo had persisted, and eventually she had been shown the plot where the prisoners who hadn't made it through their sentences lay buried: a large bare piece of ground where two or three hundred round boulders no bigger than a man's head were arranged in rows approximately five feet apart. The prisoners called it *amaTshe* and the warders simply translated this into *die Klippe*, the Stones. The boulders were all approximately the same size and of a whitish stone cut from a local quarry. Prisoners working in the quarry, when given the task of making a headstone, would shape it into a rough approximation and size of a human skull. At first glance, laid out in rows, the stones looked like a neatly organised killing field, which was a fairly accurate description of the state of affairs. Barberton wasn't a big prison, but it had more prisoner deaths than any in the country. The institutional joke among the Boer warders was that when a magistrate sentenced a black man to Barberton, he turned white. The Stones testified to the grim reality of this puerile joke.

The warder had waved his hand expansively over the stone-studded plot. 'Take you pick!' he had said, amused.

Madam Flame Flo had paid the man a pound to get three prisoners to unload the headstone from the bakkie and transport it by wheelbarrow to the Stones. Word had gotten around, and by the time the prisoners arrived, several more warders had gathered to witness the weird stone-laying ceremony for a beaten-up little boesman who wasn't worth a pinch of shit.

'*Was die Hotnot jou soetman?* Was the Hottentot your sweetheart?' one of them shouted, and the others all joined in the laughter. There was no doubt about it, kaffirs were funny buggers, but these boesmen were fucked in the head spending good money on a tombstone for a worthless piece of shit like that.

Just then a tall, fair-haired warder arrived on the scene. 'Are you the woman looking for Geel Piet's grave?' he asked, more or less politely, in Afrikaans.

'*Ja, baasie*,' Madam Flame Flo answered, not knowing what to expect from the white man.

'*Kom!*' he instructed, and started to walk to the very centre of the plot where Madam Flame Flo noticed a white boulder perhaps one-and-a-half times larger than the others, and quite nicely carved into an almost completely round ball. The warder waited for her to arrive. 'Put it here,' he said, and, turning, whistled to the prisoners who had reached the edge of the graveyard. To Madam Flame Flo's surprise the young warder dropped to his haunches and rolled the whitewashed stone away.

The headstone must have been very heavy, for the metal wheel of the barrow cut a clear rut into the hard red clay. With great difficulty the three men lifted it from the barrow and placed it where the boulder had been. It sat in the centre of the bare plot, an obscenely new and extravagant symbol set amongst the humble skull stories. There seemed nothing more to say. '*Dankie, baasie.* Can you tell me please when he died, do you know the date?'

The sergeant smiled. He had a pleasant, open face and his expression wasn't in the least condescending. 'That's easy, man. It was the night the Germans surrendered.'

Madam Flame Flo thanked the warder again as the three prisoners, laughing among themselves, left, one of them wheeling the barrow containing the rock which had now been replaced by the ludicrous tombstone.

The warder looked directly at Madam Flame Flo for the first time and offered her his hand. Surprised, she accepted it. 'My name's Gert. I'm not saying the boesman was a good man,' he grinned at the memory, 'he was a proper *skelm*, but he was also a real man. Geel Piet was the best boxing coach I ever saw.' He turned abruptly and walked away.

Madam Flame Flo turned back to the polished headstone. Behind it the green hills rose up and rolled back and tumbled into mountains blued and smudged in the high distance. It was a beautiful place for an old lag to die. '*Slaap lekker ou maat!* Sleep well, old friend,' she said quietly, and then added, 'Thanks, you hear? Thanks for everything you done for me.' Then she began to weep quietly, less for her friend than for the hopelessness of her kind, the twilight people who didn't belong, the new children of Africa spawned from the ugly, guilty lust of white for black and unwanted by both. She thought of her daughter with her fair skin and blue eyes who had escaped the tyranny of colour but who could never have a child lest it throw back and condemn her for the fraud she was.

On her return to Sophiatown Madam Flame Flo tried to re-name her liquor. She wanted to call it Geel Piet, but the name never caught on. The original name, Barberton, stood for something, and that sort of thing is not lightly put aside. Tradition in a daily start-from-scratch town like Kofifi, with few routines and even fewer laws, is important for continuity, a powerful emotional glue which holds people together. A person can't just go around changing things willy-nilly, even if the sentiment is a good one.

Barberton, and for that matter its many imitators, produced an affliction known as 'liquor flame' amongst its often poorly nourished drinkers. Liquor flame was a skin disease which resulted in the top layer of the skin peeling away. It was this affliction which gained Flo her nickname. Far from being ashamed of it, Madam Flame Flo regarded the appellation with a great deal of pride.

Madam Flame Flo had never moved from the spot Geel Piet had found for her to live. First she'd bought the room, then the house, and then the three small houses surrounding it. She had dug a septic tank and constructed a four-bedroom red-brick home with two bathrooms, where visitors would bring their children to inspect the indoor toilet. Behind the house was a large shed where the forty-four gallon drums of Barberton were brewed. Directly under the floor of this outhouse were several large tanks into which the fermented drink was strained and poured. Beside the shed, resting on its own concrete platform, was a huge round corrugated-iron rainwater tank which used the roof of the main house as its catchment area. This was the water used to make Barberton, and the whole set-up became Madam Flame Flo's brewery. Buried in the yard was a forty-four gallon drum into which the slops were emptied. This drum existed essentially as a decoy for police raids. While Madam Flame Flo paid police protection as a matter of routine, as an equal matter of routine she was regularly raided. She was too big an operator to go unnoticed; any policeman with a nose on his face could detect the slightly sour smell of the fermenting kaffir-corn and yeast simply by walking past the house.

In the strange game of corruption which existed in Sophiatown between the white police officers and the inhabitants, several unspoken rules applied. In Madam Flame Flo's case raids took place without warning so that she was obliged to pay protection to half-a-dozen street gangs. These comprised mostly teenage boys, no less vicious for their youth, and responsible for a great deal of mayhem and quite often even murder in the township. A police presence in numbers in the vicinity of Madam Flame Flo's end of Good Street would always be reported in time for her to empty the above-the-ground brewing vats into the below-the-ground tanks, and to appear innocent but for the single forty-four gallon drum conspicuously buried in the back yard. There was a second implicit law which applied in Sophiatown, this being that what is in the ground belongs to the ground. The police, after a lot of pretentious looking around, would eventually come upon the buried drum. It would be dug up and confiscated and Madam Flame Flo would be duly charged with allowing persons unknown to conceal liquor on her premises. This offence carried a biggish fine which she duly paid, though not without vehemently protesting her innocence.

The big Packard arrived in Good Street followed by a pack of yelling urchins curious to inspect the new arrivals. Madam Flame Flo, impatient to greet her sister, couldn't wait for Mama Tequila to get out of the car. She opened the back door and climbed into the rear seat as the Packard came to a halt outside her house. The two sisters embraced loudly and with copious tears.

Madam Flame Flo was already chatting as she entered the car, so that her words came out punctuated by sobs of welcome. 'The white bastards are going to take my beautiful home away! Come, my sister, your room is ready, at least you can enjoy it one last time. How are you, *liefling*? I have food, you must eat, we can still eat, though God knows how much longer before those Boer bastards take the food from out our mouths!'

Tandia, not wishing to be a part of the emotional sistering taking place in the back seat, got out of the car and was immediately surrounded by more than a dozen ragged black children who seemed to range from about seven to ten years old. Juicey Fruit Mambo was attempting to shoo them away, but these kids were city bred and they stood their ground, prepared to run only when they felt real danger which, in the way slum kids know these things, they sensed wasn't coming from Juicey Fruit Mambo's fierce-looking scowl.

'Oh my, I am so heppy you have come! We must talk plans, you hear?' Madam Flame Flo cried to Mama Tequila. 'In Sophiatown it's finish and klaar. God, I can't tell you what I been through! I'm telling you, any day now they going to come and fetch me and take me to Sterkfontein Mental Hospital. God's truth!'

'And the business? How is the business, Flo?' Mama Tequila laughed, patting her scrawny sister on the back with a heavily jewelled hand.

'That, God be thanked, is first class. With so much trouble and people losing their houses and going to Diepfontein and Meadowlands there is a lot of need. Business is good, that I got to say! But soon, no more! When they move the coloured folk out, that the end. The police already told me, no Barberton in the resettlement area. "What are the people going to drink, skokiaan?" I ask that big Dutchman, Potgieter, who is the crown sergeant at the Newlands police station. You know what he say, ousie? He says, "The government is trying to make a place for decent boesmen to live, no more blerrie shebeens, you hear, no more Barberton, no more skokiaan, we going to build a big beer hall!" That's what the dumb bugger says. So I look at him all solcastic. Since when does a coloured person drink kaffir beer? I ask him. "Here!" he says and scratches his big *dom kop*, "Maybe the authorities forgot we not mixing boesmen with black kaffirs no more. I seen it on the plans, they got a big soccer stadium and a beer hall in all the drawings!" So maybe there's a chance, hey? I ask him. That Potgieter he's the biggest crook, no way he going to run a clean show, no way, man! He looks at me sideways and his piggy blue eyes is all small in his fat face and his mouth goes like he's sucking a lemon, "Maybe you should start a brothel, hey?" he says. "Maybe that would be not such a bad thing for the boesman in the new place?" He laughs and then he says, "I seen a beer hall, but I didn't see a brothel in those plans." He picks his nose then and looks at me and then down at what he took out his nose. Sies, man! What a disgusting type, hey? "Ja, I think a brothel, that better than selling Barberton and we only charge a fixed sum every week for police protection and no fines," that's what he says to me.'

Mama Tequila laughed. 'We talk inside, Flo, I been sitting in this lousy car seat since seven this morning.'

Flo clambered out of the rear of the car backwards and Juicey Fruit Mambo began the complicated process of extracting Mama Tequila from the Packard. In the last year or so she'd put on nearly forty pounds and while getting into the car wasn't too difficult, extracting her had become somewhat of a traumatic experience for them both. First he moved Mama Tequila's legs so they protruded out of the door, then he moved around to the other side of the car. Climbing into the back, he pushed her further along the seat until her legs could reach the ground. He then moved back to Mama Tequila's side of the car and while she propped the soles of her shoes against the uppers of his boots to prevent her slipping forward, Juicey Fruit Mambo began to rock her, slowly increasing the rhythm until with a final jerk he pulled her up out of the seat. The crowd around the car applauded as Mama Tequila arrived in a vertical position. Juicey Fruit Mambo's brow was covered with beads of perspiration from the effort.

Mama Tequila acknowledged their tribute by beaming into the crowd, which now consisted of even more kids and quite a few adults as well. The original gang, the discoverers of this diversion, had a proprietorial look about them, as though they expected to be congratulated for finding so curious a spectacle on an otherwise dull Monday.

Still panting from the effort of getting out of the Packard, Mama Tequila started to walk slowly towards the house. 'Howdy folks, I do declare, it sure nice to be in this fine town of yours! Yessiree!' She looked at the shacks and shanties, leaning fences and dusty trees in the dirty street. 'It just the nicest place I ever did see!' she declared; then looking around, beamed again at the crowd. 'And I can tell, it gonna be real friendly, just like being home!'

A small gasp of appreciation went up from the crowd. In Sophiatown anything American was a very big deal. The small crowd welcoming her with their eyes decided that the enormous woman with the big, shiny American car was a celebrity, and that the beautiful young girl with her was probably also one. Someone whispered the words, 'Fillim stars!' An excited murmur swept through the crowd.

Mama Tequila, her timing as usual immaculate, took her sister by one arm and Tandia by the other and moved towards the house. 'I so excited to be here, honey!' she said in a voice loud enough for the onlookers to hear. 'My, my, now ain't that something else?' she indicated the red brick house as though she'd suddenly stepped around a corner and seen the Taj Mahal. Madam Flame Flo grinned. Mama Tequila had visited her a dozen times before at this same house, but she liked the showmanship; it couldn't do no harm anyway. Mama Tequila, still beaming, climbed the steps onto the front stoep, insisting that her sister and Tandia enter the house first. She turned at the door to face the crowd, and bringing both heavily bejewelled sets of fingers to her lips, she blew them a kiss. A spontaneous cheer broke out. Mama Tequila knew that her arrival would be the big news in town that night.

Madam Flame Flo seemed to Tandia to be everything Mama Tequila wasn't. She was thin as a wisp of morning smoke. Her voice was pitched high and she spoke rapidly. Her every movement was quick and impatient as though she was spring-loaded and would go off at the merest touch. She had prepared a huge lunch, mostly of cold meats: beef and mutton, silverside, salami, polony and cold pork sausages. Mama Tequila lost no time tucking in. She hadn't eaten since just after five that morning and declared herself to be starving. To her delight, the kitchen maid entered with a large bowl of roasted corn cobs. Sinking her fork into one end of the cob so it acted as a handle Mama Tequila ripped the hot golden seeds of corn from the husk with her teeth. Yellow butter ran down the corners of her mouth onto the napkin she had carefully folded around her neck.

Tandia was too excited to eat. Johannesburg with its yellow mine-dump mountains and the tall buildings reaching up into the sky made Durban seem like a small *dorp.* This was the big time all right! From the moment she'd been accepted by Natal University, Tandia knew where she was headed. Nothing was going to stop her. If a person made a name for herself in a place like this, she would be known in the best white circus all right! And she wanted that, though not the way Patel had craved it. Tandia would be known as the black woman who fought on even terms with the white oppressors of her people. A black who would spit in the face of apartheid. When she thought like this she would develop a glow, a burning deep within her. She wasn't even sure she understood what it was, whether love for her kind or hate for the whites, but it came increasingly and it gave her a strength which transcended even her fear of Geldenhuis.

Even Sophiatown was a surprise to Tandia. She'd never before witnessed a multiracial society and while poverty was evident everywhere, this place on the fringe of the big time had a non-interfered-with look about it. By contrast, Cato Manor, where she had been born and brought up, was an orderly urban slum kept under the heel of authority, which bred a passive resignation in its inhabitants. Cato Manor had none of the dynamism of this place on the high veld where the air seemed lighter and where the sky, a washed-out blue, seemed higher.

She'd warmed to the dusty-ankled, bright-eyed ragamuffins who'd run behind the car, yelling and cheering their progress. Some rolled hoops made from the spokeless rim of a bicycle wheel, guiding them with short sticks held into the grooved rim; others pushing skeletal motor cars shaped entirely out of bits of wire and driven by long sticks, each attached to a small wire steering wheel with which the driver turned the wheels. Catapults dangled around the necks of the kids, bouncing on their chests as they ran. Juicey Fruit Mambo had slowed right down to navigate the ruts and the puddles of dirty rainwater and the kids were thumping the back of the car with the flat of their hands as they cried a good-natured welcome.

Tandia sensed that the people, the crowd who had gathered around them when they'd stopped outside Madam Flame Flo's home, were different. For the first time she felt she belonged to something larger and more important than herself, that she was to be given a reason why her life was turning out so well. It was silly she told herself; how could she feel so much about this place? She hadn't walked more than fifty feet, the distance from the street into the dark cool house. And yet she sensed all of these things clearly. It was as though Sophiatown was the first place that made perfect sense to her in her life, this dirty little township where the spirit of her people rose above the squalor, the thuggery and the exploitation.

'So what do you think, ousie?' Madam Flame Flo leaned with her elbows on the dining-room table, her chin resting on her hands. 'What do you think about a brothel for coloured folk in the new township they calling Coronationville they making for us? Give us your honest answer. Not what you think you'd like me to hear! No soft pedalling you hear? What do you say, hey?'

Mama Tequila had settled herself down to some serious eating. 'Sshhh! Flo, not so much talk! You like a blerrie machine gun!' She had reverted to the Transvaal pronunciation of the word 'bloody', switching automatically from the more anglicised Natal 'bladdy'. She wiped her mouth with the butter-stained napkin around her neck and brought her coffee cup to her lips. She took a lingering sip from the cup. 'It all depends, Flo, what kind of whorehouse you want,' she said finally.

'The kind that makes lots of money! That the kind I want! What other kind is there?'

'Ja, of course, but in this new place you got only coloured trade. That means trouble, because you can't run a good whorehouse with only coloured people. You most likely got to run a BB-TM!'

'So, what's so wrong with that? In a BB-TM the money comes fast. No fancy overheads. Like *you* in the war. Jesus! You was raking in cash like it was going out of style!'

'Ja, jong, but soldiers and coloured people, they not the same thing. A soldier comes to a BB-TM because he's away from his home and his girl or his wife, or because his platoon they all also going. He needs a woman, he got dirty water on his chest and he want to get it off. A coloured *kerel* goes to a BB-TM when he's drunk because if he not drunk he's a natural freelancer who thinks he can get it for nothing. And when he's drunk he likes to fight and to gamble. So now what you got? You got trouble, you hear? You too old for that, Flo. Too rich also. Look! You can't open a house like Bluey Jay no more. You know how many coloureds come to Bluey Jay?' She held up three fingers. 'Three, they all rich. If I had to depend on coloureds there would be no bums bobbing in the beds, I can tell you that for sure, jong. It would be a no-go show, I'm telling you!' Mama Tequila paused and held up her hand. 'I know what you going to say and ja, I agree, here there is more coloureds than Durban. But all the same, to run a nice house you got to have rich. And also, without white you going nowhere, man! The white man is the one who likes to have black pussy! With him you can run a nice quiet house and make him pay. And you can't have no white whores for the coloured people, not because there not plenty around, but because the authorities say they can't live in this new place you going, what its name, this Coronation place? Also white whores they trouble, man, they poor whites who got no hygiene and they big friends with doctor brandy and Mary Jane!'

'Ja, okay, but what say we get only very pretty coloured girls? Just like you got at Bluey Jay. A pretty girl, no matter what colour, men always want?'

Mama Tequila arched an eyebrow. 'Flo, you know it already, a coloured man always wants what he can't get. He can get a coloured girl, he married to one! He want white pussy which is *verboten*. Even if your girls they real pretty, they still just like his wife.'

Mama Tequila took another sip from her cup before continuing. 'Flo, darling, you seen it yourself on a Saturday night! Good Street, that a damn funny name, it a good street orright! It good for pretty coloured girls and black girls who are dancing the *marabi* dance and selling freelance pussy at cut rates! Darling, in a whorehouse you got overheads. First you got to buy yourself a nice place, because if you rent, the landlord is always putting up the rent. Then you got to pay the police, not just one kind of police, you hear? You got to pay the SAPS, the Black Jacks, the Ghost Squad, the Homicide Squad, the Robbery Squad and even the Special Branch. Then the gangs; killers like Kort Boy who runs the Americans, even the tsotsi gangs so you got protection from themselves. Then you got maybe fifty people who all got their hand out. The council and the health department, you name it. In a whorehouse pay-out day is every day!'

Mama Tequila was warming to her subject. 'But all that's nothing, man! Because it's not so long before you get your first murder. Some drunk *hout kop*, wooden head, puts a knife in a girl because he think she looks like his sister or men fight over gambling and the guns come out.

'Now you got blood. When a whorehouse got blood it got trouble. No more police protection. The police, the Homicide Squad takes over and the nex' thing you in the *Rand Daily Mail* and the *Star* and you got to close down. When you start again somewhere else, every time it becomes harder 'cause now you got a rep. Soon you only get scum, only the crud comes and then it only a matter of time before someone pull the trigger and the gun is pointing at you. Bang! You dead! You a rich, dead nice-time girl!'

'Jesus!' Madam Flame Flo exclaimed. 'And I thought the shebeen business is bad! How come you never told me this before?'

'You never wanted to run a whorehouse before, my darling.' Mama Tequila leaned forward, 'Flo, you rich! Go buy yourself a nice place, get somewhere where your daughter can come sometimes to see you, somewhere where nobody can see it's happening.'

Flo sighed heavily. 'Ja, I dunno about that.'

'Ag, man, you can find a place. What about Newtown or Fordsburg, they got coloured and whites living there a long time already?'

'No, man, that all finish and klaar now! They kicking the coloureds out of Newtown and Fordsburg also, the same time they going to bulldoze Sophiatown. We all going to our own place. Indians one place, coloureds to Coronationville and the blacks going to Meadowlands and Diepkloof. That leaves the whites anywhere they want except not the places where the black and the coloured and the Indian folks been forced to live.' She laughed bitterly.

Tandia, who had been listening to the conversation, for the first time really understood what Mama Tequila had been through to get to the point where she owned and operated Bluey Jay. Maybe she wasn't a good person, but Mama Tequila was strong and resilient and a fighter. Tandia knew she too had to be all of those things if she was going to succeed. She knew that the burning inside of her was about being these things. 'Excuse me, Mama T, and also Madam Flame Flo?' she said suddenly. Mama Tequila looked up in surprise. While she had accepted Tandia as being present in the room, in terms of her conversation with her sister, Tandia had been mentally screened out. She was there to have lunch but not to be a part of the discussion. Her look of surprise turned to annoyance when Tandia added, 'I have an idea.'

Mama Tequila smiled. It was the smile the wolf gave to Red Riding Hood. The girls at Bluey Jay knew it and knew also it didn't augur well for the recipient. 'Maybe you could go take a nice walk in the sunshine, Tandy?' she said, her lips pursed.

Tandia opened her mouth and then thought better of it and began to rise from her chair. Some resilience hey? Just one Red Riding Hood smile from Mama Tequila and you weak as piss! No, bugger it! She sat down again and smiled prettily at both women. 'Swaziland! Why doesn't Madam Flame Flo open a whorehouse and a gambling place in Swaziland?' Tandia asked.

Mama Tequila and Madam Flame Flo had both stayed alive and prospered because they could think fast and on their feet. The coffee cup in Madam Flame Flo's hand dropped to the table, spilling coffee everywhere as a look of astonishment crossed her face. 'Jesus Mary and Joseph!' She turned to her sister. 'You said she was a *slimmetjie*! Jesus! That the best idea! That the best idea I ever heard in my whole life!'

Mama Tequila chuckled. Her scorn of a moment ago turned to approbation for the young girl who sat with them. 'This one is going to go a long, long way, I'm telling you, little sister, one day she going to be a somebody white people going to take a big notice of.'

Swaziland was a British Protectorate, a small mountainous country coloured red on the map which looked as though someone had taken a polite bite out of the eastern side of South Africa. It lay some four and a half hours' drive from Johannesburg and was just beginning the tedious process of being handed back by Britain to its rightful owners. The independence of Swaziland didn't trouble South Africa much, for the tiny country was and would continue to be largely dependent on South Africa for its daily bread.

Apart from forest products, sugar, iron ore and asbestos, the Swazi people had little to offer the Union of South Africa except the sweat of their backs. A part of the black labour which dug the gold in tunnels a mile below the streets of Johannesburg was Swazi. These indentured labourers were recruited to work in the mines on the Witwatersrand by the Native Recruiting Corporation for a minimum period of one hundred and eighty shifts. The Swaziland economy depended heavily on the repatriation of the money they earned. The mine labourers were paid almost no money while they worked and lived on the mine compounds. When they'd served their time – for life in the all-male dormitories where the men slept one above the other on concrete shelves and were fed like animals from giant cauldrons and who carried a copper bracelet with a number and not a name was a perfect simulation of prison – they were repatriated by overnight train to the Swaziland border, where they were paid the full amount of their six months' wages at a de-recruitment centre. The economy of this small, unimportant and very beautiful corner of Africa was based entirely on the export of sweated labour.

While there was some speculation that an independent Swaziland would be a training ground for black terrorists, the Boers consoled themselves with the knowledge that they could choke off the livelihood of the Swazi people in a matter of days should they threaten trouble or become uncooperative.

Tandia's suggestion was a stroke of genius, though it was early times yet. It might be ten years before Swaziland would be released from the paternal guidance and moral stricture of the British Colonial Service, it was time to buy land and start the business of making friends with the royal family. The King of the Swazi, King Sobhuza II, would, they felt sure, see no virtue in the South African Immorality Act and with the establishment of a brothel and casino would see an opportunity too good for his small country to miss. Mama Tequila and Madam Flame Flo instantly believed themselves to be the two people who knew just how to put this proposition to the middle-aged black monarch who preferred a leopardskin to a suit and who had been absolute tribal ruler of his people for thirty-three years.

The two women were excited, Mama Tequila just as much as Madam Flame Flo. Mama Tequila wasn't stupid; she knew that events were catching up with her at Bluey Jay. She'd be lucky if she had another ten years. The Geldenhuis affair, the biggest and most dangerous threat to Bluey Jay's existence so far, was bound to have serious repercussions as Geldenhuis set about reaping his revenge. Bluey Jay was, she knew, an anachronism, a small island of defiance in a sea of defeat. Even this was an exaggeration. Mama Tequila knew you couldn't stay open without the tacit approval of some pretty high-up officials in the government, and now they were under increasing pressure and sooner or later would have to capitulate.

In Swaziland there was a place for both sisters to start again. Mbabane, the country's mountain capital, was an ideal location for people coming from the Transvaal and Natal. All Mama Tequila's old clients would still be available to her on an occasional dirty twenty-four and the rest of the white male population could now get legit black weekend pussy no more than four hours' drive from their front door. The Van der Merwe sisters would be united at last. Flo would handle the casino and she, the one and only Mama Tequila, would run the whorehouse.

Mama Tequila wanted more time to think, and she didn't want Flo to overwork her praise for Tandia's suggestion. Tandia was after all beholden to Mama Tequila, and the big woman wasn't about to let her off the hook too easily. She intended to build up a burden of indebtedness in Tandia before the little *slimmetjie* became a lawyer. A person never knew when a lawyer might be needed. Mama Tequila wanted a good, solid debt she could cash in if the time came and the need arose.

'Ja, it is a good idea, but also it's got some problems,' Mama Tequila said in a flat voice. Flo was about to protest, but her sister raised her hand. 'Later! Later, you hear? Tonight maybe we can talk. One thing is good, with something like this you could have Stephanie with you?'

'Ag, man, I was going to tell you before about that. She wants to get married.'

Mama Tequila spread her arms out towards her sister, a look of resignation on her face. To anyone observing, as Tandia did, it would have seemed a curiously inappropriate reaction. Delight and congratulations might have been expected.

Tandia was filled with curiosity at the prospect of Madam Flame Flo's daughter being married, but the expression on Mama Tequila's face told her not to become involved. Quite suddenly, Madam Flame Flo began to cry.

'Flo, no tears, you hear!' Mama Tequila snapped.

Madam Flame Flo sniffed and blew into her napkin. 'It's hard, ousie!' she said in a tiny voice.

'I know, but crying not going to help!'

'She's, she's going to marry a Boer!' Madam Flame Flo blurted out. 'My baby is going to marry a fucking Boer!'

'It's better than a fucking kaffir!' Mama Tequila shouted at her.

'It isn't, ousie! I rather she married a tsotsi or a gangster than a verdoemde hairy back!'

'Flo, lissen! When you gave her to the nuns to bring up like a nice little white girl, when you kissed her goodbye at that convent boarding school, it was all over between you and Stephanie. It was all over, you hear? You gave her to the white world! You can't go blubbing to have her back now she wants to marry a Afrikaner!'

Madam Flame Flo avoided her sister's eye and turned suddenly to Tandia. 'How old are you, Miss Tandy?'

'Seventeen, eighteen this year,' Tandia replied.

'Nearly the same. My daughter is nineteen, this year twenty.' She smiled at Tandia. 'She's not nearly as beautiful as you, but she has white skin, blonde hair and blue eyes, dark blue like the winter sky.'

Tandia flushed. 'I'm sorry,' she stammered, 'I know how you must feel.'

Madam Flame Flo sniffed again and wiped her nose. 'Ag, it's my own fault. I deserve this,' she started to cry softly again. 'My beautiful Stephanie, she going to marry a white Boer bastard who's just like her fucking daddy!'

'Flo! You want I should call Juicey Fruit Mambo and get back in that big Packard and go home? Because if that what you want you got to just keep on like this! You want to run a brothel? Ha! You couldn't run a ring-a-ring-a-rosie contest! With Stephanie it's finish and klaar. We decided that long, long ago! You cry one more time, I'm going home, that for blerrie sure!' Mama Tequila dipped into her handbag and produced a tiny lace handkerchief. 'Here!' she snorted, holding it out to her sister.

Madam Flame Flo took the hanky and dabbed at her eyes. She was embarrassed by her outburst and at the reprimand from her older sister.

Tandia rose from her chair. 'I think I'll go for a walk,' she said quietly, in an attempt to extricate herself gracefully from the situation.

'No, please, Miss Tandy, you stay,' Madam Flame Flo sniffed, pulling her head right back. 'I'm orright now, really, it's okay, all over.' She smiled through the last of her tears. 'You can be my daughter, you hear?'

Tandia smiled back. 'What about being my Aunty? I'd like to have you as my Aunty Flo. But only if you call me Tandy.'

'That's true,' Mama Tequila chuckled. 'No more Miss Tandy, this not the right place; just Tandy from now on.'

'You got it!' Madam Flame Flo said smiling broadly. 'From now on I'm your Aunty Flo and you just plain Tandy who is beautiful and clever and has nice manners also.'

The crisis was over and Mama Tequila flipped open her cigarette case and removed a cork-tip, lit it and blew a cloud of smoke towards the ceiling. 'Ja, okay, Tandy, you go for a walk, but just be careful, you hear, all the bright boys and the tsotsis will want to make your acquaintance.'

'Juicey Fruit Mambo will want to come,' Tandia replied. She would have preferred to venture up the street alone, to feel the strange sense of freedom she'd experienced the moment they'd entered the ramshackle do-it-yourself township, but she knew Mama Tequila would expect the big black man to tag along.

'Ja, that's a damn good idea,' Mama Tequila said.

'Goodbye, Aunty Flo,' Tandia called softly to Madam Flame Flo.

Madam Flame Flo smiled. She seemed to have recovered, and she watched Tandia leave the room. 'So beautiful and so clever!' She handed the balled, wet hanky back to her sister.

Mama Tequila returned the handkerchief to her bag. 'Ja, I never seen Tandy like this before. Usually the cat got her tongue. She's a very quiet type person. I think maybe being up here on the Rand and in Sophiatown is making her different.' She turned to her sister. 'Flo, I must go lie down for my beauty sleep, you hear? I going to take three Aspro, I got a terrible headache from the drive. Is there water in my room?'

'Oh my God! I forgot the pudding!' Flo said, alarmed. 'Some pudding! Wait, you must have some. It's jelly and custard with peaches, just how you like it always!'

'No, jong, *ek is heeltemal versadig, liefling.* I don't like to eat much at lunchtime. Tonight maybe, hey?' Mama Tequila pushed her plate away, made a clearing on the table directly in front of her, and placed her handbag onto it. Then she put both her hands flat on the tablecloth and, pushing down, slowly rose from her chair. She smiled at her sister. 'We made a good start today, Flo. Here, man! This Swaziland thing, it a blerrie wonderful idea! We talk some more tonight, hey?'

'There is water for washing in your room. I'll send the kitchen girl with some nice cold ice for your sore head,' Flo said, grateful that she was back in her sister's good books.

'Flo, *moenie worry nie, alles sal reg kom, liefling!*' Mama Tequila comforted her. 'Lots can happen in young love between the diamond ring and the band of gold. And don't worry about yourself, you hear? When they going to bulldoze your house?'

'When the winter comes, June, July, maybe August. We won't have another summer in Sophiatown. This the last.'

Mama Tequila killed her cigarette in the ashtray. 'Little sister, we seen a lot of things in our time. We seen hard times and some good. But one thing I know, as long as a white policeman can be bribed – and that a long, long, time, baby – and as long as men like to get drunk and their one-eyed snake want pussy, we got no problems, only we got opportunities.' She glanced towards the door, which was something most coloured and black people seemed to do when they were about to mention the Boer government. 'Even if that bastard Strijdom tries to close us down, like he trying to close down Sophiatown! Maybe with Sophiatown he can do it. He can come in and smash everything with a big bulldozer so people's houses are just bricks and their past lies in the dust. But if he thinks he can come here and bulldoze the Van der Merwe sisters, that will be the day! He got to get up very early in the morning to do that!'

Flo was dishing out a small helping of jelly for herself. 'Maybe just a little pudding, to take with me in my room,' Mama Tequila said, and then continued. 'You know who we like, little sister? We like when you put a drop of that mercury stuff. You know, what they call it, man? Quicksilver! Remember when we was young *oubaas* we would pour some quicksilver on the linoleum and then we'd try to pick it up with our two fingers. Remember that? Well, that what we like, you and me!' Mama Tequila suddenly burst out laughing. 'As long as a man got a mouth so he can open it to drink and a one-eyed snake trying to wake up in his trousers, you and me, darling, we in business!' She took the bowl of jelly, custard and big halves of golden tinned peaches which Flo had now heaped almost to overflowing into a soup plate and, chuckling, waddled from the room.

'*Slaap lekker, ousie*,' Madam Flame Flo called after her.

'Ja, I will sleep like a baby,' Mama Tequila called back.

Tandia found herself outside in the bright sunshine. January is hot on the high veld, but at nearly six thousand feet, Johannesburg has no humidity and the air is almost always crisp and clear. Sometimes when the wind blows it raises a fine curtain of dust from the mine dumps that settles over the city and causes the skin to itch and the eyes to inflame. But these occasions are infrequent and generally the high veld climate is delightful. So at half past one on a cloudless day, despite the dirt and the piles of rubbish burning on the side of the road, the ruts and the puddles left from last night's rain in the roadway, Good Street looked bright and inviting to Tandia.

Juicey Fruit Mambo was outside beside the Packard. He'd washed it down and now it was surrounded by street urchins helping him to polish the big brown machine. They were laughing and shouting and having a high old time. Almost all the kids had a sucker stick poking from the corner of their mouths. Juicey Fruit Mambo's small-boy magic evidently worked just as well with these tough little urban kids as it did with the kids from the kraal down beside the river. He was a master of small-boy psychology, which was generally heavily slanted towards unabashed and blatant bribery.

'Have you eaten?' Tandia asked as she approached.

'Yes, Missy Tandy, plenty scoff in dis place,' Juicey Fruit Mambo answered. 'Madam Flo, she very nice madam.'

'I see you have made friends already, hey?' Tandia indicated the kids who had come to stand around the big black man and now stared shyly at her. She lifted her hand in a signal of friendship, waggling her fingers. 'Hi, everyone!'

'Good afternoon, miss!' they chorussed. It was a classroom routine which neither they nor she had expected and both parties seemed surprised at the spontaneous reaction.

Juicey Fruit Mambo grinned. 'Eh, eh, eh! Dis boys dey big skelms, but I tink dey my friend, also.' He suddenly looked serious. 'You want to go somewhere, Missy Tandy?'

'Just for a walk. You can stay if you like, I'll be all right on my own.'

Juicey Fruit Mambo looked shocked. 'Dis very bad place Missy Tandy. You not walk by yourself, plenty tsotsi boys in dis place!'

Tandia loved Juicey Fruit Mambo too much to protest, and they set off down the street followed by at least a dozen urchins of various shades, the darkest of them seemingly a full African while the lightest, despite the dirt that seemed to cover him from head to toe, was unmistakably a tousle-headed blond with blue eyes.

'Dis skelms, dey ask for me, is dis young missus a fillim star? Ja, for sure!

I say. Ja, ja, dey tell to me also, we know dis, we hear dat big fat mama how she talk Americano language!'

'Juicey Fruit Mambo! You shouldn't say such things, they'll tell grown-up people and then we'll get into trouble!'

Juicey Fruit Mambo began to laugh uproariously and all the kids joined in, not knowing why he was laughing but prepared to share in the merriment of their new friend. After all, he had bought them suckers all round at the coolies' and told them about his magic gold teeth. Which of course, they knew was a heap of crap, but a person couldn't let a good story like that go past when it came from someone who looked after a Packard and also a big, fat American fillim star and a very pretty young one who could possibly be just about anyone a person could see on the fillims.

'Maybe she's Snow White!' Flyspeck Mendoza, a dark-eyed, dark-skinned, curly-haired kid said gravely.

Dog Poep Ismali, whose father had a bicycle shop in Annadale Street, objected, 'Ag, man! Snow White wasn't a real person! She was just pitchers *drawn* with a pencil and coloured in! You can ask my sister, if you like? You mad if you think there is real people who is dwarves like Grumpy and Dopey?'

Too Many Fingers Bembi, the small black boy who looked like a pure African, giggled. 'Your stupid brother who is gezonked in the head looks like one of them dwarves and he is dopey!'

The kids all laughed, but Dog Poep Ismali, who was the cleverest in the class, ignored them. 'I think she definitely the one riding the black horse in *National Velvet*. That for sure, man!' To emphasise his certainty, he added, 'Only she was much younger then, now she's grown up some more.' Dog Poep offered this observation as though he was fitting the last piece of absolute proof into place.

They all instantly agreed with him, even those of them who hadn't seen the picture. Dog Poep had a sister who worked as an usherette at the Odin bioscope and so he was considered a bit of an authority on the fillims. Besides, they all very much wanted to believe him.

'Why you laughing, Juicey Fruit Mambo? You told them something you shouldn't have, didn't you?'

'Dis boys, dey want for you to marry,' Juicey Fruit Mambo giggled. Then he beckoned to one of the older boys. 'You tell for Missy Tandy, who you want for her to marry, okay?'

'What's your name?' Tandia asked the small boy who had stepped forward. He was too dark to pass for white. His matted hair was brown and curly and his eyes a lighter coloured brown than Bantu. His shirt was dirty and it missed two buttons and the pocket of his equally dirty shorts was torn.

Taking a raspberry sucker from his mouth the boy smiled as he answered, 'Johnny Tambourine, miss!' Then, resting his head on his shoulder, he looked up at her cheekily and asked, 'Have you come from Hollywood to marry Gideon Mandoma, miss?'

The kids must have seen how she instinctively reacted to the boxer's name, for they all started to laugh. Of course, that was it! Mandoma, the welterweight who had lost a disputed title-fight decision to Geldenhuis, must live in Sophiatown. The brown-eyed kid was talking about one of the two boxers Patel had rated higher than any other amateurs he'd seen in the ring.

'Mandoma, the welterweight? He lives here?' Tandia asked.

'Ja, miss, he's the best in the world! Welterweight champion of black Africa and also really the white champion because he was rooked!' Johnny Tambourine said this vehemently. 'It's God's truth! They *verneuked* him, miss. My uncle was there, he saw the whole fight. Mandoma won every round!'

Several of the other kids chorussed, 'It's true, miss, they rooked him!'

'They gave the title to the policeman whose name is Geldenhuis,' Dog Poep Ismali explained gravely, bringing a little sensible consideration into the emotional outburst. 'It was because Gideon Mandoma is a kaffir they wouldn't give it to him. The whites don't want a kaffir who could beat a white man, miss.'

At the mention of Geldenhuis's name Tandia had gone cold. He was still there, the dark shadow that never went away. She shook her head and skipped down the road ahead of the kids. She hadn't skipped like this since she'd been a little kid herself and it helped to erase the policeman's footprints in her mind.

'I don't even know Gideon Mandoma! How can I marry him if I don't know him?' she called back, covering her sudden apprehension with laughter.

'Easy, miss! You can meet him any time you want, he's a big friend of ours!' Johnny Tambourine, who seemed to assume the mantle as leader, called after her. Then all the kids, pushing their hoop-and-wire contraptions, took off after her yelling and laughing.

'Ja, he's our friend!' they shouted happily.

Tandia started to run down the road, her arms spread wide. 'Not today, thank you. Today I want you to show me all around the place, okay?'

Johnny Tambourine was the first to catch up with her. 'You can join our gang if you like, miss?' he offered.

Tandia stopped and turned. 'Thank you, I'd like that, that's very nice of you, Johnny!'

'Johnny Tambourine, miss, that's my name. You see my pa plays in the Harlem Swingsters with Gwigwi the clarinet player at Balanski's Picture Palace, that's how I got my name.' He was certain that Tandia would be impressed.

'Oh, I'm sorry Mr Tambourine whose first name is Johnny. I promise on my word of honour it won't happen again.'

'You can be our *nooi*!' Flyspeck Mendoza suggested, giggling.

'Of course!' Tandia replied. She looked serious for a moment. 'Unless of course you've got some other girls for sweethearts?'

'No, miss!' they all shouted.

'No, miss, only you, we only like you!' Dog Poep replied hurriedly, anxious to assure her that she was the only woman they cared sufficiently about to invite into their gang.

'Good! What must I do to be your nooi and also be in your gang?'

This seemed to bemuse them somewhat, until a small blond boy named Kaas Kop, looking down at his feet and making a circle in the earth with his dusty big toe, spoke up. 'Ag, man, nothing hard, just easy stuff like being pretty an' all that?' They all nodded their heads in rapid agreement.

'Ja, miss, that's all!' they chorussed.

Johnny Tambourine waited until the noise had died down. 'Ja, just stuff like that, you don't have to, you know, do things.'

'What sort of things, Johnny Tambourine?' Tandia asked.

He looked awkward. 'Well, like you married to us or anything. You don't have to do that, you know what married people do?'

'There's too much talk about marriage around here!' Tandia laughed. 'I'll just be your nooi, but not like we married, okay?'

They all looked serious and nodded their heads in agreement. 'And you don't have to spill blood also!' Johnny Tambourine said. 'Girls don't have to do it to belong,' he added, inventing this new rule for female membership.

'I jolly well hope not!' Tandia winced, 'I'm not at all the brave type!'

'That's okay, miss,' Dog Poep Ismali said. 'That's what we for, we can be brave for you any time you like.'

'Okay, I'll try and be the best nooi you ever had,' Tandia said graciously. 'You must call me Tandy. No other name, just Tandy! Now you got to show me around the place, you hear? Juicey Fruit Mambo and me, we want to see everything in Sophiatown, okay?'

Some of the kids raced ahead and then turned to watch Tandia and Juicey Fruit Mambo walking up Good Street towards the Odin, the largest cinema in the whole of Africa. Outside the large cinema was a poster which displayed a picture of a smiling young boxer, gloved and stripped to the waist in the classic boxing pose. The poster announced the coming Saturday night fight between Gideon Mandoma and an Irish welterweight named Terence 'Iron Jaw' McGraw. Tandia's heart began to beat faster and she knew that somehow she had to persuade Mama Tequila to take her to see the fight.

TEN

Tandia need not have worried about attending the Gideon Mandoma bout. Madam Flame Flo was a well-known Sophiatown ringside figure who never missed a fight. She knew her fighters and she knew her boxing.

She'd been taken to her first few fights by Geel Piet. She'd loved the brash boxing world, the dressing up and the American slang, the cigarette smoke, the excitement, the sweat, and of course the parties afterwards. But in the process she'd learned to love the game itself. She also saw clearly how it was a way for a coloured or black man to achieve fame and even some fortune, and the idea that black could meet white in the ring on equal terms where the best man won enchanted her. Madam Flame Flo took her boxing very seriously and the boxer she loved with a fierce pride and inner joy was Gideon Mandoma.

'I only seen him lose once, because the last fight he lost don't count. Man, he was rooked! But that first time. Magtig! What a fight. I don't think I will ever see a better one than that, even if I live to be one hundred years!'

Tandia was aware that she was talking about the same fight Patel had so often described, the fight between Gideon Mandoma and The Tadpole Angel where he had acted as referee. From Patel's countless re-tellings she knew every blow, every nuance of the contest. But now she wanted to hear it all again, hear it from fresh lips, see it with new eyes. So she said nothing and waited for Madam Flame Flo to continue.

'The Bantu, the black people, they had this thing about the white boy, the one they called the Tadpole Angel. In all his fights he always fought Boers and always he won. It was the blacks who give him this name, *Onoshobishobi Ingelosi*. That mean Tadpole Angel in Zulu. There was some other things also about this white boy. You know how superstitious the kaffirs are? I never heard the whole story but they thought, maybe because he always fought Boers and won, but I think it was something else also, they thought he was a great chief who would save them. Crazy, hey? A white kid, only about fifteen years old, a rooinek also, who was going to save *them* from the hated Boer.'

'That the first time I ever heard of a white man who is going to save the coons, not even a man, just a boy. What happened to him? Where's he now, man?' Mama Tequila asked.

'That the best part, I was coming to that,' replied Madam Flame Flo. 'He in England at the university in Oxford but he also now the British Empire Welterweight Champion and they say he going to go to America to fight for the world title later this year. That why everyone here so angry because Gideon Mandoma was rooked in his fight with the Boer Geldenhuis. You see, when the Tadpole Angel come back Mandoma or Geldenhuis is going to fight him. All the black people and the coloureds we want a re-match, we want Gideon Mandoma to fight the Tadpole Angel again.'

'For the same reason as before?' Tandia asked.

'Ja, for the blacks it's the same reason. Gideon Mandoma is a very big hero for the blacks, he is a chief, already he is very involved in the ANC freedom campaign. If he can win against the white man, then he will be *Onoshobishobi Ingelosi*, the chosen leader. For me and the other coloured people, we would like him to be leader, but also it would be the best fight possible. Last time when the white boy won, it was very close. The fight could easily have gone Mandoma's way. I'm telling you, man, it would be a fight and a half!'

Tandia wanted Madam Flame Flo to go back to the original fight. 'Aunty Flo, in the beginning, in the first fight wasn't it to decide who would be the *Onoshobishobi Ingelosi*?'

She looked at Tandia in surprise. 'You right. I forgot that. How come you know this?'

Mama Tequila laughed. 'Tandia's daddy was the ref who did that fight.'

'Jesus! Your daddy was the Indian referee, Natkin Patel? You that Patel! Then you know all about the fight between Gideon Mandoma and the Tadpole Angel!'

'Ja, but only from my father, I never heard it told by anybody else. I want to hear it from you, Aunty Flo. My father, he said the Tadpole Angel and Gideon Mandoma, they were the best amateur prospects he ever saw in his whole life. He was also training Geldenhuis for the fight with Mandoma when he died.'

It was Madam Flame Flo's turn to be amazed. 'Jesus, Mary and Joseph! It's a small world, hey? No wonder you want to meet Gideon Mandoma, it like he a part of your family and everything! Your daddy was training Geldenhuis?'

'Ja, but he thought Mandoma would win. He said, "Geldenhuis is a bladdy good welterweight, world class, if it wasn't for the Tadpole Angel and Mandoma he'd be South African champion, maybe even more, the champion of the British Empire. But the other two, they better!" He said that only a few days before he died.'

'Wragtig! He said that?' She turned to Mama Tequila. 'Jesus! What a small world, hey, ousie? Tandy who is now with you was Patel's daughter!' Her eyes shone with genuine excitement.

Tandia repeated her previous plea. 'Please, Aunty Flo, tell us about the first fight.'

'Ja, okay.' Madam Flame Flo smoothed her dress with the flat of her hands, stroking the top of her legs. 'Who knows how a kaffir's mind works? Don't ask me! The black people, they followed this white kid from when he was very young and then all of a sudden this witch doctor throws the bones and reads the smoke and she says, okay now the *Onoshobishobi Ingelosi* is a man. You know, fifteen years old, now he must prove to the people he is still the Tadpole Angel. Crazy kaffir stuff like that. So they choose Gideon Mandoma, who is a real Zulu chief and also a boxer. If the white boy wins, fair enough, he still the Tadpole Angel. If Gideon Mandoma wins he the new one and he has the power to lead the black people.'

'Gideon Mandoma,' Mama Tequila asked, 'did he also believe all this stuff?'

'Ja, of course! But not just him, everyone. Even me, a little bit. They had the fight over at the school, in the soccer field. Ten thousand people came. God's truth, two kids . . . the white one was still at school and Gideon was only sixteen years old and ten thousand people turned up for that fight.' Madam Flame Flo smiled at the memory. 'That night we sold one hundred and fifty gallons of Barberton! But only afterwards. The black people didn't drink at the fight. I'm telling you, man, it was deadly serious.'

'Maybe Gideon Mandoma will get this fight with the white guy. When you say he is coming back?' Mama Tequila asked.

'They say first he's going to fight for the world title in America, then he's coming home. August, September maybe.'

'I don't think Geldenhuis will be ready to fight by then,' she winked at Tandia. 'He had a bad car accident.' Tandia was grateful that Madam Flame Flo's concentration was on her sister so that the shrewd little woman wouldn't note her anxiety at the mention of the policeman's name.

'Ja, it was a great shame, why couldn't the bastard have died,' Madam Flame Flo rejoined. 'They say he'll be better by the end of the year. That's when he would fight the Tadpole Angel for the British Empire Welterweight title. It would be Gideon's fight if he hadn't been rooked. I admit it was a close fight, but everyone, even the *Rand Daily Mail* said it, everyone knew Mandoma won except two of the judges. Those two Boers gave it to Geldenhuis by one lousy point.'

Mama Tequila sighed. 'Ja, my little sister, if what should have been had happened, it would be a different world. The best way to win, no arguments, is to put your opponent down for a ten count. That the only way for the black man and the coloured. If it's going to be a "maybe" then it going to be the white man's maybe not the black man's maybe, that for blerrie sure!'

Saturday night on Good Street was something else, a magic six or eight hours when the people of Sophiatown forgot the trauma and the struggle of the past week, bottled and corked their tiredness and set out to celebrate the business of being alive. The Mandoma fight was on at the Odin; afterwards there would be a short political rally; and then the dance halls and the streets would fill with the jazz and jive of people having a good time. Saturday night in Sophiatown was get drunk, get laid and get dancin' time! Sunday, repenting time, was a long, long way away as the rhythm lumped into Good Street from the shacks and shebeens and good-time places.

Madam Flame Flo's house was no more than a hundred and fifty yards from the Odin, but, naturally, the Packard, which shone to within an inch of its life, was used to deliver the three women to the cinema entrance. Juicey Fruit Mambo, in his tuxedo and red bow tie, hurried round first to open the nearside door facing the cinema for Madam Flame Flo. Then he opened the door facing the street for Mama Tequila to be rocked out of the rear seat of the big car as inconspicuously as possible.

Tandia was dressed in the brilliant green cheongsam which Sonny Vindoo had made for her. With it she wore the matching high heels Heffie and Sarah had given her for Christmas. Her dark springy hair, no more than an inch long, was cut evenly over her scalp so that it looked like a sophisticated cap. From her ears two large gold hoops hung, borrowed from Madam Flame Flo. Her lips were painted a shiny, Rita-Hayworth red, and her magnificent green eyes were heightened with a touch of eyeshadow which started quite dark in the corners of her eyes and went to the palest green over the broad arch of her eyelids.

Tandia was stunningly, ravishingly beautiful, caught at the precise moment when she had become a woman. No awkward gesture or even faint trace of childhood remained. A sudden silence fell on the crowd as she stepped from the car. Then there was a gasp of appreciation as the men entering the cinema for the fight whistled and cheered loudly.

Tandia had learned a great deal about men working the bar at Bluey Jay and now she instinctively reacted to please them, dropping her gaze in a gesture suggesting a hint of shyness and tilting her head slightly as she smiled. The crowd was delighted by the glamour she added to the occasion. There were several young women in the crowd, all dressed up to the nines, but Tandia outshone them all. The crowd parted as Mama Tequila, dressed in a peacock-blue satin evening dress and turban with matching everything and Madam Flame Flo in a halter-neck, red organza dress with matching red satin high heels, walking on either side of Tandia, entered the building.

'It's showtime ladies, we all ritz, glitz and tits tonight!' Mama Tequila said happily as they were ushered by a pretty young Indian girl to the ringside seats that Madam Flame Flo had obtained from her friend and Gideon Mandoma's manager, Mr Nguni. The Indian leaned over Tandia as she was seated.

'My little brother,' she giggled, 'the one they call Dog Poep, he said you were pretty, but I didn't believe him, little brats has got some funny ideas.

But I was wrong, you the most beautiful woman I ever seen in my whole life even on the movies.'

Tandia loved the compliment but was quick to repay it. 'You too, you a very pretty girl, what's your name?'

The little usherette smiled. 'Esmeralda,' she replied.

'Esmeralda Ismali, it sounds like a song, like a love song,' Tandia said smiling. The Indian girl's eyes were wide with pleasure as she left.

Tandia found herself enjoying the atmosphere enormously as the crowd shouted, whistled and catcalled instructions and insults at the two fighters in the ring. With the main bout approaching they were impatient for the preliminary bout to end.

Johnny Tambourine, wearing a clean white cotton jacket several sizes too big for him and with a large tray of peanuts and chocolate bars held by a strap around his neck, appeared suddenly at her side. 'Hi, Tandy, everybody is saying you the most beautiful person they ever seen. I think they hundred per cent right!' he announced, and at the same time unloaded a packet of peanuts and a chocolate bar into her lap. 'It's for you, for nothing, because you our nooi and in the gang an' all,' he explained.

'Thank you, Johnny Tambourine, but you can't do this, *you'll* have to pay!'

Johnny Tambourine looked shocked at the suggestion. 'No man, never! I pinched it off another kid's tray, *he'll* have to pay.' Johnny Tambourine must have seen the look on Tandia's face and now he frowned, slightly annoyed. 'It's orright, Tandy, he isn't a member of our gang or anything like that! They done it to me lots of times when I was little.' Then he grinned, deciding to forgive her stupidity as a gang member. 'So long, I got to go now, see ya later, you hear?'

'No wait a minute! Johnny Tambourine, come back here, give me your arm.' He returned and stuck the sleeve of his white coat at her. 'Hold your arm stiff,' Tandia instructed and began to roll the sleeve neatly to just above his wrist. 'Now the other one.' She repeated the performance on the other sleeve. 'Okay, that's better now, hey?'

Johnny Tambourine grinned. 'How am I supposed to pinch stuff off other guys' trays if my hands showing?' But he was obviously pleased at the attention and aware that men from all over couldn't take their eyes off Tandia. 'Thanks, Tandy, see you after the fight. If I can pinch an eskimo pie I'll bring it!'

Tandia raised her hands in alarm. 'No! No ice cream, Johnny Tambourine!' But the small boy was already several rows away shouting, 'Peeee-nuts! Chocooo-litz! Peeeenuts!', his oversized white jacket reaching to well below his knees.

The final preliminary came to an end in a flurry of exhausted ineffectual blows and the crowd booed both fighters good-naturedly out of the ring.

A young black man with a big smile and a beautifully fitted black evening suit with a white carnation leapt into the ring. He seemed to vibrate, several parts of his body moving at the same time as though he was headed in several directions at once. He moved over to lift the microphone up into the ring, giving Tandia a pearly-white smile as he did so.

'Good evening my brothers and sisters, majietas and girls! Please give a warm welcome to the sensational Dorothy "Dotty" Masuka, the sizzling hepcat, Africa's own soul lady, the one and only yippy-woo-biddy-hi-de-ho lady, the singing sensation from Bulawayo! To accompany the first African lady of song I give you the Harlem Swingsters with the immortal clarinet of Mister Funny-face himself, the great Gwigwi!'

The crowd started to stomp and whistle and yell their heads off as half-a-dozen musicians climbed into the ring. A small, smiling man moved to the microphone as the compere hopped out of the ring. He held a clarinet in his hands, putting it to his lips as the bass started to beat out the rhythm and the alto sax pumped out a blues number slow and mournfully. He appeared to blow, but no sound came from the clarinet. He withdrew it, looked at it, tapped it with his finger as though remonstrating with it, all the while pulling funny faces. He tried and failed again as the rhythm in the background increased and the alto wailed plaintively. Finally, he moved over to the edge of the ring and, using the clarinet, pointed at Tandia, beckoning to her with his index finger to come to the edge of the stage.

Tandia was almost paralysed with fear but Mama Tequila, nudging her, whispered, 'Tandy, this your big chance, baby, go-go!' Shaking, Tandia rose and walked to the edge of the stage, to the thunderous applause and whistles of the crowd. Gwigwi brought the clarinet sideways to his lips and kissed it and then pointed to Tandia and kissed it again, whereupon he handed the instrument to her. Tandia, smiling despite her terror, brought the clarinet to her lips and kissed it lightly, handing it back to the little man. Gwigwi, smiling and miming his ecstasy, walked backwards towards the mic and, bringing the clarinet up to his lips, he blew a long, sweet, absolutely pure note that reached up, cutting through the smoke and the hubbub of the crowd, holding its distance and clarity until the cinema was completely hushed and the lone clarinet became the spirit of them all, and then fading down, slowly, perfectly controlled until it warped into a whisper hardly heard at all.

The cinema broke into wild applause and the band picked up the beat, quickened the pace and swung into Dixieland. The lights came down low until a single spot held onto the musicians in the ring; then they brightened again to show a smiling black woman in a red satin evening dress, who walked over to the microphone and began to sing with only Gwigwi's clarinet and the bass to accompany her.

I love my thing
'cause my man's my thing
Call him drink, drank, drunk . . .
he's still my thing!
He jobs for me . . .

that you wouldn't have thunk.
So I love my thing . . .
Eee . . . Ma . . . Ye . . . Mo . . . Wunk!

I love my thing
'cause my man's my thing . . .
He wins for me,
and he makes me drunk,
drunk with the love
I've fallen in!
So I love my thing . . .
Eee . . . Ma . . . Ye . . . Mo . . . Wunk!

The crowd waited half a beat after the song had ended before going wild. Tandia found her pulse racing and she could hear her heart pounding in her breast. Stop it! You don't even know him! she admonished herself. She knew Dorothy Masuka had been singing about Mandoma. Her voice was smooth and hot and suggestive and her eyes told a story of sinuous, slow, beautiful lovemaking. Tandia felt a warm stirring in her thighs and breasts that she'd never experienced before. 'Stop it! Stop it!' she demanded to herself. She brought her arms up and hugged herself and discovered she was trembling. The lights went down and in the dimness she could see the singer and the musicians climb down from the ring, but the heat within her remained, curled up inside of her like a dangerous, illicit, delicious thing.

Slowly the lights returned and the applause died down and then there was a stirring in the crowd and some spasmodic whistling and clapping as Terence 'Iron Jaw' McGraw, a pale, red-headed Irishman climbed into the ring followed by his manager and one of his seconds.

The Irish fighter wore a green silk dressing gown on the back of which was embroidered a shamrock and the initials T. McG. He walked to each side of the ring, bowing at the crowd and putting his gloves together and raising them above his head. He caught sight of Tandia in her brilliant green dress, and mistaking the colour as the sign of a fan he blew her several kisses, much to the delight of Mama Tequila and Madam Flame Flo.

'That Irish should be so lucky!' Mama Tequila boomed. 'Iron Jaw' McGraw's manager walked over and slipped the boxer's satin gown from his shoulders, whereupon the Irishman began to shadow box, throwing short left and right jabs, bobbing and weaving from an imaginary opponent and hooking into the air, grunting as each punch was thrown. He was nicely built for a welter and his pale pink shoulders were covered with fat ginger freckles, a strangely incongruous sight in the cinema filled mostly with blacks and coloureds – although there were a few white faces in the ringside seats.

Tandia could see a coloured man, a black man and a white come to sit at the judges' table. The timekeeper and referee were having an earnest conversation at the timekeeper's table. There was a sudden roar from the crowd and Tandia turned to see a huge man in evening dress coming down the aisle on her left. Behind him was Gideon Mandoma in a white satin gown down to his ankles, the satin hood almost completely covering his face.

Mandoma was looking down at his feet so that it was impossible to see him. He seemed to be oblivious of the crowd as he walked behind the huge black man whom Tandia guessed must be Mr Nguni, Madam Flame Flo's friend and Gideon Mandoma's manager. Her heart beat wildly. She had heard so much for so long about the Zulu welterweight and she could hardly believe that she was going to see him fight, see the man whom Patel had called maybe the best raw talent he had ever seen in the ring.

Mandoma had his back to her as he climbed into the ring, and as she was seated almost directly behind his corner the white satin hood continued to obscure his face from her view. The crowd had begun to chant, 'Mandoma! Mandoma! Mandoma!' 'Iron Jaw' McGraw finally went to his corner and sat down as Mr Nguni walked over, watching as his seconds taped his hands and fitted the gloves. His own manager was over in Mandoma's corner checking the same ritual on the black man.

To Tandia's surprise it was Mr Nguni who walked over to the microphone and introduced the two fighters. Madam Flame Flo leaned over and explained, 'He not just Mandoma's manager, he also the promoter.'

Mr Nguni tapped the microphone with the tips of his fingers to see whether it was alive and then; satisfied, leaned over it. 'Ladies and gentlemen,' he said in carefully enunciated English, 'tonight is an international non-title fight between the welterweight champion of Ireland, Terry "Iron Jaw" McGraw – thirty-eight professional fights, twenty-two knockouts, thirty wins, one draw, seven losses – and Sophiatown's very own black welterweight champion of Africa, Gideon Mandoma!' He paused for the applause to die down. 'Twenty-seven professional fights, twenty-six wins, twenty knockouts, no draws.' The big man paused long enough for it to have the desired effect, 'one loss.'

At the mention of Mandoma's recent defeat the crowd booed and stamped their feet. Mr Nguni was first and foremost a promoter and he was beginning to build towards the second Mandoma vs Geldenhuis fight which he knew would be a big attraction. He also felt that the better man had lost, but consoled himself with the fact that the return fight was going to be a big earner for all and sundry. Which, the way he had black boxing tied up, meant that the 'all' was him and the 'sundry' was everyone else. He passed the microphone through the ropes and climbed down from the ring without glancing back at Gideon Mandoma.

The referee stepped from the neutral corner, signalling the seconds out of the ring and the two boxers to the centre. Mandoma rose from his corner stool and his white satin gown was removed. Tandia gasped involuntarily. The black boxer was beautiful. His body shone like well-tooled leather and his muscle definition was perfect. Strong shoulders tapered to a slim, superbly muscled abdomen and waist. He had the light, well-developed legs of a true welterweight: strong in the quadriceps, lean, almost thin calves and slim ankles. Tandia was well used to the round, flattish face that distinguishes the Zulu tribe and she was surprised therefore to see that Mandoma's nose was straight and narrow and his brow and jawline were clearly pronounced in an open, handsome face. Tandia saw a flash of perfect teeth as he fitted the mouth guard into his mouth. Gideon Mandoma looked like a young chief. There was a quiet authority about the way he stood beside the referee while the Irishman danced up and down on his toes smacking one glove into the other, eyeing the black man as the two boxers listened to the pre-fight instructions.

Tandia was almost choking with excitement and her heart thumped in her breast as the two boxers returned to their corners and waited for the bell. Mandoma sat quietly on his stool while McGraw preferred to stand, appearing to be anxious to get underway. The bell went for the first round and the young Irishman rushed towards the black man, leading with three or four lefts which Mandoma took on the gloves and then attempting a rather predictable right uppercut which missed by several inches.

The Irishman stood high with his gloves held wide and fairly low in a stance which usually denotes aggression in a fighter. Mandoma was also a fighter, but by contrast he held his gloves high, almost in front of his face, his left shoulder protecting his chin. He fought in a slightly hunched-over position.

Mandoma moved to the centre of the ring, inviting the Irish boxer to come after him. The red-headed boxer moved in surprisingly fast. Feinting with the left, he hit Mandoma hard on the nose with a right. The black boxer had been waiting for the left lead that he had every right to expect, and the blow landed straight and true, a very classy straight right. A thin trickle of blood started from Mandoma's nose. He sniffed and brought his glove up to his nose as though he were trying to use the glove to wipe it. The Irishman closed in fast, thinking he'd hurt Mandoma. He led with a left which Mandoma took on the gloves and followed with a right cross which he threw too hard, pushing him slightly off balance so that he raised his chin a fraction. To a good fighter a quarter of an inch can often be enough, and Mandoma's right upper-cut seemed to come in slow motion. Moving under the Irishman's elbow, it caught him flush on the underside of the chin, rocking him on his heels and then seating him hard on the ground.

Pandemonium broke loose. So much for McGraw's iron jaw! At the count of ten, McGraw still hadn't moved. Two minutes and thirty seconds into the first round the fight was over, and Mandoma raised his gloves from where he was standing in a neutral corner to acknowledge the roar of the crowd, who had risen in their seats and were applauding wildly. A chant began in one corner of the cinema and soon it was taken up by all. Without realising it, Tandia also found herself standing and yelling the boxer's name, 'Mandoma! Mandoma! Mandoma!' She had never felt anything like it before. She wanted to laugh and cry at the same time, to hug the person beside her, to rush up into the ring and to embrace the black man, to wipe the small trickle of blood from his nose as he stood, his gloves raised high, his chest heaving and his hard brown body burnished with sweat. Mandoma was everything Patel had said he was and he was also very, very beautiful. The most beautiful human being Tandia had ever seen.

And then suddenly her perception changed. Instead of the Irishman on the canvas she saw Geldenhuis lying at Mandoma's feet. The white policeman she feared more than anyone in the world lying at the feet of the black man, bleeding and battered, the black man triumphant at last. The burning deep inside her began and welled up, the fire of it threatening to consume her. The roar of the crowd receded in her ears as though she was standing alone in the giant theatre. A stillness fixed upon her, and from the stillness she heard two words, two words that she'd never before spoken or even thought to speak, but now they sounded clear and clean like the touch of cool water on parched lips. '*Mayibuye Afrika!* Come back Africa!' Her clenched fist rose high above her head as though of its own accord as the words left her lips and danced and echoed around the giant theatre. '*Mayibuye Afrika! Mayibuye Afrika! Mayibuye Afrika!*'

Tandia's life as a terrorist had begun, born under the ring lights in the heat and sweat of a boxer's win in a palace of dreams where a black man stood over the body of a white one, his arms raised in victory. She could feel her fear for Geldenhuis turn to heat, begin to glow, first red, then white hot. Then slowly, infinitely, remorselessly, it began to cool down, to grow cold slowly over years and centuries and finally aeons and as it cooled it grew into hard, cold, hard, bitter hate and it was all the more dangerous because it was forged out of her fear.

'Come, darling, we must go.' It was Madam Flame Flo taking her by the elbow. 'You liked that, hey? Ja, I can see you liked that. You will be a fan also.' She winked and squeezed Tandia's arm. 'Maybe even more than a fan, hey? Magtig! What a boxer! Come, we must go. Later you will meet him, you can even dance with him if you want. Mr Nguni has invited us to a party at the Taj Mahal.' She turned and waited for Mama Tequila to raise herself from her seat. 'But first we go to the ANC rally, to the protest meeting at St Peter's, to Father Huddleston's.'

When the three women reached St Peter's church hall it was already crowded. The people at the protest meeting were somewhat older than the boxing crowd and a fair proportion of them were women. Some wore the green, black and yellow uniform of the ANC and carried banners protesting against the eviction notices and the demolition of Sophiatown. Most of the women were dressed in their glad rags, though even those dressed to the nines could not compare with the sheer glimmering bulk of Mama Tequila.

Madam Flame Flo was, of course, well known as one of Sophiatown's most notorious shebeen queens and in this particular company perhaps not as well liked as with the boxing crowd. Her shebeen had often enough seen the money these women worked so hard to get used by their men for the liquor which drove them crazy and chased them into the arms of the good-time girls. Many of them believed that Madam Flame Flo was letting the community down. Some, though, did call their greetings; they were the ones who knew that Madam Flame Flo gave generously to the ANC and helped in unorthodox but useful ways.

Madam Flame Flo and her party were led to the front row by a buxom woman wearing the colours of the ANC. The mood in the hall was optimistic and there was a great deal of laughter as people recognised friends and warmed to the business of the protest. Soon all the seats were taken and only standing room remained.

Father Huddleston, Sophiatown's much loved Anglican priest, standing on the slight platform at the front of the hall, looked tall and frail. The priest stood to one side of a slightly battered-looking kitchen table, his long arms clasped below his waist. He wore a priest's cassock fastened by a wide leather belt. His head was remarkable, with its pronounced jaw, thin hawk-like nose and piercing blue eyes. He had a crew cut; the barber's impatient clippers seemed to have shaved him clean to the skin from the top of his large ears to the curve beginning at the crown of his head. At the very top of his head grew a tuft of evenly clipped, thick, steel-grey hair which seemed well adapted to survive in the harsh, rarefied climate of his six foot five inch frame.

Everything about Father Huddleston suggested self-denial. He was the Model T Ford of the priesthood, a stripped-down sort of a man at the extreme opposite end of the pompous, vainglorious posturing of the clerical order. Had he been in the church of Rome he would have been a serious candidate for sainthood, an idea he would have found unnecessarily mawkish and unseemly. There was nothing saintlike in the general behaviour of Father Huddleston. He was an ordinary and often impatient man who stood his ground and had his say, fearing no one, never slow to debunk the sophistry of apartheid or to challenge the actions of the police or the authorities. In fact, his character was best summed up by Madam Flame Flo when she pointed him out to Tandia. 'That's Father Huddleston. I'm telling you, man, he's one sonofabitch of a priest.'

It was not Father Huddleston's meeting. He was simply lending the venue and opening the evening with a short prayer. The chairman of the protest meeting was a young African seated alone at the table. His name was Robert Resha and he was well known to most of the audience in his role as an ANC executive as well as sportswriter for *Drum* magazine, the urban African magazine delighted in by the blacks and held in great suspicion by the white authorities.

At the conclusion of a short prayer the entire audience sang in perfect harmony, 'Aaaahmen!' Then they moved on to sing '*Nkosi Sikelela i'Afrika*', the one-time Presbyterian hymn which has become the black national anthem of South Africa. The protest meeting had begun, and the audience waited eagerly for Robert Resha, who was known for his bold and fiery speeches.

Father Huddleston left the stage and took his place in the front row of the audience, where an empty seat awaited him. Now alone on the platform, the young black man rose quietly from where he sat at the table on the platform. He lifted his right arm high, fist clenched, thumb extended. '*Mayibuye Afrika!*' he cried.

The crowd, their own arms extended in salute, returned the cry. '*Mayibuye Afrika!*'

'My brothers and my sisters,' he began, 'tonight you will not hear from me, or Father Huddleston. Tonight we have a new speaker who is known to you all, but who is also not known to you.' He smiled. 'Because this man is a very quiet cat, this man is a man of action who has not before used words for the cause.'

There was a sigh of disappointment in the crowd. They had come to hear a fiery speech by Resha himself; now they were going to be subjected to a novice. They had put away their tiredness and dressed up for nothing.

Robert Resha raised his hand. 'Be not disappointed,' he proclaimed, using the biblical style. 'This man, he is a Zulu, with the golden voice of his people. You will remember tonight. This is my promise to you.' He turned, walked to a doorway leading from the back of the stage, and nodded at someone the crowd was unable to see.

To the sudden delight of the audience Gideon Mandoma, dressed impeccably in a navy serge suit, white shirt and red tie, stepped through the doorway. As though he was announcing a boxing match, Robert Resha threw up his arms. 'Ladies and Gentlemen, citizens of Sophiatown and all who live in Western Native, I give you my friend and all Africa boxing champion, Chief Gideon Mandoma!'

Gideon walked towards the table to the warm applause of the audience. Even the mums of Sophiatown, who couldn't have cared less about boxing, knew of Gideon Mandoma, the quiet, smiling Zulu who was black champion.

'My friends,' Gideon began slowly, his English carefully enunciated. Madam Flame Flo had told Tandia how Gideon Mandoma had educated himself by going to night school and doing a correspondence course and how, in just five years, he too had sat for and passed his matriculation examination last November, the very same examination that Tandia had passed so brilliantly.

The English that the young chief spoke was less the language of Sophiatown and more the one he'd learned from his school books. Gideon now told of his coming to Sophiatown from Zululand via Durban, where at the age of twelve he had left his kraal because of a severe drought to seek work and where, by joining the YMCA, he'd been introduced to boxing, finally coming to Johannesburg at the invitation of Mr Nguni.

'I am telling this for you, because you see I am two things in my life. I am a Zulu who was born in a kraal, who herded my father's cattle and who respected the laws of my chief. But also I am someone else,' he smiled, 'I am a majieta!' The audience laughed as he identified with the tough, cynical, street-smart young men of Sophiatown. 'Now I cannot return to my father's house, even if I am a chief and those people need me. Because now I am much more, I belong to a new tribe of Africa.' He smiled again. 'We who live in Sophiatown, Alexandra, Orlando and all the other townships, in Jo'burg, Durban, Port Elizabeth, Cape Town, even Pretoria, we are the new people. We are the new South Africans. We are not Zulus, or Pondo, Swazi, Sotho, Basuto, we are not coloured or Indian and even yes, we are not white! These things are past, they cannot be brought back. This is the new Afrika and this place . . .' He paused and looked about him as though he were looking beyond the tin walls of the church hall. 'This place is the birthplace of the new Afrika, the new South African.' He paused again and looked about the room at the serious faces looking up at him, his own face serious. Tandia could feel her heart pounding. She could see that the people around her felt the same way; not a stirring or a cough broke the silence.

'Let me tell you the ways we are different. The language we talk, it is not English, it is not Afrikaans, or Zulu, or any of the languages of the tribes. It is the language of all! Here English, there Afrikaans, here Zulu or Sotho or Fanagalo. The music we play, we call it jazz, but it is not American, it is not English or the *tickie-draai* or *boere musiek* of the Afrikaans, it is Township, township jazz. It is our music. Our ways are our ways and our thoughts are our thoughts. New ways, new thoughts. New people.

'Let me tell you why we must fight to keep these new ways. Our ways are not the ways of the Boer. This man, this white Afrikaner tribe, they do not want to be a new people. They wish always to be an old people. They believe in white superiority, this is an old way. They say the white race, the Afrikaner race is God's race and they are God's servants and we, the black people and the coloured people, we must be the servants of God's servants! It is God's will, it is God's purpose, it is so because everybody knows, God is a white man and he is on their side!'

Gideon smiled and then laughed, his brilliant smile lightening his face so that the audience found themselves chuckling with him. 'But we must not grow angry at the white, racist God-fearing government of South Africa. Because you see, what they want for themselves, they also want for us. When Dr Verwoerd and Mr Strijdom speak of apartheid, they think in their hearts they are giving us what we want! They think the Zulu is like the Afrikaner and wants only to be with the Zulu, his own tribe, and the Sotho and the Shangaan and the Pondo and the Basuto they also, they want only to be with their own kind, to talk their own language and sing their own songs and marry their own women and grow their own crops and tend their own cattle!'

Mandoma leaned forward over the table, his eyes travelling once more over the crowd. His pauses were precise. He knew how to feel the crowd and manipulate it, massage it with his voice which rose and fell, grew harsh then soft again, shot forward in a rapid spate of words and then rested until the audience silently begged for him to continue. Now he spoke quietly again. 'These Boers who believe in white superiority and race purity, they have made a fundamental error in believing that the black people also believe in this racist nonsense. They do not see that in Sophiatown and Cato Manor and Jacobs in Durban, in District Six and Windermere in Cape Town and the townships of Port Elizabeth and everywhere else where the black people huddle, we have become a new people, the new people of South Africa! We do not ask is a man coloured, or Indian or black, we do not ask his tribe, we ask only one thing!' Gideon Mandoma's voice grew low so that the audience strained to hear him. 'We ask only, is this a good man or a bad man? Is this a good woman or a bad woman? Is this a good child or a bad child?' His voice rose and grew harsh. 'Not black! Not coloured! Indian! Chinese! Not even white! We do not look at the colour of a skin, we look at the heart which beats inside the skin.'

Gideon Mandoma's voice began suddenly to tremble. He was plainly upset. 'It is this which the white man wants to kill. It is this love, it is this understanding, it is this beginning. These old white men and these old white ways want to kill the new South Africa before it becomes real. And that is why they want to destroy Sophiatown and send us all to separate places which they have built to match our colour. This township, this dirty, ugly place of tin shanties and cardboard houses, this place where a black child is already old when he is ten years old, this drunken place of whores and shebeens, of dirty streets and hungry children, of sickness and murder. This is the place where freedom has decided to make its home, where the brotherhood of man can emerge, where his colour is the colour of his heart and not his skin. This is the place the white racists must destroy before it destroys them. They will show no mercy. They will come in the night and in the early morning and they will load us onto lorries, our mattresses and our beds and our children and our cooking pots and take us to our new places. To Diepfontein and Soweto, to Coronationville. Why cannot these new places with the new soccer stadiums and the schools and the health centres be used for all the people? Clean places where a man can rest and a family can grow up without fear. But this will not be. They will not be denied the inglorious, stupid, absurd concept of separation and superiority.' Mandoma paused, allowing his words to take effect, and then he began again, his voice low and steady, the voice of a leader bringing his people together, binding their wills and their determination to his own. 'We must fight. Not because we are servants and they are masters, not because we are black and they are white. But because the human race cannot progress backwards. They are trying to return us to a time and a place that cannot exist for us. We are a new tribe, the South African tribe, and we cannot go backwards, we cannot be undone, we cannot be ignored and, in the end, we cannot be defeated!'

'*Mayibuye Afrika!*' someone shouted from the back of the hall, and soon the audience was standing, their fists in the air, shouting their defiance. Small groups of women rose and, pushing the chairs aside, began to sing and dance. Soon everybody was dancing and singing with their arms raised in the traditional salute. Gideon Mandoma was a new star in the firmament of black politics. First a chief of the Zulu tribe, now a chief of the people tribe. They had heard his power. He had the lion's breath. He had the lion's roar. He had the lion's courage and the gift of moving the people. This one was a new leader who would fight for them. From this point on he would no longer be a black boxing champion fighting to beat a white in the boxing ring. From now on he was a black champion who carried in his fists and in his mouth the message of the underclass, of the people who wanted justice for themselves and for their children – the tired, exhausted people who pulled the plough of the white man's South Africa. Gideon Mandoma would lead them to the promised land.

Tandia felt the power in the black man, the power to move and to make things happen. She would follow him. She knew she was in love with him, a thing she had thought impossible. But she also knew that she had heard the breath of the future. It had passed over her and whispered to her. She was a part of the fight, she would march beside Mandoma, she too would be a part, a fighting part of the new South Africa to come and of the new South Africans. She was not stupid enough to think it would come about through rhetoric or even violence. Geldenhuis was not an isolated, sick human being; he was in many ways, in the ways that counted when you summed up an enemy, a typical Afrikaner. He would die rather than give an inch. She saw clearly that her love was not what was needed, she would need her hate. Her hate must be equal, it must surpass that of Geldenhuis. She sensed that Mandoma was not a man who could hate enough. He would need a woman beside him who could tear at the white man's flesh with her teeth. He would need her.

'Come, darling, we are going now to the Taj Mahal,' Madam Flame Flo chuckled. 'You will meet him there, I will introduce you.' Juicey Fruit Mambo had drawn up in the Packard and was waiting to help Mama Tequila into the back. They were surrounded by the dancing women who had left the hall and now were dancing in the street. Urchins crowded around the car and suddenly Tandia felt a warm hand in her own, as what felt like a small ball of paper was pushed into her hand. She looked to see Johnny Tambourine withdrawing his hand from her own; Dog Poep Ismali, Flyspeck Mendoza and Too Many Fingers Bembi also surrounded her, and behind them stood the rest of the gang.

Tandia hardly had time to greet them when four Black Jacks, the township policemen, burst into the circle of people surrounding the car. A policeman grabbed Johnny Tambourine while the others each grabbed

Dog Poep Ismali, Flyspeck Mendoza and Too Many Fingers Bembi and started to beat them with their night sticks. The four small boys began to scream as the heavy sticks beat at their shoulders and backs and a crowd gathered around. Tandia looked quickly down into her hand and saw that she was holding several crumpled pound notes. Without even thinking about what she was doing she slipped her hand through the slit of her cheongsam which came almost to the top of her thigh, and hooking her forefinger over the top of the waist elastic, she slipped the notes into her panties. In almost one movement she turned and slashed at the face of the nearest policeman with her nails. The black policeman who had been laying into Too Many Fingers Bembi backed away clutching at his face.

'Leave him, you bastard! Leave him, you hear!' Tandia screamed at the man and turned and slashed at a second policeman, missing him as he pulled back from her sharp talons just in time.

'Stop!' The voice was a roar and the crowd, including the Black Jacks, stopped, alarmed at the sound. Juicey Fruit Mambo stood in the centre of the circle, huge and menacing. In the few seconds before the black policeman could react he opened his huge mouth and smiled, his gold incisors gleaming. The crowd gasped and then Juicey Fruit Mambo turned to the black policeman. 'Why you want to beat dis boy for your stick?' he asked in a low, threatening voice.

'They have stolen money! They have stolen money from this woman!' the Black Jack sergeant pointed to a woman who stood on the edge of the crowd. Tandia turned to look at the woman who was large and wore lipstick and bright blue eye make-up painted over her eyelids. She was gross, and Tandia knew instantly she was a street whore. She had the same look of the drunken woman who had been thrown into the police cell with her the day she had been raped.

'That's the one!' the woman shrilled, pointing at Johnny Tambourine, 'and also him and him,' she shouted, jabbing her finger at Too Many Fingers Bembi and Flyspeck Mendoza.

'Hester, you drunk you hear!' It was Madam Flame Flo's voice. She had climbed out of the Packard and, breaking into the circle, she now stood in front of the large black woman.

'I am not drunk, these boys they attacked me and they took my money. Five pounds!'

'Five pounds you earned from lying on your back!' someone, a woman's voice, called from the crowd. There was sudden laughter.

'Hester, you owe me that much. You owe me five pounds. You are clean, you hear? The debt is wiped, but only if you say, only if you tell these policemen you made a mistake?'

The sergeant spoke up. 'We must search them.' He grabbed Johnny Tambourine and pulled him towards him. Juicey Fruit Mambo's hand came down hard on the policeman's shoulder, but he was smiling.

'The boy will show you,' he said. 'All boys they show you.' Johnny Tambourine removed his shirt and then pulled the lining of his shorts out.

A single two-shilling piece landed on the dirt road together with three marbles, several lead washers, four screws and a length of string.

'I got it for selling peanuts at the fight, God's truth!' he said, stooping to pick up the coin. He stood there in his dirty khaki shorts held around his waist by an old leather belt.

'Take also the belt,' Juicey Fruit instructed. Johnny Tambourine removed his belt and held onto his shorts to prevent them from falling to the ground. Juicey Fruit stuck his thumbs into his own belt so that his trousers came away from his abdomen slightly; then he did a little wriggle, which brought laughter from the crowd. 'Make also so!' he instructed. Johnny Tambourine grinned and swivelled his hips dancing from one foot to another, playing to the crowd in a parody of a dance. Juicey Fruit Mambo turned to the police sergeant. 'You see, no money here,' he said, grinning. 'Now all boy make like same!' he declared, pointing to Flyspeck Mendoza and Too Many Fingers Bembi.

The two boys quickly followed suit, revealing pockets which contained very much the same sort of things that spilled from Johnny Tambourine's.

Madam Flame Flo brought her hands to rest on her hips. 'I open my big mouth, now I must pay, hey. These boys is innocent but still I will cancel the money you owe me, Hester. But first you must withdraw the charges, you hear?'

The big whore smiled. 'I made a mistake,' she said to the sergeant. 'All the boys in this township they look the same.'

The policeman who had been scratched by Tandia was standing directly beside the Packard, the palm of his hand covering his cheek. Mama Tequila's fat arm appeared out of the window and tugged at his sleeve. She was holding a one-pound note. 'Medical expenses,' she said. The black policeman, glancing quickly to see if they were being watched, took the money and touched the peak of his helmet.

The sergeant lifted his night stick menacingly and pushed at Hester roughly. 'Go! Go, you fat whore, before I arrest you. You are wasting the time of the police!' He turned to Madam Flame Flo. 'Your driver, he is very lucky, next time he will not be so lucky, hey.'

'Come around to the shebeen tomorrow, I will have something for you,' Madam Flame Flo said quietly. If the Black Jack sergeant had heard her he didn't react. Scowling at her, he walked away, calling to the crowd to disperse.

'Come, Tandia, come, Juicey Fruit, we must go to the Taj Mahal. I think we have enough demonstration for one night, hey?' Madam Flame Flo climbed into the back of the car with Mama Tequila. 'Let's get the hell out of here, jong . . . before the proper police come!'

'I'm sorry, Aunty Flo,' Tandia said from the front of the car. 'I didn't mean it, but they were hitting the kids!'

'You did right, Tandy, but not in Sophiatown. We just lucky they were Black Jacks and not SAP. If you attack a proper policeman like that he will shoot you, no problems!'

'Tandy! You a fucking arsehole, you hear!' Mama Tequila spat. 'You put our lives at risk, what for? For a bunch of fucking snotty-nosed kids! You must be crazy, you hear!'

'Dis boys, dey her friend, my friend also!' Juicey Fruit announced from behind the wheel.

'And you, you black bastard, you crazy also!' Mama Tequila screamed at the big black man.

Tandia remained silent and waited for more from the angry woman. Instead, Juicey Fruit started to giggle and then to laugh and Madam Flame Flo followed. Mama Tequila was also laughing as they drew up outside a large corrugated iron shed that seemed to be vibrating from the hot jazz music coming from within. They had arrived at the Taj Mahal, the biggest and the most notorious shebeen in the township.

Mama Tequila had elected to be taken home, and Juicey Fruit Mambo let Madam Flame Flo and Tandia off, promising to return before midnight. The joint was jumping as the two women entered. It was a huge tin shed with a lofted open roof which had windows set into the roof thirty feet above the floor. The lighting was indifferent and the effect was of smoke and music, noise and pink strobe lights that cut across the dancefloor in the centre, pulling the jiving couples from darkness into light and back again.

The band sat on a platform structure built at the end of the room several feet above the heads of the dancers and the drinkers. Benjo 'Gwigwi' Mrwebi who had earlier played clarinet at the fight was leading the Three Jazzalomos with Jacob 'Mzala' Lepers on the bass and Sol 'Beegeepee' Klaaste at the piano. The sound was hot and sweet and the booze was moonshine, Barberton served in jam tins. An occasional half-jack of brandy was raised quickly, furtively to the mouth, a gulp and back into the pocket, guilty blood too good to share except with your nice-time girl.

Madam Flame Flo, with Tandia in tow, worked her way through the crowd of drinkers and dancers. The tables were full, overcrowded with the nice-time girls seated on the men's laps. Those who couldn't find a table stood against the walls. It was impossible to talk, and people drank and shook and grooved to the music or found a place on the dance floor, the jazz and the noise sealing them from each other. Those who had girls danced and used their hands to touch the parts that best expressed their thoughts and smiled for the time they would spend in a dark alley afterwards when the Barberton and the dancing and the jazz had left their thighs aching for release and a crumpled pound note had passed from hand to the safety of a brassiere wet from dancing.

Madam Flame Flo, signalling for Tandia to follow, stooped slightly and passed under the band floor, opening a half-sized door cut into the wall at the back of the large shed. They squeezed through the narrow doorway and Tandia found herself in a large room with half-a-dozen tables. The room was lined and painted and on the walls in neat frames all of one size were photographs of musicians and nightclub performers. From the ceiling two large fans rotated. About thirty people sat at the tables, smartly dressed men and five pretty women in evening dress. The tables were all furnished with good glasses and bottles of brandy, gin and whisky. Despite the fact that the bandstand was only separated by a wall, the music filtering through, though loud, allowed for talk.

Mr Nguni, the tall African boxing promoter from the fight, rose from a table nearest the small doorway at which five men sat. Tandia caught a glimpse of Gideon Mandoma before the bulk of Mr Nguni blocked the table from her view. Her heart began to pound and she felt weak at the knees, as though her legs were about to give way from under her. She wet her lipstick with her tongue and swallowed hard, trying to conceal her nervousness. 'Welcome, Madam Flame Flo,' Mr Nguni said, extending his huge hand. Then turning slightly, while still holding Madam Flame Flo's hand, he greeted Tandia. 'Welcome to Sophiatown, Miss Patel, we are most happy to have you with us,' he said, smiling. 'Come, you must sit at our table. There is someone I would like you to meet.'

The big man moved aside so that Tandia and Madam Flame Flo could pass. Tandia found that she was standing almost directly in front of the table. The men, with the exception of Gideon Mandoma, half rose in their chairs before sitting back again. Gideon Mandoma rose fully from his chair.

Mr Nguni indicated the people at the table. 'You all know Madam Flame Flo?' They all nodded. Mandoma smiled and, extending his hand, shook Madam Flame Flo's.

'Nice one, Gideon, you made mincemeat of that Irishman tonight!' Madam Flame Flo said. He smiled and thanked her politely.

Mr Nguni held Tandia lightly by the elbow. 'Gentlemen, allow me to introduce Miss Tandia Patel from Durban.' Mr Nguni indicated the four men with a sweep of his hand, not bothering to introduce each individually. Tandia smiled and acknowledged the seated men, whereupon Nguni turned and placed his large hand on the boxer's shoulder. 'Miss Patel, may I introduce you to Gideon Mandoma?'

Tandia's eyes met those of Mandoma and she held his gaze. She knew she was being over-bold, that she should have glanced up at him and then away, pretended indifference, or shyness, played the shy-young-woman-meets-nice-young-man game. But she couldn't. She was held by the boxer's gaze as though mesmerised. She knew at once she had found what she wanted; she had found the antidote for Geldenhuis. She could love this man as much as she hated the other. At close quarters, Gideon Mandoma was even more beautiful than she could possibly have imagined.

Gideon Mandoma smiled, the brilliant white smile that she had seen earlier in the church hall. 'Welcome, Tandia.' He refrained from shaking Tandia's hand but instead indicated the chair beside him. 'Sit, please.' He watched as she lowered her eyes and seated herself. Then he sat back into his own chair. 'I saw you at the eviction protest meeting tonight. You are the most beautiful woman I have ever seen. Do you have courage to match your beauty?'

Tandia could feel his eyes on her as she raised her own to look at the boxer. Mandoma's expression was serious and showed no hint of condescension. He seemed to be asking a serious question and was not simply trying to humour her. 'I will take my courage from you, Gideon Mandoma,' she said quietly, 'but I will bring you something also.' Tandia paused and forced herself to look away and then lower her eyes. 'My daddy, Natkin Patel the boxing referee, he always said, to win a world championship a boxer must have hate. Without hate the pain is too much and raw courage is not enough.' Tandia looked up again and her beautiful green eyes burned fiercely into those of the black boxer. 'To win this fight for our people . . .' Tandia paused. She spoke barely above a whisper, yet her voice carried to him clearly. 'I will bring with me the hate you will need, Gideon Mandoma.'

BOOK TWO

ELEVEN

The afternoon was well advanced when Peekay wakened. Despite the lateness of the day the heat beat down on the tin roof of the round miner's hut, his home for nearly sixteen months.

It would be another month before the rains came to the Northern Rhodesian Copperbelt. One morning he'd come up from underground, his ears ringing from a night spent blasting rock, and it would be there: the hot, dry, insect-crackling night would have turned into a perfectly still, rain-misted morning. He'd remove his hard hat, unclip his miner's lamp, place it into the re-charging rack, and walk out and stand with his face held up to the pewter-coloured sky, allowing the soft drizzle to drench him, his body soaking up the first cool, wet morning for nine months. It felt so good and clean, like the beginning of the world.

But mostly the Copperbelt was like now, this last afternoon. His skin itched and felt clammy, beads of perspiration ran down his armpits, and the sheet on which he lay was damp.

Peekay stared at the ceiling fan above him. Fixed from the centre of the cone-shaped roof, it rotated in jerky movements, like a man with a slight limp forced to run for the bus. He searched around the perimeter of the fan until he found the blowfly. Almost always there was a blowfly, a big fat one with a shiny body the colours of oil spilled on water. He watched as, sensing the danger, it banked away from the fan to crash straight into the finger of God, a coil of yellow fly-paper which dangled from the ceiling.

Sweat trickled down Peekay's chest and a painful erection aimed its barrel directly at him. Virginity was a real bastard. He imagined his pointing cannon putting an end to his misery, firing directly at him, the ball whistling across his belly, over the rise of his chest, entering just under his chin, up through the roof of his mouth, the grapeshot exploding inside his head and scrambling his brains. The headline in the *Copperbelt News*: COCK CANNON KILLS OXFORD MAN IN MINING DISASTER!

His hands were swollen from the fight with the giant Botha in the Crud Bar the previous afternoon. The big man had tried to kill him in what had turned out to be an unfair contest. The huge, clumsy Afrikaner diamond driller, driven insane with the pain of a powder-headache, caused by the gelignite he'd sniffed in the course of his job, and attempting to drink himself into oblivion, and a young, fast and angry welterweight.

Peekay dwelt on the history which had brought the confrontation about: the tiny Afrikaans boarding school where, thirteen years earlier, a frightened five-year-old had been thrown in a backveld school system designed to foster a hate for the English. Here Botha, the fourteen-year-old who ruled the school and who was known as the Judge, had set about persecuting the defenceless English-speaking child.

The effect of the Judge's persecution never left Peekay and his hate had erupted on a hot afternoon a thousand miles from where it had begun. Peekay burned with mortification as he recalled his blinding anger, how he'd removed a razor-sharp pocket knife from his trousers and, straddling the unconscious Botha, had used the blade to cancel the crude swastika tattooed high up on his left arm. The retribution he'd etched with Botha's blood had been more than simple revenge; was he, too, infected with the same sick violence his childhood tormentor had shown towards him? How else could he explain the fight, this savage, appalling action?

For sixteen months Peekay had risked his life nightly blasting on a grizzly in the mines; now, as he was about to leave, like the fly banking to avoid the fan he'd flown into the finger of God.

Peekay was tired. At eighteen he ached inside with a tiredness which stretched back to the boarding school when the Judge had tried to break his small spirit. He'd barely survived that year and in the process had learned how to camouflage himself, how to protect his fragile ego. He'd never again entirely emerged from the camouflage.

Some of us hide by being so utterly normal, a digit in a sea of equal numbers; others hide from the front. Peekay had turned his childhood trauma into a succession of conquests. Only he was aware that the gifted, confident child others perceived was inwardly fearful of the retribution which came from failure. He had determined never to be beaten again, either physically or mentally. When he fought the Judge he was fighting himself.

He rose slowly from his sweat-soaked bed. He glanced down at his rigid member. This! This is a part of it! The sex urge constantly overtook him and numbed his mind. He thought of the French and Belgian whores who came over from the Congo in a chartered DC 3 every three weeks to 'service' the miners. Peekay didn't want the first time to be with a whore, having to pay for it. But now, after yesterday, he wondered why. He wasn't really any different. When it all boiled down, the law degree he was planning to take at Oxford wasn't going to turn him into a civilised man; underneath he was a cruel, animal bastard like the rest of them.

Peekay had imposed a number of conditions on the method of his deflowering. These sexual aspirations had been brought about very largely as a consequence of having read the entire collection of Mickey Spillane detective stories which he'd inherited from the previous occupant of the hut. The neatly stacked paperbacks with their lurid dime-store covers were arranged along the ledge of the only window in the hut, almost as though the books had become a part of the window. Peekay's resolve to eschew the French whores and wait until the real thing came along had been confirmed when he read how Mike Hammer, Spillane's detective hero, had seduced a beautiful and sexy heiress. He'd read that Hammer slipped his rough hands, more accustomed to fondling the butt of a snub-nosed forty-five, through the pink ribbon straps of her night lingerie, peeling them slowly over her perfect shoulders. Then he took her into his arms. Her skin was as smooth as whipped cream on a satin bedspread.

It was the final sentence which had set Peekay's blood racing. He resolved to keep his virginity intact until life delivered him just such a whipped-cream experience. For he'd convinced himself that if he could achieve a single act of perfect lovemaking, all his carnal desire would melt away and manhood would click into place like a well-oiled rifle bolt.

At eighteen Peekay was Amateur Lightweight Boxing Champion of South Africa, undefeated in one hundred and sixteen fights. He'd set his sights on becoming professional Welterweight Champion of the world.

As if this wasn't enough, he wanted more. He had brains to spare, more than he could possibly need to be a world champ, which he correctly saw as something you became and, in a matter of two or three years, were no longer. For his real future he had decided to read law at Oxford.

Peekay was aware these two ambitions were somewhat incompatible. But for almost as long as he could remember he'd been two people, or put more precisely, the same person who was thought about quite differently by two sets of people. There were those who talked about his being a future world champion and who had never heard of Oxford; and those who knew him as a brain, a small-town kid, the son of a widowed dress-maker, who had made them proud by winning a scholarship to a private school for the sons of the rich and who now had a place at Oxford University.

Somehow Peekay had managed to keep both groups in his life happy. He was highly ingenuous and people took to him easily, often taking strength from him as well as becoming loyal either to the boxer or to the brain, one or the other aspect of his personal disguise.

Only Hymie Levy, Peekay's beloved friend, believed with him that both ambitions were possible and not contradictory.

Peekay had met Hymie on their first day at boarding school and they'd remained friends. Hymie was the son of a Jew who had fled Poland just prior to Hitler's invasion and who had become a millionaire carpet manufacturer and retailer. Despite being born rich, Hymie was street smart, a loner who was naturally cautious and usually two steps ahead of most people in the thinking department. Where Peekay reached out, Hymie pulled back. Where Peekay accepted, Hymie questioned. Where Peekay trusted, Hymie was suspicious. Peekay's defence system, born out of his early boarding-school experience, made him a quiet sort of person. Hymie adopted loudness as his defence. The poor boy and the rich, the Jew and the Gentile. Together they made a formidable combination.

Parted for the year and a half Peekay had been in the mines, the bond between them was, if anything, stronger. They thought of themselves as a duo and even, in the long term, inseparable. They would both graduate in law; Hymie would manage Peekay to a world championship fight, and eventually they would practise together in Johannesburg. While Peekay had been earning money in the copper mines to pay his own way through university, Hymie had already started at Oxford.

Peekay walked over to the small paraffin fridge which stood directly under the window. He withdrew two small metal trays of ice each marked with a band-aid and sandwiched his erection between them. The shock of the ice-cold contact made him jump but it worked every time and after only a few moments he returned the ice trays to the fridge. Then he pulled on a slightly sweaty jockstrap and a pair of boxing shorts and stepped up to the speedball which hung from a central rafter just below the fan.

He began to work the beautiful tear-shaped leather ball, ignoring the pain from his swollen hands. The beautiful drumming rat-tat-tat-tat of his fists on the leather ball soon calmed his mind; although he hadn't fought for nearly eighteen months, he knew he hadn't lost any speed. His body was harder than it had ever been and his mind, after working a grizzly, was a good deal tougher. A couple of months sparring with good partners and his timing would be right on the button. He'd be ready for his first fight in England.

After twenty minutes at the speedball Peekay's entire body was a lather of sweat. But he felt good, clean. He couldn't undo yesterday. He'd go over to the cottage hospital and see Botha. Explain to him. Apologise. It probably wouldn't help but he'd do it anyway. The Boer bastard would be surprised, think Peekay was going soft; what had happened to him in the fight was fair in the violent kind of world they both shared.

He walked over to the door and took a towel from a hook. Slipping off his boxing shorts and jockstrap, he wrapped the threadbare towel around his waist and left the hut to walk over to the shower block. Tonight was his last shift underground. After tonight, the next time he went underground would be in a London tube. For some days Peekay had been trying to keep down his excitement, but now it rose in him, tingled inside of him ignoring his attempt to push it away. He did a spontaneous little dance in the dust.

Hymie met Peekay at Southampton where the Union Castle liner docked. They looked an odd combination; the blue-eyed Peekay in a cheap suit, carrying a battered suitcase, his body tanned and hard, his crew-cut just beginning to grow out; and Hymie, dark-eyed, pudgy and pale-faced, in corduroys, duffel coat and college scarf, his dark hair worn just short of a mane. They climbed into Hymie's little tan Ford Prefect and set off for Oxford.

Peekay, who had expected to find a bleak, cold England, was not prepared for the sublime shock of a perfect late September day. The idea of four distinct seasons had always fascinated him; it was tidy, clean and precise, the habits of an old and fastidious land. Now, in this quiet coming to the end of summer, there was a kind of purity which Africa could never possess, like the organ notes in a Bach cantata. Here no dust-devils danced across the cracked red earth, mocking the day-after-day thunder of Mojaji's drums as they attempted to beat the spring rains from a brazen, remorseless African sky. In this brassed and yellow autumn afternoon, England was more than Peekay had ever imagined.

TWELVE

Wisps of early morning mist sat on the surface of the Cherwell as Peekay and Hymie walked across Magdalen bridge. Hymie's car was parked in a small garage he'd rented just behind the grammar school. Despite the pale sunshine, Peekay's blood, still thin from the tropics, made it feel like the dead of winter to him. He was grateful for the fur-lined leather gloves Hymie had tossed him as they'd left their stairs. Peekay had been at Oxford a month and his life had settled into the usual student routine: lectures, tutorials and rather a lot of time spent both in the Radcliffe Camera and the Bodleian Library.

To this had been added a fairly heavy training schedule. Hymie had found a gym on the outskirts of Oxford near the Nuffield car works, where Peekay could work out with two apprentices from the Morris plant, known simply as Bobby and Eddy. Both boxed professionally. One was a middleweight, the other, like Peekay, a welter. They were country-bred, likely lads, fast enough, handy in the ring and very strong. Peekay had sharpened up, getting his timing right by boxing them both together, each taking alternate rounds. Wearing protective headgear, he'd go flat-out for six rounds four times a week.

The two Oxfordshire lads were contracted to spar for five bob a round. To keep them from becoming discouraged, Hymie secretly added a pound bonus if they could put Peekay on the canvas.

After only two weeks of intensive training, despite the heavy protective headgear they wore, Bobby and Eddy quite often found themselves on the seat of their pants in the middle of the ring. Peekay was getting back his form and by the day the appointment with Dutch Holland came around his speed was back; his punches had their old crispness and were probably landing harder. The year he had worked in the mines to build up his strength was beginning to pay off.

Neither Hymie nor Peekay was silly enough to think that a good showing against two straight-up-and-down Saturday night club fighters meant they'd get the nod from Dutch Holland, Britain's foremost fight trainer. The great man only worked with amateurs destined for the professional ring and he didn't seem over-anxious to accept the task of turning Peekay into a professional.

For his first appointment with Dutch Holland almost a year ago, Hymie had carefully prepared a portfolio of Peekay's amateur career. Holland had thumbed through this absently and stopped at the last page, which showed a ten-by-eight black-and-white photograph of Peekay in the traditional boxing pose.

'Not a bleedin' mark on him. How many fights did you say he's had, then?'

'One hundred and sixteen. He's hard to hit,' Hymie replied.

A small smile, more a smirk, appeared on Dutch Holland's face. 'Either that or he's been fightin' schoolgirls. I know a coupla lads will be happy to put a dent in that pretty-boy hooter,' he'd said, jabbing a small, pudgy finger at the photograph.

'They won't be the first to try, Mr Holland.'

'We'll see soon enough, lad,' Holland replied, but he'd reluctantly agreed to put Peekay through his paces when he eventually arrived in England.

The Thomas à Becket gym, situated above a pub from which it took its name, was on the south bank of the Thames near Bermondsey docks. Neither the pub nor the gym was open when they arrived half an hour early. A guy wearing a worn cloth cap and a woollen scarf wrapped around his neck and chin was sitting on the third from bottom step leading up to the gym. He was hunched against the cold with his hands under his armpits and looked up as Hymie and Peekay approached.

'You the two toffs the guv's been expectin' then?' It wasn't hard to see he was a pug. He possessed the best pair of cauliflower ears Peekay had ever seen and his nose had been flattened so many times it spread across his face in an arc almost as wide as his mouth. 'Which one of you gents is Mr Levy then?'

Hymie nodded. 'You the caretaker?'

The pug nodded and stood up. 'I hang about for the guv'nor. Don't expect you'll see him till half nine, though. Them two others neither.'

'Two others? The two boxers?' Peekay asked.

'Yeah, them two. I'll open the gym, but I'm warnin' you, freeze the knackers off of a brass monkey up there. By the way, me name's Fred.'

Peekay smiled. 'Nice to meet you, Fred.'

They climbed the outside stairs where Fred fumbled with a set of keys, his hands shaking badly. 'It was the war see, if it hadn't been for the flamin' war I'd a been British champ an' all.' He stopped fumbling with the keys and looked at them. 'Adolf put the kibosh on all that.' He found the key he'd been looking for and, holding it in both hands to steady it, inserted it into the lock. 'Done much fightin' then?' he asked, holding the door for them.

'A fair bit,' Hymie answered. Fred led them past two glass-partitioned offices and into the main area of the gym.

'Shit! This place smells like a wrestler's jockstrap! Can we open the windows please, Fred?'

Fred tapped what remained of his nose with his forefinger. 'That's the one good thing about me hooter, can't smell nothin'! Sorry, guv, them windows is screwed down for the winter.'

'Jesus, Fred, I'm expecting a lady! Can't you get any fresh air into this place?'

Fred looked surprised. 'This ain't much of a place for a lady, guv. Not too many ladies come by. Togger's sister sometimes and some of her friends. I'll fetch a chair for her from the guv'nor's office.'

Peekay looked at Hymie. 'What lady?'

'Harriet, she wants to meet you. Remember? I told you she's a sculptor . . . well, training to be one anyway. She's interested in boxing,' Hymie grinned. 'You know, the human body in its purest form.'

'Jesus, Hymie!'

'You'll like her, Peekay, I promise.'

Peekay sighed. 'I'm shitting myself with the prospect of two of Britain's best welterweights who've been instructed to knock my bloody head off and you decide it's time to show off your girl!'

'Them two welters, one ain't,' Fred interjected suddenly. Both of them turned, having forgotten he was still standing beside them.

'What was that?'

'Them two welters, guv, one's a middle. Turned pro this season.'

Peekay looked at Hymie. 'I thought I was being matched against a couple of welters.'

'Ja, me too,' Hymie said, a mystified look on his face. 'Better wait and see.' He turned to the ex pug. 'Fred, did a parcel come for me? It should have been addressed to the pub downstairs.'

'Yes, Mr Levy, it come yesterday, I put it in the guv'nor's office. Will I fetch it then?'

'Hello! Anyone home?' a female voice called from the door.

'Shit!' Peekay exclaimed, suddenly anxious.

Hymie patted him on the shoulder. 'Cool it,' he whispered, then he raised his voice cheerily. 'Come in Harriet!'

Hymie moved towards the door and Fred followed him, presumably to fetch the parcel or the chairs, but at the same time he removed his cloth cap. The three words spoken by Harriet told him the person at the door was a lady.

In fact, Harriet Clive wouldn't have noticed either way. Her clipped accent, the unconscious product of a good English boarding school, belied a personality in which there was no place for even the slightest pretension. As she walked towards him Peekay saw an attractive girl who wore a brilliant green polo-neck sweater under the ubiquitous blue duffel of the time. Her faded jeans disappeared into a pair of scuffed brown riding boots. She was about three inches shorter than Peekay and by the way she moved towards him Peekay could imagine a nice shape under all that heavy stuff.

Peekay smiled as Harriet approached. She threw her head back slightly and, bringing her right hand up, she brushed her fingers through a mane of chestnut hair. Then she took his hand. 'Hello, I'm Harriet Clive, I've been dying to meet you!'

Peekay's heart pounded against his will. She wasn't beautiful, not even pretty in the conventional sense, but she was unusual looking. Her perfectly ordinary brown eyes were set high above angular cheekbones. Her skin was a very light olive with both her nose and mouth seeming a little too big for an otherwise dainty, heart-shaped face.

'Hello, Harriet. Hymie tells me you're interested in boxing?'

Harriet laughed. 'The human form, rather more. I'm hoping to be a sculptor. I don't know anything about boxing.'

Peekay grinned. 'Why don't you quit while you're ahead?' He pointed to Fred who had returned carrying two bentwood chairs, one stacked on top of the other. 'As Fred says, not too many ladies come here.'

Harriet looked suddenly concerned. 'Oh? I hope you don't mind my coming?'

It wasn't what Peekay had meant and he blushed. 'No, that's not what I meant, it's nice of you to come.'

'I'll be terribly quiet.'

Harriet hadn't quite known what to expect in Peekay. Hymie had spoken of him so often she had conjured up someone she wasn't quite sure she'd like. Rather too handsome and too good at everything, particularly games. She was beastly at games. In her experience, the strong, good-looking types usually turned out to be about as interesting as boiled cabbage.

Taking Hymie's descriptions of Peekay alone, she'd decided she wasn't looking for that much perfection in a man. In fact she simply wasn't looking. Hymie came down to London reasonably infrequently, so she wasn't obliged to turn it into a grimly serious affair. He was nice to occasionally think about when he wasn't there and nice to be with when he was. Actually, she thought of Hymie as a sort of male protection device. If another man badgered her or became too persistent she could put them off with chat about her brilliant Oxford boyfriend. Brilliant Oxford boyfriends seemed always to do the trick.

Meeting Peekay at last, her preconceptions were confirmed. The lightly tanned skin, the shock of hair just beginning to grow across the forehead, the deep blue eyes, the perfectly straight nose: he looked like he'd been created from a police identification kit. It was a superior face, she decided; not quite pretty, but still the sort of idealised looks which belonged in a Rupert Brooke poem. Peekay looked like the sort who went to Harrow, flew a Spitfire, and secretly harboured a desire to be beaten by someone dressed as his childhood nanny. Finally, she decided, he was much too dull-looking to sculpt.

Harriet had been hoping for a somewhat battered face, interesting because it was still young, yet showing the premature wear and tear of a hundred hard fights. If she were to sculpt him she'd have to concentrate on his body and rearrange his face. While her mind was working on these modifications she looked up, directly into his eyes.

Peekay actually felt as though he had been pushed backwards. Her look was so open, so cool and appraising, it was like the slap of a wet towel. Suddenly his defences, so carefully developed and so easily brought into play, seemed useless. He felt vulnerable and hoped like hell it wasn't showing.

Harriet, having decided her assumptions were correct, now saw something in Peekay's eyes which told her they were not. It was as though she'd walked into a soundless place, for about him was a stillness as if she was standing in the eye of a storm. She felt the need to resist him. She must avoid being alone with him.

Fred placed the two chairs beside the ring. 'Thanks, Fred.' Hymie reached into the change pocket of his trousers. 'Do us a favour, nick down to the caff and get us a couple of bacon-and-egg sandwiches?' He handed the old man a florin and then added another shilling, 'For your trouble.'

'Thanks, Mr Levy. Wait on, I'll get your parcel.' He returned a few moments later and handed Hymie a large soft-looking parcel wrapped in brown paper and tied with string. 'I'll be off. Be all right on your own then, Mr Levy?' he asked.

'Yes, thanks, Fred.' Hymie turned to Peekay. 'It's cold in here. Wear a tracksuit when you warm up.'

'What for? I didn't bring one, just a sweatshirt and my old bottoms, like always.'

'Here, catch!' Hymie tossed the parcel to Peekay, who caught it in one hand, bringing it into his chest.

'What's this?'

'Open it. No don't! Open it in the change room. As my mom would say, health to wear!'

Peekay excused himself and, picking up his bag, walked towards a door at the far end of the gym. On the left-hand side of the door was written the word 'Change'; on the right, the word 'Room' hadn't been added. It was as though the signwriter had taken himself off for a drink in the pub downstairs and never returned to complete the job.

The room contained a single shower, a toilet with the door removed, sundry benches along the walls and one which ran down the centre. Peekay was assailed by the damp smell of soap, stale sweat and dirty wet towels. He sat on the centre bench and tore open Hymie's parcel. The label on the outside read 'Lillywhites'. Inside was a bright blue tracksuit.

He unfolded the tracksuit top and what he saw took a moment to sink in. Embroidered in yellow silk thread on the back of the tracksuit were the words, 'The Tadpole Angel'.

Levy, you bastard! he thought. You can't be serious! All that stuff was over, left behind in South Africa. They'd not even discussed it since his arrival in England. Hymie couldn't possibly want him to fight as the Tadpole Angel again.

Suddenly angry, Peekay hurled the tracksuit top against the wall and made for the door. Then he realised he'd be making a scene in front of Harriet. He retrieved the top and started to undress. He'd sort it out with Hymie later; now it was time that he started to concentrate on the business they'd come for. The tracksuit and the girl had left him distracted; he must get his mind on the bout.

Hymie and Harriet were devouring Harry's bacon-and-egg sandwiches when Peekay returned to the gym. It wasn't like Hymie to eat before noon, and the sandwiches were a sure sign he was nervous.

Peekay could feel the tension in his stomach which always came before a fight. It meant his concentration was back with him, although his stomach was tighter than usual and he knew he was a little scared. It had been more than a year since he'd stepped into a ring, other than with a sparring partner, and his whole boxing future was riding on this one work-out.

Peekay lifted his arms up high and, displaying the tracksuit, said through clenched teeth, 'Thanks, Hymie, a perfect fit!' Hymie had gone to his usual trouble but Peekay wasn't at all comfortable in it. He felt a bit ungrateful, knowing he was going to have to sort the name business out later. That is, until he suddenly realised Hymie was probably counting on him to feel rotten about making a fuss. He walked over to where the two of them sat. 'We're going to have to talk about the embroidery.'

Hymie spoke with a mouthful of egg-and-bacon sandwich. 'Sure, sure, turn round, let's have a deck.' Peekay turned to show his back. The yellow embroidery on the blue background was typical of Hymie, who loved continuity and tradition. Yellow and blue were the colours of the Barberton Blues, the prison boxing squad in the small *bush veld* town where Peekay had started as a boxer at the age of eight, and where he had been trained by his first and best boxing coach, the wily old coloured lag, Geel Piet.

'The Tadpole Angel! What a lovely name,' Harriet exclaimed.

'Now don't you start!' Peekay growled.

'Oh, but it is! There must be a story. Do tell, Peekay?'

'I think you'd better go and warm up,' Hymie said quickly, avoiding Peekay's eyes. 'Dutch Holland will be here any minute.'

Peekay could see the puzzled look on Harriet's face. 'Ask shit-face to tell you,' he said, jerking his thumb in Hymie's direction and, walking over to the wall directly behind them, he selected a skipping rope.

Peekay skipped lightly for a few minutes and then moved over to the small platform where the speedball hung. Soon a sound like the throbbing of jungle drums came from the blurred red ball and he knew his co-ordination was perfect.

A voice cut through Peekay's concentration. 'Well, that's one good thing, we won't have to worry too much about your co-ordination then will we, son?'

Ducking to avoid the flying ball, Peekay stepped off the platform. A light sweat had formed over his face and, pulling the tracksuit top over his head, he tossed it to Hymie. Then he looked directly at the man standing beside Hymie.

'Dutch, let me introduce you to Peekay,' Hymie said. His voice was calm enough, but Peekay knew he was as nervous as he was in front of the famous English trainer.

'Pleased to meet you, Mr Holland,' said Peekay.

Dutch Holland took his hand and shook it almost absently. 'Likewise, Peekay.' He nodded his head towards Hymie. 'We've heard a lot about you from your manager.' He looked Peekay up and down as a jockey might examine an unfamiliar horse. ' 'Ere, let me see your 'ands, son.'

Peekay extended both his hands. Holland took his right hand and turned it palm upwards, then back again, testing the flexibility of Peekay's wrist. Then he pushed Peekay's fingers apart, scrutinising them for past breaks or possible weakness. Folding Peekay's hand into a fist he slapped the exposed knuckles with the flat of his hand. He then repeated the process with the left hand before taking up the right again. He opened up Peekay's hand and placed his own over it. His was wider, though his fingers were shaped like small, fat, cocktail sausages and Peekay's extended well beyond them. Next he took a good look at Peekay's eyes, poking and stretching the soft tissue around them with the ball of his thumb.

Dutch Holland had the reputation for being the best cut-man in Europe and Peekay wondered how those small, pudgy, clumsy-looking fingers could be so deft with a cotton bud stick, adrenalin, and a jar of vaseline.

Peekay, who'd had very few cuts in his career, was pretty confident that Holland would find nothing wrong with his eyes. He was equally sure of his hands, though they bore several permanent scars from working in the mines. They were strong, not only from working out daily with his bare knuckles on the coarse canvas punching bag in his hut, but also from a childhood spent at Doc's piano doing five-finger exercises. They were already the hands of a pro; the scar tissue built up around his knuckles from working the big punching bag with his bare fists gave them an extra layer of protection.

'Them's grafter's 'ands, son. You supposed to be a toff from Oxford University. How'd you end up with 'ands like a bleedin' navvy?'

Hymie, standing slightly behind Dutch Holland, winked. It was obvious he'd told the famous trainer about Peekay's stint in the mines. Borrowing from the idiom, Peekay replied, 'I've done my share, Mr Holland.'

'That's good, my son. I like a grafter. All boxing is about work and boxing as a pro is about more work than you've done in your whole bleedin' life.' He placed a cocktail-sausage hand absently onto Peekay's shoulder. 'Might as well understand each other from the start. I do the shouting and you do the grafting, know what I mean?'

Peekay nodded as Hymie spoke up. 'Does that mean you'll take us on?'

Dutch Holland, a little smile on his face, jerked his head in Hymie's direction. 'Hang about! First your boy here is going to 'ave to show me if he can sort a coupla lads out in a right and proper manner.'

He pointed in the direction of the change room. Peekay turned to see two boxers wearing their sweats, with their hands already taped, walking towards them. One of them was heavily set around the shoulders as though he worked with weights, obviously a middleweight; the other, like Peekay, was probably only just a welter.

'Hang on a mo! You said two good welterweights, Dutch,' Hymie protested.

Peekay knew Hymie was protesting as a matter of course. There wasn't a great deal he could do about the situation other than call the session off, and he wasn't about to do that. 'I changed my mind,' Dutch Holland replied, but made no attempt to explain any further.

'Peekay, this is Peter Best,' Holland said. 'He's had only six fights as a pro, five KOs and a decision in his favour. He's good and he's fast and as you can see he's a middle. Peter's come along so I can see what sort of punch you carry as a fighter.'

Hymie grimaced. 'Boxer, please, Dutch. Peekay isn't some country-bumpkin fighter, a one-punch Johnny who leads with his head.'

Peekay wished Hymie hadn't interjected. He felt small next to the much larger middleweight.

'Peter, Peter, bumpkin eater!' Dutch quipped, pleased with the pun. 'We'll see about that soon enough. If your lad's a poncey little boxer and can't put a man on the canvas with both 'ands he ain't no bleedin' good to me.'

'Hello, Peter,' Peekay said. He offered his hand to Best who grunted, barely touching it. Best was dark-eyed, square-jawed with a swarth complexion, the type of looks known in Britain as black Irish. It was a face which just naturally looked unfriendly and it was obvious Best didn't do a lot to offset this initial impression. Peekay had already noted that Best's nose had been broken more than once and that he carried the pink wedge of a recently cut right eye. It was a sign of a stand-up fighter. He calculated the length of Best's arms. Best had a reach advantage of perhaps two inches; it would be difficult to hold him off so he could throw his punches from a safe distance.

'Not a man of too many words are you then, Peter?' Dutch said slapping Best lightly on the shoulder. 'You're in first against Jock of the Bushveld here, lad. Warm up and then get Togger to lace you. Wear your headgear.' He grinned. 'I don't want Peekay here to mark your pretty face.'

Dutch turned to the smaller of the two boxers. 'This is Togger Brown. He's here to test your speed. He's as good a young welter as you'll find in this or any other manor.'

Togger Brown was a ginger-haired, freckled-faced chap with a happy, open smile and friendly enough eyes. He stepped forward and shot his hand out. 'Nice to meetcha, Peekay. I don't mind admittin', you looked a tad fast yerself on the speedball an' all.'

'Hi, Togger,' Peekay smiled, relieved that Togger Brown seemed like a nice sort of guy. Togger, without waiting for Dutch Holland, stepped over, hand outstretched to Hymie. 'Nice to know you, Mr Levy.'

'Howzit!' Hymie said, greeting Togger perhaps not as warmly as he might have done. He liked to keep a small distance between himself and the boxers. Trainers and other managers didn't respect you if you acted like one of the lads.

'Righto, Togger! Get warmed up and stay warm. Your turn after Peter, lad.' Togger hadn't been able to take his eyes off Harriet since he'd entered.

Dutch Holland pointed to a box of bandages and three pairs of gloves which Fred had earlier put in the ring: two six-ounce gloves and a pair of twelves for Peter Best. At least Holland had seen to it that the bigger boxer should wear heavier gloves to cushion his punches.

Peekay sat down beside Harriet so Hymie could bandage his hands. Harriet was silent, though her eyes were excited. She'd opened up her sketch pad and she watched carefully now as Hymie fixed the bandages, noting how the tape passed high over the wrist and covered the palm while stopping short just before the first joint of the thumb and fingers. Hymie completed Peekay's left hand and Harriet lifted it carefully from Peekay's knee, feeling the texture and the tension of the binding with the ball of her thumb. She watched as it fell back naturally into his thigh, with the palm uppermost, fingers slightly curled inwards. Then she began to sketch.

Hymie held the left glove open for Peekay to insert his hand. Peekay made a fist inside the glove and pushed it against Hymie's chest so that Hymie could lace it up. He repeated the process with the right hand. Peekay got up, banging the gloves together to seat his hands firmly. This was the moment when a fight started for him, the moment his hands slipped into a pair of padded leather gloves.

The routine had always been the same from the very first time when he'd been six years old, travelling alone in the train on a two-day journey to his grandpa's new home in Barberton. Hoppie Groenewald, the train guard and Northern Transvaal Railway boxing champion, had befriended the lonely little boy. He'd brought a pair of boxing gloves into the compartment. 'With boxing, small can beat big,' he'd said, pushing the frightened child's fists into the giant gloves. It was the moment boxing came to Peekay. He'd felt the huge gloves over his hands and instinctively knew they felt right. First the left then the right, that was Hoppie's instruction that first time, and this was the order he'd insisted on ever since.

'Righto! Make it snappy, lads, let's have the two of you up 'ere then,' Dutch Holland called from inside the ring. Best and Peekay climbed up into the ring from opposite sides and moved to the centre to stand beside the trainer.

Dutch Holland was a nuggety, square-jawed sort of chap with oiled dark hair combed directly back from his brow. His hairline receded to midway down his scalp and his black, almost bushy, eyebrows swept back to give his face a slightly owlish look of reproof. A narrow vertical crease ran permanently down the centre of his brow. It added to the impression of a man who grew quickly impatient when things didn't happen the way he wanted them to.

'Three rounds, one minute between rounds, you both know the drill.' Holland looked down at Hymie seated beside Harriet, who was sketching fast, her eyes darting up and back to the paper in furious concentration. 'Mr Levy 'ere will act as timekeeper,' he said, touching the stopwatch which hung around his neck. 'At the end of three rounds Peter steps down and Togger takes over.' He lowered his voice slightly, addressing the two fighters. 'Now lads, I want a nice workout, no clinching, no unnecessary aggro. Now, Peter, we're here to see what the lad's got an' all. I want you to go hard, but no roughing up in the clinches, break clean and fast!' Best nodded and brought his right glove up to touch his nose. He sniffed noisily, looking at Peekay for the first time. Dutch Holland climbed down from the ring and, taking the stopwatch from around his neck, handed it to Hymie.

The two boxers moved over to their corners and waited for Hymie's signal. Peekay was nervous as hell. He'd waited a long time for this moment.

'Okay, ready?' Hymie looked down at the stopwatch, 'Box on!'

Peekay moved out of his corner towards a determined-looking Best. 'This guy only knows one way,' he decided. Best came straight towards him, trying to cut him off, gloves held fairly wide and low, affecting the more open stance of the professional, confident of his extra reach. If he couldn't trap Peekay in a corner he would expect Peekay to dance a little, moving him around the ring, a smaller man naturally wary of his bigger opponent, leading with a left, feeling him out.

In boxing you can quickly learn to take opportunities as they're presented to you, and the wide-open stance affected by the middleweight was a blatant show of arrogance. Peekay moved in fast and hit Best hard with a left lead to the jaw, followed by a vicious straight right, a one-two combination which set the bigger man back on his heels. Peekay was well out of harm's way as Best attempted the retaliatory right hook.

The surprise showed in his opponent's eyes. Peekay had hit him cleanly and hard with the back of the knuckles and Best was going to make the smaller man pay. But now Peekay started to box off the back foot, using the whole of the ring to stay out of trouble. It was simply a tactic to make the bigger man look bad as he threw punches and missed time and time again. If you can get a boxer to mistime his punches from the start, it can take a couple of rounds before he gets his combinations right. But Peekay knew that sooner or later Best would get him against the ropes or in a corner where he could do some real damage.

Peekay was a consummate boxer with a mind which quickly developed his opponent's faults into the pattern the fight might take if they were allowed to dictate it. Once he knew the plan he knew how to combat it. Halfway through the first round he thought he had Best set. He knew the kind of a fighter he was and what to expect. The middleweight was good with both hands. Peekay was to learn that this was a characteristic of all the Dutch Holland boxers. Best was also pretty fast, though much too dependent on a left upper-cut, a deadly punch when it connected, but when used too often, it was like sending a message via carrier pigeon: you could see it coming from a long way off. Besides, it opened him up for a right cross.

Peekay started to get inside Best, cutting off any advantage he might enjoy with his superior reach. This sudden change from boxing defensively confused the other boxer. Getting inside his opponent had two advantages: his body was exposed to a series of short, sharp, rapid-fire punches which sapped his stamina. When he attempted to retaliate, his punches had first to travel around the outside of the infighter's arms and elbows, losing a lot of sting on the way. Peekay was forcing him to shorten his punches, most of which he took on the back of his arms. In return Peekay was scoring with hard, clean shots to the body. Best's willingness to lead with his chin was to no avail. Peekay largely ignored his head. He knew that constant punishment to the body from a boxer, as fast as he was, could wear a big man down in a hurry. If the blows were set just under the heart they soon began to make their presence felt.

By the time Hymie called for the second round Peekay's breathing was even, but he noticed that Best's chest was still heaving. The fighter was gulping air in an attempt to settle himself down. Maybe the bastard isn't totally in shape, thought Peekay. This time he'll come out more carefully for sure. But Best, who must have suffered from a short memory, came at Peekay in exactly the same manner as he'd done in the opening round.

Peekay feinted with his left then hit Best hard with a right cross, pulling the blow inwards to tear at the recent cut to the fighter's eye. He'd resisted the left-right combination he'd used in the opening round in case Best set a trap for him. He pulled back out of harm's way, ducking and feinting and working the ropes as he watched the blood start to pump into Best's eye.

A boxer less intelligent than Peekay would have started to work on the eye, hoping to close it and so cut down his opponent's field of vision. Peekay knew that this would suit Best perfectly, offering his head as a target so he could land a couple of big punches which would put a lighter fighter like Peekay away.

Best's eye wasn't badly cut and Dutch would stop the bleeding between rounds, but Peekay wanted him to think he could hit him wherever and whenever it pleased him. Boxing is all about psychological control, and Peekay was working on Best's mind.

The two boxers were no longer sparring. Best was trying his hardest, with increasing frustration, to nail Peekay. The smaller boxer went back to working on the body, seating a number of good punches under the heart. Late in the second round Peekay moved Best onto the ropes and got him with an eight-punch combination which hurt him. He heard Best grunt as the middleweight pulled him into a clinch. Despite his size Best was taking a lot of punishment to the body and plainly was not liking it.' 'Come 'ere, you fuckin' bastard!' he'd invited Peekay more than once.

The two boxers were locked in a clinch when Hymie called the end of the round. Peekay released his hold of Best and stepped back, dropping his guard. Best caught him with a beautiful right upper-cut to the jaw. Peekay felt his head snap back and his knees start to buckle, but somehow he managed to stay upright.'That's for you, lad!' Best snarled.

Despite the lightness in his head, Peekay managed to smile. 'That's the only way you're going to hit me, shithead!' he called after Best, who'd moved back to his corner.

The blow had been a deliberate foul. 'You bastard!' Peekay heard Hymie shout up at Best.

Dutch Holland stepped quickly into the ring and moved over to Best. 'You stupid git! Next time you do that, lad, you're out of my stable! I told you, no aggro!' He looked over at Peekay who was standing in his corner. 'You all right, son?' Peekay nodded, his head clearing from the blow. Hymie tried to enter the ring but Peekay waved him back. The punch had hurt him, but the advantage lay in remaining cool and showing no visible signs of distress.

'Do you want to continue, Peekay?' Holland asked.

Peekay smiled. 'Sure, Mr Holland, why not?'

Dutch Holland grinned. 'Cheeky young sod!' He turned to Best and started to attend to his eye, speaking to him in an undertone. 'Now I've warned you, ain't I? Get in there and do some work, Little Lord Fauntleroy here is making you look dead ordinary, my son.'

The final round was Peekay's best. He started off working close to the bigger fighter's body and by the middle of the round the middleweight had dropped his arms to protect himself, an obvious sign that he was hurting as well as tiring. With his guard down, Peekay was able to stand back a little and punch to the head. To taunt Best he hit him everywhere except on the eye, and soon the parts of his face exposed by the headgear carried bright red patches where he'd been nailed. A thin trickle of blood ran from his nose. The big fighter's body looked untouched except for a sharp patch of red about the size of a large grapefruit under his heart where Peekay had hit him perhaps fifty times or more.

Best once again ignored Dutch Holland's caution to stay the aggro. His eyes clearly showed his fury as Peekay took the fight to him, making him miss badly. Every boxer dreams his opponent will lose his cool in the ring; nothing makes a good boxer look better than an opponent who throws caution to the winds and rushes in for the kill.

But in the end Best had enough class to last, even hitting Peekay hard twice when he moved in a little too close. They were two good punches, though he'd lost some of his speed and the blows did no more than remind Peekay in no uncertain manner to stay out of his reach. He was also grateful for the heavy gloves Best was wearing. Hymie called the end of the round just as Peekay landed another hard straight left right on the button.

Best didn't wait to touch gloves. Turning his back on Peekay, he climbed out of the ring.

Peekay looked over at Hymie and shrugged. Hymie raised his thumb without moving his hand from his lap. 'Nice one!' he mimed. Peekay's concentration had been such that he'd entirely forgotten Harriet's presence. Now, as Fred moved over to his corner handing him up a water bottle, he looked down at her, rinsing his mouth. She was still sketching, her eyes downcast onto the paper so that the lights from above the ring caught her chestnut hair, turning it into a blaze of deep coppery brown. 'She's Hymie's,' Peekay reminded himself, mentally slapping himself on the wrist. He was still a little high from the fight, delighted it had gone so well. He'd really expected Best to rough him up somewhat and counted himself lucky. He spat into the bucket Fred held up for him.

' 'Ere, more water, guv,' Fred said, handing Peekay the water bottle.

Togger Brown jumped into the ring, game as a fox terrier. He bounced around in his corner, throwing punches into the air and blowing hard, working at his aggression as Peekay took the remaining seconds to recover.

When Hymie called the start of the fourth round, what with one thing and another, there had been an almost two-minute break in between rounds. Peekay was feeling fresh, even exhilarated. He knew he'd performed better than well against the recalcitrant Best, and he was anxious to do the same in his sparring session with Togger Brown. To his opponent's surprise, Peekay faced him as a southpaw. It was an ability he'd gained as a small child under the direction of Geel Piet. The battered little coloured man believed a boxer should be as capable of leading with his right as with his left hand and Peekay had been trained this way from the very beginning. To the uninitiated, in boxing terms, it's the equivalent of being ambidextrous. A boxer who stands with his right hand and right leg forward is known as a southpaw.

Like every intelligent boxer who has watched his opponent box, Togger Brown had worked out the way he hoped to shape the fight. Now he found himself all at sea and it soon became apparent that he'd been mismatched. Towards the end of the round Peekay changed back to an orthodox stance and almost immediately put Togger onto the seat of his pants with a left-right combination.

Togger lay sprawled on the canvas and Peekay rushed over to help him up. The two punches had been so beautifully timed that he'd been almost unaware of how hard they'd been. Peekay started to lift Togger Brown to his feet, grabbing him under the armpits. Suddenly Dutch Holland was in the ring waving his arms above his head, stopping the sparring session.

Peekay held Togger around the shoulders. 'You okay?'

Togger's head was beginning to clear and he nodded, grinning. 'Jesus, Peekay! What a corker of a right hand!' He brought his glove up and sniffed, wiping his nose on the surface of the black leather.

Dutch Holland shouted to Fred to bring a bucket and sponge. Togger nudged Peekay. 'Still an' all, you gave that big bastard a good hiding,' he giggled, and whispered, 'Dutch thinks he's the big white hope. Big white dope, more like. Blimey! You didn't 'arf make him look ordinary!'

They climbed through the ropes together, though on the side opposite to where Hymie and Harriet sat. Togger Brown put his hand on Peekay's shoulder and looked serious. 'Can I box with you some more? I could learn a lot from you, I could.'

'Shit, Togger, it's all there in you. You move well, you're fast with a bloody good left lead.' Peekay shrugged and indicated the ring. 'It's just that I've been up there maybe fifty times more than you have,' he grinned. 'I've been knocked around a bit more.'

Peekay couldn't quite believe Togger Brown. His accent was straight out of a *Hotspur* comic. At first he'd thought the little freckle-faced fighter with the big smile was sending him up. He'd become accustomed to the well-varnished accents of the college proctors as well as a great many of his fellow students, but he hadn't yet attuned his ear to a broad London accent.

Fred arrived with the bucket and sponge and Dutch Holland called down to Togger to return to the ring so he could take off his headgear and gloves and check his reflexes. Peekay walked over to the side of the ring where Hymie and Harriet sat.

Hymie helped him out of the ring. 'Nice one, Peekay!' Harriet, not wanting to intrude, busied herself putting her sketch pad into her satchel. Peekay, observing her, could see that the hint of a smile played around her mouth. As Hymie lifted the protective leather headgear from his friend's head she turned towards him and looking up, fixed her eyes on Peekay. 'You were marvellous,' she said quietly.

Peekay felt suddenly light-headed. His instincts told him he was stepping into very dangerous territory. How the hell was he going to explain to Hymie he was in love with his girl?

'Can we go into my office, then, Mr Levy?' Dutch Holland said, climbing down from the ring. Hymie looked at Peekay and gave him a furtive thumbs-up sign. 'Here goes,' he whispered and then in a louder voice, 'Better have a shower, Peekay, be back in a mo.'

Peekay let himself smile at Harriet. Hymie hadn't removed his bandages and he sat down and began to pull at the tape. 'Oh! Please let me do that,' Harriet said. She unwound the bandage, winding it up carefully again as she removed it from his hand. 'What you're watching is four years of VAD training paying off at last.' She had a throaty, infectious laugh and Peekay found himself grinning stupidly. 'During the war as a kid in Norfolk I used to imagine a German flier parachuting down into the fields behind our house. I'd be the first there running across the fields in my VAD uniform and little brown bakelite first-aid suitcase banging against my knees. The Jerry would be lying there stunned and before you could say Jack Robinson I'd have bandaged him up like an Egyptian mummy. By the time the village folk would appear with their pitch forks and clubs I'd be standing between them and my captured flier. Then I'd imperiously order four of them to make a stretcher from his parachute silk. I'd be a terrific hero, of course, and have to go up to Buckingham Palace and get a medal for bravery . . . perhaps two medals, one for bravery and the other for bandaging.'

Peekay laughed. 'I used to imagine I was the Spitfire pilot who shot him down. I had no idea you were waiting below to rescue the bugger!' They laughed together. 'Thanks, Harriet, you get eleven out of ten for debandaging,' Peekay said happily.

Harriet sighed melodramatically, then threw back her head and laughed. 'I suppose I'm going to have to get used to hanging around dirty gyms waiting for a certain sweaty boxer and his manager.' She sniffed, squiffing up her nose. 'What a pong! Do they all smell like this?'

Peekay grinned. 'Only the better ones. Excuse me please, Harriet, I must pong rather myself. I'll warm down and take a shower.' On his way to the change room he felt as though he was walking on air. She's not yours! She's not yours, you fool! he insisted to himself, but it didn't help. Harriet Clive suddenly filled every nook and cranny in his mind.

Peekay entered the change room just as Peter Best was leaving. Peekay smiled and extended his hand. 'No hard feelings, Peter? Thanks for the opportunity to work out with you.'

Best did not accept Peekay's hand. Instead he jabbed his forefinger into his face and snarled, 'Listen lad! No fuckin' welterweight makes a fuckin' monkey out of me and hopes to stay fuckin' healthy. You'll get yours, mark my fuckin' words!' He brushed past Peekay and was gone.

'That's fuckin' wonderful!' Togger yelled after him, mimicking his accent. 'Remind me to nominate you for fuckin' sportsman of the fuckin' year, my son!'

'Shut up, Togger!' Peekay said, grinning broadly, bringing his finger to his lips. 'We don't want a fookin' shower-room brawl. He'll kill us! Besides, I think Hymie's about to convince your Mr Holland to take me on.' A look of mock seriousness crossed his face. 'You screw it up for me, Togger, and you're a dead welterweight!'

Togger stood nude in the middle of the room with a small tin of Johnson's Baby Powder in his hand. 'Oh, mate! From the opening bell you was never in the slightest doubt. Dutch thinks all 'is fuckin' birthdays 'ave come at once!'

'I hope you're right. Shower's cold, I suppose?' Peekay asked, attempting to make light of the compliment.

'Yeah, I suppose,' Togger said absently, then swung around. ' 'Ere! It's the middle of bleedin' winter. I mean, you 'ardly got a sweat up! Them showers is colder than fuckin' charity!'

Peekay laughed. He instinctively liked the little Londoner. He shrugged his shoulders. 'It's a nasty colonial habit, Togger.'

'Oi! I've heard about you lot, washin' all the bleedin' natural oils off of your skin with all them showers. 'Ere, lemme show you.' He lifted his left arm and upended the tin of baby powder. A cloud of powder exploded in the region of his underarm. He changed hands and repeated the process under his right arm. Then he shook the tin vigorously, rubbing the powder into his ginger-coloured short and curlies until they looked as white as Santa's beard. 'That's a British version of the winter shower,' he announced. 'You stay warm, smell like a rose and you don't 'arm your natural supply of precious body oils which stop you from ageing prematurely and being all 'orrible and wrinkled up like a boardin' 'ouse prune!'

Peekay laughed, his ribs hurting where Best had landed a brace of good punches. 'No thanks, Togger, I guess I'm doomed to premature loss of my precious body oils.'

Fred entered with the bucket and sponge from the ring and observed the two young boxers. 'Makin' friends, that's good that is,' he glanced back at the door, as though Best had only just left. 'No point in bein' like that afterwards, it don't make you no better.'

Hymie and Harriet were standing with Dutch Holland when the two young boxers emerged from the change room. Hymie was smoking a dark-brown Russian sobranie and the acrid smell of the Turkish tobacco filled the small gymnasium. It was mixed with the sweeter aroma of Dutch Holland's Cuban cigar.

'Dutch here says okay,' Hymie grinned.

Peekay whooped like a schoolboy, totally elated. 'Thank you, Mr Holland. I won't let you down, sir, I've never been surer of anything in my life.'

Dutch Holland turned to Peekay. 'If you're prepared to graft, son, I think I can promise you a crack at the British Empire title in two years, or I'm not the Flying Dutchman.'

'Sooner,' Peekay said softly.

Dutch looked surprised. 'What? What did you say, son?'

'Sooner, please, Mr Holland. I can't wait two years.'

Dutch Holland smiled. 'Sorry, lad, you can't hold a major British title until you're twenty-one, that's the law in this country.'

'Well, Mr Holland, we'll just have to miss out on it and go higher. It's not the law in America.'

Peekay was aware of the sudden silence around him. Hymie knew of course, but they'd agreed he'd say nothing about it to Dutch Holland, afraid it would frighten him away. Peekay had only spoken up now because he'd suddenly become afraid the British trainer might aim too low, content to take less than Peekay wanted.

'World?' Dutch Holland smiled, then seemed almost to chortle, which seemed a thoroughly inappropriate sound coming from his owlish face. He took a pull at his big cigar and, shaking his head incredulously, blew his cigar smoke towards the ceiling. 'The welterweight title is owned by Jake "Spoonbill" Jackson, a black boy from Louisville, Kentucky . . .' He tapped the corona with a cocktail-sausage finger. 'Now, mind, I haven't seen this lad fight, but I'm not about to quibble with the latest *Ring* magazine who rate him the best boxer, pound for pound, in the bleedin' world! And he's only twenty-three, my son!'

'It's just that we're in a hurry, Dutch,' Hymie replied quietly.

'Hurry? You've got a jet-propelled rocket up your bums, the pair of you!'

Peekay's heart was beating fast. He'd probably acted stupidly but he couldn't help himself. He had eighteen months, at the outside two years, to get a crack at the title. He'd waited long enough, by the time he'd finished at Oxford he wanted it over. Holland simply had to try to understand that, now, at the very beginning of their relationship.

Harriet had wanted to go to the Tate to see the new Jacob Epstein sculpture as well as a recently acquired Degas bronze study of a child ballet dancer. Then she and Hymie were going to drive to Berkshire to a schoolfriend's twenty-first. Peekay was taking the evening train back from Paddington to Oxford. Togger listened as they discussed which train would be best; it was a Friday night and Harriet suggested Peekay catch an early train to avoid the commuters and people going up to the country for the weekend.

Togger followed Peekay to the toilet. 'Oi, how about letting me show you the bleedin' metropolis tonight? Stay over, mate, you can doss at my place. It ain't fancy but me sister's not home, you can have her bed. Waddayasay, Peekay? We'll 'ave a few jugs, see a bit a the West End, 'ave a few laughs?'

Peekay immediately agreed. He was still elated by the outcome of the morning but now he was beginning to realise just how much the prospect of the session with Dutch Holland had played on his mind. The idea of relaxing and seeing London with Togger appealed to him enormously. Togger agreed to meet him later at a pub down the Old Kent Road with the improbable name of the World Upside Down.

'Main bar could be a titch crowded. I'll wait in the saloon bar.' Togger glanced down at Peekay's shoes, his eyes travelling upwards until they reached his face. ' 'Ere, I'll bring you some clobber. I'll be the bleedin' laughing stock if I'm seen with you lookin' like that. What size clod'oppers you take?'

Peekay looked down at his duffel coat, brown corduroys and finally at his crepe-soled brown shoes known as brothel creepers. 'Seven,' he said.

'Do the best I can. See you later then, don't be late.' Togger left them at the steps of the Tate and ran to catch a bus.

THIRTEEN

Peekay got off the Old Kent Road one bus stop too soon for the strangely named pub, but a group of women crowding around a vegetable barrow sent him on his way. 'You got off too soon for the World, love, just keep walking.'

Togger was the only man in the saloon bar; there were several older women. He had an almost empty half pint of bitter in front of him and was yacking away to the old biddies. He seemed relieved when Peekay entered nearly ten minutes late. 'Found it okay, then?' Peekay nodded. Togger turned to the ladies in the bar. 'It's been fascinating meetin' you, ladies, but I'm afraid me an' me partner here 'as got to move on to warmer climes. Don't do nothing I wouldn't do now, will yer.' Togger downed what remained of his drink, picked up a large shopping bag and took Peekay by the arm. ' 'Ere, we'll just nick into the toilet. I got your *schmutter* for tonight.'

Togger was dressed in a black suit with a three-button jacket cut very long so that it hung below his knees. The lapels and cuffs were made of black velvet and the stovepipe pants were so narrow they took the shape of his legs. From the cuffs protruded a highly shone pair of winklepicker black shoes which came to a sharp point. With his white shirt he wore a black silk tie no more than half an inch wide. 'I hope it fits, it's me mate, Tim's. He works Friday night at the docks, same as me old man. It's good clobber, tailor made an' all.'

'It's good of you, Togger.'

'Naa! Think nothing of it, mate, least I could do.'

Togger waited while Peekay changed. Tim's suit turned out to be an amazingly good fit, even the shoes felt comfortable. 'Very suave. Very bloody suave,' Togger marvelled as Peekay opened the toilet door. 'You look smashin', mate.' Togger put his hand into his pocket and produced a small green bottle. ' 'Ere, 'ave a go at this, you'll smell like a bleedin' ponce, but the girls love it!'

Peekay cupped his hands and Togger shook three or four drops of the green cologne into them. He capped the bottle as Peekay patted the after-shave onto his jowls. 'Tim got it off a queer who bought it in Paris.' Togger read the small silver label: 'Pinaud eau de toilette.' He pronounced it 'Pinord ewe de toilet'. 'It's the genuine froggie leg-opener stuff, mate, no messing about! A bird gets a whiff of this she's practically begging for it, right off!'

Peekay laughed. 'You know something, Togger, except for Harriet today and some of the girls on the boat coming over – but they were too stuck up and only went with the ship's officers – I haven't been near a chick since the last school dance which was . . . Christ, maybe two years ago.'

Togger looked genuinely shocked. He rubbed his hand through his ginger mop. 'You're kiddin' me now, ain't you, Peekay? You mean you just been wanking on your own?'

Peekay blushed, but nodded. There seemed no point in denying it. Togger laughed. 'Me grandad, he was a randy old sod, he used to say, "Ain't nothin' wrong with wankin', matter of fact, with masturbation you meets a much better class of woman!"'

Peekay laughed. 'All I meant was, it would be nice to meet a few girls for a change. The ones you see at Oxford seem to be trying their hardest to be neuter. They're not women, they're brains riding bicycles!'

'Say no more, my son. Leave it to your old mate, Togger. We'll 'ave a pint here and then we'll drop in home and give me mum her bottle and stow yer clobber. After that we'll have a feed of fish 'n' chips at a caf I know near the Elephant and Castle and then it's straight to the Streatham Locamo!' He paused for effect. 'It's Friday night, pay day, place will be wall-to-wall with top crumpet. Then, if we are not rewarded for leadin' blameless lives with a couple of first-class tarts, we'll take the tube uptown. Whaddaya reckon?'

'Lead on, MacDuff!' Peekay said happily. The teddy-boy outfit he was wearing made him feel different.

Togger picked up the shopping bag which now contained Peekay's clothes. 'You dance?' he asked. Peekay nodded. He'd learned to jive on the boat over.

Togger stopped at the off-licence to buy half a bottle of gin. 'Can't I buy that?' Peekay asked.

'Tell you what, you buy the other half.' He looked up. 'Make that a bottle of Gilbey's please, Ron.'

They walked out of the off-licence and turned right. 'It's just round the corner.' Togger tapped the brown paper packet containing the bottle of gin. 'That's good, Peekay, that'll put her out for the duration. Might as well know, mate, me mum loves gin. She's better on gin, any sort, but she likes Gilbey's best, funny old tart.'

The house had a doorway set directly onto the street, part of a double-storey terrace. The door opened into a small parlour; the air was stale and smelt slightly sour as they stepped inside. An overweight woman who looked in her fifties – it was difficult to tell – wearing a dirty housecoat and slippers, lay dozing on a couch drawn up in front of a coal fire. She opened her eyes as they entered, though her expression didn't change. It seemed to take several moments for her to focus on them. 'Sh'you, Togger?'

'Yes, mum, I brought a bottle, Gilbey's!' He turned to Peekay. 'She's on the sauce early, no use trying to talk. Me old man musta gone off early, she usually waits till he's off before she hits the bottle. Still an' all, that means the bedroom's free.'

Peekay saw how small the house was. 'Look, Togger, I'm not intruding am I?'

'No, Peekay, you're welcome. It ain't Buck House, but there's a bed for you.'

They'd moved from the parlour into the tiny scullery, where he removed a rubber hot-water bottle from a hook on the wall directly behind the sink. The bottle contained a rubber bung from the centre of which a small rubber pipe protruded for about eighteen inches. Togger removed the bung, revealing that the pipe extended into the hot-water bottle almost to its full length. He held the bottle under the tap, appearing to fill it to about one third its capacity; then he upended half the contents of the gin bottle into it. He replaced the bung, pushing it firmly into place.

'What the hell are you doing?' Peekay asked.

'Puttin' the old bird to bed. She ain't gonna budge from that couch and if I give her the bottle she'll spill it and then she'll get up in the dark and go looking for more, which she's probably got hidden somewhere, and she'll do herself mischief.' He placed the hot-water bottle carefully on the sink so that none of the contents could run out and hid the remainder of the gin in the cupboard under the sink. Then he picked up the carrier bag with Peekay's clothes. 'Hang on, I'll stow this stuff upstairs, won't be a tic!'

Peekay could hear Togger running up the stairs and the creak of boards as he moved about above him. Togger bounced down the stairs again carrying a large eiderdown and a rubber blanket over his arm. The last time Peekay had seen a rubber blanket like that had been at boarding school when he'd been five and wet his bed at night. Each morning he'd be required to take it into the showers and scrub it.

'Bring the hot-water bottle then, please mate,' Togger asked. Peekay followed Togger back into the parlour carrying the bottle, and holding the tube so none of the contents would spill.

'Who y'frr-end, love,' Togger's mum mumbled, pointing a waving finger at Peekay.

'Peekay, this is the one an' only Mrs Brown, not the original knees-up version, but the Irish one, just as good mind. Though tonight, mate, she's just a tiny bit under the weather, ain't ya, mum?'

'Nice to meet you, Mrs Brown.' Togger was so natural about the introduction that Peekay felt no awkwardness.

'How d'jado, did'cha bring t'bottle, son?'

'Only if you sit up and let me put the mat under you, mum!'

'Whaffor, Togs? I . . . I . . .' Togger's mum closed her eyes tightly, trying to force the words from her mouth. When they came they were strung together perfectly. 'I'm not goin'ter piss me pants now, son!'

'Just the same, love,' said Togger, turning to Peekay and handing the rubber mat to him, allowing the eiderdown to drop to the floor. Then he stooped down and took his mother under both arms. 'C'mon, mum, up yer come!'

Peekay placed the hot-water bottle against the edge of the hearth and quickly spread the rubber mat over the couch. Togger lowered his mother back onto it, lifting her feet up and removing her slippers. He picked up the pillow which had fallen to the floor and, puffing it up first, he placed it behind his mother's head. Then he undid the belt of her scruffy pink housecoat. ' 'Ere, Peekay, hand us the hot-water bottle, then.'

He placed it on her stomach and secured it with the belt. Then he placed his mum's left hand on the bottle and handed her the rubber tube. She took it greedily in her free hand and immediately closed her eyes. 'You're a darlin' boy,' she said, and began to suck at the tube. Peekay handed Togger the eiderdown and he wrapped it over the old girl, tucking it in under her at the back so it wouldn't fall to the floor during the night.

'Thanks, Peekay. It ain't a pretty sight, but she ain't a bad old thing really.' He put his hand on his mother's head. 'G'night, ma, sweet dreams.' He turned and, stepping over to the grate, upended a small coal bucket on the fire. The coal swallowed the embers in a tumble of black dust, but almost immediately the fire started to spit and splutter, fighting its way back. 'Righto!' Togger glanced at his watch. 'It's half six, let's be off then, place is crawlin' with crumpet by now, you mark me words.'

They arrived at the Streatham Locarno about eight. The dance hall was already packed. All the girls were dressed up to the nines and stood around in groups watching the dancers and mostly giggling. Peekay and Togger stood on the edge of the large dance floor eyeing the talent. 'May I suggest a modis opa-randy,' Togger asked.

Peekay nodded happily. 'As you say, Togger. There are some bloody nice-looking girls here.'

'Now that's just it, yer see. Getting a good sort and not a scrubber takes a fair amount of cunning. If you watch carefully you'll notice most birds go around in pairs, a pretty one and an ugly one. I dunno why this is, must have something to do with nature. But a good-looking bird always has a proper turn-off with her. A fat pimple-picker with hairy legs. Take my word for it, go fer the scrubber. Do a coupla turns with her on the floor, then ask her mate for a dance. Works every time. Her mate's happy 'cause she 'asn't been ignored, an' the good sort don't feel guilty no more for 'aving a good time, know what I mean?'

'Ja, I see what you mean,' Peekay said, looking about him. He soon spied a nice-looking blonde wearing a tight pink angora sweater, wide white skirt and black patent-leather high-heeled courts. Her hair was swept back into a ponytail. Beside her, dressed in a bright red, off-the-shoulder dress, which fitted her pudgy form rather too well, was her red-headed, big-breasted friend. 'Hey, Togger, see the dame in the white skirt, the one with the marvellous tits?' Peekay said urgently. He frowned suddenly. 'Are you certain about this theory of yours?'

Togger patted Peekay on the shoulder. 'Trust me, my son. Follow your old uncle Togger's instructions and you'll be in like bleedin' Flynn, I promise!'

Peekay moved towards the fat girl in the undersized red dress. 'May I have this dance?' he asked politely.

'Eh?' The fat girl, chewing gum, cocked her head and closed one eye to look at Peekay.

'May I have this dance?' Peekay repeated.

The girl giggled. 'Oo! Ain't you the polite one!' She turned to the girl beside her and giggled again. 'No thanks, we don't dance with toffs.'

'Hey! Who you callin' a toff, slut? This is me mate, Peekay, from South Africa. You gonna dance with him or not? Make up yer bleedin' mind, you slack tart!'

The fat girl looked surprised and then grinned at Togger. 'Oo! lovely!' She grabbed his arm. 'I bet you're a smashin' dancer an' all!' Togger was almost jerked off his feet onto the dance floor.

Peekay turned to the blonde in the angora. 'I'm a toff from Oxford University. Would you care to dance with me?'

'Don't mind if I do. I'm partial to a bit of class. I'm Doris. What's your name, then . . .? Peekay, is it?'

Doris was a top dancer and Peekay had learned enough on the boat over to cope about as well as any of the other guys on the floor. Togger was lost amongst the whirling bodies, and after twenty minutes or so, Doris pulled Peekay away from the floor. 'What'll it be, Doris?' Peekay asked.

'Ooh! Don't mind if I do. I'll 'ave a Babycham,' Doris pushed herself closely against him, and Peekay felt the curve of her left breast against his chest. His heart began to pound. They found a table and Doris sat down while a somewhat agitated Peekay went over to the bar, fighting to calm his imagination so he could take his hand out of his pocket.

Peekay had a coke while Doris toyed with her Babycham served up in a cheap champagne glass with a short straw. She smoked, using a holder, and her nails were long and painted a shiny red. Try as he might, Peekay couldn't keep his eyes off her breasts. Doris didn't seem to mind. 'If you're such a toff, how come you wearing that suit, then? That's a Ted's clobber, that is,' she laughed.

Peekay grinned. 'It belongs to Togger's mate.' He reverted back to his usual accent. 'I'm not really a toff, Doris. Togger and I are boxers and I'm a student.'

'And you're from South Africa then? What the girls like in South Africa? They all black? What's it like goin' with a black girl?'

'Jeez, so many questions. Yes, pretty; no, I don't know.'

'Come again?'

'I've never been out with a black girl.'

'Why's that, then?'

'Well in South Africa,' Peekay paused, not sure how to answer. 'Well, whites don't go out with blacks, I mean girls.'

'Why not? What's wrong with black women?'

Peekay glanced up to see whether Doris was having him on, but her question seemed perfectly innocent. 'Ja, well nothing, I suppose, it's just, well it's not the thing to do.'

'You're barmy. If you ask me, I'd like to go with a black man. I got a girlfriend who goes out with a Jamaican, he's smashin''.

Just then Togger emerged, held firmly by the arm. He was sweating and looked somewhat nonplussed. 'Oi, Peekay!' he called.

Peekay rose as they reached the table. 'What'll it be?' he asked Togger, who was standing slightly behind the big girl. Togger shook his head violently; his eyes cast heavenwards, he ran his finger across his throat. But it was too late. The big girl was already beginning to sit down. 'Ooh, Babycham!' She seemed to have forgotten that she'd earlier rejected Peekay and looked up at him, beaming.

'With a dash, please!' Peekay looked puzzled. 'My Babycham, with a little drop of brandy,' she repeated.

'Half a bitter,' Togger added wearily, borrowing a chair from an adjacent table and sitting down.

'Another Babycham, Doris?'

'Ta very much, Peekay.'

'With a dash?'

Doris giggled, giving Peekay a saucy look. Peekay was waiting at the bar when Togger appeared at his side. The barman was pulling Togger's half pint. 'Christ, Peekay, we got to scarper!' He pointed to the two Babychams on the counter, 'Know what they are?'

'They're leg-openers, dead set!'

Peekay looked pleased. 'I thought that was the general idea?'

'Oh, mate! Have a heart! Two or three of them and that Gladys is gonna rape me! She dances like a bleedin' hippo. I think me shoulder's dislocated an' all.' He took a hurried gulp from the half pint on the counter, wiping his mouth with the back of his hand. 'Plenty more where them two come from uptown.'

'Not with tits like Doris!' Peekay said, reaching for the two glasses.

'Better! I know this strip joint, I know the birds an' all. You think she's got tits!' Togger rolled his eyes. 'One girl, Geraldine, she's got bristols you can see comin' round the corner ten seconds before the rest of her arrives.'

'Jesus, Togger, I reckon a few more dances and a few more of these, I could put the hard word on Doris.'

'No doubt about it, Peekay, but I reckon our friendship couldn't stand the bleedin' strain.'

Half an hour later, after Togger had sworn on a stack of imaginary bibles that he'd call Gladys and Peekay had written down Doris's number at the Dolls' Hospital where she worked in Hammersmith, they were back on a bus headed for the West End.

'I'm telling you, Togger, this better be bloody good,' Peekay chaffed. 'By the way, I want to congratulate you. That theory of yours, it works amazingly well!'

Togger threw Peekay a sour look; then he giggled. 'Jesus, Peekay, when she grabbed me and hauled me onto the bleedin' dance floor I nearly shit meself!'

'This strip joint, what's it like?' Peekay asked.

'About the same as any other, I suppose, only I know the birds at this one, so we won't have to pay a pound a drink.'

'How much?' He was aghast.

'Well that's it, you see, it's a private club like. You pay three quid to be a member and then you buy drinks for the girls at a quid a time; that's how the management makes a crust. There's hundreds of them clubs accounting for every taste.'

Peekay's mind boggled. This was the big time all right. 'I've only got about four quid left, Togger.'

'Blimey, Peekay, we're the bleedin' cog-nos-centee. Paying's for mugs 'n' perverts. Besides, me sister works there, don't she?'

'Your sister's a stripper!' The words were out before Peekay realised what he'd said, or rather, how he'd said it.

Togger looked at Peekay with a hurt expression. Peekay grabbed his shoulder. 'I apologise Togger, I didn't mean it to sound like that. It's just that I've never been to a strip club. I've never seen a stripper!'

'And you think a stripper's on the game, is that it?'

Peekay coloured violently. 'Togger, honest, I don't know what to say. This, it's all new to me. I was brought up in the Pentecostal church, the Apostolic Faith Mission. Pastor Mulvery used to say that a girl who wears lipstick and paints her nails is a fallen woman, and as for a stripper? Shit, I don't think his imagination could stretch that far! But I'm telling you, it would simply have been another name for a whore!'

Togger grinned. 'Say no more, Peekay. It ain't unheard of for a stripper to forsake her art for the easy life on her back. You'll like me sister, she's a model really, and a doo-wap-de-wally-wally girl. Strippin's only Friday and Saturday nights. Times are hard, she's moved out from home.'

'Doo-wap-de-what?'

'A doo-wap-de-wally-wally girl! You know when the singer's beltin' out a song, the three girls who stand behind him with their 'ands out making little circles and their hips swingin', going, '*Doo-wap-de-wally-wally, doo-wap-de-wally-wally*!'

Peekay laughed. 'That's bloody marvellous, doo-wap-de-wally-wally. Wait until I tell Hymie.'

Togger was suddenly serious. 'That's the problem with me whole family. They're all *nearly* but not quite. Carmen, that's me sister, she always wanted to be a jazz singer; she *nearly* made it . . . but not quite.'

Peekay rested his hand on Togger's shoulder. 'Listen to me. I know what you're going to say, about this morning when I put you on the seat of your pants . . .'

'You're right, Peekay. Here we go again! I thought. Till this morning I reckoned I was just about the best bleedin' amateur welterweight in Britain. I ain't been beat in three years; then you come along and give me a bleedin' boxing lesson!' Togger looked up at Peekay, his eyes tearful. 'Shit, not me also? Not another member of the *nearly-but-not-fucking-quite* family of fucking Browns!' Togger tried to smile. 'Me old man was *nearly* light heavyweight champion of the Merchant Navy, but 'e got knocked out in the final round – when he was light years ahead on points.'

'Togger! Stop talking like this! We're in this together, you hear? You train with me, we're going to the top together.' Peekay shook Togger's shoulder. 'You want to know something?' Togger looked at him querulously. 'Take me, I'm so fucking scared I have to win or I'll shit myself.'

'What the hell are you talkin' about?'

Peekay paused. 'Take you, you're not scared of who you are. You're Togger Brown and proud of it. You're known around your manor, people like you, you're open to life and you let it in.' Peekay paused again. 'Even your mum, you're loving and kind to her. Let me tell you about my mum. She's a dressmaker, she worked all her life behind a Singer sewing machine. When she wasn't praying to the Lord she was working for the rich people in town, making their clothes. I had no old man and she kept us, me and my grandpa. But we didn't love her. At six I wrote her off. Ever since, I've felt guilty for not loving her, for not being a real son. You see, for reasons I'll tell you about someday, I was scared when I was a kid. Scared shitless. So I decided to hide, run away from life.'

'You're crackers, Peekay. You! Run away from life? You're going to Oxford and you just might end up world welterweight champion. Do me a favour, son!'

'No, Togger, listen to me, it's true. You can hide in two places, you can be a nobody and simply disappear into the crowd, or you can hide up front, way ahead of anybody else. But that means you can never lose. You've got to fight harder, punch better, get better marks, win, win, win! Sometimes, inside me, I feel fifty years old and always scared. Scared that they – I don't know who "they" is – that *they* will find out who I really am. They'll see the yellow streak under the winning streak, see what's really under all the camouflage.'

Togger's mouth fell open. 'Blimey, Peekay!'

'All I'm trying to say, Togger, is that you seem to be the furthermost from a *nearly-but-not-quite* personality as it is possible to get.'

Togger, his face serious, looked at Peekay. 'Thanks, Peekay. No, I mean it. Thanks for that, I appreciate your sayin' that a lot.'

'Next stop Piccadilly!' the conductor shouted.

Peekay, following Togger, was soon helplessly lost in the maze of little streets that networked London's Soho district. He was amazed at being accosted by the pros. They stood with unlit cigarettes virtually on every corner. 'Wanna a good time, darling?' It was the universal opening and, to his surprise, some of them were really very sexy. Togger appeared not to notice them, stopping at last outside a building which resembled hundreds they'd passed and which fronted, apart from four or five steps to the door and a small railed fence, directly onto the street. An outside stairway led down to a basement door about ten feet below street level, above which burned a single tiny blue globe set into a socket on the lintel of the doorway. The window beside the doorway was blacked out, though the light from the street lamp reached halfway down the steps.

They descended the steps and Togger pressed the doorbell. Almost immediately the door opened and bright light spilled over them from the interior passageway. A very large, dark-haired guy with thick brows and bad acne scars, dressed in black pants and a white tuxedo top and red bow tie, greeted them.

'Hello there, young Togger. How's tricks?' He asked in a friendly but surprisingly light voice for such a big man. 'Comin' in then?' He stepped aside, pushing his back to the wall so they could squeeze past him. 'Be a love and sign your guest in,' he said to Togger, without any affectation in his voice.

'Les, this is me mate, Peekay . . . from South Africa. He's a boxer, very handy an' all.'

Les smiled. He was missing three teeth on the left of his lower jaw so his smile looked lop-sided. 'How do, Peekay. We ain't expectin' no trouble, but you never can tell, nice to know we got a coupla likely lads on the premises.' He threw a punch at Togger, hitting him lightly on the shoulder. 'Take care now, Tiger!'

Togger wrote their names in a ledger which stood on a small table at the end of the passageway. Beside it stood a wooden plant stand from which an aspidistra sprouted. On the walls lining the passageway were several hunting prints; the wallpaper was in an art deco design and looked vaguely thirties in appearance. The effect was as though they'd entered the home of a middle-class, middle-aged couple who hadn't bothered to redecorate since their marriage. Only a small modern spotlight, which shone directly at the doorway to bring anyone entering into sharp relief, gave the game away.

The passageway led into a large room filled with a soft orangey red light from two spotlights set into the furthermost corners on either side of a small stage and bar which occupied the front wall area. The walls seemed to be painted in a gloss black and a red velvet upholstered bench ran around them. The remainder of the room was filled with small round tables, none of which seemed to take more than two people. The room was almost full, with about thirty men and a dozen women at the tables. On the bench surrounding the room sat almost as many men holding drinks, though no women. Several girls were serving, dressed in skimpy black satin dresses, the skirts not quite covering their bottoms and the fronts cut low. With this outfit they wore tiny white lace aprons and waitress caps, fishnet stockings and high heels. When they bent over the tables to serve they revealed a generous amount of panty bottom, and written across the panties in some sort of luminous paint were their names. The girl nearest to the entrance where Togger and Peekay stood appeared to be called Gerald, the 'ine' having slipped around the corner of her right buttock.

There appeared to be no band; instead a pair of speakers on either side of the small stage pumped out Dixieland.

'The red lights, they're for the skin tones, see,' Togger explained. 'Strippers always like to work under red lights, it gives 'em a sort of tanned look. You don't see all their bumps an' bruises.'

Peekay followed Togger over to the small bar which sported four chairs, all of which were empty. 'Patrons can't use the bar,' Togger explained. A small neat man in evening dress who appeared to be in his forties, his thinning blond hair greased and combed flat against his scalp, greeted them. 'Gawd, look what the cat's brought in. Who's your pretty friend, Toggalogs?' Without asking, he poured them each a brown ale, half filling the glass and placing the bottles with the remaining beer beside the glasses on the bar.

'Hello, Tony, glad to see you're your cheery self. Tony, this is Peekay, Peekay, Tony. Tony owns this cesspit.'

'Cheeky sod! Welcome to Fleshpot, Peekay,' Tony said turning to take an order from one of the girls.

'Hello there, Togger, long time no see. Where you been then, darling?' It was the girl with Gerald on her bum.

'Here, there and everywhere, kom-see, kom-sar! You know me, Geraldine, keepin' me nose clean.' Togger turned to include Peekay. 'This is Peekay, from South Africa, he's a mate of mine.'

'Pleased to meetcha, Peekay. You a boxer then?'

Peekay rose slightly awkwardly. Geraldine was pretty and she had a great bosom. 'Hello, Geraldine, nice to know you.' He looked around awkwardly, trying to keep his eyes from her spendid decolletage. 'Wow! What a place. It's all a bit much for a country boy.'

'Keep your hands off that boy, you slack tart.' Tony handed Geraldine her tray of drinks.

'Look who's talkin'!' Geraldine shot back. 'See you both later then, I'll have my numbers by half eleven, I'll buy you a drink.'

'Better get ready, darling, show time!' Tony called after her.

Togger looked surprised. 'You going on, then?'

Geraldine laughed, though a little nervously. 'It's me debut; wish me luck.'

'Break a leg,' Togger said as Geraldine left with the tray. He turned to Peekay. 'She's a nice bird, is Geraldine, very tasty. She comes down with Carmen to the gym sometimes.'

Peekay was too polite to enquire about Togger's sister and Togger didn't seem to be looking around for her. He filled his glass with the remaining brown ale from the bottle. Just then the music stopped. Togger nudged him and indicated with a nod and a look in the direction of Tony behind the bar. Peekay turned to see Tony putting a record on a gramophone. He was wearing a top hat and white gloves; a black malacca cane with a silver top rested at the side of the gramophone. Tony saw Peekay looking at him and pursed his lips in an imaginary kiss. 'You really are a very pretty boy,' he said. Then he pulled at the lapels of his coat and picked up his cane.

Tony let himself out from behind the bar and skipped up towards the small stage just as a single blues note sounded from a trumpet. He did a small dance routine on stage, no more than a dozen steps, with a tapped finale, which brought him to a halt with his arms wide. Holding his cane in one hand and his top hat in the other, the microphone adjusted exactly to his height he said, 'It's show time, boys and girls! Show time at Tony del Grado's Fleshpot! London's hot-to-trot spot, where the spirit is willing and the flesh is sleek!'

Togger spoke quietly out of the corner of his mouth. 'His real name's Arthur Higgins. His dad's a bleedin' costermonger, got a barrow down Shepherd Market!'

The trumpet sounded low and sweet as it worked the blues number and Tony, in tune with it, allowed his voice to take on a sincere note. 'In the immortal tradition of the great Gypsy Rose Lee and in the name of all the artistes from the Folies Bergères and the Lido in gay Paree we bring you, for the first time tonight at the Fleshpot, the sensational Fifi la Tombo!'

The drums cut suddenly and a new, languorously slow blues number started. The house spots dimmed and a single spot opened on the stage as the curtain opened to reveal Geraldine in a black evening gown and long black velvet gloves, the gown hugging her body and slashed to the thighs. Her routine wasn't exactly Rita Hayworth; it was mostly easy stuff, the timing not critical, but nevertheless the audience seemed to like it. Peekay found his chest feeling constricted and the tight stove-pants held his erection painfully. He pulled at his collar, trying to stay calm. Lifting his glass to his lips, his eyes fixed on Geraldine, he poured brown ale down his chin, missing his mouth by half an inch.

Geraldine finally stripped down to a small red G-string and the lights cut, leaving the room in darkness. As the curtain closed, the house spots came on to tremendous applause, even the hostesses standing up to cheer.

'I've seen a lot worse in me time,' Togger exclaimed. 'Blimey, Peekay, her bristols must be made out of bleedin' marble. Didya see how they stood straight out?'

'I didn't notice,' Peekay said, sotto voce.

Togger looked up in surprise. 'You lying bastard!'

They both broke up in laughter. 'Christ, Togger, I'd throw a world title for a night with her.'

'Oi! Steady on, lad, when you've got the world title, just imagine the birds you'll pull an' all!' Togger stood up on the crossbars of the bar stool and reached over and under the bar counter for another couple of bottles of brown ale.

Peekay laughed. 'Don't think I haven't thought about that!'

The house lights dimmed and the spot returned to rest on Tony at the microphone. The record began to play a soft continuous timpany, more a feathering of the drums than a beat, the drummer tickling the skins, making them scratch and pant. To Peekay's surprise Tony addressed the microphone quietly, his voice hardly raised. 'Ladies and Gentlemen, I bring you . . . Carmen Brown!' He reached into an inside pocket of his tails and produced a harmonica. The spot dimmed, though it remained on him, and a second spot opened up onto centre stage as the curtains lifted. Peekay could feel Togger go rigid beside him. Standing completely still, her arms raised high, wearing a white evening gown cut not very differently from the one Geraldine had worn, stood a beautiful coloured girl. Her dark hair fell to her shoulders and her skin was the colour of mimosa honey. The drum started to pick out a syncopation and Tony's harmonica blew a sharp, clean note as Carmen began to move, her slim body jerking to every drum beat and sliding to the soft roll of the harmonica. She couldn't possibly be Togger's sister. Ginger, freckled Togger. No bloody way! Her routine was the most sensuous thing Peekay had ever seen, a whipped-cream experienced way beyond anything he'd ever fantasised, but out of respect for Togger he desperately willed himself not to become aroused. But he might as well have tried to stop his heart beating. By the time her routine was complete her honey-brown body was bathed in sweat as she bumped and smoothed to the drum beat and the harmonica. The harmonica rose high and held, the drum spat a series of sharp rattat-tat-tats and cut dead as Carmen raised her hands and spread her feet wide in the same position she'd opened with, though this time she stood only in a diamante G-string and high heels. The lights went to black just as she brought her arms down and hooked her thumbs into the silver G-string, pulling downwards. The place went wild. Carmen was something else all together: erotic, wild, she easily broke every demarcation the Apostolic Faith Mission could in their wildest imaginings have laid down for penultimate sinnership.

Peekay wanted to say all sorts of things. His heart was pumping and his mouth was dry. He placed his hand on Togger's shoulder, which was still rigid, but relaxed as soon as he felt Peekay grip it, as though his friend had somehow released the tension. 'Your sister, how can she be your sister, Togger?'

'Half sister, me old man's from Haiti. He jumped ship in Bristol when he was seventeen. Me mum is Irish and 'ad a bun in the oven, which was me without a known daddy, so she hitched him to give him citizenship and make her respectable. A quid pro quo.'

'Put it there, partner,' Peekay stuck his hand out.

'What for?' Togger took his hand.

'Well, I don't know who my daddy was either!'

'Honest?' Togger laughed, 'Funny that, ain't it? I mean not knowing who your old man was. Mind, I can't explain, old Doug, that's me old man, could'na been better, he gets a bit mad sometimes when he's had a few snorts. But he's never put an 'and on Carmen or me mum, not ever, not even once. And I soon bleedin' learned to stay out the way when he'd had a few.'

'So your sister, I mean Carmen, she's younger than you?'

'Yeah, I musta been just about ready to pop outa the oven when me mum got hitched to Doug, a year and two months. We went to school together, we was like twins. That's how come I learned to box. I was always fightin' some bastard because he called Carmen a nigger, like.'

'So who's the good lookin' friend, Togger?' A female voice said suddenly behind Peekay.

'Hello, Carmo!' Togger said, smiling broadly. Togger's sister moved to stand between them, bending down she gave Togger a peck on the side of his face. 'Peekay, this is me little sister, Carmen Brown.' It was obvious from the formal way he named her and the tone of his voice that Togger was proud of the beautiful young woman who stood beside him.

'You were marvellous, Carmen. I've never seen anything as wonderful in my life,' Peekay said.

Carmen laughed. She had a big mouth and her teeth were even and white and her dark eyes danced. 'I hope you mean sexy, Peekay? I'm paid to be sexy, not wonderful! Tony del Grado's Fleshpot don't want no class acts.' She looked up at Tony, who was back behind the bar. 'Ain't that right, Tony, baby?'

'Art doesn't pay the rent, darling. We're peddling pussy not Picasso!'

'No honestly, Carmen, I'm not an expert, this is the first time I've ever seen a strip show, but you were the best by far!'

Carmen looked at Peekay in surprise. 'First time?'

'Where've you been, lovey, under a rock? I don't suppose you're still a virgin, are you?' Tony said archly.

Peekay went beetroot, unable to respond. 'Only in the sense that he hasn't been sodomised by a berk like you!' Togger shot back angrily.

'Now, now you two!' Carmen said firmly. 'Nice to know you, Peekay, we'll have a drink afterwards.' She jerked a thumb in Tony's direction, 'I've got to go and hustle drinks for the fairy with the top hat and wand.'

Just then three sharp rings sounded from a buzzer under the bar. 'Shit! Trouble! It's Les. At the door!' Tony said in alarm.

'C'mon, Peekay!' Togger flew off the stool and was heading for the passageway. Peekay followed quickly.

The door stood ajar and Les sat in the doorway, his arms covering his head. Three men were bent over him, two holding him down while one kicked him in the ribs. Togger let fly with a right which sent the kicker backwards just as Peekay caught him in a rugby tackle. The big man was forced backwards, knocking the back of his head against the wall on the far side of the steps. Peekay was up in a flash as a second man's boot landed, just missing his groin but sending him backwards into the arms of the man he'd just tackled. Fortunately the impact where he'd hit his head against the wall had dazed him and Peekay was able to leap up again towards his attacker. There wasn't room to throw a punch so, grabbing the man by the lapels of his coat, he gave him a Liverpool kiss, his forehead smashing into his assailant's face connecting with the edge of his brow and the base of his nose. The man dropped to his knees clutching at his face.

Togger was on the ground with the third man on top of him. Both the man's hands were around Togger's neck, and he was bringing his head back to kiss Togger in the face with his forehead. With Togger's head already on the ground the 'kiss' to his forehead would damn near kill him. Les got to his feet just as Peekay dived onto Togger's attacker, grabbing him in a neck-lock and pulling his head back. Les threw an upper-cut at Togger's attacker at precisely the same time as Peekay jerked the man's head away, his own head twisting sideways to take the punch from Les directly on the nose. Peekay thought he'd run into a train. Everything went black and red, but somehow he managed to hold onto the man's neck as they both went sprawling. Peekay was too dazed to hang on much longer and the man forced his arm from his neck and stood up. Through a daze of red and black lightning, his head spinning, Peekay grabbed frantically at the villain's legs, hugging them into his chest just as Togger, who'd climbed to his feet, hit the guy with a right upper-cut that came at him from the floor. Les's arm shot out, grabbed the man by the hair and jerked his head down, bringing his knee up at the same time, smashing the man's face into his knee.

'Let him fall, Peekay!' Togger shouted. Peekay released the man, who seemed to fall in slow motion, unconscious before he slumped to the floor.

Peekay crawled from out under Togger's attacker, his head clearing. He was laughing, blood pouring from his nose. Togger began to laugh and then Les. The first two attackers struggled to their feet, shaky and somewhat dazed, not sure where they were. Togger grabbed hold of the second one, and Les grabbed the bigger one, turning him around and wrenching his arm behind his back.

'Who fuckin' sent you?' demanded Les. 'Answer or I'll snap your soddin' arm off!' Behind him, Peekay giggled and Les started to laugh again. Somehow it wasn't the threat but the laughter which seemed to terrify the man.

'Nick Poultos, he paid us to do the place over,' the man panted.

'The Soho wine importer?'

'That's right.' It was the second guy who spoke. He had his hands in the air, blood pouring from his nose, down his chin and onto his white shirt front.

'G'warn, piss off you two!' Les managed a fierce expression at last. 'Take yer mate and fuck off outta here before I call the fuzz! Tell Poultos we'll be comin' for him.'

The two men lifted the third man up and between them they dragged him up the steps.

Les looked up at the people who'd gathered at street level and were watching them over the railing. 'Okay, show's over. Hoppit, ladies and gentlemen, it's all quiet on the West End front.'

Peekay covered his nose, using both hands. It hurt like hell, but he looked up at Togger and started to laugh again. The passageway was crowded with girls and some of the patrons pushed forward to see what had happened. Carmen was suddenly beside Togger, holding him fiercely by the shoulders. Togger grinned. 'I'm orright, luv.'

Carmen dropped to her knees beside the still laughing Peekay, blood from his nose running through his fingers. At her touch he stopped and moved his hands away. He saw the alarmed look on her face. 'Jesus, Peekay, the bastards have hurt you!'

Peekay grinned. 'Hi, Carmen. One hundred and sixteen fights, if you count today, one hundred and eighteen, all of them defending my dumb nose. Thank Christ it's broken at last!' He attempted to get up but Carmen held him. She pulled his head gently into her bosom, her fingers running through his hair. 'You're beautiful, Peekay, you're a beautiful man, broken nose 'an all.' She kissed him lightly on the forehead. 'Tonight you're coming home with me. It's time you broke something else as well.'

FOURTEEN

Peekay was fortunate in having E. W. White as his tutor at Oxford. White, a fellow of Magdalen, was considered one of the great tutors at law and Peekay was more than a little apprehensive when, on his second day at Oxford, he received a polite note inviting him to take tea in E. W. White's rooms the following afternoon.

The door opened to reveal a tall, angular man with dark brown eyes which belied his obviously English complexion. His hair was almost completely white, but because his eyebrows were blond, his eyes seemed incongruous, as though a hidden bloodline were surfacing. He wore grey flannels rather in need of a crease, heavy brown brogues, a light-blue cotton shirt with a slightly disarranged soft collar and a carelessly knotted club or college tie. From his bony frame hung a grey tweed jacket from which the side pockets permanently bulged, as though he was accustomed to jamming his fists into them for extended periods. He was, Peekay thought, the sort of man who would make Hymie's mum run to the kitchen for the skillet, memorising the contents of the fridge.

His eyes welcomed Peekay but he said not a word, sweeping his right hand in the general direction of one of two large leather armchairs facing a friendly-looking, but unlit fireplace.

It was a curiously mute welcome and Peekay, nervous as hell, didn't quite know how to take his tutor. He'd memorised a little speech saying how pleased he was to be taken under E. W. White's tutorial wing, but now confronting him, it didn't seem quite appropriate. His tutor radiated a calmness which an over-hasty or mumbled introduction would have disrupted.

At this point, and still without speaking, E. W. White left the study and some moments later returned wheeling a rather battered-looking tea trolley. One of the wheels of the trolley squeaked as he pushed it across the worn Persian carpet which covered most of the floor.

Peekay liked the room immediately. It was predictable and contained no disappointments. The room of a tutor at Oxford, he thought, ought to look just like this one. On two walls were a number of antique black-and-white sketches of fishing scenes – lonely, flat landscapes of willow-banked rivers at which tiny figures sat with fishing rods etched against a lowering sky. An almost equal number of pale watercolours of not dissimilar scenes in faded gold stucco frames made up the remainder of the pictures on the walls. They were uniform in size and so similar they'd probably been sold in a job lot. To Peekay's delight, mounted on the wall above the fireplace, was a glass case containing a large brown trout. Its tail curled slightly upward almost touching the top of the glass box; its jaw was set open as if about to take the angler's fly. The taxidermist's brush marks showed clearly where he had applied the lacquer too generously just below the dorsal fin. Otherwise the walls were entirely covered with books. Peekay liked the idea of a wall of books, though he was slightly disappointed that they weren't all matching tomes bound in morocco and embossed in gold. In fact, the cases were rather untidy, with books of every size and description filling every available space, some jammed sideways into the spaces left between the books and the shelf above. Small piles of books littered the floor beside the fireplace and near the door. Against the far wall was a Georgian rosewood desk and fronting it was a slightly lopsided-looking captain's chair of the swivel variety. The remainder of the room was taken up by the two large armchairs facing the fireplace, in one of which Peekay now sat. On the floor beside the other was a large hand-beaten copper ashtray, which was empty but smudged grey with powdered ash.

E. W. White brought the trolley to a halt between the two chairs and poured tea from an enormous brown enamel teapot, its spout protruding from a bright orange knitted tea cosy. Neither milk nor sugar was in evidence and Peekay was not asked if he took either. Instead E. W. White forked a wedge of lemon into Peekay's cup.

'Peekay? Just Peekay? Am I to understand that this single duosyllabic name is all that you are known by? Is this correct?'

'Yes, sir, that's right, only one name,' Peekay replied, hoping he wasn't going to probe any further.

E. W. White looked to see if Peekay was being flippant, but decided he was not. 'Splendid! You may call me E.W., which puts us on equal terms. I must say I never much believed in the English tradition whereby a child is saddled with a veritable cartouche of names. One name, it if serves to identify plainly, is quite enough, don't you think?' He continued without waiting for Peekay's reply. 'After all, there are only two parts of the human condition which matter and both of these are singular. We only have one heart and one brain. They, in the end, decide whether we are worthwhile or otherwise. The rest is simply a mixture of affectation and progenital garbage upon which we English place far too much importance. Most Frenchmen are hard put to trace their grandparents on either side.'

'Would you say that continuity and tradition are unimportant then, sir?' Peekay asked, trying out the thought.

'Only when they are the continuity of learning and concern. If a person or a nation has both a good heart and a sound head, they or it can be forgiven almost any other shortcomings. Alas, England seems, for the time being at least, to have neither.'

Peekay wasn't sure he understood. He hadn't been in England very long and wasn't much chop on British politics. 'You see, simplicity is the key to almost everything. If something can be simply stated and simply understood, it will generally translate into a working concept. Law has chosen to neglect this fundamental truth and as a result has allowed itself to become reactionary, complicated and, for the most part, unjust. Why have you chosen to study law?'

Peekay wanted desperately to impress this rather intimidating Englishman. E.W. probably saw him as just another colonial: the South African, Australian, New Zealander and Canadian – all the same, bright enough, but bred in a cultural desert – England's rather tiresome obligation to the sons and daughters of the second-rate people she'd sent abroad to tame the natives. Peekay needed to let him know he was different, his reason for being at Oxford special.

'Well, sir, my country has problems which I believe can only, in the end, be resolved through the rule of law.' It sounded rather pompous and Peekay coloured slightly.

But E.W. chuckled. 'Ha! An optimist. I expect the opposite will happen. The law will be used to prevent a solution.'

'How do you mean the opposite? Surely when a problem is solved it ought to become the law?' Peekay's mouth was dry and he was having difficulty affecting the maturity he wanted to display.

E.W's reply, when it came seemed a little terse, though Peekay may have imagined this. 'The common law, as I have indicated, is no longer simple or straightforward. Instead it is complicated, often obscure and usually costly, so it can be utilised for the most part only by rapacious men who have devised it to keep title to wealth and property and to maintain power. Poor men cannot afford it and so find themselves condemned by it. Rich men, on the other hand, cannot afford to be without it and, indeed, use the law to avoid justice. If this is true of property and individual power then it is also true of societies. The haves will fashion the law to serve themselves and to keep the have-nots from getting their share. You will know much more about this than I, Peekay, but the ideology the world is coming to know as "apartheid" is, I believe, essentially about one section of the population sustaining a lifestyle and maintaining privileges which are not available to another. Call it rich against poor, black against white. The law creates poverty for some and riches for others, slavery for the have-nots and freedom only for the rich. If you agree with me, Peekay, then explain how your precious rule of law will put such a situation to right?'

Peekay was overwhelmed. E.W. had demolished his prime reason for being at Oxford. Despite his humiliation, he admired the somewhat caustic Englishman who'd just done a complete demolition job on him. Peekay, who had thought himself on the side of the angels, was suddenly aware that in E.W.'s eyes he must seem not much better than any of his South African contemporaries.

Peekay had received a liberal education by South African standards and in the months he'd been on his own on the Copperbelt he'd grown distant from the ideas and values of most of his white South African peers. Theirs was thinking within a defined circle, with very little encouragement to step beyond its circumference. It was not that they were actively conspiring against the black people; there was simply no apparent context in which they could become aware of the need to question the concept of apartheid. Their lives were on track and the dichotomy based on colour was precise. Everyone knew where they stood. Thinking inevitably led to discomfort and perhaps even guilt. And guilt spoilt everything.

Peekay recalled a conversation he'd had with Gideon Mandoma, the young Zulu heir to a chiefdom, the man he'd fought in Sophiatown. After the fight they'd become firm friends and Peekay had arranged for the young Zulu boxer to train in Solly Goldman's gym in Doornfontein, where he himself worked out. The young Zulu had found a job as a furnace boy in a foundry which changed shifts at three in the afternoon so he could work out as a sparring partner with Peekay three days a week. Feeding a blast furnace with a shovel is hard work and the white foreman was a cruel, relentless bastard who was fond of taking his fists to the workers.

On the day the conversation took place Gideon had arrived at the gym with a split above his eye which, though dried and caked on the peripherals, showed a pink streak of bloody flesh running through its centre. The cut had obviously required stitches. Peekay had asked him how it happened. The young Zulu had tried to laugh it off but Peekay had persisted, until Gideon had shrugged and said, 'It was my turn to be beaten by the baas, Peekay.'

'How can you stand it, Gideon? Surely you must want to kill the bastard?' he had asked.

They had been gloved up, ready for a sparring session, waiting for two boxers ahead of them to relinquish the ring. Peekay was speaking in Zulu and since whites, as a general rule, do not speak an African language, there had been little fear of their being overheard.

Gideon had laughed. 'Let me tell you a story, Peekay. Once, when I was a small boy, a white farmer came to our kraal looking for women to pick beans. He carried a big basket and said that he would pay so much for every basket picked. The basket was nearly as tall as a woman, but a day begins at half-light and ends when the light is the same again; to the women it did not seem too big. The money was generous and the women agreed. He arranged to return at dawn the following day with his lorry.

'The stars still pricked the sky when the women rose. Even the herd boys still slept and the women pulled their cotton wraps tightly about the babies they carried on their backs. After whispering to the old women to rise in a short while to make the fires for the morning meal they left. They were all very happy because the drought was bad and the spring rains were late and now this unexpected good fortune had come their way and they were going to make some money.

'They worked hard all day in the hot sun, stopping only to take water or to comfort a child. The baskets were big and the beans were small and hid behind the leaves. The work was very hard, but they were happy and sang songs about the cooking pots and dress lengths they hoped one day to buy if more of this work should come their way. By sunset the beans were all picked and each took her basket to the white farmer to be paid. "I cannot pay you," he said. "Look, your baskets are not full, I agreed to pay only by the basketful." It was true,' Gideon had said, opening his forefinger and thumb, indicating about five inches. 'The beans were so far from the top in the best baskets and even a little lower in the others.'

Peekay had shaken his head; he had known in his heart that Gideon's story was not unusual, that it happened every day a thousand times over.

'We took the matter to the headman of our village and he took it to the next *indaba* with the chief,' Gideon had said. 'The chief listened. It was not an unusual story and I suppose there wasn't very much he could do. But it so happened that Inkosi-Inkosikazi, the greatest medicine man in all Africa, was from the chief's kraal. He was very old and it was thought he would soon die. It was a bit of an insult really, taking a trivial matter to such a great man, but the chief, who was wise, knew that a woman's anger makes the hut an unhappy place. He promised he would ask Inkosi-Inkosikazi if he would consider the matter of the beans. The women were contented; to have this affair of the beans looked into by the great medicine man connected them all with a great honour.

'That very night the rains came to Zululand and the women knew the spirits were on their side in the great bean affair. Even if the mighty Inkosi-Inkosikazi did no more, it was already sufficient.' Gideon Mandoma had laughed and lifted his hand about eighteen inches from the gymnasium floor. 'The young corn stood this high when a message arrived to say that Inkosi-Inkosikazi would pronounce on the matter of the beans and that the women concerned should be at the chief's kraal in two days' time. There was a great deal of excitement, women are not generally invited to attend even a small indaba.

'The news of the great indaba spread like a fire when the bush is dry. People from all over Zululand came to hear the great wizard. They brought newly fermented beer and dried tobacco and some of the precious seed *mielies* they'd been hoarding until the new season's corn was safely inside the seed baskets. Even the very old women, their backs bent double, tall sticks thumping the ground as they walked, set out for the chief's kraal.'

'Orright then, you two, stop nattering like a couple of old *yentas* and hop in the bleedin' ring,' Solly Goldman had called suddenly.

'Afterwards! You've got to promise to finish the story!' Peekay had said urgently.

Gideon had laughed, placing his hand on Peekay's shoulder. 'I do not think you are a white man, Peekay, just a white Zulu.' Then he had looked serious for a moment. 'That's why you are the Tadpole Angel.'

Peekay had spun around. 'Stop that, Gideon Mandoma! You call me that again and I'll drop you for the count, you hear?'

'Drop me? Your best punch is like a fly landing on my nose, white man!'

'Cheeky bloody kaffir!' Peekay had said in English. And they had both laughed as they moved towards Solly Goldman standing in the centre of the ring.

In South African society, the boxing ring was the only place Peekay and Gideon could meet on equal terms. Gideon, intellectually bright, with all the character and determination of a Peekay, was working in a foundry and living in a tin shanty; while Peekay sat sipping tea with his Oxford tutor.

'I know that, looking in from the outside, the rule of the law in my country makes a mockery of justice, E.W. But, equally I can't run from trying to find a solution by using the law. Without law there would be chaos in South Africa.'

'Ah, yes, chaos! How often men seem to initiate the greatest injustices and repression in the name of preventing chaos. The prevention of chaos was what brought the German people under Hitler and led to millions of Jews being crushed.'

Peekay knew that to pursue the argument would only lead to further humiliation. E.W. had probed his intellect and found him wanting. But Peekay neither knew how, nor did he want to back down gracefully, defeat meant relinquishing the central intellectual position he held for his future life.

'I'm afraid you're right, though being right doesn't help much. People such as Hymie Levy and myself have to return to South Africa to fight apartheid and, paradoxically, our only weapon is the law. The unjust, unfair and often ruthless instrument of the law is all we have.' Peekay hesitated. 'That is, short of violence, guns and bombs.'

E.W. became really interested in his new student for the first time. 'Ah, violence and guns. They are invoked as often in the name of law as they are in opposition to it. The trigger is a poor debater but the bleeding-heart liberal, filled with dogma and cant, is equally ineffective.'

Peekay wasn't sure what a bleeding-heart liberal was, but E.W.'s use of the expression suggested it was derogatory. 'I don't think I know what you mean.'

'Most revolutions, no matter how quiet, are not served well by the sympathetic intellectual who carps at the injustice of the culture but seems to live quite happily off the resultant lifestyle it affords him. The well-fed and housed white protest, lending its mouth to the black cause,' E.W. explained.

'And you see me as such?' Peekay felt hurt and humiliated. Somehow he had to make the tall man seated beside him see he wasn't the usual colonial apologist.

E.W., aware of his student's indignation sighed. 'The fuel of any revolution is injustice and heaven knows there has been enough in your country to stoke the revolutionary fires. But, as yet, I perceive your revolution as merely an intellectual idea. A few indignant members of the intelligentsia exorcising their guilt by plotting, usually without permission, on behalf of the oppressed. While this is both commendable and altruistic, it is not usually a successful ploy. The new leaders soon adopt the ways of their old masters. Witness India and Pakistan.'

E.W. looked at Peekay for a moment. 'You are not the first revolutionary to have sat in that chair. The last young chap who argued passionately about freedom from tyranny and equality of opportunity for his people, is today the tyrannical leader of a desperately oppressed nation on the same continent as your own. He has invited me on several occasions to be a guest at the presidential palace and seems genuinely surprised at my refusal. What evidence do you have that the black people in your country are ready to rise against the regime? A true revolution begins from the soil, from the grass roots. It is the final cry of despair from the ground up. Have you heard the cry "freedom"?'

E.W. was asking for hard evidence where there was none. Well, none of the sort which would satisfy a mind such as his. Africa was as unpredictable as a bomb lying in a field for years; one day it would explode, who knew when? But there were signs. Perhaps not the sort E.W. needed to become convinced, but signs nevertheless.

When Peekay had been very young his black nanny told him the story of *Igama sina kathathu*, the stork with three dances. The first dance, or starting dance, is slow and measured, done to a careful set of rules. The second dance is still measured, though somewhat faster and more inventive. The final dance is a flurry and a flutter, a wildly erratic affair in which the male stork often kills itself by breaking its own legs.

Peekay thought of the uprising of the black people in the same way. The analogy wasn't all that strange – dancing and singing were very much a part of black protest. The first dance, the dance which Peekay believed had already begun, was the muted struggle between black and white, a struggle being conducted largely through the courts. There would be trials followed by judicial sentences. The litany of justice would always be present, mostly meaningless to the recipient but painstakingly played out in form and function, precise and according to the book, the white man's book of laws.

The second dance was born of the conditions of the first, where more and more black people were driven from their homes. Already Minister Vorster was talking of separate bantustans, independent states which he referred to as 'tribal homelands', as if they represented some kind of homecoming for black refugees.

The third dance was bloody revolution, the final frenzied cry of pain, the atrocious day of reckoning, the river of blood.

Peekay saw his return to Africa as the beginning of the end of the first dance. It was still a time when the law could be challenged, where the etiquette of justice was intact and treason could still be proved. It was still a time when there was hope that some sanity might prevail.

'Yes, I think I've heard the cry "freedom". But I have to tell you in the African way, E.W. The greatest of the African medicine men told this story to the people. He was an incredibly old man, Inkosi-lnkosikazi, whose name simply means Man-Woman, denoting that he was above gender in even the male-dominated African society. His wisdom was for all the people and altogether pure.'

Peekay resumed Gideon's story, as his Zulu friend had done in the shower room in Solly Goldman's gym. 'Everyone was gathered for the great indaba. The old man began to speak in a thin piping voice which carried surprisingly to all the people present. This is what he told them.

'Once a small army of ants out foraging came across a dung beetle pushing a large ball of dung up a steep hill and making heavy work of the process. It was a time of drought and the ants were hungry. One of the ants walked politely up to the dung beetle and asked him if they could help in return for some more of this delicious dung for themselves.

'The beetle agreed readily and leisurely followed as the ants, singing happily, pushed the great ball of dung to the top of the hill.

' "We have completed the task and the sun is low in the sky, tell us where we can find some dung so that we can return with it to our homes before dark," the ants asked.

' "Hayi, hayi, hayi," the dung beetle shook his head sadly. "The dung is very far away, in a place which you cannot reach before sundown. Here, take this little bit, it will stop your hunger. Tomorrow, be at the same place just before sun-up and I will show you," the beetle promised.

'It wasn't much, but it was enough to feed their families for one night. "What an excellent beetle," the ants agreed.' Peekay paused, embarrassed. 'I'm afraid African stories are a bit long-winded, I'll try to make it short.'

'No, no, please, Peekay. I'm fascinated. Detail is colour and colour is essential to most good argument.'

'Well, the following day the ants were up early, even before sun-up, and together they hurried to meet the dung beetle. They waited and waited and the sun rose and they grew very thirsty. They had almost given up when they saw the beetle approaching, rolling another very large ball of dung before him. "Where have you been?" they cried.

'The beetle stopped pushing and looked very angry. "You are lazy. I came to this place early and you were not here. It's a good thing I am patient and am willing to give you a second chance. If you push this ball of dung up the hill again I will forgive you."

'So the ants apologised and, forming themselves into work gangs, they pushed the ball up the hill once more. They were rewarded with the same amount of dung as the previous evening, enough only for one night. Once again, the beetle promised to show them the place of the dung if they weren't too lazy to rise and meet him the next day.

'Now this beetle was a very clever *skelm* and, try as they might, they always missed him in the morning. They were then obliged to push the ball of dung up the hill in return for just enough to keep their families alive.

'Soon the ants forgot how to forage for themselves and the only way they could feed their families was to push the dung ball up the hill and receive a small portion each night.

'Time went by and they no longer questioned the beetle's authority. He owned all the dung and they accepted that they worked for him and that he could beat them if he wished or starve their children or make laws telling them where they could go or even live. The old laws and customs of the ants were destroyed and the ants were forced to live by the laws and the customs of the beetle.

'Now the ants grew very unhappy but the beetle was strong and they were weak; and besides, they now depended entirely on the beetle for their livelihood.' Peekay laughed, looking up at E.W. 'We're close to the end and I promise not to be this longwinded again.'

'Don't give up while you're ahead. I haven't listened this long to a student for years. I am suitably impressed.'

Peekay flushed at the compliment. 'Like all good stories this one has a hero. One day a young male ant was born in the ant tribe. Right from the beginning he was different. "Why can't we forage for dung ourselves? Why must we work only for the dung beetle? It is well known that the ant was here before the beetle. Why does the beetle own all the dung?" he asked.

' "Shhh!" the elders among the ants cautioned, "the beetle will hear you and come and take you away and beat you and throw you into prison." But the young ant was brave and clever and very determined and soon all the young ants gathered around him and they made a plan to get the dung, which they believed belonged to them just as much as it did to the beetle.

'That day when the beetle arrived at the spot where the worker ants would push his dung up the hill they were nowhere to be seen. He shouted and threatened and stamped his feet on the ground but nothing he did or said helped. The ants had disappeared.

'Now the beetle had a problem. If he left the dung at the bottom of the hill the ants might come in the middle of the night and steal it. He started to push the ball of dung up the hill. But he wasn't used to working hard in the hot sun and the ball was very heavy. He would push it up part of the way and then his strength would fail him and the ball would roll down the hill again.

'But the beetle was not a fool and he was also very determined. He rested for a while and gathered his strength and finally, in the cool of the evening, he began to push. All the young ants watched from the top of the hill as he pushed and pushed and this time he managed to get it almost to the brow of the hill.

' "Now!" shouted the fierce young leader and they rushed at the ball of dung and began to push it back down the hill. The beetle was exhausted but he resisted stoutly. The other ants, observing this, rushed to help the young ants. The beetle could hold the ball on the brow of the hill no longer. Inch by inch the ball began to slide backwards but the beetle would not move away. He was stubborn and he was selfish and he could not bring himself to believe that the ants were capable of overcoming him.

' "Share the dung with us equally and we will stop pushing on this side and help you on your side," the young ant cried.

'But the beetle was so used to being the baas and owning all the dung that he didn't want to share. "No!" he shouted defiantly. "Beetles are better than ants, ants are meant to work and dung beetles are expected to own dung!"

'So the ants pushed harder and the ball of dung began to roll backwards. The beetle, unwilling to jump out of the way and to lose his precious ball of dung, hung on. The ball rolled over and over with him clinging on for dear life so that his shell was cracked and he was bruised and bleeding; but still he clung to the ball of dung. When the ball of dung reached the bottom of the hill it was travelling at great speed, heading for a huge rock. The ball crashed against a rock and broke up, burying the beetle deep inside a heap of dung. The beetle was too weak and injured to crawl out of the dung. He suffocated and died, buried in shit!'

'Bravo, Peekay, a lovely allegory,' E.W. was obviously amused. 'But how does it tell us that an uprising is at hand? Is this not simply a folk story? The history of every nation is told with allegorical stories of good triumphing over evil.'

Peekay sighed inwardly. He was doing too much talking but it was too late now. He had to go on. 'Well firstly the message, or story if you like, came from the most important wizard of them all, a man who was accepted, not only by the Zulu people, but by all the tribes as the greatest of the medicine men. The story was his last; he died some weeks later. Therefore it was a message to all of the black people to take action and to do so with the absolute conviction that, in the end, they would prevail.

'But, if you understand Zulu, the message was not of a sudden uprising. What it carried was a plan. A course of action and a result. Inkosi-Inkosikazi foretold great suffering; the ball rolling down the hill with the beetle hanging on could go on for years, perhaps even decades. It also tells of the white men's determination, *their* willingness to suffer to hold on to their heritage. To the African, suffering is a familiar experience. The African people have always suffered and did so long before the advent of the white man. Suffering is an expected component of life. Shaka, the first great warrior king who forged the Zulu nation into the greatest war machine Africa has ever seen, could make an entire regiment march over a three-hundred-foot cliff to demonstrate their obedience and their loyalty. The Zulu people expect that they'll have to fight, expect that they will suffer, expect that the Boer will not capitulate easily. Nevertheless the story of the dung beetle and the ants is a blueprint, a foretelling of a future with a certainty that, in the end, the people will prevail. It is the certainty of victory which will make them fight long and hard until they win. Victory is no longer an "if"; with Inkosi-Inkosikazi's prophecy, it has become a "when".'

Peekay was conscious of how melodramatic his words must sound to this rational and totally civilised man. He looked about the slightly untidy room. He was in a perfectly ordinary study in a great seat of learning in a country where the fundamental belief was that a combination of God, Queen, good manners and a fair-minded attitude to your fellow man was a perfectly valid prescription for life and one which the rest of the world shouldn't find too difficult to grasp. Witchcraft, superstition and any of the other tenets of a primitive culture played no part in this perception.

Some fucking Oxford undergraduate he'd turned out to be! He wasn't clever at all. This place was filled with people who were light years ahead of him. Not simply the dons, most of the students as well. They spoke better, thought better and certainly argued better. Peekay felt a sudden panic. E.W. wasn't obliged to take him. 'Christ! If he rejects me, what the hell will I do?'

E.W. was silent for a long time. Finally he said slowly, 'We are all believers in magic. Very few things are wrought by logic alone. Man has always fought for improbable causes, often against impossible odds, enduring incredible hardship in the name of some truth or other. In my own way, I too succumbed to the power of a just idea, when a moment's reflection and an ounce of common sense would have shown the futility of the struggle into which I threw my puny weight.' E.W. looked a trifle embarrassed. 'I spent six months as a true believer, among other things winding bandages in Spain.'

A sudden vision of E.W's gaunt frame in an ill-fitting republican uniform in the Spanish Civil War brought a smile to Peekay's lips.

E.W. grinned. 'Well you may laugh, I readily confess to having been a ridiculous soldier, too much Quixote and not enough Hemingway. Like the peripatetic Don Quixote on his horse, I was moved from one ordnance job to another in an attempt to find something I couldn't effectively mess up. Bandages were my last stop and then our side lost. I came home just in time to be recruited into Hitler's war. On the strength of my bandage-winding experience, which obviously, in the eyes of the War Office, counted for a great deal more than a degree in jurisprudence, I spent the entire Second World War in Plymouth lecturing to young ladies in the WRNS on contraception and sexually transmitted diseases gained as an indirect result of accepting gifts of silk stockings and candy from randy American marines.'

Peekay laughed as E.W. hoped he might. He'd watched the young South African carefully. Peekay's student details, submitted to Magdalen College by his headmaster, St John Burnham, indicated that he was a champion boxer and a good all-round sportsman as well as an outstanding student, who had been shortlisted as a Rhodes scholar pending completion of his first degree. As a rule Rhodes scholars didn't impress E.W. who found them, more often than not, too busy with cricket or rugby to manage much more than a lower second.

E.W. was a man who exulted in the human mind and thought of the body as a rather clumsy method of carrying it about. Boxing, a sport which was known to damage the brain, he found both repulsive and primitive and he'd had serious reservations about accepting Peekay.

'And you? You believe in the er . . . witch doctor's prophecy, Peekay?'

'Well, yes, I suppose I do. I'm African myself. The fact that a man of Inkosi-Inkosikazi's power and intelligence, who lived his life in peace as the spirits of the dead decreed he should, would turn around and instruct the people to rise against the white man, could mean only one thing. These same spirits, the great kings, elders and the shadows of his ancestors, Shaka, Dingane and Cetewayo, had joined to ensure the outcome. By allowing the wizard of peace to carry the message of war, the ancestral shadows had cast the bones and read the smoke. The people have no choice but to respond.'

E.W. brought his hands together, the tips of his fingers touching his lips. He appeared to be deep in thought. 'I'm sure we're on the same side, Peekay. But in terms of your time at Oxford perhaps we ought to use a different term of reference. The situation in South Africa is undeniably racist, but this is by no means unique. Almost every culture practises covert racism to a greater or lesser degree. The real enemy is the denial of personal integrity for the white South African, and that of social dignity and opportunity for the black South African.

'That one tribe is thought to be superior to another is once again, common enough. In this country for centuries we've used the class system to the same effect. What makes the situation in South Africa extraordinary from the point of view of jurisprudence, is the existence of actual legislation which decrees that a person of one colour is *born* superior to a person of another colour.

'This single element of the law is the linchpin which holds everything else together. While legislation of this kind exists, corruption of the spirit is inevitable. In the next three years together you and I will *not* discuss this problem in terms of black or white, but in terms of morality, integrity and how the law, used wisely, can indeed be the universally accepted instrument of truth and become accountable for justice in a civilised society.'

This was it, a true analysis of South Africa's plight. One that cut through the bombast and the dogma and the special circumstances. Peekay was overwhelmed with admiration. This was finally what he had come for, to learn to think clearly without sentiment.

'I wish I could have said that,' Peekay said softly.

E.W. brushed away the compliment. 'And you have come to Oxford. Why?'

Peekay answered as simply as he could, 'To do what you suggest. I have come to learn how to make the law honest.'

Looking directly at his young student, E.W. said, 'I'm not sure Oxford can give you what you want, Peekay. It is not the law which keeps a people safe, but the hearts and minds of some few good men and women who are its custodians. Conventional justice, when it is not in the hearts and minds of men, has only the power to corrupt. The letter of law may be upheld but its spirit is withheld. Isn't this what you are talking about?'

Peekay laughed. 'I'm not sure. You see South Africa doesn't have *honest* racial laws which can be corrupted by dishonest and venal men. We have no custodians to see that justice is done, because justice, in racial terms, is *never* done, almost by definition cannot be done! The good guys have no precedent, no fundamentally just law upon which to anchor their arguments.' Peekay frowned, looking for another way of putting his argument. 'Because racial injustice is perfectly legal, it is like shadow boxing. When you throw a punch there is nothing to hit.'

'And making the law honest? Do you have a vision, a picture in your mind, of what this means?'

'Well, yes, it seems to me that justice should be easy to understand, a natural outcome. The prisoner, sitting alone in his cell, confronted with what he has done, should be able to admit his guilt to himself and accept the verdict because he understands he has broken his contract with a society whose laws he agreed to honour.' Peekay paused, searching for the right words. 'The law should be based on the concept of natural justice. Too often the black prisoner doesn't consider himself guilty, doesn't even understand why he is being sentenced. Too often the law itself is a denial of natural justice!'

E.W.'s eyebrows shot up. 'Good! That's good, we can use that.' When he smiled his teeth were slightly uneven and stained yellow from years of smoking a pipe. The young man seated opposite him was vulnerable and gauche, certainly an idealist, but his convictions were not entirely based on the dreary tenets of social injustice every nineteen-year-old undergraduate who pretended to think carried around like a big stick. Nor did he think he knew the answer to everything.

'Will you take me then, E.W.?' Peekay asked, concerned.

'I thought I'd indicated that earlier, my boy?'

'Well, it's just that . . . well, I wanted to make sure we get it right from the beginning.'

'What on earth do you mean, Peekay?'

'Well, you see, we white South Africans tend to have an enormous chip on our shoulders, mostly because we feel guilty, are guilty. I simply cannot afford to waste my time at Oxford trying to justify my guilt. I'd like you to accept that I'm guilty, but that I intend to do something about it.'

'My dear fellow, that will hardly do. You may be guilty wherever else you desire, the exception being in this study. Discussion is the basis of the college system, two or more inquiring minds in a small room is what

Oxford is all about. The personal tutorship you receive here is essentially why you would choose to come to Oxford. You are a boxer I believe? Here you will learn to attack and defend, the punch and counter-punch of discussion. You will win by using your intellect, it will be your only means of defeating an opponent. In this room there is no guilt. I simply won't have it!'

E.W. looked steadily at Peekay. 'We shall spend the remainder of your first term discussing natural justice.' He fumbled in the pockets of his tweed coat and produced a pipe from one pocket and a tobacco pouch and large box of Swan Vesta matches from the other. 'We may well spend the remainder of your time at Oxford discussing it. The rest of what you need to pass your examinations you can pick up in lectures and from the books I shall let you have.' He tapped the bowl of his pipe against the edge of the large copper ashtray, which gave off a loud ringing sound, and prepared to light it.

Peekay's grandfather smoked a pipe and the elaborate ritual about to take place was familiar. Finally the small study was filled with blue, molasses-flavoured smoke. Peekay knew that this was temporary, that pipes go out as a matter of ritual soon after they're lit, when they're put down, allowed to cool slightly and then taken up again. The second smoking is the meaningful one.

He sat patiently and watched his tutor, reflecting on what he had learned. Now that he was actually here, Peekay understood that he would be judged by the quality of his mind. No more sporting hero, nice guy, natural leader, the stuff of which schoolboy legends are made; here only the intellect counted.

It would be like being back with Doc. When things got tough, Doc used to say, 'Listen always on the inside, Peekay. Inside of your head, in a quiet place, is sitting waiting the answer.' He was going to enjoy E. W. White's Oxford.

E.W. removed his pipe from his mouth and placed it in the copper ashtray. Then he took one last gulp of tea and, rising, said, 'I say, what do you think of this tea?'

Peekay was somewhat taken aback. He'd just undergone an afternoon which consisted almost entirely of verbal spankings and in almost the same breath E. W. White was asking him whether he approved of his thoroughly shitty tea.

He rose, preparing to go. 'Well, it was a bit strong,' Peekay ventured.

'A chap named Goonesena whom I tutored in '47 sends it to me from Ceylon. It comes in a ten-pound plywood box beautifully sealed in tin foil, regular as clockwork every two months.' E.W. looked up at Peekay despairingly. 'I'm rather forced, as you can see, to make it in very large quantities or I should never use it up. Alas (he pronounced it 'A-laas'), what you see is a Darjeeling man, condemned forever to drink Ceylon.' He seemed genuinely upset.

Peekay had never thought very much about tea. He generally took it with milk and two sugars about mid-brown. The idea that tea should come in more than one flavour had never occurred to him.

'Ceylon is seeking independence from Great Britain. Why don't you do the same thing to them?' Peekay said, hoping he didn't sound too flippant.

E. W. White threw back his head and laughed loudly. 'I say! Well done, Peekay. Hoist with my own petard, what!' He found his pipe on the trolley and paused to re-light it. 'I think you and I are going to get along splendidly. Next week I shall require two thousand words. Please write clearly. I'd like your thoughts on the concept of natural justice and how it affects the law.'

'English law, sir?'

E.W. looked slightly taken aback. 'Why, all law, of course! I am not aware that the English are any different from any other people when they are at the receiving end of things. Natural justice is the beginning of all true justice; we shall see where it leads. I think you might profitably spend a little time in the Bodleian consulting the work of John Fawcett, though, of course, I am more anxious to read your *own* thoughts on the subject.'

E.W., skilfully moving both of them towards the door, continued his instructions. 'So, please, dear boy, not too many notations in your essay on the thoughts of men long dead. Profundity is seldom achieved by misquoting the opinions of those who cannot return to defend themselves. It is an unfortunate habit cultivated by the more modest minds at Oxford who can only impress their peers by building a bulwark of old ideas. It disguises, of course, the absence of any new ones of their own. By all means use the quotes of the dead to clear the known ground, then dare to walk the wildest unknown path. In this way we can look forward to some intellectual progress.'

At the door they shook hands formally. 'Goodbye, Peekay.' He rubbed his hands together, as though he had suddenly made up his mind about something. 'By Jove! Next time you come I shall serve you Darjeeling. I believe you have given me the courage to liberate myself!'

FIFTEEN

At the conclusion of her final year at Chelsea Arts School Harriet had applied for a grant to the National Arts Foundation, submitting two small maquettes of work she hoped to complete. The first was to be a three-quarter size study of two horses, while the other was a life-size sculpture of a boxer. Her application was successful and the grant enabled her to take a small cottage attached to an old stable with a lofted ceiling, which she hoped to convert into a studio.

The cottage, which went by the unprepossessing name of Cow Cottage, lay about five miles out of Oxford in a setting beside a small brook and amongst tall old oak trees which now stood bare and bleak against the December landscape. The doorway to the cottage was partly overgrown by a climbing white rose Peekay identified as Francis Eileste, while the garden was overgrown with sweetbriar roses and camellia fighting for a space in the pale sun with the weeds and bramble. Harriet, trudging happily around it in a pair of wellington boots, claimed to discover all manner of lovely things cowering under the onslaught of weed, winter and neglect.

Harriet, like Peekay, had grown up in the country. She had spent her childhood in Norfolk and was familiar with gardens. 'I shall have a lovely cottage garden. It's all here waiting for spring and a little love,' she exclaimed happily.

Hymie, on the other hand, was not reassured so easily. He would pass through the three acres of rolling lawns, talking about watering devices for carefully planted beds like the ones in the Levy family garden in Pretoria. He looked at it all as dispassionately as he might a small public park. 'Sure,' he said, looking disapprovingly at the stone cottage buried in weed and neglect, 'I hope you don't expect any of this love you're talking about to come from me? God made my arm to drive a gold Parker 51. Why else would He have given me thirteen of them for my barmitzvah?'

Peekay, on the other hand, was delighted. He longed to get his hands onto a bit of dark, wet earth again and, like Harriet, he could sense that the two-hundred-year-old cottage garden, given a little encouragement, would stage a magnificent comeback in the spring. He also loved the cottage, with its ancient shingle roof, green with moss and lichen, and its Headington stone walls – none too straight, so that the front door leaned decidedly to the left, as did all the windows. He pointed to the south wall of the cottage. 'It looks as though the big bad wolf stood on that side of the house and huffed and puffed and damn nearly blew it down!'

'Christ! What a mess!' Hymie snorted. 'Who are we supposed to be? The three little pigs?'

The interior of the cottage consisted of one large room with a hearth forming the centre of the northern wall which was blackened by a century or two of smoke from the open fire. The early afternoon light strained through the dirty windows, making the interior almost dark. The room hadn't been used for several years and, though dusty, was surprisingly dry and very cold. The floor was of heavy slabs of blue slate, although it was hard to tell in the semi-dark; they could equally have been brown or grey. There was no electricity and no evidence of plumbing. Water was obviously carted in from the brook.

'Jesus! Talk about cosy!' Hymie said in disgust, flicking his cigarette lighter to examine the hearth. 'Shit, Harriet, there's no bloody stove!'

The toilet, a small wooden construction, stood at the bottom of the kitchen garden beside the stream. It too leaned, though from the weight of a very old clematis, its winter-bare vine hugging the entire edifice and pushing it to the right, as if in stubborn defiance of the direction the cottage had decided to take.

The stable, which was more like a barn, was actually larger than the cottage, and the hayloft had been removed, leaving a vaulted ceiling. 'When I can get two large windows set into either side of the roof it will make a perfect studio,' Harriet explained. 'It's the only real expense actually, except for a coat of limewash inside the cottage and here and there a few tiny repairs. Otherwise the place is perfect, don't you think?'

Hymie lit a sobranie before answering. 'My grandmother on my mother's side, with only a large black frying pan on her back, fled from a shtetl in Russia where every house was a Taj Mahal compared to this dump!' He looked appealingly at Harriet. 'Do me a favour, come and live in Oxford? I tell you what. I'll buy you a bicycle so you can pedal out to this dump every day to work.'

'Oh, Hymie, can't you see how romantic it is?' Harriet exclaimed.

'Romantic? No stove! No plumbing! No bathroom! No bloody toilet! The only mod con you're going to enjoy around here is a hot and cold running nose!'

Harriet smiled. 'With a birch-log fire in the hearth, winter will soon pass and when spring comes you'll think it's a miracle, just you wait and see, Hymie Solomon Levy.'

'A miracle is right! A miracle if you're not dead in this cow of a cottage!'

Peekay was secretly glad. Harriet had asked him to pose for the boxer sculpture and he liked the idea of coming out into the country to do so. He'd known Harriet for fourteen months and had been careful to keep the relationship strictly kosher, always making sure that the three of them were together. She belonged to Hymie; but in his mind at night in bed, she belonged to him. At first he'd tried to dismiss her from his thoughts, telling himself how futile it was to allow his imagination to own her. But it didn't work. The famous Peekay mind control collapsed in a whimpering heap at the thought of Harriet in bed with him.

Peekay was not even sure, given the opportunity, that he'd have the courage anyway. His experience of women was one fantastic night with Carmen. He was hopelessly short of experience in the preliminaries. He'd been totally indulged by Carmen but in the process had received very little useful information in the preliminary kissing and feel-up department. His mind was filled with schoolboy stuff, breasts which pumped up like rocks when you felt them and nipples that stood up so you could practically roll one around in your mouth like a large plump raisin. But the practicalities of, for instance, unhooking a brassiere, were beyond him. However hard he tried to imagine it, he knew he couldn't do it.

The trouble was that Harriet was so nice. Peekay felt guilty about making love to her in his imagination. She wasn't just a stunning-looking girl you wanted to do it to. She was someone you wanted to like anyway. She was intelligent, independent and fun. She could be formidable in argument and she would kiss them both spontaneously, hug and touch and be loving, as though it was a perfectly natural thing to do. Which it was, of course; but which it also wasn't, of course.

After over a year together Peekay wasn't so sure Harriet was Hymie's girl. Harriet seemed to treat him no differently to the way she treated Peekay, and Hymie didn't seem to mind this in the least. They were seldom together alone and Hymie made no deliberate attempts to make this happen. If Hymie was sleeping with Harriet, they were going to great pains to conceal it from him.

The trouble was that he and Hymie never talked about it. It was the only thing they hadn't shared. This was mainly Peekay's fault. Because he felt the way he did about Harriet he was afraid Hymie would find out if they talked about her. Peekay wasn't sure he could hide his true feelings from his friend. So he'd gone along with the platonic bit, the two brothers and a sister thing they'd developed between them. It was infinitely better than having no Harriet in his life and Hymie seemed more than happy, even gratified by the arrangement.

Sex was the weakest link in the relationship between the two friends. Hymie had always seemed rather ambivalent about the subject. At school, when puberty had struck like lightning to keep their right hands cupped and guilty and where loud-mouthed fantasy had kept them all from going mad, Hymie had always remained cool. The contagious delirium caused by the overheating of the group's collective sexual imagination seemed to pass him by. It wasn't as though he drew apart, he simply didn't contribute. This was unusual for Hymie. In most other things his opinion played a leading role. Peekay had once bounced his fist against someone's head for suggesting Hymie was a queer. But he had to admit that when the boys woke in the morning and carried their towels to the showers draped over their rigid tent poles, Hymie always sauntered in, slack as a wind sock on a still morning, his towel slung casually over his shoulder.

If Hymie didn't take much of a physical role in the restoration of Cow Cottage, as usual he made things happen. He sent Bobby and Eddy, Peekay's two former sparring partners from the Morris Works, scrounging around builders' yards until they'd found two huge Gothic arched windows. The two boxers arrived at Cow Cottage in a Morris van 'borrowed' from the works on a Saturday morning and before mid afternoon, when the light was beginning to fade, they'd shaped two large holes in the stable roof and edged them in plywood covered with copper sheeting. The following day they'd hoisted the windows up onto the roof and fixed them neatly into place. Hymie had paid for the windows; they were Harriet's Christmas present from him. But when he'd gone to pay the lads they wouldn't hear of it.

Both boxers had become friends, particularly of Peekay. They'd become infinitely better boxers after working out with the young South African who was generous with his knowledge and was often in their corner on a Saturday night calling the tactics. They'd also met Harriet on several occasions and it was clear they approved of her thoroughly, urging Peekay in a good natured way to wrest her away from Hymie, whom they referred to as, 'the Management'.

Bobby would shake his head. 'She's a fighter's lass, lad. 'Taint no good wastin' a good sort like 'er on the Management!'

They were both originally farm lads and seemed to be able to turn their hands to most things. They'd returned the following Saturday, having again 'borrowed' a works van, and spent most of the day loading up the furniture Harriet had found in a number of second-hand locations around Oxford. They'd even been reluctant to stop for lunch, a couple of bottles of Morrell's brown ale and hunks of bread and cheese with thick wedges of freshly dug onion.

The onion was a self-sown distant relative of an antecedent onion patch and had revealed itself when Peekay turned the soil in the kitchen garden, binding it with lime and manure in preparation for the new planting they planned for spring. Peekay had also repaired the garden beds and fixed the drainage, leaving a generous clump of mint and aromatic bronze fennel and another of cotton lavender and Jerusalem sage which seemed to have thrived on the harsh times. He also left several smaller clumps of lily-of-the-valley and bright yellow winter aconite to add a spot of cheer. Against the wall of the stable forming the southern side of the kitchen garden and only a hop, step and jump from the back door of the cottage, grew damson and quince, while along the northern edge ran a badly neglected hedge of rosemary which he trimmed and weeded so that the gaps would grow back in the summer. The brook, a sprightly little stream, formed the bottom border to the garden.

By nightfall on the fourth Sunday, three weeks and a day after Harriet had told a slightly bemused farmer she'd pay him the fifty pounds a year rent in advance, she'd moved into Cow Cottage. The interior of the cottage smelt of fresh calcium and paraffin from the four hurricane lamps suspended on chains from the blackened beam which ran down the centre of the room. Two large second-hand kilims lay on the scrubbed slate floor, which had turned out to be a rich brown colour. At the end of the room, furthermost from the hearth, stood a large imitation Queen-Anne bed of oak veneer, purchased for three pounds from a dealer in Aylesbury, while in the centre rested an enormous chesterfield with broad curved arms of flat wood which looked straight out of a Noel Coward play. Two matching armchairs made up the rest of the centre of the room. The chesterfield and armchairs were covered in a red moquette edged with brass studs in the style of the thirties. The arms of the suite were badly scratched with several dark cigarette burns in the wood, but Eddy promised he'd cut the varnish back, clean it all up and re-lacquer them over the Christmas break. Further along the room near the hearth stood a fairly large scrubbed-pine kitchen table with six bentwood chairs and a kitchen dresser. Finally, sitting squat and happy in the corner to the right of the hearth was 'Bobby's Bounty', a black pot-belly stove Bobby had discovered in a gatekeeper's lodge at an entrance to the Nuffield works.

Eddy had fitted the stove with a new chimney and fixed the flue, and Bobby had set to work on it with stove black, finally buffing it up until it glowed a deep, contented black. On the door of the small stove, in raised cast-iron lettering, read the words 'Rocky Mountain Cooker' and in smaller letters below, 'Made in British Columbia: home of the Canadian Mounties'.

With the little stove had come four bags of washed coal, sufficient to last the winter, which Bobby and Eddy explained had been mysteriously placed in the back of the Morris van when they'd left it parked beside a coal truck outside a pub close to the single men's hostel where they lived.

While the handsome little cooker boasted only one plate it worked a treat and when its fat, round belly was fired up it kept the room nice and warm, even without a fire in the hearth.

Harriet had yet to add such things as bookshelves and posters and the general clutter of things that come to stay in a home, but when the hurricane lamps were lit at night, the room had a bright yellow warmth. Even in daylight, with the windows now clean, the light in the room was soft. Harriet's only initial concession to her femininity was a brilliant patchwork eiderdown on the double bed and lace curtains which framed the small cottage windows. Also, there were two huge damask pillows plumped against the bedhead in a most inviting manner.

It was eight days before Christmas when Hymie got a telegram from his father. It stated that his grandmother was dying and asked him to return home. Hymie wasn't over-fond of his Russian grandmother, which was yet another of the things he felt secretly guilty about. In a Russian Jewish family it's practically compulsory to adore your *buba* and when he'd been little his mother had scolded him for his indifference. 'Go kiss your poor buba, Hymie! God forbid, when you come back from the bioscope, who knows? Maybe she has been taken already away.'

When he'd been younger and before he'd realised that the old harridan was indestructible, he'd race home from the cinema, his heart pounding, convinced he'd see a black hearse parked in the driveway with men in long black coats and top hats carrying his dead grandmother, dressed in her full-length silver fox coat, depositing her into a coffin in the glass-sided hearse. Then, just as the hearse was about to pull away, she'd sit up suddenly and look directly at him, wagging a bony dead finger. 'Shame, boy! You didn't kiss your poor old *babushka* goodbye! Such a small thing! And me who carried already a big black frying pan on my back all the way across Roosha so you could have always nice fried fish!'

'Shit! My grandma's dying again!' Hymie announced in disgust as he read the telegram that their scout Bennett had just delivered to his rooms.

'Oh, I'm sorry to hear that, sir,' Bennett said. 'Shall I pack your bags for the tropics then?' In his mind he could see a big, fat ten-bob tip coming his way. News of a death at home always brought out the best in the undergraduates.

'Yes, thanks, Bennett, only one small suitcase.' Hymie watched as Bennett shuffled into the bedroom before he moved over to the cupboard above the fireplace and took out a bottle of sherry and two small glasses. Moving over to the window, he poured the sherry and, handing one to Peekay, he sat himself in the remaining club chair, holding the stem of the small glass in both hands. 'What a bugger! I was really looking forward to Christmas at Cow Cottage.' The disappointment was clear in his voice as he said, 'By the way, I've ordered a hamper and a Norfolk ham from Fortnum & Mason . . . and a goose!'

Peekay looked up, astounded. 'A goose!'

Hymie laughed. 'Ever since I was a kid and read *A Christmas Carol*, where Scrooge finally comes good with a fat goose for Tiny Tim's family, I've wondered what goose at Christmas tasted like. I thought we'd cook it on that terrific rotating spit Eddy made for Harriet's hearth.' Hymie was talking faster than usual to conceal his dismay.

Peekay looked at his friend. 'Christ I'm sorry, Hymie. It won't be the same without you, but maybe your grandma is, you know, on her deathbed?' Harriet had invited Bobby, Eddy, E.W. and her mother, who was divorced from her father, a marine engineer who'd gone to live in America.

'Fat bloody hope! The old cow gets ill unto death every bloody Christmas.' Hymie paused to explain. 'I think I've told you before, my old man throws this big party in our garden for all his workers. He always dresses up as Father Christmas, the only Santa in the world who says, "Oi Vey!" The moment the old witch sees his Father Christmas suit going to the dry cleaners, in late November, she starts to complain about pains in her chest. "Oh, oh, I should die already in a house where is going on a Christian feast!"

'Of course, my dad doesn't believe her. But it's bloody hopeless. My grandma goes on clutching her heart and moaning and refusing to eat. When this happens my old man has to contend with my mother. I can hear her now, "So, what you waiting for? Mama should die and where is my son? Her only grandson? She should die and then it's too late to call the air force on the phone to bring him home? Shame on you, Solomon!" '

Hymie rose from the chair and moved over to the window to re-fill his glass, waving the bottle at Peekay, who declined. Then he returned to his chair. 'It's really a cryptic message you see.' Hymie dug into the pocket of his tweed jacket and produced the scrunched-up telegram. 'Here listen! I'll read it to you the way my old man wrote it. You have to understand, for two weeks now the old harlot's been dying on him and my mum's been nagging him to the point where he can't get it up when he visits his mistress in Johannesburg.' Hymie held the piece of paper in front of him and in a deadpan voice read, 'Babushka is dying.' Then raising his voice suddenly, 'PLEEEASE COME! You see, it's a plea for help. That's why I can't ignore it. I can't let the poor old bastard down. His Christmas party for the staff is the single most important thing in his life.'

When Peekay had stopped laughing he asked, 'But how's you being there going to help?'

'Well, at least it will get my ma off his back. With me there grandma will be happy. She likes a tidy death, everything tidy and in its place, especially the only grandson.'

Peekay drove Hymie to Gatwick early the following morning to catch the BOAC Comet to Johannesburg. Hymie handed him his camel-hair overcoat as they entered the airport passenger terminal. 'Wear it if you like, you've been through an English January.'

It felt strange to Peekay seeing Hymie off, holding the soft coat over his arms and knowing that in less than twenty-four hours Hymie would be stepping out into bright sunshine, walking through a garden where tiny hummingbirds hovered like jewels above the flowers, their long beaks competing with the bees for their share of the nectar.

It had been fourteen months since Peekay had been home, a fleeting trip of only three days to say goodbye to his friends on the way to Durban to board the boat. Knowing he'd be away at least three years he wanted to see his mum and grandpa, Mrs Boxall the librarian, Miss Bornstein his teacher, Captain Smit and Gert of the prison boxing squad, and above all, his adoring Dee and Dum, the two black twin house servants who'd grown up with him and who loved him passionately. Doc, the old German professor of music and Peekay's beloved childhood mentor, was dead, but he'd walked up to his small cottage which stood alone on a *koppie* overlooking the town. Peekay had sat in Doc's marvellous cactus garden and, speaking to the giant *Pachypodium namaquanum* which now stood almost eight feet high, had told it all that had transpired and that he was finally on his way to Oxford.

Peekay wrote home often and Mrs Boxall and Miss Bornstein replied regularly. His grandfather wrote only once, a letter which named twenty-nine varieties of roses in the garden and reported precisely on the condition of each, until Peekay could smell the soft dawn fragrance of roses in a tropical garden before the heat rises and burns away the perfumed air. The old man had ended the letter as he would a conversation. Peekay could almost see his pipe going, puff, puff and the blue cloud of smoke swirling about his head. 'There's a good lad,' the last words in his letter said.

His mother too had written once for his birthday, a letter which mostly consisted of an admonishment in the name of the Lord, chastising him for his stubborn refusal to be 'born again' and ending with the words: *I am not mocked, saith the Lord*.

Dee and Dum had also written once, in Shangaan, big, crude capitals with only three lines in pencil on the page, each of them doing a line, with the last line shared. Peekay had held the page to his lips and the tears had rolled down his cheeks.

Peekay had been so anxious and preoccupied with Hymie's unexpected departure, sharing in the acute disappointment of his friend at not spending Christmas at Cow Cottage, that he was halfway back to Oxford when it struck him that he'd be alone with Harriet for the next month.

His heart began to thump. 'Oh, God! What am I going to do?' he wailed aloud to himself. He immediately began to talk himself out of all the things which raced through his head. Peekay winced as he thought of the two large pillows propped against the headboard on the big Queen-Anne bed. 'She's not interested. If she was, I'd know. She thinks of me as a brother. That's it! We're like brother and sister. Bullshit! You don't feel that way about her. Yes, but that doesn't count. It's how she feels about me! I'm her brother. She feels safe with me. Don't change that. If Hymie comes back and I've split with Harriet because, well, something went wrong what's he going to think. It's like a trust, isn't it? I mean, if I tried something and was repulsed? What would he think? He'd have every right to think I'm a bastard!'

A lump had developed in his throat and he found it hard to swallow. He lifted his bum from the car seat and, with one hand, pulled at the crotch of his pants to make more room for the severe lump which had suddenly grown there. Oh, God! Stop it! Peekay begged himself.

Christmas Day wasn't quite perfect without Hymie, but it came damn close. It had started to snow early on Christmas Eve and had continued until mid morning on Christmas Day so that the Oxfordshire countryside was suddenly transformed. To Peekay it was like a miracle, a white Christmas spent in an English cottage in the English countryside. Hymie would have moaned and pointed to the wet, slushy roads, secretly sharing in his delight.

With snow covering the ground and the roof of Cow Cottage and clinging to the Francis Eileste, the white rose, now pruned neatly back to surround the doorway, the scene indeed resembled the cover on a chocolate box. It was a scene such as might quite easily have appeared on a four-pound box Hymie's father's salesmen presented as a free gift to a customer when they'd signed up for new Wilton in the lounge.

Mrs Clive, Harriet's mother, had arrived on Christmas Eve from Norfolk in a small green Austin estate wagon which boasted wood panels on the rear section to give it a country look. The small car was loaded with stuff for the cottage: towels and linen, pots and pans, even a hessian sack of yew logs for the hearth on Christmas Day and, of course, loads of good things to eat. Together with Hymie's hamper there was enough food to feed an army, and the Christmas table was positively groaning with food as Mrs Clive fussed around it, arranging crackers and nuts. At one end of the table was a space for the goose; its rich, delicious aroma now filled the cottage and kept the hearth fire spitting, splatting and hissing.

Eddy had arrived early to supervise the goose. It was about ten o'clock when Harriet heard his motorcycle negotiating the snow-covered farm road, the engine protesting as the wheels slid and slipped in the muddy ruts. He rode his Norton around the back to the stable and Harriet, in her wellingtons, went around to meet him. His face, as well as his thick navy woollen sweater and bulky plastic over-trousers, were covered with mud. When he removed his goggles and the beanie he was wearing, two white circles around his eyes and a strip of white skin across the top of his forehead were the only clean patches remaining on his face. Harriet opened the studio door and Eddy pushed his Norton inside. At the rear door of the cottage he stopped to remove his boots and moved into the kitchen in his wet socks just as Harriet lifted a large iron kettle from the hearth.

'Here, Eddy, come and stand by the fire; you must be frozen to the bone.' Harriet poured boiling water into a large basin she'd placed on the pine table, the kettle disappearing into the cloud of steam. Eddy stood facing the hearth, rubbing his hands together and shivering. Harriet refilled the kettle from a bucket and placed it back on the hook suspended above the fire. Then she reached out and touched his mud-splashed woollen sweater. 'You're soaked!' she exclaimed. 'Raise your arms, let me take this off and rub you down, I've got an old cardigan of daddy's you can wear.'

Eddy started to pull at the thick sweater and Harriet helped him off with it, pulling it over his head. He wore no shirt or singlet under the sweater and stood naked from the waist up. She pointed to his socks. 'Off with those, they're sopping,' she commanded.

Eddy grinned. 'Harriet, you're worse than me mum!' He held onto the edge of the table and, resting the side of his foot against his knee, removed a sock, doing the same with the other sock. Harriet placed a small towel on the slate floor below the basin where he could stand, then she lifted the bucket and splashed cold water into the still steaming basin, dipping her hand into it until it was cool enough. Eddy bent over the basin and Harriet took up a towel and began to wipe his wet bent back. Eddy splashed the warm water into his face. Harriet was not only drying his torso but rubbing it hard with the coarse towel to warm him as well. Eddy was a well-built young man with the broad, muscled shoulders and narrow tapering waist of an ideal middleweight. It was a body built naturally from hard work and Harriet thought how nice it would be to sculpt. Her hands moved the wet clay around the shoulders, moulding his abdominal muscles with the pads of her thumbs, building the beautiful young body bit by bit until it became a reality under her hands.

At last Eddy rinsed the soap from his face and, standing upright, he turned to face Harriet, his eyes closed. His dark curly hair, wet at the ends, fell across his brow, his skin shone with wetness and his thick, dark eyelashes and the blue shadow of his closely shaved chin emphasised his naturally smooth olive complexion. He held out his hand for the towel but Harriet pushed his arms aside and taking his head in the towel she drew him towards her. A moment before she'd been dispassionately admiring his hard young body. Now she was suddenly hungry for him. Her lips closed slowly over his as she moved her body to stand against him. Harriet dropped the towel and brought her arms around his shoulders and slowly began to stroke his back. The young boxer didn't respond or show surprise. Harriet had moved in on him so easily that the touch of her warm lips against his wet face seemed perfectly natural.

'Come, Eddy,' she said softly, leading him the few paces across the room to the chesterfield, 'don't open your eyes, not until it's over.'

The plump goose had already begun to brown on the outside by the time Harriet's mother returned from Oxford where she'd gone to matins and stayed to attend the Christmas service at Christ Church Cathedral. And by the time Peekay, Bobby and E.W. arrived in the Ford Prefect, Hymie's goose, under Eddy's expert attention, was positively Dickensian in its perfection. It was a goose Tiny Tim's father would have been proud to serve to the Queen.

Hymie's hamper included two bottles of Chateau Margaux and a Chateau Palmer, both excellent vintages. They'd begun Christmas lunch with a bottle of Moet et Chandon. By the time Harriet's mother served the Christmas pudding everyone was pleasantly sozzled. The exceptional wine might well have been wasted on the three young boxers but E.W., who was a bit of a wine buff, held his glass up to the lamplight. 'In a great year there is a delicacy about a good Margaux and a sweet haunting perfume, which makes it undoubtedly the most exquisite claret of all.'

'There's brown ale brewed in the village I come from that I feel the same about,' Bobby declared.

They all toasted Hymie's excellent taste, the speedy recovery of his grandmother and finally, full to bursting, the four younger people staggered from the table to the chesterfield and the two welcoming armchairs. Made of sterner stuff, E.W. and Mrs Clive remained at the table and shared a bottle of excellent port that E.W. had brought with him. Harriet and Peekay sat on either side of the chesterfield and Eddy, wearing Harriet's father's old cardigan, sank deeply into one of the armchairs, while Bobby occupied the other. Too satisfied and happy to talk, they dozed.

Peekay, unaccustomed to so much wine, rose to empty his bladder. It had started snowing again and the kitchen garden was blanketed in fresh snow; the world around him was white and clean. To his delight he saw a white owl sitting on a bare branch of one of the oak trees. It sat so still, it seemed a part of the mute, ordered winterness of tree and landscape. If only Hymie was with us it would be perfect, Peekay thought. He returned to the warmth of the cottage, going first to the studio to gather up an armload of yew logs. He placed several logs on the hearth which immediately began to crackle and spit and, smiling at E.W. and Mrs Clive, who seemed remarkably happy in each other's company, he trimmed a hurricane lamp which had begun to smoke, before returning to the chesterfield.

The sharpness of the cold outside had cleared his head and heightened his senses. Peekay felt himself examining Harriet closely at the other end of the old chesterfield. She lay curled up in one corner of the large couch, her head snuggled into a bright green cushion. The light from the lamps caught her beautiful hair and gave her skin a soft, warm glow. Her eyes, closed in sleep, revealed her thick eyelashes which lay like tiny crescent moons on the brow of her cheekbones. She was achingly lovely and he felt a sudden pain just below the heart, right on the spot where you hit another boxer when you want to soften him up, so that later you can bring him slowly to his knees. Peekay had a sudden vision of an unclothed Harriet on her knees in front of him. He almost winced in an effort to rid the image from his head. 'Stop it!' he screamed in silence. 'Stop it! She's Hymie's!'

Thinking about his friend calmed Peekay down somewhat. Hymie would have arrived back in Pretoria on the day prior to the Levy's Carpet Emporium Christmas party. Peekay wondered how it had all gone, chuckling inwardly at the thought of Hymie's grandma moaning and clutching at her failing heart as the great Christian party took place in the garden outside. No doubt he'd hear all the lurid detail when Hymie returned at the beginning of the new term.

Hymie's dad's Christmas party grew more spectacular each year. Every year the Pretoria police warned that it created traffic congestion and would probably not be allowed to take place the following year. What they were really saying was that the people in the rich and influential suburb in which Hymie's parents lived had complained again that Africans had been arriving by the truckload with their families since early morning and the area wasn't safe. The police referred to the event among themselves as 'the Jew's kaffir party', but they knew it had been sanctioned 'at the very top' and that they were powerless to do anything about it unless trouble started.

Anywhere else in the world the party would have seemed a curious affair, but in South Africa it was normal enough. A fence was constructed more or less down the centre of the garden with a huge marquee on one side and a smaller one on the other, the former to serve the four thousand blacks and coloureds and the latter to accommodate the ninety white families who worked for Hymie's father. Two complete fair grounds with ferris wheel, rides and sideshows were set up, one on each side of the fence.

The only exception to the black and white dichotomy strictly observed in the Levy garden was a miniature railway track which ran around the periphery of the entire garden. Here the station was set up to cross over onto either side of the fence so children of both colours were forced to board the train together, mixing freely in the open carriages. Hymie's dad called it, 'The Freedom Train'. Dressed in his Father Christmas outfit he would get into the quarter-sized replica steam engine and drive it around the ground himself, toot-tooting happily as he passed through the white side of the garden, hugely amused at the faces of parents as they saw their children holding hands with black kids and having a high old time.

The tables in the marquees on both sides positively groaned with good things to eat, the only difference being the drinks. Only soft drink was served on the African side, as black people were not allowed to drink hard liquor outside a township beer hall. Huge turkeys and hams and roast suckling pig with potatoes and corn and all manner of other delicacies were served. The dessert tables were piled with trifles, cakes, jellies, custards, confections and dried fruits. Chefs in aprons and tall white caps served food all day long. On the black side several oxen were roasted on an open-air spit over a pit of hot coals, while on the white there was a *braai* with *boere wors*, steak and chops in a never-ending barbecue.

Solomon Levy spared no expense on presents for the kids; there were tricycles for the tots and dolls for the smaller girls and bicycles for the older boys and girls. All the expensive makes, like Raleigh and Hercules and Philips. These were a precious possession a black child could never possibly hope to buy. At the age of fifteen, childhood ended with the last of Solomon Levy's Christmas bounty, when every boy received a size twenty-eight adult bicycle and every girl a Singer sewing machine. For the black and coloured kids and for many of the poorer white ones, when they finally climbed into the lorries to be taken back to their homes in the various townships or suburbs, it was the happiest day of the whole year. For Solomon Levy it was the day every year when he paid his respects and gave thanks to Jehovah for sending him to the promised land.

It was also a day the *Broederbond*, 'bond of brothers', noted. The white supremacist, Afrikaner secret society ruled by religious fanatics, whom some said were the true power within South Africa, resolved to do something about the Jew's kaffir party. A brilliant young police lieutenant, named Geldenhuis, a member of the Broederbond, who had made his reputation as head of SAT in Durban and who had recently been promoted and moved to Pretoria, had been given the task of compiling a dossier on the carpet king. The day would come when his Jew money would no longer protect him: *I am not mocked, saith the Lord*.

SIXTEEN

Peekay grew to enjoy his Oxford tutor's company enormously. The tall, shambling English scholar, a Darjeeling man forced out of good faith to drink Ceylon, had become for Peekay the quintessential Christian gentleman and scholar. They were often seen together, always deep in discussion. The serious aspects of university life seemed to suit Peekay best; he had divided his everyday life strictly between study and training.

On one occasion, in Peekay's second year at Oxford, they had been discussing the role of the institution in public life. The tutorial had finally centred around a specific example, that of Oxford itself. To Peekay's surprise, E.W. had been quick to point out the faults of the great university.

'You must immediately forget the lofty ideals talked about so often when people mistakenly eulogise this intellectual bone yard. The human values of honesty and decency belong equally to everyone and the rest is simply social layering.' E.W. paused to light his pipe before continuing. 'So, at best, there may be a scale of values which we at Oxford hold dear for our sons and daughters. These you will hopefully learn. Most importantly, you must learn the meaning of a bore.' An amused gleam showed in E.W.'s eyes. 'Regrettably this is often the most difficult lesson of all; being a bore is an affliction found commonly among undergraduates who take Oxford and themselves much too seriously.'

Peekay understood E.W.'s tactful warning at once and blushed violently. Though, typically his tutor went on to observe, 'Alas, too often, they are aided and abetted by a certain class of don who swaddles them with catch-phrases, dogma and ready-made opinions so they gain information rather than understanding.'

'Are you saying there are no Oxford ideals?' Peekay asked, trying to conceal his embarrassment.

E.W. chuckled. 'We should always be on guard against institutional truths. Laws chipped in stone tablets belong only to God. If Oxford has a single task, it is to teach you how to think, not what to think.'

It was a nicely turned phrase, but E.W. could feel the young scholar was disappointed. Peekay wanted to believe in an ethos. It was why he had gone to the mines. The Oxford myth was a part of his dream. 'Ah, I see, you want value for your money?' E.W. teased.

Peekay flushed; as usual his tutor was right on the knocker. He'd turned down the offer of three scholarships to South African universities in order to worship at his particular shrine and now he wasn't anxious to learn that his blood, sweat and tears had been wasted. Oxford was a symbol, a milestone. It was a distance travelled with himself, a measure of his self-esteem. He didn't want it cut down to size.

'I am saddened by your disappointment, Peekay. You desire to become a pugilist of world stature. Did you not descend into the belly of earth and fire in order to attend this university?' Peekay had on one occasion described his job as a grizzly man in the mines to his tutor. Without waiting for Peekay's reply E.W. continued, 'These actions initiated by yourself will add to your sum as a man. I rather think it is you who may teach this institution a little of the process of character.'

E.W. puffed at his pipe, silent for a while. 'If you must have your money's worth, may I offer you a creed? A creed is not an institutional truth and it should never be offered gratuitously or it is immediately in danger of becoming one. There are three things I will allow that Oxford may give you.' He hesitated. 'I hope you won't find them too old-fashioned or pompous; even good creeds have the ability to sound somewhat headmasterish.' He placed his pipe into the large brass ashtray at his feet. 'The three things are these. We will endeavour to teach you to be right but not righteous, to be accurate but not dull; truth-seeking without being a pedant, accepting always that some other truth may equally exist.'

But as the year progressed Peekay became concerned about his life at Oxford. Though the principles which the great institution of learning attempted to imbue in him were noble in themselves, he sensed they were not enough for what lay ahead of him. Oxford was largely about the *game* of life and he knew the life which lay ahead of him couldn't under any circumstances be thought of as a game. He felt almost guilty thinking this way, but his instincts told him that Africa was different, that he should not be too quick to discard the ways of his childhood and the instinctive caution which is part of the survival mechanism of the continent.

The physical side of Peekay's new life was less complicated. Holland decided to take Peekay into the professional ranks immediately, though Peekay had delayed this a couple of months to meet a university obligation. Holland was certain that no amateur welterweight in Britain could go two rounds with Peekay, and he wanted to iron out several of the fighting habits amateurs acquire which do not serve them well in the professional ranks.

Peekay's stance in the ring was rather too peek-a-boo, that is to say, he held his gloves too high in the amateur way, where scoring more points than your opponent is the sole objective. Dutch Holland wanted more power in both hands, which meant Peekay had to open up his gloves in order to punch with more authority. Holland liked his boxers to know that both their hands could be relied upon to put an opponent onto the deck. A sprained or broken hand is a common enough occurrence in the ring and, after a good defence, a 'sleep-maker' in either hand is the best insurance a boxer can have. Peekay also had to learn to pace himself over ten rounds of boxing, a far more arduous task than fighting a three-rounder.

There wasn't a lot Holland could teach Peekay about the art or the skill of boxing and so he concentrated on adding power to his punch as well as teaching him other techniques he would need if he was to survive in the professional ring. This included the basic psychology of fighting, such things as how to look at the referee if your opponent is using his head to rough you up in a clinch or even, if the referee seems blind or determined to ignore this basic form of fouling an opponent, how to return the compliment in a number of subtle ways.

A charming heavyweight named Podman, from Pembroke, the president of the university boxing club, had persuaded Hymie to let Peekay box against Cambridge and Peekay had delayed turning professional to do so. There seemed nothing against the idea and it gave him a chance to win his boxing blue. But as the match drew closer Peekay became anxious.

He'd trained with the university boxers and their standard, to say the least, wasn't high. Even though Oxford wasn't favoured to win, Peekay was doubtful that the light blues would be a lot better. Hymie spoke to Podman, but the big man practically begged him to allow Peekay to remain in the team. The university club included a Welsh bantamweight named Dai Rees from Oriel College, who he believed could win. This meant Peekay, as a welterweight, came soon afterwards on the card. Two wins early in the programme might just inspire the Oxford team sufficiently to pull off the match. To persist any further would have seemed churlish and Peekay agreed to fight for the dark blues.

The match was at Oxford and Harriet attended with E.W. Dressed in a simple black dress and black court high-heeled shoes she looked older and a lot more sophisticated. Her alabaster skin needed almost no make-up, but she'd added a little dark eyebrow pencil and eyeliner together with grey eyeshadow to accent her eyes and had heightened the result by wearing a bright red, rather risque lipstick.

The large hall was packed with sporting gentlemen from both universities, though most were from Oxford. The first fight, a lightweight bout, started soon after Hymie had seated Harriet at the ringside with E.W. Immediately afterwards, he had excused himself to follow Peekay to the changing rooms. By the time the two of them emerged again, Dai Rees, the bantamweight from Oriel, had narrowly beaten his opponent on points. The teams shared a win each, the lightweight decision having gone to Cambridge. It was up to Peekay to put the home side one ahead.

Peekay had gone to great pains not to talk about his boxing at Oxford, though, inevitably, the way these things happen, the knowledge of his boxing prowess and the fact that he was about to turn professional seemed to be known to most of the home crowd.

There was an excited murmur as Peekay climbed through the ropes into the ring, though only sporadic clapping. In fact, it was the Cambridge man who received rather more applause than might have seemed a sporting away-from-home welcome. The Cambridge boxer, surprised and delighted at his reception, turned and smiled at the crowd.

He wasn't dissimilar in type to Peekay, with light hair, hazel eyes and an engaging smile. In fact, Hymie – who'd done the usual research – had discovered he'd been to Harrow and was the opening bat for Cambridge. Boxing was his not-to-be-taken-too-seriously winter sport, more a chance to gain a double blue than anything else.

'Christ! He's the full amateur,' Hymie commented from Peekay's corner. They'd already laced up and he was rubbing a little vaseline around Peekay's eyes. 'He looks as though he should be sitting in the centre of a photograph with his arms folded wearing an embroidered cap with a gold tassel.'

Peekay tried to grin. Hymie's remark was wonderfully apt, but he felt nervous about the fight. 'We should have refused Podman; I can sense the crowd are not happy with me.'

'Forget it, Peekay, just think of it as your Oxford blue.'

The Cambridge man sat in his corner, thumping his gloves together and smiling. When the referee called the two boxers together he leapt from his stool and danced towards the centre of the ring, seeming anxious to get underway. He smiled at Peekay, pushing his arm out before remembering he was wearing gloves. 'Russell . . . Jonathan Russell, how do you do?'

Peekay returned his smile and touched the extended glove. He noted the complete lack of aggression in the other man's face. 'Peekay. Nice to know you, Jonathan.' He measured the outstretched arm with his eyes, precisely calculating the Cambridge boxer's reach.

The ref, a somewhat overweight Colonel Blimp type with a ginger moustache and a clipped military accent, went through the usual catechism and wished them luck. The two boxers touched gloves for a second time and the bell sounded for the first round.

The Cambridge boxer danced round Peekay for a few moments before predictably leading with his left and then followed with a right, both punches taken on the gloves. Peekay countered with a straight left and a right cross which brought a murmur from the crowd and knocked the other boxer back a couple of paces. Peekay slammed another left into his face so that he stepped backwards into a neutral corner. The other man was wide open and Peekay hit him hard under the heart with a left-right combination, then stepped back to let the Cambridge boxer get out of trouble. It would have been too easy to put a Geel Piet eight combination together and quite possibly end the fight.

Peekay threw a desperate glance at Hymie, who answered with a shrug. The Cambridge boxer lunged forward and Peekay almost absently avoided the blow, taking it on the gloves. It was a disastrous mis-match and Peekay tried to think of ways of making the Cambridge man look good so he wouldn't be humiliated. He kept him away by pushing his left hand into his face but restrained himself from hitting his wide-open opponent with a right, even though his right hand ached to be used. Once in a while he allowed himself to be backed into the ropes where he closed up his defence, allowing the other boxer to waste a flurry of punches to the back of his arms. At least it made the light-blue boxer look busy. Towards the end of the round he pulled the Cambridge man into a clinch and as the referee stepped forward to break them up Peekay said, 'For God's sake, sir, stop the fight before this man gets hurt!'

The referee parted the two boxers and turned to the Cambridge man. 'You all right, old chap?' he asked in his polo-club accent.

'Fine thank you, sir,' the Cambridge boxer panted, grinning at the referee.

'Good show!' the referee replied.

'Please, sir?' Peekay pleaded with the referee.

'Box on, Mr . . . er, Peekay,' the big man said firmly.

Peekay shrugged and moved quickly to the centre of the ring. The crowd were beginning to boo and a slow handclap had started in the back of the hall. The Cambridge man followed after Peekay, throwing out a left which tipped Peekay's chin, allowing him to measure the precise distance to the other man's jaw.

The right hook landed precisely where it was intended. Travelling hard and upwards, it landed an inch from the centre of the Cambridge man's chin. Then the light-blue boxer staggered momentarily before dropping like a stone to the canvas.

Peekay moved quickly to go to a neutral corner so the count could commence, but the bell for the end of the round sounded before he could reach it, and he turned and ran over to the Cambridge boxer, who hadn't moved. Kneeling down beside him, he could see the stunned look in the other man's eyes as he passed in and out of consciousness.

Peekay felt sure he hadn't hurt the Cambridge boxer. The punch which took him out had landed so precisely on the point of the jaw that it would hardly be felt by the other man. When a golfer or a cricket or tennis player hits the sweet spot on the club or the bat or racquet, the timing is perfect, the stroke effortless and the result amazing; Peekay's punch was similarly skilful. At the very worst, to remind him he'd been in the ring, the Cambridge boxer would have a slightly tender jaw in the morning. It had been the best way Peekay could possibly have ended the fight without hurting his opponent. But to the onlookers it had seemed as though the Oxford boxer with the big reputation had chopped the Cambridge man down without mercy.

Peekay was suddenly aware of the hissing and booing of the crowd and he was pushed roughly aside by one of the Cambridge man's seconds who had entered the ring. 'You're a cad, sir!' he shouted.

'Shit! I should have known better,' Peekay said to himself as he rose and walked over to his corner. Taking Hymie's extended hand, he climbed through the ropes and down from the ring without waiting for the decision.

'Tough,' Hymie said sympathetically, putting his arms around Peekay. 'There was nothing else you could do, old mate.'

Peekay sighed. 'Jesus! What a shit of a way to end an amateur career.'

Ten days later Peekay received a note from Podman, the Pembroke man and president of the Oxford Boxing Club. The letter said that the Blues Committee had met and that it had been decided 'under the circumstances' not to award Peekay his blue for boxing.

Hymie was furious. 'Bloody amateurs!' he screamed.

But Peekay restrained him from taking any action. 'Forget it, Hymie, it was my fault. I didn't listen to my instincts, I knew this was a bad idea.'

Hymie, still angry, turned to his friend in disgust. 'You know something, Peekay? Fuck your instincts! If you're not bloody careful, when we get back home the hairy backs are going to eat you alive, my son!'

Despite E.W.'s warning, as his second year at Oxford went by, Peekay might well have taken Oxford too seriously. He loved the long periods of study, the lively debate and intense argument. Given half a chance he could happily have settled into a dogged routine of study and training, the business of getting his money's worth. But Hymie saw things differently.

One summer evening, after returning from a training session in London, they decided to cut through St Hilda's College so Peekay could see the Chinoiserie bridge over the Cherwell. Standing on the beautiful oriental bridge watching the slow, dreamlike flow of the river in the late twilight, Hymie remarked casually to Peekay, 'You know, this place is an investment opportunity we'll never again come across.'

Peekay laughed, taking in the tranquil river scene. 'You're a true romantic, Hymie. Do you realise, Percy Shelley may well have stood with Byron on this bridge?'

'Sure. Did you know Shelley was expelled from Oxford for lying?' Hymie replied. He turned, so that he was leaning with his back pushed against the rail of the bridge, squinting into the distance, looking downriver in the opposite direction to Peekay. 'No, man, I mean it. If we use this place properly it's money in the bank.'

'You mean the Oxford myth, exploiting the cultural cringe when we get back home?'

'That too, but that's only worth a passing lick at the icing on the cake. If anything, the bloody Boers will try to cut us down to size once we get home. Make no mistake, the Nats are in power for a long time. The brilliant hairy-back bigots from Stellenbosch University will be running the show from now on. A couple of smart-arse Anglophile Oxford graduates conducting a law practice that helps kaffirs get off won't impress them one little bit.' As usual Hymie was thinking ahead.

'The way you talk, Oxford doesn't sound like much of an investment. In what way, an opportunity?'

'Our friends. We must choose them for the future.'

Peekay turned to look at Hymie in surprise. 'You're not serious? Shit, Hymie, isn't that just a tad dry-eyed?'

Hymie laughed. 'My mom has a saying: "If a nice Jewish girl is sitting at the bus stop waiting and a Rolls Royce should happen to pass and also to stop and the back door should open, where does it say in the good book it is a sin to save a little time and take a little ride?" '

'You don't mean friends, do you? That's simply a euphemism for contacts, isn't it? We might as well have business cards printed!'

'Jesus, Peekay! You can be a bloody boring Protestant prick sometimes! You can pick up a law degree anywhere.' Hymie slapped Peekay on the arm with the back of his hand. 'Look at us! I mean, we're a couple of cultural country bumpkins who have learned enough to scale the school wall into the orchard on the other side. Only it so happens it's the Garden of fucking Eden! What are we going to do, sit cross-legged under the tree of fucking knowledge in the hope that an apple will fall into our lap?'

'As usual my learned friend makes his point forcibly, but do we have to shake every bloody apple off the tree?' Peekay replied.

Hymie was getting excited, the way he sometimes would when he wasn't getting through to Peekay. 'Let me tell you about Cecil bloody Rhodes! Okay, he's a big name around here, right? You even sat and, in my opinion, got rooked out of his scholarship. Remember?'

Peekay grinned. 'I was too young.'

Hymie ignored him. 'Cecil bloody Rhodes was a dumb-dumb! The full mahogany sideboard. When he applied for entry to Oriel the Provost lamented, "All the colleges send me their failures!" Believe me, Peekay, Cecil Rhodes didn't come here for the education. He came for the introductions, and look where they got him!'

Peekay turned back to lean against the beautiful wooden rail of the Chinese bridge. 'Just for once, Hymie, do me a favour and leave out the historical precedent. How do you propose to suck up to every half-decent brain in Oxford so they'll be beholden to us for the rest of their lives?'

'Easy, man!' Hymie said, grinning. 'Start a society!'

'Oh, great!' Peekay imitated Togger Brown, 'that's a smashin' idea, that is!' He turned to face Hymie, his expression serious. 'Do you know how many societies there are already at Oxford? If you can fart in tune you'll find a choral society celebrating its bicentennial who are prepared to cherish your skill!'

'Peekay, don't you see? This university is filled with people who don't fit in. The odd bods. Guys who've always been a pain in the arse because they're very bright in one thing and a walking disaster in everything else. They can't catch a ball, count change, kiss a girl without losing their spectacles. They disagree with everyone about everything and the idea of joining anything whatsoever is utterly repugnant to them. But, and this is my point, if you follow their later careers you discover some emerge as powerful people, while others retire into back rooms and split the fucking atom! Either way, most of them rise to the top of the milk.'

'A society for those people who positively, under no circumstances, join societies? The theory's okay, but how do you get them to join?'

'Well, they need a cause they can believe in.'

'A cause? But those guys are the original cynics.'

'Or the true believers . . . that is, if you can get through to them.'

'And just how do you propose to do that?'

'I'm working on it. Something ridiculously simple. Something they wouldn't dream of supporting in a million years!'

'You mean, something so alien to their personalities that they'd have this one thing in common with each other?'

'Yes, that's it! That's it precisely. We have to find that something! It doesn't have to be a universal truth, or last forever . . .'

Peekay turned suddenly and grabbed Hymie by the shirt front. 'No you fucking don't, Hymie! I won't do it. No bugger you, that's not fair! Piss off, you machiavellian little Hebrew.'

'Leggo my shirt!' Hymie yowled. 'You know I abhor physical violence!'

Peekay released him. 'It's not on, Hymie! You can go to hell!'

'Why not? It fits. It's no skin off your nose. And it's not as if I'm asking you to do anything you're not already doing.'

A slightly hurt expression crossed Hymie's face. 'Why are you being so unreasonable, Peekay?'

'Because it's too hard-arsed. Too bloody deliberate. It's a set-up. It's using people!'

'So? That's a sin all of a sudden?'

'Morally, yes! It's . . . it's manipulative. It's essentially vainglorious and conniving!'

'Bullshit, Peekay, it's simply filling a need. A need exists, we fill it, we benefit. There's no morality involved.'

'It's just another way of picking up the tab, Hymie.'

'Sure, I don't deny that. Give a little, take a little. But, as my dad says: "Always leave a little salt on the bread!" '

'Christ, Hymie, no more folksy aphorisms. This isn't just another scam, like at school.'

Hymie grabbed Peekay's arm and continued in an urgent voice. 'Look, I've thought it all out and honestly it's kosher. Just hear me out, will you? Your boxing supplies a much needed outlet for the aggression of these odd bods.' Hymie held his hand up. 'Okay! Don't tell me they don't need an outlet, because they do. Did you know that of the fifty or so nervous breakdowns in this place every year, most occur among the so-called brilliant loners. Those guys who get their jollies spending all day Saturday in the Bodleian pouring over old vellum!'

'I've been known to do that! And these Odd Bodleians? I'm supposed to be the saviour of these intellectual rag-bags?'

'Christ, Peekay, that's fucking brilliant! "The Odd Bodleian Society!" '

Peekay ignored Hymie's compliment, though if there was to be such a society formed, the name wasn't half bad. 'You haven't answered my question. I'm the guru?'

'No, you're the cause, I'm the guru. You give them a reason, the welterweight championship of the world. I'll give them the philosophical crap and they'll give us the smartest fan club in the history of professional boxing.' Hymie shrugged and smiled. 'See! Simple! Now everyone's rewarded!'

'And that's where the problem exists,' Peekay interrupted. 'This place is the citadel of amateurism. You know as well as I do, my being a professional boxer is the standing joke around here. The colonial oaf who brought his street-fighting past with him to Oxford. Remember, when I knocked out the guy from Cambridge they all booed!'

'Precisely, man! It's perfect! Don't you see? This is the very thing to attract the odd bods. It's in contradiction of everything their snotty-nosed cricket and rugger contemporaries stand for. Believe me, Peekay, they'll lap it up!'

'Says who?'

'You just leave it to me, my son.'

Hymie was a master in the use of haphazard time, that is: time spent apparently relaxing. He saw people in an abstract sense as time savers. To him a person was a repository of knowledge who, unlike a library, had the virtue of being available at the end of a telephone or could drop in on one. Cross-examination came naturally to him and even before he'd instituted the Odd Bodleian Society he had gathered an extraordinary collection of people around him, all of whom regarded him as a friend.

Hymie used people in an unabashed way, but never shamefully. And he was generous with his gifts, thoughtful of their needs; he never used people. To Hymie, who wouldn't accept Peekay's explanation that basically, down deep in the forgotten corner of the garden where the tall weeds grow, he was a rather nice chap, this would have been a clear indication of poor judgement and wasted human resources.

Within a month, Hymie had recruited fifty-seven members to the Odd Bodleian Society. Its first meeting took place at the Marlborough Arms in St Thomas Street just across the Isis.

The venue had been selected by Hymie for three reasons. Pubs were out of bounds to students, so the idea of a pub was immediately attractive to his members. The Marlborough Arms contained a back room large enough to accommodate the society, with a small door leading from it into a back lane should a don come snooping. Finally, Morrell's brewery was just two doors down, so the pints were guaranteed to be good.

At this first meeting Hymie had himself appointed president for life. This was less a matter of ego than of necessity, as he was the only person in the room with whom each member of the new society believed he had something in common.

The rules were simple. The cause they all stood for was the world welterweight title to an Oxford man by 1955. Attendance at Peekay's fights was the honourable intention of every member, and black tie and starched bib was mandatory on these occasions.

Peekay had pointed out to Hymie that, despite Hymie's personal charisma and the controversial nature of the society, these were probably insufficient to hold their common interest, given that they shared very few others. What was needed was some sort of mystique. In fact, a creed. It was Peekay who, searching through his own conscience for a good reason to become involved in Hymie's permanent and useful friend programme, had come up with the solution. This was to be the cornerstone of President Hymie's inaugural address.

'It gives me great pleasure to address this first gathering of the Odd Bodleian Society for the very first time,' Hymie began. He seemed unusually nervous. Hands immediately thumped on tables and someone shouted, 'Tautology!' The room immediately filled with laughter.

'Just checking to see who's not drunk,' Hymie quipped to loud boos from the audience. 'I don't need to explain why we're here. You're all here because you are about to become the brains trust of the loathsome and repugnant sport of professional boxing.' More thumping and cheering followed and Hymie waited for it to die down. 'Or so you thought!' He enunciated each word as the room became silent.

Hymie started to pace across the small space at the front of the room. He was in full control and knew he had the interest of his audience. 'The people in this room are the most brilliant at Oxford.' (More thumping.) 'The crème de la crème! Whichever country we come from, it is we who will blossom into the future.' He stopped pacing and leaned over slightly, lowering his voice. 'But! Our ultimate success will not come from our brains or our gifts.' Hymie paused, appearing to look at each of them. 'It will come from our belief in ourselves. It will come from what Peekay here calls "The Power of One!" '

'The Power of One,' Hymie repeated. He had his audience eating out of his hand. Peekay was witnessing the style which was to make Hymie famous in the courtroom, the ability to lift a jury, even one composed essentially of white bigots.

'The power of one determination! The power never to compromise your beliefs or your art or your science, to believe that you are capable of anything if you listen to the small voice, to the single truth. If you have the fortitude . . . the guts! If you have the stamina for the long haul. The power to triumph over the odds you will have to face!'

Hymie's rhetoric was effortless. 'And there will be odds!' he continued. 'Politicians and powermongers will want to buy you and direct you. They will bend and twist the universal truths and they will try to swaddle your conscience with hyperbole and rationalisation!'

As Peekay looked about the room he could see that the members' eyes were almost glazed. Talk about politicians and powermongers! Hymie was going a bit far, manipulating them, doing to them precisely what he was warning them against. What a rotten, conniving shit! But it was going down a treat.

'. . . Only a sustained and invincible belief in yourself will allow you to maintain your integrity and achieve the goals you have set for yourself.

You must be utterly determined to believe in your ability to prevail no matter what!' Hymie paused to catch his breath and the room suddenly erupted. It was powerful stuff all right. It was Hymie focussing precisely, getting to the parts of them which lauded the reason why they were different.

Christ, he's getting a bit didactic, Peekay thought. He's said enough, perhaps too much . . . the last bit, the sustained and invincible belief in yourself and the importance of your own integrity, were the things in which Peekay believed implicitly but he'd always seen them as beliefs which owned a private voice. These were quiet, determined, essential things a man might confide to a friend, a philosophical direction you have to find for yourself; they were not cheap tricks performed in public so that they might achieve gratuitous emotional rewards from an audience. Please, Hymie, stop! You've said enough! Peekay begged silently.

'You may well ask what the hell the world welterweight championship for an Oxford man has to do with all of this?' Hymie asked, dropping his voice. 'At the age of five Peekay was sent to a boarding school. He was the youngest child and the only English speaking boy in this small, viciously racist backwoods Afrikaans school. The Boer children beat him every day and bullied him mercilessly.'

Peekay closed his eyes and winced. None of this had been a part of what they'd discussed. He had never expected to witness his beloved friend being so blatantly opportunist.

'Peekay was befriended by a train conductor, who convinced the little boy that if he could learn to box, that big could beat small, that he would never again be beaten up, that he could even become the welterweight champion of the world if he believed hard enough, if he never gave up!'

Peekay had had enough.

'I say, Hymie, that's not quite fair!' He was pale with anger and his voice, though low, carried around the room.

Hymie looked at Peekay surprised. The power of his anger was palpable. His voice had been a growl, the sound of a wounded animal. Hymie's heart missed a beat. Jesus! He'd gone too far! Peekay was the most fiercely proud person he'd ever known and he'd used him. He'd done this to the person he loved the most in the world.

The room grew strangely quiet. They too had been brought up with a jolt, the spell of Hymie's rhetoric broken. Some of them looked at Peekay, their eyes showing sympathy, whether for the story they'd just heard or for the invasion of his privacy was impossible to say. These were mostly young men who knew what it was like to be a loner, to be the odd man out at school, to be the swot, the sap, the drip and the school misfit. Either way they could identify. They knew what it was like to dream privately, never daring to reveal your dream lest you be ridiculed by your peers.

The first to stand up was a smallish man with big horn-rimmed glasses named Elmer Milstein, an American from New York. He was simply known as Milstein; at Oxford, people even refused to use a name as silly as Elmer.

Milstein spoke directly to Peekay. 'Say! This thing is . . . well, it's between the two of you.' He looked around the room. 'Whaddaya say, you guys? We retire to the saloon bar until they've sorted it out?'

There was a scraping of chairs as the members of the newly formed Odd Bodleian Society rose and silently left the room, taking their half-downed pints with them.

Hymie looked up at his friend. There was nothing he could say. He had seated himself on the edge of a table and now he shrugged his shoulders. The look in Peekay's eyes was unbearable. 'Jesus! What a fuck-up,' he said helplessly.

'Why? Why, Hymie?' Peekay asked.

'Peekay, I swear to God, I'm sorry. You're right, it was vainglorious and contemptible.' Tears welled in Hymie's eyes.

'It's not that easy, Hymie. Your apology, even your tears are not enough. You were contemptuous of the people in this room. You betrayed the trust between us!' Peekay was still angry but his voice had become very calm.

Hymie looked slowly up at Peekay. His friend's eyes were cold. He could think of nothing to do but to attack. When he spoke his voice was bitter. 'It's because I'm a Jew, isn't it? Secretly you despise me. A fucking Judas! That's it, isn't it, Peekay?' The tears in Hymie's eyes brimmed, but he held his gaze steady. 'You're the only one who's allowed to lead. You with your blue eyes and the glorious two-fisted attack of the master fucking race!'

Peekay remained silent. He loved Hymie more than anyone in the world. He loved his quick mind, his generosity and even his cynicism. He knew Hymie loved him and he hated the thing he now saw in him, the fear, insecurity and guilt which made him say what he'd just said. Peekay could identify with it all and he knew how it could corrupt the soul.

They were both refugees but he was the stronger of the two. He had already been corrupted. He knew how the war had turned out. At the age of five he'd been beaten and tortured, even made to eat shit.

Hymie had never stood to fight, stood with his back to the wall. He'd always run. His fear was for the unknown and his guilt was for all the Jews who'd stayed behind to be rounded up and forced into the cattle trucks. It was time Hymie stopped running.

'Listen to me, you contemptible little bastard!' said Peekay. 'I'm going to go into that saloon bar and I'm going to call all those guys back in. Then you're going to tell them how we designed this scam. How we intended to ingratiate ourselves with the long-term plan to exploit their friendship. To use them!'

Hymie looked up alarmed. 'I couldn't do that. You can't make me do that!'

'No, that's true, I can't. You're going to have to do it for yourself!'

Hymie sniffed then reached for his handkerchief and wiped his eyes, then blew his nose. 'That's easy then, I *can't* do it.' He looked up at Peekay. 'Okay, I admit it, I'm a moral coward.' He looked down again, between his legs at the floor. 'It's all right for you, all I am is smart. I can't settle things with a pair of boxing gloves. I can't even remain silent the way you can. My silence means nothing. A silent Jew? What's that? That's an anachronism. It doesn't make me smart. It doesn't make me wise.' He looked up again, the pain showing in his eyes. 'It makes me nothing! I exist because of my fucking mouth and my head and my wit. Now you want to take the only defence I've got away from me. I'm sorry, you're asking too much, Peekay, I can't, I simply can't do it!'

Peekay shook his head. 'Hymie, none of the things you've just said about yourself are true. I wish to Christ you didn't have to carry around all this fucking emotional baggage. But if you can't face the mob, you'd better leave.'

Hymie rose. 'What are you going to do?'

'Apologise.'

Hymie grinned weakly. 'Well that's different! I can do that with you.'

Peekay sighed. 'No way, Hymie, it's on your own or not at all.'

'Fuck you, Peekay!' Hymie grabbed up his duffel coat and student's gown which lay on a chair. Crossing the room, he unlatched the doorway leading to the lane and stormed out.

Peekay sat very quietly, not even noticing the tears which ran down his cheeks. Christ, it wasn't such a bad thing. No worse than many of their scams at school. Hymie probably didn't even mean it. It had simply seemed like a good idea at the time!

But Peekay knew that somehow they'd come to a crossroads. They'd soon be returning to a country where the blacks were beginning to despair, one in which the dung beetle was demanding too much and returning too little to the worker ants. They were going to be severely tested, their integrity constantly challenged by both sides. Moral cowardice was the easiest way there was to destroy themselves.

Peekay was even beginning to have second thoughts about Oxford. He wasn't at all sure that the law he was being taught, the neat, concise rules laid out for the behaviour of a society was the intellectual ammunition he was going to need when he returned home. He sensed that to win in South Africa, even if it meant alienating both sides, the truth could not be compromised. It was going to require a strength and wisdom well beyond the careful intellectual paths of law taught at this venerable institution.

Oxford was giving him, and he felt sure would continue to give him, a great deal. But what it couldn't give him was what he'd come for. It couldn't teach him a set of rules which he could impose on his alienated society in the hope that it would make things better, like a suddenly discovered cure for a hitherto incurable disease. But he did know that the sort of compromise represented by the Odd-Bodleian fiasco, their scam, was just the way their ideals could be undermined and the aggression it would take to be a spiritual terrorist sapped and eventually dissipated.

The news from South Africa was bad. He'd already heard recently that Sophiatown, together with Cape Town's District Six, the two best-known examples of South Africa's many racially integrated communities, was going to be pulled down in the guise of slum clearance. District Six, which boasted more than a hundred years of mixed-race living, was to be converted into a whites-only community.

The words 'terrorist' and 'treason' were increasingly being used by government spokesmen to prepare the whites for the police brutality and white supremacist legislation to come. Government propaganda, carried mainly through the Afrikaner press, was growing increasingly hysterical. The second dance had begun.

They were returning to this. The law he was learning, the sweetly practised ways of civilised men, were going to be useless. Here at Oxford he was learning to play a game, and what he needed to learn was how to wage a war. It was strawberry mousse, not the diamond-hard intellectual and spiritual training they were going to need to stay alive and help to bring about change in South Africa.

It was this last point which caused Peekay to question his motives in helping to form the Odd Bodleian Society. If Hymie and he were to establish a law practice in which they hoped to win the trust of black people, they would need absolute integrity. The way in which they had gone about planning the Odd Bodleian Society demonstrated clearly that they were not yet to be trusted; it showed that they too had been infected by the virus of contempt, the white disease which was endemic in their homeland.

Peekay wiped his eyes with the back of his hand and walked towards the saloon bar. Pausing at the door he looked for Milstein. Finally he caught the American's eye. He indicated with a jerk of his head that they should all return and then went down the passage way back to the room to await their arrival.

Peekay entered the back room to find Hymie waiting. He was wearing his duffel coat and over it, his gown. He stood slightly hunched up, small and vulnerable. His unmistakably Hebraic nose, strong features and dark, swept-back hair made him look like the Rabbi in Marc Chagall's painting. Peekay's heart went out to his friend. Hymie hadn't looked up as he entered. Peekay remained silent, walking over and standing beside his friend. He nudged Hymie in the ribs. 'Welcome back, shithead!' he said, out of the corner of his mouth.

Hymie waited until they were all seated and then indicated to Peekay that he too should sit. Peekay seated himself at a table in the front of the room opposite him. The room fell silent and Hymie, clearing this throat, began.

'I owe you an apology. I have deceived you and, I believe, used you ungraciously.' Several of the students looked at each other and shrugged, their lips pursed, faces questioning. 'Ja, I can see you don't believe me,' Hymie said quickly. 'But it's true. I haven't harmed you or your reputations. Not yet anyway. But nevertheless you were being set up.' Hymie ventured a look at Peekay, but his friend had his eyes fixed on the table in front of him and was unaware of his glance.

For once in his life Hymie didn't quite know how to continue. If he told them about their intention to open a law practice designed to fight apartheid and explained how he'd hoped to manipulate them through the Odd Bodleian Society to establish a basis whereby they could be called upon in the name of friendship to help in the years to come it would make him look honourable. They might even conclude that the end justified the means.

If he revealed the second reason, the marvellous 'brains trust' publicity campaign he'd devised for Peekay's world-title bid, they might equally conclude that it sounded like fun and once again he'd be off the hook. Hymie knew that he could probably talk his way out of the predicament he found himself in. But that would be running. He was tired of running. He'd been halfway down the lane when the utter weariness of running from himself had overtaken him. Peekay was right. He had to come clean. He had to stop being scared of the grey shadows which haunted his life.

'The point is, I couldn't give a fuck about any of you! I simply wanted to bind you all into a fraternity so in the years to come I could lean on you in the name of Oxford, the Odd Bodleian Society and the successful outcome of Peekay's world-title fight. What you see in me is a supreme opportunist, a user!'

It was almost as though an electric shock had passed through the room. Suddenly they all understood. A chap named Jamie Jardine whose great grandfather had helped pioneer the China opium trade, stood up, holding his pint high, almost under his chin, his stomach pushed out. He was a fat, ginger sort of chap practically custom designed to be persecuted at any boarding school he might have attended. He was reputed to be a brilliant mathematician and a superb violinist but looked as thick as an ox and at the moment appeared somewhat inebriated.

'I say, that's a bit sniffy, old chap! A bit on the nose!' He possessed a slight lisp and his remark was delivered in a plummy public-school accent which would have been comic anywhere else.

'You're quite right, Jardine. It was contemptible,' Hymie said softly.

Jardine, who had probably never in his life been allowed to be right, stuck his premature paunch out even further at the same time lifting his chin. 'You ought to be ffrashed!' he said pompously.

There was a murmur around the room, even some laughter. 'I say, steady on, Jam Jar!' somebody called. 'You're pissed again. Sit down old chap!'

Peekay rose and turned to face the others in the room. 'We apologise to all of you. I am as much to blame as Hymie.' Peekay lowered his head. 'It was a cynical thing to do. I am deeply ashamed.'

There was the scrape of a chair as Jardine sat heavily. The room became totally, embarrassingly still. Peekay looked up again. 'May I make a suggestion?' Several heads nodded, grateful that he had broken the silence. 'That you carry on with the idea of the Odd Bodleian Society?' He paused and grinned wryly. 'I guess we're all misfits. I want to become a barrister and the world welterweight boxing champion. Frankly, I don't blame people for thinking I'm a bit strange, a bit potty.' Peekay moved over and stood beside Hymie. 'Hymie and I will, of course, resign immediately and you will naturally choose some other cause.'

Milstein jumped up and walked over to where Hymie and Peekay were standing. He turned to address the room. 'Listen you guys, I don't know how you feel, but what I've been listening to is a crock of shit!' Several of the chaps in the room grinned, relieved that the tension had been eased.

'Peekay's right, it's a damn good idea and I, for one, don't want it modified. Friendship isn't something you buy! It's not an obligation obtained through a fraternal past. It's something you feel, something you give willingly, or not at all. I've known Hymie more than a year. If he doesn't give a shit about me then he's made a damn good job of hiding this fact. He's been kind, considerate and generous to me on a number of occasions.' He turned to Peekay. 'With the greatest respect, Peekay, I joined the Odd Bodleians because of him. Personally I find boxing repugnant. On the other hand, I find your determination to prevail an inspiration. I'm sure there are others here who feel the same way.' He paused to take a breath. 'I even think I understand why Hymie acted the way he did.'

He looked about the room. 'I don't suppose I'm the only other Jew here, but I do know what it's like. You can never quite believe a Gentile can possibly like and respect you for who you are. You spend your whole goddamn life compensating. What others seem to be given willingly in comradeship and trust you have to earn, sometimes even by scheming.'

Milstein turned to Peekay. 'You're absolutely right. I've been a misfit all my life, the clever kid nobody liked. A smart-ass with all the answers. In my high-school class book, under my name it said cryptically: "Will go far!" Somebody wrote on my personal copy: "Yes please!" '

The room broke into sudden laughter and Milstein grinned. 'Anyways, I reckon we change nothing. This is the best chance I've had in my whole life to make a few good friends.' Grinning suddenly, he added, 'Whom, by the way, I intend to exploit shamelessly in years to come!' He turned back to Hymie and Peekay, 'And included among my friends is the dynamic duo, The Tadpole Angel and Attila the Rabbi!'

The room erupted into laughter and applause, with a dozen or so enthusiastic 'Hear, hears!' added. Milstein waited until the applause had died before turning to Hymie. 'Well, Mr President, aren't you going to buy your fellow Odd Bodleians an inaugural pint?'

Jam Jar rose unsteadily to his feet. 'Bloody poor show! Ought to be flogged! I'll have a pint of Morrell's special please, Mr President.'

SEVENTEEN

Harriet seldom talked to others about her work although Hymie assured Peekay that it was considered very good. She'd had an exhibition of her drawings at a small contemporary art gallery in Cambridge, and a critic from the *Manchester Guardian* had declared 'Miss Clive's charcoal sketches are both impressive and heroic with a surprising strength, which gives promise of good work to come.'

Extrovert in so many things, Harriet considered it slightly vulgar to discuss her work. But on one occasion, late in the spring term, when Peekay had agreed to model for her as the rider of the larger of the two horses, she'd talked freely about sculpture and what it meant to her. It was almost as though she was prepared to state her philosophy once only, after which the evidence would either speak for itself or remain mute.

'My father builds bridges,' she explained. 'Bridges have to be structurally sound but they can also be beautiful. People don't need to be told when a bridge is beautiful. They don't gradually acquire a taste for the way a bridge looks. They simply know it's beautiful by the way it's a part of the river or ocean landscape, a part of the early morning light and the sunset, the mist and the rain and the water which flows beneath it. Bridges are pieces of sculpture with a purpose, but nonetheless sculpture – and, like bridges, all sculpture should have a purpose.'

Peekay was sitting astride a carpenter's horse over which Harriet had folded the patchwork quilt from her bed to simulate the rounded back of a horse. She'd worked from first light until it grew too dark to see for three weeks in her stable studio and she'd almost completed the shaping of the first horse in the setting of her two horses and a rider. Now she was working on the armature of the rider, bending and shaping the thin steel rods and threading them together with wire to make the beginnings of the torso. She worked with a small pair of bolt cutters and a pair of pliers and her movements were confident and skilful.

'What do you mean by a sculpture having a purpose? Do you mean to celebrate an event, such as a great battle or a general on his horse in the park, or Lord Nelson standing on that dirty great big doric column in Trafalgar Square, that sort of thing?' Peekay asked.

'Heavens no! That's almost exactly what sculpture shouldn't be made to do. Good sculpture should please the eye because it is a part of the landscape, whether it happens to be the urban landscape or park land.' Harriet pointed to the near completed shape of the horse she'd been working on. 'See how it's standing?'

Peekay looked at the plaster-of-Paris shape of the horse standing in the centre of a tarpaulin in the middle of the studio. To the side of it was the beginning of the second slightly smaller horse. Its shape was roughly formed by an armature of steel rods covered with chicken wire; this was how the nearly completed horse beside it had started its life. Harriet had bandaged the chicken wire with strips of coarse hessian dipped in plaster-of-Paris, building up layer after layer and allowing it to dry. When it was completely built up she'd commenced to shape the plaster-of-Paris as though it was a solid medium. The effect gave the horse's appearance a solidarity and astonishing strength. It stood with its neck craned and ears swept back, its forelegs wide and firmly positioned on the ground, its rump pushed slightly backwards as though it was baulking at someone or something unseen.

'See the way it's so animated? It isn't a heroic horse on a plinth, it's a horse suddenly anxious about its forward progress. Something has arrested its attention and made it tentative. The rider will try to exert his will on the horse, make it move forward and overcome its anxiety. The drama is between the rider and the horse. It's an intensely private thing.'

'I can see that!' Peekay said, excited by the explanation. 'You're right, your horse isn't an exact down-to-the-last-tiny-detail replica of how a horse looks; it's simply a wonderful expression of how a horse feels.'

Harriet seemed pleased. 'It's the sort of horse which should be naturally set into a park among the trees with its hooves on the grass, where to the eye, it seems to belong; and where, at any distance at all, it seems to be quite real.'

'That's what you mean about a piece of sculpture having a purpose?'

Harriet nodded, her expression serious. 'The second horse, following slightly behind, will enhance the feeling, as though the bareback rider has taken the horses down to a stream to drink and they've all had a swim and now they're going home. If someone were suddenly to look up, say a little girl playing on a swing in a housing estate, and she saw my horses and rider through the trees, she'd know exactly what it would feel like if they were real, because, you see, in a sense they are real. Horses and people riding have always been a natural part of the dreaming landscape. Do you know when I first knew I wanted to become a sculptor?' Harriet asked suddenly. She stopped working on the torso and sat on an upturned tea chest. 'I was twelve and on holiday with my parents in Italy a year after the war. We'd driven into a small village in Tuscany which was reputed to have a beautiful church. My father's potty about churches. As usual the church was the main building in the piazza but this one was surrounded by huge trees, wonderful big old fig trees. It was the local saint's day, I forget which saint, and the village people were all out, playing bola, gossiping in small groups, mothers wet-nursing their babies, people seated at tables under the trees drinking wine, the men smoking. Under several of the trees stood a man playing a piano accordion, each musician taking turns to play a few chords before the others joined in so they all played the same melody.

'I can remember how hot it was, how the women sat on chairs with their skirts hauled up to their knees, fanning themselves with small paddle fans dyed pink and green, which seemed to be made of plaited bamboo and carried the name of a brand of tinned tomatoes.' Harriet laughed. 'I know I'm telling it in detail, but that's how I remember it. The people seemed so natural, so easy with themselves and, although I was only twelve, I sensed, despite the war, I mean them losing it, that nothing much had changed in their lives. There was a sort of internal combustion that worked for them collectively as though the mass was greater than the individual and time had been previously arranged and there seemed no good reason to tamper with it.

'We hadn't been long in the piazza when the bells sounded and the people started to flock towards the church. To my astonishment I realised that many of the people were pushing wheelchairs, while others hobbled towards the church on crutches. A boy of about my own age passed me pushing a man who had no legs in a wheelbarrow. They gathered around a huge stone statue of the virgin mounted on a plinth which stood outside the church. The plinth was stepped to hold hundreds of lighted candles. The enormous statue showed the virgin aloof, towering above the women, many of whom were ululating while others had thrown themselves at the base of the stepped plinth and seemed to be imploring the mother of Christ to heal their sick and cause their lame to walk again. In a few moments the piazza had changed from a natural and eternal village scene to one of frantic and frenetic people playing out an arcane ritual to the rigid, cold and unforgiving mother of God.

'It wasn't love I felt emanating from the blessed virgin. It was fear, deeply atavistic pagan fear. The church which taught love had mastered only fear. The Mother of God, who represented the warmth and continuity of motherhood, had become a monstrous apparition of power. In the piazza, with the washed-blue Italian sky above the warm cobblestones and dark shade under the giant fig trees, where moments before there had been music and laughter and soft afternoon drowsiness, now there was hysteria and madness. The hands and minds which had fashioned this virgin mother of God had been corrupted. New hands were needed, hands which would fashion a virgin to walk amongst the village people, one who nodded and smiled and stopped to listen to a bit of gossip, exchange a recipe, run her hand through a small boy's hair or comfort a mother whose child had been stillborn. A virgin mother of God with her feet on the ground.' Harriet bent down and picked up the maquette of two horses and a rider. She placed it on her lap, absently running her hands across the back of the smaller, riderless horse. 'It was at that moment, I think, that in my mind anyway, I became a sculptor.'

Peekay was silent for some time, obviously thinking about what she'd said. 'Harriet, in Africa we would call you a visionary and the people would make songs up about you and as the women shucked corn or stamped meal or fed their infants they would sing them, sing about the woman who took the feet of the mother of God and placed them on the ground.'

Harriet blushed, 'You are sweet, Peekay. The truth is, I'm fearfully retarded. While the other kids in kindergarten went on to better things, I never quite got over playing with plasticine.'

Harriet rose from the tea chest and, walking over to him, she sat astride the wooden saw horse facing him. There was only just enough room for them both and the inside of her thighs and knees touched his own. Peekay's heart began to pound furiously as Harriet rested her arms on either side of his shoulders. She leaned forward, her breasts not quite touching his chest, and, closing her eyes, she kissed him. Then she pulled back, her face only inches from his. 'Peekay, how much longer must I wait for you to ask me to make love?'

Peekay blushed furiously. A lump had grown in his throat which made it almost impossible for him to speak. 'But . . . but, you belong to Hymie,' he croaked.

Harriet looked shocked. 'I belong to me, Peekay. I love you but I'll always belong to me.' She didn't wait for Peekay's reply, aware that her response would embarrass him even further. Instead she kissed him again, slightly opening her mouth, allowing her kiss to melt softly, lovingly over his lips, opening his own so that their lips fused.

Peekay's whole body was a confusion. His mind reeled with the shame of his presumption, his heart thumped like Mojaji's drums and his maleness rose within him, the very heat of it like nothing his wildest, most erotic fantasies had ever conjured up. Mickey Spillane hadn't mentioned this part, this sudden overwhelming paralysis, when only one part of you seemed to work, draining the strength and heat from all the other parts so that the sum of everything became an urgent, blinding desire.

Harriet pulled her head away slowly, breaking the contact carefully, as though too sudden a movement might shatter something; the air around them, time, movement, distance, the kiss itself. 'When you said, "That's the only way you're going to hit me, shithead!" that was the moment . . . that was the moment I fell in love with you,' she said.

Peekay looked confused. 'Huh?'

'When Peter Best fouled you after Hymie had called the end of the round, the first day we met, that's what you said after he'd hit you. That was the moment!' Harriet began to unbutton the cardigan Peekay was wearing. It was cold in the studio and she'd made him put it on after he'd posed for a while with his torso bare. 'This old cardigan of Daddy's, it doesn't suit you at all,' she said, slipping it over his shoulders.

Peekay's arms came up to her, pulling her against him and holding her.

'Oh, oh, Harriet you're so beautiful, please, please can we make love?' His face was buried in her hair, which smelt clean and slightly perfumed.

Harriet pushed him away gently and rose, her legs still straddling the saw horse. Then she smiled a wicked little smile and lifted her arms so that Peekay could remove her sweater. Peekay stood up, oblivious of his erection, and pulled the sweater over Harriet's head, whereupon Harriet swivelled her torso so that her back was facing Peekay, her bra strap firmly clipped in the centre of a flawless, elegant back.

Peekay's hands suddenly trembled. 'Oh fuck! Push to the right . . . pull to the left! Shit no! That was when you worked from the front! Pull to the right, push to the left! Jesus!' The bra came away into Peekay's hands. For a moment he looked at either end of the bra strap, not quite believing his eyes. Then he let the bra fall from his fingers. He was in control. Harriet had turned back to face him, planting tiny kisses on his face, her fingers working at his belt buckle. Peekay's hands rose and cupped her wondrous breasts, 'Oh, oh, Jesus!' They both stepped over the saw horse together and Peekay, removing one hand, dragged the large, colourful eiderdown from it to the floor.

EIGHTEEN

Peekay's first professional fight took place at the end of April. There had been a last-minute cancellation by an English boxer named Terry Cousins who was scheduled to fight Jacques Habib, a French Algerian welterweight, in a non-title major preliminary bout at Earl's Court. Cousins's trainer, Charlie Perkins, had called Dutch Holland to say that his fighter had come down with the 'flu and had asked him if he had a welter in his stable who could fill the bill. Dutch had seen the French Algerian fight on four previous occasions and felt that Peekay, despite his lack of experience in the professional ring, could take him – or at least make a damn good fight of it.

Holland was of the school who believed it wasn't such a bad thing if a boxer lost his first professional fight, providing always that he wasn't badly hurt in a mis-match. He wanted to see Peekay blooded; he'd never had a boxer near as good, but he needed to know just how good Peekay really was.

'A young boxer can have everything in the book, dance like Fred Astaire, fast as a bleedin' rat up a drainpipe, punch like Joe Louis, Einstein's flippin' brains, but it's what he does when he's too tired for fancy footwork, too buggered to lift his arms and he's got one round to go with his opponent ahead on points. That's when you know if you've got a champ or a chump.'

Dutch had taken Peekay into the professional ranks immediately after the abortive Oxford/Cambridge bout. Now he needed someone to put real pressure on the young South African and he felt that Jacques Habib, a tough and experienced professional once ranked number one in Europe and now a little past his prime, might be just the man to sort his lad out. If Peekay looked like taking a bad hiding he would throw in the towel. The press would lambast him for creating a mis-match and the British Boxing Commission would probably hold an inquiry. But if Peekay survived it would be worth it. Even if he took a bad hiding from the Arab, provided he showed he had heart, he would still be good enough to get a crack at the British Empire title in a couple of years.

Hymie was concerned, but he trusted Holland's judgement and, as Peekay pointed out, by going higher up the ladder so early it would be that much quicker to get a shot at the world title.

Peekay had resolved to tell Hymie about Harriet and him after the fight. Apart from telling Harriet that he would confess to Hymie almost immediately, they hadn't discussed it. Peekay was anxious to avoid another blast from Harriet on the subject of her emotional independence. The mere use of the word 'confess' had raised her ire. 'You have nothing to confess! I don't belong to Hymie. You haven't stolen me. I belong to myself!' She'd stormed off in a huff, leaving Peekay scratching his head.

Harriet had called him a pompous ass and he supposed he was in a way. But he couldn't help feeling guilty and he knew he had to tell his friend. His reason for waiting until the fight was over was based on his knowledge of Hymie. Hymie would be anxious not to upset him before his first professional fight and so might too easily dismiss the affair. This would allow Peekay to get off lightly and perhaps, as a consequence, allow the issue to remain dormant and unresolved between them.

While Peekay hated the idea of hurting his friend, he felt himself morally obliged to take whatever scorn Hymie cared to dish out. He'd pinched his girl, and he was expecting Hymie to fire both barrels at him simultaneously.

Peekay knew he'd been a bit of a prick over the Odd-Bodleian affair. After all, what Hymie had done wasn't so bad. He'd merely tried to make a point by using Peekay's childhood rather cleverly in an attempt to knit a hopelessly disparate bunch of chaps into a group of boxing supporters. It was a tall order even for Hymie, but by challenging him, Peekay had completely destroyed any chances he'd had of pulling it off.

Peekay was also aware that some people saw him as too perfect, too good at everything; now with Harriet, he'd be seen as the guy who got the girl. But he didn't see himself the way others did. Rather he knew he was the one person amongst them who had been soiled, who had been corrupted. Since he'd been a small child he'd spent his life trying to get the taste of shit out of his mouth.

Peekay was beginning to understand how powerful sex was as a weapon and how, if he wasn't terribly careful, it could come between him and his beloved friend, even if Hymie accepted his affair with Harriet. He loved Harriet with a passion, but a fair part of the passion began with his loins, whereas his feelings for Hymie were born out of a steadfast friendship which had lasted longer than anything else in his life except his relationship with Doc. Not to have Hymie as his closest friend was unthinkable.

Peekay's final preliminary was at seven, an hour before the main event, a ten round light-heavyweight contest which, by coincidence, featured Peter Best's brother and a Nigerian boxer. Both were unbeaten and it promised to be a good fight, although Best, the British Empire title holder was expected to win.

Peekay's opponent, Habib, with thirty-two fights to his name, was a tough and respected welterweight who had won twenty-five of his fights, lost six and drawn one, though eighteen of his wins had been by knockout. In his last fight he'd been narrowly beated by an American negro stationed in Germany with the US Occupation Forces. The French Algerian, who at twenty-nine was a little past his prime as a fighter, was nevertheless still rated third in Europe and had to be considered very much the favourite against the unknown student from Oxford.

Such was Dutch Holland's reputation in the fight game, that Frank Mitchell, the boxing writer for the *Daily Express*, cautioned his readers to watch the young South African carefully. He commented:

Normally I'd be asking myself why the British Boxing Commission was allowing a match-up between the experienced and still highly rated welterweight French Algerian Jacques Habib and an unknown young South African boxer who goes by the unlikely name of the Tadpole Angel. But with over twenty years' experience of the fight game, I have learned to respect the judgement of the incomparable Dutch Holland, who is handling the South African boy. Holland would not have brought the young fighter who, by the way, is reading law at Oxford, against the vastly more experienced French Algerian if he wasn't expecting big things from him. Holland is a trainer known for his caution and has the reputation for bringing his fighters along carefully.

Make no mistake, my money remains firmly on the Frenchman from Algiers, who may be a little past his prime but still carries the best left hook in Europe when it connects. But I'll be watching the Tadpole Angel very carefully too, and I suggest fight fans do the same. You may find it worthwhile catching an earlier tube to Earl's Court to witness this six-rounder.

Hymie and Peekay arrived at Earl's Court just after six to find Dutch Holland and Togger waiting for them. Harriet and E.W. were there to meet them too.

'Dutch, we haven't mis-matched Peekay this time, have we?' Hymie voiced the fears they all felt.

Dutch shrugged. 'I hope not, my son. I got a reputation to keep as well, you know.' He turned to Peekay, speaking quietly. 'You and your manager better be off to the dressing room. The fight's on in half an hour. Togger wants to handle the bucket and sponge. That orright with you?'

Peekay nodded and smiled at Togger who, with Harriet and E.W., had moved closer, conscious of the tension between the three men and relieved by Hymie's sudden laughter. Togger looked gratified. 'You won't regret the decision, Peekay. I learned me spongin' technique in a bleedin' Turkish Bath in a Soho club. I can bring a dead member to life with a soapy sponge.'

Peekay laughed at Togger's crudeness. He knew, though, that Togger was worried for him. Habib was a big name to be fighting first off. Peekay could feel the familiar tightening of his stomach, but this time the tension was worse than usual. He wasn't kidding himself, he was scared and suddenly he wasn't at all sure they hadn't made a terrible mistake going in at Habib's level.

After Peekay had changed into his boxing gear, Hymie bandaged his hands and slipped on his gloves, leaving them unlaced. They were waiting for a fight steward to call them to the ring. Then Hymie fished into the pocket of his sports jacket. 'Here, I've got something for you.' Peekay looked up as Hymie continued. 'A friend of yours gave it to me with specific instructions. I saw him last Christmas in Johannesburg.' Hymie imitated the soft tones of an African speaking English. 'Tell for my brother, always when he sits on the pot, he is so still, at this time when he waiting for the fight, he must wear for this, it will make him strong. It will make him the grandson of Shaka Zulu and the son of Dingane.'

Peekay, despite his pre-fight tension, laughed. 'Gideon! How is the cheeky bugger?'

Hymie handed him a single lion's tooth on a gold chain. 'It's one of the two he wears around his neck. He's given you half his own talisman.'

Peekay looked at Hymie, his eyes wide. 'It's an incisor tooth from the lion he killed as his initiation into manhood,' he said astonished. Then Peekay frowned, suddenly dismayed. 'He's put himself in terrible danger, breaking the spell of his own protection by halving it.'

Hymie looked sharply up at Peekay. Christ, Peekay believes it, he thought to himself.

Peekay slipped the chain with the lion's tooth over his head. He was very close to tears. 'Hymie, what a wonderful thing to do!'

'Mandoma loves you, Peekay, he's your Zulu brother.'

'And the chain? It's heavy, it's gold isn't it?'

'It's from your Polish brother,' Hymie said, attempting to sound flippant. 'Your Zulu brother's also got one.' He laughed suddenly. 'We're all linked you see. I'm the big mouth and you two are the teeth!'

Just then a ring steward entered to tell them that the previous fight had one round to go. Then Togger appeared. 'Oi, I just seen the Arab! Mean-looking geezer, he's bouncin' up and down, frowin' punches like he's trying to get out the dressin' room by punchin' down the bleedin' wall!'

Hymie draped the electric-blue silk dressing gown, with the words 'The Tadpole Angel' embroidered on the back, over Peekay's shoulders. He also draped a small white hand towel around Peekay's neck as they left.

The lightweight contest before Peekay's fight was coming to an end and the crowd were excited. The two boxers, a young Irishman named Terry O'Grady, whose nose was bleeding badly, and a Cuban who called himself Sugar Boy Romero were going at each other hammer and tongs, each hoping the final round would give them the decision. The bell went and the referee, taking the judges' cards, announced the Cuban the winner. It was a result half the crowd agreed with, the other half, most of them seemingly Irish, booed loudly and stamped their feet.

Peekay could feel the tension in his stomach building further. He felt slightly nauseous and the voices around him were beginning to blur as he started to concentrate, turning inwards, his ears tuned into Hymie and Dutch, as though they were on a special frequency band in his head. He climbed into the ring. He was an unknown and not an Englishman, but as a colonial the crowd gave him a good cheer. You could sense they expected the outcome in favour of the tough and seasoned Habib. Peekay raised his right hand briefly in acknowledgement and, moving over to his corner stool, sat on the pot.

Habib had fought four times in England before and was known to the crowd as a fighter who went hard all the way. Many of them had seen him knock out his four British opponents and he'd earned their respect. A big cheer went up as he entered the ring. He raised his gloves, touching them above his head, and walked around the ring acknowledging their support. As he passed the seated Peekay he lowered a glove and clubbed him harmlessly, though somewhat arrogantly, over the ear, hoping to intimidate the young fighter. Almost without thinking Peekay stuck his leg out so the French Algerian tripped, stumbling clumsily, regaining his balance only by grabbing onto the ropes.

A roar went up from the crowd as Habib turned angrily, squaring up to Peekay and urging him to get up and fight. Except for his foot, Peekay hadn't moved and his eyes remained downcast. A buzz of excitement ran through the crowd as Habib reached his corner and stood with his back to Peekay, talking excitedly to his seconds and gesticulating towards his opponent's corner.

'Nice one,' Hymie grinned.

'You've got him angry, my son. That can't do no 'arm.' Dutch Holland walked over to the Algerian's corner to inspect his gloves, making his second take his gloves off and feeling the bandages. Then he kneaded both gloves carefully, examining them closely so that the excitable Habib became infuriated, waving his arms about indignantly.

Habib's manager had walked over to Peekay's corner to examine his gloves. He had his back to his own corner and was unaware of his fighter's pique. 'You are a very brave man,' he said to Peekay in a heavy French accent as he massaged his gloves. 'Perhaps too brave and too young, no?'

Just then there was a murmur from the crowd as fifty or so young men, dressed immaculately in starched bib and dinner suits arrived at the ringside. Hymie had observed earlier that a block of ringside seats were unoccupied and had assumed they were a group booking for fight fans who chose to arrive in time for the main light-heavyweight event.

The Odd Bodleians had gathered from all over England, interrupting the university vacation to be at the fight. Peekay's concentration was so complete that he was barely conscious of their arrival until Hymie whispered, 'The Odd Bods have arrived! It's absolutely fantastic, almost all of them are here. They're waving!' Hymie said excitedly.

Dutch was smearing vaseline over Peekay's eyebrows and ears. ' 'Ere, your toffee-nosed cheer squad's arrived,' he said morosely. Peekay looked up and, lifting his glove, he smiled and waved. The crowd had begun to whistle and boo and the Odd Bods sat down laughing, pleased by the attention they were getting.

Dutch turned to Peekay, speaking quietly. 'Take it easy now, my son.

Don't let them take your mind off what you're doing. Let him come to you. Let him do the work. Bide your time, hold him with your left, but watch his left hook, it's how he does most of his damage.'

Just then the strains of a violin cut through the pre-fight hubbub, quietening the area immediately around the ring-side. The silence spread around the stadium. Peekay couldn't believe his ears. The large form of Jam Jar was standing up in the front row with a violin, playing the overture to Doc's *Concerto for the Great Southland*. The overture was hauntingly African and picked up the feeling of a vast, sad land. Doc had written it in prison (where he was interned during the war as an enemy alien) using the five tribes who, for the most part, made up the prisoners. Each tribe took a part, the poignancy of their singing unbearably beautiful as they sang of their love for Africa. The Concerto climaxed with the Zulus singing the great song to Shaka Zulu, the mightiest of all the warriors.

The crowd had hushed as the beautiful strains of Jam Jar's violin moved to complete the overture and then picked up the opening notes of the Zulu part. The Odd Bodleians rose and came in as one, their voices rising like thunder in the hills. The rest of the audience hushed as the beauty of the male voices rose, singing of the great Zulu impi that came as wind waving in the tall grass, sweeping all before him. It ended again with the roll of thunder as the male voices in the stadium rose in triumph and then started to die down slowly until the deep hum seemed to vibrate the air about the ring. Suddenly Jam Jar's violin cut in again, picking up the refrain and bringing it to a conclusion, the male voices behind it holding the deep, humming sound and allowing it finally to die.

The audience went wild as the Odd Bodleians sat down. Peekay was not conscious that he'd risen to his feet and now the tears rolled down his cheek. He'd been scared, feeling a little overwhelmed by the fight with the highly rated Habib. The *Concerto for the Great Southland* performed by the Odd Bodleians was the strength he needed. He turned to Hymie, removing the gold chain with the lion's tooth from his neck and handing it to him. 'This fight's for Gideon,' he said softly.

Hymie had tears in his eyes as he took the talisman. 'I had no idea this was going to happen!' He withdrew a handkerchief from his pocket and wiped his eyes, '*Months ago* I'd talked about the composition and Milstein had asked me if I had the music and lyrics. I got my sister to send them over.'

Peekay sat down on the pot again, closing his eyes, regaining his concentration so that he didn't see the referee enter the ring. Dutch tapped him on the shoulder and Peekay opened his eyes, he was ready. He looked up at Habib but saw instead a black man, Jake 'Spoonbill' Jackson, welterweight champion of the world, the fastest two-fisted puncher in the world. Peekay was going in after him.

The referee called the two boxers into centre ring and Habib jumped forward, throwing punches into the air, eager to get going, his anger showing. Peekay wasn't buying the showmanship and waited a moment before moving quickly and quietly to stand beside the referee.

Both boxers waited as the Scottish referee introduced them to the crowd, using a microphone which dropped down from the ceiling. The French Algerian held his gloves high and did a little shuffle as his name was called, while Peekay briefly raised his left glove. The referee allowed the microphone to retract and spoke to the two boxers, spelling out the rules of the fight. Neither listened, they'd heard it a hundred times before. The Algerian, jerking his shoulders up and down in a relaxed manner, fixed Peekay with a grin, but Peekay made no attempt to look at him, staring instead at his feet, his hands hanging calmly at his side. As the referee told them to touch gloves Peekay looked at his opponent for the first time, his eyes giving nothing away. They returned to their respective corners to wait for the opening bell.

The crowd sensed a good fight coming up, though there must have been a great many experienced fans present who, like Mitchell of the *Daily Express*, were wondering how a young, unknown South African boxer could stand up to the tough, two-fisted attack of the experienced Arab fighter.

Peekay returned to sit on the pot, while the slightly taller Habib stood waiting in his corner. The bell sounded for the first round and the dark-eyed fighter moved like a blur towards the young blond boxer trying to force him into the neutral corner.

Peekay was fast enough to step through the gap, taking a left and a right on his gloves, turning Habib and moving backwards towards centre ring. He knew Habib wanted him on the ropes where he could rough him up early and perhaps put a few hard punches into the body. The Algerian came hard at him again, throwing a lot of leather, and Peekay was hard put to keep him out. Habib was strong and his aim was to unsettle the less experienced boxer quickly.

Habib broke away suddenly, dropping both his hands, a sign of contempt intended to throw Peekay. Perhaps he hadn't met a boxer with Peekay's speed and anticipation before. Peekay sensed the gesture coming, read the other man's thoughts through his eyes. He hit him with a straight left followed by a lightning right cross which sent the French Algerian sprawling, hitting the canvas hard.

Peekay moved quickly to a neutral corner as the ref started to count. The Algerian fighter had risen to his haunches, using the count to clear his head. At eight he stood, nodding to the ref that he was all right. The respect was back in the fight; he'd underestimated his opponent and he now knew he had a fight on his hands.

Peekay moved in quickly, but with caution. He'd hurt his opponent but his eyes were clear. It would take more than an early knock-down to intimidate the other fighter. The Algerian pushed him away with a couple of short rights, but Peekay stepped around the left that followed and caught his opponent a good blow under the heart. Habib went into a clinch, holding Peekay until the ref ordered them to break.

The first round began to take shape, Habib still the more aggressive, chasing Peekay around the ring, both boxers scoring well, neither doing any real damage. Towards the end of the round Habib caught Peekay with a right cross which sent the younger boxer several paces backwards and brought a roar from the crowd. It was a beautiful punch and Peekay felt it in his toes.

The knock-down probably gave the round to Peekay but the other boxer had seemed more aggressive. He was beginning to look impressive, as though in control, the way an experienced boxer can, often without doing a lot more than his opponent. He'd caught Peekay several times on the ropes and done some damage. He was faster than he'd looked on film and Peekay knew he had the capacity to put him away with either hand.

The second round saw Peekay staying away from the Frenchman, counter-punching and moving Habib around the ring. Peekay was a back-foot fighter who allowed his opponent to come to him so he could work out the other man's idiosyncrasies. Neither Hymie nor Dutch could pick anything about Habib's style which Peekay could use. After the knock-down the Arab boxer wasn't being careless and was putting his punches together well. He seemed to be breathing a little heavily after the first round but this could have come from the effects of the knock-down. Nevertheless Peekay determined to move him around as much as possible, making his opponent miss, keeping himself away from the ropes. Peekay managed a couple of hard hooks to Habib's body, one of which made him grunt. But it was a reasonably tame round which the Frenchman probably took with his extra aggression. Almost at the end of the round he seemed to gain confidence and was starting to be a tad liberal with his left hook; all Peekay had really managed to do was to confirm to his opponent that the novice wasn't going to be a pushover.

The third round in a six-rounder is the one in which a boxer tries to assert his authority. Peekay was clearly the faster of the two fighters with a slightly longer reach. But the French Algerian was bigger about the shoulders, stronger in the legs; he was a stand-up fighter and needed to get Peekay on the ropes where he would work on him. His tactics had been right when he'd come out for the first round; it was only his arrogance which had been his undoing.

'He's going to come out hard, lad, try to work you in close. Keep him walking, dance him, he's beginning to work a little flat-footed. If he gets a little slower, in the second half of the round take the fight to him, surprise him,' Dutch said.

Peekay had already decided Habib was a good fighter but lacked imagination. Dutch was right. If he was certain the Algerian had lost some of his speed then turning the tables on him might work.

The bell for the third round went and, as predicted, Habib came out fast and aggressive. Peekay danced him, slipping his punches, occasionally tying him up. Habib was strong and he tried to pull himself out of the clinches but Peekay held him, allowing the other fighter to waste his energy whenever possible. The older fighter was throwing so many punches that some of them were landing and hurting Peekay; but Peekay was doing enough to frustrate Habib's aggressive stand-up style and the Algerian was getting angry, which was affecting his timing. Peekay was also hitting him on the break and tying him up whenever he got in close. It wasn't what Habib expected and his frustration was making him careless. Using both hands to get at Peekay's head, Habib was leaving his torso open, whereas Peekay was laying down a pattern of punches which would begin to tell later in the fight.

Towards the end of the round, Habib decided to go for Peekay's body and brought his left hook into play, missing on several occasions. Peekay waited until he tried it just once too often. The younger fighter was perfectly balanced and positioned for the right cross. It came as though in slow motion, exploding to the side of the French Algerian's jaw. The older man staggered backwards and, moving in fast, Peekay hit him with a left to the head and another right cross; then closing in he belted him hard to the body with a left hook, following through with a hard driving right under the heart. The Algerian backed into the ropes, where he tried to grab Peekay and hold on. But the younger boxer was too fast and he hit him again with a straight left. The punch was hard, but going away so that some of the sting was missing. It was enough for Habib to grab onto the ropes and stop himself going down. Peekay moved in just as the bell went for the end of the round. He'd left his run ten seconds too late to knock Habib down, a timing mishap which could cost him the fight.

The crowd, sensing a big upset, were solidly behind Peekay, hoping for a fourth round knock-out. But in the fourth round, Habib managed to tie Peekay up, even hitting him with a left-right combination which had Peekay going for a few seconds as he back-pedalled frantically out of trouble. Yet Habib simply wasn't fast enough to capitalise on the two great punches, and Peekay was able to escape. The round came to an end and, while the crowd were now plainly on Peekay's side, the honours probably went to the French Algerian who had grown stronger and stronger as the round progressed. Peekay's inexperience showed; he'd let his quarry off the hook and, coming up for the fifth round, he seemed likely to walk into a whole heap of trouble.

In the fifth round, the Algerian had worked out Peekay's hit-and-run tactics and he began to stalk the young South African, moving him into a corner whenever he could. Peekay was mostly able to fight his way out but, towards the middle of the round, the big-shouldered Algerian nailed him with a beautiful left-right combination which put Peekay down.

Peekay had seen the punch coming but his head somehow wouldn't move. The left smashed into his mouth and the right that followed felt as though his head had been taken off. He went down fast, his bum bouncing on the surface of the ring. 'Jesus, he's nailed me. Get up! Get up!' his mind screamed. 'Christ, I've been knocked out! Get up! Get up!' But the voice in his mind came back clean and far away, as though it was an echo travelling up a long glass funnel. 'No count? There's no count! It's over, I didn't hear the count!' Peekay tried to stand but it was as though he had no legs.

Habib, elated and angry, certain that he'd hit Peekay hard enough so he wouldn't get up again, didn't move immediately to a neutral corner. Standing over Peekay he swore at him in a mixture of French and Arabic. The referee screamed at him to get into a neutral corner but the Arab remained standing over Peekay's fallen body.

The seconds gained were critical. Peekay felt the pain rush back into his legs as the count commenced at last. He still couldn't see properly but his strength was returning. 'The count! Listen for the count! Take all the time you've got! Get up at eight!' he told himself.

At the count of eight he was on his feet with enough strength in his legs to move, his eyes clear. The referee gave him a few precious seconds more as he examined him. 'Box on!' he commanded.

Habib came in fast but missed, first with a straight left and then badly with the right that followed. Peekay moved in and held him, buying the precious seconds until the referee shouted for them to break. Then Peekay switched to southpaw as he came out of the break and hit Habib with a beautiful right lead, stopping the French Algerian momentarily. Peekay was back in the fight again, and the crowd was loving his courage as he managed to weave and dance through the remainder of the round, staying out of trouble.

'Jesus, Peekay, we thought you were gone! Nice one!' Hymie said as Peekay, breathing heavily, sat down.

Dutch Holland examined his right eye, which had started to swell. 'Not much harm done,' he said, smearing fresh vaseline over the eyelid. 'At least it's not cut. How's your sight?'

Togger was sponging Peekay down, trying unsuccessfully not to look worried as Peekay sucked on the water bottle and rinsed his mouth and then spat into the bucket at his feet. 'Fine, Dutch, I can see fine. Christ, he hits hard!'

'You can't leave it to chance, my son. We reckon he's taken three. You're going to have to look very convincing in this one, lad.'

Hymie pointed to Habib, who was standing, punching his gloves together, waiting for the bell. He was still breathing hard but trying to conceal it, glaring over at Peekay. 'Look! His heart!' Hymie exclaimed. 'He's taken a lot of punishment.'

'You've marked him, lad. That's nice close work. He's hurting. Work it, work it hard, keep going under the heart,' Dutch instructed.

'As always, you'll wear him down and finish him on the ropes,' Hymie added lamely. There is a time in a close fight when there is nothing to say. Hymie was simply covering his concern with words.

Peekay understood what they were saying. He had to do more than win the round convincingly to be sure of the fight. 'He's bloody strong. I don't know whether I've got time,' Peekay replied.

'So are you, my son, fitter and stronger. The punch that put you down would have finished off any other welter in Britain.' Dutch said. He was concerned. Peekay had let the fight slip away. All Habib had to do was hang in and he could win. Dutch was no longer concerned with Peekay making a good showing; he'd seen enough already to know he had the makings of a champion, one with the skill to take him to the top. Peekay was now into the part of the fight which requires character, where the men are sorted from the boys, the would be's if they could be's. Whatever happened in the next three minutes, Dutch would have all his questions answered.

The bell went for the final round and Peekay moved into the centre of the ring. He knew he had to knock Habib out to win but the Algerian was crowding him, working up too close for a big punch. Peekay was hurting a lot, the blows from the French Algerian were remorseless. He was taking most of them on the back of the arms, and he could feel his arms starting to weaken. He needed to dig deep, deeper than he'd ever been before. Hoppie Groenewald's voice came to him suddenly. It was clean, unhurried. 'Always Peekay, remember, first with the head and then with the heart. A fighter must have himself a plan. Always a plan!'

At precisely that moment, as though Peekay and Hymie were synergised, Hymie turned to Dutch Holland, his dark eyes shining fiercely. 'Peekay will take him out, Dutch! I'm telling you, man . . . no way he's going to lose this fight!'

Dutch shook his head. 'Our lad's spent, 'e 'asn't got the punch no more to put Habib on the deck.'

Peekay switched suddenly to southpaw, as Habib moved in again. Habib expected him to back away and he held his gloves a little low, confident Peekay wasn't going to come after him. The switch in style caught him by surprise as Peekay moved forward and hit him with a left cross, followed through with a hard right.

Peekay needed those two punches to slow Habib down, to move him backwards onto the ropes. There he had to open him up, where he could work him to the body, to the spot under his heart. There was only one way. He must offer the Arab his head as a target, hope he could ride the punch, and force the Algerian to open up. He was gambling that he could read Habib, that the other fighter would follow his big punch with a left hook, miss and leave himself wide open for a hard left to the head. Habib would bring his gloves up to protect his head from the expected right hand and in doing so, he'd leave his torso open, where Peekay could hit him with everything he had under the heart. Peekay needed an eight-punch combination, a Geel Piet eight solidly into the spot to slow the other fighter right down, allow Peekay to box him, and wait for the big punch that might put him out. It was a plan which depended on Peekay reading the Algerian perfectly; but he couldn't think of a better one. If he'd underestimated the power still left in Habib's straight right, his opponent would knock him out. He had no choice; winning the round was not enough. He had to take the chance.

Peekay opened his gloves, closing them again, opening again, signalling, offering his head. Habib saw his chance as Peekay opened just a little wider, and the right smashed into Peekay's swollen eye. Perfect. The eye socket, the strongest part of the face, absorbed the power of the punch as Peekay rolled with it. Habib's left hook followed but Peekay wasn't in line for the punch. Instead his own left smashed into Habib's nose. It was the hardest punch Peekay could ever remember having thrown. Habib staggered back against the ropes, his nose broken, his good eye filling with tears. He was blinded, and his gloves came up instinctively to cover his face as Peekay knew they would. Then Peekay's right hook came from low down, with all the follow-through from his shoulder to catch the French Algerian under the heart. The left had been a spectacular punch, but it was the right hook that did the terrible damage. It was the best punch thrown all night and he could feel Habib's ribcage give as the blow ripped into his body. In went the Geel Piet eight, so fast that Habib's agonised grunt from the deadly right hook was still coming out of him when Peekay pulled back.

Habib sank to the canvas as though in slow motion. He was unconscious before his knees hit the surface of the ring. But even so, his right arm hooked around the centre rope and his left glove pushed against the canvas propping him up. He may have been out but he wasn't going to lie down.

The blood ran into Peekay's eye where Habib had hit him earlier. The eye was closing rapidly and even his good eye was less than fifty per cent effective, as though he was looking through a red haze. If Habib managed to get up from the canvas and landed half a good punch into the eye, Peekay was history; you can't fight if you can't see. Peekay felt no elation as Habib's arm dropped from the rope and he sank to the floor. For the first time in the fight he was really scared. He had nothing left.

Peekay moved quickly to a neutral corner, conscious that every second delayed gave the French Algerian time to recover. For the first time he heard the roar of the crowd. At the count of seven Habib managed to stand, using the ropes to pull himself upright. Peekay couldn't believe his eyes. He'd hit the Algerian harder than he'd ever hit anyone in his life. The punches under the heart, coming as they did, after fifty or more well-timed blows to the same spot should have taken him out for a twenty count. But the bastard was up, facing Peekay, a blood-smeared grin on his swollen face.

The referee seemed in two minds. He wasn't fooled; it was a fighter's grin. He knew Habib was hurt bad. For a moment it looked as though he was going to stop the fight. Oh God, please call it! Peekay begged silently. Please let me win! But the ref wiped Habib's gloves and signalled for the fight to continue.

Peekay closed in and pushed Habib into the ropes with two barely effective straight rights to the face. He came in so his left eye was closest to his opponent, allowing him maximum vision. Habib tried to pull Peekay into a clinch but failed, and brought his gloves up to protect his broken nose.

Peekay dug deep. He was fighting from memory, the years and years of doing it right, putting all his punches together for the maximum effect. The orthodox right hook under the heart from Peekay was almost polite it was so businesslike. Earlier in the fight it may just have stopped Habib momentarily; but now it was enough. The French Algerian grunted softly, it was almost a moan as he toppled onto the canvas. He was out cold before he hit the deck. One minute and forty-five seconds into the last round, Habib had fallen over like a sack of potatoes. The referee stood over him counting, but it was a mere formality. Habib still hadn't moved as he was counted out.

The crowd exploded with excitement and the stadium was in an uproar. They'd found a new champion. 'Angel! Angel! Angel!' they chanted.

Hymie turned to Dutch. 'What did I tell you!' he screamed. He was climbing into the ring when he felt Togger brush past him. Togger rushed over to Peekay and, grabbing him about the thighs, hoisted him off the deck.

'You was bleedin' sensational. The best, the best! The world champ!' Togger yelled. He swung Peekay around to where the Odd Bodleians were seated before putting him down. They were all on their feet yelling 'Angel! Angel! Angel!' with the crowd, their arms held high above their heads.

Hymie pointed to them, then grabbed Peekay and hugged him. 'Christ, when the Arab got up again, I think I shat my pants!'

'Me too!' Peekay gasped.

Dutch Holland remained in his corner, all his questions about Peekay answered. 'You'll do, my son, you'll do very nicely,' he said quietly to himself.

Peekay, flanked by an excited Hymie and Togger, returned to the corner. Dutch Holland looked at Peekay angrily. ' 'Ere, lad, that's living too fuckin' dangerously! Next time you offer your bleedin' noggin as a trade for a chance to knock your opponent out you better find yourself another trainer!'

In fact, it was the courage and critical judgement that showed in this very decision which made Dutch Holland finally sure he had a world champ on his hands. Dutch hoped that Peekay would never again have to repeat the tactic. Peekay had been mismatched. It was the French Algerian's arrogance and temperament which had cost him the fight. That wouldn't happen again. The next time Peekay stepped into the ring his opponent would treat him with the utmost respect. In future his skills as a boxer would decide the outcome of his fights. Nevertheless, Holland was deeply gratified that the young man in his charge had come through his baptism of fire with nothing more than a couple of black eyes and a bruised rib or two. It was a small enough price to pay to find out he had a lad on his hands who had the courage to kiss the knife. Dutch knew that from such raw material world champions are made.

Peekay held out his right hand for Hymie to remove his glove. He was stunned by Dutch Holland's reaction. His body was covered with red blotches where Habib had hit him and his right eye was closed. He winced, trying to smile. 'Shit! Nobody told me it was this hard!' he said, trying not to seem upset by his trainer's remark.

'Welcome to the professional ranks, my son. You're going to have to learn to put 'em away sooner. Saves a lot of wear 'n' tear on the old carcass,' Dutch said without smiling.

Peekay fought back his tears. Christ what do I have to do? What does the bastard want? he thought. He kept his head down so that Hymie couldn't see how upset he was and held out his left glove for his friend to remove.

'Oi! Fair go, Mr 'Olland! Peekay done marvellous! He knocked 'im bleedin' out didn't 'e? 'E's never been put down before, never!' Togger yelled, defiant and plainly upset for his friend.

Dutch Holland looked down at Togger. 'You're right son,' he said quietly. 'He's done bleedin' wonderful, but he's a toffee nose, these intellectuals can't take too much praise all at once.'

'Try starting with just a little bit, then, Dutch,' Hymie shot back at the trainer, his sarcasm plain.

'There's plenty of time for that later, Mr Levy! If the lad had ten per cent more going for him in both 'ands he'd have been enjoying an early shower. We got lots of work to do if we gonna take your man anywhere special. I haven't got no time to stand around throwin' bleedin' bouquets.'

Not wanting to show his feelings, Peekay excused himself and walked over to Habib's corner. '*Merci*,' he said, smiling, nodding his head to Habib's manager and seconds. One of them held an ice pack against Habib's face so that the Algerian fighter hadn't seen Peekay approach. '*Merci, mon ami, j'espere que je ne rencontre jamais un pugiliste qui me bat si fort que vous*,' Peekay said, in halting schoolboy French.

The second withdrew the ice pack. The French Algerian's nose was badly swollen. The bleeding from his left eye had been stemmed but the eye itself was completely closed and raised well above his cheekbone, and he could barely see out of the other eye. Habib was surprised to see Peekay, but took only a moment to smile. Sniffing back a trickle of blood which had begun again from his nose, he rose from his stool and, taking Peekay's arm, he held it aloft to cheers from the crowd.

'One day you will be world champion, Tadpole Angel,' he said, speaking in French. 'Then I will say, "*Eh bien!* He's not so great, one time I nearly knocked him out!" '

Jam Jar had invited Hymie and Peekay to the Savoy with the Odd-Bodleian crowd for a champagne supper, calling Hymie from across the ring as they were leaving for the dressing room. 'Wonderful fight, brought out positively the worst in me! Loved it!'

Hymie nodded, acknowledging his invitation, 'The singing . . . it was marvellous!' He imitated playing a violin, 'You were terrific!'

Harriet declined to accompany them to the Savoy. She hadn't realised just how much tougher professional boxing was than the amateur sport and she'd winced with every blow Peekay had absorbed. By the time the fight had ended she was exhausted and had a splitting headache. E.W., who'd travelled up from Dorset that morning for the fight, was also tired and elected to escort Harriet home in a taxi.

Harriet was anxious to be on her own. She'd seen an aspect of Peekay she'd only previously glimpsed, the ruthless determination to win. She'd been seated in the front row directly beneath Peekay when he'd taken the full impact of Habib's punch to the head in the last round and had thrown the right counter smashing the bone and cartilage in Habib's nose. She'd been watching Peekay and not the punch. The expression on his face as he landed the counter-punch had sent a shiver down her spine. It was the most primitive, ruthless fight she'd ever witnessed. In the few seconds that followed she'd seen the very core of the male animal, when he wages death with himself, the moment when he lays everything he is on the line.

By the time the party arrived at the Savoy, both Peekay's eyes were almost closed and his face was badly swollen. He had insisted that Togger and Dutch Holland accompany them, though Dutch had declined. The doorman held open the door of the cab. As they got out, Togger turned to Peekay. 'Cor, in the bleeding light you look a right berk! What you need, my son, is 'alf a gallon of bubbly poured straight down your throat.' He paused. 'I've never tasted proper Frog bubbly. What's it taste like, Hymie?'

Hymie laughed. 'It tastes civilised.'

'I know what you mean, an' all. Once when Carmen and me was little we was in St James's Park, feedin' the ducks with scraps of stale bread we pinched from home, when along come this little girl. She's dressed in a fluffy pink dress with a big ribbon around her waist and she's pushing this doll's pram, see. She stops right next to us and Carmen seen the doll in the pram. It's got big dark eyes and black hair and it's also wearin' a fluffy pink dress with a pink ribbon around its waist. I can see it's the prettiest thing Carmen ever seen, she can't take 'er eyes off of the bleedin' pram. We don't know it, because I'm watching Carmen and she's watchin' the doll, but the little girl's watchin' Carmen watching the doll. The little girl suddenly bends down and takes the doll from the pram and hands it to Carmen. "Her name is Elizabeth Jane, she's an orphan and you must be her real mummy who's come back to find her," she says, dead serious like. She turns and grabs hold of the pram, "I'm sorry, but I can't give you the pram because my other dolls need it," she says, like she's apologising an' all. Just then up comes this toff. "What *are* you doing, Margaret?" he asks.

The little girl looks up at him and I think to meself, 'ullo, 'ullo, 'ere comes a cuff behind the ear 'ole, it's time to scarper. I look at Carmen to signal her to drop the doll and run for it, but she's sort of frozen on the spot, like she's been electrocuted. "Isn't that nice, Uncle Dickie? Elizabeth Jane has found her mummy at last!" the little girl says, not a bit afraid of the big toff.

' "That's very civilised of you, my dear," the toff called Uncle Dickie says.'

At that moment the lift arrived to take them up to Jam Jar's suite and they piled into it along with several other passengers. In the manner of people in a lift they remained silent until they reached the top floor. Hymie hurried down the corridor ahead of them looking for Jam Jar's suite. 'What happened to Elizabeth Jane?' Peekay asked.

'Funny you should ask that,' Togger's expression was suddenly pained, 'she got poured into the hot water bottle. It happened only three months ago.'

'Your mum?'

'Yeah, Carmen come home and Elizabeth Jane ain't on her bed like always. Our mum is pissed, snorin' her head off. Elizabeth Jane got turned into a bottle of Gilbeys. Carmen didn't say nothing, she just packed her bags and moved out that night and she ain't been home since. I spent the whole next week goin' round every pub and pawn shop in the Old Kent Road, but it weren't no use, Elizabeth Jane had lost her bleedin' mummy again.'

NINETEEN

The following morning when Peekay awoke he hurt. His bones hurt, his muscles and joints hurt and his head hurt. But his head hurt the most, from a combination of Habib's fists and too much champagne. Both his eyes were pumped up, mere slits, the eyelids stretched and swollen, purple as aubergine.

The three young men had returned to Harriet's aunt's flat in Knightsbridge well after midnight. To Harriet's surprise it was Peekay, looking as though he'd been in a bad accident, who was supporting Hymie and Togger. As it turned out, Peekay's sobriety was only a matter of degree. She'd bathed his eyes with boracic powder and tried to persuade him to go to bed. But Peekay was too tired and too drunk to listen. Much singing and exaggerated replaying of the fight had taken place before she'd finally coaxed Togger onto a couch in the sitting-room and Hymie and Peekay onto the two beds in the second bedroom. E.W., who'd been enormously disturbed by what he'd witnessed in the ring, had taken a little pink pill and didn't stir from the safety of the tiny bedroom study. Harriet had the run of the whole flat, since her aunt was abroad – she spent her winters every year in the south of France.

In winning against Habib, Peekay had received the worst beating in his life. Despite his protests, Hymie insisted he check in to Guy's Hospital for a thorough examination. Apart from bruised ribs and bruising to the back of his arms, where he'd taken a lot of Habib's punches, the examination showed him to be in a sound condition. The young Australian intern summed up. 'We've given you a neurological examination; your reactions seem okay, the X-ray shows no broken ribs. You won, I believe? Bloody hell, I'd hate to see the other bloke. Okay, mate, if you start getting headaches, throwing up, that sort of thing, get back here fast. Blood in your urine is nothing, you can expect it for a few days, but if it persists, come back. You'll have a couple of beaut eyes for a week or two, but other than that, if you take it easy for a few days, I reckon you'll be right as rain.'

They returned to the flat and Harriet spent the latter part of the morning sketching Peekay's battered face. 'This is marvellous stuff, darling. I may never get the chance to see you like this again.'

'Christ, I hope not,' Peekay cried.

Harriet laughed. 'You're too pretty. From a sculptor's point of view you've definitely changed for the better.' She grew suddenly serious. Leaning over, she gently kissed both purple, swollen eyelids. 'Please, Peekay, darling, don't ever get hurt this badly again!'

Peekay brought his hands up to hold Harriet's head, then brought her face towards his swollen lips and kissed her deeply on the mouth. When at last they pulled away from each other they observed Hymie, propped against the door jamb, watching them from the doorway.

'Kissing it all better, are we?' He seemed to hesitate for a split second. 'Is the mouth-to-mouth resuscitation only for the boxer? There's a manager over here who's fading fast, about to expire from a terminal hangover.'

Harriet threw her head back, grinning. She didn't appear in the least embarrassed. She crossed to Hymie and kissed him on the mouth, lingering long enough for the kiss to be intimate, before drawing away. 'How about some coffee for everyone?'

She turned and walked from the room without looking back. She was wearing trousers as usual and a green cashmere sweater which showed the swell of her breasts. Despite his hangover, Peekay found himself wanting her.

'Hymie, we must talk,' he said the moment Harriet had left the room.

'Later, Peekay.' Hymie flopped into a chair. 'What we both need is a glass of champagne . . . hair of the dog.'

'Not for me!' Peekay said quickly. 'Hymie, I really need to talk to you. It's important!'

Hymie shrugged absently. 'I know you do, Peekay. We'll talk in the car on the way back to Oxford this afternoon. Last night was a mis-match. I've never seen you fight better, you were bloody marvellous. But we won't do a stupid thing like that again, will we?'

Peekay nodded silently. He knew Hymie understood why he'd agreed to fight Habib. A win against such a fighter automatically eliminated about seven opponents. These were fighters Peekay would normally have to box to get to the professional level represented by Habib. It could possibly mean getting a crack at the world title a year earlier. On the other hand, had Habib beaten him, say played with him and then knocked him out in an early round, it would have set them back disastrously, perhaps forever.

'Ja, you're perfectly right,' Peekay said finally and then added, 'For once I've got a saying, it comes from Geel Piet. I once asked him how he managed to stay alive in prison. 'Ag man, *klein* baas,' he said. 'When you're skating on thin ice you may as well tap dance.' Peekay shrugged. 'We got lucky last night.'

Hymie sprang from his chair and grabbed Peekay fiercely by the shoulders. 'For Christ's sake, Peekay! That French bastard nearly took you out. You took a hiding into the bargain and finally you had to offer him a clean shot at your jaw so you could gamble on a Geel Piet eight to take him out of the fight. That's not winning tactics! That's fucking suicide!' He paused, catching his breath. 'You're probably the most intelligent boxer in the world and certainly amongst the most skilful. If we can't win using your wit and your skill, then let's get the fuck out of the game before you suffer brain damage!' He drew back, releasing Peekay's shoulders. 'You know something, man? Dutch was right to blast you!'

Peekay didn't speak. There was nothing to say. Hymie was right. But he was also wrong. Peekay knew that he hadn't just got lucky. He'd picked his way through no-man's-land before. Sometimes you're only saved because you are prepared to die, prepared to negotiate the minefield. Sometimes danger is your friend and only ally. How could he explain, even to Hymie, that he knew with absolute certainty when he'd offered Habib his jaw, that the best punch the French Algerian was capable of throwing wouldn't knock him out. In his head Peekay was fighting for the welterweight championship of the world, whereas Habib was fighting for a purse. They are not the same thing; a dream is often lonely, but providing you're prepared to prevail, it's invincible.

It was also why Peekay knew Oxford wasn't going to give him what he was going to need in South Africa. They were going into a fight in which you had to be willing to put your life on the line every time. There could be nothing but a total commitment. He was going to go against people who wouldn't play by the tidy rules of jurisprudence, the laws set down like markings on a football field. They would change the playing field to suit themselves and the only way to beat them was to venture everything you were and everything you had to offer every time you stepped into the arena. He would always have to offer his jaw, take an instinctive risk. South Africa was going to be the final round against Habib all of the time and there was nothing at Oxford that could prepare him for that.

Harriet decided to remain in town for a few days. E.W. left shortly after breakfast to catch an early train to visit a friend in High Wycombe. He would return to Oxford in the evening in time for evensong where he always read the message at the college chapel. E.W. was quietly religious; he saw the tenets of the Christian faith as part of his life. They fitted like a pair of well-worn shoes and he made no attempt to proselytise. His God was an Englishman who wore sensible Oxford brogues, a good Irish tweed jacket and was a scholar and a gentleman.

Hymie and Peekay set out for the return to Oxford about mid-afternoon when the effects of the fight and their hangovers were less severe. The snow of Christmas had long disappeared. The countryside on the way to Oxford was ploughed and looked winter worn, with birch and elm lining the horizon like upturned witches' broomsticks against a pewter sky. Peekay thought of it as 'a crow-lonely landscape'; every once in a while the only sign of life would be a lone black crow resting high in the filigreed branches of an elm or birch, its raucous caw the one sound above the wind and engine noise.

It's funny that, he thought to himself. Africa too has its crow-lonely landscape, but instead, it is hot and harsh, with the midday sun beating the bush into silent submission, blackening the shade so that where it throws, under a tree or rock, it looks like a deep, cool hole in the sun-leached landscape. Only the anthracite crow is game enough to caw into the squinting African stillness.

'Hymie, I think you know what I'm going to say? It's about Harriet.'

'But you're going to say it anyway?'

'I can't even say it happened by mistake. That we were thrown together.'

'I'm glad you're not trying to blame it on the irresistible forces of nature.' Hymie glanced quickly at Peekay. 'Jesus, we're lucky!'

It seemed a curious remark and Peekay didn't know quite how to respond. 'Lucky?'

'Ja, for Harriet to deflower you.' He paused momentarily. 'At least we have that in common.'

Peekay sensed that Hymie wasn't angry. There was no sarcasm in his voice. 'Hymie, I know she's yours but I can't help it. I can't keep my hands off her. I can't say I'm sorry. I'd be lying. I don't know what to do.'

Hymie kept his eyes fixed on the road ahead. 'You don't understand. I'm bloody glad she accepted you and that, unlike me, you were able to make love to her.'

'Shit, Hymie, what are you saying?'

Hymie gave a wry little snort. 'I'm a phoney, Peekay. In the sex department I'm two sandwiches short of a picnic.'

Peekay was too shocked to respond. Hymie seemed to read his thoughts. 'You needn't worry, I'm not a homo!' He glanced quickly at Peekay, who despite himself, was unable to conceal his relief. 'Even that would be something. Alexander the Great was a homosexual, Michelangelo . . . the list of the greats who preferred their own sex is ten miles long. I wouldn't mind being included on it one day. You can live with knowing what you are. That's the trouble. I'm nothing. I'm fucking nothing!' He slammed down hard on the brakes and the little Ford skidded crazily for a moment, its back tyres bumping before it stopped.

Hymie cut the engine and pulled on the handbrake. 'I can't get it up! I have absolutely no desire whatsoever to fuck. Not a male or a female or even a bloody duck! Not you, whom I love more than anything in my life, not Harriet, whom I adore. Not anyone . . .' His voice trailed off. He paused, then gave a bitter little laugh. 'How does my world end? Not with a bang but with a wimp.' Even in his pain Hymie couldn't help joking.

'But you said, Harriet . . . you know, had taken your virginity?' the expression seemed old-fashioned.

'Yeah, she did. No matter how bizarre the experience, you can only lose your virginity once, thank God. We were both blotto and somehow, Christ knows, I managed to get an erection.'

'Jesus, Hymie! That means something, surely?'

Hymie shook his head. 'I don't recall what it was like. I was too pissed.

Shortly after we'd done it, or at least I *think* we'd done it, I threw up all over the sheets. Being sick was the more memorable of the two incidents. At least I remember that part. I guess I can technically claim I'm no longer a virgin, but to be honest Harriet might as well have been a knot-hole in the ironing board.'

'Hymie, I'm sorry. I'm sorry on two fronts, for your predicament and for blowing your cover. It goes without saying . . .'

'Well then, don't say it! The truth is, I'm glad. I'm glad you know. It's worried me since school that you've never questioned my obvious lack of libido. Now you know the truth.' Hymie looked up at Peekay and shrugged his shoulders, 'For what it's worth.'

'A doctor? There must be something?'

'Ja, sure, one day maybe.'

That seemed to be the end of it. In all the time Peekay had known him, this was only the second time Hymie had admitted a weakness. The business with the Odd Bodleians and now this. He knew there was no point in persisting with his sympathy, Hymie didn't operate that way. He was the most clear-eyed, clear-minded person Peekay had ever known, even more so than Doc. He would put this thing aside and get on with his mercurial life.

Hymie turned on the ignition and they pulled away, saying nothing for a while. They passed through a small village of thatched cottages just like the ones on the lids of Hymie's father's chocolate boxes. The air smelt vaguely of wood smoke and wet hay and the gardens were clothed in sombre winter greenery. In one garden, where they'd stopped at an intersection, the dry spines of summer's hollyhocks stood stark against a grey cottage wall.

'What about Harriet?' Peekay asked at last. 'We haven't resolved anything.'

Hymie grinned. 'On the Richter scale of sensitivity you haven't even made the graph-line waver. What do you mean, what about Harriet? You sleeping with her? I thought we'd discussed that?'

'Well no, not really, not our mutual relationship.'

'Ours? You mean mine? Do you want it to change?'

'No! I'd hoped things would, you know, continue,' Peekay hesitated. 'But I couldn't see how.'

Hymie grinned. 'And now you can?'

Peekay flinched inwardly. 'Yes, and now I can,' he echoed softly.

'Peekay, you have to get rid of the male notion that you own a woman. Harriet can't be owned. When sex isn't a big deal you get to see things a bit differently. You don't think with your cock all the time.'

'I say, that's a bit unfair!'

'Not at all,' Hymie contradicted. 'Consider the hours you've spent thinking about losing your virginity. About having your famous whipped-cream experience.'

Peekay was becoming distressed. While neither of them were raising their voices, they were plainly quarrelling. Harriet was squarely positioned between them. How nearly Hymie could have been right.

'Hymie, you're wrong, I didn't lose my virginity to Harriet.'

Hymie's foot involuntarily came off the accelerator and the car veered momentarily towards the wrong side of the road before he hastily corrected his steering and pushed down on the accelerator again. 'Shit, Peekay, what are you saying?'

Peekay told Hymie about the night with Togger, retelling it in some detail, taking the time to move away from the quarrel, including the funny bits, forcing Hymie to laugh.

It was a vastly expanded version of the story he'd told when he'd arrived back at Oxford with a broken nose. Then he'd simply recounted to Hymie how he and Togger had been involved in a fight in a nightclub. It had been the truth as far as it went. Peekay couldn't explain exactly, even to himself, why he'd kept the full story from Hymie. It had been so wonderful with Carmen, he instinctively didn't want to debase it. He knew Hymie would want every detail and that, in the retelling, the components of the evening would be reduced to what they probably were: a sleazy nightclub for perverts serviced by a bunch of hard-faced female drink hustlers who were willing to take off their clothes to a taped sound track so they could make the rather sad claim of being in showbiz. It hadn't been like that at all. To Peekay it had been a magical evening which could never happen again. In losing his virginity to Carmen he had also lost his innocence. Henceforth he would see the peeling paint and the purple bruises on fleshy thighs, the greasy satin skirts and shark-tooth lines of black thread where the fishnet stocking had been drawn together in hasty repair.

Finally Peekay got to the part in the story where he told Hymie of his seduction by Carmen. He had kept her relationship to Togger out of the story, sensing that Togger would want this. He painted the scene of her strip-tease, hoping that Hymie might isolate it in his imagination, the one contrast to the surrounding sleaze. But he knew, in reality, that this was unlikely. He retold the fight briefly and concluded with Carmen's offer to take him home.

'And so you see, I never got what I wanted. I might as well have lost my virginity to one of the whores in the mines. I got laid by a stripper in a cheap nightclub for drunks and perverts.' Peekay felt the sudden sting of shame as he denigrated Carmen's status and generosity in an attempt to mend Hymie's hurt.

Hymie glanced over at Peekay. In the darkness of the car cabin Peekay could only guess at his expression, but when he spoke his voice was relaxed. 'You bastard, Peekay! You kept all this from me?'

'Ja, well, you know . . .' Peekay knew Hymie wouldn't pursue it. He'd conclude Peekay was ashamed of the manner in which he'd been deflowered. 'Which brings us back to Harriet,' Peekay said, knowing he must force the discussion to some conclusion.

'I'm sorry, Peekay. I was wrong. I guess I was hurt. I wanted to think that your motive was simple penis blunder, the cock erect, blind to reason.' Then he added lamely, 'It helped explain my own inadequacy.'

'You're in love with her, aren't you, Hymie?'

Hymie was silent for a moment. 'Yes,' he paused. 'That must be hard for you to understand.'

Peekay put his hand on Hymie's shoulder. 'It would almost help if it was. But no, it isn't. I feel like a proper bastard.'

'Peekay, you are a proper bastard. Not because you stole my woman. Harriet makes up her own mind about her sleeping partner. Besides, as you now know, I was never a contender and never owned her. You're a proper bastard because you didn't see the possibility of my friendship with her outside of sex. What about all the other sensibilities? Sex doesn't make Harriet unique. Though I can't vouch for it, she's probably pretty interchangeable with a thousand women in that respect. Sex is the least unique aspect of a woman. Her uniqueness lies in dozens of other ways which attracted her to me, made me love her. You're a bastard for not understanding this fully.'

He grinned suddenly. 'Forgive me, Peekay, but when you've got an inactive dick you begin to realise that love has more to it than coitus. I hope you'll not spoil the relationship I have with Harriet by getting your aggressive cock in the way.'

Hymie had spoken without raising his voice and with his eyes mostly on the road. The afternoon had closed in and he now turned on the car lights. The darkness within the car and the throb of the engine seemed to lock them together in time.

'Pull over, Hymie. Stop the car,' Peekay asked.

Hymie braked and pulled the car over to the edge of the road. They were close to the outskirts of Oxford. Peekay embraced Hymie silently, then pulled away smiling.

Hymie laughed suddenly. 'Shit you look terrible!'

'But I feel great!' Peekay replied. 'Bloody woman, she's got us both by the short and curlies.'

Hymie laughed. 'She's only a woman. If we combine our resources and work together we may just get the better of her.'

Harriet's 'Two Horses with Naked Man' and her boxer, 'Man in Peculiar Limbo', both finished with shellac for lack of money to cast them in bronze, were exhibited in Helen Lessore's Beaux Arts Gallery in London in the summer. This was recognition that here was a new sculptor to be taken seriously. On the strength of the exhibition she'd been commissioned to make an eagle lectern for a church in Dresden, a gift from Anglo-American Catholics as a gesture of appeasement for the fire-bombing of this most beautiful of medieval German cities during World War Two. Harriet had also received a commission for a big head of Christ for St Martin's Church in Swindon.

Harriet's relationship with the two young men seemed to change little. Peekay learned to live with her fluctuating libido which seemed to become active only when she wasn't totally absorbed in her work. She seemed to share the two of them equally and if Peekay enjoyed the occasional use of her bed, Hymie was never made to feel unwanted. It was a peculiar relationship but she contrived to manage it effortlessly. Harriet had an ingenuousness about her, and as the social and working lives of the two men were almost identical, this was made all the more easy. The friends appeared more as a perfect threesome than as a loving twosome with an odd man out. Peekay's only real opportunity to be alone with Harriet was when he posed for her.

Peekay was well on the way to challenging for the British Empire Welterweight title. Dutch had scheduled a fight a month to take him up to a title fight by Christmas, a year after his match with Habib. The trainer had instituted a regime of road work to strengthen Peekay's legs and to keep him at a level of optimum fitness. Four times a week Peekay would run the five miles from Oxford to Cow Cottage, where he'd arrive in a lather of sweat and undress to pose for Harriet.

Harriet didn't seem as interested in the female form as she did the male. She readily confessed that it was the male form which gave her the impetus and energy for her purely sensuous approach to sculpture. Sometimes after making love Harriet would prop herself on one elbow and run her hand over Peekay's body. She seemed to be feeling it, though not with the practised eye of the sculptor, for her eyes were shut. She seemed to be sensing his body through the tips of her fingers and feeding the parts she touched directly into her memory.

Peekay discovered that Harriet simply couldn't resist him when his boxer's body glistened with sweat from the run. She would feel the same way watching him fight, but then her attention was directed onto the sketch pad she always carried with her. She was beginning to assemble the hundreds of sketched poses she would need for a huge tableau of boxers, twelve figures in all, six of them the same boxer in different fighting poses against six different opponents. Peekay was, of course, her consistent boxer, while his opponents would be chosen from her sketches as he worked his way up the ladder to the world welterweight championship.

Togger had also posed for one of the boxing models, Harriet sketching him in the gym when Peekay and he worked out together. He'd promised to come up to Cow Cottage in early February to 'pose proper', when he could take a couple of days off from his job as a tally clerk on the docks.

'Blimey, Peekay, you positive I've got to pose in the nuddy, in me bleedin' birthday suit, an' all? Not even a jock strap?'

'Harriet is not one to compromise, Togger.'

Togger, looking gloomily into the distance, sucked absently at his pint. 'What if I get a hard-on?' he asked suddenly.

'You get an erection, you bastard, I'll smash your teeth in,' Peekay laughed. 'It's art, Togger. One day Harriet's going to be famous and you'll be in a museum or gallery. How'd you be, standing in the Tate with a dirty great erection! Imagine a teacher brings her class in for a visit and stops next to you, "Look children, this is Togger Brown, Homo Erectus!"'

'Homo? Who's a bleedin' homo?'

They both laughed, but Togger was still worried. 'She doesn't touch ya and things, does she? I mean, run 'er hands over you to make measurements and that sorta thing? I don't think I could stand that!'

Life as a professional boxer as well as a student had to be carefully managed. While Hymie took care of all the contracts and gathered the analytical information on Peekay's opponents, Dutch required that Peekay work out three times a week in the London gym as well as fight once every month somewhere in Britain. On two occasions, Peekay had fought in Brussels and once in Paris. It meant a tight weekly schedule for Peekay, who had no intention of letting up on his studies. Despite his reappraisal of Oxford he wanted a first and this meant planning his routine very carefully. Mostly he'd drive down to London in the Ford Prefect, where he'd do a three-hour work-out, which included a sparring session, usually with Togger, but sometimes with any of the middleweights who, aware of the lesson Peekay had given Peter Best, were always anxious to get into the ring with him. Then he'd drive back to Oxford, getting back to Magdalen just before midnight.

While he had almost no time for leisure in his second year at Oxford, Togger and Peekay had formed the habit of having a pint of bitter and a game of darts in the Thomas à Becket downstairs after training.

Hymie had arranged a non-title fight with the British Empire Champion, Iron Bar Barunda, a welterweight from Ghana who now lived in the British Isles. Peekay couldn't fight for the British title because he was not twenty-one, but he could enter for the British Empire title. Both were held by Iron Bar Barunda. Barunda wouldn't put the bigger of his two titles on the line which meant Peekay couldn't get past him in the line-up for fighters he had to beat eventually to get to Spoonbill Jackson. Hymie had managed to negotiate a non-title event with virtually the whole purse going to the black boxer. If Peekay beat him, Hymie's contract stipulated that they'd get a crack at the title in December. Only three continental welterweights were rated higher than Barunda; if Peekay could get past them he was in line for a top North American fighter as well as Soap Dish Jurez, the Cuban, and Manuel Ortez, the Mexican; both of these were welters who were rated contenders for a future world title fight. The fight was to take place during the Oxford summer vacation. Peekay and Hymie had managed to stay at Harriet's aunt's flat in Knightsbridge while Peekay prepared for the fight. Harriet herself had been invited to the University at Aix-en-Provence to teach for five weeks and would miss the bout.

Harriet's Aunt Tom had grown very fond of both young men and since her return to England had become an avid boxing fan. Dressed in an immaculate dinner suit she'd attended all Peekay's fights. Her brilliant henna-coloured Eton crop could be picked out in the centre of the Odd Bodleians where she sat with a set of bongo drums between her knees and a thin black Spanish cheroot dangling from her lips. Bongo drums are not exactly African, but Aunt Tom was a skilled and versatile drummer and used it to beat out the rhythm for the *Concerto for the Great Southland*, which had by now, along with the Odd Bodleians, become a famous feature of all of Peekay's fights.

Togger and Peekay were in the Thomas à Becket after a training session when Fred, the ex-pug they'd met on their first day, approached Peekay with Dutch Holland.

'This letter come when you was away. Nice lookin' young lady bring it around.'

'Oh yes! Very ris-kay!' Togger said. ' 'Ere, you gunna open it, ain't ya?'

Peekay assumed a haughty look, mimicking Togger's accent. 'Do yer mind? This is private mail, this is.'

Togger looked crestfallen and Peekay laughed. 'Here, you open it,' he said, handing Togger the envelope.

'You serious then?'

'Ja, sure, go on, read it man.'

Togger peeled the back flap open very carefully, opening the letter inside he sniffed at it, 'Cor, it don't half pong!'

'C'mon, Togger, what's it say,' Peekay laughed.

Togger began to read.

Dear Peekay,

How are you? My brother saw you at Earls Court and says you're awfully good. You never did phone me. Maybe you did and I was out? Anyway, I remember you well. Have you got a girlfriend?

If you want you can call me at the Dolls' Hospital HAM 7295 on Wednesday we close early, 3.15. We could go for a drink or something. My mum thinks you're smashing, even if you are a toff. My dad says there's no future going with a boxer, but I told him to mind his own business!

Ta, ta, then, I must get my beauty sleep.

Love and kisses,

Doris

P.S. My best part is still in the front!

P.P.S. Now you'll think I'm being saucy!!!

'I reckon you're in like bleedin' Flynn, my son.' Togger paused, flapping his pale eyelids, 'Oh yes, very ris-kay!'

'Christ, Togger! Quit that dumb expression, will you? I know exactly what to do, I'll call her, say can she get hold of Gladys, Togger wants to know.'

'Don't you bleedin' dare! Some of me mates saw me that day we went dancin', I only just got me reputation back. Seriously, Peekay, wotcha gunna do? I mean, 'Arriet's away, ain't she? She's been gone how long, four weeks?' Togger stroked his chin, 'But I suppose you gotta stay faithful like. Mind, she has got a lovely pair a tits.'

Peekay reached over and took the letter from Togger's hands. 'I don't know, we'll see, I've got to go. Aunt Tom's taking me to the Festival Hall. Yehudi Menuhin is playing the Brahms Violin Concerto amongst other musical niceties a peasant like you wouldn't appreciate.'

Peekay arrived back at the flat in Knightsbridge just in time to change for the concert. Aunt Tom handed him a letter from Harriet, the second he'd received since she'd left for the South of France. He didn't have time to read it until he climbed into bed.

Harriet wrote well, but in snatches of thought. She'd been asked to stay another month and felt it was too good an opportunity to miss. What did Peekay think? She'd come under the influence of a sculptor named Claude Shonneborg, who'd studied under Giacomeffi. Shonneborg's name seemed to crop up much too often in the letter and Peekay hoped that Harriet's preoccupation with her work would as usual have reduced her libido to a barely flickering flame. Although by the end of the letter he'd convinced himself this was not the case and promised himself rather smugly that he'd call Doris in the morning.

'Hello, Hammersmith Dolls' 'ospital, who is it?' a young woman's voice answered.

'Howzit, Doris? It's Peekay. You know, Babychams with a dash? I got your letter.'

'Hallo, Peekay.'

Peekay cleared his throat, 'Hurrph, it just happens to be Wednesday, what say we have a drink after your work?'

'Why, that's smashin', Peekay, I'd like that very much. There's a little club just round the corner what's very nice, very quiet an' all.'

Peekay took down the address. It was too late to turn back now, he told himself. He decided to run around the perimeter of Hyde Park. It would take his mind off Harriet and the Giacomeffi apprentice, Claude Shitbag. His pulse actually quickened as he thought of the possibility of being unfaithful to Harriet. Peekay decided he'd run further, to include Kensington Gardens and to run past the round pond again. He didn't quite know why, he'd always imagined the round pond in *Peter Pan* was set amongst trees, big old oak trees and birch and elm, so that you came upon it suddenly, unexpectedly, glimpsing slivers of silver through low hanging branches. He'd been terribly disappointed to find it was simply a round pond with cement edges set into a stretch of grass, not a bit romantic, in fact as ponds go it was rather bleak and had absolutely no character and wasn't even on the Serpentine.

He wondered briefly whether Doris's tits would disappoint him the second time around. After all, he'd been a virgin when they'd seemed so wonderful. Perhaps, like the round pond, his imagination had overworked them.

Peekay arrived at the Dolls' Hospital at precisely three o'clock. The window of the shop was filled with broken dolls. Separate dolls' limbs, torsos, heads, arms and legs, a doll's graveyard. There were dolls with no eyes, hollow sockets in broken and cracked heads. Dolls with scarred and broken cheeks, dolls with only one blue eye, half open. Headless dolls and armless trunks, bits of elastic sticking out of holed armpits. They filled the window to a height of about two feet, legs and arms and faces, bodies piled together like victims of a massacre, pushed into a heap by a tyrant bulldozer.

Directly above the pile of broken bodies hung several swings made with green silk tassels suspended above the eyelevel behind a scalloped, dark green painted pelmet, its edges trimmed with gold. Across the length of the pelmet, painted in old-fashioned gold script, were the words *Dolls' Hospital*, and directly underneath in smaller, neat type, *H. Rubens, prop.* On each of the swings sat a beautifully restored doll.

The centre doll, a dark haired beauty, was the most magnificent of them all. She wore a pink organza dress with a broad ribbon of slightly darker pink velvet about her waist. Her eyes were a brilliant violet colour, and seemed to follow Peekay, as though aware of his rude curiosity. Unlike the moulded, heavy lashed, vacant expressions of the other, golden-haired dolls, the centre doll's face seemed to have been carved by a craftsman to give it a unique character. Even her limbs seemed different. Her legs and arms were chubby and realistically baby-like with her hands exquisitely carved. Her feet were contained in pink velvet slippers embroidered with gold thread, a tiny gold rose knot held the cross strap on each slipper. The doll held a plain white ivory card, about six inches by five, propped on her lap. On the card, in a large copperplate hand, was written: *Old dolls made beautiful again*.

Peekay went into the shop.

The interior was about thirty feet wide with an old-fashioned wooden mahogany counter that ran the width of the shop. Directly behind the counter were six carpenter's work benches, an old-fashioned Singer industrial sewing machine and an equally old wood working lathe.

The large room was bathed in brilliant bluish light from light boxes above each work bench. The effect was of a place with too much light, it was as though the owner of the shop could abide no shadows about him.

The shop appeared empty and the work benches deserted when a small man struggling into a navy overcoat which seemed to reach almost to the floor walked from the doorway of a small partitioned office at the furthermost point in the room. He looked up and hurried towards Peekay, doing up the top buttons of his overcoat.

'Please sir, we are closing now the shop.' He spread his hands in a gesture which seemed to suggest that, should Peekay make an objection, he regretted there was nothing he could do. He wore a homburg hat and round, old-fashioned gold-rimmed glasses, a white shirt with celluloid collar and a black silk tie.

The total appearance was of a small, neat, clean-shaven man who was being dragged down by the weight of his overcoat. The cuffs of his neatly pressed blue serge trousers showed no more than three inches below the hem of the coat.

'Good afternoon, sir, I've come to pick up Miss . . . er, Doris.' Peekay suddenly realised that he'd either forgotten or had never known Doris's surname.

The little man visibly relaxed and he dug into his overcoat pocket and triumphantly produced a pair of leather gloves, much as a conjuror might produce a live rabbit. He held the gloves up for Peekay to see and, turning, flapped them in the direction of a door at the back of the room. 'Doris? So you want Doris.' He seemed to be thinking. 'Ah yes, that is nice! Miss Mobbs! Is here a young man!' He called in a voice that carried surprisingly, even though he didn't appear to have raised it.

'Coming, Mr Rubens!' Peekay heard Doris answer back.

Mr Rubens turned back to Peekay, as though only he could possibly have heard her reply. 'She is coming,' he said reassuringly, 'you must wait now, please.' He dug his right hand into his coat pocket again. This time he produced a large bunch of keys, holding them up for Peekay to see. Peekay wasn't quite sure whether he ought to applaud.

'Thank you, sir.'

Mr Rubens nodded. 'Excuse me, young man,' and he moved over to the far end of the counter and punched the cash register open and removed a small wad of one-pound notes. He licked his thumb absently and counted the notes, aloud in German, to thirty-six.

'Thirty-six,' Peekay said suddenly. He'd been counting with the old man and surprised himself when he too declared the final tally out loud.

Mr Rubens's eyebrows shot up, 'So! You are German?' He pronounced the word *Chermin*.

Peekay was embarrassed. 'I'm sorry, sir, I didn't mean to intrude. When I was young I had a friend who taught me to count in German. It was during the war. I was just seeing if I,' he smiled, 'remembered.'

Mr Rubens looked up at Peekay sternly. Bending over the cash register his glasses had slipped halfway down the bridge of his nose and he now looked over the top of them. 'This Germin, he was a Jew?'

'No, sir, he wasn't.'

'A Germin who is not a Jew is teaching you in the war?'

Peekay didn't know why, but he felt compelled to explain to Mr Rubens that Doc hadn't been a Nazi, was the furthermost thing you could get from being a Nazi. 'He was a musician, a professor of pianoforte. It was in Africa.'

'Humph! Who played also maybe Wagner?' Mr Rubens snorted, obviously unconvinced.

'No sir, Beethoven and Mozart, he wasn't at all fond of Wagner, he found him too Teutonic. I don't think my friend was much of a German.'

'Humph!' Mr Rubens undid the top button on his overcoat and, sliding his hand into the lefthand side, withdrew a leather pocket book. He unzipped the wallet and flattening out the wad of notes slipped them full length into the pocket book, completing the task and re-zipping the wallet just as Doris appeared.

'Hello, Peekay, you two met then?'

'Well no, not officially,' Peekay said.

'Mr Rubens, this is my friend, Peekay. Peekay, this is my boss, Mr Rubens!'

'Ha! He is learning to count from Germans!' Mr Rubens said abruptly.

Doris looked from Peekay to the little man and back to Peekay, her expression bemused. Peekay shrugged almost imperceptibly. 'You better be goin' then, Mr Rubens, or you'll get to Ladbrokes too late to place a bet on the four o'clock at Epsom.'

The effect of this announcement brought a look of panic onto the little man's face. He grabbed at the region of his chest where he'd recently stowed his wallet. 'The Hans Kellerman!' he exclaimed.

'Here, give us the keys, I'll lock her away. Where's your brolly, then?' Doris sighed. 'Stay here, I'll bring that too.' She unlocked the two wooden doors which formed the back of the shop window. Leaning into the window she carefully removed the centre doll from the swing and cradled it in her arms. 'Give me the safe key, then.' She extended her hand.

Mr Rubens once again fished in his wallet and produced a surprisingly large brass key. Doris took the key and went back to the small office in the corner.

'It's a beautiful doll,' Peekay remarked to Mr Rubens.

At the sound of his voice Mr Rubens turned, surprised Peekay was still there. 'This is a Hans Kellerman. When he is making even one doll, it is not a doll, it is a miracle!'

Peekay's heart began to pound. Togger had said something about Carmen's doll having a brass plate on the sole of one foot with the 'geezer's name who made it, Hans somebody or other.'

'Did Kellerman sign his name on the dolls he made? On a brass plate on the sole of the foot?'

Mr Rubens was surprised by Peekay's question. 'You have seen a Hans Kellerman before?'

'No, just heard of one.' Instinct told Peekay to explain no further.

Doris returned and handed Mr Rubens back the key to the safe. ' 'Ere, hold your wrist out, you've forgotten your watch again.'

Mr Rubens pushed back the sleeve of his coat, taking with it the starched cuff of his shirt. Doris strapped a watch on to his wrist, about three inches above it Peekay observed a dark tattoo number on his arm.

Mr Rubens looked up at precisely that moment and saw the expression on Peekay's face. 'Already I have been counted in German, young man,' he said softly.

Doris glanced at his wristwatch before releasing his arm. 'Blimey, it's twenty-past, I'm workin' in me own time!' Turning, she approached the front doors and opening a large fuse box at the side of a door she rapidly killed half a dozen switches with the ball of her thumb, plunging the shop into darkness. She unlatched the two doors as Mr Rubens preceded them down the steps. The old man locked up the shop.

'Good night, Miss Mobbs, thank you.' He turned to Peekay and gave him a slight nod, 'Good night, young man, I think it is better that you count in English.' He walked away.

'C'mon then, Peekay!' Doris linked her arm into his and clung to him as they crossed the street. He imagined he could feel the pressure of her marvellous left tit right through his duffel coat.

TWENTY

Hymie took his finals at law in June of 1954. He'd made the decision to remain in Britain to prepare Peekay for his title fight in America towards the end of the following year. *Ring* magazine named Peekay fifth in the world rankings, but with a string of good wins to his credit it was getting close to the time when they could talk to Jake 'Spoonbill' Jackson's manager, a New York Irishman named O'Rourke, and notify the New York Boxing Commission and the World Boxing Council they intended to challenge for a title fight.

During the following year when Peekay would complete his degree, Hymie planned to travel to South Africa fairly frequently to prepare their entry into a law practice in Johannesburg. They hoped to work in practice for a year until they were admitted to the bar. When this happened they would either buy the practice outright or purchase the major share in a partnership arrangement.

Peekay had advanced up the boxing ladder and had taken the British Empire title from Iron Bar Barunda though the black man still retained his British title. Togger had also fought Iron Bar Barunda two months later and had been narrowly beaten. A return bout, this time with the British title at stake, was scheduled for September.

Trinity term at Oxford ends in June and the new university year begins with the Michaelmas term in October. In the four months between June and October Peekay had five fights, winning against all the top European welters as well as the highly rated Italian contender, Bruno Biseffi, whom he'd fought on the same bill as Togger's title fight at Harringay.

Both boxers won, Togger taking the coveted British Welterweight title from Iron Bar Barunda in a closely fought ten-rounder. It was a popular decision. Togger had developed into a very skilful boxer and was considered to be London's own. Peekay could barely contain his delight at his friend's win and later Hymie was to blame the fact that Peekay only won his fight against the Italian on points on this distraction.

Carmen had come over from Paris, where she had been working as a model, for the fight, and Hymie had taken them all to the Savoy for supper and champagne afterwards. It was here that Carmen met Harriet. Despite Peekay's fears, the two girls immediately took to each other and spent most of the evening chatting happily, Harriet deciding towards the end of the evening, when they'd all had a bit too much champagne, that she'd like to make a sculpture of Carmen.

Peekay's points win over the Italian in London had come after a string of knock-outs and the Italians took great heart by this. When Peekay fought Bisetti again, this time for the vacant European title, he faced a very partisan Turin crowd. It proved to be a damned good thing he knocked the Italian out in the ninth, for no matter how far ahead he may have been on points, the excitable Italians would never have stood for yet another points decision going to Peekay.

The win over Bisetti made Peekay the top welterweight outside of North America. Peekay became the darling of European boxing and the only boxer around who looked like bringing a world championship belt back from across the Atlantic.

The Odd Bodleians were present at every one of Peekay's fights including the one in Italy. If the Turin crowd had been somewhat partisan, this did not include the Odd Bodleians who received a standing ovation. Hymie had arranged for a record to be cut of *Concerto for the Great Southland* sung by the Odd Bodleians, which had done well in the UK and now became a great hit in Italy as well as Germany, but proved to be only a modest success in France.

In Germany it became known as a composition by the famous twenties concert pianist, Professor Karl Von Vollensteen, a romantic figure in the twenties who'd disappeared from the concert stages of Europe after a mysterious illness, never to be heard from again. The story of Doc and Peekay, much of it exaggerated, appeared in *Stern* magazine with a picture of Peekay on the cover. Doc's shadow had reached a long way from the crystal cave of Africa where he lay.

By the end of 1954, Peekay's name was beginning to appear regularly in *Ring* magazine where he was increasingly mentioned as a serious contender for the welterweight crown. Only the Cuban, Soap Dish Jurez and the Mexican welter, Manuel Ortez, remained as the bridge to Madison Square Garden in New York, and the chance to get a crack at the world champ, Jake 'Spoonbill' Jackson.

Setting up and promoting these two bridging fights, and the elimination fight with an American welterweight, took up a lot of Hymie's time in the first months of 1955. He wanted at least two of the three fights in Britain. Peekay, doing his final year at law, hadn't the time to travel either to North America or Cuba. Nor could they yet afford to go.

The fight against Soap Dish Jurez took place at Harringay Arena in North London and was a sell-out. Soap Dish proved to be well named; he was a slippery customer to handle, like Peekay a consummate boxer. It was only Peekay's power in both hands which finally wore him down, knocking him down three times in the eleventh round, whereupon the referee stopped the fight, awarding it to Peekay on a TKO.

Manuel Ortez, whom Peekay fought two months later, proved an entirely different kettle of fish. He was Habib all over again, but younger, faster and fitter. He'd gone the distance with Jake 'Spoonbill' Jackson three months earlier in an unexpected title bid and while he'd lost in the eyes of all three judges, the final points score separating the boxers had only added up to a three-round superiority for the champion.

His tearaway, non-stop fighting style was difficult to counter. A slum kid who'd fought his way out of the tin shanties of Mexico City, Ortez was as tough and determined a fighter as ever climbed into a ring. He fought as though his life depended on the outcome, which in a way, it did. Peekay had connected with half-a-dozen beautiful straight rights which should have slowed him down, but he just kept coming, forcing Peekay onto the back foot, careful to stay out of the corners where Ortez was devastatingly effective. He was a boxer who used everything he had, including his elbows and head whenever he could get away with it, which was often enough to be disconcerting, so Peekay had to be careful not to lose his cool.

But by the eleventh round Ortez had used up too many punches and taken too many hard blows to the body and he started to slow down. Midway through the final round Peekay caught him on the ropes and finished him off with a Solly Goldman thirteen. The Mexican boxer was out for the count before he hit the canvas.

Peekay was only one fight shy of a shot at the world title and *Ring* magazine recognised him as the number one contender. The following day his face appeared on the front cover of most of the Sunday papers in Britain and every Sunday paper in South Africa. He had become a national hero in both countries, the undisputed challenger for the world welterweight title.

On the *stoep* of Mr Nguni's home in Sophiatown, Gideon Mandoma held a copy of the Johannesburg *Sunday Times* up for Tandia to see. They'd both been invited to lunch and Gideon sat with Tandia on the veranda while Mr Nguni, his manager and also prominent African boxing promoter, held a business meeting with two Indians who had arrived unannounced from out of town. Juicey Fruit Mambo had the Packard parked outside the house no more than a few feet away and, as usual, was busy polishing it. He wasn't yet sure how he felt about Tandia's attraction to the Zulu boxer and if Gideon tried anything on he wanted to be around if he was needed.

'My brother will be the next world champion!' Gideon declared happily. The picture, which must have been taken at some earlier fight, showed Peekay with his arm up in a salute with the lion's tooth showing clearly around his neck. 'See, he has my luck, my brother wears my luck, he will be the next world champion, for sure, you will see!' He shook his head in admiration. 'Hayi, Hayi, Hayi, surely he is the leader of the people? He is the one, the Tadpole Angel.'

Tandia was shocked as Gideon Mandoma handed her the paper. Holding it up in front of her so he couldn't see her expression she stared angrily at the front page photograph of Peekay with his hands held high. She struggled to regain her composure so when she spoke her voice was soft, almost plaintive. 'He is a white man, Gideon. He will betray you. How can he be our leader?'

Gideon looked surprised. 'He is my brother, Tandia. His heart is not white, his heart is same like me,' he said softly.

Tandia's hand was shaking as she handed him back the paper, but Gideon didn't seem to notice. 'And you?' she asked. 'Are you not the Tadpole Angel? Patel said you were the best, even better than him, I swear it's true.'

Gideon laughed. 'This is not for me to say, Tandia. The people, they have decided. I have fought my brother and I have lost. Peekay, he is the Tadpole Angel, it is in the smoke and in the bones.'

Tandia brought her hands up and clasped her head. Despite her timidness she was a city girl and Gideon's superstition shocked her. 'My God, Gideon! You don't still believe the Sangoma?' She knew instantly she'd said the wrong thing.

Gideon Mandoma spun around. He'd known this beautiful young girl only a few months. Tomorrow she returned to Natal with Mama Tequila, where she would study law. He didn't want to fall in love with her. It wasn't convenient. It wasn't in his plans. There was too much to do. The ANC was too important, and so was his education and his boxing career. He didn't need a wife. He didn't even need a girlfriend. There were plenty of clean women he could sleep with. It was better to just send her away, forget about her. She was questioning his beliefs; the tribal blood in her had dried up, she was a city girl not afraid of the power of the spirits. Better to just send her away, to say nothing.

Gideon was a Zulu who did not allow a woman to speak to him like this, question him in these matters. He felt obliged to put her in her place. 'Shut your mouth, woman. There are things you don't understand, you hear? Peekay and me, we have suckled at the same woman's breast. Go now, I am tired of your talk!' He reached down and grabbed the newspaper from the floor. Hiding behind it, he pretended to read.

'See, already we fight over this white man. Please, Gideon, forgive me!'

Juicey Fruit Mambo was suddenly at her side. 'Go away!' she shouted at him in sudden childish frustration. Juicey Fruit backed away, stepping down the front steps slowly. He'd heard Gideon's rebuke. It was fair. Mandoma was heir to a chiefdom and a man; Tandia ought not to upset him. Nevertheless, the little Zulu had better not put a hand on her or he would break his bones.

Tandia was terrified. She loved Mandoma passionately and had done so from the first moment she'd set eyes on him in the darkened Odin cinema when he'd demolished the inept Irishman. She didn't want to lose him, although she knew she must, for the time being anyway. She would study law and come back to be at his side. She had worked it all out in her head. Please God, don't let it end like this, she thought. She *must* leave to return to Bluey Jay with her relationship with Mandoma intact, ready for the next time they met. Next to her hate, he was the most important thing in her life. She had joined the ANC, though Mandoma had insisted this be done secretly. 'You are a student, it must not be known,' he had said. 'Verwoerd's Bantu Education Act will soon remove all blacks from white education. Students who belong to the ANC will be the first to go.'

'I am sorry, Gideon. I didn't mean it, I take it back, all of it. You must forgive me, I am only a poor, stupid woman.'

Gideon lowered the paper slowly and looked sternly at Tandia. These city girls have a lot to learn about respect and the space where a man sits, he thought to himself. 'It is not right that you talk like this, Tandia. I am glad you take back your thoughts.'

Tandia broke into a brilliant smile, though she was afraid of the quiet, beautiful Zulu boxer who would one day be a chief. Despite her terror, her voice was calm and soft when she spoke. 'No, not all of them. One part I don't take back.' She took a deep breath. 'You must fight Peekay and you will win. Then *you* will be the Tadpole Angel.'

Despite himself, Gideon laughed. 'My right hand cannot fight my left hand, we are brothers.' He paused, his eyes grew soft as he looked at the beautiful young woman who stood in front of him. 'This thing will happen if it will happen, it is not for me to say. First I must fight Jannie Geldenhuis.' He grinned. 'This one, he is not my brother. I will wait until he is better, then I will fight him again. This time we shall see who is white and who is black.'

Tandia went cold. The spectre of Geldenhuis loomed up in her subconscious, almost paralysing her. Her fear of the white police lieutenant was so great that she thought him invincible. 'Please, Gideon, he is evil, you must not fight him, he has too much hate, even more than me.'

Gideon grinned. 'I do not have to read the smoke and throw the bones to know this, Tandia. I must fight him because I am a man and a Zulu, and my turn has come.'

Hymie was worried about Peekay and he took his concern to Dutch Holland. They were nailbitingly close to challenging for the world title. 'Dutch, Peekay's won the last seven fights on a KO, except his first fight with Bisetti. Each time he's been behind on points coming into the ninth round. Christ man, Peekay is one of the most skilful boxers in the world and he's having to rely on a knock-out for a win?'

'There ain't nothin' much better than a knock-out, my son. How bleedin' else do you want the lad to win? He's had fifteen pro fights, he's won thirteen by knock-out. He's beaten the best fighters in the world bar the Yanks. This weight division ain't exactly filled with chumps neither; there's more good welterweights around at the moment than you can shake a stick at.' Dutch spread his cocktail-sausage hands. 'Blimey, what's got into you? There ain't been a contender, in any bleedin' weight division, in twenty years who done what our lad's done! Not even Joe soddin' Louis.'

Hymie was not convinced. 'Dutch, listen to me, man. Jackson is a boxer, a consummate boxer. They don't come any better. Like Peekay, he's got a punch in both hands but he can box just as well. I won't say he's a better boxer than Peekay, but *Ring* magazine says he is and Budd Shulberg says he is and Nat Fleischer in an editorial last month says he's the fastest and best exponent of the skill of boxing he's ever seen. You know what he calls him? "The Ghost with a hammer in each hand!" He reckons he was coasting against Ortez. We have to accept that in terms of boxing, Jackson's practically the immaculate conception!

'Peekay's come in from behind in seven of his thirteen fights to win. And three of them have been his last four fights. With a guy like Spoonbill Jackson at the other end of your gloves that's bullshit boxing. Peekay's not going to wear him down then take him out in a late round! No bloody way!'

Dutch was reluctant to listen; he'd never taken kindly to Hymie's advice. Peekay's success had added greatly to his own prestige as a trainer, and he knew Hymie was right, but he couldn't yet bring himself to agree with his criticism. 'I'm only his trainer. You two talk all the time, why don't you talk to him, let me know what the lad says?'

Peekay was studying for his finals in June and Hymie was reluctant to talk to him about the problem. He knew Peekay wanted a first and he reasoned they'd have nearly four months after the exams with only two fights, a preliminary against a highly rated American welterweight. The likely boxer was a Marine stationed in Florida, a negro fighter originally from Harlem who went by the unlikely name of Jasper 'King Coon' Sinder. If he beat Sinder, that left the title fight.

Peekay tried not to think about the title fight, which proved impossible. You can't think about something everyday, almost every hour of your life and then dismiss it while you study for your exams. He was studying hard, working with E.W. every day, his tutor anxious for his charge to do brilliantly in his final exams. Peekay was forced to fight Ortez during the last month of cramming and he'd found it hard to concentrate on his studies as well as the fight. He'd won against the Mexican, but tediously again with a knockout in the final round. He knew Hymie was worried about him. It had been a torrid year with no easy opponents; every fight had sapped him, making it hard to recover fully for the next one. Nothing had changed, except his body was tired.

Peekay began to ready his head for Jackson, but his concentration was split. He had to get his exams out of the way first.

During Peekay's last year at Oxford Harriet increasingly drew away from him. Her study of the group of boxers, completed when Peekay had fought Bisetti, had received wide acclaim. It had been cast in bronze and purchased by the town fathers for the atrium of a new sports stadium to be built in Louisville, Kentucky.

Harriet's next commission proved to be the one on which her later international fame would be built. The same church in Dresden for whom she had created the altar piece commissioned her to do the piece she had dreamed of for so long, the Walking Madonna. The sculpture would stand nearly eight feet tall in the grounds of the new church and was by far the most important piece she had been commissioned to do.

As Harriet's creative juices rose so her libido fell. It was not that she consciously felt any differently about Peekay, but her preoccupation with the task ahead so completely filled her conscious thought and possessed her that Peekay was simply squeezed out. The Walking Madonna was the first major female piece she had done; it was also the fulfilment of a childhood dream, no different for her than the world welterweight title was for Peekay. She became almost completely introspective, the voice within her sufficient for her emotional needs.

Peekay's split with Harriet finally came halfway through March. One day, Peekay ran the five miles to Cow Cottage to find Harriet in one of her dark moods, almost unable to talk. He worked silently for an hour in the garden. It was spring and after two years of loving care the cottage garden was back to its best, though in the past weeks both of them had neglected it and it needed weeding, which Peekay now set about doing. Peekay could never quite get over spring in England. The day before he'd driven from London back to Oxford in Hymie's little Prefect. The tulips had been out in the parks in a brilliant parade of red, yellow and white. Clumps of daffodils and crocuses were growing haphazardly out of the grass while bluebells spread an azure picnic cloth under dark old oaks. Peekay had thought of the snow three months earlier, and had imagined how the flowers had waited under a cold white blanket until a day such as this one, when they'd pushed with all their might and then shaken free their pretty heads to announce that spring had officially arrived.

A shadow fell over where Peekay squatted beside a patch of sweet basil. He was pinching the small white blossom from the stems so the plants wouldn't go to seed early. He looked up to see Harriet standing beside him.

'Dear, dear Peekay, you must understand it isn't you. I love you so very much, but you must wait until this thing is out of me. I can't go to your fights anymore. I can't include your fighting in my head at present.' She paused, waiting for Peekay to react, but Peekay was too old a hand at camouflage to reveal his feelings. He was silent, gathering his thoughts so that he would say the right thing, say it sotto voce, easily, without emotion, forgiving her, understanding, his hurt completely concealed.

Finally he stood, wiping his soiled hands down the sides of his rugby shorts, like a small boy caught making mud pies. 'Don't worry, Harriet, I do understand really.' He'd put his hand out towards her, but she'd withdrawn from it, taking a step backwards.

'Please, Peekay. Please don't.'

Peekay had called the Dolls' Hospital the following day and Mr Rubens had answered. 'Where you been, young man? My chess board is waiting, Doris is waiting, Miss Hans Kellerman is waiting. One month, three days and you are not calling.'

Peekay laughed at the old man's chiding. 'Hello, Mr Rubens, how's my doll? Only two hundred more pounds to pay. How about a discount for early payment? May I speak to Doris, please?'

'Wait, I find her.' Peekay heard the clatter of the phone as he dropped the receiver onto his desk.

Peekay had enjoyed his first date with Doris. They'd had a good time and although she'd allowed him a bit of a feel-up, she wasn't going to be a pushover. At first it had been circumspect; he was in love with Harriet and although Doris did all the right things to him Peekay was able to resist the temptation. But Harriet blew hot and cold. Peekay, who was highly sexed, never quite knew how he'd find her; and finally his resolve crumbled. In his mind Harriet went to bed with him on her terms, when *she* felt like it. Doris, on the other hand, simply liked to accommodate him. Peekay was able to tell himself the meaning of the sex involved was not the same thing, that he was entitled to enjoy Doris and she him. Making love to Doris, he rationalised unfairly, was for the simple release of tension and not the sometimes almost mystical experience Harriet made of it, depending on her mood.

Besides, Peekay found he liked Doris a lot. She was funny, like Togger. She seemed to enjoy being with him, as though she was out on a special treat, though she found many of his mannerisms 'dead quaint', like taking her arm when they went up steps and holding her chair out when they went into a working man's caf for a cuppa.

They'd been out several times when Peekay first raised the question of the Hans Kellerman doll, wanting to know if it was for sale. 'Blimey, Peekay, maybe if you was a millionaire an' all, but I don't think so.'

'Why, what's so special about it? Where did the old guy get it? I mean has he always had it?'

'Funny you should ask that. About a year ago or something like that, this geezer walks into the shop with the doll. "Does we buy dolls?" he asks Mr Rubens. I'm standing behind the old man and I can see his knees start to shake, but the top half, the bit what's above the counter is cool as a cucumber. He looks-at the doll, turns it upside down, pulls at its arms and legs, then shakes it. "Ja, it is a good doll," he says, calm as you like. It's a good thing the cash register is right next to him 'cause his knees is shaking something terrible, I don't think he'd a made it on his own. He rings the register and takes out ten pound and slaps it down on the counter in front of the man. Blimey! Ten quid for a bleedin' secondhand doll? The old bugger's gorn off his rocker.' Doris laughed suddenly. 'I think the geezer who brought the doll felt the same an' all. He grabs the tenner and scarpers, like a rat up a bleedin' drainpipe. No sooner is he gone than Mr

Rubens picks up the doll and begins to cry. Hugs it to his chest, great tears runnin' down his face.'

'So you don't think he'd sell it to me?' Peekay asked.

Doris looked at him curiously. ' 'Ere, hang on a mo, we got hundreds of dolls. Why do you want that one? More particular, why do yer want a doll in the first place?'

Peekay told Doris the story of Carmen's doll. 'So I want to get it back for her,' he concluded.

'Blimey, I don't like yer chances, love. That doll means an awful lot to the old man. I'll ask him if you like?'

'No, I'll think of a plan.'

'What sort of a plan?'

'I'll think of something.'

Doris grabbed Peekay's sleeve. 'Please, anything else, but don't ask me to do it, I beg you, Peekay. It'd kill him, it would.'

'Doris, what on earth are you talking about?'

Doris looked close to tears. 'You only been nice to me because of her, haven't you? That was it all along, wasn't it?' She started to sob quietly.

'Doris! What the hell are you on about?'

'The doll! You want me to nick the 'Ans Kellerman, don'cha?' she sobbed.

Peekay threw back his head and laughed. 'Christ, no!' He put his arms around Doris and pulled her head onto his breast. 'I'm a toff from Oxford, remember. Toffs don't go around nicking other people's dolls. Here,' Peekay handed Doris his handkerchief, 'wipe your tears.' Peekay suddenly realised that if he'd asked her to steal the doll she'd have done so, that Doris loved him enough to do it.

'Doris, look at me. Your mascara's run, you look a right berk,' Peekay said, imitating Togger. He took the handkerchief from her hands and gently wiped where the mascara had run down her cheeks. Peekay sighed. 'I don't know, Doris, I can't take you anywhere,' he chided.

The following Wednesday, Peekay took an earlier than usual train to London and called Mr Rubens. 'May I have a talk with you?' he asked.

'Of course!' the old man replied. 'We both got a telephone, so talk already!'

'No, I mean, privately, away from the office. Perhaps you'll let me buy you lunch.'

'Lunch? Lunch costs money, my boy. We talk yes, but no lunch.' He gave Peekay an address, Duke's Place in the East End. 'Here is a synagogue, I will meet you two o'clock.'

Peekay arrived a little early to find Mr Rubens already waiting for him. The little man stood outside the giant doors of the ancient Great Synagogue. When he saw Peekay he pushed one half of a door open and waited with his free hand holding out a yamulka for him to take. Peekay placed the tiny skull cap on the back of his head before they entered.

Peekay's first impression of the interior was of its similarity to a church, though faintly oriental as well. He didn't know why, but he'd always thought of a synagogue as somehow different. More mysterious. He was amazed to see stained-glass windows and it was only the writing in Hebraic which suggested they were any different to the stained-glass pictures of Old Testament scenes he'd seen in a Christian cathedral.

'You are surprised I bring you here, yes?' Mr Rubens asked.

'Yes, I've never been inside a synagogue.'

'It is not so strange, I think?'

'Well, no, it's sort of like a stripped-down church, you know, without the effigies,' Peekay whispered.

'A Jew comes to the synagogue to talk. It is not necessary you talk soft, Peekay.'

'I must say it's a surprising venue.' Peekay grinned, 'I'd thought maybe a couple of ham sandwiches in a pub.' Peekay blushed suddenly. 'I'm terribly sorry, Mr Rubens!'

The old man brushed away his embarrassment.

'Tell me something, Peekay. This talk we are having, it is serious, ja?'

'Mr Rubens, I want to buy the Hans Kellerman doll from you.'

Mr Rubens was silent for some time. Then he sighed and spread his hands in a gesture of helplessness looking directly at Peekay. Ja, I think this is maybe why you are calling me. But you know this is not possible?'

Peekay's heart was beating fast. He didn't know why he was so nervous, he'd expected all along his offer would be rejected by the old man. 'Please, sir, I know the doll means a lot to you, but if you'll just let me explain why I need to buy it?'

'Please, some respect! We are not talking about a doll, we are talking about a Hans Kellerman.'

'Mr Rubens, you are not the only person who feels this way about the Hans Kellerman. Someone else loves it too!' Peekay said urgently, trying to impress his seriousness on the little man who now sat with his long coat still buttoned with his delicate white hands folded on his lap. Peekay began to tell Mr Rubens about Carmen, about how much it had meant to her, how much love had been vested in the doll and how it had been sold for a bottle of gin. Peekay concluded by recounting how Carmen had left home and how Togger searched every pawnshop in the Mile End Road and beyond in the hope of coming across Elizabeth Jane.

'Elizabet Jane, this is a name?'

'Well, it would give me a great deal of pleasure to be able to give Togger the doll so that he could return it to his sister.' Peekay paused. 'I'd expect to pay whatever it was worth, Mr Rubens.'

'Pleasure? Pay? What means this? You know what is *krystal nacht*?'

'Yes, that was when Hitler's brownshirts started breaking the shop windows of Jewish shopkeepers in Germany, early, at the very beginning, wasn't it?'

'Ja, this is so, the boychick is not so stupid. Upstairs we are sleeping, underneath is my shop, a small factory for making dolls. It is maybe two o'clock when they are coming. They are breaking the window and on the wall by the shop they are writing *Juden*.' Mr Rubens smiled sadly. 'In the morning after comes my friend, Hans Kellerman. "Nathan, we must go. You must sell your shop. I have some money, we will go to America, maybe Hollywood. In America we can make dolls. Come Nathan, it is not so bad now, but this Nazi filth, this is only the beginning. We must go!"

'Hans, you are *meshugganah*, it will pass, you will see. We are Germans, they will not harm us. Maybe they break a little glass, paint a little paint. What harm? And you are Hans Kellerman, in Germany is only one Hans Kellerman the doll maker, the genius, they will not harm you. It is nothing, you will see, it will pass.

'Hans Kellerman is shaking my hand. "Nathan, you are right. When you were the foreman at Schoenau & Hoffmeister and I was only two years an apprentice, it was you who told me to go on my own, that you can teach me no more. Always like a father, looking after me. Your family is my family. We stay together or we going together to America." Then he is giving to me a parcel. "For little Anna, your grandchild, for her birthday."

'Inside is a Hans Kellerman doll. From the world is coming orders. From also the English queen. Maybe in one year Hans Kellerman is making ten dolls. Ten dolls only in one year and he is giving the most beautiful to little Anna.

'Two more times, in 1936 and in 1938 Hans Kellerman, my friend, is coming again, "Nathan, we must go!"'

'But Germany is rich, under Chancellor Hitler my little doll factory is making good business. After they is breaking the glass I am not stupid. I make also my German foreman a partner and put on the front his name, *Horst Teintzel – Puppe Fabrik*. There is no more trouble. Little Anna is going to the gymnasium and is taking also violin lessons. My wife and daughter also, they don't want we should leave. But when Hans Kellerman is coming again in 1938, after two months I tell my friend, "You are right, it is time. We must go. We will go to America, we will go together to Hollywood!"'

Mr Rubens paused. 'But when we go to the authorities to get papers for travelling, it is not possible. "Hans, you must escape," I tell him. "You have no family, you must go, you are famous, in America they know you!" But Hans Kellerman is looking at me. "Nathan, you *are* my family, we will go together!" But comes now 1939, Germany is invading Poland and it is too late.' The old man gave a deep sigh. 'It is too late for escaping.'

Peekay grabbed Mr Rubens. Through the sleeve of his thick coat he could feel his frail arm. 'Please, Mr Rubens, you don't need to go on. I'm truly sorry I asked, I have distressed you!'

'No, no, please, we are talking. It is why we are coming here, in the house of Jehovah, it is the first time I am talking since that time.' He smiled sadly, then looking directly at Peekay, he attempted to brighten his voice. 'So? It is good to talk, ja?'

'Please, sir, I am most dreadfully ashamed, I should never have asked.'

Mr Rubens' eyes opened wide in surprise. 'Boychick, what are you saying! We have here pain and despair, and we have here love and hope. This is why we are talking. You are telling me of Fräulein Brown who is loving her Hans Kellerman and also you hope to return it. Now we must decide to who belongs this Hans Kellerman. You want only the pain should win?'

Peekay realised that he was required to take part in a bizarre debate. He felt inadequate, his emotional resources were always deeply buried. Now this old man required him to display them as a peacock might display its tail, strutting and posturing and challenging the small, brown hen called pain. He had never felt pain as Mr Rubens had, but he knew it nevertheless, was familiar with it from his childhood. But could he as easily come to terms with love? What did he know of love? It was at this moment that the bitter irony struck him, everything he knew and felt about love had been taught to him by Doc! Doc a German, a blue-eyed, once blond member of the master race.

'No, we'll talk,' Peekay replied. He was facing a challenge from the old man; he must keep the sympathy from his voice or he would lose. He realised suddenly that if he lost, Mr Rubens also lost. The outcome of the debate was the continued life of this frail German Jew.

'So, I talk, ja?'

Peekay nodded.

'In 1941 comes the SS and also, wearing the uniform from the brown shirts, Horst Teintzel, my German partner. We are packing one suitcase for each person, and after twenty minutes the SS officer is saying we must go. Little Anna she is holding her tiny suitcase; in the other hand she is holding Rebecca, the Hans Kellerman. Anna is very beautiful, blue eyes and hair the same colour as ripe wheat. The Kellerman, it has dark hair and big brown eyes, a masterpiece!'

The old man stopped talking for a moment, his eyes filling with tears. But when he spoke again his voice was steady. 'With his arms crossed so is standing Horst Teintzel by the top of the stairs. When little Anna is passing he is taking the Hans Kellerman. "Please! Please! Herr Teintzel, please give me back Rebecca!" little Anna is crying. "*Schnell Jude*!" he is saying, "Go quick, Jew!" and he is pushing little Anna by the back so.' Mr Rubens jammed the flat of his hand into the air in front of him. 'My little Anna is falling down the stairs when she is breaking her arm.'

Mr Rubens paused to explain. 'We did not know at that time what was happening to the Jews. My wife and my daughter are crying and little Anna is screaming from the pain. I am crying also, but saying to the SS officer we must take little Anna to the hospital. "Please, I beg you!" I am taking off from my finger a diamond ring. "Please take, take." The SS officer is taking the ring. "Ja, we will take her, but you cannot go there to the hospital with her! She has blue eyes and fair hair like a German. How comes this?"

'"Her father, he was German," I am saying. "Please sir, let only her mother go with her." He is calling for the corporal. "Take the child to the hospital," he says to the corporal. The SS man is putting little Anna in the automobile, her arm is hanging like a broken doll and her face is white like a sheet. "Do not say she is Jewish!" the SS officer is saying to that corporal. Then he is smiling, "She is too beautiful to be a dirty Jew!"'

'Some people is standing there, they are watching how we are going, not smiling, just looking. When he is saying this, they clap. Horst Teintzel is standing by the window upstairs. "Here, Jew, catch!" He is throwing the Hans Kellerman on the road; the beautiful bisque head is breaking in pieces, like a cup on the kitchen floor.'

There was a pause and Mr Rubens looked up slowly, speaking quietly. 'One woman in the street, she is picking up the Hans Kellerman. "Shame! How can you do such a thing to a beautiful doll!" she is shouting to Horst Teintzel.

'Teintzel is laughing. "See, it has black hair and brown eyes, it is a Jew doll!" All the people pulled back from that woman who is holding the broken Hans Kellerman. Then she is dropping it and walking away. The Hans Kellerman is lying on the road, only the back of the head is still on the body, there is no face.'

In an almost inaudible voice the little Jew added, 'Then they take us in the train, in the cattle trucks, to Buchenwald.'

Peekay knew what was to follow. The huddled mass of Jews in the cattle trucks, fighting for air, shitting where they stood or sat, some of the older people dying mercifully of heart attacks. The arrival at Buchenwald, the dogs, the huge Alsatian dogs, yapping at the heels of the hapless Jews. The sliver of bright hope at the civilised sound of the orchestra playing Strauss as the fit and the able are separated from the women and children and old people. 'Carpenters, we need carpenters! Carpenters step forward at once! Mechanics, we need mechanics!' The hoarse, violent voices of the non-commissioned officers, indifferent to the fate of their victims, practised in the routines of death. The promise of showers and medicine, the Teutonic efficiency of the operation raising their hopes. The cruelty of the journey is forgiven. 'It is wartime, trains are scarce, the authorities, they try but times are hard, the trains are for the troops, for the Russian front. Who knows? Things could be worse. On the other hand, they could be better.' The bitter humour and the desperate, comforting lies people tell among themselves when they feel the shadow of death fall over them. And in the background an old man, his prayer shawl over his shoulders, the leather phylactery on his head, as he sings the ancient prayer for the dead. He understands. He has seen the shadow. He is too old to be fooled. Too wise to waste his thin, reedy voice on hope.

'I was lucky,' Mr Rubens said at last. 'They needed carpenters, before the dolls I was a carpenter. My wife and daughter not so. Hans Kellerman not so.' His voice tailed off.

The old man sat quietly for a long time, his elegant hands like two white birds resting in his lap. After a while he looked up at Peekay. 'So now it is the turn for love and hope,' he said softly.

There was nothing Peekay could say. Carmen loved Elizabeth Jane, but how could her love for the doll compare with the pain the old man felt, the pain and the betrayal?

'Your granddaughter? Your granddaughter may be alive and she may find you?'

'Ja, this is true.'

'And that is why you want the Hans Kellerman?' The old man said nothing, not looking up from his hands. Peekay could see his shoulders were shaking as he wept, but no sound came from him.

'Love has won, Mr Rubens,' Peekay said gently, putting his hand on the old man's shoulder. 'You want the Hans Kellerman doll for the love you have for your granddaughter. Love and hope have won, they have beaten pain and despair.'

Mr Rubens agreed to sell the Hans Kellerman doll to Peekay for a thousand pounds, which was the value placed on it by Sotheby's. The money he declared would go to an orphanage in Brixton.

It was an enormous sum but Peekay had agreed to pay it in instalments. Now, with only a lead-up fight to go to the world championship, he owed just two hundred pounds.

In the background Peekay could hear Mr Rubens shouting for Doris to come to the phone. There was the sudden rattle of the receiver being picked up. 'Hello, lovely, the old man givin' you an 'ard time then?' Doris was her usual bright self. 'You better come down, he's been fussin' over his bloomin' chessboard, re-playing your last match for a month, sayin' all kinds of nasty things about the Russians.'

Peekay laughed. 'It was about time I took a game off the old bugger.' Peekay made arrangements to pick Doris up at the shop.

'Smashin', it's about bleedin' time an' all! Too much work and not enough play makes Peekay a dull boy. Tell yer what? I'll wear me new Merry Widow, it don't do me no 'arm, even if I say so meself!'

The thought of Doris in a Merry Widow bra left Peekay feeling quite faint.

TWENTY-ONE

Peekay completed his final examinations in July 1955 and felt he'd not done too badly. Oxford had treated him well and, mostly through the Odd Bodleians, he'd made friends he would keep for the remainder of his life. He was walking with E.W. in the physic garden at Magdalen in his last week at Oxford when his tutor turned to him and asked, 'Well, Peekay, we've come a long way together. Can you give me just one thing you will take from Oxford?'

Peekay thought for a few moments; he'd received so much and so little at Oxford. Not the least of what he'd gained was the wisdom of the white-haired doctor of law who'd posed the question. He'd arrived a callow youth and now, three years later, would leave a young man with a quiet assurance and a mind he'd learned to trust in a world which needed to be repeatedly questioned.

Oxford was one of the great citadels of the civilised and cultivated mind but it was ill suited to the raw keening of an Africa trying to lift itself out of generations of ignorance, suspicion, hatred and despair.

Oxford was about the detail, the cuffs and the collars and the manner and style of the buttons on the garment of civilisation, Africa had yet to know the feeling of cloth on its back.

How very nearly Peekay had become seduced by the mannerisms and accepted truths of an older world. How easy it would have been to carry a self-righteous torch into the darkness as so many others had done to no avail. But in time he'd realised it wouldn't work. Africa needed a much tougher solution than the sweet reconciliations of civilised European man. It would require a sinewed toughness and a fighting spirit which came more from the boxing ring and his understanding of the protagonists involved than from these ivy-covered portals of stone.

This was not to say that he didn't aspire to Oxford ideals. It was simply that the weapon of civilised truth wasn't a great deal of use to him in an environment which was totally corrupted by men who accepted only those truths which maintained the status quo and in which the white man was superior to the black. Peekay, with others who thought as he did, must pry justice and compassion and truth from a furnace of hate and suspicion. It would be a long, hard, slow task and required a resilience and toughness Oxford could never understand. He must be prepared to give his life if necessary.

And so when he answered E.W., it was with a careful and truthful reply which contained no mention of the doctrines and philosophies taught at the great institution of learning.

'The buildings. I'll take with me these buildings. You once said to me that Oxford was no different in many ways to any other institution of higher learning but for its tutorial system. But you forgot to mention the buildings. They add to the sum of an Oxford man. To have spent time in and about these buildings is both an education in itself and an assurance that intelligence and the spirit of man will always prevail. I have been educated by the Portland stone, the spires and the mullioned views, the gargoyles, the quiet crevices and moss-softened corners, the grandness and the piety of old stone. I shall forever remember the granite and the greatness of Oxford.'

E.W. seemed pleased by the reply. 'You have answered well, Peekay. I believe it expresses what many of us feel about this place.'

Harriet had drawn deeper and deeper into herself. Her Walking Madonna had taken almost a year from the maquette to the point when it was ready to be cast in bronze. Carmen had kept her promise and had returned to pose for the work, giving Harriet two-and-a-half weeks of her three-week holiday at Cow Cottage.

Peekay and Togger saw very little of her and when they did she talked of little else but Harriet and the Madonna. Carmen had fallen under Harriet's spell and from all accounts seemed to have overcome Harriet's desire to be alone and claimed, without affectation, that they'd talked for hours on end while she'd posed.

'For the first time in me life I feel I've got a brain, not just a body but a noggin I can use and I reckon I know how I'm gonna use it an' all.'

They'd been sitting at the bar in a small Soho pub and now she drew herself up, throwing her head back as she looked disdainfully at them both. 'In Paris I'm learnin' how to put clothes on, not take 'em off. I gotta job in a fashion house on the Faubourg St-Honoré.' Carmen paused at the look of surprise on both their faces. 'Okay, I admit, it's not too flash, a bit of sewin' and cuttin' and a bit of house modellin', but I'm learnin'.' She leaned forward grabbing Togger suddenly by the arm, her eyes shining. ' 'Ere, you remember how when I was a little nipper I used to sew all the clothes for Elizabeth Jane and later, when I was about eleven or twelve, I'd make all me own dresses? Well, now I'm learnin' to cut and design proper. I'm gonna save and save and nights I'll go to the *Polytechnique*; then I'm gonna make children's clothes, the most beautiful children's clothes in the whole bleedin' world!' Carmen was breathless with the excitement of telling them her plans, but she suddenly pulled herself upright on the stool again, afraid she'd said too much.

A large grin spread over Togger's face. 'I think we just come to the end of the nearly-but-not-quite Browns. When me boxing career's over I reckon I'm gonna invest me prize money with you, no risk!'

Carmen smiled, holding a beautifully manicured hand out to Togger. 'Put it there, partner!'

'Here's to Brown and Brown! If Hymie was here and not in New York he'd order champagne.' Peekay turned to the barman. 'Barman, a bottle of Bollinger, please!'

When the bottle was empty at last Carmen's eyes grew soft and her mood nostalgic. 'You staying in London overnight in Hymie's flat then?' she asked Peekay.

Peekay grinned. 'I reckon it's my turn to ask you home.'

On those occasions when Harriet needed someone to enter the circle of her self-imposed solitude, apart from her two-and-a-half weeks with Carmen, it was Hymie she chose. Hymie was the first person to see the completed Walking Madonna.

'Christ, Peekay,' he reported, 'it almost touches the central beam, that's bloody nearly fourteen foot from the ground. It's astonishing, a masterpiece.'

Peekay felt a little hurt that Harriet hadn't chosen him as the first to witness her triumph, but he'd more or less reconciled himself to losing her, at least while she was involved with the sculpture.

'And what of Harriet? Has the Walking Madonna changed her? Will she again be the Harriet we both know?'

'You mean will she return to you?'

Peekay didn't protest. 'Yes, I suppose I do mean that. Have I lost her, Hymie? Has she gone to you?' A new thought seemed to occur to him. 'Or have we both lost her?'

Hymie sat quietly thinking. They were in the small sitting-room of Hymie's flat overlooking Sloane Square. Finally he spoke. 'I was hoping I could tell you she was mine, Peekay. That I'd won her back. I wouldn't have minded that. All's fair in . . . Do you find that strange?'

Peekay shook his head and Hymie continued. 'You had your turn, I'd like to think now it was mine.' He grinned, 'I admit it would have given me some satisfaction! But it's not true, old son. Harriet, as I said right at the beginning and she quite emphatically maintained herself, never belonged to either of us. Not even in the least sense. Sure she loves us both. But we lie a poor second, perhaps even lower on her list of emotional needs. From now on, you will see, she will take us only on *her* terms.' Hymie sighed. 'For me that's enough. I haven't any sexual ego to get in the way, to compete. For you, I sense it will not be enough. If I appear to have grown closer to Harriet it is because I've capitulated. Utterly!' Hymie looked up and grinned. 'It's just as well you're bedding Doris with the marvellous tits, Peekay, the next physical relationship Harriet has will not be with you. It will be with whoever she is pleased to have at her moment of need, which is rare enough, like a dry creek bed taken in sudden flood and then, as suddenly, empty again.'

Peekay gave Hymie a wry grin. 'I can't say I'm not disappointed, I am. Bitterly. Even though the past year's been pretty bloody, I guess I was lucky to get what I got, not just sex, but the time spent with Harriet. It was like being plugged into electricity. She was wonderful.'

'Will you tell her that, Peekay?'

'I'll try.'

'Peekay, it isn't over. Why don't you try falling in *like* with Harriet? If Harriet was a man, let's face it, we'd be awestruck, overwhelmed by the sheer talent brought to the friendship. Try forgetting she's a woman, someone you took to bed.'

Peekay laughed. 'I can't. Hymie, I have to try to get her back. I can't simply walk away and call it a day. It wasn't just a sex thing. I admit it, I started sleeping with Doris when Harriet and I were still together, still relatively happy. If it was a sex thing it would have died then. It was, it is, a lot more.'

Hymie was silent for a moment, pulling his lower lip into his mouth. 'Peekay, she's changed, she's different.'

'Changed how? You mean the new Harriet wants a different kind of man? Older?'

'Peekay! For Christ's sake, leave it alone. Harriet's changed, that's all. I didn't say anything about a man!'

Peekay felt himself go cold. 'Carmen?'

Hymie observed that Peekay had turned white. 'You don't suppose she slept on the chesterfield for two-and-a-half weeks do you?'

'Christ! It never bloody entered my head. Harriet and Carmen sleeping together! Harriet a lesbian?'

'Hey, now! Wait a minute, Peekay, don't go jumping to conclusions! It doesn't have to be one thing or the other. I told you, the new Harriet takes what she wants when she wants it. She was modelling a female body so she got involved with it. It was simply an object of intense interest. Being intimate with Carmen, with Carmen's body, was perfectly natural for her. What I'm saying is that from now on you don't judge her, you simply accept her. Accept her as a friend. Gender has bugger-all to do with it.'

'And Carmen? Christ, I lost my virginity with Carmen.'

'Peekay, Carmen's been around. She's probably no more a lesbian than you are a homo. She's a big girl, you always knew that!'

'When did you know? Shit! Why didn't you tell me earlier?'

'Sitting on the sidelines you sometimes see the game more clearly than the players. What was I supposed to tell you? You and Harriet haven't been together for yonks.'

'Ja Hymie, but you know how I felt! For fuck's sake, it would have helped to *know*!'

Hymie took out a cigarette. He'd given up the dark brown Russian sobranies and now smoked Benson & Hedges in a small square red tin. He tapped the end of the cigarette on the lid of the tin. He realised the extent of Peekay's hurt, the crushing blow to his pride. It had taken a lot of courage for Peekay to maintain his love for Harriet. He had to play things in a lighter vein, to allow Peekay to get out from under. 'Peekay, you know what your trouble is? You're a hopeless bloody romantic! What's more you're also a horny one! Women watch you a certain way. They bed you with their eyes. When you fall in *like*, as you have done with Doris with the marvellous tits, at least you're in control. You of all people should know that achieving the things you want is all about control. Our future success against the injustice of the system when we return to the bloody fatherland is dependent on control. We will survive only because we never lose control. Remember that! Forget the romantic part, the love part, the *falling in* part. The only thing you're likely to end up falling in is shit!'

Peekay watched as Hymie lit his cigarette. For the first time in his life Peekay found himself completely at odds with him. He could understand the logic, the intellectual truth of what Hymie was saying, but it was not sufficient to convince him.

Peekay, who had spent his life camouflaged, never allowing his emotions to show, knew suddenly, hopelessly and with not a little real fear, that in the matter of love his heart was capable of ruling his head. It was a weakness against which he sensed he had no protection. It was like finding you have an incurable disease when you feel no symptoms. It was there, lurking in the womb, snapped onto the sperm, invading the egg, a gene transferred to destroy him prematurely, waiting for just the right time to manifest itself in his body.

After leaving Oxford, Peekay moved into Hymie's flat in London. He was to fight the American, King Coon Sinders just two weeks after the end of the Trinity term. Hymie had managed to arrange for the fight to take place at the US Marine base in Munich.

Hymie, through the company they'd set up to handle the financing and proceeds of the title fights, Angel Sport, sold the fight to the US military in Germany, permitting them to buy the television rights to every US base in Europe. This money he used as expenses and for the boxers' purse money. In addition he contracted the US TV network crew to film the fight for a ridiculously small amount of money, which helped to gain additional publicity in the States for the Tadpole Angel.

At last Peekay was ready to challenge Jake 'Spoonbill' Jackson. The welterweight championship of the world had all the makings; the poor boy from the South with a ninth grade education and the brilliant young law student from Oxford. A. J. Liebling, writing for the *New York Times*, referred to it as 'The Catfish and Caviar Contest'. *Sports Illustrated* were smart enough to include a reaction from the champion in the feature they ran on Peekay.

Jake 'Spoonbill' Jackson's comment was quoted verbatim:

You know what is a Spoonbill, man? A Spoonbill, he got long legs and he walks in the water and when he sees a goddamn tadpole he gobbles it up! Tell him all that education he got, it ain't gonna help. All that tadpole gonna need is enough education to count to ten, after that he with the angels . . . permanent!

Peekay had two and a half months to prepare for the world championship fight which was scheduled to take place on 27th October in Madison Square Garden. He would train initially in England and then they'd take the boat to New York to spend the final two months at a training camp in Colorado.

Jam Jar had come up with the idea of having Peekay train at the highest possible altitude. Most of the Odd Bodleians were by now experts at boxing and he reasoned that the fight might well go to the man with the most stamina. By training at the highest possible altitude and then coming down to sea level for the fight, Peekay would have extra capacity. It was a theory well worth exploiting. They'd hired the services of a small-town boxing promoter named Mike Graw to set up a camp and he'd managed to rent a small dude ranch high in the mountains near Pike's Peak in Colorado.

Dutch had been against the mountains at first. He'd brought a fighter to the States before and there was an accepted way of doing things if you were a serious contender. If you were fighting in 'The Garden' you selected a training camp not too far from the action, somewhere the more fanatical fans could visit you and – much more importantly – where the press could drop in for a story. 'The fight game in America's all about publicity, you gotta get the newspaper boys on your side. If they give you the thumbs up it's on for one an' all! The other way and you're history.'

'We'll move up to New York a week before the fight. That ought to be enough time for a press conference every day,' Hymie had suggested.

Dutch had continued to protest. 'Hymie, it ain't me. Personally I hate the bastards in the game in America. It's a dirty business and the less we have to do with them the better. But it's the lad I'm thinking of. If 'e don't know the score it's gonna throw him summink awful. All the carry-on the Yanks go in for, it gets a fighter pumped up, ready. Besides, the promoter, he's gonna insist on all the malarky, it builds up the gate.'

'Dutch, Peekay's a fast learner. A week will be sufficient. As for building up the gate, that's not included in the contract. In fact, it's one of the few bloody concessions I managed to get. They didn't think Peekay's rep carried much weight in America. People will simply come to see the shit knocked out of the Limey!'

In fact Hymie had tied up the contract for the fight some months previously when he'd made the trip to sign up King Coon Sinders, stopping for a week in New York. The contract had been on condition that Peekay won against Sinders, but apart from this clause, which was now negated, the formalities were long over when the four of them, for Togger was now included, arrived at O'Hare a week after the fight in Munich and exactly nine weeks before the title fight.

Hymie knew he had a lousy contract. Jackson's manager was a big, red-nosed, morose Irishman who smoked large, foul-smelling Philippines cigars most of the time and drank Four Roses whiskey neat. Michael O'Rourke looked like a larger version of W. C. Fields, though he had none of the great comedian's acid humour or repartee. He was stubborn and not very bright, but he knew the fight game and he was accepted in New York boxing circles.

From the beginning he'd insisted the fight be promoted by another Irishman, a millionaire scrap-metal merchant from Philadephia named Patrick O'Flynn. O'Flynn, with a consortium of New York Irish, had promoted most of Jackson's fights and O'Rourke wanted it no other way. Hymie was soon to discover why.

The deal they wanted from the start had been one-sided to say the least. The purse was set at one hundred thousand dollars with Jake 'Spoonbill' Jackson taking eighty-one thousand and Peekay, win, lose or draw, a flat nineteen thousand dollars. They would barely cover their costs. In addition, Hymie had to pay O'Flynn a further two thousand dollars for the seats occupied by the Odd Bodleians.

Hymie had little option but to go along with the deal. Jackson was established as a title holder who was expected to hang on and hang in and Hymie had to have the fight come what may.

The TV deal had been sewn up before Hymie had met with O'Rourke and O'Flynn. Both had been delighted when Hymie had capitulated with little more than a token fight except to ask for the TV rights to the fight worldwide. Both Irishmen knew they didn't have a snowball's hope in hell of interesting a major American network in the fight and they readily agreed.

Hymie wanted a second clause inserted into the contract. He wanted a return bout, win, draw or lose in the first fight, in which he guaranteed Jake 'Spoonbill' Jackson a purse of three hundred and fifty thousand US dollars in return for agreeing to contest the title in Johannesburg. There was no withdrawal clause and a three-month postponement clause which required the offending boxer to be examined by three medical practitioners from the other boxer's country before the postponement clause came into effect. The fight to take place no later than six months after the Madison Square Garden bout.

It was nearly double the largest purse for which Jackson had hitherto fought and the return bout clause was quickly drawn up by an attorney at law and inserted in the contract.

Elmer Milstein had booked the four of them in at the Plaza. He met them at Idlewild when the Pan American Boeing Stratocruiser landed at seven o'clock in the morning.

Hymie stared in astonishment at the car Elmer had brought along. 'Jesus, my old man's identity crisis is over! Just wait until Solomon Levy hears about this Lincoln. It's in such appallingly bad taste he's going to love it to death!'

TWENTY-TWO

Elmer Milstein had purchased a second-hand, twelve-seater Chevvy bus which was to take them the fifteen-hundred-mile journey through the centre of the United States to Colorado. Most of the trip would be over flatland states: through cities like Indianapolis, St Louis and Kansas City. While this meant they'd make good time, Peekay wanted to see the south. It meant catching a Greyhound bus to Atlanta and then flying from Atlanta to Kansas City to join up with the others coming across in the bus. The trip, though an additional expense, had one other advantage: it meant Peekay would only miss two days of training rather than four or perhaps five.

They were running out of time and Peekay was anxious to settle into a training routine. He'd not fought in America and he had to learn the fight culture of the place quickly. He wanted as much going for him as possible. He told himself he had to be perfectly prepared if he had a chance against Jackson, that everything mattered. Though good sparring partners mattered the most. It wasn't simply their ability, although this was very important, but also their minds. Jake 'Spoonbill' Jackson was black and from the South, Peekay could recite his boxing history in his sleep but he needed to know what made his opponent tick.

One of the sparring partners they'd hired in New York hailed originally from Atlanta, and he agreed to keep Peekay company on his trip to the South. Jerome 'Pumpkin Face' de Cresphy, so called because of his amazingly yellow skin and almost perfectly round face, had suggested checking out another young fighter from Atlanta, a Golden-Gloves winner, who'd turned pro two years earlier.

Although Jerome 'Pumpkin Face' de Cresphy was more accustomed to being called 'P.F.' than by his Christian name, Peekay reverted back to Jerome, deciding that 'P.F.' was rather too close to his own name and bound to cause confusion. The two of them caught the night bus out of the New York Greyhound terminal to Charlottesville, Virginia so they would have the benefit of travelling through most of the South in daylight.

'Ain't no prettier in the South than it is in the North, Peekay,' Jerome had insisted. 'Jus' more coloured folks and honkies.' Peekay had never heard of the term 'honky', but it served well enough to register Jerome's fear and disapproval. How could he tell him this was why he wanted to travel the South in daylight? He'd lived most of his life in a racist environment and he'd often enough heard it said that the southern states of America were no different to his own country in their treatment of the negro.

By morning they'd reached Charlottesville. They'd commandeered the long-seat at the rear of the bus and had managed to get a reasonable night's sleep. Charlottesville was closer to the Appalachian Mountains and the dawn was cold and crisp in the early fall morning as they alighted from the bus and made for the showers. They entered the large rest room and paid for a towel and a shower. Jerome stopped and looked around the clean tiled space, then he laughed softly. 'This is the last of mah freedom, this is the last place where the negro is and the nigger ain't. Nex' time we go in to a rest room, I go where it say, "Coloured Folks Only" and where there ain't no hot water and towel for hire; *you* go where it says, "Strictly White Folks", where the towels are soft and the water is steamin' and hot.'

'How the hell do you know, Jerome?' Peekay laughed. 'You're not allowed in, remember!' Peekay was being flip, trying to ease Jerome's anxiety.

Jerome laughed, his big smile splitting his round face. 'That's a good question, Peekay. When I was goin' to school I had me a job cleanin' the bus station rest rooms, evenin' shift. "How come," I said to mah pappy, "white folks' shit smell jus' same as coloured folks'. Why they got towels and hot showers and seats on their toilets?" "Son," my pappy says, "that's the million dollar question. That the one question coloured folk not supposed to ask. When coloured folk ask question, then they know for sure it's time to quit the South!" '

Around noon they passed into Tennessee and Jerome nudged Peekay. 'Time you went to sit up front, Peekay. From here out this ain't friendly country no more.'

Peekay felt awkward. He knew what was likely to happen; he also knew that by staying with Jerome he wasn't making a point. The opposite was true. Jerome was the one who stood to be hurt. Peekay would simply be branded a nigger lover; his foreign passport would get him out of trouble, but they'd take it out on 'the nigger'.

Peekay rose and moved up the bus to the front half where he sat staring out of the window, seeing nothing for a long time.

They arrived at Atlanta around ten that night and Peekay checked into a motel near the gym. Jerome had stayed on at the bus station to catch a bus to a small hamlet which he had previously described to Peekay on the journey. 'It ain't got no name, it ain't got no importance, you jus' leave the road and walk some, soon's you get near the bayou you know you're about to arrive. That's coloured folks' territory.' He'd laughed, throwing back his head. Then his face took on a serious expression for a moment. 'When I'm the champion, I'm gonna buy my mama a big house someplace where the ground is always dry.'

At eleven the following morning they met downtown at the YMCA gym for a sparring session with Peppy 'The Kid' Smith, the Golden-Gloves champ who'd turned pro and who had won six of his first eight fights, four on points, two knock-outs and a drawn bout with Jerome 'Pumpkin Face' de Cresphy. Peekay had put Jerome into the ring first so he could watch the young fighter; later they sparred together.

Peekay knew exactly what he was looking for. Hymie had spliced together all the footage they could find of Jake 'Spoonbill' Jackson and they'd watched it over and over again on a small sixteen-millimetre projector in the room they shared at the Plaza. It was the old Hymie–Peekay combination doing their homework, covering every possible aspect of the champion so that Peekay felt he knew Jackson's fighting style inside out. Almost immediately he'd been happy with Smith. The young fighter had a lightning-fast right hand but lacked a little power in the left; however, his style and fighting demeanour were very like Jackson's.

Peekay spent ten minutes or so talking to Smith, who turned out to be a shy and modest young man but with a quiet determination to make it to the top. He would make an ideal addition to the team and, at the end of their discussion, Peekay told him he was hired.

Peppy 'The Kid' Smith, the hint of a smile on his face, shook his head slowly, looking down at his still bandaged hands. 'What's the matter, Peppy, don't you want the job?'

The young man lifted his head slowly. 'Nossir, yessir, thank you, sir . . . it's my mamma, she wants to meet you before she let me go.'

Eventually Jerome managed to get out of Peppy Smith that Peekay was expected to dine with Mrs Smith in her home that evening. The young fighter gave Peekay his address and left, but then returned, shrugging his shoulders. 'Some white guys, they ain't happy 'bout drivin' there; it's best you look for a coloured man taxi driver,' he said simply.

Peekay found a florist in the foyer of his hotel and bought two dozen creamy, long stemmed roses of a type called Peace. They were one of the many varieties in his grandpa's garden and the name seemed appropriate to the occasion. Besides, Peace is a rose that opens slowly and holds its open head firm. Red or pink roses might have made a more spectacular immediate impression on Mrs Smith, but he could count on Peace to keep the goodwill going for up to a week.

The third cab to approach him was driven by a coloured man. Peekay hailed it and gave the driver Mrs Smith's address. Twenty minutes later the cab drew up outside a small, free-standing house with a neat garden. The street seemed in need of repair; the surface carried several large potholes and in front of many of the houses the grass and weeds grew tall. Every third or fourth house seemed to have a Chevvy or 'beetle-back' Ford outside on the pavement jacked up on bricks.

The houses were a job lot, more or less identical; only owner-pride separated their condition. Their front gardens were either dust bowls filled with weed or, like Mrs Smith's, were neat and tidy.

A cockerel crowed in a nearby back yard, followed by the soft 'quarrrk' of a broody hen. It was nice to know chickens had not yet been banished in this urban environment. Peekay was fond of chickens; a neighbourhood with chickens was usually settled. You can't go carting chickens all over the place.

The street was filled with children who matched the houses, some dressed with care while others were ragged, though they all seemed to be playing happily together in the late afternoon sun.

As Peekay approached the house and stepped onto the porch the door opened and a large woman appeared. She was dressed in a black satin dress with a gigantic brilliant scarlet bow attached to its front. Her thick pebble glasses seemed at first to be trying to focus on Peekay, for her head moved around to his left and then right and then over his head before steadying on him. Then Peekay realised she was looking to see if he was alone.

'Y'all come alone, Mr Peekay? Where's that bum, Jerome "Pumpkin Face" da Crecipe? What kind name that, da Crecipe? That French from down Louisiana way, for sure! My Peppy he done whup that bum, that ain't no draw'd boxing match if ever I seed one!'

'I'm afraid I wasn't there to see it,' Peekay laughed. 'But if Peppy *did* beat him he's a very promising fighter. De Cresphy is good, very good; I would have thought a draw at Peppy's age was a very creditable performance.'

'That jus' what the man sayed in the paper! Come Mr Peekay, why y'all standin' there, come, come into my house.' It seemed to Peekay less like an invitation than a demand. He followed the very large Mrs Smith into the tiny front parlour. Peekay handed her the roses and she broke into a big smile. 'You got winnin' ways, Mr Peekay. Decidedly winnin' ways!' She proceeded to count the roses, touching each with a large, fat, ringed finger.

'Why, I do declare, ain't nobody ever give me two-dozen long-stem roses before. Sit!' The fat, ringed finger, which moments before had been counting the roses, now emphasised the unexpected command by pointing in the direction of a deep overstuffed armchair. It was one of three, making up a brown vinyl suite encamped around a small coffee table covered with a white lace cloth, its tassles touching a carpet patterned in pink roses against a deep purple background. On the table was a cut-glass vase into which had been placed an arrangement of red and pink crêpe-paper roses. Beside the vase on the table lay a newspaper.

'Please, Mrs Smith, just call me Peekay, I'm not much older than Peppy.' Peekay found himself seated in the chair without quite knowing how he got there.

'You old 'nough to be the boss, Peekay. You got the drive. I can see you got the drive. Some folk got it some, some ain't got it none and some folk got 'nough to push the world 'round with their little finger. But hear me, boy! Y'all ain't gonna push the likes of me 'round, I ain't goin' nowhere, nossir!'

Peekay was embarrassed and somewhat bemused. 'Well, I don't quite know what to say, Mrs Smith. We, er . . . hadn't thought of moving you. It's your son, Peppy. Didn't he tell you?'

'Yeah, he tol' me.' She was still holding the flowers, clutching them against the large scarlet bow. She stooped and picked up the newspaper and slapped it down hard against the arm of Peekay's chair so that he jumped in alarm. 'It say here in the newspaper this is the catfish and caviar contest. That Jake "Spoonbill" Jackson, he the catfish and you, Mr Peekay, you the caviar. That's jes' another way of saying the good-for-nothing nigger is fightin' the nice, rich white boy! Well you listen up good, Mr Peekay. Peppy he catfish! His mamma she catfish! Even that bum "Pumpkin Face", he catfish! Ain't no catfish that belong helpin' caviar to win no world champion title!'

Peekay was stunned; he'd come expecting to be confronted by a slightly worried and caring mother, anxious to confirm her boy would be in good hands. A little ego massaging and all would be well, because, in fact, her boy *would* be in good hands. Now, facing this mountain of indignant opposition, he was at a loss to know how to react. He sat quietly, trying to calm his thoughts, to think of something appropriate to say.

'Ho! Cat got your tongue, boy?'

He could feel the heat coming from her large frame as though she were a generator, which, he supposed, in a way she was. The first rule of combat Peekay knew was to put your opponent on equal or inferior terms. Authority in its most basic form is two things: the way you appear and the way you talk. It is impossible to have authority standing in the nude addressing a roomful of fully clothed people. In the same sense, his small frame sunk deeply into the large vinyl chair with the quivering mass of black and scarlet female hovering over him had the same effect. Her enormous presence was calculated to reduce anything he said to pathetic drivel.

'Please, Mrs Smith, won't you sit down?' Peekay rose from his chair and indicated the chair next to him. Once down he knew it would be difficult for her to rise, she was far too big for sudden, spontaneous movement. Mrs Smith hesitated, but then sank slowly into the chair. Still clutching the roses she lowered herself into the chair by propping one arm onto the arm of the chair until a soft expulsion of air indicated she'd filled the interior. Peekay took the roses from her grasp.

'Do you know the name of this rose, Mrs Smith?' He placed the bunch on the table and seated himself on the arm of the second vinyl armchair so that he was in a position to look down at the mountainous woman.

Mrs Smith chuckled. 'A rose by any other name smell jus' as sweet!'

'That's William Shakespeare!'

'Mr Wolfson, he tell me that once when they bring me back some perfume from Paris, France. "A rose by any other name smell jus' as sweet!" My name is Rose you see.'

'Mr Wolfson?'

'That's the family where I the cook. The whole family they gone to France. Mr Wolfson he got folks in Europe, they ain't comin' back before Christmas.'

'Well, the name of this rose is "Peace". You see, Mrs Smith, I've come in peace. I didn't write that catfish and caviar nonsense. You know how the newspapers carry on? Taking something and blowing it up, pitting one side against another. You see, Mrs Smith, I'm really a lot more catfish than I am caviar. But in the end, ma'am, we're all just people, don't you think?'

Mrs Smith looked up at Peekay through her pebble glasses. She didn't seem in the least intimidated by the high ground Peekay occupied. Through the thick lenses her eyes were enormous. Peekay felt like a mouse on a rafter being watched from below by a barn owl. 'You a sweet talker, Mr Peekay.' She pointed a fat finger at the roses. 'It's true they called Peace?'

'Cross my heart!' Peekay knew he was beginning to win. It was time to change tack. 'Mrs Smith, I can understand how you feel, if Peppy can't come, well, it's disappointing. He's a wonderful young boxer, he'd learn a lot with us. But I do understand completely.'

'Now you jus' wait, Mr Caviar who turn Catfish! Who said Peppy ain't comin'?'

'Well, ah . . . I got the impression . . . well, you did?'

'Now you just listen up, young man. It ain't jus' what it says in that newspaper. Every time Peppy goes away he comes back to his mamma so thin and miserable, like a dry stick; put him across your knee, go whap an' he'd break in two pieces like he's nothin' but kindlin' wood!'

She'd walked right into Peekay's cleverly laid trap. 'Mrs Smith, why don't you come to Pike's Peak as our cook? You said the Wolfsons are overseas? I'll call Mr Graw in Denver first thing and tell him not to hire a cook. Do you think you can cook for ten men?'

Mrs Smith made a valiant effort to rise and managed to get halfway out of the chair. 'Ho, I can cook for the whole United States Marine Corps if I set my mind to it! Ten people, why, that ain't even a proper dinner party at the Wolfson residence!' She fell back into the chair, fanning her face with a large hand.

'Then it's a deal, you'll come?'

'A rose by any other name ain't so stoopid. We ain't talked 'bout the remuneration!'

'Why, what you're getting now, of course!'

'What I gettin now don't suppose I got to climb up no mountain to go to work! It don't suppose I gotta fall into no canyon! It don't suppose I gonna cook on no 'lectric range no more! It don't suppose I gotta be away from home for two months!'

'Okay, twenty-percent hardship allowance,' Peekay guessed. 'That's the usual,' he added, trying to sound convincing.

To his enormous surprise Mrs Smith rose out of her chair as though she'd been fired from a gun. 'Peppy, you come out that bedroom now, you heah! Bring mama's suitcase, the one I packed las' night; we goin' mountain climbin', sweetheart!'

The laughter in her stomach started as a low rumble that rapidly grew in intensity. Peekay started to laugh too. Soon they were clutching onto each other both of them convulsed. 'Ho, ho, ho, hee, hee, hee, you ain't no catfish, Peekay, ho, ho, hee, hee, you the virgin sturgeon, if evah I saw it!'

Peppy, a serious expression on his face, entered the small parlour struggling with an enormous old suitcase. Peekay pointed to it, his mouth open in amazement and the two of them exploded into fresh gales of laughter. Exhausted, both collapsed back into the chairs. 'Game, set and match to Mrs Smith,' Peekay said, knuckling the tears from his eyes.

'I can sing too, baby. I'm gonna throw in singing foh free.'

It was fortunate that Jerome and Peekay had left New York with what amounted to an overnight bag each. By combining the weight allowance of the four of them the airline settled for a ten dollar overweight charge on Mrs Smith's baggage. Apart from her big suitcase, she carried with her all manner of kitchen equipment starting with a griddle and frying pan, both large enough to cook enough flapjacks and fried eggs for an army.

They'd met Hymie and the rest of the New York party in Kansas City. The only other addition to the troupe was an elderly fighter's manager who claimed his name was Daddy Kocklelovsky but who was known as the shortened version, Daddy Kockle. He was a negro with snowy-white hair. He'd been born in Texas during the presidency of James A. Garfield, which made him at the most sixty-six years old.

Daddy Kockle had seen Jake 'Spoonbill' Jackson fight on several occasions and he'd taken the job in Colorado, not at all sure that the unknown Peekay wouldn't be badly mismatched in the ring. Jackson at his best was a formidable opponent; most experts believed him to be unbeatable. But after watching Peekay, the speed and intelligence of the young South African had impressed him. As the fight drew closer he became more and more convinced that the man who needed the title the most would be the ultimate winner.

One afternoon he called Peekay aside. 'Tell me, son, how bad you want to win?'

'Bad, Daddy Kockle. *Real bad!*' Peekay replied, using the Americanism for emphasis.

'Real bad ain't enough. Jackson he want *real bad* also. Tell me, you hate Jackson some, a lot, you don't hate him at all; which is it?'

'I just want what he's got, it belongs to me, the title, it's mine. But I don't hate him, Daddy!'

'Son, you got two weeks. By the time you climb in that ring you gotta hate that nigger, you hear?'

Peekay was shocked at the expression. 'Christ! I don't think of him as a nigger! He's a fighter, the world champion! I want his title. I've thought about owning that title a hundred times every day since I was six years old. I don't give a fuck who owns it, it's mine, that's all!'

'I like that, son. You got heat. That a good start. But you ain't got hate. You gotta have hate! For some other title, maybe heat enough. In a world championship it ain't. Why you think Jackson been saying those things 'bout you in the newspaper and on the radio? You saw what he said in the newspaper yesterday. He says he's buildin' up his dislike. He said he got enough already built up to put you out in the fifth round but he's buildin' on it! Dis-like! That's jus' 'nother word foh hate, sonny boy!'

'Let me tell you something! I want that title so badly my teeth hurt just thinking about it. Every muscle, every sinew, every second of my day and night is involved with winning it. It's not getting rich that matters for me. The title isn't about getting rich and driving around in a big Cadillac with my name painted on the door. It's about being free to be myself, the person hiding behind the person. I'm trapped inside myself, Daddy. The title is the doorway to my escape! That's why I'm coming down the mountain to take Jake "Spoonbill" Jackson!'

Peekay had never talked to anyone like this before and he didn't understand why he was telling Daddy Kockle now, or even if he was making any sense to the old man.

'I can't reckon too much on that, son, what's inside a man is there for his own self. But I can reckon on knowin' how a fighter get ready foh fightin'. He got to know he superior, he better! Now you lissen to me, son. What I got to say now it ain't pretty and it ain't oughta be spoke by no black man. You gonna fight a nigger. That not the same thing as fightin' a white man. A nigger got some things in his head you use right, you can whup him. Inferiority things, things he can't help hisself 'cause they borned into him. Ain't so long ago we coloured people, we been slaves. Jackson, he's a southern boy, from Kentucky. That ain't no place a coloured boy ever grow'd up brave! That's Klan territory, that's mighty fearful country. Right now, in that boy's home town, there are white folk saying, "That Nigger, he's too sassy, he got a big mouth foh a nigger. Maybe that white boy he gonna whup him good, teach him his place!" '

'Jesus, Daddy Kockle, it's nice knowing you're on my side but this is racist stuff, it's everything that repulses me!'

'Never mind no racist! You think like that, Peekay, you gonna lose! Hear me, this ain't no boxing match, this is war! What kinda war you got when you gonna love thine enemy!'

'I don't *love* Jackson, I just don't hate him because he's black. Give me some other reason to hate him!'

'Ain't no other reason. That's the strongest. That's the one reason supersedes all the others. That's the one reason ain't got logic. It's the bes' kind of hate foh a fightin' man!'

The old man shook his head, 'My granpappy he tol' me a sad tale his granpappy tol' him concernin' the slaves. He told when the Arab captured him and his brothers in his village in Africa and marched them to the ships and sold them to the white man captain of a big ship. He told how they chained them in the hold below, but the young women they put in a big cage on the deck. Then come those sailor men with a bottle and the bottle it contained blood and they drank the blood and they done raped them black women in the cage. They were raped by cannibals! Blood drinkin' cannibals who killed their men below and drank their blood!' Daddy Kockle chuckled. 'Ain't that somethin'? All the time, it ain't the black people who are the cannibals, it's the white! That's the kind of fear that lies inside the black man. That's the kind of hate. It ain't logic hate. It ain't logic fear. My granpappy he prob'ly figured out what them sailor men bin' drinking from that bottle was rum or port wine. But what his granpappy tol' him is the truth accordin' to the way he want to feel. It ain't no logical truth. That make no difference. It's the emotional truth. The emotional truth got the fear and the hate contained in it!' Daddy Kockle paused. 'That's the hate Jackson got in him! That the hate you gonna come into the ring to fight, but also the fear. Now lissen, boy, the idea! The idea is you got to make the fear in that southern black boy more than the hate. Then Jackson, he gonna be whupped!'

'Daddy Kockle, I'm going to have to take this problem to the mountain, I just don't know what to say. I'm sorry, but I can't build up an emotional reaction to Jackson based on his colour. My life, my future life, is dedicated to the proposition that all men should be born equal. What happens to them after that is up to them. But they must be given equal social and intellectual opportunity based on their minds, their skills and their personalities. When you declare a man or woman inferior, second class, because of pigmentation, then you sin beyond any possibility of redemption. That's the very point of a boxing ring; it's twenty foot by twenty foot of equal opportunity. When you climb into the ring, all you've got is your brain and your fists. If you win it's because you're the best man, not because you've been given a totally unfair advantage as a birthright!'

Daddy Kockle clucked and shook his head. 'Hallelujah! Praise the Lord! You're a good man, Peekay. But that ain't winnin' talk, that losin' talk if ever I heard it, son.'

The expression Peekay had used about taking the problem up to the mountain had been devised by Jerome. 'O-ho, Peekay he goin' to the mountains to get hisself a problem fix!'

In the bright crisp September and October afternoons in the Rockies when they'd completed training for the day Peekay would head for the mountains. Togger had accompanied him on one early occasion but they'd seen a rattlesnake on a rock catching the last of the afternoon sun and he'd decided the countryside was for the birds.

Peekay had been raised in the mountains with Doc and while the Rockies, iced with early snow, were somewhat different to the soft shouldered hills that rolled back into the high mountains which cradled the small lowveld town where he'd spent his boyhood, they nevertheless filled a deep need within him.

In the mines and during his Oxford years he'd been away from the high crags and terraces that leave a man free to think his mind clean and clear. From the dude camp he'd quickly climb through the ponderosa pine where the silvertailed squirrels darted from tree to tree, less scared at his approach than curious. Beyond the pine he'd climb through sparse clumps of sycamore and mountain ash on beyond the Alpine flora to the sharp outcrops of rock and cliff face. Twice he'd seen a lone coyote on a ridge and imagined it was the same one, an old loner who liked the privacy of the high ground where he could look at the Rockies climbing higher to the North West and the vast plains beneath him where the Sioux and the Cheyenne had once ruled and buffalo had once grazed in their tens of thousands.

Peekay would return at sunset from his mountain walks in time to take his turn chopping firewood, for it was log-sawing in the early mornings and chopping at night. Invariably he'd mention a possible solution he'd found to a problem they'd come against during the day's work-out or when they'd been discussing tactics over lunch.

A golden eagle, the first Peekay had ever seen, hovered no more than a boy's kite flight above him, so close he could see the ribbed feathers in its wingspan tipped with backlight. The eagle seemed to symbolise all that was beautiful in this magnificent country which Peekay was beginning to love enormously. The people they'd met had, for the most part, been so open, kind and hospitable that Peekay had been able to put the Jackson campaign into perspective. What he hadn't reckoned with was the power of the media, who'd grabbed the catfish and caviar analogy and were milking it to death.

Jackson had abandoned his often clever invective of earlier weeks and lately had been building on his hate thing. It was the first time a black American boxer had used the black/white dichotomy in a determined way. In the America of the mid fifties, black sportsmen were still expected to behave in a modest and submissive manner, grateful for the opportunity sport provided them to rise above their peers. It was an unstated thing, built out of a century and a half of accepting the negro as the underclass. Jackson's aggression towards his white opponent was seen as unseemly and provocative, and it was beginning to polarise fight fans along racist lines. It even had the effect of turning many of Jackson's own fans in the white Southern States against him.

The point was, if Jackson was simply building up the gate and his reputation with it, he was doing a remarkable job and the 'catfish and caviar' concept was working brilliantly. But in the last weeks he'd been pushing the concept of hate seemingly beyond the simple pyrotechnics of boxing promotion. If as Daddy Kockle insisted, rage and hate were indeed indispensable allies in the ring, then Peekay needed to do something to neutralise this advantage. Jackson's umbilical fear, passed on through generations of persecution and humiliation, was the way to do so. How to do this without being a white supremacist was the problem Peekay now faced.

The irony was, as a small boy who had himself been persecuted and humiliated, Peekay knew the kind of meaningless fear that gnaws at the lining of your gut. He had been taught by the great Inkosi-Inkosikazi, the greatest medicine man in all of Africa, to visit the night country where he could control his anxieties or solve the problems confronting him. And so, seated on a huge outcrop of rock just below the snowline in the Rocky Mountains, Peekay returned to Africa, to a primitive, deeply atavistic part of his mind, where he would seek the strength to confront Jackson's hate.

In Peekay's mind the night country was a very real place, the place of three waterfalls and ten stepping-stones in the Africa of his soul. He now prepared to enter it and closed his eyes, waiting for the stillness to come, the measured downward plunge into the night country, like the slowness of a man seen falling from a cliff at a great distance.

A sudden roar of water filled Peekay's head and he stood on a ledge above the first waterfall. Far below him the river rushed away, tumbling and boiling into a narrow gorge. Just before the water entered the gorge was the pool of the ten stepping-stones, ten anthracite teeth strung across its shimmering, gargling mouth. Inkosi-Inkosikazi spoke into the roar of the water, his voice quiet, almost gentle:

You are standing on a rock above the highest waterfall, a young warrior who has killed his first lion and is worthy now to fight in the legion of Dingane, the great impi that destroys all before it, worthy even to fight in the impi of Shaka, the greatest warrior king of all.

You are wearing the skirt of lion tail as you face into the setting sun. Now the sun has passed beyond Zululand, even past the land of the Swazi, and now it leaves the Shangaan and the royal kraal of Mojaji, the rain queen, to be cooled in the great, dark water beyond.

You can see the moon rising over Africa and you are at peace with the night, unafraid of the great demon Skohaan who comes to feed on the dark night, tearing at its black flesh until, at last, it is finished and the new light comes to stir the herd boys and send them out to mind the lowing cattle.

As Peekay stood on the rock above the highest waterfall, waiting to jump, he could see the moon rising, held huge in a star-pinned sky, a bright silver florin throwing its light down onto the ten black stepping-stones two hundred feet below, where the third waterfall crashed down.

Inkosi-Inkosikazi's voice came to him: *You must jump now, little warrior of the king.*

Peekay took a deep breath and launched himself into the night. The cool air, mixed with spray, rushed past his face. He hit the water below the first pool, sinking briefly before rising to the surface. With barely time to take a breath, he was swept over the lip of the second waterfall and then again down the third, plunging into the great roaring pool at its base. He swam strongly to the first of the great stones glistening wet and black in the moonlight. Jumping from stone to stone, he crossed the river, leaping to the pebbly beach on the far side.

Clear as an echo the great witchdoctor's voice cut through the roar of the falls. *We have crossed the dreamtime to the other side and it is done.*

Peekay opened his eyes. Above him, over the far Rockies, huge cloud castles of light rose in a sky beginning to dim for the night. He picked his way down to the dark line of ponderosa pine, sending shale sliding and small rocks tumbling ahead of him. It was turning cold, the first hint of winter coming to the high mountains. This was the last time he would go up to the mountain. Tomorrow they would leave for New York. It was exactly one week before he would climb into the ring at Madison Square Garden. One week and sixteen years of waiting to become the welterweight champion of the world.

In his head Peekay carried the line he knew would undermine Jake 'Spoonbill' Jackson's hate.

TWENTY-THREE

Hymie had spent very little time in the mountains. Most of the time he was in New York tying up details for the fight, getting the film crew organised and supervising the footage which had been shot of Peekay in training camp. It had originally been intended that the film crew would spend a month in Colorado, but a good training schedule is pretty routine and after a week they'd obtained all the footage they needed. This was good on two counts: it made up for the money Peekay had spent on air fares for himself, Mrs Smith and the two fighters flying from Atlanta to Kansas City and it left Dutch and Daddy Kockle free to run a tight, uninterrupted programme.

Peekay had entered training camp six pounds under the welterweight limit. Mrs Smith's cooking steadily took care of the deficit. No training stable ever ate better. Despite the gruelling programme, by the time they returned to New York he was a pound and a half under the correct weight, which was the strongest he'd ever been going into a fight.

Mrs Smith was a fighter's mother and was therefore conscious of diet and she'd served Peekay well.

She also realised Peekay and Dutch were helping her boy. Peekay fought hard in the training sessions but he never set out to hurt his sparring partners as some champions do and he would often enough stop when Peppy made an error of judgement and explain it to him, showing him how to avoid the trap it inevitably led to. After the seven weeks in training camp the young speed-merchant from Atlanta was starting to develop a good left-hand punch and was a much improved all-round boxer. Mrs Smith showed her gratitude by delighting their stomachs at every meal.

On one occasion Hymie had returned to the ranch with a new orchestration by St Martin in the Fields of the Odd Bodleian Choir singing the *Concerto for the Great Southland*. Mrs Smith had loved it immediately. She'd previously organised them all into a small musical group. Daddy Kockle played a nice clean clarinet and Dutch was no slouch with a mouth organ. Peppy's voice was light but clear and Jerome was a good baritone. Only Togger was almost tone deaf but this was no big deal and he was expected to sing along anyway. Seated at the ranch piano, an old upright which wasn't too badly out of tune, Mrs Smith taught Togger, Dutch and Peekay most of the well-known negro spirituals. To Peekay's surprise he knew a great many of them, coming as he did from a background of the Apostolic Faith Mission. With the advent of Hymie's new pressing the small group now learned to sing and play Doc's wonderful concerto, Mrs Smith taking the lead part with the rest of them following as the chorus. She was a skilful pianist and a superb contralto, and she sang the haunting refrains with an instinctive sense of Africa, though the music would often reduce her to tears. She would remove her pebble glasses and wipe her eyes and sniff. 'I bin visitin' my people in the great Southland of Africa. Peekay, yo' people and mine they sure got lovin' and hopin' in their voice!'

With a great fire crackling in the huge open fireplace, Mrs Smith's musical soirées proved to be among the happiest memories Peekay would take back with him from America.

It had been expected that Mrs Smith and Peppy would return to Atlanta when the camp broke up but there was simply no way she was going to miss the fight and she wrote to kin folk in Harlem to tell them to expect the two of them. Peekay had selected Jerome and Togger as the sparring partners he wished to work out with in his last week, which was basically easy stuff and a wind down to the fight. Together with Dutch, the three boxers had taken a plane from Denver to New York, leaving the others to make the long journey back in the Chevvy bus.

The Odd Bodleians had arrived, taking an entire floor of the Waldorf Astoria and sending Manhattan's socialites into a veritable whirl. The arrival of the Oxford contingent led by Aunt Tom almost guaranteed the fight would be a society affair, and Bergdorf Goodman enjoyed a sudden upsurge in business as lavish parties were hastily arranged all over town.

Jam Jar took a suite and seemed to party on from the moment he arrived. Even when he was out at the invitation of some Boston Brahmin or Sutton Place socialite, a business acquaintance or friend of the family, the party in his suite continued.

The weigh-in took place mid morning on the day of the fight at the offices of the New York Boxing Commission just up from Madison Square Garden. The auditorium with its high ceilings was crowded with people: reporters and photographers hoping for a confrontation between the two fighters, ex-fighters and hangers-on, people who hoped to be seen and who called hello loudly to others they hoped to impress.

Mrs Smith was there wearing a brilliant yellow dress with a pale blue picture hat and carrying a yellow silk parasol like a walking stick. Yellow and blue were Peekay's colours and she wore them with a huge smile as she walked with Dutch. Peppy had joined Jerome at the opposite end of the room, conscious that his mama was the only woman in the room. O'Flynn the promoter was talking to Hymie waving his hands, obviously upset over something and Elmer Milstein was talking to the unit manager of ABC Wide World of Sports who were setting up a camera.

Jake 'Spoonbill' Jackson hadn't yet arrived. It was the champ's prerogative to be late and to be weighed in first and Peekay stood quietly with Togger and Daddy Kockle. He'd made no concession to the event and wore the blue tracksuit Hymie had given him the first day they'd turned out for Dutch three years earlier. The yellow silk stitching proclaiming 'The Tadpole Angel' on the back had faded and where some of it had been worn away Mrs Smith had lovingly re-embroidered it, sitting by the fireplace in Colorado.

There was a sudden lifting of the noise level in the auditorium as Jake 'Spoonbill' Jackson entered. Jackson was a smooth-faced man with an elongated head which didn't seem in the least bit negroid. His head was completely shaved, but he'd grown a pencil-line moustache which hardly showed because his skin was so black. Now he wore a white satin dressing-gown with an American flag on the back and a plain pair of basketball boots, with the laces undone, flapping on the floor as he walked. The dirty sneaker-style boots contrasted strangely with the ritzy-looking robe. He untied and removed his robe, allowing it to fall into the hands of Michael O'Rourke, who stood directly behind him. Then he stepped out of his shoes and stood barefoot beside the scales in a pair of white satin boxing shorts. Around his waist hung his WBC World Championship Belt, a grotesque gold and enamelled affair which resembled an elaborate kidney belt. With a grin he stepped onto the machine expecting the official to commence weighing him in.

However, the small bald-headed man in charge of the scales simply waited. Jackson grinned a trifle awkwardly; unclipping the belt, he handed it to O'Rourke. He'd obviously worked up a little scene which had backfired and to cover his embarrassment he now turned to the crowd. Standing on the scales like an orchestral leader, he raised his arms.

'What a Spoonbill stork do to the Tadpole?' he yelled.

'He munch him!' the ten or so people in his retinue shouted.

'And then what he do?' Jackson shouted again.

'He crunch him!' they answered.

'And when he munch him and crunch him what he do then?'

'He swallow him down!!' The group yelled at the top of their lungs, some of them punching the air above their heads like a group of cheerleaders.

Jackson turned to Peekay, acknowledging him for the first time. 'You call me Catfish, you damn right, I Catfish!' He turned to the group once again, 'What a Catfish gonna do to a tadpole?'

'He *munch* him and *crunch* him and *swallow him down*!' they yelled back gleefully.

Jackson pointed his finger at his opponent. 'You hear me now, white boy! You hear me good, Tadpole! I'm hungry, I'm hungry, man! Tonight I gonna *eat you*!'

Peekay regarded him silently for a long moment. Then he said, 'I have only this to say to Mr Jake Spoonbill Jackson,' he paused as the whole room waited to hear his response to the champion's goading. 'If he takes his hate with him into the ring tonight I will win for . . . *hate is a slow-witted ally in the ring.'* They were the words he had been given in the night country.

The commission doctor examined them both, measuring their heartbeats and taking their blood pressure. They weighed in almost identically, Peekay just four ounces lighter than Jackson, who came in a pound under the welterweight limit. The whole procedure was all over in less than fifteen minutes. Now only waiting time remained and Peekay returned to the hotel to rest.

Dozens of telegrams had arrived from South Africa, notably from St John Burnham, Peekay's old headmaster, Gert and Captain Smith at the Barberton prison, the mayor and town council of Barberton, Miss Bornstein, Peekay's primary school teacher, Mrs Boxall and one from Gideon Mandoma which read:

Hambari ngokunakekela bafowenu ma bulala ingonyama.
Go carefully my brother and kill the lion.

Among the many telegrams were some from E.W., Harriet, from England, and one from Doris which read: *Roses are red . . . Violets are blue. Win or lose, I'll still love you! Doris xxx*

Doris with the wonderful tits, as usual, was about as subtle as a meat axe, but Peekay found he missed her rather more than Harriet.

Hymie came in and sat on Peekay's bed. 'I don't seem to have spent enough time with you, over these last eight weeks, old mate,' he grinned.

'All the time I needed, Hymie.' Peekay punched Hymie lightly on the shoulder. 'As long as you're in my corner tonight, that's all that matters.' Peekay could feel himself becoming sentimental and changed the subject quickly. 'Why were you and O'Flynn having a set-to this morning?'

Hymie explained how Aunt Tom wanted Mrs Smith in with the Odd Bodleians and O'Flynn had insisted they forfeit six seats for the space the piano would occupy or pay him two hundred and fifty dollars a seat.

'Jesus, Peekay, I usually love dealing with the Americans, they're open, honest and they make decisions fast. But the guys running American boxing are crud! It's full of hoods, hoodlums and rip-off merchants. I'll be bloody glad when you take that championship belt and piss off.'

Peekay realised what a strain it had all been for Hymie, who'd worked solidly for a year to bring the event off so that they'd end up with some money in the bank despite the lopsided purse they were getting for the fight. Peekay was going to need money to buy his share of a law practice and the often delicate negotiations had largely fallen to Hymie. 'Thank you, Hymie. I owe you a big one,' he said softly.

Hymie looked at his friend almost fiercely. 'Never! I could never begin to give you back what you've given me, Peekay. Without you I would have ended up just another rich Jew in carpet and underfelt.'

Hymie and Peekay left the hotel together, driven to the Garden in

Elmer's family Lincoln. Sensing they wished to be alone the chauffeur activated the electric window, sealing the back from the front of the car. It was a ritual the two of them had kept since the first fight they'd worked together at school. Just the two of them going through tactics, talking the fight into each other's heads. Woodrow was directed to a side entrance.

Daddy Kockle and Togger were waiting for them in the dressing room. It was big and cold place about as welcoming as a public latrine. Against the left-hand wall stood a make-up bench above which was a mirror surrounded with small naked globes, most of them either smashed or not working. Peekay entered and threw his bag on the bench which was scarred with a thousand cigarette burns. The surface of the mirror, where the mercury had blistered into brown blobs, made his face look as though it was covered in liver spots. A bentwood chair, the rattan missing from the seat and replaced by a section of plywood, stood in front of the bench. A wooden bench ran down the centre of the room and another ran across the far wall where it was stopped short by a closed door. A rub-down table rested between the centre bench and the wall opposite the mirror. From the ceiling a naked bulb of very high wattage flared concentrated white light into the room. There was absolutely nothing comfortable about the dressing room. It looked like it was; a place to leave and a place to come back to without making any impression. The door on the far wall, Togger discovered, led to a shower and toilet.

Dutch arrived, looking nervously at his watch. There was plenty of time. Togger held a small hand towel. It seemed to be a prop, to give his hands something to do for he was twisting it unknowingly into a length resembling a thick piece of rope. Only Daddy Kockle seemed relaxed and was seated on the rubbing table with his legs crossed.

Peekay started to undress. Togger, happy to find something to do, took Peekay's clothes and hung them up on a wire hanger like a valet. Peekay fitted the protector harness on, a jockstrap device with a hard, leather-covered aluminium crotch box. Then he pulled on the light blue shorts with the yellow waistline which Hymie had ordered for the fight, after which he pulled on a pair of thick socks. Leaving off his boxing boots, he moved over to the rub-down table. Daddy Kockle jumped from the table and Peekay saw he'd brought his clarinet.

Dutch started to work on Peekay's shoulders, first rubbing him down with vaseline, then taking the towel from Togger and rubbing what vaseline remained off again before starting to massage his shoulders. 'Just a light one, lad, loosen you up a bit,' he spoke softly as though only the two of them were in the room. 'Take your time tonight, build it slowly, you've got fifteen rounds.' It was advice he'd offered a hundred times before.

With half an hour to go, O'Rourke arrived to supervise the taping of Peekay's hands. He was smoking a large cigar and looked cheap and ruddy, wearing a grey pin-striped suit, a green-striped shirt with a gold collar pin, a bright green tie and a real carnation in his buttonhole. They were surprised to see him. It was usual to send the fight manager along or even the trainer to supervise the bandaging. 'I've come to do the honours meself,' he announced, smiling. 'The Garden's sold out, standing room only. Mr O'Flynn's a very happy man.'

'He ought to be, he got a grand out of me for the piano,' Hymie said.

'Well now, a piano takes a lot of space, son! At two hundred and fifty bucks a ringside seat, I reckon you got off light, my boy!'

'I'd rather you didn't call me son or boy, Mr O'Rourke. Only your fighter is further from being of Irish descent than I am and I imagine we're both grateful to our antecedents for this fact.' Hymie turned to Dutch. 'Have you got the bandages, let's get this over! Daddy Kockle, you better go do the same and check out *Munch, Crunch and Swallow's* hands.'

O'Rourke removed the cigar from his mouth, tapping ash onto the floor. 'Now, now, no hard feelings, Levy? We've come this far. It could have been worse for you, to be sure, we don't take too kindly to strangers playing on our turf.'

'Sure, Michael, you've been a perfect gentleman. Let's leave it there, shall we?'

But O'Rourke was clearly not finished yet. 'Be thankful you got a crack at the title, we could have held out, made things a lot more difficult, son.' O'Rourke stuck his chin out and pushed the cigar back into his mouth, holding it between his forefinger and thumb, waiting for Hymie to challenge him again on his use of the word 'son'.

'Hey! We're all a little tense,' Peekay exclaimed. 'Did you bring a pen, Mr O'Rourke?'

O'Rourke kept his eyes on Hymie, squinting down at him. Then he grinned, 'Sure thing, Peekay.' He removed his hand from the cigar and looking down at his left-side top pocket he withdrew a solid gold Parker, holding it up in triumph for all to see.

When Dutch had completed taping his hands, Peekay held them out for O'Rourke, who crisscrossed the bandages with his pen. He drew back. 'Okay, may the best man win, Peekay, and we all know who that is,' he said, attempting an enigmatic smile.

Hymie walked over with the Everlast gloves, offering them to the Irishman to inspect. O'Rourke shook his head, indicating that Hymie should go ahead and put them on. The gloves were a new bright red colour and soaked up the light where they curved around the fist. Hymie fitted the left glove on first, the way Hoppie Groenewald had done that first time on the train. *First with your head and then with your heart!* It was such a long time ago.

Peekay banged the two gloves together, feeling the fit. O'Rourke punched him lightly on the shoulder, then he turned and left the room.

Peekay slipped off the rub-down table and, crossing the room, sat down on the bench against the wall. Togger knelt down, slipped the soft boots onto Peekay's feet and tied the laces, taping the ends to the boots so they didn't flap around during the fight.

Daddy Kockle entered with an official who stood just outside the door holding onto the lintel with both hands and leaned in as he spoke. 'Ten minutes! The champ wants to go last. Get ready to move when you hear the ring announcer declare the result of the last fight on the undercard.'

Daddy Kockle said, 'We got a police escort to the ring, now ain't that something?'

Peekay closed his eyes, emptying his head. Doc had been dead six years, lying in the crystal cave of Africa. 'You can be it, absoloodle!' he'd said when Peekay had announced he intended to be the welterweight champion of the world. 'Every day you must say, I am champion of za world! You will see, one day you will be it.'

'Son, this for you,' Peekay heard Daddy Kockle say. 'This is the song my daddy played on his horn when something good happen.' He paused, holding the clarinet ready for his lips. 'It's called, "Crossin' over Jordan to the Other Side".'

Daddy Kockle, seated once again on the rub-down table, began to play. The sweet low sound of the clarinet climbed slowly, filling the room and calming the sharp light. The negro spiritual lifted Peekay, holding him, cradling him in its arms, rocking him, calming him, until at last it softened to an almost mute note then faded like a snowflake into nothing as it let him go.

Peekay opened his eyes and Daddy Kockle put down his instrument. 'Son, I got a whole heap of respect for you,' he said quietly.

The noise of the crowd lifted suddenly and they heard the ring announcer beginning to call the introductions. Though they'd not yet glimpsed the crowd they could feel the excitement in the Garden. The women at the ringside wearing formal gowns and the men evening suits and tuxedos. The mink from the Bronx and Harlem mixed with the silver fox from Sutton Place, and diamonds in every configuration called it a draw between bandit and banker. Boston blue blood mixed happily with prominent figures from boxing, showbiz and the Italian, Irish and black underworld. Several of the better-known TV and sporting personalities drew an excited response from the crowd as they made their way to the ringside, the loudest applause perhaps being for Joe Di Maggio of the New York Yankees.

'Time to go,' Hymie called softly, holding out the blue-and-yellow silk robe with 'The Tadpole Angel' embroidered on the back.

Peekay held his arms out for Hymie to slip the sleeves of the silk robe over them. First tying the front of the robe, Peekay put his hand on Hymie's shoulder and they walked out together to the sudden and growing roar of the crowd. Hymie could feel the slightest tremble coming from Peekay's hand. It was a good sign. The adrenalin was beginning to pump; Peekay was ready to fight.

The roar of the crowd lifted as they came into sight. There wasn't any doubt Peekay was popular, the noise had a shrillness to it, pitched high. 'The women, they love you, Peekay,' Daddy Kockle shouted. Peekay entered the ring, the lights overhead at first blinding him, so he looked into blackness as he acknowledged the audience, one glove raised above his head.

The Odd Bodleians had risen as he entered. Each wore a yellow rose in the lapel of his evening suit with a flash of blue ribbon laced through the buttonhole. Aunt Tom was dressed in a dinner suit, a brooch of canary yellow diamonds and blue sapphires clipped to her lapel.

Mrs Smith, seated at the piano, looked like an enormous party decoration in a full length, fitted evening dress made entirely of electric blue sequins. Pinned to her large bosom was a corsage of tiny yellow roses. Peekay, raising his glove, acknowledged them with a grin. Then he walked over to the rosin box in his corner and dusted the soles of his boots before sitting on the pot.

The applause as the champion entered was tumultuous; the home-grown boy was getting the acknowledgement he deserved as a great fighter. Jake 'Spoonbill' Jackson came down the aisle surrounded by his large entourage, led by half-a-dozen policemen. He climbed into the ring, jumping up and down with his arms held high above his head, twisting with each jump so that as he landed he faced a different section of the crowd. The tremendous noise hadn't stopped since he'd first appeared in the aisle.

Daddy Kockle began to massage Peekay's shoulder lightly.

'Righto, my son, let's concentrate on fightin' fifteen rounds,' Dutch said.

The ring announcer now stepped into centre ring and the microphone was lowered down to him. He was a small, bald man, dressed in a white tuxedo jacket and black evening pants. The bow tie to his white shirt was no more than half-an-inch wide but stuck out nearly six inches on either side of the tiny centre knot. The first quick impression he gave was of someone with an arrow through his epiglottis who'd had both ends sawn off for the sake of mobility and convenience.

'Ladies and gentlemen, be upstanding for the national anthem.' To everyone's surprise the usual scratched record didn't come wheezing on. Instead the opening chords of 'The Star-Spangled Banner' came from Mrs Smith at the piano where one of several microphones was located. The Odd Bodleians picked up the beautiful anthem and carried it to the crowd. It was stirring stuff and Jake 'Spoonbill' Jackson stood at attention in the centre of the ring while Peekay stood quietly in his corner. The applause was tremendous as they came to the end, the crowd conscious of the compliment they were being paid.

The crowd returned to their seats and the Odd Bodleians remained standing. The noise in the huge place died down as the prelude to the *Concerto for the Great Southland* played, merging quickly to the start of the great Zulu chant. The voice of Mrs Smith called to the chanters in song urging them to declare for the great Shaka King of the Zulus. The male voices responded. At first like distant thunder, when the great clouds on the Drakensberg are still tipped with white, then louder as the storm clouds mulled and gathered, swelling and building following the beautiful contralto voice as it called down in the valleys and up in the high mountains for the young men who had killed a lion and who had lain with a maiden to come and declare themselves for the great warrior king. Then Jam Jar, laying aside his violin, took up the calling. The voices rose in the great war cry, the blooding was coming, when the great Zulu impi would descend in waves, like wind in the grass, to crush the enemy.

Jam Jar's voice held high and then died slowly as he mourned the Zulu dead. Then it rose again as he called the living to pay homage to their fallen comrades. Softly, tenderly the deep male voices rose, like far-off thunder rolling across the valley of a thousand hills, building the sunlight, wiping the sky clean; then again the thunder of their voices rolled louder and louder until it crashed into the valley of the dead and rose again in one sudden, stricken, terrible outcry and stopped. Only the single cry of Jam Jar's violin was left to bring the chant to a close. The enemy was vanquished and the dead returned to their shadows.

For a few moments there was no sound, the crowd stunned by the impact of the chant. Then they rose as one and applauded. They all knew suddenly that this was a challenger who had come to fight for a title, if necessary to die, rather than to walk away without it.

The ring announcer raised his right hand high and, holding onto the microphone with his left, intoned, 'Under the authority of the State of New York Boxing Commission and the New York Athletic Commission, the World Boxing Council, I declare the welterweight championship of the world open to contest!'

He paused, looking over at Peekay and indicating with a jerk of his head that he should rise. 'In the blue corner, weighing one hundred and forty-three pounds and twelve ounces and wearing blue shorts, with fourteen professional engagements for thirteen knock-outs and one decision on points, the British Empire Welterweight Champion and the Welterweight Champion of Europe, the contender, from Oxford University, England and South Africa, Peekay, the Tad-a-pole Aing-el!!'

Peekay lifted his arms to acknowledge the tremendous and sustained applause. He returned to his stool and the announcer waited for the cheering to die down before he turned to face Jake 'Spoonbill' Jackson. Jackson was pumped up, already standing, his gloves held above his head, running on the spot and jumping in small, excited jerks.

'In the red corner, wearing white shorts, weighing one hundred and forty-four pounds, with thirty-two professional fights for thirty-two wins and thirty knock-outs, the undefeated genius of the square ring and welterweight champion of the world, from Louisville, Kentucky, Jake "Spoonbill" Jack-son!!'

The crowd went wild and it was nearly two minutes before they could be stilled again.

'Your referee for tonight, from Mexico City, Mr Emmanuel Sanchez.

Judges appointed by the State of New York Boxing Commission are Judge Joseph Tesoriero, Judge Mannie Mankerwitz and Judge Hoover J. Booker.'

'We got ourselves a I-talian, a Jew and a coloured man, no goddamn Irish; can't be no fairer than that!' Daddy Kockle announced, satisfied.

The referee called the two boxers into the ring and gave them the usual instructions to break at his command, to retire to a neutral corner in the event of a knock-down and not to hold in the clinches; finally, he described the deduction of points or disqualification for a foul. Peekay, as usual, looked down at his feet while Jackson stared directly at him, hoping to catch his eye and stare him down.

Sanchez directed them back to their corners: 'Come out fighteeng, boys!'

Peekay returned to his corner and Hymie removed the lion's tooth from about his neck. 'Gideon goes with you, Peekay,' he said quietly.

The warning bell sounded and then the bell and the two welterweights came out of their corners fast, Jackson covering more ground so that they met on Peekay's side of the ring. Jackson threw a left which Peekay parried and moved left, so that they now stood in the centre of the ring. Jackson threw another left and followed it with a right, Peekay taking both blows on his gloves. Jackson's stance was slightly stooped and he held his gloves wide. It was a sign of a very quick fighter who was confident he could close up in time from a left lead, no matter how fast it came. Peekay thought he might be bluffing, seeing if he could get away with the arrogance of the hit-me-if-you-can stance, at the same time trying to intimidate his opponent from the very start.

Peekay's left lead shot out so fast that Jackson had no time even to blink. It hit him square on the mouth, knocking his mouth guard half out. It wasn't a bad punch but it was a brilliant insult. Jackson backed away fast and Peekay let him go. The referee called a stop, allowing Jackson to replace his mouth guard. 'Box on, boys!' Sanchez called.

Peekay's lightning left had been sufficient to tell the other fighter he was going to have to work for every point he scored. There had been absolutely no margin of error for the punch and it hadn't needed any. It carried the hallmark of a classic boxer. Jackson's gloves closed noticeably and Peekay realised he had earned the first psychological advantage.

Some fights take time to settle down, the boxers playing out a number of ploys, each probing for weaknesses, testing a theory; but Peekay's left had come so piston straight and so clean and fast that Jackson knew instantly how perfect his opponent's timing was. The games were over and the serious fighting had begun.

The two men traded punches in the centre of the ring for a moment, each scoring, Jackson with a nice right hook and Peekay with a right cross. Both were throwing a lot of leather, but their mutual defences were superb. It was hard to find a fault in either man's technique. It was beautiful boxing and Jackson managed a pay-back for the punch on the mouth when, towards the end of the round, he caught Peekay with a long, raking right flush on the jaw which spun him around. It was a lovely punch and if Peekay hadn't been going backwards it could have done a great deal of damage. The bell went for the end of the first round without either boxer seeming to have gained any advantage.

'Can you see any weaknesses?' Peekay asked Hymie and Dutch.

'It's early times yet, my son. But he's no faster than you. If anything you've got the edge. The left to the mouth, that was magic.'

'He lifts his left shoulder up a fraction, perhaps to protect his jaw,' Hymie said.

Peekay nodded. If Hymie was right, later on in the fight when Jackson had lost a bit of speed he might not see a left cross coming at him quite as quickly. It wasn't the deadliest punch in the book, but behind the right pair of gloves it could do a lot of harm to a fighter slowing down.

The bell went for the second round. Jackson came out hard and scored well with three good punches. He was very fast and put his punches together beautifully; Peekay was hard put to keep him out. Jackson came in a second time, but Peekay tied him up. The referee called for them to break and Peekay got in a beautiful hook under the heart. It was the best punch of the fight so far and he heard Jackson grunt as it landed.

Peekay was a body puncher, preferring gradually to weaken the structure rather than to try and knock it out with one blow. Jackson's inclination was to go for the head. His speed against previous opponents had generally been enough to get through their defence and, with a knockout punch in both hands, he only needed a couple of good blows to the head to beat an opponent.

But Peekay was too fast and made him miss, which hadn't happened very often in his career. Both boxers were scoring but not doing much damage, although in the second round Jackson hit Peekay with a left jab in the eye and had the satisfaction of seeing it puff up towards the end of the round. It was a close round, but if anything it was Jackson's.

The third through to the seventh were much the same, both boxers learning quickly and punching accurately. Both were fighting at a furious pace. It was going to be a matter of who lasted the distance.

Dutch had doctored Peekay's eye and the swelling had receded. Jackson had tried getting back onto it, but each time he'd thrown a left jab, Peekay's right hook found its mark under the black fighter's heart. Jackson's skin was too dark for the familiar red blotch to show but Peekay knew it was there and Jackson too was aware of what was happening. He dropped his right just a fraction to keep Peekay out, leaving the way to his eye open. Peekay sent a good punch in, testing Jackson's eye.

They came out for the eighth round, meeting in centre ring, both fighters on their toes. Peekay opened up a cut above Jackson's eye; it wasn't big and he wasn't interested in working on it yet. The punch which had opened the eye hadn't been that hard, which meant Jackson had a weakness. Weaknesses are for exploiting later when some of the fight has gone out of your opponent. Jackson's eye would keep.

The black fighter tied Peekay up in a clinch, trying to swing him around on to the ropes. The referee called for them to break and Peekay stepped back. The left hook coming at him seemed to be in slow motion; it caught him flush on the jaw and dropped him sprawling to the canvas. Peekay felt nothing, except that his legs wouldn't work. Above him Sanchez was flicking his fingers into Peekay's face counting him out. At six the pain came into his legs and by eight he was standing, his head clear but his legs still heavy. Jackson came at him and Peekay tried to tie him up, but Jackson hit him with a right hook under the heart and down he went again. But, surprisingly, this time his legs seemed to be getting better and he rested until eight before getting up. Jackson came in hard, his hands wide again, the way he'd started out in the first round. Some guys never learn. This time the straight left from Peekay was right on the point of the chin with the full weight of his shoulder behind it, with Jackson moving into the punch. The black figure simply stopped coming forward and then seem to be propelled backwards, losing his legs from under him he landed on the seat of his pants and lay sprawling on his back. Peekay turned to move to a neutral corner when the bell went for the end of the round.

Jackson's seconds rushed out, dragging the unconscious fighter back into his corner. Jackson's eyes had opened by the time they'd seated him onto his stool. The referee signalled for a doctor but by the time the doctor had climbed into the ring his eyes were clear and he stood, ready to come out fighting.

Peekay felt better. He'd taken two of Jackson's best shots and he was still on his feet. On the other hand, if Jackson hadn't been rescued by the bell the fight would have been over. Jackson wasn't invincible. He'd keep fighting the percentage way, wearing him down, *first with the head then with the heart*; it was familiar territory for Peekay. If he could stay away from Jackson's big punch, he could play in his paddock.

The ninth round was the sort of round good fighters use to pace themselves when they know they've got a long fight on their hands. But in the tenth Jackson caught Peekay on the ropes and put in nine beautiful punches to his opponent's torso, each one slamming into him as though a hole had been punched through his rib cage; the last, a vicious left hook, seemed to lift Peekay's heart up through his rib cage, into his lungs. A terrible pain rose up from his chest, a molten substance rushing up through his mouth and nostrils like a solid object bigger than the spaces through which it was trying to escape. He didn't even sense he'd fallen, only the sensation of rushing head-first down a narrow, stainless-steel tube at great speed with light bouncing off the inside surface of the tube, burning out his eyes, a caterwauling scream echoing down the luminous tube. He came out of the other side of the tunnel like a cork forced out of a bottle, to hear the referee count to seven. To his surprise he was on his haunches with one glove resting on the canvas. But his legs held; the punishing miles running up the mountains in the high altitude were paying off. He stood upright at nine and he could see the surprise, even consternation on Jackson's face as he came in to kill him off. Nobody had ever taken a nine-punch combination from Jackson and got up off the floor.

Somehow, by hanging on grimly, using everything he knew about ringcraft and clinching whenever he could, Peekay managed to get through the remainder of the round. Jackson too was near exhaustion, or Peekay would never have got away with it. Something had to happen; neither of them was capable of fighting another five rounds. The bell went for the end of the tenth round and Peekay moved wearily to his corner.

Hymie towelled him quickly while Togger squeezed a sponge over his head, repeating the process three times so that Hymie's towelling was to no avail. Dutch grabbed a towel and wiped Peekay's head and started to work on his eye which had begun to close again. Daddy Kockle standing behind Peekay was massaging his torso around the heart, the pain of his hands working almost unbearable.

Hymie looked at Dutch and Peekay caught the look in his eye. They were going to throw in the towel. 'Don't, don't do it! We haven't begun to fight yet.'

As though on cue, Mrs Smith's piano started, picking up the very last part of the Zulu chant; instantly Jam Jar's violin cut in and the male voices rose, deep and strong, rising to a crescendo as the bell went for the eleventh round.

Jackson came out as a southpaw, obviously hoping to open up Peekay with his left. Peekay immediately changed to fight him the same way. To his surprise, the shoulder Jackson had kept up high in an orthodox stance he now dropped too low. Jackson threw a left which missed Peekay, but the right cross with which Peekay countered hit Jackson flush on the jaw. The black fighter staggered, grabbing onto the ropes. Peekay moved in and hit him two good right hooks under his heart. Jackson grabbed Peekay into a clinch and they wrestled for a few moments before the referee managed to part them.

Both fighters were oblivious to the roar of the crowd which had continued almost non-stop through the fight. They were witnessing one of the greatest title fights ever seen at the Garden and for the most part they were an audience who knew their boxing. As Jackson and Peekay broke from the clinch Jackson reverted back to an orthodox stance. He'd come off worse in the change of stance and he could feel the tremendous pain building up under his heart. Towards the end of the round Peekay got him with another hook to the heart and Jackson went down. He was in luck again; Peekay had left the punch too late and when the black fighter rose to his feet at the count of nine he had only fifteen seconds to survive to the end of the round. Going into the twelfth round they had two knock-downs each and it was still anyone's fight.

Back in the corner Dutch worked frantically on Peekay's eye, which had now completely closed. Fortunately so had Jackson's, and Dutch realised that the difference in the result of the fight might just depend on which of the two boxers saw the more clearly. Blood from internal bleeding had filled the inside of Peekay's eyelid and Dutch was trying to work it out again before it began to clot too badly, with very little result.

'Cut it, Dutch!'

'No, son, you'll wear the scar all your life; it could be dangerous.'

'For Christ's sake, Dutch! He'll nail me with his left hand if I can't see! His left is better than mine, I'm not seeing it coming half the time. Cut the eye!'

Dutch hesitated, looking to Hymie for help. Time was running out.

'You fixin' to cut that eye? You heard the man!' It was Daddy Kockle. 'Man only get one chance foh immortality; he got to do the decidin' hisself. He say cut, you cut!'

Hymie nodded and Dutch reached into his pocket for a scalpel blade. He tore at the wrapping, but, as he pulled at the paper, the blade slipped from his hands and fell to the floor outside the ring.

'Jesus, Dutch!' Hymie yelled.

Dutch shook his head. 'I ain't got a spare, lad,' he said in dismay.

Togger's hand reached out and grabbed the lion's tooth hanging around Hymie's neck. It was an incisor from a young lion, still keen-edged. He pulled it over Hymie's head. 'Cut!' he yelled.

Dutch took the tooth and sliced into the eyelid; the sudden sharp tear made Peekay wince. The blood flowed quickly, releasing the pressure from the eyelid. Dutch quickly stemmed the wound with a match-head twirled with a tiny hood of cotton wool and laced with adrenalin. He was the best cut-man in Europe and when the bell went Peekay could see clearly through an eye which was no longer bleeding.

Jackson's left eye was still up, leaving him vulnerable. Peekay was running out of energy. He didn't know how much more he could take or even dish out, whether he could get Jackson with a single punch any more. If he wasted his energy going for Jackson's head, constantly having to batter through his defence, it could be too much. Jackson had been dropped with the heart punch and it hadn't been all that hard. The punching down-under was beginning to tell. Peekay would leave the black man's head alone; he was tough as nails and it would have to be a very big punch to the cranium to put him down. Peekay knew the punch to do it just wasn't there, he'd spent it earlier in the fight. He would stick to his last, work away at the body, try to get Jackson in the fourteenth. But he'd keep the black man's eye closed, just in case.

Jackson's right eye was badly cut as well as closed, but clever boxer that he was, he kept his damaged eye on Peekay's far side. It was the intelligent thing to do but by doing so he made his first big mistake. He was certain that Peekay would use his left, swinging it round from beyond the peripheral of the closed eye where he couldn't see it coming. He knew Peekay had the punch in his left hand to put him down. Jackson was a head-hunter; he couldn't conceive of an advantage such as he was giving Peekay not being taken up. He was a superb boxer and now he made his right hand do the work, protecting his eye. Which was how Peekay figured he'd react. The straight right Jackson kept throwing to keep Peekay away from his damaged eye left the area under his heart exposed every time. Peekay was landing the left hook consistently, hitting Jackson on the spot, squeezing the juice out of him.

They fought this way for the next three rounds, both fighters concentrating on keeping the damage they'd done on the boil. Short punches, not hard, but hard enough to keep doing the work of weakening their opponent. Both were exhausted but the altitude training was beginning to pay off for Peekay; his legs were holding and he was using the breaks between the rounds well, storing up everything he had for the final two rounds.

While Jackson looked in slightly worse shape there was still nothing in the fight. Jackson had never gone fifteen rounds, his non-championship fights being fought over twelve. His title defences had always ended with a knockout inside ten rounds. Peekay too, was in no-man's-land; twelve was also his maximum. The last three rounds of a closely fought championship is all guts; the fighter with the most heart wins. The bell went for the fourteenth round and Jackson, already on his feet, came storming over to Peekay. There was little point in back-pedalling; staying out of harm's way could cost Peekay the fight. They slugged it out toe-to-toe. Jackson had worked out Peekay's tactic and was no longer protecting his eye, so Peekay hit him solidly with the left, opening up the eye badly, the blood covering Jackson's face. Should he go for a TKO? It was unlikely they'd stop the fight unless the eye looked in danger. As though reading his thoughts, Jackson changed back to protecting the eye and almost immediately caught Peekay with a beautiful right hand which put him down.

Peekay wanted an eight count; he was exhausted and the punch had made him groggy, but his head cleared quickly. He had to make the knock-down look slight, so at the count of three he was back up on his feet. He managed to tie Jackson up in a clinch until the strength returned to his legs. The referee called for them to break and Peekay moved out of trouble.

Jackson, sensing that he had Peekay, came at him with a long, raking right, but missed. Peekay hit him on the shoulder with a left, spinning him around. Jackson's right had been too hard and he'd left his torso exposed. Earlier in the fight Peekay would have put three, maybe six punches down, all of them hard, all of them within half an inch of the spot; now he put all his strength into the hook. He felt it land, enter and continue, as though Jackson's ribs had simply caved in. Jackson grunted and then sighed, falling against the ropes, his arms slung over the top. Peekay hit him with a right cross on the nose, busting it. A white-hot pain shot up his arm as his hand broke. For the second time in the fight, the bell went. Jackson was out on the ropes. The fourteenth round had been enough to win the fight for Peekay though technically he hadn't knocked Jackson out. Jackson's seconds had dragged him into his corner and were bringing him round. A doctor had climbed into the ring and was examining him.

'Stop it! Stop the fight! Stop the fuckin' fight!!' Togger was yelling hysterically at the medico. He wanted it to be over, to be Peekay's. Daddy Kockle was weeping openly.

Dutch worked on Peekay's eye. 'Steady now, my son. You've got it. Just keep stickin' him, keeping him away.' He didn't think Jackson would come out for the final round, but Dutch, the consummate professional to the last, wasn't going to raise Peekay's hopes.

Peekay began to weep silently. He didn't know why; the pain was terrible, but it wasn't the pain. He knew if Jackson came out for the final round it was all over, he couldn't fight him with a broken hand. Hymie brought his mouth to Peekay's ear. The noise from the crowd was so terrific it was the only way he could be heard. 'One more, just one more, Peekay. I love you, Peekay. Just one more. Stay on your feet, just one more round!'

Peekay drew Hymie's head down so his ear was against his mouth. 'It's all over, old mate. I've broken my hand!' he sobbed, the tears running down his cheek.

Hymie face crumbled. He choked back the tears, but they came anyway, his heart suddenly feeling the size of a pumpkin in his chest. He couldn't think, the shock was too great. Tears streamed down his face. 'Oh, God, take my life! Take anything! But don't let Jackson get out of his corner!'

The ten-second bell went for the final round and Jackson stood up. The bell went and the two fighters went into the final round. Jackson's stamina was remarkable, and Peekay tried to keep him off with his left hand, prodding at him, holding him out.

Jackson knew with a sudden certainty what had happened. It lifted him, made him strong. The white boy's hand was broken, he was defenceless. He picked at Peekay, hitting him cleanly, playing with him; there was time, he had no strength, but there was time left. He had to make sure of the big punch, he only had one left in him, maybe not even that. Weaken him down, break the white boy. Break him to his knees! He worked his mind, gathering the strength he needed. Only one punch. One to finish the fight!

But he'd left it too late. And he was careless. Knowing Peekay couldn't hit him, his gloves were wide open. Peekay's broken hand came up and connected under his heart. He heard Peekay scream with pain as the punch landed. Jackson went backwards, bouncing on the ropes; if he went down he'd never get up again. He clung on desperately, a deep red fuzz, like scarlet cotton wool, in front of his eyes, closing him down, bringing him to an end. He waited blindly for the shock of the punch which would put him away. But it never came. Peekay, groggy with the pain from his hand, was disorientated. Finally he managed to hit Jackson with a left, but the punch had no power. Jackson's knees caved in momentarily, but miraculously he stayed up, his arms hooked around the ropes. Only his courage kept him on his feet. Then he could dimly see Peekay through the red haze. Peekay threw another punch, another left; his right hand was useless, he barely had the strength to hold it above his waist. Had Jackson spat on him he'd have knocked him down. Jackson grabbed Peekay, his arms raising in slow motion, pulling his opponent into a desperate, instinctive clinch. Both boxers crashed to the floor. Both, on all fours, struggled to get up first, Peekay not having the strength in his left hand to push himself up from the floor. Finally he made it, hardly a second before Jackson. Technically it wasn't a knock-down and the referee signalled for them to fight on. The crowd was screaming for the knockout to be accepted. Peekay had won, they'd seen it clearly; it was the white boy's fight! Jackson was trying to keep his balance, swaying on his feet, the bright crimson blood from his eye splashing down onto his jet black shoulder. The two boxers faced each other a foot apart, unable to move, neither with the strength to throw another blow. The bell went and Jackson gave a small sigh and fell backwards to the floor, landing hard on the seat of his pants, eyes wide in sudden surprise, then backwards still further, hitting his head on the deck where he lay sprawled on his back, one arm stretched out the other at his side, motionless.

Peekay hadn't the strength to move and collapsed into Hymie's arms as his friend ran to embrace him, tears streaming. 'Never, never again,' Hymie wept.

The Garden was chaos; suddenly a chant started at the back, then grew: 'Pee Kay! Pee Kay! Pee Kay!' People battered the back of their seats with the palms of their hands and beat the soles of their feet on the boards, 'Pee Kay! Pee Kay! Pee Kay!' The chant grew louder; people at the ringside now stood up, throwing their fists into the air. 'Pee Kay! Pee Kay!' Society matrons and bankers shouted with good time girls, crooks, card sharps, con men, promoters and racketeers: 'Pee Kay! Pee Kay! Pee Kay!'

Jake 'Spoonbill' Jackson's people had brought him into his corner for the third time. Jackson had come round, but he was hurt badly, his nose broken, his eye badly cut and both eyes closed. He was coughing blood where his broken ribs had punctured the lung. Peekay wasn't a lot better, his eye closed, his hand, possibly his jaw and probably several ribs broken.

The ring was filled with people and the police worked frantically to clear it. It was ten minutes before the announcer was able to get to the microphone. The TV cameras were recording the chaos from their platform above and to the side of the ring.

'Ladies and gentlemen, I have the judge's decision!' The announcer was forced to repeat himself four times before the Garden grew sufficiently quiet for him to continue. 'Judge Joseph Tesoriero scores it forty-four points Jackson, forty-four points Peekay!' A roar of approval went up, though mixed with some booing. 'Judge Mannie Mankerwitz scores it forty-four Peekay, forty-four Jackson!' The roar from the crowd increased; most people would have settled for a drawn contest. The crowd hushed as the final judge's decision was announced. 'Judge Hoover J. Booker scores it forty-four Peekay, forty-five Jackson!'

There was a moment's stunned silence and then the booing began. It was clear that the crowd wasn't happy. 'The winner on points and still welterweight champion of the world, Jake "Spoonbill" Jack-a-son!' the announcer bellowed.

Chairs were being broken and the police moved in to stop the riot. Twenty police surrounded the ring holding back the crowd. Jackson rose to his feet, his hands in the air, one hand holding the elaborate championship belt. The ring was being pelted with objects and Jackson was hit by a small cushion as the boos increased. He looked about him confused; he could barely stand up and his seconds rushed to surround him. In a moment he was lost from sight in the ring.

Slowly the police gained control. The Odd Bodleians under Jam Jar's direction had stood firm. Now they started to sing, 'When the Saints go Marching in'; it was the music, perhaps more than anything, which calmed the crowd.

Peekay rose wearily; he too could barely stand. He moved over to the people surrounding Jackson, trying to get to the champion to congratulate him. Intent on protecting their man, Jackson's seconds wouldn't let him into the circle. Peekay turned to return to his corner. A TV commentator had managed to get into the ring and he now accosted Peekay.

'The crowd are obviously disappointed, they think you won, I think you won, do you think you won?' he yelled.

Peekay wanted to cry. He was empty. He'd hit bottom, there was nothing left. He felt dead inside.

'Jackson won. That was the judge's decision,' Peekay said into the microphone.

Inside him a voice cried out, protested that there was more to it than this! That he had a right to be hurt, to feel bitter, to allow himself the indulgence of suggesting it was a home-town decision. But in his mind he'd always won the title convincingly, not like this. Had he won, Jackson's side would feel as he did now. His camouflage was back.

'What will you do now, Peekay?' the man asked, disappointed, wanting the vitriol.

Peekay paused. The noise from the crowd was dying down, the police gaining control. The camera on the platform above the ring framed his face in the lens; the picture, in black and white, showed a young man with his right eye closed, deep lines of exhaustion etched down either side of his mouth, his good eye sharp, curiously untouched, incongruous, looking as it did out of a battered, broken face. But his face also registered a small, wan smile, which served to make the moment America witnessed more poignant. 'I'm going to find a quiet place where I can bawl my eyes out.' He paused and shrugged his shoulders, his mouth was close to the microphone and carried clearly, hardly above a whisper, like a small boy's. 'You see, I don't know what to do. I don't know how to fight any better than that.'

Back in the dressing room the doctor appointed by the New York Athletic Commission examined Peekay. He was a man in his fifties, wearing a cheap, baggy suit. He had a wild mop of steel-grey hair and a somewhat untidy, bushy moustache, stained yellow with cigar smoke. He looked well worn and comfortable, as though he was used to working around fighters. He handled Peekay expertly, knowing precisely what he was looking for. 'The hand is broken badly, in more than one place I should think; counting your wrist bones there are twenty-seven possibilities.' He grinned. 'It isn't possible to hit a man with a hand broken like this, hit him hard enough to lay him down. Nobody could take that much pain at once. But you did. I saw it myself. I've looked after boxers for thirty years. That was the best, the best fight I've ever seen!' He cleared his throat, embarrassed at his outburst, his voice brusque again. 'We'll need to X-ray immediately, then set it. If the broken bones are set incorrectly, your days as a fighter will be over, son.'

He put his stethoscope to Peekay's ribs, testing both sides. 'Breathe in!' Peekay took a deep breath. 'Pain? Sharp, sudden, like a knife going in?'

'No sir, just straight pain.'

'That's good, looks like none of the breaks have punctured the lung. They're probably all broken anyway, the X-ray will tell. I also want a brain scan. You took a lot of punishment about the head.' He started to pack his bag. 'Sorry I can't give you a shot of morphine to kill the pain, it will interfere with the anaesthetic. Jackson will be in hospital for several days, you'll have to join him there, at least overnight.' He walked to the door. 'He left in an ambulance, on his back. I guess you can walk out and leave in a limo . . . like the champ you are, son!'

Dutch had needed to cut the glove from Peekay's hand and now it was swollen to nearly twice its normal size. Peekay sat with the elbow cupped in his left hand, holding the hand upwards, above his heart so the blood would drain from it and relieve the pain a little. Togger was holding a towel packed with ice, making Peekay hold his broken hand in the ice as long as he could before bringing it up again. He too had cried unashamedly at the end of the fight and again when the decision had been announced. Now he stood quietly by, trying to pass on some of his love for his friend to use as emotional balm to soothe him. 'If I live ter be a hundred, I'll never see a better fight, never be more soddin' proud, Peekay.'

Daddy Kockle was standing quietly by the door, holding a large cardboard box Hymie had given him to keep. The old man was exhausted.

Hymie had been talking quietly on the phone, now he walked over to Peekay. 'Come, old mate, we've got to take you to Cedars of Lebanon.'

He grinned. 'I told Aunt Tom your hand was broken and now one of New York's foremost orthopaedic surgeons is standing by to operate on it.'

Peekay rose, he was physically exhausted and every bone in his body felt as though it was broken. He was forced to lean on Hymie as they walked towards the door. He saw Daddy Kockle looking at him. The old man's eyes were moist. 'What's in the box, Daddy Kockle? It's not big enough for my coffin.'

'Christ, I forgot!' Hymie said. 'It came on this morning's flight from London. Strict instructions from Doris, you're to open it after the fight.'

Peekay grinned. It was the Hans Kellerman doll; Mr Rubens had kept his word. 'It's for you, Togger. Open it when you get back to the hotel.'

Daddy Kockle handed Togger the box. 'For me?' Togger showed his surprise. 'Thanks, Peekay!' As Peekay didn't offer any further explanation he put the box under his arm and prepared to follow them out.

Peekay left the brightly lit room. Several people were standing in the corridor. Peekay removed his hand from around Hymie's shoulder. 'I want them to see me walking out.' He gave a wry grin, 'After all, my feet are the only bits of me which don't feel broken.' They walked down the passage followed by Dutch, Jerome, and with Togger carrying Carmen's Elizabeth Jane.

Daddy Kockle remained behind in the dressing room, seated on the rub-down table, shaking his head and clucking to himself. He glanced up into the mirror on the opposite wall, patting his snowy white hair. Only four of the twenty-four lights still shone around the perimeter. His face, blotched with the brown mercury discolouration on the mirror's surface, seemed to show every one of the sixty or more hard years of his life. He talked directly at the image in the mirror, the beginning of a smile on his face.

'Nossah! That boy, he ain't licked yet. Right now he fixin' to come back and, when he do . . . Why he gon' whup that sonofabitch! Whup him so good, he gonna lay down for a week 'foh he gets up!'

He picked up his clarinet, brought it to his mouth, and blew the sweet, clean opening notes to 'Crossing over Jordan to the Other Side'.

BOOK THREE

TWENTY-FOUR

Colonel Bokkie Venter looked down at the transfer approval notice in front of him from Pretoria. It simply stated that the application by Detective Sergeant Jannie Teunis Geldenhuis for a transfer had been approved and mentioned at the same time that he had been promoted to the Special Branch in Pretoria with the new rank of lieutenant. He was to take up duties as soon as he could be released.

Venter wasn't altogether pleased with the news. Police work is essentially about being a member of a team and Geldenhuis was by nature a secretive man who seldom asked the advice of his peers or, for that matter, showed more than cursory respect for his senior officers. It wasn't anything for which he could be reprimanded; it was just that the blond, blue-eyed policeman was too ambitious for his own good. SAT, the so-called Immorality Squad Geldenhuis ran, was deeply resented by the other divisions who accused him of headline-hunting and grand-standing.

Venter couldn't put his finger on it. On paper Geldenhuis was an exemplary police officer, but there was something about his manner which made his fellow officers dislike him and suspect his motives. Venter could see controversy ahead and controversy was something he'd spent most of his working life trying to avoid.

His appointment book showed that Lieutenant Geldenhuis was to see him at three that afternoon. He called his secretary to bring him the police officer's personal file. There'd been a lot of gossip about the nature of the young policeman's automobile accident and he wanted to bring himself up to date with the details.

At three minutes to three Lieutenant Geldenhuis presented himself to Colonel Venter's secretary. It had taken five months for him to recover from his injuries and he'd been back at work barely a month. He'd used this time to study and to pass the police examinations which allowed him to rise above the rank of detective sergeant. He'd also made real progress in learning the Zulu language.

Colonel Venter's secretary announced him on the phone and then, cradling the receiver, rose from her desk. 'The Colonel will see you now.'

Geldenhuis followed her through a small secretarial office. She stood by the door of Venter's office to let him pass. 'Coffee?' she asked. Jannie

Geldenhuis shook his head, declining. She closed the door behind him as he entered.

'Ah, sit down please, Detective Sergeant.' Venter indicated a chair.

'Thank you, sir.' Geldenhuis had been surprised at the call to see Venter; his senior officer had approved his request for a transfer and he knew of no reason why Venter would want to see him.

Now Venter half rose in his chair and extended his hand. 'Congratulations, Geldenhuis, Lieutenant Geldenhuis, it seems your career continues to prosper.'

Geldenhuis looked surprised, taking Venter's hand. 'Thank you, sir. I confess it comes as a surprise. I mean, being away for so long sick.'

'Better still, you've been promoted to the Special Branch in Pretoria,' Venter added.

This time Geldenhuis was unable to conceal his delight. 'Thank you, sir. That's even better news. It's an unexpected honour.'

Venter looked steadily at Geldenhuis for a few moments. 'I've looked at your file, Lieutenant. Your police career is commendable. It shows that in SAT you averaged two arrests a week policing the Immorality Act. It seems you have the best record in this area of any policeman in South Africa. I also note that during the period you were sick, recovering from your accident, only six arrests were made in nearly five months. Tell me, Lieutenant, why do you think this is?'

Geldenhuis sensed that there was a trap being set for him by his superior officer. 'I can't say, Colonel. I can only think that the officer who took over from me didn't utilize his contacts. This kind of work is very dependent on good information, on knowing your territory. The officer wasn't promoted from within my squad.'

'Ah yes, contacts, you're right, a policeman needs access, lots of contacts.' Venter looked down and appeared to be looking through a file placed ~~in front of hi~~m. 'How is your health? Are you fully recovered from your broken . . .?'

'Pelvis, sir.'

'Ja, pelvis. You know rumours are funny things, man. Something starts with a pelvis, a simple thing like a car accident when the driver is thrown upwards and the steering wheel snaps and breaks his pelvis. Before you know where you are, man, a word like "pelvis" turns into a word like "penis", a very similar word, don't you think, Lieutenant?'

'Yes sir,' Geldenhuis answered, his heart suddenly beating fast.

'And a thing like using your contacts, which, as you say is what every good policeman should do, turns into *using* your contacts in maybe an entirely different sort of way, hey?'

Geldenhuis had never liked Venter, who was an old-fashioned cop, the type who played everything by the book: the hear-no-evil, see-no-evil, speak-no-evil type who was always covering his arse. Now he hated the bastard. He'd applied for a transfer to get himself the hell out of Natal. Too many cops hated him. The 'accident' rumours were getting out of hand. Only recently he'd heard that a Pinetown cop's wife, one of the nurses at Durban General who'd changed his dressings from time to time, had opened her big gob to her old man. The cop whose wife blabbed had made a comment back at the station. 'Perforated pelvis? That's a bladdy funny name for a prick with tooth marks on it!' The remark had spread gleefully to every station in Natal. Now this bastard was onto it as well; he was going to make him eat shit, maybe even rescind his promotion. Geldenhuis was permanently scarred. He could never undress in front of men again. And this bastard was now going to take it out on his career. He wondered what else was in his file. If Venter had all the facts about the incident at Bluey Jay, it was enough to bury him ten times over. If he had the pictures Mama Tequila had shown him in Bayview Private Clinic he'd be out of the force before morning on a charge of miscegenation.

He tried to clear his head, to think the thing out. Surely if they had the whole story they'd have acted before now? They wouldn't have waited until he was back on duty. Venter was an old-fashioned cop, he'd have asked him to resign, not to come back. He'd have done it on the quiet, told the world that Geldenhuis was permanently disabled. Geldenhuis immediately felt a little better. Knowing your man was everything; Venter was fishing.

'Lieutenant, are you a member of the *Broederbond*?' Venter asked suddenly.

'Do I have to answer that, sir?' Jesus, membership was secret, but it wasn't illegal any more.

'You already have, Lieutenant.'

'It's a personal matter, sir.'

'Ja, sure, man, but sometimes personal matters and police matters, you know like the words pelvis and penis, they get mixed up.' Venter stood up and Geldenhuis was forced to his feet as well. 'I want you to hand over SAT to Detective Sergeant Williams and be out of Police Headquarters in a week, you hear?'

'Certainly, sir.'

'You may go, Lieutenant Geldenhuis.'

Geldenhuis replaced his cap, saluted and turned to leave. He couldn't believe it, Venter was letting him off the hook. Or was he? The file, what was in his file for later use? Geldenhuis stopped. 'Thank you, sir. Excuse me, Colonel Venter, my record, are there to be any additions?' He knew it was important to hold Venter's eyes, to show him he wasn't scared.

Venter laughed. 'Yes, of course, the fact that you used your sick leave to pass your senior police officers' exams and to learn an African language, very worthy of comment. You see, Geldenhuis, sometimes we've got friends we don't even know about ourselves, in Pretoria . . . and also other places.'

Once he was well away from Venter's office, Jannie Geldenhuis closed his eyes tightly and shook his head fiercely as though trying to rid his mind of the interview he'd just been through. At one stage he'd been certain it was all over, finish and klaar! Venter had had him by the balls and was squeezing. Thank Christ the bastard was *Broederbond* or it *would* have been all over, for sure. Then he smiled to himself. Venter was still a weak shit. If it had been him he'd have worked it up until he had a person like himself begging for mercy. Didn't the silly bastard know that the first fucking principle of police work was to compromise the other side? If you had a person compromised you had the power. Power was everything. You never knew when you'd need someone. But one thing was for bladdy sure, sooner or later you *always* did!

Then another thought occurred to Geldenhuis. Venter didn't think he was worth the trouble to compromise. Well the bastard was wrong again! He had a long fucking memory and the stupid bastard had let him off the hook. His career was intact. Special Branch was everything he wanted. He was made for it, designed by God for it! He'd show the prick what being a real policeman was all about.

When Geldenhuis had received his commendation from the Minister for Justice, a little note, written on blank halfquarto size paper had been slipped behind the official letterhead. On it, printed in biro, were just the words: 'Call Pretoria 75-4631 6 pm. Saturday.' Nothing more, no signature, nothing.

He didn't know how he knew, but somehow he just knew. He knew he was going to be invited to join the *Broederbond*. He had called the number the following Saturday, waiting until one minute to six before he gave the operator at the telephone exchange the long-distance number. The phone had rung three times before it was picked up by a voice speaking in Afrikaans.

'*Naam*?'

'Geldenhuis.'

'Christian names?'

'Johannes, Teunis.'

'Preferred name?'

'Jannie . . . Jannie Geldenhuis.' He felt a little stupid, he was a police officer, a detective sergeant and he was answering blind into a phone to someone who was filling in a form.

'Address . . . Home address and personal telephone number?'

Jannie Geldenhuis gave the voice his home address and number. 'Who am I speaking to?' he asked, strangely afraid to sound over-aggressive.

'Occupation?'

'Police officer. Look who . . . what is this?'

'Rank?'

'Detective Sergeant.'

'*Baie dankie, Speuder Sersant Geldenhuis*,' the anonymous voice thanked him and hung up.

Two weeks later he'd received a letter asking him to attend a meeting at the Hotel Edward on the esplanade. The letter asked him simply to come up to room seventy-one at half past two on 6 July and not to wear uniform.

He'd knocked on the hotel door which was opened by a big man wearing a sports coat, white shirt and tan tie. He appeared to be in his mid forties and his crew cut was already peppered with grey, though he looked fit and hard. Geldenhuis had seen him before, though he couldn't think where, but he knew immediately from the way he wore his civilian clothes that he was a police officer.

'*Kom binne asseblief, Speuder Sersant Geldenhuis*,' the man invited, holding the door open for him.

Geldenhuis entered the room to find two other men; one appeared to be in his mid fifties the other somewhat younger, perhaps a little over thirty. They were seated in a small lounge room leading onto a balcony which stood open so that you could see the yachts moored in the basin beyond.

'*My naam is Kolonel Klaasens*,' the large man said; then indicating the man on his left, '*Meneer Steyn*'; then the one on his right, '*Meneer Cogsweel*.'

Geldenhuis nodded his head and then stepped forward, shaking each of them by the hand. 'Sit, Geldenhuis,' Klaasens said brusquely, his police manner to a junior officer coming through unconsciously. The two other men hadn't risen when Jannie had extended his hand, instead taking it where they sat, though both gripped firmly in the Afrikaner manner, nodding their heads in reply to his greeting, saying nothing in return. Both were dressed in grey suits and didn't look like policemen. They were medium-sized men, Cogsweel the better dressed, his grey suit cut well, his collar neat and tie carefully knotted. He looked like a civil servant, while Steyn could have passed as a church elder or a bank manager. Neither were the sort of men you'd notice in a busy street scene.

'Do you have any idea why you are here, Geldenhuis?' Klaasens asked.

'No, sir,' Geldenhuis replied, not willing to suggest he thought they might be *Broederbond*.

'Oh? Then why did you come?'

Geldenhuis grinned. 'I am a detective, Colonel. The note I received is not uncommon in my line of work.'

'And you didn't connect it with the phone call you made two weeks ago to Pretoria?' Steyn, the older of the two men, asked.

'Well, ja, I thought it was a possibility, the postmark was Pretoria.' Geldenhuis was having a bet each way; they'd think him a fool if he didn't admit this much.

'And?' Steyn asked again.

A look of impatience crossed Jannie Geldenhuis's face. 'Look! What is this? Would someone explain, please?'

Klaasens laughed. 'The Minister is interested in you, Geldenhuis.' He indicated Cogsweel and Steyn. 'Our friends here are simply checking you out.'

'For what, sir?' Geldenhuis asked, looking somewhat bemused.

Cogsweel got up from his lounge chair. Standing, he was larger than he'd seemed, the top half of him not in proportion to his long legs. He wore a crew cut just beginning to turn grey. It was cut flat and gave his square-jawed face an almost rectangular look, the shape of a shoebox turned on its end. When he stood he was at least six foot tall. Cogsweel walked over to the window and, with his hands pushed into his jacket pockets, stood with his back to Geldenhuis, looking out over the yacht basin.

He spoke Afrikaans well, but with the slight accent of an English-speaking South African. 'We are looking for patriots, true patriots, people who put their country first, selfless people who are not afraid to take risks. We have won the first battle and the Afrikaner is back in charge of his own country again. We are making the necessary changes, consolidating, repairing the damage done by the British.' He turned and faced Jannie Geldenhuis. 'Have you heard the expression, "damage control"?'

Geldenhuis nodded. 'It's a military term.'

'Ja, that is correct. And what we are talking about is war. War against all those people and factions who would undermine the Afrikaner nation. Damage control is the business of minimising the effect our enemies have on the state.'

Steyn now spoke, though he didn't rise from his chair. 'A people are only safe when they have eyes and ears everywhere: the eyes and ears of the true patriot, the man or woman dedicated to the purity of the nation's blood. The survival of our nation is dependent on keeping both the body and the spirit of the Afrikaner from being contaminated. For three hundred years we have kept our blood pure! We have kept our belief in God. We have not broken the covenant!' He smiled suddenly, aware that he might be coming on too strong. 'Look at your eyes! They're blue, you have white hair, blond. You are the direct result of our forefathers who kept the faith. Now it is our turn to hold the torch, to serve our country, the white Afrikaner nation.'

Cogsweel seated himself again. 'You have shown yourself a man who is not afraid to take action, to become involved.'

'I am a policeman, Mr Cogsweel. That's my job.'

'Ja, but there are policemen and there are policemen. A patriot is someone who doesn't do it because it is a job, but because it is his duty to serve . . .'

'*Die Vaderland!*' Steyn said, interjecting. 'The Minister thinks you may be this sort of man, Detective Sergeant Geldenhuis.'

Jannie Geldenhuis felt his heart racing. They were telling him everything he wanted to hear. He wasn't political. Not in the sense of being a Nationalist, though he supposed he was that when it was all boiled down. But he was obsessed with the purity of his Afrikaner blood. It was what drove him in the SAT Squad; and here it was again. He could sense the power in the room and the effect that that power might have on his career. Klaasens was Special Branch; he knew because he'd picked through the filing cabinet he kept in his mind; he was also the boxing coach for the Pretoria Police Boxing Club.

'I am flattered, sir. I only hope I can justify the Minister's opinion.' Geldenhuis looked directly at Steyn, holding his eyes.

'Will you join us?' Cogsweel asked, smiling.

Geldenhuis was suddenly certain that the way he replied was critical to the outcome; if he asked whom he was joining he was in effect rejecting the ethos of the conversation which had just taken place. On the other hand, by not asking he might seem stupid, easily led.

'Thank you, I am flattered by your invitation, but there is only one organisation that truly inspires me, only one which I wish to be invited to join.'

'And that is?' Cogsweel asked quietly, a small smile creasing the corners of his mouth.

'Why, the *Broederbond*, sir.'

Cogsweel laughed, having anticipated the answer but gratified by the way Geldenhuis had neatly side-stepped the trap they'd set for him. 'Welcome to the *Broederbond*, Jannie Geldenhuis,' he said, standing, and offering the young policeman his hand.

Within a week of his transfer to the Special Branch coming through, Geldenhuis found himself reporting to Pretoria for duty.

It was curious how Geldenhuis, with his dreamy blue eyes and his hard, blank face, had an uncomfortable effect on people. It was as though they sensed he was trouble and elected to be on his side, rather than to oppose him. Geldenhuis seemed to elicit co-operation from witnesses and prisoners alike in less time even than many of the most experienced officers.

He exemplified the new kind of intelligent, hard-nosed, dedicated police officer who was entirely without compassion. It was almost as though he enjoyed the process of being hated and took pride in the little energy it took to bring most of his prisoner opponents to their knees.

Sarah, the nearest thing Mama Tequila could manage to a blonde whore, pinpointed the characteristic in Geldenhuis which, no matter how sophisticated his technique became, he never lost. 'He makes you feel like you a piece of dog shit,' was how Sarah had described his demeanour at one of Mama Tequila's Sunday morning chew-the-fat chats.

At the mention of Geldenhuis's name, Mama Tequila turned from the Aga where she was preparing scrambled eggs for her girls, folding tiny squares of bacon into the fluffy mixture. 'No more, you hear! That name is said no more in this house. Anybody say it, even once, their future is finish and klaar! No more poems about him, Sarah, no nothing. We never seen such a person at Bluey Jay, *never* you hear!'

'Yes, Mama Tequila!' they'd all chorussed. As far as the working girls were concerned, that was it; the policeman's name was expunged from their memories and, they all privately hoped, from any future experience which might involve him.

But for Tandia, a day never passed when she didn't feel the fear, the cold fist squeezing her heart at the spectre of Geldenhuis. His presence in Durban still dominated her mind. When, some months after his accident, news came that he'd been sent back to the Transvaal it was as though a great weight had lifted from her. Not just a mental thing, a physical one as well.

Juicey Fruit Mambo, driving her to university the following day, could sense the change in her. 'For why you happy, Miss Tandy?'

'Ag, man, Juicey Fruit, a badness has lifted from my heart!' Juicey Fruit Mambo seemed to understand that Tandia didn't want to explain any further.

In fact, Tandia wanted to explain further, to tell him the good news, for he shared her hatred for Geldenhuis. But her fear of Mama Tequila prevented her from mentioning Geldenhuis's name even to Juicey Fruit Mambo. She knew that, sooner or later, he would find out in his own way and they would share the joy of knowing that Geldenhuis had gone out of their lives.

Geldenhuis resumed boxing after almost a year of convalescence and in the ensuing months met a number of opponents, both local and overseas, defending his South African welterweight title successfully on two occasions, though not against Gideon Mandoma. He was now being trained by Colonel Klaasens who assumed both the role of trainer and manager in his life.

Klaasens was delighted with Geldenhuis. He was learning to know him on two fronts: as a policeman and as a boxer. He soon learned that both came together on the subject of the rooinek boxer Peekay.

Not long after Geldenhuis had moved to Pretoria and Colonel Klaasens had taken him under his charge, Geldenhuis had made a request. 'Colonel, I must fight Peekay, whatever it takes.'

'Jannie, that may not be so easy, man. They're calling the fight in New York one of the greatest welterweight contests ever fought, perhaps even the greatest. Most foreign reports say Peekay won and every South African report insists he did. In any other place in the world than New York Peekay would have got the verdict. If he wins here in Johannesburg he could make you fight ten, maybe more contenders before he lets you have a go. He may not even be around as champion by then.'

'Colonel, you don't understand. Of course I want it to be for the world title, but even if it isn't for the title, maybe only for the South African title, I want the fight, anywhere, any place, any time!'

Klaasens shook his head. 'You're asking a lot, man. Peekay has beaten you five times as an amateur; the last time he knocked you out. If I persuade the South African Boxing Board to apply for the fight, you know the rules: Peekay can chose to fight you or Mandoma, who is the black champion. Most likely he'll agree to fight the winner of an elimination fight.'

'Ja, okay, if I have to fight Mandoma again, but it's only for the right to fight Peekay.'

Klaasens looked at his boxer. 'If you get to fight the rooinek it's good you feel like this about him, it's good you hate him, but why, man? Boers hate rooineks, but not like you hate Peekay. Why?'

Geldenhuis coloured, but was forced to laugh. 'Ja, that of course, I got to admit. The first time we fought I was thirteen, he was younger. We were kids, you know our first year in high school? The posh rooinek school he went to never won, man. Rooineks can't box.'

Klaasens grinned. 'One of them can!'

'Ja, he won. It was the first time I was beaten. He beat me four more times in the next five years. Him and the Jew. I've had one hundred and twenty-seven fights altogether, amateur and pro. I've lost five times, all of them to the same guy.'

The police colonel shrugged. 'Sometimes it's like that. You know the fight game. Some guys are just wrong for you; you beat the guys who beat them, but you can't beat them. They got a style, a way of fighting that you can't manage.'

'No that's bullshit, Colonel. It's something different. Even the first time, when we were just kids, it was Boer against rooinek. With most rooinek kids, when an Afrikaner kid comes up to him and wants to fight, the rooinek runs away. You know yourself that's true. But even that first time I knew this was a rooinek who wouldn't run.'

'Ag man, that's just kid's stuff you've got to allow for the one rooinek who isn't scared.'

'No, you wrong again. Him and the Jew, they had a plan. When you get in a boxing ring there's no more place to hide. It's you and it's your opponent, nothing else matters. But with Peekay and the Jew, it was more. I could feel I was fighting for the Afrikaner people.'

'You must have felt bad losing, Jannie. I can understand how you feel.'

'It's not nice, it eats at your guts, you think about nothing else. Now he's lost himself, he'll know how it feels. I'm glad. But it will be worse when I beat him. Because he'll know, he'll know why. He'll know he was beaten by the truth, by a people who fear God and who have kept their blood pure.' Geldenhuis looked at Klaasens, suddenly furious. 'Colonel, they're scum! Him and the fat Jew, they're the scum of the earth. They're Communists and they are determined to destroy the Afrikaner people, the Afrikaner way of life.'

'And you have evidence of this?'

'Enough. I got enough! Peekay and the Jew, Hymie Levy, they're always together. The Jew wants to destroy South Africa. It was the Jews that caused the Boer War, who sucked out our blood and stole our money. They're still doing it, man! De Beers, they own all the diamonds, it all belongs to a Jew. Anglo-American, the biggest gold and copper consortium in the world, it's run by the Jews.'

'Magtig, Jannie, I also hate the Jews but there've been some good ones.

A guy like Harry Oppenheimer, he does a lot of good around the place, also Solomon Levy - just the other day he gave a whole hospital!'

'Shit, man, you make me laugh! He gave a *kaffir* hospital. A kaffir hospital that looks after children. Children's diseases and a maternity wing for black women who breed like flies! Can't you fucking see? He wants more and more blacks, so in the end they'll swarm all over us! It's part of the international Communist conspiracy to destroy the Afrikaner people.'

'Ja, I suppose you're right, I never thought of it like that.' Klaasens was still not entirely convinced. 'But Peekay? He's not a Jew and it said in the paper he comes from poor people. Just a little *dorp* in the low veld.'

'Ja, and now he's just finished at Oxford. Do you know about Oxford?' Geldenhuis asked.

'Ja, it's a university in England.'

'Peekay got a scholarship to Stellenbosch, to Witwatersrand to Natal University. Why did he have to go to Oxford? Not only that, here in South Africa it was for free. At Oxford he had to pay. Tell me that, why, man?'

'I don't know, maybe he just wanted to go overseas?'

'You just said he was a poor boy who comes from a small dorp? Whose mother is a dressmaker. You don't think he paid do you? The Jew paid! I mean no disrespect, Colonel, but that's bullshit about the mines in Rhodesia. You know why Peekay went there? To start a Communist party! You know what happened the year after he left? A strike in the Copperbelt, led by the Communist party. I know a guy, a good Boer who worked up there in the mines. He says they didn't know there was a Communist party in the mines before that! It was not even one year after Peekay left. Now the black bastards up there are demanding independence. This guy I know says the kaffirs go underground the first time and you show them a mirror. They see their face in a mirror and they scream. Now they want independence!'

'I got to admit, Jannie, you've done your homework, man. That's the sign of a good policeman. We did the right thing bringing you into the Special Branch.'

'Thank you, Colonel,' Geldenhuis said absently. He wanted to continue with his proof. 'Oxford is where all the Jews go to train to be Communists, to be traitors,' he continued. 'Why do you think they want Peekay, hey? Except that he's a rooinek, he's the perfect South African. He speaks Afrikaans as well as you and me. He can speak three African languages. He's got brains, lots of brains and maybe he'll be the world champion soon. Peekay is the perfect front for international Communism. Jews always work like that. They don't dirty their own hands.' He paused, looking at Klaasens. 'Now they're back. Peekay and the Jew, and I'm telling you something for nothing, they're the two most dangerous people in South Africa. More dangerous than the ANC or all the kaffir organisations put together!' Geldenhuis paused again, still holding the police colonel's eyes. 'You know what they play at his fights don't you?'

'No, what do you mean, music?'

'They don't play *Die Stem*, no man, the South African national anthem isn't good enough. They play a kaffir song, a song about all the tribes, the only people that isn't in it is the white man!'

'Wragtig? They don't play *Die Stem*?' Colonel Klaasens was genuinely surprised.

'You saw it, on the film of the fight? When all those Jews from Oxford stood up and sang that song with the lesbian woman in the evening suit.'

'Ja I heard that, it was beautiful, I nearly cried. Lots of people in the bioscope cried, you could hear them all over the place. Everybody clapped also. But, Jesus, I didn't know they didn't play *Die Stem*! I thought maybe they just cut it out or something, you know, off the film. The Americans, they do that.' He shook his head. 'Jesus, if I'd only known what that song was about!' Klaasens looked down and shook his head a second time, dismayed and angry with himself.

'Colonel, I want only two things, you hear? I want you to get me a fight with Peekay and I want you to let me control the Special Branch file on him and the Jew. From now on let me be personally responsible for their files. Please, Colonel, these are the two things I can do for my country, for my people, the Afrikaner people. I *can* beat him, I know it. The next time we meet in the ring I *will* beat him. God is on my side, I *will* win. Then afterwards, him and the Jew, I will destroy them before they destroy us!' Geldenhuis's voice was suddenly quiet. 'I swear it on my life.'

Klaasens looked at the young police lieutenant. 'You got the hate to do it, Jannie. I can see that. That's good, you hear? Magtig! That's very, very good, very encouraging.'

Jannie Geldenhuis was amazed he'd told Colonel Klaasens everything. He'd never spoken his thoughts out aloud before. It felt good, but he wouldn't make a habit of it. He felt sure he'd judged correctly, that he could trust Klaasens, whom he thought of as a little stupid but a fanatical Afrikaner. You don't make someone head of the Special Branch in the Transvaal if you can't trust him to keep his mouth shut. He was also a very powerful man. If anyone knew how to get the South African Boxing Board off their arse, he did. Telling Klaasens how he felt would do him no harm with the *Broederbond* either.

Geldenhuis had long since decided that Peekay's personal humiliation would begin in the ring. No matter how good Peekay was, he would be beaten. Now a black man had beaten him. This was a sign from God that it was his sacred duty to eliminate Peekay. God was in his gloves. God would be in his punches. He, Geldenhuis, would reap vengeance on Peekay. God's vengeance on traitors! He'd stalk him and destroy him.

A week later Colonel Klaasens drew him aside. 'You've been given your first assignment by the *Broederbond*, Jannie,' he said; then added, 'It's a great honour. Some people wait years, most never get a chance to serve their country directly. Cogsweel wants to see us tonight.'

He was given the assignment by the *Broederbond* to 'investigate' the black Christmas party Solomon Levy held in the grounds of his palatial home. 'It is not in the interests of our people for an event like this to take place,' was how Cogsweel put it. 'Take your time, not this year, maybe not even next, it could be in ten years' time, but you will know yourself when the time is right. Then call me.' Geldenhuis was delighted; it was God's will that he should destroy not only Peekay and the Jew, but Solomon Levy, the money pot itself.

'Cogsweel, is he, you know, the top man in the *Broederbond*?' Geldenhuis asked, as they left after dining in the private room of a restaurant in Pretoria. 'I mean, he's a rooinek isn't he?'

'Irish. His grandfather fought in the Boer War on our side. No, he's not anything very high up. But he's high enough, don't you worry, man.' He punched Geldenhuis on the arm. '*Jy is in die oog*! That's all you have to worry about; the *Broederbond* looks after its own.'

In early November 1955 Peekay and Hymie returned to Johannesburg directly from New York. Despite Peekay's loss, he returned a hero. The documentary, 'The Making of a Champion' with a quick title change to 'Fight for Your Life!' had preceded them; cut into a two-hour documentary, it had been released in every cinema in South Africa as a main attraction, and drew record crowds in both the black and white cinemas.

While Peekay held himself together in public, his camouflage intact, his defeat by Jake 'Spoonbill' Jackson was devastating for him. It ran so deep that he couldn't talk about it even to Hymie. The unthinkable had happened; he'd climbed the mountain, measured his spirit, allotting each step he took to the right amount of energy, never allowing himself to enjoy a win or even to savour a sense of triumph over an opponent. Only one thing mattered: getting to the top of the mountain, reaching the point where only the sky stretched away above him. Now he found that he'd been unsighted, that beyond the top stretched another peak; and he was completely spent.

For Peekay, welterweight champion of the world wasn't a title, it was the meaning of his life, the very principle on which he'd based his entire personality. He was too intelligent not to know it wasn't the end of the world, but his emotional grief over-ruled his logic. From the age of six, when he'd felt the huge boxing gloves slip over his small hands, he had committed himself to the single principle that the individual can move the mountain; that small can beat big; that hope and determination and singular purpose were the three powerful allies against all the odds. And now he felt betrayed. He needed something else to win and he didn't know what it was.

He'd been told a thousand times by well-meaning, sincere friends that in any other arena anywhere in the world he would have won the fight; and each time he heard this, he felt further defeated. To win by a disputed decision would have been worse for Peekay than losing. He hadn't dedicated his life to the vagary of a single judge's opinion, to luck. Winning or losing on a margin so frail that in a single pause, the time it took to take another breath, he might have come out the winner was not why he'd travelled this journey. He must win so that the thousand and the ten thousand and the million voices heard. Most of all he had to win so that *he* heard it clearly, cleanly, a clarion bell ringing in his mind. Small could beat big, good could triumph over evil.

And now he was defeated. But in Peekay's mind it wasn't Jackson who was evil. The black American boxer had simply been the peak on the mountain. When the mountain is conquered it is what it does to the climber that counts; the mountain itself doesn't change. Peekay was fighting the good and the evil in himself.

Suddenly he longed to die. To climb up into the high mountains, over Saddleback and higher still to the crystal cave of Africa, to lie beside Doc, his body held safely in the heart of the great mountain. Had his life been forfeited by his defeat he would have accepted it willingly. The effort required to get back off his knees was so great. It was a fear well beyond any he had ever experienced, for it was the first time in his life he'd reached down and come back with nothing. He had spent it all, there wasn't anything more. When he stepped into the ring with Jackson the second time he'd simply be blown away.

For the first time in years the loneliness birds returned, the great pterodactyl-like creatures with their greasy feathered wings and long, chipping beaks, their sharp eyes the colour of anthracite. He could hear their membraned wings flapping inside him, like canvas in a high wind, flapping as they squatted, laying their huge stone eggs, then fracturing them into shards of flint that began to fill up every corner of his being.

He had just five months to prepare for the next fight and he had nothing to give it. He was a loser and he had been living a lie. But Peekay could show none of this. People were flocking to the film. He was surrounded by the hyperbole of a nation who felt they'd been cheated and had decided to accept him as a hero anyway. The anticipation being built up for the return bout was immediately at fever pitch. South Africa wanted its revenge and Peekay was going to deliver it for them.

From the moment they arrived back, Hymie began the process of organising the return fight. He wanted to stage it at Ellis Park, the famous rugby and cricket ground in Johannesburg. While, in principle, the city council was only too happy to oblige, a major problem existed. Hymie and Peekay insisted that there must be the same number of seats allocated for blacks as there were for whites. Ellis Park was a white sports ground, with room for only two thousand black and coloured spectators and, for their use, a single toilet block with six urinals and three toilets. With a thirty thousand capacity crowd, half of them black, the existing toilet facilities for black people plainly weren't enough. The idea of allocating fifty per cent of the available 'Whites Only' toilet facilities to the blacks was unthinkable; and, in any case, it was against the law to do so.

The sitting member for Doornfontein, who included Ellis Park in his constituency, attempted to get a special act of parliament passed in which, for one day only, half the white toilets at Ellis Park changed colour. This was immediately thwarted by the minister representing the Department of Community Development who pointed out that this would only be constitutionally possible if half the white toilets all over South Africa became black for the same period of the fight, between four o'clock and nine o'clock in the afternoon on the 26 April. The speech, quoted directly from Hansard, was reported in all of the newspapers the following day:

If this iniquitous private members' bill is allowed to pass in this house then civilisation as we know it will have come to an end in South Africa. Decent white people will be confronted with a dilemma when trying to go to a public toilet on the afternoon and evening of 26 April 1956. All of a sudden, toilets which yesterday were white are now black. But not only that! Which toilets? Suddenly a black man will be able to walk into any white toilet he likes; when you apprehend him, all he will have to say is, 'Sorry baas, I thought this white toilet had turned into a black toilet.' 'No!' you say, 'Not this one, that one.' But which one is that one? Who are you to say which white toilet has turned black and which one has stayed white? What we have here, coming all of a sudden out of a clear blue sky, is the potential for black people to use white toilets just whenever they like! I put it to you, how would you like your daughter to use a toilet where a black woman has just two minutes before sat? Now I hear you saying it is only for one time, a few hours, but you are wrong, man. It is a precedent! Once a black man has sat on the nice clean seat of a white toilet he will think suddenly he is all high and mighty. Next thing he will be sitting at the table with his knife and fork in his hands wanting to eat with your family! One thing is for sure, there is no telling where something like this will end. As it says in the bible; 'Those who sow the wind will reap the whirlwind!'

The solution, when it came, was simple. The pupils at The Voortrekker High Technical School, an Afrikaans institution in Pretoria famous for its boxing and rugby, taking the initiative, did a crowd study during the Natal versus Transvaal provincial rugby match held at Ellis Park. They discovered the ratio of urinal users to toilet users was fifty-five to one. The major problem it seemed, therefore, was the dispersal of urine for a period of some four hours. They offered to build, in return for twenty tickets to the fight and cost of materials, three zinc temporary urinals one hundred foot in length. The city council quickly passed a by-law amending the Urban Sanitary Health Act to allow for the temporary structures to be built. The second largest problem was solved. The largest remained; permission for fifteen thousand black people to congregate in one place. The decision rested with the commissioner of police for Johannesburg and the East Rand, Major General Bul Van Breeden and the Minister of Native Affairs.

Unlike Bokkie Venter, the fifty-two-year-old Van Breeden, relatively young for the senior position he held in the police force, was a man with strong convictions who took a delight at thumbing his nose at Pretoria. He was also of the old school with very little time for the 'Hitler Youth' breed of policeman, as he referred to the young officers rising to positions of seniority in the new police force. He thought of himself as a good Afrikaner and a loyal member of the Nationalist Party but he was an exception; he was not a member of the *Broederbond* and didn't allow politics to interfere with his judgement as a policeman.

He'd also boxed at the 1924 Paris Olympics as a light heavyweight where he was defeated by an American negro named Barnstable Jones, nicknamed 'Barnstorm Jones' for his attacking style, in a memorable bout in the semi-finals.

Major General Van Breeden saw Peekay's loss to Jake 'Spoonbill' Jackson as not dissimilar to his own. Barnstorm Jones had gone on to take the gold medal in a fight which wasn't anything like as hard as the semi they'd fought. All his life the police commissioner had imagined a return fight and, in his mind, Peekay's opportunity to fight a second time for the world title was the return fight he'd wanted so badly himself.

When Hymie had requested an interview with Van Breeden and asked if he could bring Gideon's manager Mr Nguni along, he'd welcomed the opportunity to meet the young Jew who'd played such an important part in Peekay's success. Nguni was known to him as a successful businessman who controlled boxing and soccer among the black people on the Rand. He'd run a check on his local record and, apart from a minor infringement concerning a stamp on his pass two years previously, his record showed that he was straight. It was a shrewd move to bring him along.

The three men got on well and, in principle, it was agreed that the fight with an equal number of black to white fans could take place at Ellis Park. A police captain named Clive McClymont was appointed as police liaison officer for the fight and Van Breeden introduced them to him in his office.

McClymont seemed a nice, quiet sort of chap in his mid thirties and was an expert in crowd and traffic control. He'd listened quietly and then asked several intelligent questions. Hymie found he liked him immediately. The general had grinned when he'd introduced them. 'Don't worry, Mr Levy, we didn't pick McClymont because he's a rooinek, but because he is the only police officer in the traffic division who knows nothing about boxing. There's going to be a lot of heat generated over this decision, might as well have a police officer with his mind on the job, what do you say, hey?'

Hymie asked if he could give Van Breeden four ringside seats. The police general grinned broadly. 'Normally yes and thank you, Mr Levy, but we've got ourselves a hot potato issue here. Pretoria won't be happy; better make that a firm booking for four ringside seats and I'll pay for the tickets myself.' He turned to McClymont. 'Please make sure you get a personal cheque from me and deliver it to Mr Levy yourself.' Hymie grinned to himself. Major General Van Breeden was one helluva smart cop who wasn't going to let a careless detail trip him up. McClymont was his witness that his ringside seats were kosher.

Soon after they shook hands formally in the Afrikaner manner, symbolically sealing the deal. The policeman was careful to shake hands with Mr Nguni as well. He rose from his desk and walked with them to the door. 'It's a pity you couldn't have brought Peekay, I'd like to meet him,' he said as they stood waiting to depart.

'Of course! Some other time,' Hymie replied quickly. 'He's not in Johannesburg at the moment, sir. He's resting, away from it all, mending his body. Did you know he comes from Barberton?'

'Yes, I did. Yesterday he climbed to Saddleback. That's a hard climb; he's feeling a lot better, I think?'

Hymie's eyebrows shot up. The police major general seemed to know more about Peekay's whereabouts than he did.

'Ag, it's not good police work, Mr Levy. Scratch an Afrikaner and you find a blood relation just below the surface of the skin. When I knew you were coming in to see me I called Captain Smit of the Barberton prison, he is my second cousin. You probably know that he gave Peekay his first formal boxing coaching when he was seven years old. Wragtig! He worships the ground that young man walks on.'

'It's kind of you to take an interest in Peekay, sir,' Hymie said to the general.

'Ag, Mr Levy, in my business it is sometimes better to know the people involved than to assess the evidence. It is people who make things right or wrong, who make things good or bad. Allowing fifteen thousand black people and fifteen thousand white people in a sports ground where a white man is fighting a black man, on the evidence available, is asking for trouble.'

He grinned. 'But I think not. This will be the first time that the black fans will be on the white man's side. It seems to me we have a remarkable young man here. Any person who can do this in South Africa we must allow to proceed. There is more involved here than boxing.'

The police general turned to Mr Nguni. 'I am told you were the leader of the black fan club who followed Peekay and turned him into the Tadpole Angel. Is this true?'

'It is not true, sir. I am a Zulu and also I am a boxing promoter. But the legend of the Tadpole Angel, I did not make this. This is written in the smoke and in the bones. I am just taking the people to see who is the *Onoshobishobi Ingelosi*, the Tadpole Angel.'

'You people believe in this thing then? You believe a white man will come to lead the black people?'

The huge Zulu spread his hands. 'It is told who has the power, it is this one,' he said simply.

'This power? It is forever?'

'Who can say this thing? Maybe the *sangoma*, they can change this, I do not know, I am not sangoma, sir.'

'So it will be all right. I mean when Peekay fights the American negro, the blacks will behave themselves?'

'I think I can guarantee for you, it will be orright, sir, the people, they want the *Onoshobishobi Ingelosi* to win.'

'You manage the black fighter, Mandoma, don't you?' the general asked suddenly.

'Gideon Mandoma, the black Welterweight Champion of Africa, he is my fighter,' Mr Nguni said, suddenly proud.

'Black Africa!' Van Breeden answered with a slight edge to his voice. 'If I remember correctly, he was beaten by Jannie Geldenhuis, the South African Welterweight Champion.'

Mr Nguni shook his head, his grin spreading, 'Hayi, hayi, hayi! He is very clever this policeman, Geldenhuis. I don't think he wants to fight Mandoma again. Mandoma he wants to fight, but Geldenhuis will not fight I think.'

'Is that so?' Van Breeden said smiling. He pushed his chair away from his desk. 'Well Mr Levy, Mr Nguni, it's been nice to meet you both. I'm pretty sure we're in business. All you got to do now is go to the Boxing Control Board and ask them, as a formality, to get a permit from the Minister of Native Affairs.'

Two days later a letter arrived from the South African Boxing Control Board saying that their request for a mixed audience to take place at Ellis Park had been refused. No further explanation was added and a phone call to the board revealed little more, other than that they'd already sent in a letter appealing against the decision.

Hymie called Clive McClymont who arranged for a second interview with Major General Van Breeden. This time Hymie was instructed to attend alone.

The general lost no time in getting to the point. 'Look, man, I have called the minister, he is not willing to allow a mixed audience of this size.'

The general looked up at Hymie and spread his hands. 'I'm sorry, Mr Levy, my hands are tied.' He smiled. 'Things could be worse; whatever happens the fight will be a sellout, even with a white audience.'

'I guess it's a matter of conviction, general.'

'I appreciate your convictions in this matter, Mr Levy, but surely the compromise has been forced upon you? It's not of your own making. Your conscience is clear.'

Hymie laughed. 'Ha! Try telling that to Peekay.' He rose from his chair and extended his hand to the general. 'Thank you, sir, I appreciate that you did all you could to make it happen.'

Van Breeden took his hand. 'What will you do now, Mr Levy?'

'London! We'll fight in London. It will be a sell out at Wembley Stadium and the simultaneous TV hook-up will make us twice the money we can hope to make here, sir.'

The general was too wise to show surprise but he released Hymie's hand. 'That's a great pity. World championship fights don't come along every day.' He shrugged his shoulders, smacking his lips. 'It's a blerrie shame, but I don't know what else I can do.'

The general looked up suddenly, squinting slightly. He was a big man who'd more or less kept himself in shape; the grey was beginning to win in what was once jet-black hair and his dark eyebrows emphasised his intelligent, sharp brown eyes. Major General Van Breeden wore his uniform well. 'You know, maybe there is a way.' He indicated the chair. 'Sit! Let's think this out.' Hymie sat, saying nothing.

'Well, maybe we can make a deal here. Not me and you, you understand, you and me with the Special Branch.'

'How, sir?' Hymie asked, leaning forward.

'Jannie Geldenhuis, the South African Welterweight Champion, is a lieutenant in the Special Branch. Why don't we promise him a fight with Peekay after he's fought the American?'

Hymie laughed. 'Nice one, sir! Why didn't I think of that!' He frowned suddenly. 'If Peekay wins the world title from Jackson, he will only defend it once before retiring from the ring.'

'So let the fight with Geldenhuis be the once.'

'It's not quite that easy, General. Mandoma has met and beaten more fighters than Geldenhuis. Also a couple of higher-rated welterweights, for instance, the Mexican Manuel Ortez and the Italian Bruno Bisetti. Geldenhuis, you will remember, was involved in a car accident and couldn't fight for nearly fourteen months. *Ring* magazine rates him number twelve while Mandoma is rated equal ten. If Peekay become world champion, the World Boxing Council won't approve the fight.'

'What if Peekay loses to Jackson?'

'If Peekay loses to Jackson he won't fight again, no matter what.'

'I tell you what!' Van Breeden said suddenly. 'Let Geldenhuis fight Mandoma on the underbill! The winner to fight Peekay?'

Hymie stuck his hand out. 'You've got a deal, sir! If Peekay wins the title he puts it on the line against either Mandoma or Geldenhuis. Whatever happens, we still get to see who deserves to be the overall Welterweight Champion of South Africa, Geldenhuis or Mandoma.'

Later, when Hymie phoned Mr Nguni in Meadowlands where he'd built himself a rather grand new house, he said, 'Well the plan worked. Van Breeden figured it out, Gideon's got his fight with Geldenhuis.'

Nguni had thrown back his head and laughed, his big Zulu voice thundering down the phone.

He finally managed to say, 'You are very clever, Hymie. Gideon thanks you, and me also, I thank you.'

'Forget it, it wasn't clever at all. Just two businessmen who discovered they both had something to sell to each other. As my father would say, "For business like this, maybe is coming down an angel and kissing me!" '

TWENTY-FIVE

On 26 June 1955, two weeks before Peekay sat for his final exams at Oxford and when Geldenhuis had just been promoted and transferred to the Special Branch in Pretoria, the Congress of the People took place in South Africa. It was the most momentous peaceful occasion in the history of the fight against apartheid, for it brought together all the serious opposition to this heinous system of government.

As world-shattering events go, it must have seemed a modest affair. The Congress of the People had as its venue a bare, dusty stretch of ground near a place called Kliptown, a ramshackle collection of African houses, mostly shacks made of beaten tin, about ten miles southwest of Johannesburg. The veld, natural grassland, which in the early morning whitened the approaches to the village with hoar frost, had long since worn away, so the bare earth surrounding the shamble of houses and shanties was like scar tissue: hard, lifeless skin on the rump of the surrounding countryside. In the cold dawn of the June high veld mornings, its few inhabitants would emerge from their hovels, hunched over against the bitter wind, their shirts and cast-off cardigans stuffed with newspaper against the cold.

Kliptown was one of the most unpropitious places on earth and nobody seemed to know quite why it was selected for the Congress. It was a smudge of despair on the ugly apron of a large city. But, as one of the delegates told Gideon, 'It is perfect, man! Kliptown represents everything we have been given by the white man and nothing we aspire to own.'

A small tent city rose at Kliptown; everywhere the black, green and yellow colours of the ANC were on display as some three thousand delegates arrived. Doctors and lawyers, clergyman, teachers, trade unionists, businessmen, city workers and country peasants, all came to sing hymns and dance and talk and listen. They seemed not to feel the biting high veld wind or concern themselves with the sudden dust devils which came at them across the veld, irritating their eyes and leaving them feeling gritty and uncomfortable. They were freedom bent and the glory of the occasion showed in their eyes and harmonised their voices in song. It was the beginning of something – not a funeral like so many times before, but a new start, one step in the journey of a thousand miles. And so it was the happiest of all possible occasions.

For two days the meeting continued and finally the text of the great Freedom Charter was read out in Xhosa, Sesotho and English, with each clause approved by a show of hands and often a roar of delight. It didn't seem to matter that many of the clauses were patently impractical.

In a country where most black families went hungry it promised no hunger and abundant food for all. For families where two out of three children died within their first three years of life from malnutrition or disease, it promised free medicine. In a society where few people owned their homes but lived with the constant harassment of rapacious landlords and the constant threat of police eviction, it promised low rents and easy home ownership. Slums would be abolished and new houses built for everyone. Banks and mines and monopoly industries would belong to the people and every adult man and woman would have the freedom to vote and be free from discrimination.

No suggestions were put forward as to how this would be done; but Freedom Charters are written with the ink of emotion, love and hope, not with the blood, sweat and tears of practical implementation.

Late in the afternoon of the second day the police arrived. They wrote down names, searched delegates, confiscated documents and took photographs. They even confiscated the banners and two signs from the soup kitchens which read, 'Soup with meat' and 'Soup without meat'. You never could tell what might be useful in a future court of law.

But none of this mattered, the downtrodden and the dispossessed had managed to get together. The under-classes had made a stand and declared themselves. It didn't matter that the government declared the Freedom Charter to be subversive, and that the demands for full bellies, homes, free medicine and schools were claimed to be the building blocks of subversion. The people had made their presence felt. They existed. They had a charter to prove it.

There is a part of the African mind which never closes down, but lies in a patch of twilight between wakefulness and sleep, like a watchdog filtering the sounds of the environment around it. Even before the loud banging on the door of the shed and the shout, 'Open, Police!' that followed, Gideon was awake and standing upright beside his iron cot, gulping for enough breath to fight the sudden rush of adrenalin through his body. Without being fully conscious of what he was doing, he found himself pulling on an old pair of khaki shorts to cover his nudity.

'*Mina fika*, I'm coming,' he shouted, grabbing for the small torch he kept beside his bed.

'*Maak oop, polisie!*' the voice demanded again, this time in Afrikaans. With a sudden crash, the door was kicked open, swinging violently inwards on its hinges. Gideon, who'd almost reached the door, was blinded by a bright light shining directly into his eyes. The small flashlight he was holding was knocked from his hands. Clattering, it rolled under the iron cot where it cast a yellow crescent moon on the cement floor.

'*Is jou naam Gideon Mandoma?*' the voice demanded. Then almost immediately the question was repeated in English with a thick Afrikaans accent: 'Is your name Gideon Mandoma?'

'Yes, baas.'

'Ja, I can see it is you. I seen you on boxing posters.' The white police officer gave a short, high-pitched laugh, which seemed to emphasise the tension in his voice. 'I reckon your boxing days is over, man! You under arrest.'

'What for you arrest me, baas?' Gideon asked, keeping the respect in his voice, aware that the white man was nervous and that the barrel of the revolver he was pointing at him would be pushed straight into his teeth if it seemed to him the kaffir boy was being cheeky.

'You a member of the ANC, a *Comminist*, that's enough. Put out your hands, *maak gou, kaffir*!'

Gideon held out his hands for the handcuffs. 'Please baas, I want to put on my shirt.'

'No, man! Where you going you don't need a shirt!' The policeman still held the torch close to Gideon's face, making it impossible for him to see the white man's features.

'My pass, baas, it is in my coat, behind the door.'

The policeman turned to one of several black policeman behind him, momentarily diverting the torchlight from Gideon's face. Gideon caught the flash of the triple 'SB' bar on his shoulder. His heart sank. He was being arrested by the Special Branch; he was in serious trouble.

'Hey, you, Matuli, get his coat behind the door,' the white officer instructed. The black constable edged past him to get behind the door, where he removed a jacket neatly placed on a hanger, and a pair of grey flannel trousers folded over its crossbar. The black policeman removed the sports coat from the hanger and handed it to Mandoma.

'Fok!' Gideon felt a sudden stab of pain as the barrel of the policeman's revolver smashed down hard, then raked across the back of his hand and fingers. The jacket fell to the floor as Gideon clutched at his hand in pain and alarm. 'You stupid black bastard!' the white policeman screamed. 'The foking kaffir could have a foking knife or a gun in his coat! I said, get his pass book! Take it man, take it out yourself!'

The black policeman went down on his haunches and searched for Gideon's pass book. Finding it in the inside pocket of the sports coat he proffered it up to the white man.

Gideon held the damaged hand tightly, trying to squeeze the pain from it. He hadn't uttered a sound but the tears ran down his cheeks from the effort it took to contain his anguish.

The policeman handed his gun to another of the black policemen who pointed it at Gideon, holding the butt in both hands. The officer opened the pass book and examined it briefly by torchlight. The torchlight kicking back from the pages of the pass book lit the white man's face. Gideon noted that he didn't seem more than twenty years old; standing side on to him he could see that the back and sides of the white man's head were closely shaved, a barber's clipper starting at the base of his neck and cuffing tight against the skin right up to where his head disappeared into the rim of his cap. His short thick neck sat on broad shoulders and his face was wide and flat, with a wide nose and thick lips. Despite his fair skin and light eyes he had a distinctly African appearance. This one was a throwback for sure, a coloured who'd scraped in as white. One of his forebears, perhaps three or four generations ago, had hidden his sausage in the dark forbidden valley and the stubborn black gene was still throwing. Gideon knew they were the worst kind, constantly having to justify their whiteness, conscious that their skin and their eyes granted them immunity but that the moulding and the bone structure they'd inherited left other white men looking at them quizzically, turning away with a small smile when you caught them looking. 'Ja, orright, put the cuffs on him, we got the right kaffir!' He kicked the jacket which lay at his feet and it slid along the cement floor, disappearing into a dark corner beyond the arch of torchlight.

Three hours later Gideon found himself alone in a police cell. He'd been bundled into the back of a police wagon, unable to see out. They'd travelled for a while across the bumpy unmade roads of Meadowlands until he'd suddenly felt the smooth tarred surface of the main road to Johannesburg. Meadowlands is about fourteen miles from the central police cells in Marshall Square where, as a 'political', he would expect to be taken. But there was no change of light coming through the narrow air slats in the police van to indicate street lights. Then it occurred to him they might be taking him somewhere to beat him up and afterwards to leave him unconscious on the side of the road. It happened often enough as the first warning to politically minded black people not to progress any further with their affiliations.

It must have been nearly four in the morning when they drew up outside a small suburban police station on the outskirts of Pretoria. The small cell into which he'd been thrown smelled of a mixture of sweat, urine and Jeyes Fluid. Otherwise, for a 'kaffir' cell, it was remarkably clean. The toilet bucket hadn't been used, which suggested the station was quiet and probably in a good white area where blacks are required to be off the streets by nine o'clock curfew.

His right hand where the police officer had hit him with the barrel of his gun throbbed painfully and was badly swollen and Gideon had trouble moving his thumb and index finger. He guessed the fingers were broken and hoped like hell the same wasn't true of his hand.

He tried to think why he'd been arrested. After the Congress of the People the ANC had been relatively quiet. In his own case, apart from addressing his chapter in the new native township of Meadowlands at several low-key meetings, his own activities had been modest and entirely above board, most of them involving the hopeless last ditch protests at the destruction of Sophiatown. It was not as though he was one of the leaders of the movement in the new township. He was still working his way up in the ANC Youth League where, despite the promise he showed as an orator, he wasn't among the very top of the young street-smart radicals who'd grown up in the city slums. Nor was he included with the 'educated' leaders, those few young Africans who had managed a university degree at Fort Hare or, even more impressively, at Witwatersrand University. His value lay more in his role as a boxer and therefore an example of significant black achievement.

He'd attended the Congress of the People in June and his name had been taken at the raid when police had arrived during the reading of the Freedom Charter. But even this wasn't of great concern; they'd taken the names of all three thousand delegates. Besides, that was nearly eighteen months ago. Surely they wouldn't attempt to arrest all three thousand? And for what? Attending a public meeting which had been well publicised and for which a permit had been issued by the supreme court? Even for the Special Branch it seemed improbable.

And again, why a suburban police station in Pretoria? Perhaps they *had* arrested everyone – all three thousand delegates, a great many of whom came from the Rand – and the Johannesburg Fort and Pretoria Central Prison were full, so the small fry like himself got the suburban cop stations?

He didn't have long to wait. Dawn on the high veld comes early and light was just beginning to soften the square of black window set high up into the wall of the cell when two black policemen opened the door and pushed in a small table and chair. Both pieces of furniture looked as though they belonged to the station kitchen amenity; the table was covered with yellow aeroplane cloth which had been neatly tucked under at the edges and held secure with large, flat-headed brass drawing pins, while the chair was painted a bright apple green. They now took up almost half the available space and looked incongruously cheerful as they faced the bench on which Gideon sat with his back against the wall.

Twenty minutes passed and the square of light was tinged with the blue of another flawless high veld summer's day, when there was a rattle of keys at the door. A white police officer entered and closed the door behind him. Gideon had noted his lieutenant's rank and the SB insignia on the epaulettes of his uniform before he realised he was facing Geldenhuis. He'd not seen the white boxer in uniform before and the peak of Geldenhuis's cap, at first, made it difficult to see his face.

But when Geldenhuis glanced briefly over at him it was the police officer's unmistakable blue eyes which he immediately recognised. He'd often wondered about these eyes. Peekay, a white man he loved, had eyes of the same colour as Geldenhuis, yet the two sets of eyes were worlds apart.

Gideon rose from the bench and stood to attention in the customary manner, except that his head was not bowed in the obsequious way demanded by a white police officer confronting a black man.

Geldenhuis, apart from the brief glance, ignored Gideon's presence. He carried several sheets of paper which he now placed carefully on the table, squaring the sides of the paper until they made a single block positioned precisely in front of the chair. Then he pulled back the chair and sat down, removing his cap. He sighed and looked up at Gideon, nodding his head slightly. 'So Mandoma? We meet again. This time in my ring.'

Gideon wasn't sure how to reply. As a black man it would have been smart to call Geldenhuis 'baas' but as a boxer of equal merit this was difficult for him to do; however, simply to reply without acknowledging the policeman's superior status was asking for trouble. 'Yes, sir,' he murmured.

The beginning of a smile appeared on the police officer's face. 'Ag, man, you don't have to call me "sir" just "officer", that's okay by me. We boxers, hey.' Geldenhuis popped the bright brass button through the flap of the top pocket of his tunic and withdrew from it a gold Parker fountain pen. The gesture was meant to seem casual but was rather too studied and Gideon realised that the young police lieutenant was also nervous. They'd met as equals in the ring but hadn't ever met outside of it. Neither of them was sure which rules applied.

'Yes, sir,' Gideon said.

'Officer!' Geldenhuis looked up sharply.

'Yes, officer!' Gideon shot back quickly.

'See, even for a boxer, you learn quick if you try.' It was meant to be a joke and Geldenhuis smiled, but Gideon noted his eyes; those curious white man's blue eyes remained cold. Gideon smiled back at him, and to Mandoma's annoyance he felt the slightest tremble, no more than a tic at one corner of his mouth. He hoped the light was too poor for Geldenhuis to have noted it. He admonished himself silently. 'I am the loin-child of three kings; Shaka, Dingane and Cetewayo, I must show courage.' His hand throbbed painfully and he placed it behind his back so Geldenhuis wouldn't notice the swelling.

'Do you know why you here, man?' Geldenhuis suddenly asked. He hadn't raised his voice and the question seemed mildly put.

'No, sir . . . officer.'

'Well, I'm telling you it's serious, very serious, the most serious crime there is.'

Mandoma looked puzzled, 'I am not for making crime, sir?' He was having trouble remembering to say officer when he addressed Geldenhuis.

The police lieutenant let it pass. He had a dreamy, unfocussed look in his eyes and his voice was soft. 'You black people, you funny you know? You do things, bad things and then you look all innocent, like you are at a Sunday school picnic or something and all of a sudden got arrested by the police.' His eyes focussed suddenly. 'You ANC, Mandoma. I know that's not a crime, but you also a Communist, isn't that enough, man?'

'I am ANC, this is true, sir. But I am not Communist, sir!'

Geldenhuis threw back his head. 'Ha! Jus' because Communism is banned in this country *of course* you are not a Communist, but a member of the ANC is the same thing, you all Communists, everyone of you, you hear?'

'No, sir. It is not same thing.'

Geldenhuis seemed to lose interest and resumed his former unblinking look which seemed to be concentrated on a point somewhere on the wall about Gideon's head. Finally he spoke, his eyes still focussed on the same spot. You know something, Mandoma? You the luckiest kaffir in the world!' The policeman leaned forward. Resting his elbow on the table and cupping his chin in his left hand, he looked directly at him. 'Tonight we arrested one hundred and fifty-seven terrorists. All the big names; also amongst them twenty-three of the white *kaffir boeties.* The white rats from the COD who run with the blacks. Also some coloureds and Indians, the leaders from the SACPO and SAIC. You all finished, you hear? The ANC is finish, finish and klaar, we got you all on a charge of high treason!'

Gideon was deeply shocked. If what Geldenhuis said was true, it was totally unexpected. There had been some police harassment following the Congress of the People, but it had been no more than was expected, a few token arrests and a fair amount of government posturing in the press.

'I am not important, sir. I think to arrest me you have missed many, many others. The ANC can live, I think.'

'Ja, perhaps! Maybe you think you not important, but we not fools, man. If we arrest only the big names then their places will quickly be filled with you people from the Youth League.' Geldenhuis stabbed the table top with his finger. 'So we also arrested the radicals in the Youth League. We weren't born yesterday, jong!'

Gideon was one of the few people in the ANC Youth League who constantly warned that the police were to be taken seriously. A misplaced convention existed in the ANC and in particular in the more militant Congress Youth League that the Afrikaner was basically a fool, a knot-headed farmer, and that his native stupidity was best exampled by the average white Afrikaner policeman. Its members were mostly in their twenties, the product of secondary schools and the University College of Fort Hare, the black university. They were, for the most part, teachers, trade union officials, journalists and clerks, the black educated elite. Almost as a matter of necessity, these young men fed their egos by minimising their opposition. The Afrikaner government and the police became the constant butt of their jokes. Tragically they were naive enough to believe this invention of the dull-witted Afrikaner. They didn't seem to be able to grasp that, while bigotry and racism may well be stupid, it is not an automatic sign of ineptitude or incompetence. For an organisation with its back constantly to the wall the ANC's planning was haphazard and open and the police had little trouble infiltrating its ranks with informers and bringing its schemes undone. Anyone examining both sides for culpable stupidity would have been forced to conclude that the balance weighed heavily in favour of the ANC.

It was Gideon's lack of education and his cautionary attitude that kept the young radicals from allowing him a more assertive role in the Congress Youth League. They thought of him as a village African, a natural Jonah and an arch conservative. Because he had started his life as a rural African, to many of them he was a herd boy, a bush African who'd already been cowed by the white farmer's sjambok. They believed themselves street-smart urban Africans with more intelligence and sagacity than their white Afrikaner opposition. Now it was too late. The raid which had just taken place would bring the organisation to its knees. It could effectively destroy it for years to come. In the name of Communism, the Nationalist government had found a way effectively to eliminate all its enemies.

'I do not think I am lucky, sir.'

Geldenhuis grinned. 'Ja, man, the luckiest kaffir alive! You want to know why?' He smiled at Gideon, suddenly in excellent spirits. 'Simple! When they allocated the raid details I got Meadowlands and Alexandra and what's left of Sophiatown. There were twenty-three names on my list, names for my squad to apprehend and remove to the Fort.' He paused. 'Yours was there also!'

Geldenhuis seemed to expect some sort of reaction. For want of anything more appropriate to say, Gideon replied, 'Thank you, sir.'

'Ja, I think you *should* say that!' The young police lieutenant inhaled, throwing out his chest. '*Dankie, Jannie Geldenhuis . . . Lieutenant Geldenhuis*! I think you will owe me that *forever*!' He seemed impressed with his own magnanimity. 'You see, I have taken your name off the arrest list!'

Gideon Mandoma, shaking his head in disbelief, looked up at the police lieutenant. 'Haya, haya, haya! Why you are doing this for me, sir?'

'Ag, man, it's nothing. A small favour, among friends, just one good turn deserving another!'

Gideon didn't recognise the English expression but he guessed what it meant. He kept his face blank, playing dumb. 'We are not friends, you are not my brother, sir?'

Geldenhuis was somewhat taken aback by this denial that any friendship existed between them. While he knew this to be true, the white man, who takes the sycophancy of the black man for granted, doesn't expect this kind of courageous honesty. 'Boxing! We are friends in boxing. We help each other. You know? You scratch my back and I scratch yours!'

Gideon didn't have to know this expression either. His own intelligence told him that Geldenhuis would expect something in return for his release. He braced himself for the worst. 'What must I do for you, sir?'

Geldenhuis gave a visible sigh of relief. In truth, he found himself in a tremendously awkward position. If he treated Mandoma like the kaffir he was, he might possibly convey the idea that he was afraid to meet him in the ring, that he'd arrested him as a ploy to eliminate his challenge for the right to fight Peekay. Whereas the opposite was true. He was convinced he could beat Mandoma but realised that Peekay had no obligation to fight him if Mandoma was imprisoned on a charge of treason. If it became known he'd been the one to arrest Mandoma, Peekay and the Jew would almost certainly withdraw the challenge. The idea of not getting a crack at Peekay in the ring was almost more than he could bear to think about. There was no two ways about it. He had to let Mandoma go free, it was his only chance. But the black bastard didn't know this; it was the ace up his sleeve. He could undermine the fucker and make him bleed a little first while he reeled him in.

Geldenhuis picked up the gold pen in front of him and tapped the table, fidgeting with it. When he finally spoke his voice was casual. 'Look, it's simple. You go back as if nothing happened, just a misunderstanding with your pass.' He looked at his watch. 'It's five o'clock, we can drop you in an unmarked van near Meadowlands in about an hour and a half, by then it's only half past six. You can say you couldn't sleep so you went for a training run. What do you think of that idea?'

Gideon nodded, agreeing that this action would be possible without arousing suspicion. Geldenhuis, encouraged, went on. 'Nothing changes, you hear? Only now, when you go back, because of tonight's arrests, you more senior in the Congress Youth league, higher up. Maybe a year goes by, maybe ten years, you don't have to do nothing. We even arrest you a couple of times, but you too clever for us, we just stupid *japies*; the dumb police, always you get off, you the clever one, the clever black ANC leader who the police can never prosecute.' Geldenhuis without thinking about it was being patronising. 'One day, who knows?' He shrugged as though the matter was of small consequence, 'In ten years, maybe I need something, then you can help?' He paused, looking up directly at Gideon, his blue eyes ingenuous. 'This is a personal thing, two boxers who got respect for each other. Tonight I got a chance to help you; maybe some other time in the future, you'll get the same chance to pay me back?' He shrugged. 'That's all, it's simple, man.'

'Help the police?'

'No, man!' Geldenhuis hissed urgently. 'Not the police, jus' me, you hear? Only you and me know this! It's our secret.'

Gideon knew that Geldenhuis wanted to fight Peekay. He knew that he'd been beaten five times by him. Tandia had mentioned his determination to have another go at Peekay in the professional ring. What he didn't know was the true extent of the police captain's obsession.

But Mandoma realised that Geldenhuis was relying on him to show the usual ANC arrogance towards policemen. He was expecting him to agree to the conditions of his release confident that when the time came and Geldenhuis attempted to use the so called police statement against him, Mandoma would outsmart the policeman. Geldenhuis wanted the fight so he could get a crack at Peekay. He also wanted the opportunity to compromise Mandoma. What Gideon didn't know was which of these two things he wanted the most. Somehow he had to find a way to expose Geldenhuis, to show him he knew the game he was playing, but do so in such a way that the white man didn't take retribution.

He recalled how bitterly Tandia had spoken about Geldenhuis, a man who thought everything out to the exact detail, never allowing his opposition to surprise him, always ahead of the game. Geldenhuis played with a marked set of cards; he was clever and as long as he controlled the game he was almost impossible to beat. The only way to confound such a planner was to introduce a hitherto unknown element into his careful preparation, something entirely unforeseen and unexpected.

Gideon held up his swollen hand. 'There will be no fight, I think, sir. That policeman who arrest me, I think he has break my hand, also two fingers.'

Geldenhuis grew suddenly pale. His mouth worked wordlessly as his anger grew. He rose suddenly and, dropping the pen, slammed his fist hard down on the table. 'You got to fight me, you black bastard! You got to fight me, you hear?' His eyes were darting wildly about the tiny cell. 'I must fight the fucking *engelsman*! I fucking must!' He looked at Gideon again, his eyes hard. 'You fucking black bastard! You did this on purpose, you did this to stop me fighting *die verdoemde rooinek*!' He was shaking as he shouted at Gideon, white flecks of spittle at the corners of his mouth.

Gideon backed away from the onslaught until his back touched the wall behind him. He could feel the narrow bench he'd been seated at touching the back of his knees. 'No, sir, it was your policeman, he break my hand.'

It was all over in a matter of a few seconds. As suddenly as Geldenhuis had erupted he appeared to calm down somewhat. He picked up the pen and, leaning forward, looked down at the square of paper in front of him. He gripped either side of the small table to stop himself shaking. 'Shit! Shit! Shit!' The expletives coming from him sounded like sneezing. But when it was over, he was back in control. He drew himself up straight and looked up at Gideon. His eyes grew wide in surprise. Gideon was seated on the bench against the back wall grinning broadly at him.

'What you laughing at, kaffir!' Geldenhuis screamed, losing control again. He moved from behind the chair, knocking it over as he came towards Mandoma.

Gideon stopped laughing and rose, his face serious, but it was obvious he was not afraid. He raised his good hand and when he spoke his voice was quiet and controlled. 'Sit, please, Lieutenant Geldenhuis.'

To his surprise Geldenhuis found himself responding. He moved back and, picking up the chair, he righted it and sat down slowly. 'I asked you a question, man!' he repeated, but his voice had lost some of its authority.

'Lieutenant, the fight is in three months. My hand, it will be better.' Gideon paused. 'Then I will beat you.'

Geldenhuis realised he'd been duped, forced into losing control by the black fighter. But now he was sufficiently back in control not to want to respond physically again. 'That'll be the frosty Friday!' He said it the way a schoolboy might and to anyone listening it would have sounded like a light-hearted response, two friends challenging each other. Nevertheless he was deeply shocked at the sudden turn of events. One moment he had had the kaffir eating out of his hand and the next he'd lost control of the situation. He couldn't remember when last he'd been made to seem such a complete fool. A sudden hatred burned in him for the Zulu welterweight.

'I think you must let me go, Lieutenant,' Gideon said calmly. 'I think if in the newspaper they read you have arrest me for this thing and then you break my hand, I do not think the people, your people, the white people, will think it is for treason. I think they will say, "That policeman, he is afraid to fight Gideon Mandoma. Look what he do, he arrest him and he break his hand!" Haya, haya, haya, I do not think Peekay, he will fight you. He is the *Onoshobishobi Ingelosi*, he is a very strong man! I think he will not fight a coward, a Boer policeman who is afraid to fight a Zulu?' Gideon paused to let the barb find its mark. 'I think the *Onoshobishobi Ingelosi*, he will spit on you!' Gideon turned and made a spitting motion to the side.

Geldenhuis wanted to take his revolver out and put it to the black man's forehead and squeeze the trigger six times, let the whole fucking chamber go! Instead he fought down his anger and his voice was under control when he spoke. 'Come, we will drop you near Meadowlands.'

'Thank you, sir.' Gideon immediately assumed the body language of the black man facing authority, the mime of the oppressed. He had taken his insult further than he could ever have imagined possible and Geldenhuis hadn't put a bullet into him. He would keep the rest for when they met in the ring. A pair of six-ounce gloves would do the talking for him.

Gideon knew that he'd made a mortal enemy of the policeman for life and this wasn't a very intelligent thing to do. The African depends on indifference to keep him safe from the white man; any sharper focus is always dangerous. Geldenhuis would hunt him for as long as they both stayed alive. Mandoma was going to have to try to kill him in the ring. Despite his fear of the eventual outcome and the certain knowledge that Geldenhuis would never give up until he'd destroyed him, he felt good, better than he could remember feeling at any time in his life.

He grinned at Geldenhuis. 'Maybe your van can take me to Baragwanath Hospital. They can put for the plaster, then soon my hand will be better, you will see.'

TWENTY-SIX

There is a turn in the narrow mountain road about twenty minutes out of Nelspruit on the way to Barberton when suddenly the escarpment drops sharply away at your feet. Below is the bushveld proper, a valley that stretches to a line of round-shouldered hills twenty miles across. Behind these hills the high mountains rise and artists who come to paint the valley are apt to use too much cobalt when deciding the blue for them. They seem unwilling to allow the mountains to blend, as they do, almost perfectly with the sky. Unlike most valleys, this one hasn't been worn down by a patient river system and smoothed through millennia by tumultuous flood. It is pimpled with hazy purple koppies and threaded by a river that seems to meander in lazy loops as though reluctant to leave so beautiful a place. At the far side of the valley, resembling a bucketful of white pebbles carelessly scattered between the buttresses of two green hills, lies the little town of Barberton.

Peekay pulled his car into the lookout at the side of the road. The unprepossessing name of the valley is the 'de Kaap', meaning simply, 'the Cape', named for the blanket of low cloud that sometimes covers it as you descend down from the escarpment. Though this wasn't the name Peekay thought of as he sat looking across at the small town which had shaped so much of his life; he recalled the name Doc had given the valley on a day, not much different to this one, ten years before.

They'd departed before dawn and by sunrise the old man and the boy had climbed beyond the green hills and into the high mountains. The morning had been spent on a rocky *krans* looking for cacti and now they were resting in the shade of an overhanging rock waiting for the fiercest part of the noon heat to pass. Far below them, lacquered in brilliant light, the bushveld spread across the valley, its space filled so completely with the shrill of cicadas that their sound seemed to paraphrase the silence. Not that Peekay could hear them, but he knew they were there in the flat-topped fever trees throwing circles of dark shadow that looked like black holes in the heat-bright landscape. High above them a chicken hawk drifted on a thermal current, adding to the somnambulating noontime stillness.

'This valley, it begins in another place, not so long ago.' Doc pointed his walking stick across the valley and over the smudge of purple blue which marked the distant escarpment. Somehow Peekay had known he was pointing still further yet, up beyond the horn of Africa, five thousand miles to the north. This knowledge was some sort of symbiotic thing he and Doc shared.

'It begins one day, maybe three million years away. Somewhere near the Dead Sea the earth begins to shift and part. Here is happening a great fault which comes through the Gulf of Aqaba and goes south, making also the trough of the Red Sea and ploughing a deep furrow into Africa.'

Doc's eyes were slightly narrowed, as though he was straining to see into the past. 'Then also it comes to Ethiopia and splits open the mountains like a pumpkin and goes a little bit west, above Lake Nyasa.'

Doc paused, looking over at Peekay and then back across the horizon, in his mind retracing the creation of the Great Rift Valley. 'Now is coming also a volcanic eruption and making Mount Kilimanjaro. Such a beautiful strange mountain that is coming from nowhere and standing alone, six thousand metres in the sky, the highest in Africa. Great lakes come also, Albert, Edward, Kivu, Victoria, Tanganyika, some so big the moon makes only for them a special tide. At last it is enough and in Western Mozambique it stops.'

Doc held up a finger. 'Nearly and almost stopping, but not absolute!' He made several small plopping sounds with his lips. 'Some rock, just a little, is turning.' Using his walking stick Doc indicated a sharp turn to the east. 'Maybe even only some spare rocks and lava is doing this.' He repeated the soft plopping sound, seeming to indicate that this eastern turn was an afterthought, a volcanic splutter, a mere groan of shifting rock in the final progress of the great fault that had left a gaping wound four thousand miles down the spine of Africa.

'Then we are waiting a few million years before we can see what is left from this kerfuffle.' The excitement showed in Doc's pale blue eyes. He spoke as though in awe. 'What is left is this!' With his cane he swept the valley below. 'I think we will call it "God's toe mark!"' He seemed to consider this for a moment. 'Ja, this is a good name for the most beautiful place in the world, eh Peekay?'

'God's toe print?' Peekay suggested.

'Ja, this is better. God's toe print, absoloodle!'

From that moment on Peekay had always thought of himself as living in God's toe print. He opened the door of the car and went to sit on a small, dark rock, mottled with white letchin spots. The air was dry, as it always is at this time of year in the valley, and the African sun felt good on his back, seeping into the muscle and bone of him, into the tiredness and the hurt.

Waiting for him twenty miles across the valley were people he loved: Mrs Boxall, Captain Smit and Gert his great friend, Dee and Dum and his grandpa and of course his mother – though his relationship with his mother had always been a difficult one.

Peekay wondered briefly whether it would improve this time around.

His mother's tight-lipped Pentecostal piety had made much of his childhood an unequal confrontation between himself on the one side and his mother and the Lord on the other. As a small child he'd often wondered how the Lord, who seemed to be constantly required at his mother's side, found time to do anything else but be with her. With this powerful combination ranged against him Peekay had been happy to come under the altogether delightful and spiritually undemanding surrogate parentage of Doc and Mrs Boxall.

It was Captain Smit who, with Geel Piet, had been largely responsible for the physical aspect of Peekay's life, for the fight in his hands. The Afrikaner tribe are a physical people with the hardness and independence of spirit based on three hundred years of survival in a harsh and hostile wilderness. They think with their fists and their guns and believe in a God of vengeance and wrath, largely dismissing the New Testament as someone else's God gone soft.

Captain Smit's intelligence was of the kind that summed a man up, drew a line in the dirt at his feet and dared him to cross it. It was born of six generations of frontiersmen where confrontation and harsh, sudden retribution kept a man on top. A man who wasn't prepared to defend himself or his kith and kin with his fists was worthless.

He thought little of the other side of his young fighter, recognising only obliquely that Peekay was good at book learning. To him Peekay was a boxer, the best boxer he'd ever known. Only one other thing counted, his honour as a man; and Captain Smit knew Peekay was a man who could be counted on to stand with his friends.

Captain Smit had seen the championship fight at the local bioscope, not only on the night of the premiere, but also on three subsequent occasions. Twice he'd come away convinced Peekay had won and on the two other occasions he wasn't so sure. If Peekay was going to win the return fight against the American negro it would have to be through something he possessed which the black man didn't. He decided to see the film once more; this time he would 'feel' the fight with his eyes to see if he could find what it was his beloved boxer needed.

Yet, it was apparent to him this wasn't a fight in the sense that two opponents strike at each other until one drops or is accorded the winner. This was a kinetic explosion, two unstoppable but perfectly matched wills coming together, each mind determined to triumph over the other.

But could a black man's will triumph over a white man's? How could he be as intelligent? Smit's heart began to beat faster as he realised Peekay must have a weakness; this was the only plausible explanation. It had something to do with his upbringing, the part of Peekay he didn't know.

He realised, of course, that Peekay was highly intelligent, a real *slimmetjie*; you don't go getting scholarships to posh rooinek schools in Johannesburg for nothing. But, because it wasn't the sort of smart he understood, the sort you could use in a boxing ring, he hadn't taken the trouble to learn about it. Now it occurred to him that the flaw in Peekay might have something to do with his education. Too many brains could ruin a good man. He'd seen this before in the prison system; a warder who thought before he hit a kaffir was useless. Pretty soon there would be chaos around him. If you thought too long about something, that something soon ate you up.

Captain Smit's own education had been pretty basic. He'd attended a backwoods farm school, innovated by the British, who required that all children reach a primary level where they learned to read and write and do a few essential sums. Among the generally knot-headed farmers' sons he was considered brighter than most. Nevertheless he hadn't developed a lot of respect for book learning when he left at the age of eleven. As a boy he'd believed his father when he said, 'If a man can sign his name, count the number of cattle he owns, read God's meaning from the Book and sing from the hymnal, then he has all the education he will ever need.' Captain Smit came from more than 270 years of *trekboers*, backveld cattle farmers, who had first trekked east from the Cape Colony and across the Great Fish River into the wilderness less than thirty years after the colony had been established in 1652. They were the first white generation to be born on African soil and were contemptuous of the narrow, pinching ways and old-world restrictions placed on their burgher parents by the Council of Justice, a body of men appointed by the Dutch East India Company to preserve the ways of European justice in the fledgling colony. They left the carefully tended vineyards and fields of their dour Dutch and French Huguenot parents and became nomads wandering in the wilderness, men who lived by the gun and listened only to the words of a vengeful white God whose tribe they considered they'd become.

Captain Smit's grandfather lost his life in the Boer War, at the battle of Paardeberg, when a British howitzer shell exploded safely outside the perimeter of the Boer encampment, but on precisely the spot where he'd chosen to defecate. He became somewhat of a legend among his fellow commandos as the only Boer the British had managed to catch with his pants actually down.

After the Boer War Johannes, Captain Smit's father, returned to his farm. He suffered from malnutrition and chronic dysentery and his six-foot-six frame, grown to manhood in a saddle he seldom vacated, was skeletal. His dark eyes burned with fever and the fire of an enduring, all consuming hate for the British. Not yet out of his teens, Johannes the Boer found utter devastation on his return from his defeated commando. His family home and the outhouses and cattle pens had been fired and razed to the ground, a part of the British scorched-earth policy. His father's cattle had been driven away, meat for the devil General Kitchener's rapacious *khakies*, the coward women-and-children killers he called his British soldiers. His mother and all six of his brothers and sisters had been placed in a concentration camp where they'd perished, wiped out by dysentery and blackwater fever.

The embittered nineteen-year-old set about farming and raising a family, instilling into his children a congenital hate for the rooinek. This, along with the ability to shoot straight, was his only gift to his two sons. Times had changed; under British rule land was no longer cheap or for the taking and without cattle he could never hope to become more than a subsistence farmer, barely able to scratch enough from the soil to feed a barefoot wife and five ragged children.

His oldest son, Constand, had joined the prison service at the age of sixteen. The first of ten generations of his trekboer family to come out of isolation, leaving the dreaming land with its mystical tribal significance to join a gregarious white society. The young warder recruit soon discovered he was regarded as *platteland* scum. Even among his Afrikaner contemporaries he was Boer riff-raff, a poor-white person to be regarded as hardly better than a kaffir. The boots he was given for the job were the first he'd owned and when he'd been handed his uniform at the recruiting depot, he'd sniffed at it, trying to trap forever in his memory the heady camphored smell of new cloth, of clothes that he would be the first to wear.

But Constand kept his head and remembered his father's advice, that a closed mouth catches no flies, and he struggled to learn the strange new city ways. He was, in all other respects, ideally suited to his new vocation. He knew how to handle kaffirs, he was tough and could use his fists, and he could shoot straight. For all his uncouth ways, these counted in his favour in the brutal prison society he encountered, and he slowly climbed up the prison social scale, earning popularity as a handy heavyweight boxer while learning all he could of social graces and town manners. It had taken him twenty-four years to reach the rank of captain; but now, five years into his rank, he felt no need to move on. The Kommandant at Barberton prison thought of him as the finest man he'd ever had under his command and certain to replace him when he retired from the service.

Thus it was all the more surprising that Peekay, as a seven-year-old, had somehow crept past the block houses and the booby traps and the early warning systems in the mind of this prison officer to find a way past the hate to his heart. A rooinek kid had somehow reached a part of Captain Smit which he'd long thought of as dead.

Now, watching the silver screen, Captain Smit's eyes searched for a new clue. Then he saw it, and like most conundrums resolved, he wondered how he could ever have missed a sign so obvious. He'd been concentrating on Peekay and not the kaffir fighter. Behind the toughness and the skill and the intelligence there was something in the black fighter's eyes which was missing in those of his own fighter; there was an absence of 'the power' in Peekay's eyes.

He'd first seen 'the power' in his own father's eyes and then he'd watched as, one by one, it was passed from the embittered Boer farmer to his children. One moment he and his brothers and sisters were small, ragged innocents with dirt around their damp nostrils and the next, 'the power' had appeared in their eyes. They stopped playing with clay oxen and were no longer childlike.

It was simply a thing about growing up, it came to some sooner than others. It was a thing about realisation, forged from the hard ways and the righteous beatings and the hunger and the deprivation and the constant, remorseless reminder of why things were the way they were for them, for the *boere volk*.

One day, a day like any other, it would just appear, a sudden dawning realisation that to survive, to live, you needed to hate. It was hate which kept you superior, which made you different from the kaffirs at the bottom and the British at the top. Not pride or heritage or superior intelligence, just hate. Hate kept you alive, kept you in control, kept you fierce. It armed you and made you strong, made you impossible to defeat, it gave you 'the power'.

The knowledge of what was missing in Peekay's armoury had come to him through Jake 'Spoonbill' Jackson's eyes. The camera held for a moment in a close-up on the black fighter's face and, like a burst of pain slamming into his consciousness, he felt the malice of the negro boxer's hate; and all his past anger at injustice, hunger, humiliation and despair tore at Smit's chest.

Captain Smit knew Jackson's hate was enough to win the fight. He thought about Peekay, about where he'd gone wrong, about the people who'd been around him, shaping him when he was young. There was the library woman, Mrs Boxall, a genuine rooinek from England, whom he found so difficult to hate that he made a point of staying away from her. The mad old German professor who'd written a symphony around kaffir singing. *Here*, man, why would you do a thing like that, their singing always sounds just the same. Together with Miss Bornstein, the Jew teacher, these three had developed Peekay's learning intelligence. But he, *Kaptein Smit*, he'd been responsible for teaching Peekay a far more important thing, that hate comes with a power of its own. He now realised, because the kid was a rooinek, that he'd neglected this task, instinctively not wanting to give the alien child the power. He knew that hate was a fighter's sharpest sword; instead of constantly honing it, he'd allowed it to rust. *He* was the reason why Peekay had been defeated.

Peekay rose from the rock and climbed back into the car. Gunning the V8 motor, he reversed and pointed the Chevvy's nose down into the winding mountain road and home. He entered the town, its shaded streets a splash of purple jacaranda blossom as he drove up the Sheba road to his grandfather's cottage on the Berea. His family had never possessed an automobile so no original provision had been made for one and he parked the car on the road outside the small house.

Nothing seemed to have changed much, though the golden shower spilling over one side of the roof had spread into an old Pride of India tree and now almost covered it, the brilliant orange of the invading creeper and the deep purple heads of the Pride of India competing for blooming space. The old man must be getting too old to climb a stepladder or he would certainly not have allowed the one to invade the breathing space of the other. Peekay decided he'd have to put time into the garden on his grandpa's behalf, to stamp his authority on it and show it once again who was the boss.

He wondered briefly about the rose garden which rose in five terraces behind the little house. Was the old man, who saw the garden as his work alone, still up to the pruning and cutting, digging and tending it took to keep a rose garden beautiful? Perhaps Dee and Dum now helped with the lawns and the edge-trimming and the digging of rose holes?

He walked up the front steps, noting the screen door needed new wire netting; but when he opened it, its snapback hinges, acting as a surrogate door bell, squeaked as loudly as ever. The sound brought his mother hurrying from the kitchen into the tiny front parlour. In the three years since he'd seen her she'd aged faster than he'd expected. Her hair was no longer grey but quite white, which made her nose and chin appear larger. She was wearing a new black dress with a white lace collar, heavy lisle stockings and, of course, her sensible black brogues; but she appeared happy to see him and hugged him fiercely, murmuring endearments.

'Welcome home, son-boy! It's been such a long, long time, just two weeks in five years. My goodness you've grown, filled out.' She sighed, frowning slightly. 'Will you stay longer this time?' Peekay realised she'd carefully husbanded the time he'd been away. First the copper mines and then England. It was not time away, but the time spent at home that was important to her.

'Hello, mother. Yes, I hope to, I need a good rest.'

'I should jolly well think so. I am your mother after all; we are your people.' His mother's tone was a familiar mixture of concern and hurt and Peekay felt the distance they'd always maintained between each other beginning to return. 'I have prayed every day since you've been away that the Lord would bring you back to us unharmed and now I can give thanks and praise to His precious name.'

Peekay grinned. 'Well not quite unharmed. A little battered in body and spirit, but nothing a month in the hills won't cure!'

'Oh, the hills?' she sounded disappointed. 'Will you ever stop wandering around in your silly mountains?'

'And, of course, time spent with you and grandpa,' Peekay added. He pushed her gently from him, looking towards the door. 'Where is everyone, mother? Grandpa, Dee and Dum?'

'I've asked them to remain on the back stoep where we'll have tea. Those two little black imps have had tea and scones laid out since dawn. I'm sure we've used up an entire packet of Five Roses making a fresh pot every half an hour, just in case you arrived early. They've even baked a fresh batch of scones less than an hour ago, your favourite, pumpkin. They're quite beside themselves and have been impossible for days!'

'I must say I've missed them awfully, more than I can say.'

Peekay's mother cleared her throat and looked stern, an abrupt change of facial expression which made her look even older. 'There is something I want to talk to you about and I thought, if you don't mind, that we ought to get it out of the way from the start.' Without waiting for his agreement she walked over and sat primly on one of three bentwood chairs placed around Doc's Steinway which had been brought from his cottage after his death and which almost completely filled the tiny parlour. Peekay's mother sat stiffly, as one might do outside the bank manager's office, her legs together, her hands clasped on her lap.

'Whatever can it be, mother? Can't it wait?'

'No son, the Lord can't be kept waiting.'

Peekay groaned inwardly and moved to lean against the old Steinway. 'Please sit down properly. We still like to behave like nice people, even if we are country bumpkins.' Then she added primly, 'You come from very good stock, you know.'

Peekay found himself blushing. Nothing had changed. He'd taken his law degree at Oxford, fought for the championship of the world, but nothing had changed. His mother was as irksome as always. The Lord was obviously up to His neck in all this, up to His old tricks, His name used like a rapier in the dialogue about to transpire.

Peekay wanted to tell the Lord to go to buggery, to leave him alone until he felt a little stronger and better able to cope. But he knew this was impossible. When his mother brandished the sword of righteousness she had a way of pinning him down like a small winged insect on display. It surprised him that he was still capable of feeling anger and resentment, the same helpless, trapped, tight feeling in his throat and chest he always experienced when she combined with the Lord to direct his life.

He wanted to see his grandpa, but even more, he wanted to hold Dee and Dum, hug them, feel their coarse mattress-ticking shifts against him and recall the faint sweet smell of their skin mixed with a whiff of blue carbolic soap. He longed suddenly to have them giggle and weep at the same time, both hands knuckling away the tears from their darling shiny round black faces.

'Despite the fact that you have always hardened your heart to Him, you know the Lord loves you, don't you?' his mother began. Without waiting for his reply she continued, 'Loves you and cares for you. It was His will that you should go to Oxford and His hand which has been held above your head and which has guided you while you were there. Your glory has been to His greater glory. Without His love and guidance we are nothing.'

Peekay now felt slightly foolish at the anger he'd felt a moment before. She was on again about him not embracing the Lord and becoming a born-again Christian. It was the old guilt she'd always found so easy to evoke in him. He relaxed, what the hell, he hadn't been much of a son, he'd spent two weeks in five years at home. He had written dutifully, though no more than once a month. She in turn wrote him her two annual letters, for his birthday and for Christmas; and he hadn't had a tongue lashing from the Lord for nearly three years. He hoped the warning that he was a sinner and his soul was in danger of hellfire everlasting might be over quickly. He was tired from the long drive and his ribs hurt, but past experience told him that the Lord's messages were always preceded by an overture of filial love and usually took some time to come to the point. If the Lord took as long with every other sinner, it was a bloody good thing He had eternity to work with.

'I have prayed for you, for your safety and your success every day you've been away. Not just me, but the entire prayer circle at the Apostolic Faith Mission. We have prayed that the Lord would hold His hand above you, so you would walk always in His shadow. "I will walk in the shadow of the Lord and He will comfort and guide me, and be my strength",' his mother quoted smoothly.

'When you wrote to say you'd done well, we gave special thanks to Him and praised Him, for the credit was His and it was His spirit which guided you and made you successful.'

'Well, I did put in a bit of work on my own, mother,' Peekay offered with a small grin.

'Do not blaspheme, son, "I am not mocked saith the Lord." ' The warning of God's retribution was clear in her voice.

'Mother, I really am very tired, it hasn't been an easy few weeks.'

'Exactly!' his mother replied. 'Your grandfather said you didn't look well when he saw you in the bioscope. I must say you don't look too well now.'

'Mother, grandpa saw me on a movie screen at the end of fifteen rounds of boxing! It's hardly surprising I wasn't at my most chipper. My hand was broken, my ribs had been smashed, my eyes were closed and every part of my body felt as though I'd been put through a meat mincer. I was fighting against one of the world's hardest-hitting, most skilful welterweights. I was completely battered!' Merely recalling the fight brought tears to Peekay's eyes.

His mother seemed not to hear the distress in his voice. 'Ah, yes, you see the Lord was angry. He made you in His own image and you chose to defile that image. He guided you at Oxford and you returned His guidance and His compassion by entering a boxing ring and fighting a savage!'

Peekay was suddenly angry. 'Mother! How can you possibly say that? If the Lord is filled with compassion for the sinner, then he has the same compassion for the boxer as he has for the student. Besides, my opponent was no more a savage than you or I.'

His mother looked up, her expression bland, unchanged. She chose to ignore his outburst. 'He sent us a sign. We asked Him for a sign and He gave us one. In His infinite compassion and mercy He gave us a sign to use in your guidance.'

Peekay, realising he'd only been home a few minutes, swallowed hard, holding back his anger. What was it about his mother which hurt him so much? Her confrontation was inappropriate. She'd not even allowed him to greet the others. She was treating him like a small child who'd come home late. 'Mum,' he said, trying to soften his voice, 'I'm twenty-two years old. Don't you think I am old enough to guide my own life? Don't you think I ought to be allowed to see grandpa and Dum and Dee before this ridiculous conversation goes any further?'

'Oh, you find the Lord ridiculous?'

'No, mum, I find the situation you've placed me in . . . well, awkward.'

Peekay's mother looked at him and sighed. 'I'm not being cruel, sonboy. I love you very much. You are the most precious thing in my life. But the Lord cannot, must not be denied. He sent us a sign and I must deliver it now before you properly enter this house.'

Peekay remained silent, but his mother, sensing his irritation and impatience, went on, 'Do not harden your heart against the Lord, son, He too loves you even more than I do.'

Peekay sighed. 'A sign? What sort of a sign?' His words substituted for the ones in his mind which, had he said them, would have hurt her.

'It happened at the Friday night prayer meeting, the night before you were to fight the . . . er, black boy. All that day I'd been sorely troubled, my heart was heavy for you in America. Heavy as it has always been because of your boxing. The Lord has been against your boxing from the beginning, but I was weak and failed Him by allowing you to take lessons when I should have refused. Now, the Lord showed me quite clearly how the devil had taken possession of you and you were hurting people for money, just like a common thug!'

'Mother! That's not fair! From the very beginning, from the age of six, I have dreamed of being the welterweight champion of the world. You can't be that unless you turn professional.'

Peekay's mother did not react to his outburst, not even raising her voice. It was amazing how she could simply ignore his passion. 'Oh yes, we are warned that the devil is cunning, that he is clever. He began to work with you when you were still very young, teaching you how to hurt people. But the Lord, praise His blessed name, countered the work of the devil by giving you brains and by sending you to Oxford.'

'I see! The devil is responsible for my boxing and the Lord for my education. Is that it?'

Peekay's mother ignored his sarcasm. 'I rose in the early morning after praying for you all night, my heart still heavy and sorely troubled and my sorrow was still with me as I entered the prayer meeting at the Assembly that evening.'

Members of the Apostolic Faith Mission were rather fond of this kind of nineteenth-century gospelspeak. Nevertheless there was no doubting her sincerity. His mother was plainly upset.

'Please, mother, you're upsetting yourself.'

The little woman looked steadily at Peekay, her lips trembling as she forced herself to continue. 'At the Friday night meeting I stood up to witness for the Lord and asked again that He would give me a sign and that He would place His hand over you and protect you in America. We kneeled in prayer and almost immediately the Holy Spirit descended among us and Mrs Schoemann started to talk in tongues and then broke into English . . . she speaks English poorly, but her speech was flawless.'

The devil is black and has a tongue of fire and leaps to destroy the children of the lamb. His number is twice seven and one and with his hands he would destroy us, tearing at the flesh of our flesh and the bones of our bones, bruising our flesh and breaking our bones. With his right hand he will smite our firstborn and with his left hand also. His colour is black and his tongue is the fire of hate and he will triumph over the flesh of our flesh and he will vanquish him. But the Lord will place his hand beneath the feet of the vanquished and raise him up and take him from that place and anoint his head and dress his wounds and clothe him in fresh raiment and require only that he not return from that place from whence he came, for if he should do so, he will be utterly destroyed.

Peekay had heard his mother before. She could play back the complex syntax of a message delivered from the Holy Spirit, seldom missing a word. It had once occurred to him that his own ability to absorb and later recall every detail of a fight must be a different manifestation of the same inherited gift. Peekay remembered how Mrs Schoemann, whose husband ran the bioscope and was therefore definitely a sinner over whom a great many hours of prayer had been spent, was a heavyweight transmitter for the Holy Ghost. At the smallest provocation she could go off in a prayer meeting like a yard full of chickens who discover a snake in their midst.

'I don't have to tell you what Mrs Schoemann's message says, darling. You have the gift. But clearly the Lord has spoken. You have been rescued from the bottomless pit! He, in His infinite grace, has lifted you up into His everlasting arms and given you a second opportunity to repent and be washed by the blood of the lamb. His guidance is clear, you must never box again!' Peekay's mother started to weep, softly, her head bowed, a tiny white-haired lady who was the very best messenger the Holy Ghost ever had.

Peekay rose slowly and put his hand on her shoulder. He could feel her trembling beneath his touch. 'Mother, I must have two more fights. Just two more. After that, I promise, I will give up and never put on a pair of boxing gloves again.'

His mother looked up at him tearfully, her lips trembling. 'Those were not the Lord's instructions. If you fight the black man again, the black devil, it will be the end of you.' Her voice rose suddenly to overcome her distress. 'No power on earth can save you from the everlasting fires of hell!' Her shoulders shook as she pulled herself away from her son's embrace. 'Oh, oh, you are the devil's child, but also you are still *my* son, I love you so. Lord, in your infinite mercy, please grant me the strength to bear this terrible burden!'

TWENTY-SEVEN

Peekay rose before dawn and made his way through to the kitchen. To his surprise Dum and Dee lay rolled up in their blankets on a grass mat on the floor. A candle burned on the shelf above the stove and the glow of embers in the grate showed that a low fire was burning. A quarter moon of the large black cast-iron kettle was placed on the hob so as to keep it just off the boil. Both twins woke startled, the way people do when their sleeping senses have been primed with expectation.

'Why? Why are you here?' Peekay whispered. 'What has happened to your *khaya*?' He was concerned that something must have happened to their home. Doc had left everything he owned to Peekay. As it turned out, this was the entire koppie on which his tiny three-roomed cottage with its magnificent cactus garden sat. Doc's house was sufficiently above and away from the white part of town so as not to qualify as a white residential area and so Peekay gave the cottage to Dee and Dum as their home, moving only the magnificent old Steinway.

As Africans and women to boot, the law did not allow Dum and Dee to hold the title deeds. Nevertheless it had been a happy arrangement. Doc's cottage was a mansion compared to the tiny brick shed behind the stone wall in the rose nursery, which was barely large enough to contain two narrow iron beds raised up on bricks. For, while both girls confessed to be Christians, somewhere they had learned the fear most town Africans share of the *tokoloshe*, a small creature who comes in the night and climbs into bed, making young girls pregnant among other unspoken of things. The tokoloshe is just big enough to clamber with difficulty onto the average bed and a couple of bricks to raise its cast-iron legs is known to be sufficient to keep him safely out.

'You said you were going to the mountains for two days, we have come to pack your food and walk with you for the first part into the hills,' Dee said, rubbing the sleep from her eyes.

'You have slept on a hard floor. It wasn't necessary. It's all tinned stuff, bully beef, a bit of biltong, biscuits, a couple of sweet potatoes and a tin of peaches.' Peekay explained the intended contents of his rucksack in the African manner so that each item took on an importance.

'Ho, listen to the great provider of food! Would we let him who is from our kraal go into the mountains with just a tin of meat?' Dum said scornfully. 'For the first day and night you can eat well. The food we have made will not spoil in this time. Also there is a leg of mutton, it is well cooked and it will keep for two days if you keep the flies away.'

Dee turned from where she was standing at the stove. 'After that you will be home again,' she announced.

'Ho! Since when do the *izaLukazi* decide where a man goes and when he returns?' Peekay scolded, laughing.

Dee now brought him a mug of sweet, milky tea and a rusk and already Dum had the skillet sizzling on the stove with rashers of bacon plopping and splurting as though they were being prodded by a teasing finger from beneath. Two dark, shiny-skinned sausages and half a large red tomato shared the pan. With a couple of fried eggs, soft in the middle, it was one of Peekay's favourite breakfasts.

Peekay had hoped to get away quickly so as to get to the top of the first range before the sun grew too hot. Once there he'd stop for a slug of cold tea and a couple of hardtack biscuits before moving higher. There was no point now. Dee and Dum would fuss around him like a couple of old abaFazis and they'd be lucky to get away by sunrise at 5 o'clock. Still, with a big breakfast under his belt, he'd be able to keep going until noon when he hoped to arrive at the cave.

He quite liked the idea of having Dee and Dum come along. They'd take turns carrying his rucksack, balancing it on their head, chatting and laughing and pretending petulance if one took advantage and carried his rucksack for too long. They would walk with him to Pig Rock, about an hour over the foothills, before turning back.

He glanced over at his old rucksack in the corner of the kitchen. The canvas had been scrubbed and was spotless, and the tears in it had been carefully patched or cross-stitched. Both girls were excellent dressmakers, a skill they had learned from Peekay's mother. In fact, making clothes for the location women would have provided them with a far better living than being household servants, though the idea hadn't entered their heads. They were Peekay's family and would remain in his kraal, their ties to him as strong as any bloodline could possibly be.

Peekay dared not examine what they'd packed into his rucksack for the two days in the mountains; it would upset them too much to think he mistrusted their judgement. He handed Dum a small canvas bag containing a dozen crampons he'd brought from England. A look of dismay crossed her face as she recognised what they were, but then dutifully added them to his pack.

Both girls had watched the previous day as he'd tested an old climbing rope, swinging it over the branch of one of the magnificent oaks which grew so incongruously in the rose garden. With the rope they found no cause for alarm; it was standard equipment when he went into the mountains, and afterwards one of the girls coiled it carefully, attaching it, as always, to the top of his rucksack. Dum's dismay at the sight of the pitons was different; pitons confirmed that he was headed across Saddleback.

They meant Peekay was going high and would take risks. He was, they both realised, going to see Doc.

Doc's body had never been found. One day, when Peekay had still been at boarding school, he'd simply walked into his beloved hills and hadn't returned. Peekay had learned from Dee and Dum that Doc had asked them to pack food for three days and only when he hadn't returned on the fourth day had they raised the alarm through Mrs Boxall. Typically nobody officially in charge had thought to ask them when Doc had taken off and so it had been assumed by everyone that the old musician, in some sort of delirium, had wandered off during the night or early morning of the day they'd reported him missing. When they eventually discovered otherwise the conclusions they'd reached remained unchanged. Doc had simply stumbled and fallen earlier, and had been dead longer.

But Peekay instinctively knew otherwise, though he didn't share his knowledge with anyone. He'd waited until the furore over Doc's death had died down before packing a rucksack and leaving at dawn for the high mountains. He knew that Doc, always a meticulous planner, would have planned his death for months, in fact; he had cause to believe he had done so three years previously.

During the Easter holidays of Peekay's second year at school they'd found a cave, a crystal cave high up beyond Saddleback, a day's hike for the old man even then when he'd been fit and strong. Doc wanted more than anything in the world to be buried in the crystal cave of Africa, which is what they'd called their secret discovery.

Doc wanted to lie stretched out on the beautiful natural stalagmite altar they'd discovered within the cave. He'd been wildly excited by the discovery and he'd explained to a fearful Peekay how he would lie like a medieval knight in this great crystal cave cathedral, his arms folded across his breast, his legs outstretched, as the tiny drops of lime sediment fell, drop by tiny drop, upon him.

'Maybe it takes one hundred thousand years, but then also I am crystal. Imagine only, Peekay, I am Africa and Africa is me!'

Peekay knew Doc wasn't the sort of person to abandon a project as important as turning himself into crystal just because he knew it was time for him to die. So, when the search parties had given up looking for the professor's body, he'd set out to find Doc himself.

On his own the climb to the deep rainforest kloof beyond Saddleback had taken him around six hours and he'd returned home shortly after moonrise in just under five.

Dee and Dum had waited for him with two four-gallon tins of steaming hot water bubbling away on the stove ready for his bath. He'd climbed blissfully into the large tin tub, leaving his soiled clothes on the floor. Dum had entered later to empty the tin bath and take his clothes to the wash house. As usual she'd searched through his pockets where she discovered Doc's Joseph Rogers pocket knife and his gold hunter watch.

Dum's heart had beaten furiously as she realised that Peekay had found Doc. Taking the knife and the watch, together with a small tightly folded wad of paper she'd also found in Peekay's shirt pocket, she placed them under his pillow where she knew he'd find them.

Later that night she had told Dee. Holding each other, the two little teenage girls had wept themselves to sleep, for they'd loved Doc dearly. Apart from Peekay, Doc was the only person they'd ever known who'd loved them just the way they were. They also knew that Peekay, exhausted as he was from his long hike, wouldn't make a silly mistake such as leaving the objects in his pockets if he didn't want them to be found. It was, they decided, his way of saying, without incriminating them, that he'd found and taken care of Doc. They would keep Peekay's discovery secret forever and they loved him even more, if it was possible, for telling only them.

Now, nearly seven years later, Dee knew that Peekay was troubled and was going back to visit Doc in a high place in the mountains where a rope and pitons were needed. Peekay's left hand was still in plaster and it worried her to think of him climbing across the mountain crags beyond Saddleback. They could be treacherous, with mist often driving in without warning. She knew his body was not yet altogether mended; the bruising about his ribs had turned green and purple and, while his right eye was no longer swollen, there was a half-moon of bright purple below it. Above it a fresh pink scar, like a badly mended tear, showed where Jackson had worked to put it out of action. Peekay was still not as agile or as strong as he needed to be to climb high across the sheer rock face of the mountain buttresses that rolled back beyond the hills and where sometimes, even on a clear day, you could hear distant thunder and see lightning strike in the huge rocky pinnacles. She comforted herself that he was having a good breakfast and this, at least, would give him some strength.

Peekay, swallowing the last of a second mug of tea said, 'The birds are beginning to chirp in the mulberries. C'mon, it's time to go, you lazy old hippos.'

Dee giggled and hurried to the corner. Lifting the rucksack, she moved over to Dum and placed it carefully onto the head cloth Dum had placed on her head. Dum adjusted it so it was perfectly balanced and she moved away, her arms swinging freely.

A *piet kokkewiet*, always the noisiest of the early morning birds, called from one of the alien oak trees as they moved beyond the rose terraces onto a small bush path which ran past the side of the house and led straight up the rocky hill behind the house.

The hill was dotted with hundreds of aloes, each as tall as a man. They stood like mute sentinels guarding a rocky fortress at the crown of the hill, each with a menorah-like candelabra of flame-coloured blossom suggesting an exotic tribal headdress. The grass, brushing at their feet, was wet with the dawn condensation and the air was still crisp and sharp, not yet punctured with sunlight and leached with heat from a sun yet to rise above the high mountains.

They climbed together for the first hour, the two girls chatting happily, delighted to be sharing the beginning of Peekay's journey. At sunrise they reached Pig Rock and turned for home, and Peekay headed for the huge kloof some three more hours into the high mountains before he reached the base of Saddleback. There is a stillness and sureness about mountains to be found nowhere else; it is landscape that diminishes man, who, on flat land, can imagine forests and fields of ripening crops, lowing cattle and distant church bells or who, on the sea, can fashion a coracle and hoist a sail and command the wind and the surface of the sea to be his servant. But high mountains are not as easily tamed; man can burrow like a small rodent into them to hide or blast and chip vaingloriously at them, but he cannot vastly alter their shape or diminish their control of the heavens and the clouds that rise above them and the water that flows from them to replenish the earth. The mountains do not lie still, meekly submitting to the arrogant tampering, the thoughtless rearrangements of man. Instead they test his strength and courage and ignore his pompous sense of superiority over all things. When man is threatened by others of his kind he seeks the mountains, a place to disappear and to change the odds, to hide and force his enemy to pursue him on more equal terms.

By mid morning Peekay had passed over Saddleback and climbed higher beyond even the scree and tussock grass, and into the rocky crags. Towards noon he found himself between two giant cliffs that rose eight hundred feet into the air and seemed to split a mountain apart. The passageway between them was no more than six feet across at the broadest point and often no more than a foot. Half an hour later this high canyon opened up into a deep kloof of rainforest, at the far side of which rose yet another cliff face. The crystal cave of Africa, concealed from view, was midway up this opposite wall of rock, nearly two hundred feet above the forest canopy. A waterfall of thin white spray, like a bridal veil, fell from one side of the cliff and seemed to disappear directly into the top of the green forest at the far side. Peekay, who now stood high above and at the opposite end of the kloof, noted the familiar old yellowwood which thrust nearly fifty feet above the dark canopy of trees and which Doc had estimated to be a thousand years old and still growing. Beard letchin was draped from its mighty branches and Peekay tried to imagine how big it would be by the time Doc, resting on his fluted calcareous altar, had turned into pure white crystal.

It was strange; he didn't think of Doc as dead, but simply as undergoing a state of transition. The concept of Doc's metamorphism into a part of Africa itself was a willing suspension of Peekay's belief system. If Doc was alive in his mind and his unquenchable and sublime spirit dwelt within the crystal cave on the cliff opposite, then he knew he could reach him and talk to him.

Peekay descended down the steep slope into the rainforest below his feet. He worked his way through the thick undergrowth and tall tree ferns to the stream which led from the waterfall. Choosing a spot beside the stream on the far edge of the rainforest to set up camp, he spent the next hour or so clearing a patch of ground, more or less flattening it by removing the larger rocks and piling the dead branches high into the centre of the clearing. He added to the pile of dead timber until it covered the entire clearing, which he then set alight, careful to keep the flames contained within it. He allowed the fire to burn down completely and then, fashioning a broom from several leafy branches, he swept the smouldering ash evenly over the clearing. The fire would heat the ground and keep it warm for the next two hours, forcing insects, in particular scorpions, to the surface from beneath leaf mould and small rocks to be consumed in the hot ashes. Before nightfall he would sweep away the ash, leaving a clean, warm patch of earth on which to build his campfire and where he could safely spend the night.

Making the clearing had been hard, dirty work and after gathering wood for his campfire and stacking it, ready for when nightfall came, Peekay bathed in the icy mountain stream. Shivering, he found a large rock in a small clearing near his camp, where he lay naked to dry himself in the sun.

He must have fallen asleep for he woke suddenly, startled by the call of a troop of baboons high up on the cliff face. It was late afternoon. The sun had closed down over the kloof and the baboons were using the last of the afternoon light to find a high ledge in the krans above him where they could spend the night safe from the danger of a night-prowling leopard.

Peekay put his clothes on and worked quickly to sweep the ash from his clearing, whereupon he spread his groundsheet and blanket and set the rocks for his campfire. Dee and Dum had done a wondrous job of packing his rucksack and his eyes widened in amazement as he came to his food supplies. They lay at the very bottom of his rucksack, under his large Ever-Ready torch, the crampons, his groundsheet, blanket and a small canvas bag which contained salve, a snake-bite kit with a vial of Condy's Crystals, a roll of Elastoplast and a worn cake of yellow Sunlight soap. He removed a small billycan, its lid firmly jammed and then tied shut, and opened it to find it contained a thick beef stew for his dinner. Next to it in the bottom of the rucksack was a large calico bag into which the twins had placed a leg of mutton cooked with rosemary, the tiny dark flecks of rosemary leaf still clinging to the haunch. The mutton itself would have been sufficient to last him until he returned home, but there was more to come. They'd placed two eggs in a jam jar and filled it with finely chopped onion so that the onion flakes cushioned the eggs, preventing them from breaking. He searched for the can of bully beef he knew would be there; this, together with the onion and eggs was intended as his breakfast. There was also a container of coffee, a tin of condensed milk, a bar of dark chocolate, a packet of Marie biscuits and two pieces of biltong to chew on if he grew peckish during the day. Finally, there were two oranges and a fat sweet potato for his dessert.

Peekay warmed the delicious stew and ate it slowly. He hadn't bothered to stop for lunch and he was hungry. The night was filled with the noise of insects and a great moon rose, so that he could see the walls of the cliff right up to the buttress which concealed the opening of the crystal cave of Africa. Doc's spirit would be looking out over the silvered canopy of rainforest to the far mountains beyond the Swaziland border. He might even glance down to see Peekay's fire below and know he'd come back and so would visit him in his dreamtime.

The stew had warmed Peekay and he decided to skip coffee. He placed all his provisions into the calico bag and pulled the drawstring tight. Taking his torch to light the way he suspended the bag by its drawstring from a low branch over the stream. It would be safe from ants and bushbabies or anything else which chose to visit his campsite while he slept.

Returning to the fire, he reached for a stick and raked the sweet potato from the glowing embers. Rolling it onto his enamel plate he slit its steaming tummy open. Using a can opener to pierce two small holes into the top of the can of condensed milk, he placed his mouth over one hole and blew, filling the belly of the steaming sweet potato with the thick sugared milk. The intense heat from the potato caused the milk to plop and bubble and turn into caramel, impregnating the soft flesh of the sweet potato. Peekay waited for it to cool down a little before spooning the delicious confection into his mouth.

After he'd eaten he returned to the stream to wash his billycan, plate, fork and spoon, leaving them in a small running pool to rinse themselves during the night. Then he cleaned his teeth and, returning to the fire, he rubbed himself with citronella oil to ward off the mosquitos which he knew would appear in squadrons the moment the fire died out. Despite his afternoon nap, no sooner had he pulled his blanket over his head than he was asleep.

Arriving as he did in the early afternoon he could easily have scaled the cliff to the ledge outside the cave, spending an hour there before returning to his campsite. But he'd resolved not to go near the cave until morning. It had been a morning climb when they'd discovered the crystal cave of Africa. Doc always said the brain works best in the early morning, that they had merely to look about them to see that God was an early riser. Early morning was the time he'd always felt closest to Doc and he would return to him in his magic cave when the still, cool world of the high mountains was at its most benign.

Peekay woke early. Around him the rainforest was shrouded in mist and the bubbling sound of the small brook seemed louder in the dawn stillness. He rose, pulled the blanket about him, and fetched wood. In a few minutes he had a fire going and the billy boiling for coffee. He wanted to be seated on the ledge outside the cave before sun-up so that the first rays of the sun coming up directly behind him would cut through the swirling mist to reveal the great yellowwood tree and beyond it the blue smudge of mountains in the west where Swaziland lay. It was with this magnificent view that he would start his day, as though an image of perfection would prepare him for what was to come.

Except for the day when they'd discovered it, Peekay had never physically entered the cave again. After Doc's disappearance, when he'd set out to find him, he'd found the gold hunter and the old man's Joseph Rogers pocket knife together with a farewell note and a sheet of musical notation cunningly buried in a rock fault on the ledge immediately outside the cave. He knew immediately that Doc, who had trained him so carefully in the art of observation, had expected him to find these last small tokens of his love and, by the act of concealing them outside, did not wish him to enter the cave.

Nor would he enter the cave this time. It was Doc's mystical crystal cathedral and he alone belonged within it. Peekay would visit him again by jumping the stepping stones in the night country. He sipped at his coffee, taking it strong and black, allowing it to warm his stomach, deciding to forgo breakfast. Leaving the warmth of the fire he fixed his torch to his belt, together with half-a-dozen crampons and his climbing hammer and rope, and walked into the mist-shrouded rainforest towards the cliff and the crystal cave of Africa. It was difficult going and he made a fair amount of noise; at one point he disturbed a forest *duiker*, the tiny buck disappearing noisily into the undergrowth.

Peekay was a fairly experienced climber and the two hundred or so feet to the ledge was not overly difficult. Nevertheless he needed to be careful, his hand was still in plaster and parts of the rock face were wet; visibility was down to a few feet. On several occasions he needed to use the rope and pitons and it took him almost an hour to get to the ledge beside the cave. The sun rising over the cliff above him was cutting away the mist which covered the rainforest canopy far below him and he could see the outline of the giant yellowwood begin to appear almost level with his eyeline as he seated himself, his legs crossed and tucked under him, his hands perfectly relaxed in his lap. He would sit perfectly still, building his concentration by the very act of his stillness, his mind going deeper and deeper into himself, his eyes seeing everything yet nothing as his mind focussed inwardly.

He'd been sitting like this for about twenty minutes when he saw the snake appear. Its flat black head and a part of its body rose like a black periscope over the lip of the ledge until, swaying slightly, it was poised level and no more than eighteen inches from Peekay's eyes. He could see directly into the huge snake's anthracite eyes on either side of its wedged head and its darting tongue seemed to have a life of its own as it flicked and tested the air for vibrations to tell it of danger.

Peekay's concentration was so complete that he wasn't sure whether what he was witnessing was an apparition. The snake seemed too big for a black mamba which, fully grown, is usually around six feet long. Judging from the breadth of its neck this snake was considerably larger. He felt no fear as his mind measured the part of the snake in front of his eyes, concluding that the deadly reptile was more than ten foot in length. If it struck him, the poison would paralyse his nervous system in less than fifteen minutes and he would die of a massive trauma within an hour.

The black mamba vision had come to him before in his life, always as a warning when he was in danger. Now, deep into his own head, he was unable to tell whether the snake was real or imagined.

The sudden bark of a baboon on the cliff face somewhere above him tore the stillness, its echo exploding across the kloof. The snake, who must have sensed danger, triggered by the unexpected noise, struck. Inside Peekay's head the entire action took place in slow motion; the reptile's jaws opening, showing their bright yellow lining and the fangs riding out of their scabbards, then the slight whipping motion as the mamba drew back, and the seemingly infinite time it took for the whiplash strike.

In fact the process happened in a blur of light and Peekay's reactions must have been equally fast. As the huge snake struck, Peekay's right hand rose instinctively to protect his face. The mamba's needle-sharp fangs sank deeply into the plaster cast as Peekay's left hand came up to grip the mamba behind the head, his thumb pushing the wedge-shaped head down hard into the dirty plaster.

Peekay, without knowing how, found himself standing upright, holding the deadly mamba, its open jaws forced into his right hand, its powerful body wriggling like a muscled whip with its end still over the edge of the ledge. His mind was working surprisingly cleanly and, while his heart was pounding furiously with the rush of adrenalin through his system he realised immediately that if he pulled the snake's deadly jaws clear of his hand he might not have the strength in his left hand to prevent it from striking again. He moved towards the edge of the ledge. This was his best chance. He'd tear the snake's head free from the plaster and release his left hand over the ledge. The fall was almost two hundred feet directly downwards and the huge serpent would dash itself against the jagged outcrop of rock before it hit the forest canopy a hundred and fifty feet below. He moved forward to the edge of the ledge just as the snake's tail rose above it and whipped tightly around his legs.

The realisation that he was trapped struck him like a physical blow and his mind misted with uncertainty as the fear welled up in him, threatening to overwhelm him. The huge snake, its entire length whipped about him, was very strong. Using Peekay's own body as a purchase, it was attempting to force his left hand backwards. But Peekay held its head and jaws pushed deeply into his encased hand. The surface of the plaster where the fangs had entered was wet with the venom milked from the poison ducts behind the snake's hooked fangs. It was sufficient to kill ten men.

Peekay stood helpless. For some reason he couldn't explain the valley below and the distant mountains seemed to be etched more sharply than he'd ever seen them. Everything was suddenly closer, as though seen through a powerful telescope. The rising sun had vaporised the mist in the kloof below and the yellowwood tree stood clear against a perfectly blue morning sky. He could see the lacework quality of the beard letchin that hung from its branches. For no reason whatsoever the great tree's botanical name popped into his head, *Podocarpus falcatus*, Outeniqua yellowwood. It was all a part of the bizarre moment in which he realised that in this deadly waiting game, the snake would outlast him.

The troop of baboons higher up barked raucously and then as suddenly stopped, silent as they left their night shelter and went about their way. Below him in the forest canopy the birds chattered and called to each other. The soft *kooka-roo-kooka-roo* of a bush dove reached Peekay as he stood helplessly on the high, cold, limestone shelf outside the crystal cave of Africa knowing the strength was going out of his left hand and that it was only a matter of time before the snake would be free to strike again.

Fear was beginning to cloud his mind again and he fought it, driving it back, trying to regain the bright clarity of moments before. He was going to die, that was for sure; the pain in his thumb was becoming unbearable, spearing up his right arm into his shoulder like a red-hot poker. He could feel the muscles in his forearm and upper arms begin to weaken. Suddenly his fear turned to an emotion of intense aversion which, in turn, became absolute hate for the creature which was going to kill him. He thought to bite through the snake's thick neck, to hack through it with his teeth. He looked down at the loathsome creature with its huge jaws locked around his hand. The snake's eyes were open, but appeared sightless; they formulated no plans, they were incapable of intelligence. Instinct alone would drive its tiny reptile brain to resist and make it strike again.

As suddenly as the hate for the creature had grown in him it was gone and in the calm it left, Doc's voice came clearly to Peekay. *Ja that's good, Peekay, now you have seen what is hate. Hate is something that is coming from fear. This snake, it cannot hate, but you can hate because you can fear. Think, Peekay, think what you know about this snake? It is a reptile, it is cold-blooded, all night it is lying under a rock where it is cold. It must be hungry, a snake, a big snake like so, it must warm itself in the sun before it likes to move. But it is hungry and comes early to find the bats in the cave. This snake cannot move so fast, because its metabolism is slowed down. Think also this, you have milked already the venom, see how it runs over your right hand. This snake is empty, the last drops of poison, they are already out of the sacks behind the fangs and in your right hand. These are the facts, ja? Now you must weigh your courage. If you show no fear, if you conquer your fear and you bend slowly to the ground and put the head of the snake on the ground near the opening of the cave and you take your hand away from behind the head . . .*

The voice changed, it was no longer Doc's, but the high whine of Inkosi-Inkosikazi. *The head, bring the head down slowly to the ground, release your left hand, take away his eyes, the poison is all in your right hand!* The old wizard gave a maniacal chuckle at the clever way he'd paraphrased Doc's instructions. *See now if the great devil iNyoka will enter the cave to the bats. Or will it turn and strike you, white boy? Maybe there is still some poison in its fangs?*

Doc's steady, reassuring voice broke in. *Ah, Peekay, when you know this then you will be the champion of the world, absoloodle!*

Peekay bent from the waist, releasing the pressure of his left thumb very gradually as he placed his right hand on the stone at his feet while pointing the snake's head to the end of the shelf and in the direction of the cave opening. To his surprise the snake didn't seem to sense the release of pressure on the back of its head. Peekay rubbed the ball of his thumb down the smooth hard head, gently massaging it as he loosened his grip around the snake's neck.

Slowly the snake disengaged its jaws from the plaster and its head slid over the inert hand, its enormous black body unwinding slowly from around Peekay's legs, sliding after it. The head of the great snake reached the end of the ledge before the last of its body slid over Peekay's motionless hand. Ten feet away from where Peekay now crouched its head rose six or eight inches from the rock surface, its neck swaying slightly in the air over the ledge, tongue flicking incessantly, faster than a human can blink, as though it had a life of its own, a small, black electric creature which lived in the reptile's mouth. Then its neck arched and its head lowered again and dipped below the ledge, moving onto a narrow shelf of rock that led to the concealed entrance of the crystal cave of Africa.

Peekay's heart began to pound furiously, robbing him of breath as he watched the body of the deadly reptile follow until the last of its tail disappeared over the end of the limestone shelf. The adrenalin was surging through him again and it took every ounce of his remaining willpower to sit still instead of trying to climb down the cliff face with his broken right hand and his weakened left arm. He would need to remain on the cliff face until his strength returned.

Peekay made several attempts to leave the ledge, but his knees would begin to shake and his legs seemed too weak to support him. The snake would feed on the bats in the outer chamber of the great crystal cave and then two possibilities for it existed. It would return the way it had come, passing back over the ledge and down the cliff face to find a warm rock below on which to sleep, or it would come to wait on the ledge until the sun struck the face of the cliff, where it would remain sleeping all morning and deep into the afternoon until the cliff was once more in shadow, when it would return down the cliff face to conceal itself under a warm rock at its base.

The day was not turning out the way Peekay had planned it. He had thought to take himself down into the night country and, as he had done many times before, jump the ten stones across the river, where he hoped his trance might take him into the crystal cave of Africa where he could talk with Doc. Instead, as he jumped the final stone across the roaring moonlit gorge in his transcendental consciousness, the snake had come to him in slow motion, ripping away the veiled fabric of his imagination and hurling him back into conscious presence. He was not sure now whether it was Doc or the great medicine man Inkosi-Inkosikazi who had come to him. The voice had been Doc's but the sequence, the liaison between his subconscious and conscious minds, had been typically the work of the old witchdoctor.

Peekay realised suddenly that both had played a part in what had happened, that contained in him was an ambivalence: part Doc with his precise, reasoning European mind, and part the ancient black man of Africa with his powerful wizardry. He was the mind-child of both. It was this strange dichotomy which the people saw and responded to when they called him the Tadpole Angel. Both beings had reached out with their different wisdom to answer the urgent questions on his mind, both men were *his shadows*, destined to watch over him.

What was it Doc had said? *You can hate because you can fear.* Peekay knew he could fear, had feared, still feared; he'd been running since he was a child. If he could conquer the fear, would that be stronger than hate? Was that what Inkosi-Inkosikazi meant when he challenged him to lay the snake's head down? *See now if the great devil iNyoka will enter the cave of bats. Or will he turn and strike you?* Then Doc's quiet reassuring voice: *Ah, Peekay, when you know this you will be the champion of the world, absoloodle!*

And then it came to Peekay. He must confront his fear, and when he had done so he must confront the hate that was brought against him; but not with the head as he had taught himself to do, as Oxford had taught him to do, but with his heart. He must fight fear and hate with his heart. And to do so he must learn to feel hate so that he could destroy it, know it for what it was. That was the power, the power of one. He began to feel that he could fight again, that he could come back.

TWENTY-EIGHT

By the end of January Peekay was fit and well, his body mended. He'd spent a lot of time in the mountains and he was physically hard and superbly conditioned. The time spent outside the boxing ring had been good for him. As a professional he'd been fighting without a break for three years and, in the constant effort to shorten the time to the title, there had been no easy bouts of the kind trainers seek to spell their fighters, with the result that his body had taken a great deal of punishment.

After his visit to the crystal cave of Africa Peekay began to work on his fear, starting at the most obvious point, its physical aspects. He took to the mountains for days on end, sleeping rough and seeking the most difficult kranse to scale, often without rope or crampons, testing his courage on the sheer rock face, his hand now out of plaster, the tips of his groping fingers often his only anchor against certain death.

Captain Smit had tried on several occasions to broach the subject of Peekay's need to hate, his need to acquire 'the power', but he was not an articulate man and he lacked the skill to put it in such a way that it didn't seem like mystical nonsense, the pathetic superstition of an ignorant dirt farmer's son. When Peekay had asked him if he'd seen anything in the fight which might help him to defeat Jackson, he'd grunted, 'Ja, there is something, but I'm still thinking it out, jong.'

In fact he'd spoken about it at length to Gert, who'd immediately understood. Gert was also from the North Western Transvaal, the fiery core of the Afrikaner hate for the English. He was fifteen years younger than Captain Smit and had grown up when times had been somewhat better economically, though essentially his background was similar to Smit's. Although Gert didn't share the pathological hate for the rooinek to anything like the extent of his superior, he understood it well enough and recognised 'the power' as the factor which had most enabled the Afrikaners to persist and to overcome so that they were now beginning to be back on top again.

'Kaptein, it's useless, man. You can't make a guy like Peekay feel "the power". It's not just that he's a rooinek, lots of rooineks know how to hate. It's . . . it's, well, he doesn't think like us; the old musician taught him different. He even loves kaffirs. I'm telling you man, you know those two kaffir girls, those twins who are the servants at his place, he loves them. I don't mean, you know, physically or anything, I mean he loves them like you love a brother or a sister, even more. Geel Piet too, Peekay loved that old bastard.'

Captain Smit nodded, then added, 'He was a blerrie good boxing coach for Peekay, he taught him well.'

'Ja, well, Peekay still loves him for it.'

'Ja, but kids they like that. They don't see the colour sometimes 'till quite late. That's why you got to teach them early.'

'No, Kaptein, not loved, *loves*! The other day he asked me if he could go to The Stones. I didn't tell him about the tombstone that mad *Hotnot* woman brought down from Johannesburg, "*vir die geel man*". He found it and just stood and said nothing, stood there among all the kaffir graves next to this big black marble tombstone biting his lip and looking up into the hills, and the tears were rolling down his cheeks. Jesus! He was blubbing for Geel Piet! A yellow man who wasn't worth a pinch of baboon shit! How you going to teach someone like that to hate a kaffir in time for the big fight?'

It had been Gert who'd finally brought up the subject with Peekay. They'd been in the prison workshop where Peekay was watching Gert making a hunting knife. The big raw-boned sergeant was good with his hands and could make almost anything from bits of scrap iron. He was cutting leather rings to form the handle of the knife which had started out life as a Dodge truck rear spring. The elegant brass escutcheon was already fitted into place at the blade end of the shaft and the end piece, designed to hold the leather rings into place and form the end of the handle, was a tiny brass death's head which Peekay had been absently tossing a few inches into the air and catching again as they spoke. Gert tried to keep his voice light, as though he was making a casual observation which Peekay could ignore if he wished. 'Kaptein Smit. He's been thinking.'

Peekay caught the brass head and spun round to face him. 'What? Tell me, Gert, what does he think?' Gert could sense the tension in his voice.

'It's not easy, jong. You know it's not easy for an Afrikaner to talk about some things.'

'Fuck, Gert, don't give me all that introspective *platteland* crap! What did he tell you?'

Gert grinned, but his voice was serious as he spoke. 'Peekay *ou maat*, it's not that easy. He wants you to learn to hate. He says it's his fault, he never taught you.'

Peekay sighed and shrugged his shoulders. 'Ja, I've been told before, in America. But I've only had the opportunity to hate one person in my life, a big Afrikaner called the Judge. And at the time I was only five and I was so shit scared of him I clean forgot to hate him. Then later, in the copper mines, I caught up with him and got even by beating the shit out of the bastard; and then I hated myself for being such a stupid prick, for thinking that beating someone senseless would do me some good. All it did was humiliate me and make me feel, you know, dirty, unworthy, a bigger shit than the guy I just smashed!'

'Revenge can be sweet, Peekay. Sometimes it's the only way to clean things out.'

'Bullshit, Gert!'

Gert laughed. 'No, it's not bullshit, Peekay. That's what you don't understand!' He hesitated. 'For an Afrikaner the need to avenge ourselves has been what's kept us going. *'N oog vir 'n oog*, an eye for an eye, that's what the Bible says. Hate keeps you sharp, it drives you, it gives you power and a direction, it's also what keeps you standing up when you should be dead. That's what Kaptein Smit is talking about, man.'

'I hear what you're saying, Gert. I just don't know how to get it. How do I develop a hate for Jackson, an American negro? If anything I admire him, he comes from a dirt-poor Southern family who've had their arse kicked by the white honkies for generations. Those white bastards in the South are as bad as we are, worse perhaps; not too many blacks these days get strung up on a tree in South Africa for looking sideways at a white woman. Jackson's illiterate and he's had a shit life where he's had to fight everything; hunger, cruelty, prejudice and the business of being a nigger boxer, which, like here, means you eat shit until you prove you can knock the shit out of everyone else. Christ, Gert, I don't hate him, I admire him!'

Gert shrugged. 'He's still a black kaffir, Peekay! The Bible says he's the son of Ham, a drunkard and a fornicator, destined to be a hewer of wood and a drawer of water. He's dirt, the Bible says so, it gives you permission to hate him.'

Gert smiled. 'But that doesn't mean you can't also admire him. At the battle of Blood River the Zulus came in waves like wind in the grass; they'd run for thirty miles, beating their asegais against their shields and stamping their feet on the ground until the air trembled and the earth shook. Then they fought all day and all night; wave after wave of brave warriors were cut down by the Boer guns, but still they came. A man can admire that. But just think about it; if they'd broken through the laager what do you think would have happened, hey? Let me tell you? They would have raped the women and afterwards slit their throats and they would have grabbed the babies by the feet and smashed their brains out on a rock.'

Gert spat and then wiped the back of his hand across his mouth. 'You can admire them as fighters, as warriors, but they still savages, kaffirs, and it is your *duty* to hate them.' Gert paused again before adding, 'Jesus, Peekay! If you can't learn to hate a blerrie kaffir, even an American kaffir, then there's something very fucking wrong with you!'

Peekay looked down at his hands, at the small brass skull which rested in his right hand. 'Christ, Gert, when is all this hate going to end? This whole country is haemorrhaging with hatred!'

'Peekay, can't you see? The kaffir hates you! Kaptein Smit saw it first!

We both went back to the bioscope and saw the fight again and I saw it too. Wragtig! I'm telling you, man! It was plain as the nose on my face. For fuck's sake, Peekay, wake up *ou maat*, you're walking around in a *dwaal*. Jackson's hate won the title for him!'

Peekay sighed and closed his hand around the lump of brass, his fingers automatically exercising his recently damaged hand by running the death's head through them as a penitent might an amber necklace.

'Gert, I know you think I've gone crazy or something, huh? But just give me a chance, just let me explain how I feel, then maybe you can understand how difficult it is for me to go into the ring against Jackson with the same kind of hate you say he used against me. Will you let me try to do that?'

'Here, Peekay, I dunno, man. Sure, go ahead, but I dunno that I'll be able to understand it all. I'm not educated like you, I like to keep things simple in my head.'

'Okay, but promise me only one thing, whatever I say, whether you believe it or you think it's a load of bullshit, we're still friends, hey?'

Gert thought for a moment and then extended his hand. They shook hands silently but Peekay could see his friend's eyes were deeply troubled.

Peekay began slowly. 'When I went overseas, I mean to the university, I thought I'd find people, maybe even a whole nation which was free of prejudice. But, of course, I was wrong. The English were no better than the rest of us. The English working-class mother points out the runny-nosed kids from the Irish family who live further down the lane and warns her children not to play with them. When her kids ask, "Why, mummy?" she replies, "They're dirty, you'll catch something bad. Stay away from them, they're different from you!" Or if it isn't the Irish, it's the middle-class mother talking about the working-class family at the end of the street. Prejudice is a universal condition, whether it's the colour of your skin, the difference in your accent, the length of your nose, the way you dress or the food you eat.

'Here in South Africa we cut things neatly and mostly along racist lines: black, white, coloured, coolie, English, Afrikaner. All simple, clear divisions we can focus on. But I started to realise that it doesn't begin like this, that anybody can be the target for prejudice, all you have to be is *too* something. Too short, too fat, too clever, too big, too small, too slow, too new, too different from what others think of as normal.'

Peekay paused and looked up at Gert who was still working slowly on the knife, though Peekay could feel that he was concentrating hard, trying to follow what he was saying. 'The tragedy of the human condition is that the very things that make us interesting and culturally important and progressively brilliant are our differences; and these are also the principle reasons for our prejudices.'

Gert shook his head slowly. 'Here, Peekay, I never thought of it like that. What you saying is the things we like most about ourselves are the things other people hate the most about us?'

'Well, ja, more or less, it isn't quite as black and white as that, hate isn't simply the product of differences, it's the result of fear. The differences we *fear* most; even though these fears are often totally irrational, they are the cause of our racism and our hate.

'The Afrikaner is not prepared to accept that the black man is a rational and intelligent human being no different to any other. His fear has convinced him that a black skin is the outward sign of the black man's primitive ways. The whites fear that at any moment they will all be murdered in their beds by servants they've known and trusted since childhood. Isn't that right?'

'What are you saying, Peekay? That a man who will murder his brother for sixpence will all of a sudden become an upstanding citizen?'

'Well yes, Gert, as a matter of fact, I am. That is, if we can remove the fear and remove the hate, then it won't, *can't* happen like that.'

'And how are we going to do that?' Gert asked. 'Next Sunday from the pulpits of every Dutch Reformed Church shall we shout, *Allies is vergewe, julle is almal ons broeders en susters, ek sal julle lief en julle moet my terug lief?* All is forgiven, you are my black brothers and sisters and I will love you and you must love me back! Is that how it will happen?'

'Well, ja, in a manner of speaking that's about it. The only way to eliminate prejudice is to eliminate the differences which create the fear and, with the fear gone, the hatred will go too. We must integrate our society. If we don't, if we continue the way we are going with the blacks, in the end they will have no choice, in the end they will get "power".'

Gert went rigid. He tried to hide the shock of Peekay's pronouncement. It was clear to him now that Peekay was mad or, at least, temporarily insane, that the fight with Jackson had somehow damaged his brain. His voice was tight as he spoke. 'And with "the power" they will win? Is that what you telling me, Peekay?'

'No, with hate nobody can win; in the end hate creates only losers, Gert.' Peekay's voice pleaded, 'Can't you see, it's just like this place. The prisoners are brutalised and so, of course, they behave as you would expect them to. When you cut hope from the heart the hole you leave is filled with the worms of hate. Hate for you, hate for the system, but even more destroying, a putrefying hate of yourself. When you hate yourself you want to destroy yourself. That is you want to destroy your own kind.'

'Kaffirs always been like that, Peekay. Last week we got a prisoner to hang who chopped off the hands of his daughter to take to the witchdoctor to make a powerful potion, *umuThi*, for a tribal war. This was a township kaffir, not a kaffir from the *bundu*! Magtig, Peekay, they always been brutalised. Kaffirs don't get bad in prison, they already like that, they savages, blood, death, cruelty, that's their way, man!'

'Jesus, Gert, can't you see. Life is no different to prison. The life we give the black people, the poverty, injustice, cruelty, the places we make them live, the crime that goes on around them, that is prison! We brutalise these people from the moment they're born. We've been doing it to them for three hundred years. For fuck's sake, what do you expect?'

'Well then, man, it's too late. If they like that they not going to change now. I'm telling you, show a kaffir kindness and next thing you know you got more trouble than you can handle. Kaffirs understand only one thing, the sjambok or a gun. If you understand anything about a black kaffir you never show him any compassion, because if you do, sooner or later you dead and he pisses on your grave.'

Peekay sighed. He knew it was useless, but he had to try. 'Gert, would you say that the Afrikaners are a violent people?'

Gert thought about this for a moment. 'With everyone, or jus' kaffirs?'

'No, as people. Are they violent?'

'No way, man, we a God-fearing people. We a kind people. You know lots of Afrikaners, Peekay, you answer that one yourself.'

'Personally? Ja, I think they're a generous and kind people, Gert. That is, if I think about them as Afrikaners, meaning you are different from me.'

'That's not true. You think about it a lot. You're a rooinek, Peekay, even if you wanted to, the Afrikaners wouldn't let you think we are no different from you. We are different and we don't want to be the same.'

'Okay, I think about it. But my experience has been mostly a pleasant one.'

'You see, I'm right.'

'Would you say the black man thinks of you as a good people who are not violent?'

Gert grinned. 'Jesus, Peekay, I already told you, kaffirs is different. They more like animals, they don't understand kindness, animals chop off their little daughters' hands for strong *muthi*. They don't know what is good. They violent people and when we dealing with them we got to be violent people also. You think we would have survived three hundred years in the veld if we were kind to the kaffirs?

'We are a *boere* tribe, a white tribe and the strongest tribe, and we understand the law of Africa, kill or be killed, *kragdadigheid*. That's the way it's always been. Kaffirs don't expect kindness. They know if they do wrong they get the sjambok.'

'Like a dog?'

Gert ignored Peekay's remark. 'If they do more wrong we put them in prison, if they do more even than that we hang them.'

'Like the Zulu nursery rhyme, *One, two, three, a policeman caught me, I died, Mama cried, now I'm free*!' Tell me? What happens if they live good, blameless lives?'

'Then we leave them alone, of course.'

'That's not true, Gert! We restrict their movement. We make them carry passes. We harass them from the moment they're born. We cram them into the world's most horrific slums where they die like flies of all the diseases of neglect. We pin them down in their tribal lands which is the poorest land, over-populated, over-grazed and a fraction – less than thirteen per cent – of the total land mass of South Africa. We pay them a below subsistence wage so they remain on the edge of starvation. Two years ago when the rains were good our white, government-subsidised farms produced a milk glut; we poured the surplus milk into the sea while our blacks were starving in the slums of our major cities. We tear their families apart as a matter of course, husband from wife and children from parents. We watch their small children die of kwashiorkor and their elderly of enteric dysentery and TB. Those we bother to educate are trained to be slaves, taught by teachers who are barely educated themselves. We give them no say in the future, even their own. We allow them no skills or trades to compete in the workplace above that of the lowest white man. We offer them no hope and no place in their own country beyond that of servant to a white master. That's what we do to them when they live good, blameless lives! That's our idea of justice before we show our teeth and demonstrate our anger and hate.'

'Justice? That's a funny word man. Ask any Boer about justice, we know about British justice, they say that supposed to be the best kind.' Gert spoke slowly, deliberately. 'I am a Boer, Peekay. When I was born, the English were on top; the Afrikaner was nothing, a crushed, defeated people. My father was a dirt-poor farmer and all my uncles left the land and went to work in the mines on the Rand, the mines which belonged to the Englishman and the Jews.

'But my pa said if we *never* forgot, if we swore revenge every day of our lives the first thing when we woke up and if we learned to hate enough, one day we would win; *die volk* would be on top again. When Malan came into power in 1948 my pa was so happy on election night, he had a heart attack. You were away at school, but my *ousis* phoned from the police station and I drove most of the night and was at his bedside just before dawn.

'He'd been unconscious all night but I hadn't been sitting beside his bed for long when he reached out and pulled at my sleeve. He spoke softly, he was a big man with a great white beard, but now his voice was like a small child. "Gert, my son, *die volk het gewen*! The beloved country is yours again. *Nou sal alles reg kom* . . . Hold it tight, never give it up, there will be no second chance. God is with His people again." '

'But how will you win, Gert? More and more gun and more and more sjambok. You know why the Boers won the last election? They won it in bed. Afrikaners now outnumber the English-speaking South Africans; your revenge over the British was plotted between the sheets! That's okay, that's what the voting system is all about, the majority point of view wins – providing, of course, that it's white. Enough Afrikaners bought Malan's shit about it being time to return to the laager, to prepare against *die swart gevaar*, the black danger, when the blacks would rise up and murder us all in our beds: this time, not with the rattle of shields and the stamping of feet until the earth trembles, but silently on padded feet. Like the Bible says, *They will come like a thief in the night.* Isn't that how Malan put it? Shadows in the night, they will come to slit our throats. The spectre of *die bloed smoor*, choked by blood, was a sure-fire vote-winner not only on the *platteland* but in the cities as well.'

Peekay drew his breath, he was excited and angry but knew he must calm down, that Gert would grow impatient and his natural good manners forsake him. 'But think about this, Gert. When the Boer War ended there were about four million Africans and about one million whites. Now fifty years later there are ten million Africans and three million whites. That's not too bad really, with enough sjambok and gun the odds are still okay. By the year two thousand, less than fifty years from now, there will be thirty-five million Africans and five and a half million whites. Will we hold them with a sjambok and a gun then? Will hate be enough to arm your fear when the impis of the dispossessed come at the white man in endless waves like wind in the grass?'

Suddenly Gert raised the hunting knife and plunged the blade into the surface of the work bench. The large knife vibrated from the impact. '*Jy praat kak!* You talk shit,' he spat. 'At the battle of Blood River four hundred and seventy Boers held off ten thousand Zulus! The odds were a hundred to one, our hate held then, it will hold again! With modern weapons on our side and only sticks and stones on their side, those odds are no different to Blood River!'

'They will get guns and if we don't give them hope they will be trained by someone, somewhere to use them. Gert, *ou maat*, it is not just South Africa, all of black Africa stirs. Colonialism of every sort is coming to an end. In the whole of Africa, in West Africa, Tunisia, Kenya, both Rhodesias, Angola and Mozambique there are about two hundred million Africans and four million whites. And in all these places the black man is questioning the laws which justify the concept of white supremacy.'

Peekay paused. 'I once asked my friend Gideon Mandoma, you know, the black welterweight, whether he respected the laws of South Africa? He looked at me and then he slowly shook his head, "The only law is the law that is in a man's heart. There is no white man's law in my heart, Peekay."

'That's about it, Gert. Until we have the same law in every South African's heart we have no country and we have no future. Gert, please listen! It's my country too! Like the black people and the coloured people, I too would like to have a say in its future, don't you see, we're all brothers and sisters! Christ, Gert, I am about to become an advocate, a lawyer and, like Gideon Mandoma, I cannot feel the law of this land in my heart.'

Gert's voice suddenly sounded a warning. 'Don't speak like that, Peekay! I heard what you said the first time, that we must all fuck kaffir woman so we all end up the same. If we all *hotnots* then we going to love each other all of a sudden. You talking shit, you hear? A *boesman* isn't much better than a kaffir; some are worse even, *skollies* and drunks and liars, the coloured people are shit, the scum of the earth!'

His hand shot out and he pulled the knife from the bench and used the point of the blade to prick the inside of his arm just below his wrist. A trickle of dark blood appeared immediately and Gert watched it as it ran down his wrist towards his elbow which now rested on the work bench.

'That's Afrikaner blood, little *boetie*, I will willingly die to keep it pure.' His voice was menacing, though hardly above a whisper. 'If you don't fight with me then I will kill you too, Peekay!' He picked up a piece of grey cotton wadding from the work bench and wiped the blood from his arm. 'I love you, Peekay. You are my little brother, but I will kill you just the same. If it is necessary to preserve Afrikanerdom we will drown this country in blood!'

Peekay rose and grabbed Gert by the shoulder. He had to reach up to do so, the prison sergeant was six feet three and weighed two hundred and sixteen pounds. 'Take it easy, *ou maat*! Remember, we promised at the beginning of this talk that we'd stay friends. Try to remember, I love my country just as much as you do.'

Gert sniffed and gave a bitter laugh. 'No, Peekay, you've said that twice now, but you lie. You have other ties. You have just returned from England where you finished your education. Inside you there is still a Britisher, still a *verdoemde rooinek*. When the trouble comes you can leave and go and live in England or Canada or Australia, you can start a new life, be someone else, somewhere else. Me, I'm a Boer, I don't speak English so well, I don't speak Dutch or French at all, it is three hundred years since my forebears spoke those languages. For three hundred years I have belonged to the Afrikaner tribe and we have kept our bloodline pure. When the shit hits the fan, you can run away, you will run away, but my tribe will have to stay and fight. We have no place to go. *Dit is hier of dood*, it's here or dead.'

'Maybe that's why we have to stop the hating now, before it's too late,' Peekay said softly.

'You might as well try to stop the sun coming up tomorrow morning, Peekay.'

Peekay returned the tiny brass death's head to the work bench and Gert picked it up and screwed it onto the end of the handle. The leather grip had been roughly shaped, though it hadn't yet been sanded and polished; nevertheless it was a beautiful piece of work. 'It's magnificent, Gert.'

Gert looked up and grinned, breaking the tension between them. 'Good! I'm glad you like it, Peekay. It's a coming-home present for you. You better learn how to use it to kill. With your *kaffir boetie* politics you're going to need to protect yourself with something better than your fists, even if you do end up the welterweight champion of the world.'

Peekay gripped Gert by his arm, 'Thanks, *ou maat*, I shall treasure it. No hard feelings hey? When I've fought Jackson I'm going to defend my title only once, against Geldenhuis or Mandoma. After that, like I told you, I'm going to be an *advokaat*, a barrister. I just want you to know that I'm not on the white side or the black side, but on the side of all South

Africans.' Peekay grinned. 'And so you can see, I'm on my ace, up shit creek with a broken stick as a paddle!'

Gert laughed, glad that the tension had passed between them, glad also that Peekay had stopped in time, for as an Afrikaner he knew he could never back down. 'I guess I'm going to have to tell Captain Smit you a hopeless case, hey? No way you going to learn to hate that black American bastard in time for the title fight.'

But Gert was wrong. Peekay was beginning to understand the hate he was against. While he'd always seen hate as an evil and repulsive force which must – his nice, clean, rational mind told him – lead to destruction, he hadn't seen how powerful it was and how it could be channelled. Gert's hate could be focussed; he exercised it in the same way as he did his love and lived with it as easily. Whereas Peekay's initial hate for the Judge had become fear which was mindless and totally unfocussed, Gert's hate, Jackson's hate, was a force they could use, it *was* the force they used to create fear, the unreasoning fear that weakened Peekay, made him vulnerable to the hate Jackson would bring into the ring with him. He could look into the blind eyes of hate and in their reflection see his own fear, which was just as blind, just as senseless but was totally useless as an emotional force.

Peekay returned to Johannesburg at the end of January to prepare for the world title. He set up a training camp which he could share with Mandoma, each acting as sparring partner for the other while Gideon worked with Solly Goldman as his trainer and Peekay with Dutch Holland. Several local black, coloured and white sparring partners were selected on an ad hoc basis, though Togger was brought out from London to act as a principle sparring partner. Hymie had selected a small farm in Elandsfontein, some fifteen miles outside Johannesburg, as the training camp and Peekay, Gideon and Togger shared the same bunkhouse which caused some comment in the newspapers. Peekay when asked about this by a visiting reporter had replied, 'The closest you can get to a man is in a boxing ring. You share his sweat and his breath and his arms and his chest. You don't get much closer when you make love to a woman. He doesn't snore so why would I be concerned about sharing a room with him?'

The South African papers made much of this, the most blatant headline being: PEEKAY SAYS OKAY TO SLEEP WITH BLACK MAN! which appeared in a Bloemfontein paper. But the ongoing quarrel was more the fact that Peekay had elected to train with Mandoma. Almost to a man, the sports pages cried foul! The Peekay camp, they maintained, was giving the Bantu fighter an unfair advantage over Geldenhuis, in that he came under the eye of the world-famous trainer, Dutch Holland, and also enjoyed the services of Solly Goldman, South Africa's foremost trainer.

It was even mooted in parliament that a law should be passed preventing people of mixed race sparring together. In fact, five years later, just such a law was passed.

Peekay was asked about this in an interview he'd given with the press just prior to going into training camp. 'It's perfectly true that Mandoma will benefit from working with Dutch Holland, though he's been under the training of the great Solly Goldman for several years already and Solly remains his trainer. It seems to me that a black fighter of Mandoma's class has none of the infrastructure and training facilities the South African Police College have made available to Jannie Geldenhuis. Mandoma has to work for a living and when he's in training camp he isn't earning. Working out with us means he'll be eating the right food and getting the right sort of rest and I get the best sparring partner I could possibly hope for. I'm delighted with the arrangement, wouldn't you be?'

Baasie Pienaar, South Africa's foremost sportswriter stood up. 'Good morning, Baasie,' said Peekay. 'I believe you attended the New York fight? I'm sorry I didn't see you to say hello.'

Baasie Pienaar grinned. 'You did better than that, Peekay, you gave me the best fight I will probably ever see.' He cleared his throat. 'I happen to think, like you in New York, Mandoma got a bum steer last time he fought Geldenhuis. There's been a lot in the paper about it being unfair that he's sharing your camp; I just want to say, personally I'm glad.' There was a murmur of surprise in the room. *Die Vaderland* was the leading Afrikaans newspaper and, politically speaking, the mouthpiece for the government. 'Because I'm a reporter, I also have a question,' Pienaar went on. 'Geldenhuis says he'll take Mandoma in the seventh. Do you have any comment?'

Peekay laughed. 'He's a brave man, Mandoma is the most under-rated welterweight in the world. But why don't you ask Mandoma yourself.' He pointed to the back of the room where Gideon was standing with Togger.

Gideon took a couple of steps towards the front of the room. 'Mr Pienaar for two years already we have been wanting for dis fight. Always Mr Nguni he asks, "Please Mr Geldenhuis, why you not want to fight the black champion of Africa?" But always he say, "No!".'

Peekay saw the look in Mandoma's eyes when he talked about Geldenhuis. It was the same thing he'd seen in Gert's. His eyes had gone blank, turned inward, focussed on his hate; even his voice seemed to take on a menacing tone, giving a fierceness to his words which was not actually contained in what he said. 'I am very, very hungry for dis fight. I do not think I will lay down in round seven.' Gideon gave the white reporters a huge smile, but behind its humour Peekay could hear the snarl of the lion, his talisman. 'I am a Zulu, I am chief, I do not think in the ring I have to lay down for dis policeman. In the ring he has only got gloves on his hands same like me, there is no sjambok and there is no revolver.'

The room broke up in uproar and Peekay terminated the interview. The reporters left, they all had their afternoon headline. Pienaar walked over to Gideon. 'Nice one, Mandoma,' he said quietly.

The *Johannesburg Star* was first on the streets. MANDOMA ACCUSES GELDENHUIS OF POLICE BRUTALITY! Baasie Pienaar's paper, *Die*

Vaderland, ran the headline, PEEKAY RATES MANDOMA WORLD BEATER. Hymie was delighted; things were hotting up, in terms of promoting the fight. Nothing they could have dreamed up as a publicity stunt could have had anywhere near the same impact on boxing fans. Geldenhuis had obligingly come back with a comment which, paraphrased, said that in or out of the ring, his hands, with or without gloves, were enough to give the black man a hiding.

Tickets for the fight had gone on sale the day before and in two days the thirty thousand reserved seats for the fight had been sold out. Hymie was assured of sufficient profit to pay Jackson the huge win-or-lose purse he'd promised him to fight in South Africa and sufficient to pay Mandoma and Geldenhuis the biggest purse either had ever earned.

TWENTY-NINE

On the morning of 26 April, an English-speaking announcer on Springbok breakfast radio called the thirty-thousand crowd expected at Ellis Park the largest gathering of blacks and whites in one place since the British fought the Zulu at the battle of Isandhlwana in 1879.

The remark had been intended flippantly, but, inasmuch as it was a fight which brought both sides together, the symbolism was there for all who wished to see it; and in South Africa that was just about everyone. The old fears were working overtime; the flames fanned by an eager media who imbued the event with the drama of a high-noon shoot-out. Make no mistake, this was no less a battle for race superiority than any other fought against the kaffirs.

At Ellis Park a white rope ran like a snake down the bleachers and cut across the rugby field to end in the centre of either side of the ring and, by doing so, dividing the entire park in half. This was dubbed 'the wall' by the press and was designed to separate the black fans from the white – no less a wall than one made of granite blocks.

The crowd control designed for the fight seemed to be the usual overkill. A black policeman would stand every ten feet on the African side of the white rope with his back to the white spectators looking directly into the black crowd for troublemakers and a white one would stand between him and the next black policeman with his back to the black fight fans. The white police officers all carried revolvers and police batons which hung from their Sam Browne belts, while the black constables were armed with riot sticks.

The fight had been sold out for nearly three months. Nevertheless African ticket-holders started to arrive at dawn and seemed content to sit on the pavement outside the grounds where there was much singing of the Chant as the good-humoured crowd waited for the gates to open at 1 o'clock.

The Mandoma versus Geldenhuis fight was scheduled for four o'clock in the afternoon, a ten-rounder followed at a quarter past six by the world-title fight.

It was late autumn in Johannesburg, a glorious time of crisp mornings and bright, cloudless days when it remains reasonably light until almost seven in the evening. Johannesburg, with its high altitude, grows quite chilly soon after sunset, and a great many of the Africans had brought blankets with them. Red is a favourite colour and by five o'clock the African side of the field was splashed with scarlet.

Closer to the time of the first major fight the African cognoscenti began to appear, most of them in evening suits and some even in tails. There were few women amongst them; even the gangsters and gamblers had decided to leave their molls behind, the importance of the fight and the prestige of owning a ringside ticket being too great to waste on a woman. Although some white women appeared on the opposite side of the ring, this too was made up largely of white men.

It was a surprise therefore when, half an hour before the first fight, three women appeared on their own and started to make their way across the short strip of no-man's land leading from one of the entrances under the stands to the ringside seats.

The excited black crowd, anxious to applaud anything on their side which seemed in the least bit worthy of attention, started to cheer at the perfectly splendid sight which appeared below them.

Thin as a rake in a glittering red diamante fishtail gown, and wearing a short mink jacket to which was pinned an enormous corsage of purple orchids, was Madam Flame Flo, the famous shebeen queen from Sophiatown. Beside her, big as a circus tent, dressed in a pink satin dress with plunging neckline and wearing a pink fur stole as big as a small blanket, was Mama Tequila. On her head rested a satin turban shaped like a beehive and embroidered with a thousand tiny mirrors. From the centre of the turban, clipped down under a huge circular diamante broach, were three pink ostrich feathers. It was a sight to make the seventeen thousand African men in the stadium positively drool with admiration.

Walking behind both women in a simple white crepe evening dress and a satin stole came Tandia Patel. It was immediately apparent to the black crowd that she was extraordinarily beautiful.

The Bantu crowd began to clap, drumming their feet on the wooden floor of the stands so that the sound had the resonance of a hundred drum rolls. The white side rose to their feet, anxious to see what was happening, and thirty thousand eyes trained on the three women crossing towards the ringside seats.

'Jesus, *ousis*! We got the spotlight!' Madam Flame said in alarm.

Mama Tequila chuckled, her giant breasts rolling like twin mountains in an earthquake. 'Honey, jes keep yoh head high, what *we* got now we came here to get!' She stopped and turned, waiting for Tandia to catch up to her. 'You walk tall now, sugar, this your fight too, baby!' Mama Tequila was in her full American mode and loving every moment.

Tandia was quite certain she was about to die. She was terrified that Gideon Mandoma might be somewhere looking out at her and that he would not approve. Her fear of disobeying Mama Tequila fought with her natural modesty. She was Mandoma's woman now and a law student, but the huge old whore still completely dominated her. Though Gideon and she were an item, she saw almost nothing of him; during the university vacations she was expected to work at Bluey Jay and it was only when the brothel closed down after Christmas and she came with Mama Tequila up to the Rand to stay with Madam Flame Flo that they could be together. Madam Flame Flo had moved from Sophiatown to Meadowlands and Tandia had to rely on Juicey Fruit Mambo to drive her to see Gideon.

Their relationship was still very tentative and mostly based on politics. She hadn't even slept with him. Once when he'd brought up the subject she'd been terrified but had agreed, though there hadn't been a place they could do it. She knew she must, that to consolidate the relationship it was necessary, but she told herself they'd do it after she graduated at law, when she came to live in Johannesburg.

For the black crowd the three glittering women had added a dimension of class to the day's proceedings. They could savour in advance the pleasure they'd get from relating, perhaps twenty years hence, the story of how they'd been present at the two greatest fights in history. Now they could include in the long preliminary the two *abaFazi* who shone like the sun on water and the beautiful young one.

Hymie and Peekay, unseen by the crowd, were seated in the enclosed members' stand watching the crowd. Jackson had made a great fuss of being photographed entering through the gate for blacks only, pointing to the sign with one hand and pinching his nose in disgust with the other, the whites of his eyes showing in mock horror.

'Christ, Peekay, look at that!' Hymie exclaimed suddenly. He passed his binoculars to Peekay. 'Get a deck of the two women coming towards us on the black side!'

Peekay, looking through the glasses, started to grin immediately. 'She's wonderful! Oh, Hymie, they're sensational. I wonder who they are? You don't suppose they're Jackson supporters do you?'

Peekay suddenly let out a gasp followed by the short, sharp expletive. 'Shit!'

Hymie's grin changed to sudden alarm. 'What is it? Here, let me see,' he said, reaching for the glasses. He now saw the third woman who had caught Peekay's attention.

He focussed on Tandia. She was absolutely ravishing. Her green eyes set into a classically proportioned honey-coloured face seemed to be looking directly at him through thick black lashes. Her slightly parted lips gave her a rather bewildered, totally ingenuous expression.

Hymie lowered the binoculars and turned to look at Peekay, who sat with his chin cupped in his hands, his elbows resting on his knees. He wore a slightly stunned expression. 'Shit no, Peekay!' he whispered. 'Not now, not ever! For Christ's sake, she's coloured!'

Peekay gave Hymie a wry grin. 'Maybe she's American? I could go and live in America?'

Hymie laughed. 'Forget it Peekay, we've got a fight on our hands. If she's Jackson's girl you're going to have to knock him over first. Come on, it's time to see Gideon. You promised him and I promised Mr Nguni, no matter how busy I was, I'd personally make sure you'd be there to wish Gideon good luck.'

In fact, Hymie had been as busy as a one-armed wallpaper hanger and had found himself doing just about everything leading up to the title fight. From the beginning when they'd had the kerfuffle about segregating Ellis Park and the debacle over the toilets, seating had been the major problem. Right up to the end, even though half the ringside seats had been sold to black people, the trustees of Ellis Park were still demanding that they be reserved exclusively for whites. When this wouldn't wash, they'd demanded an extra sixty seats for white patrons.

In a gesture of appeasement, Hymie had managed to get a travelling theatrical company to hire him a dozen wooden stage units, designed to build an outdoor stage. The trustee seats were placed on these, affording them a grand, if not intimate, ringside viewing platform. Hymie's gesture was lost on the furious trustees who, to a man, hated him for sticking up for the rights of the 'coons'.

One more seating problem occurred on the morning of the fight. O'Rourke, Jackson's manager, had approached Hymie, pointing out that his party hadn't been allocated seats together and demanding that something be done about it.

Jake 'Spoonbill' Jackson's entourage consisted of twelve people. Three of them would be in his corner but the remainder, five black Americans and four white, were not prepared to be separated along racial lines. Hymie pointed out that he had no choice, that the law required the separation, but that he'd placed them in the front row on the side of the ring divided by the rope. In effect, they were all in the same row with only a two-inch rope dividing the five blacks from the four white Americans.

'It's the principle, me boy!' O'Rourke demanded in a sanctimonious voice. 'It may be a bit of a rope to you, but it's a wall as high as Everest itself to me and the boys. We do come from the land of the free you know!'

O'Rourke had gone to some pains to avoid Hymie during the week the Jackson party had been in town. The snub had started at the airport where Hymie, caught up in an emergency, sent Solly Goldman to welcome him and transport the entourage from Jan Smuts airport to a magnificent old mansion set on fifteen acres of land which he'd staffed and provisioned fully as their training camp.

O'Rourke had refused to take Hymie's call when later he'd phoned to welcome him to South Africa. 'Tell him, if he can't come to the airport to welcome us, I can't come to the telephone to talk to him,' was the message carried back to Hymie by one of Jackson's people. Hymie grinned, recalling the non-existent welcome they'd received when they'd arrived in New York for the first title fight.

O'Rourke and Jackson had made themselves freely available to the press. Jackson, concentrating on Peekay, claiming there were no more surprises in the white man's limited attack, prophesied that the fight would end in a knock-out in the seventh, the same round Geldenhuis had forecast for Mandoma. He was unaware of the special relationship Peekay enjoyed with black fight fans and it was clear that most of his name calling was predictably meant to win the sympathy of South Africa's black people.

On the other hand, O'Rourke took every opportunity to be critical of just about everything. His first act had been to fire the entire black staff working at the training camp, claiming they were spies placed by Hymie. Now, on the final morning, he was making a fuss about the seating arrangements and, in the process, hugely enjoying Hymie's discomfort.

Hymie phoned General Van Breeden and requested permission for the Americans to be seated in any order they wished on either side of the rope. Van Breeden chuckled into the phone. 'You know something, Hymie? Sometimes I think we're all going crazy! Ja man, no problems. Wait, I'll get Captain McClymont to fix it with the senior police officer in charge of ringside crowd control.'

Hymie waited as the general summoned McClymont on his office intercom and then came back on the phone. 'You can put a negro on either side of me if you like.' He chuckled again. 'Pretoria already think I've sold out to the kaffirs by allowing them to see the fight in the first place.'

Half an hour before the Geldenhuis versus Mandoma fight the ringside seats were full. The huge ground was packed to the heavens and though it was still light, the ring lights had been turned on, casting a phosphorescent glow some twenty feet beyond the ring.

Mr Nguni's concern to have Peekay visit Gideon Mandoma before the fight was a very real one. Two days before the fight, Gideon had suddenly insisted he must go to Zululand, to his home in one of the many hills behind the Tugela River. He wished to go alone, accompanied only by a driver from his own clan.

When Mr Nguni informed Solly Goldman of Gideon's departure he wasn't at all happy. He didn't like to have any fighter he was training out of his sight for the final forty-eight hours, a time which he regarded as psychologically the most important. Nguni had persuaded him that the visit was essential, but privately he was also worried. He knew that, surrounded by his extended family, Gideon might easily lose the razor-edge concentration he required as a fighter. He had offered to have Gideon's particular *umNgoma*, witchdoctor, driven up to Johannesburg to personally attend to him, or even to obtain the services of any of the famous sangoma who operated in Soweto.

Gideon's reply had been simple. 'He is too old to leave his fireplace, but he is the one who can see me with his heart.'

Mr Nguni understood perfectly. What Gideon was saying in effect was that not only was the *umNgoma* he wished to see able to cast the necessary spells, but there existed an intimate relationship between them as well.

Relationships and trust in a time of battle are enormously important to the Zulu warrior, who has less a fear of dying than of letting down his brother who fights valiantly at his side to protect him. In exactly the same way, it was crucial to Gideon to have Peekay with him just before he entered the ring against Geldenhuis.

Peekay entered Gideon's dressing room a quarter of an hour before the fight was due to start. 'I see you, Gideon,' he said quietly as he walked in.

Gideon looked up and smiled his brilliant white smile, extending his already bandaged hand and greeting Peekay in the double-fisted African handshake. 'I see you, Peekay,' he said shyly.

'The drought is not yet broken in the Tugela?' Peekay asked. He too spoke in a reserved way, as though it had been some time since they'd met, even though he'd seen Gideon just two days previously.

'It is very, very bad, Peekay, the cattle are dying, there is no more grass.'

'And the river? The river is holding?'

'Only pools. The cattle must walk far and they are weak.'

The reason for Peekay's formal greeting was simple enough. In Zulu terms Gideon had been away, not so much on a journey as on a transformation. In tribal eyes he was changed. He'd returned a somewhat different person after being with his shadows and the shadows of his tribal ancestors. These were still with him, his guardian angels; they would protect him during the fight, and due respect must be shown to them. By greeting him traditionally Peekay was acknowledging Gideon's changed state of being and was formally acknowledging and honouring the presence of his shadows.

After a while Gideon smiled, signalling his preparedness to get down to a normal conversation. Peekay returned his smile and the two boxers reached out and touched hands shyly with the tips of their fingers, each lightly brushing the inside of the other's palm.

'I have brought you something, Gideon,' Peekay said softly. 'You must close your eyes.' Peekay took the gold chain with the lion's tooth from around his neck and looped it over the black boxer's head so that it joined its twin already around his neck. 'Your strength has served me well, my brother; now it must return to you and stay with you forever. It is your manhood and your destiny as foretold to you by your *umNgoma*.'

Immediately the chain with the lion's tooth fell over his neck, Gideon knew it was the other half of the charm which spelled his coming to manhood. The bandaged fingers of his right hand reached up to hold the tooth and when he opened his eyes they were filled with emotion.

'Haya, haya!' he said, shaking his head, bewildered at Peekay's generosity. He could say no more. Peekay had guessed correctly; the witchdoctor who had attended him had questioned the breaking of his strength, the dividing of his manhood spell. He would have cast spells and made potions to compensate for the missing charm. Now, moments before the fight with Geldenhuis, Peekay had made him whole by returning it to him and had used the correct words in his presentation and by doing so, made it possible for him to accept the return of a gift he had once given himself.

'I see you with my heart, Peekay,' he said at last, these awesomely personal words sealing the acceptance.

'It has always been yours, Gideon. It was only *yayinto yernilingo*, a magical loan. I needed it for the strength it gave me to get to the world title; now it must return to make your strength complete.' Peekay hesitated for a moment before adding, '*My okumiselwe khona*, my destiny, is foretold; I must go with the snake and not with the lion. The snake is my talisman as the lion is yours.'

Gideon looked into Peekay's eyes. 'This snake, it is *uMamba*, the black one?'

Peekay nodded and Gideon gave a low whistle. 'This *iNyoka*, it is very powerful. The lion rips and tears to make a kill but its death-making is not certain and often the prey will break free. But *uMamba* strikes near the heart; the poison works slowly but there is no escape, death is certain.'

Peekay could see that his new talisman made perfect sense to Gideon. Apart from his courage, Peekay was not the lion type in the ring. This new talisman his shadows had found for him was perfect and, like the return of his own, a wonderful omen for the fight.

'You will be very powerful tonight, Gideon,' Peekay grinned. 'The *iBhunu*, the Boer, will be in for a big surprise. You have doubled your power. Before was enough to beat Jannie Geldenhuis; now you are truly a man who goes with his shadows into the ring and is invincible!'

'Haya, haya, Peekay, I hear you. But Geldenhuis will not come easy, he has great hate.'

'And your hate?'

'It is different, it is an old hate passed on to me by my shadows; it cannot go away but it does not feed on raw meat like the *amaBhunu*.'

Geldenhuis had never trained harder for a fight. He was superbly fit and confident, and had every reason to be. On paper, the fights he'd had leading up to this contest were of a somewhat better quality to those fought by Mandoma. He knew this would hold him in good stead against the black man, whom he hoped had been lured into a false sense of his own ability by a string of comparatively easy wins against fairly mediocre opponents. It rankled him enormously that Gideon was placed above him in the world rankings on the basis of having defeated Soap Dish Jurez, the Cuban, the only really classy fight the kaffir had had in a year.

The Special Branch had given him three months on light duties, which, in effect, meant full-time training. Two of his sparring partners were young white fighters on their way up, both middleweights, so he could get used to a physically stronger, harder punching opponent like Gideon Mandoma. His third sparring partner was a young Zulu who fought a lot like Gideon. Of the three sparring partners the young Zulu was the least skilled but the toughest, a non-stop battler whose fighting name was the Black Tornado.

While Geldenhuis sparred in the normal way with the two white middleweights, the black fighter was used to sharpen the policeman's aggression. Geldenhuis would work him over as hard as he could, building up his hate. The young Zulu fighter, though tough as nails, was no match for the policeman's skill in the ring. Geldenhuis would often knock him down; though in the three months the Zulu had endured these hidings, the policeman had been unable to knock him out. Tom Majombi, the Black Tornado's real name, was too proud to simply lie down like any sensible pug when he'd taken enough punishment. Day after day, the black fighter took a terrible pounding at the police lieutenant's hands, and in the final week of training the white boxer's aggression and hate had sharpened to the point where he beat the young African so severely that he started to bleed from his ears. Geldenhuis was ready.

Now, with the entrance of the Afrikaner policeman into the ring, the band struck up *Die Stem*, the South African National Anthem which means 'The Voice'. Geldenhuis stood in the centre of the ring as the fifteen thousand white people sang; the entire audience stood. He'd never fought in front of a crowd even one-fifth as big and he would remember the moment for the remainder of his life. The beautiful words of the anthem reached his soul; at that moment, Jannie Geldenhuis knew what it was to be an Afrikaner, and his pride and joy and love overwhelmed him so that he stood with tears running down his cheeks. He was fighting for more than just a chance to get to Peekay; he was fighting the same fight his ancestors had been fighting for three hundred years. He was fighting to keep his blood pure, he was fighting for the survival of his race. The Zulu would have to kill him to win.

Gideon entered the ring to a tremendous roar from the crowd. He too stood in the centre of the ring while the black anthem *NKosi Sikelela i'Afrika*, 'God Bless Africa', was played by the band, this time accompanied by fifteen thousand black voices. The white audience, who for the most part had remained seated, was awestruck by the sound. This was an Africa they didn't know, this was a voice they hadn't heard, and it was both chilling and beautiful.

Gideon stood with his gloves raised, turning to the crowd. He too had never boxed to a crowd like this before and he felt great pride in the black people who had come to see him fight. They were giving him a hero's welcome and they made him strong; the black champion of Africa wanted the white title as well. His mind flashed back to the prison cell where Geldenhuis had completely lost his cool when he thought Gideon had broken his hand and he would be denied the fight and thus the opportunity to get to Peekay. Tonight he would be denied that opportunity again; the judges were the same international panel selected to judge the world championship bout. There would be no pigment decisions, the best man would win. Gideon knew that the shadows were with him, even the great Shaka and Dingane. He was fighting for his people, for their dignity and honour and the greatness of their hearts.

The referee called them both into the centre of the ring and neither man looked at each other as they received instructions.

Tandia, seated directly below the ring in the front row, was overwrought before the fight began between the man she loved the most and the man she hated the most in the world. Of the two emotions, hate was the stronger and with it fear. In her mind Geldenhuis was invincible and she was terribly afraid for Gideon. She was close to tears, and by the time the bell went for the opening round she held Madam Flame Flo's hand in a fierce grip, her whole body shaking.

The first round was torrid enough, with both fighters standing toe to toe, both boxing well and keeping the other out. Geldenhuis hit Mandoma with a beautiful right hand towards the end of the round, sending him back several paces; then he'd come in fast, hoping to put another couple of good punches in, but Gideon tied him up and the bell went. If anything it was this single punch which separated the two fighters in the first round.

The second and third rounds were not dissimilar, both boxers trying to get on top, punching hard and accurately but seldom penetrating the other's defence. It was surprising that after three rounds no pattern seemed to be emerging. But the fans were getting their money's worth; neither man would back down and the pace of the fight was too fast to last.

The fourth round was Geldenhuis's best. He came out early and caught Gideon again with a right to the jaw. Gideon went down, though he was up at the count of four, not staying down, as Solly had advised him for an eight count. Geldenhuis was all over him and it wasn't until halfway through the round that he began to even things out. The fourth round ended with a definite advantage for Geldenhuis, although he'd thrown an awful lot of leather trying to nail the black man and he was showing the first signs of slowing down.

Five and six saw the fight beginning to change. Gideon was punching the more accurately of the two fighters, landing more often. Fought at a slightly slower pace, it was easier to see what was happening and the crowd began to sense that the black man was starting to get on top. It was the first time Tandia released Madam Flame Flo's hand; six rounds had ended and the seventh was the one when Geldenhuis had promised he'd put Gideon away. Now Gideon was starting to look the better boxer.

Forecasting your opponent's demise is good for pre-fight publicity but in boxing it comes back to haunt you too often. History will tell that by the seventh round Mandoma had Geldenhuis where he wanted him. Geldenhuis came out strong, determined to keep his promise, but seemed to almost run into a hard left to his jaw. It was a dumb punch but he was badly hurt and he dropped like a stone, a bewildered look on his face. He rose at the count of eight but he was very groggy on his feet, whereupon Mandoma set about the task of working his body, working the policeman onto the ropes and ripping punches into him just below the heart.

Geldenhuis seemed to have no counter for these deadly short blows and he rapidly weakened. It almost looked as though he was only staying on his feet because Mandoma wanted to keep him upright.

The bell went and Mandoma was met at his corner by an excited Solly Goldman. 'You could have put him away, why, why? You could have put him away in the seventh, turned the books on him!'

'I want him for one more round, this next round is for Tandia,' Gideon said. He turned to Togger, who was acting as one of the seconds. He grinned, raising his glove as Togger was about to insert his mouth-guard. 'Please, Togger, you go tell her this round is for her.'

'It's my pleasure, Gideon, a looker like that. She your girlfriend, then?'

Gideon nodded as Solly pushed him up. 'It's not over yet, my son. You get in there and box. It's not over until the man counts ten!' He was furious at Gideon's break in concentration.

But it was. Right at the start of the following round Mandoma hit Geldenhuis hard and put him down again. When Geldenhuis got up at eight he stumbled around the ring as Mandoma pushed him about with his left hand, though without following through with the right. The black fighter taunted the policeman, dropping his gloves and showing Geldenhuis his jaw, making the police lieutenant miss simply by bobbing and weaving around. Then, towards the end of the round he dropped him four times in quick succession. 'This one is for Shaka!' he said coming after Geldenhuis and putting him down. Geldenhuis stayed down for a count of seven, then rose. The referee examined him and let the fight continue. Ten seconds later Gideon put him down again; 'For Dingane!' he spat as he walked away to a neutral corner. The third time Geldenhuis went down, Gideon waited until he rose and let the white man pull him into a clinch. 'That was for my mother, white man!'

Geldenhuis grinned and spat out his mouth-guard and spoke through his broken mouth. 'You better kill me now, jong. Because if you don't, you a dead kaffir!' Then he spat, sending a spray of blood and spittle into Gideon's face.

With fifteen seconds to go in the eighth Mandoma positioned Geldenhuis with his back to the front row of black ringside seats, working him onto the ropes. Then he hit the helpless policeman with a straight left, knocking him backwards hard into the ropes so that his shoulders and arse opened up the top and middle rung. Gideon followed with a looping right hand which caught Geldenhuis on the left underside of his jaw, knocking him completely through the ropes. 'That's for me!' he hissed.

Then Gideon did something for which he would never be forgiven by the whites; he spat at the sprawling Geldenhuis. For a split second there was complete disbelief in the crowd, both black and white; then the roar rose on the black side of the rope. They'd witnessed the impossible; black had openly shown its contempt for white. The ants had defied the dung beetle.

The policeman landed backwards on his arse, skidding with the momentum and coming to rest at Tandia's feet in the front row. His head jerked violently and blood from his nose arched towards her in slow motion, splashing over the skirt of her white gown, like a Japanese brush-drawing of a sprig of cherry blossom. Though unconscious, his eyes were open and he appeared to be looking directly up at her.

Tandia screamed as a roaring panic filled her head. She didn't see Geldenhuis at her feet, instead her mind exploded into a vision of a pink room where she knelt naked, bent over the edge of a bed covered with pink satin. She fainted, slumping against Mama Tequila.

Both Captain Smit and Gert had witnessed Gideon Mandoma's head come back and move forward again in what was unmistakably a spitting action directed at the fallen Geldenhuis. Smit had to bring his mouth up to Gert's ear and shout to be heard above the roar of the black crowd. 'That fokken kaffir has "the power". Somebody is going to have to kill him or he's going to be big trouble!' Gert nodded, hearing but not attempting to reply.

The black crowd was on its feet, their fists raised. '*Amandla! Amandla!* Power! Power!' they chanted. The white police drew their revolvers and the black constables, trained in crowd control, suddenly appeared holding riot shields, which had been resting all the while at their feet. They raised their fighting sticks in readiness to charge. '*Amandla! Amandla!*' the black crowd chanted, oblivious to the danger they faced from the police. Some of the white crowd had risen, ready to move out in a hurry.

Gideon stood in a neutral corner as the referee commenced to count Geldenhuis out, finally crossing his arms and scissoring the air with his open palms to indicate that the fight was over.

It was the traditional moment in boxing when the winner leaps into the air and holds his hands high in victory as he circles the ring, and all hell breaks loose in the crowd. But Gideon Mandoma did no such thing. Instead he took three steps to the centre of the ring where he stood at rigid attention with his head bowed, as if in sorrow, his gloves brought together over his scrotum.

The effect on the black crowd was instantaneous. By some sort of osmosis his will imposed itself on the crowd and they grew silent almost in the time it took to catch a breath. Then the young Zulu chief's voice rang out clear and sharp, echoing through the giant stadium, '*ukuBekezela abakowethu*! Patience my brothers!'

The crisis was over. Moments later, the referee from Cuba raised Gideon's right hand and the ecstatic black crowd acknowledged him with waves and waves of roared approval, their aggression of a moment before turned to a fierce and benign love for the new leader who had been revealed to them.

General Van Breeden leaned over to Captain Smit on his left. 'Wragtig! Did you see that, hey? Tonight a new Dingane is born, you mark my words!'

Geldenhuis was back on his feet, his arms around the necks of two of his seconds who helped him back into the ring. This brought a spontaneous cheer from the white crowd as well as steady applause from the black. He moved jerkily towards Mandoma, his legs clearly unsteady; they started to give way again just as he reached the black boxer. Gideon grabbed him, preventing him from going down. Flashlights popped everywhere as the black man held the white in a macabre embrace.

THIRTY

After the Mandoma win, the preliminaries to the title bout were close to magical. The black crowd, buoyed by Gideon's brilliant victory, were in the mood for more. Jackson had come out first, carrying a huge American flag and followed by his entourage. This had caused terrific excitement and the crowd had been generous in their applause. Things American were popular in the African townships and, against any other white opponent, the American would undoubtedly have been the black favourite.

When Peekay, accompanied by Hymie, walked out onto the field from the entrance under the members' stand, the tension was almost unbearable. The huge black crowd, unwilling to wait for the opening wail of the great Gwigwi's clarinet to lead them, broke into spontaneous song. Seventeen thousand voices lifted in harmonious greeting as the Chant to the Tadpole Angel rose like thunder into the evening air.

It was spine-chilling stuff and many of the whites would later swear they'd felt the hair standing up on the back of their necks. The Chant continued until Peekay climbed into the ring and sat on the pot in his corner.

'Christ, Peekay, stop bawling,' Hymie said into the sudden silence as the voices rose one last time and then suddenly cut dead. It was obvious that he too was enormously moved.

Almost immediately the obese figure of Jam Jar rose up on the white side of the ringside audience. The opening strains of his violin carried over the loudspeakers and twenty-eight Odd Bodleians, led by the small, neat figure of Aunt Tom, stood over half-a-dozen microphones as they commenced to sing the *Concerto for the Great Southland*.

The beautiful voices of the Oxford men rose in chorus and almost immediately the blacks came in. First the Xhosa; the concerto rising higher and higher under the huge stadium seemed to expand with the sound. The same was true of the Sotho, Ndebele and Swazi as they picked up the theme and the audience went with it. Finally, when the great chorus of the Zulus came, the huge stadium filled with the fulminous sound as five thousand Zulu men rose to stamp their feet as they took the great tribal song into their chests and wound it upwards into the heavens itself. The thunder rolled over the stadium and surrounded the people, lifted them up, rose high and crashed down on them as the impi of Shaka and Dingane swept down from the hills like wind in the grass.

For one moment, all of South Africa stood together united in the storm of love, both black and white drenched until no colour or creed or worthwhile difference existed. All, for a few moments, felt *the possibility*, the possibility of one land and one purpose and the perfect harmony of one people.

General Van Breeden, seated beside Captain Smit, wept openly; and directly opposite them, on the black side of the rope, Mama Tequila, Madam Flame Flo and Tandia did the same. The bitter, sad land paused from the hating and reached up and touched the face of God who, for a few moments, stayed His vengeance and stilled His wrath.

When the opening chords of the Star-Spangled Banner played for Jackson and immediately after it, *Die Stem* for Peekay, they came almost as a relief to an emotion which, if it had been allowed to endure, would have burst the hearts of the huge crowd. Peekay seemed to be in a daze, even when the Mexican referee called the stats for both fighters and brought the fighters together into the centre of the ring, where Jackson, taking advantage of the ref's poor English, spat out, 'I'm gonna whup your ass, whitey'. Peekay appeared not to hear him as he returned to his corner. With a huge roar from the crowd the bell sounded for the opening round and Peekay moved almost casually to meet a fiercely advancing Jackson.

Jackson came at him hard and Peekay prepared to snap his concentration into focus. There was a diamond-hard pin of light that seemed to move around his head as though spotlighting the next move, reading his opponent's mind. But this time all he could hear was his mother's voice, 'I am not mocked, saith the Lord'. Jackson hit him hard with a straight left, surprised that he'd made it through his opponent's defences so easily. He followed with a lightning right which connected high on Peekay's head but which nevertheless knocked him backwards. Peekay didn't seem able to focus; he was boxing blind, not reading Jackson. It was like lifting your hand and finding your fingers don't work any more. He moved frantically on the back foot, trying to stay out of trouble, his mind a blank, instinct alone defending him. The end of the round came and Jackson was clearly on top.

'What the hell's the matter?' Hymie shouted.

'I don't know, I'm not seeing it, it's not flowing.'

'For Christ's sake, Peekay, you know it backwards, every rhythm, every combination, they're pre-programmed in your head, they have to happen!'

'Stay on the back foot son, stay outta trouble till it starts to come,' Dutch said calmly, but he was worried. He'd never seen Peekay like this.

The next two rounds were the same. Jackson was clearly starting to move in on Peekay, getting through his defences. Peekay's timing was way out and it was all he could do to stay out of trouble.

In the fourth round the voice in his head started again. First it was Mrs Schoemann's voice speaking in tongues, the weird cacophony of words that made no sense. Jackson was beginning to hit him almost at will; it was only Peekay's instinctive skill that was minimising the effect of the punches. He saw the right hand coming but there was nothing he could do about it; it landed on the point of his jaw and he went down, the voices reaching a crescendo. He lay there, the voices going faster and faster in his head like a tape recorder speeded up. At eight, the number was the only thing he could make out in the gabble of sound in his head. He stood. Somehow he managed to get through the round.

Hymie was shaking him. 'Peekay! What's the matter, what's happened?' Peekay didn't answer. 'Christ, he's out on his feet we better throw in the towel,' he heard Dutch say, 'The lad's going to get hurt bad.'

'No!' was all Peekay could manage. His head seemed to be clearing; the bell went and he went out to meet a Jackson who now wore a tight grin on his face.

The American stalked Peekay and put him down in the fifth round. The voices were back, this time his mother's. *The devil is black and has a tongue of fire and leaps to destroy the children of the lamb. His number is seven and with his hands he will destroy you, tearing at the flesh of our flesh and the bones of our bones.* Jackson was going to take him in the seventh. When was that? The next round. Peekay danced, trying to stay out of trouble. Jackson's glove kept coming. Like a steam shovel, like a piston, bang, bang, bang, but it wouldn't be until seven. *The Lord is not mocked . . . With his right hand he will smite our firstborn and with his left also. His colour is black and his tongue is the fire of hate and he will triumph over the flesh of our flesh and he will vanquish him.* Jackson hit Peekay with a right, an insult; he hit him leading with a right and then followed with a left upper-cut, and as Peekay hit the floor the bell went for the end of the round. Hymie and Togger rushed to bring him back to his corner, but by the time they reached the corner Peekay's legs were beginning to return to him. He hadn't laid a decent punch on Jackson for three rounds, the fight was a fiasco. Dutch held the smelling salts under his nose and Peekay came to, shaking his head violently. There was a stillness in the crowd that was awesome; they were seeing their man demolished, destroyed by the furious black American.

Tandia couldn't watch any more and had her head buried in Mama Tequila's huge breasts. Peekay was Gideon's friend, Gideon idolised him and she was seeing the black American do to him what in her imagination she had seen Geldenhuis do to Gideon. Madam Flame Flo was shaking her head. 'He was so marvellous, that first time in Sophiatown, he was so marvellous!' There were tears in her eyes.

Now Peekay waited for the bell to go for the seventh. Dutch had worked hard to close a small cut above his eye. 'Son, what's on your mind? We're fighting for a world title! Wake up, you're taking a hiding, you have to lift your work rate! Watch his left, it's setting you up too often for a straight right; use your feet, don't let him set you up!' He was trying to stay calm and not show the edge of panic in his voice.

Peekay spat into the bucket Togger held out to him and handed the water bottle back to him. He was still breathing hard as he looked up at Hymie. His face, which so few boxers had ever managed to hit, was a mess, the flesh puffy and raw with the eye Dutch had worked on starting to close. 'I can't see it, I can't see the fight in my head, Hymie. I'm blacked out, just voices, my mother's voice, it's as though a light in my head has gone out.'

The bell sounded and Peekay rose to see the bull-like Jackson coming at him, his shoulder muscles polished with sweat, hunched to get the most power from the punches he was beginning to throw almost at will. The negro's face was virtually untouched and there was kill in his eyes, like a predator certain he has his quarry cornered.

Peekay managed to parry his left lead and move out of the way of the right which followed. He spent most of the round on the back foot trying to slip Jackson's punches and when the black boxer grew frustrated and attempted to move him onto the ropes he tied him up. Nevertheless the American managed to hurt him with two beautiful punches under the heart. Somehow, though both punches were capable of putting him down, Peekay stayed on his feet. But the voice was back. '*I am not mocked! His colour is black and his tongue is fire . . . flesh of our flesh . . . with his right hand he will smite . . . he will be utterly destroyed, utterly destroyed!*'

'The lad is finished, Hymie, he could take a terrible hiding, you *must* use the towel!'

'No, Dutch! No way! We're not stopping the fight, not unless he says so!' Hymie had never seen Peekay like this, he'd never before witnessed him humiliated in the ring, a feeling which he knew would be infinitely worse for Peekay than the physical damage he'd endured in the first fight with Jackson. The black boxer was making a fool of him and Hymie wanted to scream at him to stop, to take the title and go away and never come back again. He felt devastated, as though he found himself caught in a nightmare from which he couldn't wake and seemed helpless to control.

'He's fightin' like a zombie, Hymie,' Solly Goldman hissed. 'It's gotta stop, son!'

Hymie looked at Togger, who had no say in the matter anyway. 'Don't, Hymie, please don't!' The little fighter's blind trust in Peekay was still miraculously intact. 'He'll come out of it, just give him a chance!' Togger was crying.

'Peekay decides!' Hymie shouted again; it was as though by repeating his denial he could shout down an inner voice which urged him to throw in the towel. 'That is, if he makes it through this round!'

The bell went for the end of the round. Peekay dragged himself back and slumped wearily into his corner. Dutch massaged his shoulders as Togger handed him the water bottle. It was pointless offering Peekay advice, he was finished. He only hoped Jackson wasn't going to toy with him, make him eat crow. 'Easy now lad, Hymie wants to talk to you,' he said, knowing that he and Peekay had come to the end of the road, that Peekay would never fight again.

Hymie scowled, hating Dutch Holland. 'Peekay, how are you? What do you reckon?'

Peekay, spitting the water he'd taken from Togger into the bucket, shook his head. 'I can't . . . get my mother's voice . . . out of my head . . . she . . . she said things . . . bad things about this fight.' His chest was heaving and the words came out between gasps like a small boy who's been running away from a bully and finds the safety of a grown up he knows.

Suddenly a black arm pushed Togger's bucket aside and Mandoma looked into Peekay's face. The Zulu's eyes blazed and he was shaking as he started to talk, spitting venom in Zulu. 'You white bastard! I shit in your mouth. You want to take it from me! You want to stop me from being *the one*! If *you* lose this fight, *I* lose my chance!' He grabbed Peekay by the throat. 'You coward, you are not *uMamba*, the great snake, you are a worm who feeds on dead flesh! I spit on your shadows!'

Togger and Dutch grabbed at Gideon and pulled the black fighter away. Peekay hadn't moved. Even when Mandoma grabbed at his throat his eyes remained fixed, as though he was in a trance. As if triggered by the word '*uMamba*' the giant black snake rose up in his vision, the flat wedge-shaped head so close he expected its darting, flicking tongue to touch the bridge of his nose, the tiny, flat, remorseless eyes looking into his own. The sudden highpitched cackle in Peekay's head was the voice of Inkosi-Inkosikazi. *The head, bring the head down slowly to the ground, release your left hand, you must take away his eyes, the poison is all in your right hand.*

As suddenly as it had appeared, the snake's head dipped below Peekay's line of sight. There was a sudden rush of wind through the leaves of the giant yellowwood tree above the forest canopy and then the bell for the eighth round sounded. Peekay rose. He could see Jackson coming towards him, he could see the hate in his eyes. The light in Peekay's head went on and the shape of the fight yet to come was clearly etched in his mind. He could handle the hate. The fear had gone as he moved towards his dancing opponent, who was wearing a huge malicious smile.

Jackson held the smile, dancing round Peekay, waiting to plant a combination that would put him down. He'd lost all respect for him but for one thing. Peekay should have stayed down long ago, he was a tough sonofabitch. And then Peekay's beautifully timed left hand came out like a jab of lightning, smashing through the smile on Jackson's face and sending his mouthguard flying, breaking three teeth. Peekay was back in the fight.

The ref stopped to retrieve Jackson's mouthguard and Jackson spat out the broken teeth into his hand. The crowd had come alive, not believing what they'd just seen. Jackson grinned; he'd been careless, a lucky shot. He hadn't expected a punch like that to still be in the white man, but he was pretty sure he'd sapped most of Peekay's strength and he could now take anything the white man could dish out. He was still strong, although he was beginning to feel the effects of the altitude and was taking a little longer to recover between rounds. There was plenty of time left, he told himself; Peekay couldn't go beyond ten. But Peekay continued to land hard, clean punches that snapped his head back. The white man was working to his head; that wasn't his style, he was a body man. Now they were coming; sharp, clean, hard, into the nose, into his mouth – and then, towards the end of the round, Peekay drew blood again as he caught him with a mercurial right cross which opened up the old wound above his right eye, tearing a gash almost completely across the soft tissue below his eyebrow. The round was Peekay's, the first he'd won.

The next round wasn't exactly fireworks. The American tried to finish Peekay off but Peekay tied him up and on the break managed to hit him consistently to the head, banging away at the tissue above the broken eye. Peekay was resting, regaining his strength. Jackson's cut-man had worked frantically with adrenalin between rounds to close the gash above his eye. Peekay was working it, ripping his punches across the eye so that now it was taking a lot of internal blood and closing fast. Peekay wasn't trying to put Jackson away, but he was slowly beginning to bring Jackson's head to the ground and the crowd sensed that, miraculously, the tide was beginning to turn in the fight.

By the end of the tenth round Peekay was on top and he'd opened Jackson's left eye as well. In the following, the eleventh, Peekay closed it almost completely and Jackson was left with no more than thirty per cent vision in both eyes as Peekay, growing stronger by the minute, began to put his punches together brilliantly.

Dutch couldn't believe what he'd seen. Hymie was grinning and Solly and Togger were falling over each other to sponge and water Peekay. Dutch was still cool. 'All you do is hold him for the next two, work him up. You're too far behind to win on points, lad. You got to take him out in the thirteenth or fourteenth. Save your strength, you've taken a fair bit of punishment, save it for the big one.'

When the bell went for the end of the eleventh round the crowd was screaming and hadn't let up between rounds. Peekay was taking the fight to the American and giving the rapidly tiring Jackson a boxing lesson. It was almost as though they'd been allocated six rounds each to beat the living daylights out of each other. Jackson was plainly weary when they reached the end of the round. Peekay had kept at his head, putting the punches in with his left hand.

'Shit, they're cutting Jackson's eyes,' Togger yelled.

'Good!' Dutch said. 'There's too much old scar tissue, they'll cut. But listen, lad, if you can bang them shut again, that's the end. They won't be able to open them up again!' He tried to keep his voice calm. 'Listen carefully, son. The American has to try and take you out in this next round, he has no bleedin' choice! If he can hang on he'll win on points but he knows he can't. Dance him lad, stay out of clinches, keep off the ropes. If you can put a coupla good hard 'uns into the eyes to close them for good, that's all it'll take – then stay away, you hear me now. You're on top, you can get him in the next round. There's plenty of time, you've got three rounds up your sleeve.'

The twelfth round was perhaps the greatest in both men's careers. Jackson put Peekay on the canvas in the first fifteen seconds with a beautiful right cross. Peekay was on his feet at the count of six but shaky on his pins. Jackson came at him again and put him to the floor again with a sharp left which seemed to travel no more than eight inches but caught Peekay on the point of the jaw.

Peekay lay sprawled looking up at Jackson. Everything seemed fine except that he couldn't move. Inkosi-Inkosikazi's insane, high-pitched cackle filled his head . . . *The poison is in your right hand*! Almost immediately the feeling returned to his legs and he was standing at the count of eight. Jackson took him onto the ropes where Peekay tied him up. The ref called for them to break and Peekay came out of the break as a southpaw, leading with his right hand instead of his left.

Jackson went down to a right-left combination moments later. It was the first of three knock-downs for Jackson in the twelfth. Later Baasie Pienaar would write in *Die Vaderland*:

> *Jackson, who'd fought brilliantly for the first ninety seconds of the twelfth, now seemed to have no counter for the southpaw switch of Peekay. The Tadpole Angel hit the black fighter one hundred and fifteen times in the remainder of the round, which included the three trips to the canvas. It was the most remorseless attack led with a right hand that I have ever witnessed. The Angel hits hard and clean and has a KO punch in both hands even this late in a fight, though the same punches earlier in the fight would have put the American away half a dozen times. Nevertheless they were still good punches and Jackson must have a head like Mount McKinley; how he managed to get back on his feet and see the round out this sportswriter will never know.*

The thirteenth round lasted only thirty-two seconds before Jackson took a perfect right cross on the nose, smashing it. The punch forced him backwards where he grabbed frantically at the ropes to stop himself going down. His entire body was exposed for a few moments and Peekay exploded a Solly Goldman thirteen-punch combination into the American which was so fast, perfect and complete that it would be talked about by boxing aficionados for years to come. Jackson simply pitched forward, sprawling on the canvas; then he rolled over once, his arms outstretched as though he'd been crucified. It was obvious, even from the furthermost row in the highest stand, that he wasn't going to get to his feet again for a long, long time.

Peekay moved to a neutral corner to wait for the Mexican referee to count Jackson out. It was all over. The small boy had conquered his fear. It had been enough to overcome the hate and the power that came with it. The long journey, begun at the age of six, was completed. Peekay was the undisputed welterweight champion of the world. 'Thank you, Hoppie Groenewald, wherever you may be,' Peekay said quietly to himself.

The crowd erupted and chaos reigned. Then, as suddenly, the hum of the Chant began to break through the tumult as fifteen thousand Africans rose up and danced in the stands, their arms raised in the victory salute. Suddenly the greater part of the white crowd joined them and turned and hugged each other and they too danced; white hands reached out past the police and over the rope to join hands with black. While the rope held and the policemen remained at the ready, it might as well not have been there at all; that is the peculiar thing about happiness, it comes from the heart and not from the head and when it demands to be shared it can't be separated by ropes, walls or least of all, by guns and three-foot fighting sticks which shatter kneecaps.

Peekay's dressing room was mayhem as he lay on a massage table while Dutch worked on him. Hands reached out to touch him, shouting their good wishes, and the room seemed filled with the dinner suits of the Odd Bodleians, including Aunt Tom. Some of the Oxford men had only arrived the previous day in South Africa and now shared the ecstasy of winning.

Jam Jar was playing his fiddle in between taking deep swigs from a bottle of Chivas Regal which he passed out to anyone who seemed inclined to partake. Van Breeden, Smit and Gert, grinning from ear to ear, were standing nearest to Peekay trying to make themselves heard.

'I've never seen anything like it! I never seen anything like it, you were dead, Peekay! *Wragtig!* I never seen anything like it!' Captain Smit repeated, his voice hoarse from shouting. Gert, as usual, said nothing, but his pride in Peekay showed in his eyes and you would have needed a charge of buckshot to blast the grin off his face.

Solly Goldman was walking around the room collaring anyone he could find to listen. 'Six years ago, I taught him. I never seen 'im use it, I never seen anyone use it, it was impossible they said, too difficult. Solly, they said, there's not enough time to seat thirteen good 'uns home! Then tonight I seen the Solly Goldman thirteen-punch combination win the championship of the whole world!'

It took Hymie almost half an hour to clear the room. He'd arranged for four buses to take the Odd Bodleians and other invited guests to Pretoria where a victory celebration for two hundred guests was arranged at Solomon Levy's palatial home. The ever-efficient Captain McClymont had laid on a police escort to accompany the buses. As well, he arranged for four motorcycle cops to escort Peekay and Hymie when they were due to depart an hour or so later, after the police had dispersed the main part of the crowd.

The moment the room was clear Peekay told Dutch he felt better. Dutch lifted him gently to a sitting position. 'Peekay, I'm not much with words, son. I've handled a lot of lads, good 'uns too. I don't mind sayin' I thought you was gone in the seventh. That was the bravest comeback by a fighter I've ever seen and what's more, my son, five of the last seven rounds, well, I doubt I'll ever see better boxing.' He towelled Peekay's shoulders. 'I still don't believe I saw that thirteen-punch combo, it was the fucking immaculate conception. You was magic, son!'

Peekay grinned. 'Thank you, Dutch. There was a lot of work in those winning rounds. I shall always be grateful. One more fight to go. I know your contract is up but I hope you'll agree to train me?'

Dutch Holland cleared his throat. 'Now's a lousy time to tell you, Peekay.'

Peekay looked up quickly. The sudden jerk of his neck sent a stab of pain down his right shoulder. 'Tell me what, Dutch?'

'Son, I'm a professional trainer; win, lose or draw, the next fight with Mandoma is your last.'

'So?' Peekay was too tired to be polite.

'Mr Nguni has asked me to train Gideon Mandoma. If he wins against you he's going to have a big career in the ring. Even if he doesn't, the title will be vacant and I think he could take Jackson or any of the other top contenders.'

Only Hymie, had he been present, would have seen Peekay's reaction and known that Dutch Holland's announcement was like a sudden kick in the scrotum. 'Dutch, that's great! Solly Goldman has had a hard time playing second fiddle and I'll be happy to go back to him.' Peekay extended his hand. 'I shall miss you in my corner.'

'Peekay, you make me feel a right berk.'

'Dutch, I owe tonight to Mandoma. Had he not interfered in the break before the eighth, Christ knows what would have happened. Nothing was going for me.' Peekay rose from the massage table, wincing from the effort. 'I understand your decision, Dutch. It seems only right that Gideon should have the services of the best fight trainer in the world.'

Peekay wondered whether Hymie knew of Dutch's decision. He felt betrayed and his gut was taut with anger but he was buggered if he was going to let on to the Englishman. He wondered to himself why Holland couldn't have waited for just one more fight? Mr Nguni must have made him a terrific offer. Peekay made a note never to underestimate the black fight manager again, and smiled once more to conceal his thoughts. 'No hard feelings, Dutch.'

Holland smiled back, relieved. Then he draped the small towel he was carrying over Peekay's head and took his hand. 'Keep warm, son,' he said, 'I promised I'd make a champ outta you and I done that; not too many trainers part with their fighters when they're at the top.'

Togger entered the dressing room at that moment. Peekay beckoned him over and whispered in his ear. Togger nodded and left the room. Peekay removed his gown, boxing shorts and jockstrap and moved painfully into the shower cubicle.

The doctor who had examined him immediately after the fight pronounced his nose broken and also several suspected broken ribs. His face was swollen but seemed to have responded well to the ice packs Dutch had used on him immediately after the fight. Apart from a black eye where Jackson had cut him, his face was almost back to normal. If anything, despite the pounding Jackson had given him in the first six rounds, he was in a lot better shape physically than after the New York fight.

Peekay was out of the shower with a towel around his waist when Togger returned and closed the door behind him. 'He's waiting outside, Peekay,' he said.

Peekay walked to the door and opened it, pulling Gideon into the room. Dutch had left and Solly, together with Hymie and Togger, stood silent, not sure for a moment what was going to happen. Then Peekay hugged the black fighter and both of them started to laugh.

'Shit, Peekay! Don't do that to me!' Hymie yelled, holding his heart in mock consternation. 'I thought World War Three was about to start!'

Peekay grinned. 'You think I'm crazy? This black bastard had an easy fight, he could probably go another ten rounds!' He turned back to Gideon and put a hand on either shoulder, looking into the eyes of the black boxer. 'Thank you, my brother, it is your title, you broke the *isiBango*, the spell, so my shadows could come to my rescue; it is you who are *the one*.'

'Haya, haya, Peekay, this is nice but it is not the truth. You are still the *Onoshobishobi Ingelosi*; the people have seen you tonight. They are very, very happy.'

'Then you will come to the celebration in Pretoria? It is as much for you as it is for me.'

Gideon looked grave for a moment. 'Hymie has invited me, but I am with some other people.' He switched suddenly from Zulu to English. 'Me also, I must go home with them.'

'How many people? One hundred, two hundred, your whole *isigodi*? You are a very big hero tonight, Gideon Mandoma!'

Gideon laughed, his marvellous white teeth showing. 'Three *abaFazi* and a driver! They are all.'

'Three women! Haya, haya! They are the victory gifts to the chief, hey?'

Gideon brought both hands up and covered his mouth, laughing. 'Only one is *isiXebe*, my sweetheart, Peekay.'

'Bring them all along then, you hear? Mr Nguni will be there, you will not be alone with all the white people.' Gideon seemed pleased. 'Thank you, Hymie, we will come.'

Peekay touched Gideon lightly on the shoulder. 'The *iBhunu* was outclassed, you deserve a crack at the world title and I'm bloody glad it's you and not that shit Geldenhuis.' Peekay turned and reached for a clean, freshly laundered shirt which hung on a wire hanger from a hook on the wall.

Gideon seemed to hesitate for a moment. 'Peekay?'

'Ja?'

'I meant what I said, you know, in the ring?'

Everything hurt as Peekay turned slowly to face Gideon. He measured him with his eyes, just the suggestion of a smile at the corners of his mouth. 'Ja, I know, but you're going to have to fight a lot harder than you did against the policeman or you're going to end up with more than shit in *your* mouth, black man.'

Gideon grinned. 'Your testicles are two dead frogs, white man!'

'Already you have found three women to cower behind, kaffir!' Peekay shot back.

They broke into simultaneous laughter, Peekay holding his recently strapped ribs, wincing with pain between his laughter. It was obvious that Gideon knew nothing of the plan to have Dutch Holland train him for the title fight.

The party was well underway when Peekay and Hymie arrived, but someone must have seen them coming for the band struck up 'For he's a jolly good fellow!' the moment they entered. Peekay had to endure this embarrassment as the two hundred or more people present joined in song. He spent the first half an hour greeting people before he excused himself to go upstairs to Hymie's room to phone home.

Fifteen minutes later he came downstairs again, and it was nearly midnight before he finally found himself alone again. He was dog tired; the elation at being the new world champion was beginning to wear off and his body was growing stiff and sore as his metabolism slowed down. He waited until nobody seemed to be looking before opening a french window and slipping quietly into the garden.

Outside it was bright moonlight and he filled his lungs with the crisp autumn air. Peekay found himself standing in Solomon Levy's rose garden and he bent over a yellow rose, tipped with saffron. Cupping his hands on either side of the half-opened bloom he directed the exquisite perfume to his swollen nose, surprised and delighted that he could still capture the faint familiar perfume which reminded him of home and of his grandpa's rose garden. When earlier he'd called home his mother was unavailable to talk to him, but the old man had grunted his pleasure and told him, 'There's a good lad,' about six times, so Peekay knew that he was hugely delighted. Then his grandpa had said that Mrs Boxall and Miss Bornstein as well as old Mr Bornstein and old Mr McClymont, and Mr Andrews and Kommandant Kruger from the gaol – in fact everyone who was anyone and a lot of people who weren't – had called to say how delighted they were and how proud the town felt and that if he called, to tell him they wanted to be remembered to him. Peekay's grandpa chuckled. 'Georgie Hankin called to read me his front page in tomorrow's *Goldfields News*, it says: PEEKAY! MORE FAMOUS THAN JOCK OF THE BUSHVELD!'

'Mr Peekay?'

It was a young female voice and Peekay, surprised, straightened up, turning in the direction it came from. Standing in the soft moonlight stood the most beautiful creature he'd ever seen. He knew instantly it was the girl he'd seen crossing towards the ringside before Gideon's fight, though now she wore a green evening gown, her perfect shoulders, the colour of new honey, bare in the bright, cold moonlight.

'Roses, you like roses? The welterweight champion of the world likes roses!' There was laughter and real surprise in her voice.

Peekay pointed to the yellow rose. 'It's named Macreadie Sunset and is a variety bred by the Macreadie family who, for two hundred years, created some of England's most famous roses. This one is my grandpa's favourite, it's a very old variety and goes back to George the First.'

Peekay reached into his pocket and withdrew the small pocket knife which had once belonged to Doc. He opened the blade, which was worn from constant honing, and bending over the rosebush he carefully cut the rose from the main stem. It was autumn, and he left a bud point at the end of the stem so that it would grow another branch to replace the one he'd removed. Then he expertly worked the half-dozen thorns off the stem of the rose using the side of his thumb, rendering it smooth and harmless. 'I suppose we ought to introduce ourselves, although I guess you already know who I am.'

Tandia extended her hand. 'Tandia Patel, I'm a second-year law student from Natal University and . . .' she smiled and added a little breathlessly, 'I'm also Gideon Mandoma's girlfriend.'

Peekay's heart missed several beats, though he managed to conceal his dismay. 'Would he mind very much if I gave you this rose, Miss Patel?' he asked, looking into her marvellous eyes.

Tandia laughed. There was an attractive shyness to her laughter, as though she was holding some of it back. 'Maybe he'll want to fight you, Mr Peekay?'

'Peekay, please!' he grinned at Tandia. 'I guess he'll be doing that soon enough anyway.' He handed her the rose. 'So, what say we give him a proper excuse, Tandia?'

She took the rose and brought it to her nose, closing her eyes as she inhaled its perfume. 'It has a beautiful smell. You seem to know a lot about roses?'

Peekay grinned. 'I know a lot about roses, boxing, a little about law and nothing about you.'

Tandia dropped her eyes, looking down at the rose she held. 'Me? There is nothing to tell.' She shivered involuntarily.

'You're cold, Tandia. Come, we'd better go inside.'

'Oh, but I've disturbed you!'

'I can't think of a nicer way to be disturbed. Have you eaten?'

'No, I've been too excited . . . well, nervous really.'

'Don't be. I haven't eaten either and I'm suddenly ravenous. C'mon, let's go before Gideon comes looking for us. I've had all the fighting I can handle for one night. What I don't need is an angry Zulu warrior!'

Tandia put her hand lightly on Peekay's shoulder. 'Peekay, you were wonderful! My father said you were the best. You and Gideon, the two best prospects he'd ever seen. He said you'd be world champion one day. I only wish he'd been there tonight.'

'Your father?'

'Ja, he was a referee, he handled your first fight with Gideon in Sophiatown, when you were just kids.'

'That Patel! The Durban referee? Why that's absolutely amazing! You're Indian then?'

'No, half. My mother was a Zulu.' As though anticipating his next question she quickly added, 'Both my parents are dead.'

They'd reached the door and Peekay paused. 'I'm sorry to hear that, Tandia.'

'Ag no, please, it wasn't like that. My mother died when I was a baby and my father, well it was . . . a strange relationship.'

'If I may say so, they made a beautiful baby,' he paused, looking directly at Tandia. 'I mean that's strictly a professional observation, one lawyer to another, you understand.'

'Why, thank you, my learned colleague,' Tandia replied, dropping her gaze from his.

Christ, she's beautiful, Peekay thought.

Tandia was amazed at how relaxed she felt in Peekay's presence. She'd observed him slip through the french window into the garden and had decided suddenly to follow him. The decision set her heart pounding and she was conscious of the male eyes which followed her as she moved across the room. The eyes of the South African whites, slightly guarded, afraid to look at her openly and the looks of the Odd Bodleians, open and frank in their admiration. On the way to Pretoria they'd stopped at Madam Flame Flo's new house in the coloured suburb of Meadowlands so she could change out of her bloodstained evening gown into the green one. She knew she looked sexy.

Although Tandia had largely grown out of her shyness at Bluey Jay, away from home she was reserved. At university she was thought to be aloof. Many of the male undergraduates fantasised amongst themselves about her. One or two of the braver and wealthier ones had jokingly suggested to her that they drive the six hours to Lourenco Marques in Mozambique which was Portuguese territory, where no colour bar existed, and spend the weekend. This was always couched as a joke but she knew that the slightest friendliness on her behalf would result in it becoming a reality in their minds. The assumption underlying everything, of course, was that she was a coloured so her virtue would be easily compromised.

At first she'd been too intimidated to be blatantly rude and had simply remained silent, which had only made things worse. One day, when one of the more loutish, wealthy final-year law students named Lew Holt, who fancied himself and who drove a red MG convertible and played rugby for Natal, had been persisting for several days with the idea of a weekend away, she'd turned and smiled at him. 'You'll have to ask my brother,' she said sweetly.

Holt was obviously taken aback at Tandia's reply but, true to form, recovered quickly. 'When? Where?' he asked cheekily. Tandia could see his mind working. 'How much?' he asked again.

Tandia wanted to die on the spot, but the years at Bluey Jay had conditioned her and she remained smiling disarmingly at the stupid prick, though, if Holt hadn't been thinking with his one-eyed snake he'd have seen that her eyes were cold and hard, filled with her loathing for him. 'What is your question? *When* can you see him? Or, *where* can you see him? Or *how much*?'

The law student grinned. 'All three, Tandia,' he replied. He looked around furtively and then tried to put his arm around her shoulders, but she backed away from him, though still smiling.

'I'll ask him. Meet me at morning recess tomorrow in the main quad.'

The following day Tandia gave him a location on the old road to Umhlanga Rocks and told him to be there at precisely two o'clock. 'There will be a Packard parked at the side of the road. My brother will be the driver. Please go alone.'

Tandia had hoped that the silly bastard would get the message and not turn up, but Mama Tequila was right; the one-eyed snake is not known for its brains, and Lew Holt looked completely ingenuous as he carefully noted her instructions.

Later, around four o'clock, when Juicey Fruit Mambo picked Tandia up at the gates of Natal University, he gave her his usual grin. 'I see you, Miss Tandy,' he said saluting her, then, taking her books as usual, he opened the back rear door of the Packard for her to get in.

They drove off in silence, which was unusual for Juicey Fruit Mambo who was always curious about Tandia's day. Halfway home to Bluey Jay Tandia could bear it no longer. 'Well, what happened?' she asked.

Juicey Fruit laughed. 'What happen for between mans, Miss Tandy. I not for you want to know dis thing.'

'You didn't kill him, did you?' Tandia asked, suddenly alarmed.

'Haya, haya, haya,' Juicey Fruit Mambo shook his head. 'Den de policeman he come and dere be many, many problems and dey take me away and who is going to drive for you?'

'Thank you, Juicey Fruit. Maybe that will teach the bugger a lesson.'

Juicey Fruit thought this was very funny and laughed uproariously, as though Tandia had made a huge joke. 'What are you laughing at, Juicey Fruit?' Tandia asked.

'I tink dis boy he need a big, big, lesson for driving.' Juicey Fruit turned to look at Tandia, the whites of his eyes showing large. 'Same like Geldenhuis. I tell him, "Baas, dis car, it is very, very dangerous, look dere is no roof!" '

Tandia squealed in delight. 'Juicey Fruit, not his red MG?'

Two days later Lew Holt was back on campus sporting his left arm in plaster, though otherwise he seemed unhurt. He busily told everyone at law school about his accident and about how the MG had been totalled coming around a bend at eighty on the old road near Umhlanga Rocks. It seemed he'd missed the turn and taken it straight into a large syringa tree.

A day or so later Tandia saw him ahead of her on campus and she ran to catch up with him, arriving breathless. 'Gee, Lew, I heard about your accident!' Holt could hardly believe his eyes, Tandia seemed genuinely distressed.

'Fuck off, kaffir!' he growled.

Tandia smiled sweetly. 'Still an' all, hey, it could have been a lot worse, don't you think? Only a broken arm? You were lucky, man. If I were you I'd tell all my friends about that particular bend in the road, you don't want them running into the same tree now, do you?'

Tandia hadn't only learned how to look sexy from Mama Tequila. Over the years at Bluey Jay she'd watched the old woman carefully, observing how she knew when to be soft and when to be hard. For Mama Tequila a compromise was a gesture you made on the way to achieving something else; no indiscretion, no matter how small, was left unpunished in the end. The Lew Holt incident was the first time Tandia had ever hit back and it consolidated this principle for her.

Now, as she went back into the house with Peekay, she found herself surprisingly at ease, even excited by being with him. She'd expected some sort of contest, the male thing trying to assert itself and dominate her immediately. She would naturally comply with it, stroke the ego presented to her by the white boxer, play on the aspect of forbidden fruit, both as a coloured and as Gideon's woman.

Peekay, she knew from Gideon, was liberated. Gideon said he simply didn't see colour. This made him vulnerable. He was the welterweight champion of the world as well as a brilliant young graduate from Oxford, Mr Nice Guy. He'd be bending over backwards not to show any skin bias and would also be over-anxious to appear modest and unassuming. But Tandia also knew that in the end the one-eyed snake in him would win. That would come later, that would be her ultimate weapon. Tandia knew it was important for her to make an impression on Peekay, and on the Jew also. Think ahead, she told herself. Think the bad things that can happen, because they will, for sure. Think them out and have a plan of action. You must know who to know long before you need to know them. It was more of Mama Tequila's advice; and it was what had given her the courage to follow Peekay through the french windows to confront him in the rose garden.

She'd found him smelling a rose, standing in the moonlight, his face battered and his nose broken, smelling a rose, happy to be by himself. She didn't know quite what she'd expected, but smelling a rose wasn't an acceptable discovery. She'd watched him in the clear, bright, cold night. There was a quietness about him, a lack of tension, like being in a warm, clean place. Yet she could feel the power.

Tandia was an expert on power. Most power, she'd observed, was based on hating, though some was driven by ambition or triggered by wealth or arrogance or both. Power was about getting something, making people bend to your will, imagining something and then making it happen no matter what.

The power she sensed around the white man putting his broken nose into the petals of a yellow rose was different; it was infectious and seemed to swell and recede as though it was trying to include her within its spectrum. There seemed nothing complex about it; it was singular but simple, it made no demands on her and it made her feel safe.

Tandia could never remember feeling completely safe; maybe when she was very young on Patel's knee when he was boasting to someone about her green eyes. The closest she could get to the feeling she now experienced was when she sat in the branches of the big old fig tree which grew beside her upstairs window at Bluey Jay. The tree seemed to be the only place in the world which was her own. In all the time she'd been at Bluey Jay nobody had ever seen her seated within its leafy canopy or discovered her secret. She had become so obsessed with the idea of its importance to her life that she waited, often until two or three in the morning, before she climbed out onto the branch where she would sit and think until the dawn came up and put the shine back onto the surface of the sweeping river that formed one boundary of Bluey Jay. Then she would creep silently back to bed, her head filled with enough cleanness to see her through another day. The aura she now felt around Peekay made her feel the same way. This made her very suspicious and decidedly uncomfortable.

He was white and gifted, brilliantly educated and a sporting genius. The white rose of South Africa's European culture would open its petals to him. There would be nothing he couldn't have: wealth, beauty, position and power. Nothing was beyond his reach; his skin was white and his eyes were blue and he would wake up between crisp, clean sheets every morning for the remainder of his life.

Gideon said he was a white man who didn't see colour. In such things Gideon was a fool. White men like Peekay didn't need to see colour; truth and justice and understanding were abstract virtues for them and if, in the end, nothing changed, you sighed and laid your noble head down, satisfied you'd done your best. It was no less a crock of shit in the end than the policeman with a salivating alsatian at his side and a sjambok in his hand.

Tandia hated all white men except Magistrate Coetzee and Dr Rabin. And this white man for whom she felt such a strange attraction was possibly the worst of them all. She should have known all along. When Peekay was still a boy Patel had eulogised him. Patel always ended up admiring the biggest white bastard in the pack.

And so, seemingly in a matter of minutes, Tandia, having felt herself invaded, built her hate back up again, layering it with reminders, insights and the phantasmagoria of loathing until it regained its comfortable thickness. It had all been done by a white man who'd barely spoken to her, but who'd cut a yellow rose from a bush, removed the thorns from its slender stem with a practised flick of his thumb and quietly and politely handed it to her before inviting her to dine with him.

Peekay and Hymie were a part of Tandia's long-term plan. She would graduate at the end of the year and, from what Gideon had told her, the law practice the two Oxford men were about to open seemed just the sort of place she'd like to join, the first rung in the ladder she would have to climb so she could get even with the world.

Tandia was only just nineteen and she saw herself as a terrorist and a Communist, though she'd not yet effected any acts, even small ones, of terrorism or joined a secret cadre. This didn't stop her seeing herself as totally committed to the overthrow of the white South African regime and the implementation of a socialist state.

Unlike Gideon, who saw a South Africa where blacks shared power with the other racial groups on the basis of a universal franchise, which meant a black prime minister and a black majority, Tandia believed in the Africa for Africans movement with its uncompromising cry, 'Hurl the white man into the sea!' In fact, she would sometimes make Juicey Fruit Mambo drive her down to the harbour where she would stand on the sea wall built to contain the yacht basin, imagining a continuous line of whites being marched over the edge and into the sea. 'Good riddance bad rubbish!' she would shout into the crashing waves, her fist raised in the ANC salute.

There is a time in most thinking adolescent lives when we are granted the gift of absolute certainty, when all is known to us and a position on everything is willingly taken, with no possibility of compromise. Tandia, no less than Peekay, believed in truth and justice, but the difference between them was that her Africa included no whites and insisted on revenge before the Freedom Charter could become a reality.

When she first talked to Gideon about terrorism he'd been reluctant to discuss the topic. But after his arrest and interrogation by Geldenhuis on the night of the farcical national raid in the name of the Suppression of Communism Act and with the subsequent Treason Trial at present underway, he'd started to think differently. He was one of the leaders of the ANC Youth League who now talked openly about an armed struggle against apartheid. 'We are not ready yet, but its time will come and then we will call it *Umkonto we Sizwe*, The Spear of the Nation,' he told her. Five years later, when in December 1961 the first acts of sabotage announced the formation of *Umkonto we Sizwe*, the young black activist lawyer, Tandia Patel, was secretly sworn in as the first female member.

THIRTY-ONE

The lower end of Fox Street, just opposite the Johannesburg Magistrates Courts is a dingy part of town where at sunset the streets go suddenly empty. Newspapers blow across the pavements and the smell of garbage and the rancid fat of cheap cafés pervades the atmosphere. In the vacant blocks sow-thistle grows among the torn-down building debris. But it was handy for Africans coming into court and that's why Peekay chose it for their law chambers.

Hymie would have preferred more fashionable chambers, but Peekay insisted that although whites would come to scungy rooms for good legal advice, blacks would be intimidated by oak panelling, carpets on the floor and rows and rows of leather-bound tomes – all the plush and hush of the legal profession.

Nevertheless Solomon Levy insisted on carpeting the offices, as well as the long corridor leading to them, with his very best red British Axminster. In the end, the black people *were* intimidated. They would often remove their shoes before walking down the pontifical corridor, or if they wore no shoes, when they saw the brilliant red carpet they paused to wash the soles of their feet at the courtyard tap before entering the building.

The law firm of Levy, Peekay & Partners became known in African as '*inDawo ye cansi elibomvu*', the place of the red mat, and after a while it was shortened to 'Red'. By 1958, when Gideon and Tandia both joined the firm, it was not uncommon for an African plaintiff, asked by a magistrate whether he had counsel, to proclaim proudly, 'Yes, baas, I am standing on the red mat!'

An African arrested at a political rally or taken at home during a night raid would jam his feet against the buckboard of the kwela-kwela and resist being thrown into the back of the police van until he was sure someone within earshot had heard him scream, '*ukuBizwa Bomvu!* Call Red!'

Peekay's reputation as a defender of the black people had a spectacular beginning in a preliminary hearing before Magistrate Coetzee, the recently appointed chief magistrate of Johannesburg, in which he sought to indict two police officers on a charge of murder. Because of the high profiles of the people involved, it was a hearing which kept the nation hurrying out to the front lawn for the morning newspaper and gave the black people their first tangible evidence that the *Onoshobishobi Ingelosi*, the Tadpole Angel, was their true defender now that he was grown to adulthood. As the case came to court and continued for nearly three years it established the Red Mat's reputation among the people and also saw Tandia Patel introduced as Peekay's junior counsel.

Two days after Peekay was crowned Welterweight Champion of the World he and Hymie were admitted to the South African Bar. The following day he received a call from Madam Flame Flo, whom he'd met briefly at the Levys' party.

'Peekay, I'm sorry to bother you, I suppose you very busy you and all?' she began.

Peekay laughed. 'Madam Flame Flo, I have a desk, a telephone and a law degree. Somehow I know they all go together but I'm not sure how. So far I haven't been given the opportunity to give even *free* advice. What can I do for you?'

'Well, I dunno, man, first let me tell you the story. Yesterday I got a call from a doctor at Baragwanath Hospital about a young black boxer who has been brought in with a bad ear infection. He was a young boy who used to help around the shebeen in Sophiatown, a tribal kid who became quite a good boxer under the name the Black Tornado. He doesn't have anyone here, you know, his own people, so when they asked for next of kin, he gave my name. Well, the doctor said the ear came from his having been badly beaten. Well, I mean, man, he's a boxer, so I didn't think much about it. The doctor told me the boy said he had some money in the Post Office, but they wanted me to guarantee his hospital fees.' Madam Flame Flo paused. 'Well, I mean, man, you can't just go guaranteeing people all over the place, so I said I'd come out and see him. Well, to cut a long story short, it turns out this boy, whose name is Tom Majombi, was the black sparring partner for Jannie Geldenhuis leading up to the fight with Gideon and the damage they done to his ears, it wasn't just an accident.'

'You mean there was malicious intent?' Peekay asked.

'I dunno what you call it, jong, but I'm telling you something for nothing, it was on purpose!'

Peekay agreed to go out and see Tom Majombi, taking a Nagra tape recorder with him.

Peekay drove over to the huge black hospital in Soweto. It turned out that Tom Majombi appeared to have lost the hearing in his left ear and complained of a ringing sensation in his head, with a great deal of pain. Peekay immediately agreed to pay for the X-rays needed to check whether permanent brain damage had occurred, and for any other medication Majombi might need.

Peekay spoke to the Zulu fighter in his own language. 'The *iBhunu* punches very hard, I think? With heavy sparring gloves and with your headgear on, he is still able to make your ears bleed?'

Tom Majombi laughed. 'The gloves I wore were heavy, but the ones he wore were for fighting; six-ounce gloves and there was no headgear for me, only for the *iBhuni*.'

The young black fighter went on to explain that when no outside witnesses were present he was not permitted to wear a headguard. The idea was to closely simulate the effect of a real fight, with the Zulu boxer wearing the heaviest possible sparring gloves, permitted to fight back as hard as he liked.

Majombi boasted quietly about how he had refused to go down, but admitted he was no match for the brilliant Geldenhuis. Day after day, he took a lot of punishment to the head with no protection. He recalled how Colonel Klaasens, Geldenhuis's trainer, called this aggressive sparring '*bloed krag*', blood power, and boasted it was designed to feed his fighter's hate for the kaffir boy, Mandoma.

Despite his apparent stupidity for not playing possum in the ring when he'd had enough, Tom Majombi proved to be an intelligent young man who would be able to handle himself in the witness box. Peekay felt sure he could bring either a legal indictment against Geldenhuis or at the very least have him and his trainer up before the South African Boxing Board tribunal for disciplinary action and compensation to the young black fighter. Before he left Peekay gave instructions that Tom Majombi was to get the best possible treatment available. He signed a commitment to pay and he left.

The following morning Peekay called the hospital to enquire about the results of the X-ray and he was told that the Zulu boxer had been removed to Pretoria Prison Hospital for further observation. The young intern who'd originally called Madam Flame Flo came to the phone and told Peekay that a kwela-kwela had arrived to remove the young boxer less than two hours after Peekay's visit. He'd been powerless to prevent the removal or even to ask that the Zulu boxer be taken by ambulance, so he'd sent a request to the superintendent of the prison hospital for X-rays to be taken, though he was extremely doubtful that this would be done. Peekay told him to keep the duplicate paperwork of Tom's admission and to hide it.

'Haya, they are not stupid,' the African doctor replied laconically, then added 'these *amaBhunu* are from the Special Branch. The admission papers and medical notes have been confiscated; no record exists of Tom Majombi's stay at Baragwanath.'

'There must be something. Look for it, we may need it later, doctor.'

After he put the phone down, Peekay turned to Hymie.

'The bastards have got Tom Majombi. He was supposed to have been taken to the Pretoria Prison Hospital but I've checked and they have no admission for anyone of the name. Tom Majombi has been abducted by the police, forcibly taken out of a hospital without being arrested. We've checked all the local police stations. In effect he's been kidnapped.'

'Can the police be charged with kidnapping?' Hymie asked.

'The point is he's disappeared and we know he was taken by the police. But I can't get any leads from that point. It can only be Special Branch and it can only be Klaasens and Geldenhuis.'

'But we have no proof.'

'We have his testimony on tape. That's not a bad start.'

'Look, I'll call Van Breeden. Moving against a policeman of Klaasen's rank could be bloody difficult; he may help, though I don't see why he should.'

'Jesus, Hymie, if it was a white boxer!'

'Okay, okay! I'll call him.'

The police major general listened and promised to call him back. He did so an hour later, suggesting Hymie drop round to de Villiers Square to see him.

Hymie was shown directly in to see Van Breeden and the policeman came straight to the point. 'Listen, Hymie, it's not so easy. I've got Colonel Klaasen's record, he's head of Special Branch in Pretoria, a member of the *Broederbond* and was *Ossewa brandwag.* He's also on the executive board of the Police College and his record shows him to be an exemplary officer. I'm telling you now, I'm not prepared to move against him even if the evidence was better than it is. We've checked both Baragwanath and the Prison Hospital in Pretoria; nobody of the name of your Zulu boxer appears to have been admitted. My advice to you is to forget the whole thing; the boy is not charged with anything and will be safe if we just let the whole thing die down. If you stir things up, who knows? People disappear all the time.'

'Sir, Peekay won't buy that answer.'

'With the greatest respect, this incident with the black boxer, if it was reported to a local police station it is doubtful the sergeant would take it seriously enough to make even a phone call. Peekay has to grow up! This is South Africa, the Nationalist government has been in for nine years and looks like being in for ever. Justice for a black man is not the same as for a white. Peekay would do well to understand this.'

'General, I appreciate your time and I hear what you say. I assure you Peekay isn't trying to prove anything or big-note himself, but in matters such as this he thinks with his heart. He'll march on Pretoria Prison personally unless I can give him some sort of assurance that Tom Majombi hasn't been abducted and is getting the best possible attention.'

'You mean he'll bring the matter up with the press, don't you?'

Hymie nodded. Van Breeden sighed. 'Okay, tell him I'll call Colonel Klaasens and drop a hint to him that we know there is a black person, a Zulu boxer by the name of . . .' Van Breeden looked down at the pad in front of him.

'Majombi, Tom Majombi,' Hymie said.

'Ja, okay, I have it here, Tom Majombi. This should be enough to keep him safe. I can almost personally guarantee it.'

'I am grateful to you, sir.' Hymie was genuinely appreciative of Van

Breeden's help. He pushed his chair back ready to rise, conscious that Van Breeden had made time in his day for something so trivial it probably wouldn't normally even appear in the charge book of a district police station, but which nevertheless now involved the tedious business of the police investigating the police.

'Hymie, don't go for a moment.'

Hymie sat back in his chair again. 'Yes, sir?'

'I don't scare easily and I don't much like being threatened. In this country there are a million Tom Majombis and, depending on your viewpoint, each has a genuine grievance against the white man, the police, the system and the state. You would be well advised to stop tilting at windmills because, I'm telling you, you won't win!' Van Breeden smiled. 'I have a feeling that the law firm of Levy and Peekay is going to be a very big pain in the arse. Particularly the Peekay part. Will you do me a favour?'

'Well, that depends, sir.'

'Spoken like a true lawyer. But even good lawyers need friends and I'm beginning to feel you're going to need your share of contacts in the right places. Do you understand me, Hymie?'

'Well, it still depends, general.'

'Both you and that difficult little welterweight partner of yours seem destined not to make too many friends among the lower ranks of the police force or magistrates or even the higher echelons of the judiciary.' Bul Van Breeden smiled again. 'The two of you will make a lot of noise and get your names in the paper, but you won't change anything. Let me tell you something for nothing, man! In the end the black people will despise you and the Nationalists will ignore you. And if they can't ignore you they'll find a way to silence or eliminate you.' Van Breeden leaned forward over his desk, serious now. 'There are new laws being drafted right at this moment. One of them allows the government to retain anyone in custody for as long as it likes without trial. Another allows them to place a person under house arrest. He or she is confined to their own home and may not meet with more than three people at a time. It can happen to anyone for any reason at any time.'

'Sir, I'm a Jew. The last time that sort of law existed my people was damn near eliminated.'

'I want you to keep the line open between us, Hymie. I want to be able to pick up the phone and call you and have you do the same for me.' The policeman smiled. 'A special phone. Your office phone and your house phone will be tapped, that I can guarantee, not by my department, but by the Special Branch.'

Three weeks after Peekay first visited Majombi in hospital the Zulu boxer was found dead on the side of a lonely farm road midway between Johannesburg and Pretoria. The death of the black man had been reported to the Meadowlands police station who had sent out a police truck to pick up the body and remove it to the morgue. Tom Majombi was just another dead kaffir in a day that would usually produce four or five of the same.

A small crowd as usual gathered outside the township mortuary as the two Black Jacks pulled the corpse from the police van. A brown paper bag had been pulled over Tom Majombi's head and tied with a piece of string around his neck, so that faceless, he resembled a limp, dark, dusty scarecrow. A head bag was easier to use and cheaper than a body bag and served the same basic purpose, to avoid identification in the event that the dead man was someone of political importance whom the crowd might recognise.

Johnny Tambourine and Dog Poep Ismali pushed to the front of the crowd gathered around the police van. Their families, along with the rest of the gang, had been forcibly moved from Sophiatown to Meadowlands and Moroka. Now the two boys stared at the body and Dog Poep Ismali jabbed Johnny Tambourine in the ribs. 'Hey look, it's Tom Majombi,' he announced in a loud whisper.

'How can you tell?' Johnny Tambourine whispered back.

'The tattoo, see the tattoo on his arm!'

Etched on the deep brown forearm of the young Zulu fighter in the familiar midnight blue of tattoo ink was the name Black Tornado, Tom Majombi's fighting name.

The news of the boxer's death was soon on the township streets and, as always, reached Madam Flame Flo by nightfall. She called Peekay and he went directly to the morgue. It was after five and the white man who was responsible for the morgue, a large Boer named Klopper, at first refused to admit him.

'It's after hours, man, tell him to come back tomorrow,' Klopper had told the black clerk who'd come to tell him a white man was making an enquiry. Occasionally a white would come to the mortuary looking for a black servant whom the family may have been fond of, but Klopper didn't like this. They were *kaffir boeties* and not to be encouraged. But then he'd glanced down at the card the black man had handed him and had seen Peekay's name. 'Here, man, why didn't you say so, this is the Welterweight Boxing Champion of the whole world!' He hurried out to meet Peekay.

Peekay identified Majombi's body. 'When does the doctor perform the autopsy, Meneer Klopper?' he asked.

'Ag, man, we don't worry too much.' Klopper waved his hands, indicating the fifteen or so bodies lying on the cement floor of the mortuary. 'When you seen one stab wound you seen them all. The doctor comes in for half an hour, maybe sometimes forty minutes, every day and writes out certificates for the coroner.'

'And if there isn't any stab wound?'

'Man, then it's only one of two things, a heart attack or the spoke.'

'Spoke?'

'Ja, man, a bicycle spoke is a major murder weapon. Come I'll show you.' He walked over to the body of a young male and turned him over onto his stomach. The man was naked and there appeared to be no marks on his body. Klopper went down on his haunches and pointed to a tiny red spot between the first and second vertebrae at the base of the neck. 'The victim is pushed forward and a sharpened bicycle spoke is pushed in. His spine is cut. He's dead in ten seconds, maybe less, and there's no mark, no noise. Here in Soweto, Advocate Peekay, the spokesman is the hired killer. A good spokesman is higher up than a gunman. He can kill a kaffir in a crowd and nobody will notice; they just think the man fell down or something.'

'Tom Majombi, how did he die?'

'Ag man, I haven't looked. Tomorrow the doctor will say maybe.'

'Maybe is not sufficient, Meneer Klopper. I would like to bring my own doctor, two doctors.'

Klopper was visibly upset. 'We have a government doctor. We don't like other people sticking their nose in our business, Advocate.'

'Meneer Klopper I'd appreciate your co-operation in this matter. Tom Majombi was a boxer, I'm a boxer. In the ring a boxer is just a boxer,' Peekay explained.

'But outside he's just a kaffir again,' Klopper added.

'Please, I don't want to bring a court order, it just makes more paperwork for you.'

Klopper scratched his chin. 'I don't know, man, it's highly irregular.'

'Perhaps they can come in, say, two hours before your pathologist comes, that way there is no confrontation?'

Klopper thought about this for a while. 'Okay, man, you must be here half past seven tomorrow morning.'

Peekay had challenged the coroner's finding in court. The government pathologist's report simply showed 'death by causes unknown'. However the evidence by the two independent specialists told a different story. Both indicated that the morgue examination was too superficial and, after the government pathologist had seen Majombi, they had caused the body to be moved to a private hospital where they'd performed an exhaustive autopsy.

Klopper hadn't mentioned the visit of the two private medical men prior to the government's pathologist's arrival, thinking not to upset him. Now the government found itself totally compromised as the evidence showed that Tom Majombi had died of a massive brain haemorrhage, the result of a middle-ear infection caused by a ruptured eardrum.

It was three weeks from the time Peekay had seen the boxer in hospital to the discovery of his body, and from the report it was also obvious that he hadn't been treated since his original hospital diagnosis.

Dr Dinkelman, the forensic surgeon who'd been present at the autopsy, was asked to explain in court at the preliminary hearing how massive brain damage, sufficient to cause death, could occur as a result of middle-ear infection. The surgeon showed how repeated punching to the naked ear by a soft boxing glove would compress air inside the canal which, unable to escape outwards, would blow inwards into the eardrum which would eventually rupture. If the rupture wasn't attended to it would set up a middle-ear infection which would eventually lead to brain haemorrhage and death.

It was this single point on which Peekay's potential right to have his case heard rested.

'This middle-ear infection, is it painful, Dr Dinkelman?' he asked.

'Extremely, the man would be in a great deal of pain,' the doctor replied.

'So much pain that he would be likely to seek medical attention?'

'Almost undoubtedly.'

Peekay turned to Magistrate Coetzee. 'May I suggest, your honour, that the reason why Tom Majombi didn't seek medical attention at this stage was that he was incarcerated somewhere?'

The counsel for the government, a senior police prosecutor named Opperman, objected. 'This is conjecture, your honour; there is no evidence to say the deceased was incarcerated.'

Peekay sighed. 'Your honour, I am trying to establish the degree of pain suffered by the deceased. I will rephrase the question.' He turned to the doctor in the witness stand. 'Is it possible, doctor, that Mr Majombi would simply grin and bear his condition? A Zulu stoic, far braver than you or I?'

Dinkelman frowned. 'No, sir, even if he was able to stand the pain of an untreated middle-ear infection, what would follow the initial infection would be impossible for him to sustain in silence. The man would have been in the most dreadful agony.'

'Thank you, Dr Dinkelman. One or two more questions, please.'

'Is it one or two?' Opperman asked, laughing. 'In a South African court we like to be precise, Mr Peekay!' He was trying to take the mickey out of Peekay, pointing up his inexperience to the court.

Peekay brought his finger to his nose, rubbing the tip, but ignored Opperman's remark and continued. 'Apart from intense pain, what would be the outward signs of such a condition?'

'Night sweats at first, then a high fever and shivering; severe vomiting; finally delirium.'

'And you said that the infection eventually travels to the brain. How long would this process take?'

The coroner rubbed his chin. 'If the conditions in which the entire infection took place were unhygienic . . .'

'As in a prison cell?' Peekay said.

'Objection!' Opperman sighed.

'You were establishing the degree of pain, not the whereabouts of the deceased, Mr Peekay,' Magistrate Coetzee said. He was a big drowsy-looking man, recently transferred from Durban where he'd been Chief Magistrate to take the same position on the Rand. Peekay was quickly learning to respect him. 'Objection sustained,' the big man added in a tired voice.

'Please continue, doctor,' Peekay asked Dinkelman.

'Well, yes, where was I now . . .'

'You were talking about conditions, unhygienic conditions,' Peekay reminded him.

'Ja, okay, under unhygienic conditions we could expect the prognosis to go from onset to termination in three weeks to a month.'

'The deceased appeared at the Baragwanath Outpatients a week after he claimed he'd first felt the pain. He was found dead nearly three weeks later. Does this fit with a typical prognosis, doctor?'

'If what you tell me is correct, then certainly,' Dinkelman answered.

Opperman laughed. He was enjoying himself. Not bothering to address himself through Magistrate Coetzee or even to rise, he pointed his pencil at Peekay: 'Mr Peekay, I must object. You are young and this is, I believe, your first case.' His tone was tinged with sarcasm. 'We are not in the habit of *planting* evidence, even if this clever technique is taught in England where, I believe, you received your legal training. *You* have alleged that the deceased turned up at the Baragwanath Outpatients. There is no evidence to prove this was ever so!'

Magistrate Coetzee looked up. 'Mr Peekay, are you trying to establish the time it took for the native boy to die, or is your point that someone deliberately interfered with his attempt to be treated in a hospital and that this interference was the direct cause of his death?'

'Your honour, my learned colleague may regard this case as one simply involving a dead black man. Or as Mr Klopper put it earlier in this preliminary hearing, "Listen, man, I can't be responsible for every dead kaffir now, can I?"' Peekay mimicked Klopper perfectly. 'Nevertheless, I intend to prove that Mr Majombi did register at the hospital and was diagnosed with an inner-ear complaint and that shortly thereafter he was forcibly removed by the Special Branch on the instructions of a senior police officer who I am prepared to name in this court.'

'That will not be necessary, Advocate,' Magistrate Coetzee said.

'I am asserting that people under the direction of this man caused the deceased to be taken in a police van to a place or places unknown, where he was unable to ask for, or was refused, treatment for his condition, and as a direct consequence died an agonising and unnecessary death.'

Peekay paused, and appeared to be rubbing the point of his nose with the tip of his forefinger, a gesture for which he would become famous in the years to come. 'When the Red man touches his nose everybody watch out!' the Africans would say of him later, for they learned that the gesture always signalled an unexpected turn in events.

Now Peekay began again slowly. 'I admit I may be clumsy and lack the sagacity of my learned colleague, whom I note feels so much at ease in this court room that he considers himself free to confront me directly without addressing himself through the bench. However, must I conclude that where *he* was trained there is a distinction made between the sanctity of a black life and a white?'

Magistrate Coetzee sighed. 'We are not here to be lectured on the sanctity of life, Advocate. Will you kindly stick to the point.' Though the magistrate's expression didn't change, he liked the young lawyer who refused to be intimidated by Opperman, a notorious bully who took great delight in putting young counsel in their place. 'Would the counsel for the deceased now show the court any evidence he has to prove, or at least to strongly suggest beyond reasonable doubt, that the deceased, Tom Majombi, was a patient in Baragwanath Hospital,' the magistrate instructed.

Peekay turned to his law clerk, who was acting as his junior. The man handed him an envelope which Magistrate Coetzee instructed the clerk of the court to retrieve. 'Your honour, I submit a letter signed by myself on the day in question, in the presence of a doctor and nurse authorising any extra medical attention Mr Majombi would require and for which I guaranteed payment.' He turned to his clerk again, who handed him a manila folder. 'The carbon copy, in other words, the hospital copy of the letter you have, is contained in this file which I now also submit to this court as further evidence. You will note that in this letter the patient's name and address appears and specific details are given of his prognosis and of the treatment required.'

Opperman jumped to his feet. It was obvious Peekay had caught him unawares. 'Counsel requests permission to study this document, your honour,' he said.

'Advocate Opperman, may I remind you that this is a preliminary hearing. The evidence will be assessed by me alone.' Opperman was suddenly aware that he'd underestimated his young adversary. This was the third and, most likely, the final day of the hearing and Opperman had relaxed, confident that if any evidence existed which would show that the kaffir boxer had been admitted to hospital the young, inexperienced lawyer would have revealed it long before now. On more than one occasion during the hearing he'd been neatly caught in a verbal trap of Peekay's making. In his mind he'd made light of this; without any real evidence, it would take more than a clever young tongue to outwit him. Now his expression showed real enmity towards the young advocate, a sure sign to Magistrate Coetzee that the ground had been taken from under his feet.

'I'd like to validate this document, your honour. As you know, it is relatively easy to reproduce material of this nature. What's in a receipt? A few hastily scribbled words, such a thing is easy to forge. Nobody knows this better than you, your honour!'

Magistrate Coetzee looked up over the top of his glasses at the government lawyer. 'Advocate Opperman, if I am such a expert on forgery, then I would also be in a position to know whether the document seems genuine. In which case, I take it you will be satisfied with the court's decision on this matter?'

Opperman sat down heavily. 'Certainly, your honour.'

Magistrate Coetzee had mixed feelings about the new evidence. He was now sufficiently convinced by Peekay's conduct during the hearing that some prima-facie evidence existed against the police for conspiracy and that there was also sufficient cause for charges to be laid against Geldenhuis and Klaasens for assault leading to the death of the young black boxer. On the other hand, cases against members of the police force usually ended up in a horrible shit fight and he hated the idea of ruling for the crown that the two senior policemen in the Special Branch of the South African police force had a case to answer.

Magistrate Coetzee knew nothing of the hate which Geldenhuis felt for Peekay, but he knew how difficult it would be for a young barrister's career if he earned the enmity of the police force at the outset. Peekay would almost certainly lose his case; but win or lose he could expect a rocky road ahead in his career.

The tired old magistrate hoped that it might be otherwise for the young lawyer; but he told himself that if he knew anything about men, Peekay wasn't going to give up easily. Momentarily he wished that he wasn't so old and cynical and that his gout didn't play up as much as it did. He would have liked to keep the hearing in the Magistrates Courts and preside over it himself. It would have given him the opportunity to match wits against the young advocate who carried a flaming sword and a fine mind into battle. He told himself he would also, in the process, have tried very hard to see that justice was done.

But Magistrate Coetzee had too much brandy under his belt and too many years on the bench to want to take on a trial which could last who knows how long? His transfer from Durban to Johannesburg was his last before he retired and he wanted his remaining few years to be as peaceful as possible. At his age he knew better than to be caught in the crossfire. He had fifty acres waiting for him in the Eastern Transvaal where his land formed part of a bend in the Crocodile River. There, small buck and guinea fowl and an occasional warthog came to drink at sunset and when you lay at night in bed you could hear the distant crash of the rapids as the water swept across the rocks in a bend in the river.

Magistrate Coetzee comforted himself that he could look forward with some anticipation to following the ensuing court case. He would take great pleasure in watching the way this upstart from Oxford would conduct it. On the other hand, the young advocate was about to make a lot of trouble for everyone, trouble which could be avoided if Magistrate Coetzee now ruled that insufficient evidence existed for the case to go on trial. The police would be happy and, in the long run, he'd be doing the young rooinek lawyer a real favour. Personally he wasn't under any illusions; a Bantu death, no matter how you looked at it, wasn't equal to a white one. Why then should he care? His duty in this matter was plain: he would serve Pretoria best by declaring that no proper evidence existed to justify a trial.

At the end of the third day's hearing, at two in the afternoon, immediately after the court had returned from luncheon recess, Magistrate Coetzee announced that, in the opinion of the court, a prima-facie case existed against the two members of the South African police force, Lieutenant J. Geldenhuis and Colonel N. J. P. Klaasens, together with persons unknown, for conspiring to abduct a patient from his hospital bed and, as a result, to cause him such grievous bodily harm as to lead to his death.

Peekay had won the right to go to trial.

For Jannie Geldenhuis the news was devastating. His defeat by Mandoma had left him severely depressed, to the point where he'd considered taking his own life. He knew he would never step into the ring with Peekay and to add to this, he would now have to appear for cross-examination before the man he hated the most in the world. He, Jannie Geldenhuis, a brilliant young lieutenant in the police force would have to stand in the dock, not as an officer of the law, but as someone whose reputation and career was on trial. And what for? For the death of a stinking black kaffir, a meat bag whom they'd tossed into a cell because he'd been stupid enough to talk to Peekay and Mandoma. What the fuck did the black bastard expect? They'd paid him good money to be a sparring partner. In his sick head, Geldenhuis told himself that Tom Majombi had been a plant. How else would Peekay have known about him? He had gone directly to Baragwanath the day Majombi had been admitted. It was too bloody neat. It was a conspiracy, a conspiracy to make sure that he never got a chance to fight Peekay. Majombi was a deliberate plant, he'd been feeding Mandoma information prior to the fight. The reason he'd lost was because Tom Majombi had told Gideon about his weaknesses. The rooinek and the Jew had framed him. Jesus! He and Klaasens had played right into Peekay's hands! By stupidly allowing the Zulu fighter to die in an isolated police cell, there was now no possibility of proving that such a conspiracy had existed. Geldenhuis felt sick at the stupidity he had shown.

The more Geldenhuis thought about it, the more convinced he became that *he* was the victim and not Tom Majombi. What did they care about another shit black fighter? It had to be a set-up! Otherwise why would Peekay agree to pay Majombi's hospital expenses? Since when do white guys go around paying the hospital fees for kaffirs they don't even know?

Geldenhuis shook his head, disgusted with himself. If only he'd realised sooner, he would have made the black bastard confess. He was suddenly angry again. It was fucking Klaasens! He'd assumed control of the abduction and in the process he'd totally fucked things up.

Geldenhuis told himself that had he been in charge he'd have thought it out. He'd have discovered the plot. Klaasens hadn't even talked to Majombi. Christ! That was fundamental police stuff, routine, the sort of information you fall over without even trying when you're conducting an interrogation. He would have kept Majombi alive to confess in court and then later quietly killed the black bastard.

Geldenhuis winced at the stupidity of the whole thing. The rooinek and the Jew had played him for a sucker. Now Peekay had him crucified. He, Jannie Geldenhuis, was indicted on a fucking murder charge!

When the young policeman had fitted all the pieces together his physical reaction to his total dismay was a compulsion to throw up. The vomiting and retching continued for an hour until he was so weak he sank to his knees in front of the toilet with his head hanging into the bowl. Every time he threw up he swore to God that, come what may, he would spend the remainder of his life dedicated to the destruction of Peekay. The kaffir didn't matter; he'd get Mandoma anyway; but it was Peekay and the Jew – above all, Peekay. He wouldn't rest until he'd killed him, but before he did that he would humiliate him. He would find a way to discredit him in the eyes of everyone, to totally destroy him.

Finally someone found Geldenhuis unconscious, with his head resting in the toilet basin, his hair swimming in his own sick.

Magistrate Coetzee set a date for the trial to come before a judge six months ahead. Peekay immediately filed for a further three-month postponement so that he could defend his welterweight title against Gideon Mandoma. His request was rejected by the chief magistrate and Peekay faced the prospect of going into court three days after the first defence of his title.

Peekay's title defence proved to be as big an affair as the fight with Jake 'Spoonbill' Jackson, though this time the home crowd was torn between the Tadpole Angel and the charismatic young chief, Gideon Mandoma.

Gideon had meanwhile fought Togger Brown in Orlando stadium for the British Empire title. Peekay and Solly Goldman were in Togger's corner; Dutch Holland, who'd moved over to train Gideon after Peekay's world title fight, handled the black boxer with Mr Nguni. Mandoma's aggressive punching, especially with the left hand, proved too strong for the mercurial Togger; Gideon defeated him fairly convincingly by knocking him out in the thirteenth round of the scheduled fifteen-round fight.

Dutch Holland now owned fifteen per cent of Gideon which, if Gideon made it to the world title, would prove to be a nice little earner for him. Peekay had persuaded Gideon to allow Hymie to draw up his new contract; when all was said and done, Hymie had managed by a combination of implied threats and cajoling to get Mr Nguni to agree to a maximum of twenty per cent for himself with all out-of-pocket expenses exceeding twenty per cent of the gate coming from his cut.

At the outset Mr Nguni had opposed the new arrangement although, properly handled, it was a decent enough cut. Peekay was hugely surprised when he discovered that Gideon's manager had previously owned seventy-five per cent of the black boxer.

Peekay confronted Gideon when he'd heard of Mr Nguni's cut. 'Gideon, how did you get this insane contract? You're not stupid.'

Gideon laughed. 'It was a long time ago. I was sixteen years old and hungry. Nguni, he told me to touch the pencil and he would feed and clothe me and put money in my pocket. It is the same with all his fighters and soccer players also.' He looked at Peekay. 'Nguni is a chief, but he is also *namandla* and he has many, many cattle. He is very powerful; these boys they come from his *isigodi*, they must do what he says.'

'And you?'

Gideon drew back, puffing up. 'No, Bra! I am same like him, I am chief, I am not from his *isigodi*. That paper, it was because I was hungry and still *umfana*, but I am not a boy now, now it will be okay, you will see.'

Hymie asked Peekay not to make a fuss about the other black sportsmen until they'd sorted out Gideon's contract with Mr Nguni. He patiently persuaded the black boxing manager that, should Gideon become world champion, Mr Nguni stood to be infinitely better off. Furthermore, Gideon could well defend his title as many as a dozen times. The profit opportunity represented was a hundred times greater than seventy-five per cent of a good undercard fighter.

Hymie felt a little foolish explaining all this to the huge black man. Mr Nguni was a shrewd and resourceful businessman and Hymie told himself he would have seen the advantages immediately. Why was he making him spell things out so laboriously in front of Peekay and Gideon? What was Nguni up to? Mr Nguni seemed reluctant at first to agree. What he seemed to be baulking at was the principle that his fighter would receive the bigger share of the prize money. It was essentially a matter of face.

Peekay was aware that it wasn't the money but the percentages which concerned Mr Nguni. They made Gideon of greater importance than himself in the partnership. 'Peekay pointed out to Mr Nguni that Gideon was a chief in his own right, that the contract in the tribal sense was between two equals and that therefore a precedent existed for the uneven split.

Although nothing had been said, Peekay was certain Mr Nguni would be aware he was prepared to hold up the contract for the title fight indefinitely unless he agreed to Hymie's proposed contract. Nevertheless, he was surprised when Mr Nguni seemed suddenly to capitulate and accept his argument of the equality of two chiefs and also, without equivocation, all the clauses that Hymie had drawn up to protect Gideon's principal sum.

Mr Nguni was no fool. He knew Peekay held the better hand. His only concern was not to lose face in front of Gideon. Zulus talk and if it got out that Gideon's *isigodi* had got the better of his, he would be shamed. This he prevented by making Hymie spell out the deal in Gideon's presence and also by forcing Peekay to use the precedent of the two equal chiefs. The huge Zulu was an ambitious man with long-term plans for himself, most of which relied heavily on the possibility of Gideon becoming the world champ. Hymie was right, he'd end up making more money anyway, even though he controlled a smaller share of Gideon. But, for the time being anyway, money alone wasn't at the root of his ambition.

To be the manager of a world champion was a position Mr Nguni wanted more than anything. It would put him on a par with the black American fight promoters, which in the eyes of South Africa's black people, would earn him enormous kudos. But it would do something else as well. Mr Nguni's secret political ambitions had very little to do with the ANC's struggle for freedom, which he basically saw as a waste of time. He wanted to be seen as a black man among important white people in the capitals of the world. This would do a great deal for his future status in the white political arena.

Mr Nguni was a hard-eyed realist. Come the black revolution, he was confident that he could buy the political leverage he needed. Revolutions always need money and when the time came he would trade it for power, which in turn would earn him more money. It was all very simple. Keep your nose clean and don't confront either side, the ANC or the white government. But what about the other consideration? What if the revolution didn't come? What if the *amaBhunu*, the Boers, won the fight again, as seemed more than likely? Already they were talking in Pretoria of creating separate bantustans, separate independent countries for the various black tribes. The Zulu tribe was three million strong, nearly one quarter of the total black population. When the time came for the independent state of the Zulu people, they would need a president. This president would have to be carefully chosen. He would need to be a chief in his own right, a man of impeccable credentials who outwardly seemed to be his own man, acceptable to his own people, both the migrants from the townships and the peasants on the land. It would also help if he appeared independently wealthy, a man of the world who believed in the capitalist system and was respected by the white political leaders of other countries. But, above all, he would need to be someone the white government in Pretoria could trust. President Nguni had a nice ring to it.

In the meantime Mr Nguni appeared to eschew politics. The ever-smiling black promoter appeared essentially as a sporting man who, through the promotion of boxing and soccer, was beginning to be favourably noticed by the Pretoria government. In fact, a dossier already existed on him in Pretoria.

Zulu Nguni – Mathew. Born: Masinga, Zululand, 1920. Tribal Chief (Minor) Pass No: ZU 00 73152 T/N. Occupation: Sports Promoter – Boxing, Soccer. Also manager, Zulu Mandoma – Gideon, South African Welterweight Champion, British Empire Champion (ANC Youth League.) Social history: No personal political history. Good race relations, White/Black. Youth development programme. Property: Independent means. Property, 3 houses, Moroka, Meadowlands, Masinga (Z'land). Cattle owner. State Police Clearance. Category AAA.*
See Zulu Mandoma G.-ANC Transvaal. Ref. Youth League – Political File.

Included with these cryptic notes were several transcripts from speeches, mostly of a sporting nature. The most notable was a transcript taken from a remark in parliament by the Minister for Sport:

> *That Nguni, he's a proper sportsman. I'm telling you, he's a good black man, the sort of native you can talk to if you want something done in the townships. Not a political type, but he's a natural leader, a chief in his own right. If we had more like him things would go better with the native people all round.*

Among the black people, even most of the township people, Peekay's first title defence became a deadly trial to see whether Mandoma would beat Peekay and so lay claim to being the *Onoshobishobi Ingelosi*, the Tadpole Angel. For them the fight had a mystical importance well beyond boxing and it became the major topic of conversation in the weeks and the months leading up to the fight. The trial against Geldenhuis and the police colonel Klaasens had convinced many of the blacks that Peekay was their leader. No person had ever taken a Special Branch policeman to court on behalf of a black man, not even an important black man. The very fact that Tom Majombi had been a nobody was proof that the *Onoshobishobi Ingelosi* was there to protect and to fight for them. A great many of the fans came to the fight wanting Peekay to win.

When Peekay entered the ring, the Chant to the Tadpole Angel thundered around the old Jabulani stadium where the fight was held; and now even a great many of the white supporters joined in. They had learned the lyrics on Springbok radio where, after Peekay had won the world championship, it had risen to number one on the hit parade. It was a magical moment which brought Peekay close to tears. He stood together with Mandoma in the centre of the ring as the Chant came to an end and Gideon suddenly moved and lifted Peekay's hand and held it aloft.

This was a different kind of fight. Even those who had come to see the white man smash the kaffir or the other way around, now realised that what they were going to see were two boxers with enormous pride who wouldn't give an inch, a white man and a black one who respected each other, who openly referred to each other as brothers, so that in some parts of the Afrikaner press both were actively despised.

Both had motive enough to win. Peekay wanted to retire the undefeated champion of the world and Gideon Mandoma, the herd boy from the hills and mountain peaks of Zululand, who had used his fists to get to the pinnacle, wanted to fight a man who, after beating Jackson, had been described by *Ring* magazine as the greatest boxer pound-for-pound in the world. If Gideon became the world champion he would be the first black boxer out of Africa ever to have done so.

The referee, a New Yorker who had officiated at two Joe Louis title fights, called the two boxers together and went through the usual ho-hum. The bell went and Peekay and Mandoma forgot that they'd ever been friends as they moved towards each other.

Mandoma was a natural fighter who came forward all the time. It had served him well against Geldenhuis, because he too fought off the front foot, but against Peekay it wasn't such a good idea. A straight-line fighter is easier to hit, he doesn't bob and weave and move about. Peekay's speed was such that he could nail Gideon more often. In the first round Peekay moved off the back foot as usual but he was making Gideon miss and nailing him in reply, though because he was moving back his punches lacked real steam. However, in terms of points he won the round quite easily.

In the second round Mandoma's timing was still out. He was trying too hard, trying for a big punch, and Peekay was too elusive and too fast. Peekay was beginning to put his punches together, working the familiar pattern to Mandoma's body. Mandoma hit Peekay several times with a good straight left and a right upper-cut coming off the ropes, the best punch of the fight so far. Peekay grinned, a sure sign that he'd been hurt. Mandoma came after him and received a beautiful straight left on the nose, making it bleed. The second round, despite the harder punching by Gideon, was also clearly Peekay's.

The third and the fourth round were the same. Gideon seemed to be no match for the hugely skilled world champion. Peekay was boxing beautifully, his feet a miracle of economy, lovely to watch. Mandoma, who was also a very fast boxer, was being made to look slow. The fight was going perfectly to plan and Hymie and Solly were delighted.

When Gideon came in after the fifth, a round which Dutch thought he'd probably shared with Peekay, the English trainer spoke to him. 'You're doing all right, son, but Peekay can dance all night. You've got to slow him down, get him on the ropes, clinch him, hold him as long as you can and, when you come off the rope, try to hit him first. He nails you going away. Go for him fast, a left-right as you come off the ropes. You have the shoulders, push him away; don't let him get away, you make the break for him then hit him on the break.'

In the sixth round the tactic worked well. Gideon would tie Peekay up as often as he could and move him onto the ropes. Twice he hit him with a glorious left-right combination as he pushed him away; once he thought he had Peekay going, but the bell saved the white fighter. The sixth round was Gideon's.

The tactic was working well for Gideon although he had to take a few torrid punches to get close enough to Peekay to tie him up. But once he had him on the ropes he was the stronger of the two fighters and he was doing a lot of damage close up, his short inside punches carrying more power than Peekay's. The seventh round was Gideon's too, and the crowd began to sense that the fight had evened up.

But the tactic couldn't last too long with a fighter as intelligent as Peekay and by the eighth round Peekay was starting to move forward, hitting Mandoma fast and clearing out, avoiding the clinch. Late in the round Mandoma walked into a left-right combination that put him on the canvas. Peekay would have stayed for the eight count, but Gideon was on his feet immediately, too proud to take the rest. It was a mistake.

Almost immediately Peekay hit him with a long raking right, pushing him against the ropes; he wasn't quite quick enough from the recent knock-down to recover and Peekay planted three beautiful punches under his heart. Gideon went down again, this time taking the full eight count before he stood up. The bell went as the two boxers moved towards each other.

The ninth round showed the superb boxer Mandoma was. He came out on the attack and hit Peekay with a beautiful right cross, slamming into the side of the jaw. Peekay crashed to the canvas. At four Peekay hadn't moved and by seven he had only just managed to get to his knees. Peekay could only barely hear the referee counting and he felt himself slipping down the silver tunnel. At nine he was on his legs but plainly shaky. The ref examined him and allowed the fight to continue. Mandoma came in fast for the kill and Peekay managed to tie him up. But not for long; as the ref called for them to break, Mandoma pushed him away and hit him to the head with a good left-right combination. Peekay went down again. He was up at nine, but he knew he couldn't take very much more. *Dance klein baas, dance; when you dance they don't think you hurt.* It was Geel Piet's voice coming to him as a child.

Peekay didn't know where it came from. His legs felt like lead but he was on his toes, allowing his legs to do the thinking, years of training making them work instinctively. Gideon was trying too hard, trying to finish the fight. With twenty seconds to go he drew back on his right a little too far to follow a good left jab and Peekay, seeing the opening, hit him with a perfect right hand, smashing into his chin. Mandoma hit the floor so hard he actually bounced. He was up at nine and hung on grimly for the remaining few seconds before the bell went. Both fighters were exhausted. They'd fought each other to a standstill. Both sat in their corners knowing that they'd spent it all, that there were no more tricks. From now it was heart; there was nothing else to give.

Some people claimed that both fights against Jack 'Spoonbill' Jackson were Peekay's greatest, but there were others who were adamant that the last five rounds of the Mandoma versus Peekay title was the all-time great.

It proved to be one of the toughest fights ever witnessed in South Africa. Both men were exhausted, but they came out for the tenth. They started to fight toe to toe, too tired to move about the ring. Both went down during the round and got up and fought again. The fight had evened up, with perhaps Peekay just ahead on points.

There were those in the audience who'd seen Peekay's comeback against Jackson and who said to themselves that Mandoma couldn't withstand the courage of the white boxer, that he'd go before Peekay. But they reached round fourteen and Mandoma had been down seven times and Peekay six. They were still standing in the centre of the ring trading punches.

The crowd was hysterical. Something had to give. Each time one of the boxers went down there was a huge sigh, as though the crowd was sure it was the end; then there was a roar as the fighter got to his feet. Peekay had broken Mandoma's nose and closed one of his eyes, though Dutch had kept it working well enough for him to keep fifty per cent of his sight. Solly was not as skilled, and Peekay's right eye was completely closed.

Early in round fourteen Peekay put Mandoma down again with a left and felt a sharp pain in his hand. Mandoma got to his feet and Peekay tried to put another good one home but his left hand was hurting like hell every time he used it. Mandoma was gone, he was simply hanging on. Peekay was forced to lead with the right and Mandoma managed to survive, to keep his opponent's gloves away from his heart, for he knew that one more good punch under the heart and he was history. Peekay as usual had judged the fight to perfection; he was going to take him out in the final round. Towards the end of the fourteenth, Peekay landed another hard left and gasped as the pain shot up through his arm into his shoulder. His arm fell to his side and Mandoma hit him with a right just as the bell went.

Peekay was too exhausted to speak as Solly and Hymie worked on him. 'You just have to get through the round, you're ahead on points, just keep him off this last round, Peekay,' Hymie said, working on his shoulders.

'That's the ticket, my son, you don't have to put him down, just stay away,' Solly echoed.

'It's Jackson all over again,' Peekay gasped at last. 'I've broken my hand again.'

'Oh, Jesus, no!' Hymie gasped. 'Are you sure?'

'You've got the skill, just run, run from him,' Solly cried.

'I haven't got the legs, Solly.'

Peekay came out as a southpaw. It wasn't a surprise to Mandoma, they'd worked it too often sparring, but Gideon wondered why. He was so exhausted that it was all he could do to try to find the punch he'd need to take Peekay out. Time was running out. Halfway through the final round, Peekay put Mandoma down again with a good right hand, but there wasn't enough power in it to keep him on the floor. The Zulu had Peekay in the corner leaning on him when he heard Dutch shout, 'His hand, his left hand is broke!' Gideon came out of the clinch, moving back to the centre of the ring. Peekay's hand was broken; he couldn't hit him with a left. Peekay's left was the only hand that could put him down; he was safe. All he had to do was find the last punch. Peekay moved up to him and Gideon went onto the back foot, allowing Peekay to push him onto the ropes.

With thirty seconds to go in the fight, Peekay had Gideon on the ropes. He just had to hang on. The referee called for them to break and Peekay hung on. 'Break!' he heard the referee shout. He hung on a little longer. 'Break!' the command came again. The seconds were ticking by. Peekay stepped back but managed to drive a right under the black man's heart, then moved away. The black man's right upper-cut came from nowhere. Peekay didn't even see it coming. It connected flush to the champion's jaw and Peekay dropped like a stone to the canvas.

Gideon Mandoma moved two tottering steps to a neutral corner, barely able to stand. The final right hand from Peekay to the heart was catching up with him and he was blacking out in flashes. He held desperately onto the ropes, supporting himself, trying to stop his knees from collapsing under him. At the count of ten and as the crowd went wild Gideon tried to raise his glove, but releasing the rope was all it needed and his knees collapsed from under him. He pitched forward, face first onto the canvas. Both men lay unconscious but it was Gideon Mandoma who was the new Welterweight Champion of the World.

Still today there are white people and black who were present at the fight who argue that Peekay threw the fight, that he wanted Gideon Mandoma to be the next Welterweight Champion of the World. But it wasn't true. The young Zulu chief had just one more punch left in him and Peekay simply hadn't seen it coming.

The result of the fight should have settled the matter of leadership. Gideon was now champion of the world and the mantle of *Onoshobishobi Ingelosi*, the mystical leader of the black people, was expected to fall on him. It was what Mr Nguni wanted and had been careful to spread around before the fight. Initially it seemed that the people had accepted the new leader.

White South Africans love to think of Africans as predictable and simple-minded, though nothing could be further from the truth. The mantle which mystically befell the white boy as a leader of great importance was not lightly given away. A convocation of five of the country's most powerful witchdoctors, one each from all the major tribes, met in Moroka township to discuss the matter. These *abaNgoma* were not only men of the dead spirits, they were also astute elders of their tribes, and it did not escape them that Gideon Mandoma was a Zulu, the tribe which had successfully conquered all the other tribes excepting the Xhosa.

In the matter of tribes it was always the Zulus who differed in opinion or who thrust their point of view to the front. The fact that a white boy had been chosen to lead was so remarkable as to be beyond their doing and even beyond their magic, for none of them would have willingly brought such a thing about. On the other hand, assuming that the leadership was now taken from the white and returned to the black, this was not a decision to be made in haste. Many pots of beer would need to be consumed and much looking into the entrails of freshly slaughtered animals and throwing of bones and reading of the smoke and re-telling and examining of the ancient prophecies and legends must take place first.

The elders met during the day on a soccer field. It was more a patch of bare earth with two rickety posts at either end, but it was large enough for the people to come and sit as the old men discussed the way of this thing between the white *Onoshobishobi Ingelosi* and the young Zulu chief, Mandoma.

Finally, after many days they signalled that they were ready to give the verdict. A feast was prepared for that night and Mr Nguni supplied three oxen to be roasted. Thirty male members of each of the tribes were invited to be present at the feast, to carry the decision back to the people. The feast again took place on the dusty soccer field under the stars, although the soft coal the people burn in the townships creates a haze that blots out the sky and cancels the stars nightly. The five old men sat on *indaba* mats covered with jackal-skin karosses around a fire built in the centre of the field. In a semicircle around them sat the tribal representatives and behind the old men, roasting on three great wooden spits over beds of glowing coals, were the three oxen. The smell of the slowly roasting meat filled the night air.

One by one the old men rose to speak. They spoke of the beginning of the mystery; of how a small white boy had brought comfort to the prisoners in the country's most notorious prison, how he had made tobacco appear where there had been no tobacco before and how the words of the prisoners had flown through him to their kraals to bring comfort to their women and children; how on one great night he had brought all the tribes together and blended them by taking their tribal songs and making one great song of the people; and then he had made the stars fall from the sky. Finally they told of how he had fought the *amaBhunu*, the Boers in the ring, and had never lost to them. Not once. Now he was fighting for the black man, Tom Majombi, who was dead, but the white one was fighting the Boers for his shadow so that he might rest peacefully with his ancestors' spirits. Is this not the sign of a great mystical leader of great courage? He who will fight to restore the spirit of a dead man to him? These were surely the signs of greatness which cannot be lightly exorcised from the *Onoshobishobi Ingelosi*.

Mr Nguni, fortified with half a bottle of brandy, stood up and asked to speak. He was taking a tremendous chance, but his generous gift of the oxen and a constant supply of kaffir beer all week made him feel entitled to talk and gave him the confidence to do so. 'Was it not spoken once that the conquest by Mandoma of the *Onoshobishobi Ingelosi* was to be the principal sign that the power had passed over? Was it not true that the first time when the sangoma declared they must fight to see if the white one still has the power, they did so in Sophiatown and the *Onoshobishobi Ingelosi* defeated Mandoma in front of the people and so the greatness was still in him? Now again, they have fought and this time it is Mandoma who has won. This he has done again in front of the people. Does this not mean that the shadows and the spirits have spoken differently this time?' Mr Nguni sat down, satisfied he'd said enough, noting from the nods and 'hayas' emanating from the audience that most of them agreed with him.

There was a long silence from the old men until at last the great Swazi medicine man and high witchdoctor Somojo, who took his name from a witchdoctor who belonged to the great legend which began across the Zambesi when time was pale grey and not yet black with the age of things, spoke. Among the assembled doctors he was the most powerful. His peppercorn skull was white and the whites of his eyes were tobacco brown, bloodshot at the edges and watered with age. 'Was it not true that the fight was even, as of two well-matched warriors?' he asked.

'Haya! It is true,' the crowd answered.

'Was it not true that towards the end the *Onoshobishobi Ingelosi* was beginning to win?'

'It is as you say!'

'Was it not true that the Zulu Mandoma unleashed a mighty blow which brought his opponent crashing to the ground where he lay *ukungezwa*, unable to get up?'

'Yes! Everything you say, great one, it is so, he was unconscious!'

'Was it not true that when the *Onoshobishobi Ingelosi* lay, a count of ten was made?' The old witchdoctor crouched suddenly, his long neck pushed forward like an ancient tortoise as he turned slowly to look at them all, his shrill voice counting to ten on his fingers. Then, shooting both hands above his head, his fingers splayed, he cried, 'Suddenly at the count of ten the Zulu Mandoma was struck by a blow unseen and fell to the ground and lay *ukungezwa* beside the *Onoshobishobi Ingelosi*?'

'Oh, oh, oh!' the crowd moaned their amazement. 'He was struck and he fell forward. It is as you say!'

The old man looked around him, his rheumy eyes taking them all in and finally coming to rest on Mr Nguni. 'I ask you this then. Who was he that struck the last blow?'

A gasp of astonishment passed over the crowd. The shadows which guarded over the *Onoshobishobi Ingelosi* were so powerful that they could strike his opponent to the ground even when he himself was unconscious.

'The *Onoshobishobi Ingelosi*, he struck the last blow!' the crowd shouted. 'He is still *the one*!'

'It is the rule that at the count of ten the fight is over, he who is standing is the winner!' Mr Nguni shouted angrily, emboldened by the brandy.

There was a shocked silence as the crowd turned to look at him. Nguni towered over the diminutive witchdoctor. He was also a man of power who had many cattle and was said to have great wealth; he was also a chief, but to speak to the great Somojo in such a manner was inviting disaster.

'This rule? It is a white man's rule,' the old man spat.

Mr Nguni knew immediately that he was trapped. He had swallowed the gourd of quick anger and now was being made to vomit its contents up again. 'Yes, it is a white man's rule,' he said ruefully.

The old man stabbed his finger accusingly at Mr Nguni. 'Ho! In this black man's heart there rests a white man's rules?'

There was silence from the crowd as the old man waited for Mr Nguni to speak. Finally the huge Zulu looked up. 'It is not a rule in my heart,' he said slowly.

The old man raised his fly switch, his voice a shrill warning, 'Who wishes to challenge "the power" of the *Onoshobishobi Ingelosi*? Who would have us pass "the power" on to the Zulu chief, Mandoma?' The old man glared at the crowd, waiting to see if anyone would respond.

'We have read this in the smoke and in the throwing of the bones. It is also in the entrails as it was told in the great legends.' He looked at Mr Nguni. 'He who would change this will be struck dead by the same unseen hand that struck Zulu Mandoma at the counting of ten.' He directed a toothless grin at Mr Nguni. 'That is the black man's rule!'

'Haya! Haya!' the crowd exclaimed, shaking their heads in fear and wonderment.

The old man was a high witchdoctor, the highest of the high, who had taken the leopardskin and the jackal kaross of the greatest of them all, the ancient and venerable Inkosi-Inkosikazi. But more than this; on his deathbed the great medicine man had passed the gold coin of ancestry to Somojo the Swazi. The title of high witchdoctor is not a capricious decision, it comes to him who is the most worthy and it is decided by the ancient coin of gold about his neck.

Somojo began slowly walking up and down in front of the *indaba* mats and glaring at the assembled men. 'There is more to this matter than the business of the fight, which is merely an affair between young men of equal valour.' The old man's arthritic, simian claw reached into the leopardskin cloak and withdrew a leather bag which hung about his neck. His hands trembled as he withdrew a small gold coin not much larger than a blazer button. He displayed the ancient, slightly misshapen coin in his open palm. With an excited murmur the crowd surged forward, compulsively drawn to the tiny gold object. The old man's fingers snapped over the coin and the crowd drew back as though rebuked. 'This is the coin of the *strange ones* from that time; this is the magic coin of the high witchdoctor which speaks only the truth for those who hold its power in their hands. About this coin there is a legend that dips its ancient hands deep into the corn basket of time, each grain of corn a year, until two thousand grains have run through the dark fingers of time.

'At this time there came to the land of the Zambesi huge canoes with oars that stuck from their bellies like the skeletons of a great fish and from the centre of these grew large poles, higher than the centrepole of the king's great *indaba* hut, and from the poles hung great white karosses to catch the wind. From the belly of the great canoe a hundred times the size of even the biggest war canoe came the *strange ones.* Their skin was pink and their eyes were the colour of the sky and their hair was long and fell to their shoulders, some as pale as flax and others like the gold of ripe corn and yet others with hair as red as the deeper glow of breath on embers. Some wore beards while others were smooth faced, but on their arms and legs grew the same fine thick hair which shone in the sun.

'Upon their heads they wore close-fitting helmets of metal of a kind unseen before, the tops of which were shaped like the beak of the hornbill, pointing both front and back, with plumes of hair and sometimes feathers. Over their torsos they wore scales of metal rings extending to a metal flap which hung like a small apron over their private parts and which jingled as they walked so that it was always known when they were coming. Under this flap of metal their hips were girded with a skirt of cloth or soft leather and on their feet they wore leggings to their knees, these extending down to form sandals of strong, thick leather. Strapped from a broad leather belt which further protected their intestines hung a sword of a metal never seen before, harder and sharper and stronger than any stone or copper, and sharper than shaved hippo bone or flinted rock. About their wrists they wore bracelets of tooled leather studded with shining metal studs to ward off the blows of knopkieries and each carried a mighty axe of the same metal as the sword, shaped like a slice of a melon with the haft set into two metal shafts set into the concave side of the axe. The blade of this great head-chopping instrument was sharper than a young lion's teeth.

'These strange pink creatures came with their women and children and they subdued the black tribes and took slaves and some left in their ships and returned again and again, each time taking slaves and bringing others of their kind back with them when they returned, until they made a great empire. With the black people as their slaves they dug deep into the earth for copper and iron,' the old witchdoctor opened his hand to show the coin, 'and the precious yellow metal which they prized above all else.'

A low moan escaped from the crowd, like the dry crackle of a man's dying breath. They all knew of the white man's greed for gold and the tyranny the precious metal had brought them all.

Somojo the high witchdoctor stopped pacing and hopped from one leg to another as though the ground beneath his feet was hot and he could only bear to stand for so long on one spot. 'The empire of the *strange ones* who came and lived as rulers became known as the *Ma-iti* though it was commonly known that they called themselves the "Children of the Star". They claimed to have descended from a star that fell to earth and took a young woman of the *strange ones*, mated with her and had many sons of a great fierceness who spread across the earth. The shining blueness of their eyes was the light of the stars burning through a daylight sky and it was this which gave them power over all the dark-eyed people of the world.'

A man drew closer to the fire carrying fresh logs and a bundle of branch twigs. He moved forward stooped as though trying not to intrude into the ambient circle of witchdoctors. He hurriedly placed fresh logs onto the embers and then threw the armful of branch twigs atop the fire, brought from who knows where, because there are no trees in Moroka township. The fire snapped and crackled as the twigs flared in short fierce blazes of yellow flame, snatching at the smallest twigs at the tributaries of each branch then, as suddenly, dying away, a twist of white smoke where a moment before the flame had been. Beneath the brief pyrotechnics of dry branch and twig the embers licked slow tongues of flame over the surfaces of the new logs, slowly wrapping them into themselves, turning the mute wood into heat and flame and life.

'Like all things based on murder, oppression and theft the empire of the *strange ones* fell into corruption. Their great empire was drifting on the canoe of time towards the rapids of oblivion when a slave was born among the *strange ones.* His eyes were of the bluest hue, like the clean, high winter sky, but his hair was dark and his skin the colour of tanned leather. He was the son of a black slave woman and a male from the *strange ones*, though he too was a slave, for such was the corruption and decay of the empire that they had made slaves of some of their own people who in the past had questioned their wrong ways. This child, born of the black and the white, was named Lumukanda and it was he who when he was still young rose up and brought the miserable remnants of the people together and destroyed the two empires of the *strange ones.* A child of the star led the desperate starveling tribes against the *strange ones* and he conquered them and utterly destroyed them. Then he set fire to their great cities and wiped out the marks of where they had been, like a man's foot wipes out the mark of an overnight fire in the dust of the new morning.'

The crackle of fire, as the new wood caught and grew the flames, was the only sound to be heard as the people listened to the words of Somojo the great witchdoctor. The flickering light from the fire lit his wizened monkey face as he brought the great tale to a close. 'Then Lumukanda the *strange one* gathered all the remnants of all the tribes and moved the people from the Zambesi, south to the river of the Limpopoma; and when he reached this and came to a deep gorge which led to a place to cross he called the tribes to himself. Behind him rose a great cliff and he stood with his back to the cliff and he pointed to the land across the river. "Go into these lands where the grass is sweet and make it your own; multiply and live in peace," he commanded.

'Then the witchdoctor Somojo came to him. "Great one, will you not come with us?" he asked. Lumukanda turned and pointed to the great cliff where a small waterfall fell to its side. "High on this cliff to the right of that waterfall there is a cave. I shall climb to its entrance and dwell there with the great Snake God where my spirit will remain to watch over you. If the *strange ones* should return with their blue eyes and their hair the colour of ripe corn and they would take you into slavery, I will come down from the cave and return to all the tribes and I will deliver you from their bondage and the tyranny of their greed." Then Lumukanda placed a gold coin into the hand of Somojo. "This is the coin of your ancestry and the sign that I, the child of the star, will come when I am needed," he said.'

The high witchdoctor paused, waiting for the weight of the words of the great legend to be felt upon the bent backs of the hushed crowd seated around the witchdoctors on the soccer ground. Then slowly he pointed to the night sky and in a shrill, high voice asked, 'Did not the stars fall from the heavens when the *Onoshobishobi Ingelosi* brought the tribes together for the singing of the great song of Africa?'

There was a gasp from the crowd as they finally comprehended what the old man was saying. Many of the men grabbed handfuls of dust and wiped it on their foreheads; others rocked on their haunches at the awesomeness of the prophecy. Somojo the great Swazi witchdoctor folded his spindly legs down slowly to sit on the jackal-skin kaross under a sky where the heavens were shrouded by the smoke of the township fires and the night smelt of roasting meat and the slightly sour odour of fermenting kaffir beer.

Mr Nguni didn't remain behind for the feast, he was fiercely disappointed at the outcome. 'The fly-blown old fart in his tattered leopardskin cloak has ruined everything!' he thought bitterly. His immediate plans were in disarray; had Gideon been given 'the power' then he, Nguni, the one who controlled him, would have seen his own power and prestige spread throughout the land.

But Mr Nguni knew better than to try to change things or, from this point on, ever to openly oppose Peekay. By morning the whole country would know of the decision to retain the white *Onoshobishobi Ingelosi* and there would be no way he could confound it. His mouth was dry with the coppery taste of defeat on his tongue. Somojo the great witchdoctor, the old Swazi pimp, had openly rebuked him and made him eat the meal of humiliation in front of all the tribes.

But Mr Nguni was also an African. In his head he might well reject the old man's silly warnings, but he felt the expensive brandy in his stomach turn sour and in his heart he trembled mightily. He would have to step on the surface of this problem with great care, or he would sink into oblivion.

THIRTY-TWO

Red, despite its quickly earned reputation, remained small and for the first two years comprised Hymie and Peekay and two other people: first, a law clerk named Mr Bottomley-Tuck who was in his fifties and was an alcoholic who would sip quietly from a small silver hip flask of brandy (constantly refilled) all day so that by five in the evening when he went home to a bleak flat and an ageing mother in Rosebank he was generally half shickered. But he knew his torts and his way around the Johannesburg courts better than anyone in South Africa and was indispensable to both young men. The second was the general dogsbody, Chronic Martha who later, when they'd grown big enough to need one, ran the switchboard. Martha too was a good worker, though she suffered from chronic hayfever and seemed always to be on the verge of catching a cold which never quite arrived. She was rather fat and wore glasses and thought Mr Bottomley-Tuck was a disgusting old man because he suffered from mouth ulcers and would sometimes take his false teeth out and stand them in a glass on his desk. He'd sometimes forget them when he went home and Chronic Martha, whose final job each night was to tidy the offices, would come across them, 'All pink and white and yukky, like they alive in the glass and if a person put their finger in they'd bite you!'

After two years, when both Hymie and Peekay were snowed down with work, they advertised for a junior partner and a law clerk, the clerk to be trained in law. To both Peekay and Hymie's surprise Gideon begged for the clerk's job. It seemed insane; he had already defended his world title some four times and was, by African standards anyway, extremely well off. The job of law clerk under Bottomley-Tuck promised to begin by being a glorified messenger boy. But he proved to them that he wanted the job and they gave it to him, though not expecting it to last. Because Red was increasingly known as a law firm that represented the non-European element in criminal jurisprudence they expected very little response for the junior partnership. It wasn't a fashionable position and in career terms promised to be a disaster. They were amazed at the response from young barristers and lawyers from all over the country. Peekay and Hymie spent almost three weeks processing the candidates, reducing the one hundred and fifty replies to twenty which they gave to Bottomley-Tuck to interview. He narrowed these down to the finalists. He'd selected only four.

Tandia, who hadn't come through the back door but had applied in the normal way, was one of them. As Bottomley-Tuck had no idea who she was and was a confirmed bachelor Hymie and Peekay were forced to take her application seriously, though they both felt inclined to treat her candidature warily. Peekay left the final interview to Hymie, aware that from the first day he'd met her he was stricken.

This fact alone made Hymie reluctant to take the initial interview any further. However, he couldn't ignore her results with Bottomley-Tuck and the fact that she'd won the university medal as the top law graduate with the third highest marks ever obtained for jurisprudence.

Tandia had been driven up from Durban by Juicey Fruit Mambo for the interview and had stayed with Madam Flame Flo who had recently moved from Meadowlands to the town of Vereeniging.

Tandia badly wanted to work with Red. When Gideon had been employed as a law clerk she'd been shattered, realising that it was unlikely they'd employ her as well. When called up for an initial interview she'd been ecstatic, but soon came down when confronted only by a somewhat inebriated Mr Bottomley-Tuck. On the trip home she'd cried several times, convinced that Peekay and Hymie weren't interested and had fobbed her off with the funny little man who was half cut, but who nevertheless had given her a torrid interview after she'd completed the written paper. Nothing Juicey Fruit Mambo could say cheered her up and she'd immediately applied for a position with the Durban Urban Planning Authority.

When a month later a letter had arrived from Hymie saying that of the one hundred and fifty people who'd originally applied she was one of four to be selected for a final interview, she could hardly believe her luck. Immediately she began to see the problems, however. She was a woman. A coloured. Gideon's friend. She had to move. She wouldn't be in a position to buy into the practice. She was too inexperienced. All of these things she discussed endlessly with Juicey Fruit Mambo on the trip up to Johannesburg.

Juicey Fruit would listen as though considering every point carefully and then he'd declare his verdict. You are number one, Missy Tandy, they no say no to you. He said this with such conviction that he gave Tandia enough courage for at least thirty miles until the next doubt grew from a dear blue sky like cumulus cloud and Juicey Fruit Mambo was thrown into another bout of deep and meaningful listening.

But what Hymie saw was a young and beautiful woman immaculately – if somewhat cheaply – dressed, who appeared confident and assured.

'Tandia, I want you to understand that our previous knowledge of you in any capacity doesn't count *for* you, Hymie grinned. 'It may even count *against* you, though I hope not. Let me ask you the first obvious question. Why do you want this position?'

'Because I need a job,' Tandia answered simply.

The reply bowled Hymie over. Each of the other three candidates had gone into a long explanation involving politics, the law and their need to do something to expunge their guilt. Hymie had mentally sat back waiting for the well-turned phrases and the conscience-stricken reasons to pour out. Now he laughed. 'That is perhaps the best answer I've had to that question. Do you mind if I probe a bit?'

Tandia smiled, her brilliant green eyes coming alive. She really was a devastatingly beautiful woman and Hymie saw how, if her brains matched her looks, she could be a terrible thorn in the side of the racist law profession. He grinned to himself; in haute couture clothes, hair properly styled, speech pattern modified somewhat to a more cultured accent, Tandia Patel would be dynamite, something to throw at the smug and pompous white legal profession. 'Why did you become a lawyer, Tandia?' Hymie now asked.

Tandia looked at Hymie directly. 'Because I was clever and because I know how to hate.'

In two replies Hymie had been totally surprised. The woman in front of him wasn't that much younger than him and Peekay and she was playing for real. She was either totally ingenuous or very clever, and Hymie was quite sure it was the latter. 'The law is not about sides, Tandia. It is above your personal politics. You will need to see it that way.'

Though the interview lasted an hour Tandia's reply to this was what got her the job: 'When it is in South Africa, then I will,' she said simply.

Tandia Patel was hired as the new junior partner in Levy, Peekay & Partners. As Hymie put it to Peekay, 'I had no choice, it was no contest. She sees with a perfectly clear pair of eyes. We simply have to have her, she's tougher than both of us put together.'

On 7 March 1960, almost exactly three years after Magistrate Coetzee had concluded that Peekay had a prima-facie case against Colonel Klaasens and Lieutenant Geldenhuis for the abduction and murder of Tom Majombi, the last of three verdicts was handed down by Mr Justice Petzer of the Court of Criminal Appeal.

In an editorial the day following the court decision, the *Cape Argus* summed up the general feeling amongst the black people and also the fair-minded element of the white South African public by writing:

> *Over a period of three years we have witnessed two police officers, Lieutenant Geldenhuis and Colonel Klaasens, receive a trial by jury which resulted in a murder conviction. Since this original sentence we have seen two further trials, in which no jury sat, where murder has been reversed to manslaughter and finally manslaughter to a misdemeanour which has been further trivialised by a fine of ten pounds. Justice is not only blind in South Africa, it has also become totally deaf; finally, it is senile.*

Two days after Judge Petzer's decision Geldenhuis was returned to duty, and just twenty-four hours after returning to his post at Special Branch in

Pretoria he was transferred to the police district of Vereeniging, some thirty-five miles from Johannesburg.

The period over which the Majombi trial was conducted had not proved a happy one for Geldenhuis. He'd been placed on clerical duties away from the real action of the Special Branch and his promising career had suffered accordingly. His only consolation had been that he had access to the Red File which concerned itself with the movement of the principals of Levy & Peekay. His transfer to Vereeniging was, in effect, a censure for the young policeman who, despite his acquittal, had become too hot to handle and needed a period in the comparative wilderness to cool down.

Though nothing was ever said, his defeat by Mandoma had also affected the way his senior officers regarded him. From a potential world champion he'd become just another boxer, and one who'd made a series of unfortunate headlines over a protracted murder trial. In addition he'd suffered a second defeat, this time at the hands of Togger Brown, when he again boxed as the undercard to the world title fight between Peekay and Mandoma. In all, he'd caused too much embarrassment even for a police force which is not easily embarrassed.

The posting to Vereeniging was ideally suited for a career censure when you don't want it to look that way. To a prying media, the move could be explained as an important posting for a promising young police officer while, in truth, it amounted to several steps down the road to oblivion.

Vereeniging is an industrial satellite town on the Rand where the giant Sasol state-owned petrochemical works involved in the task of converting coal to petroleum, a technology the South African government was perfecting in the event of a future Middle East oil embargo against South Africa, is located. The government regarded the giant works as a potential terrorist target and designated the Vereeniging district as a small, though separate, Special Branch responsibility.

Despite its potential sensitivity the district had enjoyed almost total freedom from the sort of unrest which was becoming commonplace in African townships. The job prospects for Africans in the area were good, not only at the refinery, but also in the light industry which had developed in the district. The large model township which housed the black workers was noted for its law-abiding black people. In fact, it was this very reputation for quietness which caused Madam Flame Flo to move to the township. After the mass government eviction from Sophiatown she'd moved to Meadowlands, but when her daughter's white husband got a job at the Sasol refinery in Vereeniging, she saw the move as an opportunity to be closer to her at last. She and Mama Tequila still planned to set up business in Swaziland, so Vereeniging was a temporary move for Madam Flame Flo. Nevertheless she built a nice house in the African township with two spare bedrooms, one for Mama Tequila which contained a king-size Ebenezer Snoozer inner-spring mattress spread over two divan bases. The bedroom also sported its own bathroom with a shower, an essential requirement, as Mama Tequila was too large to get in and out of a bathtub on her own.

From this neat cottage, with its eight-foot corrugated-iron fence surrounding the back yard, Madam Flame Flo ran a quiet little shebeen which opened only during the day for the more serious drinkers. This dalliance with her old lifestyle was more to stay out of mischief and as an opportunity to fraternise with the locals than to make any serious money. It proved to be the perfect set-up; the shebeen provided good liquor but no gramophone music or dancing so the good-time girls, who usually slept during the daylight hours, stayed away. Madam Flame Flo had given up brewing the dreaded Flame which attracted far too much trouble. With smuggled bottle-store liquor the shebeen practically ran itself and allowed her plenty of time to visit her daughter and her two grandchildren, which she did twice each week by posing as the coloured lady who came in to do the sewing and the heavy cleaning.

At the time of the Geldenhuis transfer Mama Tequila was up from Durban visiting her sister. She was unaware of the proximity of the police lieutenant or she would almost certainly have mentioned his presence to her sister, warning her to stay away from him. Madam Flame Flo was already, of course, aware of Geldenhuis from the murder trial which she herself had set in train more than three years previously.

Geldenhuis was no fool and saw the move to Vereeniging for what it was. Outwardly he'd recovered from his extreme angst and inwardly from the almost suicidal frustration which had culminated in his vomiting fit and collapse in the toilet. But his bitterness against Peekay consumed him. He was famous for being able to keep his feelings under control but now his rage was always near the surface and he would lash out at the slightest provocation.

In his tunic pocket Geldenhuis kept a single gold-plated pistol bullet with the nose suitably filed into a dum-dum configuration and when his inner anxiety grew too unbearable he would finger the bullet, reminding himself that it was reserved for his mortal enemy, that sooner or later the time must come when he held Peekay squarely in the sights of his police revolver.

In his imagination they would be alone and he would make Peekay go down on his knees and beg for his life. They would make a deal and he would insist that Peekay fight him, properly in a ring, and he would fight Peekay until he'd knocked him unconscious. Then Peekay would recover and the place would be in darkness and he'd stand up in the boxing ring as the lights went on. Standing in the ring would be a huge, ugly, syphilitic black whore in the nude. He would force Peekay to undress and then he would hold the gun to the back of his head and make him go down on the mountain of black kaffir flesh. When he was down there with his head in the hair and the stink of her thighs he would pull the trigger, blowing away the back of his enemy's head with the gold dum-dum bullet.

The spectre of the grotesquely naked black whore was buried deep in his subconscious. It was a major part of his hate for the blacks and his fanatical response to the traditional Afrikaner call of *bloed gevaar*, blood danger. It would surface when he fantasised about the gold bullet and the demise of Peekay. He was careful not to dwell on the manner of Peekay's death, allowing himself the fantasy only in extreme frustration, for the memory which seemed to live in tandem with the fantasy, so that the one always conjured up the other, was too painful for him to bear.

He was six years old, in the back of his father's butcher shop in Doornfontein. He'd sneaked into the cold-storage room where the hindquarters and dressed sides of beef were hung from great hooks attached to wheels on three separate rails which ran along the ceiling. It was forbidden territory but he found the temptation irresistible. He'd walk out of the blazing sun and suddenly find himself in a cool, dark world. On Tuesdays in particular, when the beef and the dressed mutton and the creamy pink porkers arrived from the abattoir, the cool room would be full to bursting with the smaller carcasses of lamb and pig and calf. The huge sides of beef would be stacked, one on top of the other, on the floor against the wall on the furthermost side from the door, where they would remain until there was sufficient room to hoist them onto hooks. Jannie used to love to climb to the top of these stacked sides of beef and lie across the top, his cheek placed against the cool, soft flesh.

The insulated door was too heavy for him to open on his own and he'd wait for one of the butcher's lads to open it and, when they were busy hoisting or slicing from a carcass, he'd slip in and hide, waiting for the moment when they'd depart, switching off the light as they left and leaving him in the cool, dark, secret place. Later, when someone returned, he'd quietly slip out again. Occasionally he'd be caught and receive a severe thrashing from his angry father.

Jannie's father was a large, irascible and impatient man who was disappointed at his small-boned eldest son, blaming his tiny, long suffering, slightly dark-skinned wife for his undersized offspring. When he'd had a few drinks, which was often enough, he'd refer to her in the family as the 'bushman'. Indeed, to race-obsessed eyes in constant search for tainted blood, she appeared to have a touch of the tar brush which had become more pronounced as she bore him four children, each of them sapping her vitality and leaving the prettiness of youth behind her while etching the distinctive features of her ancestors more sharply on her careworn face. Jannie's blond hair and pale blue eyes, inherited from his father, was all that saved him from his father's ultimate wrath. At least the dwarf looks like a proper Boer, his father would say when he was drunk.

One hot Monday afternoon when he'd slipped unnoticed into the cold room and was lying on the long, cool slabs of beef the door slid open and the light went on. He only just had sufficient time to scramble down from the stack of beef and hide elsewhere when he heard his father's gruff voice and the higher-pitched giggle of a woman. From where he hid Jannie could just see what was going on. To his surprise the woman with his father was black, a young black woman with large buttocks which wobbled as she walked. Without undue ceremony the woman walked over to the stack of beef and straddled the carcasses, her huge bottom facing towards his father. Jannie watched as his father removed his butchers belt and apron and then unbuckled his real belt and let his trousers fall to his ankles. He was amazed at the enormity of his father's engine as it stiffened. He'd had his own tiny version do the same thing often enough, but he'd never imagined it could possibly grow so huge or look so dangerous and ugly. His father pulled the skirt of the woman's dress up over her back and unceremoniously mounted her, pushing and grunting. The black woman made no noise of her own, her huge bottom moving only to accommodate the thrusts of the white man who grunted and farted once, calling her filthy names, his thick fingers kneading into the flesh of her huge black bottom. Finally, urgently, with a loud groan he became suddenly possessed and then as quickly came down to panting silence as though he was suddenly exhausted; his hands were still, no longer kneading the woman's purple flesh.

Jannie watched as his father dismounted and used his apron to wipe himself before he pulled up his trousers and buckled on his heavy leather butcher's belt and knife sporran which contained a slicing and boning knife.

To Jannie's dismay his father turned and walked directly towards where he hid, crouched between two dressed sheep carcasses and directly behind a large pig, the pig's pink snout only inches from his own nose. Jannie's father stopped and, removing the larger of the two knives from his belt, he cut quickly around the neck of the pig until its head was attached to its pink body only by the spinal cord. With a grunt the huge man snapped the spine where the neck met the skull and neatly severed it with the boning knife, removing it from the carcass. The head came away in his hands to reveal Jannie's frightened face staring up at him.

The butcher gave no sign of recognising his son. Indeed, for a few moments, as he walked away with the pig's head held by its purple-pink ears, Jannie believed his father hadn't seen him, that the unexpected image of his son crouched behind the pig's carcass somehow hadn't registered. He remained crouched where he was, too frightened to move. 'Here, take this, kaffir!' he heard his father say, then add, 'Go out the back, come back next week same time!'

Then the woman's timid voice. '*Dankie, baas.*'

The small boy's terror rose as he heard his father's footsteps which finally came to a halt directly in front of him. The butcher wore black workman's boots and their caps were dirty with grease, to which bits of sawdust clung. Jannie saw a small piece of meat, a piece of white and pink spotted mince, caught in between the shoelaces of the left boot. Then the headless pig's carcass was pushed aside and his father's hand shot out, grabbing him by his hair, yanking him to his feet.

Jannie was too terrified even to scream, though the pain was horrific. His father released his grip on his hair and grabbing him by his shirt front he hoisted him into the air. Holding him with one hand aloft he hooked the back of his shirt into the hook from which the headless pig already hung. Then he eased Jannie down so that his small body was completely encased by the carcass of the pig.

His father had yet to say a word and Jannie was too frightened to scream. The big man drew the boning knife from its leather apron holster and sliced into the pig's thighs on either side of the boy's throat. 'Just like a Jew can't eat pork, so a Boer can't have a kaffir woman, that's why a kaffir is so *lekker.* Your papa likes to be nice to kaffir women. When you grow up you will see, you will too! You saw nothing, boy, you hear?' He ran the back of the blade across the small boy's throat.

The butcher returned two hours later, when Jannie was blue. His teeth were chattering and he was beginning to pass out from the cold. He removed his six-year-old son from the hook and left him in the sun in the yard at the back of the butcher shop to thaw out.

It was the visual metaphor conjured up in his head immediately after he'd pulled the imaginary trigger to blow Peekay apart that sometimes compensated Geldenhuis for his own nightmare. In his sick mind he would savour the scene that followed in his imagination. He could see the homicide squad arriving. After surveying the scene they might even suspect it was him, but as he'd killed the black whore as well, there would be no clues. He'd ordered the gold-plated, .45-calibre bullet from an American mail-order company in Jacksonville Alabama nearly three years ago and he'd never shown the bullet with its filed nose to anyone, preferring it to lie warm to the touch and secret in his pocket where he could reach down and finger it. The boys in the murder squad would look down at the blown away white man's head between the black whore's thighs and smile, and one of them would be sure to smirk and make the obvious crack. Forever afterwards people would talk about Peekay the rooinek lawyer . . . *whose brains were wasted on useless black cunts.*

Jannie Geldenhuis found himself head of the Vereeniging Special Branch in charge of nothing in particular. Although there was a great amount of unrest in other parts of South Africa over the government's infamous 'endorsing out' laws, Vereeniging's model African township was quiet as always.

As a member of the Special Branch Geldenhuis wasn't involved in regular police duties, his brief being essentially political, concerned with demonstrations, sabotage and anti-government activity.

The murder trial had knocked him about severely and he would have been almost happy to be away from the spotlight had, for instance, someone else rather than Peekay been involved in his prosecution. What ate at him was not the original conviction for murder, but the fact that his trial and the publicity it had caused had allowed Peekay to rise to prominence as a brilliant young barrister while, at the same time, leading to his own ignominious demise. Added to this, the new posting had removed him from daily contact with the Red File and the long-planned revenge the meticulously researched details within it represented for him.

From the inception of the law partnership Geldenhuis had been keeping tabs on the daily movements of Levy & Peekay. The two young barristers were under constant surveillance and for the past year this had also involved Gideon Mandoma who'd joined as an articled clerk. Mandoma and also the coloured whore, Tandia Patel, who'd graduated from law school in Durban to join Red as a junior, already had secret police files of their own which were as carefully annotated and updated as those of Peekay and Hymie. Hymie was proving the most difficult to keep tabs on; he was involved more in the world of business and finance which was by its very nature secretive; also, he seemed to exercise a natural caution which often made his movements hard to follow.

Peekay was different. His work was in the courts and he seemed to attract publicity without necessarily seeking it. The cases he took on were often considered hopeless and his clients unlikely to be able to pay, although Hymie would see to it that the firm always had one big corporate litigation case going. 'Peekay, you've got to help finance our legal charity work with a bit of corporate robbery,' Hymie would tell him. Peekay proved to be as astute and tough in this area as he was in the other and, more and more, large companies involved in litigation were seeking his services.

It infuriated Geldenhuis when large corporations, some even run by Afrikaners, such as the Volkskas Bank, would retain Red. On more than one occasion, accompanied by Colonel Klaasens, he would pay a discreet visit to such a company and sometimes with good results, though often enough it was the two men's connection with the *Broederbond* which made more of an impression on the company directors than their official status as police officers.

Despite these efforts Peekay and Hymie seemed to have more legal work in the corporate sector than they could conveniently handle. Sometimes, to their enormous chagrin, the board of directors of a large company would find themselves unexpectedly facing a coloured woman who chain-smoked as she asked them rapid-fire questions and who showed a grasp of the problems involving their brief which confounded her beguiling looks, leaving most of them in open-mouthed disbelief after she'd departed.

Peekay and Hymie would wait for the inevitable phone call to come through on the day after Tandia had visited a company to report on the initial brief given to Levy & Peekay. The reaction was almost always the same. The chairman was disappointed, the company had expected a principal of Levy & Peekay to represent them.

The dialogue which followed became a familiar litany. Typical of such incidents was a phone call intended for Peekay but received instead by Hymie. The caller's name was Jordaan and he was chairman of a medium-sized mining exploration group. Jordaan, after the usual pleasantries, spoke of his disappointment at not receiving the services of a principal of Levy & Peekay.

'But Miss Patel is a principal, Mr Jordaan,' Hymie replied.

There was a pause as Jordaan absorbed this first shock. A coloured woman was a principal of a Johannesburg law practice? What the hell was he getting his company mixed up in? 'Ja, okay, but you know what we mean, Mr Levy,' he said, recovering quickly.

'You see, we have only men on the board. A woman lawyer would be awkward.' Jordaan paused then added, 'Especially with a mining company!'

'Your case, Mr Jordaan? I understand it involves a dispute with a group of cotton farmers over damming a river in a small catchment area to supply water for a bauxite mine you intend to open?'

Hymie could almost hear the sigh of relief on the other end, 'Ja, that's right, I'm glad you know the details, Mr Levy.'

'We all read the notes from the initial brief, Mr Jordaan. Your case will be heard in the Lands Court. As far as I understand, women are perfectly at liberty to represent a disputation in this court?'

'Well, ja, I suppose, but these matters are not of concern for a woman, we'd feel safer with a male lawyer, you know, well it's just that mining . . . it's a man's business,' Jordaan repeated.

'Are you suggesting that a woman's mind isn't capable of understanding how a sluice system works or how many gallons of water you require to process a ton of bauxite ore?' Hymie waited expectantly; it was around this time that the threat would come.

It came from Jordaan, right on cue. 'Mr Levy, I'm a plain man, a miner. We thought Mr Peekay was going to take the case, that's all! If this is not so and you personally also refuse to represent us, then we will make other arrangements!'

Hymie knew Jordaan as anything but a plain man and if he'd ever shovelled a spadeful of dirt it had been to plant a commemoration tree at some girls' school or outside a new corporation building. Hymie's voice was dismissive. 'Yes, of course, you must do that, Mr Jordaan, but, as I said before, it places us in a damned awkward spot.'

'I don't see that at all, my company wants to brief *you* or Mr Peekay! Not some . . . some unknown . . .'

'Kaffir girl?' Hymie interjected softly.

'No, lawyer! Some unknown lawyer! We are not racist, we just want to win our case.'

'Ah ha! that's just it, Mr Jordaan. You see, the partners have reviewed your brief as we do with all important litigation. We believe you have a difficult case, though not an impossible one to win. What you're going to need is a clear strategy, yet one which is likely to catch your opposition by surprise. Miss Patel has come up with just such a strategy. She has done her initial research and is now thoroughly familiar with your brief. We believe she is the person most suited to the successful conclusion of your case.' Hymie's tone was deliberately a little pompous, though still extremely polite. At this point he paused just a fraction longer than might be expected before continuing, 'It would be unthinkable to remove my colleague from your case. More even than this, it would be a matter of such poor legal judgement as to be reprehensible. As you put it, you want to win and so, of course, do we.'

Hymie's calming voice together with his good manners made it difficult for the managing director of the mining company to retain his aggressive manner on the phone. But Jordaan wasn't a pushover, prepared, as many others had been, to capitulate and accept Tandia onto their case.

'Nevertheless I must insist, Mr Levy,' Jordaan said stubbornly.

Hymie's voice was buttery with assurance. 'Well, if you insist, Mr Jordaan, of course we accept our dismissal as your counsel in the best legal spirit though, in parting, I hope you will agree this is not due to any legal incompetence on behalf of our female partner?'

Hymie held the receiver closer to the Nagra tape recorder winding silently beside him. 'Of course not, Mr Levy! No hard feelings, you hear? Naturally we expect to pay you for the work she has already done.'

'Thank you, Mr Jordaan, but that will not be necessary. Our initial briefing is always without charge and as the partner who did the subsequent work has proved personally, though not professionally, unsuitable to you, it would not be appropriate to send you an account for our services.'

Jordaan's voice sounded relieved that the matter was resolved. 'Thank you, Mr Levy. I hope you understand, this has not been easy for me?'

'Please! Think no more about it, Mr Jordaan. You have released Miss Patel from all obligation to your company; we owe each other nothing and you are free to engage any advocate you wish.'

'Yes, thank you, Mr Levy. I'm glad we were able to resolve this little matter without acrimony.'

'Mr Jordaan!' Hymie replied expansively, 'This is the legal profession. We don't take things personally. When Miss Patel accepts the brief to represent the group of cotton farmers against you, I know you will understand this is a perfectly professional thing for her to do?'

Of the four people who most obviously represented Red – Peekay, Hymie, Tandia and Gideon, Jannie Geldenhuis concerned himself perhaps the least with Tandia. He still had the original confession he'd forced out of her at the Cato Manor police station, admitting that she was a whore. When the time came it alone would be enough to completely discredit her. He also had the personal matter of Bluey Jay to resolve and this too he would bring to a head when the time was right. But, after Peekay, Gideon Mandoma was Geldenhuis's most constant source of concern; though once again, it wasn't the Zulu boxers well-documented and rapid rise in the ANC which concerned him most (the police informers, planted as moles within the ANC, could be relied upon to keep him informed). Rather, it was Mandoma's ambition to be something else. This aspect of Mandoma's life completely puzzled the young police lieutenant.

Gideon Mandoma was apparently seriously concerned with the job of being a law clerk with Levy & Peekay and with part-time university attendance to gain his LLB degree at Witwatersrand University.

Geldenhuis prided himself that if you stuck with an apparent conundrum long enough, eventually the riddles in a plot presented their solutions politely to you. People were predictable and if you studied them sufficiently you could discern their personal patterns. Everything has a pattern, every human being has an intellectual thumb print. 'Why?' Geldenhuis would ask himself. Why would Gideon go to work every morning when he'd successfully defended his title five times? By most white standards and by all black ones, he was filthy rich. Most boxers, even the white ones, squander their money and when they're not in training have a good time. Mandoma's actions were against everything he knew about African behaviour. Gideon had everything he needed to be powerful among his own people; he was a folk hero and he was rich. Africans saw education only as a means of achieving the kind of status Gideon already enjoyed a hundred times over.

Geldenhuis didn't believe that Africans were altruistic; history had showed that the tribes killed each other for power and material possession – cattle and land. In modern black society this had become money and influence. If Gideon already had all these things, including a rapidly growing respect in the ANC, why then would he make things hard for himself by working as a humble clerk in a law firm?

One afternoon during the second trial, Opperman, the police advocate defending them, was droning on about what constituted abduction and, in particular, abduction of a black man whom the lawyer contended might simply have walked out of Baragwanath Hospital himself: 'Because, your honour, that's what the Bantu people do all the time! They get treated and then, during the night sometime, they abscond so they don't have to pay the bill!' It was old ground and Geldenhuis had heard it all before and so he'd turned his attention to the riddle of Mandoma's involvement with Red. And then it came to him. Of course! Gideon was thinking long term. The Zulu chief was thinking way ahead to when he was much older and an African lawyer with many years of service to his people. Geldenhuis gasped inwardly at the audacity of the idea. Mandoma was preparing to be the first black prime minister of South Africa!

The idea shocked him beyond belief and later in the police car as they drove back to Pretoria he mentioned it to Colonel Klaasens. 'I think I've worked it out. Why would a world boxing champion want to be the kaffir boy who makes the tea and carries messages around the place?' He looked steadily at Klaasens. 'You want to know why? I'm telling you something for nothing. Mandoma sees himself one day as the first black prime minister of South Africa and what's more, so does Peekay and the Jew!'

Klaasens laughed but then stopped abruptly and suddenly looked serious, as though he too had come to a realisation. 'No, Jannie, you're wrong!' He paused. 'He wants to be the president! We going to be a republic pretty soon, they're all talking about it in Pretoria. Verwoerd wants the British off his back. The black bastard thinks eventually their side will win in this country and he's making early plans, he wants to be the first black president!' He paused, his finger raised dramatically. 'Not just him, that *kaffir boetie* bastard, Peekay, *he's* the one who sees himself as the fucking prime minister!'

Geldenhuis was almost bowled over by the logic of the remark. It was all the more surprising coming from Klaasens, an impulsive and therefore dangerous man, but not a deep thinker. Geldenhuis simply hadn't thought it through; the pattern fitted both men perfectly. The Zulu chief who rose to the top of the black nation and won the respect of the other tribes as a boxer and later as a lawyer; brilliant Oxford-trained advocate who'd always been the champion of the black people. In a multiracial South Africa with a white minority which, initially anyway, possessed the wealth and industrial muscle, it made almost perfect sense! Geldenhuis secretly blamed his senior officer for preparing him incorrectly for the Mandoma fight. They'd concentrated on working for Mandoma's head, believing he cut easily around the eyes, that if hit consistently they would pump up and close down. But Mandoma took everything Geldenhuis managed to throw at his head and in the end was able to see clearly enough to slam the policeman clear through the ropes. He flushed just thinking about the humiliation. He was going to nail Mandoma, but the case against the Zulu boxer would be tighter than a nun's twat. He wasn't stupid and he wasn't Klaasens. He'd do it by the book and he'd put the bastard away for ever where they could break his spirit and turn the would-be president of South Africa into a gibbering black monkey.

Jannie Geldenhuis found some consolation in the fact that in Vereeniging he'd run his own show and be away from the day-to-day contact he'd endured for almost three years with Klaasens. But he'd make sure he kept in touch with and on the right side of the big bastard. The police colonel remained his only direct access to the Red File. Geldenhuis gained a great deal of comfort from the fact that Klaasens hated Peekay almost as much as he did himself; he would happily help to put Mandoma away as well, so he'd take a special interest in the surveillance of the people involved in Red. Tandia he could handle himself. And as for the Jew? Well, he had a special surprise for him. Furthermore, Klaasens could be relied upon to respond to 'suggestions' by the more imaginative Geldenhuis when it came to tactics against their common enemy. In the end Vereeniging might not be such a backwater after all.

THIRTY-THREE

In late March, Mama Tequila had come up to the Rand to see a specialist about her gall stones and was staying with Madam Flame Flo in Vereeniging. Her stay coincided with the national campaign by the PAC for the abolition of the hated pass laws which, more than any other, made Africans prisoners on constant probation in their own country.

The campaign announced by Robert Sobukwe, the charismatic Pan African Congress leader on Friday, 18 March, was to be a strictly non-violent affair and, as he explained it, was the first step to achieving 'freedom and independence' for the black people by 1963. It involved leaving passes at home as a legitimate protest.

Tandia secretly liked the aggressive Sobukwe, despite Gideon's disapproval of the PAC. The Congress was growing rapidly as a pro-Africanist organisation made up mostly of young black radicals a lot more militant than the ANC old guard of Chief Luthuli and Professor Matthews. The PAC's 'Africa for the Africans' policy was gaining a lot of popularity among urban blacks, particularly in the Western Cape, the Eastern Province and parts of the Southern Transvaal.

As the white government came to show less and less concern for its African people so many Africans came to believe that a South Africa ruled by a black majority should have no place in it for the white man. Robert Sobukwe promised freedom and independence by 1963 and his anti-pass laws campaign was to be his first major show of strength and defiance.

Late that Friday Tandia and Peekay had returned from court and were sitting with Gideon in what passed for the boardroom at Red, a waist-high, partitioned-off area where everyone tried to get together at morning and afternoon tea. Hymie was out and the firm's messenger, Tom 'Ace' Temba, always left early on a Friday for soccer practice with his team the Moroka Swallows. Chronic Martha, now the switchboard operator, had gone home sick with laryngitis.

Tandia and Peekay had arrived to find Gideon making an awful hash of working the tiny antiquated switchboard. It was five minutes to five and Tandia decided they'd all had enough for the day so she switched the board to night switch before joining the others in the boardroom, where they now sat, sipping the strong black percolated coffee Peekay usually made and served out of large tin mugs. It was the first opportunity they'd had to discuss Sobukwe's announcement. The PAC leader had announced that the protest would begin within seventy-two hours which probably meant on Monday morning.

Tandia was excited about the event. 'It's good! I'm telling you, something's being done, at last. I only wish the initiative had come from the ANC, that's all.'

'Tandy, Robert Sobukwe's call for a non-violent campaign over passes is too early,' Peekay replied. 'The ANC is right, nobody's ready. There has yet to be a Treason Trial decision; the infrastructure isn't in place. The PAC will be lucky to get fifty thousand demonstrators out on the streets. They are going to be made to look ridiculous.'

Tandia tossed back her head, showing her impatience, her green eyes sharp. 'A revolution can afford to look ridiculous, Peekay. There are no rules, this isn't the Gentlemen-versus-Players cricket match. In the ANC book, it's always too early, too late or too something! That's the trouble with them, they're so careful they've practically disappeared from the political scene. At least Sobukwe wants action!'

Peekay blushed. Tandia was having a shot at him, the white man from Oxford trying to teach the black people how to conduct a revolution by the rules. It was true, he seemed to be always pulling her back a notch. Tandia was proving to be a very bright lawyer but not always a mature one. There was so much hate in her and so much injustice going on around her that she'd often rush into things without fully thinking of the consequences. If the firm had agreed to work on every case she wanted to take to court Red would have been totally snowed under with petty session work. As it was, Peekay was allowing her to do much too much, and Hymie complained frequently that she left no time in her court diary for the profitable corporate work they all needed to do in order to pay the bills.

Peekay was reminded that Magistrate Coetzee had called him several days earlier, ostensibly to discuss an altered date for a murder hearing coming up. After they'd settled on a new date Peekay could sense that the man on the other end of the telephone wasn't finished.

'Is there anything else, Magistrate Coetzee?' He'd developed a great deal of respect for the gruff Afrikaner with the brandy balloon nose.

'Ja, maybe, I don't know.' The magistrate sounded uncertain.

'Something I can do to help, magistrate?'

'About your junior, I see her a lot around the court of petty sessions.'

'Ja, that's true, she's trying to win everything at once for every one with a beef against society,' Peekay grinned.

'She's very talented, it's a waste! She's a lot more clever than you think, man!' The magistrate rang off with only a cursory '*Totsiens*'.

Peekay had been puzzled. Coetzee was the chief magistrate of Johannesburg; how could he possibly know of, or even care about the progress of a young female coloured lawyer doing work in the court of petty sessions?

When he'd asked Tandia she'd shrugged. 'He knows Mama Tequila. He used to be a magistrate in Durban.' Her reply had been too studied, her beautiful green eyes looked up at him just a little too ingenuously. Peekay had made a note to look into it.

He'd met Mama Tequila and Madam Flame Flo, of course, on several occasions since the night of the world championship fight. Peekay wasn't stupid and when Mama Tequila explained that she ran a nursing home and that Madam Flame Flo was a retired businesswoman in the liquid refreshment business, he was aware both were not exactly walking the tightrope of an honest living. But he knew better than to probe any further. He had also discovered the attachment Madam Flame Flo had for Geel Piet, and so had solved the riddle of the black granite tombstone raised so proudly among The Stones. He admired her enormously for that, and had come to see both sisters as Tandia's family. But he sensed there were parts of Tandia even her surrogate family couldn't reach.

There were a great many things about Tandia he simply didn't know, things which seemed to drive her remorselessly, for she worked impossibly long hours and apart from attending fights and meetings of the ANC with Gideon, seemed to have no personal life whatsoever. Occasionally she'd admit to having spent part of a Sunday with Madam Flame Flo, but that was about all. For Tandia, life was her legal work and she'd often work all Saturday afternoon and all day Sunday on the briefs piled up on her desk, far too many for her own good.

Peekay was too honest with himself to deny that his interest in the beautiful young lawyer was somewhat tempered by his personal feelings. He kept reminding himself that Tandia, except for that first night in Solomon Levy's rose garden, hadn't given him the slightest encouragement and obviously regarded him as a friend and professional colleague, but no more than this. Even becoming her friend hadn't been easy. Tandia knew little of the mechanics of friendship; she was tentative and suspicious, both characteristics concealed by the clever guise of seeming to be shy. It was Peekay's friendship with Juicey Fruit Mambo which had finally won her over. Juicey Fruit Mambo and Peekay would chat together in Zulu for hours like two old women washing clothes on the rocks down by the river. Juicey Fruit Mambo's hate for all whites was such, that if he decided he liked Peekay, then it was perfectly safe for her to do so as well. But respecting and even liking a white man like Peekay came pretty low on Tandia's list of priorities, even though it was a friendship that could be useful to her. Tandia had plans and the law was the vehicle which would take her where she was going. Gideon was exactly the right person on whose arm she wanted to be seen for all sorts of reasons, with love only a small part of them. When she'd first heard Gideon speak and had seen him fight against the Irishman in Sophiatown she'd believed herself to be in love. Now she realised it had been a young girl's infatuation for a larger-than-life hero. She'd fallen for his quiet assurance, his power in the ring and his way with words. She didn't doubt his intelligence and sometimes his amazing perception, but his wasn't a mind like Peekay's that cut like a knife and saw the concepts in your head almost before you'd started to shape them properly – or even a Hymie who always seemed to have thought everything out in advance.

Gideon's mind didn't have the discipline of an education and it was still locked into the old tribal ways. Tandia was an urban creature, her African heritage essentially an intellectual acquisition. Secretly Tandia knew Gideon for what he was, a tribal Zulu who would always regard her as a woman and therefore inferior, in the African manner. Peekay, on the other hand, was trouble of the sort no coloured person needed, let alone one with an ambition and mission as deadly serious as her own. She could use both men but she could sleep with only one; and him only when she could find no way to avoid it.

Tandia sensed Peekay's attraction to her. Mama Tequila had taught her too well; she knew how a hungry, one-eyed snake could ride rampant over even the most acute intelligence. Thus she reasoned that Peekay must not be given the slightest encouragement.

Mama Tequila had seen them together at Solomon Levy's party after the world championship fight and had kept a close eye on them since then. One time, at Madam Flo's home in Vereeniging, she'd taken Tandia aside. 'Lissen, Tandy, the white boy, he is eating you with his eyes. That's a very clever person, also some man, I'm telling you! But still a man you understand? Right now his one-eyed snake is still under control, but I don't know for how long, jong!'

'Ag, Mama Tequila, don't worry, he's not my type,' Tandia had replied, trying to dismiss the old woman's remarks. She was aware that Mama Tequila missed nothing and would pin her down if she wasn't very careful. 'Anyhow, you know I'm with Gideon.'

Mama Tequila sighed. She looked up at Tandia, her small, almost black eyes bright pinpricks in the great pink and blue bulge of her made-up eyelids. 'The kaffir is okay, a world champion, and now also he has some money. But he's in politics, kaffir politics, next week the *boere* will catch him and lock him away for ten years! What will you do then?'

'Mama, Gideon is Welterweight Champion of the World. They wouldn't dare! We'd . . . Peekay, I mean the firm, we'd have them in court and make a fool of them in front of the world!'

Madam Flame Flo entered the room and sat down quietly. It was as though she sensed Tandia's discomfort and wanted to lend her support just by being in the same room. But Mama Tequila didn't seem to notice her sister's presence.

'Ja, for sure, next week comes along some Joe Palooka from Chatanooga and knocks him down and then he's not welterweight champion no more, he's just another kaffir who's in a lot of trouble with the police. Believe me, for black boxing heroes the memory is short but the forgettery is long! Lissen, Tandy, I told you before, it's no use thinking you some lah-di-dah snot-nosed lawyer, you a coloured person the same as Flo here and me! You also beautiful and you a *slimmetjie*, clever as anything, man, but in the end that make no difference, you still walking pussy. You still bait for the one-eyed snake!'

'Mama, I don't have to be like everyone else! Not every coloured girl is like that! Mama, *you* know what happened! You know how I feel!' A tear ran from Tandia's eye and she brushed it away with the back of her hand.

Mama Tequila appeared not to notice Tandia's distress. Her voice grew impatient. 'Tandy, you stupid or something, hey? That the precise point I'm making! You finish and klaar in the love department, twice you got hurt, no man's going to get through to you now! I'm not talking about love, I'm not talking even about being a whore who works for money, I'm talking about exchanging! Pussy can be a cash register and it can be a weapon but it can also be something else. For God's sake, Tandy, you a lawyer, man! You should understand. Pussy, it also a means of negotiation, the only way a woman has of exchanging goods for services rendered! Every woman who ever lived, one way or another, been forced to do that. What God put there is not to enjoy, it's your collateral! Magtig! He put it there neat and nice between your legs for your own survival!'

'A woman doesn't have to take everything in life lying down.' Tandia knew it was useless arguing, but she felt suddenly dirty and inferior and she'd worked very hard not to feel either of these things ever again. Mama Tequila was taking her back to where she never wanted to be again. Tandia turned suddenly on Mama Tequila; her eyes flashed. It was the first time she'd ever seriously answered her back.

'Mama, I've got brains and I've got hate and that's got to be enough! For three hundred years the white man has been throwing black women on their backs and plundering them, taking what he wants. It's time women fought back. When the revolution comes and the underpeople win, the blacks and the coloureds and the Indians, then their women, you and I and Aunty Flo and Sonny Vindoo's wife and all the black women, we'll still be inferior! We'll trade one master for another, we'll still have to take everything a man wants on our backs!' Tandia paused, close to tears. 'Mama, I hate sex! I sleep with Gideon, but I don't like it! I sleep with him because I love him and the man you love expects you to lie on your back for him. But I'm not going to sleep with Peekay! If I do that, then I lose everything! I'm just another kaffir woman to be plundered by the white man!'

Madam Flame Flo clasped her hands together and drew them into her chest. '*Here*, Tandy! That's the best speech I ever heard!' She turned to Mama Tequila. '*Ousis*, did you hear that? Did you hear what Tandy jus' said, hey? She's right, one hundred per cent! We women must fight now or those black bastards going to do exactly the same to us as the white bastards already done!' She turned to Tandia, an indulgent smile on her face. 'Magtig, what a clever lawyer you going to be Tandy, we very proud of you, you know.'

Mama Tequila snorted suddenly. 'All I got to say further on this matter is there is not going to be a revolution and what you saying, Tandy, that lawyer's bullshit, man!'

Now as Tandia sat with Peekay and Gideon sipping coffee, she wondered if Mama Tequila wasn't right. The ANC under Chief Luthuli and Professor Matthews was in good, God-fearing Christian hands, old tired hands and old tired legs that limped from one crisis to another. What was it Luthuli said the other day? *I have knocked on the white man's door and I have waited, patiently, but no one has answered.* Something like that. It was nice Zulu rhetoric, but the Boers in Pretoria would still be chortling over the old man's naivety. Gideon called him, 'The great Induna, the Father of the Nation'. The black people didn't need a father, they needed a lean and hungry fighter with sharp teeth, someone who wouldn't knock at the door but kick it down instead. In the absence of anyone else, Sobukwe would have to do. Even if the campaign for the abolition of the pass laws failed, it was another blow struck, another kick at the still firmly closed door of apartheid. If the black people kicked long and hard enough the door jamb would finally give.

Peekay took a deliberate swig of coffee from his mug. 'What do you reckon. Gideon, do you think Sobukwe can pull this pass thing off?'

Gideon seemed to consider for a time. It was a characteristic Tandia used to love about him, it made everything he said seem wise, but now she wasn't so sure it wasn't simply a mannerism and a fairly calculated one at that. 'That Sobukwe, he talks and he promises, but he doesn't organise. His people think things just happen. You blow a whistle and the people rise up and burn their passes and go to the police and put out their hands like so . . .' Gideon proffered his hands to Tandia, '. . . and say, "Arrest me, please, baas, I have burned my pass." It doesn't happen like this. That I can tell you every time . . . for sure!'

Tandia's eyes flashed. 'We know what's going to happen, the government is going to ban the ANC and the PAC and then it will be too late!'

Gideon laughed, shaking his head. This time there was no hesitation in his answer. 'I do not think they can do this thing. The ANC is very very old, since 1912, you cannot ban such a organisation.'

His manner was pedantic and condescending and Tandia felt a tiny knot of anger in her stomach. But she didn't respond, she was getting much too excited. Magistrate Coetzee had suggested the notion to her outside a cafe near the courts where they regularly met for a chat and a cup of coffee. As Tandia was not allowed to sit in a Whites-Only cafe, he'd buy coffee in two paper cups together with two huge doughnuts and they'd stand on the pavement and chat while they drank the coffee and finally licked the sticky sugar off their fingers.

Old Coetzee was a constant source of valuable information and his suggestion that the ANC might be banned by the government had to be taken seriously. Nevertheless Tandia wasn't sure how to use it. It would be impossible to reveal her source and she was fairly certain she wouldn't be taken seriously if she proposed it simply as something she felt.

'Wait a minute, Tandia, why did you say that? What have you heard?' Peekay looked directly at her, his eyes slightly narrowed, the way he did when he sensed something. Tandia demurred, not wanting to fight Gideon on the issue. 'Ag, nothing Peekay, it was just a silly "just suppose"!' 'Just supposes' were things Peekay encouraged in the office when they were discussing a case. The wildest 'Just suppose . . . ?' would often give them a valuable insight into a case or the character of a witness. Now she watched to see if Peekay scratched his nose, a certain sign that he felt he was onto something and wasn't prepared to let it go. Hastily she added, 'It's, well, just that we have the government on the run at Langa. Robert Sobukwe may be too impatient but I wish the ANC had the same guts as him. Look at what the PAC are doing in Langa.'

Langa was an African township in the Western Cape originally built to house 5,000 people and which now housed 25,000 of which 20,000 qualified as 'new' bachelors – men who had been split (cleaved was a better word) from their families, men who were condemned to poverty and forced to return to their so-called tribal homeland.

Langa was in a crisis situation and the PAC had sent its organisers in to stir the pot and exploit the tension among the disconsolate men. They had done this so effectively that the possibility of a black uprising was being taken seriously by parliament, who ordered up troops with Saracen armoured cars and paramilitary police. Even the air force with Sabre jets and Harvard bombers was on emergency standby. How they intended using the aircraft was anyone's guess, but it was into this overheated atmosphere that Robert Sobukwe, the leader of the PAC, had devised his organisation's hastily contrived national campaign for the abolition of the hated pass laws.

Monday, 21 March was a bright highveld late summer morning with just a hint of autumn in the air. Juicey Fruit Mambo didn't need to get up early so he slept in late. He'd had a bit too much beer the night before and when he'd wakened as usual at six his head was sore; so he'd turned over, pulled his blanket over his head and gone back to sleep, waking finally around eight and feeling somewhat better.

Madam Flame Flo's house girl had left him a pot of meat and *phutu*, maize meal cooked light and fluffy with plenty of salt, and she'd added two ears of roasted con. When Juicey Fruit got up, he sat in the sun in the back yard eating quietly and reading the *Sunday Times.* He looked for things in it to talk to Tandia about, hoping also he might find a court case in which Red was involved. He'd followed the Geldenhuis murder trial for three years, searching the papers every day for news. When Peekay secured a verdict of guilty (which was later overturned) he'd simply helped himself to a bottle of Mama Tequila's brandy from the Bluey Jay supply and wandered off down to the river and got himself joyfully plastered, keeping the entire African village awake all night. When he'd returned about noon the next day Mama Tequila had chastised him, 'It was a rotten party without you, you hear! We all got drunk with happiness and here you are doing it on your own down by the river, you got no consideration, Edward King George Juicey Fruit Mambo!'

About mid morning, when he'd finished reading the paper, he went out to inspect the Packard. The beautiful pink car gleamed under an open-sided car port which Madam Flame Flo had had specially built for their visits.

Juicey Fruit Mambo realised that more people than ought to were passing the house. It was a Monday; the people should be at work and the children at school. Why were so many of them walking towards the centre of the township? He stopped and leaned over the roof of the Packard. 'Where are you going, what is all the excitement?' he called to a passing group of high-school students dressed neatly in their freshly pressed uniforms.

The group stopped and a boy of about sixteen raised his arm and gave the thumbs-up, freedom salute of the Pan-Africanist. '*Izwe Lethu!* Our Land!' he shouted, clearly excited. 'Have you not heard, Bra? We are going to the police station without our passes! Maybe they will arrest us,' he added, puffing out his chest, 'but we don't care. Sobukwe says they can't arrest everyone, so we must all do it all at once, then the police can't do anything, man!'

Juicey Fruit Mambo grinned, showing his two pointed gold incisors, then he shook his head. 'Haya! haya! Sobukwe, he said this thing? The police they can always do something. Maybe they will beat you with a sjambok, or they will bring in the dogs or even tear gas and the water gun machine!' He pointed to an aeroplane flying high overhead. 'Maybe they will bomb you!' he laughed. 'The *amaBhunu*, they can always do something!'

'*Izwe Lethu!* Today is the first step to freedom!' a young school girl in the group shouted out. Then she started to giggle, so they all began to laugh, though Juicey Fruit Mambo could sense there was hope in their laughter; they really believed. 'Kids, they're all crazy!' he thought to himself.

Like Tandia, Juicey Fruit Mambo was an ANC man, though privately he also thought of them as a bunch of no-hopers. He was also surprised at the demonstration; he'd heard Madam Flame Flo tell Mama Tequila that the township was always quiet, even when there was trouble elsewhere. He'd first heard Robert Sobukwe's call to action on the car radio, then, only an hour or so before, he'd read an editorial in the Sunday paper. It was one of the subjects he'd tucked away in his mind to talk to Tandia about. The editorial had suggested there would be trouble in the Western Cape, near Langa and also in some areas of the Southern Transvaal, particularly Orlando township in Johannesburg where Sobukwe himself would lead a group to the police station. The paper anticipated the whole thing would be a bit of an anti-climax but that the police, given seventy-two hours warning by Sobukwe himself, would be heavily armed and ready for anything.

Juicey Fruit Mambo set about waxing the Packard and soon forgot about the people heading for the demonstration. In his mind he was rehearsing the conversation he would have with Tandia later when they'd drive to Alexandra township for supper before returning to Vereeniging.

Juicey Fruit Mambo missed Tandia terribly. For nearly five years he'd taken her to school and later to university and back every day. She'd sit up in the front seat of the old Packard with him and chat all the way home to Bluey Jay. Because she'd been shy and a misfit and so somewhat isolated both at school and later at Natal University, she would use Juicey Fruit Mambo as her sounding board. They always spoke in Zulu, which he had taught her. She'd talk to him about her lessons and later her lectures and Juicey Fruit, whom Tandia had taught to read and write, took these conversations very seriously. And because he was the only one who actually wanted to hear her talk, Tandia developed a technique of explaining her studies to the huge Zulu so that he could, at least in part, understand them. He was probably the only chauffeur in South Africa who could recite the complete legal torts as a Catholic might recite the catechism.

Tandia didn't know it at the time but these daily lessons with Juicey Fruit Mambo had taught her to explain often quite complex ideas in a simple and direct manner. Many of her clients were illiterate and for the most part completely ignorant of the law, and she became famous for her simple and articulate explanations. She was known among them as *umlomo ubomvu ocacisay*, the red mouth who explains. Like so many African nicknames it was a clever combination of ideas; it told people Tandia was a member of the Red team, at the same time it gave them a physical characteristic to latch onto, the bright lipstick she always wore, and finally it told them what she was famous for. Not bad in four words.

Juicey Fruit worried daily about Tandia's safety in Johannesburg and had no trust whatsoever in the boxer Mandoma, even if he was a Zulu. He reasoned that Gideon was a midget and that he could crush him with one hand. What use was a midget when half a dozen tsotsis came at her? Now he grinned at the thought of how he'd solved the problem of her safety.

His love for kids had paid off when, after three days of the previous week spent driving around Meadowlands, Orlando and Moroka townships, stopping and asking teenagers everywhere, he finally located the whereabouts of Johnny Tambourine.

He didn't recognise Johnny Tambourine when he drew up in the pink Packard outside a shop in Moroka, but he had no need to worry. The moment he opened his mouth to speak Johnny stepped forward. Juicey Fruit Mambo didn't have the sort of face you forgot in a hurry. The tall young man who stepped up to the car had a serious expression on his face.

'Long time no see, Bra.' He spoke quietly with no animation.

Johnny Tambourine was now a tall, lean teenager of sixteen who wore the familiar baggy pants cut down to nothing at the ankles, open-necked floral shirt and cardigan of the tsotsi. On his head he wore the ubiquitous 'tsotsi' itself, the English working man's cloth cap. Juicey Fruit Mambo hid his disquiet at finding Johnny Tambourine was a tsotsi, but after his initial surprise, he realised that it had been inevitable and was, now that he thought about it, perfect. That is, providing he could get the gang to go along with his plans.

Juicey Fruit Mambo broke into an enormous smile. He was dressed in a dark grey suit with a white shirt and brilliant pink tie to match the Packard; he was looking sharp. 'I see you, Johnny Tambourine!' He stuck his large hand out of the car window and Johnny Tambourine took it, his own hand disappearing into the huge black fist.

Johnny Tambourine didn't return the traditional Zulu greeting, nor did he affect the two-phase grip. He didn't go in for that shit . . . I see you, you see me, everybody sees everybody, then the cows and the hens and on and on for ten minutes or more before any business you've come for takes place! That sort of talk was for the peasants. He remembered the huge man standing in front of him clearly but that was a long time ago when he'd been a little snotnose with a bicycle wheel hoop. He wondered what the big bastard wanted after all these years? His expression remained sober as he spoke. 'I hear you want me, Bra?'

If Juicey Fruit Mambo felt insulted by Johnny's poor manners he showed no sign. He'd lived in a township himself and knew the kids had no respect for the old ways. He released his grip on Johnny's hand and waited while the three other tsotsi youths moved up to the car. The handshake had broken the ice and the three others seemed more friendly.

'Remember me, Dog Poep Ismali?' a light-skinned youth asked cheekily and then grinned at Juicey Fruit Mambo, taking his hand and shaking it silently. Juicey Fruit Mambo also offered his hand to Flyspeck Mendoza, who was the smallest of the three by far and dragged one leg slightly as he walked. He wore spectacles and seemed a very serious type, not at all the kind to be a tsotsi. Too Many Fingers Bembi hung back a little, but when Juicey Fruit Mambo extended his hand his face broke into a huge white smile and he gripped it in the African manner, the only one of the three boys to do so.

Juicey Fruit Mambo scratched his head as though thinking, his fingers tapping down the length of the long jagged scar which crossed his shining pate. Then he suddenly patted his scalp, indicating hair. 'The white one. Where is the white one?'

'Kaas Kop? He crossed over,' Johnny spat.

Juicey Fruit clearly didn't understand the expression and looked querulous. 'He is in gaol?'

'No, man, his skin, it was white like his hair, so he crossed over. He went to Cape Town where nobody knows him. He's white shit now, dog shit dried in the sun!'

The other three laughed, it was clear that Johnny Tambourine was still their leader. Juicey Fruit considered this news for a moment. 'That is enough punishment, now he must live with that fear.'

'I hear you been asking all over the place for me?' Johnny said, kicking at the dirt. He seemed ready to talk and as he looked up he brushed a fly from his face. Juicey Fruit Mambo noticed that three fingers of his left hand seemed deformed, as though they'd been badly smashed and hadn't been properly set again.

'This is true, Johnny Tambourine, I have come to make you keep your promise.'

'Promise?' Johnny Tambourine laughed, drawing his head back arrogantly, 'We are tsotsi, we snatch bags, pick pockets, mug and rob. Sometimes we get in a bit of housebreaking and theft, but we never make promises,' he boasted. 'That is why we are tsotsi, you can never trust us!'

Juicey Fruit Mambo opened the door and stepped from the car. 'First you are a man, Johnny Tambourine. Then you are a tsotsi. Is it the man or the tsotsi who does not keep promises?' He towered nearly a foot above the already tall youth.

The movement from Johnny Tambourine was amazingly fast. The knife came from somewhere, he opened the blade with his teeth and the thrust of it came towards Juicey Fruit Mambo, seemingly in one smooth lightning movement. But it wasn't fast enough. Juicey Fruit Mambo grabbed him by the wrist and appeared simply to turn him upside down. One moment he was standing with a knife in his hand and the next the knife spun from it and Johnny Tambourine hit the dirt as though he'd suddenly, on a whim, decided to dive into the dust head first.

'Ho!' Juicey Fruit Mambo grinned. 'Now I have seen the tsotsi, can I please talk to the man?'

Dog Poep Ismali, Too Many Fingers Bembi and Flyspeck Mendoza took a step backwards, ready to run. Nobody had ever seen anything like Juicey Fruit Mambo before. He'd 'flipped' Johnny Tambourine without even appearing to move from the spot.

Johnny Tambourine rose slowly, dusting his pants with both hands, his eyes downcast. He walked over and picked up the long open-bladed pocket knife and snapped it closed, dropping it into a pocket of his neatly pressed tsotsi pants. Finally he looked up, measuring Juicey Fruit with his eyes as though nothing had happened. The look showed he was still not afraid. Juicey Fruit Mambo liked what he saw a lot. Maybe he'd come to the right place.

'The *man* will keep his promise,' Johnny Tambourine said quietly.

Juicey Fruit asked for a meeting the following day, promising to bring beer.

'Carling Black Label, that's what we drink, Bra. Bring a case, tsotsi are big beer drinkers!' Flyspeck Mendoza chipped in.

The following day they met again under one of the few remaining large trees in Moroka township. Someone had built a crude bench all the way around the trunk of a large old leadwood tree. It was strange to find a leadwood at this altitude but the old tree looked well set, its dark grey bark rough looking with its characteristic longitudinal furrows and irregular transverse cracks. In fact the entire tree had a grey appearance which suited the bleak landscape of the township.

The five of them sat under the tree. There were a few other people about, all of them youths of roughly the same age. 'Don't worry, those guys are my operators, real cowboys; they'll watch for the police.' Johnny Tambourine looked at Juicey Fruit Mambo and nodded his head towards the Packard. 'The Black Label?'

Juicey Fruit Mambo's mouth fell open. 'Haya, Johnny Tambourine, here in the open? We will drink here under this tree?'

'I told you man, those are my men, we'll know long before a Black Jack can come near.'

They sat down under the tree drinking beer, Juicey Fruit opening the bottles in a flash with a gold incisor. Flyspeck Mendoza produced a large zol and they shared the joint between them, the marijuana making them feel cool and relaxed. When they'd each drunk a couple of bottles of beer and the zol was down to a finger nip, Juicey Fruit Mambo opened up the subject of why they were there.

'Johnny Tambourine, Flyspeck Mendoza, Dog Poep Ismali and Too Many Fingers Bembi,' Juicey Fruit Mambo spoke each name slowly and with great respect, as though they were men of substance and purpose, and the gesture was not lost on the four boys. 'You remember Tandy?' Each of them nodded, smiling at his own memory of the days in Sophiatown when they'd met what they thought must be a beautiful film star.

'She was a great *unine*, we talk about her still sometimes,' Johnny Tambourine confessed.

'She is a member of your gang. It is a long time now but she agreed, you agreed also. Time does not change these things, my brothers,' Juicey Fruit said rather ponderously.

Dog Poep Ismali laughed. 'She will be the prettiest tsotsi in tsotsidom!'

This sent them all into gales of laughter. The dope was having its effect and the giggles had set in. 'Now she is a lawyer in Jo'burg.'

'Yes, we know, Bra. She is called "the red mouth who explains", and she is the world champion Gideon Mandoma's sweetheart,' Flyspeck Mendoza said; then he added, 'He is still our friend.'

'Haya! You have seen them together, you have spoken to her?' Juicey Fruit asked.

Too Many Fingers Bembi shook his head. 'No, he is big time now. We do not see him, only in the movies or when he rides in a big open Cadillac.'

'He has a Cadillac, a big open car?' Juicey Fruit said, impressed.

'No, Bra, it is a car that belongs to other people, big-time gangsters I think, but when he wins he drives in the back of this car and people come from all over to see him,' Dog Poep Ismali said.

'He is the best world champion of any weight any time in world history!' Flyspeck declared.

'I think maybe Peekay, the *Onoshobishobi Ingelosi*, he is better,' Juicey Fruit Mambo said mischievously.

'Never!' they all chorussed. 'He beat him hollow! He knocked him out!' Too Many Fingers Bembi protested, getting quite upset.

It was Johnny Tambourine who brought the meeting to order again. 'How must we help Tandy?' he asked, the whites of his eyes red from smoking the zol.

Juicey Fruit Mambo opened four more bottles of beer and handed one each to the boys before de-capping another for himself. Then he told them the story of Tandia and why she hated Geldenhuis. The treatment of Tandia at the hands of the police officer was a familiar enough story and each of them understood how such a thing could happen. They only really became deeply interested when Juicey Fruit spoke of the murder trial and how Peekay had nailed Geldenhuis and gotten a conviction for murder against the policeman which, naturally, had subsequently been quashed. But Geldenhuis was determined to get Peekay and with him Tandia.

'She is fighting for the rights of the people and she knows too much about him. He will try to kill her someday; she must be protected.'

'How can we protect her?' said Johnny Tambourine.

'She is living in Meadowlands. You can watch her house. If they are going to get her they will come to the house. They will not do anything in public, except maybe in a crowd. If she is in a crowd at a protest or maybe at an ANC meeting, you must be near her, you must watch the people around her, that is when they will try to get her!' Juicey Fruit Mambo put his hand into his pocket and withdrew a wad of banknotes held together with a rubber band. 'Here is two hundred pounds, it is all the money I have.'

Two hundred pounds was nearly four years' salary for the average black working man and it represented a fortune. In fact it was everything in cash money Juicey Fruit Mambo owned, his entire retirement fund put together one note at a time.

Johnny Tambourine removed the rubber band and counted off sixty single one-pound notes. He handed ten to each of the boys and put ten into his own pocket. 'Expenses! Ten pounds each for expenses, Bra,' he said, being practical. 'You do not have to pay us, but there will be expenses.' He held up the remaining pound notes. 'We will need a gun and some ammo.' He returned the rubber band to the roll and handed what remained of the stash back to Juicey Fruit Mambo. 'We will do this job, we will keep this promise.' They all solemnly shook hands on the deal and arranged to meet at Tandia's house in Meadowlands the following Monday evening when Juicey Fruit Mambo would drive Tandia home and reveal his protection plan to her and re-acquaint her with the four boys.

It was nearly one o'clock by the time Juicey Fruit Mambo had finished polishing the Packard. People had been passing all morning and his curiosity had grown. The township police station was no more than a fifteen-minute walk from Madam Flame Flo's house and Juicey Fruit Mambo enjoyed the stroll in the sun. It was one of those marvellous high veld late summer days when the air is polished clean and sits warm on your back and the sky is blue, the colour of a much-washed cotton shirt – though it was the time of year when a storm could build up in minutes. Seemingly from nowhere the big cumulo-nimbus clouds would build in the late afternoon. If you went indoors for a moment you'd sense from the change of light that something had happened and then when, minutes later, you came out again, there were the towering castles of grey tinged with white, real estate for Gods and frightening giants to live in. Rain would come down in torrents. First a sharp 'ting!' like a pellet on the iron roof, then half a dozen more and the preliminaries were over; down it came, crashing, so you couldn't hear yourself speak, filling the gutters and flooding the dirt roads, each drop heavy with malice, washing away the red topsoil and generally behaving badly. Then, as suddenly, it would stop, leaving the whole place polished in the bright evening sun, the sky even bluer than before. That was a high veld rain storm for you, full of braggadocio but not very big in the long-term department.

Juicey Fruit Mambo was surprised at the size of the crowd as he moved down Seeiso Street towards the police station at the top end of the township. Everywhere people were singing and dancing and shouting '*Izwe Lethu!*', raising their arms in the thumbs-up salute and generally having an excellent demonstration. If you wanted a peaceful demonstration with a bit of class you couldn't have asked for a better one. People were carrying placards, neatly printed by schoolchildren. You could see everyone had been up late by lamplight the previous night, parents exclaiming in astonishment at the work of their kids, who had made placards not just protesting against the pass laws – when you had a good demonstration going there wasn't much point in reserving it for just one thing when there were so many inequalities available. Placards covered the whole gamut of protest: *Down with Bantu Education. We want BETTER homes, Free Education, Equal Work for Equal Pay, Down with Unjust Laws! We want Freedom of Speech, Down with Removal of People! Down with Bosses, Freedom for All, Let our leaders Speak of Freedom now! Down with Passes, Passes must go! Passes put people in gaol. Pass laws Break Family Life. Pass laws are Enemy No 1 of the People.* Juicey Fruit Mambo observed that the 'down with' posters were the most popular.

The demonstration was unusual for another reason; no police with leashed Alsatian dogs walked among the crowd. In fact, not a policeman, black or white, was to be seen anywhere on the African side of the high-security fence which surrounded the squat red police station building. It was not until Juicey Fruit Mambo broke through to the front that he saw the two Saracen armoured vehicles with machine guns mounted on their turrets. Here the police station was surrounded by policemen carrying sten guns and an occasional rifle; there looked to be about two-hundred-and-fifty or so white constables, although there may have been others inside. Some were dressed in ordinary everyday police uniform while others wore the not-yet familiar combat fatigues and soft cloth caps which gave them the look of German Panzer troops. These were obviously the police recruited overnight from outside the area in anticipation of trouble in the township; they looked young and inexperienced. Most of the police were chatting, smoking, and watching the crowd. They carried belts of ammunition around their shoulders and you could just see they thought they looked tough. It was obvious they'd decided the crowd was peaceful and that nothing unforeseen was about to occur.

Near the gate on the right leading into the police station compound was an area of no-man's-land about ten yards wide. Every once in a while, to the cheering of the crowd, a young man would run into the clearing, place his pass on the ground and set it alight. This was sheer bravado; the PAC instruction was for the men to leave their passes at home and offer themselves up for arrest as not having their passes on them, an offence which led to imprisonment. They were to stand with hands held out, waiting for the police to walk over and handcuff them and take them away. But by the time Juicey Fruit Mambo arrived, too many people had been arrested this way and the police were simply ignoring the gestures and even the foolhardy burning.

After each such burning a white police sergeant with a blond crew cut would pick up a megaphone and say, 'That's all right, burn away, man! We have your pitcher on our camera and we will get you another time. Without a pass we will find you because, man, you going nowhere, no job, no place to live, you a nobody!' The crowd would laugh in response to this warning and even the police sergeant seemed to be enjoying himself.

But he was right of course, and the crowd grew less enthusiastic about destroying the one document that at least allowed them to stay in the township and work. The peaceful demonstration was beginning to fizzle a bit, though everyone seemed happy enough. Overhead the planes circled and every once in a while a Sabre jet would dive, coming in low over the crowd, the ground trembling with the shock waves it made, but it had the opposite effect to that intended and seemed to add to the carnival effect of the demonstration. The people remained unafraid. The big bad wolf had huffed and puffed to no avail. Everyone was a bit pleased with themselves; the point had been made and nearly five thousand people had turned up in a township that never protested. It was a show of strength, some claimed, far more significant than that shown in Langa or even Evaton, where a crowd of twenty thousand people had been dispersed earlier in the day when the same Sabre jets and Harvard bombers dived menacingly low over them. 'Those Evaton people scare easy, man! There will be no more peaceful townships, the government has been warned!' people were saying to each other as they prepared to go home for a late lunch.

It was about half past one when an old man, using a long smooth stick to lean on, hobbled into the clearing in front of the police station. He was diminutive and so old and poorly dressed that many of the people started to laugh. He approached the gate, nearer to the police station than most of the pass burners had ventured and, in the manner of very old people, he came to a slow halt and turned stiffly, looking over his shoulder at the crowd. Then he took his pass from a threadbare coat which hung well below his knees and slowly brought it up so that eventually he held it aloft, above his shoulders.

Juicey Fruit watched fascinated. The old man must have been in his eighties, and he had a scrawny tuft of white beard and snowy white hair. He looked like a country person, his clothes clean though in rags and his body bent from the sort of work a man does in the fields or walking all his life behind a plough, his bones welded stiff by arthritis and the years of sleeping hard on a grass mat. Now the old man lowered himself into a crouched position, leaning heavily on the stick. He placed his pass on the ground and then the stick; and, taking a box of safety matches from his coat pocket, with trembling hands he tried to set his passbook alight.

The crowd were enchanted by the sight and were cheering and chanting 'Afrika!', showing the thumbs-up sign and shouting '*Izwe Lethu!*' A small group near the fence on the left of the police station, where a couple more Saracens were parked, their machine guns trained on the crowd, started to sing *NKosi Sikelela i'Afrika*.

But, as so often happens with gestures, the old man's hands trembled too much or the breeze which had suddenly risen was too strong, for he was unable to light the document. Juicey Fruit Mambo, observing his predicament, rushed forward and bent down beside him.

'You are brave as a lion, my father. You have the courage of a bull elephant, but your hands are old, I will help you. Give me your pass and I will add it to my own and together we will light the fire which will show the white devils our contempt!'

Juicey Fruit Mambo took his passbook from the inside pocket of his jacket and, picking up the old man's grubby pass, he helped him back to his feet. Then he stooped to pick up the stick. It was of a dark wood and smooth as satin to the touch. This is a stick which was a very good friend to this old man, he thought, and turned the stick around so that the more pointed end reached his shoulder. 'We will hold this burning of our passbooks up to the heavens, my father.' The old man barely came to Juicey Fruit Mambo's waist as the huge Zulu punched a hole through the passes so they rested on the end of the beautiful old stick.

The crowd were showing their delight at the sight of the huge black man, with his front teeth missing and the two pointed gold incisors flashing in his mouth, and the ragged little man. It was a metaphor not lost on them; the age and endurance of Africa taken together with the hugeness and strength of the African people. At that moment they knew they could win. If it took a hundred or even a thousand years they would win. The roar from the crowd was becoming deafening.

The mood of the white men guarding the police station changed and they hastily stubbed out their cigarettes and held their sten guns at the ready, releasing the safety locks. The machine guns fixed to the turrets of the Saracens arced over the crowd in a silent warning. There was nothing except the increased noise level to suggest the crowd was getting out of control; the two kaffirs in front burning their passes seemed to have captured its imagination. The big guy with the bald head in the well-tailored suit, he must be somebody important, a PAC organiser or something. The sergeant who'd been on the megaphone entered the police station and in an immortal statement not intended in the least to be funny, reported to Lieutenant Geldenhuis, 'Sir, the natives are becoming restless. Better you come and speak to them. They are expecting someone from Pretoria, a senior person. Is someone coming?'

Jannie Geldenhuis finished the last of his coffee before rising and walking out of the station. He was pretty sure that the crowd was under control, there were none of the usual signs that political agitators were working them up. No stones had been thrown and few among the crowd even carried sticks. He was anxious to keep the status quo; he didn't want it to appear on his record that the quietest township on the Rand had erupted into chaos almost immediately it had come under his control.

In fact, he'd been unhappy about the extra recruits and the presence of the Saracens. These new men were raw, not accustomed to crowd control. It was the usual overkill by the people in Pretoria. The last thing he wanted was a senior officer from Pretoria trying to take over. He removed his revolver from his holder and slipped off the catch, more as a gesture to his own men than as an intended threat to the crowd.

Juicey Fruit Mambo produced his zippo lighter and, removing the top, he poured a little lighter fluid on the passbooks. Then he replaced the top and, activating the lighter, held it carefully to a corner of the passbooks, waiting until he was sure they were well alight. Then he lofted them high into the air above him to the delight of the crowd. 'Look, my father, your gesture is not wasted, the people, all the people they salute and respect you,' he shouted down to the old man.

At this precise moment Geldenhuis stepped out of the police station. He would later replay in his mind what had happened, but in truth he was never quite sure. Something in his brain snapped and he was suddenly standing naked and back in the pink room at Bluey Jay with a screaming Tandia crouched over the pink satin bed in front of him. Blood ran from his penis and he was in terrible pain. The door into the room crashed down and a huge, snarling black man with two gold incisor teeth, his eyes popping with madness and his great hands stretched out to reach for his neck, was coming towards him. He reached for his police revolver on the carpet, knowing he was about to be killed. The explosion roared in his head as he fired in a crouched position. The firing seemed to go on and on and when the mist cleared in front of his eyes the crowd was fleeing and bodies lay everywhere. A machine gun from one of the Saracens was still raking the bodies lying in the dust. They jerked, animated by the impact of the automatic fire as the hot ballistic teeth ripped into them. Some black people sat in the dirt, still alive, screaming from their wounds. One huge woman held her hands cupped in her lap; they were filled with her own intestines. She didn't scream; her shoulders shook as she sobbed, a small private sobbing ceremony for the death enveloping her in the hot afternoon sun.

Juicey Fruit Mambo lay face down, his body covering the old man's. Part of his head had been torn away by a dumdum bullet which would have killed him instantly. There was a stir, as though miraculously the huge black man still moved; then the ancient little man rose from under him and brushed the dirt from his ragged coat. With one hand held to his back, he stooped to pick up the stick which had fallen from Juicey Fruit Mambo's grasp; the passbooks still burned and he brushed them off the end of the stick where they continued to burn, a tiny sacrificial fire. Then he rested the stick on Juicey Fruit Mambo's heart, holding it upright. 'I invite your spirit to enter the sacred stick,' he said quietly. 'Come, I will take you home.' Then he stood upright again facing the Sharpeville police station. Slowly, his neck stiff as a turkey cock, his rheumy eyes passed along the line of white policemen as he raised his clenched fist into the air, his thin reed-like voice cut through the silence. '*Lumukanda ehla!* Come back, Lumukanda!' And the white men who stood wrapped in the silence of their slaughter, their guns still smoking, knew something had happened, something had changed in Africa for ever.

It was quarter to two on a cloudless late summer day in the once peaceful township of Sharpeville. The world would never be the same again. Somojo, the greatest of all the African witchdoctors, leaning heavily on the spirit stick which carried Juicey Fruit Mambo back to his shadows, hobbled away, picking his way through the dead bodies, most of which had been shot in the back. Around the old man's neck hung a tiny leather bag. He could feel the comforting thump of it against his chest cavity as the ancient gold coin within it knocked against him. He spoke to the stick in his hand. 'You have not died in vain, spirit of a brave man, I have called and it is time! It is time for Lumukanda, the child of the morning star, to return.' Somojo the Swazi, the greatest of all the living witchdoctors, made this promise to Juicey Fruit Mambo.

Later that afternoon, when they'd loaded the sixty-nine dead into the back of two trucks for the mortuary, holding them by the arms and legs and swinging them, then letting them go so they landed on an awkward pile of arms and legs and blood-soaked torsos, a thunderstorm struck. The usual thing: quick as anything, big clouds arriving out of nowhere, a typical late summer high veld storm. It did what such a storm always does; rushed in, a fearful conniption of water, wind and muddy fuss. When it was over, all the blood which had soaked into the hard ground in front of the Sharpeville police station had been washed away.

That night the sky was more beautiful than usual with the stars so close you could almost reach up and touch them. This was unusual; the soft coal the people burn in their cooking fires in the townships mists the evening sky with smog which blocks out all but the most determined stars. But the rain had somehow washed the sky clean and the stars above Meadowlands were as bright as they are in the bush. Johnny Tambourine, Too Many Fingers Bembi, Flyspeck Mendoza and Dog Poep Ismali waited outside Tandia's house for Juicey Fruit Mambo to bring her home in the Packard. Too Many Fingers Bembi suddenly pointed upwards, 'Look! Over there, a falling star!' he shouted excitedly.

THIRTY-FOUR

Peekay was utterly devastated by the news of Sharpeville. For him it was the end of hope and the beginning of a deep fear that insanity was going to win in the beloved country. The killing fields had come back to South Africa; hostilities had broken out again in the three-hundred-year war based on greed, fear and revenge.

Peekay found himself facing a terrible moral dilemma. A liberal South African who believed in justice, a sense of fairness and the rights of every man, woman and child to an equal place in a society based on freedom of opportunity – in the post-Sharpeville South Africa it could only be thought of as the ridiculous credo of a hopeless dreamer.

The black people had had enough, and Peekay's love for them was swept away in the torrent of hurt, anger and betrayal they felt. Now they demanded the right to avenge the injustice and to play by the same cynical rules of vengeance as those used against them.

On the day following the massacre, Peekay accompanied a distraught Tandia to the mortuary near Sharpeville. When they arrived hundreds of people were waiting around the squat red-brick building to claim their dead. They were mostly women, their eyes swollen from weeping, some with their men and rather more with small, runny-nosed children clutching at their skirts.

Under similar circumstances, a white crowd would have been loud and demanding, impatient with the tedious paperwork performed by a battery of clerks recruited from elsewhere who sat under the bluegum trees behind portable tables. It was well into the morning yet none of the bodies had been processed for release and some of the people had been waiting since dawn. But Africans are familar with the despair of waiting and they'd come expecting no less. The people of Sharpeville had not yet indulged in the luxury of anger; overcome with grief they waited, confused and beaten in the still hot autumn day, for the white man to restore their dead to them.

Peekay, who'd phoned earlier for an appointment, arrived with Tandia at precisely eleven o'clock to be met by the white mortuary official, Klopper.

Klopper had a nickname among the Africans, who called him '*Inkosi Asebafa*, Lord of the Dead'. He liked this name a lot and lost no opportunity explaining it to any white person he might meet. Klopper was about as big in the dead-body business as you could get and held absolute power in Soweto which, he was fond of pointing out, housed Africa's largest mortuary.

His presence in Sharpeville on temporary transfer from Soweto to take charge of body sorting was an indication of how seriously the government regarded the matter of the previous day's massacre. Klopper was not easily intimidated and he wouldn't stand for any nonsense. He was just the sort of man to have on hand when you were thinking of having a massacre and wanted a calm, orderly aftermath.

Peekay had met him before when he'd been a witness in the Tom Majombi case. Klopper seemed to him to be a man obsessed with death, though in his mind he seemed only to equate it with the black people. He had witnessed so many violent and unnatural deaths – the stabbings, mutilations, muggings, ritual murders, clubbings and domestic beatings which make up the daily count of the dead in the black townships – that he seemed to have forgotten that people die of natural causes, or for that matter, that white people die at all.

He didn't see the Sharpeville massacre as any more than destiny catching up with another sixty-nine kaffirs. It wouldn't have occurred to him to blame the white police officers involved for the incident. White men do their duty and sometimes kaffirs become dead as a consequence. There was nothing wrong with that.

He was standing outside the mortuary scratching his balls and enjoying the late morning sun when Peekay and Tandia drew up. Klopper was an obese, ruddy-complexioned man who, despite being completely bald, gave the impression of being overly hirsute. He affected an untidy beard roughly trimmed about two inches below his chin. Coming up to meet it, as though it was stuffing spilling out of a rent in his chest, a wild tuft of white hair mixed into his beard. His arms, too, were covered with thick, almost matted black hair and the short sleeves of his open-neck shirt were rolled as far up his arms as they'd go so his biceps appeared to balloon out of them like Popeye arms. He was at least six feet tall but possessed the legs of someone a foot shorter, so his ballooned torso seemed precariously balanced, as though it was always about to topple from its unsteady and undersized pinning. This impression was reinforced by a strong smell of brandy, suggesting that he might be somewhat tipsy. Klopper looked dangerous, as though he had been designed for violence.

He drew his right hand from his trouser pocket and raised it casually in greeting at Peekay and Tandia's approach. '*Goeie more, Advokaat*, it's a nice day after the rain last night, hey?' Klopper's voice was cheerful, though his greeting seemed to ignore Tandia completely.

'Good morning, Meneer Klopper,' Peekay said, smiling, though his voice was formal. He turned to Tandia. 'May I introduce you to Miss Patel, my legal partner.'

Klopper offered his hand to Peekay, still ignoring Tandia. The two men shook hands briefly whereupon Klopper's fat fingers plunged back into the interior of his khaki trousers to resume their jiggling. His head slightly to one side, squinting, he examined Peekay, as though trying to read his thoughts. Finally he smiled, showing a lot of gold in his mouth but no laughter in his small, black eyes. 'If you want trouble you must go some place else, you hear? The trouble here is over yesterday already. Today is all peace and quiet.'

Tandia felt the anger rise up in her. It wasn't Kopper's rudeness – she was prepared for that – but this mocking tone. She'd cried for Juicey Fruit Mambo most of the previous night and by early morning she was back in control of herself. By the time Peekay picked her up in Hymie's Mercedes for the drive to Vereeniging, he'd been surprised at her composure.

But now, simply by opening his mouth, this huge, stupid Boer with his fat guts spilling over his belt and his fingers working his elasticised testicles brought back her distress. He seemed to typify everything Juicey Fruit Mambo despised. Even in death this gross human had dominion over him. She struggled to fight back her tears, but the anger she felt threatened to overpower her. 'Tonight!', she comforted herself, 'tonight Gideon meets to launch *Umkonto we Sizwe*, Spear of the Nation. Please God let them allow me to be the first woman to join!' she prayed silently.

She'd left Peekay's flat in Hillbrow very early that morning. Gideon had been called to an all-night ANC meeting and Peekay had taken her to his flat in Hillbrow from the office soon after the news of Sharpeville had come through. He'd spent the night trying to comfort and calm her. Tandia had been too distraught to resist when Peekay had held her in his arms and rocked her and soothed her with quiet, reassuring words.

At one stage he'd tried to sing her to sleep with a Zulu lullaby. He had a nice voice, clean and unselfconscious and the melody with its beautiful Zulu words was so hauntingly familiar that she fantasised that her own Zulu mother must have used it, sung to her when she was an infant.

Later, when the sparrows were beginning to chirp in the eaves directly above his top-floor window, when Peekay thought she'd fallen asleep, he stretched her out and covered her with a blanket and slipped a pillow under her head. Then she'd felt his lips touch her brow as he whispered, 'Sleep now, sweet Tandia. Sorrow has a season, but it will pass.' Then she'd heard the squeak of a loose floorboard under the carpet as he tiptoed from the room; soon after, she'd heard the shower running.

With Peekay out of the room, Tandia started to cry again, this time not knowing whether it was for Juicey Fruit Mambo or herself. Peekay's barely sensed kiss and the manner of his words were the gentlest thing she could ever remember happening to her. They contrasted so with Gideon's words when, less than an hour after the news of the Sharpeville massacre, Madam Flame Flo had phoned to say that Juicey Fruit Mambo was among the dead. Tandia had become almost hysterical and Gideon made very little attempt to comfort her. 'Tandia, Mambo was a Zulu. He died like a Zulu should die. I would be happy to die like him. He will be happy, his shadows will be happy and the people of his *isigodi*, they will be happy. There is no need for grief!' He'd spoken as though he was giving her an instruction, a lesson in how he expected her to behave; and then, without touching her, he'd left her for an urgent meeting at Moroka township.

Soon after dawn, despite Peekay's protests that he must take her all the way to Meadowlands, Tandia insisted he only drive her to Johannesburg Central where she proposed to take a non-European taxi home. When Peekay had looked upset, she'd explained, 'Peekay, they rise early in the townships. By now the place is bustling with people hurrying to catch an early train. What do you think my neighbours will think if I arrive at my doorstep at dawn dropped off in a big black car by a white man?'

Peekay grinned, suddenly understanding. 'About what my neighbours would think if they'd seen you leaving my doorstep at dawn?'

'No wonder you're such a crackerjack barrister!' Tandia said, trying to sound cheerful.

Tandia needed to go home to bathe, to change into a black dress, and to pick up a brief she'd been working on. Peekay would pick her up around mid morning, using the intervening time to get a court order to have Juicey Fruit Mambo's body removed for burial in Zululand. This would normally have been extremely difficult, if not impossible in the time, but it had been quickly arranged after a phone call to Magistrate Coetzee.

The taxi had only just pulled away and she was fumbling in her bags for the keys to her house when a youth of about sixteen appeared suddenly at her side. Tandia gave a start.

'Hi Tandy, long time no see.' The boy had a nice smile and it was obvious he was friendly. Then Tandia recognised him.

'Johnny Tambourine!' Despite her distress she was glad to see him.

'When we heard about Sharpeville and you didn't come with Juicey Fruit Mambo last night, I told the others to go away. I thought, for sure, something bad has happened.'

'Oh, Johnny they killed him. They shot him!' She began to cry again.

'Don't cry, Tandy,' Johnny Tambourine put his hand on her shoulder and, taking the key she was holding from her hand, he opened the front door of her little house. 'Sit, I'll get you some water or something.' He looked about him, trying to decide where the kitchen might be.

'Thank you, Johnny, I'm fine,' Tandia sniffed, rubbing her swollen eyes. 'I must look a mess,' she smiled through her tears. 'I didn't know you'd seen Juicey Fruit Mambo. Please sit, I'm being rude.' She moved to sit on the edge of a small sofa and pointed to a chair.

'Ja, only yesterday, we made a deal, we done some business.' Johnny sat casually on the arm of a chair that matched the design of the sofa, crossing his legs to show a pair of bright red socks which matched his cardigan. He seemed a young man very much in control.

'Business? You had some business with Juicey Fruit Mambo?'

Johnny Tambourine scratched his head, then realised he was still wearing his cap. He removed it from his head, placing it on the chair beside him. 'Ja, we got a contract to look after you. Me an' Dog Poep Ismali an' Flyspeck Mendoza an' Too Many Fingers Bembi, all four, we going to protect you from now on; it's all agreed and signed for.'

Despite considerable effort on her part, Tandia was unable to persuade Johnny Tambourine that she was perfectly safe on her own. Exhausted from lack of sleep and in some exasperation, she'd finally agreed to a trial week under the protection of the four boys. It was another wonderful, typical ham-fisted Juicey Fruit Mambo scheme wrought out of his love for her and the least she could do was pretend to go along with it until the boys grew tired of the game and went back to loitering, three-card scams, mugging and petty theft.

Johnny Tambourine considered that his job had started right there and then and he'd come with her in the car to Sharpeville, sitting quietly in the back seat of the car while she and Peekay confronted Klopper.

'We've come to identify one of the deceased and to arrange for the removal of his body, Meneer Klopper,' Peekay said politely to the large man.

Klopper removed his hands from his trouser pockets and to their surprise came to attention; then he lifted himself onto his toes, which caused him to wobble dangerously as he leaned over them. The entire performance was meant to intimidate. 'I must say, man, you don't look like a relation of anybody we got here, Advokaat.' Klopper stabbed a blunt finger in Tandia's direction, acknowledging her presence for the first time. 'Not her too! We only got black kaffirs here. Who was it who died? The garden boy or the house girl at your place, hey?'

Peekay removed an envelope from the jacket of his suit. 'He was a friend,' he said quietly. He handed the envelope to the big man. 'It contains a court order entitling me to make a positive identification and gives me authority to remove the body.'

Klopper smiled. Taking the envelope and holding it by the corner he tapped it several times into the open palm of his left hand. 'That's nice. A friend, hey? A white man who has black kaffir friends,' he squinted down again at Peekay, 'That Tom Majombi, you know the kaffir who become dead in the Geldenhuis trial, he was your friend also, hey?' He laughed suddenly and turned to Tandia. 'I would be careful if I was his friend, you hear? All his kaffir friends, they become dead!' He stressed the word kaffir, making it obvious that it included her. He continued to look at Tandia, a thin smile on his fat face. 'You hear what I'm saying?'

Tandia held his stare. It was an impertinence she might not have been allowed had they been alone. Even now, the years of conditioning made her feel guilty. Guilty for what? She wasn't sure, for being born? Why was it she felt this life-or-death need to hold the fat white man's insolent stare? How could this animal intimidate her? Klopper ignored the flap of the envelope he was holding and, without looking, nipped a corner with his thumb nail and began tearing about a quarter of an inch off the top, his fingers working deliberately as though he was in no hurry to open it.

Tandia held his gaze, though the need to look away was becoming almost irresistible. She felt like a small bird mesmerised by a snake and, inwardly, she was screaming for the eye contact to come to an end. When Klopper had torn a thin sliver of paper off the top end of the envelope he finally dropped his gaze, inserting a fat thumb and forefinger pincer-like into the envelope to withdraw the court order. He unfolded the paper and appeared to look at it for a moment. 'Edward King George Juicey Fruit Mambo?' He read it slowly and aloud. Then without looking up he added, '*Here*, man, some kaffirs got blerrie funny names!'

'*Inkosi Asebafa*, Lord of the Dead! That's not a funny name?' Peekay shot back.

Tandia grinned and Klopper looked at him coldly, his small dark eyes hostile. His voice was clipped as he spoke. 'You done your homework as usual, I see, Advokaat. Most of the dead here, you know, they haven't got any papers.' He grinned, seeming to brighten up. 'They left their passes at home, that's what this whole kerfuffle is all about, man! Do you have papers for the kaffir who has become dead?'

'No, I don't, but we can identify him quite easily.'

'Identify him?' Klopper looked surprised. 'You can't identify a kaffir without papers, man!'

Peekay sighed. He could have kicked himself for making the crack about Klopper's African name. 'The deceased is quite distinctive looking, he has two gold-capped incisor teeth and a large zig-zag scar across his skull.'

'Gold teeth and a zig-zag skull? We got no one who become dead who looks like that!'

Klopper's response was clumsy. Peekay knew instantly that the Boer knew all along that they'd come for Juicey Fruit Mambo.

'I'm sure you have, Meneer Klopper, he's very large, six eight, six ten maybe? You couldn't miss him.'

Klopper's voice was casual, almost uninterested as he spoke. 'Oh, that one? Ja, I remember now! It was the zig-zag head, when you said about the zig-zag head, that got me mixed up.' He paused just long enough for the effect, looking directly at Tandia. 'That part was blown away when he become dead.'

Tandia gasped and Peekay put his hand around her shoulder and squeezed her lightly. It was an involuntary action and a mistake and he saw the triumphant smirk on Klopper's face. 'We have an ambulance coming, Meneer Klopper,' Peekay withdrew his arm from around Tandia's shoulders and looked at his watch, 'any minute now. I'd like to sign for him please!'

Klopper shook his head as though he was genuinely regretful. 'I'm sorry, any other one you can have. Just say a name and you can have any other kaffir who has become dead yesterday, but not this one. The kaffir with the sharp gold teeth, I definitely got strict instructions from high up not to release him.' He handed the court order back to Peekay.

'This is ridiculous, Klopper!' Peekay said, dropping all pretence at politeness. 'I've got a court order, until it's rescinded it's valid. Who gave you the order to retain the deceased?'

Klopper seemed not in the least upset by Peekay's pointed manner. He could quite easily have told Peekay to mind his own business, but instead he smiled, 'As a matter of fact a friend of yours, Advokaat. A good friend of yours,' he grinned, enjoying the moment. 'Lieutenant Geldenhuis, it was him, he personally left the instructions.'

'Jannie Geldenhuis? Lieutenant Jannie Geldenhuis?' Peekay corrected.

'Ja, I think it will soon be Kaptein Geldenhuis. It was a brave thing that he done yesterday against all those drunk, *dagga*-smoking, murdering black bastards!'

'Brave thing!' Tandia could contain herself no longer, 'Jesus! Can you believe it?'

Klopper turned surprisingly quickly for a man his size and stabbed his finger at Tandia, 'Hey! You! Kaffir! You shut your mouth, you hear? You take God's name in vain again you in lots of trouble!'

Tandia looked at him defiantly then turned and walked back to the car, too distraught and angry to remain with Peekay. Johnny Tambourine opened the door from inside and she sat beside him. Inside the car she gave vent to her feelings. She was snorting with indignation: her nostrils flared as she fought to keep down her anger, 'I'll kill him, I'll kill the fat white pig!' she hissed.

Johnny Tambourine put his hand on Tandia's shoulder and chuckled pleasantly, 'That's why you got us, Tandy,' he said quietly. 'Hey man! I told you, we got a contract.'

From the seam running down the side of his shaped tsotsi trousers Johnny Tambourine withdrew a sharpened bicycle spoke. 'Me, really I'm a knife man. Flyspeck Mendoza, he's the professional, he can use a spoke, cut spine with it better than a surgeon. When the time comes, Flyspeck will do it for you.'

Tandia shuddered, 'Johnny, you mustn't do it! Klopper's just an ignorant Boer, there are thousands like him.'

'He's dog shit in the sun, Tandia!'

'Johnny you're here to protect me; that doesn't mean you've got to kill everyone who insults me! *Here*, I'm a coloured person, a black like you; if we did that, in one month all the white people in South Africa would be dead!'

Peekay knew better than to follow after Tandia. He'd already compromised himself earlier by physically touching her in the presence of Klopper. The fat mortician would have seen it as a weakness, even worse, a perversion, and would have totally lost respect and become wholly recalcitrant.

'Can I get Geldenhuis on the phone? Do you have a number?'

Klopper indicated the mortuary building directly behind him with a jerk of his head. 'He's in there; wait here, I'll go and ask him if he'll see you.'

A few minutes later Geldenhuis came out of the building, adjusting his cap as he walked into the sunlight. 'Howzit, Peekay?'

'*Goed*, Jannie,' Peekay answered, equally casually, in Afrikaans.

'What you want?' Geldenhuis asked bluntly, reverting to that language.

Peekay produced the court order and held it out to Jannie Geldenhuis. 'It's a court order giving me authority . . .'

Geldenhuis cut across him impatiently. 'Ja, Klopper here told me. But why do you want this kaffir, what's he to you?'

'He was a friend, he's also a Zulu, I want to give him a proper burial.'

Geldenhuis looked directly at Peekay. 'Don't play games with me, you hear? You know he was a terrorist!'

Peekay laughed, surprised. 'What? Juicey Fruit Mambo? Don't be bloody ridiculous!'

'I know this kaffir, he works for a coloured woman called Mama Tequila. Do you know her?'

'Ja, I know her. The deceased was her chauffeur, that's not a crime.'

'No, man, before that, in 1947 he was in a gang that tried to blow up a pylon for the main power line from Durban to Pietermaritzburg. We keeping him for fingerprints, also we got a photographer coming down from Pretoria to take his picture.'

Peekay laughed. 'Jesus, Jannie, you people never give up, do you? Tandia's told me about the case. The police were made a laughing stock! It turned out to be a group of white guys. Juicey Fruit Mambo happened to be nearby on his way to a hospital where he worked!' He paused, 'But it didn't stop your lot from smashing in his skull when they threw him down a stairway and knocking out his front teeth in an attempt to get him to confess!'

Jannie Geldenhuis looked up at Peekay, 'I wouldn't believe everything that coloured bitch told you or, for that matter, hasn't told you! The police case was badly prepared, he, whatzisname, Juicey Fruit Mambo, was guilty all right; today that wouldn't have happened, I'm telling you, man!'

Peekay brought his forefinger to the tip of his nose. 'Hey, wait a minute, Jannie, what are you saying . . . hasn't told me yet?'

Geldenhuis laughed. 'You think you know everything, don't you? You always so fucking smart! Well you don't, you hear? You know nothing!'

'Miss Patel is a colleague, a partner and a lawyer with an impeccable reputation, that's all I need to know about her.'

'Miss Patel? Who are you calling miss? Miss, like she's a somebody, like she's a white person! The black bitch is a whore and I can prove it,' Geldenhuis spat.

Peekay was suddenly terribly angry. 'Who are you calling a whore, Geldenhuis?' A tiny voice in the back of his head told him to stop; danger lay ahead. But he couldn't leave it there and just back down. He suddenly knew he was in love with Tandia, that he wanted to smash Geldenhuis's face in, defend her against his vile accusations. He gritted his teeth, fighting for control, his entire body shaking with the effort.

'You fucking her!' Geldenhuis grinned, pulling his head back slightly, delighted. 'Jesus! Peekay's fucking a black whore!'

Geldenhuis was fast enough to see the left coming, but it was only a feint. Peekay's right hand smashed into his jaw, almost lifting him from the ground, and he sat down hard and then rolled in the dirt. There was a cry of astonishment from the Africans waiting under the bluegum trees and a solitary black constable came running up. The people, alerted by Tandia's return to the car, had been watching; someone in the crowd had recognised her and the *Onoshobishobi Ingelosi* when they'd arrived. Now they saw the Tadpole Angel knock the hated Lieutenant Geldenhuis down and they were too astonished to do anything but gasp. Had it been anyone else they would have scattered, running from the trouble to come, but they now saw Peekay's presence as a sign and they held their ground.

Geldenhuis lay still as Klopper ran over to him but before the big man could lift him up he sat up and shook his head. '*Is jy okay?*' Klopper asked anxiously.

Geldenhuis pushed his arm aside and waved the black policeman back; then he rose a little unsteadily to his feet. The policeman ran over and retrieved Geldenhuis's cap and, dusting it first with the back of his hand, handed it to his superior who placed it back on his head. A bright trickle of blood ran from the corner of Geldenhuis's mouth. He wiped at it with the back of his hand and then looked up, grinning triumphantly. 'I've got you, Peekay!' He turned to Klopper, 'You witnessed it, an unprovoked attack on a police officer!'

'Ja, I'm your witness, I saw the whole thing, Lieutenant.' Klopper's voice was unctuous, anxious to collaborate.

'You know what is the stupid part, Peekay? You hit me for nothing, I can prove it. I can prove she's a whore.'

Klopper's arm went around Peekay as he stepped towards Geldenhuis. 'No more, you hear!' The fat man's strength was enormous as he held Peekay. Some of the Africans had moved closer and the men among them were starting to look angry.

Geldenhuis hadn't slept the previous night. He still couldn't quite believe that he'd been responsible for the first shot, the fatal shot which had killed Juicey Fruit Mambo. The whole thing had a dreamlike quality. He'd realised later that in the subsequent chaos nobody seemed to know he'd started the massacre. What had kept him sleepless was the certainty that his career was finished. He'd been the Special Branch man on the spot, responsible for maintaining order during the protest and he'd failed. Coming after everything else, he was certain that this time he was doomed.

But he showed none of this anger outwardly as he fixed his pale blue eyes on Peekay who was being held in a bear hug by Klopper. At the very least he should smash his fist into Peekay's face. In his imagination he could hear the crunch of bone and cartilage as he flattened his nose.

But this moment too passed and he was back in control. He was too good a police officer to waste the opportunity with a piece of gratuitous revenge when Peekay had so much more ultimately coming to him.

'You'd better come inside, man.' Geldenhuis paused, 'Into the office . . . or I can place you under arrest here, you can suit yourself.' He was still panting a little from the shock of the punch though the blood had ceased to run from his mouth. Tandia and Johnny Tambourine came running up. Klopper still held Peekay, who'd made no attempt to struggle. 'Let him go, man,' Geldenhuis said to Klopper, 'I can defend myself.' He turned to Tandia, 'Get back to the car and wait, you hear? Take the kaffir boy with you!'

Tandia looked questioningly at Peekay. 'It's okay, Tandia, we're just going to the office for a chat; wait for me, I shan't be long.'

Geldenhuis grinned, his voice over-familiar, 'Do as you told now, Tandy.'

Tandia, pale and frightened, stood her ground. 'What's going on, Peekay?'

'Lieutenant Geldenhuis said something to me and I took exception to it. What I did was stupid; it's okay, just wait for me in the car.'

Tandia knew immediately that Peekay had come to her defence, that he'd hit Geldenhuis because of something he'd said about her. 'Lieutenant, do you intend to press charges?' She was surprised at the firmness of her voice.

Geldenhuis gave a short, dismissive laugh. 'I'm a boxer, I should have known better, man. I thought he was going to hit me with a left hook!' His voice was almost friendly as he added, 'I just want to talk with Peekay, in the office, do you mind?'

'If you're going to arrest him he's entitled to a lawyer,' Tandia persisted.

'Then if he's arrested, I'll call you, you hear?' He turned to Klopper, 'You too, stay outside, calm these kaffirs down, get things going but don't let anybody in the mortuary while we're there, we got things to talk about.' He turned and walked towards the door, Peekay following him. Geldenhuis stopped before entering the building, brushing the dirt from the back of his pants. He turned again, looking back at Klopper. 'Nobody comes in, you hear? Not even you!'

The big Boer nodded and, turning to Tandia and Johnny Tambourine, indicated with a dismissive sweep of his hands that they should return to the car. Then he did the same to the Africans who'd gathered around, '*Buyela emuva!* Go back!' he yelled. It was an expression he used a lot and it was one of no more than a dozen instructions he'd learned in Zulu in over thirty years of dealing with black people on a day-to-day basis.

Peekay followed Geldenhuis into a small office. 'Close the door, man,' Geldenhuis said. 'Sit down.' He indicated a bentwood kitchen chair, one of two beside a table. He removed his cap and placed it on top of a brown manila file lying on the table. He hadn't been quite quick enough and Peekay read the single word 'Mambo' scrawled quite large on the cover.

Peekay hadn't addressed Geldenhuis directly since he'd punched him. Now he said, 'That was a bloody stupid thing to do, Jannie, but I don't wish to apologise; understand, I'd do it again under the same circumstances.' He should have left it at that, but he was still angry. 'You bastards think you can say anything, do anything, but you can't. Miss Patel may just be another kaffir to you, but she's a colleague and a young advocate with a brilliant career ahead of her. You can hide behind your policeman's badge as much as you like, but she's the future and your bullets and your bullying and your *baasmanskap* isn't going to change that. When you pulled the trigger you put an end to hope for a reconciliation. You declared war!'

'Who said I pulled the trigger?' He spoke calmly enough, not giving anything away, but instantly Peekay knew that it was Geldenhuis who had fired the first shot and who had killed Juicey Fruit Mambo.

'It doesn't matter who pulled the trigger; Sharpeville was your operation.'

Geldenhuis grinned. 'Like you, man, I'd do it again under the same circumstances; my men were in danger!'

'Ja, that seems clear, three hundred men armed with sten guns, two Saracen armoured weapon carriers with machine gun turrets, an eight-foot high riot fence between you and the crowd, which consisted of as many women and schoolchildren as it did men. The dangerous weapons they carried were sticks attached to protest banners. I imagine you were in mortal danger!'

Geldenhuis looked over at Peekay calmly. 'You talking shit! You wasn't there, man, I was. Save your questions for the inquiry, we going to charge all the wounded for inciting violence. I have no doubt you and that black whore will be in court for the defence.'

Peekay gritted his teeth, but this time he didn't react to the policeman's taunt. 'We'll be there,' he said quietly.

Without thinking, Geldenhuis rubbed his chin; then he took his wallet from the pocket of his police tunic. He opened it and produced a small square of paper. He handed the square to Peekay, 'Here, read it, now let's see who's telling lies.'

Peekay opened the tiny square of paper carefully and slowly read the confession Geldenhuis had forced out of the frightened teenager at the Cato Manor police station all those years ago. Peekay folded the page again and without saying anything he returned it to Geldenhuis.

'Tandy and me go back a long time,' Geldenhuis said smugly, enjoying the effect of the innuendo as he replaced the paper into his wallet.

Peekay leaned on the table and brought his fingers up to his lips. He was silent for a while. 'Tell me, Geldenhuis, this confession. I see it's typed; was it part of a statement of arrest?'

'Ja, you could say that.'

'I see, but there is no record of Miss Patel having been arrested and charged with prostitution. Had there been, she could never have been admitted to the bar.'

'Ja, well, there were no charges.'

'Why not? Thirteen is the age of consent for Africans and coloured women. If that is a voluntary confession she should have been charged for prostitution.'

'Ag man, I forget now, there were other circumstances, she wasn't charged, just brought in for questioning.'

Peekay's forefinger touched his nose lightly 'Other circumstances? I take it there is a record somewhere, a transcription of these other circumstances? An adequate reason why a young girl prostitute is allowed to go free after signing an official admission of guilt?'

Geldenhuis sighed impatiently. 'I'm not stupid, Peekay. You know the police make deals all the time. That document is signed by a police officer and a black police constable witness. Maybe, because it's not official, in a court of law you can make mincemeat of it! Inadmissible evidence and all that.' He leaned back in his chair, fanning himself with his wallet. 'Who gives a fuck! It's got Tandia's signature on it and mine and a reliable witness and, published in a newspaper, people will draw their own conclusions! The first female black lawyer, she's big news, man! And I can destroy her credibility any time I like.'

'Why?' Peekay asked, his manner almost absent-minded.

'Why what?' Geldenhuis returned.

'Why, all those years back, would you have gone to that much trouble?'

'Simple! I already told you. Young girls like that. She was pretty and not stupid. They go on the game, sooner or later they shack up with an important gang leader and suddenly you on the inside, you got a reliable informer.'

'So Miss Patel is your personal informer?'

Geldenhuis realised too late that Peekay had him trapped. It was so quick, none of the niceties he'd expected, just one sharp, deadly verbal thrust: *So Miss Patel is your personal informer?* If he lied and claimed that Tandia was his informer then Peekay would confront her and she'd be forced to clear herself by telling of the incident in the pink room at Bluey Jay. If he told the truth, that Tandia had never been in his service as an informer, Peekay would become equally curious as to why he would blackmail a schoolgirl who was making a few bob on the side as a prostitute. There was only one obvious reason and you didn't have to be Sherlock Holmes to figure it out.

Jannie Geldenhuis felt as though he was going to choke; both ways he ended up being seen as a sexual pervert. It was the one thing he couldn't bear anyone to find out, least of all Peekay. He felt a sudden chill come over him, a bone marrow coldness as a sudden vision of the childhood experience in the cold room of his father's butcher's shop etched itself sharply in his mind.

Peekay looked up, his face without expression, waiting for the policeman's reply. He was suddenly terribly confused; he couldn't believe that Tandia was a plant, a police informer, it simply didn't make sense. Yet he'd seen the note, and Geldenhuis was in a perfect position to blackmail her. 'Are you telling me Miss Patel is in your pay?' he asked again.

Jannie Geldenhuis smiled blandly at Peekay, concealing his emotions. He was in charge here, not Peekay. He was not here to be cross-questioned by the rooinek lawyer. 'No more questions. Save your questions for the courts, advocate. Let me ask you some questions now. This man, Juicey Fruit Mambo, why was he at Sharpeville; this person comes from Durban. He has a record as a terrorist; why does he suddenly show up at Sharpeville which is a small township, not even important and thirty-five miles from Johannesburg?'

'That's quite easy to answer. His employer, whom we both know as Mama Tequila, has a sister who lives near here. She was visiting her sister and no doubt he was curious and went along to the demonstration for a look.' Peekay paused, shrugging his shoulders. 'The rest you know.'

If Geldenhuis was surprised by this news he didn't show it. 'Have we not got a wider conspiracy here? Funny how the visit comes about just when there is a major demonstration planned isn't it? A demonstration in a township that is known for being peaceful, for not normally joining into this sort of thing?'

'Hang on! What are you trying to say? That Mama Tequila is a covert terrorist? Or that Juicey Fruit Mambo is an agent provocateur? Or that someone else is pulling the strings and made it convenient for him to be up here when the protest was planned? Which is it to be?'

'The law is the law, if people break the law they going to get into trouble.' Geldenhuis pointed his finger at Peekay, stabbing it in the air several times to make his point. 'You know what you are, Peekay? You're the lowest type there is, the kind of white man who wants to destroy all that we've built up, you want to tear down a decent God-fearing people. You want to hand back to the dirty, ugly, stupid and primitive black man what my ancestors fought three hundred years to win. I'm warning you, man, that kaffir with the gold teeth in there was number one. And if you're fucking Tandia Patel, you're number two!' He lifted his head, looking up at the ceiling, 'Jesus! Imagine the headlines!' He looked back at Peekay, 'Please, man, do it! Please give me the chance to string you up by your balls in front of the public. It would be the best day of my whole fucking life!'

'You know what your problem is, Jannie? You could never beat me in the ring. You simply weren't good enough.' Peekay pointed to the policeman's gun. 'And now, because you lack the skill with your head and your hands, you want to even the score with that!' He felt a little foolish taunting him, but he hoped it would work.

Geldenhuis jumped to his feet, kicking the chair away from behind him. 'Any time, you hear? Any place! You name it, I'll be there, with or without gloves!' His face, contorted with rage, was two inches from Peekay's.

'Christ, Geldenhuis, back there with Klopper you fell for the oldest trick in the book, a feint with the left hand followed by a right. Don't insult me! Go pick on some defenceless black man and gun him down at a peaceful protest!'

Peekay got ready to block the punch he felt sure was coming. Geldenhuis's face had gone white as chalk and his pale blue eyes made him look as though they were fitted into a porcelain mask. It was not the first time Peekay had witnessed naked aggression; he'd faced hate and rage in the ring often enough, but this was different. Strangely he felt better for it. Now he knew what he was up against, he'd flushed the enemy out. He'd have to keep scoring off the Afrikaner, try to keep him off balance. That way the police themselves would watch him, tie his hands, afraid that if Geldenhuis came after any of them too openly the media would cry foul and Red would make a fool of them in court. As long as he could keep alive the policeman's determination to vindicate himself utterly in everyone's eyes, to show the world he was the better man by trying publicly to humiliate Peekay, they were all more or less safe. He had to keep needling him in public so as to keep the enemy in the open. Geldenhuis hunting them without the need to vindicate himself in public was much too dangerous.

But Geldenhuis had one more surprise for him. He pulled back, suddenly smiling, and Peekay could feel the tension leave the policeman. Peekay realised that the lightning ferocity and the incredible calm, all within moments, was what made the policeman such a remarkable and feared interrogator, this schizoid ability to be hot and cold, two people at once.

Geldenhuis quietly resumed his seat and, pushing his cap aside, he opened the manila folder. 'Do you have a good picture of the deceased?' he asked calmly.

'Not personally, but I'm sure we could find one easily enough,' Peekay replied.

'In that case I will release his body to you. We have a photographer coming from Pretoria to take the pictures of all the dead, that's why the relatives are having to wait outside. He's late, he was supposed to be here by eight o'clock.'

'You mean we're going to have to wait?'

'No I just said, get me a good picture. Even if we took a picture of this person,' he tapped the manila file, 'it wouldn't be any good, he's only got half of his head with him.' Geldenhuis said this sotto voce, not attempting to score a point; he was a police officer doing his job. He rose from the chair. 'C'mon, you'll have to officially identify him. I'll take his fingerprints at the same time.'

Predictably, the first thing that hit Peekay as they entered the mortuary was the smell. He had no idea that human bodies could develop such a stench in so short a period. The smell of putrefaction filled the room. He clutched at his stomach with one hand and covered his nose and mouth with the other as he turned to rush out again, but Geldenhuis grabbed him by the shoulder halting him.

'Dead kaffirs stink, hey? Just stand still for a moment and breath normally.' Peekay turned back again to face the room and, reaching for his handkerchief, he placed it over his nose. Geldenhuis showed no reaction to the stench.

The room was in semi-darkness, like being under a heavy canopy of trees. It wasn't large and if you looked carefully you could pick out most of the detail, though it contained no windows. Light entered from two skylights in the roof, both of which had been painted white in an attempt to insulate the heat coming in; two large extractor fans whirred on either side of the skylights.

The room seemed completely filled with the dead, laid out side by side on the polished cement floor, each corpse touching the other with a narrow corridor running down the centre and another, even narrower, along the wall leading to where they stood at the doorway. The corpses which were identified were covered with a green sheet from which two naked feet extended into the centre isle. On each left big toe was tied a manila label bearing the dead person's name. Those of the dead who had no identification, those who'd done as instructed and left their passes at home, were also covered, though this time their feet were covered and their faces exposed awaiting identification by their relatives. It was all very neat and tidy; Klopper obviously ran a tight ship.

The far wall appeared to be made of glass insulator bricks in the centre of which was set a white enamel door about twice the size of a normal oven door. Set in line with the door and extending about eight feet out into the room was a ramp of the sort you sometimes see in loading depots where cases are pushed along metal coasters set between rails. The oven-like structure was obviously the incinerator for the unclaimed dead, and the ramp was for the smooth delivery of a body through the enamel door into its interior. Near the oven door, completely covered by several of the green morgue sheets, was what appeared to be a mound about five feet high.

'Can we do this quickly, please?' Peekay gasped.

'Ja, but we have a problem,' Geldenhuis pointed to the green mound. 'Klopper didn't have room for everyone, you know, to lay them out all neat. These are crisis conditions, this place is only built for a few stiffs. So, well, man, some they still in that pile. If Zulu Mambo, the Bantu you looking for isn't here,' his hand swept along the row of bodies, 'then you going to have to find him in that pile over there. Mostly over there is the bits and the bad sights. A machine gun, it can cut right through a person, also some of the guys, they used dum-dum bullets.'

Peekay removed the handkerchief; his expression was incredulous. 'You bastard, Geldenhuis!'

Geldenhuis shrugged. 'I'm sorry, we can't let anyone in to help you. No black people are allowed in until we have taken all the photographs.

Maybe you'll be lucky, maybe he's here, all neat in a row,' he paused, rubbing the point of the chin where Peekay had hit him, 'but I don't think so.'

Peekay was trapped and he trembled as he walked down the centre aisle looking into the faces of the dead. There was a constant hum of flies in the room which he hadn't noticed as he'd entered and now he saw them clustered about the eyes and crawling around and into the open mouths of the dead who, apart from being covered with a sheet, had received no special attention. The blood from their internal haemorrhaging had caked around their mouths and necks. Peekay brushed a bloated fly from his face.

'We spray them with Doom, but the buggers come back, I don't know where they come from.' Doom was a popular brand of insecticide; under the circumstances it seemed an appropriate name.

Peekay came to the end of the long lines of the dead, knowing Juicey Fruit Mambo would not be among them but nevertheless forcing himself to look at each face. Here was the legacy of hate, the ultimate punishment for mothers and fathers and children who'd dared to hope they might be free in the country of their birth. Finally he reached the cloth-covered mound of the dead. The green sheeting was heavily stained with large brown patches of dried blood and in one place the brighter red of a fresh seepage. Peekay stood trembling, lacking the courage to pull back the sheets. Finally he did so and what he saw would be part of a recurring nightmare from which he'd wake screaming for the remainder of his life.

Peekay would dream he was standing on the pavement looking into the window of Mr Rubens' Doll Factory in Hammersmith, looking down at the bits of broken doll, torsos and legs and arms and cracked and broken bisque heads lying higgledy-piggledy on top of each other in the window. Then, as he watched, the scene in the window would transform into this Sharpeville pile of the dead above which, seated on a single swing, was Geldenhuis. He wore a doll's wig and a pretty pink doll's dress embroidered across the bodice with blue forget-me-nots and tiny white roses, his feet in white calf-length cotton socks and shod with black patent-leather kiddies' shoes, his toes turned inward in the manner of a small child. Geldenhuis would look at him, his eyes wide and incredulous. He'd say, 'We spray them with Doom, but the buggers come back, I don't know where they all come from!' Then he'd smile and a bright trickle of blood would run from the corner of his mouth.

On the top of the pile lay a huge woman, her legs wide open; her crotch and stomach had been blown away and viscera had been pushed back into the gaping wound. The elastic bottoms of her pink crêpe-de-chine bloomers with tattered fragments of bloody cloth attached still dug into her thighs, though her dress and the rest of the bloomers had been torn away. Except for the bizarre garters, her enormous body lay naked from the waist down. Propping it up were heads and arms, legs and torsos

– though piled up the way they were, at all angles, they didn't look like bodies, more like components, a junk heap of rejected human parts.

Peekay knew he was going to be sick and he grabbed at the oven door set into the wall, only just managing to swing it open and lean over the delivery ramp before vomiting into its interior. He remained like this for some time, continuing to heave when at last he withdrew his head he was totally distraught, his body bent forward almost double, shaking violently.

Geldenhuis watched Peekay as he threw up into the interior of the cremation oven, then he slowly withdrew his Smith & Wesson .38 calibre service revolver from its holster. Pushing to the left, he opened the chamber, removing the bullet in the chamber nearest to the barrel. He reached into his trouser pocket, his hands closing around the warm, familiar shape of the single gold square-nosed bullet. He slid it silently into the vacant hole in the revolving chamber of the revolver and carefully pushed the chamber back. When he cocked the gun the gold dum-dum bullet would line up with the barrel to blow half of Peekay's head away.

The coldness had come back, the terrible cold that seemed to seep down into his marrow. This place; the plan was working perfectly, it was even better than his fantasy of finding a boxing ring. He hadn't planned to kill him, just to humiliate him. But now as he saw the way things were turning out, he knew it was a certain sign from God that he was right. He was alone with Peekay; the black whore lay there ready for him on top of the sides of beef, just like the vision he'd been given. The cold grew more intense. Things were becoming mixed up in his head, blurred. He was in the cold room behind his father's butcher's shop. It must be a Tuesday, the carcasses were stacked up against the end wall. It was only right, his father must be punished, what he was doing was terribly wrong, he was committing a mortal sin, he was doing it with a black woman and so he must die. It was the only way to save South Africa, to do his duty as an Afrikaner and as a white man! But he was too cold, his finger was frozen on the trigger, slowly he lowered the gun and tried to still his shivering body.

Peekay stood stooped over, panting, his hands resting on his knees. 'I'm a coward, I can't do it!' he gasped, without looking up. Then he began to sob softly, a great sorrow welling up in him, a terrible sadness for his whiteness, for his pale eyes and hair like straw which marked him as a vicious killer, a member of the *strange ones.* Slowly his fear began to leave him; the great hollow places it left behind were filled instead with grief. His grieving was for the mother, the great, warm mother of Africa with a washing basket on her head filled with freshly laundered clothes smelling of sunlight, the flash of her white teeth as she laughed and gobbled up the gossip of the day, the slow perambulation of her massive thighs. He mourned for the woman who cradled her soft brown children in her massive arms, her skin like velvet and her song sweet as goats' milk mixed with honey. He pulled her as gently as he could from the top of the pile and laid her on the ground. Then his grief turned back as he lifted a child, no more than eight years old, his small, innocent face serene in death, as though he'd fallen asleep and was being carried in the arms of a loving father to his bed. Peekay laid him down as well, not even seeing the gaping hole in his chest. His grief moved the people one by one and laid them gently down. At last, at the very bottom, lay Juicey Fruit Mambo, his two gold incisor teeth intact in his huge broken head. Peekay bent down and lifted his shoulders off the ground and then he sat and cradled Edward King George Juicey Fruit Mambo in his arms and wept and wept.

THIRTY-FIVE

Juicey Fruit Mambo was buried according to tribal rights and rituals, with the slaughter of two oxen killed so that their bellowing would awaken his shadows to come for him. The meat from the two great beasts was hung inside his childhood *khaya*, huge strips of meat hanging mostly from the centre pole, drenching the small round hut in blood.

Very early on the day of the ceremony two Swazi warriors arrived in a battered pick-up and requested permission to enter the lands of the Zulu and then specifically to visit Juicey Fruit Mambo's *isigodi*, his district or neighbourhood. The two strangers handed the *umNgoma* presiding over the burial ceremony a long sheath made of the fresh hide of an ox which still carried the beast's hair, mostly black with a splash of white near the top of its six-foot length. The two men were anxious to depart; they were deep into alien territory and when pressed to take a calabash of kaffir beer they did so, gulping the traditional thick, sour-tasting beer quickly before making elaborate excuses to depart. The sheath was from the great Somojo, the old man who had presided at Juicey Fruit Mambo's death at Sharpeville, and within it was the magic stick which contained his spirit. The spirit stick meant that Juicey Fruit Mambo could now be properly returned to his shadows to live with his ancestors in the land of the Zulu.

The funeral was a big affair, attended by a great many people from his *isigodi*, and some from other places. It lasted a day and a night of dancing, feasting and excessive drinking, all at the expense of Mama Tequila, who, too sad and distraught to attend herself, instructed Tandia to see that it was a funeral to be remembered for ever.

'Tandy, darling, I want everything first class, you understand, nothing slipshod, just the best, you hear? All of a sudden I wish we could be a *catlicks* like Ruth, then we could pay the Pope to make him the patron saint of motor cars!'

Gideon came and this was thought a great honour even though he did not belong to the same *isigodi* as Juicey Fruit Mambo.

A great many orations took place, for the Zulu people like to remember and to build things up so that all who are present should be given the correct impression. When it came to Gideon's turn to speak he was careful with his form; country people like things to be done correctly and he thanked his rival chief for his welcome and paid homage to Juicey Fruit Mambo's clan.

'Zulu Mambo was a warrior of great distinction who had the heart of a lion,' he went on to say. 'All his life he spat in the face of the *amaBhunu*, the Boers, and he suffered greatly at their hands. But he was a proud man from a fiercely proud clan.'

'Haya, haya!' the crowd sighed, pleased with the compliment.

'They tried to break his spirit, but they couldn't do this. In the end he defied the police guns and the great motors of steel that wear guns that spit bullets like a hailstorm. He stood and he cried out, "White man, I want my freedom back, I have come to take it back!" '

The crowd moaned and the women started to ululate; this was their tribesman and the champion of the world was talking about his bravery. 'And they heard him, the *amaBhunu* heard his cry, but their hearts were stone like always and stone hearts cannot hear the truth. They killed him.'

A great howl went up and a moaning even from the men. The Boer's heart of stone was well known to all.

'But it was too late,' Gideon said, bringing them to silence. 'When the teeth of the bullets tore into his great chest, it was too late, the call for freedom was out and its echoes were in the hills and the valleys and it rose above the crashing sounds of the spitting guns. The people have heard Zulu Mambo's call and they will answer, they will answer with *Umkonto we Sizwe*, the Spear of the Nation. The time to answer with the spear has come. It is the beginning and because Zulu Mambo has made this beginning for all, it is the beginning of the end of the tyranny of the white man. The name of the place where our brother made the great call for freedom will ring around the world as a mighty blow rings on metal. The drums of freedom are sounding, we cannot turn back now, we cannot be stopped!'

For a hundred years the people of Zululand will talk about the funeral of the great warrior Zulu Mambo. How it took fifty men to dig his grave, the same fifty men with ropes singing a chant to a dead warrior as they lowered him into his grave seated behind the wheel of a great pink automobile, dressed in a grey suit, white shirt, pink tie and chauffeur's cap which cunningly covered the wound of his noble death. Covering his eyes were the dark glasses for looking into the setting sun; on his hands were white gloves of the finest leather which held firmly to the steering wheel. They would tell the story of how the great warrior Zulu Mambo drove himself to the place of his ancestors with his shadows, who had come on foot to fetch him, resting comfortably in the back seat of the huge automobile, laughing and chatting away happily. Right to the very end that one was a Zulu who showed a lot of class.

And now when the dust devils come and play willy-nilly across the dry land the herd boys laugh and point as they watch from the hilltops, 'There goes Edward King George Juicey Fruit Mambo, that is the dust of his parting, his roaring away in his great pink Packard!' And sometimes they can follow his dust cloud for miles. Haya! they think, one day I'll be just like him!

When Tandia, Gideon and Peekay were ready to depart, the witch-doctor, who had presided at the burial ceremony, handed Tandia a tiny leather bag worked so thin that the cream-coloured uncured leather was almost opaque. The bag, no bigger than her thumb, was made from the hide of one of the sacred oxen slaughtered for Zulu Mambo's burial rituals. 'Take what's inside and wear it around your neck if you do this, then he who is now with his shadows will protect you always.'

In the car driving back from Zululand Tandia took the tiny leather sack from her bag and tapped the contents gently into the palm of her hand. First one and then the second of the gold caps which had covered Juicey Fruit Mambo's incisor teeth fell out. She looked down at the two tiny pieces of gold and wept quietly for the last time for the only person who had always loved her selflessly.

In the days and weeks immediately after Sharpeville the country was in an uproar with strikes and protest marches occurring everywhere. This time the world sat up and took notice and the Johannesburg stock exchange hit an all-time low. Whites in their thousands mobbed travel agents and the United States, Australian, Canadian and New Zealand embassies were flooded with requests for immigration papers.

A week after Sharpeville, with the country almost brought to a standstill, Magistrate Coetzee called Tandia from a telephone box near the Magistrates Courts. From where he stood he could see the dilapidated building with its four windows on the first floor where Red had its offices. He could as easily have walked across but he couldn't take the chance of being seen. Besides, there wasn't much time; he had to take a chance that the Red telephone wasn't tapped.

When Tandia came to the phone Magistrate Coetzee spoke urgently. 'Listen, man, Tandy, the government has declared a state of emergency! This morning I signed warrants for the arrest of ninety-seven so-called activists here in Johannesburg,' he paused, 'you know I don't take sides in these things, but Gideon Mandoma's name was among them. Geldenhuis came personally to pick up the warrant for him, *jy moet gou maak*, there is not much time.' Then he added, 'I don't know how to advise you, but like I suggested might happen, in a week's time they are going to ban the ANC and PAC, they will become outlawed organisations. For your own sake perhaps you should resign now. Later, who knows, it might be useful to have done so?' He replaced the receiver without saying goodbye.

Tandia called Johnny Tambourine to her office and told him to meet them with an unmarked car from Levy's Carpet Emporium at the usual place. Months previously the four boys, who as tsotsis knew the city drains well, had located a manhole in the centre of the small rear courtyard to the Red building. They entered it and found it led to a main storm-water channel that was almost dry when it wasn't raining and easy to walk along. They'd checked all the manholes out until they'd found one in a quiet back street four city blocks away which they'd marked; another was marked nine blocks away. The four of them, Hymie, Peekay, Tandia and Gideon were the only people at Red to know about the escape route which, except for several practice runs, had never so far been used. A small storage shed was built over the manhole with a permanent covered walkway from the main building to the shed so that they couldn't be observed from the roof of a surrounding building.

Tandia went through to the tiny cubbyhole which served as Gideon's office and asked him if he'd come through to Peekay's small office. Gideon saw the look of concern on her face and rose immediately, 'What is it, Tandy?'

'Trouble. Come quick, you may have only minutes. There is a warrant out for your arrest. Geldenhuis!' She was shaking slightly and Gideon could see that she was scared.

Tandia quickly outlined Magistrate Coetzee's conversation to Peekay. 'I've organised a car and we'll use the drain. Johnny Tambourine will be waiting at the manhole in half an hour.'

'Not *we*, Tandia. Just Gideon!' Peekay said.

Tandia was shocked. 'I must go with him, Peekay!'

'No! You cut down his chances. If he's caught you're implicated.'

'He's right, Tandy,' Gideon said.

'Bullshit! The government have declared war, they're going to ban the ANC, Coetzee told me. If you have to go underground I'm in this fight too!'

'Tandy, you're more useful where you are. We have to have some people who are clean. We've discussed it, remember?' Gideon said.

'You can use Peekay. I'm a member of *Umkonto.* We have to fight, you can't stop me.'

Gideon spoke slowly. 'I am the head of *Umkonto*, its chief. You will remain here and you will not come with me, you hear?' It was a different Gideon talking; he was perfectly calm but there was no mistaking the authority in his voice and Tandia actually took a step backwards.

Her head downcast, looking at her fingernails, she said softly, 'Yes, sir.'

Peekay looked at his watch. 'You better scram.' He embraced Gideon. 'I see you with my heart, Gideon,' and drew away. 'You two would like a few moments alone, I'm sure.' He walked over to the door and closed it behind him.

'What will you do? Where will you go?' Tandia asked.

Gideon smiled. 'We have planned for this moment a long time. I will be in touch, but don't worry if you don't hear from me for a while. You can tell Peekay anything you hear from me, but no one else, not even one of us, not even *Umkonto.* You understand?'

Tandia nodded. 'Please Gideon, please let me fight?'

'I must go,' he said, as though he hadn't heard her. He moved towards the door then paused. 'There will be lots of time and lots of pain. The

Boers are going to give us a terrible hiding at first. Your time will come, Tandia.'

Tandia ran over and kissed him, but Gideon pushed her away. 'No, Tandy, that's over. When we come to the end of this thing, we'll see.'

'Gideon! I love you,' Tandia cried.

'Tandia, you promised you would do my hating for me. I need your hate now. Don't love me, *hate for me*!' He closed the door and was gone.

'You Zulu bastard!' Tandia spat at the door. 'You think a woman can't fight!'

Gideon moved around the country evading detention and addressing young black South Africans who were being recruited to *Umkonto we Sizwe*. These meetings were known as 'the midnight cadres' because most of them took place in secret after midnight and never involved more than fifty young men and women, selected to attend a freedom lecture with 'General' Mandoma.

The title of general was an honorarium given to Gideon by his young recruits who spoke of him as 'General Mandoma, the undefeated champion of the world'. It was stirring stuff and with his own charisma and undoubted power with words, Gideon was quickly seen as the head of a terrorist army in the making.

But Gideon was a general without experience. The ANC had not anticipated guerrilla warfare with the white South African regime, believing right up to the time of Sharpeville that one day soon they would sit around the negotiating table. Gideon had not been given permission to recruit or train and no meaningful retaliatory infrastructure existed. The techniques of urban and rural guerrilla warfare were practically unknown to them. The ANC were strictly amateurs coming up against a hardened and highly experienced paramilitary police force led by the Special Branch whom they knew shot to kill.

After having been on the run for nearly eight months, Gideon was to be sent to Algeria to learn how to organise guerrilla groups and urban fighting units. The Algerians had offered to train the ANC in the business of fighting a superior and better organised force, all the technique and know-how they had gained fighting the French for their independence.

Peekay arranged to see Gideon just before his departure. This last meeting, which would follow a typical midnight cadre talk so that there would be no suspicion of Gideon's departure even among his own people, was to take place in a church hall in the heart of Wesselton African Township on the outskirts of Ermelo, a smallish town in the Eastern Transvaal.

Peekay hadn't seen his friend for nearly two months and, as it was a week into December, among other things he carried with him several Christmas presents, though his most important reason for seeing Gideon was to give him the British passport prepared in Kenya for him. Peekay's visit to Gideon also concerned Tandia. In the aftermath of Sharpeville she had become hopelessly overloaded with work. The South African government was prosecuting the Sharpeville wounded and even members of the families of the dead. Several days before his final meeting with Gideon Peekay had confronted Hymie, questioning his priorities.

Hymie had remained very quiet while Peekay talked and Peekay soon realised he'd spoken thoughtlessly. Hymie looked at him steadily. 'Have you any idea what you and Tandia bring into this company in fees every year?'

'Not really. Look, I'm sorry, Hymie, I spoke out of turn. You're right, I guess I don't think about it much, there's so much bloody work to do.'

'There was a time when money was important to you, Peekay, when you were too conscious of not having it. Now you've gone the other way. Why is it that you can never do anything more or less moderately? Let me tell you how much the two of you earned last month; about sufficient to keep the switchboard operating!'

'I'm sorry, Hymie, but you know the nature of the work. These people can't pay!'

Hymie brushed the comment aside. 'I have two talents, old son: I know how to make money and I reckon I'm a half decent sort of a barrister. You appear to only have one: an ability to fight injustice without any thought of material gain. Our other partner, the pretty one, is so preoccupied she wouldn't even bother to eat if we didn't insist on her having a square meal once a day here in the office so we can talk. She thinks a statement is something the police take down, not something we send out. It was great when you were both doing some corporate work, the firm actually made a bob or two, enough on several occasions to pay for the electricity and maybe even the stationery and lunches!'

Hymie sighed. It was more a quick intake of air than a sigh, for Hymie never sighed. 'However, that all ended with Sharpeville. No legal firm was ever more aptly named, we have been in the red since the day we opened our doors.' Hymie's monologue was delivered with typical machine gun rapidity and now he slowed down. 'Peekay, altruism costs a great deal; we also serve who only stand around and make money! The fight for freedom in this man's republic is a very expensive business; every time you lose a civil case your client has costs awarded against him.'

Peekay was deeply ashamed and he hugged Hymie, apologising, 'You know Hymie, I forget sometimes that without your genius I'd probably be a hack lawyer in a small town somewhere, another Don Quixote tilting at windmills, fighting cases for washerwomen.'

'So what's new? Talking about washerwomen, your clothes . . . how long is it since you bought a new suit and all the stuff that goes on under it?' Hymie pointed at Peekay's somewhat shabby attire. 'I recall you bought that grey suit at Macey's in New York after the first title fight!'

Hymie dressed beautifully. His suits were made by a short, rotund Jewish tailor in Saville Row known as Mr Emms, who believed that with the invention of the belt to replace what he called 'suspenders' the art of tailoring had come to an end. 'You're a successful barrister and you dress like a tramp!'

Peekay gave Hymie a wry grin. 'Some successful barrister! I have a string of noteworthy, even glorious defeats against my name. No barrister ever earned a bigger reputation with a poorer record. Christ, I sometimes wonder what the hell we're trying to do, Hymie? Yesterday, as I was walking back here from court a young guy stopped me. He wasn't any older than Johnny Tambourine; he asked me for a light. "Sorry, I don't smoke," I replied. "That's okay, I don't want a light anyway. I just want to say something to you. My mother, she thinks you are a hero, because you have defended my father. Last night, the police, they came to my house, 'Your father is dead,' they say, 'He committed suicide. He jumped from the fifth-floor window of John Vorster Square, you must come an' fetch his body!' " The young guy was suddenly crying, "Fuck you, white man! Why you come to help him? Maybe if you don't come they would have beaten him and put him in Johannesburg Fort, but one day he would have come back to us!" Dammit, Hymie, I feel as though I'm achieving nothing. Pretoria is laughing at us, that is if they even notice the Jew, the rooinek bastard and the coloured bitch.'

'The fat Jew!' Hymie corrected. 'You're wrong, Peekay. There is a belief in the Jewish faith that in every generation a "just man" is born, someone who is incorruptible, the perfect innocent. The just man is sent to keep the chosen people on the rails, to prod their consciences and allow no compromises with the faith. By all definitions he's probably a perfect pain in the arse, but the Jews believe that without a just man they would not survive, that the light of Judaism would go out.' He paused. 'That's what we are, the last of the just men in South Africa. If we give up then the light goes out. They must be made to feel remorse.'

'Ha-bloody-ha! Do you think Geldenhuis feels remorse? He thinks of only one thing, vengeance! They're obsessed with blood, *bloed renheid!* blood purity. If we are watchdogs of justice they don't hear us yapping at their ankles. I sometimes think Nguni has more influence on the outcome of things than we do.'

'I've been meaning to talk to you about that, Peekay. Nguni is getting increasingly difficult to handle. He arrives at Angel board meetings pretty sozzled on brandy. He's getting more and more rapacious, he keeps demanding a larger share of the action but isn't prepared to put up any capital. I must say, he seems to have rather a lot of clout with the various quasi government committees.'

Peekay laughed. 'Hymie, you're beating about the bush. What you're saying is that you think Nguni is in the pay of Pretoria. The share we gave him in Angel Sport after the Jackson fight was supposed to be the carrot to keep him close to us. What if he's using his position to spy on us? Tell him to go to buggery!'

Hymie nodded. 'His share in the firm is what's financing Soweto bus company he started three years ago without us knowing. Without the income from Angel Sport he'd be up the spout.'

'Transport? He'd need a government concession for that.'

'Precisely. It's not the sort of thing they hand out willynilly.' Hymie sighed, 'I'm glad you agree we get rid of him.' He paused momentarily, 'What about his friendship with Tandia?'

Peekay knew precisely what Hymie meant. Nguni had used the excuse of Gideon's absence to start squiring Tandia, saying that he was responsible for showing her the ways of the African people. Tandia had been happy to go along with him. While she claimed at every opportunity to be unashamedly black, carrying a pass like any other black woman, she was conscious that her looks prevented her from being wholly accepted by the important echelons of black male society. Peekay watched in dismay as she seemed to spend most of her infrequent spare time with Nguni, seeming almost to see him as a father figure.

Peekay shrugged. 'Tandia's a big girl, she'll understand.'

'I hope you're right,' Hymie said.

Peekay knew Hymie too well not to realise what he was saying. He was asking him whether there was something about Tandia he ought to know. He'd shared his doubts about Mr Nguni for this very reason. Peekay knew he was abusing Hymie's trust by not confiding his concern about Tandia to him.

After Sharpeville, Peekay knew he was besotted with Tandia. It was only by supreme willpower that he could maintain his concentration in court when the going grew tedious. Sometimes he would sneak into her courtroom and sit in the gallery and listen to her. Tandia in a courtroom became transformed she moved around in a black gown as though it was the costume of a queen, elegant and her gestures beautiful to watch. Her mind was as sharp as a whiplash and she commanded great respect from men who would have spat on her rather than light her cigarette outside the courtroom.

Peekay would wake in the morning his whole mind filled with her. He'd lie still, hardly daring to breathe, so that the notion of her lying in his arms remained undisturbed. At night his last thoughts would be of her and often he would find that his cheeks were wet with tears he hadn't even felt. Peekay was profoundly in love and there was nothing he could do about it.

Tandia sensed his feelings towards her and they filled her with fear. Her emotional defences where infinitely greater than Peekay's, besides which the thought of loving him was so fraught with danger and self-destruction that her mind couldn't entertain an idea so positively futile. She had believed herself in love with Gideon but over the weeks he'd been away from her, while she worried enormously for his safety, she found that she missed him less and less emotionally. She had decided that love for a man was something she could never have, that it had been eliminated from her psyche, that her brutalised past had branded her, searing the tenderness and love in her and leaving only scar tissue. In addition, the idea of sex with a white man, any white man, filled her with revulsion.

Nevertheless, sometimes when she looked at Peekay and he was unaware of her, she felt a strange compulsion to touch him. He was so strong and so vulnerable at the same time. His was a kind of innocence she couldn't believe possible in a human being. Tandia didn't know whether she wanted to shake him or hold him, but she knew he was different, different to any person she'd known – and that the difference was extraordinarily attractive while at the same time infuriating.

Peekay was in a high old mess with nobody to turn to, not even Hymie, who'd warned him off on the very first day they'd seen Tandia crossing the football stadium towards the boxing ring in the centre of Ellis Park.

Peekay's love for Tandia and his knowledge of Geldenhuis's letter tore at him remorselessly. He even thought to confront Tandia and tell her that Geldenhuis had shown him her signature on the statement and that he didn't care, that it didn't make the slightest difference. But, if he was mistaken, if there was some other explanation, his suspicion was such a blatant sign of mistrust in her that she would have every right to despise him for it, a thought he couldn't bear.

Suspicion feeds upon itself like a cancer and Tandia's relationship with Magistrate Coetzee now seemed to take on a sinister new meaning for Peekay. He found himself watching her with Coetzee and with Mr Nguni, as much as he was privy to either of these relationships. He became confused, not knowing whether he did so from jealousy or to spy on her. Either way he hated himself, hated what it was doing to him.

Doc had said, 'Every fact has two sides, it depends always from what side you are coming!' Peekay knew this to be true. Looked at from one side, Tandia had always shown the utmost dedication to the cause of justice for the black people and had been totally loyal to him and Hymie, while Magistrate Coetzee had proved a just and marvellous mentor.

Peekay was too good a lawyer not to examine the second interpretation, the facts seen from the opposite perspective. These could also be made to make almost perfect sense if you thought of it as a clever, patient and determined police operation designed, in the end, to trap Hymie, Gideon and himself and bring about their destruction.

But, much as he respected Geldenhuis, he couldn't bring himself to believe that the young police captain (Geldenhuis received promotion after Sharpeville) had the necessary clout to put something like this into place on his own. He thought about Klaasens, but quickly dismissed him too; the publicity the police colonel had received at the Tom Majombi murder trial would have made him too high on the suspect list. Any half-competent lawyer, using revenge as the true motive for their capture, would leave the police case open to ridicule in ten minutes in front of the bench.

And then, on the way to Wesselton township to see Gideon and to bid him farewell, driving along a stretch of road between Bethal and Ermelo, it struck Peekay. General Van Breeden, Police Commissioner for Johannesburg. He was the missing ingredient!

Almost from their first day back home Van Breeden had been involved with them. He'd been the influence behind allowing Ellis Park to be the venue for the fight and it had been his interference which had allowed an equal black audience to attend. Over the years the likeable and capable police commissioner had maintained a friendly relationship with both of them, though more particularly with Hymie, who maintained an unlisted telephone in his home where the two men could contact each other at any time.

Tandia, Mr Nguni, Magistrate Coetzee and Van Breeden, with Geldenhuis playing the overt role of hunter and later to distract attention from the others; these four made an almost perfect flip-side of the coin.

'Jesus! Stop it Peekay,' he commanded himself. South Africa had become such a place of hate, suspicion and fear that his imagination was running away from him. Why was it that the most demented, the most evil scenario always seemed to be the most likely? People were always seeing a conspiracy where none existed, making connections which were dubious to say the least. He spent half his life in court disproving conjecture. The police prosecutors could see connections which were so completely tenuous as to be absurd, yet they'd often spend days building on them, heaping them with innuendo and often helping them along with false witness. He was indulging in the behaviour of a Geldenhuis, the Special Branch mentalities which believed everyone was guilty until proven innocent.

It all hinged on the original confession by Tandia to being a prostitute. Peekay decided to ask Gideon whether Tandia had ever talked to him about it. He thought it was unlikely, but people in love will often clear the emotional deck; it was too important not to try.

It would be tricky trying to maintain his loyalty to both Gideon and Tandia and not to send Gideon away disenchanted or to provoke him to an emotional defence of his woman. But Peekay was desperate for some sort of reassurance and he felt he had to try. He told himself there were other reasons as well. Because it had been a natural assumption after Gideon's escape that Tandia would be watched by the Special Branch it had been suggested that he make no attempt to contact her. But love takes enormous and often foolish chances and Peekay didn't know whether Gideon had tried to see her despite this warning. Tandia also knew about Gideon's departure to Algeria. Perhaps .Gideon himself was in terrible danger and should be warned. If Geldenhuis knew of his imminent departure, he would strike immediately, pulling out all stops to find him, issuing a border and airport alert and sealing off the borders to South Africa with extra men and helicopters.

In actual fact, two of the half-dozen Special Branch black men delegated to watch Tandia since Gideon's disappearance had been hospitalised by unseen assailants, believed to be tsotsis. In each case robbery had been assumed to be the motive, and as the muggings had taken place several miles from where Tandia lived and when the men had been off duty, it was assumed by Geldenhuis to be a coincidence, though nonetheless one to watch carefully. Peekay noted this as yet another contradiction to Tandia's guilt. If Johnny Tambourine and his boys were active, surely this was another sign of her innocence?

Approaching Ermelo and Wesselton township, Peekay stopped to pick up a small barefooted kid of no more than twelve who'd been waiting by arrangement on a lonely strip of road outside the town. The small, serious-faced boy, who wore only a pair of ragged khaki shorts, looked at him a little fearfully from the side of the road as he responded shyly to the password Peekay gave him, his eyes showing big in the bright moonlight as Peekay asked him his name. 'It is Simon, sir,' he answered proudly in English. Peekay later learned from Simon's father that his son had been waiting for him beside the road for eleven hours and had gone without supper. Simon climbed into the front of the car and seated himself on the edge of the seat, his back straight as a ram-rod with both his hands holding onto the dashboard. He gave Peekay shy directions to a place under a willow tree beside a small river, really more a *spruit*, where he could conceal his car. From there they walked the mile or so into the dark township.

General Mandoma, the undefeated champion of the world, had just risen to speak and the kids, some no more than fifteen, rose to their feet chanting, 'General! General! General!' as he stood ready to address them. He saw Peekay enter and silently motioned him to sit at one of two vacant chairs set at the back of the room. Gideon held his hand up for silence and when they'd quietened down and seated themselves, sitting cross-legged on the floor, he opened up with a huge smile. A Gideon Mandoma smile was something to see; it had the effect of the sun coming from behind a cloud and it immediately transferred to the people around him, so that the kids returned his smile spontaneously, leaning forward, drawn impulsively towards him.

Hymie called Gideon's smile his secret weapon. 'If they ever catch you, Gideon, our defence will be a piece of cake. We'll say nothing and simply have you smile at the jury once every hour!'

Now Gideon began, his expression one of mock seriousness. 'Yes, I am a general, that is true. The white authorities already accept this, they call me, "The General Nuisance"!' The smile came again and, coupled with this simple corny quip, it brought the house down. Gideon could count on another fifty soldiers joining 'The Spear'.

Now his face grew serious. 'I am a general whose army is made up of barefooted amateurs. My automatic weapons are flick knives and sharpened bicycle spokes, my artillery is stones and, in a battle charge, my bayonets are sharpened sticks!' He paused, looking at his audience. 'But we will learn, my brothers! We will learn, my sisters! We will sharpen your teeth, comrades, and make your hands familiar with the explosion "plastic" and we will show you how to make a bomb from an old alarm clock and stuff found on this town's junk heap and how a beer bottle filled with paraffin and an old rag can be your hand grenades against the police.'

There was a murmur of excitement around the room. Gideon changed tack suddenly. 'This unlikely force, this barefoot army of freedom, it can run partly on courage but it also needs money. We are not rich, we do not have taxes and goldmines to finance our fight, but we will ask the people to give.' He paused. 'The white people!' Mouths fell open in surprise and a murmur rose from the small crowd. 'There are those amongst you who are already skilled at helping white people to give; your fingers know the feel of pockets and crawl as quickly as spiders into handbags.' Gideon looked over at the dozen or so young tsotsis in the audience who stood together in a bunch at the back. 'Gentlemen, from tonight you are our bankers, from Wesselton native township,' he raised his hands and wiggled his fingers, 'from your fighting fingers, *Umkonto we Sizwe* need one hundred pounds a week!'

The crowd gasped. This was a great deal of money, the weekly wages for twenty-five families. A tall, gangly youth stepped forward. He was dressed in typical tsotsi fashion. 'We will bring you two hundred, General!' he called. The crowd cheered and beat their hands against the cement floor and the dozen or so tsotsi boys glowed with pride. It was the first time these tough street waifs had felt needed in their lives; the idea of fighting for freedom by simply 'doing their own thing' was enormously appealing.

Gideon looked serious. 'Some of you will be caught and go to prison. If you find yourself in prison look for the ANC leader. If there is no ANC leader there,' Gideon shook his head, 'Haya! I don't think this is possible, but if there isn't then ask for the PAC, it doesn't matter, *Umkonto we Sizwe* or *Poqo*, we are all fighting for the same thing, we all eat with the same spoon.' Gideon quoted an old Xhosa proverb, *'Umuntu ngumuntu ngomnye*, People are people through other people. In prison you will learn things, new things you can use. You will also teach things, things you already know how to do on the street. If you go to prison you must use the time well, so when you come out your teeth will be sharp with malice for our oppressors!' Gideon made the act of going to prison seem a worthy one. 'Prison for our soldiers is like going to the white man's boarding school, a private college; the *amaBhunu*, the Boers, will supply the food, the clothes and the classrooms and we will all go willingly to our daily lessons.'

There was a great deal of laughter over this, though it was laughter mixed with fear. Everyone knew how brutal existence for a black man was in a South African prison. Peekay marvelled at Gideon's way with the people. 'Some of you will die,' Gideon said simply. He turned his palms up in an elegantly simple gesture, which looked more like a blessing than a shrug. 'It is in the nature of a soldier to die.' His voice changed and grew soft. 'But dying is not easy. You will sit alone in the death cell when the great dawn of no tomorrow comes and you will think, "I am alone! My brothers have forsaken me!" But you will not be alone; soon you will hear the singing, the singing of those around you who have wakened with the dawn to thank you and bid you farewell.' Gideon's voice was now only a whisper, 'People are people through people.'

The room was silent and unabashed tears could be seen in the eyes of many in the audience. 'This is no time to cry, my comrades, we are going together on a journey,' Gideon smiled his wonderful smile once more. 'One day we will be free. We will come out of our houses one morning and the air will be sharp and clean and we will smell the wood smoke of the morning cooking fires and we will fill our lungs with the breath of freedom! And you will say, each one of you, "I remember, I was there when it all began." '

Gideon changed the mood as abruptly as he had done before, turning to Peekay who sat mesmerised. What a great barrister Gideon would make; what a tremendous leader he was becoming.

'We have with us tonight a friend,' Gideon gestured to Peekay at the back of the hall. 'I went against our custom and did not introduce him to you at the beginning, this is because he isn't here!' The crowd laughed, but only the youngest amongst them turned to look at Peekay.

'I know it is difficult for some of you to understand, but not all whites are against us. There are some who work with us. Some of you will know of the work which is done by my friend Peekay for the people, the work which is done by Red. Peekay has put himself in danger by coming here tonight, but now you can see his face and see his heart. If you are in trouble in the fight for freedom and the police catch you, because you have joined *Umkonto* and because you are a freedom fighter, you can call Peekay. He will come to you in prison and he will fight for you in the courts.'

The tall youth who had volunteered to double the weekly tithe for the township now asked, 'How will we let you know, how will we tell you we have been caught?'

Gideon chuckled, 'You are not alone now. You are *Umkonto we Sizwe*; we will know and then the *Onoshobishobi Ingelosi* will know,' he snapped his fingers, 'Just like that!'

Gideon brought the meeting to a close and a great many of the audience came up to him simply to touch him before they departed, their fingers touching his hand or some part of his anatomy lightly, briefly, not expecting a response. It was as though by actually touching him they gained the power and confidence they needed; the concept of *people are people through people* was operating instinctively in them. Gideon's was a rag-tag army based on trust and not on fear.

'Come, my brother, we can talk now. A woman here has cooked some food, we must go now to that hut.' The two men walked together through the township in the moonlight, the people who had attended the meeting gliding past them silently. They came to a small shack and

Gideon knocked politely at the door. A large woman opened it quietly and they entered. Inside the shack was divided by a curtain behind which must have been the sleeping quarters for whoever occupied it.

Gideon pointed to the curtain, an eyebrow raised in question. 'It is only me here. My husband and my two boys they are in gaol,' the woman said. 'I have cooked food and I will go now.' She touched them each lightly on the hand and left the shack.

A tiny table was set in the centre of the room lit with a hurricane lamp. On it sat a pot of *phutu*, stiff mealiemeal porridge, and a smaller one of meat and gravy together with two enamel plates and spoons. A pot of tea, a can of Ideal milk, a cup without a handle used as a sugar bowl, and two tin mugs were placed on the centre of the table. Both men began to eat in the African way, spooning meat and gravy into the plates and taking the stiff porridge from the pot with their fingers, dousing it in the gravy before bringing it to their mouths. They were both ravenous and neither spoke as they ate.

After they'd eaten Peekay produced several packages from his bag. He handed one to Mandoma. 'Here, it's your Christmas present. It's something I own which I want you to carry with you always.'

Gideon took the parcel. 'Who knows where I will be on Christmas day, may I open it now?'

'Of course!'

Gideon unwrapped the small parcel. Inside, resting in a beautiful hand-tooled leather scabbard, was the hunting knife Gert had made for Peekay.

'My sincerest hope is that you never have to use it, but if you do, my hand is on it with you, Gideon. When you strike, you strike for me as well.'

Gideon withdrew the blade from its scabbard and felt the balance of the knife in his hand. 'It is beautiful, but the skull, the skull on the handle, it means it is a killing knife.'

'I am sorry, Gideon, it's not much of a Christmas gift.'

'It is a gift of concern and protection, that makes it a gift of love, I will keep it always with me, Peekay.' Gideon put the remaining gifts from Hymie and Tandia aside to open later. Peekay withdrew a passport from the inside pocket of his jacket and offered it to Gideon. 'It is a British passport obtained through Kenya. Hymie brought it back with him from London yesterday. You'll have to get used to your new name.' He handed Gideon an envelope. 'Inside you'll find your new birth certificate, it indicates you were born in a mission hospital and educated at a mission school in Kitale which is a northern outpost of Kenya's white highlands.' Peekay put his hand on Gideon's shoulder. 'Well, you old bastard, at last you're going off to a very selective boarding school to be educated.'

Gideon chuckled, deep down in his throat as though it came from his stomach. 'Tell Hymie thanks, the people will honour him some day for this.'

Peekay interrupted. 'Please Gideon, Oliver Tambo is organising your travel details outside South Africa. I don't want to know how you leave or how you get to Algeria.'

Gideon shook his head and laughed softly. 'Haya, haya, Peekay, there is so much to learn about being a freedom fighter.' He looked at Peekay. 'In the boxing ring it's so easy, so clean, one on one, your fists, your heart and your head. The bell goes, you fight and in the end the man with the most skill and the most courage,' he laughed softly as though thinking, 'maybe even the man with the last punch wins.'

Peekay grinned, 'That's all it took, you bastard, you saved it up special!'

Gideon laughed, 'I have not told you about this punch, from where it came. When I was very small, I was a herd boy and every morning we would go out and milk the cows and bring in the milk. I longed to grow up and come to the big city and be somebody. Every afternoon when it was time to bring the cattle in we would take them first to the river to drink and then we would have the competition for the boots.'

Gideon looked down at his shiny shoes and wiped a spot of dirt off his left toecap with a casual brush of his hand. 'There was an old man who worked in Durban and every year he would come back to his home on holiday for two weeks and he would bring a pair of boots. His baas would give him these old boots to wear on his holidays and he would give the herd boys the old boots the baas gave him to wear before, the last time he came. These boots they had done a lot of walking and there were big holes in the soles, but they were city boots, the guy among us who wore them, he was the king of the herd boys, if only for that day.

'Every night when we came to the river for the cattle to drink, we would put one of the boots up on a rock and count fifty steps and each boy would take two stones. The boy who hit the boot wore them home and all the next day until sunset, then we would come again to throw stones for the boots.

'All day, while I watched the cattle alone on the mountain, I would throw stones. I would put a small rock, the size of a boot, on a big rock and count fifty steps and throw at it. When I could no longer lift my arm because it had become very, very sore I would start with my other hand. Always I would throw until I could not lift this arm also, then I would start on the other again. Soon I was the one who almost always wore the boots.

'I was very proud and all the other guys respected me because I always won fair and square. When I beat you, Peekay, for the title, that last punch, I had nothing left, but in my head I said, "My arms they are stronger than his, he has never thrown for the boots, he has already got the boots. I have one stone left, one last throw." That's what won the title for me.'

They sat in silence for a moment, two friends who knew each other well. Then Peekay cleared his throat. 'Gideon, there is something.'

Gideon replied softly, 'Haya, Peekay, yes, I can feel this thing, your heart is heavy, heavy! What is this something?'

'It's Tandia.'

Gideon chuckled. 'You are in love, I have known this thing a long time.'

Peekay looked shocked. 'I cannot deny this, Gideon. But I know it is impossible! You are my friend and even if I fought you for her, the law says I cannot have her.'

'The law cannot stop a man and a woman. The law of nature is stronger than the law of the *amaBhunu* . . . At the mission school when I was young, once the teacher was reading from the Bible. It was a hot afternoon and I was nearly asleep, but I remember the words so very well.' Gideon paused and then, almost as though he was a schoolboy again, started to recite: ' "Show me the way of an eagle in the air, show me the way of a snake on the rock and show me the way of a man with a maid, when I know these three things, then all things are known unto me!" '

Peekay grinned, 'Thank you, Gideon, but I am not in the woman-stealing business. You quote from the Bible and I will quote you a Zulu proverb, "The heart is a hunter who does not seek permission from the herd to hunt." I think it means roughly the same thing but, nonetheless, unless Tandia herself decides otherwise she will, I'm sure, be waiting for you when you get back.'

Gideon shook his head. 'Peekay, I know Tandia and I know Nguni. That Zulu, he was my manager since I was an *umfana*. Since I fought you that first time in Sophiatown. That man, he is a big pain, he would give a headache to an Aspro!'

Peekay laughed. Gideon was trying to put him at his ease and now he continued, 'I cannot be angry with Nguni, he is very greedy; to have a beautiful woman on your arm is good for business. The people they look at you and they know you are rich and have a lot of power, that's what a beautiful woman can do for a guy. I have done this also, but when the time comes I will take a woman from my own kraal, it is the Zulu way. A woman from another *isigodi* but from my own tribe who can give me sons, the sons of a chief. When I return, Tandia will not be waiting for me, that is for sure, my brother.'

Peekay had never heard Gideon speak like this before. It had never occurred to him that Gideon might take a village woman for his wife. Gideon had the potential to be a future leader of South Africa and Tandia, a beautiful and intelligent wife of mixed blood, would have been politically perfect as his partner. Peekay now realised that it was precisely Gideon's grass-roots personality that made him so effective as a leader. He had a foot in both camps; he was a sophisticated and highly successful urban African who had not forsaken his tribal roots. He could reach his people at any level without having to pretend to be anyone but himself.

Now Gideon looked at Peekay and shrugged, 'Tandia too, she wants something from Nguni, she wants acceptance, the respect of the elders, it is important for her to climb into her black skin.' He looked up at Peekay, his eyes filled with concern for his friend. 'This time I am glad there is a bad law which says a black woman and a white man they cannot make love.' He paused again, biting his lower lip. 'Tandia cannot love a man, Peekay. Inside her something it has happened, I don't know what is this thing. Even if the law was not there, she is not the woman for you. She cannot make you happy, man!'

'Gideon, I can't think about her, but I also can't stop thinking about her; it is a nightmare and now there is something else.' Peekay took a deep breath and told Gideon what had transpired with Geldenhuis.

' . . . And then he showed me a statement, a piece of paper signed by Tandia when she was just a kid. Geldenhuis is in a perfect position to blackmail her, to ruin her life and therefore to force her to be an informer.'

Gideon looked at Peekay. He spoke quickly, but there was anger and hurt in his eyes. 'I don't want to hear this! Not from you, Peekay. If Tandia was a white woman, would you believe this? Because she is black, you think maybe . . . maybe that white policeman he is right?' He made a fist and clenched his jaw. 'You believe this dog shit when he shows you a piece of paper!' By now Gideon was shouting, his shoulders shaking with rage.

Peekay was shocked. He put his hand on Gideon's shoulder but the black man knocked it away. He tried again, and again Gideon pushed Peekay's hand away. 'Please Gideon, listen to me! I . . . I don't know what to believe! I'm in love with Tandia, I'm a white man and if I fall in love with her I destroy her! Destroy everything! So it's simple. I'm a big boy, I know what to do. I can handle that. I *have* to handle it!' Peekay paused, catching his breath. 'In the end it concerns only me and I can learn to live with that. But now there is this thing, this statement. This isn't just me any more. This is everything I care about! You whom I love, Hymie whom I love, the things we are fighting for. Those people in Sharpeville who died. What do I do? Say nothing? Keep hoping it's all bullshit? Another Geldenhuis trap?' He paused again. 'But what if it isn't? If that bastard has got her nailed down? Tell me, what the fuck do I do? If I remained silent, said nothing and it all happened? What if Geldenhuis does have Tandia on a string?'

Gideon's voice was cold and angry and he spoke in Zulu. 'Every black woman is a whore in the eyes of people like Geldenhuis! Every little black girl ever born is supposed to be waiting to spread her legs the first time she gets near a white boy. That's what we're fighting. When it comes down to it, that's what apartheid is all about! This single, terrible fear within the white man's mind that the black whore will tempt his sons and destroy his bloodline.

'But what about temptation? Well, Afrikaners know all about temptation, they tell us all the time they are a deeply Christian people. Temptation is the work of the devil, temptation is evil. And what colour is evil?' Gideon gave Peekay a bitter smile, 'Evil is black, of course. So when the white man feels his temptation, he knows it is the work of the devil! And when he rejects temptation, separates himself from it, what is that?' Gideon laughed scornfully, 'That is God's mercy. Separation . . . apartheid, is therefore the work of God!'

The anger had left Gideon's eyes, but now there was a sadness and his voice remained urgent. 'Can't you see, Peekay? Can't you see, what we're fighting is *your* fear. And when *you* think Tandia may be guilty, it is *your* own guilt you are feeling.' He stabbed his finger at Peekay, 'You say you love this woman? This black woman? What is it you love? Her body? Her long legs and nice tits? Her arse? Her beautiful face? Her smile? Or is it something else? Something that makes her Tandia? Her dedication to truth and honesty? Her courage? Her desire for fairness and justice for all of the people? Her ability to fight like a tiger for all of these things? Her determination to be better, stronger, quicker in her mind than those who oppress us? Even her hate? Sometimes you can even love a person's hate! Tandia is black. *She* knows *she* is not a white, she is not afraid of herself; that piece of paper she signed when she was a child, it is not *her* guilt on that piece of paper, it is the guilt of Geldenhuis. Geldenhuis is carrying his own guilt around on that piece of paper.' Gideon's voice grew suddenly strident again. 'It is not possible for him to use it against her, blackmail her, because, listen to me, Peekay, she is not guilty!'

THIRTY-SIX

Captain Geldenhuis was a hero to a great many of the white population after Sharpeville, where he exemplified for them the concept of *kragdadigheid*, the concept of white supremacy through punitive power. The knowledge that white people were represented by a government who would take no nonsense and were prepared to act against *die swart gevaar*, the black danger, brought them a great deal of comfort.

The Special Branch was usually portrayed by the press as a unit working against political targets, and a great many South Africans felt their methods were justified; they were, after all, matched against black activists, 'terrorists', and the end justified the means. In fact the great majority of their work was at a grass-roots level. Typical of everyday Special Branch work was the case of Katie Kembeni, a woman from Mofolo, a sub-division of Soweto, who had been killed when she refused to be endorsed out of her township home back to a so-called homeland. When the authorities arrived forcibly to remove her and her three small children, they arrested her husband on the spot, alleging a pass infringement. They forced him to watch in the custody of two policemen as the family's possessions were loaded onto a truck and his three children dumped on top of them. His wife Katie fought them furiously and was physically restrained, handcuffed and dragged kicking to where her husband Alfred stood, his face wet with tears.

Katie broke loose just as the truck carrying her children started to move away. She ran to the front of the truck, blocking its way, whereupon the truck shot forward, knocking her down and only coming to a halt when its back wheel ran over her head. She lay on the road in front of her three small children, tyre-marks across her crushed skull, blood haemorrhaging from her mouth.

Of the fifty or more people who'd witnessed the entire episode only three could be persuaded to make statements and agree to appear as witnesses. Two of these withdrew after they'd both been severely beaten up by hired thugs who broke into their homes in the middle of the night. The third, a young boy of seventeen, had simply disappeared, 'gone bush' for fear of what might happen to him.

Geldenhuis was handling the case for the police in court and it was he who rose to cross-examine Alfred Kembeni, the woman's husband. 'Is it true that you were a member of the ANC before it was outlawed?'

'No, baas, I am not a member.'

'Listen, man, I did not say you are a member. The ANC is now outlawed. I said you *were* a member.'

Tandia raised her hand, 'Objection, your honour, in the nomenclature of African spoken English my client's reply means the same thing.'

The magistrate looked up. 'I must remind you, Miss Patel, that because your client can't speak Afrikaans this court is already accommodating him in the English language. Now you want us to accommodate him in African English, whatever that is supposed to be!'

There was laughter in the court and the magistrate seemed pleased with his bon mot. Tandia replied, 'With the greatest respect, your honour, my client has not been accommodated, as you put it. If you were standing in the dock in his place and your case was being heard in the Sotho language you would be in the same situation as he now faces.'

This time there was a stunned silence in the court. Even the Africans present didn't dare to laugh. 'Counsel will refrain from addressing the bench in this matter and from attempting to make a mockery of accepted court procedure! Counsel will apologise to this court. Objection overruled.'

'Yes, your honour, I apologise.'

Geldenhuis grinned as he repeated the question to Alfred Kembeni. 'Were you a member of the ANC?'

'No, sir.'

Geldenhuis consulted a pad. 'Are you Alfred Kembeni of one thousand and three Motjuwadi Street, Mofolo?'

'No, sir.'

'We know this is your address, you hear?' Geldenhuis snapped, without addressing his remarks through the bench.

Tandia rose. 'Your honour, my client has been forcibly removed by the authorities from this address to a single man's hostel. He is correct in saying this is not his address.'

'Your honour, I have not got time to waste. We have a list of all past ANC members, his name is on this list!'

'Objection, your honour. The evidence please. May we see this list and the name of the plaintiff specified on it?'

Geldenhuis looked over at Tandia, his face expressionless. 'Your honour, counsel knows this information is classified.'

'In that case, your honour, I object to the accusation Captain Geldenhuis has made. He has no evidence he can show to this court which proves that the plaintiff was a member of the ANC.'

The magistrate, a small bald man named Dreyer with over-large horn-rimmed glasses, the heavy frames chosen, Tandia suspected, to give him an air of authority, looked at her now. 'I will sustain your objection on a point of law. But I must point out it has come to a sorry state of affairs when a senior police officer is virtually said to be telling a lie. Objection sustained!'

Tandia sighed. What the magistrate was telling her was that he accepted Geldenhuis's accusation that Alfred Kembeni was a past member of the ANC and so might be correctly described as a political agitator.

Later Tandia recalled Alfred Kembeni to the stand. 'Mr Kembeni, will you please tell the court what Sergeant Bronkhorst of the Special Branch shouted to Thomas Motlana, the driver of the removal truck, as your wife stood screaming directly in the path of the already moving truck?'

'He say, "Petrol! Push the Petrol, down!" '

'Thank you. Can you now point to the man who said this?'

Alfred Kembeni pointed to a medium-sized man with thinning hair and thick, wide sideburns down almost to the point of his chin. He was wearing civilian clothes, a cheap, greenish-coloured sports jacket with a large brown check running through it, a white shirt and a somewhat vulgar painted tie. The shirt was obviously too small for him and strained over a pronounced gut. Tandia had watched him during the morning when Geldenhuis had put him on the witness stand. He'd constantly touched and pulled at his tie until eventually he could tolerate it no longer and loosened the collar button, pulling the tie down away from it. He was obviously under instructions to wear a tie with his civilian clothes and was showing Geldenhuis that he couldn't be pushed around. Plain-clothes policemen are a special breed accustomed to doing things their own way, and the gesture with the tie probably meant that the plain-clothes sergeant didn't take too kindly to instructions. He was the kind of independent-minded police witness she liked.

Bronkhorst appeared to be in his early forties, of florid complexion, with a flat nose and peculiar mud-coloured eyes, the whites of his eyes only two or three shades lighter then the flat brown centre. As Hymie might have put it, 'It is a face not to like.' But now, as the black man pointed to him, Bronkhorst grinned, showing a mouth filled with gold dental work.

'Thank you, Mr Kembeni, you may step down.' Tandia turned to Dreyer. 'You honour, I request permission to return my client to the witness stand at a later time.'

'Permission granted.'

'And once again, your honour, I ask that the accused, Thomas Motlana, be excused from this court during the time I cross-examine Sergeant Bronkhorst, the second accused.'

The little magistrate looked over at Geldenhuis who nodded, agreeing. 'Would the sergeant of the court please temporarily remove the accused Thomas Motlani from this court!'

'Thomas Motlana, your honour,' Tandia corrected. 'I now ask permission from this court to put Sergeant Bronkhorst on the stand?'

Tandia was used to the way white police officers stood in the witness box when she confronted them. As far as they were concerned she was a cheeky kaffir, a black bitch who had no right to be in a court of law, let alone to address questions to a white man. The contempt on their faces always gave her a nice warm feeling; a man trying to express his feelings outwardly tends not to listen as carefully as he ought and now the almost imperceptible sneer on the face of Bronkhorst brought an inward smile.

The clerk of the court produced the Bible and commenced to administer the oath to Sergeant Bronkhorst. Standing in front of the witness box Tandia paused for almost a minute, as though she was thinking. It was a technique she'd discovered which, for some reason, brought out the anger in white Afrikaner witnesses and it worked particularly well with members of the police force.

'Sergeant Bronkhorst,' Tandia said at last, 'tell the court what you were doing at the home of Alfred Kembeni on or around three o'clock in the afternoon of 5 December last year.'

'Ja, okay man, but you don't have to tell me the time and the date, I already know when it was.' Bronkhorst grinned and looked around the court expecting people to smile. Observing the hard-eyed look on the face of Jannie Geldenhuis, he brought a hand up to his tie knot and cleared his throat. 'We got a call from the B-A-D,' he spelt the letters out, the irony of the acronym long since lost on him, but then added, 'Bantu Administration and Development. They said this Bantu woman Katie Kembeni was endorsed out, but she was telling everyone around the place that she wasn't going to go, that there was no way she was going to the Transkei.'

'Did you arrive before Bad?'

Dreyer sat up suddenly and brought his gavel down. 'If counsel wishes to use an abbreviation for Bantu Administration and Development, a very senior government department, then you may do so by spelling out the initials, B-A-D!' He turned to the court stenographer. 'You will write it down in full, the full title of this department, you hear?' He turned to Bronkhorst. 'You may give the court your answer.'

'Well no, that's not the procedure. In a case like this they send a removal truck and we come in it together.'

'Is that so that the Special Branch are not seen to be a component of the removal?' Tandia asked.

'Ja, that's right, when they think there might be trouble a plain-clothes man goes along just in case.' He paused and then added, 'In an EO, an Endorse Out,' he corrected, 'we try to keep the police presence low-key, a couple of Black Jacks, that's all. Mostly people co-operate with the authorities.'

'And the lorry, the removal truck, what sort of a lorry was this?'

Bronkhorst looked bemused and shrugged again. He was feeling safe and he'd undone his collar button again, inching his tie down. 'A Dodge I think. But what do you mean? Are you asking, was it a one ton, a *bakkie* or bigger? It was a big lorry, a three ton, like you would use for a removal.'

'I apologise, sergeant, I haven't made myself clear. To whom did this lorry belong?'

'Oh, I see what you mean now! It was a GG, a "government garage", you know? It was a three-ton GG that belonged to B-A-D.'

'Used in an EO?' Tandia said quickly as the court erupted into laughter.

'Write that down fully again, Miss De Jager,' Dreyer instructed the stenographer, 'Government Garage, Bantu Administration and Development and Endorse Out!'

Tandia suddenly changed tack. 'Thank you, Sergeant Bronkhorst. I now want to take you to the point of departure after the deceased Mrs Katie Kembeni had been arrested and handcuffed, with her furniture and her children loaded onto the back of the lorry. I understand you were sitting in the front passenger seat?'

'Ja, that's right.'

'I want you to listen carefully to my question.' Tandia paused, one of her extra-long pauses. 'What were your exact words to the driver of the lorry as the vehicle was moving forward and you observed Mrs Kembeni standing screaming directly in front of it?'

'Objection!' Geldenhuis called, 'It has not been established that the accused saw this woman. In the noise and the confusion he could easily have been looking elsewhere.'

'Objection,' Tandia said. 'Counsel for the accused is attempting to put words into the mouth of this witness.'

Dreyer brought his gavel down hard. 'Objection sustained on both counts. Both counsel will abstain from attempting to confuse or instruct the accused!'

'I am not confused, your honour,' Bronkhorst said.

Tandia smiled. 'Let me put it another way then. When you shouted at the driver . . .'

'Objection!' Geldenhuis called.

Tandia sighed. 'When you spoke . . . you did speak to the driver?' Bronkhorst nodded. 'When you spoke to the driver, what were the exact words you used to him?'

'Ja, thank you, I'm glad you asked this question because it wasn't like he said, you know, like the Bantu witness Kembeni said. I didn't speak the way he said, I said it without raising my voice. I said, "Petrol. Push the petrol down." ' Bronkhorst looked around the courtroom as though addressing everyone present. 'This is not the same as saying' he raised his voice and shouted, "Petrol! Push the petrol down!" ' He paused after his shout and waited a moment before saying quietly, 'You see I was talking about the choke! I was asking him to push the choke in.'

There was a burst of disbelieving laughter from the court and Dreyer was forced to use his gavel and call for silence.

Tandia smiled at Bronkhorst. 'I am not a mechanical person, sergeant. The choke? The petrol!? What is the connection?'

'Ja, okay, I will explain.' Bronkhorst, not in the least phased by the laughter, seemed to be enjoying himself. 'When it's cold, in the winter, you know in the mornings, and you want to start an engine you got to give it more petrol, you have to open the valve to the distributor more, so you've got what is called a choke. It's usually on the dashboard just under the steering wheel so you can pull it out, it's just a button on the end, a little lever, and you pull it out and when you start the engine you pump the accelerator a couple of times to pump more petrol which goes in the distributor and the engine starts and won't stall because it's getting extra petrol. That's why you call it the petrol because, you see, what you doing is feeding the engine more petrol. When I said, "Petrol. Push the petrol down," I meant for the driver to push in the choke.'

'I see, and why should he do that?' Tandia asked.

'Well kaffir drivers, I mean Bantu drivers, they leave the choke out and forget to push it back and it races the engine and wastes a helluva lot of petrol. It's just something you do automatically, when you get in a lorry with a Bantu driver, you look at the choke and if it's out, you make him push it in.' He paused, looking around the court, and then added, 'The government tells us all the time we mustn't waste petrol. If the Arabs want they can cut off our petrol any time they like. We making our own at Sasol, outside Vereeniging, out of coal, but it's not yet enough. Petrol must not be wasted!' He offered this gratuitous advice seemingly to all the court and appeared to be very pleased with himself.

'Let me see now, sergeant. You are about to leave, there is a lot of shouting, confusion and panic, yet you calmly give the driver an instruction to push in the choke?'

'Who's panicking?' Bronkhorst asked, pulling his head back and raising his eyebrows. 'Maybe them, but not me. As far as I am concerned it was a routine job.'

'Yet a moment ago you said, people usually co-operate?'

'Ja, with EOs, but I'm a plain-clothes officer, panic and shouting you come across all the time, man.'

'You said a choke is needed in the cold weather, in the mornings in winter, but it was half past three in the afternoon on 5 December last year, not exactly winter? Why would you instruct the driver to push in the petrol, the . . . er, choke?'

Bronkhorst grinned. 'That's the whole point I'm trying to make, man! You see, the black people, when they drive they just use the choke any time, summer, winter, any time they get in a lorry, when they start an engine they use the choke, then they leave it on, sticking out full throttle. It wastes a helluva lot of petrol. Sometimes they miles down the road when they remember to push it in again. Sometimes they don't even remember.'

Tandia noted the look of relief on Geldenhuis's face. He'd seen what was coming and was relieved. Bronkhorst had been smart enough not to fall into Tandia's trap. 'Thank you, Sergeant Bronkhorst, you have been very patient. Perhaps you will help me a little more to understand?'

Tandia used one of her long pauses and the police sergeant dropped his answer neatly into her deliberate silence: 'Certainly.'

'Thank you. You are in the cabin of the lorry now, moving forward, and you tell the driver in a calm voice to push the choke in. What were your words again?'

'Petrol. Push the petrol down,' Bronkhorst said, grinning.

'And you didn't see Mrs Katie Kembeni standing in front of the truck screaming up at you?'

'Ja, that's right, man, I didn't see her.'

'And hear, you didn't hear her screaming?'

'I was looking at the driver, concentrating on the choke, there was lots of noise, lots of women screaming and shouting, I didn't take any notice.'

'But with all the noise going on, all the confusion, you were still able to say to the driver in a quiet voice, "Petrol. Push the petrol down"?'

The court was hushed as Tandia waited for Bronkhorst's answer, but again the policeman didn't panic. 'The windows were closed in the lorry, we do that in case somebody throws something inside. I was looking down at the choke, my eyes were not on the road in front. What happened was all in a couple of seconds, I was pointing to the choke and then I looked at the driver and said, "Petrol. Push the petrol down."'

'And he didn't understand you and put his foot on the petrol, I mean, of course, the accelerator. No doubt he was looking at you and not at the road either?' Tandia said.

'Ja, that's perfickly true.' Bronkhorst said, feigning surprise. 'You can ask him yourself if you like. He was looking straight at me when he put his foot down, I can testify to that fact.'

Tandia smiled brightly at Bronkhorst. 'I'm sure you will, Sergeant. You spoke to him in a quiet, reasoning voice and he panicked and slammed his foot down hard on the petrol, the accelerator?'

'Ja, I dunno why he did that, maybe he was panicking a little from the crowd, you know, the noise and all the onlookers.'

'Was this the noise he couldn't hear because the cabin windows were closed and the onlookers he couldn't see because he was looking directly at you?'

Bronkhorst drew his head back impatiently. 'The noise had been going on a long time, he knew it was there outside, his eyes were on me only a matter of a few seconds while I talked, it must have been then when the woman, Mrs Kembeni, escaped from custody of the Black Jack and came to the front of the lorry.'

Tandia swung away from the witness box, her black advocate's gown swirling around with her movement to reveal a smart tailored black suit underneath. With her black high-heel shoes she looked perfectly stunning. 'Thank you, Sergeant Bronkhorst.' She turned to Magistrate Dreyer. 'I have no further need for Sergeant Bronkhorst, your honour. Now I would like to call Thomas Motlana to the stand.'

Dreyer used his gavel again. 'The accused may stand down, call Thomas Motlana,' he said, getting the black man's name right on this occasion.

Tandia was quick with Motlana, simply starting at the point where the police sergeant had spoken to him, asking the black driver what he had heard. Predictably the black man repeated the words, sotto voce, in a similar vein to the sergeant. As Sergeant Bronkhorst had said, his attention was drawn from the front of the truck to the policeman's face and he had reacted automatically, thinking the sergeant meant the accelerator. He'd put his foot down on the petrol and the truck shot forward, killing Katie Kembeni. Tandia then asked Motlana if he drove the same lorry all the time, to which he replied that he didn't, but used any one of five lorries; he'd been given the Dodge GG 1728 for this particular job.

After the driver Thomas Motlana had been excused from the witness stand Tandia returned to the bench and retrieved a file. With the file under her arms she walked over to the bench and, opening it, she withdrew two sheets of paper. 'Your honour, I submit for the scrutiny of this court three documents. The first is a government bulletin dated 10 August 1964, directing that during the summer months until 1 May, all government vehicles over a one-ton limit must have their choke cable removed to conserve petrol!'

A murmur rose from the court. 'This second document is an affidavit from the government garage in Randfontein. It stipulates that all GG vehicles over three tons on the road this summer comply with this instruction. And furthermore,' Tandia removed a small receipt from the file. 'I have here the mechanic's time sheet which shows that GG 1728, a blue Dodge three-ton vehicle, the property of Bantu Administration and Development, had its choke cable removed by government mechanic D. Du Plooy on 28 November 1964, one week before the incident.

'Your honour, I submit that both the accused could not have acted as they have claimed and that Sergeant Bronkhorst *did* instruct driver Thomas Motlana in a voice intended to be instantly obeyed, with the words, "Petrol! Push the petrol down!" meaning to place his foot hard down on the accelerator in order to run over Mrs Katie Kembeni, and that doing this he is directly responsible for having committed a deliberate act of premeditated murder!'

In his summing up Magistrate Dreyer admitted that due care had not been taken by the driver of the truck due to the noise and urgency of the situation at the time, that Sergeant Bronkhorst may have mistaken any one of several round buttons on the dashboard for the choke. He added that Captain Geldenhuis, counsel for both the accused, had demonstrated this by pointing out that the sergeant was not familiar with the layout of a Dodge three-ton truck, that the driver had indeed misinterpreted the police sergeant's instructions and while his attention was momentarily diverted he'd reacted somewhat in panic by placing his foot down hard on the accelerator.

He declared Bronkhorst not guilty and Motlana guilty of manslaughter but with mitigating circumstances. The driver was given a six-month suspended sentence and fined ten pounds. Two weeks after the trial Alfred Kembeni was endorsed out and sent back to the Transkei.

Both Peekay and Tandia began to despair. They were fighting cases in which the evidence had patently been tampered with by the police or witnesses had been intimidated, tortured or murdered, but more and more even the best argued defence was simply being ignored in court. Magistrates such as Dreyer were commonplace and patently sympathetic to the activity of the Special Branch; it was becoming increasingly difficult to prepare a case with precision and care when the court lists showed one of these men presiding.

Every time they lost one of the old guard, men such as Magistrate Coetzee, he was replaced by someone who soon showed his *Broederbond* background and responded to the honour the government had bestowed on him in appointing him to the bench with bigotry and blatantly racially motivated decisions.

When, despite all the forces ranged against them, Red successfully challenged the meaning of a law and won an important case, within a few weeks of the victory the law would be changed, thus eliminating the legal precedent involved.

Finally Peekay and Tandia lost Magistrate Coetzee, or to put it more correctly Magistrate Coetzee retired to his beloved farm on a bend of the Crocodile River, near Barberton, in the Eastern Transvaal. The South African Bar Association held a reception for him and gave him silver plate, the ubiquitous tray with the EPNS stamp on the back and the usual fatuous dedication on the front:

J. H. Coetzee
In grateful appreciation for thirty-five years on the bench.

The girls at Bluey Jay sent him a case of his favourite Cape brandy and a poem penned by Sarah which read:

Magistrate Coetzee
We love you so
We hear it's time
for you to go
From now on it's free
if you feel randy . . .
But if you don't,
enjoy the brandy!

Mama Tequila also sent him the Boer Mauser, the old rifle that had been such an important part of his dalliance with Sarah.

The people of Soweto collected enough money to purchase a blue

Fordson tractor and a red disc plough. A brass plate fitted to the side of the engine read:

For the Induna Coetzee
Who ploughed the land for the seeds of freedom for all the people.
From the citizens of Soweto.

The Special Branch heard about this proposed gift and reported it to Pretoria who 'suggested' to Magistrate Coetzee that the gift was unacceptable and that it should be turned down. Magistrate Coetzee, however, accepted the gift with humility and with a speech which was widely quoted, calling for understanding and compassion from the legal system.

Alas, the small blue tractor never reached its destination; it was sent by rail and offloaded onto a railway siding near Magistrate Coetzee's small farm. When he came to collect it someone had taken a ten-pound hammer to both it and the disc plough, destroying them beyond repair. Scrawled on the ground beside the battered little tractor were the two words, *kaffir boetie.*

Though the small brass plate had received more than one direct hit, the words on it were still legible and Magistrate Coetzee unbolted it, straightened it out in his workshop, polished it with Brasso and screwed it to the front door of his small farmhouse. He polished it himself every week, not allowing the black woman who looked after the house and cooked for him to touch it.

Two weeks after the incident with the tractor and plough, and six weeks after his retirement, the old magistrate was placed under house arrest. The government had simply waited for his talk to the people of Soweto to grow cold before they placed a restraint order on him forbidding him to communicate with the press and confining him to his farm and a once-a-week visit into Barberton to do his shopping, where he was not allowed to be in the presence of more than one person at a time.

When Tandia heard of the detention notice, with Johnny Tambourine at the wheel of her Volkswagen she drove down to Magistrate Coetzee's farm called *Eendrag*, which means unity and harmony, in the sense of all the people being together of one accord.

Tandia and Johnny Tambourine left Johannesburg after lunch and arrived at the farm just on sunset. The old man was sitting on the stoep with a decanter of brandy and he stood to welcome Tandia, formally shaking her by the hand. When Tandia introduced Johnny Tambourine he did the same; Magistrate Coetzee's grip was firm and his smile was welcoming.

'I must apologise, but I am under house arrest. As you probably know I may not see more than one person at a time.'

Johnny looked around him expecting to see someone, a security man, posted to watch the old man.

Magistrate Coetzee laughed. 'No, no, there is no one here. Only us and my servant at the back. You must indulge an old man, after thirty-five years as a man of the law I tell myself this is stupid, but then again another part of me says, "Coetzee, the law is still the law!" and this other part of me always wins. I have asked the old woman who looks after me to give you a nice supper and there is a clean room with a new mattress and blankets on the bed in the servants' quarters for you to stay tonight.'

Johnny Tambourine grinned. He didn't know quite what to make of the craggy old man with the bulbous nose as red as a turkey's crop. 'It's okay, man, I'm a guy who can look after myself.'

Magistrate Coetzee grinned back. He'd probably never been spoken to in such a familiar way in his entire life. 'Two months ago in my court, talk like that would have earned you the sjambok. You're a cheeky bloody kaffir, Johnny Tambourine, but I'm glad you're here to look after Miss Tandy as well!'

Johnny Tambourine laughed. The honours were even, the old man hadn't tried to patronise him. He gave Magistrate Coetzee an informal salute and wandered off to the back of the house with Tandia's overnight bag. This place was so quiet. He'd become aware of the silence the moment he'd turned off the high whine of the VW's air-cooled engine. He could feel it, it was a distinctly spooky sort of quiet, a nothing-is-happening-in-this-place sort of silence. No engine noises, bicycle bells, car engines, the sudden cry of a child, the sharp bounce of a tennis ball as the kids played soccer in the street, the laughter of people, the sudden roar of a bus passing, the coal man rattling along in his donkey cart, the repetitive notes of a mine worker strumming his guitar and the call of the woman mealie vendor with her golden cobs of roast corn carried in a white enamel dish on her head. Already he was missing Soweto.

The only noises Johnny Tambourine heard now were from the birds and insects. Christ, there must be a hundred things around here to bite a person! Like snakes! He'd heard how snakes like the cool and came into people's houses in the country and sometimes even got into your bed.

Johnny Tambourine was so busy scanning the bush beyond the yard that he didn't notice a large black hen pecking away in his path. The hen, alarmed at his sudden approach, jumped into the air with a 'Schwark!', its feathers flapping. Johnny Tambourine's feet also left the ground and Tandia's bag went flying; he seemed to pedal the air for a moment, like a Tom and Jerry cartoon, before he realized it was only an old black hen.

That was it! That was the trouble with coming into the bush, all of a sudden a guy has to live like a fucking peasant! Looking out for things he doesn't even know about. Sounds don't make sense any more. You couldn't even trust a hen to sound right. No wonder all the guys from the country wanted to come into the city. It was definitely dangerous out here, the most dangerous place he'd ever been.

Johnny Tambourine retrieved Tandia's bag and opened the screen door leading into the kitchen at the back of the house.

'I see you, Mother,' he said politely to the old woman bent over a scrubbed pine table kneading a large lump of dough, her quick black hands disappearing into the white dough and then out again.

The old woman didn't look up at his entrance. 'Tell me, my son,' she asked, 'where you come from, are the people afraid of hens?'

Tandia sat on the stoep with Magistrate Coetzee. It was like being back at Bluey Jay on a Sunday morning when everyone slept. So quiet and peaceful. You could see the riverbank and then the cool glint of the setting sun on water beyond.

A flock of guinea fowl appeared at the water's edge. It was too far to see them clearly but she'd seen them often enough when she'd been on walks with Juicey Fruit Mambo into the hills around Bluey Jay. The guinea fowl was a pretty bird, the size of a smallish hen with a bright grey-purple head and a hornlike cockscomb sweeping back from its small beak. It possessed sharp little beady eyes, a lot more suspicious than a hen's. Grey feathers, patterned with minute white dots, swept back smoothly into a beetle-backed body to gave it the appearance of a church elder, which was further characterised by the way it walked. Guinea fowl seemed to rock slightly as they walked on their short blue legs, always on the move, never pausing, busy as anything.

Magistrate Coetzee spoke quietly. 'Sometimes, if you're lucky, you see a small-buck, a little duiker or an old warthog couple who come down to drink. But usually they wait till dark, then you hear them grunting, just like ordinary pigs. Maybe I should get some pigs? They tell me pigs are easy to look after.' His voice trailed off.

'What will you farm, Magistrate Coetzee?' Tandia asked. There was no sign of any farming around her and they seemed almost entirely surrounded by natural bush.

'You know in every Afrikaner there is a farmer waiting to come out, we are a people of the land, just like the Bantu. But for me it is more an idea in the head, a race memory, a coming back to my roots. It is the land that matters. I don't think I want to farm, to grow things.' He indicated the bush around him. 'At my age it seems pointless to compete with God. I think I'll just sit on my stoep and drink brandy, grow a beard – a proper voortrekker beard - and grow old properly.' He chuckled and placed his empty glass beside the decanter. 'Thank you, my dear, for your nice letter about the tractor.'

'Peekay and I were both terribly upset when we read about it in the papers.'

Magistrate Coetzee chuckled. 'Ag, Tandy it's probably a good thing, if I had the tractor standing out there in the shed I'd feel I had to use it. My old bum is more used to sitting on the bench than on a tractor seat trying to grow something I don't need and only have to worry about.' He turned slightly in his wicker chair and pointed to the small brass plate which shone brightly on the door. 'It wasn't the tractor and the plough, though God knows it was a generous gesture from poor people, but that, the inscription they put on the side of the tractor, that has made my whole life worthwhile.'

Tandia rose and examined the small plate screwed to the door. The indentations from the hammer blows it had received could be clearly seen, though they didn't interfere with the inscription etched into the plate.

Tandia turned suddenly, her heart beating fiercely. She was standing directly behind Magistrate Coetzee as she spoke. 'Sir, I know you could have almost any lawyer in South Africa to represent you when you challenge the government's banning order, but I would be tremendously honoured if you would let me act for you.' It was the reason she'd come to see the old man, but now she found she was trembling. Old Coetzee, for she suddenly thought of him like this, was a great magistrate, but underneath he was still an Afrikaner. How would he feel about a black girl defending him in court?

Standing behind the old man, she couldn't see his expression and he was quiet for a long time. Tandia didn't dare move. At last Old Coetzee spoke. 'Tandy, I am touched beyond words. You have given me hope, hope that one day our beloved country will come out of its madness and all the tribes can live together in peace. But until that time we have only the instrument of the law,' he paused, 'which I know is becoming a very blunt instrument, but it is all we've got, it is the last bit of sanity left.' He half turned his head. 'Come here, child, come where I can see you.'

Tandia moved to stand in front of the wicker chair where he sat. 'You are a very good lawyer and I am enormously proud of you. While I don't honestly think Pretoria will allow me to appeal, I accept your offer. I would be proud to be represented by you.'

Tandia gave a squeal of delight and without thinking she stooped and kissed Old Coetzee on the cheek. The old man grinned. 'Magtig, you are pretty!' He leaned forward and, lifting his glass, proffered it to Tandia. 'Here, pour me a brandy just like old times at Bluey Jay.'

Tandia poured Old Coetzee another snort, holding it up to the setting sun.

'They were good times, Tandy.' He took the brandy from her. 'You know that old Mauser, the old Boer rifle Sarah would give me when I came to Bluey Jay?'

Tandia nodded, not sure how much to admit she knew. 'Well, Mama Tequila sent it to me when I retired, together with a case of my favourite brandy and a nice little poem from Sarah.'

Tandia was trying hard to contain her laughter. She had a fair idea what the poem might be like. Then Old Coetzee started to chuckle and she began to laugh with him, two people laughing naturally and easily, no self-consciousness between them, two old friends sharing the the past. 'If we lose the case I'll take that old gun up to Pretoria and shoot Minister Vorster's balls off, hey Tandy?'

After a while Old Coetzee grew silent. She sensed that they'd stirred too many thoughts between them and he wanted to be on his own to settle them down again. 'It's getting dark and we must leave at dawn,' Tandia said. 'I have a petty sessions case scheduled for two o'clock tomorrow. May I take a walk around?'

'Tandia, you do too much, leave the little cases for someone else.'

Tandia laughed. 'I can't this time. It's Johnny Tambourine's aunt, she's been cheated over the cost of her dead husband's headstone.'

The old man made as though to rise from his seat, but Tandia stayed him with her hand. 'No, please stay where you are, Magistrate, I just want to nosey-park around the yard. I've been sitting in the car for four hours.'

Magistrate Coetzee's farm wasn't really a farm, just a little house with a nice stoep and a low roof with the ground beaten hard around it. A few small trees were planted in scooped-out hollows so they could be hand watered until they grew strong enough to make it on their own. A large round corrugated water tank with a pipe that pumped water up from the river stood at the far side of the house and further back was an open-sided garage and shed with a corrugated-iron roof. A green International pick-up stood parked under it with a white hen standing on its bonnet. To the left were the servants' quarters, two corrugated-iron rooms with wooden doors and a window cut out of the iron, hinged at the top so it could be pulled out and propped open with a branch which rested against the corrugated-iron wall below each window. It was late spring. Tandia had spent her childhood in a shed not dissimilar and she knew that on a hot night it would be like an oven.

Further along the yard was a fowl run, stakes cut from the bush and driven into the ground and then covered with chicken wire to a height of about six feet, with the wire bending and extended over the top as well to keep the chickens safe from hawks. Inside was the cabin and the front mudguards of an old rusted lorry, its doors still intact, the window and windshield glass long since removed. Tandia imagined it must serve as shelter for the hens. The gate to the run stood open, and Tandia observed how the hens were returning voluntarily, each pausing momentarily at the open gate, one leg raised, head slightly cocked as though listening for an instruction to proceed, then a quick, bold step into the safety of the chicken run. Finally the old rooster arrived, his head darting around as though checking his harem to see if anyone was missing.

A fat black hen with a flash of henna-coloured feathers about her breast came hurrying up, clucking ten to the dozen with eight tiny mottled yellow-and-black chicks cheep-cheeping and frantically moving about her. She hurried into the coop and moved under one of the rusted mudguards, spreading her wings wide. In a few moments the chicks gathered around her legs and her wings swept downwards so they disappeared into her undercarriage. With a soft 'Schwark' she settled down for the night, grateful to get the weight off her legs.

Tandia was about to return to the house when she noticed an overgrown and disused farm road to the right of the yard which appeared to lead to the top of a small rise. Old Coetzee's house was built two-thirds up this slope rising from the river and now Tandia wondered what might be concealed behind the top of the slope; though in the far background she could see a ridge of koppies, the middle ground was lost to her. There was still sufficient light for her to see and she walked the thirty or so yards to the top of the rise where, to her surprise, she discovered that the road continued for another hundred yards or so into a dip in the landscape which then led up to the green ridge of rock, aloe and the brighter, lighter green of early summer thorn bush.

At the end of the road stood a large old farmhouse fronted with two gables in the Cape Dutch tradition. The walls stood intact though its roof was missing; the crossbeams were mostly still in place, though the corrugated-iron sheets had been stripped from them, perhaps to be used in Old Coetzee's far smaller and less appealing new house.

The house was built on a high solid rock foundation probably quarried from the ridge which rose up behind it, so that its front stoep was fifteen or so feet from the ground with wide steps leading up to it. It had never been a grand house, but it had the look of a home which had bred two or three generations of solid burghers in its time, a house built to last as long as it was needed. Its thick whitewashed walls seemed to defy its hapless state, like an ageing bull elephant fallen on hard times but with his pride still intact. Silhouetted against the setting sun it looked as though it was merely waiting to get a new roof and a few new window panes and wasn't really standing idle and useless in the landscape. It seemed a used, happy house accustomed to the smell of baking and the cries of children and the aroma of pipe tobacco, a house in which to be born and in which to spend old age. To the left of the house stood the remains of an orchard; a dozen orange trees, two large mango trees, an avocado tree, and a single tall leafless stump of an old paw paw, its top dried out, like a twist of brown paper.

Almost nothing remained of the front garden except for two coffee bushes, a tall moonflower tree growing under one of the gables and a huge old frangipani covered in white and yellow blossom, which as Tandia drew closer perfumed the evening air around her. Closer yet she could see that the coffee bushes, with their small, dark, shiny leaves, were covered in brilliant red coffee beans. The bushland had taken over the remainder of what must once have been a garden, but this didn't make the approach to the house seem in the least untidy or even uninhabited. Rather it looked as though someone had, very sensibly, allowed the bush to create a natural landscape about the lovely old home.

At Bluey Jay when, in the early mornings with everyone asleep, she sat in the safety and quietness of the branches of the old fig tree beside her upstairs window, Tandia imagined a house like this, safe and quiet and beautiful, confident in its surroundings, a place where she could belong to herself completely.

It was growing too dark to continue up the steps and she turned back, though her heart was beating with excitement. She must own this house and restore it. She knew it was impossible; she was an African and forbidden to own property – she couldn't even live in it for more than seventy-two hours at a time, and even then she needed a permit to visit the area. But it didn't matter. Peekay could own it if Magistrate Coetzee would sell, just the house and the few trees around it and access to it through his property in perpetuity.

Tandia realised with a shock that for the first time since she had been raped at Patel's grave, the fear and the hate wasn't with her. It had taken an old house with its roof open to the sky to give her hope. Hope? She shivered suddenly; someone had just walked over her grave. Hope was the most frightening feeling she'd ever experienced. It meant she had to try and stay alive when the odds were stacked against her. It meant she and Gideon and Peekay had to win.

Tandia realised that she'd never thought about victory based on hope, rather on inflicting a defeat predicated on revenge. Peekay's dreams of harmonious integration were too altruistic for her; Gideon's were too ambitious for himself; and Hymie's were too practical and mercantile. When the day came, and if she was still alive, she wanted to be on the volunteer list of judges who would pronounce the sentences which would break the spirit of Geldenhuis and his arrogant tribe of murderers forever.

How could there be forgiveness in her heart? How do you forgive the barrel of a gun up your anus? How do you forgive a boot planted on your neck? How do you forgive being handcuffed and then entered like a dog? *Jesus a virgin! The-black-bitch-is-a-fucking-virgin!* How do you forgive the dum-dum bullet that blew Juicey Fruit Mambo's brains out? How do you forgive Sharpeville? How do you forgive the twenty-seven of your clients, or the witnesses who came forward for them, who died in the custody of Geldenhuis and his Special Branch or left after a few hours, free to go without being charged, but in ambulances, gibbering idiots with permanent brain damage? How do you forgive Tom Majombi, the human punch bag, abducted from hospital to lie in the most terrible pain in a dark cell for three weeks while an abscess ate at his brain until it killed him in an explosion of pus? How do you forgive a white tribe who educates the black one only to be his servant? Not only to clean but to lick his boots as well? How do you forgive the prison the black people are born into and remain in all the days of their lives?

Now she wondered what had happened to her. How could it be that no human, despite the great kindness she had been shown by many, had been able to reach her, yet her personal road to Damascus could well prove to be a clump of old bricks and stones and roofless rafters standing in a patch of African wilderness against a setting sun? They spoke of her deep need to belong to somewhere and something which she'd never before dared to admit to herself. From the time she was raped she'd seen herself as black, the opposite to white. Inferior, the opposite to superior. Shackled, the opposite to being free. Her blackness was an actual and emotional classification which substituted as an identity. Her personality was secondary to her status.

But in truth she was a middle child, neither one thing nor another, the bastard orphan of the old Africa and the legitimate child of the South Africa yet to come. She couldn't be classified as a new house, but was instead an old one changed to accommodate the new family of South Africa. She was this old house mended and with a new roof. Tandia smiled inwardly, enjoying the metaphor.

Then she snorted to herself in disgust. She must be going crazy! She was beginning to sound as stupid as Peekay! It was much better to hold onto the hard, cold reality of revenge than attempt to grasp a tenuous and amorphous hope. That old house had been built by vicious racists who'd murdered and plundered for the land it stood on. In the Africa of her future revenge, it must not be allowed to stand.

Old Coetzee was still on the stoep when she returned. It was almost dark and the old woman had hung a storm lantern on a hook on the rafter directly above the small wicker table on which stood the brandy decanter. 'Sit, Tandy.' Old Coetzee had straightened in his chair as she approached. The old man's voice was slurred and he was well on his way to being drunk, though he made no attempt to apologise for this. Tandy had, after all, seen him like this at Bluey Jay often enough before.

Tandia sat quietly in the chair next to him. 'Excrement!' Old Coetzee said suddenly, holding his glass high up in the air in front of him. 'I have spent my life in excrement!' Then he brought the brandy to his lips and drained the glass. His eyes were closed and he held the empty glass in both hands resting on his stomach, appearing to be asleep.

The woman appeared. 'Excuse missus, the dinner, it is ready.'

Tandia nodded her head towards Old Coetzee and the black woman shook her head. 'He will not eat tonight.' Her voice was without emotion, a statement of fact.

Tandia followed her through the small, almost dark, house to the kitchen. It smelt of the two kerosene lanterns which bathed the room in a soft yellow light. The woman brought her a plate of cold lamb, tomatoes, and cold roast potatoes, also placing a jar of mustard pickles on the table in front of her. 'You want coffee?' the woman asked.

Tandia shook her head. 'No thank you, but could you call the young man who came with me please?'

The woman sighed heavily. She removed her apron, folding it carefully over a chair beside the wood stove in the corner, and shuffled out, the screen door leading to the back yard banging sharply after her.

Tandia was struck by the loneliness of the house, its complete absence of human spirit. She was an expert in the business of loneliness and she realised that, quite apart from the banning order which confined Old Coetzee to this house, he'd cut himself off anyway. This silent, almost morose woman he'd chosen to look after him was a part of his isolation; it was as though he'd come to this lonely little farm to do some sort of penance.

Johanna returned with Johnny Tambourine and then entered the interior of the house. Shortly afterwards they heard a series of coughs and snuffles as she guided Old Coetzee to his bedroom, from the sound of her progress probably half carrying him most of the way. A few minutes later she returned to the kitchen where she picked up a white enamel dish covered and tied at the top with a cheese cloth. 'Goodnight, missus,' she said and nodded to Johnny Tambourine.

After she'd departed Johnny said; 'Tandia, let's get the hell out of here hey? We can go now, after you have eaten.'

'Don't think I'm not tempted, Johnny Tambourine, the old man's *gestonkered*. But he'll be up at dawn. I have to get instructions from him, we're challenging his banning order.'

'I don't like it, man, it's spooky in that room and hot!'

'Ja, I saw earlier; you'll have to push that big corrugated iron window open. It will be nice and cool then.'

'Are you crazy, man? You know what is this place? You standing in the world headquarters of the black mamba! Snakes, man, they can come right into your bed!'

'I'm sorry, Johnny, we can't go tonight, but we'll leave early, try to get to Barberton by seven o'clock. We'll be home before afternoon. I think I'll go to bed now.'

Tandia laughed at the irony; the environment in which Johnny Tambourine lived his everyday life was one of the most dangerous in the world and here he was, terrified at the prospect of spending a night in the country.

Johnny took both the lanterns in the kitchen down and Tandia followed him into the interior of the house. He handed her one of the lanterns and Tandia whispered goodnight, though judging from the snores coming from the closed door opposite, Old Coetzee was dead to the world. She was saddened at the thought that putting Old Coetzee to bed was probably the last thing his servant girl did before going home at night, like putting the cat out.

Johnny lay awake for a long time in his tin room. He'd taken one of the lanterns with him and it stood on the floor beside the bed, filling the air with the paraffin. It was unbearably hot and the sweat ran from his naked body and soaked into the bare mattress, leaving it damp and clammy. There was a three-inch gap between the end of the door and the cement floor and he'd used his blanket to stuff it tightly; a snake could easily make it through a gap like that. He longed to push the large window open but his fear of what might enter the room uninvited from the dangerously wild outside was too great. Eventually, though, he must have dozed off, for he awoke with a start, jerking upright in bed.

The light from the kerosene lamp gave the room an eerie glow and he had to squint to make out the time on his watch face. It was just after two o'clock in the morning and he was almost certain he'd heard the sound of a car engine. He sat still for a moment allowing his pounding heart to come to a rest as he listened to the sounds of the night outside. He could hear the rush of water over the rapids and the sounds of frogs in the reeds acting as basso profundo to the higher pitched sounds of crickets and other night insects. But nothing came to him which sounded vaguely human.

Johnny Tambourine had slept most of his life with one mental eye open and he knew the feel of danger. He hurriedly pulled on his trousers and put on his shirt, leaving it unbuttoned. In his bare feet he moved over to the door and pulled at the blanket with his toes, drawing it away from the bottom of the door, which he opened slowly about six inches. The moon was a large watermelon slice, two-thirds full in the sky and he'd never seen as many stars in his life. He was amazed at how light it seemed; details showed sharper than in street light. He looked down to the back of the house which lay quiet and still, its white, moonlight-bright walls sharply outlined, one side thrown into shadow. The chorus of frogs down at the river stopped suddenly and the higher pitch of the crickets filled the void. It was crazy, the old guy should have a dog. Who ever heard of a farmhouse without a dog? The old guy was asking for trouble. Johnny Tambourine remembered how he'd tried to lock the kitchen door when he'd left Tandia but, to his consternation, there had been no key in the lock. Everything about this place was crazy.

He concentrated on the side of the house thrown into shadow, trying to read its darkness. He knew from experience of a thousand alleys that if you concentrated hard enough and kept looking without panicking you could see into shadow. Then he saw a figure crouched low at the corner of the house. 'Christ, Tandia!' He hoped it was a burglar, he could cope easily with a single guy trying to break in.

Johnny Tambourine reached into his trouser pocket for his knife. Bringing it to his teeth he opened the long, sharp blade, then inched the door open a little further. The figure moved out of the shadow still crouching low and then he saw two others. They were directly behind the first man and now they too moved into the light. 'Shit! Special Squad!' The blackened faces were outlined in balaclavas pulled over their heads; they wore old clothes, but white men don't wear cast-off clothes the way Africans do. And terrorists go barefoot like village men, they don't wear identical brown sandshoes. But it was the way they crouched, elbows on their knees, in a particular manner the black people call *hlalaphansi*. Black people don't crouch quite like that. He couldn't see any guns, but they'd be armed for sure and it was open ground between where he stood and the back of the house – open in bright moonlight. They'd cut him to pieces if he was crazy enough to run at them, which he wasn't.

One of the men rose quickly and, half crouching, moved to the kitchen door. He inserted a small jemmy near the latch and Johnny Tambourine heard the soft crack as the door was levered open. What happened next was all over in seconds; the men crouched at the dark corner of the house moved quickly towards the kitchen door, each carrying what looked like a small package.

Then a flare of a match or cigarette lighter was touched to each package, and all three started to run from the house. Johnny Tambourine, shouting at the top of his voice, also started to run, though towards the house, closing his knife and returning it to his pocket. Before he'd run halfway across the yard the kitchen filled with roaring flame as the petrol bombs exploded within it.

Johnny Tambourine went straight down the side of the farmhouse and through the front door. The house had already filled with smoke but the flames had not yet reached Tandia's room. Opening her bedroom door and rushing to her bed, he jerked her to her feet; then half carrying her he propelled her down the hallway which was already in flames. He crossed the front parlour and pushed her screaming onto the stoep where she fell sprawling. Then he turned and rushed back into the smoke-filled house. The flames had reached the parlour and he beat at them with his hands as he made his way back down the hallway to Coetzee's room. The moment he opened the door the flames, pulled into the room by the draught created by the open window, entered the small room and enveloped the bed where Coetzee lay on his back fully dressed.

Johnny Tambourine lifted Coetzee from the bed, the adrenalin pumping through his body making the two-hundred-pound lift effortless. The open window was no more than three or four steps away and Johnny, his shirt in flames, dumped the still unconscious body of the magistrate through the window and dived through it himself.

He jumped up instantly, pulling his shirt off and then dragging the heavy body of the white man clear, rolling him on the ground and then picking up handfuls of soft dust and dousing out the last of the flames licking at his khaki shirt and trousers. Coetzee hadn't moved and Johnny Tambourine thought for a moment that the fall from the window might have killed him. Then he heard a soft groan as the old man opened his eyes.

Johnny Tambourine examined the seared flesh of his arms and torso. 'Shit! I risked my life to save a Boer? It must be the bush, it makes a man crazy!' he said aloud.

THIRTY-SEVEN

Peekay picked up the *Johannesburg Star*, turning quickly to the classified section. For the past three weeks he'd been doing the same thing each morning and now he saw what he was looking for:

This little piggy went to market
This little piggy had a beer alone
This little piggy climbed a peak
And this little piggy came home.

Gideon was back! The coded message conveyed that Gideon would be crossing the border from the Portuguese side into Swaziland and that Peekay should be alone at the marketplace at Pigg's Peak, a small town in Swaziland. He would indicate his presence by placing a case of Lion beer in the back of the car and the assignation would take place in four days' time at four o'clock in the afternoon.

Peekay worried about Gideon's return. He'd tried in his letters to persuade him to stay away, to lead from the outside. The courts were full of ANC and PAC men who'd been captured, who'd shown themselves no match for the Special Branch. Informers were everywhere and Peekay feared his friend's life would be wasted on a senseless act of terrorism.

But Gideon was coming back. Coming through Swaziland was a peculiar route. His face was famous in the Portuguese territory, he'd fought twice in Lourenco Marques so he'd be easily recognised by the locals. The only advantage was that it was less than four hours from the border to Pigg's Peak and from there they could cross at Bulembu and come into South Africa through Barberton, country Peekay knew intimately.

Still it was chancy. Then it occurred to him that Gideon was travelling without the knowledge of the ANC. This would cut down the likelihood of informers alerting the Special Branch. Coming through Lourenco Marques also had the added advantage that Gideon would come straight off a ship and be across the border in less than two hours.

Peekay still hoped to convince Gideon not to return when he met him face to face. The three partners had all but concluded that what Peekay and Tandia were doing, in terms of achieving justice, was very nearly pointless, that by going overseas and beginning the task of working for sanctions against South Africa they would, in the long run, have a far greater chance of bringing the apartheid regime to its knees. When the whites saw their way of life being eroded they would be less inclined to support a fanatical racist regime. Greed is nearly always the best persuader.

Peekay wanted only one more thing, a second crack at Jannie Geldenhuis: an opportunity to get the infamous police captain on the stand again, preferably on a charge of murder.

This time Peekay was vastly more experienced and, while he expected to lose the case regardless of how blatantly he proved the policeman's guilt, he was confident that he could use the courtroom as a stage to expose, for the entire world to see, the perfidy, cruelty and moral corruption of apartheid. He simply needed to trap Geldenhuis one more time.

Peekay knew this wouldn't be easy. The policeman was watching him as carefully as he was waiting for Geldenhuis to make an error of judgement. Hymie tried desperately to persuade him that it was a foolhardy plan. Hymie was getting close to despair; he'd calculated the odds of their remaining safe from the new laws which seemed specially designed for their demise and he'd concluded that time was running out for Peekay and Tandia in particular, but really for all of them.

Just a week before Peekay read Gideon's message in the *Star* he'd tried to force Peekay to look at the case rationally. 'Listen to me, this isn't like last time when we nailed the bastard with Tom Majombi! The law has been doctored to the point where as long as Geldenhuis kills black people in the name of the Special Branch he's safe as a house. He isn't going to do anything he can't justify as police work.'

'Ja, I know, Hymie, but sooner or later he has to do something we can nail him on personally. You can't just be evil in one way and good in all other respects; sooner or later he has to act on his own, do something which he can't justify in the name of the law. Guys like him always do.'

Peekay looked anguished. 'Hymie, I know you think part of it is getting even for Tandia. But I promise it isn't that! I mean, if it was, I dare say, with the contacts we have, we could plan some sort of ultimate revenge, then we could all leave South Africa and in the best of all worlds I could try to persuade Tandia to love me enough to marry me legally. You could marry Harriet and we'd all live happily ever after, spreading truth and justice and persuading the world to bring sanctions against the government in Pretoria.'

Peekay stopped, rubbing his forehead with the butt of his hand as though he was trying to expunge what he was about to say next. 'But that's just what it isn't! I want the world to see what we see, that Jannie Geldenhuis isn't an isolated madman, but a part of the logical offspring of a country where one section of the population has gone mad! We may not all be like Geldenhuis, but in any other country he would be either in prison or under severe psychiatric treatment in an institution. In our country he is a Godfearing citizen, who reads the lesson in church on Sunday and who is about to be promoted to colonel by a grateful government. He is a media personality, a famous policeman who keeps our children safe from the pathological fears of their insane parents. Geldenhuis is there because we appointed him; it is our collective insanity which allows him, and the thousands like him, to be who they are!'

'Peekay, I tremble in my very boots when I hear you talk like this. Let's at least put a deadline on leaving South Africa.' Hymie laughed grimly. 'My people have an instinct for knowing when to move. The only time we denied that instinct we paid too big a price. Let's put a time on leaving and I'll get Red sorted out so we don't lose too much. What do you say?'

Peekay shook his head. 'Hymie, I don't know. I don't know that I can leave just like that with nothing to show for ten years as a barrister. Less than nothing! My country is in ten times worse shape now than it was when we left Oxford. We have contributed bugger all!'

Hymie grew suddenly angry. 'Arsehole! You're showing all the signs of being a martyr. You know what you want to make me do? You want to make me puke! You've done everything a man can do for his country except die for it! If you want to do that, then go ahead, most of the whites will breathe a sigh of relief because you're no longer there to prick at their collective consciences. The blacks will mourn you for a day or two and then you'll just be another white liberal who got swallowed up in their plight. You won't even be useful dead! A white man dying for the cause of South Africa's blacks wouldn't even make a useful martyr!'

The conversation had ended there, but Peekay knew Hymie was right; it was only a matter of time before the government delivered the blow which would put them out of the game. Geldenhuis was holding all the aces. Now as he sat reading the paper and thinking of Gideon's return he wondered how he might persuade Tandia to come with them. She agreed that they'd become a useless appendage to the justice system but she wanted to go underground to fight. Perhaps if he could also persuade Gideon she'd see the need to get out, but Peekay was fairly certain both would elect to stay and fight even knowing that the odds were stacked against them. He despaired at the thought of Geldenhuis on the loose with Tandia on her own without the protection of Red. He simply couldn't see how he could possibly leave without her.

Tandia he knew had no hope as a freedom fighter; she was too well known, too conspicuous. She'd play straight into the hands of a waiting Geldenhuis, who had already made one recent attempt on her life with the fire-bombing of Magistrate Coetzee's farmhouse.

Though no incontrovertible proof existed that Geldenhuis had been responsible for the attack on the lonely farmhouse, Too Many Fingers Bembi, who took it in turns with Dog Poep Ismali to watch the police captain, had reported that he'd left in his car at eight o'clock on the night of the bombing in the company of two other men, a sergeant and a corporal in the Special Branch. They'd been dressed in civilian clothes and carried three canvas tote bags. One of the men also carried a two-gallon tin of petrol. They'd stowed the bags and the petrol in the boot of the police captain's blue 1957 Chevvy sedan and taken off.

When Too Many Fingers Bembi returned to the block of flats the following morning at seven o'clock, just shortly before Geldenhuis usually left for work, the blue Chevvy was parked outside. It was caked in dust and the front mudguard had been dented; he'd placed his hand on the bonnet to discover it was still warm.

There was no way they could prove the police captain's involvement, of course. There were no fingerprints at the scene of the crime and Johnny Tambourine was the only witness. Cross-examined, his evidence of what he'd purported to have seen in the dark would count for little, although his picture did appear in all the newspapers as the 'boy' who'd saved the lives of the famous retired magistrate currently under house arrest and the beautiful coloured lawyer who would soon be representing him in court.

So the case was closed. The police stated that they believed the people responsible for the fire were the ones who had destroyed Magistrate Coetzee's tractor and disc plough. They felt sure that when they solved the first crime they'd resolve the second. And no, they were no closer to solving the first.

One good thing did come from the incident. Though Tandia subsequently lost her appeal against Magistrate Coetzee's house arrest, his sentence was lifted one week after his eight-week stay in hospital. The old man never returned to live at Eendrag, but took a room in a private house in Barberton. He would often drive the half hour out to his farm in the bend of the Crocodile River. He would pass the burnt-out ruins of his old home without so much as a glance and continue past it up the eroded and barely visible road, over the slight rise to what he now called Tandia's house.

Here he would park the International under the frangipani tree, kill the engine and sit quietly for a few moments inhaling the soft perfumed air around him. Then he'd climb slowly from the pick-up, taking his old Boer War Mauser with him up the grand steps to the stoep. Seated on a deck chair, he would pass the afternoon away in the excellent company of a good bottle of brandy. Occasionally he'd bring the Mauser up and squint down its sights. He never fired a shot, even though the gun had been restored to mint condition and the chamber was always loaded. He told himself he didn't want to destroy the tranquillity of a perfectly good afternoon or even for a moment drown out the sound of the river as it turned into rapids at the wide bend that marked the boundary of his own land.

One night nearly six months after leaving hospital he didn't return home at his usual time soon after sunset. Mrs Boxall, the town's librarian, who was his landlady and who'd grown rather fond of the old man, waited until eight o'clock before she called Gert from the prison.

Gert arrived in a prison car a short time later and together they'd driven the half hour out to Eendrag. As Mrs Boxall would later tell it to Peekay, they found Magistrate Coetzee seated in his deck chair on the stoep in the bright moonlight, the old rifle over his lap and the smell of the moonflowers and frangipani strong in the night air.

At first they both thought he was asleep. His great red nose actually shone by the light of the full moon. Then Mrs Boxall saw that the bottle of Cape brandy was still half full. 'He wouldn't fall asleep until the bottle was empty,' she whispered to Gert. She knew suddenly he was dead, but strangely she didn't feel in the least upset; it seemed such a pleasant way to die.

'Mrs Boxall, I wonder, could you do me a favour?' Gert asked suddenly.

'Of course, Gert.'

'Well, man, I think we leave the old *kerel* here tonight, hey? Then tomorrow morning we can send the ambulance.'

Mrs Boxall was puzzled, though she knew Gert was far too sensible not to have a good reason. 'Yes, of course, whatever you say.'

Gert walked to the edge of the stoep and looked up into the brilliant night sky pinned with a million stars. 'He was *'n regte oubaas*, they don't make his kind any more,' he paused. 'I jus' got a feeling inside me he wants to spend his last night under the stars of an African night on his own farm, with his rifle at his side. It's the proper way, the way every Boer wishes to die.'

Magistrate Coetzee was found to have no relations and in his will he left the farm to Peekay to be held in trust for Tandia. With his last will and testament he'd included a note for Tandia written in his beautiful copperplate hand:

My dear Tandy,
you are the future and I am very proud of you. You will see, there will come a time when the house you build on Eendrag will be for all the children of the beloved country.
Though the fight will be hard, your rewards will be astonishing.
Never give up, never compromise, the future belongs to you.
Johannes H. Coetzee - Magistrate

Peekay left for Barberton after breakfast on the day he was to meet Gideon at Pigg's. He stopped briefly at the library to say hello to Mrs Boxall and then drove up to the Berea to see his family.

He received the usual joyous reception from the black twins. Even his mother seemed delighted to see him; she'd mellowed considerably since he'd obeyed the Lord and given up boxing. Peekay now supported the family financially and she no longer needed to sew and had grown quite plump from all the morning and afternoon teas she attended witnessing in His name and generally doing the Lord's work. If only he would stop wasting his talent on black murderers and terrorists and become a judge, a born-again judge, she would have the perfect son. She, in conjunction with the Lord, was working on this during their 'quiet time' every day.

Peekay explained that he could only stay a couple of hours and was on his way to Swaziland, news which was met with a great deal of consternation, particularly from the twins who'd rushed to the kitchen to rustle up a batch of pumpkin scones. Peekay wasn't going to chance bringing Gideon over the border, he'd bring him back over the mountains on foot, and so he got the twins to pack two sets of bush clothes. Then he told Dee and Dum to take food enough for two meals out to Eendrag farm where they would find a motor car parked outside the old house. 'The boot will be open; put the food in the boot.'

'We will wait for you, so we can cook you a proper meal,' Dum said. Peekay forbade them to do so and their bottom lips dropped simultaneously in an exact and unconscious duplicate expression of dismay.

Peekay called Gert at the prison and asked if he could borrow his half-ton utility and if he'd meet him at Eendrag farm. Gert didn't question him when they met, he understood that if an explanation was necessary Peekay would have made it. Peekay arranged to have Gert pick up his bakkie at an Indian store two miles into the border on the Swaziland side in two days' time, the keys left with the Indian storekeeper. Dropping Gert off at the prison, he left just after two in the afternoon for the drive over the mountains to Swaziland.

The road to Havelock is winding and not well used, so that Peekay felt he had the mountains to himself. It was an early spring day in September and the sky was an intense blue, turning the crags and bluffs around him to grey. The winter tussocks which grew on the high slopes shone silver with the late season, making a dreaming landscape around him. He imagined the stillness beyond the whining engine of the truck: the crystal cave of Africa was no more than a few miles from the road he travelled and he thought of Doc, the knight errant of Africa, his long thin body stretched out on his white throne.

Sudden tears welled in Peekay's eyes. 'Doc, the madness has won in the beloved country,' he said, looking up into the mountains. He pulled over and cut the engine, his tears making him unable to see the winding road. The total stillness swept around him and enclosed him as though drawing him into the dreaming time where Doc lay in his cave. 'Doc, please help me to fight the madness,' he whispered.

Peekay crossed the border and the road deteriorated almost immediately so that it took almost forty minutes to reach the little town of Pigg's Peak. He drove to the general store, bought a case of Lion beer and a carton of cigarettes and returned to the car. Then he drove to the open marketplace where twice a week the women from the villages brought produce for sale. He placed the beer in the back of the truck and the cigarettes in the glove compartment, got back in and waited. It was five minutes to four in the afternoon.

A few minutes later an African, wearing a shabby khaki army greatcoat, perhaps in his fifties, opened the door on the passenger side and climbed in. He smelt pretty ripe and Peekay extended his hand. The black man took it, and they shook hands in the traditional African double-grip manner. 'My name is Julius,' the black man said slowly in English, pausing between each word.

'Peekay, my name is Peekay. Thank you for being on time to meet me,' Peekay said in Siswati. The older man was delighted and threw back his head and laughed, showing only four yellowed teeth in his mouth. 'Now I know you are the *Onoshobishobi Ingelosi*, you speak all the languages of the people!' He pointed to four young men who stood outside waiting. 'Please, we can give for these boys a lift, they go to the same village.'

Peekay readily agreed and the four young guys, laughing among themselves, climbed into the truck.

Peekay turned on the ignition. 'Where are we going, Julius?'

'We are going to see Somojo. It is near the great mountain Bulembu, I think maybe one hour.' Julius held up his forefinger. It was almost back to the border he'd just come from, though Julius had no way of knowing this.

'Somojo? The great sangoma?' Peekay was surprised, the greatest of the living medicine men seldom saw whites.

'He said we must bring the *Onoshobishobi Ingelosi* to him.'

Peekay had expected that Gideon might be in hiding in a friendly village where they would have to deal with a clan chief and he'd brought three good white collarless cotton poplin shirts with him. The shirts were of the old-fashioned kind intended for starched collars; worn collarless, with a traditional stud to hold the neck together, they were much favoured by older African men of some standing. They were not a gift worthy of the great Somojo, Peekay thought; he would need to apologise profusely when he presented them.

They arrived at sunset and Peekay was taken to a reception hut, a round beehive construction made of woven grass held into a conical shape by saplings, known as a '*guga*'. A woman brought him a huge old Victorian porcelain basin and jug filled with water for him to wash. The floor was covered with a freshly woven grass mat; a small three legged stool in the very centre of the room was the single piece of furniture in the round hut. At the door was an earthenware water pot of dark clay with a small drinking calabash floating on top of it.

The four young guys brought out the case of beer, his canvas overnight bag and sleeping bag and placed these within the hut. Then they squatted beside the doorway, talking in an animated manner, enjoying the importance of the occasion. From their conversation they appeared to know nothing of Gideon but had simply gone along to bring Peekay to Somojo's kraal. It seemed unlikely that they'd simply cadged a lift or they would have moved on after they'd arrived. Then it occurred that they were there to guard him in the event that they had been followed.

Julius, too, hadn't mentioned Gideon. Peekay walked out to the bakkie and retrieved the carton of cigarettes from the glove box. He broke out a pack and he handed it to the boys who were delighted and divided the pack between them, each lighting a cigarette and keeping the remaining four, sticking two behind each ear.

Using his rolled-up sleeping bag as a pillow, Peekay lay on the grass mat which was new and still smelt of the sweetness of the meadow. When it had grown dark in the hut and Peekay had been kept waiting an hour or so, sufficiently long for the old witchdoctor to assert his importance, a small boy came to fetch him. Carrying the three white poplin shirts, Peekay stepped out into the early evening. The village was a big one with perhaps fifty beehive huts built around a cattle kraal enclosure of wooden stakes and thorn-tree scrub. The cattle were being driven into the safety of the kraal for the night by the herd boys, one of whom was cracking a whip and really acting the boss. Outside the huts, fires were beginning to crackle and snap as women fed green thorn-bush branches into them. The smell of smoke, cattle dung and dust, the sound of the lowing cattle, the barking and yapping of the scrawny yellow mongrels and the laughter of the women as they prepared the evening meal filled the air and seemed to Peekay to be an altogether fitting way to close down a long and tiring day.

The small boy ran ahead of him. Moving between huts, scattering chickens who'd not yet flown to their roosts for the night. They came to a path on the edge of the village and Peekay followed the child up it. It was getting dark, as it does quickly after sunset in those parts where the high mountains snaffle the light. They came to a clearing completely enclosed with a high wooden fence made of heavy stakes. The child stopped at the opening to the enclosure and pointed inwards; then he turned and ran for his life back down the way they'd just come. Peekay turned and watched as the darkness swallowed the child up.

The small compound contained three beautifully constructed traditional conical huts, one large central one and a smaller one to each side of it. A fire burned outside the large hut and two jackal-skin karosses were spread over grass mats beside the fire. Almost immediately a young woman appeared from one of the smaller huts and silently invited Peekay to sit, pointing to one of the karosses.

Peekay removed his shoes and sat cross-legged, placing the white shirts on his lap. Outside the compound a frog began to croak and almost immediately the night was filled with the the sound of frogs responding. Peekay had seen no water but guessed there must be a dam or stream nearby. He heard the sound of coughing coming from the large hut, then hawking and the pause of someone spitting. Then he made out the irascible voice of an old man saying something he couldn't quite hear.

Moments later the great Somojo stood at the entrance, being led by a second young African woman. He was a tiny little man, bent over with age, wrapped entirely in a bright purple blanket. He allowed himself to be led to the kaross next to Peekay where the first young woman waited for him. Together they placed him on the soft warm fur and pulled the blanket around him so that only his ancient head appeared above the purple mound. He sniffed and smacked his toothless gums; his rheumy eyes appeared not to see and his chest wheezed so that he gave the impression of someone who wonders where he is and is completely confounded as to how he got there.

The Swazis are small and lightly built, a mountain people, but Somojo was positively tiny and took up hardly more room than if the blanket alone had been carelessly dropped to the ground. It was hard to believe that this old man was one of the most powerful black men in Africa, the greatest of all the medicine men alive, the wizard of all the wizards. When the drums of Africa carried his name, kings and paramount chiefs trembled for the power of his witchcraft. It was said that he could turn day-old chickens into hawks and hawks into mighty eagles with wings that cast a shadow over the sun. Stories were told of how he could make the great black mamba dance on the last three inches of his tail, how he had reached through the king's chest, when King Sobhuza II was just a young boy, and pulled out his heart, making an incantation and putting it back in front of the eyes of all his counsellors, how the king had fathered seventy sons in the ensuing forty years and each year came more, each a mightier warrior than the last. At night, late, a white owl came to sit on the roof of his hut and if any man saw this great white bird, in seven days he would die of a madness which would make him take a knife and tear his own entrails from his stomach. Somojo's cures were legendary and his prophecies so profound that no great tribal decision from the Congo River down could take place until he had seen the sacred smoke, thrown the bones, examined the entrails of a red jackal and given his approval or sanction. The curse of Somojo the great was worse than death because it meant when death came there would be no return to the shadows of the dead man's clan. The dead one would become a ghost who wandered alone in the spirit world, howling in crags and mountain peaks, cursed and utterly forlorn, never again to sit beside a fire drinking beer in the company of his shadows in the spirit world.

Like Inkosi-Inkosikazi before him, Somojo was very rich and had travelled throughout the country in a great black Mercedes 600. He no longer travelled now, though, and the last time he had left his home in the mountains of Swaziland had been when he appeared at Sharpeville. His great black car had been given to the king and now he lay each night on his jackal-skin kaross between two young princesses from the royal kraal who kept his old bones warm and attended to his every need.

One of these young women brought two gourds of *mqomothi*, maize beer, and handed one to Peekay.

'I thank you, *inKosazana*,' Peekay said, addressing her by her title of princess. The young woman smiled shyly, surprised at this expression of respect coming from a white man. Then she kneeled and held the second gourd of beer to the great Somojo's mouth, feeding him the thick concoction as one might a small child. Peekay wondered if the old man was senile, for he'd given no sign that he was aware of his presence. He drank the sour beer, trying desperately not to pull a face and waited, for he dared not say a word until he had been formally recognised by the great medicine man.

One of the young women appeared with a tin plate piled high with stiff maize porridge, known as *iPhalishi*, a small bowl of meat, and another bowl of peppered yams and greens picked in the wild. She placed these in front of Peekay. The second maiden appeared with food for Somojo and together the two young women proceeded to hand feed the old man, rolling the stiff porridge into tiny balls and chewing his meat for him before placing it in his mouth.

There is a moment in the high mountains that is like no other experience on earth. It comes when a full moon rises suddenly from behind the black outline of the high crags and peaks and lights the night world. It is a moment of moments, a sudden great golden orb that hangs so close above the peaks that the women in the mountain kraals rush from their huts to sing a song to encourage it to remain where it is and not to roll down the peaks and set the world on fire. The song is like a children's nursery rhyme and is meant to show proper respect as well as flatter the Lord Full Moon so he doesn't get any crazy ideas about coming down the mountain side to have a look at how things are going on earth and, in the process, do all manner of damage.

Lord, Full Moon
Stay high in your mountain sky
Great eye of bone and golden light
watch the wily demon night
Stay high, stay high!

Peekay finished his simple meal and waited for the great Somojo to complete his own. It was now quite dark and only the embers from the fire threw a little light, though only sufficient to outline the old man and his two handmaidens. A grunt came from Somojo; the two women rose and, taking the plates, returned to the cooking hut. At that moment the moon came up and the young women came out of the cooking hut again, sang the rising moon song and then returned.

The moon hung huge and golden above the great Bulembu which rose up in front of Peekay. A voice came from Somojo, a thin, clear voice; though of an old, old man, it contained no cackle of infirmity. 'I see you *Onoshobishobi Ingelosi*, you have been witness to our dead and your tears have been our tears and your voice our voice and now your seed shall be our seed and you shall father a son and he will be a man for all Africa and his name shall be Lumukanda, child of the morning star.'

Peekay was deeply moved by Somojo's unexpected words. 'I see you, great Lord Somojo and I thank you for allowing me to sit on your kaross and beside your fire.' He rose to his knees and, crawling over to the old man, he placed the three shirts beside him. '*Makhosi*, please accept this unworthy gift.' The fire spluttered as old fires sometimes do, catching up into a few moments of licking flame and lighting the old witchdoctor's tiny simian face. Peekay saw Somojo's eyes were rolled back and he appeared to be in a deep trance. Somojo's hands, like dry twigs in winter, emerged from the top of the blanket and he withdrew a leather cord to the end of which was attached a small leather bag not much bigger than the top half of a man's thumb.

The old man held the tiny bag in front of him so that it dangled from the leather thong. Slowly his eyes rolled back until the whites disappeared and he was looking directly at Peekay, his eyes like soft, bright raisins.

'Take it, wear it, it is the golden coin of Lumukanda.'

Peekay was astonished beyond belief. This was the most sacred of all the things that ever were to the black people. 'I cannot, Somojo, it is an honour beyond me, too great for my status, much too great for a white skin, I cannot take this from you.'

The old man's expression didn't change. 'You are not taking it, it is bringing you. It will come back to me, you must do as I say and wear it around your neck, it will know when to come back,' he repeated.

Peekay took the small leather bag, cupping his hands in the African manner to receive it. Somojo dropped it into his hands. His tiny, skeletal hands fluttered briefly in the air and then, like trapdoor spiders, they retreated back into the blanket. Somojo closed his eyes and Peekay knew he was dismissed.

Peekay crawled back to the kaross and put his shoes on, stooping low until he judged that he was sufficiently far from the old man to rise with respect. Then he made his way in the moonlight along the path back to the village.

At dawn Peekay was awakened by a cock who seemed to be crowing on the roof of his hut. He stooped to get out of the guga and felt the unaccustomed tug of the leather bag around his neck. He crawled out into the light, feeling a little stiff from having slept on the floor in his sleeping bag. Outside the mist hung low over the village and he could barely make out the outline of the cattle kraal, though he heard the bell of a lead cow and the soft cries of the herd boys as the cattle lowed, ready to be taken out to graze. He removed the leather thong from his neck and gently pulled the drawstrings of the tiny bag, tapping the contents into the palm of his hand. The coin was heavy, nearly a quarter of an inch thick, and smooth with generation upon generation of handling, so that it was only roughly round and resembled a pebble in shape. On its face were the very vaguest markings, which appeared almost as tiny scratches on the surface. The gold coin shone in the early morning light and Peekay was totally awed by the sight of it, he'd been afraid to remove it from the bag in the dark and now as he looked at the most precious relic in Africa, south of the Congo River, he began to tremble. It was the most powerful magic he had ever been near and the soft morning light catching it seemed to give the tiny coin, no bigger than his thumbnail a heartbeat of its own. Peekay was frightened about its meaning. He put the coin back into its tiny bag and tucked it under his shirt. If any African knew he possessed it he would kill him instantly; it was unimaginable that it could ever come into white hands, no matter what the circumstances.

A fire burned low outside his hut and he placed a couple of pieces of wood onto it adding a few twigs to make the embers flare. Peekay stood hunched over the fire, rubbing his hands above the flames. He was grateful for the padded anorak he wore. It was an old one he'd bought for Pike's Peak when they'd trained in the US for the first title fight and he'd often used it in the mountains at home and when he'd first returned. Now he was glad to have it on, a familiar garment to cloak his terror and his awe.

He'd returned to his hut the evening before hoping he might receive news of Gideon, though he wasn't sure that after his confrontation with the ancient witchdoctor he could go through the emotional reunion of a meeting with his friend. Now, standing in the dawn light in the mist shrouded mountain village, he wondered to himself what the day might bring.

The woman who had brought him the basin and jug the previous day now brought him a mug of dark tea sweetened with honey. '*Ngiya bonga, Mama*, I thank you, mother.' Peekay said, taking the steaming mug from her in both hands. The woman left quietly, melting into the mist.

Peekay looked up from his cup to see a man wrapped tightly in a blanket approaching him in the mist. It was only when Gideon was within twenty feet of the fire that Peekay recognised him and, dropping the cup so that the tea spluttered furiously in the hot coal, he rushed to embrace his friend. Gideon brought his blanket around both of them and hugged him, the village echoing with their laughter.

'I see you, Gideon,' Peekay said; then he glanced quickly at the black man beside him, though he could hardly see him through his sudden tears. 'I have missed you, with my heart, but in my head I wish you hadn't returned.'

'I am a soldier now, Peekay. I have no choice, comrade,' Gideon said softly, his voice also showing his emotion.

Peekay sniffed, then laughed. 'Comrade? That's a habit you'd better get out of bloody fast, kaffir. Just the word itself could get you twenty years!' As he'd expected Gideon was dressed in old clothes, dirty and heavily patched, and on his head he wore an ancient grease-stained felt hat, misshapen and tattered, which he'd pulled almost over his eyes so he had to raise his chin to see Peekay. While the clothes he wore were perfect for the anonymity he needed on the road, Peekay said, 'Jesus, Gideon. You smell like a gorilla's armpit. How long have you been travelling rough?'

Gideon chuckled. 'Not long, my brother. I exchanged them for my suit when I got off the boat. The old man who wore them thought I had gone mad. But it is good for me to feel like this, it will do me no harm; it is like wearing the skin of my countrymen again. Algeria and Europe spoiled me; I was beginning to think I was a somebody.'

'Welcome home then, and take off that bloody hat. You're talking to a white man you understand!'

Gideon pulled the tattered felt hat off his head. 'Shit, I'd forgotten, it's too easy to die where we are going.'

'I thought you went to Algeria to learn how to survive in a war zone?'

'They taught me twenty ways to kill a man, but nothing about surviving amongst killers. It's not going to be easy being a kaffir again. I can't even be Gideon Mandoma, Welterweight Champion of the World. I'm just a kaffir like I was when I was lashing coal for the furnace.'

'That's good, that way you *may* stay alive; your anonymity is everything now. I have brought you clothes, old clothes for the mountains, but clean at least.' Peekay looked down at Gideon's feet. Gideon wore a pair of tackies, the sandshoes well scuffed but still durable. 'Your tackies will last going over Saddleback. We really ought to make an early start. We'll stay the night in the old farmhouse outside Barberton, the place Magistrate Coetzee left Tandia. Then tomorrow morning you will drive as my chauffeur to Johannesburg. If I cannot do it right now, I warn you that on the mountains and at Eendrag I will try to persuade you to go back, Gideon. I have money and a plane ticket out of Lourenco Marques to London with me.'

'Haya, haya, Peekay,' Gideon said, shaking his head sadly, 'we cannot go back. It is too late to turn back now. I have come to fight, there is no other way the *amaBhunu* can be made to understand.'

THIRTY-EIGHT

In December the Solomon Levy Carpet Emporium held its annual Christmas party and Solomon Levy gave the entire first three weeks of the month over to the preparations for it.

Hymie called Peekay early one morning in the second week of December. 'Have you read the papers, old son?' he asked. Peekay had been out early for a run and confessed he was only just out of the shower and hadn't.

'Simon Fitzharding, you know, the BBC producer guy I told you about who's doing the thing on the old man's Christmas party, said something dumb on a radio programme yesterday and it's on the front pages of all the morning papers.'

'Dumb? What did he say?'

'The stupid prick announced over the air that the Solomon Levy Christmas party was the only true example of Christianity and the true spirit of Christmas to be found in South Africa.'

Peekay laughed. 'He's probably right.'

'Well the shit's hit the fan! That bloody Christmas party! It's too high profile anyway. Did you see the stuff in the *Outspan* and *Die Huisgenoot*?'

'Ja, Tandia showed me in the office, it was pretty spectacular. But, so what's new? It's the same every year, your old man has a natural instinct for getting publicity. Have you called him about Fitzharding's gaff?'

'Ja, before you. He thinks it's the greatest publicity ever. He's besotted with the idea of this BBC documentary. He spends most of the day in that ridiculous little engine going around the garden blowing its steam whistle and shouting "Camera, action!" '

Peekay laughed. 'Sorry Hymie, I know it isn't funny, but there's something very bizarre about the BBC choosing to show a Christmas bash by one of South Africa's foremost Jews in order to demonstrate to the world that the African Christ has been put back into Christmas.'

Over the years Solomon Levy's Christmas party for the employees of the Levy carpet empire had become an annual media event and, because of the BBC documentary, this Christmas party of 1966 promised to be a bigger and more extravagant affair than ever. In the mid-November issue of the *Outspan*, South Africa's traditional English household magazine, there appeared an article which among other things catalogued the gifts the children would receive at his Christmas party. It also included a special article on the design of the now-famous black dolls which were created by the London doll firm of Rubens and Brown.

Doris with the wonderful tits had married Togger Brown and they'd gone into partnership with Mr Rubens to establish a doll factory. The traditional Shirley Temple doll had been replaced by a beautiful new doll with a magnificent bisque head, which was rapidly earning a worldwide reputation in the toy department of better department stores. It was referred to in the toy trade as a 'Rubens-Kellerman' doll.

The *Outspan* article told how the beautiful dolls had been patterned on the world-famous Hans Kellerman German doll and how each was dressed in one of ten outfits designed by Carmen Brown's haute couture shop for children in Paris.

The six-page article, in colour, also showed a picture, taken the previous year, of two five-year-old girls at the Solomon Levy Christmas party, one black and the other white, standing on tiptoe on either side of the dividing fence exchanging their dolls. Under the picture ran the caption, *Two little dolls cross the colour barrier on tiptoe.*

The following week *Die Huisgenoot*, a slightly more politically inclined Afrikaans equivalent of the *Outspan*, featured the same picture of the little girls in a leading article, but this time the headline read: *Prominent Pretoria Jew defies apartheid policy*! The following week's issue of the same magazine contained several letters from readers vowing never to purchase a carpet from a Solomon Levy Carpet Emporium ever again.

When these letters were translated to him, Solomon Levy immediately wrote a letter of his own.

Dear Customers,

It hurts me to think only last week some of my very good Afrikaner friends are writing in this magazine about 'Again'. They say they will NEVER buy carpet from me AGAIN.

I beg your pardon! A Solomon Levy Carpet Emporium broadloom (a nice Christmas special, 35% off!) is NOT an 'Again' carpet!

To those people who are writing to insult the quality of my best broadloom with this 'Again' talk, I only have this to say – you should all go to that place where it's so hot they got only asbestos carpet on the floor!

Yours in pile, shag and broadloom, believe me, only the best! Also, Happy Christmas, God Bless!

Alles van die beste,
Solomon Levy
President, Solomon Levy Carpet Emporiums –
Solomon's carpet is a wise decision.

The big party as usual was to take place on the last Saturday before Christmas and the preparations for it started at daybreak on the first of December when an army of workmen moved in. For the next three weeks there would be a great deal of coming and going. The tracks for the miniature railway had to be laid, the fence which divided the black from the white needed to be built, *braaivleis* pits prepared and the huge spits where several whole oxen would be roasted set up. In the final week two identical carnivals with flying swings, a big dipper, dodgem cars and all the usual side shows would be erected.

To Solomon Levy the toy train was the most important of all, and the tracks for the miniature railway were the very first thing to be done on the estate. These followed around the complete perimeter of the gardens except for a detour through his prize-winning dahlia garden on the black side and famous rose garden on the white.

The old man was determined to make the Christmas of 1966 the best ever. The BBC had selected his party for the Africa segment of its Christmas day programme, 'Christmas with Children Around the World'. He was tremendously excited about this, and imagined at once that the Queen of England would be watching the programme on Christmas day, seated on her throne with Axminster on the floor, and there he would be, driving the train in his new lightweight Father Christmas outfit.

Simon Fitzharding, a rather pompous Englishman who was known at the BBC as an awful hack, had been the only director available to cover the Africa segment of the documentary and he couldn't believe his luck. Solomon had insisted he move from his second-rate, BBC-budget hotel, and take over an entire wing of the large house, where he found himself treated like royalty.

After this splendid reception he simply hadn't the heart to tell the excited Solomon Levy that Africa had been allotted exactly five minutes of the one-hour programme and that, furthermore, because Africa started with an 'A' it would appear at the opening of the documentary – a nice compliment in one way, but also the scene over which the title and opening credits would appear.

Simon Fitzharding also had a BBC budget which gave him very few options. He'd settled on the Solomon Levy Carpet Emporium Party almost immediately because it was a single location – a splendid one at that – it was multiracial, it cut down on expenses, it offered unstinting co-operation and, in fact, it had everything he needed to succeed.

He made the decision to put most of his efforts into one grand opening sequence. The opening shot, he decided, would be Solomon in all his glory as the Father Christmas engine driver coming towards camera in the little engine with all its carriages loaded with toys. The sequence would culminate in Father Christmas Solomon Levy drawing his engine into the station where all the children waited for their presents. The final shot would show two little girls, a black and a white, holding their appropriate dolls and looking wide-eyed into the future.

Simon Fitzharding, though perhaps not a very inspired film maker, was nevertheless a perfectionist and with Solomon Levy he had a willing actor on his hands. Over the final week they'd practised the action at least fifty times until the timing was perfect.

Jannie Geldenhuis was in his office in John Vorster Square at his usual time of half past seven when he read about the proposed BBC documentary of the Jew's annual party in the morning papers. He'd also read the recent *Die Huisgenoot* article with rising apprehension. It was seven years since he'd been sworn into the *Broederbond* and had vowed to fix the fat Jew's Christmas party. Now it had finally got out of hand and, he knew, in the eyes of the *Broederbond*, that this could be seen as partially or even entirely his fault. The matter of the Jew's kaffir Christmas party should have been settled years ago.

In the intervening years Solomon Levy had become one of South Africa's leading philanthropists. He gave equally to both English-speaking and Afrikaans-speaking charities, as well as many African and coloured ones, though notably never to the Indian community whom he regarded as deadly competitors in the carpet business. In short, Solomon Levy had become an extremely difficult target.

Geldenhuis picked up the phone and dialled a number in Pretoria. Finally, after the phone had rung more than a dozen times a voice at the other end simply said, 'Ja?'

'*Jakkals*,' Geldenhuis replied.

'Your number?' The voice demanded in Afrikaans.

'*Een en tagtig*.'

'*Jou moeder se voorname*?'

'Anna, Sophie,' Geldenhuis replied, giving his mother's christian names.

'*Wag*,' the voice said, instructing him to wait.

He held on for ten minutes before the original voice returned, still speaking in Afrikaans. 'Are you calling about a certain kaffir Christmas party?'

'*Ja*.'

'*Wag*,' the voice instructed again.

This time he didn't have to wait long before there was a new voice, which he thought he recognised, though it had been a long time since he'd been briefed. '*Jakkals?*'

'*Ja, meneer?*'

'You may proceed with maximum impact.' The phone went dead.

Jannie Geldenhuis felt his heart pounding. 'Shit!' They wanted Solomon Levy killed! 'Jesus!' And he'd been afraid he'd get a negative response. Censured for not having undertaken the task long before. At best he thought they'd simply tell him to create a disruption and make it look like an attack from religious fanatics or an extreme right-wing element: create enough of a disaster, kill a few kaffirs.

Geldenhuis was delighted with his Christmas present from the *Broederbond*. Maybe he could work it so he got Hymie and Peekay as well;

also, why not Tandia? At one stage or another they had to be standing together. A bomb in the right place, that's all it would take.

But Jannie Geldenhuis knew he was daydreaming. He could get a couple of his men into the grounds, that wouldn't be too hard – there were carpenters and technicians everywhere, even planting a bomb with a timing device wouldn't be impossible. But on the day the place would be crawling with children, white children. His chances of getting the four people he most wanted to kill all together on the black side was negligible.

Besides, while he didn't care particularly about killing Hymie, he wanted Peekay and Tandia alive for two reasons. He hoped they would lead him to Gideon Mandoma. The sudden increase in terrorist activity and rumours from his informers gave him reason to believe that Gideon was back in South Africa. And, most importantly, he had a personal vendetta to settle with both Peekay and the black bitch.

He'd already broken Tandia as a teenager; what had happened then was child's play. Now she would be really something to work on, all the old fears to bring back, new ones to work on. Breaking down her beauty alone, that would be something. Now, when she was so terribly guilty, breaking her now would be a most exquisite pleasure. His brains against hers, his arrogance against her fear, his hate against her hate. The re-enactment of that day at Bluey Jay, only this time with his ending.

But, more even than her, there was Peekay. He could taste Peekay like blood in his mouth. Geldenhuis dreamed of reducing both Peekay and Tandia down to shit, for he knew both were guilty of the most terrible crimes against his Afrikaner nation for which they must both die. He also believed in his heart that they were guilty of miscegenation, the most heinous crime of them all, that struck at the very roots of the survival of the white tribe in Africa. With Peekay there was the physical thing as well, the man on man.

Just as Peekay dreamed of getting Jannie Geldenhuis into court for a showdown in front of the world media, so Geldenhuis dreamed of getting Peekay into the ring. The need physically to get the better of the hated rooinek had never left him. He knew that while most weeks Peekay kept himself in reasonable shape with a couple of hard games of squash and two or three long runs in the early morning, he worked much too hard to be in the really top condition he needed to fight. Besides, he hadn't put on a glove since the night he'd lost the title to Mandoma. He was probably ten pounds over the welterweight limit and not nearly as strong or in the same sort of shape as Geldenhuis knew himself to be.

Geldenhuis spent most of the day after his phone call to Cogsweel at the *Broederbond* working on how he might eliminate Solomon Levy without leaving any trace as to the identity of his assassins. And when he opened the evening paper he couldn't quite believe his luck. In the paper was a picture of the little engine. In the background, on what appeared to be a door, was the name of an engineering company, J. Poulos Pty, Ltd. Beside the photograph of the train was a plan of the Levy gardens showing the entire topography of the estate and the exact layout of the train tracks. The plan had been prepared to scale by a qualified draughtsman so that the grounds could be correctly laid out for the Christmas party and for the film crew to work from. Apparently the train had gone in for some last-minute repairs and there was some concern as to whether it would be ready in time.

The idea of sabotaging the toy train had already occurred to Geldenhuis but he'd quickly dismissed the idea. He couldn't be sure of blowing up the engine without killing the white children in the carriages. Now, as he read an interview with one of the cameramen hired by Simon Fitzharding, his excitement increased. In the interview the cameraman explained the opening film sequence for the BBC documentary when Solomon Levy would be alone in the train filled with toys during one complete loop of the tracks.

Geldenhuis had all the information he needed to formulate a plan. The newspaper had presented it to him on a plate. Checking the Pretoria telephone directory he located the address of the engineering company. Geldenhuis had long since learned to trust simple ideas and he knew if he could get into the engineering works for less than twenty minutes he could go a long way to bringing the assassination of Solomon Levy to a successful conclusion.

With most of the equipment he needed in a small canvas sports bag he left just after three in the afternoon in an unmarked car for the forty-mile drive to Pretoria. With him he took a plain-clothes black detective from the Special Squad who had no idea as to the purpose of their journey and who was simply required to act on instructions when they got there.

They arrived in the general area of the engineering works, which was in one of the older industrial suburbs of Pretoria, just before five o'clock, having stopped along the way to Pretoria at three hardware shops where Geldenhuis sent the black detective in to make several small purchases. The factories in the area closed at four and now the dirty back streets were completely deserted.

Geldenhuis stopped the car half a block from where the engineering works was situated and, with the black detective, he went to work on a well-rehearsed routine. The police captain grabbed a tyre iron and spanner and slipped the hubcap from the rear driver's side wheel. He started to undo the nuts while the black man removed the jack and spare tyre. The detective quickly seated the jack and raised the tyre while Geldenhuis removed the tyre nuts and finally the tyre itself. Together they fitted the spare, tightened the nuts again and lowered the jack. When the weight of the car was taken by the spare tyre it was shown to be almost completely deflated, with only sufficient air in it to keep the tyre from riding directly on the wheel rim. It would drive safely enough for the half a block it needed to travel.

Geldenhuis wiped his hands on a piece of cotton waste and removed a pair of blue workman's overalls from the back seat of the car which he climbed into and quickly buttoned up. Then he reached back into the car for the canvas sports bag in which he'd placed their several purchases.

With a cursory nod to the black man, he slid the canvas bag over his arm and held up both hands, fingers wide, indicating ten minutes, whereupon he started to walk in the direction of the engineering works.

He soon found the place he was looking for, a large iron shed or workshop, roughly the height of a three-storey building with the name 'J. Poulos Pty, Ltd. Industrial & Heavy Engineering' in large white letters painted halfway up and across its entire windowless front. A massive set of double sliding doors, perhaps twenty feet high and almost as wide, were set into the centre of the building and opened by sliding along heavy greased steel tracks fitted above and set into the cement floor below the doors. Cut into the farthest corner of the left-hand door, like a pet's door in the kitchen, was a small door raised about a foot from the ground and only large enough for a man to enter the huge workshop if he stooped right over. It too was made of corrugated iron and was obviously only used when, as now, the large doors were closed. To his surprise the small door stood slightly ajar; it must be used by the night watchman, who was seated rather grandly in a crude imitation of a heavy old squared-off club armchair, made entirely from packing-case planks. The black man sat in the evening sunlight and appeared to be mending a pair of trousers which were draped over his knees.

'God is on my side,' Geldenhuis thought, observing the open door, 'the fat bastard was meant to die.' He waited out of sight against the wall of an adjoining property until he heard the car approaching. The road ran some fifty feet from where the watchman was seated and, as the black detective drew to a halt, the watchman looked up from his sewing.

The plain-clothes detective got out from behind the wheel. Geldenhuis could see that he had one arm in a sling as he walked over to examine the rear tyre. 'Shit!' the detective said in a voice loud enough to carry to the watchman.

The watchman rose and put down the pair of trousers he'd been repairing, walking over to the car. 'You have a puncture,' he said in Zulu, pointing to the offending tyre.

'Haya, haya, I have a big problem!' the black detective tapped the sling on his right arm, 'My elbow, it is cracked, I can drive, but this tyre, I cannot change this tyre, my arm is not so strong.'

The night watchman scratched his head and looked somewhat bemused. 'It is a big problem, my brother,' he said rather sheepishly. 'Also I do not know this thing for changing tyre.'

The detective laughed. 'Give me only your strength, brother, I will show you, then next time you will know. It is good to know this thing.'

'Ja, it is good,' the night watchman agreed, 'you will show me, I will help you.' It was still completely light and, in his mind, his duties as a night watchman only really started after dark. He liked the idea of learning how to change a tyre. You never knew when such a skill could be useful, maybe one day he would work in a garage?

Geldenhuis watched as, using his left hand, the detective opened the boot and indicated the spare tyre. He waited until the night watchman was crouched beside the flat tyre; the detective stood directly behind him so that if he turned suddenly his view of the engineering works would be blocked by the black policeman's legs.

Geldenhuis threw the canvas bag over the wall and vaulted it himself, dropping lightly to the other side. He covered the distance to the small door in less than ten seconds, walking quickly on rubber soles. He pushed carefully at the door which opened easily without a sound; stooping, he entered into the interior of the building.

To his surprise, once inside he could see quite easily. Sixty feet above his head, beyond the steel crossbeams from which hung six set-ups of heavy block and tackle equipment, were several large skylights. Almost immediately he saw the small engine standing directly outside a small works office built at one end of the building. Geldenhuis approached the tiny locomotive and as he drew closer he noted the name, 'Poulos Pty, Ltd.' painted in fairly large letters on the door of the office directly behind the engine. This was the sign he'd seen in the newspaper photographs, saving him the need to make any enquiries as to the whereabouts of the engine and thus avoiding anyone remembering a telephone call at some later date.

Geldenhuis worked quickly. From the canvas bag he removed a six-inch aluminium single cigar canister which had been packed with plastic explosive and was already fitted with a fuse which protruded about six inches from a hole cut into the rounded top of the cigar container. It was about a twelve-second fuse, its detonator buried deep within the plastic explosive.

In Geldenhuis's hand the small cigar bomb didn't look much but it packed enough wallop to blow the engine in front of him sky high. He removed a lump of cotton waste and a small tin of lighter fluid, and doused the waste with the fluid. Then, lying on his stomach, he pushed his hands behind the left-hand front wheel of the engine until he could run his fingers along the front axle. He wiped the axle clean, the lighter fluid removing any film of grease there might be on it. He waited a few moments for it to dry before he removed from his pocket a tiny tube of a new Japanese instant glue which had just come onto the market. He spread a thin line of glue along the side of the cigar canister, pressing down hard and emptying the entire tube as he traced its point along the length of the canister. He then attached the canister to the centre of the hidden side of the front axle, holding it for a minute or so until the instant glue attached it, leaving his hands free. He wiped the silver aluminium canister clean, using a freshly doused wad of cotton waste. He then removed a roll of electrical tape and taped the canister firmly to the axle, making it impossible to shake loose. Finally he led the short fuse along the axle, taping it completely so that the dark electrician's tape concealed the white fuse, allowing only the last teased end of the fuse to rest no more than a quarter of an inch from the inside rim of the front wheel.

It was awkward work and he skinned his knuckles several times, cursing quietly to himself. He wasn't unduly worried about being discovered; if for any reason the night watchman became suspicious and attempted to investigate, the black detective had instructions to kill him – simply rendering him unconscious would mean someone would know they'd been there. Geldenhuis was a professional and he knew not to hurry a job as critical as this one. The charge would lie hidden for more than two weeks before it was to be exploded and, in the meantime, it had to be capable of withstanding dozens, perhaps hundreds of trips in the little train.

Next Geldenhuis removed a small tin of Estapol, a clear plastic lacquer, and using a new one-inch paintbrush he painted the inside rim of the wheel with the lacquer. Reaching into the bag, he withdrew a flat tobacco tin which he opened to reveal about fifty two-inch strips of highly flammable magnesium tape, which he began to lay carefully into the wet plastic lacquer until they covered the entire inside circumference of the train wheel. By morning the plastic lacquer would be dry, fixing the strips tightly to its surface. Finally he doused a fresh wad of cotton waste in lighter fluid and wiped the surface of the electrician's tape carefully, as well as any metal areas he may, inadvertently, have touched to leave a fingerprint.

Geldenhuis remained on his stomach and, using the torch, he inspected the outside of the wheel he'd doctored. Even from a distance of a few inches nothing showed on the outside of the train. The job was complete. He rose confident that unless someone with a probing torch lying on their stomach as he had just done knew exactly where to look, the engine would have to be flipped onto its back with its wheels in the air to see where the tiny bomb was concealed.

He tidied up quickly, returning everything to the canvas bag. Finally he inspected the floor to see whether he'd left anything behind. Returning once more to lie on his stomach he pointed the torch to shine it under the engine. His eye caught a single magnesium strip which lay on the floor directly under the inside of the wheel. He recovered it and slipped it into the pocket of his overalls.

Geldenhuis glanced at his watch. It was almost fifteen minutes since he'd entered the building, less time than it required to get a novice to change a tyre, but time to leave. He took one final glance at the shiny little green engine with *The Solomon Levy Magic Carpet Express* lettered in gold along its side. Christ! The fat Jew bastard could have anything in the world and he spent his time playing engine driver! To Geldenhuis there was something sinful about this. A man ten times richer than the president who dressed up in a Father Christmas outfit to play toy train driver and give kaffirs expensive presents was definitely sick. Bastards like that deserved to die.

He moved quietly over to the door. The two black men were still hunched over the wheel with their backs to him. Stooping, Geldenhuis let himself out. He moved quietly along the front and then down the side of the building and quickly crossed the back area of the works and scaled the wall. He set out to walk to the pick-up point he'd arranged, about a mile away on the main highway.

Geldenhuis was delighted with the way things had gone. It was copybook stuff and he hadn't even had to break in to do it. Now all he needed to do was to find someone who'd been invited to attend the kaffir Christmas party so that he could prepare the bomb's triggering method at the right moment. He grinned to himself. God was good, it was payback time. He knew just the man for the job.

THIRTY-NINE

Just after midnight on the day of the Solomon Levy Carpet Emporium Christmas party the *braaivleis* barbecue pits were lit. By dawn, with the wood reduced down to beds of glowing coals, the huge spits, each carrying a whole ox, were moved into place. By mid morning the delicious smell of roasting meat filled the air.

The air crackled with the excitement of the carnival, the screams, whirrings, whooshing and thumping of the dodgem cars, the flying swings, the big wheels and the calliope music of the carousels. Everything was for free as many times as you liked and the very thought of it pumped the heart full of good-time juice. The children rushed around in circles and chased each other about, just to wear off a little energy so they wouldn't completely burst into tiny pieces from the happiness of things.

Just on three thousand employees and two hundred other guests attended the Solomon Levy Carpet Emporium Christmas party. Lorries and buses began to arrive from dawn onwards on this day of days and the people in the upper-crust suburb surrounding the big house were wakened early by the singing of black people packed like gaily papered chocolates into the back of open lorries and rickety buses passing their clipped, manicured and aloof properties. To the indignant people who lived around the Levy estate the day was known as 'Kaffir Christmas' and each year they signed a petition to the council and the police to abolish it.

Many families had travelled hundreds of miles overnight to get to the party while others had been on the road since long before dawn. Shower blocks and marquees were set up to headquarters these distance travellers and to provide a little early morning respite for already exhausted parents.

The baby-feeding and medical clinic, staffed by a dozen nurses and two doctors, opened at six and already waiting as the day's first patient was a five-year-old from Germiston named Tiger Joe. Fat tears streamed down his little black face as a young female doctor examined him while his ma, a giant woman wearing a huge mauve picture hat, puffed out her cheeks and continued to scold the little boy for causing the neat pink gap where he'd lost three front teeth falling off a stationary carousel pony.

Breakfast, an unofficial event which the caterers had learned over the years to provide, was served to the early arrivals. There were mugs of scalding sweet white tea, a couple of hundred loaves of white bread, a hundred yards of cold sausages, huge brown pots of soup-bone gravy and, of course, to go with it, mountains of stiff white mealie pap, steaming in giant black three-legged, round-tummied kaffir pots.

The experienced mothers among the early arrivals dressed their children in their second-best outfits for the morning mayhem, hauling them back in by the ear around eleven for a good scrub and general repairs in the shower block where they changed into their party best, outfits which had taken months to pay for with every spare penny the family could scrape together. The children wore socks as white as driven snow, patent-leather shoes like Shirley Temple's, a flutter of petticoats and pretty organza dresses in limes and yellows, pinks and greens with huge ribbons to match. Little boys in sailor suits walked stiffly in unaccustomed shoes that creaked with newness. Older children in their school uniforms, pressed and starched, with trouser creases and gym frock pleats perfect, concealed little pieces of flannel cloth in their pockets to keep their polished shoes up to optimum presentation at all times.

A few minutes before noon the people on the black side of the fence started to converge on the tiny train station, where a microphone had been placed on the platform. The five hundred or so children and parents on the white side were drawn to the toy station as well. It was from here that Solomon Levy would officially declare the festivities open and, much more importantly, announce that lunch was ready to be served from a dozen great marquees and roasting pits.

They all knew the routine; a shorter-than-short speech from Solomon who, on this one occasion every year, always seemed lost for words; then the world's most sumptuous feast; and at precisely two o'clock, to a shrill 'toot-toot!' from the little engine, the most successful Jewish Father Christmas in creation would circle the grounds bringing with him the most wonderful gifts imaginable.

This year though, to accommodate the needs of Simon Fitzharding's endlessly rehearsed documentary, the open train carriages would be filled with Christmas gifts instead of children and Solomon would arrive at the station to the final chorus of 'Hark the Herald Angels Sing', performed by two hundred children of all the colours of Africa.

In the matter of security Hymie had ignored his father's protests and instigated a huge security operation. Upon arrival at the gate every guest, regardless of colour, was required to show a specially produced employee or guest identification disc. Finally, to the embarrassment of many of the white employees and the good-natured laughter of the black, who were more accustomed to the indignity, every guest was searched by uniformed security men and women. The high-walled estate was ringed with a private army of security men, who also mingled freely with the crowd, watching for a would-be assassin.

And, of course, the little engine came under the scrutiny of Hymie's team who wanted it pulled apart but Solomon, whose final week of rehearsals in the little engine had been constantly disrupted by the security men working on the track, wouldn't hear of it. He was heartily sick of his son's paranoia and agreed only to an inspection of the train.

Mama Tequila, too fat to move more than a few yards on her own, stayed sitting in a huge old swing chair in the rose garden where she could quietly watch the children passing in the train without having to attempt to carry her huge frame about the place. The children and lunch was all she cared about – and the fact that Solomon Levy had sent her a personal letter inviting her to come. For lunch she could rely upon Madam Flame Flo to dart into the food marquee like a cheeky sparrow and emerge, chirping excitedly, with a couple of plates piled high with the choicest titbits. She'd practically starved herself at breakfast: six pieces of toast and three eggs, with a pot of coffee. Flo had fussed and worried for her, but she was reserving extra room for lunch. Solomon, who referred to food as 'nosh', knew almost as much about pleasing a person's stomach as she did.

Mama Tequila was wearing a red sequined gown and a huge red Laughing-Cavalier picture hat festooned with two magnificent white ostrich feathers. Her chubby fingers were a vulgar splash of diamonds as she fanned herself with a delicate little Japanese paper fan. Where she sat among the roses, with the swing chair moving back and forth, she glimmered, glittered, sparkled and shimmered in thousands of tiny bombbursts of light. The swing chair was situated close to a long and beautiful rose arbour festooned with climbing pink roses to make a natural tunnel of blossoms through which the train travelled. Children would see her as the train emerged from the arbour and squeal with delight. It was as though she was an unexpected sideshow placed in amongst a bed of roses to surprise them. Halfway through the morning a rumour started that Mama Tequila was Mother Christmas, after which the children waved and smiled and cheered and blew kisses at her. The presents had yet to be given out and they reasoned that if Mother Christmas was anything like their own ma, it was just as well to be nice as pie and show no disrespect.

Mama Tequila was beginning to feel decidedly peckish. She was happy when noon came, the funfair stopped abruptly and the train was halted for Solomon Levy to make his welcoming speech. She knew Flo would soon be chirping at her side with the first of several plates piled high with her favourite food.

She listened as the public address system whistled and then crackled. A voice said, 'Testing, testing, one . . . two . . . three . . .' and then with a final tear of static grew silent. The next voice she heard was that of Mr Nguni who spoke in Zulu to the crowd, though only for a moment. She couldn't understand him but she guessed he was simply calling the crowd to attention for Solomon's welcome. Trust him to get in there somewhere. She didn't like the big black man, nor did she trust him. More than once she'd chastised Tandia for going out with him; he was creepy, a black man you couldn't read, who laughed too much and showed too many white teeth. That would be a one-eyed snake that would be very cruel and careless with a girl, you could tell just by looking at the bastard. Tandia had told her that nothing had ever happened between them, that he was like her father. 'A father you don't need, a Big Daddy, yes, that more like it, but only if he likes to give diamonds, you hear? Does he give you diamonds?'

'He takes me places, I meet people I couldn't normally meet, people who are important to me,' Tandia protested.

'Meeting kaffirs is never important to any one, skatterbol,' Mama Tequila had said, ending the discussion.

Now she heard Solomon Levy clear his throat briefly and she imagined him standing at the microphone in his blue blazer with the bright brass buttons and beret. Flo had left ten minutes earlier to get a good place in the lunch queue.

'My friends, happy Christmas!' Solomon Levy's voice suddenly boomed out over the loudspeaker. 'Thank you for comink to my house. Thank you, also, for helping me to make the business. This year you are gettink a bonus, one month's pay!' Mama Tequila could hear the loud cheer from the crowd and Solomon Levy waited for it to die down. 'My pleasure,' he said quietly, 'you are all makink me very proud.' His voice brightened suddenly, changing tack. 'Also, children, I got here a letter from Father Christmas, comink direct the north pole!' Mama Tequila heard the scrunch of paper over the microphone and Solomon began to read. '*Dear children at Solomon Levy Carpet Emporium, Thank you all za nice letters you are writing. Don't vorry, I got for sure everything. I hope you are being also good boys and girls because two o'clock sharp I'm coming wit' my train by Mr Solomon Levy's house! Maybe you can be zere?*'

Mama Tequila could hear the squeals of delight from the children and she imagined how they'd be hugging each other. Their parents too, with the knowledge of a double pay packet coming in at Christmas time, would be feeling very good. Solomon Levy now ended the letter, 'Yours sincerely, Father Christmas. North Pole, za world, za universe!' There was a great deal of clapping and laughter and he concluded simply by saying, 'Okay, my friends! Now we eat. Enjoy please a little lunch.'

Simon Fitzharding's film crew had hardly been noticed during all the morning's excitement and the cameramen had used the time for pick-up shots, filming the oxen roasting on the spits, the chefs preparing the tables groaning with good food and generally keeping an eye out for a 'cute' shot.

Now the cameramen, grips and sound men stood by for a final briefing from the BBC director who, in a manner of speaking, had caused the entire security kerfuffle. The plan was simple and had been rehearsed a hundred times. The unit stood by, bored; they'd long since stopped listening to the Englishman with the hot potato in his mouth. There was very little that could go wrong. Both cameras would be mounted on platforms; there was a small one that allowed the cameraman to operate six feet above the heads of the crowd and looked directly into the train station. It was fitted with a four-to-one zoom lens so it could pan as Father Christmas Solomon Levy made his triumphant arrival from the direction of the rose garden. This same camera would also be used for the medium and close-up shots of the choir. The second unit, placed on the black side, was mounted on a much higher camera platform with the latest twelve-to-one zoom lens to pull focus and follow the entire progress of the little engine around the estate.

The platform on the taller tower had been built fairly high so that Hymie's security men could man it as well, with radio contact to their plain-clothes people in the crowd. Solomon Levy's train ride was the next obviously critical moment in the entire security operation. For six minutes he would be alone and totally exposed with a crowd of three thousand or so people lining the tracks.

Peekay had permission to share the platform as he wanted to take pictures to send to Doris and Togger and Harriet in England. Later he'd also get the snaps for Mr Rubens, the schmaltzy shots the old man adored, showing wide-eyed kids hugging their Rubens-Kellerman dolls.

Peekay was as anxious as everyone else involved in the security operation, but he played no active role in it and the team had been so thorough that, as the day wore on, they'd all begun to relax a little. Hymie had given him a Nikon with the very latest telephoto lens for his birthday a year previously and he found he enjoyed messing about with it. He'd spent a lot of time taking pictures with Doc's old Hasselblad as a child and privately he fancied himself as a bit of a photographer. How the old man would have loved this Nikon, Peekay thought as he set the camera on its tripod and squinted through the powerful lens, deciding on the mandatory shots he would take when the little train finally got under way.

Now, with a few minutes to go, he watched the crowd through the camera's telephoto lens. The little green train would start in the dahlia garden on the black side where it was concealed from the crowd. Below him he could see Solomon Levy in his Father Christmas outfit flapping his hands about and, Peekay imagined, being a general nuisance to the security men who were loading the train with the pretend Christmas packages. This year Solomon needed no padding for his Father Christmas outfit and Peekay thought to himself that the old bugger really ought to go on a diet. The carriages were almost loaded with the beribboned boxes and assortment of bicycles, scooters, tricycles and dolls sticking out among them.

Peekay turned the lens towards the station. The platform was crowded with the children's choir which spilled over onto two stands, one on either side of the strange-looking little building. Next he turned the tripod and camera to face the distant rose garden. This was a shot he didn't want to miss; the little engine at this point was a hundred yards from the end of its journey when it entered a long arbour of brilliant pink climbing roses. He began to focus when he realised that Mama Tequila was in the background slightly to the side of the rose arbour. He adjusted the lens to bring her into sharp focus. The huge woman appeared to be asleep. Peekay grinned to himself, he'd seen Mama Tequila tuck in before and he had no illusions about the size of the lunch she would have consumed. Even at the distance of some two hundred and fifty yards he imagined he could see her huge bosoms heaving under her shimmering red dress. He fired off a shot of the dozing Mama Tequila and flipped the camera ratchet to the next frame.

There was a sudden excited roar from the crowd as the little engine gave two shrill whistles and emerged from the dahlia garden. Peekay pulled his camera tripod around and checked his pad, quickly adjusting the lens of the camera by hand without bringing his eye to the lens. When he looked into the camera, to his satisfaction he saw his focus was bang-on as he fired off the shot. He removed the camera from the tripod and followed the little engine around, pulling focus and taking random shots. Then he suddenly realised that he'd been so intrigued by Mama Tequila that he hadn't completed focussing on his third set-up, the little train emerging from the rose arbour.

There was still a couple of minutes to go and he positioned the camera tripod and fixed the Nikon to it. He brought his eye to the camera and worked the powerful telephoto lens. The lens sharpened into focus and to his enormous surprise he saw Mr Nguni on his haunches beside the track halfway down the rose arbour. Peekay sharpened focus on his crouching figure; the big man was fairly deep into the arbour and it would have been almost impossible to see him by eye at the distance Peekay was standing. Peekay fired off a shot. The shutter blinked and in the fraction of a second it went from light to dark and back again he knew with a blinding realisation what Mr Nguni was doing.

Peekay turned from the camera tripod and reached the top of the ladder leading up to the platform in three steps. He half climbed and half skidded down the ladder, jumping the last ten rungs to hit the ground running.

'What is it?' he heard one of the security men call from the top of the platform.

'A detonator on the track!' Peekay yelled, but already he was yards away, running hard. He had to run around a small copse of trees and down a sideshow alley. Two teenage girls, walking between tents, didn't see him coming and his shoulder collected one of them and knocked her spinning. He reached the open lawns and made for the rose arbour. People seeing him coming jumped out of his way, though some he dodged and others he pushed aside as he ran. His head was pounding and he could taste blood in his mouth where he must have bitten his tongue. The sound of the children singing in Zulu came to him clearly, like a car passing suddenly with its radio on too loudly; then he lost it, his own furious panting drowning out all sound. By the time he'd reached the centre fence the little train was behind the big house and heading for the rose garden. He reached the front of the arbour just as the engine entered the other side. Seconds later he heard two shots go off, one a split second after the other. A moment later a dense white smoke came from the front wheel of the engine, which seemed to be flaring with an intensely bright blue flame.

'Jump!' he screamed at Solomon Levy. 'Jump!!'

The old man was too shocked to respond and he flapped his hands wildly, beating at the magnesium smoke billowing into his face. Peekay ran towards him and, turning so that he was running with the train, he tried to pull Solomon Levy from the carriage. But Solomon wearing a bullet-proof vest was a snug fit, and in his panic he held onto the sides of the cabin. 'Stand up! Try to stand up!' Peekay screamed. The old man was gulping for air, his eyes popping out of his head; he was totally panic stricken and beyond response. Peekay beat down at his fists which were white-knuckling the sides of the engine, but still Solomon clung on. Peekay brought his hands around Solomon's thick throat and started to strangle him. With a cry Solomon brought his hands up and Peekay released his grip, slipping his arms under the old man's armpits and jerking with all his strength against the movement of the train. With Solomon's foot now off the throttle, the train started to slow down. For a few desperate moments nothing happened and then Solomon Levy was dragged clear of the cabin. They hit the ground hard at the same moment that the engine emerged from the arbour; then Peekay lost his hold on the old man. Both of them seemed to bounce and then roll wildly, the momentum of the fall hurling them over a small embankment and clear of the engine. With a deafening roar the bomb exploded, sending the little engine high into the air. It landed on its snout and somersaulted three times to land on its back in a rose bed fifty feet away.

Peekay was already on his feet by the time the first of the security men reached the scene. He was bleeding slightly from the mouth but seemed to be all right, though his head spun furiously and the sound of the explosion at such close range had momentarily deafened him. Had they not been below the sound when the explosion went off it might well have burst their eardrums. He was also finding it difficult to focus, catching only glimpses of a man moving towards him. He felt the man grab his shoulder; the man's mouth opened like a fish under water but he made no sound. Peekay nodded, unable to speak and the man turned and ran towards Solomon Levy who lay motionless against a small tree. The top of his Father Christmas outfit had been torn away by the explosion, showing the bullet-proof vest, half on and half off his hairy stomach. Peekay's eyes were beginning to focus a little better, though they still seemed to snapshoot the scene around him, like a cinema projector with its speed out of synchronisation. People seemed to be running from everywhere.

His vision cleared, but now it was as though he could see everything with the clarity of slow motion. Hymie moved up to him, touched his face with the flat of his hand, sobbing; he said something which Peekay couldn't hear then moved towards his father. Tandia rushed up and grabbed him; she seemed to be sobbing in little gasps, grabbing him about the waist and burying her head in his chest. He tried to bring his arms up to embrace her but they wouldn't work. There was no pain, but they simply wouldn't respond to the message his brain was sending to them. Solomon Levy's legs seemed to be at strange angles and Peekay wondered vaguely whether they were broken. Nothing made a lot of sense. Hymie returned and hugged them both, tears streaming down his cheeks, his lips moving soundlessly. Someone threw a blanket over his shoulder and he tried to hold it but his arms still refused to move. Then, as though someone had thrown a switch in his head, the sound came back on and he could hear. It was the most fortuitous piece of timing in his life, for Tandia was looking up at him, her green eyes bright with tears, 'Peekay, I love you,' she said and started to sob quietly, her head against his chest. Then he was looking into the pale face of a blonde woman in a white coat with an untidy wisp of hair across her forehead who had the same pale blue eyes as Jannie Geldenhuis.

'Let me take a look at you?' the woman said in Afrikaans. Then she let out a short expletive, '*Here, jou been!*' She pointed to his left leg.

Peekay's head was almost clear and he realised he hadn't imagined Tandia's words. He glanced almost casually at his leg, looking down over Tandia's shoulder. He felt no pain whatsoever so he was surprised to observe that the bottom half of his khaki trousers had been torn and below it the knee was totally soaked in blood.

The woman doctor was on her haunches, ripping the material away. A deep gash ran from just under his knee to his ankle and looked as though it had been sliced open with a boning knife, the top layer of skin folded back to expose the tendons of his ankles and his calf muscle. With a sudden rush, the pain appeared in his shoulders as though his arms had been jerked out of their sockets, though there was still no pain from his leg. 'I can't stitch it here, you'll have to go in the ambulance,' the doctor said rising. 'I'll give you a tetanus injection, also one to kill the pain.'

'*Dankie, doktor. Hoe gaan dit met die ou kerel?*' Peekay asked. He had a violent headache but his mind was now lucid and his concern was for Solomon Levy.

'Both his legs appear to be broken and his collarbone. We'll have to watch his heart, that's all,' the doctor replied. She looked directly at him and sniffed; with an almost imperceptible nod of her head, she indicated Tandia. 'It's none of my business, you hear, but people are looking,' she said, loud enough for Tandia to hear.

Shocked, Tandia pulled away from Peekay. 'Don't! Please don't go!' Peekay cried. He tried to stretch his arm towards Tandia but the pain was too great. Tandia stood three feet from him; her hands covering her face in shame.

The woman doctor stepped between Peekay and the distraught Tandia, blocking her from his view. 'Come now,' she said, 'You can't stay any longer on that bad leg.' She called over a couple of medics carrying a stretcher. '*Kom hier, maak gou, jong!*'

Whatever the doctor had given Peekay to kill the pain was making him feel very woozy. Johnny Tambourine had appeared just as they were putting him into the ambulance. 'Look after Tandia, Johnny!' he shouted up at him.

'She's a mess, man! Mama Tequila is dead,' Johnny said, making no attempt to soften the news.

'Stay with her, Johnny, take my car, take them home to Madam Flame Flo's house in Vereeniging. Stay there, I'll call tonight or get over.' He had to fight to keep his concentration and his eyelids were becoming impossibly heavy. The ambulance attendants were trying to close the door. The news of Mama Tequila's death was suddenly too much and his mind shut it out. He suddenly remembered the camera on the tower, his lawyer's mind asserting itself. 'Johnny, my camera! It's on the tower, get it!' he shouted; he was too woozy to realise how callous and unfeeling he must have sounded to Johnny Tambourine.

'Shit, why is it always us who die,' he heard Johnny Tambourine say as the ambulance doors closed him from view.

Peekay awoke just after dawn and lay listening to the sparrows chirping outside. The nylon curtains were drawn but the window showed as a contrasting square of pale light in the dark hospital room. The bird noises told him he was probably on the ground floor. 'Good, I can walk out,' he thought, 'walk out and find a phone box and call Hymie.' This thought was, of course, a nonsense but his mind was still blurry from the sedation he'd received and it had taken up more or less where it had left off with Johnny Tambourine in the ambulance. A thought formed in his head. 'Tandia? She said she loved me?' Then he wondered if it was something he'd dreamed. His mind began to clear, the outline of his thoughts sharpening. He could vaguely remember arriving at the hospital, the strips of pale purple neon light passing above him as he was wheeled down a long corridor, then nothing more. Now it was all coming back to him, like animated bits of a jigsaw puzzle falling into place by themselves. He felt the shock of Mama Tequila's death for the first time and sudden tears blinded him and ran down his cheeks. He tried to move his hand up to wipe at them and realised both his arms lay across his chest cradled in a sling which was tied around his neck. He was feeling lousy, he tried to sniff away the tears and his head still ached, but the pain was familiar. His body had been badly battered before and he knew he'd be okay in a week or so when the bruising and stiffness worked out of his muscles. His left leg was stiff and sore but it wasn't throbbing.

He was propped up against a pile of cushions in a half seated position. He tried to look for a call button; his throat was dry and he needed a glass of water. He became conscious that his neck was in a brace and that he couldn't move his head either to the left or right; his entire torso was a slab of dull pain. Then Peekay felt a hand touch him gently on the right shoulder. 'You all right, old mate?' Hymie rose from the chair beside the bed where he'd dozed off and moved over to look at Peekay. He needed a shave and his eyes were red with dark rings about them; they seemed set back too far into his pale face. He'd never seen Hymie looking so exhausted.

Peekay tried to smile. It was difficult to get the first word past his lips; his throat was dry and sore from swallowing blood where he'd broken a tooth in the fall. 'You look like hell, Hymie,' he croaked at last.

Hymie grinned. 'Look who's talking.' He walked round to the console on the other side of the bed and poured a glass of water and held it for Peekay to drink. The water felt wonderful and though it hurt a little to swallow, it cleared his throat.

'How's the old man?'

'I checked an hour ago, he's sleeping. He's off the critical list.' Hymie grinned again. 'He's so swathed in bandages and plaster of Paris that he looks like the Michelin man. The doc says all that blubber and the stupid vest we made him wear probably saved his life a second time when he took the fall.' Hymie was talking too fast, trying to over-ride the exhaustion in his voice.

'Hymie, you're beat. You're going to have to get some rest. What's the time?'

'No, really, I'm fine, I've been dozing most of the night.' Hymie looked at his watch. 'Ten past five.'

'You've got to get some sleep,' Peekay insisted. The need to concentrate was making his head throb. 'We've got a hell of a day ahead of us.'

'We? That's a joke, you're going nowhere mate, that's for sure!'

'Hymie? Have you contacted Tandia?'

'Ja, I called late last night. The doctor gave Madam Flame Flo a heavy sedative and she was asleep. Tandia was pretty broken up, but having to look after the old girl was probably a good thing. Johnny Tambourine is still with her.'

'My camera? Did he pick it up?'

Hymie looked quizzical. 'Camera?'

'I'm not sure he heard me, I asked him to get my Nikon from the camera tower. It holds a picture of Mr Nguni placing a detonator on the track.'

Hymie's head jerked back in surprise. 'Nguni? Jesus!'

'He placed a couple of detonators on the train track. They set off some sort of highly inflammable material, probably phosphorus. No, the flame was blue,' Peekay recalled suddenly, 'magnesium! It was probably magnesium. It would have fired a short fuse and set off the bomb.'

'We've got to get him before the police do. They'll want to interview me today and if I don't tell them it was Nguni, when we get him into court as a witness it will be obvious I withheld evidence from the police.'

'Witness? How do you mean, you just said you saw him?' Hymie's usually quick mind was a fraction slow, but then he realised what Peekay meant. 'Shit, you don't mean Special Branch? Geldenhuis?'

'It's not such a leap to take. Nguni was paying back a favour to someone. Why otherwise would he be implicated in a plot to assassinate your old man? He wouldn't do something like that on his own.'

Hymie drew breath through his teeth. 'If you're right and Geldenhuis realises Nguni's been identified, he's going to be one dead black man before nightfall,' he said.

'Exactly.'

Hymie looked at his watch. 'I'll call Tandia and ask Johnny Tambourine about the camera; it's still early but I guess she'll understand. I'll also call Pretoria; if Johnny didn't get it, let's pray it's still on the platform.'

'Hymie, I've got to get out of here. Don't put up a fuss, can you send a car around for me?'

'Ja, okay, but only late this afternoon. You've got to get a little rest at least.'

'You too, we'll meet at five o'clock at Red. If Tandia's in any sort of shape she ought to be at Red with us.'

Hymie nodded, then stopped at the doorway. 'Peekay, about yesterday, my old man . . .'

Peekay cut him short, 'Don't, Hymie, don't say it!' he laughed. 'I can't stand a mawkish Yid!'

FORTY

People talked about Peekay's incredible rescue for months afterwards and they told of how the bomb could have killed hundreds of children, exaggerating his bravery and suggesting somehow that he'd not only rescued Solomon Levy, the famous Jewish multi-millionaire, from certain death, but had somehow diverted the train, preventing the bomb from exploding in the dead centre of the children's choir.

But only rarely, when the story was in the hands of a more responsible teller, and even then always as an afterthought, would they mention the incredible fluke: how the sheered-off head of a tiny bolt, no bigger than the pinkie on a man's hand, had flown off the exploding engine, entered the right eye and lodged in the brain of a fat old coloured woman who was sitting in the rose garden. Some storytellers would even add that she'd brought her bizarre death upon herself, pointing out that there was a notice put there, as plain as the nose on your face, which said nobody was supposed to go in the rose garden.

There were never less people and more flowers at a single funeral. Mama Tequila's grave was piled fourteen feet high and ten yards across with the most expensive wreaths you could imagine, though few of the cards accompanying these floral tributes carried names on them. People who didn't want to be remembered, remembered in their hundreds.

To everyone's surprise, except Tandia and Madam Flame Flo, Mama Tequila turned out to be Dutch Reformed Church. The young *dominee*, not long out of Stellenbosch University, where he'd scored high on theology and zero for street smart, didn't know what to make of the whole thing. The entire front of the church and the extensive lawns on either side were covered in floral tributes but only thirteen people and an Indian photographer came to the funeral service and only twelve to the graveyard.

The six girls were there of course, with Hester hiccuping with grief throughout the service and Rachel elbowing her in the side, though she too had a good cry with all the other girls; and so were Doctor Louis Rabin and Mr Dine-o-mite, who'd done his crying previously and whose eyes were red with grief. Then there was the projectionist from the Odeon cinema, Ismail Naidoo, who nobody had ever seen before but who told how Mama Tequila had brought a double chocolate ice cream cone to his projection booth every Wednesday for twenty-five years.

Madam Flame Flo, Tandia, Peekay and Hymie made up the thirteen, or fourteen if you counted Sonny Vindoo's driver – who would have counted himself but didn't know whether he had a right to do so. And of course there was Mr Dine-o-mite's son, who took pictures of the floral tributes which he tried to sell to a newspaper syndicate. Photographers can't really be counted in these things, you can't be a serious mourner with a camera stuck up your nose.

Mama Tequila turned out to be enormously wealthy and left a diamond ring for every one of the girls, including Tandia, and a trust fund which granted the girls an income for the remainder of their lives. They also received the money she'd invested on their behalf, which was enough to buy them houses and set them up in good marriages. However, in her will, which had been dictated to Tandia at Red, in a part Tandia didn't read to the girls on the day, Mama T, the realist to the end, said, 'I'm telling you, man, I'll be very surprised if they all go straight and narrow. A working girl is a working girl, it's very hard to make a new life standing on your feet all day in front of a hot stove, to keep a man, when you can make him keep you on your back in a warm bed.' Finally, in an announcement which shocked even the girls, but when you thought about it was a pretty good thing to do, she placed Bluey Jay under the trusteeship of Dr Louis Rabin and Sonny Vindoo together with a trust fund to run it as a private drug, alcohol and VD clinic for the treatment of coloured and African street women. Mama Tequila hadn't forgotten her beginnings or forsaken her less fortunate sisters, though she was buggered if she was going to help those white sluts.

The meeting at Red scheduled at five o'clock on the day after the explosion had finally taken place at eight in the evening, Peekay having taken a little longer than he'd expected to sign himself out of hospital and Tandia having been unwilling to leave Madam Flame Flo until she'd given her supper and put her to bed with a strong sleeping potion.

Hymie opened the meeting, the first part of which was attended by the two senior security men who'd been responsible for the overall surveillance of the Levy property and who had wanted to strip the small engine. One was an ex-Pretoria CID detective named Swart and the other an ex-Scotland Yard Detective Sergeant named Brown who had been on the London Metropolitan Bomb Squad before migrating to South Africa. They were briefed on the significance of the Nguni identification and its implications that the Special Branch might be behind the plot to assassinate Solomon Levy.

Brown gave a low whistle. 'You've got the perfect lead and you can't use it. These Special Branch chappies are usually pretty hard to nail anywhere their sort operate. It's always tough going in against the police, but it's twice as hard against the political bods, they've got carte blanche. You're going to have to find this Mr Nguni and get him to confess before you hand him over.'

Peekay laughed. 'That won't be sufficient to get an indictment. The chances are he'll never get as far as the witness box and we won't be able to prove the tape wasn't obtained under extreme duress. Besides, a black man's evidence doesn't carry a lot of weight with an all-white jury. The Special Branch are heroes to the whites in this country and, if it's the guy we believe who's behind Nguni, he's practically a national hero.'

'We need to have Nguni on the day in court so he can be cross-examined,' Tandia added, 'and we need to have his confession on tape. Somehow we need to keep him from the Special Branch in the meantime.' She paused, then added, 'Or he'll die falling out of a window trying to escape.' Tandia was mortified by the Nguni incident and although she had been enormously distressed by the death of Mama Tequila she had made a point of phoning both Peekay at the hospital and Hymie at home to say how she regretted not taking their advice to stay away from him. They had both repeatedly warned Tandia that they believed Nguni was not to be trusted, but she'd persisted with the relationship, declaring that he had never done anything to deserve her mistrust and had been having a tough time with his transport business lately. This was true and both Hymie and Peekay had reaffirmed this in an effort to comfort her.

'Mr Nguni left his house in Moroka township about four o'clock yesterday afternoon and he hasn't returned. I have the information from Johnny Tambourine whom I have asked to put out feelers in Soweto,' Tandia said. Peekay was gratified; despite her distress she'd been acting as a professional and doing her share of the work.

'Do you think he'll go bush?' Swart asked.

'I don't know,' Hymie replied, 'while I can't elaborate, there are a lot of people out there looking for him. Nguni's face is pretty well known among the black people. He may try to get out of the country.'

Peekay turned to the two security men, changing the subject. 'Have either of you had a chance to take a look at the engine. Can you tell us anything about the bomb?'

Hymie interjected. 'Just a moment, Peekay, before our friends answer, I'd like to say something. I know you must be feeling pretty rotten about the bomb, but I want it made perfectly clear that you *did* warn me about the engine, you *did* want to take it apart and you did not guarantee its safety. I am entirely to blame; the decision not to take the engine apart was mine.' Hymie looked over at Tandia. 'The death of Mama Tequila is on my conscience, Tandia.'

Tandia looked up shocked. 'You mustn't, Hymie! You are not to blame for the evil, the terrible evil in people that makes them do things like this. I am the stupid one, I refused to listen to your warnings about Mr Nguni.'

'Nobody is to blame for anything; now *please*, can we get on with my question?' Peekay was being deliberately insensitive. This wasn't the time for self-recriminations. Peekay was proud of the way Tandia was holding herself together. Apart from a wan smile when he'd commiserated with her, she'd contained her emotions when she'd arrived. How he ached to hold her in his arms, to stroke her and tell her he loved her.

'Thank you for your remarks, Mr Levy, though I must say I feel pretty upset with myself,' Brown said. He then explained how the bomb had been devised and how the detonator had ignited the magnesium strips glued to the inside of the train wheel and how they'd flared, lighting the fuse and setting off the plastic. 'It was extremely clever because it was so simple: a pot of glue, magnesium strips and a bit of electrician's tape. The whole thing could have been put together in less than twenty minutes by a relative amateur. The bomb must have been placed when the train was sent to the engineering works for spray painting and modifications.'

'Do the police know this?' Hymie asked.

'I couldn't say so, sir. Certainly they didn't hear it from me. They cordoned off the entire area and threw me off the site as soon as their own explosives men arrived. Which is fair enough, I would have done the same thing myself. I'm pretty sure it won't take them long to come to the same conclusion.'

'We should try to get to the engineering works first, sir,' Swart said. 'It's a long shot, but he or they may have left a calling card.'

'How are we going to get to look around the engineering works without a warrant to make a search?' Hymie asked.

Mr Swart answered, they'd obviously already worked out a plan. 'Tomorrow we'll be there when the place opens. I'll walk in and I'll simply act like the police officer I used to be, ask if I may look around and if my partner,' he turned towards Brown, 'can ask the engineers a few questions.' Swart grinned. 'If it doesn't work or if the police have already been, well we haven't broken any law I know about, man.'

Despite the fact that the ANC, through Gideon's people, were alerted, Mr Nguni simply disappeared into thin air. A security man at the gate on the day of the picnic could recall him leaving, but he wasn't sure whether it was before or after the explosion. After three or four days Peekay began to suspect the worst, that Geldenhuis had got to him and Mr Nguni was dead.

A week after the explosion Peekay received a call from Mr Nguni's wife, a timid country woman named Martha who was well born and therefore acceptable where it mattered in African tribal society, but who had no place in his public life and who played the traditional and subservient role in his household. Peekay had met her a few times over the years when he'd been at Mr Nguni's home and he'd always made a point of going into the kitchen and talking to her.

'*Ninjani*, Martha,' Peekay said, using the more common township greeting.

Martha returned his greeting shyly, 'I greet you, baas, Peekay,' and then added in a soft, concerned voice, 'My husband, he has not come home, we have not seen him for one week.'

'Ja, Martha, Hymie too, he has been worried, your husband missed a board meeting yesterday. When did you see him last?'

'He came home in the afternoon when he came from baas Hymie's house in Pretoria, but he left again soon in his car.'

'Did he not say anything to you?'

'He does not tell me when he is going, but when he is going far away he tells me,' the woman answered simply.

'But this time he didn't tell you?'

'That is why I am worried. When he goes far away he always tells me. When he goes only one day or two, he doesn't tell me. Now he has gone away one week already!'

'Did he pack a suitcase or take anything?'

'No, everything is in the bedroom.'

'Money, did he take any money?'

'Haya, haya, I cannot say this, I do not know where he is keeping his money.'

'Do you want me to call the police, Martha?'

There was a pause at the other end of the line before Martha Nguni answered, 'He will be very, very angry, baas Peekay, but I think also you must call.'

As a matter of course Peekay identified the time and date of his conversation with Martha Nguni on the tape recorder plugged into the phone and then called the Phomolong police station and reported Mr Nguni missing.

Two days later two detectives from the Special Branch in Pretoria arrived to interview Peekay and Hymie and asked them if they had any reason to suspect Nguni may have been involved in the explosion. Hymie pointed out to the two men that Mr Nguni was a business partner with a great deal to lose and absolutely nothing to gain by such an act, that to suspect him was ludicrous.

They then asked why Peekay hadn't informed them at the same time he'd informed the police at Moroka township and Peekay said he hadn't connected the two incidents, but that now obviously the police had. 'Is Nguni, for some reason, under suspicion?' he asked. One of the detectives replied that this wasn't the case, that they were simply exploring every possibility. The two Special Branch men left apparently satisfied and Peekay hoped to hell he'd been convincing. The official report that he was missing now made it possible for the police to instigate a real, if only pretended, search for the black man and as long as this wasn't connected with the explosion by Hymie or himself, or openly by the police, Geldenhuis would feel relatively safe, even if Mr Nguni was genuinely on the loose and trying to escape from the Special Branch.

Several weeks and then a couple of months went by and Mr Nguni still hadn't surfaced. By this time Red was convinced he was dead and the best chance they'd ever had to get Jannie Geldenhuis had been frustrated, probably by Geldenhuis himself. The Nguni connection had not been made by the newspapers and so the disappearance of the well-known black man had only been paid minor attention by the media. Nguni had a relatively low profile to the whites and was only really known in boxing circles. In due course the police announced they had no new information but were pursuing their enquiries, the usual official euphemism for a case book which was about to be closed or at least given a low priority.

Peekay's shoulders mended quite quickly to the point where he could use his arms, but the muscles still pained him a good deal and had grown weak from lack of use. He decided to go back to the gym to build up his strength and to regain a modicum of fitness. The Rand Club to which he belonged had a small gym which would have suited this purpose perfectly but he chose instead to return to Solly Goldman's boxing gym.

The two men embraced warmly when Peekay arrived at the sleazy downtown gym. 'It's good to 'ave ya back, my son,' Solly said. Then trying to cover his obvious emotion he rubbed his hands together. 'Right, Champ, give us a coupla months and I'll 'ave ya ready for a shot at the bleedin' title.'

Peekay smiled. He saw Solly from time to time, but not often enough. The inventor of the Solly Goldman thirteen punch combination had been one of the more important people in Peekay's life. Now he held Solly at arm's length pretending to examine him. 'You know, Solly, when I started with you at fifteen you wore that same frayed brown striped tie to hold up those same baggy grey flannel trousers. I'm not sure it wasn't even the same sweatshirt, I swear I remember that egg stain!'

Peekay started working with weights trying to build up his shoulder muscles where they'd been torn by the explosion. But one thing led to another and in a couple of months he was spending time with the young fighters in the gym most nights after he was finished at Red, boxing with them in the ring, demonstrating punches and correcting their technique. He was never one to do anything by halves and he began to put a lot more into his early-morning road work, building his wind and his legs. Pretty soon he was back to the welterweight limit and his body was hard and fit again.

Almost four months after the explosion and the death of Mama Tequila, Tandia got a telephone call late one afternoon from Madam Flame Flo: 'Listen, Tandy, I know you already coming over Thursday but something funny has come up, jong. Do you think you could come and see me tonight?'

'It will have to be late, Auntie Flo. About nine o'clock, I'll get Johnny Tambourine to drive me. No I won't, I'll drive myself and stay the night.'

'No, man, bring him, he can stay in the room in the yard. What I got to say, maybe he can help.'

Tandia was working on a case with Peekay and she'd set aside two hours that evening to go through the briefing with him. She glanced at her watch; it was nearly six o'clock, he'd be coming in any minute. She fumbled in her handbag for her compact. Peekay was the last guy in the world who would notice whether she'd put on fresh lipstick or not, but the operation of fixing her make-up helped her confidence. Ever since the death of Mama Tequila she'd been awkward; no, not so much awkward, but on edge, nervous, when she was alone with Peekay.

Nothing had been said about the afternoon of the explosion when, in her panic and distress, she'd blurted out her love for him. In fact, later when she'd had the courage to face the incident herself she was genuinely surprised at her outburst. Her love for him was so fraught with impossible implications that she'd buried it deep in her subconscious.

Tandia was not a dreamer. Mama Tequila had taught her to keep her eyes focussed on the hard edge of reality, only to gamble with resources she was prepared to lose. Loving Peekay, no matter how covert, was well beyond any such resources, and when she'd declared her love for him immediately after the explosion, it was her heart and not her head which had betrayed her. She was determined that this should never happen again.

Peekay had tried on several occasions to talk with her when they'd appeared to be alone but she'd resisted, either leaving the room on some hastily fabricated excuse or talking over him about some or other legal concern. She could see his frustration, but she had to lead in this matter. She was stronger than him and knew that even the smallest declaration of his reciprocal love, the merest suggestion, would lead to disaster.

Mama Tequila's death had had a surprising effect on her. She found that she'd relied on the old woman more than ever she'd thought possible. Mama Tequila was like an old coastal freighter; battered and weathered by the storms of life, it always knew the quickest way to a safe port or the best way to ride out a storm. You could focus on her, knowing that she'd calculated the odds and prepared for the disaster at the slightest sign of a change in the barometer reading.

The old girl had also been proved right about Nguni. The black tycoon's demise had shattered Tandia's confidence in men even further and added to the awkwardness she felt with Peekay and Hymie. There hadn't been the slightest suggestion from either partner that her friendship with him had delayed Angel Sport's disassociation with the black businessman, but she now knew this to be true. Nguni would not have been present at the Solomon Levy Christmas party had Hymie acted when he'd first decided to do so. Tandia tormented herself with this and with the fact that Mama Tequila might still be alive had she not been so stubborn about her relationship with Nguni.

It concerned her that she was still looking for Patel's approbation, that she'd never been able to do without him in her life, that she'd always needed a father figure, an older man; Juicey Fruit Mambo, Dr Rabin, Magistrate Coetzee and finally Mr Nguni. The little girl who had been starved so early of the love of her father seemed to spend her life trying to regain it, the wonderful safety of a love that was protective without being physical.

Despite his outward appearances of gentleness, Peekay was a man with needs who would want to possess her for herself, body, mind and soul. He was a possessor of a one-eyed snake she couldn't ignore.

All the other men, the father figures in her life, had wanted something from her, Juicey Fruit Mambo to protect her, Dr Rabin to assuage his Jewish guilt and feed his intelligence, Magistrate Coetzee to confound his own racist beliefs and, finally, the ambitious and calculating Nguni who wanted her to sharpen his aspirations and show off in front of his peers.

Peekay would want nothing and everything and everything was much too much. Tandia told herself she would not give herself to Peekay ever. It was making him understand this without coming out and declaring it bluntly to him, making him somehow understand that what was going on between them was unrequited love, that she would not be going to England with him should they decide to leave, that she had already been drawn into the fight for freedom beyond the passive and almost useless pursuit of the law. She was tired of tilting at windmills and the time had come for her to join Gideon and to take direct action.

Tandia now realised that her love for Gideon had been an infatuation which she had allowed to grow into a habit. Now that this pressure had been taken from her she liked him even more as her leader. Though she'd only seen him once since his return, his work was everywhere and, under his command, *Umkonto we Sizwe* was beginning to look like a concerted and determined force.

Tandia told herself that her need to hate was infinitely more important than any other emotional commitment she might have in her life and that with Nguni she had finally sloughed off her need for even a father figure in her life. She was on her own and her teeth were sharp. For the time being this was enough, she had all the emotional baggage it was possible to carry.

She made sure that the briefing to Peekay filled the two hours she'd allowed for it and when they concluded and Peekay asked her if she could stay a little longer she was able to plead her visit to Madam Flame Flo.

'Tandia, we must talk. You've been avoiding me ever since the explosion.' They'd taken to referring to it as 'the explosion' to avoid the pain of Mama Tequila's death. 'I want you to know that I . . .'

'Peekay, it was a mistake! An emotional outburst brought on by my anxiety at the time; my relief that you were alive was such that my mind found the wrong words. Please, Peekay, as a friend I cherish you more than I can say.' Tandia took a deep breath, looking directly at him, 'But that's all there can ever be between us.'

Johnny Tambourine picked her up at eight o'clock and they set out for the hour or so's drive to Vereeniging. Madam Flame Flo gave them the usual big welcome. She set the table for supper and invited Johnny Tambourine to join them. The little woman always prepared a feast and he'd been thinking about it most of the way from Johannesburg.

Madam Flame Flo allowed them to eat before she talked, fussing over Tandia, making her eat more than she would have done on her own. When she'd served coffee she relaxed for the first time and began to talk.

'You remember the Taj Mahal night club?' she asked Tandia.

Tandia smiled. 'How could I ever forget it; that's where I met Gideon.'

'Well I never told you, but Mr Nguni and a woman named Baby Shabooti and myself, we owned it. I don't want to go in to the details, but it never worked, the three of us. I was convinced that Nguni, who was responsible for the hard spirits we bought from outside and smuggled in, was taking a cut and not sharing it, so I sold my share to Baby Shabooti.

She and Nguni, they had a thing, so it was okay between them. When Sophiatown was no more she opened a lot of shebeens in Soweto and made a lot of money and built a big house, the biggest in the whole place, double storey with everything hot and cold. I'm telling you, man, you name a convenience she got it, even two of it! She and Nguni, they broke up I thought after the Taj Mahal. But yesterday she calls me on the telephone. Maybe she calls me once a year, maybe not even so much. She tells me she wants me to sign a paper.' Madam Flame Flo looked up. 'A long time ago we bought a garage, you know a service station, and when we broke up they paid me my share okay, but I forgot to sign the paper. Now she wants me to sign. "Ja, of course," I say, "no problems, I'm going over to Meadowlands Friday, I'll come by your house and sign." "No!" she says, like I caught her by surprise, "I'll send it over to you." '

Madam Flame Flo looked at them expectantly. 'Is that all?' Tandia asked, 'She didn't say any more?'

'Tandy, that's enough, man! That woman she spends her life showing off her house. She is the biggest brag artist in Soweto! It wouldn't surprise me one of these days she sells tickets! Guided tours to see the bathroom taps! If she didn't want me to come to her place so she can rub my nose in what she got, the new velvet curtains, maybe a new lounge suite, everything matching, then there is something wrong, man. I'm telling you something for nothing, there is something very funny going on, jong.' She took a deep breath, 'You know what's going on?' Tandia and Johnny both looked at *her* expectantly. 'You go in that house, you find Nguni!'

'That's a big leap in logic, Auntie Flo,' Tandia said.

'Never mind logic, you hear? I'm telling you I'm right! But I also did something else. I called two friends who see her sometimes, you know once a month maybe. We talked about this and that, then I asked, "How's Baby Shabooti?" They both said the same thing, they haven't been to her place for four months!' Madam Flame Flo clapped her hands together gleefully, 'You want to make a bet I'm right, hey?'

The four boys waited until Baby Shabooti left in her big Pontiac convertible, sitting in the back with the hood down, her chauffeur even wearing a cap, before they approached the house. Johnny Tambourine walked round to the back door, tapping politely on the wire screen door. Directly behind it was a burglar-proof door of steel bars and he could see a fat woman, no doubt the cook, working at the stove. She turned at the sound of his tapping to look at him.

Johnny stood with his cap in both hands. 'Please mama, I am looking for work?'

The big woman wiped her hands on her apron and approached the door. 'There is no . . .'

Johnny Tambourine removed the cap with his left hand so that she was looking directly into the gun. 'Open the door, mama, you will not be hurt.'

The woman, eyes big with fright, unlocked the burglar proof door.

Johnny whistled sharply and entered. Flyspeck and Dog Poep emerged from the side of the house and entered the kitchen with him. Dog Poep was carrying a canvas bag and both were wearing balaclavas over their faces. Too Many Fingers Bembi had been left outside to warn them with a sharp whistle should anyone approach.

'Are you alone? Who else is here?' Johnny asked.

'A man, he is sleeping in the big bedroom. Please do not kill me,' she pleaded.

'Take her and tie her up, not here – someplace, maybe the bathroom,' Johnny said to Dog Poep. He said to the woman, 'Please mama, do not scream or make a noise and we will not harm you, you understand?'

Johnny and Flyspeck found the room they were looking for after the third try. They opened the door quietly to see Nguni fast asleep on a double bed. Both waved at their noses; the room smelled of brandy and sick and Nguni was either asleep or passed out on the double bed. He'd kicked the blankets off and lay in the nude, his huge stomach rising and lowering with each breath. He was snoring horribly and seemed to have gained weight since the last time they saw him. The boys looked at each other, grinning. They couldn't believe their luck. Nguni was out to the world and there would be plenty of time to set up.

They crept to either side of the bed and Johnny Tambourine nudged an old-fashioned porcelain chamber pot half-filled with sour sick under the bed with his toe. He whispered to Flyspeck to set the tape recorder up. An empty bottle of Cape brandy stood on the console beside the bed and another half filled, but there didn't seem to be a glass.

When Flyspeck was ready, Johnny Tambourine reached over and slapped Nguni hard across the face. To his surprise the huge man grunted but remained asleep. 'Jesus, he's unconscious, man,' Johnny said in a loud whisper. Flyspeck brought back his hand, indicating that Johnny should hit him again. This time the blow was even harder. Nguni jerked up and his eyes opened, though his face showed no surprise and his eyes were unfocussed. Johnny hit him again with the flat of his hand and, grunting, Nguni came to.

'Who? Who are you?' he said thickly, not yet seeing the gun.

'Sit up, Nguni!' Johnny said.

Nguni opened his mouth, about to protest when he saw the gun and gave a start, his eyes suddenly huge in his head. He pulled himself up into a sitting position, his eyes never once leaving the gun Johnny Tambourine held. Then he looked up slowly, his lips gibbering with fright. But then, just as quickly, his expression changed.

'It's you, Johnny Tambourine! I thought it was Special Branch. Put your gun away, man, we can talk.' He snapped the gold Rolex off his fat wrist and handed it to Johnny Tambourine. 'Here, take it, I am your friend,' he smiled.

Johnny took the watch and handed it to Flyspeck. It felt heavy, people said it was real gold. 'We are not friends, Nguni.'

The large black man must have had the constitution of an ox for he seemed to have recovered instantly, though his eyes were completely bloodshot and his skin puffy from drink. 'Johnny, Tandy is my friend, you are my friend.'

'No more, man! You killed Mama Tequila.'

Nguni actually chuckled, his stomach wobbling. 'Why would I do that?' he said, his voice amused.

'No bullshit, Nguni. We have proof.' Johnny was bluffing. Tandia had simply told him that he was the prime suspect.

'What proof?' Nguni said, raising his head slightly and sticking his jaw out. He was gaining confidence by the second. 'You are lying, Johnny Tambourine! If this was so, they would have said it in the newspapers.'

Nguni cursed himself. He was still drunk, he'd slipped, his mind wasn't working fast enough, he'd virtually admitted his guilt. He tried to recover, hoping the boys were not very bright. 'I left that place before the explosion.'

'Why did you run away? Because you are guilty!' Johnny replied for him.

Nguni shook his head slowly. 'Haya, haya, Johnny, it was my business. There were people who wanted money from me, I couldn't pay them.' He spread his hands. 'That is the simple reason, man. I am hiding from these people.'

Johnny sighed, 'Nguni, we are tsotsi, not lawyers or the police, we do not ask how is a thing? Why?' He pointed the muzzle of his gun in Flyspeck's direction. 'My friend here has been hired by Tandia. He is a killer, a hired gun. But Tandia doesn't want to kill you. "Don't kill him, Johnny," she says. "Tell him only, if he makes a confession we will let him go. If he does not, we will tell Geldenhuis where he is."'

At the mention of Geldenhuis's name Nguni jerked backwards hitting his head hard against the bed-head. It was so sudden as to be almost ridiculous. The giant Zulu was suddenly out of bluff, unable to hold himself together any longer.

'That whore!' he spat.

Johnny and Flyspeck froze, not believing what they'd heard. 'What? What did you say?' Flyspeck said. It was the first time he had spoken.

'Geldenhuis has a paper, a confession, when she was a schoolgirl she was a whore, *isiFebe*!' He started to laugh. 'That Geldenhuis, he is a very clever man, so clever he got me a bus transport licence for Soweto. It is not possible for a black man to have a licence, but he fixed it for me.' He spread his hands, squinting up at Johnny Tambourine and Flyspeck Mendoza. 'You can work for me, I will pay you well. One day I will be the richest black man in Africa!' He seemed to find this last statement very amusing and started to laugh again, his laughter turning almost immediately into a fit of coughing.

Nguni leaned forward, his head bent towards his knees. Flyspeck didn't even think, the spoke came out of the seam of his trousers and entered the first and second vertebrae, his wrist turning to sever the nerve and cut through the soft, pulpy tissue. Nguni was dead without having moved. He simply sat slumped over his huge black belly.

'Shit!' Johnny said.

Flyspeck shrugged and grinned. 'He bad-mouthed Tandy, man!'

'Dog Poep heard them and came running into the room. 'What happened? What's the matter?' He stared at them both. Johnny Tambourine and Flyspeck Mendoza were pointing at the huge buckled shape of Mr Nguni and pissing themselves with laughter.

Johnny Tambourine, Dog Poep Ismali, Too Many Fingers Bembi and Flyspeck Mendoza, with the help of Gideon's people, crossed the border into Mozambique to join a terrorist training squad. Or that's what Tandia thought, but halfway across the Komati River Flyspeck Mendoza lost the grip of the guide who was holding him and panicked. He couldn't swim and, being the smallest, the water came up to his neck. He disappeared under the swift-flowing current, came up thrashing and disappeared again as the river current carried him off. Several minutes later and several hundred yards downstream he was washed up unconscious on a part of the bank covered with reed. The villagers guiding the boys across called him with the soft hoot of a river owl, which was the signal to keep them together in the dark. Two of them came back and searched the riverbank to no avail, and they assumed he was drowned.

Flyspeck Mendoza regained consciousness just before dawn and climbed up the riverbank, not knowing which side he was on. He started to walk and skirted the lights of a town, which unbeknown to him was Komatipoort. When the sun came up he slept, and travelled all of the next night. At dawn, hungry and footsore, he came to a farm where he waited until sun-up and then asked the farmer for work. The farmer asked him for his work papers and when Flyspeck said he'd lost them the farmer grinned and said he could work for his food, but no pay. And so he became a slave.

Flyspeck was a city boy, a bad guy who stayed up late and rose around noon, a hired gun. He had a bad leg from a knife fight and he'd never worked a day in his life. The farmer took the gold Rolex he was wearing and then beat the living shit out of him. He continued to do so daily with a sjambok until Flyspeck was working quite well for a city boy with a bad limp.

But at night in the dark cell, no different to a prison, where the farmer kept all the vagrants – who turned out to be just about everyone who worked on the farm – he sharpened the end of a bicycle spoke he'd stolen, using a small slab of slate-stone. Though he was exhausted from the dawn-to-dusk work and the others around him fell asleep within minutes of eating their evening meal of mealie pap and watery gravy, Flyspeck forced himself to stay awake long enough each night to do a little honing.

For almost two months, night after night, he worked in the pitch blackness until the point of the spoke was smooth and narrow and sharp as a needle and the sides felt like satin to his touch. The time had come for Flyspeck Mendoza to depart.

Two days later the tractor broke down in a field where they were sowing potatoes and the Boer climbed down and buried his head in the engine. Then he sent his boss boy back to the shed for something. The boss boy laid his sjambok over the back of the tractor and walked quickly away. Suddenly the Boer was alone in the field with only his slave workers, his head in the tractor engine and the top three vertebrae deliciously exposed on the base of his red, sunburned neck.

The spoke went in so cleanly that the Boer let out a soft 'pffft!' like a long sigh. To anyone watching, he would have appeared just like before, on his knees with his head in the tractor engine. Only this time he was dead and the beautiful spoke was already back down the seam of Flyspeck's ragged trousers. Flyspeck reached down and unclipped the Rolex from his wrist and put it in his pocket. Then he picked up his bag of seed potatoes and walked to the end of the field and he just kept walking. Two days later the police caught him on the outskirts of Barberton where he was arrested and thrown into gaol to await trial.

Flyspeck Mendoza confessed readily to the murder of the Boer, but he'd not used his proper name when he'd asked the Boer for employment. His fingerprints were sent to Pretoria to the Department of Native Affairs which keeps the fingerprints of every African over the age of sixteen. A month later he was indicted for murder a second time, this time under his correct name which, because it showed up on a computer check of wanted persons, was also sent to the Special Branch. Finally it arrived on the desk of the youngest colonel in the history of the South African police force.

Colonel Jannie Geldenhuis didn't take long to make the connection between Flyspeck Mendoza, the death of Mr Nguni, and the disappearance of the four boys. The Rolex watch found on Flyspeck was instantly identified as having belonged to Mr Nguni. The Boer who'd been murdered on a farm about twenty miles outside Komatipoort had died in exactly the same way as Nguni had done. He was also sure that Tandia was behind the murder somewhere – otherwise why would all four boys, Johnny Tambourine in particular, have found him when a national manhunt had failed? Johnny Tambourine was her chauffeur and minder; she had to be involved somewhere. Even if Tandia was only aware of the murder and hadn't reported it to the police she could be indicted.

The more Geldenhuis looked at the file on Johnny Tambourine, the more excited he became. Flyspeck Mendoza was a lifelong friend, they did everything together. The four boys, he discovered, all worked for Tandia. He had to find out if Nguni had said anything before he'd died. Geldenhuis grew suddenly cold. He had to find out whether she had anything and if she did he had to compromise her so that it couldn't be used.

How Geldenhuis handled the kaffir on the murder charge at present in Barberton gaol was critical if he was to compromise Tandia. He picked up the phone and a voice answered, 'Constable Vermaas.'

'Vermaas, look up your prison directory and tell me the name of the Kommandant at Barberton prison.'

'Yes, Colonel,' Stoffel Vermaas answered. A couple of minutes later he called back. 'Colonel Smit, sir. Do you want me to call him for you?'

'*Asseblief, ja*,' Geldenhuis thanked the operator and waited for the call to come through from Barberton.

There was a click in Geldenhuis's ear. '*Smit hier*,' a voice said on the other end of the phone.

Geldenhuis identified himself to the prison officer. 'Not *the* Jannie Geldenhuis, the boxer?' Smit asked.

'Ja, I boxed a little,' Geldenhuis laughed, 'a long time ago.'

'We take our boxing pretty seriously down here, Colonel. What can I do for you?'

Jannie Geldenhuis explained to Smit what he wanted.

'Ja, of course, Colonel, we will make everything available and ready for your arrival. But, just one thing; prison regulations state that a prison officer must be present if an interrogation takes place within the prison. I cannot allow you to interrogate with only your own people in the room.'

Geldenhuis cursed under his breath; he was dealing with a small-town yokel who played by the book. 'This is a Special Branch case, Kommandant, we do not require supervision with the work we do,' he said, a hint of sarcasm in his voice.

'Nevertheless, Colonel, I must insist.'

Geldenhuis was too good an operator to push it any further. He sighed heavily so that Smit would hear him on the other end. 'As you wish, Smit.'

'Colonel Smit, Colonel!' Smit corrected, his voice suddenly hard.

Geldenhuis realised at last that he wasn't dealing with a fool and softened his voice immediately. 'I'm sorry, Colonel, here in Special Branch we do a lot of undercover work, we get a bit careless with titles. If you will make a man available we'd like one who has been involved in getting information out of a prisoner himself, if you understand what I mean?'

Geldenhuis wasn't too worried. He'd have preferred to have Flyspeck Mendoza on his own with a couple of his own men, but Barberton prison was a place with a notoriously tough reputation and, anyway, in his experience, warders in country prisons didn't exactly play by the rules. He'd sweet-talk the prickly kommandant when they got there.

Smit called Gert immediately after the phone call. 'We've got Jannie Geldenhuis, the boxer and Special Branch Colonel coming down from Johannesburg tomorrow early to interrogate the kaffir who murdered the Boer from Komatipoort. I've told him you will attend.'

'Yes, Colonel,' Gert replied, 'Do we want the interview on tape?' Though he and Smit had been friends for twenty years they generally kept things formal during working hours.

Colonel Smit looked up at Gert. 'You know who called yesterday?'

'No, sir?'

'Peekay. He's going to defend the kaffir murderer. He phoned to say he's coming down the day after tomorrow to see this Flyspeck kaffir.'

'*Here*, man, why?' Gert asked, amazed. 'It's open and shut, the man has confessed.'

'That's just what I said. He wants to expose the conditions on the farms. Blacks without papers used as slaves. This guy who got murdered, he says he's been doing it a long time.'

'Jesus! So what's new? It's been going on three hundred years!'

Smit looked up again. 'You know, Gert, I love Peekay like my own son, but I don't think he's going to make old bones, he doesn't know where to draw the line.'

'That's what made him champion of the whole world, he never knew when he was beaten,' Gert said, though it was plain he was as concerned for Peekay as Smit was.

Smit cleared his throat. The subject of Peekay was too painful to discuss even with Gert. Peekay was the only truly innocent man he'd ever known and he found it a distressing experience coming to terms with this kind of truth. He admitted to himself that if he hadn't known him as well as he did he would despise him for it. Smit knew about fanatics; his own people, the volk, were often as fanatical and totally unreasonable and unreasoning. But you couldn't put Peekay in the same category. Peekay didn't hate the Afrikaner people or the kaffirs or anyone for that matter, he hated injustice. He couldn't see the grey shades, the reasons, the necessities for things to be as they were and this made him dangerous to a system which Smit himself supported. But it made him doubly dangerous to people like Jannie Geldenhuis, and Colonel Smit knew how people like Geldenhuis were and how they reacted when they were threatened.

'Ja, on second thoughts, we'll let Colonel Geldenhuis and his people in alone with the kaffir. If he's going to have to smack him round a bit to get whatever he wants from the bastard we don't want to be the people to stand in the way of justice. But tape the interview, Gert. Put a two-hour tape on and let it run; if he does something stupid and the coon dies, we want to be covered. But also, man, if they ask if we taping, just look stupid, let him think the *japies* from the *platteland* don't go in for that sort of thing.'

FORTY-ONE

Tandia was arrested in the early hours of the morning and given five minutes to dress. It was the second time in her life she'd been roughly pushed into the back of a kwela-kwela, a police van, and taken into custody. In the ensuing years the frightened teenager had become a great beauty and a famous barrister, yet nothing, she told herself, had changed. She was still a kaffir and Geldenhuis, her original tormentor, still had his boot on her neck.

The back of the police van had the sharp pungency of African sweat and the sour smell of beer mash as though earlier in the night a drunk had vomited. In fact, Tandia concluded, this was precisely what had happened, for the floor and the wooden seat on which she sat were wet, suggesting that the back of the van had recently been hosed out. The wetness now added to the cold, though she was not sure whether she shivered from the damp, dark cold interior of the van or from her own sense of misery.

For some reason the siren on the van would wail intermittently, for fifteen seconds or so every few minutes. She wondered if it was intended to intimidate her; there couldn't be much traffic at this time of the morning nor, she imagined, was her arrival urgent.

After a while they slowed down and stopped. She heard the police driver talking to someone. They must have arrived at the gate into the huge, grey granite structure of the John Vorster Square police headquarters. The van moved off slowly again and proceeded for what seemed like only a few yards before it stopped. Moments later Tandia heard the passenger door slam and then the sudden rattle of the lock on the rear door of the van. The door opened and the detective sergeant who'd arrested her stood waiting. 'Get out now, please, miss,' he instructed. Tandia half stooped and climbed out, the air outside cold and fresh on her face after the smell of the van. He held a pair of handcuffs. 'I've got to do this, it's procedure, I should really have done it when we arrested you.'

Tandia nodded, holding up her wrists. It was dark but if the policeman had looked carefully he might just have made out the slight discolouring around her wrists which were the scars from the last time she'd worn handcuffs.

She expected to be finger-printed and formally charged but instead she was led down a long corridor into a brightly lit room which, under normal circumstances, would have seemed like a joke. It contained a powerful light with a larger than usual frosted bulb in the centre of the ceiling. A single wooden upright chair stood directly under it. A polished honey-coloured cork linoleum covered the floor and muffled her footsteps as she entered. The walls of the fairly large room were painted a light apple green. It was so obviously an interrogation room that it seemed to belong in the pages of a Dick Tracy comic book. The door was painted a glossy brown and on it was lettered in white:

Interview Rm.1. Europeans only.
Onderhoud Km.1. Slegs Blankes.

Tandia pointed to the door. 'You've brought me to the wrong place. I do not suffer from the affliction of being white, constable.' She was using the last of her courage, for she could feel her bowels beginning to constrict; the well-known barrister was quickly dissolving into the small frightened teenager sitting in the play chair at Cato Manor police station.

The white female constable who'd taken over from the detective sergeant when they'd arrived at John Vorster didn't bother to reply. 'You can sit if you like,' she said, standing at the door and pointing to the lone chair. She was so nondescript in appearance that she almost defied description; she was twenty pounds overweight and the hem of her light-blue drill skirt was a good four inches higher on one side than the other.

'I'd like to use the toilet, please,' Tandia asked.

The female constable looked confused, then annoyed. 'The non-European toilets are on the other side of "C" block. There's no time, man.'

Tandia pointed to the chair. 'If I can sit on that white person's chair, why not on a toilet seat?'

The woman seemed to hesitate again; then she jerked her head. '*Kom, maak gou, jong*,' she said, telling Tandia to hurry. Tandia followed her down a corridor to a women's toilet. 'Leave open the door,' the female constable instructed. She stood directly in front of the open door looking into the toilet, her heavy brown stockinged legs slightly apart and her hands clasped behind her back.

They returned to the room and Tandia seated herself on the chair. The constable closed the door and left her, having first made her remove her shoes and confiscated her handbag and wristwatch. Placing the watch into the bag and taking both shoes and bag with her she placed them in the corridor directly outside the door. Then, using both hands, she pulled at the door which closed slowly. Tandia realised it was nearly six inches thick and must be sound-proofed. As the door clicked to a close a small red light went on above the lintel and she noted a telephone receiver fixed to the wall where it had been hidden by the open door.

Tandia longed suddenly for the calming effect of a cigarette. 'Hold yourself together, nothing's happened yet,' she said to herself, though she could feel the constriction in her chest and the leaden feeling in her stomach as her terror began to mount. It was oppressively hot in the room and she rose from the chair and removed the cardigan and then the sweater she wore under it. She was wearing a fashionably short green woollen shift which, she now realised, showed her figure. Soon this, too, became too warm and she was conscious of her clammy overheated body. Her scalp itched as the perspiration gathered on her brow.

She wiped herself down with a discarded sweater but the perspiration soon returned as she paced the room, fanning herself with both hands. She was becoming increasingly distressed. Finally after what seemed like an hour or more, with a rattle and a soft 'phffft', the door opened and Geldenhuis stood framed in the doorway.

'*Here*, but it's hot in here,' he said, blowing through his teeth and fanning his face with his right hand. He turned and spoke to someone in the corridor, 'Tell them to take down the heat, you hear?' Then turning to her he smiled, 'Good morning, Tandy. I'm sorry about the heating, I told them they mustn't let you get cold.' He grinned, 'You know cops, they always over-react!'

Tandia sniffed, 'That was considerate of you, Colonel Geldenhuis.' She was surprised at the hint of sarcasm in her voice.

Geldenhuis took a step into the room, 'Now don't be like that, Tandy!' There was a grin on his face but his pale blue eyes were cold and seemed not to move, as though they were permanently locked into place. He turned. 'Bring a table and another chair!' he called at the open door.

Almost immediately two black constables appeared, one carrying a table and another carrying a chair. It was obvious to Tandia that they'd been waiting outside for permission to enter. The single chair placed directly under the light had been a ploy to unsettle her. Jannie Geldenhuis was dressed in full uniform, though he wore no cap and he carried a flat plastic zip-up folder under his left arm. He put the folder on the table which had been placed away from the light with the original chair moved to one side of it and the second chair placed on the other side.

Tandia was surprised. She hadn't seen Geldenhuis in uniform for several years and in it he took on a different dimension. If the uniform was meant to intimidate her it had slightly the opposite effect. As a uniformed policeman he tended to be the Geldenhuis who had terrorised the child. As long as she could hold on to her adult status, her lawyer's mind, Tandia told herself she could overcome these old fears. The uniform he wore would help her to keep this in mind. What she needed to fear far more was the plain-clothes Geldenhuis where the evil and the private madness lay.

Had she known why Geldenhuis had appeared in uniform she would have recoiled from him in horror.

'You know why we've arrested you?' Geldenhuis asked suddenly, though his voice was still relaxed.

'On a conspiracy charge,' Tandia said. 'It won't hold up.'

'Ja, that's right. But you're wrong, it will.' His voice tightened a fraction. 'Sit please, Tandy.' He pointed to the chair and waited for her to sit. 'So, after all these years here we are at the beginning again, hey?'

'Only in one respect, colonel. This is the second time you have placed me under wrongful arrest. I would like to make a phone call please.'

'Maybe later, it's still early in the morning,' he glanced at his watch. 'Hey man, it's only six o'clock; your boyfriend, Peekay, will still be out running.' It was the first hint of animosity and Tandia braced herself.

'My partner is in Barberton today. I would like to call Hymie Levy.'

The policeman's lips puckered, 'Ja, that's right, I remember now. I was down there yesterday, they told me he was coming.'

'I've read the warrant, colonel, could you please explain how it involves me?'

Geldenhuis held Tandia's eyes. 'Very simple. We have incontrovertible proof that you were aware of the killing and the identity of the killer of Samuel Nguni.'

'That is not true!' Tandia burst out, the volume of her protest betraying her nervousness.

'That is not for you to say, the court will decide.'

'Will you show me your supporting evidence?' Tandia asked, trying to keep her voice calm.

'Ja, maybe I will, maybe I won't, it all depends . . .'

'On what?'

'What do you think?'

'On whether I co-operate? I am no more implicated in Samuel Nguni's murder than you are.' Tandia was feeling safer; if Geldenhuis kept it to legal matters she could cope.

From the time he'd placed the plastic folder on the table Geldenhuis started to pace the length of the room, his arms behind his back, his whole attitude seemingly relaxed, never actually looking at Tandia. His manner was almost courtroom procedure, with her seated in the witness box and him prowling the floor as he cross-examined. Now, for the first time, he moved up close and placed his hands on the edge of the table opposite to her, leaning slightly forward so that he was almost directly above her, dominating the space they occupied, forcing Tandia to keep her eyes downcast. 'Co-operation, in our business that's a very important word, wouldn't you say, Tandy? Without co-operation we would be in a lot of trouble. But mostly, people, they're good, they co-operate with the police. Sometimes they need a little help, but mostly they're pretty good.'

Tandia realised that Geldenhuis was using standard authority structure, a slightly patronising, though initially impersonal manner backed by an acute awareness in the victim of the authority behind it.

She told herself she would need to keep the dialogue on an equal footing as long as she possibly could. 'I cannot co-operate by pleading guilty, colonel.'

Geldenhuis moved even closer to her, raising his voice suddenly, so that she jumped involuntarily, looking up at him. 'I am not a fool, Tandy. I know that!' The expression on the policeman's face changed instantly and he smiled. 'There are lots of sorts of co-operation.' He paused. 'And each kind has, you know, its reward.'

'And what sort of co-operation did you have in mind . . .' she paused for less than a second before adding, 'Colonel Geldenhuis?'

Geldenhuis realised that she was up to most of his tricks, that Tandia wasn't some ingénue with whom he could toy. But he had a long way to go yet and if she thought she knew where he was coming from, all the better. 'Well let me see now, Tandy, first we have to put our cards on the table. I show you the cards I got hey? Then you show me what you got.'

Tandia forced herself to smile, 'I'm afraid I'm not very good at card games, colonel.'

'Ag, man, it's easy, I'll teach you how to play. It's very simple, really. The one with the best cards wins.' He walked over to the door and closed it.

Tandia followed him with her eyes, noting again the small red light that went on above the door the moment it shut. 'I am not aware of having any cards,' she said, raising her voice so Geldenhuis could hear her.

He turned and walked over to the table. 'No, man, that's not true, you will see when we play the game you have a good hand.' Geldenhuis picked up the plastic folder on the desk and unzipped it. He withdrew two neatly typed pages and, leaning over, placed them in front of Tandia. 'I am putting my first card down. This is known as an ace. Take your time . . . read it.' He turned and started to pace again.

Tandia began to read the transcript which was headed up in the standard manner of a confession notice. After a few paragraphs she looked up and waited for Geldenhuis, who had his back to her, to turn. 'This is a police verbal, Colonel Geldenhuis.'

'Ja, and that's just the start.'

Geldenhuis dug into the folder again and produced a newspaper photo of Johnny Tambourine taken when he had been written up as the boy who had saved Tandia and Magistrate Coetzee's lives. 'We have positive identification from the cook.'

Tandia ignored him. She read through the documents, trying to seem the lawyer she was, although inwardly she was filled with misgiving.

'. . . and then man, my Bra comes to me. We are going to hit Nguni he says.'
P: 'How do you mean hit? To hit with your fist?'
Mendoza: 'No, baas, hit is like a hit-man. We must kill this Nguni guy. He is a bad cat, man.'
P: 'Why must you kill him. Did he tell you why?'
Mendoza: 'For what he did to Mama Tequila.'
P: 'Why would he do that? Was this Mama Tequila a relation or something?'
Mendoza: 'Ja, my Bra says because he killed Mama Tequila . . . Tandy's friend, when he exploded the bomb.'
P: 'Did he say she knew what he was going to do?'

Mendoza: 'Ja, I think she knew.'
P: 'Think?'
Mendoza: 'She knew.'

When she came to the end, Tandia looked up at Jannie Geldenhuis. 'Colonel Geldenhuis, I don't know what you're trying to do, but this verbal isn't worthy of you. Peekay was in Barberton today interviewing Flyspeck Mendoza. If the prisoner has been over-enthusiastically interviewed by your people this will come out in the evidence. Even the South African courts don't like police verbals obtained under duress and that leak like a sieve. I never knew of Nguni's murder until after it happened. What you're trying to do is clear up Nguni's murder and implicate me in some sort of treasonable conspiracy.'

Geldenhuis rose from the chair, and perched on the corner of the table. He reached down and retrieved the two pages in front of her and returned them to the plastic folder. Finally he leaned over and patted Tandia lightly on the shoulder. 'You're good, Tandy,' he chuckled, 'But I already knew that. I admit, maybe we had to do a few things to get this kaffir boy to talk, but the lowveld court where they're going to hold the trial won't worry about a little thing like that. We're giving them a double murder confession – that's not something that happens every day, a kaffir who has killed two white men. Magtig! What a trial for the district court! Don't you worry, I can make this confession stick all the way, man.' Geldenhuis paused. 'Your boyfriend can do what he likes, I've got a signed confession.' He reached into his pocket and withdrew the gold Rolex watch. Tandia recognised it immediately. Nguni would brag about it to everyone who would listen; it had cost him six thousand American dollars. 'This was found in the pocket of the accused, it is Nguni's watch.' He leaned over and touched Tandia lightly under the chin, grinning. 'And now I've also got you, skatterbol. What do you think your boyfriend can do about that, hey?'

Tandia was repulsed by Geldenhuis touching her and she wanted to jerk her head away, but she didn't have the courage to do so. This was the third time he'd referred to Peekay as her boyfriend and she couldn't continue to ignore him. 'Please, colonel, do not refer to Peekay as my boyfriend, it's not true!'

Geldenhuis opened the folder and withdrew a ten-by-eight-inch photograph, the size which would normally be submitted as evidence in court. He tossed it carelessly in front of Tandia, not saying a word. Tandia looked down at the picture without picking it up. The black-and-white print was grainy, having been blown up quite a lot from the original sixteen-millimetre negative, but it clearly showed Tandia with her arms around Peekay and her head on his chest.

Tandia's mouth fell open. 'The explosion! It happened after the explosion. Peekay is my friend, I was terribly upset!' she protested.

Geldenhuis's hand shot out and grabbed her by the throat. 'You are fucking him, you hear? Fucking him!! You fucking him at the Jew's house. The Jew bastard who loves kaffirs, he should have died! That bomb should have killed the fucking bastard!'

His voice had started low but now he was shouting, his eyes wild, as though he'd gone suddenly mad, and the corners of his mouth twitched. It was all so astonishingly quick that pure fright had not yet caught up with Tandia. Geldenhuis was choking her and she clawed at his hands, but they were enormously strong for a man his size and the clamp around her throat grew tighter until she started to black out in flashes. As suddenly as he'd attacked her he released his grip, standing up and walking away from the table. He cleared his throat, lifting his chin slightly and adjusting his tie. Then he produced a folded handkerchief and dabbed at the corners of his mouth.

Tandia's head was bent over the table and she was coughing violently, trying at the same time to regain her breath. Tears streamed from her eyes, blinding her. Geldenhuis turned suddenly and pointed his finger at her, taking a step towards the table again. Her tears prevented her seeing him clearly but she instinctively flinched, expecting another attack. But he moved no closer to her. When he spoke his voice seemed to have gained a level of control, though it was still angry. 'You think you so bladdy clever, you two. Two big-time lawyers always in the papers. To me you just a kaffir, you hear? A stinking black kaffir! You think you can do anything you like, that we just all *japies*, hairy backs, stupid Afrikaners, you think it's a joke. You think keeping our blood pure, it's a joke, don't you?'

'It's not a joke,' Tandia rasped, her voice barely audible.

'Hey? What did you say, kaffir?' Geldenhuis took another step closer to the table, his voice menacing. Tandia pulled back, involuntarily bringing her hands up in front of her face.

'It's not a joke, colonel,' Tandia repeated. She was having difficulty speaking.

'What do you mean by that, kaffir?'

Tandia was frightened and her throat burned terribly. She realised dimly that what was happening was not part of the way Geldenhuis had planned things, that he'd lost control. 'Nothing, Colonel Geldenhuis. I meant nothing,' she whimpered.

He sniffed, wiping his nose with the back of his hand, turning away and then immediately turning back again. 'What would you know about racial purity, hey? You part a kaffir and you part a bladdy *charra* and now you want to do it with a white man so your children will be part of us too! Your filth will come into our blood!' He took a step up to the table and reached over to retrieve the photograph, waving the picture in Tandia's face. 'You fucking him, you bitch, and you got to be punished!'

It was the word 'punished' which acted as the trigger. The vision of his father in the butcher's cold room, his large hairy white flanks bent over the huge buttocks of a black woman, suddenly overwhelmed Geldenhuis. It was his duty, his sacred duty before God to keep the purity, to prevent the blacks from turning them all into bastards and half-castes, into the scum of the earth! His hand shot out to grab her again and Tandia jerked back, over-balancing her chair and landing hard on her back, hitting the back of her head on the cork floor.

For a moment Tandia lay stunned. Then she felt the boot on her neck. The fear rose up in her, a dark animated ghost which started from nowhere and filled her entire being. She was back in the cemetery at Cato Manor; in her mind she heard his voice, a younger voice, but still his. *You report this you dead meat, you hear?*

'Get up, you black bitch,' she heard Geldenhuis say, though his voice seemed to come from a distance. Tandia lay perfectly still, his boot still on her neck. Then it lifted but she still didn't respond. 'Up!' he shouted and the toe of his boot landed in the small of her back. The pain drove up her spine but she managed to stifle the scream so that it came out as a choking, gasping sound. Still she didn't move, her fear rendering her totally powerless. Now it was a huge wave washing over her senses and drowning them in its roar.

Geldenhuis reached down and grabbed Tandia by the hair, jerking her head from the ground. 'On your knees, kaffir!' He pulled hard and Tandia felt an explosion of pain in her head as it was drawn upwards. Her eyes remained tightly closed, her traumatised mind still obeying his order in the cemetery a dozen years before. Tandia had no sense of time, she was no longer aware of where she was, her body simply responding to his commands.

Geldenhuis released her hair and still she kept her eyes closed. His words in the graveyard repeated over and over again like a gramophone record stuck in one place. She could hear him panting above her and then his voice again, 'Open your eyes, kaffir!'

Tandia opened her eyes. Geldenhuis stood in front of her, his legs slightly apart; in one hand he held his police revolver and in the other his deformed erection. 'Kiss it better!' he commanded, bringing the barrel of the gun to her forehead. Tandia moved her head forward, her lips touching him. 'Properly better, man!' She felt the barrel of the gun push into the side of her head. Tandia opened her mouth and took him in. Above her Geldenhuis began to whimper; then she felt his body shudder and then he pulled away from her.

Geldenhuis walked halfway across the room, adjusting himself and replacing his revolver. Then he took his handkerchief out and, without unfolding it, wiped the sweat from his face. He walked over to the phone beside the door. Lifting the receiver he waited, then spoke into it. 'Bring water, drinking water and a glass.' He turned, remaining beside the phone. 'Get up, pick up the chair and sit down!' he commanded.

When the water came he walked over to the table, placed the glass down and filled it, pushing it across the table towards her. In a solicitous voice he said, 'Drink, Tandy, it will help your throat.'

Tandia drank greedily, though the glass chattered against her teeth and she had to hold it in both hands. Her throat hurt to swallow. She put the glass down empty, not looking at Geldenhuis who had brought his chair back to the table and now sat opposite her. He took the empty glass and removed his handkerchief; unfolding it, he wiped the interior of the glass, then he half filled it, drinking himself, though only half the water in the glass.

'That's the difference between us an' you people, we always get even. We never forget. That's why we on top and you on the bottom. Now you and me, we even again, quits.' Geldenhuis paused. 'What's the matter? You think something terrible happened? When you bit me in Durban, that's when something terrible happened. What happened just now, that was fair, you hear? Very fair. I should have killed you for what you did to me. I thought about it a lot. But in the end I am a Afrikaner, we are a fair people. I got even, but I did it fair. You can count yourself very lucky you not dead, man.'

Tandia looked directly at Geldenhuis. She spoke slowly at first, her voice coming out slightly hoarse. 'Since the first day you came into my life you've tried to make a whore of me, Jannie Geldenhuis. But it won't work, you'll never do it.' She sniffed, 'You can't make a whore out of someone who isn't one. But what you just made me do, that won't make you better, because you can't make a man out of someone who isn't one!'

Geldenhuis laughed but Tandia could see in his pale blue eyes that she'd struck home. It was the first time she'd seen confusion in them and she wasn't afraid of him attacking her again; the demon in him was temporarily spent.

'I suppose you think Peekay is a man? Sies! A white man who does it with kaffirs!' he said, but the smile on his face wasn't secure and he lowered his eyes, unable to hold hers.

'I know nothing of Peekay's sexual proclivities, Colonel Geldenhuis, but I now count you among the kaffir fuckers!'

The shock on the police colonel's face was enormous. It was as though he'd walked unexpectedly into a right thrown from way back behind the shoulder; his face seemed to physically crumble, his jaw went slack and he grabbed onto the edge of the table with both hands as though he was preventing himself from falling. Tandia panicked, his sudden reaction triggering the delayed shock of the past hour of horror. She knew suddenly that he was going to kill her and she jumped from her seat and flung herself at the door, hammering at it with her fists. 'Open the door! Open the door!! Please! Please!!' she screamed. Then she saw the phone on the wall and grabbed it, 'Open the door! Please open the door!' she screamed again down the receiver. She turned, weeping with shock, expecting Geldenhuis to leap upon her and instead saw him seated at the table looking at her, the expression on his face benign.

'Come and sit down, Tandy,' he said quietly. 'No one will open the door.'

Her heart still beating violently, Tandia returned to her seat. Geldenhuis seemed perfectly relaxed, one hand on the table the other on his lap. 'Sit, we haven't finished talking yet.

Tandia sat, avoiding his eyes. 'Look at me,' he said. Tandia lifted her head to look at him and his hand shot up from his lap and pushed the gun against her forehead and pulled the trigger. The empty gun clicked a fraction before Tandia's scream, her hand grabbing at her neck in fright. Geldenhuis was even prepared for this and slapped her across the face, cutting the scream cold and preventing the hysteria rising up in her. 'See, there are no bullets,' he said.

Geldenhuis put the revolver back in its holster and then looked up at her again. 'You have broken your neck chain,' he said, pointing to the thin gold chain lying on the table. He reached over and picked it up, examining the two small pointed gold teeth attached to it. 'There is no escape, we always get even in the end,' he said impassively, then placed the chain back on the table in front of Tandia. 'Tandy, look at me.' Tandia raised her eyes slowly, expecting anything and was surprised to see that Geldenhuis wore a hurt expression. He shook his head slowly, 'You don't understand, do you? You have co-operated with me, Tandy, even if we didn't play our game of cards hey? Never mind, some other time; now you must get your reward.' Jannie Geldenhuis reached over for the plastic folder and withdrew the two foolscap pages of transcript. 'I could have made it stick,' he boasted and tore the manuscript in half. Then he tore it again and again until little squares of paper covered the table in front of him. Finally he looked up and Tandia knew instantly that the policeman had returned. His eyes were hard as he spoke. 'I'm going to get you, Tandy. You and Peekay. But fair and square. Also Mandoma and the Jewboy. All four. You are trying to destroy my country and my people and you will hang for treason.' He pointed to the bits of paper scattered over the table. 'Tonight we fixed one more thing; you and me, we quits now.' Geldenhuis turned to Tandia. 'Will you do me a favour?'

Tandia was exhausted and enormously distressed, but she held herself together, not sure that they'd come to the end of the bizarre and terrifying night. Geldenhuis could as easily snap again and so she was careful to mollify him now. 'I will try, what do you want me to do?'

'Tell Peekay about what happened.'

Tandia looked at Geldenhuis in alarm. 'Why?' she asked, astonished .

Geldenhuis spoke impassively. 'Ja, well, you see if you try to bring a charge against the police for molesting you, Detective Sergeant Koekemoer and his two coons who brought you in will swear to the court you resisted arrest. A bruise like you going to have on your neck and maybe a mark on your back, that's consistent with resistance and necessary subsequent restraint.' Geldenhuis seemed to be smiling to himself as he placed his elbows on the table and began to gather together the tiny pieces of paper, pushing them into a neat pile between his cupped hands. Finally he looked up at Tandia, the smile still on his face. 'So, tell Peekay he can have his revenge in the boxing ring. Tell him he can come any time, you hear? Any time he likes. I'm ready.'

Peekay had been in Barberton on the night of Tandia's arrest, seeing Flyspeck Mendoza at the prison. He'd arrived to find that Flyspeck had been brutally tortured by Colonel Geldenhuis the previous day so that now one eye sagged half an inch lower in the eye socket, his nose was broken and most of his teeth were missing. But the little guy swore to Peekay that he hadn't confessed to Nguni's murder, which is what Geldenhuis wanted him to do. Peekay had spent most of the day seeing to it that Flyspeck received adequate medical attention and so decided to remain overnight and leave for Johannesburg at dawn the following morning.

Though Gert and Colonel Smit had been helpful, they had little sympathy for Peekay's client. In their book a self-confessed murderer takes what comes to him, even if it ends up being a bastard like Geldenhuis. Peekay got into town by nine in the morning and went directly to Red. Chronic Martha met him with a message to call Tandia at his Hillbrow flat. Tandia had a key, for she would often go there to work on a case when she didn't want to be disturbed. It was convenient, no more than ten minutes by taxi from the office. Peekay called immediately and Tandia answered.

'Peekay, I thought you'd be here,' she sounded distressed.

'I spent the night in Barberton. What's wrong Tandy?'

'Can you come please, Peekay?' she said in a tiny voice.

'Hang on, I'll be right there.'

'Tandia, you look bloody awful, what's happened?' Peekay said, dropping his briefcase and running towards her as he entered the flat. Tandia had attempted to smile as Peekay walked in but the sustained effort to remain in control of her emotions was too great and now, for the first time since she'd left Geldenhuis and John Vorster Square that morning, she was unable to push the horror of the night sufficiently away from her and her bottom lip began to quiver.

The detective sergeant had put her into a non-European taxi just after half past seven that morning. He'd paid the driver and instructed him to take her home to Soweto. A block along she'd re-directed the driver to Hillbrow, to Peekay's flat. The taxi driver took one look at Tandia and without saying a word changed direction. Ten minutes later she arrived at the flat. 'He gave me too much money,' the driver said.

'Your lucky day,' Tandia said, crossing the road. She'd rung the bell and when there had been no reply, she'd let herself in to Peekay's flat. He'd obviously not returned from Barberton. She panicked suddenly. Why had she come directly to him? She thought about retreating, returning home. Nobody need know. She was strong enough. Mama Tequila would have told her to get off her sweet arse and go to work.

She went directly to the bathroom and turned on the shower, scrubbing herself from head to toe, washing the lather off her body and starting again until she had repeated the process three times. She felt sure she would never feel clean again in her life. She'd taken a spare toothbrush she'd found in Peekay's bathroom cabinet into the shower with a tube of paste and she did the same thing, cleaning her teeth three times and spitting the foam violently at her feet in the shower.

She was still dry-eyed as she towelled herself and fixed her make-up; then she called the office just after half past eight when Chronic Martha opened the switchboard. Her concentration kept lapsing and her attention span grew shorter and shorter as her panic grew. She'd been pushing it away ever since she'd left Geldenhuis but now it began to seep through her fingers. She thought again about running away, keeping what had happened to herself. She'd learn to live with last night, she always had in the past. It was one more hate, one more score to settle. But this time she knew it was more than this. The police colonel's threat to destroy them was real; they were all in danger. She must talk to Peekay and in doing so she would have to tell him what had taken place at John Vorster Square.

How would Peekay react when she told him what Geldenhuis had done to her? How could she begin to tell him? She didn't have those kinds of words, she'd never shared an intimacy in her life with a man. Only once with another human being, Sarah. In Sarah's bed all those years ago. She'd never forgotten the touch, the loveliness of the touch of someone else's hand caring about her, gentling her spirit. It was a warmth she'd felt for a few stolen early mornings and then never again.

Gideon had been Tandia's only lover. His lovemaking was masculine and direct; she expected no more, it suited her and meant she didn't have to pretend. She hadn't allowed Nguni to touch her and he, in turn, hadn't persisted; this had been one of the main reasons why she had continued to go out with him.

Peekay had kissed her just once, thinking she was asleep, after Juicey Fruit Mambo's death, and the touch of his lips on her brow was like nothing she had felt before. Now she wanted it again, like a little girl who wants a hurt kissed better. When she'd called him from Barberton hospital after the fire bombing at Eendrag, Magistrate Coetzee's farm, he'd been barely able to reply, his voice choked with emotion and relief at her safety. It was then that she had begun to realise he was fundamental to her life. When she'd seen him lying dazed in the smoke and chaos of the explosion at the Christmas party her heart, empty for so long, had suddenly filled, like water rising up from an underground stream, rising from the bottom of an empty well and splashing over the lip, all in a time frame faster than her mind could comprehend. In that moment she was totally without fear and she'd run to him and held her head against him and brought her arms around him. For a few dazzling minutes before the doctor's asinine voice had torn her from this completeness, she'd known what it felt like to be totally in love.

Now Tandia waited for Peekay to return, not knowing what to expect, not knowing what to do, but returning blindly to him, knowing instinctively that if she pushed the hurt and the anger and the loathing back into her one more time it would corrupt her spirit to the point where even the hate she felt couldn't sustain her need to live.

Peekay sat beside her and put his arm around her and pulled her into his chest. She couldn't look at him, dared not look. 'Tandy, please, tell me?' He pushed her gently away from him, took her face in his hands and made her look at him. At last the tears came, the tears for what Geldenhuis had done to her, the tears for Patel and the tears for herself as Peekay held her in his arms and stroked her and started the healing of her with his strong hands.

When finally Tandia was able to control herself sufficiently to speak she looked up at Peekay. 'Last night I was arrested by Geldenhuis.'

The shock on Peekay's face was enormous. 'Arrested? How? Why?'

'Peekay, we are in danger. He tried to indict me for complicity in Nguni's murder. He had a verbal supposedly taken from Flyspeck Mendoza, accusing me of ordering the murder.'

'It's not true, Tandy. I spoke to Flyspeck yesterday. They tortured him, but they got nothing!'

Tandia sighed. 'It was only an excuse, Peekay. It is a long, long story, but you and Hymie are in danger so I must tell it.' Tandia looked up at Peekay and burst into tears again.

'Come Tandy, you don't have to say anything.'

'No, I must.' She began to talk, telling Peekay of the rape after Patel's funeral. She spoke quietly going through every detail, as though the words were in braille etched into her mind and she was running her fingers over them and saying them out aloud. There was a flatness to her voice, as though by keeping it in a monotone she could hold the emotion she felt at bay. She spoke without looking up at Peekay, until she paused to blow her nose, and then she saw that tears were running down his face as he looked at her, his love for her so intense that she could feel it burning into her. He felt a terrible shame that he'd doubted her, that Geldenhuis had so easily conned him with the confession.

Tandia talked on and on, finally coming to the arrest, despite her distress not sparing herself or working shy of the sordid detail.

Peekay felt a deep, dark presence rise up in his soul, a need to destroy so great that his entire body shook. He grew so pale that Tandia grew fearful. But what Tandia was witnessing was the coming of hate to Peekay, the destruction of innocence. The power of hate roared into him like a white-hot furnace, consuming everything; he disappeared into it, a silent scream of vengeance shouting in the flames. Nothing of him was spared by the consuming fire; only the scream remained, the single violent scream of hate. Slowly he started to control it, to hold its gnashing teeth from his heart.

It was the same feeling he'd experienced when suddenly confronted by the Judge in the mines. The hate which had been bottled up in him all the years of his childhood had burst like a ripe boil and he'd beaten the huge man senseless. He'd pushed the incident back into his subconscious; never allowing it to surface. It was the single moment in his life of which he was monstrously ashamed, knowing he had been no better than his oppressors, that within him there was a darkness.

Now the need to strike out blindly, to inflict a physical hurt, senseless and violent, had returned. If he allowed it to grow it would bind into a knot that would fill his being, a giant serpent of hate writhing within him.

Tears ran down his cheeks as he fought to control the desire to smash Geldenhuis, to take a club to him and pulp his head for all the hurt and suffering his kind brought upon others. But Peekay knew that the spirit of an evil dragon slain in this way simply enters the heart of its slayer where it eats from the inside to destroy him. That the killing had to stop in the beloved country. That men and women must see that the world is not simply the domain of the cruel, vicious and rapacious. That good can grow from the killing fields and that justice was a mighty sword that could work for their side.

'Geldenhuis wants a fight, Tandy. Nothing would give me greater pleasure than to beat the shit out of him in the ring, if only to try a little to make up for the brutality and humiliation his kind have imposed on others, on you! But it won't do anything of the sort. When I step into the ring I accept that his way is right, that violence is the only revenge. But we have to stop believing in the right of might, we must get him on our own terms. Just once, in this wretched country's history, I promise you, justice will be seen to be done!'

A week later, Gideon was captured along with six other *Umkonto we Sizwe* terrorists attempting to blow up a government fuel depot on the outskirts of Johannesburg. The depot wasn't of particular strategic importance but was located close to a very up-market white suburb and the explosion was designed to shatter windows for a mile around and to burn conspicuously, a part of the campaign designed by Gideon to undermine the confidence of whites in the ability of the police ultimately to protect them from black aggression.

But, as so often happened in the past, the Special Branch, under the leadership of Colonel Jannie Geldenhuis, proved worthy of this task and the six terrorists were allowed to disarm the three guards patrolling the depot and to cut the wire and enter. Police waiting inside caught them with fifty pounds of common mining gelignite, cordtex for linking up the explosives, half a pound of semtex plastic explosive and two fairly sophisticated timing devices in case one failed. They were totally surrounded and out-gunned. Gideon conceded without a fight.

Geldenhuis personally arrested Gideon, pulling his arms behind his back and borrowing a pair of handcuffs to do the job. Gideon was unarmed except for a knife on his belt which Geldenhuis now removed. 'You had your chance, Mandoma. I told you in the ring to kill me; now it's my turn. But first I have something to return to you.' The police colonel's head drew back and he spat in Gideon's face.

Gideon laughed, spit running down his cheek. 'I am sorry I spat at you, Geldenhuis. You are not worthy of a black man's spit.' Gideon saw the police colonel's face contort and the left hand coming, but there was nothing he could do to avoid the fist which smashed into his face. Gideon steeled for the second blow; a boxer instinctively follows through and the right now smashed into the side of his jaw. He stood panting, waiting for Geldenhuis to hit him again, but the policeman held back. Gideon's nose was bleeding and he could taste blood in his mouth. He grinned. 'Your right hand was never any good, Geldenhuis!' He paused momentarily. 'Not like Peekay, he's got a right you have to respect, man!'

The morning papers, having completed printing at midnight, ran an additional two-page supplement on Mandoma's capture which was on the streets by half past seven. Though Gideon wasn't the official leader of the ANC he was looked upon, particularly by the young blacks, as the man who would eventually lead them to victory. To the whites his arrest represented a high water mark in the campaign against terrorism and they applauded the brilliant Colonel Geldenhuis who'd brought it about.

Hymie called Peekay, who had been at Johannesburg Fort since three in the morning trying to get access to Gideon and had only just returned home. 'Peekay, we've got Geldenhuis just about nailed down, let's move now. With Gideon's capture the bastard has become a national hero. Two of the morning papers speak of him as a future general. If we move quickly and bring a charge of murder against Geldenhuis it should force the state to postpone Gideon's treason trial until the court has heard the murder charges against him.'

Their case against Geldenhuis was almost complete. Mr Bottomley-Tuck, the chief legal clerk at Red, had obtained a set of Geldenhuis's fingerprints simply by applying for them through the cryptics department in Pretoria. These were sent to London where they were found to match those on a tube of glue found by Brown during his search at Poulos Industrial & Heavy Engineering. The glue type also matched the glue used to attach the bomb to the metal surface inside the train engine.

Another piece of proof surfaced closer to the trial. Peekay obtained a warrant to search Geldenhuis's flat and Swart and Brown discovered a pair of overalls hanging behind the kitchen door. In the left pocket lining of the overalls was a thin piece of wire about three inches long, resembling the filament which runs through the centre of magnesium tape. This exactly matched the tiny sample taken from the train engine. On further examination in a laboratory a small part of the hem of the pocket lining was found to be stained a pinkish colour; this was analysed as magnesium of the same type used to fire the wheel of the little train.

Red was ready to pounce.

FORTY-TWO

Colonel Jannie Geldenhuis was arrested by two of General Van Breeden's men leaving the office just after six in the evening. The warrant charged him with the murder of Sophie Van der Merwe (Mama Tequila) and the attempted murder of Solomon Moshe Levy.

The arrest of Geldenhuis was a bitter blow for *die volk*, who regarded the police colonel as *Die vuis van regverdigheid*, the fist of righteousness, a white knight who single-handedly stood between them and the black hordes. Churches throughout the country asked their congregations to pray for the safe deliverance of Colonel Jannie Geldenhuis from the forces of evil and from the anti-Christ whose hand was so clearly in evidence.

On the afternoon of the day following the arrest, General Van Breeden was summoned to Pretoria by the Department of Justice and from there he was taken to see Balthazar Johannes Vorster, the Minister for Justice and of Police and Prisons.

Bul Van Breeden was ushered politely, though almost silently, into the minister's office by his male secretary. Vorster was a large, bull-necked man. He sat at his desk signing documents as the secretary tapped lightly on the door. '*Kom!*' the minister said; then, still not glancing up, 'Sit!' as General Van Breeden entered.

Bul Van Breeden had known Vorster for a number of years and, had they met on a casual basis, they would have referred to each other by Christian name. But Vorster, who was widely tipped to be the next prime minister, was a stickler for procedure in his ministerial capacity and it was obvious to Bul Van Breeden that he was on anything but a casual visit.

'Good morning, Minister,' Bul Van Breeden said, taking the chair at the desk. The fact that he hadn't been ushered into the minister's lounge to wait for a formal interview boded badly. Vorster was an impatient and outspoken man with the usual politician's long and spiteful memory.

'Colonel Geldenhuis, why have you arrested him?' he asked suddenly.

'Because I was satisfied that a prima-facie case exists that he has committed a murder.'

'Prima facie! That's hardly proof positive! And you didn't think to inform me first?'

'No, Minister. Colonel Geldenhuis is not of sufficient rank to have made that necessary.'

'Good God, man, must I remind you that I am the Minister for Police also! The man is a brilliant young police officer. He exemplifies the best things in the force. He stands for something important in the white community. He has just captured, at great risk to his life, the most wanted terrorist in the country! He's a national hero, man! And you go and arrest him as a *murder* suspect!' The minister brought his fist down hard. 'How do you know that this so-called murder wasn't an accident brought about in the course of the man's official duty?'

Bul Van Breeden's voice was very quiet when he spoke. 'I hope you don't mean that last statement, Minister?'

'Grow up, Van Breeden!' Vorster shouted.

Bul Van Breeden rose up from his chair. 'Is that all, Minister?' he said, standing to attention. He was having difficulty controlling his anger.

Vorster clicked his tongue in annoyance and then sighed. 'Sit down, we are not finished yet.'

Van Breeden returned to the overstuffed high-backed chair in front of the minister's desk. 'I want you to make an arrangement, General,' Vorster said.

'What sort of arrangement?' Van Breeden was still angry.

The Minister for Justice ignored his question. 'The arrest of Colonel Geldenhuis, taken together with the treason trial of Mandoma and the five others, is going to have international ramifications.' He leaned back in his chair. 'It's a delicate time for the republic, you understand? Britain and America and some of the more important European countries, Germany in particular, are talking of imposing trade sanctions. The treason trial will be bad enough, but if it is held in conjunction with a murder trial involving Colonel Geldenhuis it would greatly enhance the cause of our enemies overseas and has the potential to do great harm to the republic. London reports people gathering outside South Africa House – and it's the middle of the blerrie night in London!' Vorster picked up a pencil from the desk and pointed it towards Van Breeden. 'Tell me, General, how compelling is the prima-facie evidence against Geldenhuis? Can this whole thing not be pinned on the kaffir, what's his name?'

'Nguni.'

'Ja, Nguni.'

'I don't think so, Minister. The evidence outlined to me by Advocate Peekay is precise and very detailed and seems to implicate Geldenhuis categorically.'

Vorster grunted. 'Him again! Why is it always him! Can we not bring some sort of injunction against the man?'

'Not one that would stand up in court.'

'Well, what then? What do you recommend?'

Bul Van Breeden looked surprised. 'Recommend, Minister? I am a police officer, I deal with the law. Advocate Peekay hasn't broken the law!'

'Yes, yes I know that, man,' Vorster said impatiently, then adding,

'When something involves the security of the state we all have to expect a few twists and bends in the straight and narrow road of legal precedent.'

'I could arrest Advocate Peekay on a DWT, detention without trial, but Minister, I don't recommend it. You would be adding a great deal of fuel to an already blazing fire,' he said.

Vorster appeared to be leafing through a file in front of him and Van Breeden realised it was his own dossier. 'Hmm, I see here you are a known friend of Hymie Levy, the partner of Advocate Peekay, himself an advocate?' Vorster looked up. 'Can we not do business with this Jewish friend of yours?'

'I'm sure you can talk to him, Minister.'

Vorster seemed to be thinking for a moment, tapping the end of the pencil on the edge of his desk. Finally he looked up at the policeman. 'I want you to arrange a meeting, a casual meeting that never took place, you understand?' He straightened up and closed the file in front of him. 'I want Advocates Peekay and Levy and the coloured girl to be present.'

'You mean Advocate Patel, Minister?'

'Ja, her. Make it a private dinner, at your house. One of my people will be there to brief you.'

'Brief, Minister? We will be receiving orders?'

'To put a proposition to your friends,' Vorster corrected. 'And, General, I charge you with the task of making sure no record exists of it having taken place, if you know my meaning?'

'Certainly, Minister.' General Van Breeden rose.

'Oh, and let my secretary know the venue first thing in the morning. Can you see yourself out, General? I think you know the way.'

Bul Van Breeden called Hymie on his return to Johannesburg an hour later and arranged for dinner the following evening, simply saying it was important and inviting Peekay and Tandia as well.

The three partners arrived promptly at eight. Van Breeden met them at the door of his modestly stylish home in a suburb called Saxonwold. 'We have a "guest" from Pretoria,' he said in an undertone. 'I'm afraid everything's "Mr" tonight, the complete protocol.' He ushered them down the hall into the living room. 'Hettie is visiting her sister and it's the maid's night off. I hope you don't mind a cold collation?'

A tall thin man with rimless glasses on a head roughly the dimensions of a shoe box standing on its end stood up as they entered the living room. He was dressed in a blue pinstriped suit, a white shirt and a light blue rayon tie. He appeared to be about forty, though his perfectly square crew cut was already quite grey. 'I'd like you to meet Mr Cogsweel from Pretoria.'

'Graham Cogsweel,' the tall man said, shaking hands all round.

Supper was a finger affair eaten on their laps and it passed quickly enough with Hymie and Bul Van Breeden keeping the conversation going. Tandia offered to make coffee and after she'd poured for everyone Van Breeden addressed them briefly.

'Frankly, I'm not totally sure why I've invited you here tonight, though I have some idea.' He looked at the tall government man enquiringly.

'It serves no practical purpose for you to know,' Cogsweel answered, smiling thinly. His accent suggested one of the better private schools somewhere in Natal and though he hadn't been exactly talkative during supper he'd kept his end up and was obviously an intelligent person. Judging from his slightly didactic manner, Hymie concluded that he was probably a lawyer.

'Okay, just as you wish,' the general said, 'I haven't a lot more to add other than to suggest we listen to what Mr Cogsweel has to say.' He leaned forward and recovered his coffee cup from the table beside him.

Cogsweel took a hurried sip from his own cup, then placed it on the coffee table. 'I'm sorry we have to go through all this cloak-and-dagger stuff, it isn't really as it seems,' he said, immediately confirming to them all that it was indeed what it seemed. 'It's just that this is an unofficial meeting, no notes are being taken and no record kept.' He spread his hands. 'If we can't make any progress then I'll . . .' he smiled, 'slip silently back into the night!'

'A very cloak-and-dagger expression,' Hymie laughed. Peekay and Tandia smiled; the man from Pretoria was making such an obvious attempt to play it down.

'I'll come straight to the point,' Cogsweel said. 'We are led to believe that the case against Colonel Jannie Geldenhuis is substantial?'

'Surely that's for the courts to decide,' Tandia said quickly.

Cogsweel looked over, obviously surprised that she'd spoken. In talking he'd looked mostly at Hymie, on whom Pretoria had directed him to concentrate. 'Well, we'd hoped to avoid this, you know, happening.'

The people in the room were stunned. 'What? The case coming to court?' Hymie asked astonished.

'Ja, it's not in the ultimate interest of the state.'

Peekay started to laugh. 'I'm bloody sure it isn't,' he said.

'Gentlemen,' Cogsweel said and then quickly added, 'and Miss Patel, I am appealing to you as South Africans. This case has the potential to damage our overseas relations at a time when things are very delicately poised for the government. The prime minister himself is involved in this matter.'

Peekay snorted. 'And what if we refuse you, Mr Cogsweel?'

They all waited. Cogsweel turned his hands upwards. 'It's still early times, let me talk some more. You will note that we haven't questioned your evidence? At a preliminary hearing we could examine your evidence *very, very* closely!'

'We are *very, very* used to that happening, Mr Cogsweel,' Tandia shot back.

'But we want to negotiate in good faith,' Cogsweel continued. 'We are going to accept that your evidence is compelling and try to reach a compromise before we find ourselves lost in a legal wrangle.'

'Hold it right there!' Peekay said. 'We are appearing on behalf of two parties. The sister of the deceased victim and Mr Solomon Levy! We are quite used to legal wrangles and certainly we believe our evidence indicting Colonel Geldenhuis is compelling. But it *isn't* open for discussion or for bargaining! We are *not* prepared to discuss anything, with you or the minister for justice or even the bloody prime minister or anyone else outside a court of law!'

Cogsweel looked at Hymie, who shrugged. 'I guess that's the end of our discussion, Mr Cogsweel.' He raised one eyebrow. 'Time to slip silently into the night?'

But the man from Pretoria was made of sterner stuff and wasn't to be denied. 'I respect your point of view, Advocate Peekay. Your encounters with our government over the years may have left you somewhat disaffected. I admit it isn't always easy to understand the ways of Pretoria.'

'Please don't patronise me, Mr Cogsweel.'

'Oh but I'm not! Politics and politicians often confound me as well. Can I change the subject for a moment?' Cogsweel said suddenly. Then without waiting for their agreement, he continued, 'Let me talk about the other case, the treason trial. You people in this room are the defending lawyers. It's interesting isn't it how in this case it is the government who has the compelling evidence. There appear to be no mitigating circumstances; the six men have already been charged with treason and they will certainly be convicted.'

Peekay moved forward in his chair as though to speak and Cogsweel held up his hand. 'No please, advocate, there is no possibility of any other verdict.' He paused and they all knew what he was about to say. 'The sentence for treason is death. Gideon Mandoma and the other five men will certainly die; your defence, no matter how provocative or brilliant, is purely academic. Nothing will prevent Mandoma going to the gallows.'

Peekay started to rise. 'I think we've heard enough, Mr Cogsweel.' Hymie and Tandia also began to move out of their seats when Tandia saw Peekay bring his forefinger up and lightly touch his nose.

'Jesus, Mandoma in exchange for Geldenhuis!' His voice was barely above a whisper, but they all heard him.

'A simple swap,' Cogsweel said, rising and pulling at the lapels of his suit jacket, and then flicking at the left-hand lapel with his hand. 'You have twenty-four hours to decide. There can be no discussion. Mandoma will be allowed to escape, providing he undertakes to leave the country. The other five will receive ten-year sentences. You will agree to withdraw all your evidence against Colonel Geldenhuis.' Cogsweel glanced towards Bul Van Breeden and, putting his hand into the inside breast pocket of his suit, he withdrew an envelope and handed it to the police general. 'This is an instruction from Brigadier General du Plooy. In it he asks that you carry out the government's wishes in this matter as though the instruction had come from him personally.' Cogsweel smiled his thin smile, 'Which, I suppose they have, in a manner of speaking.' He turned to the others.

'Please convey your decision to the general here before eight o'clock tomorrow night.'

Cogsweel stooped and picked up a brown felt hat from beside his chair. He placed the hat on his head, adjusting the brim. 'Please, don't anyone get up,' he said. He moved over to each of them and shook them formally by the hand, only just touching the tips of Tandia's fingers. Then he walked to the doorway of the room as Van Breeden rose to accompany him to the front door. 'No, no, I can see myself out, General.' Cogsweel looked over at Hymie. 'Now it's time for me to slip silently into the night, Mr Levy.' He smiled, turned and was gone.

'Mama Tequila always said, a man who wears a brown hat has trouble with his one-eyed snake!' Tandia said, not sure why she'd made a statement so entirely inappropriate, though they all laughed, which somewhat eased the shock they felt.

Van Breeden shook his head, '*Here*, man! You must believe me. I had no idea.'

'Bul, you must excuse us, it looks as though it's going to be a long night,' Hymie said as they heard the sound of Cogsweel's car driving away.

The three partners left soon afterwards and went directly to Hymie's apartment where Hymie perked a large pot of coffee. They hadn't spoken much in the car, each involved with their own thoughts.

'First,' Hymie said, 'we ought to set the rules, decide what constitutes a decision from all of us? Or do we have one already, are we all prepared to simply say yes or no?'

'No, I've got problems. I need to talk them out,' Peekay said.

'Ja, me too,' Tandia added.

'Well then, do we decide by unanimous vote, or what?'

'We've always resolved things unanimously, why should we change now?' Tandia asked.

'Because I'd be bloody surprised if it doesn't get personal,' Peekay grinned, 'and I want to leave here still loving you both.'

'Ah, I see, you are not inclined to vote with a simple "yes" to the government's offer?' Hymie asked.

'No, I have to talk. It isn't that easy.'

'Okay, but it has to be unanimous,' Hymie said. 'Peekay, you start.'

'I know I'm going to sound like a bit of a prick, but swopping Geldenhuis for Gideon is too easy. When we went to Oxford it soon became clear to me that the law E.W. taught wasn't the law I was going to find when we returned. Our law has never been colour blind, it has always judged pigment. But in the ten years we've been practising we have seen a madness come into it. Innocent people die every day on the gallows and murderers go free to kill again, to kill in the name of the law! That a man as vile and loathsome as Geldenhuis, the man who fired the first shot at Sharpeville, can become the youngest colonel in the history of the South African police force proves my point. If it was simply a matter of letting him go free to save Gideon's life, a swap, it would be easy. But it isn't! That's precisely what it isn't!' Peekay's voice was filled with emotion. 'It's joining the madness! It's allowing ourselves to be a part of it, part of this dreadful conspiracy!'

'Hang on a mo, Peekay! This decision involves just the sort of universal integrity that makes man decent. It allows us to return life to a man who has gone to war and is prepared to die to defeat an evil system, to replace it with your kind of justice,' Hymie cried.

'Let me finish, Hymie! Then you can go for your life. Man's highest single collective achievement is the application of natural justice to society, his greatest defeat is when he destroys it. If that sounds didactic I don't apologise. If mankind forsakes this single premise, then we are doomed as a species!' Peekay looked up at Hymie. 'You're right, Gideon is at war, a righteous war, but nevertheless one in which the consequences were clear to him. He has always known that if he was captured he would die. By swapping him for Geldenhuis we are making a mockery of the very principles for which he is prepared to die. I don't think Gideon would find this acceptable. I'm not at all sure I do either.' Peekay's voice trailed off, full of emotion.

'You'd have made an excellent God, Peekay,' Hymie laughed. Then he turned to Tandia. 'I am going to take the position of Solomon; hear all the evidence first and then capitalise on it. Your turn next, Tandy?'

Tandia sat with her shoes off and her legs curled up under her. 'I don't share Peekay's respect for the law. But then I have never seen it operate so that the scales of justice gave me and my kind an equal weighting. Frankly, the law stinks! I use it because, though a blunt and stupid weapon, it is the only one we have – the country of the blind where the one-eyed man is king. My other choice would be to do what Gideon is . . . was doing. And you both know that I've thought more than once about that! All my life I have seen evil triumph over good. Even when we win a case against the state it isn't because justice has triumphed, or good has beaten evil, it's because our proof is so overwhelming that the state can't afford to be shown up for what it is, or some corrupt or incompetent magistrate or judge will be exposed – and that's only when, despite the best efforts of the bench, we manage to get away with a jury who don't suffer from collective brain damage. From where I sit, hate always wins! Always! Geldenhuis's hate beats me, beats you, beats Gideon! The only way we're going to destroy his kind – and that means the white racist regime in South Africa – is by using the same weapon they use, hate and fear! It's the only thing they understand! But to do this we need leaders who are prepared to take up arms and wage a relentless and ceaseless war of attrition until the last racist is burned out of the system. Gideon Mandoma is a charismatic leader who can get the people behind him and he's not afraid to take up arms, not afraid to kill! For once the black people have a leader who doesn't want to sit on the *indaba* mat and talk platitudinous crap with the hairy backs! If we manage to get a murder conviction against Geldenhuis, and even that isn't certain, all we do is create a vacancy for the next bastard from the queue stretching from Pretoria to Cape Town! Quite apart from Gideon being my loving friend, my country cannot afford to lose him. You can stick your principles, Peekay. I want him released so we can wage war!'

Tandia was shaking by the time she was finished and very close to tears. She had never spoken like this in her life before. All her life her hurt and her hate had been folded up and locked away inside her heart.

Peekay wasn't surprised. Tandia's uncompromising feelings were no less rigid than those of Gert or Colonel Smit and he told himself he had no right to expect that they should be.

'Phew!' Hymie said. 'And you, Tandia Patel, would have made an excellent Old Testament prophet! I think I'm going to have a good brandy after that. Will you join me?'

Tandia attempted a smile, though she was still somewhat overwrought. 'Yes please, Hymie, I need it more than you do!' She was conscious that she might have alienated Peekay, even lost his affection, and she felt a stab of actual pain in her breast at the thought of this. But, for the first time in her life, she'd spoken the burning in her belly, she'd released the fist that clamped her heart, she'd let the hate surface. More than this, she'd shouted it. She had opened the doors of the dark little room and spread the carefully folded sheets of her hate out so that they billowed in the wind. Hate was the driving force which had kept her going through the years of despair and misery, through the deaths of Juicey Fruit Mambo and of Mama Tequila; now, at last, she'd articulated the source of her power and she felt suddenly whole and strong.

Hymie handed Tandia a brandy balloon and Tandia brought it up to her lips. The sharp, bright fumes of the brandy struck her nostrils and then she felt the warm glow expand throughout her breast as she took the first sip. Even brandy tastes better, she thought to herself. She ventured a glance at Peekay who sat with his eyes downcast. She was in love with a dreamer, an impossible dreamer. He actually believed in good as a force, despite everything, he still believed. How did he do that? Tandia didn't know whether to laugh or to cry, all she knew was that she loved him and that, curiously, she could keep her love in a separate compartment to her hate, that both could co-exist within her.

'Well, we're in trouble. We're split. My task is to convince one of you to change your mind,' Hymie said, coming to sit on the arm of the leather couch beside Tandia. He looked into the brandy balloon as he started to speak, as though he saw within it a truth he was about to pronounce. 'I think you're both missing the point,' he said quietly. 'We have been placed in a position which will decide the lives of two men. That pompous idiot Cogsweel was right in one thing, our chances are almost nil in terms of saving Gideon from the gallows. If he is found guilty of treason, as he almost certainly will be, there can be only one result. Our case against Geldenhuis, despite what Pretoria may try to do, is strong enough to get a conviction, particularly if we've got the world media watching. In other words, if things remain as they are, two men are going to die. Or, if we agree to the swap, two men remain alive.' Hymie looked up from the brandy balloon. 'Don't you see? We've been given the power over life and death! Don't think of these two lives as belonging to Mandoma and Geldenhuis, a freedom fighter and a cruel, corrupt member of the secret police. See them as two men, any two men. We are being asked to sentence them to death or release them. Can we honestly put on the black cap and pronounce sentence so as not to damage the precious principle of natural justice? In the end natural justice has to exist in the hearts of man! That means in my heart, your heart, Peekay and yours, Tandy! It doesn't begin in a society, it begins with each of us. Is Mama Tequila's death paid for if Geldenhuis dies? If my father had died, would I feel recompensed when they strung Jannie Geldenhuis up on a piece of rope? I don't think so!' Hymie gulped at his brandy and then continued, 'When the British liberated the death camp at Dachau they found scribbled on one of the latrine walls these words, *Together since the world began, the madman and the lover.* The concept that we can prevent murder by murdering is barbaric and strains the quality of natural justice so that it is rendered useless! I violently disagree with Tandia's point of view, though I think I can understand it. I know a great many Jews feel the same way about the German people. But, Peekay, I cannot reconcile *your* justice with the qualities of mercy and compassion, which are surely the very cornerstones of natural justice? If we make the decision not to make the swap between these two nameless men, we deny the very principle on which your case rests. Our choice is not between justice or tyranny; it is far more fundamental, we must choose between the madman and the lover in each of us.'

The room was very quiet for what seemed like a long time, then Peekay looked up. 'I agree,' he said simply.

Hymie walked over and kissed his friend on the brow. Then he brightened suddenly. 'Why don't you both sleep here tonight? Tandia, you can get up early and take a taxi home. I have a special reason.' He paused and then pronounced the single word, 'kippers'. He turned back to Peekay. 'I've had half a dozen of the loathsome creatures flown out from Fortnum & Mason as a special treat.' He turned to explain to Tandia. 'They're a predilection he learned from Doris with the wonderful tits and I'm even willing to have the whole place stink for days. After all, what are friends for, if they can't tolerate the odd *really* nasty habit between each other?' Hymie grinned, and Tandia knew that what he was telling her, despite having heard how she felt, was that he loved her.

'What are kippers?' she asked.

Peekay looked at her. 'Taken together with eggs and tomatoes, the ultimate breakfast experience. If you will share my kippers, Tandy, all is forgiven!'

FORTY-THREE

The one good thing about escaping from custody with police permission is that you don't have to run for your life expecting a bullet in your back. Gideon escaped from the police kwela-kwela which was taking him from Pretoria Prison to court (or that's what they told him on the morning). He hadn't been told of the plan and was more than a little confused when the police van stopped and appeared to be making a complicated turn in a narrow road, moving back and forwards several times before coming to a halt in an opposite direction.

He could smell dust in the interior of the van and the scrunch of tyres told him they were off the tarred road. Next he heard the rattle of the chain as the back doors were unlocked, flinging bright daylight into the dark van.

'Get out, *maak gou, jong!*' a white police officer ordered.

'What for?' Gideon asked, remaining seated.

'*Uit, kaffir!*'

Gideon looked out of the back of the van to see they'd pulled up on a lonely dirt road, in what looked a little like a kloof, for there was a krans rising steeply on either side of the road which stretched back to the end of two koppies then turned abruptly to the left.

They're going to kill me, was his first thought as he sheltered his eyes, stooping and stepping out into the blinding December morning.

'What are you going to do?' he asked querulously, convinced he was experiencing the final minutes of his life.

'Here, man.' A second officer handed him the large padlock lock from the back door of the van, 'hold this so your fingerprints are on it, make sure, also your thumb, okay?'

'What are you going to do?' Gideon asked again, taking the lock in his 'cuffed hands and doing as the officer required.

The officer took back the lock carefully and placed it hanging open on the hasp. 'Okay, fuck off kaffir!' the first police officer instructed.

'Then you will shoot me!' Gideon cried.

'You escaping officially, man! Go on, *voetsek*!' The officer pointed down the dirt road with a sweep of his hand.

Gideon held up his hands showing his handcuffs. If he was going to die he wanted to die unshackled. 'Can you make loose my hands, please? You can put them back after you have killed me,' he said to the policeman.

'No way, man! You can't escape with your hands free, it's not right if you got no handcuffs on, it makes the police look blerrie silly. Now run, jong! Or I bring the sjambok, you hear?'

'How can I pick the lock and escape when I'm wearing handcuffs?' Gideon asked sensibly.

'Hey! You trying to be cheeky, kaffir?' The second officer stepped forward, his face menacing, his forefinger held under Gideon's nose. Gideon backed away, then turned suddenly and started to run down the road, zigzagging frantically, expecting the bullet in his back any moment. But all he heard were the two policemen laughing. He couldn't leave the road; the rocky slopes on either side of it would have slowed him down and made him a sitting duck as he attempted to climb to safety.

'Hey, kaffir! You drunk or something?' Peekay stepped into the middle of the road, grinning broadly. Gideon looked fearful; there was no recognition on his face, his memory was smudged with fear. He glanced backwards to see the police van pulling away, moving in the opposite direction. 'Whoa!' Peekay caught him at the same moment as his mind snapped out of panic. The two men embraced, Gideon panting frantically, his head on Peekay's shoulder. 'I see you, my brother,' Peekay said, patting Gideon on the back as though he was a small child who needed comforting.

Gideon pulled away at last. 'I don't know . . . how is it . . . this thing . . . Peekay?' he said in English, gasping out the words.

They reached the car and Peekay opened the door on the passenger side, taking a pair of bolt cutters from the floor. 'I hope to hell I know how to use these things. The guy in the hardware shop showed me, but I couldn't exactly explain to him why I wanted them. So here goes!' With some trouble Peekay finally managed to remove the handcuffs and, placing them in the glove compartment, said, 'We'll throw them into a river somewhere.'

Gideon rubbed his wrists, 'When I'm prime minister, remind me not to make you Minister for Industry!' They both fell about laughing, their tension escaping like a suddenly punctured inner-tube.

'There's a cold chicken, some fruit and two cokes on the back seat. Help yourself, I even brought paper napkins!'

They drove directly to Swaziland crossing the border at Havelock where they showed the travel permits Peekay had obtained in Johannesburg. After this simple formality they continued on down the road for about a mile when Peekay saw Julius. Despite the heat he was still in his ancient army greatcoat, standing waiting for them beside the road.

Peekay drew up beside the little man. Julius stood to rigid attention and gave the thumbs-up salute. '*Sakubona, uJenene! Amandla*! Greetings, General! Power!'

'It is twice now you have helped the people. You are now an officer in

Umkonto we Sizwe,' Gideon announced solemnly, placing his hand on Julius's shoulder.

Julius, overcome, started to cry. 'Officers don't cry!' Peekay said, trying not to laugh.

'You've lost another tooth, old man! You better be careful, you don't have too many to spare.'

'It's okay, officers in *Umkonto we Sizwe* are often toothless,' Gideon laughed.

'Usually after they've been interviewed by the Special Branch.'

Julius seemed to think this was enormously funny and cackled a great deal, though the tears continued to run down his cheeks. 'Haya, haya!' he said at last. 'The woman who shares my blanket buys only gristle, my teeth are not good fighters!' He got into the back of the car, immediately filling it with rich pungency. Then he produced a Swaziland passport from somewhere inside his army coat and handed it to Gideon. 'Your passport, General, it has also in it a visa for Tanzania.'

Gideon examined the passport which looked well used and had a number of exit stamps as well as the entry and departure stamps of several African countries. His name and picture looked as well worn as the rest of the document. It was an excellent forgery.

They stopped at Pigg's Peak for Julius to get off and catch the bus to Bulembu, back to his village. Peekay got out of the car and walked around to the boot where he removed a large box with a cellophane window forming most of the lid. It was a cashmere blanket in a brilliant scarlet. 'It is for Somojo, Julius. Last time I came with empty hands.'

'*Ngiya bonga Inkosi*,' 'Thank you, Lord. You are well remembered in the village. I am always there when you need me.'

Gideon and Peekay arrived at Matsapa airport on the outskirts of Manzini in plenty of time for the three o'clock Heron flight to Salisbury, the capital of Southern Rhodesia. Peekay handed him a ticket, several loose bank notes and a small book of travellers' cheques. The two friends embraced. 'Here we go again, my brother, *hamba kahle*, go well.'

Gideon was too moved to reply and his eyes welled up with tears. He turned and walked towards the small plane, not looking back. Even from the back he looked like a fighter. 'So long, champ,' Peekay whispered, 'keep punching, you hear?' The lump in his chest was about to burst and he hurried back to the car.

Peekay drove into Manzini to call Tandia long distance from the post office. Then he called home to Barberton to tell his mother to expect him for the night. Dum answered the phone, picking up the receiver and immediately announcing in slow monosyllabic English, 'We are very, very sorry, the missus is gone for having tea by missus . . . Oost . . . Oos . . .' She hesitated, obviously having trouble getting her tongue around the name of the lady Peekay's mother was visiting.

'Missus Oosthuisen! It's me, you silly *umFazi*!' Peekay laughed, feeling suddenly better as Dum squealed with delight at the sound of his voice.

The news of Gideon's escape would be on the evening news and he was grateful he wouldn't be in Johannesburg to deal with an over-excited press. A dose of Dee and Dum innocence was just the sort of cheer-up medicine he needed before the farce of the Geldenhuis murder trial which was to begin in two days.

The less said about the trial the better. Geldenhuis was acquitted and the judge granted his lawyers permission to sue Red for wrongful arrest. Jannie Geldenhuis was restored to his rank and was back on the job a week later. In church congregations throughout the land prayers of thanks were offered to a merciful God who had once again demonstrated that, in crucial matters, He was prepared to step in and see that the right thing was done by His children. Colonel Jannie Geldenhuis was booked for nearly a year's church appearances.

Flyspeck Mendoza was found guilty and sentenced to death, but his case exposed the slavery and brutality on many white backveld farms, and the government was forced to open an inquiry.

Just before dawn, on 15 January 1967, Peekay, Tandia and Hymie stood silently outside Pretoria Prison. As the moon began to fade and the first light appeared Peekay heard the words of Inkosi-Inkosikazi in his head. 'You can see the moon rising over Africa and you are at peace with the night, unafraid of the great demon Skokiaan, who comes to feed on the dark night, tearing its black flesh until, at last, it is finished and the new light comes to stir the sleeping herd boys and send them out to mind the lowing cattle.'

As the light came to the dark prison so came the voices of the black inmates as they began to sing their brother to his death. The marvellous voices of Africa, sometimes soft and low and sometimes thundering, carried down the cold, polished, disinfected corridors of iron as the inmates sang the hymns of praise in their cells. Then, as six o'clock approached, their voices rose in the final choruses of the *Concerto to the Great Southland*. First the Sotho, then the Ndebele, followed by the Swazi and the Shangaani, and finally the Zulu voices rose, huge and awesome as they sung the victory song of the great Shaka, using the flats of their hands to bang on the steel doors of their cells as the mighty Zulu impi had done with their feet to make the earth thunder. Then, as the hour struck, all the tribes came together, humming the glorious finale, the refrain of each of the tribes. The huge prison vibrated with the deep, haunting male voices and the wardens stood in silent awe as the kid, who had no tribe, was sung to glory by all the tribes. At six o'clock precisely, Little Flyspeck Mendoza's neck was snapped and he was torn from the tree of life.

With the star missing, and the anti-apartheid world celebrating the escape of Mandoma, the international media stayed away from the treason trial of the other five men on the truism that nobody comes to the pantomime to see the fairies. Thus the government almost achieved its aim as the trial chugged to its inevitable and prearranged ending. But on the final day the prosecution dropped a bombshell. One of the prisoners had turned state's witness and they asked permission from the bench to put him on the witness stand.

The prisoner who'd decided to sing was an ex-mine boy named Samson Mungazela, who had served as boss boy to a diamond driller on Randfontein Consolidated Mines and was the explosives expert on Gideon's team. He'd been hurt in an accident underground several years previously and had been given a job in the High Explosives Depot on the surface. It was he who had supplied Tandia and Johnny Tambourine with gelignite when Tandia visited the mine compound once a week in her capacity as free legal adviser to the migrant black mine workers.

Tandia had always parked in the same spot, reversing her beetle-backed Volkswagen into a small alley between two mine buildings which could be approached from the rear without being observed. The smuggled sticks of gelignite would then be placed under the rear seat while she was away from the car.

Tandia had never told Peekay and Hymie that she had been actively transporting explosives for *Umkonto we Sizwe* for three years, and that apart from being its first recruited female member she was the highest-ranking woman in the resistance movement.

The prosecuting barrister, a brilliant contemporary of Peekay's named Martinus Kriel, asked for permission to put Mungazela in the witness box. 'The accused has evidence, your honour, which we believe is pertinent to this trial.'

Peekay rose immediately. 'Objection, your honour, the witness has already testified to this court and my learned colleague for the prosecution has commenced the summary of the state's case against the accused.'

Tandia had passed a note to Peekay as he sat down. It said, *Object! Mungazela could implicate me!* Peekay's heart stood still. What had Tandia been involved in?

Kriel picked his words carefully. 'Your honour, we believe that by cross-examining this witness again we can prove that a member of the counsel for defence is directly implicated in a culpable way in the indictment for which we are prosecuting counsel.'

'Objection!' Peekay called. But he was hardly heard in the uproar which followed Kriel's statement.

'Order! Order!' Judge Boshoff shouted using his gavel repeatedly, but it was nearly a minute before the courtroom was brought to silence again. 'There is no need for you to object, Advocate Peekay. I will do so myself. What the counsel for the prosecution is indicating is highly irregular and should not be handled in this manner.' He turned to the jury. 'I require the jury to retire from this court until they are recalled. Both senior counsel will then approach the bench.' He brought his gavel down once again. 'This court is adjourned for fifteen minutes!'

Peekay and Kriel stood before the judge's bench. 'We will retire to my chambers for ten minutes at which time, Advocate Kriel, you had better have some answers,' Boshoff said.

'Yes your honour,' Kriel said.

'Kriel, you dirty bastard!' Peekay hissed as they followed Boshoff. 'If you had something like this on me you should have taken it to the Public Prosecutor!'

Kriel smiled, 'It's not on you, Peekay, it's on your partner!'

The judge asked them to enter and told Peekay to close the door. 'I ought to report you to the Law Society. I may still do so, Counsellor Kriel. Explain!' he demanded.

'Your honour, the police prosecutor presented us with evidence during the luncheon adjournment which implicates Peekay's colleague Miss Patel strongly in matters that could be construed as treasonable and relate directly to this case. It seemed appropriate to give notice of this in court today.'

'The police prosecutor? Was this the arresting officer Colonel Geldenhuis?'

'Yes, your honour.'

Kriel was too sure of himself, Pretoria was clearly behind him. Peekay had to play for time and try to abort Mungazela's evidence. 'Your honour, I believe my learned colleague has designed this entire affair to engender speculation. He knows this is unacceptable evidence in your court. It's a cheap shot at my colleague and I take enormous exception to it! He knows the correct procedure is to take his accusation to the public prosecutor!'

Judge Boshoff looked hard at both men. 'I am giving you until nine o'clock tomorrow morning, an hour before this court convenes. You will both of you report to me in my chambers, you hear? You, Kriel, to satisfy me that you can substantiate the testimony of your witness. And you, Peekay, to assure me that your junior counsel is not, to the best of your knowledge, involved other than as your second counsel in this trial.'

Peekay saw the tiny smirk on Kriel's face and he knew that the barrister had achieved what he'd set out to do, to give himself a little more time, and more importantly, to have the evidence against Tandia accepted at the treason trial. Geldenhuis would have his revenge.

When he and Tandia stepped out of the court fifteen minutes later, bulbs flashed everywhere and reporters crushed around them, shouting questions. Fortunately they'd both wanted to work in the car that morning so Hercules, the Red driver, had brought them to Pretoria. Now he waited for them outside the court and they were able to make their escape.

Tandia broke down in the car, not because of what she'd done, but because she'd deceived Peekay and Hymie. Gulping back tears, she told Peekay of her work as a member of *Umkonto we Sizwe.*

Peekay handed her his handkerchief. 'Tandy, dry your tears. One stick of dynamite or a thousand, it doesn't make any damn difference, the charge is still treason if it can be proved you supplied Gideon's people, your people. You're a terrorist, so the deception of both Hymie and myself is academic.'

'Peekay, you and Hymie are the only two people I've ever entirely trusted and now I've betrayed that trust,' Tandia cried.

Peekay held her hand. 'Tandia, we're all fighting for the same thing. The question now is not one of recrimination, it's whether we fight or flee. Nothing else matters. What are our chances of discrediting Samson Mungazela when I cross-examine tomorrow?'

'When you cross-examine? You're going to tell the judge in chambers I'm innocent? Peekay, if it comes out you perjured yourself it'll be the end of your legal career!'

'Tandia, listen! If there's a good chance I can get the judge to dismiss Mungazela's evidence we can kill the thing stone dead tomorrow. Jannie Geldenhuis is panicking. If he'd done this the slow way and used the proper procedures it could be a bloody sight worse.'

Tandia shook her head. 'Peekay, if Mungazela has talked, and we know he has, it couldn't be any worse. When we get into Red I'm going to have to use Hymie's clean phone to make at least ten calls, if it isn't already too late. Geldenhuis will be able to bring in fifteen, maybe twenty, men in the explosives cadre of *Umkonto*; some are going to crack, they always do! And like Samson Mungazela I'm the ace they hold, the only thing with which they can bargain. If they know Samson's confessed, why would they hold back; they don't know their collaborating evidence is the vital difference! Jannie Geldenhuis must be convinced . . .' Tandia's voice trailed off and she shivered involuntarily, though as much from disgust as fear, '. . . that he's got me on a plate.'

Hercules coughed politely. 'What is it?' Peekay asked him in Zulu.

'The police, they are following us, sir.'

Peekay didn't bother to look through the rear window. Hercules had an uncanny instinct for police. The old black man was more than a chauffeur to them all. He'd been in Solomon Levy's family since Hymie's childhood, driving Hymie to kindergarten and ever since, and finally becoming the driver for Red where he was greatly beloved.

'Hercules, listen carefully, you're going to have to go shopping when we get to Johannesburg. When you drop us at Red go straight to John Orrs.' Peekay turned to Tandia. 'Write down your shoe size for a pair of tackies, the size of jeans you wear, two shirts, a warm sweater, also a couple of changes of underwear – practical stuff, cotton, that won't rub you – enough for two days. Add three pairs of thick woollen socks. You've got toilet things in the office, haven't you? Write anything else you're going to need. Cigarettes?'

Tandia nodded and, taking a yellow legal pad from her briefcase, started to write. 'Put two blankets and two towels on the list as well,' Peekay said. Tandia didn't ask any questions; she knew there could be no possibility of going home, that all their places would be under twenty-four-hour surveillance by men from the Special Branch. Peekay was making plans for her to get away immediately. She knew he wouldn't talk in the car; Hercules wouldn't blab but he was an elderly man and, under interrogation, could break.

Peekay added a few items of food to the list and handed it to Hercules, adding a fifty-rand note with it for the food. 'Hercules, give this list to the manager and tell him to give you the stuff immediately and to put it on my account. I have written all this on the note as well. Then when you've bought the food take the car to the carpet depot and exchange it with a Solomon Levy Carpet Emporium car, but make sure it doesn't have anything written on the door. Put all the stuff in the boot and bring the car to the manhole. Make sure you fill it with petrol first. Don't go back to Red. Go straight to the manhole and be waiting at the usual place by a quarter to six tonight. Do you understand?' Peekay said all of this in Zulu.

'I understand. What sort of food do you want me to buy, baas Peekay?' Hercules asked.

'I've writ . . .' Peekay hesitated for a fraction of a second, realising Hercules didn't want to say he couldn't read. 'Get a cold chicken, some bread, salami, maybe a tin of canned peaches, Nescafe and condensed milk. Don't forget a tin opener and matches.'

'I hate salami!' Tandia said.

Peekay grinned. 'Okay, no salami, Hercules. Get a tin of bully beef, two tomatoes and an onion, also a small billycan, make it two, one for water.' He turned to Tandia, 'I'll make you Doc's favourite, you're in for a treat.'

Tandia didn't want to tell Peekay that she hated bully beef even worse than salami. The light banter had eased the tension a little and she tried to prepare her mind for what lay ahead.

Hymie was waiting for them in the boardroom when they arrived. 'Christ, the place is surrounded with cops. I've phoned home, there are a couple of guys watching the block, I imagine it's the same with your places.' He took Tandia in his arms and hugged her.

'We're going to have to get you out, Tandy.' Hymie had heard the story from a reporter on the *Star* who'd called him for comment and he'd obviously reached the same conclusion as Peekay.

Tandia nodded. 'But look, my own people can try to get me out, it's crazy for you two to be involved!'

'We are your own people, Tandy, and we are involved,' Peekay said quietly. 'If I thought you had a better chance of getting out of the country with them I'd agree for your sake, but I don't. Your face is well known and Gideon isn't here to see things go right.'

'There's no chance of an international flight, Tandy.' Jan Smuts will have been alerted. Hymie glanced at his watch. 'If we could find a private field perhaps a small plane over the border, but it's nearly four o'clock, it would be too dark to get off the ground by the time we get there. Besides, air traffic control would have been alerted. But if we can get you to Swaziland we can have a Heron waiting for you on the ground at Matsapa to fly you to Nairobi; from there you can catch a flight to London.'

Peekay glanced at his watch. 'If we leave soon we may make it to the lowveld by car, but from the Nelspruit turnoff to Barberton we can anticipate a police road block; it's a side road and the only logical place to stop traffic without disrupting a major highway.' Peekay paused, thinking. 'Geldenhuis will expect us to try to get out by light plane so he will already have covered the smaller airports but he can't put out an alert or road blocks on the national highway until we're officially wanted, which will be after you appear in court tomorrow. By that time we'll be into the mountains.'

'What about the other way through Hectorspruit, the Matsamo entrance?' Hymie asked. 'It's quicker, isn't it?'

'Too risky, I don't know where they'd put the road block and it's unfamiliar country for me if we have to try and go through the bush to get over the border. If I can get us across the de Kaap valley I can take Tandy over the mountains. It's only eighteen miles or so, but it's tough going. Tandy's unfit and not used to climbing; it may take us two days, but once we're into the high mountains, it's going to be bloody difficult for anyone to follow us.'

'Two days! Shit, Peekay, that's a long time for a city girl to be roughing it!'

Tandia laughed. 'I love the mountains, man! Juicey Fruit Mambo and I would often spend all day in the Drakensberg.'

'It's going to be a bit tougher, you didn't smoke forty cigarettes a day in those days. Hymie, there is no better place to hide, I'd rather we took a little longer and were sure, don't you reckon?'

'Well, as far as we know, Jannie Geldenhuis is no mountain man,' Hymie replied. 'Frankly I'd feel much better if Tandy was in the first-class section of the four fifteen BOAC flight to London.'

Peekay went over to the phone, called Barberton long distance and asked to speak to Colonel Smit. Smit's secretary put him through. '*Hoe gaan dit*, Peekay? What can I do for you?' he asked.

Peekay took a deep breath, hoping his voice would sound casual. 'Colonel, what I'm asking you to do tonight will be illegal by tomorrow morning.'

Smit was silent on the other end of the phone. '*Here*, Peekay, I just heard the four o'clock news on the radio.' There was a pause. 'Is it true what they saying?'

'Colonel, it's a Geldenhuis trap, a conspiracy. I need a favour.'

There was another longish pause and then Smit said, 'Peekay, tomorrow is a long time in a man's life. What is legal today is all the information a man can act on. What is it, man?'

Peekay sighed with relief. 'Colonel, could Gert meet me, us, in the prison van with half-a-dozen black warders dressed as prisoners already in the back?'

'Ja, I suppose that can be arranged, where?'

'At a small place called Schagen, it's a little railway station, about eight, ten miles up from Nelspruit.'

'Ja, I know where is Schagen. What time?'

'Around ten o'clock tonight.'

Peekay knew that Kommandant Smit and Gert would have to wrestle furiously with their consciences. Just about any way they looked at it they would see Tandia, if the allegations were true, as a traitor to their country. A black traitor. He was asking them to give aid to a terrorist. Peekay would not have been surprised if Smit refused, though he knew he'd keep his mouth shut. But he also knew he had one thing going for him. An Afrikaner with Smit or Gert's background valued and honoured friendship above all else.

'I will ask Gert, Peekay,' Smit said, then paused for a moment. 'If he won't do it, I'll be waiting for you at Schagen tonight, son.'

'Thank you, Colonel.'

Smit's voice came back over the line. 'Peekay, you're a bloody fool, you hear? Don't do it, man! You are risking your life for a kaffir girl!'

'No, Colonel, for a friend,' Peekay said softly and hung up.

Next he called home and spoke to his mother briefly. Then, somewhat to her chagrin, he asked to speak to one of the twins.

'You know, I sometimes think you love them more than your own mother, son,' she said in a hurt voice.

'Mum, it's just a bit of business.' He heard the receiver being put down and his mother calling. A minute or so later Dee, breathing heavily from having run, answered. 'You are coming to see us, ja?' she asked in Shangaan, her excitement coming through.

'Listen Dee, I can't explain, but pack my rucksack as if I was going away for two days into the mountains. Put in everything for a high climb. Also my boots and mountain clothes. Don't forget the medicine box and the square torch, the one that fits on my belt. Then both of you meet me at four o'clock tomorrow morning at *Itshe Ingulube*, where you used to turn back for home when you came with me part way into the mountains.'

'There is something wrong, Peekay. I can feel it, my skin is sore with your trouble. There is something wrong, you must tell me!' Dee repeated, her voice was urgent.

'No, Dee, just do as I say. Meet me at the place we named Pig Rock before dawn. The path is good up to that point and you can use the torch in the dark. Oh, and bring extra drinking water! I must go now, I'll see you in the morning. Go well, Dee!' Peekay put down the receiver and turned to Tandia. 'I think we ought to be going soon.'

Peekay had anticipated Geldenhuis pretty accurately, the policeman had indeed assumed that they would attempt to get Tandia out by light plane, though, in case they tried the obvious, he had his men alerted at Jan Smuts Airport. Before Kriel had even stood up in court he had men headed for every private or municipal airport within a hundred miles of Johannesburg. Flight Control had been alerted to report any private or small aircraft flying out of the Transvaal, Natal or the Orange Free State filing a flight plan which took them within fifty miles of any South African border.

He'd also anticipated the Swaziland plan and had arranged for road blocks from 6 o'clock in the evening onwards, three miles into the Barberton turn-off from Nelspruit and two miles out of Hectorspruit on the road to the border post. Though it seemed unlikely that Peekay would choose any of the further six entrances into Swaziland he'd nevertheless alerted the local border police at each of them.

He'd done the same thing for Basutoland and Bechuanaland. The border into Rhodesia and Portuguese territory was already well guarded and here he'd simply issued an alert. This time Jannie Geldenhuis believed he had Tandia boxed in, trapped at Red or within the confines of the city or Soweto. Three police cars surrounded the block ready to tail her should she leave the building. All these precautions may have seemed over-elaborate but he knew Peekay was as clever as trick shit and he wasn't taking any chances.

Geldenhuis cursed himself for not having done the initial interviews with the Treason Six. But because of his suspension from the case after his own arrest, he only got back to the prisoners after his acquittal and Gideon's escape. He quickly saw his mark among the five remaining prisoners; it was the kaffir with the withered arm, Samson Mungazela, who seemed to lack the resolve of the others and responded a lot quicker to pain. When he implicated Tandia, Geldenhuis quite simply thought all his Christmases had come at once. He had the kaffir girl at last! Now all he had to do was get her boyfriend!

Samson Mungazela also spilled a dozen other names and Geldenhuis followed this up with four arrests within hours; by dawn, after a little physical persuasion, he had collaborating evidence from two of his suspects, which was all he needed. He was confident that Tandia would be forced into court in the morning where the world would witness her humiliation and also see Peekay's reactions as Kriel tore his girlfriend to pieces in the witness box.

Peekay and Tandia left Red five minutes apart, walking under the coverway across the rear courtyard into the tiny storage shed and down into the storm water drain below. Both of them were dressed in the white overalls of the Johannesburg municipal maintenance workers. Ten minutes later they emerged onto a back street two blocks from Red and walked to a vacant building lot where Hercules sat in an unmarked brown Chrysler sedan.

The evening traffic was heavy all the way along the Rand to Pretoria and Tandia hid on the back seat with a blanket covering her. They repeated this performance through every small town they went through until they reached the tiny deserted station at Schagen at a quarter to ten that night and parked the car under a large kaffirboom tree. A few minutes later they heard a truck slowing down as it turned off the highway and changed up from low gear as it gathered speed again. A couple of minutes later the prison van loomed up and drew to a halt beside them.

Both Colonel Smit and Gert got out, though only Gert was in uniform. They could hear the black warders chatting in the back of the van and Gert shouted to them to shut up. Peekay greeted his two friends quietly as they shook hands, indicating Tandia who stood a little apart. It was bright moonlight and she could see the two men quite clearly. To Peekay's surprise they both stepped up to her and shook her by the hand. '*Goeienaand, Tandia,*' Smit said formally while Gert, smiling easily, took Tandia's hand.

Tandia smiled. '*Baie dankie,*' she said simply, thanking the two officers for coming. She had changed into jeans and blouse and wore the new socks and sand-shoes Hercules had bought for her, putting the suit she'd worn in court into the boot.

Peekay still wore his business suit, though he'd removed the jacket. It was almost a full moon and the subtropical evening was warm, but he knew that towards dawn it would get very cold and he'd added his jacket to the stuff they'd piled onto the hood of the car to take with them.

'You were right, Peekay, there's a road block about three miles in along the Barberton road. They're Nelspruit guys, but none of the police we know, probably Special Branch.' Gert said in an undertone. 'We stopped and talked a bit; they're stopping all incoming traffic.' He glanced over at Tandia. 'They know who they looking for and showed us a magazine picture.'

'Okay, let's get going, man. You never know what eyes are around, even in the dark. Where are we taking you?' Smit asked.

'Gert knows, Colonel. To the farm, Eendrag, you know Magistrate Coetzee's old farm.'

Gert opened the back of the large van, shining his torch into the interior where half-a-dozen black warders dressed in prison uniform sat. They immediately stood up as the doors opened, grinning into the torchlight.

Gert explained to them that if the van was stopped by the police and opened they were to stand up and conceal the presence of Tandia. To Peekay's enormous surprise, he used the name *Onoshobishobi Ingelosi*. There was a murmur of amazement from the men at the mention of the mystical Peekay, who was the special legacy of Barberton prison.

No more than about twenty minutes after they'd left, driving down the escarpment into the valley which Doc had named 'God's toe print,' the van slowed and drew to a halt. The men in the back of the van stood up immediately, pushing Tandia and Peekay to the back of the cabin end where they crouched. They heard a voice say in Afrikaans, 'Police!'

Then Gert saying, 'Ja, we saw you before coming out.'

Then the second voice again, 'No, man, we the new shift. You from Barberton prison?'

'Ja, ten prisoners from the lock-up in Nelspruit. A fight in the location over a shebeen woman. Kaffirs are crazy, man!'

'We'll have to look,' the policeman said. Peekay held Tandia's hand, squeezing it in the dark. The sound of his heart seemed to fill the whole van. He pulled Tandia close to him so that her body touched his and he felt her trembling.

'What for! Don't be blerrie ridiculous, the kaffirs in there are some of them still drunk!' Smit said.

'This is Colonel Smit, our kommandant,' Gert said, then added, 'We don't want a shooting, man! Kaffirs like this are dangerous.' He paused 'Here, you open it!' Gert must have offered the keys to the back of the van to the police officer.

There was a pause; then a second voice, one they hadn't heard before said, 'What's going on here?'

'I've got ten kaffirs in the back, they been arrested after a fight in the Crocodile River valley native location and they mostly still drunk. If you want to open the back, sergeant, you better take your gun, you know what kaffirs are like when they been drinking skokiaan!'

There was a sudden banging on the side of the van and Tandia nearly fainted, but it came from the inside. 'Haja! Policeman! *Buya lapa!* Come here!' one of the black men in the van shouted and the others all laughed and began to bang on the side, shouting obscenities. Moments later the van pulled away and after a short while the men all sat down again convulsed with laughter and congratulating Peekay on his magic as they all chatted on happily. A few miles further on they heard a hand banging against the back of the driver's cabin; it was Colonel Smit telling Peekay they were approaching the turn-off to Eendrag.

'We must go soon, my brothers,' Peekay said to the men in the van. 'I thank you for what you have done and my ancestors thank you also.' They all responded, 'Haya, *Onoshobishobi Ingelosi*, it is a great honour.' Then one of them, starting slowly, began the first high single note that begins the chant to the Tadpole Angel, when the boss boy in a gang calls them to the song. He held the note which deepened down and down as it neared its end until it vibrated in the back of the prison van. Then the voices of the others came in to pick up the first words of the chant. Soon the van was filled with the haunting melody of the great fighter who came for the people.

The van stopped and Peekay and Tandia got out while the men still sang. Then their leader called them to a final chorus and their voices ended with a sudden thud, an expulsion of air from deep within their chests as though a hundred picks had hit the ground at the same time.

They stood in the moonlight, the two Afrikaners, the coloured, the rooinek and the black men, all the colours of Africa for one moment in perfect harmony. Colonel Smit shook Peekay's hand, then suddenly the huge man embraced him, pulling the little welterweight into his chest. 'My God, little *boetie*, be careful!' As quickly as he'd held him he let him go, his voice tight with emotion.

Gert took Peekay's hand. 'Go quickly into the mountains, Peekay. I'll only feel safe when I know you're up past the foothills.' He squeezed Peekay's shoulder, 'You the best, you hear?' Peekay was too overwhelmed to speak, but it wasn't necessary for him to say anything; they both knew how he felt.

The two men both shook Tandia's hand, wishing her luck. She wondered what was really going on in their heads. They so obviously loved Peekay that the fact that she was placing him in danger must have made them feel enormous animosity towards her. But they showed none of this to her. Both men climbed quickly into the van and with a scrunch of tyres they pulled off the shoulder of the road and went on their way. The back of the van was now open and the men called, '*Hamba kahle, Inkosi, Inkosazana.* Go well, my Lord and Princess.' Peekay and Tandia watched until they could no longer see the tiny wink of the red tail-lights and then turned down the dirt road leading to Eendrag half a mile away.

The bushveld lay silver in the bright moonlight and they could hear the sound of the river in the distance, where it took a bend and the water flowed over rock to make the rapids. Tandia had only been here once, she'd not even come down when the old man had left the property to Peekay in trust for her. But now as they walked up the rutted road, each on a tyre path with the grass on the centre island grown high and almost to their waists, she felt as though she was coming home.

They passed the burned-down cottage where the walls stood naked and sheets of twisted corrugated iron collapsed inwards, like a toy box filled with untidy bits and pieces. They continued over the small rise and there stood Tandia's ghosted house of Africa against the ridge, its white gables and the sweep of the steps leading up to it clear in the moonlight. As they approached she smelt the moonflower blossoms and the frangipani which hung in the still air as if to perfume her arrival home. They climbed the steps and stood on the stoep looking out at the silver ribbon of river where, in the moonlight, the water turned white as it took the wide bend and turned into the rapids. Tandia, who was running for her life, had suddenly never felt safer. Peekay stood at her side and Africa was all around her, clean and perfect. Calm flooded her and seemed to invade the very bones in her body. Though the African night was filled with sounds, it was also perfectly still. Peekay, as though instinctively understanding, turned and took her in his arms. His mouth closed over hers. After what seemed like her whole life he lifted his head. 'Tandia, I love you,' he said.

Tandia suddenly wanted this man with a fierceness that physically hurt. It was a feeling she'd never experienced and it rushed into her hands. The calmness of the moments before Peekay had taken her into his arms was gone; now an urgency grew in her as she tore at her blouse and then her jeans. Tandia made no attempt to calm the feeling within her, or to delay in getting her clothes off and then helping Peekay to remove his own. She pulled at his shirt, breaking a button as the others came loose. Around his neck he wore a leather thong with a small bag attached to it that she'd never seen before. Getting his shirt off, even though he was attempting to help her, almost brought her to panic, as though the moment would pass and she'd be left with nothing. Peekay spread the blankets they'd brought and suddenly he lay with her and was loving her, his lips moving over her, his hands urgent and caring, trying to gather up all of her at once. Then he was inside her and she rose up and was carried away, floating on the perfumed air over the distant rapids which roared white water over rock. Then they were quiet again; she lay perfectly still, perfectly silent, bathed in the perfume of frangipani and moonflowers in the shining African night. Tandia cried softly and Peekay kissed her tears and held her and sssh'd her, kissing the lids of her eyes until he'd magicked her into a deep exhausted sleep.

FORTY-FOUR

At about the same time as Gert and Colonel Smit were turning the prison van into the short road leading to Schagen station Jannie Geldenhuis left John Vorster Square and went home. The police colonel was dog-tired; he'd been interrogating the four black men they'd brought in that afternoon. He badly needed sleep and when a report came through at half past nine that the lights were still burning in the Red boardroom he was confident he'd won the first round and forced Tandia and Peekay to appear before Justice Swart in the morning.

At a quarter past four in the morning Geldenhuis was awakened by Koekemoer, the duty sergeant on the phone. 'Sir, we have a report in from the Nelspruit police.'

Geldenhuis was instantly awake. 'Ja, quick, what?'

'They've found a brown sixty-five Chrysler with "TJ" plates parked at a place called Schagen, which is a small railway station about eight or ten miles before you get to Nelspruit.'

'Have they forced it, looked inside, checked the registration?'

'We've done that, sir. It's registered to the Solomon Levy Carpet Emporium.'

'Shit!' Geldenhuis cried.

'They've forced the boot and discovered a woman's skirt and jacket and high-heeled shoes. It seems pretty certain. The suit fits the description of the stuff Tandia Patel was wearing in court today, I mean, yesterday.'

'They may have transferred to another vehicle. Have you checked the road block on the Barberton road?'

'Yes, sir, every vehicle coming in since six o'clock last night has been stopped and searched.'

'I'm coming in. What's the time? Okay, it will be light by six o'clock, call Police Air Command. I want a Piper Cherokee with pilot on standby and cleared for take-off to Barberton by seven o'clock. Call the Barberton police. No, don't! That whole fucking town thinks Peekay is Jesus Christ! Call Nelspruit, it's only thirty miles away, they can make it in plenty of time.'

Geldenhuis had made his first big mistake. He was a city boy and he'd assumed that two towns so close and both in the lowveld would share the same sort of environment. But Barberton is a mountain town, its topography quite different from the savannah grasslands and undulating hills of the Nelspruit area. He was recruiting a bunch of plainsmen for territory that even mountain men respect. 'Tell the senior officer I want ten men, if they've got them, and a sergeant, all white and fit and fully armed; also a good kaffir tracker, explain they're going to be climbing, to wear fatigues. If they've got dogs, bring them also, we can let them get a scent off the clothes *the terrorist* left in the car.' Geldenhuis no longer referred to Tandia by her name but by the words *the terrorist*, in the same way as a hunter might refer to '*the lion*': she was something he was hunting to kill. Her personality dimensions no longer existed for him; his task was to destroy her. In his mind she was already dead meat. 'What time did they find the car?' he asked.

The sergeant was reluctant to tell Geldenhuis the truth, but his superior always found out. 'Just after midnight, Colonel.'

'What? And you called me now! Four hours later?' Geldenhuis was suddenly furious, 'Jesus fucking Christ, Koekemoer! We could have been in Barberton by now!'

'Colonel! The call came through the main switch and wasn't transferred to the operations room. I didn't know about it! They filed it for your morning report.'

'They? Who? Find out who took the message!'

'I've done that already, Colonel. Officer Stoffel Vermaak. He came onto the switchboard on the eleven o'clock shift and didn't read his standing instructions until just before I called you.'

'Put him on report, he's a boxer isn't he? Yes, that's right, a middle. Still, put him on report! Bladdy idiots like that don't belong in the police force! I'll be in in forty minutes. Call off the other road blocks. Jesus no! Don't do that! The car near Nelspruit could be a decoy. Call Nelspruit again, tell them to put a road block on the Havelock road, halfway up between Barberton and the Swaziland border. If they say it's not their district, tell them we've cleared it in Pretoria.' Geldenhuis changed the subject. 'Has Hymie Levy left Red?'

'Yes, Colonel. We followed his Mercedes home about midnight. We have people in the front and back of his place and the car is still parked underneath the building.'

'Jesus, how much does that mean? You had people front and back of Red and Peekay and *the terrorist* managed to walk out under your bladdy noses! What about the driver, what's his name, Hercules?'

'We haven't seen him since he dropped the two of them off at Red at fourteen hundred hours yesterday.'

'Check his home, I don't remember his surname. If he isn't home, bring him in when he gets in.'

Sergeant Koekemoer was surprised, it wasn't like Jannie Geldenhuis to forget the surname of the Red chauffeur, Hercules. The police colonel was so well versed in the three Red partners and every circumstance of their daily lives; forgetting the surname of the black man who drove them regularly was definitely not a good sign.

Koekemoer worshipped Jannie Geldenhuis and was, perhaps, the only person in the police force who did. He was worried about him. Lately, Geldenhuis had complained occasionally of a headache and hadn't seemed quite as sharp. He hadn't been near the boxing ring, or even into the police gym since his acquittal. It was as though the anger in him, which these days always seemed at the point of boiling over, was clouding his judgement. Increasingly he'd lash out violently and several black prisoners had died at his hands before they'd confessed. Which wasn't like him at all.

Geldenhuis came back on the line. 'One last thing. Make a note to call a guy named Cogsweel in Pretoria at eight o'clock. I want authority to talk to the army base commander at Komaatipoort. His number is in the code book in central security, I'll phone through now and give them my clearance number.' Geldenhuis slammed the receiver down. Peekay woke Tandia at half past three in the morning. She tried to sit up but discovered she'd been wrapped in a cocoon of blankets. The moon was still bright in the sky and there was as yet no sense of the coming morning. Peekay unwrapped her blankets. 'It's very cold, Tandy, put on your sweater when you dress.' Tandia realised with surprise that she was naked and clung to a blanket, pulling it up over her breasts as she sat up. Peekay laughed. 'Too late for that, darling. You are quite the most beautiful woman in the world anyway, you shouldn't be allowed to wear clothes!'

'You're supposed to love me for my brains, Counsellor!'

Peekay knelt down beside her and kissed her gently. 'But I do! Good morning, beloved Tandia. Your brains, body and spirit, all of you, I love with a deep passion.'

Tandia couldn't quite believe she'd made love! Physically loving Peekay had played no part in her romancescape. Physical love wasn't an aspect of her life she cared to remember. With the exception of Gideon, her body had only ever been violated by a man. Now, inexplicably, all that had changed.

'Peekay, last night was? We did . . .? I'm not still asleep?'

Peekay kissed her again. 'No, but you've got to get up, we have to be gone in half an hour.' He rose, turned and walked over to the end of the stoep where Tandia was surprised to see the embers of a small fire. He returned moments later with a small billycan which smelled of onions. Tandia was ravenous, she hadn't eaten since the luncheon adjournment the previous day. 'No plates! Hercules remembered a spoon and a fork, two tin mugs, but no plates.'

Tandia ate from the can, a mixture of bully beef, tomato and onions. She hated bully beef, but the concoction Peekay had prepared for her was delicious. Perhaps being in love makes you like bully beef, she thought. She ate half the contents of the can and handed it to Peekay.

'No, please, finish it! I ate during the night, cold chicken. There's still some left, would you prefer it?' Tandia shook her head, getting stuck into the remaining bully beef with gusto. 'There's a small running stream behind the house, get dressed, you can wash and I'll put on water for coffee.'

By the time Tandia returned from the stream the sky in the east was beginning to show the faintest indication of light, a narrow strip against the horizon, as though the night had developed a silver rind. Peekay handed her a mug of coffee, white and sweetened with condensed milk. Putting his arm around Tandia, he pointed to a star just above the horizon. 'See the big star on the horizon, that's the morning star. As a kid I would sometimes wake up just before dawn and frantically climb the path up the hill behind our house and sit on a big rock at the top and wait to see if I could see the exact moment when the morning star went out. But I never could. I'd watch and watch until my eyes started to water. Then always, when I couldn't stand it any more and blinked, when I looked again it was gone!' Peekay laughed softly, 'But it was back again the next day, squatting there just above the horizon and due east, always in the same spot waiting to disappear on me again. I used to think it knew all about me and was playing a game it was very good at and which it was determined I would never win.'

'Peekay, do you think one day we can rebuild this house and you and I could live here in a South Africa where it isn't a crime for a black woman to be terribly in love with a white guy?'

Peekay turned Tandia towards him and pulled her into his chest, almost spilling her coffee. 'If I didn't think that, Tandy, I don't think I'd want to live. I don't want to make our life in England. We are African, this is where the sweetness and the bitterness lies for us. This land has been sick for so long I sometimes think it will never recover, that the sickness is terminal. But I know it will. My nanny, Gideon's mother, used to say, "There is a season for sorrow and then it will pass." When it passes we'll come back and restore this house; like the beloved country it has solid foundations. It will be our house, the house for all Africa.' He kissed her again.

It was nice hearing the words. Tandia could almost believe them when Peekay spoke them. Dreamers are like that, they can make you believe things. They believe the morning star is playing with them. She found it was nice believing, even easy, if only for these few moments.

Peekay pushed her gently from him, his tone lighter as he spoke. 'Okay, kid, let's kick the dust. It's half an hour's walk to where Dee and Dum are meeting us; drink your coffee and let's vamoose!' He stooped down and, picking up a blanket, started to fold it, gripping the edge of the blanket in his mouth and bringing the two ends together.

Dee and Dum were waiting for them when, just after half past four, they arrived at Pig Rock. It had been light for twenty minutes but was still cold, the early sunlight not yet bright enough to warm them. The twins saw them coming and ran squealing to meet them, each of them grabbing Peekay by a hand and dancing about him like young girls, though they were women in their mid thirties. 'Stop!' Peekay said laughing, 'Where are your manners? This is Tandia, who I have talked to you about many times.'

Dee and Dum stopped and turned to Tandia, both held their arms out and they hugged her simultaneously. The gesture was one of total openness and generosity; they were including her into their circle, for they instinctively guessed that Peekay loved this beautiful woman. 'Welcome, our sister,' they said simultaneously, as though they'd rehearsed the line. But Peekay knew it wasn't rehearsed; he'd seen them do it all their lives, as if they shared a collective brain, or at least a connected one. He doubted very much if the two girls could exist apart from each other for more than a few hours, though he couldn't remember them ever apart for even this long.

Tandia liked them immediately; she was amazed by the process of falling in love. She found that she was able to let her defences down and allow the warmth of Dee and Dum to come straight through to her. It was like a rebirth.

'Thank you, my sisters,' she said, hugging them back.

'Come on, you silly *izaLukazi*! Tandy and me must be gone, the sun will be high in a minute. Where are my mountain clothes?'

'We have brought everything. More than you asked!'

'We can't carry more. We have to travel light. Tandy isn't accustomed to the mountains.'

'That is why we are coming,' Dee said.

Peekay looked stern. 'No, Dee, you can't!'

Dee stood directly in Peekay's path, her legs firmly planted, slightly apart, arms folded. She seemed suddenly like a big woman, though he could never remember ever seeing her like this. Dum now stood beside her, unconsciously striking the same pose. 'You are in danger! You who belong to us, who is our flesh and our heartblood, you cannot tell us a lie!' Dum cried.

'No, you cannot tell us a lie. It is in our skin, it is hurting us all over!' Dee said and both of them started to rub their folded arms and roll their shoulders, moaning softly.

'We will carry for you!' Dum said suddenly. She pointed at Tandia. 'Tandy is beautiful, but she has no legs for the mountains. Her ankles, look at them, pfft! They could snap like a chicken bone! If she falls, if she hurts her leg, who will carry her?'

Peekay had to admit they had a point. Tandia was both unfit and unaccustomed to the sort of climbing they would need to do. The likelihood of her spraining her ankle or falling was considerable. Peekay knew the twins could walk all day, that even if they had to carry Tandia in a stretcher, they'd make it over the top.

'What about the missus?' Peekay asked, thinking of his mother's objections.

'We have written a letter!' Dee spoke in English, 'Gon wun day missus pliz, Dee, Dum,' she said proudly, repeating the exact words in the note they'd left for his mother.

'She will be angry,' Dum added, 'but you are our heartblood! There is danger in our kraal, we *must* be with you.'

'Okay!' Peekay said, making his mind up suddenly. If they could distribute the weight between them so that Tandia carried nothing they would make better time and there would be less likelihood of her injuring herself.

The twins wiped tears away, dabbing their eyes with identical gestures, as though they'd been choreographed. 'Thank you, Peekay,' they said, their voices soft and loving, 'we will protect you.'

Peekay loved them both fiercely, but now he frowned, hiding his feelings. 'Now! Where are my mountain clothes?' He looked down with distaste at the rumpled grey pinstripe lawyer's suit he was wearing.

'They are on the Pig Rock,' both girls shouted.

Peekay went up to the rock to find his mountain clothes laid out on it, his old shirt and khaki pants ironed and starched. His anorak too had been washed within an inch of its life with precise creases down the centre of both sleeves. His thick grey socks were laid side by side, lined up perfectly with both toes pointing in the same direction. His climbing boots were waterproofed with fresh dubbin and his old khaki cloth hat, torn and mended a hundred times also bore the signs of having been starched and ironed. Even his belt and the worn and scuffed sheath of his hunting knife were polished. He climbed into the clothes which were not uncomfortable despite the liberal starching they'd received, but he felt stupidly neat in the perfectly creased khaki trousers which had been patched in a dozen places.

The girls took the blankets Peekay had brought along and quickly redistributed the stuff in Peekay's rucksack plus the provisions they'd brought, folding the blankets around it so that they ended up with two neat bundles tied at the top. These they lifted to their heads, where they balanced easily, leaving their hands free. Peekay's rucksack now contained only his mountain gear, spikes, climbing hammer, and small axe as well as a torch and Doc's battered binoculars. Hanging over the top of his rucksack was a coil of rope. It all felt light and comfortable as they set out.

Peekay allowed Dee and Dum to set the pace, placing Tandia between them. They were both experienced bush walkers, accustomed to the mountain terrain and would set a pace which would allow Tandia to continue far longer without a rest than if he attempted to do the same thing. By the end of the day they would have travelled further than if he tried to hurry them along the easy bits and nurse Tandia up the steeper slopes. Mountain climbing is like digging; you end up with a deeper hole if you go at it at a steady pace.

By half past six they were over the foothills and about to begin the climb into the high mountains. Tandia had kept up well, but Peekay could see she was tired and needed a rest. Dee and Dum seemed simultaneously to reach the same decision for they stopped. Dee took a thermos of tea out of a bundle and Dum a flask of water and a couple of cups. She poured water for Tandia first, filling the tin mug. 'Drink it all, Tandy. You have lost much water already.'

Tandia drank gratefully and handed the empty cup back to Dum. 'Thank you, Dee,' she said.

Dum held the mug out allowing Dee to fill it with hot, sweet tea. She handed it to Tandia, 'I am Dum,' she said.

'I will call you both, "Dum-dee-dum!" Then I won't get it wrong!' Tandia laughed.

As they'd set off Peekay had spoken to the twins in the Shangaan language with which Tandia was not familiar. 'We have five, maybe six hours' lead; you must take this city woman as fast as you can, but do not break her. We are going over Saddleback to Swaziland.'

'In one day?' Dee asked.

'It depends how well Tandy lasts. But as far as you can take her.'

The twins nodded, knowing their task, knowing that how they judged the journey could mean Peekay's life, for they now felt the danger around him strongly. It smelt of death and of hate; they knew their heartblood was running from a great and calamitous evil.

The climb to Saddleback normally took five hours from the end of the foothills. On the very top of Saddleback there was a small plateau, about three hundred yards across, like a bald patch, torn by the wind from the leeward side of the mountain. It was composed mostly of rock and scree and tuft grass and the wind usually blew at gale force across it. It was totally exposed but it was the only way across the high mountains on foot. After they were across it Peekay knew they would be safe, they'd be on the rainy side of the mountains and, if necessary, could leave the path and conceal themselves within the dense mountain scrub and even in the rainforest in the high kloofs.

Ten minutes later they started to climb again, this time in earnest. Two and a half hours later, with stops of five minutes every half hour to rest Tandia, they reached a spot where Peekay could see the valley for the last time. He took the binoculars from his rucksack and focussed them. In the deep blue distance the de Kaap valley looked peaceful; in one or two places smoke rose straight up where a small bush fire burned and a scud of low cloud lay just below the far escarpment. Then he heard the faint sound of a small aircraft, a buzz like an angry bee rising in the clear morning. Sound carries remarkably far in the mountains. He looked carefully, scanning the length of the valley until he finally saw it, a Piper Cherokee still fairly high but heading towards the town which was concealed, tucked below the foothills. Geldenhuis had arrived.

If it took the police colonel an hour to get underway, they had about three and a half hours' lead. Peekay made a rough calculation; if Tandia didn't crack they would make it over the top, but only just. His only concern was to get over Saddleback; concealed in the deep mountain scrub the police would be no match for him unless they had a bloody good black tracker, and even then he felt confident that he could avoid his pursuers.

A police transport vehicle and squad car was waiting at the small airport when Geldenhuis arrived. Beside them stood seven white police constables and a sergeant, formed into a rough squad. The sergeant brought them to attention and saluted. 'Sergeant Maritz, Colonel!'

'Stand your men at ease, Sergeant,' Geldenhuis said. He was dressed in fatigues and carried a police semi-automatic rifle slung over his shoulder. He wore no pistol on his webbing belt; in its place was a hunting knife whose leather handle was topped with a death's head. Some knives rest peacefully on a man's hips, mere decoration or affectation, used for cutting fishing line or sharpening twigs. Even though its blade wasn't visible this wasn't that kind of knife. It was purpose built, the kind of knife a man would give a name and would also speak to, but always with respect in his voice.

'Is there anyone here who knows this country?' Geldenhuis asked.

'Yes, sir, we have a black tracker who says he knows it well. He looked over to a middle-aged African who was seated under a nearby syringa tree. '*Buya lapa*!' he called in Fanagalo. The man scrambled to his feet and came running over. He was a little man dressed in an old army greatcoat and he smiled, showing only four yellow teeth in his mouth. 'He's a Swazi and he says he comes from up near Havelock on the Swazi border; he says he knows the mountains round here very well.'

'You mean he's not your regular police tracker?'

'No, Colonel, this isn't our area; the Nelspruit area is flatter country, our trackers don't come over this way.'

'What about the local police?'

'Well, Colonel, if I may say so, they're not too pleased about this. I mean, us people from Nelspruit police taking over an' all.' He pointed to the little Swazi who now stood fifteen or so feet from them, waiting to be asked to step forward, 'They sent this guy.'

Geldenhuis said, 'Okay, fuck them!' He ignored the little black man and turned to the map. 'Let's see if the kaffir knows what he's talking about.'

'There are several paths up through the foothills but they all seem to eventually converge going through this gorge; after this it's straight up over the top, a single path. We have to get to them somewhere between this gorge and the top of Saddleback. If they get over the top the kaffir says you can forget it, it's dense bush and scrub and from what I understand, Peekay knows the country well from when he was a kid.'

Geldenhuis turned the map upside down and called the little Swazi over. 'Show us where to go,' he demanded in Zulu, pointing to the map.

The little Swazi looked at the map. 'Even if you turn it the right side up I can't read it, baas,' he said in Siswati. 'For reading maps I am no good.'

Geldenhuis grinned despite himself, at least the bastard wasn't a fool. 'Explain then how we go,' he demanded.

'There are four ways, baas. One is longest, but it is shortest, because the path is good. All the paths they come to a gorge, then same path all the way over the mountain.'

'How many hours to the top?'

The black man seemed to think for a moment, counting on the fingers of one hand. 'Six, six hours I think, baas. It is very, very hard.'

'The top of the mountain where the path crosses, is it very rocky?'

'No, baas, by that mountain is only grass by the top,' Julius ran his hand over his head. 'Like the baas head.'

'Well, the kaffir seems to know his way. It's six hours to Saddleback.' He turned to the men, 'Have you brought enough food and water? Remember you've got to come back as well.' Geldenhuis grinned, looking up at the high mountains, 'Have a good climb, you hear.'

'You won't be coming, Colonel?' Sergeant Maritz asked, surprised.

'Ja, I'll see you up there.' Geldenhuis didn't explain any further. 'Okay, man, now I want to talk about *the terrorist*.' He cleared his throat. 'You already know there are two of them, a woman and a man who is supposed to be a pretty big hero around these parts, you all know who I am talking about. I don't want to mention his name because when a man turns against his country the only name you can call him is a dog. A fucking mongrel! I'd like them taken alive. But I'd rather they were dead than free.' He sighed, 'Okay, you know how I feel? That's why I'm not using the local police for this job. If we kill their hero, it's bad public relations for the Barberton police and I don't want the whole fucking town up in arms. But someone who aids a known terrorist to escape is a terrorist too! If any of you feel differently about this then say so now, you hear?'

Geldenhuis looked at the men standing in front of him. 'This isn't police work, man! This is fighting for your country! You are helping to rid South Africa of the scum!' He waited, looking at each of them, but the men kept silent, most of them with their eyes downcast. 'Okay, I'm waiting for a helicopter to come up from the military base at Komaatipoort. We're going to try to squeeze the bastards between me and you guys coming up. I'll land on Saddleback and ambush them if they manage to get that far before you reach them. Okay, you better get going. Good luck.' Geldenhuis turned to the sergeant beside him and shook his hand, 'Thank you for your co-operation, Sergeant Maritz. If we pull this one off I'll see all your men get a commendation from Pretoria.'

The men marched off and one of them, a corporal named Shorty Bronkhorst who was known as the station wit, snorted, 'The bastard thinks he's John fucking Wayne!'

Captain Julius Dube had come down from Bulembu, crossing into South Africa to do some serious shopping in Barberton. It wasn't quite as close as Pigg's Peak on his side of the border, but he wanted a double bed and inner-spring mattress. To go with his newfound military status he'd paid the *lobola*, bridal price, for a second wife, a young and nubile *intombi* from a good family. Their wedding gift to themselves was to be the bed, a status symbol probably closer to a general than a captain, but Julian was ambitious.

However, the choice of double beds with inner springs in Pigg's Peak was decidedly limited. Barberton was three times as close as Mbabane, the Swazi capital, and also likely to prove a better shopping venue. Julius was fairly careless about borders and while his papers were in order he failed to get a required stamp from the police station on the South African side of the frontier. He'd come down from Havelock in the bus and had passed a police road block on the road but had thought nothing of it. Later, having selected a bed and mattress and arranged for it to be brought up by lorry to the Bulembu border post in two days, he'd celebrated at a shebeen in the native location where one or two jam tins of *mqombothi* too many had made him conspicuous. He'd been picked up by the local police and accommodated in a cell for the night.

The routine for being caught was standard, he'd be sjamboked (five lashes to discourage future temporary immigration) then put on the bus to Havelock, handcuffed to the bus seat and the key given to the driver. When they got to Havelock the bus driver would deliver him to the local police sergeant who would come out and officially unlock him, give him a stiff kick up his already very blistered backside and escort him to the border.

Julius had been waiting at the sergeant's desk to be released and his wallet and sundry shopping returned to him before being taken out into the yard of the police station to get sjamboked and put on the bus. Then the call had come through to the front desk from the Nelspruit police asking for a black tracker who knew the local mountains.

Captain Dube was not a man to be easily daunted. He was a mountain man born and bred. He'd once been a tracker in the Swaziland police; besides he knew these particular mountains like the back of his hand. He'd also heard Peekay's name mentioned in the conversation and details as to why a tracker was required. The *Onoshobishobi Ingelosi* was in a great deal of shit and Julius wasn't the sort of officer who walks away from a crisis. The rest was astonishing, even to a smooth operator like himself. He wondered fleetingly whether Somojo had a hand in it somewhere, seeing as the *Onoshobishobi Ingelosi* was involved. The white police sergeant seemed angry with the police from Nelspruit and when Julius, who like all Africans kept every official paper he'd ever received, had shown him his honourable discharge notice from The Royal Swaziland Police Constabulary he'd given him the job of taking the police contingent from Nelspruit over the mountains. The sergeant had also let him off the mandatory sjambok on the basis that it might inhibit his walking speed.

Thus Captain Julius Dube's finest hour had been thrust upon him as though miraculously. He could already see his next promotion and wondered to himself whether a rank existed somewhere above a captain but below a general. Julius knew one thing for sure; it was going to be a very long day in the mountains for the Boer policemen, and their chances of reaching Saddleback were about the same as his of growing a fresh set of molars.

Though nothing untoward happened, the six hours it had taken them to get to the gorge had been very difficult for Tandia. They'd stopped for ten minutes every hour and reaching the gorge they had taken half an hour for lunch. Tandia had by this time just about had enough. Peekay removed her shoes and allowed her to bathe her feet in the icy mountain stream before he examined them for blisters. In choosing sand-shoes for her to wear he'd shown his experience. Tackies are the best walking shoes for this kind of country, they're comfortable, don't need to be broken in, are soft enough not to cause blistering and will accommodate swollen feet simply by adjusting the laces. To his surprise, though her feet were swollen, the skin wasn't broken. He smeared her toes in vaseline before putting on a pair of fresh socks for her. Peekay knew that if her feet could last, she could, though clearly she was close to a state of collapse. They had two hours' climbing to go and Geldenhuis would be closing in fast. The twins too were tired; they'd put on a fair bit of weight over the years and while they often went into the mountains this was serious climbing for anyone. He noticed that Dee was limping as she walked to the water to fill their water bottles and discovered she'd cut her foot when she'd slipped on a section of miner's blue shale when they'd passed an abandoned mine digging; she'd jammed it against a sharp outcrop of rock. She'd continued on, ignoring the cut and not wanting to delay their progress. Peekay cleaned the rather nasty three-inch wound, picking the tiny bits of shale out of it with a pair of tweezers and finally dousing it with iodine to kill any infection. The iodine stung horribly and tears ran down Dee's cheeks, but she never said a word, simply biting her lip. Dum suffered with her; tears also ran down her cheeks and she stood by her sister biting her lip as well, seeming genuinely to be experiencing the same pain Dee felt. Peekay padded the wound thickly with gauze and wrapped it tightly, using almost the whole spool of two-inch wide elastoplast. Though Dee limped slightly he knew she wouldn't let her foot slow them down, and she refused to lighten the burden on her head.

Peekay made his calculations. If they could cover the slope ahead in two hours, a climb which usually took a little over one hour from the gorge, they'd be over the top at half past two, half an hour ahead of Geldenhuis and his men. It wasn't much of an advantage, but it would be enough if he was careful.

Halfway up the slope was a place where he could stop and see into the valley approaching the gorge below them, where the three good paths to the gorge began to converge. Anyone coming along any of them would be clearly visible through the binoculars. If the valley was empty, he knew they were in trouble. Geldenhuis would have made it through the valley and into the gorge. The maximum pace he could expect from Tandia wouldn't get them over the top; the police trackers would reach them twenty minutes before they could achieve their goal.

They set out once again to climb out of the gorge and onto the final slope, the twins in front with Tandia just ahead of Peekay so he could steady her. Despite the cold her body was soaked with perspiration and she was forced to stop every twenty feet to gain her breath. Though nothing was said Tandia was conscious that they were losing ground rapidly and that Geldenhuis couldn't be too far away. But her legs simply wouldn't carry her more than twenty paces at a time and sometimes far less. Her chest hurt terribly and on several occasions she was sure she was going to have a heart attack. At first she'd cried softly, but soon she didn't even have the energy for that and became convinced that every step she took would be her last.

Halfway up the slope to the top and more than an hour after they'd left the gorge Peekay halted them. Focussing his binoculars he pulled the valley beyond the gorge into focus. He saw almost immediately that it was empty and his heart sank. Geldenhuis had made it into the gorge below, they were finished.

Then Peekay caught a tiny glint of metal on the edge of the vista contained within the glasses and he swung the binoculars to his right. He gasped as his eyes adjusted to the sudden movement. Then he started to laugh, his laughter building until it echoed against the hills about him. Finally he turned to the three women, his face creased in a huge grin, 'God is good, children, if we can just keep on our feet we're going to make it. The opposition, God knows how, has become confused!'

Peekay had seen the police trackers coming down a valley parallel to the one which worked its way to the entry of the gorge. Ten years before there had been access between the two valleys through a second narrow gorge but it had been filled with a massive rock slide. In about ten minutes Geldenhuis and his men would find it impossible to continue. Though the two valleys were less than half a mile apart a sheer cliff face separated them and it would take nearly two hours for the men to retrace their steps. He couldn't believe his extraordinary luck; the path to the mountain slide was well known locally, a favourite destination for hardened climbers. It was common knowledge there was no longer a way through to the big gorge and he couldn't imagine how such a mistake could be made, unless it was deliberate.

Greatly cheered, Peekay talked Tandia up the slope, sometimes it seemed by inches. Nearly two and a half hours later they sat within fifty feet of the top. 'The last bit is tricky, so we'll rest for half an hour before crossing, Tandia. It's a bit windy up top so we'll stop here.' Given the choice, Peekay would have liked to cross, just to know that they would be out of immediate danger where they had more than one option. But the final fifty feet was almost sheer and he was doubtful Tandia would make it without a rest. The luxury of the extra two hours they'd gained on Geldenhuis made it an easy decision. He chose an overhanging rock that cut into the side of the mountain as shelter. There was room under it to spread a blanket where Tandia could lie.

Tandia was crying softly, her courage completely exhausted. The fact that she was fifty feet from the top meant nothing; it might as well have been a mile. Peekay removed her shoes and her jeans; lying her on a blanket, he began to massage her legs. She cried out in agony at the ouch of his hands against the knotted quads and calf muscles. Peekay continued to work on them for nearly an hour, a lot longer than he'd hoped to stop. But he realized that if he couldn't get her moving again they'd be trapped anyway. The mistaken path taken by their pursuers had most certainly saved them from capture and possibly saved heir lives.

Captain Julius Dube led the Nelspruit police patrol right up to the rock slide, gasping in pretend horror when they'd come around a corner path and faced the mountain of rubble. 'Haya, haya!' he'd exclaimed, holding his hands to his head. The disaster was immediately apparent to them all and Julius had prepared himself for the thrashing he was about to receive. The men were tired and had been pushed at a hard pace by him as he'd deliberately attempted to wear them out.

'Jesus! What happened here!' Sergeant Maritz shouted. The rock slide, though a decade old, had torn most of the side of a mountain away. The rock fall had been much too calamitous for vegetation to have taken over and the slide they looked at seemed as though it could have happened the day before yesterday. But the men from Nelspruit, who were not even local Nelspruit guys, most of them transferred from all over the place, knew nothing of this and even less of the way of mountains, where it might take a thousand years and a million rainfalls washing silt into the rock to cover a fall like this one with grass and bush. Maritz, though plainly exasperated, judged the predicament they found themselves in to be an honest mistake and Captain Julius Dube began seriously to believe that the hand of the great Somojo was apparent in all of this. Everything he'd done with the *Onoshobishobi Ingelosi* had turned out successfully, as well as being very profitable. He also knew that the great *makhosi*, Somojo, had blessed the white man with the special gifts. He, Julius Dube, was having the one great day of his life which the spirits promised to every man who lives on this earth.

Maritz, trying to contain his exasperation in front of his men, took a swig from his water flask and, rinsing his mouth, spat it out. 'How far back is it to get onto another path?' he enquired of Julian.

'Haya, baas, it is very, very, far. I think two hours also!'

'*Fok! Ons moet nog twee ue loop tot die groot kloof!* Still two hours from the big gorge!' he said in dismay to his tired men, who'd already had about as much time in the mountains as they felt they'd ever need.

The men all groaned and Shorty Bronkhorst observed, 'John Wayne is going to have to hold the fucking pass alone.'

No one thought this was very funny. It was half past one and they still had three hours to go to the top. Peekay and his kaffir girl would be in

Swaziland drinking a second cup of tea by then, Maritz thought to himself. 'We'll stop for fifteen minutes,' he said, 'it's not going to make that much difference now.'

Geldenhuis had waited nearly six hours for the helicopter to arrive from the army base at Komaatipoort and he was getting worried. He wanted to be well in place to ambush Peekay and Tandia when they came over the top and it was nearly three o'clock already. He was cursing himself; the men would be closing in and he wasn't in place. He wanted Peekay and Tandia for himself. He hadn't yet decided whether he would kill them, but he wanted the option to do so before the men arrived so that he could claim they'd made a run for it. He was nearly crying with frustration when he heard the beat of the chopper's blades and five minutes later it landed. But then the pilot had to refuel and go through an entire checking procedure before they took off.

The pilot was a colonel himself so Geldenhuis couldn't pull rank, which was the usual procedure when the police and the army worked together. It's deliberate, he thought to himself, these army bastards don't like to take orders from a cop, they've deliberately sent a fucking colonel to checkmate me! What's more the shit is a rooinek! He felt like hitting somebody, but there were no kaffirs handy.

The pilot had introduced himself simply as Robin Winter, not observing his rank but not saluting as well, so that the police colonel knew from the start they were quits. He spread a map on the grass and Geldenhuis explained their destination. Winter was far from impressed, looking up from the map into the mountains as though he was making an instant judgement. 'The up-draughts in that range are notorious, Colonel. A chopper like this one can drop two or three hundred feet with no prior indication. Landing on top of Saddleback could be suicidal.' He checked the wind speed averages marked on his flying map. 'The winds up there are gale force.' He looked at his watch and then back at the high mountains. 'At least there's no cloud, though I expect it will come up soon.' He seemed to be making up his mind. 'We've got time for only one pass. After that I'm out of there, old son,' he said cheerfully, but Geldenhuis knew he meant it.

Geldenhuis wanted to hit the pompous bastard; almost six hours to get up from his base at Komaatipoort and he wasn't even guaranteeing he'd put him down on the top of Saddleback. Fuck it! He'd make the bastard do so at gunpoint. 'Thanks, Colonel Winter, let's go, man,' he said keeping his voice even; it was fifteen minutes past three.

Ten minutes later Peekay saw the helicopter approaching. They'd just prepared themselves to leave. The helicopter circled once above them at about five hundred feet and then disappeared. It came around again half a minute later, this time lower, and he could see Geldenhuis at the open door with his rifle pointed at the pilot. The chopper disappeared from view and they heard it faintly above the howl of the wind as its engines went into a higher pitch. Then they lost its sound, but it returned, the blades whining at an even higher pitch. Moments later the chopper passed low over them, banking sharply with only the pilot in it. They were only ten minutes from the top, fifty lousy feet. Peekay could see the panic in the eyes of the twins and Tandia looked at him. 'It's all over isn't it, Peekay?'

Peekay's mind was working too rapidly to grasp the despair they felt. He turned to the twins. 'Go over now. When the policeman stops you, he will ask if you have seen us. Tell him we are just ten minutes ahead, that you saw us ahead of you as you came up from the gorge. He will come after us, thinking we are ahead. Now listen carefully. The path divides into a fork on the other side. Tell him the one going to Swaziland is the right-hand path, then take the left one yourself. Wait for us after one mile of walking. Hide in the bush in case he comes.'

Dee and Dum picked up their bundles and balanced them carefully, though with the wind they had to hold onto them with one hand. Now that Peekay had told them what he wanted they were not frightened. They turned to leave and Peekay walked over to them and kissed them both. The last time he had kissed them he was five years old. Dee and Dum's faces lit up into a brilliant smile, for that's what it seemed like, a single smile on two faces, as though the smile came out of both of them. 'You are our heartblood, Peekay,' they said together.

Geldenhuis was surprised to see the two women coming across the open ground towards him. He was still searching for the path when they suddenly emerged over the top fifty yards from where he stood. They appeared not to see him and he shouted. '*Buya lapa, abaFazi*! Come here, women!' But his voice was torn from him by the howling wind, which was now buffeting the women's skirts as they used both hands to steady the bundles on their heads.

Geldenhuis ran towards them, covering the fifty yards fairly quickly, though it was difficult against the wind. He'd jumped from the helicopter six feet from the ground and Winter had put everything into the blades to get himself out. He stopped beside them now, panting. Both women looked amazed at seeing him, the whites of their eyes huge in their faces. They pulled back from him afraid.

'Do not be afraid of the gun, I am a policeman,' he shouted.

'We are afraid, Inkosi!' Dum shouted back.

'I won't harm you, I am in a hurry.' Geldenhuis was not conscious of the irony of this remark. 'Tell me, have you seen two people? One a white man? Maybe ahead of you?' He'd turned his back to the wind, standing parallel to the two women so that he could talk quite normally.

The two women turned to each other, talking rapidly in a language he couldn't understand.

'What is that you are saying, hey?' Geldenhuis said.

'We have seen him, Inkosi,' Dee said.

'He is with a woman, Inkosi,' Dum added.

'How long ago?'

The twins seemed to be thinking. 'I think not so long, Inkosi.

'I think twenty minutes.' Each twin held up ten fingers.

Geldenhuis grinned; then his expression changed and he looked at them strangely. 'Are you two twins?'

'Yes, Inkosi,' the twins said together.

It explained the hands going up together. He'd heard of that happening with twins. 'Which way is it to the Swaziland border?' Geldenhuis asked.

'We will show you, Inkosi,' Dee said.

'Did you hear any men coming behind you?'

'No, Inkosi, we did not hear,' they both said.

It was amazing, Geldenhuis thought, they seemed to have one mind. They turned back into the teeth of the wind and set out for the other side of the plateau. Geldenhuis was jubilant. Peekay and Tandia would be exhausted and he was fresh; they couldn't be more than a few hundred yards away and the trackers hadn't caught up. He had them to himself.

When they got to the edge of the plateau and dropped over the side the wind seemed to stop. Fifty feet further on the path divided and the two kaffir women stopped. One of the women pointed to the right-hand path. 'It is this one, Inkosi.'

'To Swaziland? This path goes to Swaziland?' Geldenhuis repeated.

'Ja, ja, it is this one, Inkosi,' the second woman said.

They had nice manners, Geldenhuis thought, these bush kaffirs, not like the cheeky black bastards in the city. He was amazingly relaxed. He knew he'd come up to Peekay from behind. If he'd seen the helicopter he'd know it couldn't land in the wind and would have seen it fly away again. He set off down the path the two women had indicated. He wouldn't run, there was plenty of time.

Dee and Dum took the path to the left. Too afraid to stop and hug each other, they moved forward as quickly as their tired legs would take them, fearful that the policeman with the gun might return, fearful also of Peekay crossing in case the man came back. But they'd always done as Peekay asked and now they hurried to where they would anxiously wait for him.

Peekay and Tandia climbed to the edge of the plateau and watched as the twins reached the other side with Geldenhuis and disappeared. Peekay waited another minute before they set out. It took them nearly ten minutes to cross in the gale-force winds.

But by that time Dee was dead.

Geldenhuis had followed the path at a steady trot, covering a couple of hundred yards along the rocky descent in as many minutes. His mind was concentrating hard, but there was something nagging at him. He knew from past practice to listen to it. This was an instinct that was never wrong. He scratched at his mind, even stopping once to try to think the concern to the surface of his consciousness. A little later he passed a patch of soft sand, smoothed by the previous night's rain; it would have been impossible to avoid it if one were walking along the path, yet there were no footprints. He came to another a little further along and it too was virginal. Then it happened! Shit! African twins are very rare. Twins are regarded as bad *muthi*, bad medicine, and, even today, the weaker of the two twin babies is left outside the village. It was not uncommon to find a small black infant on a rubbish dump in the townships, a twin left to die. Then it hit him like a thunderclap! The two black women were Peekay's twins. It was in his file. He'd grown up with black twins! Geldenhuis turned and retraced his steps down the path. Turning down the second pathway he ran steadily until he saw the twins. 'Stop!' he shouted. Dee and Dum saw him and panicked. They dropped their bundles and started to run. Geldenhuis ran after them, not even seeing the bundles which had rolled off the path. He lost sight of them and then saw them ahead of him again, still on the path. The stupid women hadn't run into the cover of the bush. He stopped, went down onto one knee and, taking quick aim, fired. The bullet tore into Dee's back, killing her instantly .

Dum stopped and turned, screaming. She flung herself onto Dee's lifeless body, then rose and ran into the dense bush on the side of the path. Geldenhuis fired off three more shots, missing her. He ran up to the black girl's body; he could hear the second kaffir girl crashing through the bush. He kicked at Dee's body, knowing instantly that she was dead. '*Jou moel!*' He looked into the bush where he could hear Dum. Jesus, it's just a kaffir girl! he said to himself. I must be going crazy, thinking about going after a kaffir girl. He'd worked out Peekay's ploy. As usual it was shit smart. The two women had been sent ahead as a decoy and to misdirect him. He'd fired the four shots while Peekay and Tandia were coming across the plateau and the howl of the wind had killed the sound. All he had to do was wait. It was just how he'd imagined it would be; even the dead kaffir woman. He brought his boot under the hem of Dee's dress, lifting it. He'd make Peekay die the way he'd always fantasised it. *The terrorist* could watch and then he'd kill her.

Geldenhuis pulled Dee's body off the pathway, covering the blood on the path by kicking dust over it with his boot. There wasn't much time and he found an outcrop of rock just off the path and waited.

Peekay and Tandia came down the path glad to be away from the wind, Tandia walking slowly but a little easier. Geldenhuis saw them coming and steadied his rifle. Peekay was in front shielding Tandia. He aimed low at his hip just as Peekay saw one of the bundles lying at the side of the pathway. Peekay turned and dived at Tandia, knocking her over into the bush beside the path just as Geldenhuis squeezed the trigger. The bullet caught Peekay high in the shoulder, just below the collarbone.

Peekay felt no pain. He rolled off the path and leapt to his feet, grabbing Tandia's hand and pulling her. 'Up! Get up!' he screamed. Tandia somehow managed to get to her feet and they stumbled down the slope into the dense scrub, disturbing the boulders which clattered down the mountain slope in front of them.

Somehow Peekay managed to get Tandia a hundred yards or so down the densely wooded slope. Then he stopped. They'd come to an outcrop of rock in high grass which appeared to form a small hollow to one side. He pushed Tandia into it and crept in beside her. Tandia's breathing was coming in rasps and Peekay held her to him. Then he realised that blood was dripping onto her shoulder. He put his hand up, feeling the hole in his shoulder for the first time.

They could hear Geldenhuis crashing around some distance to their right. Peekay pushed Tandia from him. Seeing the blood, she brought her hand up over her mouth, stifling her scream. Geldenhuis was moving further away. He'd be quiet for a few moments, obviously listening for them, then they'd hear him moving again. It was impossible this high up on the slopes not to disturb loose shale and rocks as you walked.

Peekay knew Geldenhuis would go back to the path soon, not taking the chance of getting lost. Then he would see the blood and know he'd wounded Peekay and he'd come down more carefully, following the blood spoor. 'Listen, Tandia, we don't have much time. I know a place near here, maybe a mile and a bit where I can hide. I'm going to draw Geldenhuis away, make him follow me. Don't worry, I know the country, he doesn't, he won't get me, I promise.' Peekay tried to grin; his shoulder was starting to throb badly.

Tandia flung herself at him. 'Peekay, you're going to die! If you're going to die I want to die too!' She sobbed against his chest.

'Tandy! Listen, you can make it!' Peekay whispered urgently. 'When Geldenhuis comes after me wait five minutes, then go back to the path. You've got five miles to go, it's mostly downhill. In two hours you'll be in Swaziland. Ask the first person you see to take you to the village of Somojo, every Swazi knows where that is.' He reached into his shirt and removed the leather strap around his neck with the tiny leather bag attached to it. It was the gold coin of Lumukanda. 'Take this, Tandy.' Peekay placed it over her head so that it sat with the gold chain on which hung Juicey Fruit Mambo's gold eye-teeth. 'When you get to the village give it to one of the young women who serve Somojo. It's important, do you understand?' Tandia nodded, her eyes tearful again. Peekay took his wallet from his top pocket. 'There's money in there. When you get to the village ask for Julius Dube, he's one of our people, also a captain in *Umkonto.* He'll take care of the rest!'

'I don't want to go,' Tandia pleaded.

Peekay was suddenly angry. 'Go! You must go! Otherwise they win! You understand? Otherwise Geldenhuis and all he stands for wins!'

Tandia nodded, sniffing, and Peekay rose. 'It will be all right, darling. Move out with me, go to the right for fifty yards, then wait quietly. He'll come after the blood, after me. When you see him pass this spot wait five minutes then move back to the path.' He kissed Tandia, holding her with his good arm. 'I love you, Tandia. You are my whole life!'

Tandia started to weep. 'Peekay, I love you! Please, don't leave me.'

'Tandia, you must make it! You must hang on. Whatever happens, you must get through.' Peekay smiled, 'Tandia, about last night. If you're pregnant, you know, just if? If it's a boy, will you call him just one name? Just Lumukanda.' Peekay repeated the name, 'Lumukanda, child of the morning star!' He kissed her deeply. 'Goodbye, beloved Tandia,' he said softly. Moments later they set off together. Peekay squeezed her hand and released it, Tandia moved to the right and he, making a fearful racket to hide her movement, moved downwards and to the left, away from the rock outcrop where they'd been hiding.

Geldenhuis had done just as Peekay had thought he might. He retraced his steps to the pathway and soon he discovered the blood trail; then he heard the two of them crashing to his left in the dense bush directly below him. He followed the sound for nearly ten minutes, soon finding more blood. Whichever of the two of them he'd hit wasn't going to get too far. He knew Tandia was exhausted but that Peekay wouldn't leave her. The madness in him made him feel totally confident, a lion stalking his prey. It was better this way, he had to work for his kill. He would enjoy it the more for the effort it had taken.

Peekay was no more than a mile and a half away from the crystal cave of Africa. As he walked he cut a length of rope from where it sat on the top of his rucksack and made a quick sling for his arm, cushioning the rope with a handful of tough mountain grass. He dabbed at the blood on his shoulder, laying the spoor for Geldenhuis until he judged he was sufficiently far from Tandia for her to get away. The men following her wouldn't reach Saddleback before nightfall, that was, if they'd been foolish enough to continue beyond the gorge. Trapped in the high mountains for the night they'd freeze to death even in midsummer.

After an hour it was time to lose Geldenhuis. Peekay had moved around in a large circle, climbing gradually higher. Geldenhuis would never find the path again. It was half past four, he had an hour and a half before sunset. The deep kloof of rainforest he was going to was hidden in a crease of a mountain abutting Saddleback and he worked his way towards it. Geldenhuis was managing to keep on his track and he could hear him coming up behind him.

The shrub was becoming more sparse as they climbed higher. Twice Geldenhuis caught sight of Peekay and took a shot at him. But it was almost impossible to fire up the mountain slope; his optical perspectives were out and he missed by a large margin. By now Geldenhuis realised that Peekay was on his own. But it didn't matter, it was Peekay he wanted. He laughed to himself. When the chips were down Peekay had deserted the kaffir girl, the white man in him asserting itself. Peekay's blood spoor had stopped but he could hear him and occasionally see him. His quarry was in country where it wasn't too hard to track him.

Peekay was beginning to feel slightly nauseous from loss of blood; he was growing weaker but enough strength remained. The wound was clean; under the collarbone and out the other side, smashing a hole through the shoulder blade. His arm was getting very stiff and painful but he'd torn his sleeve, plugging the bleeding, though he could feel his back was wet, sticky with blood. Peekay came at last to the narrow gap between the two high cliffs. It was here that he hoped finally to lose Geldenhuis. It was well concealed and in the shadow of the towering rock, a place you could pass fifty times and not see. He slipped into the darkness of the narrow opening, moving quietly. Soon he was on the other side looking down into the rainforest below. On the side opposite to him was the cliff face that contained the crystal cave. To the right of the concealed entrance to the cave the bridal veil fell, the fine white spray of water turning pink in the late afternoon sun. Below him the huge old yellowwood tree stood high above the canopy of trees, the way it had stood sentinel for six hundred years, maybe more.

Peekay moved slowly down the slope, his bad shoulder making it difficult and painful to do so. He was sweating, the sweat cold, coming from the pain. Twice he stopped to hear if he was being followed but he heard nothing. It took him fifteen minutes to get to the floor of the forest below and he stopped briefly at the stream to drink. He was growing weak but he knew he must somehow get to the ledge beside the cave, get into the crystal cave to Doc. Peekay knew that he was losing too much blood, that by morning he'd be unconscious and too weak to climb out of the kloof. He had somehow to find the strength to climb up to the cave, to lie beside Doc. He moved through the dark cover of the trees reaching the base of the cliff. 'Please, Doc, give me the strength,' he cried softly, looking up at the rock face towering above him. 'Just one more time, give me the strength I need.'

Peekay took off his rucksack, gingerly pulling its blood soaked strap off his left shoulder. His movements were slow, conserving his strength. He didn't panic; panic races the blood. He took half-a-dozen climbing spikes and the tiny hammer and fitted them into his belt. He also took the torch and attached it as well. He started up the rock face moving slowly, judging every move. His shoulder had started to bleed profusely as he demanded work from the arm; his teeth cut through his lower lip from the pain. Sometimes he was so dizzy he was forced to stand with his back to the cliff to prevent himself falling.

Geldenhuis lost Peekay. He'd caught sight of him for a moment as they worked across a ridge but then they approached a huge towering bluff and Peekay had vanished. He knew he must be in the vicinity; beyond the huge bluff the mountain fell sheer for a thousand feet. Peekay had disappeared into the rock. It was getting late, in less than an hour it would be sunset. Night comes quickly in the mountains. He wasn't even sure if he knew his way back. But he was past caring. Nothing else mattered to him now but the kill. He was so close, he could smell the death he was going to bring about. For forty minutes he searched, passing the entrance a dozen times before seeing the blood spot and looking into the dark, narrow fissure in the cliff face. He had to slide in sideways. At first the entrance didn't appear to lead anywhere, just a huge fissure in the towering cliff and then, as his eyes grew accustomed to the softer light, he saw another drop of blood. He moved on, squeezing through the narrowest bit which wasn't much wider than his body turned sideways. Suddenly he was looking down into a kloof of rainforest. In the centre a huge tree rose above all the others; at the far end, a cliff with a waterfall to its right held the kloof in its lap. He saw where Peekay had made his descent and then more blood.

Geldenhuis was able to follow the blood spoor down to the floor of the rainforest below. Once he reached the rainforest floor he lost it, but he kept going; moving along the stream he found another spot of blood on a rock. It was dark and still under the canopy of trees but he forced his way up the stream towards the waterfall. When he reached it he moved along the cliff face to his right, choosing it instinctively. He'd lost the blood trail but then he saw Peekay's rucksack and, looking up, he saw the blood on the cliff face above him; it was smeared over parts of the rock face where Peekay's shoulder had wiped against the rock. Geldenhuis could see clearly how to make the climb, but he would have to do so without his rifle. He placed it on the rock and felt to make sure the knife was on his belt. He began to climb, moving as quietly as possible up the bloodstained rock.

Peekay had finally reached the ledge. He was totally exhausted. The wound had torn further and he was bleeding profusely. He was too weak to do anything about it. He could feel the setting sun on his face as he lay there, trying to gather sufficient strength to venture onto the six-inch ledge which led to the cave entrance. He would have to wait a while and gather his strength, harvesting every little bit until he had sufficient for the last short journey, the precarious ledge, the crawl down the narrow tunnel into the bat cave and then into the crystal cave of Africa itself, where Doc lay waiting for him, his long body turning slowly into crystal, into Africa itself, the blood and the muscle and the spirit of him entering into the mystic land. He would lie with Doc, they'd be together again. If only he could find the strength. The ledge was warm and it seemed a nice place to be. He could see the dark smudge of mountains in the distance silhouetted against the red sky of a setting sun. Those mountains were in Swaziland, Tandia would be there by now. Tandia had made it.

Peekay must have passed out, or perhaps he was dreaming, because he wakened to see a face standing above him. It looked like Jannie Geldenhuis. Only it wasn't. It was a Jannie Geldenhuis who had gone mad. The face above him was going to kill him. He followed the face's hand and saw the knife Gert had made for him, the death's head knife. He'd given it to Gideon, but now it was on the belt of the mad face of Geldenhuis. The blade drew out, sharp and beautiful, as keen to strike as death itself, the blade made into a miracle from a Dodge truck spring, deadly and cunning in Gert's brilliant hands. A spring under a Dodge truck that had gone mad and turned into a killer blade. That was funny. The knife came up and Peekay began to laugh. The knife Gert made to protect him from hate; he'd given it to Gideon because the hatred against him was bigger, he needed Gert's blade more to equal the odds against him. But he should have known, hate cannot live in a good man's hands for long, hate has to find the fingers it knows. The knife had found the hate it needed in the grip of the white policeman's madness. Now Gert's knife was going to kill Peekay. In the end hate was going to win. You had to laugh. He'd been wrong after all. In the end, blind ignorant hate with a knife in its hand had triumphed over love and compassion which always came open-handed. The blade came up into a high arc, beautiful against a blood-red sky.

A shadow passed slowly over Peekay as Dum moved up the ledge behind Geldenhuis. She snarled like an animal, lifting him off his feet, her white teeth flashing as they sunk into his throat, hurling herself off the ledge with Geldenhuis pulled tightly against her body. Peekay heard him scream and then the crash of their bodies, the black and the white, as they smashed onto the rocks a hundred and fifty feet below where their blood mixed and flowed together at the base of the great altar of rock. *Together since the world began, the madman and the lover.*

Peekay lay still for a long time. The moon came up, full and glorious, a bright florin of light in the African night. He'd always liked the full moon. He was back in the night country. He stood on the rock above the top waterfull ready to jump. 'You must jump now, little warrior of the king,' he heard Inkosi-Inkosikazi say.

Peekay launched himself into the silver air. This time he seemed to float and the old witchdoctor's voice came to him again, but from a distance. 'You are wearing the skirt of the lion tail as you face into the setting sun. Now the sun has passed beyond Zululand, even past the land of the Swazi and now it leaves the Shangaan and the royal kraal of Mojaji, the rain queen, to be cooled in the great dark water beyond.

'You can see the moon rising over Africa and you are at peace, unafraid of the great demon Skokiaan who comes to feed on the night, tearing its black flesh until at last it is finished and there is light again and the people sing softly in the morning.'

Peekay saw the journey, the bittersweet journey from the beginning, from the soft warm black breasts that suckled him, the warm taste of milk, more than you could drink if you tried your hardest. He heard the click of the train wheels carrying him to the east, a small child frightened as a butterfly. *Small can beat big, you must remember only one thing, little boetie, first with the head and then with the heart.* It was Hoppie's voice coming to him as he flew higher and higher . . . Grandpa Chook, Geel Piet, *Dance, klein baas, that way they think you not hurt.* Captain Smit, E.W., Hymie, who would love him now? Beautiful Hymie . . .

Such a fortunate life . . . Peekay rose higher and higher, floating on the silver night above Africa. He passed over a village, a high mountain village where the yellow moon clung to the peaks and the bluffs. Below him in a tiny mound of scarlet cashmere Somojo sat, his grizzled head clear in the firelight. He was in a trance. 'A woman has come into the village, Somojo, a woman of no tribe,' one of the princesses said quietly. 'She gave me this and told me she must bring it to you.' Somojo's tiny hand, bony as an ancient monkey's claw, rose from the scarlet blanket and she placed the leather pouch within it. 'You are wrong, my child,' the old, old man moaned softly. 'The mother of the morning star belongs to every tribe. Lumukanda is back with us.'